THE
LUDLUM
TRIAD

ROBERT LUDLUM

THE LUDLUM TRIAD

 RANDOM HOUSE NEW YORK

The Holcroft Covenant was originally published in 1978 by
Richard Marek Publishers. Copyright © 1978 by Robert
Ludlum

The Matarese Circle was originally published in 1979 by
Richard Marek Publishers. Copyright © 1979 by Robert
Ludlum.

The Bourne Identity was originally published in 1980 by Richard
Marek Publishers. Copyright © 1980 by Robert Ludlum.

*Grateful acknowledgment is made to the following for permission
to reprint previously published material:*

Associated Press: An article of July 7, 1975 that appeared in
Associated Press. Used by permission.

The New York Times: Portion of front page of a July 11, 1975
article that appeared in *The New York Times.* Copyright ©
1975 by The New York Times Company. Reprinted by
permission.

Library of Congress Cataloging-in-Publication Data

Ludlum, Robert
  The Ludlum triad.

  I. Title.
PS3562.U26A6 1989   813'.54   89-8472
ISBN 0-394-57610-1

Manufactured in the United States of America
98765432
First Edition

CONTENTS

INTRODUCTION

It's very difficult for an author to write an introduction for such a volume as this without sounding pretentious—which I am not. I know who I am and what I am, nothing more and I hope not a great deal less.

I am an entertainer, albeit one with the temerity to deal frequently with serious ideas, or concepts or—as we say in the theater, where I came from—the "spines" of drama. Simple things like the abuse of power, the conspiracies of manipulators, the debasers of the public weal, the sanctimonious screamers hell-bent on transforming their personal morality into everyone else's legality, the bastards of the social contract who corrupt the agreements between the governing and the governed. Not exactly buck-and-wing stuff.

Yet, although privileged to have received a decent education, I am certainly no scholar in those areas that so disturb me—nay, outrage me. Therefore, like a painter with his oils, I can only interpret my impressions and reactions with words, expressing themes through the depiction of *people* framed in a succession of scenes that form the stories in which they are intensely involved. That may not make sense to the arbiters of literature, but it does to me. Then again, I come from the theater and we've always been suspect. "They tell their demon stories with mirrors and smoke! Beware the *jongleurs!*"

Yet again to paraphrase Bernard Shaw, that most literary and glorious of playwrights-cum-footnotes, if a writer is to get across his ideas, he must first *entertain.* For without entertainment, his audience diminishes in direct proportion to his numbing sermonics. So to my writer's mind, to entertain is a perfectly legitimate priority as long as there is a concept behind the entertainment. For me it is a necessity.

This said, what *were* the concepts—the ideas or the spines—behind the three novels in this volume? What compelled the storyteller to commit so many months of energy and sweat into their inventions? Were the concepts worth it? (Obviously, to me they were.) Were they conveyed? (Oddly enough, to me it both did and did not matter. I simply had to have them. If, for many, the stories stand by themselves as acceptable entertainment, so be it, and I'm grateful. But I doubt they would without the concepts.)

So let's examine them—briefly, for heaven's sake.

The Holcroft Covenant: The concept for this novel was literally handed to me, if not on a silver platter, certainly in the presence of a silver server at Simpson's restaurant in London during a late-night supper nearly fifteen years ago. And fourteen years later the unbelievable happened. I was sent a videotape of a documentary pieced together by two English film producers exclusively using newsreel footage from Nazi Germany that all but confirmed the long-discredited theory that was the premise for *The Holcroft Covenant*. Let's go back.

As was arranged, my wife, Mary, and I had dinner with my British publisher, who brought along a retired intelligence officer from MI6, England's counterpart of our Central Intelligence Agency. As anxious as I was to talk with a man of his vast experience during the "hot years," I soon learned that he was equally determined to "chat" with me regarding a World War II intelligence operation I described as having taken place in Scotland in a previous novel. Apparently my fiction was somewhat too close to the facts, and since the "facts" were still classified, his curiosity had been aroused—as well as the curiosity of several others in the Foreign Office, he ominously added with great charm and ice-cold eyes.

My *God*, I thought to myself, he wants to send me to the Old Bailey! Do they still hang people here? In public? The children won't like that. Even Mary might be upset.

After several whiskies—all *right*, more than several—accompanied by a carefully if fitfully constructed explanation of how I *invented, made up, formulated, fabricated* the Scotland operation, he accepted my innocence. He probably thought that someone with my limited intellectual powers couldn't elicit a secret from a compulsive government leaker, or conversely, having heard one, would misinterpret it totally.

Regardless, the cold eyes warmed up, the charm remained constant, and along with a brandy—all *right*, brandies—he agreed that the basis for all intelligence operations under extreme stress was the extension of the imagination . . . under extreme stress. It was a conclusion we both stole from William Stephenson, the man called Intrepid. Then the MI6-er reminisced. He said that frequently the imagination went too far, into the realm of the improbable, if not the impossible, and had to be held in check.

"For instance, there was a rumor out of Bremerhaven that Hitler's fanatics had arranged for hundreds of so-called Aryan infants to be sent to all points of the Western world by submarines, planes, trains, to families who expected them. The object, of course, was the birth of the Fourth Reich years from now. We traced it down. Worthless, nothing to it."

Nothing? *Everything!* Good Lord, what a *spine!* My head was spinning, my writer's mind racing. Before the brandies were finished my concept was in place. My German is so limited it's practically nonexistent, but I knew the word for children—*kinder*, as in kindergarten, and I somehow recalled the word for the sun—*Sonne*, every fanatic's dream of a new day when he alone will bathe in its melodramatic early light. *Operation Sonnenkinder*. And then, to illuminate the blind spots in that blinding sunlight, *what if* there was a specific *Sonnenkind* who had no idea he was one of the chosen, that, in fact, he was to be manipulated into being the catalyst for the emergence of the Fourth Reich, for he was so completely above suspicion?

Dinner over, Mary and I returned to the hotel and I began scribbling. I couldn't help it. I started an outline.

"What are you doing?" asked my bride of then some twenty-four years.

"Nobody's going to hang *me* in public, not for this! No Brit in black robes and a white wig is going to send *me* to the gallows. Not for *this!*"

"What *are* you talking about?"

"I got it straight from one of their own. Maybe I'll make *him* a *Sonnenkind.*"

"Good night."

Thus was born *The Holcroft Covenant.*

Yet this explanation would not be complete without explaining the aforementioned documentary, which is still in my possession. It was sent to me by a gifted Hollywood producer who somehow unearthed it in Europe, and subsequently and brilliantly weaved into a screenplay for a television film. It is called simply and chillingly: *Of Pure Blood.*

Through newsreel and propaganda footage, producers Clarissa Henry and Marc Hillel filmically depict (with British commentary) the existence of the *Lebensborn,* a biological operation created and promulgated by Heinrich Himmler with Adolf Hitler's messianic benediction. Aryan children were "produced" in "breeding farms." Selected S.S. officers were ordered to copulate with blond-haired, blue-eyed women—who, oddly enough, considering the Führer's racial insults, were, in the main, Polish women. The mothers and their offspring were pampered beyond belief in a disastrously disintegrating wartime economy, and then, dozen by dozen, score by score, hundreds by hundreds—thousands by thousands?—the children disappeared. After the war, a number of the mothers of the *Lebensborn*—not many, to be sure, for they were checkmated by the *Odessa;* they had slept with the Nazi—began asking questions: What had happened to their children?

The International Red Cross, operating with extraordinary diligence and patience from its headquarters in Geneva, Switzerland, came up with a few answers.

France, England, Austria, Brazil; these were documented. How many other destinations were there?

Truth? Fiction? Where does one end and the other begin?

The Matarese Circle: The Trilateral Commission? Mr. David Rockefeller came up with a hell of a title. Do you remember when the name first surfaced in the early seventies and the more paranoid among us wrapped it in all manner of conspiratorial motives? Of course, I knew better—once more from my theater experience. No director worth his Equity, SAG, or AFTRA card would cast the handsome, elegant, brilliant, *steely-eyed* Sir David as the overlord of a secret society in search of global power. Instead, the smart director opts for the innocent persona of an Eddie Albert or a Hume Cronyn. See what I mean? (I hope D.R. has a sense of humor because I'd like to think I still have a friend at Chase Manhattan.) No, the Trilateral Commission was and is a group of high-minded, highly visible men and women of international stature who represent the combined interests of the United States, Europe and Japan—the three sides of the triangle. They are, of course, influential, but they cannot set national policies, for, to the best of my knowledge, no one elected them to represent their governments pursuant to the commission's judgments.

But wait! Suppose such elections were not necessary; suppose the genesis of such an organization was not in the 1970s but, instead, in the 1870s—and it *was* secret. Suppose, rather than a renowned banker from a prominent family constantly in the media spotlight, the creator of this organization was a distant visionary, isolated from the world on, say, an island, a huge landmass of an island—say, Corsica. That visionary would have to be a great *padrone,* an empire builder who looked far beyond his own life span in the tradition of the true nineteenth-century barons of industry. He would be the founder of an infrastructural global dynasty that would shape the financial centers of the world for its own interests in ways never dreamed of by the Rothschilds in Europe. Whoever controls a government's economy ultimately controls the government.

Now, *there* was a story! And with a concept that served my particular paranoia regarding the manipulators of the marketplace. And to move us through the complexities of the plot while simultaneously emphasizing its universal peril, another idea joined forces with the primary concept. How better to do it than with two people, each possessing a consummate hatred of the other, forced to recognize that their personal conflicts were dwarfed by the spreading cancer that was enveloping both the East and the West.

They would be two mature superbly trained intelligence officers, one from Washington, the other from Moscow, each having caused the death of his adversary's loved ones. Their mutual loathing would have to be dramatically illustrated through flashbacks, perhaps, showing the pain each had suffered by the other's hand, thus illuminating the universal pain experienced by any human being, regardless of moral, political or religious convictions. Stripped to the essentials, we think, we perceive, we love, we hate. It's only *in extremis* that we choose the paths we instinctively believe we should take, hoping beyond our rational ability to hope, praying to whatever gods or non-gods we can conjure up, that we have chosen the right tracks to follow.

In this way, I felt, with two such figures, larger than life, perhaps, but no more than ordinary in their feelings, could the pervasive evil of the *Matarese* (or, as they say in Corsica, the *Mataresa*) be brought into full and devastating focus.

That's how *The Matarese Circle* came about.

The Bourne Identity: The origins of this novel were the stuff of which fiction is made, but I assure you it wasn't fantasy but fact. I know because it happened to me. I lost approximately four hours of my life and found a character. Let's go back.

This odd tale begins one evening in 1978 with a gentleman named Pierre Salinger, a most talented fellow whom I've never met but to whom I am indebted. You see, several years previously I had written a book entitled *The Chancellor Manuscript,* and for the French translation, *L'homme qui fit trembler l'Amérique,* Mr. Salinger, who lives in Paris, provided a wonderful introduction. On this particular evening my wife noticed in the "TV Highlights" of a newspaper that Mr. Salinger was broadcasting from Vienna. Although the time conflicted with another engagement, we decided to "arrive late" so as to watch the former White House press secretary—sort of a remote *thank you,* as it were.

During the broadcast, Mr. Salinger made note of the fact that the terrorist and assassin-for-hire, Carlos the Jackal, had been spotted in Vienna but had once again escaped the dragnet. I was both fascinated and repelled. Fascinated by the terrible legend, repelled by the news that he had not been caught, that he was free to kill again, as he surely would—and did.

The broadcast over, I went into my office and began making notes for myself. Mary pulled me away to attend the function we had previously scheduled and on the way there I told her what I had in mind. Stripped to its essentials, it was: *What would be the most credible scenario for the capture of Carlos the Jackal? How could it be done? How could this killer of killers be drawn out and taken?* I think my wife was as excited as I was by the premise because we returned home early and I stayed up half the night working on the concept.

Now, we must, as they say in screenplays, Fade Out and Fade In on the next morning. I was between novels, so contrary to my normal working routine I joined Mary for coffee on the sun porch. She eyed me with suspicion and even pulled her concentration away from The *New York Times* crossword puzzle—in itself an act of supreme self-denial.

"You're not dressed and you haven't shaved," she said.

"You're very observant," I replied. "And we're not heading out to Ascot for strawberries and cream, either."

"But you *are* going into town," she rejoined.

"Since when?"

"Since yesterday afternoon, dummy, when Ed was here. You and he agreed to meet tomorrow morning in New York. He made phone calls and set up the appointment and *this* is 'tomorrow morning.' "

"I knew one day that damned puzzle would drive you into the trees. Ed wasn't here yesterday afternoon."

"Of course he was."

"Of course he wasn't."

"Then just who *was* that attractive man who kept drumming his fingers on the table while you explained the irrelevance of filling out stubs in a checkbook because the bank did that kind of thing."

"The logic's incontestable, but Ed wasn't here."

For the sake of the gentle readers' gentle ears, I shall employ that time-honored parenthesis [*expletives deleted*], and state simply that I picked up the sun-porch phone to confirm my wife's certifiability for a room made of thick sponge rubber. The "Ed" in question was my manager before an early retirement (for which some say I was exclusively responsible) and his lovely wife, Norma, is Mary's co-conspirator in all things, especially the *Times* crossword puzzles. (Can you imagine a call placed from Kowloon, Hong Kong to Long Island, New York, because "I'm stuck on thirty-five across?" It happened.)

"Hello there, Ed, old boy!" saith I, chuckling in my superior knowledge. "How are you, buddy?"

"I'm fine. How are you, and perhaps more to the point, *where* are you?"

"At home, just finishing coffee," I answered, a hollow sickness spreading through my stomach.

"You'd better get a move on, Robert. The traffic on the highway can be pretty heavy."

"The appointment . . . right?"

"They'll be here in an hour."

"Right!"

"By the way, tell Mary I'm sorry I ate all the shrimp yesterday, but I loved the sauce."

"Right!"

Hanging up, I looked across at my wife, who pretended to be engrossed in that lousy, ill-begotten, nefarious, infamous crossword puzzle (do you get the idea that I can't do them?) and bolted from my chair. The fact that she did not indulge in the insidious game of I-told-you-so is just one more reason among several thousand that we've been married for thirty-eight years. Why, from her point of view, I can't possibly answer.

Nevertheless, on my way upstairs I slunk into my office for a moment and gazed at the voluminous notes I'd made the night before. At that moment the terrible realization hit me. It was more frightening than I can rationally explain, for there was no rational explanation. I had *lost* an entire afternoon, my mind had blotted it out! Then, suddenly, as I stared down at those yellow legal pages filled with illegible handwritten script, I knew I'd found the key to a character who became Jason Bourne. *Amnesia.*

As with the addendum to *Holcroft,* I must digress here, if for no other reason than to thank a great many people. In 1980, on a television talk show, I recounted this experience, and as a result received several hundred letters, many from doctors, explaining my temporary loss of memory, and I thank all of you who wrote. The majority concurred with what I had learned from the professional advice I had sought. No big deal; it's a common occurrence among people of my Type A, who tend to work compulsively in long stretches without reasonable breaks from intense concentration. Translation: The guy's not too smart in the pacing department. Don't put him in a marathon.

So here was a concept, a "spine" for a novel that got bent out of shape by an unforeseen event over which I had no control. I could not have wished for a better intrusion.

Finally, I must return to my opening statement. It *is* difficult to write an introduction of this kind because an author's self-doubts, which are constant, can be fueled by the nagging question, *Does anybody really care how he writes a book?*

Just get on with it, chum. Nevertheless, in attempting to do what was asked of me, it brought back vibrant memories, some still startling, others intriguing, many amusing—all in the broadest sense, satisfying. Together they form a large part of the canvas that is the story of my experiences as a writer. More important, it reminded me of how very, very fortunate I am. Thank you for making it possible.

—Robert Ludlum
January 1989
Florida

THE
HOLCROFT
COVENANT

For Michael and Laura—

A lovely, talented, wonderful couple

PROLOGUE

The hull of the submarine was lashed to the huge pilings, a behemoth strapped in silhouette, the sweeping lines of its bow arcing into the light of the North Sea dawn.

The base was on the island of Scharhörn, in the Helgoland Bight, several miles from the German mainland and the mouth of the Elbe River. It was a refueling station never detected by Allied Intelligence and, in the cause of security, little known among the strategists of the German High Command itself. The undersea marauders came and went in darkness, emerging and submerging within several hundred feet of the moorings. They were Neptune's assassins, come home to rest or going forth to press their attacks.

On this particular dawn, however, the submarine lashed to the dock was doing neither. For it, the war was over, its assignment intrinsic to the origins of another war.

Two men stood in the well of the conning tower, one in the uniform of a commanding officer of the German Navy, the other a tall civilian in a long dark overcoat—the collar turned up to ward off the North Sea winds—yet hatless, as if to defy the North Sea winter. Both looked down at the long line of passengers who slowly made their way toward the gangplank amidships. As each passenger reached the plank, a name was checked off against a list, and then he or she was led—or carried—aboard a submarine.

A few walked by themselves, but they were the exceptions. They were the oldest, some having reached their twelfth or thirteenth birthdays.

The rest were children. Infants in the arms of stern-faced army nurses, who surrendered their charges to a unit of navy doctors at the plank; preschoolers, and early graders clutching identical traveling kits and one another's hands, peering up at the strange black vessel that was to be their home for weeks to come.

"Incredible," said the officer. "Simply incredible."

"It's the beginning," replied the man in the overcoat, his sharp, angular features rigid. "Word comes from everywhere. From the ports and the mountain passes, from the remaining airfields all over the Reich. They go out by the thousands. To every part of the world. And people are waiting for them. Every-where."

"An extraordinary accomplishment," said the officer, shaking his head in awe.

"This is only one part of the strategy. The entire operation is extraordinary."

"It's an honor to have you here."

"I wanted to be. This is the last shipment." The tall civilian kept his eyes on the dock below. "The Third Reich is dying. These are its rebirth. These are the *Fourth* Reich. Unencumbered by mediocrity and corruption. These are the *Sonnenkinder.* All over the world."

"The children . . ."

"The Children of the Damned," said the tall man, interrupting. "They are the Children of the Damned, as millions will be. But none will be like these. And these will be everywhere."

1

JANUARY 197—

"Attention! Le train de sept heures à destination de Zürich partira du quai numéro douze."

The tall American in the dark-blue raincoat glanced up at the cavernous dome of the Geneva railway station, trying to locate the hidden speakers. The expression on his sharp, angular face was quizzical; the announcement was in French, a language he spoke but little and understood less. Nevertheless, he was able to distinguish the word *Zürich;* it was his signal. He brushed aside the light-brown hair that fell with irritating regularity over his forehead and started for the north end of the station.

The crowds were heavy. Bodies rushed past the American in all directions, hurrying to the gates to begin their journeys to scores of different destinations. None seemed to pay attention to the harsh announcements that echoed throughout the upper chambers in a continuous metallic monotone. The travelers in Geneva's *Bahnhof* knew where they were going. It was the end of the week; the new mountain snows had fallen and the air outside was crisp and chilling. There were places to go, schedules to keep, and people to see; time wasted was time stolen. Everyone hurried.

The American hurried, too, for he also had a schedule to keep and a person to see. He had learned before the announcement that the train for Zürich would leave from track twelve. According to the plan, he was to walk down the ramp to the platform, count seven cars from the rear, and board at the first entrance. Inside, he was to count again, this time five compartments, and knock twice on the fifth door. If everything was in order, he would be admitted by a director of

La Grande Banque de Genève, signifying the culmination of twelve weeks of preparations. Preparations that included purposely obscured cablegrams, transatlantic calls made and received on telephones the Swiss banker had determined were sterile, and a total commitment to secrecy.

He did not know what the director of La Grande Banque de Genève had to say to him, but he thought he knew why the precautions were deemed necessary. The American's name was Noel Holcroft, but Holcroft had not been his name at birth. He was born in Berlin in the summer of 1939, and the name on the hospital registry was "Clausen." His father was Heinrich Clausen, master strategist of the Third Reich, the financial magician who put together the coalition of disparate economic forces that insured the supremacy of Adolf Hitler.

Heinrich Clausen won the country but lost a wife. Althene Clausen was an American; more to the point, she was a headstrong woman with her own standards of ethics and morality. She had deduced that the National Socialists possessed neither; they were a collection of paranoiacs, led by a maniac, and supported by financiers interested solely in profits.

Althene Clausen gave her husband an ultimatum on a warm afternoon in August: Withdraw. Stand against the paranoiacs and the maniac before it was too late. In disbelief, the Nazi listened and laughed and dismissed his wife's ultimatum as the foolish ravings of a new mother. Or perhaps the warped judgment of a woman brought up in a weak, discredited system that would soon march to the step of the New Order. Or be crushed under its boot.

That night the new mother packed herself and the new child and took one of the last planes to London, the first leg on her journey back to New York. A week later the Blitzkrieg was executed against Poland; the Thousand Year Reich had begun its own journey, one that would last some fifteen hundred days from the first sound of gunfire.

Holcroft walked through the gate, down the ramp, and on to the long concrete platform. *Four, five, six, seven.* . . . The seventh car had a small blue circle stenciled beneath the window to the left of the open door. It was the symbol of accommodations superior to those in first class: enlarged compartments properly outfitted for conferences in transit or clandestine meetings of a more personal nature. Privacy was guaranteed; once the train was moving, the doors at either end of the car were manned by armed railway guards.

Holcroft entered and turned left into the corridor. He walked past successive closed doors until he reached the fifth. He knocked twice.

"Herr Holcroft?" The voice behind the wood panel was firm but quiet, and although the two words were meant as a question, the voice was not questioning. It made a statement.

"Herr Manfredi?" said Noel in reply, suddenly aware that an eye was peering at him through the pinpoint viewer in the center of the door. It was an eerie feeling, diminished by the comic effect. He smiled to himself and wondered if Herr Manfredi would look like the sinister Conrad Veidt in one of those 1930s English films.

There were two clicks of a lock, followed by the sound of a sliding bolt. The door swung back and the image of Conrad Veidt vanished. Ernst Manfredi was a short, rotund man in his middle to late sixties. He was completely bald, with a pleasant, gentle face; but the wide blue eyes, magnified beyond the metal-framed glasses, were cold. Very light blue and very cold.

"Come in, Herr Holcroft," said Manfredi, smiling. Then his expression changed abruptly; the smile disappeared. "Do forgive me. I should say *Mister* Holcroft. The *Herr* may be offensive to you. My apologies."

"None necessary," replied Noel, stepping into the well-appointed compartment. There was a table, two chairs, no bed in evidence. The walls were wood-paneled; dark-red velvet curtains covered the windows, muffling the sounds of the figures rushing by outside. On the table was a small lamp with a fringed shade.

"We have about twenty-five minutes before departure," the banker said. "It should be adequate. And don't be concerned—we'll be given ample warning. The train won't start until you've disembarked. You'll not have to travel to Zürich."

"I've never been there."

"I trust that will be changed," said the banker enigmatically, gesturing for Holcroft to sit opposite him at the table.

"I wouldn't count on it." Noel sat down, unbuttoning his raincoat but not removing it.

"I'm sorry, that was presumptuous of me." Manfredi took his seat and leaned back in the chair. "I must apologize once again. I'll need your identification. Your passport, please. And your international driver's license. Also, whatever documents you have on your person that describe physical markings, vaccinations, that sort of thing."

Holcroft felt a rush of anger. The inconvenience to his life aside, he disliked the banker's patronizing attitude. "Why should I? You know who I am. You wouldn't have opened that door if you didn't. You probably have more photographs, more information on me, than the State Department."

"Indulge an old man, sir," said the banker, shrugging in self-deprecation, his charm on display. "It will be made clear to you."

Reluctantly, Noel reached into his jacket pocket and withdrew the leather case that contained his passport, health certificate, international license, and two A.I.A. letters that stated his qualifications as an architect. He handed the case to Manfredi. "It's all there. Help yourself."

With seemingly greater reluctance, the banker opened the case. "I feel as though I'm prying, but I think . . ."

"You should," interrupted Holcroft. "I didn't ask for this meeting. Frankly, it comes at a very inconvenient time. I want to get back to New York as soon as possible."

"Yes. Yes, I understand," said the Swiss quietly, perusing the documents. "Tell me, what was the first architectural commission you undertook outside the United States?"

Noel suppressed his irritation. He had come this far; there was no point in refusing to answer. "Mexico," he replied. "For the Alvarez hotel chain, north of Puerto Vallarta."

"The second?"

"Costa Rica. For the government. A postal complex in 1973."

"What was the gross income of your firm in New York last year? Without adjustments."

"None of your damned business."

"I assure you, we know."

Holcroft shook his head in angry resignation. "A hundred and seventy-three thousand dollars and change."

"Considering office rental, salaries, equipment and expenses, that's not an altogether impressive figure, is it?" asked Manfredi, his eyes still on the papers in his hands.

"It's my own company and the staff is small. I have no partners, no wife, no heavy debts. It could be worse."

"It could be better," said the banker, looking up at Holcroft. "Especially for one so talented."

"It could be better."

"Yes, I thought as much," continued the Swiss, putting the various papers back in the leather case and handing it to Noel. He leaned forward. "Do you know who your father was?"

"I know who my father *is*. Legally, he's Richard Holcroft, of New York, my mother's husband. He's very much alive."

"And retired," completed Manfredi. "A fellow banker, but hardly a banker in the Swiss tradition."

"He was respected. *Is* respected."

"For his family's money or for his professional acumen?"

"Both, I'd say. I love him. If you have reservations, keep them to yourself."

"You're very loyal; that's a quality I admire. Holcroft came along when your mother—an incredible woman, incidentally—was most despondent. But we split definitions. Holcroft is once removed. I referred to your natural father."

"Obviously."

"Thirty years ago, Heinrich Clausen made certain arrangements. He traveled frequently between Berlin, Zürich, and Geneva, beyond official scrutiny, of course. A document was prepared that we as"—Manfredi paused and smiled—". . . as biased neutrals could not oppose. Attached to the document is a letter, written by Clausen in April of 1945. It is addressed to you. His son." The banker reached for a thick manila envelope on the table.

"Just a minute," said Noel. "Did those certain arrangements concern money?"

"Yes."

"I'm not interested. Give it to charity. He owed it."

"You may not feel that way when you've heard the amount."

"What is it?"

"Seven hundred and eighty million dollars."

Holcroft stared at the banker in disbelief; the blood drained from his head. Outside, the sounds of the huge station were a cacophony of muted chords, barely penetrating the thick walls of the car.

"Don't try to absorb it all at once," said Manfredi, placing the letter to one side. "There are conditions, none of them, incidentally, offensive. At least, none we're aware of."

"Conditions? . . ." Holcroft knew he could hardly be heard; he tried to find his voice. "What conditions?"

"They're spelled out very clearly. These vast sums are to be channeled into a great good for people everywhere. And, of course, there are certain benefits to yourself personally."

"What do you mean there's nothing offensive that you're . . . 'aware of'?"

The banker's magnified eyes blinked behind his glasses; he looked away briefly, his expression troubled. He reached into his brown leather briefcase, which lay at the corner of the table, and pulled out a long, thin envelope with curious markings on the back side; they were a series of four circles and appeared to be four dark coins affixed to the border of the flap.

Manfredi held the envelope across the table, under the light. The dark circles were not coins but waxed seals. All were intact.

"Following the instructions given to us thirty years ago, this envelope—unlike your father's letter here—was not to be opened by directors in Geneva. It is separate from the document we prepared, and to the best of our knowledge, Clausen was never aware of it. His own words to you would tend to confirm that. It was brought to us within hours after the courier delivered your father's letter, which was to be our final communication from Berlin."

"What is it?"

"We don't know. We were told it was written by several men aware of your father's activities. Who believed in his cause with great fervor; who considered him in many ways a true martyr of Germany. We were instructed to give it to you with the seals unbroken. You were to read it before you saw your father's letter." Manfredi turned the envelope over. There was writing on the front side. The words were in German and written by hand. "You are to sign below, so to state that you received it in the proper condition."

Noel took the envelope and read the words he could not understand.

Dieser Brief ist mit ungebrochenem Siegel empfangen worden. Neuaufbau oder Tod.

"What does it say?"

"That you've examined the seals and are satisfied."

"How can I be sure?"

"Young man, you're talking with a director of La Grande Banque de Genève." The Swiss did not raise his voice but the rebuke was clear. "You have my word. And, in any event, what difference does it make?"

None, reasoned Holcroft, yet the obvious question bothered him. "If I sign the envelope, what do you do with it?"

Manfredi was silent for several moments, as if deciding whether or not to answer. He removed his glasses, took a silk handkerchief from his breast pocket, and cleaned them. Finally he replied. "That is privileged information. . . ."

"So's my signature," interrupted Noel. "Privileged, that is."

"Let me finish," protested the banker, putting back his glasses. "I was about to say it was privileged information that can't possibly be relevant any longer. Not after so many years. The envelope is to be sent to a post-office box in Sesimbra, Portugal. It is south of Lisbon, on the Cape of Espichel."

"Why isn't it relevant?"

Manfredi held up the palms of his hands. "The post-office box no longer exists. The envelope will find its way to a dead-letter office and eventually be returned to us."

"You're sure?"

"I believe it, yes."

Noel reached into his pocket for his pen, turning the envelope over to look once again at the waxed seals. They had not been tampered with; and, thought Holcroft, what difference *did* it make? He placed the envelope in front of him and signed his name.

Manfredi held up his hand. "You understand, whatever is contained in that envelope can have no bearing on our participation in the document prepared by La Grande Banque de Genève. We were not consulted; nor were we apprised of the contents."

"You sound worried. I thought you said it didn't make any difference. It was too long ago."

"Fanatics always worry me, Mr. Holcroft. Time and consequence cannot alter that judgment. It's a banker's caution."

Noel began cracking the wax; it had hardened over the years and took considerable force before it fell away. He tore the flap open, removed the single page, and unfolded it.

The paper was brittle with age; the white had turned to a pale brownish yellow. The writing was in English, the letters printed in an odd block lettering that was Germanic in style. The ink was faded but legible. Holcroft looked at the bottom of the page for a signature. There was none. He started reading.

The message was macabre, born in desperation thirty years ago. It was as though unbalanced men had sat in a darkened room, studying shadows on the wall for signs of the future, studying a man and a life not yet formed.

From this moment on the son of Heinrich Clausen is to be tested. There are those who may learn of the work in Geneva and who will try to stop him, whose only purpose in life will be to kill him, thus destroying the dream conceived by the giant that was his father.

This must not happen, for we were betrayed—all of us—and the world must know what we really were, not what the betrayers showed us to be, for those were the portraits of traitors. Not us. And particularly not Heinrich Clausen.

We are the survivors of Wolfsschanze. We seek the cleansing of our names, the restoration of the honor that was stolen from us.

Therefore the men of Wolfsschanze will protect the son for as long as the son pursues the father's dream and returns our honor to us. But should the son abandon the dream, betray the father, and withhold our honor, he will have no life. He will witness the anguish of loved ones, of family, children, friends. No one will be spared.

None must interfere. Give us our honor. It is our right and we demand it.

Noel shoved the chair back and stood up. *"What the hell is this?"*

"I've no idea," replied Manfredi quietly, his voice calm but his large, cold blue eyes conveying his alarm. "I told you we were not apprised. . . ."

"Well, *get* apprised!" shouted Holcroft. "Read it! Who *were* these clowns? Certifiable *lunatics?"*

The banker began reading. Without looking up, he answered softly. "First cousins to lunatics. Men who'd lost hope."

"What's *Wolfsschanze?* What does it mean?"

"It was the name of Hitler's staff headquarters in East Prussia, where the attempt to assassinate him took place. It was a conspiracy of the generals: Von Stauffenberg, Kluge, Höpner—they were all implicated. All shot. Rommel took his own life."

Holcroft stared at the paper in Manfredi's hands. "You mean it was written thirty years ago by people like that?"

The banker nodded, his eyes narrowed in astonishment. "Yes, but it's not the language one might have expected of them. This is nothing short of a threat; it's unreasonable. Those men were not unreasonable. On the other hand, the times *were* unreasonable. Decent men, brave men, were stretched beyond the parameters of sanity. They were living through a hell none of us can picture today."

"Decent men?" asked Noel incredulously.

"Have you any idea what it meant to be a part of the Wolfsschanze conspiracy? A bloodbath followed, thousands massacred everywhere, the vast majority never having heard of Wolfsschanze. It was yet another final solution, an excuse to still all dissent throughout Germany. What began as an act to rid the world of a madman ended in a holocaust all its own. The survivors of Wolfsschanze saw that happen."

"Those survivors," replied Holcroft, "followed that madman for a long time."

"You must understand. And you will. These were desperate men. They were caught in a trap, and for them it was cataclysmic. A world they had helped create was revealed not to be the world they envisioned. Horrors they never dreamed of were uncovered, yet they couldn't avoid their responsibility for them. They were appalled at what they saw but couldn't deny the roles they played."

"The well-intentioned Nazi," said Noel. "I've heard of that elusive breed."

"One would have to go back in history, to the economic disasters, to the

Versailles Treaty, the Pact of Locarno, the Bolshevik encroachments—to a dozen different forces—to understand."

"I understand what I just read," Holcroft said. "Your poor misunderstood storm troopers didn't hesitate to threaten someone they couldn't know! 'He will have no life . . . no one spared . . . family, friends, children.' That spells out murder. Don't talk to me about well-intentioned killers."

"They're the words of old, sick, desperate men. They have no meaning now. It was their way of expressing their own anguish, of seeking atonement. They're gone. Leave them in peace. Read your father's letter . . ."

"He's *not* my father!" interrupted Noel.

"Read Heinrich Clausen's letter. Things will be clearer. Read it. We have several items to discuss and there isn't much time."

A man in a brown tweed overcoat and dark Tirolean hat stood by a pillar across from the seventh car. At first glance, there was nothing particularly distinguishing about him, except perhaps his eyebrows. They were thick, a mixture of black and light-gray hair that produced the effect of salt-and-pepper archways in the upper regions of a forgettable face.

At first glance. Yet if one looked closer, one could see the blunted but not unrefined features of a very determined man. In spite of the pockets of wind that blew in gusts through the platform, he did not blink. His concentration on the seventh car was absolute.

The American would come out of that doorway, thought the man by the pillar, a much different person from the American who went in. During the past few minutes his life had been changed in ways few men in this world would ever experience. Yet it was only the beginning; the journey he was about to embark on was beyond anything of which the present-day world could conceive. So it was important to observe his initial reaction. More than important. Vital.

"*Attention! Le train de sept heures . . .*"

The final announcement came over the speakers. Simultaneously, a train from Lausanne was arriving on the adjacent track. In moments the platform would be jammed with tourists flocking into Geneva for the weekend, the way Midlanders scrambled into Charing Cross for a brief fling in London, thought the man by the pillar.

The train from Lausanne came to a stop. The passenger cars disgorged; the platform was again packed with bodies.

The figure of the tall American was suddenly in the vestibule of car seven. He was blocked at the doorway by a porter carrying someone's luggage. It was an irritating moment that might have provoked an argument under normal circumstances. But the circumstances were not normal for Holcroft. He expressed no annoyance; his face was set, unresponsive to the moment, his eyes aware of the physical confusion but not concerned with it. There was an air of detachment about him; he was in the grips of lingering astonishment. This was emphasized by the way he clutched the thick manila envelope between his arm and his chest, his hand curved around the edge, his fingers pressed into the paper with such force they formed a fist.

It was the cause of his consternation, this document prepared a lifetime ago. It was the miracle *they* had waited for, lived for—the man by the pillar and those who had gone before him. More than thirty years of anticipation. And now it had surfaced at last!

The journey had begun.

Holcroft entered the flow of human traffic toward the ramp that led up to the gate. Although jostled by those around him, he was oblivious of the crowds, his eyes absently directed ahead. At nothing.

Suddenly, the man by the pillar was alarmed. Years of training had taught him to look for the unexpected, the infinitesimal break in a normal pattern. He saw that break now. Two men, their faces unlike any around them, joyless, without curiosity or expectation, filled only with hostile intent.

They were surging through the crowds, one man slightly ahead of the other. Their eyes were on the American; they were after him! The man in front had his right hand in his pocket. The man behind had his left hand concealed across his chest, beneath his unbuttoned overcoat. The hidden hands gripped weapons! The man by the pillar was convinced of that.

He sprang away from the concrete column and crashed his way into the crowd. There were no seconds to be lost. The two men were gaining on Holcroft. They were after the envelope! It was the only possible explanation. And if that were the case, it meant that word of the miracle had leaked out of Geneva! The document inside that envelope was priceless, beyond value. Beside it, the American's life was of such inconsequence that no thought would be expended taking that life. The men closing in on Holcroft would kill him for the envelope *mindlessly,* as if removing a disagreeable insect from a bar of gold. And *that* was mindless! What they did not know was that without the son of Heinrich Clausen the miracle would not happen!

They were within yards of him now! The man with the black-and-white eyebrows lunged forward through the mass of tourists like a possessed animal. He crashed into people and luggage, throwing aside everything and everyone in his path. When he was within feet of the killer whose hand was concealed under his overcoat, he thrust his own hand into his pocket, clutching the gun inside, and screamed directly at the assailant:

"Du suchst Clausens Sohn! Das Genfer Dokument!"

The killer was partially up the ramp, separated from the American by only a few people. He heard the words roared at him by a stranger and spun around, his eyes wide in shock.

The crowd pressed rapidly up the ramp, skirting the two obvious antagonists. Attacker and protector were in their own miniature arena, facing each other. The observer squeezed the trigger of the gun in his pocket, then squeezed it again. The spits could barely be heard as the fabric exploded. Two bullets entered the body of Holcroft's would-be assailant, one in the lower stomach, the other far above, in the neck. The first caused the man to convulse forward; the second snapped his head back, the throat torn open.

Blood burst from the neck with such force that it splattered surrounding faces, and the clothes and suitcases belonging to those faces. It cascaded downward, forming small pools and rivulets on the ramp. Screams of horror filled the walkway.

The observer-protector felt a hand gripping his shoulder, digging into his flesh. He spun; the second attacker was on him, but there was no gun in his hand. Instead, the blade of a hunting knife came toward him.

The man was an amateur, thought the observer, as his reactions—instincts born of years of training—came instantly into play. He stepped sideways quickly—a bullfighter avoiding the horns—and clamped his left hand above his assailant's wrist. He pulled his right hand from his pocket and gripped the fingers wrapped around the knife. He snapped the wrist downward, vising the fingers around the handle, tearing the cartilage of the attacker's hand, forcing the blade inward. He plunged it into the soft flesh of the stomach and ripped the sharp steel diagonally up into the rib cage, severing the arteries of the heart. The man's face contorted; a terrible scream was begun, cut off by death.

The pandemonium had escalated into uncontrollable chaos; the screaming increased. The profusion of blood in the center of the rushing, colliding bodies fueled the hysteria. The observer-protector knew precisely what to do. He threw up his hands in frightened consternation, in sudden, total revulsion at the sight of the blood on his own clothes, and joined the hysterical crowd racing away like a herd of terrified cattle from the concrete killing ground.

He rushed up the ramp past the American whose life he had just saved.

Holcroft heard the screaming. It penetrated the numbing mists he felt engulfed in: clouds of vapor that swirled around him, obscuring his vision, inhibiting all thought.

He tried to turn toward the commotion, but the hysterical crowd prevented him from doing so. He was swept farther up the ramp and pummeled into the three-foot-high cement wall that served as a railing. He gripped the stone and looked back, unable to see clearly what had happened; he did see a man below arch backward, blood erupting from his throat. He saw a second man lunging forward, his mouth stretched in agony, and then Noel could see no more, the onslaught of bodies sweeping him once again up the concrete ramp.

A man rushed by, crashing into his shoulder. Holcroft turned in time to see frightened eyes beneath a pair of thick black-and-white brows.

An act of violence had taken place. An attempted robbery had turned into an assault, into a killing, perhaps. Peaceful Geneva was no more immune to violence than were the wild streets of New York at night, or the impoverished alleyways of Marrakesh.

But Noel could not dwell on such things; he could not be involved. He had other things to think about. The mists of numbness returned. Through them he vaguely understood that his life would never again be the same.

He gripped the envelope in his hand and joined the screaming mass racing up the ramp to the gate.

3

The huge aircraft passed over Cape Breton Island and dipped gently to the left, descending into its new altitude and heading. The route was now southwest, toward Halifax and Boston, then into New York.

Holcroft had spent most of the time in the upstairs lounge, at a single chair in the right rear corner, his black attaché case against the bulkhead. It was easier to concentrate there; no straying eyes of an adjacent passenger could fall on the papers he read and reread, again and again.

He had begun with the letter from Heinrich Clausen, that unknown but all-pervading presence. It was an incredible document in itself. The information contained in it was of such an alarming nature that Manfredi had expressed the collective wish of the Grande Banque's directors that it be destroyed. For it detailed in general terms the sources of the millions banked in Geneva three decades ago. Although the majority of these sources were untouchable in any contemporary legal sense—thieves and murderers stealing the national funds of a government headed by thieves and murderers—other sources were not so immune to modern scrutiny. Throughout the war Germany had plundered. It had raped internally and externally. The dissenters within had been stripped; the conquered without, stolen from unmercifully. Should the memories of these thefts be dredged up, the international courts in The Hague could tie up the funds for years in protracted litigations.

"Destroy the letter," Manfredi had said in Geneva. "It's necessary only that you understand why he did what he did. Not the methods; they are a complication without any conceivable resolution. But there are those who may try to stop you. Other thieves would move in; we're dealing in hundreds of millions."

Noel reread the letter for perhaps the twentieth time. Each time he did so, he tried to picture the man who wrote it. His natural father. He had no idea what Heinrich Clausen looked like; his mother had destroyed all photographs, all communications, all references whatsoever to the man she loathed with all her being.

Berlin, 20 April 1945

My Son.
    I write this as the armies of the Reich collapse on all fronts. Berlin will soon fall, a city of raging fires and death everywhere. So be it. I shall waste no moments on what was, or what might have been. On concepts betrayed, and the triumph of evil over good through the treachery of morally bankrupt leaders. Recriminations born in hell are too suspect, the authorship too easily attributed to the devil.

Instead, I shall permit my actions to speak for me. In them, you may find some semblance of pride. That is my prayer.

Amends must be made. That is the credo I have come to recognize. As have my two dearest friends and closest associates who are identified in the attached document. Amends for the destruction we have wrought, for betrayals so heinous the world will never forget. Or forgive. It is in the interest of partial forgiveness that we have done what we have done.

Five years ago your mother made a decision I could not comprehend, so blind were my loyalties to the New Order. Two winters ago—in February of 1943—the words she spoke in rage, words I arrogantly dismissed as lies fed her by those who despised the Fatherland, were revealed to be the truth. We who labored in the rarefied circles of finance and policy had been deceived. For two years it was clear that Germany was going down to defeat. We pretended otherwise, but in our hearts we knew it was so. Others knew it, too. And they became careless. The horrors surfaced, the deceptions were clear.

Twenty-five months ago I conceived of a plan and enlisted the support of my dear friends in the Finanzministerium. Their support was willingly given. Our objective was to divert extraordinary sums of money into neutral Switzerland, funds that could be used one day to give aid and succor to those thousands upon thousands whose lives were shattered by unspeakable atrocities committed in Germany's name by animals who knew nothing of German honor.

We know now about the camps. The names will haunt history. Belsen, Dachau, Auschwitz.

We have been told of the mass executions, of the helpless men, women and children lined up in front of trenches dug by their own hands, then slaughtered.

We have learned of the ovens—oh, God in heaven—ovens for human flesh! Of the showers that sprayed not cleansing water but lethal gas. Of intolerable, obscene experiments carried out on conscious human beings by insane practitioners of a medical science unknown to man. We bleed at the images, and our eyes burst, but our tears can do nothing. Our minds, however, are not so helpless. We can plan.

Amends must be made.

We cannot restore life. We cannot bring back what was so brutally, viciously taken. But we can seek out all those who survived, and the children of those both surviving and slaughtered, and do what we can. They must be sought out all over the world and shown that we have not forgotten. We are ashamed and we wish to help. In any way that we can. It is to this end that we have done what we have done.

I do not for a moment believe that our actions can expiate our sins, those crimes we were unknowingly a part of. Yet we do what we can—I do what I can—haunted with every breath by your mother's perceptions. Why, oh eternal God, did I not listen to that great and good woman?

To return to the plan.

Using the American dollar as the equivalent currency of exchange, our goal was ten million monthly, a figure that might appear excessive, but not when one considers the capital flow through the economic maze of the Finanzministerium at the height of the war. We exceeded our goal.

Using the Finanzministerium, we appropriated funds from hundreds of sources within the Reich and to a great extent beyond, throughout Germany's ever-expanding borders. Taxes were diverted, enormous expenditures made from the Ministry of Armaments for nonexistent purchases, Wehrmacht payrolls rerouted, and monies sent to occupation territories constantly intercepted, lost. Funds from expropriated estates, and from the great fortunes, factories, and individually held companies, did not find their way into the Reich's economy but, instead, into our accounts. Sales of art objects from scores of museums throughout the conquered lands were converted to our cause. It was a master plan carried out masterfully. Whatever risks we took and terrors we faced—and they were daily occurrences—were inconsequential compared to the meaning of our credo: Amends must be made.

Yet no plan can be termed a success unless the objective is secured permanently. A military strategy that captures a port only to lose it to an invasion from the sea a day later is no strategy at all. One must consider all possible assaults, all interferences that could negate the strategy. One must project, as thoroughly as projection allows, the changes mandated by time, and protect the objective thus far attained. In essence, one must use time to the strategy's advantage. We have endeavored to do this through the conditions put forth in the attached document.

Would to the Almighty that we could give aid to the victims and their survivors sooner than our projections allow, but to do so would rivet attention to the sums we have appropriated. Then all could be lost. A generation must pass for the strategy to succeed. Even then there is risk, but time will have diminished it.

The air-raid sirens keep up their incessant wailing. Speaking of time, there is very little left now. For myself and my two associates, we wait only for confirmation that this letter has reached Zürich through an underground courier. Upon receipt of the news, we have our own pact. Our pact with death, each by his own hand.

Answer my prayer. Help us atone. Amends must be made.

This is our covenant, my son. My only son, whom I have never known but to whom I have brought such sorrow. Abide by it, honor it, for it is an honorable thing I ask you to do.

Your father,
HEINRICH CLAUSEN

Holcroft put the letter facedown on the table and glanced out the window at the blue sky above the clouds. Far in the distance was the exhaust of another aircraft; he followed the streak of vapor until he could see the tiny silver gleam of the fuselage.

He thought about the letter. Again. The writing was maudlin; the words were from another era, melodramatic. It did not weaken the letter; rather, it gave it a certain strength of conviction. Clausen's sincerity was unquestioned; his emotions were genuine.

What was only partially communicated, however, was the brilliance of the plan itself. Brilliant in its simplicity, extraordinary in its use of time and the laws of finance to achieve both execution and protection. For the three men understood that sums of the magnitude they had stolen could not be sunk in a lake or buried in vaults. The hundreds of millions had to exist in the financial marketplace, not subject to discontinued currency or to brokers who would have to convert and sell elusive assets.

Hard money had to be deposited, the responsibility for its security given to one of the world's most revered institutions, La Grande Banque de Genève. Such an institution would not—could not—permit abuses where liquidity was concerned; it was an international economic rock. All the conditions of its contract with its depositors would be observed. Everything was to be legal in the eyes of Swiss law. Covert—as was the custom of the trade—but ironbound with respect to existing legalities, and thus current with the times. The intent of the contract—the document—could not be corrupted; the objectives would be followed to the letter.

To permit corruption or malfeasance was unthinkable. Thirty years . . . *fifty* years . . . in terms of the financial calendar was very little time, indeed.

Noel reached down and opened his attaché case. He slipped the pages of the letter into a compartment and pulled out the document from La Grande Banque de Genève. It was encased in a leather cover, folded in the manner of a last will and testament, which it was—and then some. He leaned back in the chair and unfastened the clasp that allowed the cover to unfold, revealing the first page of the document.

His "covenant," Holcroft reflected.

He skimmed over the words and the paragraphs, now so familiar to him, flipping the pages as he did so, concentrating on the salient points.

The identities of Clausen's two associates in the massive theft were Erich Kessler and Wilhelm von Tiebolt. The names were vital not so much for identifying the two men themselves as for seeking out and contacting the oldest child of each. It was the first condition of the document. Although the designated proprietor of the numbered account was one Noel C. Holcroft, *American*, funds were to be released only upon the signatures of all three oldest children. And then only if each child satisfied the directors of La Grande Banque that he or she accepted the conditions and objectives set forth by the original proprietors with respect to the allocation of the funds.

However, if these offspring did not satisfy the Swiss directors or were judged to be incompetent, their brothers and sisters were to be studied and further judgments made. If all the children were considered incapable of the responsibility, the millions would wait for another generation, when further sealed instructions would be opened by executors and by issue yet unborn. The resolve was devastating: *another* generation.

The legitimate son of Heinrich Clausen is now known as Noel Holcroft, a child, living with his mother and stepfather in America. At the specific date chosen by the directors of La Grande Banque de Genève—not to be less than thirty years, nor more than thirty-five—said legitimate son of Heinrich Clausen is to be contacted and his responsibilities made known to him. He is to reach his coinheritors and activate the account under the conditions set forth. He shall be the conduit through which the funds are to be dispensed to the victims of the Holocaust, their families and surviving issue. . . .

The three Germans gave their reasons for the selection of Clausen's son as the conduit. The child had entered into a family of wealth and consequence . . . an *American* family, above suspicion. All traces of his mother's first marriage and flight from Germany had been obscured by the devoted Richard Holcroft. It was understood that in the pursuit of this obscurity a death certificate had been issued in London for an infant male named Clausen, dated February 17, 1942, and a subsequent birth certificate filed in New York City for the male child Holcroft. The additional years would further obscure events to the point of obliteration. The infant male Clausen would someday *become* the man Holcroft, with no visible relationship to his origins. Yet those origins could not be denied, and, therefore, he was the perfect choice, satisfying both the demands and the objectives of the document.

An international agency was to be established in Zürich, which would serve as headquarters for the dispersal of the funds, the source of the funds to be held confidential in perpetuity. Should a spokesman be required, it was to be the American, Holcroft, for the others could never be mentioned by name. Ever. They were the children of Nazis, and their exposure would inevitably raise demands that the account be examined, that its various sources be revealed. And if the account *was* examined, its sources even hinted at, forgotten confiscations and appropriations would be remembered. The international courts would be swamped with litigations.

But if the spokesman was a man without the Nazi stain, there would be no cause for alarm, no examinations, no demands for exhumation or litigation. He would act in concert with the others, each possessing one vote in all decisions, but he alone would be visible. The children of Erich Kessler and Wilhelm von Tiebolt were to remain anonymous.

Noel wondered what the "children" of Kessler and Von Tiebolt were like. He would find out soon.

The final conditions of the document were no less startling than anything that preceded them. All the monies were to be allocated within *six months* of the release of the account. Such an imposition would demand a total commitment from each of the offspring, and that was precisely what the depositors demanded: total commitment to their cause. Lives would be interrupted, sacrifices required. The commitments had to be paid for. Therefore, at the end of the six-month period and the successful allocation of the funds to the victims of the Holocaust, the Zürich agency was to be disbanded and each descendant was to receive the sum of two million dollars.

Six months. Two million dollars.

Two million.

Noel considered what that meant to him personally and professionally. It was freedom. Manfredi had said in Geneva that he was talented. He *was* talented, but frequently that talent was obscured in the final product. He'd had to accept assignments he would have preferred not to take; had to compromise designs when the architect in him dictated otherwise; had to refuse jobs he wanted very much to do, because financial pressures prohibited time spent on lesser commissions. He was turning into a cynic.

Nothing was permanent; planned obsolescence went hand in hand with depreciation and amortization. No one knew it better than an architect who once had a conscience. Perhaps he would find his conscience again. With freedom. With the two million.

Holcroft was startled by the progression of his thoughts. He had made up his mind, something he had not intended to do until he'd thought things through. Everything. Yet he was reclaiming a misplaced conscience with money he had convinced himself he was capable of rejecting.

What *were* they like, these oldest children of Erich Kessler and Wilhelm von Tiebolt? One was a woman; the other, a man, a scholar. But beyond the differences of sex and profession, they had been a part of something he had never known. They'd been there; they'd seen it. Neither had been too young to remember.

Each had lived in that strange, demonic world that was the Third Reich. The American would have so many questions to ask.

Questions to ask? *Questions?*

He had made his decision. He had told Manfredi he would need time—a few days at least—before he could decide.

"Do you really have a choice?" the Swiss banker had asked.

"Very much so," Noel had replied. "I'm not for sale, regardless of conditions. And I'm not frightened by threats made by maniacs thirty years ago."

"Nor should you be. Discuss it with your mother."

"What?" Holcroft was stunned. "I thought you said . . ."

"Complete secrecy? Yes, but your mother is the single exception."

"Why? I'd think she'd be the last . . ."

"She's the first. And only. She'll honor the confidence."

Manfredi had been right. If his answer was yes, he would by necessity suspend his firm's activities and begin his travels to make contact with the offspring of Kessler and Von Tiebolt. His mother's curiosity would be aroused; she was not a woman to let her curiosity lie dormant. She would make inquiries, and if, by any chance—however remote—she unearthed information about the millions in Geneva and Heinrich Clausen's role in the massive theft, her reaction would be violent. Her memories of the paranoiac gangsters of the Third Reich were indelibly printed on her mind. If she made damaging disclosures public, the funds would be tied up in the international courts for years.

"Suppose she isn't persuaded?"

"You must be convincing. The letter is convincing, and we'll step in, if need be. Regardless, it's better to know her position at the outset."

What would that position be? Noel wondered. Althene was not your run-of-the-mill mother, as mothers were understood by this particular son. He knew very early in life that Althene was different. She did not fit into the mold of the wealthy Manhattan matron. The trappings were there—or had been. The horses, the boats, the weekends in Aspen and in the Hamptons, but not the frantic chase for ever-expanding acceptance and social control.

She'd done it all before. She'd lived in the turbulence that was the European thirties, a young, carefree American whose family had something left after the crash and were more comfortable away from their less-fortunate peers. She had known the Court of St. James's as well as the expatriate *salons* in Paris . . . and the dashing new inheritors of Germany. And out of those years had come a serenity shaped by love, exhaustion, loathing, and rage.

Althene was a special person, as much a friend as a mother, that friendship deep and without the need for constant reaffirmation. In point of fact, thought Holcroft, she was more friend than mother; she was never entirely comfortable in the latter role.

"I've made too many mistakes, my dear," she had said to him once, laughing, "to assume an authority based on biology."

Now he would ask her to face the memory of a man she had spent a great deal of her life trying to forget. Would she be frightened? That wasn't likely. Would she doubt the objectives set forth in the document given him by Ernst Manfredi? How could she, after reading the letter from Heinrich Clausen. Whatever her memories, his mother was a woman of intellect and perception. All men were subject to change, to remorse. She would have to accept that, no matter how distasteful it might be to her in this particular case.

It was the weekend; tomorrow was Sunday. His mother and stepfather spent the weekends at their house in the country, in Bedford Hills. In the morning he would drive up and have that talk.

And on Monday he would take the first steps on a trip that would lead him back to Switzerland. To an as yet unknown agency in Zürich. On Monday the hunt would begin.

Noel recalled his exchange with Manfredi. They were among the last words spoken before Holcroft left the train.

"The Kesslers had two sons. The oldest, Erich—named for the father—is a professor of history at the University of Berlin. The younger brother, Hans, is a doctor in Munich. From what we know, both are highly regarded in their respective communities. They're very close. Once Erich is told of the situation, he may insist on his brother's inclusion."

"Is that permitted?"

"There's nothing in the document that prohibits it. However, the stipend remains the same and each family has but one vote in all decisions."

"What about the Von Tiebolts?"

"Another story, I'm afraid. They may be a problem for you. After the war the records show that the mother and two children fled to Rio de Janeiro. Five or six years ago they disappeared. Literally. The police have no information. No address, no business associations, no listings in the other major cities. And that's unusual; the mother became quite successful for a time. No one seems to know what happened, or if people do, they're not willing to say."

"You said two children. Who are they?"

"Actually, there are three children. The youngest, a daughter, Helden, was born after the war, in Brazil, obviously conceived during the last days of the Reich. The oldest is another daughter, Gretchen. The middle child is Johann, the son."

"You say they disappeared?"

"Perhaps it's too dramatic a term. We're bankers, not investigators. Our inquiries were not that extensive, and Brazil is a very large country. *Your* inquiries must be exhaustive. The offspring of each man must be found and scrutinized. It's the first condition of the document; without compliance, the account will not be released."

Holcroft folded the document and put it back in his attaché case. As he did so, his fingers touched the edge of the single sheet of paper with the odd block lettering written by the survivors of Wolfsschanze thirty years ago. Manfredi was right: They were sick old men trying to play their last desperate roles in a drama of the future they barely understood. If they had understood, they would have appealed to the "son of Heinrich Clausen." Pleaded with him, not threatened him. The threat was the enigma. Why was it made? For what purpose? Again, perhaps, Manfredi was right. The strange paper had no meaning now. There were other things to think about.

Holcroft caught the eye of the stewardess chatting with two men at a table across the way and gestured for another scotch. She smiled pleasantly, nodded, and indicated that the drink would be there in moments. He returned to his thoughts.

The inevitable doubts surfaced. Was he prepared to commit what amounted to a year of his life to a project so immense that his own qualifications had to be examined before the children of Kessler and Von Tiebolt were examined—if, indeed, he could find the latter? Manfredi's words came back to him. *Do you really have a choice?* The answer to that question was both yes and no. The two million, which signified his own freedom, was a temptation difficult to reject, but he could reject it. His dissatisfactions were real, but professionally, things were going well. His reputation was spreading, his skills acknowledged by a growing number of clients who in turn told potential clients. What would happen if he suddenly stopped? What would be the effect should he abruptly withdraw from a dozen commissions for which he was competing? These too were questions to be considered deeply; he was not ruled by money alone.

Yet, as his mind wandered, Noel understood the uselessness of his thoughts. Compared to his . . . covenant . . . the questions were inconsequential. Whatever his personal circumstances, the distribution of millions to the survivors of an inhumanity unknown in history was long overdue; it was an obligation impossible to dismiss. A voice had cried out to him through the years, the voice of a man in agony who was the father he had never known. For reasons he was incapable of explaining to himself, he could not be deaf to that voice; he could not walk away from that man in agony. He would drive to Bedford Hills in the morning and see his mother.

Holcroft looked up, wondering where the stewardess was with his drink. She was at the dimly lit counter that served as the bar in the 747's lounge. The two men from the table had accompanied her; they were joined by a third. A fourth man sat quietly in a rear seat, reading a newspaper. The two men with the stewardess had been drinking heavily, while the third, in his search for camaraderie, pretended to be less sober than he was. The stewardess saw Noel looking at her and arched her eyebrows in mock desperation. She had poured his scotch, but one of the drunks had spilled it; she was wiping it up with a cloth. The drunks' companion suddenly lurched back against a chair, his balance lost. The stewardess dashed around the counter to help the fallen passenger; his friend laughed, steadying himself on an adjacent chair. The third man reached for a drink on the bar. The fourth man looked up in disgust, crackling his paper, the sound conveying his disapproval. Noel returned to the window not caring to be a part of the minor confusion.

Several minutes later the stewardess approached his table. "I'm sorry, Mr.

Holcroft. Boys will be boys, more so on the Atlantic run, I think. That was scotch on the rocks, wasn't it?"

"Yes. Thanks." Noel took the glass from the attractive girl and saw the look in her eyes. It seemed to say, *Thank you, nice person, for not coming on like those crashing bores.* Under different circumstances he might have pursued a conversation, but now he had other things to think about. His mind was listing the things he would do on Monday. Closing his office was not difficult in terms of personnel; he had a small staff: a secretary and two draftsmen he could easily place with friends—probably at higher salaries. But why in heaven's name would Holcroft, Incorporated, New York, close up shop just when its designs were being considered for projects that could triple its staff and quadruple its gross income? The explanation had to be both reasonable and above scrutiny.

Suddenly, without warning, a passenger on the other side of the cabin sprang from his seat, a hoarse, wild cry of pain coming from his throat. He arched his back spastically, as if gasping for air, clutched first his stomach, then his chest. He crashed into the wooden divider that held magazines and airline schedules and twisted maniacally, his eyes wide, the veins in his neck purple and distended. He lurched forward and sprawled to the deck of the cabin.

It was the third man, who had joined the two drunks at the bar with the stewardess.

The next moments were chaotic. The stewardess rushed to the fallen man, observed him closely, and followed procedure. She instructed the three other passengers in the cabin to remain in their seats, placed a cushion beneath the man's head, and returned to the counter and the intercom on the wall. In seconds a male flight attendant rushed up the circular staircase; the British Airways captain emerged from the flight deck. They conferred with the stewardess over the unconscious body. The male attendant walked rapidly to the staircase, descended, and returned within a few moments with a clipboard. It was obviously the plane's manifest.

The captain stood and addressed the others in the lounge. "Will you all please return to your seats below. There's a doctor on board. He's being summoned. Thank you very much."

As Holcroft sidestepped his way down the staircase, a stewardess carrying a blanket climbed quickly past him. Then he heard the captain issue an order over the intercom. "Radio Kennedy for emergency equipment. Medical. Male passenger, name of Thornton. Heart seizure, I believe."

The doctor knelt by the prone figure stretched out on the rear seat of the lounge and asked for a flashlight. The first officer hurried to the flight deck and returned with one. The doctor rolled back the eyelids of the man named Thornton, then turned and motioned for the captain to join him; he had something to say. The captain bent over; the doctor spoke quietly.

"He's dead. It's difficult to say without equipment, without tissue and blood analysis, but I don't think this man had a heart attack. I think he was poisoned. Strychnine would be my guess."

The customs inspector's office was suddenly quiet. Behind the inspector's desk sat a homicide detective from New York's Port Authority police, a British Airways clipboard in front of him. The inspector stood rigidly embarrassed to one side. In two chairs against the wall sat the captain of the 747 and the stewardess assigned to its first-class lounge. By the door was a uniformed police officer. The detective stared at the customs inspector in disbelief.

"Are you telling me that two people got off that plane, walked through sealed-off corridors into the sealed-off, guarded customs area, and *vanished?*"

"I can't explain it," said the inspector, shaking his head despondently. "It's never happened before."

The detective turned to the stewardess. "You're convinced they were drunk, miss?"

"Not now, perhaps," replied the girl. "I've got to have second thoughts. They drank a *great* deal; I'm certain of it; they couldn't have faked that. I served them. They appeared quite sloshed. Harmless, but sloshed."

"Could they have poured their drinks out somewhere? Without drinking them, I mean."

"Where?" asked the stewardess.

"I don't know. Hollow ashtrays, the seat cushions. What's on the floor?"

"Carpeting," answered the pilot.

The detective addressed the police officer by the door. "Get forensic on your radio. Have them check the carpet, the seat cushions, ashtrays. Left side of the roped-off area facing front. Dampness is enough. Let me know."

"Yes, sir." The officer left quickly, closing the door behind him.

"Of course," ventured the captain, "alcoholic tolerances vary."

"Not in the amounts the young lady described," the detective said.

"For God's sake, why is it important?" said the captain. "Obviously they're the men you want. They've vanished, as you put it. That took some planning, I daresay."

"Everything's important," explained the detective. "Methods can be matched with previous crimes. We're looking for anything. Crazy people. Rich, crazy people who jet around the world looking for thrills. Signs of psychosis, getting kicks while on a high—alcohol or narcotics, it doesn't matter. As far as we can determine, the two men in question didn't even know this Thornton; your stewardess here said they introduced themselves. Why did they kill him? And, accepting the fact that they did, why so brutally? It *was* strychnine, Captain, and take my word for it, it's a rough way to go."

The telephone rang. The customs inspector answered it; listened briefly, and handed it to the Port Authority detective. "It's the State Department. For you."

"State? This is Lieutenant Miles, NYPA police. Have you got the information I requested?"

"We've got it, but you won't like it. . . ."

"Wait a minute," Miles broke in. The door had opened and the uniformed officer had reappeared. "What have you got?" Miles asked the officer.

"The seat cushions and the carpet on the left side of the lounge are soaked."

"Then they were cold sober," said the detective, in a monotone. He nodded and returned to the telephone. "Go ahead, State. What won't I like?"

"Those passports in question were declared void more than four years ago. They belonged to two men from Flint, Michigan. Neighbors, actually; worked for the same company in Detroit. In June of 1973 they both went on a business trip to Europe and never came back."

"Why were the passports voided?"

"They disappeared from their hotel rooms. Three days later their bodies were found in the river. They'd been shot."

"*Jesus!* What river? Where?"

"The Isar. They were in Munich, Germany."

One by one the irate passengers of Flight 591 passed through the door of the quarantine room. Their names, addresses, and telephone numbers were checked off against the 747's manifest by a representative of British Airways. Next to the representative was a member of the Port Authority police, making his own marks on a duplicate list. The quarantine had lasted nearly four hours.

Outside the room the passengers were directed down a hallway into a large cargo area, where they retrieved their inspected luggage, and headed for the doors of the main terminal. One passenger, however, made no move to leave the cargo area. Instead, this man, who carried no luggage, but had a raincoat over his arm, walked directly to a door with thick, stenciled printing on the panel.

U.S. CUSTOMS. CONTROL CENTER
AUTHORIZED PERSONNEL ONLY

Showing identification, he stepped inside.

A gray-haired man in the uniform of a high-ranking customs official stood by a steel-framed window, smoking a cigarette. At the intrusion, he turned. "I've been waiting for you," he said. "There was nothing I could do while you were quarantined."

"I had the ID card ready in case you weren't here," replied the passenger, putting the identification back into his jacket pocket.

"Keep it ready. You may still need it; the police are all over the place. What do you want to do?"

"Get out to that aircraft."

"You think they're there?"

"Yes. Somewhere. It's the only explanation."

The two men left the room and walked rapidly across the cargo area, past the numerous conveyor belts, to a steel doorway marked NO ADMITTANCE. Using a key, the customs official opened it and preceded the younger man with the raincoat through the door. They were inside a long cinderblock tunnel that led to the field. Forty seconds later they reached another steel door, this one guarded by two men, one from U.S. Customs, the other from the Port Authority police. The gray-haired official was recognized by the former.

"Hello, Captain. Hell of a night, isn't it?"

"It's only begun, I'm afraid," said the official. "We may be involved, after all." He looked at the policeman. "This man's federal," he continued, angling his head at his companion. "I'm taking him to the five-ninety-one aircraft. There may be a narcotics connection."

The police officer seemed confused. Apparently his orders were to allow no one through the door. The customs guard interceded.

"Hey, come on. This man runs all of Kennedy Airport."

The policeman shrugged and opened the door.

Outside a steady rain fell from the black night sky as pockets of mist rolled in from Jamaica Bay. The man with the customs official put on his raincoat. His movements were swift; in the hand beneath the coat held over his arm had been a gun. It was now in his belt, the buttons at his waist unfastened.

The 747 glistened under floodlights, rain streaking down its fuselage. Police and maintenance crews were everywhere, distinguished from one another by the contrasting black and orange of their slickers.

"I'll build your cover with the police inside," said the customs official, gesturing at the metal steps that swept up from the back of the truck to a door in the fuselage. "Good hunting."

The man in the raincoat nodded, not really listening. His eyes were scanning the area. The 747 was the focal point; thirty yards from it in all directions were stanchions connected by ropes, policemen at midpoints between them. The man in the raincoat was within this enclosure; he could move about freely. He turned right at the end of the parallel ropes and proceeded toward the rear of the aircraft. He nodded to the police officers at their posts, slapping his identification open casually to those whose looks were questioning. He kept peering through the rain into the faces of those entering and leaving the plane. Three quarters around the plane, he heard the angry shout of a maintenance crewman.

"What the fuck are you *doing?* Get that winch secure!"

The target of the outburst was another crewman, standing on the platform of a fuel truck. This crewman had no rain slicker on; his white coverall was drenched. In the driver's seat of the truck sat another crewman, also without rain apparel.

That was *it,* thought the man in the raincoat. The killers had worn coveralls beneath their suits. But they had not taken into consideration the possibility of rain. Except for that mistake, the escape had been planned brilliantly.

The man walked over to the fuel truck, his hand on the gun concealed beneath his raincoat. Through the rain he stared at the figure beyond the truck window, in the driver's seat; the second man was above him, to his right on the platform, turned away. The face behind the window stared back in disbelief, and instantly lurched for the far side of the seat. But the man in the raincoat was too quick.

He opened the door, pulled out his revolver and fired, the gunshot muted by a silencer. The man in the seat fell into the dashboard, blood streaming out of his forehead.

At the sound of the commotion below, the second man spun around on the steel platform of the truck and looked below.

"*You!* In the *lounge!* With the newspaper!"

"Get inside the truck," commanded the man in the raincoat, his words clear through the pounding rain, his gun concealed behind the door panel.

The figure on the platform hesitated. The man with the gun looked around. The surrounding police were preoccupied with their discomfort in the downpour, half blinded by the floodlights. None was observing the deadly scene. The man in the raincoat reached up, grabbed the white cloth of the surviving killer's coverall, and yanked him into the frame of the open door of the fuel truck.

"You failed. Heinrich Clausen's son still lives," he said calmly. Then he fired a second shot. The killer fell back into the seat.

The man in the raincoat closed the door and put his gun back into his belt. He walked casually away, directly underneath the fuselage toward the roped-off alleyway that led to the tunnel. He could see the customs official emerging from the 747's door, walking rapidly down the steps. They met and together headed for the door of the tunnel.

"What happened?" asked the official.

"My hunting was good. Theirs wasn't. The question is, what do we do about Holcroft?"

"That's not our concern. It's the Tinamou's. The Tinamou must be informed."

The man in the raincoat smiled to himself, knowing his smile could not be seen in the downpour.

4

Holcroft got out of the taxi in front of his apartment on East Seventy-third Street. He was exhausted, the strain of the last three days heightened by the tragedy on board the flight. He was sorry for the poor bastard who'd had the heart attack, but furious at the Port Authority police who treated the incident as if it were an international crisis. Good Lord! *Quarantined* for damned near four hours! And all passengers in first class were to keep the police informed of their whereabouts for the next sixty days.

The doorman greeted him. "A short trip this time, Mr. Holcroft. But you got a lot of mail. Oh, and a message."

"A message?"

"Yes, sir," said the doorman, handing him a business card. "This gentleman came in asking for you last night. He was very agitated, you know what I mean?"

"Not exactly." Noel took the card and read the name: PETER BALDWIN, ESQ.; it meant nothing to him. WELLINGTON SECURITY SYSTEMS, LTD. THE STRAND, LONDON, W1A. There was a telephone number underneath. Holcroft had never heard of the British company. He turned the card over; on the back was scribbled ST. REGIS HOTEL. RM. 411.

"He insisted that I ring your apartment in case you'd gotten back and I didn't see you come in. I told him that was crazy."

"He could have telephoned me himself," said Noel, walking toward the elevator. "I'm in the book."

"He told me he tried, but your phone was out of order." The elevator door closed on the man's last words. Holcroft read the name again as the elevator climbed to the fifth floor. Peter Baldwin, Esq. Who was he? And since when was his phone out of order?

He opened his apartment door and reached for the light switch on the wall. Two table lamps went on simultaneously; Noel dropped his suitcase and stared in disbelief at the room.

Nothing was the same as it was three days ago! *Nothing.* Every piece of furniture, every chair, every table, every vase and ashtray, was moved into another position. His couch had been in the center of the room; it was now in the far-right corner. Each sketch and painting on the walls had been shifted around, none where it had been before! The stereo was no longer on the shelf; instead it was neatly arranged on a table. His bar, always at the rear of the living room, was now at the left of the door. His drafting board, usually by the window, was now by itself ten feet in front of him, the stool somewhere else—God knew where. It was the strangest sensation he had ever had. Everything familiar, yet not familiar at all. Reality distorted, out of focus.

He stood in the open doorway. Images of the room as it had been kept reappearing in front of his eyes, only to be replaced by what was in front of him now.

"What *happened?*" He heard his own words, unsure they were his at first.

He ran to the couch; the telephone was always by the couch, on a table at its right arm. But the couch had been moved, and the telephone had not been moved with it. He spun around toward the center of the room. Where was the table? It was not there; an armchair was where the table should be. The telephone was not there, either! *Where* was the telephone? Where was the table? Where the *hell* was the *telephone?*

It was by the window. There was his *kitchen* table by the *livingroom* window, and the telephone was on top of it. The large center window that looked out at the apartment building across the wide courtyard below. The telephone wires had been taken out from under the wall-to-wall carpeting and moved to the window.

It was crazy! Who would take the trouble to lift tacked-down carpeting and move telephone wires?

He raced to the table, picked up the phone, and pressed the intercom button that connected him to the switchboard in the lobby. He stabbed the signal button repeatedly; there was no answer. He kept his finger on it; finally, the harried voice of Jack the doorman answered.

"All right, all right. This is the lobby. . . ."

"Jack, it's Mr. Holcroft. Who came up to my apartment while I was away?"

"Who came what, sir?"

"Up to my *apartment!*"

"Were you robbed, Mr. Holcroft?"

"I don't know yet. I just know that everything's been moved around. Who was here?"

"Nobody. I mean, nobody *I* know of. And the other guys didn't say anything. I'm relieved at four in the morning by Ed, and he's off at noon. Louie takes over then."

"Can you call them?"

"Hell, I can call the police!"

The word was jarring. "Police" meant questions—*Where had he been? Whom had he seen?*—and Noel was not sure he wanted to give any answers.

"No, don't call the police. Not yet. Not until I see if anything's missing. It might be someone's idea of a joke. I'll call you back."

"I'll call the other guys."

Holcroft hung up. He sat on the wide windowsill and appraised the room. *Everything.* Not a single piece of furniture was where it had been before!

He was holding something in his left hand: the business card. PETER BALDWIN, ESQ.

"*. . . he was very agitated, you know what I mean? . . . he insisted I ring your apartment . . . your phone was out of order. . . .*"

ST. REGIS HOTEL. RM. 411.

Noel picked up the phone and dialed. He knew the number well; he lunched frequently at the King Cole Grill.

"Yes? Baldwin here." The voice was British, the greeting abrupt.

"This is Noel Holcroft, Mr. Baldwin. You tried to reach me."

"Thank heavens! Where are you?"

"Home. In my apartment. I just got back."

"Back? From where?"

"I'm not sure that's any of your business."

"For God's sake, I've traveled over three thousand miles to see you! It's dreadfully important. Now where *were* you?"

The Englishman's breathing was audible over the phone; the man's intensity seemed somehow related to fear. "I'm flattered you came all that distance to see me, but it still doesn't give you the right to ask personal questions. . . ."

"I have *every* right!" broke in Baldwin. "I spent twenty years with MI Six, and we have a great deal to talk about! You have no idea what you're doing. No one does but me."

"You *what? We* what?"

"Let me put it this way. Cancel Geneva. *Cancel* it, Mr. Holcroft, until we've talked!"

"Geneva? . . ." Noel felt suddenly sick to his stomach. How would this Englishman know about Geneva? How *could* he know?

A light flickered outside the window; someone in an apartment directly across the courtyard was lighting a cigarette. Despite his agitation, Holcroft's eyes were drawn to it.

"There's someone at the door," Baldwin said. "Stay on the phone. I'll get rid of whoever it is and be right back."

Noel could hear Baldwin put the telephone down, then the sound of a door opening and indistinguishable voices. Across the courtyard, in the window, a match was struck again, illuminating the long blond hair of a woman behind a sheer curtain.

Holcroft realized there was silence on the line; he could hear no voices now. Moments went by; the Englishman did not return.

"Baldwin? Baldwin, where are you? *Baldwin!*"

For a third time a match flared in the window across the way. Noel stared at it; it seemed unnecessary. He could see the glow of a cigarette in the blond woman's mouth. And then he saw what was in her other hand, silhouetted behind the sheer curtain: a telephone. She was holding a telephone to her ear and looking over at his window—looking, he was sure, at him.

"*Baldwin?* Where the hell *are* you?"

There was a click; the line went dead.

"*Baldwin!*"

The woman in the window slowly lowered the telephone, paused for a moment, and walked away, out of sight.

Holcroft stared at the window, then at the telephone in his hand. He waited until he got the active line, then redialed the St. Regis.

"I'm sorry, sir, room four-eleven's telephone seems to be out of order. We'll send someone up right away. May I have your number and we'll give it to Mr. Baldwin."

. . . your phone was out of order. . . .

Something was happening that Noel did not understand. He knew only that he would not leave his name or number with the operator at the St. Regis. He hung up and looked again at the window across the courtyard. Whatever light there had been was gone. The window was dark; he could see only the white of the curtain.

He pushed himself away from the windowsill and wandered aimlessly about the room, around familiar possessions in unfamiliar locations. He was not sure what to do; he supposed he should see if anything was missing. Nothing seemed to be, but it was difficult to tell.

The telephone buzzed: the intercom from the lobby switchboard. He answered it.

"It's Jack, Mr. Holcroft. I just spoke to Ed and Louie. Neither of 'em know anything about anyone going up to your place. They're honest guys. They wouldn't screw around. None of us would."

"Thanks, Jack. I believe you."

"You want me to call the police?"

"No." Noel tried to sound casual. "I have an idea someone at the office was playing a joke. A couple of the fellows have keys."

"I didn't see anybody. Neither did Ed or—"

"It's okay, Jack," interrupted Holcroft. "Forget it. The night I left we had a party. One or two stayed over." It was all Noel could think of to say.

Suddenly it occurred to him that he had not looked in his bedroom. He went there now, his hand reaching for the light switch on the wall.

He expected it, but it was still a shock. The disorientation was now somehow complete.

Again, each piece of furniture had been moved to a different position. The bed was the first thing that struck his eye; it was oddly frightening. No part of it touched the wall. Instead, it was in the center of the room, isolated. His bureau stood in front of a window; a small writing desk was dwarfed against the expanse of the right wall. As had happened minutes ago, when first he'd seen the living room, the images of what his bedroom looked like three days ago kept flashing before him, replaced by the strangeness of what he now observed.

Then he saw it and gasped. Hanging down from the ceiling, strapped together with dull black tape, was his second telephone, the extension cord snaking up the wall and across the ceiling to the hook that held it.

It was spinning slowly.

The pain shifted from his stomach to his chest; his eyes were transfixed on the sight, on the suspended instrument revolving slowly in midair. He was afraid to look beyond, but he knew he had to; he had to understand.

And when he did, his breath came back to him. The phone was in the direct path of his bathroom door and the door was open. He saw the curtains billowing in the window above the basin. The steady stream of cold wind was making the telephone spin.

He walked quickly into the bathroom to shut the window. As he was about to pull the curtains, he saw a brief flash of illumination outside; a match had been struck in another window across the courtyard, the flare startling in the darkness. He looked out.

There was the woman again! The blond-haired woman, her upper body silhouetted beyond another set of sheer curtains. He stared at the figure, mesmerized by it.

She turned as she had turned before, and walked away as she had walked away minutes ago. Out of sight. And the dim light in the window went out.

What *was* happening? What did it mean? Things were being orchestrated to frighten him. But by whom and for what purpose? And what had happened to Peter Baldwin, Esq., he of the intense voice and the command to cancel Geneva? Was Baldwin a part of the terror, or was he a victim of it?

Victim . . . *victim?* It was an odd word to use, he thought. Why should there be any victims? And what did Baldwin mean when he said he had "spent twenty years with MI Six"?

MI Six? A branch of British intelligence. If he remembered correctly, MI *Five* was the section that dealt with domestic matters; *Six* concerned itself with problems outside the country. The English CIA, as it were.

Good God! Did the British know about the Geneva document? Was British intelligence aware of the massive theft of thirty years ago? On the surface, it would appear so. . . . Yet that was not what Peter Baldwin had implied.

You have no idea what you're doing. No one does but me.

And then there was silence, and the line went dead.

Holcroft walked out of the bathroom and paused beneath the suspended telephone; it was barely moving now, but it had not stopped. It was an ugly sight, made macabre by the profusion of dull black tape that held the instrument together. As if the phone had been mummified, never to be used again.

He continued toward the bedroom door, then instinctively stopped and turned. Something had caught his eye, something he had not noticed before. The center drawer of the small writing desk was open. He looked closer. Inside the drawer was a sheet of paper.

His breathing stopped as he stared at the page below.

It couldn't *be.* It was *insane.* The single sheet of paper was brownish yellow. With *age.* It was identical to the page that had been kept in a vault in Geneva for thirty years. The letter filled with threats written by fanatics who revered a martyr named Heinrich Clausen. The writing was the same; the odd Germanic printing of English words, the ink that was faded but still legible.

And what was legible was astonishing. For it had been written more than thirty years ago.

> Noel Clausen-Holcroft
> Nothing is as it was for you. Nothing
> Can ever be the same. . . .

Before he read further, Noel picked up an edge of the page. It crumbled under his touch.

Oh, God! It *was* written thirty years ago!

And that fact made the remainder of the message frightening.

The past was preparation, the future is committed to the memory of a man and his dream. His was an act of daring and brilliance in a world gone mad. Nothing must stand in the way of that dream's fulfillment.

We are the survivors of Wolfsschanze. Those of us who live will dedicate our lives and bodies to the protection of that man's dream. It will be fulfilled, for it is all that is left.

An act of mercy that will show the world that we were betrayed, that we were not as the world believed us to be.

We, the men of Wolfsschanze, know what the best of us were. As Heinrich Clausen knew.

It is now up to you, Noel Clausen-Holcroft, to complete what your father began. You are the way. Your father wished it so.

Many will try to stop you. To throw open the floodgates and destroy the dream. But the men of Wolfsschanze do survive. You have our word that all those who interfere will be stopped themselves.

Any who stand in your way, who try to dissuade you, who try to deceive you with lies, will be eliminated.

As you and yours will be should you hesitate. Or fail.

This is our oath to you.

Noel grabbed the paper out of the drawer; it fell apart in his hand. He let the fragments fall to the floor.

"Goddamned maniacs!" He slammed the drawer shut and ran out of the bedroom. Where was the telephone? Where the *hell* was the goddamned *telephone?* By the window—that was it; it was on the *kitchen* table by the fucking *window!*

"Maniacs!" he screamed again at no one. But not really at no one: at a man in Geneva who had been on a train bound for Zürich. Maniacs might have written that page of garbage thirty years ago, but now, thirty years later, other maniacs had delivered it! They had broken into his home, invaded his privacy, touched his belongings. . . . God knows what else, he thought, thinking of Peter Baldwin, Esq. A man who had traveled thousands of miles to see him, and talk with him . . . silence, a click, a dead telephone line.

He looked at his watch. It was almost one o'clock in the morning. What was it in Zürich? Six? Seven? The banks in Switzerland opened at eight. La Grande Banque de Genève had a branch in Zürich; Manfredi would be there.

The window. He was standing in front of the window where he had stood only minutes ago, waiting for Baldwin to come back on the phone. The *window.* Across the courtyard in the opposite apartment. The three brief flares of a match . . . the blond-haired woman in the window!

Holcroft put his hand in his pocket to make sure he had his keys. He did. He ran to the door, let himself out, raced for the elevator, and pushed the button. The indicator showed that the car was on the tenth floor; the arrow did not move.

God damn it!

He ran to the staircase and started down, taking the steps two at a time. He reached the ground floor and dashed out into the lobby.

"Jesus, Mr. Holcroft!" Jack stared at him. "You scared the shit out of me!"

"Do you know the doorman in the next building?" shouted Noel.

"Which one?"

"Christ! That one!" Holcroft gestured to the right.

"That's three-eighty. Yeah, sure."

"Come on with me!"

"Hey, wait a minute, Mr. Holcroft. I can't leave here."

"We'll only be a minute. There's twenty dollars in it for you."

"Only a minute. . . ."

The doorman at three-eighty greeted them, understanding quickly that he was to give accurate information to Jack's friend.

"I'm sorry, sir, but there's no one in that apartment. Hasn't been for almost three weeks. But I'm afraid it's been rented; the new tenants will be coming in. . . ."

"There *is* someone there!" said Noel, trying to control himself. "A blond-haired woman. I've *got* to find out who she is."

"A blond-haired woman? Kind of medium height, sort of goodlooking, smokes a lot?"

"Yes, that's the one! Who is she?"

"You live in your place long, mister?"

"What?"

"I mean, have you been there a long time?"

"What's that got to do with anything?"

"I think maybe you've been drinking. . . ."

"What the hell are you talking about?! Who *is that woman?*"

"Not *is*, mister. *Was*. The blond woman you're talking about was Mrs. Palatyne. She died a month ago."

Noel sat in the chair in front of the window, staring across the courtyard. Someone was trying to drive him crazy. But why? It did not make sense! Fanatics, maniacs from thirty years ago, had sprung across three decades, commanding younger, unknown troops thirty years later. Again, *why?*

He had called the St. Regis. Room four-eleven's telephone was working, but it was continuously busy. And a woman he had seen clearly did not exist. But she did exist! And she was a part of it; he *knew* it.

He got out of the chair, walked to the strangely placed bar, and poured himself a drink. He looked at his watch; it was one-fifty. He had ten minutes to wait before the overseas operator would call him back; the bank could be reached at two A.M., New York time. He carried his glass back to the chair in front of the window. On the way, he passed his FM radio. It was not where it usually was of course; that was why he noticed it. Absently, he turned it on. He liked music; it soothed him.

But it was words, not music, that he heard. The *rat-tat-tatting* beneath an announcer's voice indicated one of those "all-news" stations. The dial had been changed. He should have known. *Nothing is as it was for you. . . .*

Something being said on the radio caught his attention. He turned quickly in the chair, part of his drink spilling onto his trousers.

". . . police have cordoned off the hotel's entrances. Our reporter, Richard Dunlop, is on the scene, calling in from our mobile unit. Come in, Richard. What have you learned?"

There was a burst of static followed by the voice of an excited newscaster.

"The man's name was Peter Baldwin, John. He was an Englishman. Arrived yesterday, or at least that's when he registered at the St. Regis; the police are contacting the airlines for further information. As far as can be determined, he was over here on vacation. There was no listing of a company on the hotel registry card."

"When did they discover the body?"

"About a half hour ago. A maintenance man went up to the room to check the telephone and found Mr. Baldwin sprawled out on the bed. The rumors here are wild and you don't know what to believe, but the thing that's stressed is the method of killing. Apparently, it was vicious, brutal. Baldwin was garroted, they said. A wire pulled through his throat. An hysterical maid from the fourth floor was heard screaming to the police that the room was drenched with—"

"Was robbery the motive?" interrupted the anchorman, in the interests of taste.

"We haven't been able to establish that. The police aren't talking. I gather they're waiting for someone from the British consulate to arrive."

"Thank you, Richard Dunlop. We'll stay in touch. . . . That was Richard Dunlop at the St. Regis Hotel, on Fifty-fifth Street in Manhattan. To repeat, a brutal murder took place at one of New York's most fashionable hotels this morning. An Englishman named Peter Baldwin . . ."

Holcroft shot out of the chair, lurched at the radio, and turned it off. He stood above it, breathing rapidly. He did not want to admit to himself that he had heard what he had just heard. It was not anything he had really considered; it simply was not possible.

But it *was* possible. It was real; it had happened. It was death. The maniacs from thirty years ago were not caricatures, not figures from some melodrama. They were vicious killers. And they were deadly serious.

Peter Baldwin, Esq., had told him to cancel Geneva. Baldwin had interfered with the dream, with the covenant. And now he was dead, brutally killed with a wire through his throat.

With difficulty, Noel walked back to the chair and sat down. He raised his glass to his lips and drank several long swallows of whisky; the scotch did nothing for him. The pounding in his chest only accelerated.

A flare of a match! Across the courtyard, in the window! There she was! Silhouetted beyond the sheer curtains in a wash of dim light stood the blond-haired woman. She was staring across the way, staring at *him!* He got out of the chair, drawn hypnotically to the window, his face inches from the panes of glass. The woman nodded her head; she was slowly *nodding her head!* She was telling him something. She was telling him that what he perceived was the truth!

. . . *The blond woman you're talking about was Mrs. Palatyne. She died a month ago.*

A dead woman stood silhouetted in a window across the darkness and was sending him a terrible message. Oh, Christ, he was going *insane!*

The telephone rang; the bell terrified him. He held his breath and lunged at the phone; he could not let it ring again. It did awful things to the silence.

"Mr. Holcroft, this is the overseas operator. I have your call to Zürich. . . ."

Noel listened in disbelief at the somber, accented voice from Switzerland. The man on the line was the manager of the Zürich branch of La Grande Banque de Genève. A *directeur,* he said twice, emphasizing his position.

"We mourn profoundly, Mr. Holcroft. We knew Herr Manfredi was not well, but we had no idea his illness had progressed so."

"What are you talking about? What happened?"

"A terminal disease affects individuals differently. Our colleague was a vital man, an energetic man, and when such men cannot function in their normal fashions, it often leads to despondency and great depression."

"What *happened?*"

"It was suicide, Mr. Holcroft. Herr Manfredi could not tolerate his incapacities."

"Suicide?"

"There's no point in speaking other than the truth. Ernst threw himself out of his hotel window. It was mercifully quick. At ten o'clock, La Grande Banque will suspend all business for one minute of mourning and reflection."

"Oh, my *God. . . ."*

"However," concluded the voice in Zürich, "all of Herr Manfredi's accounts to which he gave his personal attention will be assumed by equally capable hands. We fully expect—"

Noel hung up the phone, cutting off the man's words. *Accounts . . . will be assumed by equally capable hands.* Business as usual; a man was killed, but the affairs of Swiss finance were not to be interrupted. And he *was* killed.

Ernst Manfredi did not *throw* himself out of a hotel in Zürich. He was *thrown* out. Murdered by the men of Wolfsschanze.

For God's sake, *why?* Then Holcroft remembered. Manfredi had dismissed the men of Wolfsschanze. He had told Noel the macabre threats were meaningless, the anguish of sick old men seeking atonement.

That had been Manfredi's error. He had undoubtedly told his associates, the other directors of La Grande Banque, about the strange letter that had been delivered with the wax seals unbroken. Perhaps, in their presence, he had laughed at the men of Wolfsschanze.

The match! The flare of light! Across the courtyard the woman in the window nodded! Again—as if reading his thoughts—she was confirming the truth. A dead woman was telling him he was right!

She turned and walked away; all light went out in the window.

"Come back! Come *back!"* Holcroft screamed, his hands on the panes of glass. "Who *are* you?"

The telephone beneath him buzzed. Noel stared at it, as if it were a terrible thing in an unfamiliar place; it was both. Trembling, he picked it up.

"Mr. Holcroft, it's Jack. I *think* I may know what the hell happened up at your place. I mean, I didn't think about it before, but it kinda hit me a few minutes ago."

"What was it?"

"A couple of nights ago these two guys came in. Locksmiths. Mr. Silverstein, on your floor, was having his lock changed. Louie told me about it, so I knew it was okay. Then I began to think. Why did they come at night? I mean, what with overtime and everything, why didn't they come in the daytime? So I just called Louie at home. He said they came *yesterday.* So who the hell were those other guys."

"Do you remember anything about them?"

"You're damned right I do! One of them in particular. You could pick him out in a crowd at the Garden! He had—"

There was a loud, sharp report over the line.

A *gunshot!*

It was followed by a crash. The telephone in the lobby had been dropped!

Noel slammed down the receiver and ran to the door, yanking it open with such force that it crashed into a framed sketch on the wall, smashing the glass. There was no time to consider the elevator. He raced down the stairs, his mind a blank, afraid to think, concentrating only on speed and balance, hoping to God he would not trip on the steps. He reached the landing and bolted through the lobby door.

He stared in shock. The worst had happened. Jack the doorman was arched back over the chair, blood pouring out of his neck. He had been shot in the throat.

He had interfered. He had been about to identify one of the men of Wolfs-schanze and he had been killed for it.

Baldwin, Manfredi . . . an innocent doorman. Dead.

. . . *all those who interfere will be stopped. . . . Any who stand in your way, who try to dissuade you, who try to deceive you . . . will be eliminated.*

. . . *As you and yours will be should you hesitate. Or fail.*

Manfredi had asked him if he really had a choice. He did not any longer.

He was surrounded by death.

5

Althene Holcroft sat behind the desk in her study and glared at the words of the letter she held in her hand. Her chiseled, angular features—the high cheekbones, the aquiline nose, the wide-set eyes beneath arched, defined brows—were as taut, as rigid, as her posture in the chair. Her thin, aristocratic lips were tight; her breathing was steady, but each breath was too controlled, too deep, for normalcy. She read Heinrich Clausen's letter as one studying a statistical report that contradicted information previously held to be incontrovertible.

Across the room, Noel stood by a curving window that looked out on the rolling lawn and gardens behind the Bedford Hills house. A number of shrubs were covered with burlap; the air was cold, and the morning frost produced intermittent patches of light gray on the green grass.

Holcroft turned from the scene outside and looked at his mother, trying desperately to conceal his fear, to control the occasional trembling that came upon him when he thought about last night. He could not allow the terror he felt to be seen by his mother. He wondered what thoughts were going through her head, what memories were triggered by the sight of the handwritten words in blue ink put down by a man she once had loved, then had grown to despise. Whatever she was thinking, it would remain private until she chose to speak. Althene communicated only that which she cared to convey deliberately.

She seemed to sense his gaze and raised her eyes to his, but only briefly. She returned to the letter, allowing a briefer moment to brush away a stray lock that had fallen from the gray hair that framed her face. Noel wandered aimlessly toward the desk, glancing at the bookcases and photographs on the wall. The room reflected the owner, he mused. Graceful, even elegant; but, withal, there was a pervading sense of activity. The photographs showed men and women on horses at the hunt, in sailboats in rough weather, on skis in mountain snow. There was no denying it: There was an undercurrent of masculinity in this very feminine room. It was his mother's study, her sanctuary where she repaired for private moments of consideration. But it could have belonged to a man.

He sat down in the leather chair in front of the desk and lighted a cigarette with a gold Colibri, a parting gift from a young lady who had moved out of his apartment a month ago. His hand trembled again; he gripped the lighter as tightly as he could.

"That's a dreadful habit," said Althene, her eyes remaining on the letter. "I thought you were going to give it up."

"I have. A number of times."

"Mark Twain said that. At least be original."

Holcroft shifted his position in the chair, feeling awkward. "You've read it several times now. What do you think?"

"I don't *know* what to think," said Althene, placing the letter on the desk in front of her. "He wrote it; it's his handwriting, his way of expressing himself. Arrogant even in remorse."

"You agree it's remorse then?"

"It would appear so. On the surface, at any rate. I'd want to know a great deal more. I have a number of questions about this extraordinary financial undertaking. It's beyond anything conceivable."

"Questions lead to other questions, mother. The men in Geneva don't want that."

"Does it matter what they want? As I understand you, although you're being elliptical, they're asking you to give up a minimum of six months of your life and probably a good deal more."

Again, Noel felt awkward. He had decided not to show her the document from La Grande Banque. If she was adamant about seeing it, he could always produce it. If she was not, it was better that way; the less she knew, the better. He had to keep her from the men of Wolfsschanze. He had not the slightest doubt Althene would interfere.

"I'm not holding back any of the essentials," he said.

"I didn't say you were. I said you were elliptical. You refer to a man in Geneva you won't identify; you speak of conditions you only half describe, the oldest children of two families you won't name. You're leaving out a great deal."

"For your own good."

"That's condescending and, considering this letter, very insulting."

"I didn't mean to be either." Holcroft leaned forward. "No one wants that bank account even remotely connected with you. You've read that letter; you know what's involved. Thousands and thousands of people, hundreds of millions of dollars. There's no way to tell who might hold *you* responsible. You were the wife who told him the truth; you left him because he refused to accept it. When he finally realized that what you said *was* true, he did what he did. There may be men still alive who would kill you for that. I won't let you be put in that position."

"I see." Althene drew out the phrase, then repeated it as she rose from her chair and walked slowly across the room to the bay window. "Are you sure that's the concern the men in Geneva expressed?"

"They—he—implied it, yes."

"I suspect it was not the only concern."

"No."

"Shall I speculate on another?"

Noel stiffened. It was not that he underestimated his mother's perceptions— he rarely did that—but, as always, he was annoyed when she verbalized them before he had the chance to state them himself.

"I think it's obvious," he said.

"Do you?" Althene turned from the window and looked at him.

"It's in the letter. If the sources of that account were made public, there'd be legal problems. Claims would be made against it in the international courts."

"Yes." His mother looked away. "It's obvious, then. I'm amazed you were allowed to tell me anything."

Noel leaned back in the chair apprehensively, disturbed at Althene's words. "Why? Would you really do something?"

"It's a temptation," she answered, still gazing outside. "I don't think one ever loses the desire to strike back, to lash out at someone or something that's caused great pain. Even if that hurt changed your life for the better. God knows mine—ours—was changed. From a hell to a level of happiness I'd given up looking for."

"Dad?" asked Noel.

Althene turned. "Yes. He risked more than you'll ever know protecting us. I'd been the fool of the world and he accepted the fool—and the fool's child. He gave us more than love; he gave us our lives again. He asked only love in return."

"You've given him that."

"I'll give it till I die. Richard Holcroft is the man I once thought Clausen was. I was so wrong, so terribly wrong. . . . The fact that Heinrich has been dead these many years doesn't seem to matter; the loathing won't go away. I do want to strike back."

Noel kept his voice calm. He had to lead his mother away from her thoughts; the survivors of Wolfsschanze would not let her live. "You'd be striking back at the man you remember, not the man who wrote that letter. Maybe what you saw in him at first was really there. At the end, it came back to him."

"That would be comforting, wouldn't it?"

"I think it's true. The man who wrote that letter wasn't lying. He was in pain."

"He deserved pain, he caused so much; he was the most ruthless man I ever met. But on the surface, so different, so filled with purpose. And—oh, *God*—what that purpose turned out to be!"

"He changed, mother," interrupted Holcroft. "You were a part of that change. At the end of his life he wanted only to help undo what he'd done. He says it: 'Amends must be made.' Think what he did—what the three of them did—to bring that about."

"I can't dismiss it; I know that. Any more than I can dismiss the words. I can almost hear him say them, but it's a very young man talking. A young man filled with purpose, a very young, wild girl at his side." Althene paused, then spoke again, clearly. "Why did you show me the letter? Why did you bring it all back?"

"Because I've decided to go ahead. That means closing the office, traveling around a lot, eventually working out of Switzerland for a number of months. As the man in Geneva said, you wouldn't have accepted all that without asking a lot of questions. He was afraid you'd learn something damaging and do something rash."

"At *your* expense?" asked Althene.

"I guess so. He thought it was a possibility. He said those memories of yours were strong. 'Indelibly printed' were his words."

"Indelibly," agreed Althene.

"His point was that there were no legal solutions; that it was better to use the money the way it was intended to be used. To make those amends."

"It's possible he was right. If it can be done. God knows it's overdue. Whatever Heinrich touched, very little of value and truth was the result." Althene paused, her face suddenly strained. "You were the one exception. Perhaps this is the other."

Noel got out of the chair and went to his mother. He took her by the shoulders and drew her to him. "That man in Geneva said you were incredible. You are."

Althene pulled back. "He said that? 'Incredible'?"

"Yes."

"Ernst Manfredi," she whispered.

"You *know* him?" asked Holcroft.

"It's a name that goes back many years. He's still alive then."

Noel did not answer her question. "How did you know it was he?"

"A summer afternoon in Berlin. He was there. He helped us get out. You and I. He got us on the plane, gave me money. Dear *God*. . . ." Althene disengaged herself from her son's arms and walked across the room, toward the desk. "He called me 'incredible' then, that afternoon. He said they would hunt me, find me. Find us. He said he would do what he could. He told me what to do, what to say. An unimpressive little Swiss banker was a giant that afternoon. My God, after all these years . . ."

Noel watched his mother, his astonishment complete. "Why didn't he say anything? Why didn't he *tell* me?"

Althene turned, facing her son but not looking at him. She was staring beyond him, seeing things he could not see. "I think he wanted me to find out for myself. This way. He was not a man to call in old debts indiscriminately." She sighed. "I won't pretend the questions are put to rest. I promise nothing. If I decide to take any action, I'll give you ample warning. But for the time being I won't interfere."

"That's kind of open ended, isn't it?"

"It's the best you'll get. Those memories are, indeed, indelibly printed."

"But for now you'll do nothing?"

"You have my word. It's not lightly given, nor will it be lightly taken back."

"What would change it?"

"If you disappeared, for one thing."

"I'll stay in touch."

Althene Holcroft watched her son walk out of the room. Her face—so tense, so rigid, only moments ago—was relaxed. Her thin lips formed a smile; her wide eyes were reflective, in them a look of quiet satisfaction and strength.

She reached for the telephone on her desk, pressed the single button *O*, and seconds later spoke.

"Overseas operator, please. I'd like to place a call to Geneva, Switzerland."

He needed a professionally acceptable reason to close up Holcroft, Incorporated. Questions of substance could not be asked. The survivors of Wolfsschanze were killers for whom questions were too easily construed as interference. He had to disappear legitimately. . . . But one did *not* disappear legitimately: One found plausible explanations that gave the appearance of legitimacy.

The *appearance* of legitimacy.

Sam Buonoventura.

Not that Sam wasn't legitimate: He was. He was one of the best construction engineers in the business. But Sam had followed the sun so long he had blind spots. He was a fifty-year-old professional drifter, a City College graduate from Tremont Avenue, in the Bronx, who had found a life of instant gratification in the warmer climes.

A brief tour of duty in the Army Corps of Engineers had convinced Buonoventura that there was a sweeter, more generous world beyond the borders of the United States, preferably south of the Keys. All one had to be was good—good in a job that was part of a larger job in which a great deal of money was invested. And during the fifties and sixties, the construction explosion in Latin America and the Caribbean was such that it might have been created for someone like Sam. He built a reputation among corporations and governments as the building tyrant who got things done in the field.

Once having studied blueprints, labor pools, and budgets, if Sam told his employers that a hotel or an airport or a dam would be operational within a given period of time, he was rarely in error beyond four percent. He was also an architect's dream, which meant that he did not consider himself an architect.

Noel had worked with Buonoventura on two jobs outside the country, the first in Costa Rica, where if it had not been for Sam, Holcroft would have lost his life. The engineer had insisted that the well-groomed, courteous architect from the classy side of Manhattan learn to use a handgun, not just a hunting rifle from Abercrombie & Fitch. They were building a postal complex in the back country, and it was a far cry from the cocktail lounges of the Plaza and the Waldorf, and from San José. The architect had thought the weekend exercise ridiculous, but courtesy demanded compliance. Courtesy, and Buonoventura's booming voice.

By the end of the following week, however, the architect was profoundly grateful. Thieves had come down from the hills to steal construction explosives. Two men had raced through the camp at night, they'd crashed into Noel's shack as he slept. When they realized the explosives were not there one man had run outside, shouting instructions to his accomplice.

"*¡Matemos el gringo!*"

But the *gringo* understood the language. He reached his gun—the handgun provided by Sam Buonoventura—and shot his would-be killer.

Sam had only one comment: "Goddamn. In some cultures I'd have to take care of you for the rest of your life."

Noel reached Buonoventura through a shipping company in Miami. He was in the Dutch Antilles, in the town of Willemstad, on the island of Curaçao.

"How the hell *are* you, Noley?" Sam shouted, over the phone. "Christ, it must be four, five years! How's your pistol arm?"

"Haven't used it since the *colinas,* and never expect to use it again. How are things with you?"

"These mothers got money to burn down here, so I'm lighting a few matches. You looking for work?"

"No. A favor."

"Name it."

"I'm going to be out of the country for a number of months on private business. I want a reason for not being in New York, for not being available. A reason that people won't question. I've got an idea, Sam, and wondered if you could help me make it work."

"If we're both thinking the same thing, sure I can."

They *were* thinking the same thing. It was not out of the ordinary for long-range projects in faraway places to employ consulting architects, men whose names would not appear on schematics or blueprints but whose skills would be used. The practice was generally confined to those areas where the hiring of native talent was a question of local pride. The inherent problem, of course, was that all too frequently the native talent lacked sufficient training and experience. Investors covered their risks by employing highly skilled outside professionals who corrected and amended the work of the locals, seeing the projects through to completion.

"Have you got any suggestions?" Noel asked.

"Hell, yes. Take your pick of half a dozen underdeveloped countries. Africa, South America, even some of the islands here in the Antilles and the Grenadines. The internationals are moving in like spiders, but the locals are still sensitive. The consulting jobs are kept separate and quiet; graft is soaring."

"I don't want a job, Sam. I want a cover. Someplace I can name, someone I can mention who'll back me up."

"Why not me? I'll be buried in this motherlode for most of the year. Maybe more. I've got two marinas and a full-scale yacht club to go to when the hotel's finished. I'm your man, Noley."

"That's what I was hoping."

"That's what I figured. I'll give you the particulars and you let me know where I can reach you in case any of your high-society friends want to throw a tea dance for you."

Holcroft placed his two draftsmen and his secretary in new jobs by Wednesday. As he suspected, it was not difficult; they were good people. He made fourteen telephone calls to project-development executives at companies where his designs were under consideration, astonished to learn that of the fourteen, he was the leading contender in eight. Eight! If all came through, the fees would have totaled more than he had earned during the past five years.

But not two million dollars; he kept that in the back of his mind. And if it was not in the back of his mind, the survivors of Wolfsschanze were.

The telephone-answering service was given specific instructions. Holcroft, Incorporated, was unavailable at the time for architectural projects. The company was involved in an overseas commission of considerable magnitude. If the caller would leave his name and number . . .

For those who pressed for further information, a post-office box in Curacao, Netherlands Antilles, under the name of Samuel Buonoventura, Limited, was listed. And, for the few who insisted on a telephone number, Sam's was to be given.

Noel had agreed to phone Buonoventura once a week; he would do the same with the answering service.

By Friday morning, he had an uneasy feeling about his decision. He was taking himself out of a garden he had cultivated to walk into an unfamiliar forest.

Nothing is as it was for you. Nothing can ever be the same.

Suppose he could not find the Von Tiebolt children. Suppose they were dead, their remains no more than graves in a Brazilian cemetery? They had disappeared five years ago in Rio de Janeiro; what made him think he could make them reappear? And if he could not, would the survivors of Wolfsschanze strike? He was afraid. But fear itself did not cover everything, thought Holcroft as he walked to the corner of Seventy-third Street and Third Avenue. There were ways to handle fear. He could take the Geneva document to the authorities, to the State Department, and tell them what he knew of Peter Baldwin and Ernst Manfredi and a doorman named Jack. He could expose the massive theft of thirty years ago, and grateful thousands over the world would see to it that he was protected.

That was the sanest thing to do, but somehow sanity and self-protection were not so important. Not now. There was a man in agony thirty years ago. And that man was his rationale.

He hailed a cab, struck by an odd thought, one he knew was in the deep recesses of his imagination. It was the "something else" that drove him into the unfamiliar forest.

He was assuming a guilt that was not his. He was taking on the sins of Heinrich Clausen.

Amends must be made.

"Six-thirty Fifth Avenue, please," he said to the driver as he climbed into the cab. It was the address of the Brazilian Consulate.

The hunt had begun.

6

"Let me understand you, Mr. Holcroft," said the aging attaché, leaning back in his chair. "You say you wish to locate a family that you won't identify. You tell me this family immigrated to Brazil sometime in the forties and, according to the most recent information, dropped from sight several years ago. Is this correct?"

Noel saw the bemused expression on the attaché's face and understood. It was a foolish game perhaps, but Holcroft did not know any other one to play. He was not going to name the Von Tiebolts before he reached Brazil; he was not going to give anyone the chance to complicate further a search that had enough disadvantages at the start. He smiled pleasantly.

"I didn't quite say that. I asked how such a family might be found, given those circumstances. I didn't say I was the one looking."

"Then it's a hypothetical question? Are you a journalist?"

Holcroft considered the medium-level diplomat's question. How simple it would be to say yes; what a convenient explanation for the questions *he* would ask later. On the other hand, he'd be flying to Rio de Janeiro in a few days. There were immigration cards to be filled out, and a visa, perhaps; he did not know. A false answer now might become a problem later.

"No, an architect."

The attaché's eyes betrayed his surprise. "Then you'll visit Brasília, of course. It is a masterpiece."

"I'd like to very much."

"You speak Portuguese?"

"A bit of Spanish. I've worked in Mexico. And in Costa Rica."

"But we're straying," said the attaché, leaning forward in his chair. "I asked you if you were a journalist, and you hesitated. You were tempted to say you were because it was expedient. Frankly, that tells me you are, indeed, the one looking for this family that has dropped from sight. Now, why not tell me the rest?"

If he was going to consider lying in his search through this unfamiliar forest, thought Noel, he'd better learn to analyze his minor answers first. Lesson one: Preparation.

"There isn't that much to tell," he said awkwardly. "I'm taking a trip to your country and I promised a friend I'd look up these people he knew a long time ago." It was a variation on the truth and not a bad one, thought Holcroft. Perhaps that was why he was able to offer it convincingly. Lesson two: Base the lie in an aspect of truth.

"Yet your . . . *friend* has tried to locate them and was unable to do so."

"He tried from thousands of miles away. It's not the same."

"I daresay it isn't. So, because of this distance, and your friend's concern that there could be complications, shall we say, you'd prefer not to identify the family by name."

"That's it."

"No, it isn't. It would be far too simple a matter for an attorney to cable a confidential inquiry-of-record to a reciprocating law firm in Rio de Janeiro. It's done all the time. The family your friend wants to find is nowhere in evidence, so your *friend* wants you to trace them." The attaché smiled and shrugged, as if he had delivered a basic lecture in arithmetic.

Noel watched the Brazilian with growing irritation. Lesson three: Don't be led into a trap by pat conclusions casually stated. "You know something?" he said. "You're a very disagreeable fellow."

"I'm sorry you think so," replied the attaché sincerely. "I want to be of help. That's my function here. I've spoken to you this way for a reason. You are not the first man, God knows, nor will you be the last, to look for people who came to my country 'sometime in the forties.' I'm sure I don't have to amplify that statement. The vast majority of those people were Germans, many bringing to Brazil great sums of money transferred by compromised neutrals. What I'm trying to say is simply put: Be careful. Such people as you speak of do not disappear without cause."

"What do you mean?"

"They have to, Mr. Holcroft. *Had* to. The Nuremberg Tribunals and the Israeli hunters aside, many possessed funds—in some cases, fortunes—that were stolen from conquered peoples, from their institutions, often from their governments. Those funds could be reclaimed."

Noel tensed the muscles of his stomach. There *was* a connection—abstract, even misleading, under the circumstances, but it was there. The Von Tiebolts were part of a theft so massive and complex it was beyond accounting procedures. But it could not be the reason they had vanished. Lesson four: Be prepared for unexpected coincidences, no matter how strained; be ready to conceal reactions.

"I don't think the family could be involved in anything like that," he said.

"But, of course, you're not sure, since you know so little."

"Let's say I'm sure. Now, all I want to know is how I go about finding them—or finding out what happened to them."

"I mentioned attorneys."

"No attorneys. I'm an architect, remember? Lawyers are natural enemies; they take up most of our time." Holcroft smiled. "Whatever a lawyer can do, I can do faster by myself. I do speak Spanish. I'll get by in Portuguese."

"I see." The attaché paused while he reached for a box of thin cigars on his desk. He opened it and held it out for Holcroft, who shook his head. "Are you sure? It's Havana."

"I'm sure. I'm also pressed for time."

"Yes, I know." The attaché reached for a silver table lighter on the desk, snapped it, and inhaled deeply; the tip of the cigar glowed. He raised his eyes abruptly to Noel. "I can't convince you to tell me the name of this family?"

"Oh, for Christ's sake . . ." Holcroft got up. He'd had enough; he'd find other sources.

"Please," said the Brazilian, "sit down, please. Just a minute or two longer. The time's not wasted, I assure you."

Noel saw the urgency in the attaché's eyes. He sat down. "What is it?"

"La comunidad alemana. I use the Spanish you speak so well."

"The German community? There's a German community in Rio—is that what you mean?"

"Yes, but it's not solely geographical. There's an outlying district—the German *barrio,* if you will—but that is not what I refer to. I'm speaking of what we call *la otra cara de los alemanes.* Can you understand that?"

"The 'other face' . . . what's underneath, below the German surface."

"Precisely. 'The underside,' you might say. What makes them what they are; what makes them do what they do. It's important that you understand."

"I think I do. I think you explained it. Most were Nazis getting out of the Nuremberg net, bringing in money that wasn't theirs; hiding, concealing identities. Naturally, such people would tend to stick together."

"Naturally," the Brazilian said. "But you'd think after so many years there'd be greater assimilation."

"Why? You work here in New York. Go down to the Lower East Side, or Mulberry Street or up to the Bronx. Enclaves of Italians, Poles, Jews. They've been here for decades. You're talking about twenty-five, thirty years. That's not much."

"There are similarities, of course, but it's not the same, believe me. The people you speak of in New York associate openly; they wear their heritages on their sleeves. It is not like that in Brazil. The German community pretends to be assimilated, but it is not. In commerce, yes, but in very little else. There is a pervading sense of fear and anger. Too many have been hunted for too long; a thousand identities are concealed daily from everyone but themselves. They have their own hierarchy. Three or four families control the community; their huge Germanic estates dot our countryside. Of course, they call them Swiss or Bavarian." Once more the attaché paused. "Do you begin to grasp what I'm saying? The consul general will not say it; my government will not permit it. But I am far down the ladder. It is left to me. *Do* you understand?"

Noel was bewildered. "Frankly, no. Nothing you've said surprises me. At Nuremberg they called it 'crimes against humanity.' That kind of thing leads to a lot of guilt, and guilt breeds fear. Of course such people in a country that isn't their own would stay close to each other."

"Guilt *does* breed fear. And fear in turn leads to suspicion. Finally, suspicion gives birth to violence. That's what you must understand. A stranger coming to Rio looking for Germans who have disappeared is undertaking a potentially dangerous search. *La otra cara de los alemanes.* They protect each other." The attaché picked up his cigar. "Give us the name, Mr. Holcroft. Let *us* look for these people."

Noel watched the Brazilian inhale the smoke from his precious Havana. He was not sure why, but he felt suddenly uneasy. *Don't be led into a trap by pat conclusions casually stated. . . .* "I can't. I think you're exaggerating, and obviously you won't help me." He stood up.

"Very well," said the Brazilian. "I'll tell you what you would find out for yourself. When you get to Rio de Janeiro, go to the Ministry of Immigration. If you have names and approximate dates, perhaps they can help you."

"Thanks very much," said Noel, turning toward the door.

The Brazilian walked rapidly out of the office into a large anteroom that served as a reception area. A young man sitting in an armchair quickly got to his feet at the sight of his superior.

"You may have your office back now, Juan."

"Thank you, Excellency."

The older man continued across the room, past a receptionist, to a pair of double doors. On the left panel was the great seal of the República Federal de Brasil; on the right was a plaque with gold printed that read OFÍCIO DO CÔNSUL GENERAL.

The consul general went inside to another, smaller anteroom that was his secretary's office. He spoke to the girl and walked directly to the door of his own office.

"Get me the embassy. The ambassador, please. If he's not there, locate him. Inform him that it's a confidential matter; he'll know whether he can talk or not."

Brazil's highest-ranking diplomat in America's major city closed the door, strode to his desk, and sat down. He picked up a sheaf of papers stapled together. The first several pages were photocopies of newspaper stories, accounts of the killing on British Airways flight 591 from London to New York, and the subsequent discovery of the two murders on the ground. The last two pages were copies of that aircraft's passenger manifest. The diplomat scanned the names: HOL-CROFT, NOEL. DEP. GENEVA. BA #577. O. LON. BA #591. X. NYC. He stared at the information as if somehow relieved that it was still there.

His telephone hummed; he picked it up. "Yes?"

"The ambassador is on the line, sir."

"Thank you." The consul general heard an echo, which meant the scrambler was in operation. "Mr. Ambassador?"

"Yes, Geraldo. What's so urgent and confidential?"

"A few minutes ago a man came up here asking how he might go about locating a family in Rio he had not been able to reach through the usual channels. His name is Holcroft. Noel Holcroft, an architect from New York City."

"It means nothing to me," said the ambassador. "Should it?"

"Only if you've recently read the list of passengers on the British Airways plane from London last Saturday."

"Flight five-ninety-one?" The ambassador spoke sharply.

"Yes. He left that morning from Geneva on British Airways, and transferred at Heathrow to five-ninety-one."

"And now he wants to locate people in Rio? Who are they?"

"He refused to say. I was the 'attaché' he spoke with, naturally."

"Naturally. Tell me everything. I'll cable London. Do you think it's possible—" The ambassador paused.

"Yes," the consul general said softly. "I think it's very possible he is looking for the Von Tiebolts."

"Tell me everything," repeated the man in Washington. "The British believe those killings were the work of the Tinamou."

Noel felt a sense of *déjà vu* as he looked around the lounge of the Braniff 747. The colors were more vivid, the uniforms of the aircraft's personnel more fashionably cut. Otherwise, the plane seemed identical to that of British Airways flight 591. The difference was in attitude. This was the Rio Run, that carefree holiday that was to begin in the sky and continue on the beaches of the Gold Coast.

But this was to be no holiday, thought Holcroft, no holiday at all. The only climax awaiting him was one of discovery. The whereabouts or the nonwhereabouts of the family Von Tiebolt.

They'd been in the air for more than five hours. He had picked his way through a dismissable meal, slept through an even more dismissable film, and finally decided to go up to the lounge.

He had put off going upstairs. The memory of seven days ago was still discomforting. The unbelievable had happened in front of his eyes; a man had been killed not four feet from where he'd been sitting. At one point he could have reached over and *touched* the writhing figure. Death had been inches away, unnatural death, chemical death, murder.

Strychnine. A colorless crystalline alkaloid that caused paroxysms of unendurable pain. Why had it happened? Who was responsible and for what reason? The accounts were specific, the theories speculative.

Two men had been physically close to the victim in the lounge of Flight 591 from London. Either one could have administered the poison by way of the victim's drink; it was presumed one had. But again, why? According to the Port Authority police, there was no evidence that the two men had ever known Thornton. And the two men themselves—the suspected killers—had met *their* deaths by gunshot in a fuel truck on the ground. They had disappeared from the aircraft, from the sealed-off customs area, from the quarantine room, and themselves been murdered. Why? By whom?

No one had any answers. Only questions. And then even the questions stopped. The story faded from the newspapers and the broadcasts as dramatically as it had appeared, as though a blackout had been called. Again, why? Again, who was responsible?

"That was scotch on the rocks, wasn't it, Mr. Holcroft?"

The *déjà vu* was complete. The words were the same but spoken by another. The stewardess above him, placing the glass on the round Formica table, was attractive—as the stewardess on Flight 591 had been attractive. The look in her eyes had that same quality of directness he remembered from the girl on British Airways. The words, even to the use of his name, were uttered in a similar tone, only the accent varied. It was all *too* much alike. Or was his mind—his eyes, his ears, his senses—preoccupied with the memory of seven days ago?

He thanked the stewardess, almost afraid to look at her, thinking that any second he would hear a scream beside him and watch a man in uncontrollable agony lunge out of his seat, twisting in spastic convulsions over the divider.

Then Noel realized something else, and it discomforted him further. He was sitting in the same seat he had occupied during those terrifying moments on Flight 591. In a lounge constructed identically with that lounge a week ago. It was not really unusual; he preferred the location and often sat there. But now it seemed macabre. His lines of sight were the same, the lighting no different now from the way it was then.

That was scotch on the rocks, wasn't it, Mr. Holcroft?

An outstretched hand, a pretty face, a glass.

Images, sounds.

Sounds. Raucous, drunken laughter. A man with too much alcohol in him, losing his balance, falling backward over the rim of the chair. His companion reeling in delight at the sight of his unsteady friend. A third man—the man who would be dead in moments—trying too hard to be a part of the revelry. Anxious to please, wanting to join. An attractive stewardess pouring whisky, smiling, wiping the bar on which two drinks had been reduced to one because one had been spilled, rushing around the counter to help a drunken passenger. The third anxious man, embarrassed perhaps, still wanting to play with the big boys, reaching. . . .

A *glass. The* glass! The single, remaining glass on the bar.

The third man had reached for that glass!

It was scotch on the rocks. The drink intended for the passenger sitting across the lounge at the small Formica table. Oh, my *God!* thought Holcroft, the images racing back and forth in sequence in his mind's eye. The drink on the bar—the drink a stranger named Thornton had taken—had been meant for *him!*

The strychnine had been meant for *him!* The twisting, horrible convulsions of agony were to be *his!* The terrible death assigned to *him!*

He looked down at the glass in front of him on the table; his fingers were around it.

That was scotch on the rocks, wasn't it? . . .

He pushed the drink aside. Suddenly he could no longer stay at that table, remain in that lounge. He had to get away; he had to force the images out of his mind. They were too clear, too real, too horrible.

He rose from the chair and walked rapidly, unsteadily, toward the staircase. The sounds of drunken laughter weaved in and out between an unrelenting scream of torment that was the screech of sudden death. No one else could hear those sounds, but they pounded in his head.

He lurched down the curving staircase to the deck below. The light was dim; several passengers were reading under the beams of tiny spotlights, but most were asleep.

Noel was bewildered. The hammering in his ears would not stop, the images would not go away. He felt the need to vomit, to expunge the fear that had settled into his stomach. Where was the toilet? In the galley . . . behind the galley? Beyond the curtain; that was it. Or was it? He parted the curtain.

Suddenly, his eyes were drawn down to his right, to the front seat of the 747's second section. A man had stirred in his sleep. A heavyset man whose face he had seen before. He did not recall where, but he was sure of it! A face creased in panic, racing by, close to his. What was it about the face? Something had made a brief but strong impression. What *was* it?

The *eyebrows;* that was it! Thick eyebrows, the coiled, matted hair an odd mixture of black and white. Salt-and-pepper eyebrows; *where* was it? Why did the sight of those strangely arresting brows trigger obscure memories of another act of violence? Where *was* it? He could not remember, and because he could not, he felt the blood rushing to his head. The pounding grew louder; his temples throbbed.

Suddenly, the man with the thick, coiled eyebrows woke up, somehow aware that he was being stared at. Their eyes locked; recognition was absolute.

And there was violence in that recognition. But of *what? When? Where?*

Holcroft nodded awkwardly, unable to think. The pain in his stomach was knifelike; the sounds in his head were now cracks of thunder. For a moment he forgot where he was; then he remembered and the images returned. The sights and sounds of a killing that but for an accident would have claimed his life.

He had to get back to his seat. He had to control himself, to stop the pain and the thunder and the pounding in his chest. He turned and walked quickly beyond the curtain, past the galley, up the aisle to his seat.

He sat down in the semidarkness, grateful there was no one beside him. He pressed his head into the rim of the chair and closed his eyes, trying with all his concentration to rid his mind of the terrible sight of a grotesque face, screaming away the last few seconds of life. But he could not.

That face became *his* face.

Then the features blurred, as if the flesh were melting, only to be formed again. The face that now came into focus was no one he recognized. A strange, angular face, parts of which seemed familiar, but not as a whole.

Involuntarily, he gasped. He had never seen that face but suddenly he knew it. Instinctively. It was the face of Heinrich Clausen. A man in agony thirty years ago. The unknown father with whom he had his covenant.

Holcroft opened his eyes, which stung from the perspiration that had rolled down his face. There was another truth and he was not sure he wanted to recognize it. The two men who had tried to kill him with strychnine had themselves been murdered. They had interfered.

The men of Wolfsschanze had been aboard that plane.

7

The clerk behind the desk of the Pôrto Alegre Hotel pulled Holcroft's reservation from the file. A small yellow message envelope was stapled to the back of the card. The clerk tore it off and handed it to Noel.

"This came for you shortly past seven o'clock this evening, senhor."

Holcroft knew no one in Rio de Janeiro, and had told no one in New York where he was going. He ripped open the flap and drew out the message. It was from Sam Buonoventura. He was to return the overseas call as soon as possible, regardless of the hour.

Holcroft looked at his watch; it was nearly midnight. He signed the register and spoke as casually as he could, his mind on Sam.

"I have to telephone Curaçao. Will there be any trouble at this hour?"

The clerk seemed mildly offended. "Certainly not with our *telefonistas*, senhor. I cannot speak for Curaçao."

The origins of the difficulty notwithstanding, it was not until one-fifteen in the morning that he heard Buonoventura's rasping voice over the line.

"I think you've got a problem, Noley."

"I've got more than one. What is it?"

"Your answering service gave my number to this cop in New York, a Lieutenant Miles; he's a detective. He was hot as hell. Said you were supposed to inform the police if you left town, to say nothing about leaving the country."

Christ, he had forgotten! And now he understood just how vital those instructions were. The strychnine was meant for him! Had the police reached the same conclusion?

"What did you tell him, Sam?"

"Got hot myself. It's the only way to handle angry cops. I told him you were off in the out-islands doing a survey for a possible installation Washington was interested in. A little bit north, we're not too far from the Canal Zone; it could mean anything. Nobody talks."

"Did he accept that?"

"Hard to tell. He wants you to call him. I bought you time, though. I said you radioed in this afternoon and I didn't expect to hear from you for three or four days, and I couldn't make contact. That's when he yelled like a cut bull."

"But did he buy it?"

"What else could he do? He thinks we're all fucking-A stupid down here, and I agreed with him. He gave me two numbers for you. Got a pencil?"

"Go ahead."

Holcroft wrote down the numbers—a Port Authority police telephone and Miles's home—thanked Buonoventura, and said he'd be in touch next week.

Noel had unpacked during the interminable wait for the Curaçao connection. He sat in a cane-backed chair in front of the window and looked out at the night-white beach and the dark waters beyond, reflecting the bright half moon. Below, on that isolated section of the street bordering the ocean walkway, were the curving, black-and-white parallel lines that signified the Copacabana, the golden coast of Guanabara. There was an emptiness about the scene that had nothing to do with its being deserted. It was too perfect, too pretty. He would never have designed it that way; there was an absence of character. He focused his eyes on the windowpanes. There was nothing to do now but think and rest and hope he could sleep. Sleep had been difficult for the past week; it would be more difficult now. Because he knew now what he had not known before: Someone had tried to kill him.

The knowledge produced an odd sensation. He could not believe that there was someone who wanted him dead. Yet someone had to have made that decision, had to have issued the order. Why? What had he done? Was it Geneva? His covenant?

We're dealing in millions. Those were not only the dead Manfredi's words;

they were his warning. It was the only possible explanation. The information had got out, but there was no way to know how far it had spread, or who was affected by it, who infuriated. Or the identity of the unknown person—or persons—who wanted to stop the release of the Geneva account, to consign it to the litigations of the international courts.

Manfredi was right: The only moral solution was found in carrying out the intent of the document drawn up by three extraordinary men in the midst of the devastation their own monster had created. *Amends must be made.* It was the credo Heinrich Clausen believed in; it *was* honorable; it *was* right. In their misguided way, the men of Wolfsschanze understood.

Noel poured himself a drink, walked over to the bed, and sat down on the edge, staring at the telephone. Next to it were the two numbers written on a hotel message pad, given to him by Sam Buonoventura. They were his links to Lieutenant Miles, Port Authority police. But Holcroft could not bring himself to call. He had begun the hunt; he had taken the first step in his search for the family of Wilhelm von Tiebolt. Step, hell! It was a giant leap of four thousand air miles; he would not turn back.

There was so much to do. Noel wondered whether he was capable of doing it, whether he was capable of making his way through the unfamiliar forest.

He felt his eyelids grow heavy. Sleep was coming and he was grateful for it. He put down the glass and kicked off his shoes, not bothering with the rest of his clothes. He fell back on the bed and for several seconds stared at the white ceiling. He felt so alone, yet knew he wasn't. There was a man in agony, from thirty years ago, crying out to him. He thought about that man until sleep came.

Holcroft followed the translator into the dimly lit, windowless cubicle. Their conversation had been brief; Noel had sought specific information. The name was Von Tiebolt; the family, German nationals. A mother and two children—a daughter and a son—had immigrated to Brazil on or about June 15, 1945. A third child, another daughter, had been born several months later, probably in Rio de Janeiro. The records had to contain *some* information. Even if a false name was used, a simple cross-check of the weeks involved—two or three either way— would certainly unearth a pregnant woman with two children coming into the country. If there were more than one, it was his problem to trace them. At least a name, or names, would surface.

No, it was not an official inquiry. There were no criminal charges; there was no seeking of revenge for crimes going back thirty years. On the contrary, it was "a benign search."

Noel knew that an explanation would be asked of him, and he remembered one of the lessons learned at the consulate in New York: *Base the lie in an aspect of truth.* The family Von Tiebolt had relations in the United States, went the lie. People who had immigrated to America in the twenties and thirties. Very few were left, and there was a large sum of money involved. Surely, the officials at the *Ministério do Imigração* would want to help find the inheritors. It was entirely possible that the Von Tiebolts would be grateful . . . and he, as the intermediary, would certainly make known their cooperation.

Ledgers were brought out. Hundreds of photostats from another era were studied. Faded, soiled copies of documents, so many of which were obviously false papers purchased in Bern and Zürich and Lisbon. Passports.

But there were no documents relating to the Von Tiebolts, no descriptions of a pregnant woman with two children entering Rio de Janeiro during the month of June or July in 1945. At least, none resembling the wife of Wilhelm von Tiebolt. There were pregnant women, even pregnant women with children, but none with children that could have been Von Tiebolt's. According to Manfredi, the daughter, Gretchen, was twelve or thirteen years old; the son, Johann, ten. Every one of the women entering Brazil during those weeks was accompanied either by a husband or a false husband, and where there were children, none—not *one*—was more than seven years of age.

This struck Holcroft as being not only unusual but mathematically impossible. He stared at the pages of faded ink, at the often illegible entries made by harried immigration officials thirty-odd years ago.

Something was wrong; his architect's eye was troubled. He had the feeling he was studying blueprints that had not been finished, that were filled with minute alterations—tiny lines erased and changed, but very delicately, so as not to disturb the larger design.

Erased and changed. *Chemically* erased, *delicately* changed. That was what bothered him! The birthdates! Page after page of miniature figures, digits subtly altered! A 3 became an 8, a 1 a 9, a 2 a 0, the curve retained, a line drawn down, a zero added. Page after page in the ledgers, for the weeks of June and July of 1945, the birthdates of all the children entering Brazil had been changed so that none was born prior to 1938!

It was a painstakingly clever ruse, one that had to be thought out carefully, deliberately. Stop the hunt at the source. But do it in a way that appeared above suspicion. Small numbers faithfully—if hastily—recorded by unknown immigration personnel more than thirty years ago. Recorded from documents, the majority of which had been long since destroyed, for most were false. There was no way to substantiate, to confirm or deny, the accuracy. Time and conspiracies had made that impossible. Of course there was no one resembling the Von Tiebolts! *Good Lord,* what a deception!

Noel pulled out his lighter; its flame would provide more light on a page where his eye told him there were numerous minute alterations.

"*Senhor!* That is forbidden!" The harsh command was delivered in a loud voice by the translator. "Those old pages catch fire easily. We cannot take such risks."

Holcroft understood. It explained the inadequate light, the windowless cubicle. "I'll bet you can't," he said, extinguishing his lighter. "And I suppose these ledgers can't be removed from this room."

"No, *senhor.*"

"And, of course, there are no extra lamps around, and you don't have a flashlight. Isn't that right?"

"*Senhor,*" interrupted the translator, his tone now courteous, even deferential. "We have spent nearly three hours with you. We have tried to cooperate fully, but as I'm sure you're aware, we have other duties to perform. So, if you have finished . . ."

"I think you made sure of that before I started," broke in Holcroft. "Yes, I'm finished. Here."

He walked in the bright afternoon sunlight, trying to make sense out of things, the soft ocean breezes caressing his face, calming his anger and his frustration. He strolled on the white boardwalk overlooking the immaculate sand of Guanabara Bay. Now and then he stopped and leaned against the railing, watching the grown-up children at their games. The beautiful people, sunning and stunning. Grace and arrogance coexisted with artifice. Money was everywhere, evidenced by the golden, oiled bodies, too often too perfectly formed, too pretty, all flaws concealed. But again, where was character? It was somehow absent on the Copacabana this afternoon.

He passed that section of the beach that fronted his hotel and glanced up at the windows, trying to locate his room. For a moment he thought he had found it, then realized he was wrong. He could see two figures behind the glass, beyond the curtains.

He returned to the railing and lit a cigarette. The lighter made him think about the thirty-year-old ledgers so painstakingly doctored. Had they been altered just for him? Or had there been others over the years looking for the Von Tiebolts? Regardless of the answer, he had to find another source. Or other sources.

La comunidad alemana. Holcroft recalled the words of the attaché in New York. He remembered the man's saying there were three or four families who were the arbiters of the German community. It followed that such men had to know the most carefully guarded secrets. *Identities are concealed every day. . . . A stranger coming to Rio looking for Germans who have disappeared is undertaking a potentially dangerous search . . .* "la otra cara de los alemanes." *They protect each other.*

There was a way to eliminate the danger, Noel thought. It was found in the explanation he had given the translator at the Ministry of Immigration. He traveled a great deal, so it was plausible that someone somewhere had approached him, knowing he was flying to Brazil, and asked him to locate the Von Tiebolts. It had to be a person who dealt in legitimate confidentiality, a lawyer or a banker. Someone whose own reputation was above reproach. Without analyzing it deeply, Holcroft knew that whoever he decided upon would be the key to his explanation.

An idea for a candidate struck him, the risks apparent, the irony not lost. Richard Holcroft, the only father he had ever known. Stockbroker, banker, naval officer . . . father. The man who had given a wild young mother and her child a chance to live again. Without fear, without the stain.

Noel looked at his watch. It was ten minutes past five—past three in New York. Midafternoon on a Monday. He did not believe in omens, but he had just come upon one. Every Monday afternoon Richard Holcroft went to the New York Athletic Club, where old friends played gentle squash and sat around thick oak tables in the bar and reminisced. Noel could have him paged, talk to him alone— ask for help. Help that was to be rendered confidentially, for confidentiality was not only the essence of the cover but the basis of his protection. Someone, *anyone*, had contacted Richard Holcroft—man of stature—and asked him to locate a family named Von Tiebolt in Brazil. Knowing his son was going to Rio, he quite logically asked his son to make inquiries. It was a confidential matter; it would not be discussed. No one could turn away the curious with greater authority than Dick Holcroft.

But Althene was not to be told. That was the hardest part of the request. Dick adored her; there were no secrets between them. But his father—damn it, *step*father—would not refuse him if the request was based in genuine need. He never had.

He crossed the smooth marble floor of the hotel lobby toward the bank of elevators, oblivious of sights and sounds, his concentration on what he would say to his stepfather. As a result, he was startled when an obese American tourist tapped his shoulder.

"They calling you, Mac?" The man pointed toward the front desk.

Behind the counter the clerk was looking at Noel. In his hand was the familiar yellow message envelope; he gave it to a bellhop, who started across the lobby.

The single name on the slip of paper was unknown to him: CARARRA. There was a telephone number below, but no message. Holcroft was bewildered. The lack of a message was unusual; it was not the Latin way of doing things. Senhor Cararra could phone again; he had to reach New York. He had to build another cover.

Yet, in his room, Holcroft read the name again: CARARRA. His curiosity was aroused. Who was this Cararra that he expected to be called back on the basis of a name alone, a name the man knew meant nothing to Holcroft? In South American terms it was discourteous to the point of being insulting. His stepfather could wait a few minutes while he found out. He dialed the number.

Cararra was not a man but a woman, and from the sound of her low, strained voice she was a frightened woman. Her English was passable but not good; it did not matter. Her message was as clear as the fear she conveyed.

"I cannot talk now, senhor. Do not call this number again. It is most not necessary."

"You left it with the operator. What did you expect me to do?"

"It was a . . . *êrro.*"

"*Yerro?* Mistake?"

"Yes. A mistake. I will call you. *We* will call."

"What about? Who are you?"

"*Mais tarde!*" The voice descended to a harsh whisper and was abruptly gone with the click of the line.

Mas tarde . . . mas tarde. Later. The woman would call him again. Holcroft felt a sudden hollowness in his stomach, as sudden as the abrupt disappearance of the frightened whisper. He could not recall when he had heard a woman's voice so filled with fear.

That she was somehow connected with the missing Von Tiebolts was the first thought that came to his mind. But in what way? And how in God's name would she know about *him?* The feeling of dread came over him again . . . and the image of the horrible face contorted in death, thirty thousand feet in the air. He was being observed; strangers were watching him.

The whine of the telephone receiver interrupted his thoughts; he had forgotten to hang up. He depressed the button, released it, and made the call to New York. He needed his protection quickly; he knew that now.

He stood by the window, staring out at the beachfront, waiting for the operator to call him back. There was a flash of light from the street below. The chrome of a car grille had caught the rays of the sun and reflected them skyward. The car had passed that section of the boardwalk where he had been standing only minutes ago. Standing and absently glancing up at the hotel windows, trying to spot his room.

The *windows*. . . . The angle of *sight.* Noel moved closer to the panes and studied the diagonal line from the spot below—where he had been standing—to where he stood now. His architect's eye was a practiced eye; angles did not deceive him. Too, the windows were not that close to one another, befitting the separation of rooms in an oceanfront hotel on the Copacabana. He looked up at *this* window, thinking it was not his room because he saw figures inside, behind the glass. But it *was* his room. And there *had* been people inside.

He walked to his closet and stood looking at his clothes. He trusted his memory for detail as much as he trusted his eye for angular lines. He pictured the closet where he had changed clothes that morning. He had fallen asleep in the suit he had worn from New York. His light-tan slacks had been on the far right, almost against the closet wall. It was habit: trousers on the right, jackets on the left. The slacks were still on the right, but not against the wall. Instead, they were several inches toward the center. His dark-blue blazer was *in* the center, *not* on the left side.

His clothes had been searched.

He crossed to the bed and his open attaché case. It was his office when he traveled; he knew every millimeter of space, every compartment, the position of every item in every slot. He did not have to look long.

His attaché case had been searched as well.

The telephone rang, the sound an intrusion. He picked it up and heard the voice of the Athletic Club's operator, but he knew he could not ask for Richard Holcroft; he could not involve him. Things were suddenly too complicated. He had to think them through.

"New York Athletic Club. Hello? Hello? . . . Hello, Rio operator? There's no one on the line, Rio. Hello? New York Athletic Club. . . ."

Noel replaced the receiver. He had been about to do something *crazy*. His room had been searched! In his need for a cover in Rio de Janeiro, he had been about to lead someone directly to the one person closest to his mother, once the wife of Heinrich Clausen. What had he been *thinking* of?

And then he realized that nothing was wasted. Instead, another lesson had been learned. *Carry out the lie logically, then reexamine it, and use the most credible part.* If he could invent a reason for such a man as Richard Holcroft to conceal the identity of those seeking the Von Tiebolts, he could invent the man himself.

Noel was breathing hard. He had almost committed a terrible error, but he was beginning to know what to look for in the unfamiliar forest. The paths were lined with traps; he had to keep his guard up and move cautiously. He could not permit himself a mistake like the one he had nearly made. He had come very close to risking the life of the father that was, for one he had never known.

Very little of value or truth ever came from anything he touched. His mother's words, and like Manfredi's, meant as a warning. But his mother—unlike Manfredi—was wrong. Heinrich Clausen was as much a victim as he was a villain of his time. The anguished letter he had written while Berlin was falling confirmed it, and what he had done confirmed it. Somehow his son would prove it.

La comunidad alemana. Three, four families in the German community, the arbiters who made irreversible decisions. One of them would be his source. And he knew exactly where to look.

The old, heavyset man with thick jowls and steel-gray hair, cut short in the fashion of a Junker, looked up from the huge diningroom table at the intruder. He ate alone, no places set for family or guests. It seemed strange, for as the door was opened by the intruder, the voices of other people could be heard; there were family and guests in the large house, but they were not at the table.

"We have additional information on Clausen's son, Herr Graff," said the intruder, approaching the old man's chair. "You know about the Curaçao communication. Two other calls were made this afternoon. One to the woman, Cararra, and the second to a men's club in New York."

"The Cararras will do their job well," said Graff, his fork suspended, the puffed flesh around his eyes creased. "What is this club in New York?"

"A place called the New York Athletic Club. It is—"

"I know what it is. A wealthy membership. Whom was he calling?"

"The call was placed to the location, not to a person. Our people in New York are trying to find out."

The old man put down his fork. He spoke softly, insultingly. "Our people in New York are slow, and so are you."

"I beg your pardon?"

"Undoubtedly among the members will be found the name of Holcroft. If so, Clausen's son has broken his word; he's told Holcroft about Geneva. That is dangerous. Richard Holcroft is an old man, but he is not feeble. We always knew that if he lived long enough, he might be a stumbling block." Graff shifted his large head and looked at the intruder. "The envelope arrived in Sesimbra; there is no excuse. The events of the other night had to be clear to the son. Cable the Tinamou. I don't trust his associate here in Rio. Use the eagle code and tell him what I believe. Our people in New York will have another task. The elimination of a meddling old man. Richard Holcroft must be taken out. The Tinamou will demand it."

8

Noel knew what he was looking for: a bookstore that was more than a place to buy books. In every resort city there was always one major shop that catered to the reading requirements of a specific nationality. In this case, its name was A Livraria Alemão: the German Bookshop. According to the desk clerk, it carried all the latest German periodicals, and Lufthansa flew newspapers in daily. That was the information Holcroft sought. Such a store would have accounts; someone there would know the established German families in Rio. If he could get just one or two names. . . . It was a place to start.

The store was less than ten minutes from the hotel. "I'm an American architect," he said to the clerk, who was halfway up a ladder, rearranging books on the top shelf. "I'm down here checking out the Bavarian influence on large residential homes. Do you have any material on the subject?"

"I didn't know it was a subject," replied the man in fluent English. "There's a certain amount of Alpine design, chalet-style building, but I wouldn't call it Bavarian."

Lesson six, or was it seven? Even if the lie is based in an aspect of truth, make sure the person you use it on knows less than you do.

"Alpine, Swiss, Bavarian. They're pretty much the same thing."

"Really? I thought there were considerable differences."

Lesson eight or nine. Don't argue. Remember the objective.

"Look, to tell you the truth, a rich couple in New York are paying my way here to bring back sketches. They were in Rio last summer. They rode around and spotted some great homes. They described them as Bavarian."

"Those would be in the northwest countryside. There are several marvelous houses out there. The Eisenstat residence, for example; but then, I think they're Jewish. There's an odd mixture of Moorish, if you can believe it. And, of course, there's the Graff mansion. That's almost too much, but it's really spectacular. To be expected, I imagine. Graff's a millionaire many times over."

"What's the name again? Graff?"

"Maurice Graff. He's an importer; but then, aren't they all?"

"Who?"

"Oh, come now, don't be naive. If he wasn't a general, or a muckedy-muck in the High Command, I'll piss port wine."

"You're English."

"I'm English."

"But you work in a German bookstore."

"Ich spreche gut Deutsch."

"Couldn't they find a German?"

"I suppose there are advantages hiring someone like myself," said the Britisher cryptically.

Noel feigned surprise. "Really?"

"Yes," replied the clerk, scaling another rung on the ladder. "No one asks me questions."

The clerk watched the American leave and stepped quickly down from the ladder, sliding it across the shelf track with a shove of his hand. It was a gesture of accomplishment, of minor triumph. He walked rapidly down the book-lined aisle and turned so abruptly into an intersecting stack that he collided with a customer examining a volume of Goethe.

"Verzeihung," said the clerk under his breath, not at all concerned.

"Schwesterchen," said the man with the thick black-and-white eyebrows.

At the reference to his lack of masculinity, the clerk turned. "You!"

"The friends of Tinamou are never far away," replied the man.

"You followed him?" asked the clerk.

"He never knew. Make your call."

The Englishman continued on his way to the door of an office at the rear of the store. He went inside, picked up the telephone, and dialed. It was answered by the aide of the most powerful man in Rio.

"Senhor Graff's residence. Good afternoon."

"Our man at the hotel deserves a large tip," said the clerk. "He was right. I insist on talking to Herr Graff. I did precisely as we agreed, and I did it superbly. I've no doubt he'll be calling. Now, Herr Graff, please."

"I'll pass along your message, butterfly," said the aide.

"You'll do no such thing! I have other news I'll tell only to him."

"What does it concern? I don't have to tell you he's a busy man."

"Shall we say a countryman of mine? Do I make myself clear?"

"We know he's in Rio; he's already made contact. You'll have to do better than that."

"He's still here. In the store. He may be waiting to talk to me."

The aide spoke to someone nearby. The words, however, were distinct. "It's the actor, mein Herr. He insists on speaking to you. Everything went as scheduled during the past hour, but there seems to be a complication. His countryman is in the bookshop."

The phone passed hands. "What is it?" asked Maurice Graff.

"I wanted you to know that everything went exactly as we anticipated. . . ."

"Yes, yes, I understand that," interrupted Graff. "You do excellent work. Now, what's this about the *Engländer?* He's there?"

"He followed the American. He was no more than ten feet from him. He's still here, and I expect he'll want me to tell him what's happening. Should I?"

"No," replied Graff. "We are perfectly capable of running things here without interference. Say to him that we're concerned he'll be recognized; that we suggest he remain out of sight. Tell him I do not approve of his methods. You may say you heard it from me personally."

"*Thank* you, Herr Graff! It will be a pleasure."

"Yes, I know it will."

Graff handed the telephone back to his aide. "The Tinamou must not let this happen," he said. "It starts again."

"What, mein Herr?"

"All over again," continued the old man. "The interference, the silent observations, one upon the other. Authority becomes divided, everyone's suspect."

"I don't understand."

"Of course you don't. You weren't there." Graff leaned back in his chair. "Send a second cable to the Tinamou. Tell him that we request he order his wolf back to the Mediterranean. He's taking too many risks. We object, and cannot be responsible under the circumstances."

It took several phone calls and the passage of twenty-four hours, but word that Graff would see him finally came, shortly past two o'clock the next afternoon. Holcroft leased a car at the hotel and drove northwest out of the city. He stopped frequently, studying the tourist map provided by the rental agency. He finally found the address, and swung through the iron gates into the ascending drive that led to the house at the top of the hill.

The road leveled off into a large parking area of white concrete, bordered by green shrubbery that was broken up by flagstone paths leading through groves of fruit trees on either side.

The clerk at the bookstore had been right. The Graff estate was spectacular. The view was magnificent: plains nearby, mountains in the distance, and far to the east the hazy blue of the Atlantic. The house itself was three stories high. A series of balconies rose on both sides of the central entrance: a set of massive double doors—oiled mahogany, hinged with large, pitted triangles of black iron. The effect *was* Alpine, as if a geometric design of many Swiss chalets were welded into one and set down on a tropical mountain.

Noel parked the car to the right of the front steps and got out. There were two other automobiles in the parking area—a white Mercedes limousine and a low-slung, red Maserati. The Graff family traveled well. Holcroft gripped his attaché case and camera and started up the marble steps.

"I'm flattered our minor architectural efforts are appreciated," said Graff. "It's natural, I suppose, for transplanted people to create a touch of their homeland in new surroundings. My family came from the *Schwarzwald*. . . . The memories are never far away."

"I appreciate your having me out here, sir." Noel put the five hastily drawn sketches back into his attaché case and closed it. "I speak for my client as well, of course."

"You have everything you need?"

"A roll of film and five elevation sketches are more than I had hoped for. Incidentally, the gentleman who showed me around will tell you the photographs were limited to the exterior structural detail."

"I don't understand you."

"I wouldn't want you to think I was taking pictures of your private grounds."

Maurice Graff laughed softly. "My residence is very well protected, Mr. Holcroft. Besides, it never crossed my mind that you were examining the premises for purposes of theft. Sit down, please."

"Thank you." Noel sat opposite the old man. "These days some people might be suspicious."

"Well, I won't mislead you. I did call the Pôrto Alegre Hotel to see if you were registered. You were. You are a man named Holcroft from New York whose reservation was made by a reputable travel agency that obviously knows you, and you use credit cards cleared by computers. You entered Brazil with a valid passport. What more did I need? The times are technically too complicated for a man to pretend to be someone he's not, wouldn't you agree?"

"Yes, I guess I would," replied Noel, thinking that it was the moment perhaps to shift to the real purpose of his visit. He was about to speak, but Graff continued, as if filling an awkward silence.

"How long will you be in Rio?" he asked.

"Only a few more days. I have the name of your architect, and naturally I'll consult with him when he's free to see me."

"I'll have my secretary telephone; there'll be no delay. I have no idea how such financial arrangements are made—or, indeed, if there are any—but I'm quite sure he'd let you have copies of the plans if they would be helpful to you."

Noel smiled, the professional in him aroused. "It's a question of selective adaptation, Mr. Graff. My calling him would be as much a matter of courtesy as anything else. I might ask where certain materials were purchased, or how specific stress problems were solved, but that'd be it. I wouldn't ask for the plans, and I think he'd be reluctant to say yes if I did."

"There would be *no* reluctance," said Graff, his bearing and intensity a reflection of a military past.

... *If he wasn't a general, or a muckedy-muck in the High Command, I'll piss
port wine.* ...

"It's not important, sir. I've got what I came for."

"I see." Graff shifted his heavy frame in the chair. It was the movement of
a weary old man toward the end of a long afternoon. Yet the eyes were not weary;
they were strangely alert. "An hour's conference would be sufficient, then?"

"Easily."

"I'll arrange it."

"You're very kind."

"Then you can return to New York."

"Yes." It was the moment to mention the Von Tiebolts. Now. "Actually,
there's one other thing I should do while I'm here in Rio. It's not terribly
important, but I said I'd try. I'm not sure where to begin. The police, I imagine."

"That sounds ominous. A crime?"

"Quite the contrary. I meant whichever department of the police it is that
could help locate some people. They're not in the telephone directory. I even
checked unlisted numbers; they don't have one."

"Are you sure they're in Rio?"

"They were when last heard from. And I gather the other cities in Brazil were
checked out, again through the telephone companies."

"You intrigue me, Mr. Holcroft. Is it so important these people be found?
What did they do? But then you said there was no crime."

"None. I know very little. A friend of mine in New York, an attorney, knew
I was coming here and asked me to do what I could to locate this family.
Apparently it was left some money by relatives in the Midwest."

"An inheritance?"

"Yes."

"Then perhaps legal counsel here in Rio . . ."

"My friend sent what he termed 'inquiries of record' to several law firms down
here," said Noel, remembering the words of the attaché in New York. "There
weren't any satisfactory responses."

"How did he explain that?"

"He didn't. He was just annoyed. I guess the money wasn't enough for three
attorneys to get involved."

"Three attorneys?"

"Yes," replied Noel, astonished at himself. He was filling a gap instinctively,
without *thinking*. "There's the lawyer in Chicago—or St. Louis—my friend's
firm in New York, and the one down here in Rio. I don't imagine what's
confidential to an outsider is confidential between attorneys. Perhaps splitting a
fee three ways wasn't worth the trouble."

"But your friend is a man of conscience." Graff arched his brows in appreciation. Or something else, Holcroft thought.

"I'd like to think so."

"Perhaps I can help. I have friends."

Holcroft shook his head. "I couldn't ask you. You've done enough for me this afternoon. And, as I said, it's not that important."

"Naturally," said Graff, shrugging. "I wouldn't care to intrude in confidential matters." The German looked over at the windows, squinting. The sun was settling above the western mountains; shafts of orange light streamed through the glass, adding a rich hue to the dark wood of the study.

"The name of the family is Von Tiebolt," said Noel, watching the old man's face. But whatever he expected to find, nothing could have prepared him for what he saw.

Old Graff's eyes snapped open, their glance shooting over at Holcroft, filled with loathing. "You are a *pig,*" said the German, his voice so low it could barely be heard. "This was a trick, a devious ruse to come into my house! To come to me!"

"You're wrong, Mr. Graff. You can call my client in New York. . . ."

"*Pig! . . .*" the old man screamed. "The Von Tiebolts! *Verräter!* Below filth! Cowards! *Schweinhunde!* How *dare* you!"

Noel watched, mesmerized and helpless. Graff's face was discolored with rage; the veins in his neck were at the surface of his flesh, his eyes red and furious, his hands trembling, gripping the arms of the chair.

"I don't understand," said Holcroft, getting to his feet.

"You understand . . . you *garbage!* You are looking for the Von Tiebolts! You want to give them life again!"

"They're *dead?*"

"Would to the Almighty they *were!*"

"Graff, listen to me. If you know something—"

"*Get out of my house!*" The old man struggled up from the chair and screamed at the closed door of the study. "Werner! *Komm' her!*"

Graff's aide burst through the door. "*Mein Herr? Was ist—*"

"Take this impostor away! Get him out of my house!"

The aide looked at Holcroft. "This way. *Quickly!*"

Noel reached down for his attaché case and walked swiftly toward the door. He stopped and turned to look once more at the enraged Graff. The old German stood like a bloated, grotesque manikin, yet he could not control his trembling.

"Get out! You are *contemptible!*"

The final, searing accusation shattered Noel's self-control. It was not he who was contemptible; it was the figure of arrogance in front of him, this swollen image of indulgence and brutality. This monster who betrayed, then destroyed, a man in agony thirty years ago . . . and thousands like him. This *Nazi.*

"You're in no position to call me names."

"We'll see who's in what position. Get *out!*"

"I'll get out, General, or whatever the hell you are. I can't get out fast enough, because now I understand. You don't know me from the last corpse you bastards burned, but I mention one name and you can't stand it. You're torn apart because you know—and I know—that Von Tiebolt saw through you thirty years ago. When the bodies piled up. He saw what you *really* were."

"We did not conceal what we were! The world knew. There was no deception on our part!"

Holcroft stopped and swallowed involuntarily. In his burst of anger, he had to seek justice for the man who had cried out to him from the grave; he had to strike back at this symbol of the once-awesome might and decay that had stolen a father from him. He could not help himself.

"Get this clear," said Noel. "I'm going to find the Von Tiebolts, and you're not going to stop me. Don't think you can. Don't think you've got me marked. You haven't. I've got *you* marked. For exactly what you are. You wear your Iron Cross a little too obviously."

Graff had regained control. "Find the Von Tiebolts, by all means. We'll be there!"

"I'll find them. And when I do, if anything happens to them, I'll know who did it. I'll brand you for what you are. You sit up here in this castle and bark your orders. You're still pretending. You were finished years ago—before the war was over—and men like Von Tiebolt knew it. They understood, but you never did. You never will."

"Get *out!*"

A guard raced into the room; hands grabbed Noel from behind. An arm plunged over his right shoulder and down across his chest. He was yanked briefly off his feet and pulled backward out of the room. He swung his attaché case and felt the impact on the large, weaving body of the man dragging him through the door. He rammed his left elbow into the stomach of that unseen body and kicked viciously, jabbing his heel into his attacker's shin bone. The response was immediate; the man yelped; the grip across Noel's chest was momentarily lessened. It was enough.

Holcroft shot his left hand up, grabbing the cloth of the extended arm, and pulled forward with all his strength. He angled his body to the right; his right shoulder jammed into the chest that rose behind him. His assailant stumbled. Noel rammed a last shoulder block into the elevated chest, throwing his attacker into an antique chair against the wall. Man and delicate wood met in a crushing impact; the frame of the chair collapsed under the weight of the body. The guard was stunned, his wide eyes blinking, his focus temporarily lost.

Holcroft looked down at the man. The guard was large, but his bulk was the most threatening part of him. And the bulk was just that; like old Graff, a mountain of flesh packed under a tight-fitting jacket.

Through the open door Holcroft could see Graff start for the telephone on his desk. The aide he had called Werner took an awkward step toward Noel.

"*Don't,*" said Holcroft. He walked across the large hallway toward the front entrance. On the opposite side of the foyer several men and women stood in an open archway. None made a move toward him; none even raised his voice. The

German mentality was consistent, thought Noel, not unhappy with the realization. These minions were awaiting orders.

"Do as I've instructed," said Graff into the telephone, his voice calm, with no trace of the fury he had exhibited only minutes ago. He was now the general officer issuing commands to an attentive subordinate. "Wait until he's halfway down the hill, then throw the gate switch. It's vital that the American thinks he has escaped." The old German hung up and turned to his aide. "Is the guard hurt?"

"Merely stunned, mein Herr. He's walking around, shaking off the effects of the blow."

"Holcroft is angry," mused Graff. "He's filled with himself, exhilarated, consumed with purpose. That's good. Now he must be frightened, made to tremble at the unexpected, at the sheer brutality of the moment. Tell the guard to wait five minutes and then take up pursuit. He must do his job well."

"He has his orders; he's an expert marksman."

"Good." The former *Wehrmachtsgeneral* walked slowly to the window and squinted into the final rays of the sun. "Soft words, lover's words . . . and then sharp, hysterical rebukes. The embrace, and the knife. One must follow the other in rapid succession until Holcroft has no judgment left. Until he can no longer distinguish between ally and enemy, knowing only that he must press forward. When finally he breaks, we'll be there and he'll be ours."

9

Noel slammed the huge door behind him and walked down the marble steps to the car. He swung the automobile into reverse, so that his hood faced the downhill drive out of the Graff estate, pressed the accelerator and headed for the exit.

Several things occurred to him. The first was that the afternoon sun had descended behind the western mountains, creating pockets of shadows on the ground. Daylight was disappearing; he needed his headlights. Another concern was that Graff's reaction to the mention of the Von Tiebolts had to mean two things: The Von Tiebolts were alive, and they were a threat. But a threat to what? To whom? And where were they?

A third was more of a feeling than a specific thought. It was his reaction to the physical encounter he had just experienced. Throughout his life he had taken whatever size and strength he possessed as a matter of course. Because he was large and relatively well coordinated, he never felt the need to seek physical challenge except in competition against himself, in bettering a tennis game or besting a ski slope. As a result, he avoided fights; they struck him as unnecessary.

It was this general attitude that had made him laugh when his stepfather had insisted he join him at the club for a series of lessons in self-defense. The city was turning into a jungle; Holcroft's son was going to learn how to protect himself.

He took the course, and promptly forgot everything he had learned when it was over. If he had actually absorbed *anything*, he had done it subconsciously.

He *had* absorbed something, reflected Noel, pleased with himself. He remembered the glazed look in the eyes of the guard.

The last thought that crossed his mind as he turned into the downhill drive was also vague. Something was wrong with the front seat of the car. The furious activity of the last minutes had blurred his usually acute eye for such things, but something about the checkered cloth of the seat cover bothered him. . . .

Terrible sounds interrupted his concentration: the barking of dogs. Suddenly, the menacing faces of enormous long-haired black shepherds lunged at the windows on both sides of the car. The dark eyes glistened with hatred and frustration; the fur-lined, saliva-soaked jaws slapped open and shut, emitting the shrill, vicious sounds of animals reaching a quarry but unable to sink their teeth into flesh. It was a pack of attack dogs—five, six, seven—at all windows now, their paws scratching against the glass. An animal leaped up on the hood, its face and teeth against the windshield.

Beyond the dog, at the base of the hill, Holcroft saw the huge gate beginning to move, the movement magnified in the beams of his headlights. It was starting the slow arc that would end with its closing! He pressed the accelerator against the floor, gripped the wheel until his arms were in pain, and drove at full speed, swerving to his left, through the stone pillars, missing the steel gate by inches. The dog on the hood flew off to the right in midair, yelping in shock.

The pack on the hill had pulled up behind the gate in the darkening twilight. The explanation had to be that a high-frequency whistle—beyond human ears— had caused them to stop. Perspiring, Noel held the pedal against the floorboard and sped down the road.

He came to a fork in the countryside. Did he take the right, or the left? He could not recall; absently he reached for his map on the seat.

That was what had bothered him! The map was no longer there. He took the left fork, reaching below the seat to see if the map had fallen to the floor. It had not. It had been removed from the car!

He arrived at an intersection. It was not familiar; or, if it was, the darkness obscured any familiarity. He turned right, out of instinct, knowing he had to keep going. He kept the car at high speed, looking for anything that he could relate to the drive out from Rio. But the darkness was full now; he saw nothing he remembered. The road made a wide, sweeping curve to the right and then there was a sharp, steep incline of a hill. He recalled no curve, remembered no hill. He was lost.

The top of the hill flattened out for approximately a hundred yards. On his left was a lookout, bordered by a parking area enclosed by a chest-high wall fronting the cliff. Along the wall were rows of telescopes with round casings, the type activated by coins. Holcroft pulled over and stopped the car. There were no other automobiles, but maybe one would come. Perhaps if he looked around he could get his bearings. He got out of the car and walked to the wall.

Far below in the distance were the lights of the city. Between the cliff and the lights, however, there was only darkness. . . . No. Not total darkness; there was a winding thread of light. A road? Noel was next to one of the telescopes. He inserted a coin and peered through the sight, focusing on the weaving thread of light he presumed was a road. It was.

The lights were spaced far apart; they were street lamps, welcome but out of place in a path cut out of the Brazilian forests. If he could reach the beginning of that road. . . . The telescope would move no farther to his right. Goddamn it! Where did the road begin? It *had* to be. . . .

Behind him he heard the sound of an engine racing up the hill he had just climbed. Thank God! He would stop the car, if he had to stand in the middle of the road to do it. He ran from the wall, across the concrete, toward the tarred pavement.

He reached the edge and froze. The car lunging over the final incline into the lookout area was a white Mercedes limousine. The same car that stood gleaming in the afternoon sun on top of another hill. Graff's car.

It stopped abruptly, tires screeching. The door opened and a man got out. In the reflecting spill of the headlights he was recognizable: Graff's guard!

He reached into his belt. Holcroft stood paralyzed. The man raised a gun, aiming at him. It was unbelievable! It could not be happening!

The first gunshot was thunderous; it shook the silence like a sudden cracking of the earth. A second followed. The road several feet away from Noel exploded in a spray of rock and dust. Whatever instincts remained beyond his paralysis, his *disbelief,* commanded him to run, to save himself. He was going to die! He was about to be killed in a deserted tourist lookout above the city of Rio de Janeiro! It was insane!

His legs were weak; he forced himself to race toward the rented car. His feet *ached;* it was the strangest sensation he had ever felt. Two more gunshots filled the night; there were two more explosions of tar and concrete.

He reached the car and fell below the door panel for protection. He reached up for the handle.

Another gunshot, this one louder, the vibration deafening. Accompanying the detonation was another kind of explosion, one that rang with the violent smashing of glass. The car's rear window had been blown out.

There was nothing else to do! Holcroft pulled the door open and leaped inside. In panic he turned the ignition key. The engine roared; his foot pressed the accelerator against the floor. He jammed the gearshift into drive; the car bolted forward in the darkness. He spun the wheel; the car swerved, narrowly missing impact with the wall. His instincts ordered him to switch on the headlights. In a blur he saw the downhill road, and in desperation he aimed for it.

The descent was filled with curves. He took them at high speed, sliding, skidding, barely able to hold the car in control, his arms aching. His hands were wet with sweat; they kept slipping. Any second he fully believed he would crash; any moment now he would die in a final explosion.

He would never remember how long it took, or precisely how he found the winding road with the intermittent streetlights, but at last it was there. A flat surface heading left, heading *east,* the road into the city.

He was in dense countryside; tall trees and thick forests bordered the asphalt, looming up like the sides of an immense canyon.

Two cars approached from the opposite direction; he wanted to cry with relief at the sight of them. He was approaching the outskirts of the city. He was into the suburbs. The streetlights were close together now, and suddenly there were cars everywhere, turning, blocking, passing. He never knew he could be so grateful to see traffic.

He came to a traffic light; it was red. He was again grateful—for its actually being there, and the brief rest it brought him. He reached into his shirt pocket for his cigarettes. *God,* he wanted a cigarette!

A car pulled alongside him on his left. He stared once more in disbelief. A man beside the driver—a man he had never seen before in his life—had rolled down his window and was raising a pistol. Around the barrel was a perforated cylinder—a silencer. The unknown man was aiming the gun at him!

Holcroft recoiled, ducking his head, spinning his neck, yanking the gearshift, plunging the accelerator to the floor. He heard the terrible spit and the crash of glass behind him. The rented car sprang forward into the intersection. Horns blew crazily; he swerved in front of an approaching automobile, turning at the last second to avoid a collision.

The cigarette had fallen from his lips, burning a hole in the seat.

He sped into the city.

The telephone was moist and glistening with sweat in Noel's hand. "Are you *listening* to me?" he shouted.

"Mr. Holcroft, calm down, *please.*" The voice of the attaché at the American Embassy was disbelieving. "We'll do everything we can. I have the salient facts and we'll pursue a diplomatic inquiry as rapidly as possible. However, it *is* past seven o'clock; it'll be difficult reaching people at this hour."

"Difficult to *reach* people? Maybe you didn't *hear* me. I was damn near killed! Take a look at that car! The windows were blown out!"

"We're sending a man over to your hotel to take possession of the vehicle," said the attaché matter-of-factly.

"I've got the keys. Have him come up to my room and get them."

"Yes, we'll do that. Stay where you are and we'll call you back."

The attaché hung up. *Christ!* The man sounded as if he had just heard from an irritating relative and was anxious to get off the phone so he could go to dinner!

Noel was frightened beyond any fear he had ever known. It gripped him and panicked him and made breathing difficult. Yet in spite of that sickening, all-pervasive fear, something was happening to him that he did not understand. A minute part of him was angry, and he felt that anger growing. He did not want it to grow; he was afraid of it, but he could not stop it. Men had attacked him and he wanted to strike back.

He had wanted to strike back at Graff, too. He had wanted to call him by his rightful name: monster, liar, corrupter . . . *Nazi.*

The telephone rang. He spun around as if it were an alarm, signifying another attack. He gripped his wrist to steady the trembling and walked quickly to the bedside table.

"Senhor Holcroft?"

It was not the man at the Embassy. The accent was Latin.

"What is it?"

"I must speak with you. It is very important that I speak with you right away."

"Who is this?"

"My name is Cararra. I am in the lobby of your hotel."

"Cararra? A woman named Cararra called me yesterday."

"My sister. We are together now. We must both speak with you now. May we come up to your room?"

"No! I'm not seeing anyone!" The sounds of the gunshots, the explosions of concrete and glass—they were all still too sharp in his mind. He would not be an isolated target again.

"Senhor, you *must!*"

"I *won't!* Leave me alone or I'll call the police."

"They can't help you. We can. We wish to help you. You seek information about the Von Tiebolts. We have information."

Noel's breathing stopped. His eyes strayed to the mouthpiece of the telephone. It was a trap. The man on the phone was trying to trap him. Yet, if that were so, why did he announce the trap?

"Who sent you here? Who told you to call me? Was it Graff?"

"Maurice Graff does not talk to people like us. My sister and I, we are beneath his contempt."

You are contemptible! Graff held most of the world in contempt, thought Holcroft. He breathed again and tried to speak calmly. "I asked you who sent you to me. How do you know I'm interested in the Von Tiebolts?"

"We have friends at Immigration. Clerks, not important people. But they listen; they observe. You will understand when we speak." The Brazilian's words suddenly accelerated; the phrases tumbled awkwardly. Too awkwardly to be studied or rehearsed. *"Please,* senhor. *See* us. We have information and it is

information you should *have*. We want to help. By helping you, we help ourselves."

Noel's brain raced. The lobby of the Pôrto Alegre was always crowded, and
there was a certain truth in the bromide that there was safety in numbers. If
Cararra and his sister really knew something about the Von Tiebolts, he had to
see them. But not in an isolated situation, not alone. He spoke slowly.

"Stay by the reception desk, at least ten feet in front of it, with both hands
out of your pockets. Have your sister on your left, her right hand on your arm.
I'll be down in a little while, but not in the elevator. And you won't see me first.
I'll see you."

He hung up, astonished at himself. Lessons *were* being learned. They were
basic, no doubt, to those abnormal men who dealt in a clandestine world, but
new to him. Cararra would not have his hand gripped around a gun in his pocket;
his sister—or whoever she was—would not be able to reach into a purse without
his noticing. They would have their attentions on the doorways, not the elevators,
which of course he would use. And he would know who they were.

He walked out of the elevator in a crowd of tourists. He stood briefly with
them, as if one of the party, and looked at the man and woman by the front desk.
As instructed, Cararra's hands were at his side, his sister's right hand linked to
her brother's arm, as if she were afraid to be set adrift. And he *was* her brother;
there was a distinct similarity in their features. Cararra was in his early thirties,
perhaps; his sister, several years younger. Both dark—skin, hair, eyes. Neither
looked at all imposing; their clothes were neat but inexpensive. They were out
of place among the furs and evening gowns of the hotel's guests, aware of their
awkward status, their faces embarrassed, their eyes frightened. Harmless, thought
Holcroft. Then he realized he was making too fast a judgment.

They sat in a back booth of the dimly lit cocktail lounge, the Cararras across
the table from Noel. Before they'd gone inside, Holcroft had remembered that
the embassy was supposed to call him back. He told the desk that if the call came,
it was to be relayed to him in the lounge. But only the embassy—no one else.

"Tell me first how you learned I was looking for the Von Tiebolts," said Noel
after their drinks arrived.

"I told you. A clerk at Immigration. The word was passed discreetly, last
Friday, among the sections, that an American would be coming in asking about
a German family named Von Tiebolt. Whoever took the request was to call in
another, a man from the *polícia do administração*. That's the secret police."

"I know what it is. He called himself a 'translator.' I want to know why *you*
were told."

"The Von Tiebolts were our friends. Very close friends."

"Where are they?"

Cararra exchanged a brief look with his sister. The girl spoke.

"Why do you look for them?" she asked.

"I made that clear at Immigration. It's nothing out of the ordinary. They were
left some money by relatives in the United States."

Brother and sister again looked at each other, and again the sister spoke. "Is it a large amount of money?"

"I don't know," replied Holcroft. "It's a confidential matter. I'm merely a go-between."

"A what?" Again the brother.

"*Un tercero,*" answered Noel, looking at the woman. "Why were you so frightened on the telephone yesterday? You left your number, and when I called you back, you told me I shouldn't have. Why?"

"I made a . . . mistake. My brother said it was a bad mistake. My name, the telephone number—it was wrong to leave them."

"It would anger the Germans," explained Cararra. "If they were watching you, intercepting your messages, they would see that we called you. It would be dangerous to us."

"If they're watching me now, they know you're here."

"We talked it over," continued the woman. "We made our decision; we must take the risk."

"What risk?"

"The Germans despise us. Among other things, we are Portuguese Jews," said Cararra.

"They think like that even now?"

"Of course they do. I said we were close to the Von Tiebolts. Perhaps I should clarify. Johann was my dearest friend; he and my sister were to be married. The Germans would not permit it."

"Who could stop them?"

"Any number of men. With a bullet in the back of Johann's head."

"Good *Christ,* that's crazy!" But it was not crazy, and Holcroft knew it. He had been a target high in the hills; gunshots still rang in his ears.

"For certain Germans such a marriage would be the final insult," said Cararra. "There are those who say the Von Tiebolts were traitors to Germany. These people still fight the war three decades later. Great injustices were done to the Von Tiebolts here in Brazil. They deserve whatever can be done for them. Their lives were made most difficult for causes that should have died years ago."

"And you figured I could do something for them? What made you think that?"

"Because powerful men wanted to stop you; the Germans have a great deal of influence. Therefore you, too, were a powerful man, someone the Graffs in Brazil wanted to keep from the Von Tiebolts. To us that meant you intended no harm to our friends, and if no harm, you meant well. A powerful American who could help them."

"You say the 'Graffs in Brazil.' That's Maurice Graff, isn't it? Who is he? What is he?"

"The worst of the Nazis. He should have been hanged at Nürnberg."

"You know Graff?" asked the woman, her eyes on Holcroft.

"I went out to see him. I used a client in New York as an excuse, said he wanted me to look over Graff's house. I'm an architect. At one point, I mentioned the

Von Tiebolts, and Graff went out of his mind. He began screaming and ordered me out. When I drove down the hill, a pack of attack dogs came after the car. Later, Graff's guard followed me. He tried to kill me. In traffic, the same thing happened again. Another man shot at me from a car window."

"Mother of God!" Cararra's lips parted in shock.

"We should not be seen with him," said the woman, gripping her brother's arm. Then she stopped, studying Noel closely. "If he's telling the truth."

Holcroft understood. If he was to learn anything from the Cararras, they had to be convinced he was exactly who he said he was. "I'm telling the truth. I've also told it to the American Embassy. They're sending someone over to take the car as evidence."

The Cararras looked at each other; then both turned to Holcroft. His statement was the proof they needed; it was in their eyes.

"We believe you," said the sister. "We must hurry."

"The Von Tiebolts are alive?"

"Yes," said the brother. "The Nazis think they are somewhere in the southern mountains, around the Santa Catarina colonies. They're old German settlements; the Von Tiebolts could change their names and melt in easily."

"But they're not there."

"No. . . ." Cararra seemed to hesitate, unsure of himself.

"Tell me where they are," pressed Noel.

"Is it a good thing you bring to them?" asked the girl, concern in her voice.

"Far better than anything you can imagine," replied Holcroft. *"Tell* me."

Once again, brother and sister exchanged glances. Their decision was made. Cararra spoke. "They are in England. As you know, the mother is dead. . . ."

"I didn't know," said Noel. "I don't know anything."

"They go by the name of Tennyson. Johann is known as John Tennyson; he is a journalist for a newspaper—the *Guardian.* He speaks several languages and covers the European capitals for the paper. Gretchen, the oldest, is married to a British naval officer. We don't know where she lives, but her husband's name is Beaumont; he is a commander in the Royal Navy. Of Helden, the youngest daughter, we know nothing. She was always a little distant, a bit headstrong."

"Helden? It's an odd name."

"It fits her," said Cararra's sister softly.

"The story is that her birth certificate was filled out by a doctor who did not speak German, who did not understand the mother. According to Senhora von Tiebolt, she gave the child's name as 'Helga,' but the hospital staff was rushed. They wrote down 'Helden.' In those days, one did not argue with what was written on papers. The name stayed with her."

"Tennyson, Beaumont. . . ." Holcroft repeated the names. "England? How did they get out of Brazil and over to England without Graff finding out? You say the Germans have influence. Passports were needed; transportation had to be arranged. How did they do it?"

"Johann . . . John . . . he's a remarkable man, a brilliant man."

"*A homen talentoso,*" added his sister, her strained features softening with the words. "I love him very much. After five years we still love each other."

"Then you've heard from him? From them?"

"Every now and then," said Cararra. "Visitors from England get in touch with us. Never anything written on paper."

Noel stared at this man riddled with fear. "What kind of world do you live in?" he asked incredulously.

"One where your own life can be taken," answered Cararra.

It was true, thought Noel, as a knot of pain formed in his stomach. A war that was lost thirty years ago was still being fought by those who had lost it. It had to be stopped.

"Mr. Holcroft?" The greeting was tentative, the stranger standing by the table not sure he had the right party.

"Yes, I'm Holcroft," said Noel warily.

"Anderson, American Embassy, sir. May I speak with you?"

The Cararras rose as one from the table and sidestepped out of the booth. The embassy man stepped back as Cararra approached Holcroft.

Cararra whispered, "*Adeus, senhor.*"

"*Adeus,*" the woman whispered also, reaching out to touch Noel's arm.

Without looking at the man from the embassy, brother and sister walked rapidly out of the lounge.

Holcroft sat beside Anderson in the embassy car. They had less than an hour to get to the airport; if the ride took any longer, he would miss the Avianca flight to Lisbon, where he could transfer to a British Airways plane for London.

Anderson had agreed—reluctantly, petulantly—to drive him.

"If it'll get you out of Rio," Anderson had drawled, "I'll go like a greased pig in a slaughterhouse and pay the speeding tickets from my per diem. You're trouble."

Noel grimaced. "You don't believe a word I've said, do you?"

"Goddamn it, Holcroft, do I have to tell you again? There's no car at the hotel; no window's been blown out. There's no record of your even renting a car!"

"It was there! I rented it! I saw Graff!"

"You *called* him. You didn't *see* him. To repeat, he says he got a call from you—something about looking at his house—but you never showed up."

"That's a lie! I was there! After I left, two men tried to kill me. One of them I saw . . . hell, I *fought* with . . . inside his place!"

"You're juiced, man."

"Graff's a fucking Nazi! After thirty years, he's *still* a Nazi, and you people treat him like he's some kind of statesman."

"You're damn right," said Anderson. "Graff's very special material. He's protected."

"I wouldn't brag about it."

"You've got it all backward, Holcroft. Graff was at a place called Wolfsschanze in Germany in July in 1944. He's one of the men who tried to kill Hitler."

There was no blinding sunlight outside his hotel window now; no golden, oiled bodies of grown-up children playing in the white sands of the Copacabana. Instead, the London streets were mottled with drizzle, and gusts of wind swept between the buildings and through the alleys. Pedestrians rushed from doorways to bus queues, train stations, pubs. It was that hour in London when Englishmen felt sprung from the coils of daylight drudgery; making a living was not living. In Noel's experience no other city in the world took such pleasure at the end of the workday. There was a sense of controlled exhilaration in the streets, even with the rain and the wind.

He turned from the window and went to the bureau and his silver flask. It had taken nearly fifteen hours of flying to reach London, and now that he was here, he was not sure how to proceed. He had tried to think on the planes, but the events in Rio de Janeiro were so stunning, and the information gathered so contradictory, that he felt lost in a maze. His unfamiliar forest was too dense. And he had just begun.

Graff, a survivor of Wolfsschanze? One of the *men of Wolfsschanze?* It wasn't possible. The men of Wolfsschanze were committed to Geneva, to the fulfillment of Heinrich Clausen's dream, and the Von Tiebolts were an integral part of that dream. Graff wanted to destroy the Von Tiebolts, as he had ordered the death of Heinrich Clausen's son on a deserted lookout above Rio and from a car window in a city street at night. He was no part of Wolfsschanze. He could not be.

The Cararras. They were complicated, too. What in heaven's name prevented them from leaving Brazil? It was not as though the airports or the piers were closed to them. He believed what they had told him, but there were too many elementary questions that needed answers. No matter how he tried to suppress the idea, there was something contrived about the Cararras. What *was* it?

Noel poured himself a drink and picked up the telephone. He had a name and a place of work: John Tennyson; the *Guardian.* Newspaper offices did not close down at the end of the day. He would know in minutes if the initial information given him by the Cararras was true. If there was a John Tennyson writing for the *Guardian,* then Johann von Tiebolt had been found.

If so, the next step according to the Geneva document was for John Tennyson to take him to his sister Gretchen Beaumont, wife of Commander Beaumont, Royal Navy. She was the person he had to see; she was the oldest surviving issue of Wilhelm von Tiebolt. The key.

"I'm terribly sorry, Mr. Holcroft," said the polite voice over the phone at the

Guardian's news desk, "but I'm afraid we can't give out the addresses or telephone numbers of our journalists."

"But John Tennyson does work for you." It was not a question; the man had already stated that Tennyson was not in the London office. Holcroft merely wanted a direct confirmation.

"Mr. Tennyson is one of our people on the Continent."

"How can I get a message to him? Immediately. It's urgent."

The man at the desk seemed to hesitate. "That would be difficult, I think. Mr. Tennyson moves around a great deal."

"Come on, I can go downstairs, buy your paper, and see where his copy's filed from."

"Yes, of course. Except that Mr. Tennyson does not use a byline. Not in daily despatches; only in major retrospectives. . . ."

"How do *you* get in touch with him when you need him?" broke in Holcroft, convinced the man was stalling.

Again there was the hesitation, a clearing of the throat. *Why?* "Well . . . there's a message pool. It could take several days."

"I don't *have* several days. I've got to reach him right away." The subsequent silence was maddening. The man at the *Guardian* had no intention of offering a solution. Noel tried another trick. "Listen, I probably shouldn't say this . . . it's a confidential matter . . . but there's money involved. Mr. Tennyson and his family were left a sum of money."

"I wasn't aware that he was married."

"I mean *his* family. He and his two sisters. Do you know them? Do you know if they live in London? The oldest is—"

"I know nothing of Mr. Tennyson's personal life, sir. I suggest you get in touch with a solicitor." Then, without warning, he hung up.

Bewildered, Holcroft replaced the phone. Why such a deliberate lack of cooperation? He had identified himself, given the name of his hotel, and for several moments the man at the *Guardian* seemed to listen, as if he might offer help. But no offers came, and suddenly the man had ended their conversation. It was all very strange.

The telephone rang; he was further bewildered. No one knew he was at this hotel. On the immigration card he'd filled out on the phone he had purposely listed the Dorchester as his London residence, not the Belgravia Arms, where he was staying. He did not want anyone—especially anyone from Rio de Janeiro—to be able to trace his whereabouts. He picked up the receiver, trying to suppress the pain in his stomach.

"Yes?"

"Mr. Holcroft, this is the front desk, sir. We've just learned that your courtesy basket was not delivered in time. We're dreadfully sorry. Will you be in your room for a while, sir?"

For God's sake, thought Noel. Millions upon millions were being held in

Geneva, and a desk clerk was concerned about a basket of fruit. "Yes, I'll be here."

"Very good, sir. The steward will be there shortly."

Holcroft replaced the phone, the pain in his stomach subsiding. His eyes fell on the telephone directories on the bottom shelf of the bedside table. He picked one up and turned the pages to the letter *T.*

There was an inch and a half of Tennysons, about fifteen names, no John but three *J*'s. He'd start with those. He lifted up the phone and made the first call.

"Hello, John?"

The man on the line was Julian. The other two *J*'s were women. There was a Helen Tennyson, no Helden. He dialed the number. An operator told him the phone was disconnected.

He turned to the directory with the letter *B.* There were six Beaumonts in London, none indicating any rank or affiliation with the Royal Navy. But there was nothing to lose; he picked up the phone and started dialing.

Before he finished the fourth call, there was a knock at the door; his basket of English courtesy had arrived. He swore at the interruption; put the phone down, and walked to the door, reaching into his pocket for some change.

Two men stood outside, neither in steward's uniform, both in overcoats, each with hat in hand. The taller of the two was in his fifties, straight gray hair above a weathered face; the younger man was about Noel's age, with clear blue eyes, curly reddish hair, and a small scar on his forehead.

"Yes?"

"Mr. Holcroft?"

"Yes."

"Noel Holcroft, United States citizen, passport number F-two-zero-four-seven-eight—"

"I'm Noel Holcroft. I've never memorized my passport number."

"May we come in, please?"

"I'm not sure. Who are you?"

Both men held black identification cases in their hands; they opened them unobtrusively. "British Military Intelligence, Five branch," the older man said.

"Why do you want to see me?"

"Official business, sir. May we step inside?"

Noel nodded uncertainly, the pain returning to his stomach. Peter Baldwin, the man who had ordered him to "cancel Geneva," had been with MI Six. And Baldwin had been killed by the men of Wolfsschanze because he had interfered. Did these two British agents know the truth about Baldwin? Did they know Baldwin had *called* him? Oh, *God*, telephone numbers could be traced through hotel switchboards! They *had* to know! . . . Then Holcroft remembered: Baldwin had *not* called him; he had come to his apartment. Noel had called him.

You don't know what you're doing. I'm the only one who does.

If Baldwin was to be believed, he had said nothing to anyone. If so, where was the connection? Why was British Intelligence interested in an American named Holcroft? How did it know where to find him? *How?*

The two Englishmen entered. The younger, red-haired man crossed rapidly to the bathroom, looked inside, then turned and went to the window. His older associate stood by the desk, his eyes scanning the walls, the floor, and the open closet.

"All right, you're inside," Noel said. "What is it?"

"The Tinamou, Mr. Holcroft," said the gray-haired man.

"The what?"

"I repeat. The Tinamou."

"What the hell is that?"

"According to any standard encyclopedia, the Tinamou is a ground-dwelling bird whose protective coloring makes him indistinguishable from his background; whose short bursts of flight take him swiftly from one location to another."

"That's very enlightening, but I haven't the vaguest idea what you're talking about."

"We think you do," said the younger man by the window.

"You're wrong. I've never heard of a bird like that, and don't know any reason why I should have. Obviously, you're referring to something else, but I don't make the connection."

"Obviously," interrupted the agent by the desk, "we're not referring to a bird. The Tinamou is a man; the name is quite applicable, however."

"It means nothing to me. Why should it?"

"May I give you some advice?" The older man spoke crisply, with an edge to his voice.

"Sure. I probably won't understand it anyway."

"You'd do far better cooperating with us than not. It's possible you're being used, but frankly we doubt it. However, if you help us now, we're prepared to assume that you *were* being used. I believe that's eminently fair."

"I was right," said Holcroft. "I don't understand you."

"Then let me clear up the details and perhaps you will. You've been making inquiries about John Tennyson, born Johann von Tiebolt, immigrant to the UK roughly six years ago. He is currently employed as a multilingual correspondent for the *Guardian.*"

"The man at the *Guardian* desk," interrupted Noel. "He called you—or had someone call. That's why he stalled, why he went on the way he did, then cut me off. And that goddamned fruit; it was to make sure I didn't go out. What *is* this?"

"May we ask why you're trying to find John Tennyson?"

"No."

"You've stated, both here and in Rio de Janeiro, that a sum of money is involved. . . ."

"*Rio de!* . . . Jesus!"

"That you're an 'intermediary,' " continued the Englishman. "That was the term you used."

"It's a confidential matter."

"We think it's an international one."

"Good God, why?"

"Because you're trying to deliver a sum of money. If the ground rules are followed, it amounts to three quarters of the full payment."

"For what?"

"For an assassination."

"Assassination?"

"Yes. In the data banks of half the civilized world, the Tinamou has a single description: 'assassin.' 'Master assassin,' to be precise. And we have every reason to believe that Johann von Tiebolt, alias John Tennyson, is the Tinamou."

Noel was stunned. His mind raced furiously. An assassin! Good God! Was that what Peter Baldwin had been trying to tell him? That one of the Geneva inheritors was an assassin?

No one knows but me. Baldwin's words.

If they were true, under no condition could he reveal his real reason for wanting to find John Tennyson. Geneva would explode in controversy; the massive account would be frozen, thrown into the international courts, his covenant destroyed. He could not allow that to happen; he knew it now.

Yet it was equally vital that his reasons for seeking Tennyson be above suspicion, beyond any relationship to—or cognizance of—the Tinamou.

The Tinamou! An assassin! It was potentially the most damaging news possible. If there was any truth in what MI Five believed, the bankers in Geneva would suspend all discussions, close the vaults, and wait for another generation. Yet any decision to abort the covenant would be for appearance's sake. If Tennyson *was* this Tinamou, he could be exposed, caught, severed from all association with the Geneva account, and the covenant would remain intact. Amends *would* be made. According to the conditions of the document, the older *sister* was the key—she was the eldest surviving child—not the brother.

An assassin! Oh, *God!*

First things first. Holcroft knew he had to dispel the convictions of the two men in his room. He walked unsteadily to a chair, sat down, and leaned forward.

"Listen to me," he said, his voice weak in astonishment. "I've told you the truth. I don't know anything about any Tinamou, any assassin. My business is with the Von Tiebolt *family*, not a particular member of the family. I was trying to find Tennyson because I was told he was Von Tiebolt and worked at the *Guardian.* That's all there is to it."

"If so," said the red-haired man, "perhaps you'll explain the nature of your business."

Base the lie in an aspect of truth.

"I'll tell you what I can, which isn't a great deal. Some of it I pieced together myself from what I learned in Rio. It *is* confidential, and it *does* concern money." Noel took a deep breath, and reached for his cigarettes. "The Von Tiebolts were left an inheritance—don't ask me by whom, because I don't know, and the lawyer won't say."

"What's the name of this lawyer," asked the gray-haired man.

"I'd have to get his permission to tell you," answered Holcroft, lighting his cigarette, wondering whom in New York he could call from an untraceable pay phone in London.

"We may ask you to do that," said the older agent. "Go on, please."

"I found out in Rio that the Von Tiebolts were despised by the German community there. I have an idea—and it's only an idea—that somewhere along the line they opposed the Nazis in Germany, and someone, perhaps an anti-Nazi German—or Germans—left them the money."

"In America?" asked the red-haired man.

Noel sensed the trap and was prepared for it. *Be consistent.* "Obviously, whoever left the Von Tiebolts money has been living there for a long time. If he, or they, came to the United States after the war, that could presume they had a clean bill of health. On the other hand, they could be relatives who came to the States years ago. I honestly don't know."

"Why were you chosen as the intermediary? You're not a lawyer."

"No, but the lawyer's a friend of mine," replied Holcroft. "He knows I travel a lot, knew I was going to Brazil for a client. . . . I'm an architect. He asked me to call around, gave me some names, including Rio's Immigration people."

Keep it simple; avoid complication.

"That was asking quite a bit of you, wasn't it?" The red-haired agent's disbelief was in his question.

"Not really. He's done me favors; I can do him one." Noel drew on his cigarette. "This is crazy. What started out as a simple . . . well, it's just crazy."

"You were told Johann von Tiebolt was John Tennyson and that he worked in London, or was based in London," said the older man, his hands in his overcoat pockets, looking down at Noel. "So, as a favor, you decided to make the trip from Brazil to the UK to find him. As a *favor.* . . . Yes, Mr. Holcroft, I'd say it was crazy."

Noel glared up at the gray-haired man. He remembered Sam Buonoventura's words: *I got hot myself. . . . It's the only way to handle angry cops.*

"Now just a minute! I didn't make a special trip from Rio to London for the Von Tiebolts. I'm on my way to Amsterdam. If you check my office in New York, you'll find that I'm doing some work in Curaçao. For your benefit, it's Dutch, and I'm going to Amsterdam for design conferences."

The look in the older man's eyes seemed to soften. "I see," he said quietly. "It's quite possible we drew the wrong conclusions, but I think you'll agree the surface facts led us to them. We may owe you an apology."

Pleased with himself, Noel suppressed the urge to smile. He had adhered to the lessons, handled the lie with his guard up.

"It's okay," he replied. "But now I'm curious. This Tinamou. How do you know it's Von Tiebolt?"

"We're not certain," replied the gray-haired agent. "We were hoping you'd provide that certainty. I think we were wrong about that."

"You certainly were. But why Tennyson? I guess I should tell the lawyer in New York. . . ."

"No," interrupted the Englishman. "Don't do that. You must not discuss this with anyone."

"It's a little late for that, isn't it?" Holcroft said, gambling. "The 'matter' *has* been discussed. I'm under no obligation to you, but I do have an obligation to that lawyer. He's a friend."

The MI-Five men looked at each other, their mutual concern in the exchange.

"Beyond an obligation to a friend," the older man said, "I suggest that you have a far greater responsibility. One that can be substantiated by your own government. This is a highly classified, intensely sensitive investigation. The Tinamou is an international killer. His victims include some of the world's most distinguished men."

"And you believe he's Tennyson?"

"The evidence is circumstantial, but very, very strong."

"Still, not conclusive."

"Not conclusive."

"A few minutes ago you sounded positive."

"A few minutes ago we tried to trap you. It's merely a technique."

"It's damned offensive."

"It's damned effective," said the red-haired man with the scar on his forehead.

"What's the circumstantial evidence against Tennyson?"

"Will you hold it in the strictest confidence?" asked the older agent. "That request can be transmitted by the highest law-enforcement officials in your country, if you wish."

Holcroft paused. "All right, I won't call New York; I won't say anything. But I want information."

"We don't bargain." The younger man spoke offensively, cut off by a look from his associate.

"It's not a question of a bargain," said Noel. "I said I'd reach a member of the family, and I think I should. Where can I contact Tennyson's sisters? One's married to a commander in the navy named Beaumont. The lawyer in New York knows that; he'll try to find her if I don't. It might as well be me."

"Far better that it's you," agreed the gray-haired man. "We're convinced that neither woman is aware of her brother's activities. As near as we can determine, the family are estranged from one another. How seriously, we don't know, but there's been little or no communication. Frankly, your showing up is a complication we'd rather not be burdened with. We don't want alarms raised; a controlled situation is infinitely preferable."

"There won't be any alarms," said Noel. "I'll deliver my message and go about my business."

"To Amsterdam?"

"To Amsterdam."

"Yes, of course. The older sister is married to Commander Anthony Beaumont; she's his second wife. They live near Portsmouth, several miles north of the naval base, in a suburb of Portsea. He's in the telephone directory. The younger girl recently moved to Paris. She's a translator for Gallimard Publishers, but she's not at the address listed with the company. We don't know where she lives."

Holcroft rose from the chair and walked between the two men to the desk. He picked up the hotel pen and wrote on a page of stationery.

"Anthony Beaumont . . . Portsmouth. . . . Gallimard Publishers. . . . How do you spell 'Gallimard'?"

The red-haired agent told him.

Noel finished writing. "I'll make the calls in the morning and send a note to New York," he said, wondering to himself how long it would take to drive to Portsmouth. "I'll tell the lawyer I reached the sisters but was unable to contact the brother. Is that all right?"

"We couldn't persuade you to drop the entire matter?"

"No. I'd have to say why I dropped it, and you don't want that."

"Very well. It's the best we can hope for, then."

"Now, tell me why you think John Tennyson is this Tinamou. You owe me that."

The older man paused. "Perhaps we do," he said. "I reemphasize the classified nature of the information."

"Whom would I tell it to? I'm not in your line of work."

"All right," said the gray-haired man. "As you say, we owe you. But you should know that the fact that you've been told gives us a certain insight. Very few people have been."

Holcroft stiffened; it wasn't difficult to convey his anger. "And I don't imagine too many have had men like you knock on their doors and been accused of paying off assassins. If this were New York, I'd haul you into court. You *do* owe me."

"Very well. A pattern was uncovered, at first too obvious to warrant examination until we studied the man. For several years, Tennyson consistently appeared in or near areas where assassinations took place. It was uncanny. He actually reported the events for the *Guardian*, filing his stories from the scene. A year or so ago, for example, he covered the killing of that American in Beirut, the embassy fellow who was, of course, CIA. Three days before, he'd been in Brussels; suddenly he was in Tehran. We began to study him, and what we learned was astonishing. We believe he's the Tinamou. He's utterly brilliant and, quite possibly, utterly mad."

"What did you find out?"

"For starters, you know about his father. One of the early Nazis, a butcher of the worst sort. . . ."

"Are you sure about that?" Noel asked the question too rapidly. "What I mean is, it doesn't necessarily follow. . . ."

"No, I suppose it doesn't," said the gray-haired agent. "But what does follow is, to say the least, unusual. Tennyson is a manic overachiever. He completed two university degrees in Brazil at the age at which most students would have been matriculating. He has mastered five languages; speaks them fluently. He was an extremely successful businessman in South America; he amassed a great deal of money. These are hardly the credentials of a newspaper correspondent."

"People change; interests change. That *is* circumstantial. Pretty damned weak, too."

"The circumstances of his employment, however, lend strength to the conjecture," said the older man. "No one at the *Guardian* remembers when or how he was employed. His name simply appeared on the payroll computers one day, a week before his first copy was filed from Antwerp. No one had ever heard of him."

"Someone had to hire him."

"Yes, someone did. The man whose signature appeared on the interview and employment records was killed in a most unusual train accident that took five lives on the underground."

"A subway in London. . . ." Holcroft paused. "I remember reading about that."

"A trainman's error, they called it, but that's not good enough," added the red-haired man. "That man had eighteen years' experience. It was bloody well murder. Courtesy of the Tinamou."

"You can't be sure," said Holcroft. "An error's an error. What were some of the other . . . coincidences? Where the killings took place."

"I mentioned Beirut. There was Paris, too. A bomb went off under the French minister of labor's car in the rue du Bac, killing him instantly. Tennyson was in Paris; he'd been in Frankfurt the day before. Seven months ago, during the riots in Madrid, a government official was shot from a window four stories above the crowds. Tennyson was in Madrid; he'd flown in from Lisbon just hours before. There are others; they go on."

"Did you ever bring him in and question him?"

"Twice. Not as a suspect, obviously, but as an expert on the scene. Tennyson is the personification of arrogance. He claimed to have analyzed the areas of social and political unrest, and followed his instincts, knowing that violence and assassination were certain to erupt in those places. He had the cheek to lecture us; said we should learn to anticipate and not so often be caught unawares."

"Could he be telling the truth?"

"If you mean that as an insult, it's noted. In light of this evening, perhaps we deserve it."

"Sorry. But when you consider his accomplishments, you've got to consider the possibility. Where is Tennyson now?"

"He disappeared four days ago in Bahrain. Our operatives are watching for him from Singapore to Athens."

The two MI-Five men walked into the empty elevator. The red-haired agent turned to his colleague.

"What do you make of him?" he asked.

"I don't know," was the soft-spoken reply. "We've given him enough to send him racing about; perhaps we'll learn something. He's far too much of an amateur to be a legitimate contact. Those paying for a killing would be fools to send the money with Holcroft. The Tinamou would reject it if they did."

"But he was lying."

"Quite so. Quite poorly."

"Then he's being used."

"Quite possibly. But for what?"

11

According to the car-rental agency, Portsmouth was roughly seventy miles from London, the roads clearly marked, the traffic not likely to be heavy. It was five past six. He could be in Portsea before nine, thought Noel, if he settled for a quick sandwich instead of dinner.

He had intended to wait until morning, but a telephone call made to confirm the accuracy of the MI-Five information dictated otherwise. He reached Gretchen Beaumont, and what she told him convinced him to move quickly.

Her husband, the commander, was on sea duty in the Mediterranean; tomorrow at noon she was going on "winter holiday" to the south of France, where she and the commander would spend a weekend together. If Mr. Holcroft wished to see her about family matters, it would have to be tonight.

He told her he would get there as soon as possible, thinking as he hung up that she had one of the strangest voices he had ever heard. It was not the odd mixture of German and Portuguese in her accent, for that made sense; it was in the floating, hesitant quality of her speech. Hesitant or vacuous—it was difficult to tell. The commander's wife made it clear—if haltingly so—that in spite of the fact that the matters to be discussed were confidential, a naval aide would be in an adjoining room. Her concerns gave rise to an image of a middle-aged, self-indulgent *Hausfrau* with an overinflated opinion of her looks.

Fifty miles south of London, he realized that he was making better time than he had thought possible. There was little traffic, and the sign on the road, reflected in the headlights, read PORTSEA—15 M.

It was barely ten past eight. He could slow down and try to collect his thoughts. Gretchen Beaumont's directions had been clear; he'd have no trouble finding the residence.

For a vacuous-sounding woman, she had been very specific when it came to giving instructions. It was somehow contradictory in light of the way she spoke, as if sharp lines of reality had suddenly, abruptly, shot through clouds of dreamlike mist.

It told him nothing. He was the intruder, the stranger who telephoned and spoke of a vitally important matter he would not define—except in person.

How *would* he define it? How could he explain to the middle-aged wife of a British naval officer that she was the key that could unlock a vault containing seven hundred and eighty million dollars?

He was getting nervous; it was no way to be convincing. Above all, he had to be convincing; he could not appear afraid or unsure or artificial. And then it occurred to him that he could tell her the truth—as Heinrich Clausen saw the truth. It was the best lever he had; it was the ultimate conviction.

Oh, God! Please make her understand!

He made the two left turns off the highway and drove rapidly through the peaceful, tree-lined suburban area for the prescribed mile and a half. He found the house easily, parked in front, and got out of the car.

He opened the gate and walked up the path to the door. There was no bell; instead there was a brass knocker, and so he tapped it gently. The house was designed simply. Wide windows in the living room, small ones on the opposite, bedroom side; the facade, old brick above a stone foundation—solid, built to last, certainly not ostentatious and probably not expensive. He had designed such houses, usually as second homes on the shore for couples still unsure they could afford them. It was the ideal residence for a military man on a military budget. Neat, trim, and manageable.

Gretchen Beaumont opened the door herself. Whatever image she had evoked on the telephone vanished at the sight of her; it disappeared in a rush of amazement, with the impact of a blow to his stomach. Simply put, the woman in the doorway was one of the most beautiful he had ever seen in his life. The fact that she was a woman was almost secondary. She was like a statue, a sculptor's ideal, refined over and over again in clay before chisel was put to stone. She was of medium height, with long blond hair that framed a face of finely boned, perfectly proportioned features. Too perfect, too much in the sculptor's mind . . . too cold. Yet the coldness was lessened by her large, wide eyes; they were light blue and inquisitive, neither friendly nor unfriendly.

"Mr. Holcroft?" she asked in that echoing, dreamlike voice that gave evidence of Germany and Brazil.

"Yes, Mrs. Beaumont. Thank you so much for seeing me. I apologize for the inconvenience."

"Come in, please."

She stepped back to admit him. In the doorway he had concentrated on her face, on the extraordinary beauty that was in no way diminished by the years; it was impossible now not to notice the body, emphasized by her translucent dress. The body, too, was extraordinary, but in a different way from the face.

There was no coldness, only heat. The sheer dress clung to her skin, the absence of a brassiere apparent, accentuated by a flared collar, unbuttoned to the midpoint between her large breasts. On either side, in the center of the swelling flesh, he could see her nipples clearly, pressing against the soft fabric as if aroused.

When she moved, the slow, fluid motion of her thighs and stomach and pelvis combined into the rhythm of a sensual dance. She did not walk; she glided—an extraordinary body screaming for observation as a prelude to invasion and satisfaction.

Yet the face was cold and the eyes distant; inquisitive but distant. And Noel was perplexed.

"You've had a long trip," she said, indicating a couch against the far wall. "Sit down, please. May I offer you a drink?"

"I'd appreciate it."

"What would you care for?" She held her place in front of him, momentarily blocking his short path to the couch, her light-blue eyes looking intently into his. Her breasts were revealed clearly—so close—beneath the sheer fabric. The nipples were taut, rising with each breath; again in that unmistakable rhythm of a sexual dance.

"Scotch, if you have it," he said.

"In England, that's whiskey, isn't it?" she asked, walking toward a bar against the wall.

"It's whiskey," he said, sinking into the soft pillows of the couch, trying to concentrate on Gretchen's face. It was difficult for him, and he knew she was trying to make it difficult. The commander's wife did not have to provoke a sexual reaction; she did not have to dress for the part. But dress for it she had, and provoke she did. Why?

She brought over his scotch. He reached for it, touching her hand as he did so, noting that she did not withdraw from the contact but, instead, briefly pressed his curved fingers with her own. She then did a very strange thing; she sat down on a leather hassock only feet away and looked up at him.

"Won't you join me?" he asked.

"I don't drink."

"Then perhaps you'd prefer that I don't."

She laughed throatily. "I have no moral objections whatsoever. It would hardly become an officer's wife. I'm simply not capable of drinking or of smoking, actually. Both go directly to my head."

He looked at her over the rim of the glass. Her eyes remained eerily on his, unblinking, steady, still distant, making him wish she'd look away.

"You said on the phone that one of your husband's aides would be in an adjoining room. Would you like us to meet?"

"He wasn't able to be here."

"Oh? I'm sorry."

"Are you?"

It was *crazy*. The woman was behaving like a courtesan unsure of her standing, or a high-priced whore evaluating a new client's wallet. She leaned forward on the hassock, picking at an imaginary piece of lint on the throw rug beneath his feet. The gesture was foolish, the effect too obvious. The top of her dress parted, exposing her breasts. She could not have been unaware of what she was doing. He had to respond; she expected it. But he would not respond in the way she anticipated. A father had cried out to him; nothing could interfere. Even an unlikely whore.

An unlikely whore who was the key to Geneva.

"Mrs. Beaumont," he said, placing his glass awkwardly on the small table next to the couch, "you're a very gracious woman and I'd like nothing better than to sit here for hours and have a few drinks, but we've got to talk. I asked to see you because I have extraordinary news for you. It concerns the two of us."

"The two of *us?*" said Gretchen, emphasizing the pronoun. "By all means talk, Mr. Holcroft. I've never met you before; I don't know you. How can this news concern the two of us?"

"Our fathers knew each other years ago."

At the mention of the word "father," the woman stiffened. "I have no father."

"You had; so did I," he said. "In Germany over thirty years ago. Your name's Von Tiebolt. You're the oldest child of Wilhelm von Tiebolt."

Gretchen took a deep breath and looked away. "I don't think I want to listen further."

"I know how you feel," replied Noel. "I had the same reaction myself. But you're wrong. *I* was wrong."

"Wrong?" she asked, brushing away the long blond hair that swung across her cheek with the swift turn of her head. "You're presumptuous. Perhaps you didn't live the way we lived. Please don't tell me I'm wrong. You're in no position to do that."

"Just let me tell you what I've learned. When I'm finished, you can make your own decision. Your knowing is the important thing. And your support, of course."

"Support of what? Knowing what?"

Noel felt oddly moved, as if what he was about to say were the most important words of his life. With a normal person the truth would be sufficient, but Gretchen Beaumont was not a normal person; her scars were showing. It would take more than truth; it would take enormous conviction.

"Two weeks ago I flew to Geneva to meet with a banker named Manfredi. . . ."

He told it all, leaving out nothing save the men of Wolfsschanze. He told it simply, even eloquently, hearing the conviction in his own voice, feeling the profound commitment in his mind, the stirrings of pain in his chest.

He gave her the figures: seven hundred and eighty million for the survivors of the Holocaust, and the descendants of those survivors still in need. Everywhere.

Two million for each of the surviving eldest children, to be used as each saw fit. Six months—possibly longer—of a collective commitment.

Finally, he told her of the pact in death the three fathers made, taking their lives only after every detail in Geneva was confirmed and iron bound.

When he had finished, he felt the perspiration rolling down his forehead. "It's up to us now," he said. "And a man in Berlin—Kessler's son. The three of us have to finish what they started."

"It all sounds so incredible," she said quietly. "But I really don't see why it should concern me."

He was stunned at her calm, at her complete equanimity. She had listened to him in silence for nearly half an hour, heard revelations that had to be shattering to her, yet she displayed no reaction whatsoever. *Nothing.* "Haven't you understood a word I've said?"

"I understand that you're very upset," said Gretchen Beaumont in her soft, echoing voice. "But I've been very upset for most of my life, Mr. Holcroft. I've been that way because of Wilhelm von Tiebolt. He is nothing to me."

"He *knew* that, can't you see? He tried to make up for it."

"With money?"

"More than money."

Gretchen leaned forward and slowly reached out to touch his forehead. With her fingers extended, she wiped away the beads of perspiration. Noel remained still, unable to break the contact between their eyes.

"Did you know that I was Commander Beaumont's second wife?" she asked.

"Yes, I heard that."

"The divorce was a difficult time for him. And for me, of course, but more so for him. But it passed for him; it will not pass for me."

"What do you mean?"

"I'm the intruder. The foreigner. A breaker of marriages. He has his work; he goes to sea. I live among those who don't. The life of a naval officer's wife is a lonely one in usual circumstances. It can become quite difficult when one is ostracized."

"You must have known there'd be a degree of that."

"Of course."

"Well, if you knew it? . . ." He left the question suspended, not grasping the point.

"Why did I marry Commander Beaumont? Is that what you mean to ask?"

He did not want to ask *anything!* He was not interested in the intimate details of Gretchen Beaumont's life. Geneva was all that mattered; the covenant, everything. But he needed her cooperation.

"I assume the reasons were emotional; that's generally why people get married. I only meant that you might have taken steps to lessen the tension. You could live farther away from the naval base, have different friends." He was rambling, awkwardly, a little desperately. He wanted only to break through her maddening reserve.

"My question's more interesting. Why did I marry Beaumont?" Her voice floated again; it rose quietly in the air. "You're right; it's emotional. Quite basic."

She touched his forehead again, her dress parting once more as she leaned forward, her lovely, naked breasts exposed again. Noel was tired and aroused and angry. He *had* to make her understand that her private concerns were meaningless beside Geneva! To do that, he had to make her like him; yet he could not touch her.

"Naturally it's basic," he said. "You love him."

"I loathe him."

Her hand was now inches from his face, her fingers a blur at the corner of his eyes—a blur because their eyes were locked; he dared not shift them. And he dared not touch her.

"Then why did you marry him? Why do you stay with him?"

"I told you. It's basic. Commander Beaumont has a little money; he's a highly respected officer in the service of his government, a dull, uninteresting man more at home on a ship than anywhere else. All this adds up to a very quiet, very secure niche. I am in a comfortable cocoon."

There was the lever! Geneva provided it. "Two million dollars could build a very secure cocoon, Mrs. Beaumont. A far better shelter than you have here."

"Perhaps. But I would have to leave this one in order to build it. I'd have to go outside—"

"Only for a while."

"And what would happen?" she continued, as if he had not interrupted. "Outside? Where I'd have to say yes or no. I don't want to think about that; it would be so difficult. You know, Mr. Holcroft, I've been unhappy most of my life, but I don't look for sympathy."

She was infuriating! He felt like slapping her. "I'd like to return to the situation in Geneva," he said.

She settled back into the hassock, crossing her legs. The sheer dress rose above her knees, the soft flesh of her thigh revealed. The pose was seductive; her words were not.

"But I have returned to it," she said. "Perhaps awkwardly, but I'm trying to explain. As a child I came out of Berlin. Always running, until my mother and my brother and I found a sanctuary in Brazil that proved to be a hell for us. I've floated through life these past years. I've followed—instincts, opportunities, men—but I've followed. I haven't led. I've made as few decisions as possible."

"I don't understand."

"If you have business that concerns my family, you'll have to talk to my brother, Johann. He makes the decisions. He brought us out of South America after my mother died. He is the Von Tiebolt you must reach."

Noel suppressed his desire to yell at her. Instead, he exhaled silently, a sense of weariness and frustration sweeping over him. Johann von Tiebolt was the one member of the family he had to avoid, but he could not tell Gretchen Beaumont why. "Where is he?" he asked rhetorically.

"I don't know. He works for the *Guardian* newspaper, in Europe."

"Where in Europe?"

"Again, I have no idea. He moves around a great deal."

"I was told he was last seen in Bahrain."

"Then you know more than I do."

"You have a sister."

"Helden. In Paris. Somewhere."

All the children will be examined . . . decisions made.

Johann had been examined and a judgment had been made—rightly or wrongly—that disqualified him from Geneva. He was a complication they could not afford; he would draw attention where none could be permitted. And this strange, beautiful woman on the hassock—even if she felt differently—would be rejected by Geneva as incompetent. It was as simple as that.

Paris. Helden von Tiebolt.

Absently, Noel reached for his cigarettes, his thoughts now on an unknown woman who worked as a translator for a publishing house in Paris. He was only vaguely aware of the movement in front of him, so complete was his concentration. Then he noticed and he stared at Gretchen Beaumont.

The commander's wife had risen from the hassock and unfastened the buttons of her dress to the waist. Slowly, she parted the folds of silk. Her breasts were released; they sprang out at him, the nipples taut, stretched, swollen with tension. She raised her skirt with both her hands, bunching it above her thighs, and stood directly in front of him. He was aware of the fragrance that seemed to emanate from her—a delicate perfume with a sensuousness as provoking as the sight of her exposed flesh. She sat down beside him, her dress now above her waist, her body trembling. She moaned and reached for the back of his neck, drawing his face to hers, his lips to hers. Her mouth opened as she received his mouth; she sucked, breathing rapidly, her warm breath mixed with the juices that came from her throat. She put her hand on his trousers and groped for his penis . . . hard, soft, hard. *Harder.* She became suddenly uncontrollable; her moans were feverish. She pressed into him. Everywhere.

Her parted lips slid off his mouth and she whispered. "Tomorrow I go to the Mediterranean. To a man I loathe. Don't say anything. Just give me tonight. Give me *tonight!*"

She moved away slightly, her mouth glistening, her eyes so wide they seemed manic. Slowly, she rose above him, her white skin everywhere. The trembling subsided. She slid a naked leg over his and got to her feet. She pulled his face into her waist and reached for his hand. He stood up, embracing her. She held his hand in hers, and together they walked toward the door of the bedroom. As they went inside, he heard the words, spoken in that eerie, echoing monotone.

"Johann said a man would come one day and talk of a strange arrangement. I was to be nice to him and remember everything he said."

12

Holcroft awoke with a start, for several seconds not sure where he was; then he remembered. Gretchen Beaumont had led him into the bedroom with that incredible statement. He had tried to press her, tried to learn what else her brother had said, but she was in no state to answer clearly. She was in a frenzy, needing the sex desperately; she could concentrate on nothing else.

They had made love maniacally, she the aggressor, writhing on the bed at fever pitch, beneath him, above him, beside him. She'd been insatiable; no amount of exploration and penetration could gratify her. At one point she had screamed, clasping her legs around his waist, her fingers digging into his shoulders long after he was capable of response. And then his exhaustion had caught up with him. He'd fallen into a deep but troubled sleep.

Now he was awake, and he did not know what had interrupted that sleep. There'd been a noise, not loud, but sharp and penetrating, and he did not know what it was or where it came from.

Suddenly, he realized he was alone in the bed. He raised his head. The room was dark, the door closed, a dim line of light at the bottom.

"Gretchen? . . ." There was no reply; no one else was in the room.

He threw the covers off and got out of the bed, steadying his weakened legs, feeling drained, disoriented. He lurched for the door and yanked it open. Beyond, in the small living room, a single table lamp was on, its light casting shadows against the walls and the floor.

There was the noise again! A metallic sound that echoed throughout the house, but it did not come from inside the house. He ran to a living-room window and peered through the glass. Under the spill of a streetlamp he could see the figure of a man standing by the hood of his rented car, a flashlight in his hand.

Before he knew what was happening, he heard a muffled voice from somewhere else outside, and the beam of light shot up at the window. At him. Instinctively, he pulled his hand up to shield his eyes. The light went out, and he saw the man race toward a car parked diagonally across the street. He had not noticed that car, his concentration so complete on his own and on the unknown man with the flashlight. Now he tried to focus on this automobile; there was a figure in the front seat. He could not distinguish anything but the outline of the head and shoulders.

The running man reached the door on the street side, pulled it open, and climbed in behind the wheel. The engine roared; the car shot forward, then skidded into a U-turn before it sped away.

Briefly, in the wash of light from the streetlamp, Noel saw the person in the seat next to the driver. For less than a second the face in the window was no more than twenty yards away, racing by.

It was Gretchen Beaumont. Her eyes stared ahead through the windshield, her head nodding as if she were talking rapidly.

Several lights went on in various houses across from the Beaumont residence. The roar of the engine and the screeching of the tires had been a sudden, unwelcome intrusion on the peaceful street in Portsea. Concerned faces appeared in the windows, peering outside.

Holcroft stepped back. He was naked, and he realized that being seen naked in Commander Beaumont's living room in the middle of the night while Commander Beaumont was away would not be to anyone's advantage, least of all his own.

Where had she gone? What was she doing? What was the sound he had heard?

There was no time to think about such things; he had to get away from the Beaumont house. He turned from the window and ran back to the bedroom, adjusting his eyes to the dim light, trying to find a light switch or a lamp. He remembered that in the frenzy of their lovemaking, Gretchen had swung her hand above his head into the shade of the bedside light, sending it to the floor. He knelt down, groping until he found it. It was on its side, the bulb protected by the linen shade surrounding it. He snapped it on. Light filled the room, its spill washing up from the floor. There were elongated shadows and patches of darkness, but he could see his clothes draped over an armchair, his socks and shorts by the bed.

He stood up and dressed as rapidly as he could. Where was his jacket? He looked about, remembering vaguely that Gretchen had slipped it off his arms and dropped it near the door. Yes, there it was. He walked across the room toward it, glancing briefly at his reflection in the large mirror above the bureau.

He froze, his eyes riveted on a photograph in a silver frame on the bureau. It was of a man in naval uniform.

The *face*. He had seen it before. Not long ago. Weeks . . . days, perhaps. He was not sure where from, but he was certain he knew that face. He walked to the bureau and studied the photograph.

It was the eyebrows! They were odd, different; they stood out as an entity in themselves . . . like an incongruous cornice above an undefined tapestry. They were heavy, a thick profusion of black-and-white hair interwoven . . . salt and pepper. Eyes that blinked open suddenly, eyes that stared up at him. He remembered!

The plane to Rio de Janeiro! And something else. The face from that moment on the plane to Brazil prodded another memory—a memory of violence. But a blurred, racing figure was all he recalled.

Noel turned the silver frame over and clawed at the surface until he loosened the backing. He slid it out of the groove and removed the photograph. He saw minute indentations on the glossy surface; he turned it over. There was writing.

He held it up to catch the light and, for a moment, stopped breathing. The words were German: NEUAUFBAU ODER TOD.

Like the face in the picture, he'd seen these words before! But they were meaningless to him; German words that meant nothing . . . yet he had seen them!

Bewildered, he folded the photograph and stuffed it into his trouser pocket.

He opened a closet door, shoved the silver frame between folded clothes on the shelf, picked up his jacket, and went into the living room. He knew he should get out of the house as fast as he could, but his curiosity about the man in the photograph consumed him. He had to know *something* about him.

There were two doors, in the near and far walls of the living room. One was open and led to the kitchen; the other was closed. He opened it and walked into the commander's study. He turned on a light; photographs of ships and men were everywhere, along with citations and military decorations. Commander Beaumont was a career officer of no mean standing. A bitter divorce followed by a questionable marriage might have created messy personal problems for the man, but the Royal Navy had obviously overlooked them. The latest citation was only six weeks old: for outstanding leadership in coastal patrols off the Balearic Islands during a week of gale-force seas.

A cursory look at the papers on the desk and in the drawers added nothing. Two bank books showed accounts in four figures, neither more than three thousand pounds; a letter from his former wife's solicitor demanded property in Scotland; there were assorted copies of ships' logs and sailing schedules.

Holcroft wanted to stay in that room awhile longer, to look more thoroughly for clues to the strange man with the odd eyebrows, but he knew he dared not. He had already tested the situation beyond reason; he had to get out.

He left the house and looked across the way, up to the windows that only minutes ago had been filled with lights and curious faces. There were no lights now, no faces; sleep had returned to Portsea. He walked rapidly down the path and swung the gate open, annoyed that the hinges squeaked. He opened the door of the rented car, and quickly got behind the wheel. He turned the key in the ignition.

Nothing. He turned it again. And again and again. Nothing!

He released the hood and raced to the front of the car, not worried about the noise; worried about something far more serious. There was no reason for the rented car's battery to be worn down, but even if it were, there would still be a faint click in the ignition. The light of the streetlamp spread over the exposed engine, showing him what he was afraid he might find.

The wires were cut, severed at their source with a surgeon's precision. No amount of simple splicing would start the car; it would have to be towed away.

And whoever was responsible knew that an American would be without means of travel in an unfamiliar area in the middle of the night. If there were taxis in this outlying suburb, it was doubtful they'd be available at that hour; it was past three o'clock. Whoever immobilized the car wanted him to stay where he was; it had to follow that others would come after him. He had to run. As far and as fast as he could . . . reach the highway . . . hitch a ride north, out of the area.

He closed the hood. The sharp, metallic noise echoed throughout the street. He was grateful it had done so before.

He started up the block toward the traffic light; it was not operating now. Crossing the intersection, he began walking faster, then broke into a run. He tried to pace himself; there was a mile and a half before he reached the highway. He was sweating, and he could feel the knot in his stomach forming again.

He saw the lights before he heard the furious pitch of the engine. Up ahead, directly ahead on the straight road, the glare of headlights came out of the darkness, drawing closer so rapidly that the automobile had to be traveling at tremendous speed.

Noel saw an opening to his right, a space between a line of waisthigh privet hedge, an entrance to another path to another doorway. He dived through it and rolled into the dirt beneath the shrubbery, wondering if he'd been seen. It was suddenly very important for him not to be involved with Gretchen Beaumont. She was a dismissable enigma, an unhappy, highly erotic . . . beautiful woman. But in herself a threat to Geneva, as was her brother.

The approaching car raced by. He had not been seen. Then the sound of the roaring motor was replaced by the screeching of tires. Holcroft crawled halfway through the break in the hedge, his face turned to his left, his eyes focused on the block behind him.

The car had stopped directly in front of the Beaumont house. Two men leaped from the car and raced up the path. Noel could hear the squeaking of the gate hinges. There was no point in remaining where he was; it was the moment to run. Now he heard the tapping of the door knocker a hundred yards away.

He moved to his right on his hands and knees, along the sidewalk, by a privet hedge, until he was in the shadows between the streetlamps. He got to his feet and ran.

He kept running straight ahead, up the dark, tree-lined street, block after block, corner after corner, hoping to God he would recognize the first turn to the highway when he came to it. He cursed cigarettes as his breath became shorter and turned into pain-filled gasps; sweat poured down his face and the pounding in his chest became intolerable. The rapid cracks of his own footsteps on the pavement frightened him. It was the sound of a man running in panic in the middle of the night, and that man in panic was himself.

Footsteps. *Racing* footsteps. They were his, but *more* than his! Behind him, steady, heavy, gaining on him. There was someone running after him! Someone running in silence, not calling his name, not demanding that he stop! . . . Or was his hearing playing tricks on him? The hammering in his chest vibrated throughout his entire body; were his footsteps echoing in his ears? He dared not turn, *could* not turn. He was going too fast—into light, into shadow.

He came to the end of yet another block, to another corner, and turned right, knowing it was not the first of the turns that would take him to the highway, but turning anyway. He had to know if there was someone behind him. He raced into the street.

The footsteps *were* there, the rhythm different, not his own, closer, ever closer, shortening the distance between them. He could stand it no longer; and he could run no faster. He twisted his waist, trying to look over his shoulder.

It was there; *he* was there! The figure of a man silhouetted in the light of a streetlamp on the corner. A stocky man, running in silence, shortening the gap, only yards away.

His legs aching, Noel hammered his feet on the surface in a final burst of speed. He turned again, his panic complete.

And his legs gave out, tangled in the chaos and the terror of the chase. He plunged headlong onto the street, his face scraping the asphalt, his extended hands icelike and stinging. He twisted over on his back, instinctively raising his feet to ward off his assailant—the silent, racing figure that shot out of the darkness and was suddenly over him.

Everything was a blur; only the thrashing outlines of arms and legs silhouetted in the darkness penetrated his sweat-filled eyes. And then he was pinned. An enormous weight was crushing his chest, a forearm—like a heavy iron bar—was across his throat, choking off all sound.

The last thing he saw was a hand raised high, a dark claw in the night sky, a curved hand that held an object in it. And then there was nothing. Only a huge chasm filled with wind. He was falling toward unseen depths in darkness.

He felt the cold first. It made him shiver. Then the dampness; it was everywhere. He opened his eyes to distorted images of grass and dirt. He was surrounded by wet grass and mounds of cold earth. He rolled over, grateful to see the night sky; it was lighter to his left, darker to his right.

His head ached; his face stung; his hands were in pain. Slowly he raised himself and looked around. He was in a field, a long flat stretch of ground that appeared to be a pasture. In the distance he could see the faint outlines of a wire fence— barbed wire strung between thick posts ten or twenty yards apart. It *was* a pasture.

He smelled cheap whiskey or rancid wine.

His clothes were drenched with it, his shirt sopping wet, sending the awful fumes into his nostrils. His *clothes* . . . his wallet, his money! He rose unsteadily to his feet and checked his pockets, both hands stinging as he plunged them into the moist cloth.

His wallet, his money clip with the bills in it, his watch—all were there. He had not been robbed, only beaten unconscious and taken away from the area where the Beaumonts lived. It was crazy!

He felt his head. A bump had formed, but the skin was not broken. He had been hit with some kind of padded blackjack or pipe. He took several awkward steps; he could move, and that was all that mattered. And he could see more clearly now; it would be morning soon.

Beyond the fence there was a slight rise in the ground, forming a ridge that extended as far as he could see in both directions. Along the ridge he saw highway lights. He started across the field, toward the fence and the ridge and the highway, hoping to convince a driver to give him a ride. As he climbed over the fence, a thought suddenly occurred to him. He checked his pockets again.

The photograph was gone!

A milk truck stopped and he climbed in, watching the smile of the driver fade abruptly as the stench filled the cab. Noel tried to make light of it—a predicament brought on by an innocent American's having been taken in by some very sharp British sailors in Portsmouth—but the driver found nothing amusing. Holcroft got out at the first town.

It was an English village, the Tudor architecture of the square marred by a profusion of delivery trucks in front of a roadside stop.

"There's a telephone inside," said the milkman. "And a gents' room, too. A wash would do you no harm."

Noel walked into the sight and sounds of the early-morning truckers, the smell of hot coffee somehow reassuring. The world went on; deliveries were made and small comforts accepted without particular notice. He found the washroom, and did what he could to minimize the effects of the night. Then he sat in a booth next to the pay telephone on the wall and had black coffee, waiting for an angry trucker to conclude an argument with an angrier dispatcher on the other end of the line. When the call was finished, Noel got out of the booth and went to the phone, Gretchen Beaumont's telephone number in his hand. There was nothing to do but try to find out what happened, try to reason with her, if, indeed, she had returned.

He dialed.

"Beaumont residence." A male voice was on the line.

"Mrs. Beaumont, please."

"May I ask who's calling?"

"A friend of the commander. I heard Mrs. Beaumont was leaving today to join him. I'd like her to take a message to him."

"Who is this, please?"

Noel replaced the receiver. He did not know who had answered the phone; he knew only that he needed help. Professional help. It was possibly dangerous for Geneva to seek it, but it was necessary. He would be cautious—very cautious—and learn what he could.

He rummaged through his jacket pockets for the card given him by the MI-Five men at the Belgravia Arms. There was only a name—Harold Payton-Jones—and a telephone number. The clock on the wall read ten minutes to seven; Noel wondered if anyone would answer the phone. He placed the call to London.

"Yes?"

"This is Holcroft."

"Oh, yes. We wondered if you'd ring up."

Noel recognized the voice. It was the gray-haired intelligence agent from the hotel. "What are you talking about?" Noel said.

"You've had a difficult night," the voice said.

"You *expected* me to call! You were there. You were watching!"

Payton-Jones did not respond directly. "The rented car's at a garage in Aldershot. It should be repaired by noon. The name's easily remembered; it's Boot's. Boot's Garage, Aldershot. There'll be no charge, no bill, no receipt."

"Wait a minute! What the hell is this? You had me followed! You had no right to do that."

"I'd say it was a damned good thing we did."

"You were in that car at three o'clock this morning! You went into Beaumont's house!"

"I'm afraid we weren't and we didn't." The MI-Five man paused briefly. "And if you believe that, then you didn't get a very good look at them, did you?"

"No. Who were they?"

"I wish we knew. Our man got there closer to five."

"Who ran after me? Who bashed my head in and left me in that goddamned field?"

Again the agent paused. "We don't know anything about that. We knew only you had left. In a hurry, obviously, your car immobilized."

"It was a setup! I was the pigeon!"

"Quite so. I'd advise you to be more cautious. It's both tasteless and dangerous to take advantage of the wife of a commander in the Royal Navy while her husband's at sea."

"Bullshit! The commander's no more at sea than I am! He was on a plane to Rio less than two weeks ago. I saw him! He's got something to do with the Von Tiebolts."

"Most assuredly," replied Payton-Jones. "He married the oldest daughter. As to his being on an aircraft two weeks ago, it's preposterous. He's been in the Mediterranean for the past three months."

"No! I *saw* him! Listen to me. There was a photograph in the bedroom. I took it. It was him! And something else. There was writing on the back. In German."

"What did it say?"

"I don't know. I don't speak German. But it's goddamned unusual, don't you think?" Holcroft stopped. He had not meant to go this far. In his anger, he had lost his control! *Goddamn it!*

"What's unusual?" asked the agent. "German is Mrs. Beaumont's native tongue; the family's spoken it for years. An endearing phrase, words of devotion to or from her new husband? Not unusual at all."

"I guess you're right," said Noel, backing off. Then he realized he had retreated too quickly. The MI-Five man was suspicious; Noel could sense it in his next words.

"On second thought, perhaps you should bring the photograph to us."

"I can't. I don't have it."

"I thought you said you took it."

"I don't have it now. I . . . I just don't have it."

"Where are you, Holcroft? I think you should drop in and see us."

Without consciously making the decision, Noel pressed down the lever, severing the connection. The act preceded the thought, but once it was done, he understood clearly why he did it. He could not ally himself with MI Five, he could not solidify any relationship whatsoever. On the contrary, he had to get as far away from British Intelligence as was possible. There could be no association at *all*. MI Five had *followed* him. After they had told him they would leave him alone, they had gone back on their word.

The survivors of Wolfsschanze had spelled it out: *There are those who may learn of the work in Geneva . . . who will try to stop you, deceive you . . . kill you.*

Holcroft doubted that the British would kill him, but they *were* trying to stop him. If they succeeded, it was as good as killing him. The men of Wolfsschanze did not hesitate. *Peter Baldwin, Esq. Ernst Manfredi. Jack.* All dead.

The men of Wolfsschanze would kill him if he failed. And that was the terrible irony. He did not *want* to fail. Why couldn't they understand that? Perhaps more than the survivors of Wolfsschanze, he wanted to see Heinrich Clausen's dream realized.

He thought of Gretchen Beaumont, follower of instincts, opportunities, and men. And of her brother, the arrogant, brilliant multilingual newspaperman who was suspected of being an assassin. Neither would be remotely acceptable to Geneva.

There was one child left. Helden von Tiebolt—now Helden Tennyson—currently living in Paris. Address unknown. But he had a name. "Gallimard."

Paris.

He had to get to Paris. He had to elude MI Five.

13

There was a man in London, a stage designer, who'd had a brief vogue as a decorator among the wealthy on both sides of the Atlantic. Noel suspected that Willie Ellis was more often hired for his outrageous personality and his talents as a raconteur than for any intrinsic abilities as an interior decorator. He had worked with Willie on four occasions, vowing each time never to do it again but knowing each time that he probably would. For the truth was that Noel liked Willie immensely. The mad Englishman was not all artifice and elegance. Underneath, in quiet moments, there was a thinking, talented man of the theater who knew more about the history of design than anyone Holcroft had ever met. He could be fascinating.

When he was not outrageous.

They had kept in touch over the years, and whenever Noel was in London, there was always time for Willie. He had thought there would be no time this trip, but that was changed now. He needed Willie. He got the number from London information and dialed.

"Noel, my friend, you're out of your mind! No one's up but those stinking birds and street cleaners."

"I'm in trouble, Willie. I need help."

Ellis knew the small village where Holcroft was calling from and promised to be there as soon as he could, which he estimated would be something close to an hour. He arrived thirty minutes late, cursing the idiots on the road. Noel climbed into the car, taking Willie's outstretched hand as well as his characteristic abuse.

"You're an absolute mess and you smell like a barmaid's armpit. Keep the window open and tell me what the hell happened."

Holcroft kept the explanation simple, giving no names and obscuring the facts. "I have to get to Paris, and there are people who want to stop me. I can't tell you much more than that except to say that I haven't done anything wrong, anything illegal."

"The first is always relative, isn't it? And the second is generally subject to interpretation and a good barrister. Shall I assume a lovely girl and an irate husband?"

"That's fine."

"That keeps me clean. What stops you from going to the airport and taking the next plane to Paris?"

"My clothes, briefcase, and passport are at my hotel in London. If I go there to get them, the people who want to stop me will find me."

"From the looks of you, they're quite serious, aren't they?"

"Yes. That's about it, Willie."

"The solution's obvious," said Ellis. "I'll get your things and check you out. You're a wayward colonial I found in a Soho gutter. Who's to argue with my preferences?"

"There may be a problem with the front desk."

"I can't imagine why. My money's coin of the realm, and you'll give me a note; they can match signatures. We're nowhere near as paranoid as our cousins across the sea."

"I hope you're right, but I've got an idea the clerks have been reached by the people who want to find me. They may insist on knowing where I am before they let you have my things."

"Then I'll tell them," said Willie, smiling. "I'll leave them a forwarding address and a telephone number where your presence can be confirmed."

"What?"

"Leave it to me. By the way, there's some cologne in the glove compartment. For Christ's sake, use it."

Ellis made arrangements for the whiskey-soaked clothes to be picked up by the cleaners and returned by midafternoon, then left the Chelsea flat for the Belgravia Arms.

Holcroft showered, shaved, put the soiled clothes in a hamper outside the door, and called the car-rental agency. He reasoned that if he went for the car in Aldershot, MI Five would be there. And when he drove away, the British would not be far behind.

The rental agency was not amused, but Holcroft gave them no choice. If they wanted the automobile back, they would have to pick it up themselves. Noel was sorry, but there was an emergency; the bill could be sent to his office in New York.

He had to get out of England with as little notice as possible. Undoubtedly, MI Five would have the airports and the Channel boats watched. Perhaps the solution was to be found in a last-minute ticket on a crowded plane to Paris. With any luck, he'd reach Orly Airport before MI Five knew he had left England. The shuttles to Paris were frequent, the customs procedures lax. Or he could buy two tickets—one to Amsterdam, one to Paris—go through the KLM gates, then on some pretext come back outside and rush to the Paris departure area, where Willie held his luggage.

What was he *thinking* of? Ruses, evasions, deceptions. He was a criminal without a crime, a man who could not tell the truth, because in that truth was the destruction of so much.

He began to perspire again, and the pain returned to his stomach. He felt weak and disoriented. He lay down on Willie's couch in Willie's bathrobe and closed his eyes. The image of melting flesh came back into focus. The face emerged; he heard the cry clearly, and he fell asleep, the plaintive sound in his ears.

He woke suddenly, aware that someone was above him, looking down at him. Alarmed, he whipped over on his back, then sighed in relief at the sight of Willie standing by the couch.

"You've had some rest, and it shows. You look better, and God knows you smell better."

"Did you get my things?"

"Yes, and you were right. They were anxious to know where you were. When I paid the bill, the manager came out and behaved like a rep-company version of Scotland Yard. He's mollified, if confused. He's also got a telephone number where you're currently in residence."

"In residence?"

"Yes. I'm afraid your reputation hasn't been vastly improved, unless you've had a change of heart. The number's for a hospital in Knightsbridge that doesn't get a *P* from National Health. It specializes in venereal diseases. I know a doctor there quite well."

"You're too much," said Noel, standing. "Where are my things?"

"In the guest room. I thought you'd want to change."

"Thanks." Holcroft started toward the door.

"Do you know a man named Buonoventura?" Ellis asked.

Noel stopped. He had sent Sam a three-word cablegram from the airport in Lisbon: BELGRAVIA ARMS LONDON. "Yes. Did he call?"

"Several times. Quite frantically, I gather. The hotel switchboard said the call came from Curaçao."

"I know the number," said Holcroft. "I have to get in touch with him. I'll put the call on my credit card."

It was five minutes before he heard Sam's rasping voice and less than five seconds before he realized it was not fair to ask the construction engineer to lie any longer.

"Miles isn't fooling around anymore, Noley. He told me he's getting a court order for your return to New York. He's going to serve it on the owners down here, figuring they're American. He knows they can't force you to go back, but he says they'll know you're wanted. It's a little rough, Noley, because you're not on any payroll."

"Did he say why?"

"Only that he thinks you have information they need."

If he could get to Paris, Noel thought, he would want Buonoventura to be able to reach him, but he did not want to burden him with an address. "Listen, Sam. I'm leaving for Paris later today. There's an American Express office on the Champs-Elysées, near the avenue George Cinq. If anything comes up, cable me there."

"What'll I tell Miles if he calls again? I don't want to get my ass burned."

"Say you reached me and told me he was trying to find me. Tell him I said I'd get in touch with him as soon as I could. That's all you know." Noel paused. "Also tell him I had to get to Europe. Don't volunteer, but if he presses, let him know about the American Express office. I can phone for messages."

"There's something else," said Sam awkwardly. "Your mother called, too. I felt like a goddamned idiot lying to her; you shouldn't lie to your mother, Noley."

Holcroft smiled. A lifetime of deviousness had not taken the basic Italian out of Sam. "When did she call?"

"Night before last. She sounds like a real lady. I told her I expected to hear from you yesterday; that's when I started phoning."

"I'll call her when I get to Paris," said Noel. "Anything else?"

"Isn't that enough?"

"Plenty. I'll be in touch in a few days, but you know where to cable me."

"Yeah, but if your mother calls, I'm going to let her know, too."

"No sweat. And thanks, Sam. I owe you."

He hung up, noticing that Willie Ellis had gone into the kitchen, where he had turned on the radio. One of Willie's attributes was that he was a gentleman. Noel sat by the phone for several moments, trying to figure things out. His mother's call was not surprising. He had not spoken with her since that Sunday morning in Bedford Hills nearly two weeks ago.

Miles was something else again. Holcroft did not think of the detective as a person; he had no face or voice. But Miles had arrived at certain conclusions; he was certain of that. And those conclusions tied him to three deaths connected with British Airways Flight 591 from London to New York. Miles was not letting go; if he persisted, he could create a problem Noel was not sure he could handle. The detective could ask for international police cooperation. And if he did, attention would be drawn to the activities of a United States citizen who had walked away from a homicide investigation.

Geneva would not tolerate that attention; the covenant would be destroyed. Miles had to be contained. But *how?*

His unfamiliar forest was lined with traps; every protective instinct he possessed told him to turn back. Geneva needed a man infinitely more cunning and experienced than he. Yet he could not turn back. The survivors of Wolfsschanze would not permit it. And deep in his own consciousness he knew he did not want to. There was the face that came into focus in the darkness. He had to find his father and, in the finding, show the world a man in agony who was brave enough and perceptive enough to know that amends must be made. And brilliant enough to make that credo live.

Noel walked to the kitchen door. Ellis was at the sink, washing teacups.

"I'll pick up my clothes in a couple of weeks, Willie. Let's go to the airport."

Ellis turned, concern in his eyes. "I can save you time," he said, reaching for a china mug on a shelf. "You'll need some French money until you can convert. I keep a jarful for my bimonthly travels to the fleshpots. Take what you need."

"Thanks." Holcroft took the mug, looking at Willie's exposed arms beneath rolled-up sleeves. They were as powerful and muscular as any two arms he'd ever seen. It struck Noel that Willie could break a man in half.

The madness started at Heathrow and gathered momentum at Orly.

In London he bought a ticket on KLM to Amsterdam, on the theory that the story he gave MI Five had been checked out and considered plausible. He suspected it had been both, for he saw a bewildered man in a raincoat watch him in astonishment as he raced out of the KLM departure gates back to Air France. There Willie was waiting for him with a ticket for a crowded plane to Paris.

Immigration procedure at Orly was cursory, but the lines were long. As he waited, Noel had time to study the milling crowds in the customs area and beyond the swinging doors that led to the terminal proper. Beyond those doors he could see two men; there was something about them that caught his attention. Perhaps it was their somber faces, joyless expressions that did not belong in a place where people greeted one another. They were talking quietly, their heads immobile, as they watched the passengers walk out of customs. One held a piece of paper in his hand; it was small, shiny. A photograph? Yes. A photograph of *him.*

These were not the men of Wolfsschanze. The men of Wolfsschanze knew him by sight; and the men of Wolfsschanze were never seen. MI Five had reached its agents in Paris. They were waiting for him.

"Monsieur." The customs clerk stamped Holcroft's passport routinely. Noel picked up his luggage and started toward the exit, feeling the panic of a man about to walk into an unavoidable trap.

As the doors parted, he saw the two men turn away to avoid being noticed. They were not going to approach him; they were going to . . . *follow* him.

The realization gave painful birth to an unclear strategy. Painful because it was so alien to him, unclear because he was not sure of the procedures. He only knew that he had to go from point *A* to point *B* and back again to *A*, losing his pursuers somewhere in the vicinity of *B*.

Up ahead in the crowded terminal he saw the sign: LIGNES AÉRIENNES INTÉRI-EURES.

France's domestic airline shuttled about the country with splendid irregularity. The cities were listed in three columns: ROUEN, LE HAVRE, CAEN . . . ORLÉANS, LE MANS, TOURS . . . DIJON, LYON, MARSEILLES.

Noel walked rapidly past the two men, as if oblivious of all but his own concerns. He hurried to the Intérieures counter. There were four people ahead of him.

His turn came. He inquired about flights south. To the Mediterranean. To Marseilles. He wanted a choice of several departure times.

There was a flight that landed at five cities in a southwest arc from Orly to the Mediterranean, the clerk told him. The stops were Le Mans, Nantes, Bordeaux, Toulouse, and Marseilles.

Le Mans. The flight time to Le Mans was forty minutes. Estimated driving time, three, three and a half hours. It was now twenty minutes to four.

"I'll take that one," Noel said. "It gets me to Marseilles at just the right time."

"Pardon, monsieur, but there are more direct flights."

"I'm being met at the airport. No point in being early."

"As you wish, monsieur. I will see what is available. The flight leaves in twelve minutes."

Five minutes later, Holcroft stood by the departure gate, the *Herald Tribune* opened in front of him. He looked over the top of the page. One of the two somber-faced Britishers was talking with the young lady who had sold him his ticket.

Fifteen minutes later the plane was airborne. Twice Noel wandered up the aisle to the lavatory, looking at the passengers in the cabin. Neither of the two men was on the aircraft; no one else seemed remotely interested in him.

At Le Mans he waited until the departing passengers got off the plane. He counted; there were seven of them. The replacements began coming on board.

He grabbed his suitcase from the luggage rack, walked quickly to the exit door and down the metal steps to the ground. He went inside the terminal and stood by the window.

No one came out of the plane; no one was following him.

His watch read seventeen minutes to five. He wondered if there was still time to reach Helden von Tiebolt. Again he had the essence of what he needed—a name and a place of work. He walked to the nearest telephone, thankful for Willie's jar of franc notes and coins.

In his elementary French, he spoke to the operator. *"S'il vous plaît, le numéro de Gallimard à Paris . . ."*

She was there. Mademoiselle Tennyson did not have a telephone at her desk, but if the caller would hold on, someone would get her on a line. The woman at the Gallimard switchboard spoke better English than most Texans.

Helden von Tiebolt's voice had that same odd mixture of Portuguese and German as her sister's but it was not nearly so pronounced. Too, there was a trace of the echo Noel remembered so vividly in Gretchen's speech, but not the halting, once-removed quality. Helden von Tiebolt—Mademoiselle Tennyson—knew what she wanted to say and said it.

"Why should I meet with you? I don't know you, Mr. Holcroft."

"It's urgent. Please, believe me."

"There's been an excess of urgencies in my life. I'm rather tired of them."

"There's been nothing like this."

"How did you find me?"

"People . . . people you don't know, in England, told me where you worked. But they said you didn't live at the address listed with your employer, so I had to call you here."

"They were so interested they inquired where I lived?"

"Yes. It's part of what I have to tell you."

"Why were they interested in me?"

"I'll tell you when I see you. I *have* to tell you."

"Tell me now."

"Not on the phone."

There was a pause. When the girl spoke, her words were clipped, precise . . . afraid. "Why exactly do you wish to see me? What can there be that's so urgent between us?"

"It concerns your family. *Both* our families. I've seen your sister. I've tried to locate your brother—"

"I've spoken to neither in over a year," interrupted Helden Tennyson. "I can't help you."

"What we have to talk about goes back over *thirty* years."

"No!"

"There's money involved. A great deal of money."

"I live adequately. My needs are—"

"Not only for *you,*" pressed Noel, cutting her off. "For thousands. Everywhere."

Again there was the pause. When she spoke, she spoke softly. "Does this concern events . . . people going back to the war?"

"Yes." Was he getting through to her at last?

"We'll meet," said Helden.

"Can we arrange it so we . . . we—" He was not sure how to phrase it without frightening her.

"So we won't be seen by those watching for us? Yes."

"How?"

"I've had experience. Do exactly as I say. Where are you?"

"At the Le Mans airport. I'll rent a car and drive up to Paris. It'll take me two or three hours."

"Leave the car in a garage and take a taxi to Montmartre. To the Sacré-Coeur cathedral. Go inside to the far end of the church, to the chapel of Louis the

Ninth. Light a candle and place it first in one holder, then change your mind and place it in another. You'll be met by a man who will take you outside, up to the square, to a table at one of the street cafés. You'll be given instructions."

"We don't have to be *that* elaborate. Can't we just meet at a bar? Or a restaurant?"

"It's not for your protection, Mr. Holcroft, but mine. If you're not who you imply you are, if you're not *alone,* I won't see you. I'll leave Paris tonight and you'll never find me."

14

The granite, medieval splendor of Sacré-Coeur rose in the night sky like a haunting song of stone. Beyond the enormous bronze doors, an infinite cavern was shrouded in semidarkness, flickering candles playing a symphony of shadows on the walls.

From near the altar, he could hear the strains of a *Te Deum Laudamus.* A visiting choir of monks stood in isolated solemnity, singing quietly.

Noel entered the dimly lit circle beyond the apse that housed the chapels of the kings. He adjusted his eyes to the dancing shadows and walked along the balustrades that flanked the entrances to the small enclosures. The rows of scattered candles provided just enough light for him to read the inscription: LOUIS IX. Louis the Pious, Louis the Just, Son of Aquitaine, Ruler of France, Arbiter of Christendom.

Pious. . . . Just. . . . Arbiter.

Was Helden von Tiebolt trying to tell him something?

He inserted a coin in the prayer box, removed a thin tapered candle from its receptacle, and held it to the flame of another nearby. Following instructions, he placed it in a holder, then seconds later removed it and inserted it in another several rows away.

A hand touched his arm, fingers gripped his elbow, and a voice whispered into his ear from the shadows behind him.

"Turn around slowly, monsieur. Keep your hands at your side."

Holcroft did as he was told. The man stood not much over five feet six or seven, with a high forehead and thinning dark hair. He was in his early thirties, Noel guessed, and pleasant-looking, the face pale, even soft. If there was anything particularly noticeable about him, it was his clothes; the dim light could not conceal the fact that they were expensive.

An aura of elegance emanated from the man, heightened by the mild fragrance of cologne. But he acted neither elegantly nor softly. Before Noel knew what was happening, the man's hands were jabbed into both sides of his chest, and strong fingers spanned the cloth in rapid movements, descending to his belt and the pockets of his trousers.

Holcroft jerked backwards.

"I said, be still!" the man whispered.

In the candlelight, by the chapel of Louis IX, in the cathedral of Sacré-Coeur, on the top of Montmartre, Noel was checked for a weapon.

"Follow me," said the man. "I will walk up the street to the square; stay quite far behind. I will join two friends at an outside table at one of the street cafés, probably Bohème. Walk around the square; take your time; look at the artists' work; do not hurry. Then come to the table and sit with us. Greet us as if we are familiar *faces*, not necessarily *friends*. Do you understand?"

"I understand."

If this was the way to reach Helden von Tiebolt, so be it. Noel stayed a discreet distance behind the man, the fashionably cut overcoat not hard to follow among the less elegant clothes of the tourists.

They reached the crowded square. The man stood for a moment, lighting a cigarette, then proceeded across the street to a table beyond the sidewalk, behind a planter filled with shrubbery. As he had said, there were two people at the table. One was a man dressed in a ragged field jacket, the other a woman in a black raincoat, a white scarf around her neck. The scarf contrasted with her very dark, straight hair, as dark as the black raincoat. She wore tortoise-shell glasses, framed intrusions on a pale face with no discernible makeup. Noel wondered if the plain-looking woman was Helden von Tiebolt. If she was, there was little resemblance to her sister.

He started his stroll around the square, pretending interest in the artworks on display everywhere. There were canvases with bold dashes of color and heavy, un-thought-out lines, and bulging wide eyes of charcoal-rendered children . . . cuteness and swiftness and artificiality. There was little of merit; nor was there meant to be. This was the tourist marketplace, the bazaar where the bizarre was for sale.

Nothing had changed in the Montmartre, thought Holcroft, as he threaded his way around the last turn toward the café.

He walked by the planter and nodded at the two men and the woman seated at the table beyond. They nodded back; he proceeded to the entrance, walked in, and returned to the "familiar faces, not necessarily friends." He sat down in the empty chair; it was beside the dark-haired woman with the tortoise-shell glasses.

"I'm Noel Holcroft," he said to no one in particular.

"We know," answered the man in the field jacket, his eyes on the crowds in the square.

Noel turned to the woman. "Are you Helden von—? Excuse me, Helen Tennyson?"

"No, I've never met her," replied the dark-haired woman, looking intently at the man in the field jacket. "But I will take you to her."

The man in the expensive overcoat turned to Holcroft. "You alone?"

"Of course. Can we get started? Helden . . . Tennyson . . . said I'd be given instructions. I'd like to see her, talk for a while, and then find a hotel. I haven't had much sleep during the past few days." He started to get up from the table.

"Sit down!" The woman spoke sharply.

He sat, more out of curiosity than in response to command. And then he had the sudden feeling that these three people were not testing him; they were frightened. The elegantly dressed man was biting the knuckle of his index finger, staring at something in the middle of the square. His companion in the field jacket had his hand on his friend's arm, his gaze leveled in the identical direction. They were looking at someone, someone who disturbed them profoundly.

Holcroft tried to follow their line of sight, tried to peer between the crisscrossing figures that filled the street in front of the café. He stopped breathing. Across the street were the two men he thought he had eluded at Le Mans. It didn't make sense! No one had followed him off the plane.

"It's *them,*" he said.

The elegantly dressed man turned his head swiftly; the man in the field jacket was slower, his expression disbelieving; the dark-haired woman studied him closely.

"Who?" she asked.

"Those two men over there, near the entrance to the restaurant. One's in a light topcoat, the other's carrying a raincoat over his arm."

"Who are they?"

"They were at Orly this afternoon; they were waiting for me. I flew to Le Mans to get away from them. I'm almost sure they're British agents. But how did they know I was *here?* They weren't on the plane. No one followed me; I'd *swear* to it!"

The three exchanged glances; they believed him, and Holcroft knew why. He had picked out the two Englishmen himself, volunteered the information before being confronted with it.

"If they're British, what do they want with you?" asked the man in the field jacket.

"That's between Helden von Tiebolt and myself."

"But you think they *are* British?" pressed the man in the jacket.

"Yes."

"I hope you're right."

The man in the overcoat leaned forward. "What do you mean you flew to Le Mans? What happened?"

"I thought I could throw them off. I was convinced I *had.* I bought a ticket to Marseilles. I made it clear to the girl at the counter that I had to get to

Marseilles, and then picked a flight that had stops. The first was Le Mans, and I got off. I saw them *questioning* her. I never said anything *about* Le Mans!"

"Don't excite yourself," said the man in the field jacket. "It only draws attention."

"If you think they haven't spotted me, you're crazy! But how did they *do* it?"

"It's not difficult," said the woman.

"You rented a car?" asked the elegantly dressed man.

"Of course. I had to drive back to Paris."

"At the airport?"

"Naturally."

"And naturally, you asked for a map. Or at least directions, no doubt mentioning Paris. I mean, you were not driving to Marseilles."

"Certainly, but lots of people do that."

"Not so many, not at an airport that has flights to Paris. And none with your name. I can't believe you have false papers."

Holcroft was beginning to understand. "They checked," he said in disgust.

"One person on a telephone for but a few minutes," said the man in the field jacket. "Less, if you were reported having left the plane at Le Mans."

"The French would not miss the opportunity of selling an empty seat," added the man in the elegant coat. "Do you see now? There are not so many places that rent cars at airports. The make, the color, the license, would be given. The rest is simple."

"Why simple? In all Paris, to find *one car?*"

"Not *in* Paris, monsieur. On the road *to* Paris. There is but one main highway; it is the most likely to be used by a foreigner. You were picked up outside of Paris."

Noel's astonishment was joined by a sense of depression. His ineptness was too apparent. "I'm sorry. I'm really sorry."

"You did nothing intentionally," said the elegant man, his concentration back on the Englishmen, who were now seated in the first booth of the restaurant in the middle of the square. He touched the arm of the man in the field jacket. "They've sat down."

"I see."

"What are we going to do?" asked Holcroft.

"It's being done," answered the dark-haired woman. "Do exactly what we tell you to do."

"Now," said the man in the expensive coat.

"Get up!" ordered the woman. "Walk with me out into the street and turn right. Quickly!" Bewildered, Holcroft rose from his chair and left the café, the woman's fingers clasped around his arm. They stepped off the curb.

"To the right!" she repeated.

He turned to his right.

"Faster!" she said.

He heard a crash of glass behind them, then angry shouts. He turned and looked back. The two Englishmen had left the booth, colliding with a waiter. All three were covered with wine.

"Turn right again!" commanded the woman. "Into the doorway!"

He did as he was told, shouldering his way past a crowd of people in the entrance of yet another café. Once inside, the woman stopped him; he whirled around instinctively and watched the scene in the square.

The Englishmen were trying to disengage themselves from the furious waiter. The man in the topcoat was throwing money on the table. His companion had made better progress; he was under the trellis, looking frantically to his left—in the direction Holcroft and the girl had taken.

Noel heard shouts; he stared in disbelief at the source. Not twenty feet from where the agents stood was a dark-haired woman in a shiny black raincoat, wearing thick tortoise-shell glasses and a white scarf around her neck. She stood yelling at someone loudly enough to draw the attention of everyone around her.

Including the Englishmen.

She stopped abruptly and began running up the crowded street, toward the south end of Montmartre. The British agents took up the chase. Their progress was slowed unexpectedly by a number of young people in jeans and jackets who seemed to be purposely blocking the Englishmen. Furious shouts erupted; then he could hear the shrill whistles of the *gendarmes*.

Montmartre became pandemonium.

"Come! *Now!*" The dark-haired woman—the one at his side—grabbed Noel's arm again, and again propelled him into the street. "Turn left!" she ordered, pushing him through the crowds. "Back where we were."

They approached the table behind the planter box. Only the man in the expensive overcoat remained; he stood up as they drew near.

"There may be others," he said. "We don't know. Hurry!"

Holcroft and the woman continued running. They reached a side street no wider than a large alley; it was lined with small shops on both sides, the dimly lit store fronts providing the only light in the block.

"This way!" said the woman, now holding Noel's hand, running beside him. "The car is on the right. The first one by the corner!"

It was a Citroën; it looked powerful but undistinguished. There were layers of dirt on the body, the wheels were filthy and caked with mud. Even the windows had a film of dust on them.

"Get in the front! Drive," commanded the woman, handing him a key. "I'll stay in the back seat."

Holcroft climbed in, trying to orient himself. He started the engine. The vibrations caused the chassis to tremble. It had an outsized motor, designed for a heavier car, guaranteeing enormous speed for a lighter one.

"Go straight toward the bottom of the hill!" said the woman behind him. "I'll tell you where to turn."

The next forty-five minutes were blurred into a series of plunges and sudden turns. The woman issued directions at the last second, forcing Noel to turn the wheel violently in order to obey. They sped into a highway north of Paris from a twisting entrance road that caused the Citroën to lurch sideways, careening off the mound of grass that was the center island. Holcroft held the wheel with all his strength, first straightening the car and then weaving between two nearly parallel cars ahead.

"Faster!" screamed the dark-haired woman in the back seat. "Can't you go *faster?*"

"Jesus! We're over ninety-five!"

"Keep looking in your mirrors! I'll watch the side roads! And go *faster!*"

They drove for ten minutes in silence, the wind and the steady high-pitched hum of the tires maddening. It was *all* maddening, thought Noel as he shifted his eyes from the windshield to the rearview mirror to the side-view mirror, which was caked with dirt. What were they *doing?* They were out of Paris; whom were they running from *now?* There was no time to think; the woman was screaming again.

"The next exit; that's the one!"

He barely had time to brake and turn the car into the exit. He screeched to a halt at the stop sign.

"Keep going! To the left!"

The split seconds of immobility were the only pause in the madness. It began again: the accelerated speed over the dark country roads, the sudden turns, the commands barked harshly in his ear.

The moonlight that had washed over the splendor of Sacré-Coeur now revealed stretches of rock-hewn farmland. Barns and silos loomed in irregular silhouettes; small houses with thatched roofs appeared and disappeared.

"There's the road!" yelled the woman.

It was a dirt road angling off the tarred surface over which they traveled; the trees would have concealed it if one did not know where or when to look. Noel slowed the Citroën and turned in. The entire car shook, but the voice behind him did not permit more cautious driving.

"Hurry! We have to get over the hill so our lights won't be seen!"

The hill was steep, the road too narrow for more than one vehicle. Holcroft pressed the accelerator; the Citroën lurched up the primitive road. They reached the crest of the hill, Noel gripping the steering wheel as if it were uncontrollable. The descent was rapid; the road curved to the left and flattened out. They were level again.

"No more than a quarter of a mile now," said the woman.

Holcroft was exhausted; the palms of his hands were soaked. He and the woman were in the loneliest, darkest place he could imagine. In a dense forest, on a road unlisted on any map.

Then he saw it. A small thatched house on a flat plot of ground dug out of the forest. There was a dim light on inside.

"Stop here," was the command, but it was not rendered in the harsh voice that had hammered into his ears for nearly an hour.

Noel stopped the car directly in front of the path that led to the house. He took several deep breaths and wiped the sweat from his face, closing his eyes briefly, wishing the pain would leave his head.

"Please turn around, Mr. Holcroft," said the woman, no stridency in her tone.

He did so. And he stared through the shadows at the woman in the back seat. Gone were the shining black hair and the thickrimmed glasses. The white scarf was still there, but now it was partially covered by long blond hair that cascaded over her shoulders, framing a face—a very lovely face—he had seen before. Not *this* face, but one like it; delicate features modeled lovingly in clay before a chisel was put to stone. This face was not cold and the eyes were not distant. There was vulnerability and involvement. She spoke quietly, returning his stare through the shadows.

"I am Helden von Tiebolt, and I have a gun in my hand. Now, what do you want of me?"

15

He looked down and saw a tiny reflection of light off the barrel of the automatic. The gun was pointed at his head, the bore only inches away, her fingers curved around the trigger.

"The first thing I want," he said, "is for you to put that thing away."

"I'm afraid I can't do that."

"You're the last person on earth I'd want to see hurt. You've got nothing to fear from me."

"Your words are reassuring, but I've heard such words before. They were not always true."

"Mine are." He looked into her eyes through the dim light, holding his gaze steady. The tenseness of her expression diminished. "Where are we?" Noel asked. "Was all that craziness necessary? The riot in Montmartre, racing around the country like maniacs. What are you running from?"

"I might ask the same question of you. You're running, too. You flew to Le Mans."

"I wanted to avoid some people. But I'm not afraid of them."

"I also avoid people, and I *am* afraid of them."

"Who?" The specter of the Tinamou intruded on Noel's thoughts; he tried to push it away.

"You may or may not be told, depending upon what you have to say to me."

"Fair enough. Right now you're the most important person in my life. That may change when I meet your brother, but right now, it's you."

"I can't imagine why. We've never met. You said you wanted to see me over matters that could be traced back to the war."

" 'Traced back to your father' would be more specific."

"I never knew my father."

"Both our fathers. Neither of us knew them."

He told her what he had told her sister, but he did not mention the men of Wolfsschanze; she was frightened enough. And he heard his words again, as if echoes from last night, in Portsea. It *was* only last night, and the woman he spoke to now was like the woman then—but only in appearance. Gretchen Beaumont had listened in silence; Helden did not. She interrupted him quietly, continuously, asking questions he should have asked himself.

"Did this Manfredi show you proof of his identity?"

"He didn't have to; he had the papers from the bank. They were legitimate."

"What are the names of the directors?"

"The directors?"

"Of the Grande Banque de Genève. The overseers of this extraordinary document."

"I don't know."

"You should be told."

"I'll ask."

"Who will handle the legal aspects of this agency in Zürich?"

"The bank's attorneys, I imagine."

"You imagine?"

"Is it important?"

"It's six months of your life. I'd think it would be."

"Our lives."

"We'll see. I'm not the oldest child of Wilhelm von Tiebolt."

"I told you when I called you from Le Mans," said Holcroft, "that I'd met your sister."

"And?" asked Helden.

"I think you know. She's not capable. The directors in Geneva won't accept her."

"There's my brother, Johann. He's next in age."

"I know that. I want to talk about him."

"Not now. Later."

"What do you mean?"

"I mentioned on the phone that there had been an excess of urgencies in my life. There has also been an excess of lies. I'm an expert in that area; I know a liar when I hear his words. You don't lie."

"Thank you for that." Noel was relieved; they had a basis for *talking*. It was his first concrete step. In a way, in spite of everything, he felt exhilarated. She lowered the gun to her lap.

"Now we must go inside. There's a man who wants to speak with you."

Holcroft's exhilaration crashed with her words. He could not share Geneva with anyone but a member of the Von Tiebolt family. "No," he said, shaking his head. "I'm not talking with anyone. What I've discussed with you is between us. No one else."

"Give him a chance. He must know that you don't mean to hurt me. Or hurt others. He must be convinced that you are not part of something else."

"Part of what?"

"He'll explain."

"He'll ask questions."

"Say only what you wish to say."

"No! You don't understand. I can't say *anything* about Geneva, and neither can you. I've tried to explain—"

He stopped. Helden raised the automatic. "The gun is still in my hand. Get out of the car."

He preceded her up the short path to the door of the house. Except for the dim light in the windows, it was dark. The surrounding trees filtered the moonlight to such a degree that only muted rays came through the branches, so weak they seemed to disintegrate in the air.

Noel felt her hand reaching around his waist, the barrel of the gun in the small of his back.

"Here's a key. Open the door. It's difficult for him to move around."

Inside, the small room was like any other one might imagine in such a house deep in the French countryside, with one exception: Two walls were lined with books. Everything else was simple to the point of primitiveness—sturdy furniture of no discernible design, a heavy old-fashioned desk, several unlit lamps with plain shades, a wood floor, and thick, plastered walls. The books were somehow out of place.

In the far corner of the room sat an emaciated man in a wheelchair. He was between a floor lamp and a short table, the light over his left shoulder, a book in his lap. His hair was white and thin, combed carefully over his head. Holcroft guessed he was well into his seventies. In spite of his gaunt appearance, the face was strong, the eyes behind the steel-rimmed spectacles alert. He was dressed in a cardigan sweater buttoned to the throat, and a pair of corduroy trousers.

"Good evening, Herr Oberst," said Helden. "I hope we didn't keep you waiting too long."

"Good evening, Helden," replied the old man, putting the book to one side. "You're here and obviously safe. That's all that matters."

Noel watched, mesmerized, as the gaunt figure put his hands on the arms of the wheelchair and rose slowly. He was extremely tall, over six feet two or three. He continued speaking in an accent obviously German and just as obviously aristocratic.

"You're the young man who telephoned Miss Tennyson," he said, not asking a question. "I'm known simply as *Oberst*—colonel—which was not my rank, but I'm afraid it will have to do."

"This is Noel Holcroft. He is an American, and he is the man." Helden took a step to her left, revealing the gun in her hand. "He is here against his will. He did not want to talk with you."

"How do you do, Mr. Holcroft?" The colonel nodded, offering no hand. "May I ask why you're reluctant to speak to an old man?"

"I don't know who you are," replied Noel as calmly as he could. "Further, the matters I've discussed with Miss . . . Tennyson . . . are confidential."

"Does she agree?"

"Ask her." Holcroft held his breath. In seconds he would know how convincing he had been.

"They are," said Helden, "if they are true. I *think* they are true."

"I see. But you must be convinced, and I am the devil's advocate without a brief." The old man lowered himself back into the wheelchair.

"What does that mean?" asked Noel.

"You won't discuss these confidential matters, yet I must ask questions, the answers to which could allay our anxieties. You see, Mr. Holcroft, you have no reason to be afraid of me. On the contrary, we may have a great deal to fear from you."

"Why? I don't know you; you don't know me. Whatever it is you're involved with has nothing to do with me."

"We must *all* be convinced of that," said the old man. "Over the telephone you spoke to Helden of urgency, of a great deal of money, of concerns that go back more than thirty years."

"I'm sorry she told you that," interrupted Noel. "Even that's too much."

"She said very little else," continued the colonel. "Only that you saw her sister, and that you're interested in her brother."

"I'll say it again. It's confidential."

"And finally," said the old man, as if Holcroft had not spoken, "that you wished to meet secretly. At least, you implied as much."

"For my own reasons," said Noel. "They're none of your business."

"Aren't they?"

"No."

"Let me summarize briefly, then." The colonel pressed the fingers of his hands together, his eyes on Holcroft. "There's urgency, a great sum of money, matters traced back three decades, interest in the offspring of a ranking member of the Third Reich's High Command, and—most important, perhaps—a clandestine meeting. Doesn't all this suggest something?"

Noel refused to be drawn into speculation. "I have no idea what it suggests to you."

"Then I'll be specific. A trap."

"A trap?"

"Who are you, Mr. Holcroft? A disciple of ODESSA? Or a soldier of the Rache, perhaps?"

"The ODESSA? . . . or the . . . what?" asked Holcroft.

"The *Rache,*" replied the old man sharply, pronouncing the word with phonetic emphasis.

"The *'Rah-kuh'?* . . ." Noel returned the cripple's penetrating stare. "I don't know what you're talking about."

Oberst glanced at Helden, then pulled his eyes back to Holcroft. "You've heard of neither?"

"I've heard of the ODESSA. I don't know anything about the . . . *'Rah-kuh'* . . . or whatever you call it."

"Recruiters and killers. Yet both recruit. Both kill. The ODESSA and the Rache. The pursuers of children."

"Pursuers of children?" Noel shook his head. "You'll have to be clearer, because I haven't the vaguest idea what you're saying."

Again, the old man looked at Helden. What passed between them Holcroft could not decipher, but Oberst turned back to him, the hard eyes boring in as if studying a practiced liar, watching for signs of deception—or recognition. "I'll put it plainly to you," he said. "Are you one of those who seek out the children of Nazis? Who pursue them wherever they can be found, killing them for revenge—for crimes they never committed—making *examples* of the innocent? *Or* forcing them to join you. Threatening them with documents portraying their parents as monsters, promising to expose them as offspring of psychopaths and murderers if they refuse to be recruited—destroying what lives they have for the insanity of your cause? These are the people who seek the children, Mr. Holcroft. Are you one of them?"

Noel closed his eyes in relief. "I can't tell you how wrong you are. I won't tell you any more than that, but you're so wrong it's incredible."

"We have to be sure."

"You can be. I'm not involved in things like that. I've never heard of those kind of things before. People like that are sick."

"Yes, they're sick," agreed Oberst. "Don't mistake me. The Wiesenthals of this world search out the real monsters, the unpunished criminals who still laugh at Nürnberg, and we can't object; that's another war. But the persecution of the children must stop."

Noel turned to Helden. "Is this what you're running from? After all these years, they're still after you?"

The old man answered. "Acts of violence take place every day. Everywhere."

"Then why doesn't anyone know about it?" demanded Holcroft. "Why aren't there stories in the newspapers? Why are these things kept quiet?"

"Would . . . 'anyone,' as you put it, really care?" asked the colonel. "For the children of Nazis?"

"For God's sake, they were *kids.*" Again Noel looked at Helden. "Is what I saw tonight part of this? You have to *protect* each other? Is it so widespread?"

"We're called the 'children of hell,' " said the Von Tiebolt daughter simply. "Damned for what we are and damned for what we're not."

"I don't *understand* it," protested Holcroft.

"It's not vital that you do." The old soldier once again got up slowly, trying, thought Noel, to rise to his former imposing height. "It's only important that we be convinced you are from neither army. Are you satisfied, Helden?"

"Yes."

"There's nothing more you wish me to know?"

The woman shook her head. "I'm satisfied," she repeated.

"Then so am I." The colonel extended his hand to Noel. "Thank you for coming. As Helden will explain, my existence is not widely known; nor do we want it to be. We would appreciate your confidence."

Holcroft took the hand, surprised at the old man's firm grip. "If I can count on yours."

"You have my word."

"Then you have mine," Noel said.

They drove in silence, headlights knifing the darkness. Holcroft was behind the wheel, Helden in the front seat, beside him, directing him by nodding wearily, pointing to the turns. There was no screaming now; there were no harsh commands barked at the last second. Helden seemed as exhausted from the events of the night as was he. But the night was not over; they had to talk.

"Was all that necessary?" he asked. "Was it so important for him to see me?"

"Very much so. He had to be convinced you weren't part of the ODESSA. Or the Rache."

"What exactly are they? He spoke as if I should know, but I don't. I didn't really understand him."

"They're two extremist organizations, sworn enemies of each other. Both fanatic, both after us."

"Us?"

"The children of Party leaders. Wherever we are; wherever we've scattered to."

"Why?"

"The ODESSA seeks to revive the Nazi party. The disciples of ODESSA are everywhere."

"Seriously? They're for real?"

"Very real. And very serious. The ODESSA's recruiting methods range from blackmail to physical force. They're gangsters."

"And this . . . 'Rah-kuh'?"

"*Rache.* The German word for 'vengeance.' In the beginning it was a society formed by the survivors of the concentration camps. They hunted the sadists and the killers, those thousands who were never brought to trial."

"It's a Jewish organization, then?"

"There are Jews in the Rache, yes, but now they're a minority. The Israelis formed their own groups and operated out of Tel Aviv and Haifa. The Rache is primarily Communist; many believe it was taken over by the KGB. Others think Third World revolutionaries gravitated to it. The 'vengeance' they spoke of in the beginning has become something else. The Rache is a haven for terrorists."

"But why are they after *you?*"

Helden looked at him through the shadows. "To recruit us. Like everyone else, we have our share of revolutionaries. They're drawn to the Rache; it represents the opposite of what they're running from. For most of us, however, it's no better than the Party at its worst. And on those of us who won't be recruited, the Rache uses its harsher tactics. We're the scapegoats, the fascists they're stamping out. They use our names—often our corpses—to tell people Nazis still live. Not unlike the ODESSA, it's frequently 'recruit or kill.' "

"It's *insane,*" said Noel.

"Insane," agreed Helden. "But very real. We say nothing; we're not anxious to call attention to ourselves. Besides, who would care? We're Nazi children."

"The ODESSA, the Rache. . . . No one I know knows anything about them."

"No one you know has any reason to."

"Who's Oberst?"

"A great man who must remain in hiding for the rest of his life because he had a conscience."

"What do you mean?"

"He was a member of the High Command and saw the horrors. He knew it was futile to object; others had, and they were killed. Instead, he remained, and used his rank to countermand order after order, saving God knows how many lives."

"There's nothing dishonorable in that."

"He did it the only way he could. Quietly, within the bureaucracy of command, without notice. When it was over, the Allies convicted him because of his status in the Reich; he spent eighteen years in prison. When what he did finally came out, thousands of Germans despised him. They called him a traitor. What was left of the Officer Corps put a price on his head."

Noel, remembering Helden's words, said, "Damned for what he was and damned for what he wasn't."

"Yes," she answered, pointing suddenly to a turn in the road she'd nearly missed.

"In his own way," said Noel, turning the wheel, "Oberst is like the three men who wrote the Geneva document. Didn't it occur to you?"

"It occurred to me."

"You must have been tempted to tell him."

"Not really. You asked me not to."

He looked at her; she was looking straight ahead, through the windshield. Her face was tired and drawn, her skin pale, accentuating the dark hollows beneath her eyes. She seemed alone, and that aloneness was not to be intruded upon lightly. But the night was *not* over. They had things to say to each other; decisions had to be made.

For Noel was beginning to think that this youngest child of Wilhelm von Tiebolt would be the one selected to represent the Von Tiebolt family in Geneva.

"Can we go someplace where it's quiet? I think a drink would do us both good."

"There's a small inn about four or five miles from here. It's out of the way; no one will see us."

As they swung off the road, Noel's eyes were drawn to the rearview mirror. Headlights shone in the glass. It was an odd turn off the Paris highway, odd in the sense that there were no signs; an unmarked exit. The fact that a driver behind them had a reason to take this particular exit at this particular time seemed too coincidental for comfort. Holcroft was about to say something when a strange thing happened.

The lights in the mirror went out. They simply were not there any longer.

The inn had once been a farmhouse; part of the grazing field was now a graveled parking lot bordered by a post-and-rail fence. The small dining room was through an archway off the bar. Two other couples were inside; the people were distinctly Parisian, and just as obviously having discreet dinners with companions they could not see in Paris. Eyes shot up at the newcomers, no signs of welcome in the glances. A fireplace filled with flaming logs was at the far end of the room. It was a good place to talk.

They were shown to a table to the left of the fire. Two brandies were ordered and delivered.

"It's nice here," said Noel, feeling the warmth of the flames and the alcohol. "How did you find it?"

"It's on the way to the colonel's. My friends and I often stop here to talk among ourselves."

"Do you mind if I ask you questions?"

"Go ahead."

"When did you leave England?"

"About three months ago. When the job was offered."

"Were you the Helen Tennyson in the London directory?"

"Yes. In English, the name 'Helden' seems to require an explanation, and I was tired of having to give one. It's not the same in Paris. The French don't have much curiosity about names."

"But you don't call yourself 'Von Tiebolt.'" Holcroft saw the flash of resentment on her face.

"No."

"Why 'Tennyson'?"

"I think that's rather obvious. 'Von Tiebolt' is extremely German. When we left Brazil for England, it seemed a reasonable change."

"Just a change? Nothing else?"

"No." Helden sipped her brandy and looked at the fire. "Nothing else."

Noel watched her; the lie was in her voice. She was not a good liar. She was hiding something, but to call her on it now would only provoke her. He let the lie pass. "What do you know about your father?"

She turned back to him. "Very little. My mother loved him, and from what she said, he was a better man than his years in the Third Reich might indicate. But then, you've confirmed that, haven't you? At the end, he was a profoundly moral man."

"Tell me about your mother."

"She was a survivor. She fled Germany with nothing but a few pieces of jewelry, two children, and a baby inside her. She had no training, no skills, no profession, but she could work, and she was . . . convincing. She started selling in dress shops, cultivated customers, used her flair for clothes—and she had that—as the basis for her own business. Several businesses, actually. Our home in Rio de Janeiro was quite comfortable."

"Your sister told me it was . . . a sanctuary that turned into a kind of hell."

"My sister is given to melodramatics. It wasn't so bad. If we were looked down upon, there was a certain basis for it."

"What was that?"

"My mother was terribly attractive. . . ."

"So are her daughters," interrupted Noel.

"I imagine we are," said Helden matter-of-factly. "It's never concerned me. I haven't had to use it—whatever attractiveness I may have. But my mother did." "In Rio?"

"Yes. She was kept by several men. . . . We were kept, actually. There were two or three divorces, but she wouldn't marry the husbands involved. She broke up marriages, extracting money and business interests as she did. When she died, we were quite well off. The German community considered her a pariah. And, by extension, her children."

"She sounds fascinating," said Holcroft, smiling. "How did she die?"

"She was killed. Shot through the head while she was driving one night."

The smile faded abruptly. Images returned: a deserted lookout high above the city of Rio; the sounds of gunfire and the explosions of cement; the shattering of glass. . . . *Glass.* A car window blown out with the spit of silenced gunshot; a heavy black pistol leveled at his head. . . .

Then the words came back to him, spoken in the booth of a cocktail lounge. Words Holcroft had believed were ridiculous, the products of unreasonable fear.

The Cararras, brother and sister. The sister, dearest friend and fiancée of Johann von Tiebolt.

He and my sister were to be married. The Germans would not permit it.

Who could stop them?

Any number of men. With a bullet in the back of Johann's head.

The Cararras. Dear friends and supplicants for the ostracized Von Tiebolts. It suddenly struck Noel that if Helden knew how the Cararras had helped him, she might be more cooperative. The Cararras had risked their lives to send him to the Von Tiebolts. She would have to respond to that confidence with her own.

"I think I should tell you," he said. "In Rio it was the Cararras who contacted me. They told me where to start looking for you. They were the ones who told me your new name was Tennyson."

"Who?"

"Your friends, the Cararras. Your brother's fiancée."

"The Cararras? In Rio de Janeiro?"

"Yes."

"I've never heard of them. I don't know any Cararras."

16

The tactic blew up in his face with the impact of a backfired rifle. Suddenly Helden was wary of him, apprehensive of saying anything further about her family.

Who were the Cararras?

Why had they told him things that were not true?

Who sent them to him? Her brother had no fiancée, nor any best friend whom she could recall.

He did not claim to understand; he could only speculate as truthfully as possible. No one else had come forward. For reasons known only to them, the Cararras had created a relationship that did not exist; still, it made no sense to call them enemies of the Von Tiebolts. They had reached him for the purpose of *helping* the two sisters and the brother who had been driven from Brazil. There were those in Rio—a powerful man named Graff, for one—who would pay a great deal of money to locate the Von Tiebolts. The Cararras, who had much to gain and very little to lose, had not told him.

"They wanted to help," Noel said. "They weren't lying about that. They said you'd been persecuted; they did want to help you."

"It's possible," said Helden. "Rio is filled with people who are still fighting the war, still hunting for those they call traitors. One is never sure who is a friend and who is an enemy. Not among the Germans."

"Did you know Maurice Graff?"

"I knew who he was, of course. Everyone did. I never met him."

"I did," Noel said. "*He* called the Von Tiebolts traitors."

"I'm sure he did. We were pariahs, but not in the nationalistic sense."

"What sense, then?"

The girl looked away again, lifting the brandy glass to her lips. "Other things."

"Your mother?"

"Yes," replied Helden. "It was my mother. I told you, the German community despised her."

Again Holcroft had the feeling she was telling him only part of the truth. He would not pursue it now. If he gained her confidence, she would tell him later. She *had* to tell him; whatever it was might have an effect on Geneva. Everything affected Geneva now.

"You said your mother broke up marriages," he said. "Your sister used almost the same words about herself. She said she was shunned by the officers and their wives in Portsmouth."

"If you're looking for a pattern, I won't try to dissuade you. My sister is quite a bit older than I. She was closer to my mother, watched her progress, saw the advantages that came mother's way. It wasn't as if she was oblivious of such things. She knew the horror of Berlin after the war. At the age of thirteen she slept with soldiers for food. American soldiers, Mr. Holcroft."

It was all he had to know about Gretchen Beaumont. The picture was complete. A whore, for whatever reasons, at thirteen. A whore—for whatever other reasons—at forty-five-plus. The bank's directors in Geneva would rule her out on grounds of instability and incompetence.

But Noel knew there were stronger grounds. The man Gretchen Beaumont said she loathed, but lived with. A man with odd, heavy eyebrows who had followed him to Brazil.

"What about her husband?"

"I barely know him."

She looked away again at the fire. She was frightened; she *was* hiding something. Her words were too studiedly nonchalant. Whatever it was she would not talk about had something to do with Beaumont. There was no point in evading the subject any longer. Truth between them had to be a two-way matter; the sooner she learned that, the better for both of them.

"Do you know anything about him? Where he came from? What he does in the navy?"

"No, nothing. He's a commander on a ship; that's all I know."

"I think he's more than that, and I think you know it. Please don't lie to me."

At first, her eyes flashed with anger; then, just as rapidly, the anger subsided. "That's a strange thing to say. Why would I lie to you?"

"I wish I knew. You say you barely know him, but you seem scared to death. *Please.*"

"What are you driving at?"

"If you know something, tell me. If you've heard about the document in Geneva, tell me what you've heard."

"I know nothing. I've heard nothing."

"I saw Beaumont two weeks ago on a plane to Rio. The same plane I took from New York. He was following me."

He could see fear in Helden's eyes. "I think you're wrong," she said.

"I'm not. I saw his photograph in your sister's house. His house. It was the same man. I stole that photograph and it was stolen from me. After someone beat the *hell* out of me for it."

"Good *lord*. . . . You were beaten for his *photograph?*"

"Nothing else was missing. Not my wallet or my money or my watch. Just his picture. There was writing on the back of it."

"What did it say?"

"I don't know. It was in German, and I can't read German."

"Can you remember any of the words?"

"One, I think. The last word. T-O-D. *Tod.*"

" 'Ohne dich sterbe ich.' Could that be it?"

"I don't know. What does it mean?"

" 'Without you I die.' It's the sort of thing my sister would think of. I told you, she's melodramatic." She was lying again; he knew it!

"An endearment?"

"Yes."

"That's what the British said, and I didn't believe them either. Beaumont was on that plane. That picture was taken from me because there was some kind of message on it. For Christ's sake, what's going *on?*"

"I don't know!"

"But you know *something.*" Noel tried to control himself. Their voices were low, almost whispers, but their argument carried over to the other diners. Holcroft reached across the table and covered her hand. "I'm asking you again. You know something. Tell me."

He could feel a slight tremble in her hand. "What I know is so confusing it would be meaningless. It's more what I sense than what I know, really." She took her hand from his. "A number of years ago Anthony Beaumont was a naval attaché in Rio de Janeiro. I didn't know him well, but I remember him coming to the house quite often. He was married at the time, but interested in my sister—a diversion, I suppose you might call it. My mother encouraged it. He was a high-ranking naval officer; favors could be had. But my sister argued violently with my mother. She despised Beaumont and would have nothing to do with him. Yet only a few years later we moved to England and she married him. I've never understood."

Noel leaned forward, relieved. "It may not be as difficult to understand as you think. She told me she married him for the security he could give her."

"And you believed her?"

"Her behavior would seem to confirm what she said."

"Then I can't believe you met my sister."

"She was your sister. You look alike: both beautiful."

"It's my turn to ask you a question. Given that beauty, do you really think she would settle for a naval officer's salary and the restricted life of a naval officer's wife? I can't. I never have."

"What do you think, then?"

"I think she was forced to marry Anthony Beaumont."

Noel leaned back in the chair. If she was right, the connection was in Rio de Janeiro. With her mother, perhaps. With her mother's murder.

"How could Beaumont force her to marry him? And why?"

"I've asked myself both questions a hundred times. I don't know."

"Have you asked her?"

"She refuses to talk to me."

"What happened to your mother in Rio?"

"I told you: She manipulated men for money. The Germans despised her, called her immoral. Looking back, it's hard to refute."

"Was that why she was shot?"

"I guess so. No one really knows; the killer was never found."

"But it could be the answer to the first question, couldn't it? Isn't it possible that Beaumont knew something about your mother that was so damaging he could blackmail your sister?"

Helden turned her palms up in front of her. "What could possibly *be* so damaging? Accepting everything that was said about my mother as being true, why would it have any effect on Gretchen?"

"That would depend on what it was."

"There's nothing conceivable. She's in England now. She's her own person, thousands of miles away. Why should she be concerned?"

"I have no idea." Then Noel remembered. "You used the words 'children of hell.' Damned for what you were, and damned for what you weren't. Couldn't that apply to your sister as well?"

"Beaumont isn't interested in such things. It's an entirely different matter."

"Is it? You don't know that. It's your opinion he forced her to marry him. If it isn't something like that, what is it?"

Helden looked away, deep in thought now, not in a lie. "Something much more recent."

"The document in Geneva?" he asked. Manfredi's warning repeated in his ears, the specter of Wolfsschanze in his mind.

"How did Gretchen react when you told her about Geneva?" asked Helden.

"As if it didn't matter."

"Well? . . ."

"It could have been a diversion. She was too casual—just as you were too casual when I mentioned Beaumont a few minutes ago. She could have expected it and steeled herself."

"You're guessing."

It was the moment, thought Noel. It would be in her eyes—the rest of the truth she would not talk about. Did it come down to Johann von Tiebolt?

"Not really guessing. Your sister said that her brother told her a man would 'come one day and talk of a strange arrangement.' Those were her words."

Whatever he was looking for—a flicker of recognition, a blink of fear—it was not there. There was *something,* but nothing he could relate to. She looked at him as if she herself were trying to understand. Yet there was a fundamental innocence in her look, and that was what *he* could not understand.

" 'A man would come one day.' It doesn't make sense," she said.

"Tell me about your brother."

She did not answer for several moments. Instead, her eyes strayed to the red tablecloth; her lips parted in astonishment. Then, as if she were coming out of a trance, she said, "Johann? What's there to say?"

"Your sister told me he got the three of you out of Brazil. Was it difficult?"

"There were problems. We had no passports, and there were men who tried to stop us from obtaining them."

"You were immigrants. At least, your mother, brother, and sister were. They had to have papers."

"Whatever papers there were in those days were burned as soon as they served their purpose."

"Who wanted to stop you from leaving Brazil?"

"Men who wanted to bring Johann to trial."

"For what?"

"After mother was killed, Johann took over her business interests. She never allowed him to do much when she was alive. Many people thought he was ruthless, even dishonest. He was accused of misrepresenting profits, withholding taxes. I don't think any of it was true; he was simply faster and brighter than anyone else."

"I see," said Noel, recalling MI Five's evaluation—"over-achiever." "How did he avoid the courts and get you out?"

"Money. And all-night meetings in strange places with men he never identified. He came home one morning and told Gretchen and me to pack just enough things for a short overnight trip. We drove to the airport and were flown in a small plane to Recife, where a man met us. We were given passports; the name on them was Tennyson. The next thing Gretchen and I knew we were on a plane for London."

Holcroft watched her closely. There was no hint of a lie. "To start a new life under the name of Tennyson," he said.

"Yes. Completely new. We'd left everything behind us." She smiled. "I sometimes think with very little time to spare."

"He's quite a man. Why haven't you stayed in touch? You obviously don't hate him."

Helden frowned, as if she were unsure of her own answer. "Hate him? No. I resent him, perhaps, but I don't hate him. Like most brilliant men, he thinks he should take charge of everything. He wanted to run my life, and I couldn't accept that."

"Why is he a newspaperman? From all I've learned about him, he could probably own one."

"He probably will one day, if that's what he wants. Knowing Johann, I suspect it's because he thought that writing for a well-known newspaper would give him a certain prominence. Especially in the political field, where he's very good. He was right."

"Was he?"

"Certainly. In a matter of two or three years, he was considered one of the finest correspondents in Europe."

Now, thought Noel. MI Five meant nothing to him; Geneva was everything. He leaned forward.

"He's considered something else, too. . . . I said in the Montmartre that I would tell you—and *only* you—why the British questioned me. It's your brother. They think I'm trying to reach him for reasons that have nothing to do with Geneva."

"What reasons?"

Holcroft kept her eyes engaged. "Have you ever heard of a man they call the Tinamou?"

"The assassin? Certainly. Who hasn't?"

There was nothing in her eyes. Nothing but vague bewilderment. "I, for one," said Noel. "I've read about killers for hire and assassination conspiracies but I've never heard of the Tinamou."

"You're an American. His exploits are more detailed in the European press than in yours. But what has he got to do with my brother?"

"British Intelligence thinks he may *be* the Tinamou."

The expression on Helden's face was arrested in shock. So complete was her astonishment that her eyes were suddenly devoid of life, as noncommittal as a blind man's. Her lips trembled and she tried to speak, unable to find the words. Finally, the words came. They were barely audible.

"You can't be *serious.*"

"I assure you, I am. What's more to the point, the British are."

"It's outrageous. Beyond anything I've ever heard! On what basis can they possibly *reach* such a conclusion?"

Noel repeated the salient points analyzed by MI Five.

"My *God,*" said Helden when he had finished. "He covers all of Europe, as well as the Middle East! Certainly the English could check with his editors. He doesn't *choose* the places they send him to. It's preposterous!"

"Newspapermen who write interesting copy, who file stories that sell papers, are given a very free hand when it comes to the places they cover. That's the case with your brother. It's almost as though he knew he'd gain that prominence you spoke of; knew that in a few short years he'd be given a flexible schedule."

"You can't *believe* this."

"I don't know what to believe," said Holcroft. "I only know that your brother could jeopardize the situation in Geneva. The mere fact that he's under suspicion by MI Five could be enough to frighten the bankers. They don't want that kind of scrutiny where the Clausen account is concerned."

"But it's unjustified!"

"Are you sure?"

Helden's eyes were angry. "Yes, I'm sure. Johann may be a number of things, but he's no killer. The viciousness starts again: The Nazi child is hounded."

Noel remembered the first statement made by the gray-haired MI-Five man:

For starters, you know about the father. . . . Was it possible Helden was right? Did MI Five's suspicions come from memories and hostilities that went back thirty years to a brutal enemy? *Tennyson is the personification of arrogance. . . .* It was possible.

"Is Johann political?"

"Very, but not in the usual sense. He doesn't stand for any particular ideology. Instead, he's highly critical of them all. He attacks their weaknesses, and he's vicious about hypocrisy. That's why a lot of people in government can't stand him. But he's no assassin!"

If Helden was right, Noel thought, Johann von Tiebolt could be an enormous asset to Geneva, or, more specifically, to the agency that was to be established in Zürich. A multilingual journalist whose judgments were listened to, who had experience in finance . . . could be eminently qualified to dispense millions throughout the world.

If the shadow of the Tinamou could be removed from Johann von Tiebolt, there was no reason for the directors of La Grande Banque de Genève ever to learn of MI Five's interest in John Tennyson. The second child of Wilhelm von Tiebolt would be instantly acceptable to the bankers. He might not be the most personable man alive, but Geneva was not sponsoring a personality contest. He could be an extraordinary asset. But first the Tinamou's shadow *had* to be removed, British Intelligence suspicions laid to rest.

Holcroft smiled. *A man would come one day and talk of a strange arrangement. . . .* Johann von Tiebolt—John Tennyson—was waiting for him!

"What's funny?" said Helden, watching him.

"I have to meet him," answered Noel, ignoring the question. "Can you arrange it?"

"I imagine so. It'll take a few days. I don't know where he is. What will you say to him?"

"The truth; maybe he'll reciprocate. I've got a damn good idea he knows about Geneva."

"There's a telephone number he gave me to call if I ever needed him. I've never used it."

"Use it now. Please."

She nodded. Noel understood that there were questions left unanswered. Specifically, a man named Beaumont, and an event in Rio de Janeiro that Helden would not discuss. An event connected to the naval officer with the heavy black-and-white eyebrows. And it was possible that Helden knew nothing about that connection.

Perhaps John Tennyson did. He certainly knew a lot more than he told either sister.

"Does your brother get along with Beaumont?" asked Holcroft.

"He despises him. He refused to come to Gretchen's wedding."

What *was* it? wondered Noel. Who was the enigma that was Anthony Beaumont?

17

Outside the small inn, in the far corner of the parking area, a dark sedan rested in the shadow of a tall oak tree. In the front seat were two men, one in the uniform of the English navy, the other in a charcoal-gray business suit, his black overcoat opened, the edge of a brown leather holster visible beneath his unbuttoned jacket.

The naval officer was behind the wheel. His blunt features were tense. The eyebrows of black-and-white hair arched just noticeably every now and then, as if prodded by a nervous tic.

The man beside him was in his late thirties. He was slender but he was not thin; his was the tautness that comes with discipline and training. The breadth of his shoulders, the long muscular neck, and the convex line of a chest that stretched his tailored shirt were evidence of a body honed to physical precision and strength. Each feature of his face was refined and each coordinated with the whole. The result was striking, yet cold, as if the face were chiseled in granite. The eyes were light blue, almost rectangular, their gaze steady and noncommittal; they were the eyes of a confident animal, quick to respond, the response unpredictable. The sculptured head was covered by a glistening crown of blond hair that reflected the light of the distant parking-lot lamps; above this face, his hair had the appearance of pale-yellow ice. The man's name was Johann von Tiebolt, for the past five years known as "John Tennyson."

"Are you satisfied?" asked the naval officer, obviously apprehensive. "There's no one."

"There *was* someone," replied the blond man. "Considering the precautions taken since Montmartre, it's not entirely surprising there's no one now. Helden and the other children are quite effective."

"They run from idiots," said Beaumont. "The Rache is filled with Marxist subhumans."

"When the time comes, the Rache will serve its purpose. Our purpose. But it's not the Rache I'm concerned with. I want to know who tried to kill him." Tennyson turned in the shadows, his cold eyes glaring. He slammed his hand on the top of the leather dashboard. "Who tried to *kill Clausen's son?*"

"I swear to you, I've told you everything we know! Everything we've learned. It was *not* a mistake on our part."

"It was a mistake because it nearly happened," replied Tennyson, his voice quiet again.

"It was Manfredi; it *had* to be Manfredi," continued Beaumont. "It's the only explanation, Johann. . . ."

"My name is John. Remember that."

"Sorry. It *is* the only explanation. We don't know what Manfredi said to Holcroft on that train in Geneva. It's possible he tried to convince him to walk away. And when Holcroft refused, he sent out the orders for his execution. They failed in the station because of me. I think you should remember that."

"You won't let me forget it," interrupted Tennyson. "You may be right. He expected to control the agency in Zürich; that could never be. So the removal of assets totaling seven hundred and eighty million dollars became too painful an exercise."

"Just as the promise of two million is an irresistible temptation to Holcroft, perhaps."

"Two million he banks only in his mind. But his death will come at *our* hands, no one else's."

"Manfredi acted alone, believe that. His executioners have no one to take orders from now. Since the hotel room in Zürich, there've been no further attempts."

"That's a statement Holcroft would find impossible to accept. . . . There they *are.*" Tennyson sat forward. Through the windshield, across the parking area, he could see Noel and Helden coming out of the door. "Do the colonel's children meet here frequently?"

"Yes," answered Beaumont. "I learned of it from an ODESSA agent who followed them one night."

The blond man coughed a quiet laugh; his words were scathing. "ODESSA! Caricatures, who weep in cellars over too many steins of beer! They're laughable."

"They're persistent."

"And they, too, will be useful," said Tennyson, watching Noel and Helden get into the car. "As before, they will be the lowest foot soldiers, fed to the enemy's cannon. First seen, first sacrificed. The perfect diversion for more serious matters."

The Citroën's loud, outsized engine was heard. Holcroft backed the car out of its slot, then drove through the entrance posts onto the country road.

Beaumont turned on the ignition. "I'll stay a fair distance behind. He won't spot me."

"No, don't bother," said Tennyson. "I'm satisfied. Take me to the airport. You've made the arrangements?"

"Yes. You'll be flown on a Mirage to Athens. The Greeks will get you back to Bahrain. It's all military transport, UN-courier status, Security Council immunity. The pilot of the Mirage has your papers."

"Well done, Tony."

The naval officer smiled, proud of the compliment. He pressed the accelerator; the sedan roared out of the parking lot into the darkness of the country road. "What will you do in Bahrain?"

"Make my presence known by filing a story on an oil-field negotiation. A prince of Bahrain has been most cooperative. He has had no choice. He made an arrangement with the Tinamou. The poor man lives in terror that the news will get out."

"You're extraordinary."

"And you're a devoted man. You always have been."

"After Bahrain, what?"

The blond man leaned back in the seat and closed his eyes. "Back to Athens and on to Berlin."

"Berlin?"

"Yes. Things are progressing well. Holcroft will go there next. Kessler's waiting for him."

There was a sudden burst of static from a radio speaker beneath the dashboard. It was followed by four short, high-pitched hums. Tennyson opened his eyes; the four hums were repeated.

"There are telephone booths on the highway. Get me to one. Quickly!"

The Englishman pressed the accelerator to the floor; the sedan sped down the road, reaching seventy miles an hour in a matter of seconds. They came to an intersection. "If I'm not mistaken, there's a petrol station around here."

"Hurry!"

"I'm sure of it," said Beaumont, and there it was, at the side of the road, dark, no light in the windows. "Damn, it's closed!"

"What did you expect?" asked Tennyson.

"The phone's inside. . . ."

"But there is a phone?"

"Yes. . . ."

"Stop the car."

Beaumont obeyed. The blond man got out and walked to the door of the station. He took out his pistol and broke the glass with the handle.

A dog leaped up at him, barking and growling, fangs bared, jaws snapping. It was an old animal of indeterminable breed, stationed more for effect than for physical protection. Tennyson reached into his pocket, pulled out a perforated cylinder, and spun it on to the barrel of his pistol. He raised the gun and fired through the shattered glass into the dog's head. The animal fell backward. Tennyson smashed the remaining glass by the latch above the doorknob.

He let himself in, adjusted his eyes to the light, and stepped over the dead animal to the telephone. He reached an operator and gave her the Paris number that could connect him to a man who would, in turn, transfer his call to a telephone in England.

Twenty seconds later he heard the breathless, echoing voice. "I'm sorry to disturb you, Johann, but we have an emergency."

"What is it?"

"A photograph was taken. I'm very concerned."

"What photograph?"

"A picture of Tony."

"Who took it?"

"The American."

"Which means he recognized him. Graff was right: Your devoted husband can't be trusted. His enthusiasm outweighs his discretion. I wonder where Holcroft saw him?"

"On the plane, perhaps. Or through the doorman's description. It doesn't matter. Kill him."

"Yes, of course." The blond man paused, then spoke thoughtfully. "You have the bank books?"

"Yes."

"Deposit ten thousand pounds. Let the transfer be traced through Prague."

"KGB? Very good, Johann."

"The British will suffer another defection. Friendly diplomats will argue among themselves, each accusing the other of a lack of candor."

"*Very* good."

"I'll be in Berlin next week. Reach me there."

"So soon Berlin?"

"Yes, Kessler's waiting. *Neuaufbau oder Tod.*"

"*Oder der Tod,* my brother."

Tennyson hung up and stared through the night light at the dead animal on the floor. He had no more feeling for the clump of lifeless fur than for the man waiting in the car. Feelings were kept for more important things, not for animals and misfits—regardless of how devoted either might be.

Beaumont was a fool, a judgment contained in a dossier sent from Scotland to Brazil years ago. But he had a fool's energy and a fool's sense of surface accomplishment. He had actually become an outstanding naval officer. This son of a *Reichsoberführer* had climbed the ladder of Her Majesty's Royal Navy to the point where he was given vital responsibility. Too much for his intellect; that intellect needed to be directed. In time, they had projected that Beaumont might become a power within the Admiralty, an expert consulted by the Foreign Office. It was an optimum situation; extraordinary advantages could be handed to them through Beaumont. He had remained a *Sonnenkind;* he was permitted to live.

But no more. With the theft of a photograph, Beaumont was finished, for in that theft was the threat of scrutiny. There could be no scrutiny whatsoever; they were too close, and there was still too much to accomplish. If Holcroft gave the photograph to the wrong people in Switzerland, told them of Beaumont's presence in New York or Rio, military authorities might be alerted. Why was this outstanding officer so interested in the Geneva document? The question could not arise. This son of the *Reichsoberführer* had to be removed. In a way, it was a pity. The commander would be missed; at times he'd been invaluable.

Gretchen knew that value. Gretchen was Beaumont's teacher, his guide . . . his intellect. She was enormously proud of her work, and now she called for Beaumont's death. So be it. They'd find another to take his place.

They were everywhere, thought Johann von Tiebolt as he walked to the door. Everywhere. *Die Sonnenkinder.* The Children of the Sun, never to be confused with the damned. The damned were wandering refuse, entitled to nothing.

Die Sonnenkinder. Everywhere. In all countries, in all governments, in armies and navies, in industry and trade unions, commanding intelligence branches and the police. All quietly waiting. Grownup children of the New Order. *Thousands.* Sent out by ship and plane and submarine to all points of the civilized world. So *far* above the average—confirmed every day by their progress everywhere. They were the proof that the concept of racial superiority was undeniable. Their strain was pure, their excellence unquestioned. And the purest of all, the most excellent of all, was the Tinamou.

Von Tiebolt opened the door and stepped outside. Beaumont had driven the sedan fifty yards down the country road, headlights out. The commander went by the book; his training was apparent in everything he did—except when his enthusiasm overrode his discretion. That enthusiasm would now cost him his life.

Tennyson walked slowly toward the sedan. He wondered absently how it all had begun for Anthony Beaumont. The son of the *Reichsoberführer* had been sent to a family in Scotland; beyond that Tennyson had never inquired. He had been told of Beaumont's tenacity, his stubbornness, his singleness of purpose, but not of how he had been sent out of Germany. It was not necessary to know. There'd been thousands; all records were destroyed.

Thousands. Selected genetically, the parents studied, families traced back several generations for organic and psychological frailties. Only the purest were sent out, and everywhere these children were watched closely, guided, trained, indoctrinated—but told nothing until they grew up. And even then, not all. Those who failed to live up to their birthright, who showed weakness or gave evidence of being compromised, were never told, only weeded out.

Those that remained were the true inheritors of the Third Reich. They were in positions of trust and authority everywhere. Waiting . . . waiting for the signal from Switzerland, prepared to put the millions to immediate use.

Millions funneled judiciously, *politically.* One by one, nations would fall in line, shaped internally by the *Sonnenkinder,* who would have at their disposal extraordinary sums to match and consolidate their influence. Ten million here, forty million there, one hundred million where it was necessary.

In the free world the election processes would be bought, the electorates having fewer and fewer choices, only echoes. It was nothing new; successful experiments had already taken place. Chile had cost less than twenty-seven million, Panama no more than six. In America, Senate and congressional seats were to be had for a few hundred thousand. But when the signal came from Switzerland, the millions would be dispensed scientifically, the art of demographics employed. Until the Western world was led by the grown-up children of the Reich. *Die Sonnenkinder.*

The Eastern bloc would be next, the Soviet Union and its satellites succumbing to the blandishments of their own emerging bourgeoisie. When the signal came, promises would be made and people's collectives everywhere would suddenly realize there was a better way. Because, suddenly, extraordinary funds would be available; austerity could be replaced by the simple dislocation of loyalties.

The Fourth Reich would be born, not confined to the borders of one or two countries but spread all over the world. The Children of the Sun would be the rightful masters of the globe. *Die Sonnenkinder.*

Some might say it was preposterous, inconceivable. It was not; it was happening. Everywhere.

But mistakes were made, thought Tennyson, as he approached the sedan. They were inevitable, and just as inevitable was the fact that they had to be corrected. Beaumont was a mistake. Tennyson put the pistol back in his holster; it would not stay there long.

He walked around the car to the driver's window; it was rolled down, the commander's face turned in concern. "What was it? Is anything wrong?"

"Nothing that can't be fixed. Move over, I'll drive. You can direct me."

"Where to?"

"They said there's a lake somewhere in the vicinity, not more than eight or ten kilometers away. It was difficult to hear; it was a bad connection."

"Only lake near here is just east of Saint-Gratien. It's nearer twelve to fifteen."

"That must be the one. There are forests?"

"Profuse."

"That's the one," said Tennyson, getting into the car as Beaumont moved over on the seat. "I know the headlight codes. You tell me where to go; I'll concentrate on the lamps."

"Seems odd."

"Not odd. Complicated. They may pick us up along the way. I'll know what to look for. Quickly, now. Which direction do we go?"

"Turn around, to begin with. Head back to that dreadful road; then turn left."

"Very well." Tennyson started the engine.

"What *is* it?" Beaumont asked. "It must be a bloody emergency. I've heard a four-dash signal only once before, and *that* was our man at Entebbe."

"He wasn't our man, Tony. He was our puppet."

"Yes, of course. The Rache terrorist. Still, he was our *connection,* if you know what I mean."

"Yes, I know. Turn here? Left?"

"That's it. Well, for God's sake, *tell* me! What the devil's going on?"

Tennyson steadied the car and accelerated. "Actually, it may concern you. We're not sure, but it's a possibility."

"*Me?*"

"Yes. Did Holcroft ever spot you? See you more than once? Be aware that you were following him?"

"*Spot* me? Never! Never, never, *never!* I swear it."

"In Geneva? Think."

"Certainly not."

"In New York?"

"I was never within a mile of him! Impossible."

"On the plane to Rio de Janeiro?"

Beaumont paused. "No. . . . He came through a curtain; he was quite drunk, I think. But he took no notice, no notice at all. I saw him; he didn't see me."

That was it, thought Tennyson. This devoted child of the Reich believed what he had to believe. There was no point in discussing the matter any further.

"Then it's all a mistake, Tony. A wasted half hour. I talked with your wife, my dear sister. She said you were much too discreet for such a thing to have happened."

"She was right. She's *always* right, as you well know. Remarkable girl. Regardless of what you may think, ours was not purely a marriage of convenience."

"I know that, Tony. It makes me very happy."

"Take the next right. It goes north, toward the lake."

It was cold in the forest, colder by the water. They parked at the end of a dirt road and walked up the narrow path to the edge of the lake. Tennyson carried a flashlight he had taken from the glove compartment of the sedan. In Beaumont's hand was a narrow shovel; they had decided to build a small pit fire to ward off the chill.

"Will we be here that long?" Beaumont asked.

"It's possible. There are other matters to discuss, and I'd like your advice. This is the east shore of the lake?"

"Oh, yes. A good rendezvous. No one here this time of year."

"When are you due back at your ship?"

"Have you forgotten? I'm spending the weekend with Gretchen."

"Monday, then?"

"Or Tuesday. My exec's a good chap. He simply assumes I'm prowling around on business. Never questions if I'm a day or so late."

"Why should he? He's one of us."

"Yes, but there are patrol schedules to be observed. Can't muck them up."

"Of course not. Dig here, Tony. Let's have the fire not too near the water. I'll go back and watch for the signals."

"Good."

"Make the hole fairly deep. We wouldn't want the flames too obvious."

"Righto."

Fire. Water. Earth. Burned clothing, charred flesh, smashed and scattered bridgework. John Tennyson walked back over the path and waited. Several minutes later he removed his pistol from the holster and took a long-bladed hunting knife from his overcoat pocket. It would be a messy job, but necessary. The knife, like the shovel, had been in the trunk of the sedan. They were emergency tools, and always there.

A mistake had been revealed. It would be rectified by the Tinamou.

18

Holcroft sipped coffee and looked out at the cold, bright Paris morning. It was the second morning since he had seen Helden, and she was no nearer reaching her brother than she was the night before last.

"He'll call me; I know he will," she had told him over the phone minutes ago.

"Suppose I go out for a while?" he had asked.

"Don't worry. I'll reach you."

Don't worry. It was an odd remark for her to make, considering where he was and how he got there—how *they* got there.

It had been an extension of the madness. They had left the country inn and driven back to Montmartre, where a man had come out of a doorway and relieved them of the Citroën; they had walked through the crowded streets, past two sidewalk cafés where successive nods meant they could return to Noel's rented car.

From Montmartre she had directed him across Paris, over the Seine, into Saint-Germain-des-Prés, where they had stopped at a hotel; he had registered and paid for the night. It was a diversion; he did not go to his room. Instead, they had proceeded to a second hotel on the rue Chevalle, where a soft-drink sign provided him with a name for the registry: N. Fresca.

She had left him in the lobby, telling him she would call him when she had news of her brother.

"Explain something," he had said. "Why are we doing all this? What difference does it make where I stay or whether or not I use my own name?"

"You've been seen with me."

Helden. Strange name, strange woman. An odd mixture of vulnerability and strength. Whatever pain she had endured over the years she refused to turn into self-pity. She recognized her heritage, understood that the children of Nazis were hounded by the ODESSA and the Rache and they had to live with it: damned for what they were and damned for what they were not.

Geneva could help these children; *would* help them. Noel had settled that for himself. He identified with them easily. But for the courage of an extraordinary mother, he could be one of them.

But there were other, more immediate concerns. Questions that affected Geneva. Who was the elusive Anthony Beaumont? What did he stand for? What really happened to the Von Tiebolts in Brazil? How much did Johann von Tiebolt know about the covenant?

If anyone had the answers it was Johann . . . John Tennyson.

Holcroft walked back to the window; a flock of pigeons flew over a nearby roof, fanning up into the morning wind. The Von Tiebolts. Three weeks ago he had never heard the name, but now his life was inextricably involved with theirs.

Helden. Strange name, strange girl. Filled with complications and contradictions. He had never met anyone like her. It was as if she were from another time, another place, fighting the legacies of a war that had passed into history.

The Rache. The ODESSA . . . *Wolfsschanze.* All fanatics. Adversaries in a bloodbath that had no meaning now. It was over, *had* been over for thirty years. It was dead history, finished.

The pigeons swooped down again, and in their mass attack on the rooftop, Noel suddenly saw something—understood something—he had not before. It had been there since the other night—since his meeting with Herr Oberst—and he had not perceived it.

It was *not* over. The war itself had been revived. By Geneva!

There will be men who will try to stop you, deceive you, kill you. . . .

The ODESSA. The Rache. *These* were Geneva's enemies! Fanatics and terrorists who would do anything to destroy the covenant. Anyone else would have exposed the account by appealing to the international courts; neither the ODESSA nor the Rache could do that. Helden was wrong—at least, partially wrong. Whatever interest both had in the children of party leaders was suspended to fight the cause of Geneva! To stop *him.* They had learned about the account in Switzerland—somehow, somewhere—and were committed to blocking it. If to succeed meant killing him, it was not a decision of consequence; he was expendable.

It explained the strychnine on the plane—a horrible death that was meant for him. The terror tactics of the Rache. It clarified the events in Rio de Janeiro— gunshots at a deserted lookout and a shattered car window in the night traffic. Maurice Graff and the psychopathic followers of Brazil's ODESSA. They knew— they *all* knew—about Geneva!

And if they did, they also knew about the Von Tiebolts. That would explain what had happened in Brazil. It was never the *mother;* it was Johann von Tiebolt. He was running from Graff's ODESSA; the protective brother saving what was left of the family, spiriting himself and his two sisters out of Rio.

To live and fulfill the covenant in Geneva.

A *man will come one day and talk of a strange arrangement. . . .* And in that "strange arrangement" was the money and the power to destroy the ODESSA—and the Rache—for certainly these were legitimate objectives of the covenant.

Noel understood clearly now. He and John Tennyson and a man named Kessler in Berlin would control Geneva; they would direct the agency in Zürich. They would rip out the ODESSA wherever it was; they would crush the Rache. Among the amends that had to be made was the stilling of fanatics, for fanatics were the fathers of murder and genocide.

He wanted to call Helden, to tell her that soon she could stop running—they could *all* stop running—stop hiding, stop living in fear. He wanted to tell her that. And he wanted to see her again.

But he had given his word not to call her at Gallimard, not to try to reach her for any reason. It was maddening; *she* was maddening, yet he could not break his word.

The telephone. He had to call the American Express office on the Champs-Elysées. He had told Sam Buonoventura he would check for messages there.

It was a simple matter to get messages by telephone; he had done so before. No one had to know where he was. He put down his coffee and went to the phone, suddenly remembering that he had a second call to make. His mother. It was too early to call her in New York; he'd reach her later in the day.

"I'm sorry, monsieur," said the clerk at the American Express office. "You must sign for the cables in person. I'm very sorry."

Cables! Noel replaced the phone, annoyed but not angry. Getting out of the hotel room would be good for him, would take his mind off the anticipated call from Helden.

He walked along the rue Chevalle, a cold wind whipping his face. A taxi took him across the river, into the Champs-Elysées. The air and the bright sunlight were invigorating; he rolled the window down, feeling the effects of both. For the first time in days he felt confident; he knew where he was going now. Geneva was closer, the blurred lines between enemies and friends more defined.

Whatever was waiting for him at the American Express office seemed inconsequential. There was nothing he could not handle in New York or London. His concerns were now in Paris. He and John Tennyson would meet and talk and draw up plans, the first of which would be to go to Berlin and find Erich Kessler. They knew who their enemies were; it was a question of eluding them. Helden's friends could help.

As he got out of the taxi, he looked over at the tinted-glass window of the American Express office, and was struck by a thought. Was the refusal to read him his messages over the phone a trap? A means of getting him to show himself? If so, it was a bit obvious, and no doubt a tactic of British Intelligence.

Noel smiled. He knew exactly what to say if the British picked him up: John Tennyson was no more an assassin than he was, and probably far less of one than a number of MI-Five personnel.

He might even go a step further and suggest that the Royal Navy take a good, long look at one of its more decorated officers. All the evidence pointed to the probability that Commander Anthony Beaumont was a member of the ODESSA, recruited in Brazil by a man named Graff.

He felt he was falling through space, plunging downward, unable to catch his breath. His stomach was hollow and pain shot through his lower chest. He was gripped by combined feelings of grief and fear . . . and anger. The cablegram read:

YOUR FATHER DIED FOUR DAYS AGO STOP UNABLE TO CONTACT YOU STOP
PLEASE RESPOND BY TELEPHONE BEDFORD HILLS STOP

MOTHER

There was a second cable, from Lieutenant David Miles, New York Police Department.

THE RECENT DEATH OF RICHARD HOLCROFT MAKES IT IMPERATIVE YOU
CONTACT ME IMMEDIATELY STOP PROFESSIONALLY I RECOMMEND YOU
SPEAK TO ME BEFORE REACHING ANYONE ELSE STOP

There were the same two telephone numbers Buonoventura had given him in Rio de Janeiro, and six—*six*—follow-up inquiries listed by day and hour since the original message had been received at the American Express office. Miles had checked twice a day to see if his message had been picked up.

Noel walked up the Champs-Elysées, trying to collect his thoughts, trying to control his grief.

The only father he had ever known. "Dad" . . . "my *father,*" Richard Holcroft. Always said with affection, with love. And always with warmth and humor, for Richard Holcroft was a man of many graces, not the least of which was an ability to laugh at himself. He had guided his son—stepson—no, *goddamn it,* his *son!* Guided but never interfered, except when interference was the only alternative.

Oh, God, he was *dead!*

What caused the sharp bolts of pain—pain he understood was part of the fear and the anger—was implied in Miles's cable. Was he somehow responsible for Richard Holcroft's death? Oh, *Christ!* Was that death related to a vial of strychnine poured into a drink thirty thousand feet over the Atlantic? Was it woven into the fabric of *Geneva?*

Had he somehow sacrificed the father he had known all his life for one he never knew?

He reached the corner of the avenue George V. Across the broad intersection that teemed with traffic he saw a sign above awnings that stretched the length of the sidewalk café: FOUQUET's. It was all familiar to him. To his left was the Hôtel George V. He had stayed there, briefly, a year ago, courtesy of an extremely wealthy hotelman who had delusions, later proved to be just that, of duplicating its exterior in Kansas City.

Holcroft had struck up a friendship with the assistant manager. If the man was still there, perhaps he'd let him use a telephone. If telephone calls *were* traced back to the George V, it would be a simple matter to learn about them. And a simpler matter to leave misleading information regarding his whereabouts.

Anticipate.

"But, of course, it's my pleasure, Noel. It's so good to see you again. I am chagrined you do not stay with us, but at these prices, I don't blame you. Here, use my office."

"I'll charge the calls to my credit card, of course."

"I'm not worried, my friend. Later, an *apéritif,* perhaps?"

"I'd like that," said Noel.

It was ten-forty-five, Paris time. Quarter to six in New York. If Miles was as anxious as his message implied, the hour was insignificant. He picked up the phone and placed the call.

Noel looked at Miles's message again.

THE RECENT DEATH OF RICHARD HOLCROFT . . . PROFESSIONALLY I RECOM-
MEND YOU SPEAK TO ME BEFORE REACHING ANYONE ELSE . . .

The recommendation had an ominous tone; the "anyone else" had to mean his mother.

He put the paper down on the desk and reached into his pocket for Althene's cablegram.

YOUR FATHER DIED FOUR DAYS AGO . . . UNABLE TO CONTACT YOU . . .

The guilt he felt at not having been with her nearly matched the guilt and the fear and the anger that consumed him when he considered the possibility that he was responsible for the death. Possibility? He *knew* it; he *felt* it.

He wondered—painfully—if Miles had reached Althene. And if he had, what had he said to her?

The telephone rang.

"Is this Noel Holcroft?"

"Yes. I'm sorry you had trouble reaching me. . . ."

"I won't waste time going into that," interrupted Miles, "except to say you've violated federal laws."

"*Wait* a minute," broke in Noel, angrily. "What am I guilty of? You found me. I'm not hiding."

"*Finding* you after trying to locate you for damn near a week is called flagrantly ignoring and disregarding the law. You were not to leave the city of New York without telling us."

"There were pressing personal matters. I left word. You haven't got a case."

"Then let's try 'obstruction of justice.' "

"What?"

"You were in the lounge of that British seven-forty-seven, and you and I both know what happened. Or, should I say, what *didn't* happen?"

"What are you talking about?"

"That drink was meant for you, not Thornton."

Holcroft knew it was coming, but his knowing it did not lessen the impact. Still, he was not about to agree without a protest. "That's the craziest goddamn thing I've ever heard," he said.

"Come on! You're a bright, upstanding citizen from a bright, upstanding family, but your behavior for the past five days has been stupid and less than candid."

"You're insulting me, but you're not saying anything. You mentioned in your message—"

"We'll get to that," interrupted the detective. "I want you to know whose side you're on. You see, I want you to cooperate, not fight."

"Go ahead."

"We traced you to Rio. We spoke to—"

"You *what?*" Had Sam turned on him?

"It wasn't hard. Incidentally, your friend Buonoventura doesn't know. His cover for you didn't wash. He said you were in a boat out of Curaçao, but Dutch immigration didn't have you in the territory. We got a list of the overseas telephone numbers he called and checked the airlines. You were on Braniff out of New York, and you stayed at a Pôrto Alegre Hotel in Rio."

The amateur could not match the professional. "Sam said you called a couple of times."

"Sure did," agreed Miles. "You left Rio and we wanted to find out where you went; we knew he'd get in touch with you. Didn't you get my message at the hotel in London?"

"No."

"I'll take your word. Messages get lost."

But that message had not been lost, thought Noel. It had been stolen by the men of Wolfsschanze. "I know where I stand now. Get to the point."

"You don't *quite* know," Miles replied. "We talked to the embassy in Rio, to a man named Anderson. He said you told him quite a story. How you were trapped, chased, shot at. He said he didn't believe a word of it; considered you a troublemaker and was glad to get you out of Brazil."

"I know. He drove me to the airport."

"Do you want to tell me about it?" asked the detective.

Noel stared at the wall. It would be so easy to unburden himself, to seek official protection. The faceless Lieutenant Miles was a symbol of authority. But he was the wrong symbol in the wrong place at the wrong time. "No. There's nothing you can do. It's been resolved."

"Has it?"

"Yes."

Neither spoke for several seconds. "All right, Mr. Holcroft. I hope you change your mind, because I think I can help you. I think you *need* help." Miles paused. "I now make a formal request for your return to the City of New York. You are considered a prime witness in a homicide and intrinsic to our jurisdiction interrogations."

"Sorry. Not now."

"I didn't think you would. So let me try informally. It concerns your father."

The terrible news was coming, and he could not help himself. He said the words quietly. "He was killed, wasn't he?"

"I didn't hear that. You see, if I did, I'd have to go to my superior and report it. Say you said it without provocation. You drew a conclusion that couldn't possibly be based on anything I said to you. I'd have to request extradition."

"Get off it, Miles! Your telephone message wasn't subtle! 'The recent death,' et cetera; 'professionally speaking, I recommend,' et cetera! What the hell am I supposed to think?"

Again, there was a pause from the New York end. "Okay. It's checkmate. You've got a case."

"He was murdered, wasn't he?"

"We think so."

"What have you said to my mother?"

"Nothing. It's not my jurisdiction. She doesn't even know my name. And that answers my next question. You haven't talked to her yet."

"Obviously. Tell me what happened."

"Your father was in what can best be described as a very unusual accident. He died an hour later, at the hospital, as a result of the injuries."

"What was the accident?"

"An old man from the Bronx lost control of his car near the Plaza Hotel. The car went wild, jumped the curb, and plunged into a crowd of people on the sidewalk. Three were killed instantly. Your father was thrown against the wall; actually, he was pinned, almost crushed."

"You're saying the car aimed for him!"

"Hard to tell. There was mass confusion, of course."

"Then what *are* you saying?"

Miles hesitated. "That the car aimed for him."

"Who was the driver?"

"A seventy-two-year-old retired accountant with an inflamed heart, a pacemaker, no family at all, and a license that expired several years ago. The 'pacer' was shorted in the accident; the man died on the way to the hospital."

"What was his connection to my father?"

"So far, no definite answers. But I've got a theory. Do you want to hear it?"

"Of course!"

"Will you come back to New York?"

"Don't press me. What's your theory?"

"I think the old guy was recruited. I think there was someone else in that car, probably in the back seat, holding a gun to his head. During the confusion, he smashed the pacer and got away. I think it was an execution made to look like a freak accident in which more than the target got killed."

Noel held his breath. There had been another "freak accident." A subway in London had gone out of control, killing five people. And among those killed was the only man who could shed light on John Tennyson's employment at the *Guardian.*

It was bloody well murder. . . .

The thought of a connection was appalling. "Aren't you reaching, Miles?" Holcroft asked.

"I said it was a theory, but not without some support. When I saw the name Holcroft on the accident report, I did a little digging. The old man from the Bronx has an interesting history. He came to this country in 'forty-seven, supposedly a penniless Jewish immigrant, a victim of Dachau. Only he wasn't penniless, as half a dozen bank-books show, and his apartment is a fortress. Besides which, he made thirteen trips to Germany and back since he got here."

Beads of perspiration broke out on Noel's forehead. "What are you trying to say?"

"I don't think that old guy was ever near Dachau. Or if he was, he was part of the management. Almost no one knew him in his apartment building; no one ever saw him in a synagogue. I think he was a Nazi."

Holcroft swallowed. "How does that connect him to my father?"

"Through you. I'm not sure how yet, but through you."

"Through me?" Noel felt the acceleration of his heartbeat.

"Yes. In Rio, you told Anderson that someone named Graff was a Nazi and tried to kill you. Anderson said you were crazy on both points, but I don't. I believe you."

"I was mad as hell. I didn't *mean* to tie one into the other. It was a misunderstanding. . . ." Noel sought desperately to find the words. "Graff's paranoid, a hot-tempered German, so I called him a Nazi, that's all. He thought I was making sketches, taking pictures of his grounds. . . ."

"I said I *believed* you, Holcroft," broke in the detective. "And I've got my reasons."

"What are they?" Noel knew he could barely be heard; he was suddenly afraid. His father's death was a warning. The Rache. The ODESSA. Whichever, it was another *warning.* His mother had to be protected!

Miles was talking, but Holcroft could not hear the detective; his mind raced in panic. Miles had to be stopped! He could not be allowed near Geneva!

"Those men on the plane who tried to kill you were German," Miles explained. "They used passports taken off two Americans killed in Munich five years ago, but they were German; the dental work gave them away. They were shot at Kennedy Airport; their bodies were found in a fuel truck. The bullets that killed them came from a German Heckler and Koch nine-millimeter pistol. The silencer was made in Munich. Guess where that little old man traveled when he went to Germany—at least on the six trips we were able to trace."

"Munich," whispered Noel.

"That's right. Munich. Where it all began and where it's still going on. A bunch of Nazis are fighting among each other thirty years after that goddamn war is over, and you're right in the middle of it. I want to know *why.*"

Noel felt drained, swept by exhaustion and fear. "Leave it alone. There's nothing you can do."

"There's something I might be able to *prevent,* goddamnit! Another murder."

"Can't you understand?" said Holcroft, in pain. "I can say it because he *was* my father. Nothing can be resolved in New York. It can only be resolved over here. Give me time; for the love of God, give me *time.* I'll get back to you."

"How long?"

"A month."

"Too much. Cut it in half. You've got two weeks."

"Miles, *please* . . ."

There was a click on the line; the connection in New York was severed.

Two weeks. Oh, God, it wasn't possible!

But it *had* to be possible. In two weeks he had to be in a position to stop Miles from going further. He could do that with the resources in Geneva. A philanthropic agency with assets of seven hundred and eighty million dollars would be listened to—quietly, in confidence. Once the account was freed, arrangements could be made, understandings reached, cooperation given and received. The ODESSA would be exposed, the Rache destroyed.

All this would happen *only* when three acceptable offspring presented themselves to the bank in Geneva. It *would* happen, Noel was convinced of that, but until then he had to protect his mother. He had to reach Althene and convince her that for the next few weeks she had to disappear.

What could he say to her? She'd never obey him. She'd never listen to him if she believed for an instant her husband had been murdered. What in God's name could he *say* to her?

"Allo? Allo, monsieur?" The voice of the operator floated out from the telephone. "Your call to New York—"

Holcroft hung up so quickly he jarred the instrument's bell. He could not talk to his mother. Not now. In an hour or so, not now. He had to think. There was so much to think about, so much to do.

He was going mad.

19

"He'll go mad," said the blond-haired man into the telephone at Hellenikon Airport, in Athens. "He must have heard the news by now. It will be a strain that may tear him apart; he won't know what to do. Tell our man in Paris to stay close to him for the next twenty-four hours. He must not return to America."

"He won't," said Gretchen Beaumont, thousands of miles away.

"You can't be sure. The psychological stresses are building properly; our subject's in a delicate frame of mind. However, he can be guided. He's waiting for me; he sees me now as his answer to so many things, but the string must be drawn tighter. I want him to go to Berlin first. For a day or two. To Kessler."

"Shall we use his mother? We could plant the idea with her."

"No. Under no circumstances must she be touched. It would be far too dangerous."

"Then how will you suggest Berlin?" asked Gretchen Beaumont, in England.

"I won't," answered John Tennyson, in Athens. "I will convince our sister to lead him to that conclusion. She's trying to reach me, of course."

"Be careful with her, Johann."

"I will."

Holcroft walked along the concrete bank of the Seine, unaware of the biting winds that came off the river. An hour ago he had been filled with confidence; now he felt lost. He knew only that he had to keep moving, clear his head, make decisions.

He had to reevaluate some matters, too. An hour ago the one man he believed he could count on was Helden's brother. That judgment was suspect now. A runaway car on a New York street that took the life of the only father he had ever known was too similar to an unexplained disaster in a London subway.

The man was killed in a most unusual accident that took five lives. . . . MI Five.

An execution . . . a freak accident in which more than the target got killed. David Miles, NYPD.

The meeting with Tennyson was suddenly *not* the answer to everything; the shadow of the Tinamou had appeared again. A *man would come one day and talk of a strange arrangement.* Tennyson was waiting for him, but perhaps he was waiting for the wrong reasons. Perhaps he had sold out their covenant for a higher price.

If he had, he was as responsible for Richard Holcroft's death as surely as if his foot had been on the accelerator and his hands on the wheel. Should that be the case, Tennyson would not leave the meeting alive. The son would kill for the father; he owed Richard Holcroft that.

Noel stopped and put his hands on the concrete wall, astonished at himself . . . at his thoughts. He was actually projecting himself into the role of a killer! His covenant was extracting a cost more terrible than anything he had considered.

He would confront Tennyson with the facts as they had been given to him. He would watch the son of Wilhelm von Tiebolt closely. The truth or the lie: It would be in Tennyson's words, in his eyes. Holcroft hoped to God he would recognize it.

One step at a time. His mind was clearing. Each move had to be considered carefully; yet that caution could not slow him down.

First things first, and first there was the indisputable fact that he could no longer move freely, carelessly. The most deadly warning of all had been given him: the killing of a loved one. He accepted that warning in fear and in rage. The fear would make him careful; the rage would give him a degree of courage. It *had* to; he was depending on it.

Next was his mother. What could he say that she would accept without being suspicious? Whatever it was, she had to believe him. If she thought for an instant that her husband's death was the work of men spawned by the Third Reich, she would raise her voice in fury. And her first cry would be her last. What could he say to her that would sound plausible?

He started walking again, absently, his eyes unfocused. As a result, he collided with a short man strolling in the opposite direction.

"Excuse me. *Pardon, monsieur,*" Noel said.

The Frenchman had been glancing at a newspaper; he shrugged, and smiled pleasantly. *"Rien."*

Noel stopped. The Frenchman reminded him of someone. The round, pleasant face, the spectacles.

Ernst Manfredi.

His mother had respected Manfredi, still owed the Swiss banker a great debt. Perhaps he could speak to Althene through Ernst Manfredi, invent an explanation given him by the banker. Why not? The words would not be contradicted; Manfredi was dead.

It was Manfredi who had been concerned for his old friend Althene *Clausen. He* had been frightened for her. He had been afraid that during the coming weeks, while the extraordinary account in Geneva was being released, Clausen's name would surface. There would be those who remembered a headstrong young woman who left her husband in revulsion, whose words became the basis for Heinrich Clausen's moral conversion. A conversion that resulted in the theft of hundreds of millions. Dormant hostilities might be aroused, revenge sought against that woman.

It was *Manfredi's* fear that she had to respect. The old banker knew more than either of them, and if he had thought it best that she disappear for a while, until the impact of the account's release was diminished, she should take his advice. A sick old man about to end his life did not draw frivolous conclusions.

The explanation made sense; it was consistent with their conversation in Bedford Hills three weeks ago. His mother would see that consistency. She would listen to the "words" of Ernst Manfredi.

Instinctively, Noel glanced over his shoulder to see if anyone was following him. It had become a habit. Fear made him careful; rage gave him a certain strength. He wanted very much to see an enemy. He was getting used to his unfamiliar forest.

He headed back to the hotel. He had rushed out of the George V in panic and bewilderment, avoiding the assistant manager, needing the cold air of the streets to clear his head. Now he would accept an aperitif and ask to make another transatlantic call. To his mother.

He walked faster, stopping abruptly twice, turning quickly. Was anyone there? It was possible. A dark-green Fiat had slowed down a block behind. *Good.*

He crossed the street rapidly, went into the front entrance of a sidewalk café, and emerged seconds later from an exit that led out to the avenue George V. He walked up the block, stopping at a newstand for a paper.

He could see the green Fiat careening around the corner near the café. It stopped abruptly. The driver parked at the curb and lowered his head. *Good.* It was suddenly made clear to Noel what he would do after the aperitif and the call to Althene.

He would see Helden. He needed a gun.

Von Tiebolt stared at the mouthpiece of the pay phone in the Athens airport, his lips parted in shock.

"What did you say?" he asked.

"It's true, Johann," said Helden in Paris. "British Intelligence thinks you may be the Tinamou."

"How extraordinary." The astonished blond man drew out the word. "And outrageous!"

"That's what I said to Holcroft. I told him you were being hounded for the things you write . . . and because of who you are. Who *we* are."

"Yes, I imagine so." Von Tiebolt could not concentrate on his sister's reasoning; he gripped the receiver in anger. An error had been made somewhere; steps had to be taken immediately to correct it. What had led MI Five to *him?* Every track had been covered! But then, he could produce the Tinamou at will; it was his final strategy. No one was more trusted than the suspect who produced the hunted killer. This was the ultimate tactic of his creation. He might have to employ it sooner than he thought.

"Johann, are you there?"

"Yes, sorry."

"You *must* meet Holcroft as soon as possible."

"Of course. I'll be in Paris in four or five days. . . ."

"Not until then?" interrupted Helden. "He's very anxious."

"It's quite impossible."

"There's so much more to tell you. . . ." She told him of the account in Geneva; of the agency in Zürich that would dispense hundreds of millions; of the American son of Heinrich Clausen; of Erich Kessler in Berlin; of the Von Tiebolts in Rio. Finally, haltingly, she repeated the words uttered by their sister: A *man will come one day and talk of a strange arrangement.* "Did you say that?" she asked her brother.

"Yes. There's a great deal you've never been told. I didn't know when or how it would happen, only that it would. I spoke to Gretchen earlier. This Holcroft saw her the other night. I'm afraid she wasn't much help to him. We have a commitment as profound and as moving as anything in recent history. Amends must be made . . ."

"That's what Holcroft said," broke in Helden.

"I'm sure he did."

"He's frightened. He tries not to show it, but he is."

"He should be. It's an enormous responsibility. I have to learn what he knows in order to help."

"Then come to Paris now."

"I can't. It's only a few days."

"I'm worried. If Noel's what he says he is, and I see no reason to doubt him—"

" 'Noel'?" asked the brother, with mild surprise.

"I like him, Johann."

"Go on."

"If he's the one that's to bring the three of you to the directors of La Grande Banque, then nothing can happen in Geneva without him."

"So?"

"Others know that. I think they know about the account in Switzerland. Terrible things have happened. They've tried to stop him."

"Who?"

"My guess would be the Rache. Or the ODESSA."

"That's doubtful," said John Tennyson. "Neither is capable of keeping such extraordinary news quiet. Take a newspaperman's word for it."

"The Rache kills; so does the ODESSA. Someone tried to kill Noel."

Tennyson smiled to himself; errors had been made, but the primary strategy was working. Holcroft was being pounded on all sides. When everything came together in Geneva, he'd be exhausted, completely malleable. "He must be very cautious, then. Teach him the things you know, Helden. As much as you can. The tricks we've all learned from one another."

"He's seen some of those tricks," said the girl, a soft, compassionate laugh in her voice. "He hates using them."

"Better than ending up dead." The blond man paused. The transition had to be casual. "Gretchen mentioned a photograph, a picture of Beaumont. She thinks Holcroft took it."

"He did. He's convinced he saw Beaumont on the plane from New York to Rio. He thinks he was following him. It's part of what he'll tell you."

So it *was* the plane, thought Tennyson. The American was more observant than Beaumont had wanted to believe. Beaumont's disappearance would be explained in a matter of days, but it would be difficult to explain the photograph in Holcroft's possession if he showed it to the wrong people in Switzerland. The fanatic commander had left too obvious a trail, from Rio to the Admiralty. They had to get the photograph back. "I don't know what to say to that, Helden. I never liked Beaumont. I never trusted him. But he's been in the Mediterranean for months. I don't see how he could have left his ship and turned up on a plane out of New York. Holcroft's wrong." Tennyson paused again. "However, I think Noel should bring the photograph with him when we meet. He shouldn't be carrying it around. Nor should he talk about Beaumont. Tell him that. It could lead people to Gretchen. To us. Yes, I think it would be a good idea if he brought the photograph with him."

"He can't do that. It was stolen from him."

The blond man froze. It was *impossible*. None of *them* had taken the photograph! No *Sonnenkind.* He'd be the first to know. Someone *else?* He lowered his voice. "What do you mean, 'stolen from him'?"

"Just that. A man chased him, beat him unconscious, and took the picture. Nothing else, just the photograph."

"*What* man?"

"He didn't know. It was night; he couldn't see. He woke up in a field miles away from Portsmouth."

"He was attacked in Portsmouth?"

"About a mile from Gretchen's house, as I gather."

Something *was* wrong. Terribly wrong. "Are you sure Holcroft wasn't lying?"

"Why should he?"

"What *exactly* did he tell you?"

"That he was chased by a man in a black sweater. The man hit him with a blunt weapon and took the photograph out of his pocket when he was unconscious. Just the photograph. Not his money or anything else."

"I see." But he did *not* see! And it was the unseen that disturbed him. He could not convey his fears to Helden; as always, he had to appear in total control. Yet he had to search out this unseen, unknown disturbance. "Helden, I'd like you to do something . . . for all of us. Do you think you could arrange to take a day off from work?"

"I imagine so. Why?"

"I think we should try and find out who it is that has so much interest in Holcroft. Perhaps you might suggest a drive in the country, to Fontainebleau or Barbizon."

"But why?"

"I have a friend in Paris; he often does odd jobs for me. I'll ask him to follow you, very discreetly, of course. Perhaps we'll learn who else takes the trip."

"One of our people could do it."

"No, I don't think so. Don't involve your friends. Herr Oberst should not be a part of this."

"All right. We'll start out around ten in the morning. From his hotel. The Douzaine Heures, rue Chevalle. How will I know the man?"

"You won't. He'll pick you up. Say nothing to Holcroft; it would upset him needlessly."

"Very well. You'll call me when you get to Paris?"

"The minute I arrive, *meine Schwester.* "

"*Danke, mein Bruder.* "

Tennyson replaced the phone. There was a last call to make before he boarded the plane to Berlin. Not to Gretchen, now; he did not want to speak with her. If Beaumont's actions proved to be as disastrous as they appeared, if in his recklessness he had impeded the cause of Wolfsschanze, then all the strings that led to him and through him to Geneva would have to be severed. It was not an easy decision to make. He loved Gretchen as few men on earth loved their sisters; in a way that the world disapproved of because the world did not understand.

She took care of his needs, satiated his hungers, so that there were never any outside complications. His mind was free to concentrate on his extraordinary mission in life. But that, too, might have to end. Gretchen, his sister, his lover, might have to die.

Holcroft listened to Althene's last words, stunned at her equilibrium, astonished that it had been so easy. The funeral had been yesterday.

"You do what you must, Noel. A good man died needlessly, foolishly, and that's the obscenity. But it's over; there's nothing either of us can do."

"There's something you can do for me."

"What's that?"

He told her of Manfredi's death—as the Swiss believed it had happened. An old man wracked with pain, preferring a quick end to prolonged suffering and infirmity. "The last thing he did as a banker was to meet with me in Geneva."

Althene was silent for a moment, reflecting on a friend who once meant a great deal to her. "It was like him to fulfill an agreement as important as the one he brought to you. He wouldn't leave it to others."

"There was something else; it concerned you. He said you'd understand." Holcroft held the telephone firmly and spoke as convincingly as he could. He expressed Manfredi's "concerns" about those who might remember a headstrong woman many believed responsible for the conversion of Heinrich Clausen, and for his decision to betray the Reich. He explained that it was entirely possible that there remained fanatics who might still seek revenge. Manfredi's old friend Althene Clausen should not risk being a target; she should go away for a while, where no one could find her in the event Clausen's name surfaced. "Can you understand, mother?"

"Yes," answered Althene. "Because he said it to me once before, several hundred years ago. On a warm afternoon in Berlin. He said they would look for us then, too. He was right; he's right now. The world is filled with lunatics."

"Where will you go?"

"I'm not sure. Take a trip, perhaps. It's a very good time for it, isn't it? People are so embarrassingly solicitous about death."

"I'd rather you went someplace where you were out of sight. Just for a few weeks."

"It's easy to be out of sight. I have a certain expertise in that. For two years after we left Berlin, you and I kept moving. Until Pearl Harbor, actually. The Bund's activities were too varied for comfort in those days; it took its orders from the Wilhelmstrasse."

"I didn't know that," said Holcroft, moved.

"There's a great deal—No matter. Richard put an end to it all. He made us stop running, stop hiding. I'll let you know where I am."

"How?"

His mother paused. "Your friend in Curaçao, Mr. Buonoventura. He was positively reverential. I'll let him know."

Holcroft smiled. "All right. I'll call Sam."

"I never did tell you about those days, did I? Before Richard came into our lives. I really must; you might be interested."

"I'd be very interested. Manfredi was right. You are incredible."

"No, dear. Merely a survivor."

As always, they said rapid goodbyes; they were friends. Noel walked out of the assistant manager's office. He started across the George V lobby, toward the bar, where his friend was waiting with aperitifs, then decided to take a short detour. He crossed to the huge window to the left of the entrance and peered out between the folds of the red velvet drapes. The green Fiat was still down the street.

Noel continued across the lobby toward the bar. He would spend a quarter of an hour in pleasant conversation with the assistant manager, during which he would impart some very specific, if erroneous, information, and ask a favor or two.

And then there was Helden. If she did not call him by five o'clock, he would telephone her at Gallimard. He had to see her; he wanted a gun.

"Four or five *days?*" exploded Holcroft into the phone. "I don't want to wait four or five days. I'll meet him anywhere! I can't waste time."

"He said he wouldn't be in Paris until then and suggested you go on to Berlin in the meantime. It would only take you a day or so."

"He knew about Kessler?"

"Perhaps not by name, but he knew about Berlin."

"Where was he?"

"At the airport in Athens."

Noel remembered. *He disappeared four days ago in Bahrain. Our operatives are watching for him from Singapore to Athens:* British Intelligence would have its confrontation with John Tennyson imminently, if it had not taken place already. "What did he say about the British?"

"He was furious, as I knew he would be. It's not unlike Johann to write an article that would embarrass the Foreign Office. He was outraged."

"I trust he won't. The last thing any of us want is a newspaper story. Can you call him back? Can I call him? He could fly in tonight. I could pick him up at Orly."

"I'm afraid not. He was catching a plane. There's only a number in Brussels; it's where he picks up his messages. It took him nearly two days to get mine."

"Goddammit!"

"You're overwrought."

"I'm in a hurry."

"Noel . . ." Helden began haltingly. "I don't have to work tomorrow. Could we meet? Perhaps go for a drive? I'd like to talk."

Holcroft was startled. He wanted to see *her.* "Why wait until tomorrow? Let's have dinner."

"I can't. I have a meeting tonight. I'll be at your hotel at ten o'clock tomorrow morning. In the afternoon you can fly to Berlin."

"Are you meeting your friends?"

"Yes."

"Helden, do something for me. I never thought I'd ask this of anyone, but . . . I want a gun. I don't know how to go about getting one, what the laws are."

"I understand. I'll bring it. Until morning."

"See you tomorrow." Holcroft hung up and looked at his open attaché case on the hotel chair. He could see the cover of the Geneva document. It reminded him of the threat from the men of Wolfsschanze. *Nothing is as it was for you. . . .* He knew now how completely true that was. He had borrowed a gun in Costa Rica. He had killed a man who was about to kill him, and he never wanted to see a gun in his hand again, for as long as he lived. That, too, was changed. Everything was changed, because a man he never knew had cried out to him from the grave.

20

"Do you like mountain trout?" asked Helden, as she handed him the automatic in the front seat of his rented car.

"Trout's fine," he said, laughing.

"What's funny?"

"I don't know. You hand me a gun, which isn't the most normal thing for a person to do, and at the same time you ask me what I'd like for lunch."

"One has nothing to do with the other. I think it might be a good idea if you took your mind off your problems for a few hours."

"I thought you wanted to talk about them."

"I do. I also wanted to know you better. When we met the other night, you asked all the questions."

"Before I asked those questions, you did all the yelling."

Helden laughed. "I'm sorry about that. It was hectic, wasn't it?"

"It was crazy. You have a nice laugh. I didn't know you laughed."

"I do quite frequently. At least twice a month, regularly as clockwork."

Holcroft glanced at her. "I shouldn't have said that. I don't imagine you find much to laugh at."

She returned his look; a smile was on her lips. "More than you think, perhaps. And I wasn't offended. I'm sure you think me rather solemn."

"Our talk the other night wasn't designed for a barrel of laughs."

"No, it wasn't." Helden turned, both hands on her knees beneath the pleated white skirt on the seat. There was a gamine quality about her Noel had not noticed before. It was reinforced by her words. "Do you ever think about them?" she asked.

"Who?"

"Those fathers you and I never knew. What they did was so incredible, such an act of daring."

"Not just one act. Hundreds . . . thousands of them. Each different, each complicated, going on for months. Three years of manipulations."

"They must have lived in terror."

"I'm sure they did."

"What drove them?"

"Just what . . ." Noel stopped, not knowing why he did so. "Just what Heinrich Clausen wrote in his letter to me. They were shocked beyond anything we can imagine when they learned about the 'rehabilitation camps.' Auschwitz, Belsen— it blew their minds. It seems incredible to us now, but remember, that was 'forty-three. There were conspiracies of silence."

Helden touched his arm; the contact was brief, but it was firm. "You call him Heinrich Clausen. You can't say 'father,' can you?"

"I *had* a father." Noel stopped. It was not the moment to talk at length about Richard Holcroft; he had to control himself. "He's dead. He was killed five days ago in New York."

"Oh, *God.* . . ." Helden stared at him; he could feel the intensity of her concern. "Killed? Because of Geneva?" she asked.

"I don't know."

"But you think so."

"Yes." He gripped the wheel and was silent. A shell was forming, and it was an awful thing.

"I'm sorry, Noel. I don't know what else to say. I wish I could comfort you somehow, but I don't know how."

He looked at her, at her lovely face and at the clear brown eyes filled with concern. "With all your problems, just saying that is enough. You're a nice person, Helden. I haven't met too many people like you."

"I could say the same . . . nice person."

"We've both said it. Now, what about that trout? If we're going to take a few hours off, why not tell me where we're going?"

"To Barbizon. There's a lovely restaurant in the center of the town. Have you ever been to Barbizon?"

"Several times," said Noel, his eyes suddenly on the small rectangular mirror outside the window.

There was a dark-green Fiat behind them. He had no idea whether it was the same car that had waited for him yesterday on the avenue George V, but he intended to find out—without alarming Helden. He slowed down; the Fiat did not pass. Instead, it veered into the right lane, allowing another car to come between them.

"Is something wrong?" asked Helden.

Holcroft depressed the accelerator. The automobile lurched slightly at the slower speed. "No, not really. I had trouble with this damn thing yesterday. It needs a carburetor adjustment, I think. Every now and then there's an air lock. It passes if you nurse it."

"You sound very efficient."

"I'm a fair mechanic. You don't take jobs in Mexico and points south unless you are." He stepped on the pedal and held it down; the car sped forward.

He could see the green Fiat in the rearview mirror now. It swerved to the left, passing the intervening car, then returned to the right lane, behind them. The question was answered. They were being followed.

His fear was making him cautious. Whoever was in that Fiat was indirectly involved with Richard Holcroft's death; he was certain of it. And he was going to trap that man.

"There. Everything's fine now," he said to Helden. "The air lock's passed. Lunch in Barbizon sounds like a hell of a good idea. Let's see if I remember the way."

He did not. On purpose. He took several wrong turns, covering his mistakes with laughter, insisting the whole French countryside had been changed around. It became a silly game with a deadly serious objective: He had to see the face of the man in the Fiat. In Paris that face had been obscured behind a windshield and a cloud of cigarette smoke; he had to be able to recognize it in a crowd.

The Fiat's driver, however, was no amateur. If he was bewildered by Noel's aimless turns and shifting speeds, he gave no indication of it, staying a discreet distance behind them, never allowing the gap between them to become too close. There was a disabled car on a narrow road south of Corbeil-Essonnes; it was a good excuse to stop. Holcroft pulled alongside to see if he could help; the driver of the Fiat had no choice. He drove swiftly past the two parked cars. Noel looked up. The man was fair, his hair light brown; and there was something else: splotches, or pockmarks, on the man's cheek.

He would know that face again. That was all that mattered.

The driver of the disabled car thanked Holcroft, indicating that help was on the way.

Noel nodded and started up again, wondering if he'd see the green Fiat soon. Would it be in a side road, waiting for him, or would it simply emerge from nowhere and appear in the rearview mirror?

"That was a very nice thing to do," said Helden.

"We ugly Americans do nice things every once in a while. I'll get back on the highway."

If the green Fiat was in a side road, he did not see it. It was simply there, in his mirror, on the highway. They got off at the Seine-et-Marne exit and drove into Barbizon. The green Fiat stayed far behind, but it was there.

Their lunch was a strange mixture of ease and awkwardness: brief starts and abrupt stops; short conversations begun, suddenly suspended at midpoint, the purpose unremembered. Yet the ease was in their being together, physically close to each other. Holcroft thought she felt it as surely as he did.

This sense of closeness was confirmed by something Helden did, obviously without thinking about it: She touched him repeatedly. She would reach over briefly and touch his sleeve, or, more briefly, his hand. She would touch him for emphasis, or because she was asking a question, but she touched him as if it were the most natural thing in the world for her to do. And it was natural for him to accept her touch and return it.

"Your brother didn't discuss Beaumont?" he asked.

"Yes, he did. He was very angry. Everything about Beaumont angers him. He thinks you were wrong about seeing him on the plane, though. He wanted you to bring the photograph. I told him you didn't have it. He was furious."

"About the photograph?"

"Yes. He said it might be dangerous. It could lead 'people,' he said, to Gretchen, to you. To Geneva."

"I think the answer's simpler. The Royal Navy's no different from any other military organization. The officers protect each other."

"My promiscuous sister, you mean?"

Holcroft nodded; he really did not want to discuss Gretchen Beaumont, not with Helden. "Something like that."

She touched his fingers. "It's all right, Noel. I don't sit in judgment where my sister's concerned." Then she took away her hand, embarrassed. "What I mean is, I have no right. . . . No, I don't mean that, either. I mean where you are concerned, I have no right. . . ."

"I think we both know what you mean," interrupted Holcroft, covering her hand with his. "Feel free to have a right. I think I like it."

"You make me feel foolish."

"Do I? It's the last thing I want to make you feel." He pulled back his hand, and followed her glance out the window. She was looking at the small stone pond on the terrace, but his attention did not remain where hers did. His gaze rose to several groups of tourists strolling in the Barbizon street beyond the gates of the restaurant. The man with the light-brown hair and pockmarked face was standing motionless on the far sidewalk. A cigarette was in his mouth, what appeared to be an artist's brochure in his hands. But the man was not looking at the brochure. His head was raised slightly, his eyes angled over at the entrance of the restaurant.

It was time to make his move, thought Noel. His rage was rekindled; he wanted that man.

"I've got an idea," he said as casually as he could. "I saw a poster by the door that—in my schoolboy French—I think said *Fête d'Hiver*. Someplace called Montereau-something-or-other. Isn't that a kind of carnival?"

"The *fête* is, not the village. It's about seven or eight miles south of here, I think."

"What is it? The carnival, I mean."

"Fêtes d'hiver? They're quite common and usually run by the local churches. As a rule, they're associated with a saint's day. It's like a flea market."

"Let's go."

"Really?"

"Why not? It might be fun. I'll buy you a present."

Helden looked at him quizzically. "All right," she said.

The bright afternoon sunlight bounced off the side-view mirror in harsh reflections, causing Holcroft to squint and blink repeatedly, trying to rid his eyes of blind spots. The dark-green Fiat appeared now and then. It was far behind them, but never out of sight for very long.

He parked the car behind a church, which was the focal point of the small town. Together he and Helden walked around the rectory to the front and into the crowds.

The village square was typically French, the cobblestone streets spreading out like irregular spokes from an imperfect wheel, old buildings and winding sidewalks everywhere. Stalls were set up in no discernible order, their awnings in various stages of disrepair, crafts and foodstuffs of all descriptions piled on counters. Shiny platters and a profusion of oilcloth caught the rays of sun; shafts of light shot through the crowd. This *fête* was not aimed at the tourist trade. Foreigners belonged to the spring and summer months.

The man with the pockmarked face was standing in front of a stall halfway across the square. He was munching on a piece of pastry, his eyes darting in Holcroft's direction. The man did not know he had been spotted; Noel was certain of that. He was far too casual, too intent on eating. He had his targets under surveillance; all was well. Holcroft turned to Helden, at his side.

"I see the present I want to get you!" he shouted.

"Don't be silly. . . ."

"Wait here! I'll be back in a few minutes."

"I'll be over there"—she pointed to her right—"at the pewter display."

"Fine. See you soon."

Noel began edging his way through the crowd. If he could weave enough, slouch enough, and make sufficiently quick movements, he could reach the edge of the mass of colliding bodies without the light-haired man's seeing him. Once on the cobblestone sidewalk beyond the crowd, he could inch his way around to within yards of the pastry stall.

He reached the sidewalk; the man had not seen him get there. He had ordered another piece of pastry and was eating it absently, rising on the balls of his feet, peering anxiously over the heads of the crowd. Abruptly, he seemed to relax and settle back, his attention only half on his targets. He had spotted Helden; apparently he was convinced that if he could see her, her companion would not be far away.

Noel feigned a suddenly lame ankle and limped around the border of the crowd, his new injury allowing him to bend over in pain. There was no way the man could see him now.

Noel was directly behind the pastry stall, no more than ten yards from it. He watched the man closely. There was something primitive about him as he stood there motionless, eating deliberately, every now and then stretching to make sure his quarry was still in sight. It struck Holcroft that he was watching a predator. He could not see its eyes, but somehow he knew they were cold and alert. The thought made him angry, raising images in his mind of such a man seated behind a driver, a gun perhaps at the driver's head, waiting for Richard Holcroft to emerge on a New York sidewalk. It was the sense of ice-cold, deadly manipulation that enraged him.

Noel lunged into the crowd, his right hand gripping the automatic in his pocket, his left extended in front of him, fingers taut. When Noel touched him, it would be a grip the light-haired man would never forget.

Suddenly he was blocked. *Blocked!* As he parted the shoulders of a man and a woman in front of him, a third figure met him head on, cross-checking him with its body, its face turned away. He was being stopped deliberately!

"Get out of my way! Goddammit, let go of me!"

He could see that his shouts, or his English, or both, had alarmed the light-haired man, just feet away, who spun in place, dropping his pastry. His eyes were wild; his face was flushed. He spun again and forced his way through the crowd, away from Noel.

"Get out of—!" Holcroft could feel it before he saw it. Something had sliced through his jacket, ripping the lining above his left pocket. He looked down, his eyes unbelieving. A knife had been thrust at his side; had he not twisted his body, it would have penetrated!

He grabbed the wrist holding the knife, pushing it away, afraid to let go, crashing his shoulder up into the chest of the man who held it. Still the man kept his face hidden. Who *was* he? There was no time to think or wonder; he had to get the terrible knife away!

Noel screamed. He bent over, his enemy's wrist vised in both his hands, the blade thrusting about in the crowded space, his whole body writhing, twisting into those surrounding him. He yanked the fist with the blade extending from it, then smashed it down with his full weight, falling to the street as he did so. The blade fell away, clattering on the stone.

Something crashed into his neck. Suddenly dazed, he still knew what it was; he had been hit with an iron pipe. He lay curled up in terror and confusion, but he could not stay down! Instinct made him lurch up; fear made him hold his place, waiting for an attack, prepared to fend it off. And rage made him seek out his attackers.

They were gone. The body that belonged to the unseen face was gone. The knife on the ground was gone! And all around him people backed away, staring at him as if he were deranged.

My God! he thought, with a terrible awareness. If they would kill him, they would kill Helden! If the man with the pockmarked face was protected by killers, and those killers knew he had spotted their charge, they would assume that Helden had spotted him, too. They would go after her! They would kill *her*, because she was part of his trap!

He broke his way through the circle of onlookers, and dodged a hundred angry arms and hands in the direction he instinctively remembered she'd indicated only minutes before. A stall that was selling some kind of pitchers, or plates, or . . . pitchers, plates, *pewter*. That was it! A stall with pewter. Where was it?

It was there, but she was not. She was nowhere to be seen. He ran up to the counter of the stall and shouted.

"A woman! A blond woman was here!"

"*Pardon? Je ne parle pas—*"

"*Une femme. . . . Aux cheveux blonds. Elle a été ici!*"

The vendor shrugged and continued polishing a small bowl.

"*Où est elle?*" shouted Holcroft.

"*Vous êtes fou! Fou!*" yelled the stallkeeper. "*Voleur! Police!*"

"*Non! S'il vous plaît! Une femme aux—*"

"*Ah,*" broke in the vendor. "*Une blonde. Dans ce sens.*" He gestured to his left.

Holcroft pushed himself away from the stall and raced into crowds again. He pulled at overcoats and jackets, making a path for himself. Oh, Christ, he had *killed* her! His eyes searched everywhere, every corridor, every pair of eyes, every thatch of hair. She was nowhere.

"*Helden!*"

Suddenly, a fist hammered into his right kidney, and an arm shot over his shoulder, locking itself around his neck, choking the air out of his throat. He slammed his right elbow into the body of his assailant, now behind him, now dragging him backward through the crowd. Gasping for air, he jammed his left elbow into the hard, twisting figure holding him, then his right again. He had caught his attacker in the rib cage; the lock around his throat loosened for an instant, and that instant was enough. He spun to his left, his fingers digging into the forearm around his neck, and pulled downward, throwing his assailant over his hip. Both men fell to the ground.

Noel saw the face! Beneath the unruly crop of red hair was the small scar on the forehead, and beneath it the angry blue eyes. The man was the younger of the two MI-Five agents who had questioned him in his London hotel. Noel's rage was complete; the madness based in a terrible error had gone unchecked. British Intelligence had intruded, and that intrusion might well have cost Helden her life.

But *why?* Why here in an obscure French village? He had no answers. He knew only that this man whose throat he now clutched was his enemy, as dangerous to him as the Rache or the ODESSA.

"Get *up!*" Holcroft struggled to his feet and pulled at the man. His mistake was in momentarily releasing the agent. Without warning, a paralyzing blow hammered into his stomach. His eyes spun out of focus, and for several moments he was aware only of being yanked through a sea of astonished faces. Suddenly he was slammed against the wall of a building; he could *hear* the impact of his head on the hard surface.

"You goddamn fool! What the devil do you think you're doing? You were nearly killed back there!"

The MI-Five man did not scream, but he might as well have, so intense was his tone. Noel focused his eyes; the agent had him pinned. The man's forearm was again pressed against his throat.

"You son of a bitch!" He could barely whisper the words. "You're the ones who tried to kill me. . . ."

"You're a certifiable lunatic, Holcroft! The Tinamou wouldn't *touch* you. I've got to get you out of here."

"The Tinamou? Here?"

"Let's go!"

"*No!* Where's Helden?"

"Certainly not with us! Do you think we're crazy?"

Noel stared at the man; he was telling the truth. It was all insane. "Then someone's taken her! She's gone!"

"If she's gone, she went willingly," said the agent. "We tried to warn you. Leave it alone!"

"No, you're wrong! There was a man—with pockmarks on his face . . ."

"The Fiat?"

"Yes! Him. He was following us. I went after him and his men caught me. They tried to kill me!"

"Come with me," ordered the agent, grabbing Holcroft's arm and propelling him down the sidewalk.

They reached a dark narrow alleyway between two buildings. No ray of sunlight penetrated; everything was in shadow. The alley was lined with garbage cans. Beyond the third garbage can on the right, Noel could see a pair of legs. The rest of the figure was hidden by the receptacle.

The agent pushed Noel into the alley; four or five steps were all that were needed to get a clear view of the upper part of the body.

At first glance, the man with the pockmarked face appeared to be drunk. In his hand he clutched a bottle of red wine; it had spilled into the crotch of his trousers. But it was a different red from the stain that had spread over his chest.

The man had been shot.

"There's your killer," said the agent. "Now will you listen to us? Go back to New York. Tell us what you know and leave it alone."

Noel's mind churned; mists of confusion enveloped him. There was violent death in the skies, death in New York, death in Rio, death here in a small French village. The Rache, the ODESSA, the survivors of Wolfsschanze. . . .

Nothing is as it was for you. . . .

He turned to the MI-Five man, his voice no more than a whisper. "Don't you understand? I *can't*. . . ."

There was a sudden skirmish at the end of the alleyway. Two figures raced by, one propelling the other. Commands were shouted—gutteral, harsh, the words not distinguishable but the violence clear. Cries for help were cut short by the sound of flesh against flesh, vicious slaps repeated again and again. And then the blurred figures were gone, but Holcroft could hear the scream.

"Noel! *Noel!* . . ."

It was Helden! Holcroft found his mind again and knew what he had to do. With all his strength, he slammed his shoulder into the side of the agent, sending him crashing over the garbage can that concealed the dead body of the man with the pockmarked face.

He ran out of the alley.

21

The screams continued, how far away he could not tell, so boisterous were the crowds in the village square. Music issued from a number of concertinas and cornets. Pockets of space were formed for couples, skipping, twirling, turning, in countryside dances. The *fête d'hiver* was now a carnival.

"*Noel! Noel.* . . ."

Up the curving sidewalk to the left of the square—the cries came from that direction! Holcroft ran wildly, colliding with a pair of lovers embracing against a wall. *There.*

"*Noel!*"

He was on a side street lined with three-story buildings. He raced down it, hearing the scream again, but no words, no name, only a scream cut short by the impact of a blow that produced a cry of pain.

Oh, *God,* he had to find—

A *door!* A door was partially open; it was the entrance to the fourth building on the right. The scream had come from there!

He ran to it, remembering as he drew near that he had a gun in his pocket. He reached in and pulled it out, thinking as he held it awkwardly in his hand that he had never really looked at the weapon. He did so now, and for an instant he stopped and stared at it.

He knew little about handguns, but he knew this one. It was a Budischowsky TP-$_{70}$ Autoloading Pistol, the same type of gun Sam Buonoventura had lent him in Costa Rica. The coincidence gave him no confidence; rather, it made him sick. This was not his world.

He checked the safety and pulled the door open, staying out of sight. Inside was a long, narrow, dimly lit corridor. On the left wall, spaced perhaps twelve feet from each other, were two doors. From what he remembered of this type of structure he had to presume that there were identically spaced doors on the right wall; he could not see them from where he stood.

He darted into the entrance, the gun held steady in front of him. There were the two doors on the right wall. Four doors. Behind one of them Helden was a captive. But which one? He walked to the first door on the left and put his ear to it.

There was a scratching sound, erratic, unfamiliar. He had no idea what it was. Cloth, fabric . . . the tearing of cloth? He put his hand on the knob and twisted it; the door swung free and he opened it, his weapon in firing position.

Across the dark room was an old woman on her knees, scrubbing the floor. She was in profile, her gaunt features sagging, her arm working in circles on the soft wood. She was so old she neither saw him nor heard him. He closed the door.

A black ribbon was nailed to the door on the right. A death had taken place behind that door; a family was in mourning. A death behind *that* door. The thought was too unnerving; he listened.

This was it! A struggle was going on. Heavy breathing, movement, tension; inside that room there was desperation. Helden was behind that door!

Noel stepped back, his automatic leveled, his right foot raised. He took a deep breath, and, as if his foot were a battering ram, he drove it into the wood to the left of the knob. The force of the blow sent the door crashing inward.

Inside, on a filthy bed, were two naked teenagers, a dark-haired boy on top of a fat, fair-skinned girl, the girl's legs spread up toward the ceiling, the boy lying between them, both hands on her breasts. At the sound of the crash and the sight of the stranger, the girl screamed. The boy spun off her, rolling onto the floor, his mouth open in shock.

The crash! The sound of the crash was an alarm. Holcroft ran into the corridor and raced to the next door on the left. There was no time to be concerned about anything but finding Helden. He slammed his shoulder into the door, twisting the knob awkwardly with his left hand, his right gripping the handle of the gun. There was no need for force; the door gave way.

Noel stood in the door frame, for an instant feeling ashamed. Against the wall by a window was a blind man. He was an old man and he was trembling at the unseen, unknown violence that had invaded his dark privacy.

"*Nom de Dieu . . .*" he whispered, holding his hands in front of him.

The sound of racing footsteps came from the hallway, footsteps that grew louder—the sound of a man not simply running but running frantically, leather slapping against wood. Holcroft turned quickly, in time to see the figure of the MI-Five agent rush past. There was a crash of glass from somewhere outside. Noel lurched out of the blind man's room, looking to the left, where the crash had come from; there was sunlight streaming through an open door at the end of the corridor. Its panes of glass had been painted black; he had not seen it in the dim light.

How did the agent know a door was there? Why had he kicked it open and raced outside? Did the MI-Five man think *he* had gone out that way? Instinct told him the agent would not give him that much credit; he was an amateur, a lunatic. No, he was after someone else.

It could be only Helden! But Helden was behind the door across from the blind man's room; it was the only place left. It *had* to be. The agent was wrong!

Holcroft kicked the door in front of him; the lock broke, the door swung open, and he rushed inside.

It was empty, had been empty a very long time. Layers of dust were everywhere . . . and there were no footprints. No one had been inside that room for weeks.

The MI-Five man had been right. The amateur had not known something that the professional had perceived.

Noel ran out of the empty room, down the dark corridor, through the shattered door, and out into a courtyard. On the left was a heavy wooden door that led back to the side street. It was open, and Holcroft raced through it. He could hear sounds of the carnival from the square, but they were not the only sounds. Far down the deserted street to his right he could hear a scream, cut off now as it had been cut off before. He ran in the direction of the scream, in Helden's direction, but he could see no one.

"Get *back!*" The command came from a recessed doorway.

There was a gunshot; above him stone shattered and he could hear the sickening whine of a ricocheting bullet.

Noel threw himself to the ground, onto the hard, irregular surface of the cobblestones. As he broke his fall, his finger touched the trigger of his gun. It fired, the explosion next to his face. In panic, he rolled over and over toward the recessed doorway. Hands grabbed him, pulling his body into the shadows. The man from British Intelligence, the young man with the scar on his forehead, yanked him back against the stone entranceway.

"I repeat! You're a goddamned fool! I should kill you myself and save them the trouble." The agent was crouched against the wall; he inched his face to the edge.

"I don't *believe* you," said Noel. "I don't believe *any* of this. Where is she?"

"The bastard's holding her across the way, about twenty yards down. My guess is he's got a radio and has contacted a car."

"They're going to *kill* her!"

"Not now they won't. I don't know why, but that's not what they have in mind. Perhaps because she's his sister."

"Get off that! It's *wrong;* it's crazy! I told her; she reached him. He's no more this Tinamou than you are. And he's mad as hell. He'll probably write something for his paper, make you, the Foreign Office, the whole damned British government, look like assholes!"

The MI-Five agent stared at Holcroft. His look was that of a man studying the ravings of a psychopath, equal parts curiosity, revulsion, and astonishment. "He *what?* You what?"

"You heard me."

"My *God*. . . . Whoever you are, whatever you're involved with, you're not remotely connected with any of this."

"I told you that in London," said Noel, struggling to sit up, trying to find his breath again. "Did you think I was lying?"

"We knew you were lying; we just didn't know why. We thought you were being used by men wanting to reach Von Tiebolt."

"For what?"

"Make a blind contact, neither side exposing itself. It was a fair cover: money in America, left for the family."

"But for *what?*"

"Later! You want the girl, I want the bastard who's got her. Listen to me." The agent gestured at the automatic in Noel's hand. "Do you know how to use that?"

"I once had to use a gun like it. I'm no expert."

"You don't have to be; you'll have a large target. If I'm right, they've got a car cruising the area."

"Don't you?"

"No, I'm alone. Now listen to me. If a car drives up, it'll have to stop. The second it does I'm going to dash over to that doorway across the street. As I'm running, cover me by shooting directly at the car. Aim for the windscreen. Hit the tires, the radiator. I don't care what, but try to get the windscreen. Shoot it up; immobilize the damned car, if you can; and pray to God that the locals stay away at that fucking winging in the square."

"Suppose they don't, suppose someone—"

"Try not to hit him, you ass!" broke in the Englishman. "And keep your fire to the right side of the car. *Your* right. Expose yourself as little as possible."

"The *right* side of the car?"

"Yes, unless you want to hit the girl, which, frankly, I don't give a piss about. But I want *him*. Of course, if I'm wrong, none of this applies, and we'll have to think of something else."

The agent's face was pressed against the stone. He inched it forward, peering down the street. The unfamiliar forest belonged to such men, not to well-intentioned architects. "You weren't wrong back in that old building," Noel said. "You knew there was another way out."

"A second exit. No one worth his pecker would allow himself to be trapped inside."

Once more the professional was right. Noel could hear the screeching of tires; an automobile careened around an unseen corner and drew rapidly closer. The agent stood up, gesturing for Noel to follow. He looked around the edge of the entranceway, his forearm angled across his chest, his pistol in his hand.

There was a second screech of tires; the automobile came to a stop. The agent shouted at Holcroft as he leaped from the doorway, firing his pistol twice at the car, and raced across the street.

"*Now!*"

It was a brief nightmare, made intensely real by the shattering sounds and the frantic movement. Noel was actually *doing* it. He could see the automatic in front of him, at the end of *his* arm, being held in *his* hand. He could feel the vibrations that traveled through his body each time he squeezed the trigger. *The right side of the car. Your right. Unless—*He tried desperately to be accurate. Amazed, he saw the windshield shatter and crack; he heard bullets enter the door; he heard the screams of a human being . . . and then he saw that human being fall out of the door and onto the cobblestones beside the car. It was the driver; his arms were extended in front of him; blood poured out of his head and he did not move.

Across the street he could see the MI-Five man come out of a doorway, crouching, his pistol out in front of him. Then he heard the command:

"Release her! You can't get out!"

"*Nie und nimmer!*"

"Then she can go with you! I don't give a piss! . . . Spin to your right, miss! *Now!*"

Two explosions, one right after the other; a woman's scream echoed throughout the street. Noel's mind went wildly out of focus. He raced across the pavement, afraid to think, afraid to see what he might see, to find what he dared not find, for his own sanity.

Helden was on her knees, trembling, her breathing a series of uncontrollable sobs. She stared at the dead man, splayed on the pavement to her left. But she was *alive;* that was all he cared about. Noel ran to her and fell down beside her, pulling her shivering head into his chest.

"Him. . . . *Him,*" Helden whispered, pushing Noel away. "Quickly."

"What?" Noel followed her look.

The MI-Five agent was trying to crawl; his mouth opened and closed; he was trying to speak and no sound emerged. And over the front of his shirt was a spreading stain of red.

A small crowd had gathered at the entrance to the square. Three or four men stepped forward tentatively.

"Get him," said Helden. "Get him quickly."

She was capable of thinking and he was not; she was able to make a decision and he was immobile. "What are we going to do? Where are we going to go?" was all he could say, not even sure the words were his.

"These streets, the alleys. They connect. We have to get him away."

"*Why?*"

Helden's eyes bored into his. "He saved my life. He saved yours. *Quickly!*"

He could only do as he was ordered; he could not think for himself. He got to his feet and ran to the agent, bending over him, their faces inches apart. He saw the angry blue eyes that floated in their sockets, the mouth that struggled to say something but could not.

The man was dying.

Noel lifted the agent to his feet; the Englishman could not stand, so he picked him up, astonished at his own strength. He turned and saw Helden lurching toward the automobile at the curb; the motor was still running. Noel carried the agent over to the shot-up car.

"I'll drive," Helden said. "Put him in the back seat."

"The windshield! You can't see!"

"You can't carry him very far."

The next minutes were as unreal to Holcroft as the sight of the gun still in his hand. Helden made a swift U-turn, careening over the sidewalk, swerving out to the middle of the street. Sitting beside her, Noel realized something in spite of the panic. He realized it calmly, almost dispassionately: He was beginning to adjust to this terrible new world. His resistance was wearing down, confirmed by the fact that he *had* acted; he had *not* run away. People had tried to kill him. They had tried to kill the girl beside him. Perhaps that was enough.

"Can you find the church?" he asked, now amazed at his own control.

She looked at him briefly. "I think so. Why?"

"We couldn't drive this car even if you could see. We have to find ours." He gestured through the cracked glass of the windshield; steam was billowing from the hood. "The radiator was punctured. Find the church."

She did, mostly by instinct, driving up the narrow streets and alleys that connected the irregular spokes that spread out from the village square. The last few blocks were frightening. People were running beside the car, shouting excitedly. For several moments Noel thought it was the shattered windshield, riddled with bullet holes, that drew the villagers' attention; it was not. Figures rushed by toward the hub of the square; the word had spread.

Des gens assassinées! La tuerie!

Helden swung into the street that passed the church rectory and fronted the entrance to the parking lot. She turned in and drove up beside the rented car. Holcroft looked in the rear seat. The MI-Five man was angled back in the corner, still breathing, his eyes on Noel. He moved his hand, as if to draw Noel closer.

"We're switching cars," said Holcroft. "We'll get you to a doctor."

"Listen . . . to me first, you ass," whispered the Englishman. His eyes strayed to Helden. "Tell him."

"Listen to him, Noel," she said.

"What is it?"

"Payton-Jones—you have the number?"

Holcroft remembered. The name on the card given him by the middle-aged, gray-haired intelligence agent in London was Harold Payton-Jones. He nodded. "Yes."

"Call him. . . ." The MI-Five man coughed. "Tell him what happened . . . everything."

"You can tell him yourself," said Noel.

"You're a piss ant. Tell Payton-Jones there's a complication we don't know about. The man we thought was sent by the Tinamou, Von Tiebolt's man . . ."

"My brother's *not* the Tinamou," cried Helden.

The agent looked at her through half-closed lids. "Maybe you're right, miss. I didn't think so before, but you may be. I only know that the man who followed you in the Fiat works for Von Tiebolt."

"He followed us to protect us! To find out who was after Noel."

Holcroft spun in the seat and stared at Helden. "You know about him?"

"Yes," she replied. "Our lunch today was Johann's idea."

"Thanks a lot."

"Please. You don't understand these things. My brother does. I do."

"Helden, I tried to trap that man! He was killed!"

"What? Oh, my *God* . . ."

"That's the complication," whispered the agent, speaking to Noel. "If Von Tiebolt's not the Tinamou, what is he? Why was his man shot? Those two men, why did they try to take *her?* Kill *you?* Who were they? This car . . . trace it." The Englishman gasped; Noel reached over the seat but the agent waved him away. "Just listen. Find out who they were, who owns this car. They're the complication."

The MI-Five man was barely able to keep his eyes open now; his whisper could hardly be heard. It was obvious that he would die in moments. Noel leaned over the seat.

"Would the complication have anything to do with a man named Peter Baldwin?"

It was as though an electric shock had jolted the dying man. His eyelids sprang open; the pupils beneath came briefly back from death. *"Baldwin?* . . ." The whisper echoed and was eerily plaintive.

"He called me in New York," said Holcroft. "He told me not to do what I was doing, not to get involved. He said he knew things that no one else knew. He was killed an hour later."

"He was telling the *truth!* Baldwin was telling the truth!" The agent's lips began to tremble; a trickle of blood emerged from the corner of his mouth. "We never believed him; he was trading off *nothing!* We were sure he was *lying.* . . ."

"Lying about what?"

The MI-Five man stared at Noel; then, with effort, shifted his gaze to Helden. "There isn't time. . . ." He struggled pathetically to look again at Holcroft. "You're clean. You must be . . . you wouldn't have said what you just said. I'm going to trust you, both of you. Reach Payton-Jones . . . as fast as you can. Tell him to go back to the Baldwin file. Code Wolfsschanze. . . . It's Wolfsschanze."

The agent's head fell forward. He was dead.

22

They sped north on the Paris highway as the late-afternoon sun washed the countryside with rays of orange and cold yellow. The winter sun was the same everywhere: It was a constant. And Holcroft was grateful for it.

Code Wolfsschanze. It's Wolfsschanze.

Peter Baldwin had known about Geneva. He had tried to tell MI Five, but the doubters in British Intelligence had not believed him.

He was trading off nothing!

What was he trading *for?* What was the bargain he sought? Who *was* Peter Baldwin?

Who *had been* Peter Baldwin?

Who was Von Tiebolt . . . Tennyson?

If Von Tiebolt's not the Tinamou, what is he? Why was his man shot? Why did they try to take her? Kill you?

Why?

At least one problem was put to rest: John Tennyson was *not* the Tinamou. Whatever else the son of Wilhelm von Tiebolt was—and it might well be dangerous to Geneva—he was not the assassin. But then, who was he? What had he done to become involved with killers? Why were men after him—and, by extension, his sister?

The questions kept Noel's mind from dwelling on the last hours. He could not think about them; he would explode if he did. Four men killed—one by him. Killed by gunfire in the back street of a remote French village during a carnival. Madness.

"What do you think 'Wolfsschanze' stands for?" asked Helden.

"I know what it stands for," he said.

She turned, surprised.

He told her—everything he knew about the survivors of Wolfsschanze. There was no point in concealing facts now. When he had finished, she was silent. He wondered if he had pushed her too far. Into a conflict she wanted no part of. She had said to him only a few days ago that if he did not do as she instructed, if he was not who he said he was, she would leave Paris and he would never find her. Would she do that now? Was the threat of Wolfsschanze the final burden she could not accept?

"Are you afraid?" he asked.

"That's a foolish question."

"I think you know what I mean."

"Yes." She leaned her head back on the seat. "You want to know if I'll run away."

"I guess that's it. Will you?"

She did not reply for several moments; nor did he press her. When she spoke, there was the echoing sadness in her voice—so like her sister's and yet so different. "I can't run away any more than you can. Morality and fear aside, it's simply not practical, is it? They'd find us. They'd kill us."

"That's pretty final."

"It's realistic. Besides, I'm tired of running. I have no energy left for it. The Rache, the ODESSA, now Wolfsschanze. Three hunters who stalk each other as well as us. It's got to end. Herr Oberst is right about that."

"I came to the same conclusion yesterday afternoon. It occurred to me that if it weren't for my mother, I'd be running with you."

"Heinrich Clausen's son," said Helen reflectively.

"And someone else's." He returned her look. "Do we agree? We don't get in touch with this Payton-Jones?"

"We agree."

"MI Five'll look for us. They have no choice. They had a man on us; they'll find out he was killed. There'll be questions."

"Which we can't answer. We were followed; we did not follow."

"I wonder who they were? The two men," he said.

"The Rache, I would think. It's their style."

"Or the ODESSA."

"Possibly. But the German spoken by the one who took me was odd. The dialect wasn't recognizable. He was not a Münchner, and certainly not a Berliner. It was strange."

"How do you mean?"

"It was very gutteral, but still soft, if that makes sense."

"Not too much. Then you think they were from the Rache?"

"Does it matter? We've got to protect ourselves from both. Nothing has changed. At least, not for me." She reached over and touched his arm. "I'm sorry for you, though."

"Why?"

"Because now you are running with us. You're one of the children now—*die verwünschten Kinder*. The damned. And you've had no training."

"It seems to me I'm getting it in a hurry."

She withdrew her hand. "You should go to Berlin."

"I know. We've got to move quickly. Kessler has to be reached and brought in; he's the last of the"—Holcroft paused—"the issue."

She smiled sadly at the word. "There's you and my brother; you're both knowledgeable, both ready to move. Kessler must be made ready, too. . . . Zürich is the issue. And the solution to so much."

Noel glanced at her. It did not take much to perceive what she was thinking. Zürich meant resources beyond imagination; surely a part of them would be used to curb, if not eliminate, the fanatics of the ODESSA and the Rache. Holcroft knew that she knew he had witnessed their horrors for himself; a one-third vote was hers for the asking. Her brother would agree.

"We'll make Zürich work," he said. "You can stop running soon. We can all stop."

She looked at him pensively. Then she moved over on the seat next to him and put her hand through his arm and held it. She laid her head on his shoulder, her long blond hair falling over his jacket.

"I called for you and you came to me," she said in her odd, floating voice. "We nearly died this afternoon. A man gave his life for us."

"He was a professional," replied Noel. "Our lives may have been incidental to him. He was after information, after a man he thought could give it to him."

"I know that. I've seen such men before, such professionals. But at the last, he was decent; many aren't. They sacrifice others too easily in the name of professionalism."

"What do you mean?"

"You're not trained; you would have done as he told you. You could have been used for bait, to draw fire. It would have been easier for him to let you take the bullets, and then me. I wasn't important to him. In the confusion he might have saved his own life and gotten his man. But he saved us."

"Where shall we go in Paris?"

"Not Paris," said Helden. "Argenteuil. There's a small hotel on the river. It's lovely."

Noel raised his left hand from the wheel and let it fall on the hair that cascaded down his jacket. "You're lovely," he said.

"I'm frightened. The fear has to go away."

"Argenteuil?" he mused. "A small hotel in Argenteuil. You seem to know a lot of places for someone who's been in France for only a few months."

"You have to know where they don't ask questions. You're taught quickly; you learn quickly. Take the Billancourt exit. Please hurry."

Their room overlooked the Seine, with a small balcony beyond the glass doors directly above the river. They stood for a few minutes in the night air, his arm around her, both of them looking down at the dark waters. Neither spoke; comfort was in their touch.

There was a knock on the door. Helden tensed; he smiled and reassured her.

"Relax. While you were washing up I ordered a bottle of brandy."

She returned his smile and breathed again. "You should really let me do that. Your French is quite impossible."

"I can say 'Remy Martin,'" he said, releasing her. "Where I went to school it was the first thing we learned." He went inside toward the door.

Holcroft took the tray from the waiter and stood for a moment watching Helden. She had closed the doors to the balcony and was staring out the windows at the night sky. She was a private woman, a lonely woman, and she was reaching out to him. He understood that.

He wished he understood other things. She was beautiful; it was the simple truth, and needed no elaboration. Nor could she be unaware of that beauty. She was highly intelligent, again an attribute so obvious no further comment was necessary. And beyond that intelligence she was familiar with the ways of her shadow world. She was street-smart in a larger sense, in an international sense; she moved swiftly, decisively. There had to have been dozens of times when she used sex to get an advantage, but he suspected it was used in cold calculation: Buyer beware, there is nothing but a body for you to take; my thoughts are mine; you'll share none of them.

She turned from the glass doors; her eyes were soft, her expression warm and yet still distant, still observing. "You look like an impatient maître d' waiting to escort me to my table."

"Right this way, mademoiselle," said Noel, carrying the tray to the small bureau across the room and placing it on top. "Would the lady care for a table by the water?" He moved a small chaise in front of the glass doors and faced her, smiling and bowing. "If the lady would care to be seated, brandy will be served, and the fireworks will begin. The torchbearers on the boats await only your presence."

"But where will you sit, my attractive *garçon?*"

"At your feet, lady." He leaned over and kissed her, holding her shoulders, wondering if she would withdraw or push him away.

Whatever he expected, he was not prepared for what happened. Her lips were soft and moist, parted as if swollen, moving against his, inviting him into her mouth. She reached up with both her hands and cupped his face, her fingers gently caressing his cheeks, his eyelids, his temples. Still her lips kept moving, revolving in desperate circles, pulling him into her. They stood together. He could feel her breasts pressed against his shirt, her legs against his, pushing into him, matching strength for strength, arousing him.

Then a strange thing happened. She began to tremble; her fingers crept around his neck and dug into his flesh, holding him fiercely, as if she were afraid he might move away. He could hear the sobs that came from her throat, feel the convulsions that gripped her. He moved his hands to her waist and gently pulled his face from hers, forcing her to look at him.

She was crying. She stared at him for a moment; pain was in her eyes, a hurt so deep Noel felt he was an intruder watching a private agony.

"What is it? What's the matter?"

"Make the fear go away," she whispered plaintively. She reached for the buttons on her blouse and undid them, exposing the swell of her breasts. "I can't be alone. Please, make it go *away.*"

He pulled her to him, cradling her head against his chest, her hair beneath his face soft and lovely, as she was soft and lovely.

"You're not alone, Helden. Neither am I."

They were naked beneath the covers, his arm around her, her head on his chest. With his free hand, he kept lifting the strands of her long blond hair, letting them fall to cover her face.

"I can't see when you do that," she said, laughing.

"You look like a sheep dog."

"Are you my shepherd?"

"I have a staff."

"That's dreadful. You have a dirty mouth." She reached up with her index finger and tapped his lips. He caught her finger between his teeth and growled. "You can't frighten me," she whispered, raising her face above his, depressing his tongue playfully. "You're a cowardly lion. You make noises, but you won't bite."

He took her hand. "Cowardly lion? *The Wizard of Oz?*"

"Of course," she answered. "I loved *The Wizard of Oz.* I saw it dozens of times in Rio. It's where I began to learn English. I wanted so to be called Dorothy. I even named my little dog Toto."

"It's hard to think of you as a little girl."

"I was, you know. I didn't spring full flower. . . ." She stopped and laughed. She had raised herself above him; her breasts were in front of his face. His hand instinctively reached for the left nipple. She moaned and covered his hand, holding it where it was as she lowered herself back down on his chest. "Anyway, I *was* a little girl. There were times when I was very happy."

"When?"

"When I was alone. I always had a room to myself; mother made sure of that. It was always in the back of the house or the apartment; or, if we were in a hotel, it was separate, away from my brother and sister. Mother said I was the youngest and should not be disturbed by the hours they kept."

"I imagine that could get pretty lonely. . . ."

"Oh, *no!* Because I was *never* alone. My friends were in my mind, and they would sit in chairs and on my bed and we'd talk. We would talk for hours, telling each other our secrets."

"What about school? Didn't you have flesh-and-blood friends?"

Helden was silent for a moment. "A few, not many. As I look back, I can't blame them. We were all children. We did as our parents told us to do. Those of us who had a parent left."

"What did the parents tell them?"

"That I was a Von Tiebolt. The little girl with the silly first name. My mother was . . . well, my mother. I think they thought my stigma was contagious."

She may have been branded with a stigma, thought Noel, but her mother was not the cause of it. Maurice Graff's Odessa had more important things on its mind. Millions upon millions siphoned off their beloved Reich to be used by traitors such as Von Tiebolt for a massive apology.

"Things got better when you grew up, didn't they?"

"Better? Certainly. You adjust, you mature, you understand attitudes you didn't as a child."

"More friends?"

"Closer ones, perhaps, not necessarily more. I was a poor mixer. I was used to being by myself; I understood why I was not included at parties and dinners. At least, not in the so-called respectable households. The years curtailed my mother's social activities, shall we say, but not her business interests. She was a shark; we were avoided by our own kind. And of course the Germans were never really accepted by the rest of Rio, not during those years."

"Why not? The war was over."

"But not the embarrassments. The Germans were a constant source of embarrassment then. Illegal monies, war criminals, Israeli hunters . . . it went on for years."

"You're such a beautiful woman, it's difficult to think of you . . . let's say, isolated."

Helden raised herself and looked at him. She smiled, and with her right hand pushed her hair back, holding it at the base of her neck. "I was very stern-looking, my darling. Hair straight, wrapped in a bun, large glasses and dresses always a size too large. You wouldn't have looked at me twice. . . . Don't you believe me?"

"I wasn't thinking about that."

"What then?"

"You just called me 'my darling.' "

She held his eyes. "Yes, I did, didn't I? It seemed quite natural. Do you mind?"

He reached for her, his answer his touch.

She sat back on the chaise, her slip serving as a negligee; she sipped the brandy. Noel was on the floor beside her, leaning against the small couch, his shorts and open shirt taking the place of a bathrobe. They held hands and watched the lights of the boats shimmering on the water.

He turned his head and looked at her. "Feeling better?"

"Much better, my darling. You're a very gentle man. I haven't known many in my life."

"Spare me."

"Oh, I don't mean that. For your information, I'm known among Herr Oberst's ranks as *Fräulein Eiszapfen.*"

"What's that?"

" 'Icicle.' 'Mademoiselle Icicle.' At work, they're convinced I'm a lesbian."

"Send them to me."

"I'd rather not."

"I'll tell them you're a faggot in drag who uses whips and bicycle chains. They'll run at the sight of you."

"That's very sweet." She kissed him. "You're warm and gentle and you laugh easily. I'm terribly fond of you, Noel Holcroft, and I'm not sure that's such a good thing."

"Why?"

"Because we'll say good-bye and I'll think of you."

Noel reached up and held the hand that still touched his face; he was suddenly alarmed. "We just said hello. Why good-bye?"

"You have things to do. I have things to do."

"We both have Zürich."

"*You* have Zürich. I have my life in Paris."

"They're not mutually exclusive."

"You don't know that, my darling. You don't know anything about me. Where I live, how I live."

"I know about a little girl who had a room to herself and saw *The Wizard of Oz* dozens of times."

"Think kindly of her. She will of you. Always."

Holcroft took her hand from his face. "What the hell are you trying to say? Thanks for a lovely evening, now good-bye?"

"No, my darling. Not like that. Not now."

"Then what *are* you saying?"

"I'm not sure. Perhaps I'm just thinking out loud. . . . We have days, weeks, if you wish them."

"I wish them."

"But promise me you'll never try to find where I live, never try to reach me. I'll find you."

"You're married!"

Helden laughed. "No."

"Then, living with someone."

"Yes, but not in the way you think."

Noel watched her closely. "What am I supposed to say to that?"

"Say that you'll promise."

"Let me understand you. Outside of where you work, there's no place I can reach you. I can't know where you live, or how to get in touch with you?"

"I'll leave a number of a friend. In an emergency she'll reach me."

"I thought I was a friend."

"You are. But in a different way. Please, don't be angry. It's for your own protection."

Holcroft remembered three nights ago. In the midst of her own anxieties, Helden had been worried about him, worried that he had been sent by the wrong people. "You said in the car that Zürich was the solution to so much. Is it the answer for you? Could Zürich change the way you live?"

She hesitated. "It's possible. There's so much to do. . . ."

"And so little time," completed Holcroft. He touched her cheek, forcing her to look at him. "But before the money's released, there's the bank in Geneva and specific conditions that have to be met."

"I understand. You've explained them, and I'm sure Johann knows about them."

"I'm not so sure. He's laid himself open to a lot of speculation that could knock him out of the box."

"Knock him where?"

"Disqualify him. Frighten the men in Geneva; make them close the vaults. We'll get to him in a minute. I want to talk about Beaumont. I think I know what he is, but I need your help to confirm it."

"How can I help?"

"When Beaumont was in Rio, did he have any connection with Maurice Graff?"

"I have no idea."

"Can we find out? Are there people in Rio who would know?"

"Not that I know."

"God damn it, we've got to learn. Learn everything we can about him."

Helden frowned. "That will be difficult."

"Why?"

"Three years ago, when Gretchen said she was going to marry Beaumont, I was shocked; I told you that. I was working at the time for a small research firm off Leicester Square—you know, one of those dreadful places that you send five pounds to and they get you all the information you want on a subject. Or a person. They're superficial, but they do know how to use sources." Helden paused.

"You checked on Beaumont?" asked Noel.

"I tried to. I didn't know what I was looking for, but I tried. I went back to his university records, got all the available information about his naval career. Everything was filled with approvals and recommendations, awards and advancements. Why, I can't tell you—except that there seemed to me to be an inconsistency. I went farther back to find out what I could about his family in Scotland."

"What was the inconsistency?"

"Well, according to the naval records, his parents were quite ordinary. I got the impression they were rather poor. Owners of a green-grocery or a florist shop in a town called Dunheath, south of Aberdeen, on the North Sea. Yet, when he was at university—Cambridge, by the way—he was a regular student."

"Regular? . . . What should he have been?"

"On scholarship, I would think. There was need, and he was qualified, yet there were no applications for a scholarship. It seemed odd."

"So you went back to the family in Scotland. What did you learn?"

"That's the point. Next to nothing. It was as if they had disappeared. There was no address, no way to reach them. I sent off several inquiries to the town clerk and the postal service—obvious places people never think of. The Beaumonts were apparently an English family who simply arrived in Scotland one day shortly after the war, stayed for a few years, then left the country."

"Could they have died?"

"Not according to the records. The navy always keeps them up to date in case of injury or loss of life. They were still listed as living in Dunheath, but they had left. The postal service had no information at all."

It was Holcroft's turn to frown. "That sounds crazy."

"There's something more." Helden pushed herself up against the curve of the chaise. "At Gretchen's wedding, there was an officer from Beaumont's ship. His second-in-command, I think. The man was a year or two younger than Beaumont, and obviously his subordinate, but there was a give-and-take between them that went beyond friendship, beyond that of officer to officer."

"What do you mean, 'give-and-take'?"

"It was as if they were always thinking exactly alike. One would start a sentence, the other might finish it. One would turn in a particular direction, the other would comment on what the first was looking at. Do you know what I mean? Haven't you seen people like that? Men like that?"

"Sure. Brothers who are close, or lovers. And often military men who've served a long time together. What did you do?"

"I checked on that man. I used the same sources, sent out the same inquiries, as I had with Beaumont. What came back was extraordinary. They *were* alike; only the names were different. Their academic and military records were almost identical, superior in every way. They both came from obscure towns, their parents undistinguished and certainly not well off. Yet each had gone to a major university without financial aid. And each had become an officer without any prior indication that he was seeking a military career."

"What about the family of Beaumont's friend? Were you able to locate them?"

"No. They were listed as living in a mining town in Wales, but they weren't. They hadn't been there in years, and no one had any information about them."

What Helden had learned was consistent with Noel's theory that Anthony Beaumont was an ODESSA agent. What was important now was to take Beaumont—and any "associates"—out of the picture. They could not be allowed to interfere further with Geneva. Perhaps he and Helden were wrong: Perhaps they should reach Payton-Jones and let Beaumont become his problem. But there were side issues to consider, among which was the danger of British Intelligence's reopening the Peter Baldwin file, going back to Code Wolfsschanze.

"What you've told me fits in with what I've been thinking," Noel said. "Let's go back to your brother. I have an idea what happened in Rio. Will you talk about it now?"

Helden's eyes widened. "I don't know what you mean."

"Your brother learned something in Rio, didn't he? He found out about Graff and the Brazilian ODESSA. That was why he was hounded, why he had to get out. It wasn't your mother, or your brother's business dealings, or anything like that. It was Graff and the ODESSA."

Helden slowly let out her breath. "I never heard that, believe me."

"Then what was it? Tell me, Helden."

Her eyes pleaded with him. "Please, Noel. I owe you so much; don't make me pay like this. What happened to Johann in Rio has nothing to do with you. Or with Geneva."

"You don't know that. I don't know that. I just know that you have to tell me. I have to be prepared. There's so much I don't understand." He gripped her hand. "Listen to me. This afternoon I broke into a blind man's room. I smashed the door in; the sound was awful—sudden and loud. He was an old man and, of course, he couldn't see me. He couldn't see the fear in my own eyes. His hands shook and he whispered a prayer in French. . . .

"For a moment I wanted to go to that man and hold his hands and tell him I knew how he felt. You see, he *didn't* see the fear in my eyes. I'm frightened,

Helden. I'm not the sort of person who crashes into people's rooms, and shoots guns, and gets shot at. I can't turn back, but I'm scared. So you've got to help me."

"I want to; you know that."

"Then tell me what happened in Rio. What happened to your brother?"

"It's simply not important," she said.

"*Everything's* important." Noel stood up and crossed to the chair where he had thrown his jacket. He showed Helden the torn lining. "Look at this. Someone in that crowd this afternoon tried to put a knife in me. I don't know about you, but that's never happened to me before; it's just not something I know anything about. It petrifies me . . . and it makes me goddamned angry. And five days ago in New York, the man I grew up with—the only man I ever called my father—walked out on a sidewalk and was killed by an 'out-of-control car' that *aimed* for him and crushed him against a building! His death was a warning. For *me!* So don't talk to me about the Rache, or the ODESSA, or the men of Wolfsschanze. I'm beginning to learn all about those sick sons of bitches, and I want every last one of them put away! With the money in Zürich, we can do that. Without it, no one'll listen to us. It's an economic fact of life. You don't dismiss people who have seven hundred and eighty million dollars. You *listen* to people like that." Holcroft let the jacket fall to the floor. "The only way we'll get to Zürich is to satisfy the bank in Geneva, and the only way to reach Geneva is to use our heads. There's no one really on our side; there's just us. The Von Tiebolts, the Kesslers . . . and one Clausen. Now, what happened in Rio?"

Helden looked down at the torn jacket, then back at Noel.

"Johann killed someone."

"Who?"

"I don't know—I really don't. But it was someone important."

23

Holcroft listened to her, watching for false notes. There were none. She was telling him what she knew, and it was not a great deal.

"About six weeks before we left Brazil," Helden explained, "I drove home one night after a seminar at the university; we lived out in the countryside then. There was a dark-colored limousine in front, so I parked behind it. As I walked up to the porch, I heard yelling from inside. There was a terrible fight and I couldn't imagine who it was; I didn't recognize the one screaming. He kept yelling things like 'killer,' 'murderer,' 'it was you' . . . things like that. I ran inside and found

Johann standing in the hallway in front of the man. He saw me, and told the man to be still. The man tried to strike Johann, but my brother is very powerful; he held the man's arms and pushed him out the door. The last words the man screamed were to the effect that others also knew; that they would see Johann hanged as a murderer, and if that didn't happen, they'd kill him themselves. He fell on the steps, still screaming, then he ran to the limousine, and Johann went after him. He said something to him through the window; the man spat in my brother's face and drove off."

"Did you ask your brother about it?"

"Naturally. But Johann wouldn't discuss it other than to say the man was mad. He had lost a great deal of money in a business venture and had gone crazy."

"You didn't believe him?"

"I wanted to, but then the meetings began. Johann would be out until all hours, away for days; he behaved quite abnormally. Then, only weeks later, we flew to Recife with a new name and a new country. Whoever was killed was very rich, very powerful. He had to be to have friends like that."

"You have no idea who the man was inside your house that night?"

"No. I'd seen him before, but I couldn't remember where, and Johann wouldn't tell me. He ordered me never to bring up the matter again. There were things I should not be told."

"You accepted that?"

"Yes. Try to understand. We were children of Nazis, and we knew what that meant. It was often best not to ask questions."

"But you had to know what was going on."

"Oh, we were taught; make no mistake about it," said Helden. "We were trained to elude the Israelis; they could force information from us. We learned to spot a recruiter from the ODESSA, a maniac from the Rache; how to get away, how to use a hundred different tricks to throw them off."

Noel shook his head in amazement. "Your everyday training for the high-school glee club. It's crazy."

"That's a word you could use three weeks ago," she said, reaching for his hand. "Not now. Not after today."

"What do you mean?"

"In the car I said I felt sorry for you because you had no training."

"And I said I thought I was getting it in a hurry."

"But so little, and so late. Johann told me to teach you what I could. I want you to listen to me, Noel. Try to remember everything I tell you."

"What?" Holcroft felt the strength of her grip and saw the concern in her eyes.

"You're going to Berlin. I want you back."

With those words she began. There were moments when Noel thought he might smile—or, worse, laugh—but her intensity kept him in check; she was deadly serious. That afternoon four men had been killed. He and Helden might easily have been the fifth and the sixth victims. So he listened and tried to remember. Everything.

"There's no time to get false papers; they take days. You have money; buy an extra seat on the plane. Stay alert, and don't let anyone sit next to you; don't get hemmed in. And don't eat or drink anything you didn't bring with you."

His mind briefly raced back to a British 747 and a vial of strychnine. "That's a suggestion I won't forget."

"You might. It's so easy to ask for coffee or even a glass of water. Don't."

"I won't. What happens when I get to Berlin?"

"To any city," she corrected. "Find a small hotel in a crowded district where the main business is pornography, where there's prostitution, narcotics. Front desks never ask for identification in those areas. I know someone who'll give us the name of a hotel in Berlin. . . ."

Her words poured forth, describing tactics, defining methods, telling him how to invent his own variations. . . .

False names were to be used, rooms switched daily, hotels changed twice a week. Phone calls were to be placed from public booths, never from hotel rooms, never from residences. A minimum of three changes of outer clothing, including hats and caps and dissimilar glasses, were to be carried; shoes were to have rubber soles. These were best for running with a minimum of sound, for stopping and starting quickly, and walking silently. If questioned, he was to lie indignantly but not arrogantly, and never in a loud tone of voice. That kind of anger triggered hostility, and hostility meant delay and further questions. While flying from airport to airport, a gun was to be dismantled, its barrel separated from the handle, the firing pin removed. These procedures generally satisfied the European customs clerks: Inoperable weapons did not concern them; contraband did. But if they objected, he was to let them confiscate the gun; another could be purchased. If they let the weapon through, he was to reassemble it immediately, in the toilet stall of a men's room.

The street. . . . He knew something about the streets and crowds, he told Helden. One never knew enough, she replied, telling him to walk as close to the curb as possible, to be ready to dash out among the traffic at any sign of hostility or surveillance.

"Remember," she said, "you're the amateur, they're the professionals. Use that position; turn your liability into an asset. The amateur does the unexpected, not because he's clever or experienced but because he doesn't know any better. Do the unexpected rapidly, obviously, as if confused. Then stop and wait. A confrontation is often the last thing surveillance wants. But if he does want it, you might as well know it. Shoot. You should have a silencer; we'll get you one in the morning. I know where."

He turned, stunned, unable to speak. She saw the astonishment in his eyes. "I'm sorry," she said, leaning forward, smiling sadly and kissing him.

They talked through most of the night, the teacher and the pupil, lover and lover. Helden was obsessed; she would invent situations and then demand that he tell her what he would do in the hypothetical circumstances.

"You're on a train, walking through a narrow corridor; you're carrying important papers. A man comes toward you from the opposite direction; you know him; he's the enemy. There are people behind you; you can't go back. What do you do?"

"Does the man—the enemy—want to hurt me?"

"You don't know. What do you do? Quickly!"

"Keep going, I guess. Alert, expecting the worst."

"No, my darling! The *papers*. You've got to protect them! You trip; you fall to the floor!"

"Why?"

"You'll draw attention to yourself; people will help you up. The enemy won't make his move in that situation. You create your own diversion."

"With *myself,*" said Noel, seeing the point.

"Exactly."

It went on, and on, and on, until the teacher and the pupil were exhausted. They made quiet love and held each other in the comfort of their warmth, the world outside a faraway thing. Finally, Helden fell asleep, her head on his chest, her hair covering her face.

He lay awake for a while, his arm across her shoulders, and wondered how a girl who'd been entranced by *The Wizard of Oz* had grown up to become so skilled a practitioner in arts of deception and escape. She was from another world, and he had entered that world with alarming speed.

They awoke too late for Helden to go to work.

"It's just as well," she said, reaching for the phone. "We have shopping to do. My supervisor will accept a second day of illness. I think she's in love with me."

"I think I am too," said Noel, letting his fingers trace the curve of her neck. "Where do you live?"

She looked at him, smiling as she gave the number to the operator. Then she covered the mouthpiece. "You'll not extract vital information by appealing to my basic instincts. I'm trained, remember?" She smiled again.

And was maddening again. "I'm serious. Where do you *live?*"

The smile disappeared. "I can't tell you." She removed her hand from the telephone and spoke rapidly in French to the Gallimard switchboard.

An hour later they drove into Paris, first stopping at his hotel, to pick up his things, then moving on to a district profuse with second-hand-clothing stores. The teacher once more asserted her authority; she chose the garments with a practiced eye. The clothes she selected for the pupil were nondescript, difficult to spot in a crowd.

A mackinaw and a brown topcoat were added to his raincoat. A battered country walking hat; a dark fedora, its crown battered; a black cap whose visor fell free of the snap. All were well worn. But not the shoes; they were new. One pair with thick crêpe soles; a second, less informal, whose leather soles were the base for a layer of rubber attached by a shoemaker down the street.

The shoe-repair shop was four blocks away from a shabby storefront. Helden went in alone, instructing him to remain outside. She emerged ten minutes later with a perforated cylinder, the silencer for his automatic.

He was being outfitted with uniforms and the proper weapon. He was being processed and sent into combat after the shortest period of basic training one could imagine. He had seen the enemy. Alive and following him . . . and then dead in the streets and alleyways of a village called Montereau-faut-Yonne. Where was the enemy now?

Helden was confident they had lost him for a while. She thought the enemy might pick him up at the airport, but once in Berlin, he could lose that enemy again.

He *had* to. She wanted him back; she would be waiting.

They stopped at a small café for lunch and wine. Helden made a final phone call and returned to the booth with the name of a hotel in Berlin. It was in the *Hurenviertel,* that section of the city where sex was an open commodity.

She held his hand, her face next to his; in minutes he would go out on the street alone and hail a taxi for Orly Airport.

"Be careful, my darling."

"I will."

"Remember the things I've told you. They may help."

"I'll remember."

"The hardest thing to accept is that it's all real. You'll find yourself wondering, why me? why this? Don't think about it; just accept it."

Nothing is as it was for you. Nothing can ever be the same.

"I have. I've also found you."

She glanced away, then turned back to him. "When you get to Berlin, near the hotel, pick up a whore in the street. It's a good protective device. Keep her with you until you make contact with Kessler."

The Air France 707 made its final approach into Tempelhof Airport. Noel sat on the right side of the plane, in the third seat on the aisle, the space next to him unoccupied.

You have money; buy an extra seat . . . and don't let anyone sit next to you; don't get hemmed in.

The ways of survival, spoken by a survivor, thought Holcroft. And then he remembered that his mother had called herself a survivor. Althene had taken a certain pride in the term, her voice four thousand miles away, over the telephone.

She had told him she was taking a trip. It was her way of going into hiding for several weeks, the methods of evasion and concealment learned more than thirty years ago. God, she *was* incredible! Noel wondered where she would go, what she would do. He would call Sam Buonoventura, in Curaçao, in a few days. Sam might have heard from her by then.

The customs inspection at Tempelhof was swift. Holcroft walked into the terminal, found the men's room, and reassembled his gun.

As instructed, he took a taxi to the *Tiergarten* park. Inside the cab, he opened his suitcase, changed into the worn brown topcoat and the battered walking hat. The car stopped; he paid the fare, got out, and walked into the park, sidestepping strollers, until he found an empty bench, and sat down. He scanned the crowds; no one stopped or hesitated. He got up quickly and headed for an exit. There was a taxi stand nearby; he stood in line, glancing around unobtrusively to see if he could spot the enemy. It was difficult now to single out anything or anyone specifically; the late-afternoon shadows were becoming longer and darker.

His turn came. He gave the driver the names of two intersecting streets. The intersection was three blocks north and four blocks west of the hotel. The driver grinned and spoke in thickly accented but perfectly understandable English.

"You wish a little fun? I have friends, *Herr Amerikaner.* No risk of the French sickness."

"You've got me wrong. I'm doing sociological research."

"*Wie?*"

"I'm meeting my wife."

They drove in silence through the streets of Berlin. With each turn they made, Noel watched for a car somewhere behind them that made the same turn. A few did, but none for any length of time. He recalled Helden's words: *They often use radios. Such a simple thing as a change of coat or the wearing of a hat will throw them off. Those receiving instructions will look for a man in a jacket and no hat, but he is not there.*

Were there unseen men watching for a certain taxi and a certain passenger wearing certain clothing? He would never know; he knew only that no one appeared to be following him now.

During the twenty-odd minutes it took to reach the intersection, night had come. The streets were lined with gaudy neon signs and suggestive posters. Young fair-haired cowboys coexisted with whores in slit skirts and low-cut blouses. It was another sort of carnival, thought Holcroft, as he walked south for the prescribed three blocks, toward the corner where he would turn left.

He saw a prostitute in a doorway, applying lipstick to her generous mouth. She was in that indeterminate age bracket so defiantly obscured by whores and chic suburban housewives—somewhere between thirty-five and forty-eight, and losing the fight. Her hair was jet black, framing her pallid white skin, her eyes deep, hollowed with shadows. Beyond, on the next block, he could see the shabby hotel's marquee, one letter shorted out in its neon sign.

He approached her, not entirely sure what to say. His lacking German was not his only impediment: He had never picked up a whore in the streets.

He cleared his throat. "Good evening, Fräulein? Can you speak English?"

The woman returned his look, coolly at first, appraising his cloth topcoat. Then her eyes dropped to the suitcase in his right hand, the attaché case in his left. She parted her lips and smiled; the teeth were yellow. *"Ja mein* American friend. I speak good. I show you a good time."

"I'd like that. How much?"

"Twenty-five deutsche marks."

"I'd say the negotiations are concluded. Will you come with me?" Holcroft took his money clip from his pocket, peeled off three bills, and handed them to the woman. "Thirty deutsche marks. Let's go to that hotel down the street."

"Wohin?"

Noel gestured at the hotel in the next block. "There," he said.

"Gut," said the woman, taking his arm.

The room was like any room in a cheap hotel in a large city. If there was a single positive feature, it was to be found in the naked light bulb in the ceiling. It was so dim it obscured the stained, broken furniture.

"Dreissig Minuten," announced the whore, removing her coat and draping it over a chair with a certain military élan. "You have one half hour, no more. I am, as you Americans say, a businessman. My time is valuable."

"I'm sure it is," said Holcroft. "Take a rest or read something. We'll leave in fifteen or twenty minutes. You'll stay with me and help me make a phone call." He opened the attaché case and found the paper with the information on Erich Kessler. There was a chair against the wall; he sat down and started to read in the dim light.

"Ein Telefonanruf?" said the woman. "You pay thirty marks for me to do nothing for you but help you *mit dem Telefon?"*

"That's right."

"That is . . . *verrückt!"*

"I don't speak German. I may have trouble reaching the person I've got to call."

"Why do we wait here, then? There is *Telefon* by the corner."

"For appearances, I guess."

The whore smiled. "I am your *Deckung."*

"What?"

"You take me up to a room, no one asks questions."

"I wouldn't say that," replied Noel uneasily.

"It's not my business, mein Herr." She came over to his chair. "But as long as we're here . . . why not have a little fun? You paid. I'm not so bad. I once looked better, but I'm not so bad."

Holcroft returned her smile. "You're not so bad at all. But no thanks. I've got a lot on my mind."

"Then you do your work," said the whore.

Noel read the information given to him by Ernst Manfredi a lifetime ago in Geneva.

Erich Kessler, Professor of History, Free University of Berlin. Dahlen district.

Speaks fluent English. Contacts: University telephone—731-426. Residence—824-114. Brother named Hans, a doctor. Lives in Munich. . . .

There followed a brief summary of Kessler's academic career, the degrees obtained, the honors conferred. They were overwhelming. The professor was a learned man, and learned men often were skeptics. How would Kessler react to the call from an unknown American who traveled to Berlin without prior communication to see him about a matter he would not discuss over the telephone?

It was nearly six-thirty, time to find out the answer. And to change clothes. He got up, went to his suitcase, and took out the mackinaw and the visored cap. "Let's go," Noel said.

The prostitute stood by the phone booth while Holcroft dialed. He wanted her nearby in case someone other than Kessler answered, someone who did not speak English.

The line was busy. All around he could hear the sounds of the German language—emphatic conversations as couples and roving packs of pleasure seekers passed the telephone booth.

He wondered. If his mother had been anyone but Althene, would he be one of those outside the glass booth right now? Not where he was right *now*, but somewhere in Berlin, or Bremerhaven, or Munich? Noel Clausen. German.

What *would* his life have been like? It was an eerie feeling. Fascinating, repulsive . . . and obsessive. As if he had gone back in time, through the layers of his personal mist, and found a fork in a fog-bound road he might have taken but did not. That fork was reexamined now; where would it have led?

Helden? Would he have known her in that other life? He knew her now. And he knew that he wanted to get back to her as soon as he could; he wanted to see her again, and hold her again, and tell her that . . . *things* . . . were going to be all right. He wanted to see her laugh and have a life in which three changes of outer clothing and guns with silencers were not crucial to survival. Where the Rache and the ODESSA were no longer threats to sanity and existence.

A man answered the telephone, the voice deep and soft.

"Mr. Kessler? Doctor Kessler?"

"I shan't cure any diseases, sir," came the pleasant reply in English, "but the title is correct, if abused. What can I do for you?"

"My name is Holcroft. Noel Holcroft. I'm from New York. I'm an architect."

"Holcroft? I have a number of American friends and, of course, university people with whom I correspond, but I don't recognize the name."

"No reason for you to; you don't know me. However, I have come to Berlin to see you. There's a confidential matter to discuss that concerns the two of us."

"Confidential?"

"Let's say . . . a family matter."

"Hans? Did something happen to Hans?"

"No. . . ."

"I have no other family, Mr. Holcroft."

"It goes back a number of years. I'm afraid I can't say more over the telephone. Please, trust me; it's urgent. Could you possibly meet me tonight?"

"Tonight?" Kessler paused. "Did you arrive in Berlin today?"

"Late this afternoon."

"And you want to see me tonight. . . . This matter must, indeed, be urgent. I have to return to my office for an hour or so this evening. Would nine o'clock be satisfactory?"

"Yes," said Noel, relieved. "Very satisfactory. Anyplace you say."

"I'd ask you to my house, but I'm afraid I have guests. There's a *Lokal* on the Kurfürstendamm. It's often crowded, but they have quiet booths in the back and the manager knows me."

"It sounds perfect."

Kessler gave him the name and address. "Ask for my table."

"I will. And thanks very much."

"You're quite welcome. I should warn you: I keep telling the manager that the food is grand. It isn't, really, but he's such a pleasant fellow and good to the students. See you at nine o'clock."

"I'll be there. Thanks again." Holcroft put the phone back in its cradle, swept by a sudden feeling of confidence. If the man matched the voice over the telephone, Erich Kessler was intelligent, humorous, immensely likable. What a relief!

Noel hung up and smiled at the woman. "Thanks," he said, giving her an additional ten marks.

"Auf wiedersehen." The whore turned and walked off. Holcroft watched her for a moment, but his attention was suddenly drawn to a man in a black leather jacket halfway down the short block. He stood in front of a bookstore, but he was not interested in the pornography displayed in the window. Instead, he was staring directly at Noel. As their eyes met, the man turned away.

Was he one of the enemy? A fanatic from the Rache? A maniac of the ODESSA? Or perhaps someone assigned to him from the ranks of Wolfsschanze? He had to find out.

A confrontation is often the last thing surveillance wants. But if he does want it, you might as well know it. . . .

Helden's words. He would try to remember the tactics; he would use them now. He felt the bulges in the cloth of his mackinaw; weapon and silencer were there. He pulled the visor of his cap free of its snap, gripped the handle of his attaché case, and walked away from the man in the black leather jacket.

He hurried down the street, staying close to the curb, prepared to race out into the traffic. He reached the corner and turned right, walking swiftly into a crowd of spectators watching two life-size plastic manikins performing the sex act on a black bearskin rug. Holcroft was jostled; his attaché case was crushed against his leg, then pulled, as if being yanked aside by a victim of its sharp corners. . . . Yanked, pulled—*taken;* his attaché case could be taken, the papers inside read by those who should never read them. He had not been totally stupid; he had removed Heinrich Clausen's letter and the more informative sections of the Geneva document. No figures, no sources, only the bank's letterhead and the names—meaningless legal gibberish to an ordinary thief, but something else entirely to the extraordinary one.

Helden had warned him about carrying even these, but he had countered with the possibility that the unknown Erich Kessler might think him a madman, and he needed fragments, at least, to substantiate his incredible story.

But now, if he *was* being followed, he had to leave the case in a place where it would not be stolen. Where? Certainly not at the hotel. A locker in a train station or bus depot? Unacceptable, because both were accessible; such places would be child's play for the experienced thief.

Besides, he needed those papers—those fragments—for Erich Kessler. Kessler. The *"Lokal." The manager there knows me. Ask for my table.*

The pub on the Kurfürstendamm. Going there now would serve two purposes: On the way, he could see if he was actually being followed; once there, he could either stay or leave his case with the manager.

He pushed his way into the street, looking for an empty taxi, glancing behind him for signs of surveillance—for a man in a black leather jacket. There was a cab in the middle of the block. He ran toward it.

As he entered, he spun around quickly. And he saw the man in the black leather jacket. He was not walking now. Instead, he was in the saddle of a small motorbike, propelling it along the curb with his left foot. There were a number of other bikes in the street, cruising in and out between the traffic.

The man in the black leather jacket stopped pushing his machine, turned away, and pretended to be talking with someone on the sidewalk. The pretense was too obvious; there was no one responding to his conversation. Noel climbed in the cab and gave the name and address of the pub. They drove off.

So did the man in the black leather jacket. Noel watched him through the rear window. Like the man in the green Fiat in Paris, this Berliner was an expert. He stayed several car lengths behind the taxi, swerving quickly at odd moments to make sure the object of his surveillance was still there.

It was pointless to keep watching. Holcroft settled back in the seat and tried to figure out his next move.

A confrontation is often the last thing surveillance wants. . . . If he does . . . you might as well know it.

Did he want to know it? Was he prepared for confrontation? The answers were not easy. He was not someone who cared to test his courage deliberately. But in the forefront of his imagination was the sight of Richard Holcroft crushed into a building on a sidewalk in New York.

Fear provided caution; rage provided strength. The single answer was clear. He wanted the man in the black leather jacket. And he would get him.

24

He paid the driver and got out of the cab, making sure he could be seen by the man on the motorbike, who had stopped down the block.

Noel walked casually across the pavement to the pub and went inside. He stood on a platformed staircase and studied the restaurant. The ceilings were high, the dining area on a lower floor. The place was half full; layers of smoke were suspended in the air, and the pungent smell of aromatic beer drifted up the staircase. From the speaker system, Bavarian *Biermusik* could be heard. The wooden tables were placed in ranks throughout the central area. The furnishings were heavy, massive.

He saw the booths Kessler had described. They were along the rear wall and the sides: tables flanked by high-backed seats. Running across the fronts of the booths were brass rods holding red-checked curtains. Each booth could be isolated from its surroundings by drawing a curtain across the table, but with the curtains open one could sit at almost any booth and observe whoever came through the door at the top of the staircase.

Holcroft descended the stairs to a lectern at the bottom and spoke to a heavyset man behind it. "Pardon me, do you speak English?"

The man looked up from the reservation book in front of him. "Is there a restaurateur in Berlin who doesn't, sir?"

Noel smiled. "Good. I'm looking for the manager."

"You've found him. What can I do for you? Do you wish a table?"

"I think one's been reserved. The name is Kessler."

The manager's eyes showed immediate recognition. "Oh, yes. He called not fifteen minutes ago. But the reservation was for nine o'clock. It is only—"

"I know," interrupted Holcroft. "I'm early. You see, I've got a favor to ask." He held up the attaché case. "I brought this for Professor Kessler. Some historical papers lent him by the university in America where I teach. I have to meet some people for an hour or so, and wondered if I could leave it here."

"Of course," said the manager. He held out his hand for the case.

"You understand, these are valuable. Not in terms of money, just academically."

"I'll lock them in my office."

"Thank you very much."

"*Bitte schön.* Your name, sir?"

"Holcroft."

"Thank you, Herr Holcroft. Your table will be ready at nine o'clock." The manager nodded, turned, and carried the attaché case toward a closed door under the staircase.

Noel stood for a moment considering what to do next. No one had entered since he had arrived. That meant the man in the leather jacket was outside, waiting for him. It was time to bait the trap, time to corner that man.

He started up the staircase, suddenly struck by a thought that made him sick. He had just done the most stupid thing he could think of! He had led the man in the black leather jacket directly to the spot where he was making contact with Erich Kessler. And to compound that enormous mistake, he had given his own name to the manager.

Kessler and *Holcroft. Holcroft* and *Kessler.* They were tied together. He had revealed an unknown third of Geneva! Revealed it as clearly as if he had taken out a newspaper ad.

It was no longer a question of whether he was capable of setting the trap. He *had* to do it. He had to immobilize the man in the black leather jacket.

He pushed open the door and walked on to the sidewalk. The Kurfürstendamm was lit up. The air was cold, and in the sky above, the moon was circled by a rim of mist. He started walking to his right, his hands in his pockets to ward off the chill. He passed the motorbike at the curb and continued to the corner. Ahead, perhaps three blocks away, on the left side of the Kurfürstendamm, he could see the outlines of the enormous Kaiser Wilhelm Church, floodlights illuminating the never-to-be-repaired, bombed-out tower, Berlin's reminder to itself of Hitler's Reich. He would use the church as his landmark.

He continued walking along the tree-lined pavement, slower than most of the strollers around him, stopping frequently in front of store windows. He checked his watch at regular intervals, hoping to give the impression that the minutes were important, that perhaps he was pacing himself to reach a rendezvous at a specific time.

Directly opposite the Kaiser Wilhelm Church, he stood for a while at the curb, under the glare of a streetlight. He glanced to his left. Thirty yards away the man in the black leather jacket turned around, his back to Holcroft, watching the flow of traffic.

He was there; that was all that mattered.

Noel started up again, his step faster now. He came to another corner and looked up at the street sign: SCHÖNBERGSTRASSE. It angled off the Kurfürstendamm and was lined with shops on both sides. The sidewalks seemed more crowded, the strollers less hurried than those on the Kurfürstendamm.

He waited for a break in the traffic and crossed the street. He turned right on the sidewalk, staying close to the curb, excusing himself through the strollers. He reached the end of the block, crossed over into the next, and slowed his walk. He stopped, as he had stopped on the Kurfürstendamm, to gaze into the store-front windows, and he checked his watch with growing concentration.

He saw the man in the leather jacket twice.

Noel proceeded into the third block. No more than fifty feet from the corner there was a narrow alley, a thoroughfare between the Schönbergstrasse and a parallel street about a hundred yards away. The alley was dark and dotted along its sides with shadowed doorways. The darkness and the length were uninviting, obvious deterrents for pedestrians during the evening hours.

But this alley, at this time, was the trapping ground, an unlit stretch of concrete and brick into which he'd lead the man who followed him.

He continued walking down the block, past the alley, toward the corner, his pace quickening with every stride, Helden's words resounding in his ears.

The amateur does the unexpected, not because he's clever or experienced but because he doesn't know any better. . . . Do the unexpected rapidly, obviously, as if confused. . . .

He reached the end of the block and stopped abruptly under a streetlight. As if startled, he looked around, pivoting on the sidewalk, a man undecided but one who knew a decision must be made. He stared back toward the alleyway and suddenly broke into a run, colliding with pedestrians, entering the alley—a man in panic.

He ran until the darkness was nearly full, until he was at midpoint in the alley, shadows upon shadows, the lights at either end distant. There was a delivery entrance of some sort—a wide metal door. He lunged toward it, spinning into the corner, his back pressed against steel and brick. He put his hand into his jacket pocket and gripped the handle of the automatic. The silencer was not attached; it was not necessary. He had no intention whatsoever of firing the weapon. It was to be but a visible threat and, at first, not even that.

The wait was not long. He could hear racing footsteps and thought as he heard them that the enemy, too, knew about rubber-soled shoes.

The man ran by; then, as if sensing a trick, he slowed down, looking about in the shadows. Noel stepped out of his hidden corner, his hand in his jacket pocket.

"I've been waiting for you. Stay right where you are." He spoke intensely, frightened at his own words. "I've got a gun in my hand. I don't *want* to use it, but I will if you try to run."

"You did not hesitate two days ago in France," said the man in a thick accent, his calm unnerving. "Why should I expect you to stop now? You're a pig. You can kill me, but we will stop you."

"Who are you?"

"Does it matter? Just know that we will stop you."

"You're with the Rache, aren't you?"

In spite of the darkness, Noel could see an expression of contempt on the man's face. "The Rache?" he said. "Terrorists without a cause, revolutionaries no one wants in his camp. Butchers. I'm no part of the Rache!"

"The Odessa, then."

"You'd like that, wouldn't you."

"What do you mean?"

"You'll use the Odessa when the time comes. It can be blamed for so much. You can kill so easily in its name. I suppose the irony is that we'd kill the Odessa as quickly as you would. But you're the ones we want; we know the difference between clowns and monsters. Believe me, we'll stop you."

"You're not making sense! You're not part of Wolfsschanze; you couldn't be!"

The man lowered his voice. "But we are all part of Wolfsschanze, aren't we? In one way or another," he said, a challenge in his eyes. "I say it again. You can kill me, but another will take my place. Kill him, another his. We *will* stop you. So shoot, Herr Clausen. Or should I say, son of Reichsführer Heinrich Clausen."

"What the hell are you talking about? I don't want to kill you. I don't want to kill anybody!"

"You killed in France."

"If I killed a man, it was because he tried to kill me."

"*Aber natürlich,* Herr Clausen."

"Stop calling me that."

"Why? It's your name, isn't it?"

"No! My name is Holcroft."

"Of course," said the man. "That was part of the plan. The respected American with no discernible ties to his past. And if anyone traced them, it would be too late."

"Too late for what? Who *are* you? Who sent you?"

"There is no way you can force that from me. We are not part of your plan."

Holcroft took the gun from his pocket and stepped closer. "What plan?" he asked, hoping to learn something, *anything.*

"Geneva."

"What about Geneva? It's a city in Switzerland."

"We know everything, and it's finished. You won't stop the eagles. Not this time. We will stop *you!*"

"*Eagles? What* eagles! Who's 'we'?"

"Never. Pull the trigger. I won't tell you. You won't trace us."

Noel was perspiring, though the winter night was cold. Nothing this enemy said made sense. It was possible that an enormous error had been made. The man in front of him was prepared to die, but he was not a fanatic; there was too much intelligence behind the eyes. "Not with the Rache, not with the ODESSA. For God's sake, why do you want to stop Geneva? Wolfsschanze doesn't want to stop it; you must know that!"

"Not *your* Wolfsschanze. But we can put that fortune to great use."

"No! If you interfere, there won't be anything. You'll never get the money."

"We both know that doesn't have to be."

"You're wrong! It'll go back into the ground for another thirty years."

The unknown enemy drew himself up in the shadows. "That's the flaw, isn't it? You put it so well: 'back into the ground.' But, if I may be permitted, there'll be no scorched earth then."

"No what?"

"No scorched earth." The man stepped backward. "We've talked enough. You had your chance; you have it still. You can kill me, but it will do you no good. We have the photograph. We're beginning to understand."

"The *photograph?* In Portsmouth? *You?*"

"A most respected commander in the Royal Navy. It was interesting that you should take it."

"For Christ's sake! Who *are* you?"

"One who fights you, son of Heinrich Clausen."

"I told you—"

"I know," said the German. "I should not say that. In point of fact, I shall say nothing further. I will turn around and walk out of this alleyway. Shoot, if you must. I am prepared. We are all prepared."

The man turned slowly and began walking. It was more than Noel could stand.

"Stop!" he yelled, pursuing the German. Then grabbing his shoulder with his left hand.

The man spun around. "We have nothing further to say."

"Yes, we do! We're going to stay here all night, if we have to! You're going to tell me who you are and where you came from and what the hell you know about Geneva and Beaumont and—"

It was as far as he got. The man's hand shot out, his fingers clasping Noel's right wrist, twisting it inward and downward as his right knee hammered up into Holcroft's groin. Noel doubled forward in agony, but he would not let go of the gun. He shoved his shoulder into the man's midsection, trying to push him away, the pain in his testicles spreading up into his stomach and chest. The man brought his fist crashing down into the base of Holcroft's skull, sending shock waves through his ribs and spine. But he would not relinquish the gun! The man could not have the gun! Noel gripped it as if it were the last steel clamp on a lifeboat. He lurched up, springing with what strength he had left in his legs, wrenching the automatic away from the man's grip.

There was an explosion; it echoed through the alley. The man's arm fell away, and he staggered backward, grabbing his shoulder. He had been wounded, but he did not collapse. Instead, he braced himself against the wall and spoke through gasps of breath.

"We'll stop you. And we'll do it our way. We'll take Geneva!"

With those words he propelled himself down the alley, clawing at the wall for support. Holcroft turned; there were figures clustered about the alley's entrance on the Schönbergstrasse. He could hear police whistles and see the coruscating beams of flashlights. The Berlin police were moving in.

He was caught.

But he could *not* be caught! There was Kessler; there was Geneva. He could not be detained now!

Helden's words came back to him. *Lie indignantly . . . with confidence . . . invent your own variations.*

Noel shoved the automatic in his pocket and started toward the Schönbergstrasse, toward the slowly approaching flashlights and the two uniformed men who held them.

"I'm an American!" he yelled in a frightened voice. "Does anyone speak English?"

A man from the crowd shouted, "I do! What happened?"

"I was walking through here and someone tried to rob me! He had a gun but I didn't know it! I shoved him and it went off. . . ."

The Berliner translated quickly for the police.

"Where did he go?" asked the man.

"I think he's still there. In one of the doorways. I've got to sit down. . . ."

The Berliner touched Holcroft's shoulder. "Come." He began leading Noel out through the crowd toward the sidewalk.

The police yelled into the dark alleyway. There was no response; the unknown enemy had made his escape. The uniformed men cautiously continued forward.

"Thanks very much," said Noel. "I'd just like to get some air, calm down, you know what I mean?"

"*Ja.* A terrible experience."

"I think they've got him," added Holcroft suddenly, looking back toward the police and the crowd.

The Berliner turned; Noel stepped off the curb, into the street. He started walking, slowly at first, then found a break in the traffic and crossed to the sidewalk on the other side. There he turned and ran as fast as he could through the crowds, toward the Kurfürstendamm.

He had done it, thought Holcroft, as he sat, coatless and hatless, shivering on a deserted bench within sight of the Kaiser Wilhelm Church. He had absorbed the lessons and put them to use; he had invented his own variations and eluded the trap he had set for another, but which had sprung back, ensnaring himself. Beyond this, he had immobilized the man in the black leather jacket. That man would be detained, if only to find a doctor.

Above all, he had learned that Helden was wrong. And the dead Manfredi— who would not say the names—had been wrong. It was not members of the ODESSA, nor of the Rache, who were Geneva's most powerful enemies. It was another group, one infinitely more knowledgeable and deadlier. An enigma that counted among its adherents men who would die calmly, with intelligence in their eyes and reasonable speech on their tongues.

The race to Geneva was against three violent forces wanting to destroy the covenant, but one was far more ingenious than the other two. The man in the black leather jacket had spoken of the Rache and the ODESSA in terms so disparaging they could not have sprung from envy or fear. He had dismissed them as incompetent butchers and clowns of whom he wanted no part. For he was part of something else, something far superior.

Holcroft looked at his watch. He had been sitting in the cold for nearly an hour, the ache in his groin still there, the base of his skull stiff with pain. He had stuffed the mackinaw and the black-visored cap into a refuse bin several blocks away. They would have been too easy to spot if the Berlin police had an alarm out for him.

It was time to go now; there were no signs of the police, no signs of anyone interested in him. The cold air had done nothing for his pain, but it had helped clear his head, and until that had happened he dared not move. He could move now; he had to. It was almost nine o'clock. It was time to meet with Erich Kessler, the third key to Geneva.

25

The pub was now crowded, as he expected it would be, the layers of smoke thicker, the Bavarian music louder. The manager greeted him pleasantly, but his eyes betrayed his thoughts: Something had happened to this American within the last hour. Noel was embarrassed; he wondered if his face was scratched, or streaked with dirt.

"I'd like to wash up. I had a nasty fall."

"Certainly. Over there, sir." The manager pointed to the men's room. "Professor Kessler has arrived. He's waiting for you. I gave him your briefcase."

"Thanks again," said Holcroft, turning toward the door of the washroom.

He looked at his face in the mirror. There were no stains, no dirt, no blood. But there was something in his eyes, a look associated with pain and shock and exhaustion. And fear. That's what the manager had seen.

He ran the water in the basin until it was lukewarm, doused his face and combed his hair and wished he could take that look out of his eyes. Then he returned to the manager, who led him to a booth at the rear of the hall, farthest from the room's activity. The redchecked curtain was drawn across the table.

"Herr Professor?"

The curtain was pulled aside, revealing a man in his mid-forties with a large girth and a full face framed by a short beard and thick brown hair combed straight back over his head. It was a gentle face, the deep-set eyes alive, tinged with anticipation, even humor.

"Mister Holcroft?"

"Dr. Kessler?"

"Sit down, sit down." Kessler made a brief attempt to rise as he held out his hand; the contact between his stomach and the table prevented it. He laughed and looked at the pub's manager. "Next week! *Ja*, Rudi? Our diets."

"Ach, natürlich, Professor."

"This is my new friend from America. Mr. Holcroft."

"Yes, we met earlier."

"Of course you did. You gave me his briefcase." Kessler patted Noel's attaché case, next to him on the seat. "I'm drinking scotch. Join me, Mr. Holcroft?"

"Scotch'll be fine. Just ice."

The manager nodded and left. Noel settled back in the seat. Kessler exuded a kind of weary warmth; it was an expression of tolerance from an intellect constantly exposed to lesser minds but too kind to dwell on comparisons. Holcroft had known several men like that. Among them were his finest teachers. He was comfortable with Erich Kessler; it was a good way to begin.

"Thanks so much for seeing me. I've got a lot to tell you."

"Catch your breath first," said Kessler. "Have a drink. Calm down."

"What?"

"You've had a difficult time. It's written all over your face."

"It's that obvious?"

"I'd say you were that distraught, Mr. Holcroft."

"It's Noel. Please. We should get to know each other."

"A pleasant prospect, I'm sure. My name is Erich. It's a chilly night outside. Too cold to go without an overcoat. Yet you obviously arrived without one. There's no checkroom here."

"I *was* wearing one. I had to get rid of it. I'll explain."

"You don't have to."

"I'm afraid I do. I wish I didn't, but it's part of my story."

"I see. Ah, here's your scotch."

A waiter deposited the glass in front of Holcroft, then stepped back and drew the red-checked curtain across the booth.

"As I said, it's part of the story." Noel drank.

"Take your time. There's no hurry."

"You said you had guests at your house."

"A guest. A friend of my brother's, from München. He's a delightful fellow, but long-winded. A trait not unknown among doctors. You've rescued me for the evening."

"Won't your wife be upset?"

"I'm not married. I was, but I'm afraid university life was rather confining for her."

"I'm sorry."

"She's not. She married an acrobat. Can you imagine? From the academic groves to the rarefied heights of alternating trapezes. We're still good friends."

"I think it would be difficult not to be friendly with you."

"Oh, I'm a terror in the lecture rooms. A veritable lion."

"Who roars but can't bring himself to bite," said Noel.

"I beg your pardon?"

"Nothing. I was remembering a conversation I had last night. With someone else."

"Feeling better?"

"That's funny."

"What is?"

"That's what I said last night."

"With this someone else?" Kessler smiled again. "Your face seems more relaxed."

"If it was any more relaxed, it'd be draped over the table."

"Perhaps some food?"

"Not yet. I'd like to start; there's a great deal to tell you, and you're going to have a lot of questions."

"Then I shall listen carefully. Oh, I forgot. Your briefcase." The German reached beside him and lifted the attaché case to the top of the table.

Holcroft unlocked the case, but did not open it. "There are papers in here you'll want to study. They're not complete, but they'll serve as confirmation for some of the things I'm going to tell you."

"Confirmation? Are the things you say you must tell me so difficult to accept?"

"They may be," said Noel. He felt sorry for his good-natured scholar. The peaceful world he lived in was about to collapse around him. "What I'm going to say to you may interrupt your life, as it has mine. I don't think that can be avoided. At least, I couldn't avoid it, because I couldn't walk away from it. Part of the reason was selfish; there's a great deal of money involved that will come to me personally—as it will come to you. But there are other factors that are much more important than either you or me. I know that's true, because if it weren't, I'd have run away by now. But I won't run. I'm going to do what I've been asked to do because it's *right*. And because there are people I hate who want to stop me. They killed someone I loved very much. They tried to kill another." Holcroft stopped suddenly; he had not meant to go this far. The fear and the rage were coming together. He had lost control; he was talking too much. "I'm sorry. I could be reading a lot of things into all this that don't belong. I don't mean to frighten you."

Kessler put his hand on Noel's arm. "Frightening me isn't a concern. You're overwrought and exhausted, my friend. Apparently, terrible things have happened to you."

Holcroft drank several swallows of whiskey, trying to numb the pain in his groin and his neck. "I won't lie. They have. But I didn't want to start this way. It wasn't very bright."

Kessler removed his hand from Noel's arm. "Let me say something. I've known you less than five minutes, and I don't think being bright is relevant. You're obviously a highly intelligent man—a very honest one, too—and you've been under a great strain. Why not simply start at the beginning without worrying how it affects me?"

"Okay." Holcroft put his arms on the table, his hands around the glass of whiskey. "I'll begin by asking you if you've ever heard the names Von Tiebolt and . . . Clausen."

Kessler stared at Noel for a moment. "Yes," he said. "They go back many years—to when I was a child—but of course I've heard them. Clausen and Von Tiebolt. They were friends of my father's. I was very young, around ten or eleven. They came to our house frequently, if I recall, at the end of the war. I *do* remember Clausen; at least I think I do. He was a tall man and quite magnetic."

"Tell me about him."

"There's not much I can remember."

"Anything you can. *Please.*"

"Again, I'm not sure how to put it. Clausen dominated a room without making any effort to do so. When he spoke, everyone listened, yet I don't recall his ever raising his voice. He seemed to be a kind man, concerned for others, but extremely strong willed. I thought once—and remember, these were the thoughts of a child—that he was someone who had lived with much pain."

A man in agony had cried out to him. "What kind of pain?"

"I have no idea; it was only a child's impression. You would have to have seen his eyes to understand. No matter whom he looked at, young or old, important or not, he gave that person his full concentration. I do remember that; it was not a common trait in those days. In a way, I picture Clausen more clearly than I do my own father, and certainly more than Von Tiebolt. Why are you interested in him?"

"He was my father."

Kessler's mouth opened in astonishment. "You?" he whispered. "Clausen's *son?*"

Noel nodded. "My natural father, not the father I knew."

"Then your mother was . . ." Kessler stopped.

"Althene Clausen. Did you ever hear anyone speak of her?"

"Never by name, and never in Clausen's presence. Ever. She was spoken of in whispers. The woman who left the great man, the American enemy who fled the fatherland with their—You! You were the child she took from him!"

"Took *with* her, *kept* from him, is the way she puts it."

"She's still alive?"

"Very much so."

"It's all so incredible." Kessler shook his head. "After all these years, a man I remember so vividly. He was extraordinary."

"They were all extraordinary."

"Who?"

"The three of them. Clausen, Von Tiebolt, and Kessler. Tell me, do you know how your father died?"

"He killed himself. It was not unusual then. When the Reich collapsed, a lot of people did. For most of them it was easier that way."

"For some it was the only way."

"Nürnberg?"

"No, Geneva. To protect Geneva."

"I don't understand you."

"You will." Holcroft opened his attaché case, took out the pages he had clipped together, and gave them to Kessler. "There's a bank in Geneva that has an account that can be released for specific purposes only by the consent of three people. . . ."

As he had done twice before, Noel told the story of the massive theft of over thirty years ago. But with Kessler, he told it all. He did not, as he had done with Gretchen, withhold specific facts; nor did he tell the story in stages, as he had with Helden. He left out nothing.

". . . monies were intercepted from the occupied countries, from the sales of art objects and the looting of museums. Wehrmacht payrolls were rerouted, millions stolen from the Ministry of Armaments and the—I can't remember the name, it's in the letter—but from the industrial complex. Everything was banked in Switzerland, in Geneva, with the help of a man named Manfredi."

"Manfredi? I remember the name."

"It's not surprising," said Holcroft. "Although I don't imagine he was mentioned too frequently. Where did you hear it?"

"I don't know. After the war, I think."

"From your mother?"

"I don't think so. She died in July of 'forty-five and was in the hospital for most of the time. From someone else . . . I don't know."

"Where did you live, with your father and mother dead?"

"My brother and I moved in with our uncle, my mother's brother. It was lucky for us. He was an older man and never had much use for the Nazis. He found favor with the occupation forces. But please, go on."

Noel did. He detailed the conditions of competence required by the directors of La Grande Banque de Genève, which led him into the dismissal of Gretchen Beaumont. He told Kessler of the Von Tiebolts' clouded migration to Rio, the birth of Helden, the killing of their mother, and their eventual flight from Brazil.

"They took the name of Tennyson and have been living in England for the past five years. Johann von Tiebolt is known as John Tennyson. He's a reporter for the *Guardian.* Gretchen married a man named Beaumont and Helden moved several months ago to Paris. I haven't met the brother, but I've . . . become friends with Helden. She's a remarkable girl."

"Is she the 'someone else' you were with last night?"

"Yes," replied Holcroft. "I want to tell you about her, what she's gone through, what she's going through now. She and thousands like her are part of the story."

"I think I may know," said Kessler. *"Die Verwünschte Kinder."*

"The what?"

"The *Verwünschten Kinder. Verwünschung* is German for a curse. Or one damned."

"The Children of the Damned," said Noel. "She used the expression."

"It's a term they gave themselves. Thousands of young people—not so young now—who fled the country because they convinced themselves they couldn't live with the guilt of Nazi Germany. They rejected everything German, sought new identities, new life-styles. They're very much like those hordes of young Americans who left the United States for Canada and Sweden in protest against the Vietnam policies. These groups form subcultures, but none can really reject their roots. They *are* German; they *are* American. They migrate in packs and cling together, taking strength from the very pasts they've rejected. The proddings of guilt are a heavy burden. Can you understand?"

"Not really," said Holcroft. "But then, I'm not built that way. I'm not going to take on a guilt that isn't mine."

Kessler looked into Noel's eyes. "I submit you may have. You say you won't run from this covenant of yours, yet terrible things have happened to you."

Holcroft considered the scholar's words. "There may be some truth in that, but the circumstances are different. I didn't *leave* anything. I guess I was selected."

"Not part of the damned," said Kessler, "but part of the chosen?"

"Privileged, anyway."

The scholar nodded. "There's a word for that, too. Perhaps you've heard of it. *Sonnenkinder.*"

"*Sonnenkinder?*" Noel frowned. "If I remember, it was in one of those courses I didn't exactly shine in. Anthropology, maybe."

"Or philosophy," suggested Kessler. "It's a philosophical concept developed by Thomas J. Perry, in England in the nineteen-twenties, and before him by Bachofen, in Switzerland, and by his disciples in München. The theory being that the *Sonnenkinder*—the Children of the Sun—have been with us throughout the ages. They're the shapers of history, the most brilliant among us, rulers of epochs . . . the privileged."

Holcroft nodded. "I remember now. They were ruined by that privilege of theirs. They became depraved, or something. Incestuous, I think."

"It's only a theory," said Kessler. "We're straying again; you're an easy man to talk to. You were saying about this Von Tiebolt daughter that life is difficult for her."

"For all of them. And more than difficult. It's crazy. They're running all the time. They have to live like fugitives."

"They're easy prey for fanatics," agreed Erich.

"Like the ODESSA and the Rache?"

"Yes. Such organizations can't function efficiently within Germany itself; they're not tolerated. So they operate in other countries where disaffected expatriates such as the *Verwünschten Kinder* have gravitated. They want only to stay alive and vital, waiting for the chance to return to Germany."

"Return?"

Kessler held up his hand. "Please God, they never will, but they can't accept that. The Rache once wanted the Bonn government to be an arm of the Comintern, but even Moscow rejected them; they've become nothing more than terrorists. The ODESSA have always wanted to revive Nazism. They're scorned in Germany."

"Still, they go after the children," said Noel. "Helden used the phrase 'damned for what they were, damned for what they weren't.' "

"An apt judgment."

"They should be stopped. Some of that money in Geneva should be used to cripple the ODESSA and the Rache."

"I wouldn't disagree with you."

"I'm glad to hear that," said Holcroft. "Let's get back to Geneva."

"By all means."

Noel had covered the objectives of the covenant and defined the conditions demanded of the inheritors. It was time to concentrate on what had happened to *him*.

He began with the murder on the plane, the terror in New York, the rearranged apartment, the letter from the men of Wolfsschanze, the telephone call from Peter Baldwin and the subsequent brutal killings it engendered. He spoke of the flight to Rio and a man with thick eyebrows: Anthony Beaumont, ODESSA agent. He told of the doctored records at Rio's Department of Immigration and the strange meeting with Maurice Graff. He emphasized MI Five's intrusion in London and the astonishing news that British Intelligence believed Johann von Tiebolt was the assassin they called the Tinamou.

"The *Tinamou?*" broke in Kessler, stunned, his face flushed. It was his first interruption of Holcroft's narrative.

"Yes. You know something about him?"

"Only what I've read."

"I gather some people think he's been responsible for dozens of assassinations."

"And the British think it's Johann von Tiebolt?"

"They're wrong," said Noel. "I'm certain they know it now. Something happened yesterday afternoon that proves it. You'll understand when I come to it."

"Go on."

He touched briefly on the evening with Gretchen, the photograph of Anthony Beaumont. He went on to Helden and Herr Oberst, then to the death of Richard Holcroft. He described the calls between himself and a detective in New York named Miles, as well as conversations with his mother.

He told of the green Fiat that had followed them to Barbizon, and the man with the pockmarked face.

Then came the madness of the *fête d'hiver.* How he had tried to trap the man in the Fiat and had himself nearly been killed.

"I told you a few minutes ago the British were wrong about Tennyson," Noel said.

"Tennyson? Oh, the name Von Tiebolt assumed."

"That's right. MI Five was convinced that everything that happened in Montereau, including the man with the pockmarked face who was following us, was the work of the Tinamou. But that man was killed; he *worked* for Von Tiebolt; they *knew* that. Helden even confirmed it."

"And," interrupted Kessler, "the Tinamou would not kill his own man."

"Exactly."

"Then the agent will tell his superiors. . . ."

"He can't," broke in Noel. "He was shot saving Helden's life. But identifications will be made; the British will piece it together."

"Will the British find the agent who died?"

"Word will get back to them. It has to. The police were everywhere; they'll find his body."

"Can he be traced to you?"

"It's possible. We fought in the square; people will remember. But as Helden put it: We were followed; we didn't do the following. There's no reason why we should *know* anything."

"You sound unsure."

"Before the agent died, I decided to mention Baldwin's name to him, to see if I could learn anything. He reacted as if I'd fired a gun in front of his face. He pleaded with Helden and me to get in touch with a man named Payton-Jones. We were supposed to tell him everything that happened, tell him to find out who attacked us, who killed Von Tiebolt's man, and most important, to tell MI Five he believed it was all related to Peter Baldwin."

"To Baldwin? He'd been with MI Six, you said?"

"Yes. He'd gone to them some time ago with information about the survivors of Wolfsschanze."

"Wolfsschanze?" Kessler repeated the name softly. "That was the letter Manfredi gave you in Geneva, the one written over thirty years ago."

"That's right. The agent said we were to tell Payton-Jones to go back to Baldwin's file. To 'code Wolfsschanze.' That was the phrase he used."

"In his phone call to you in New York, did Baldwin mention Wolfsschanze?" asked Kessler.

"No. He said only that I should stay away from Geneva; that he knew things no one else knew. Then he went to answer the door and he never came back."

Kessler's eyes were colder now. "So Baldwin had learned about Geneva and this Wolfsschanze's commitment to it."

"How much he learned we don't know. It could be very little, just rumors."

"But these rumors are enough to stop you from going to MI Five. Even the advantage of warning them that Beaumont is ODESSA could be too great a price. The British would question you and the girl at length; there are a thousand ways, and they're experts. Baldwin's name might surface and they would go back to his file. You can't take that chance."

"I came to the same conclusion," said Holcroft, impressed.

"Perhaps there's another way to get Beaumont away from you."

"How?"

"The ODESSA is loathed here in Germany. Word to the proper people could result in his removal. You'd never have to reach the British yourself, never have to risk Baldwin's name coming to light."

"Could that be arranged?"

"Unquestionably. If Beaumont's really an ODESSA agent, a brief message from the Bonn government to the Foreign Office would be enough. I know any number of men who could send it."

Relief swept over Holcroft. One more obstacle was being removed. "I'm glad we met . . . that you're you and not somebody else."

"Don't be too quick to make that judgment. You want my answer. Will I join you? Frankly, I—"

"I don't want your answer yet," interrupted Noel. "You were fair with me, and I have to be fair with you. I'm not finished. There was tonight."

"Tonight?" Kessler was disturbed, impatient.

"Yes. The last couple of hours, in fact."

"What happened . . . tonight?"

Noel leaned forward. "We know about the Rache and the ODESSA. We're not sure how much *they* know about Geneva, but we're damned sure what they'd do if they knew enough. We know about the men of Wolfsschanze. Whoever they are, they're crazy—no better than the others—but in their own strange way they're on our side; they want Geneva to succeed. But there's someone else. Someone—*something*—much more powerful than the others. I found that out tonight."

"What are you saying?" The tone of Kessler's voice did not change.

"A man followed me from my hotel. He was on a motorbike and stayed with my taxi across Berlin."

"A man on a motorbike?"

"Yes. Like a damned fool I led him here. I realized how stupid that was, and knew I had to stop him. I managed to do it, but I never meant it to happen the way it did. He was no part of the Rache, no part of the ODESSA. He hated them both, called them butchers and clowns. . . ."

"He called them . . ." Kessler was silent for a moment. Then he continued, regaining part of the composure he had lost. "Tell me everything that happened, everything that was said."

"Do you have any ideas?"

"No. . . . Not at all. I'm merely interested. Tell me."

Holcroft had no difficulty remembering it all. The chase, the trap, the exchange of words, the gunshot. When he had finished, Kessler asked him to go back to the words he and the man in the black leather jacket had said to each other. Then he asked Noel to repeat them again. And again.

"Who was he?" Holcroft knew that Kessler's mind was racing ahead of his. "Who *are* they?"

"There are several possibilities," said the German, "but obviously they're Nazis. Neo-Nazis, to be precise. Descendants of the party, a splinter faction that has no use for the ODESSA. It happens."

"But how would they know about Geneva?"

"Millions stolen from the occupied countries, from Wehrmacht payrolls, from the Finanzministerium. All banked in Switzerland. Such massive manipulations could not be kept completely secret."

Something bothered Noel, something Kessler had just said, but he could not put his finger on it. "But what good would it do them? They can't get the money. They could only tie it up in the courts for years. Where do they benefit?"

"You don't understand the hard-core Nazi. None of you ever did. It's not merely how he can benefit. It's of equal importance to him that others do *not* benefit. That was his essential destructiveness."

There was a sudden, loud commotion outside the booth. A single crash, then several; followed by a woman's scream that triggered other screams.

The curtain across the booth was yanked aside. The figure of a man loomed suddenly in the open space and plunged forward, falling over the table, his eyes wide and staring, blood streaming from his mouth and his neck. His face was contorted, his body wracked with convulsions; his hands lurched over the surface of the table, gripping the sides between Holcroft and Kessler. He whispered, gasping for air, *"Wolfsschanze! Soldaten von Wolfsschanze!"*

He raised his head in the start of a scream. His breath was forced out of him, and his head crashed down on the table. The man in the black leather jacket was dead.

26

The next moments were as bewildering to Noel as they were chaotic. The screaming and the shouting grew louder; waves of panic spread throughout the pub. The blood-soaked man had slipped off the table and was now sprawled on the floor.

"Rudi! *Rudi!*"

"Herr Kessler! Come with me!"

"Quickly!" yelled Erich.

"What?"

"This way, my friend. You can't be seen here."

"But he's the one!"

"Say *nothing*, Noel. Please, take my arm."

"What? Where? . . ."

"Your briefcase! The papers!"

Holcroft grabbed the papers and shoved them into the case. He felt himself being pulled into a circle of onlookers. He was not sure where he was being taken, but that it was away from the dead man in the black leather jacket was enough. He followed blindly.

Kessler pulled him through the crowd. In front of Kessler was the manager, parting the bodies in their path, the path that led to a closed door beneath and to the left of the staircase. The manager took a key from his pocket, opened the door, and rushed the three of them inside. He slammed the door shut and turned to Kessler.

"I don't know what to say, gentlemen! It's terrible. A drunken brawl."

"No doubt, Rudi. And we thank you," replied Kessler.

"*Natürlich.* A man of your stature can't be involved."

"You're most kind. Is there a way outside?"

"Yes. My private entrance. Over here."

The entrance led into an alleyway. "This way," Kessler said. "My car's on the street."

They hurried out of the alley into the Kurfürstendamm, turning left on the sidewalk. To the right, an excited crowd had gathered in front of the pub's entrance. Farther on, Noel could see a policeman running up the street.

"Quickly," said Kessler.

The car was a vintage Mercedes; they climbed in. Kessler started the engine, but did not idle it. Instead, he put the car in gear and sped west.

"That man . . . in the jacket . . . he was the one who followed me," Holcroft whispered.

"I gathered as much," answered Kessler. "He found his way back, after all."

"My *God,*" cried Noel. "What did I *do?*"

"You didn't kill him, if that's what you mean."

Holcroft stared at Kessler. "What?"

"You didn't kill that man."

"The gun went off! He was shot."

"I don't doubt it. But the bullet didn't kill him."

"What *did* then?"

"Obviously you didn't see his throat. He had been garroted."

"Baldwin in New York!"

"Wolfsschanze in Berlin," answered Kessler. "His death was timed to the split second. Someone in that restaurant, outside the booth, brought him to within feet of our table and used the noise and the crowd to cover the execution."

"Oh, Jesus! Then whoever it was . . ." Noel could not finish the statement; fear was making him ill. He wanted to vomit.

"Whoever it was," completed Kessler, "knows now that I am part of Geneva. So, you have your answer; for I have no choice. I'm with you."

"I'm sorry," said Holcroft. "I wanted you to have a choice."

"I know you did, and I thank you for it. However, I must insist on one condition."

"What's that?"

"My brother, Hans, in Munich, must be made part of the covenant."

Noel recalled Manfredi's words; there were no restrictions in this respect. The only stipulation was that each family had one vote. "There's nothing to prevent him, if he wants to."

"He'll want to. We are very close. You'll like him. He's a fine doctor."

"I'd say you were both fine doctors."

"He heals. I merely expound. . . . I'm also driving aimlessly. I'd ask you out to my house, but under the circumstances I'd better not."

"I've done enough damage. But you should get back as soon as you can."

"Why?"

"If we're lucky, nobody'll give your name to the police, and it won't matter. But if someone does—a waiter or anybody who knows you—you can say you were on your way out when it happened."

Kessler shook his head. "I'm a passive man. Such thoughts would not have occurred to me."

"Three weeks ago they wouldn't have occurred to me, either. Let me off near a taxi stand. I'll go to my hotel and get my suitcase."

"Nonsense. I'll drive you."

"We shouldn't be seen together anymore. That's asking for complications."

"I must learn to listen to you. When will we see each other, then?"

"I'll call you from Paris. I'm meeting with Von Tiebolt in a day or so. Then the three of us have to get to Geneva. There's very little time left."

"That man in New York? Miles?"

"Among other things. I'll explain when I see you again. There's a taxi on the corner."

"What will you do now? I doubt there are planes at this hour."

"Then I'll wait at the airport. I don't want to be isolated in a hotel room." Kessler stopped the car; Holcroft reached for the door. "Thank you, Erich. And I'm sorry."

"Don't be, my friend Noel. Call me."

The blond-haired man sat rigidly behind the desk in Kessler's library. His eyes were furious, his voice strained and intense as he spoke.

"Tell me again. Every *word*. Leave out nothing."

"What's the *point?*" replied Kessler from across the room. "We've gone over it ten times. I've remembered everything."

"Then we shall go over it ten more times!" shouted Johann von Tiebolt. "*Thirty* times, *forty* times! Who *was* he? Where did he come from? Who were the two men in Montereau? They're linked; where did all three come from?"

"We don't *know,*" said the scholar. "There's no way to tell."

"But there is! Don't you see? The answer's in what that man said to Holcroft in the alley. I'm certain of it. I've heard the words before. It's there!"

"For God's sake, you *had* the man." Kessler spoke firmly. "If you couldn't learn anything from *him,* what makes you think we can from anything Holcroft said? You should have broken him."

"He wouldn't break; he was too far gone for drugs."

"So you put a wire to his throat and threw him to the American. Madness!"

"Not madness," said Tennyson. "Consistency. Holcroft must be convinced that Wolfsschanze is everywhere. Prodding, threatening, protecting. . . . Let's go back to what was said. According to Holcroft, the man wasn't afraid to die. What was it? '. . . I am prepared. We are all prepared. We will stop you. We will stop Geneva. Kill me and another will take my place; kill him, another his.' The words of a fanatic. But he wasn't a fanatic; I saw that for myself. He was no ODESSA agent, no Rache revolutionary. He was something else. Holcroft was right about that. Something *else.*"

"We're at a dead end."

"Not entirely. I have a man in Paris checking on the identities of the bodies found in Montereau."

"La Sûreté?"

"Yes. He's the best." Tennyson sighed. "It's all so incredible. After thirty years, the first overt moves are made, and within two weeks men come out of nowhere. As if they'd been waiting along with us for three decades. Yet they do not come out in the open. Why not? That is the sticking point. Why *not?*"

"The man said it to Holcroft in the alley. 'We can put that fortune to use.' They can't get it if they expose Geneva's sources."

"Too simple; the amount's too great. If it was money alone, nothing would prevent them from coming to us—to the bank's directors, for that matter—and negotiating from a position of strength. Nearly eight hundred million; from their point of view, they could demand two thirds. They'd be dead after the fact, but they don't know that. No, Erich, it's not the money alone. We must look for something else."

"We must look at the other crisis!" Kessler shouted. "Whoever that man was, tonight, whoever the two men were in Montereau, they're secondary to our most immediate concern! Face it, Johann! The British know you're the Tinamou! Don't sidetrack that any longer. They know you're the Tinamou!"

"Correction. They *suspect* I'm he; they don't know it. And as Holcroft so correctly put it, they'll soon be convinced they're wrong, if they're not convinced already. Actually, it's a very advantageous position."

"You're mad!" screamed Kessler. "You will jeopardize *everything!*"

"On the contrary," said Tennyson calmly. "I will solidify everything. What better ally could we have than MI Five? To be certain, we have men in British Intelligence, but none so high as Payton-Jones."

"What in the name of God are you *talking* about?" The scholar was perspiring; the veins in his neck were pronounced.

"Sit down, Erich."

"No!"

"Sit down!"

Kessler sat. "I won't tolerate this, Johann."

"Don't tolerate anything; just listen." Tennyson leaned forward. "For a few moments, let's reverse roles; I'll be the professor."

"Don't push me. We can handle intruders who won't show themselves; they have something to hide. We can't handle this. If you're taken, what's left?"

"That's flattering, but you mustn't think that way. If anything should happen to me, there are the lists, names of our people everywhere. A man can be found among them; the Fourth Reich will have a leader, in any event. But nothing *will* happen to me. The Tinamou is my shield, my protection. With his capture, I'm not only free of suspicion, I'm held in great respect."

"You've lost your senses! You *are* the Tinamou!"

Tennyson sat back, smiling. "Let's examine our assassin, shall we? Ten years ago you agreed he was my finest creation. I believe you said the Tinamou might well turn out to be our most vital weapon."

"In *theory*. Only in theory. It was an academic judgment; I also said that!"

"True, you often take refuge high up in your cloistered tower, and that's how it should be. But you were right, you know. In the last analysis, the millions in Switzerland cannot serve us unless they can be put to use. There are laws everywhere; they must be circumvented. It's not as simple as it once was to pay for a Reichstag, or a block of seats in Parliament; or to buy an election in America. But for us it is nowhere near as difficult as it would be for others; that was your point ten years ago, and it is more valid today. We are in a position to make extraordinary demands on the most influential men in every major government. They've *paid* the Tinamou to assassinate their adversaries. From Washington to Paris to Cairo; from Athens to Beirut to Madrid; from London to Warsaw and even to Moscow itself. The Tinamou is irresistible. He is our own nuclear bomb."

"And he can claim *us* in the fallout!"

"He could," agreed Tennyson, "but he won't. Years ago, Erich, we vowed to keep no secrets from each other, and I've kept that vow in all matters except one. I won't apologize; it was, as they say, a decision of rank, and I felt it was necessary."

"What did you do?" asked Kessler.

"Gave us that most vital weapon you spoke of ten years ago."

"How?"

"A few moments ago you were quite specific. You raised your voice and said *I* was the Tinamou."

"You *are!*"

"I'm not."

"What?"

"I'm one half of the Tinamou. To be sure, the better half, but still only half. For years I trained another; he is my alternate in the field. His expertness has been taught, his brilliance acquired; next to the real Tinamou, he's the best on earth."

The scholar stared at the blond man in astonishment . . . and with awe. "He's one of us? *Ein Sonnenkind?*"

"Of course not! He's a paid killer; he knows nothing but an extraordinary life-style in which every need and appetite is gratified by the extraordinary sums he earns. He's also aware that one day he may have to pay the price for his way of living, and he accepts that. He's a professional."

Kessler sank back in the chair and loosened his collar. "I must say, you never cease to amaze me."

"I'm not finished," replied Tennyson. "An event is taking place in London shortly, a gathering of heads of state. It's the perfect opportunity. The Tinamou will be caught."

"He'll be what?"

"You heard correctly." Tennyson smiled. "The Tinamou will be captured, a weapon in his hands, the odd caliber and the bore markings traceable to three previous assassinations. He will be caught and killed by the man who has been tracking him for nearly six years. A man who, for his own protection, wants no credit, wants no mention of his name. Who calls in the intelligence authorities of his adopted country. John Tennyson, European correspondent of the *Guardian.*"

"My *God,*" whispered Kessler. "How will you do it?"

"Even you can't know that. But there'll be a dividend as powerful as Geneva itself. The word will go out, in print, that the Tinamou kept private records. They haven't been found, and thus can be presumed to have been stolen by someone. That someone will be ourselves. So, in death, the Tinamou serves us still."

Kessler shook his head in wonder. "You think exotically; that's your essential gift."

"Among others," said the blond man matter-of-factly. "And our newfound alliance with MI Five may be helpful. Other intelligence services may be more sophisticated, but none are better." Tennyson slapped the arm of the chair. "Now. Let's get back to our unknown enemy. His identity is in the words spoken in that alley. I've heard them! I know it."

"We've exhausted that approach."

"We've only begun." The blond man reached for a pencil and paper. "Now, from the beginning. We'll write down everything he said, everything you can remember."

The scholar sighed. "From the beginning," he repeated. "Very well. According to Holcroft, the man's first words referred to the killing in France, the fact that Holcroft had not hesitated to fire his pistol then. . . ."

Kessler spoke. Tennyson listened and interrupted and asked for repetitions of words and phrases. He wrote furiously. Forty minutes passed.

"I can't go on any longer," said Kessler. "There's no more I can tell you."

"Again, the *eagles,*" countered the blond man harshly. "Say the words exactly as Holcroft said them."

"Eagles? . . . 'You won't stop the eagles. Not this time.' Could he have meant the Luftwaffe? The Wehrmacht?"

"Not likely." Tennyson looked down at the pages in front of him. He tapped his finger at something he had written down. "Here. 'Your Wolfsschanze.' *Your* Wolfsschanze. . . . Meaning ours, not theirs."

"What are you talking about?" said Kessler. "We *are* Wolfsschanze; the men of Wolfsschanze are *Sonnenkinder!*"

Tennyson ignored the interruption. "Von Stauffenberg, Olbricht, Von Falkenhausen, and Höpner. Rommel called them 'the true eagles of Germany.' They were the insurrectionists, the Führer's would-be assassins. All were shot; Rommel, ordered to take his own life. *Those* are the eagles he referred to. *Their* Wolfsschanze, not ours."

"Where does it lead us? For God's *sake,* Johann, I'm exhausted. I can't go on!"

Tennyson had covered a dozen pages of paper; now he shuffled them, underlin-

ing words, circling phrases. "You may have said enough," he replied. "It's here
. . . in this section. He used the words 'butchers and clowns,' and then, 'you won't
stop the eagles.' . . . Only seconds later, Holcroft told him that the account would
be tied up for years, that there were conditions . . . 'the money frozen, sent back
into the ground.' The man repeated the phrase 'back into the ground,' saying it
was the flaw. But then he added that there would be 'no scorched earth.'
'Scorched earth.' 'There will be no . . . *scorched earth.'* "

The blond man's upper body tensed. He leaned back in the chair, his sculptured face twisted in concentration, his cold eyes staring rigidly at the words on
the paper. "It couldn't be . . . after all these years. Operation Barbarossa! The
'scorched earth' of Barbarossa! Oh, my God, the Nachrichtendienst. It's the
Nachrichtendienst!"

"What are you talking about?" Kessler said. " 'Barbarossa' was Hitler's invasion
of Russia, a magnificent victory."

"He called it a victory. The Prussians called it a disaster. A hollow victory,
written in blood. Whole divisions unprepared, decimated. . . . 'We took the land,'
the generals said. 'We took the worthless, scorched earth of Barbarossa.' Out of
it came the Nachrichtendienst."

"What was it?"

"An intelligence unit. Rarefied, exclusively Junker, a corps of aristocrats. Later,
there were those who thought it was a Gehlen operation, designed to sow distrust
between the Russians and the West. But it wasn't; it was solely its own. It loathed
Hitler; it scorned the Schutzstaffel—'SS garbage' was the term it used; it hated
the commanders of the Luftwaffe. All were called 'butchers and clowns.' It was
above the war, above the party. It was only for Germany. *Their* Germany."

"Say what you mean, Johann!" shouted Kessler.

"The Nachrichtendienst survives. It's the intruder. It wants to destroy Geneva.
It will stop at nothing to abort the Fourth Reich before it's born."

27

Noel waited on the bridge, watching the lights of Paris flicker like clusters of tiny
candles. He had reached Helden at Gallimard; she had agreed to meet him after
work on the Pont Neuf. He had tried to persuade her to drive to the hotel in
Argenteuil, but she had declined his offer.

"You promised me days, weeks, if I wished," he said.

"I promised us both, my darling, and we'll have them. But not Argenteuil. I'll
explain when I see you."

It was barely five-fifteen; the winter night descended on Paris quickly, and the chill of the river wind penetrated him. He pulled up the collar of his secondhand overcoat to ward off the cold. He looked at his watch again; its hands had not moved. How could they have? No more than ten seconds had elapsed.

He felt like a young man waiting for a girl he had met at a country club in the summer moonlight, and he smiled to himself, feeling awkward and embarrassed, not wanting to acknowledge his anxiety. He was not in the moonlight on some warm summer's night. He was on a bridge in Paris, and the air was cold, and he was dressed in a secondhand overcoat, and in his pocket was a gun.

He saw her walking onto the bridge. She was wearing the black raincoat, her blond hair encased by a dark-red scarf that framed her face. Her pace was steady, neither rapid nor casual; she was a lone woman going home from her place of work. Except for her striking features—only hinted at in the distance—she was like thousands of other women in Paris, heading home in the early evening.

She saw him. He started walking toward her, but she held up her hand, a signal for him to remain where he was. He paid no attention, wanting to reach her quickly, his arms held out. She walked into them and they embraced, and he felt warm in the comfort of being with her again. She pulled her head back and looked at him, then pretended to be firm, but her eyes smiled.

"You must never run on a bridge," she said. "A man running across a bridge stands out. One strolls over the water; one doesn't race."

"I missed you. I don't give a damn."

"You must learn to. How was Berlin?"

He put his arm around her shoulder and they started toward the quai Saint-Bernard, and the Left Bank. "I've got a lot to tell you, some good, some not so good. But if learning something is progress, I think we've taken a couple of giant steps. Have you heard from your brother?"

"Yes. This afternoon. He called an hour after you did. His plans have changed; he can be in Paris tomorrow."

"That's the best news you could give me. At least, I think it is. I'll let you know tomorrow." They walked off the bridge and turned left along the riverbank. "Did you miss me?"

"Noel, you're mad. You left yesterday afternoon. I barely had time to get home, bathe, have a very-much-needed night's sleep, and get to work."

"You went home? To your apartment?"

"No, I—" She stopped and looked up at him, smiling. "Very good, Noel Holcroft, new recruit. Interrogate casually."

"I don't feel casual."

"You promised not to ask that question."

"Not specifically. I asked you if you were married, or living with someone—to which I got a negative to the first and a very oblique answer to the second—but I never actually promised not to try and find out where you live."

"You implied it, my darling. One day I'll tell you, and you'll see how foolish you are."

"Tell me now. I'm in love. I want to know where my woman lives."

The smile disappeared from her lips. Then it returned, and she glanced up at him again. "You're like a little boy practicing a new word. You don't know me well enough to love me; I told you that."

"I forgot. You like women."

"They're among my best friends."

"But you wouldn't want to marry one."

"I don't want to marry anyone."

"Good. It's less complicated. Just move in with me for the next ten years, exercisable options on both sides."

"You say nice things."

They stopped at an intersection. He turned Helden to him, both his hands on her arms. "I say them because I mean them."

"I believe you," she said, looking at him curiously, her eyes part questioning, part fearful.

He saw the fear; it bothered him, and so he smiled. "Love me a little?"

She could not bring the smile to her lips. "I think I love you more than a little. You're a problem I didn't want. I'm not sure I can handle it."

"That's even better." He laughed and took her hand to cross the street. "It's nice to know you don't have all the answers."

"Did you believe I did?"

"I thought you thought so."

"I don't."

"I know."

The restaurant was half filled with diners. Helden asked for a table in the rear, out of sight of the entrance. The proprietor nodded. It was apparent that he could not quite fathom why this *belle femme* would come into his establishment with such a poorly dressed companion. In his eyes was the comment: things were not going well for the girls of Paris these days. Nights.

"He doesn't approve of me," said Holcroft.

"There's hope for you, though. You grew in his estimation when you specified expensive whiskey. He grinned; didn't you see?"

"He was looking at my jacket. It came from a somewhat better rack than the overcoat."

Helden laughed. "That overcoat's purpose was not high fashion. Did you use it in Berlin?"

"I used it. I wore it when I picked up a whore. Are you jealous?"

"Not of anyone accepting an offer from you dressed like that."

"She was a vision of loveliness."

"You're lucky. She was probably an ODESSA agent and you've come down with a social disease, as planned. See a doctor before you see me again."

Noel took her hand. There was no humor in his voice when he spoke. "The ODESSA's no concern of ours. Neither is the Rache. That's one—or two—of the things I learned in Berlin. It's doubtful either of them knows anything about Geneva."

Helden was stunned. "But what about Beaumont? You said he was ODESSA, that he followed you to Rio."

"I think he is ODESSA, and he did follow me, but not because of Geneva. He's tied in with Graff. Somehow he found out I was looking for Johann von Tiebolt; *that* was why he followed me. Not Geneva. I'll know more when I speak to your brother tomorrow. Anyway, Beaumont'll be out of the picture in a few days. Kessler's taking care of it. He said he'd make a call to someone in the Bonn government."

"It's that simple?"

"It's not that difficult. Any hint of ODESSA, especially in the military, is enough to start a battery of inquiries. Beaumont'll be pulled in."

"If it's not the ODESSA, or the Rache, who is it?"

"That's part of what I've got to tell you. I had to get rid of the mackinaw and the cap."

"Oh?" Helden was confused by the non sequitur.

He told her why, playing down the violence in the dark alleyway. Then he described the conversation with Kessler, realizing as he came to the end that he could not omit the murder of the unknown man in the leather jacket. He would tell her brother about it tomorrow; to withhold it from Helden now would serve no purpose. When he had finished, she shuddered, pressing her fingers into the palm of her hand.

"How *horrible*. Did Kessler have any idea who he was, where he came from?"

"Not really. We went over everything he said a half-dozen times, trying to figure it out, but there wasn't that much. In Kessler's opinion he was part of a neo-Nazi group—descendants of the party, Kessler called them. A splinter faction that has no use for the ODESSA."

"How would they know about the account in Geneva?"

"I asked Kessler that. He said that the sort of manipulations required to get that money out of Germany couldn't have been kept as quiet as we think; that someone somewhere could have learned about it."

"But Geneva is *based* on secrecy. Without it, it would collapse."

"Then it's a question of degree. When is a secret a secret? What separates confidential information from highly classified data? A handful of people found out about Geneva and want to stop us from getting the money and using it the way it's supposed to be used. They want it for themselves, so they're not going to expose it."

"But if they've learned that much, they know they can't get it."

"Not necessarily."

"Then they should be told!"

"I said as much to the man in the alley. I didn't convince him. Even if I had, it wouldn't make any difference now."

"But don't you see? Someone has to reach these people—whoever they are—and convince them they gain nothing by stopping you and my brother and Erich Kessler."

Holcroft drank. "I'm not sure we should do that. Kessler said something that bothered me when I heard it, and it bothers me now. He said that we—the 'we,' I guess, meaning all of us who haven't studied the subject that closely—never understood the hard-core Nazi. From the Nazi's point of view, it wasn't simply a question of how *he* could benefit; it was just as important to him that others *do not* benefit. Kessler called it the 'essential destructiveness.' "

Helden's frown returned. "So if they're told, they'll go after you. They'll kill the three of you, because without you, there's no Geneva."

"Not for another generation. That's motive enough. The money goes back into the vaults for another thirty years."

Helden brought her hand to her mouth. "Wait a minute; there's something terribly wrong. They've tried to kill you. *You*. From the beginning . . . *you.*"

Holcroft shook his head. "We can't be certain—"

"Not *certain?*" broke in Helden. "My God, what more do you want? You showed me your jacket. There was the strychnine on that plane, the shots in Rio. What more do you want?"

"I want to know who was really behind those things. That's why I have to talk to your brother."

"What can Johann tell you?"

"Whom he killed in Rio." Helden started to object; he took her hand again. "Let me explain. I think we're in the middle—*I'm* in the middle—of two fights, neither having anything to do with the other. Whatever happened to your brother in Rio has nothing to do with Geneva. That's where I made my mistake. I tied everything into Geneva. It's not; it's separate."

"I tried to tell you that," said Helden.

"I was slow. But then, no one's ever fired a gun at me, or tried to poison me, or shoved a knife in my stomach. Those kinds of things play hell with your thinking process. At least they do mine."

"Johann is a man of many interests, Noel," she said. "He can be very charming, very personable, but he can also be reticent. It's part of him. He's lived a strange life. Sometimes I think of him as a gadfly. He darts quickly from one place to another, one interest to another, always brilliantly, always leaving his mark, but not always wishing that mark to be recognized."

" 'He's here, he's there, he's everywhere,' " interrupted Holcroft. "You're describing some sort of Scarlet Pimpernel."

"Exactly. Johann may not tell you what happened in Rio."

"He has to. I have to know."

"Since it has nothing to do with Geneva, he may disagree."

"Then I'll try to convince him. We *have* to find out how vulnerable he is."

"Let's say he is vulnerable. What happens then?"

"He'd be disqualified from taking part in Geneva. We know he killed someone. You heard a man—a wealthy, influential man, you thought—say he wanted to see your brother hanged for murder. *I* know he tangled with Graff, and that means the ODESSA. He ran for his life. He took you and your sister with him, but he ran for *his* life. He's mixed up in a lot of complications; people are after him, and it's not unreasonable to think he could be blackmailed. That could shake Geneva; it could corrupt it."

"Do the bankers have to be told?" asked Helden.

Noel touched her cheek, forcing her to look at him. "I'd have to tell them. We're talking about seven hundred and eighty million dollars; about three men who did something remarkable. It was their gesture to history; I really believe that. If your brother puts it in jeopardy, or causes it to be misused, then maybe it's better that those millions get locked up for the next generation. But it doesn't have to be that way. According to the rules, you're the one who'd be the Von Tiebolt executrix."

Helden gazed at him. "I can't accept that, Noel. It must be Johann. Not only is he more qualified to be a part of Geneva; he deserves it. I can't take that from him."

"And I can't give it to him. Not if he can hurt the covenant. Let's talk about it after I see him."

She studied his face; he felt awkward. She took his hand from her cheek and held it. "You're a moral man, aren't you?"

"Not necessarily. Just angry. I'm sick of corruption in the rarefied circles of finance. There's been an awful lot of it in my country."

" 'Rarefied circles of finance'?"

"It's a phrase my father used in his letter to me."

"That's odd," said Helden.

"What is?"

"You've always called him Clausen, or Heinrich Clausen. Formal, rather distant."

Holcroft nodded, acknowledging the truth of her remark. "It's funny, because I really don't know any more about him now than I did before. But he's been described to me. The way he looked, the way he talked, how people listened to him and were affected by him."

"Then you do know more about him."

"Not actually. Only impressions. A child's impressions, at that. But in a small way I think I've found him."

"When did your parents tell you about him?"

"Not my parents, not my . . . stepfather. Just Althene. It was a couple of weeks after my twenty-fifth birthday. I was working then, a certified professional."

"Professional?"

"I'm an architect, remember? I've almost forgotten."

"Your mother waited until you were twenty-five before she told you?"

"She was right. I don't think I could have handled it when I was younger. Good Lord. Noel Holcroft, American boy. Hot dogs and french fries, Shea Stadium and the Mets, the Garden and the Knicks; and college and friends whose fathers were soldiers in the big war, each one winning it in his own way. That fellow's told his real father was one of those heel-clicking sadists in the war movies, Christ, that kid would flip out."

"Why did she tell you at all, then?"

"On the remote chance that I'd find out for myself one day, and she didn't want that. She didn't think it would happen. She and Dick had covered the traces right down to a birth certificate which said I was their son. But there was another birth certificate. In Berlin. 'Clausen, male child. Mother—Althene. Father—Heinrich.' And there were people who knew she'd left him, left Germany. She wanted me to be prepared if it ever surfaced, if anyone for any reason ever remembered and tried to use the information. Prepared, incidentally, to deny it. To say there'd been another child—never mentioned in the house—who had died in infancy in England."

"Which means there was another certificate. A death certificate."

"Yes. Properly recorded somewhere in London."

Helden leaned back against the booth. "You and we are not so different after all. Our lives are full of false papers. What a luxury it must be not to live that way."

"Papers don't mean much to me. I've never hired anyone because of them, and I've never fired anyone because someone else brought them to me." Noel finished his drink. "I ask the questions myself. And I'm going to ask your brother some very tough ones. I hope to God he has the answers I want to hear."

"So do I."

He leaned toward her, their shoulders touching. "Love me a little?"

"More than a little."

"Stay with me tonight."

"I intend to. Your hotel?"

"Not the one in rue Chevalle. That Mr. Fresca we invented the other night has moved to better lodgings. You see, I've got a few friends in Paris, too. One's an assistant manager at the George Cinq."

"How extravagant."

"It's allowed. You're a very special woman, and we don't know what's going to happen, starting tomorrow. By the way, why couldn't we go to Argenteuil? You said you'd tell me."

"We were seen there."

"What? By whom?"

"A man saw us—saw you, really. We don't know his name, but we know he was from Interpol. We have a source there. A bulletin was circulated from the Paris headquarters with your description. A trace was put out for you from New York. From a police officer named Miles."

28

John Tennyson walked out into Heathrow Airport's crowded arrivals area. He walked to a black Jaguar sedan waiting at the curb. The driver was smoking a cigarette and reading a book. At the sight of the approaching blond man, the driver got out of the car.

"Good afternoon, Mr. Tennyson," said the man, in a throaty Welsh accent.

"Have you been waiting long?" asked Tennyson, without much interest.

"Not very," answered the driver, taking Tennyson's briefcase and overnight bag. "I presume you wish to drive."

"Yes, I'll drop you off along the way. Someplace where you can find a taxi."

"I can get one here."

"No, I want to talk for a few minutes." Tennyson climbed in behind the wheel; the Welshman opened the rear door and put the luggage inside. Within minutes they had passed the airport gates and were on the highway to London.

"Did you have a good trip?" asked the Welshman.

"A busy one."

"I read your article about Bahrain. Most amusing."

"Bahrain's amusing. The Indian shopkeepers are the only economists on the archipelago."

"But you were kind to the sheikhs."

"They were kind to me. What's the news from the Mediterranean? Have you stayed in touch with your brother on board Beaumont's ship?"

"Constantly. We use a radiophone off Cap Camarat. Everything's going according to schedule. The rumor circulated on the pier that the commander was seen going out in a small boat with a woman from Saint-Tropez. Neither the boat nor the couple have been heard from in over forty-eight hours, and there were offshore squalls. My brother will report the incident tomorrow. He will assume command, of course."

"Of course. Then it all goes well. Beaumont's death will be clearcut. An accident in bad weather. No one will question the story."

"You don't care to tell me what actually happened?"

"Not specifically; it would be a burden to you. But basically, Beaumont overreached himself. He was seen in the wrong places by the wrong people. It was speculated that our upstanding officer was actually connected to the ODESSA."

The Welshman's expression conveyed his anger. "That's dangerous. The damn fool."

"There's something I must tell you," said Tennyson. "It's almost time."

The Welshman replied in awe. "It's happened, then?"

"Within two weeks, I'd guess."

"I can't believe it!"

"Why?" asked Tennyson. "Everything's on schedule. The cables must begin to go out. Everywhere."

"Everywhere. . . ." repeated the man.

"The code is 'Wolfsschanze.' "

"Wolfsschanze? . . . Oh God, it's come!"

"It's here. Update a final master list of district leaders, one copy only, of course. Take all the microdot files—country by country, city by city, each political connection—and seal them in the steel case. Bring the case personally to me, along with the master list, one week from today. Wednesday. We'll meet on the street outside my flat in Kensington. Eight o'clock at night."

"A week from today. Wednesday. Eight o'clock. With the case."

"And the master list. The leaders."

"Of course." The Welshman brought the knuckle of his index finger to his teeth. "It's really come," he whispered.

"There's a minor obstacle, but we'll surmount it."

"Can I help? I'll do anything."

"I know you will, Ian. You're one of the best. I'll tell you next week."

"Anything."

"Of course." Tennyson slowed the Jaguar at the approach of an exit. "I'd drive you into London, but I'm heading toward Margate. It's imperative that I get there quickly."

"Don't worry about me. God, man, you must have so much on your mind!" Ian kept his eyes on Tennyson's face, on the strong, chiseled features that held such promise, such power. "To be here now; to have the privilege to be present at the beginning. At the rebirth. There's no sacrifice I wouldn't make."

The blond man smiled. "Thank you," he said.

"Leave me anywhere. I'll find a taxi. . . . I didn't know we had people in Margate."

"We have people everywhere," said Tennyson, stopping the car.

Tennyson sped down the familiar highway toward Portsea. He would reach Gretchen's house before eight o'clock, and that was as it should be; she expected him at nine. He'd be able to make sure she had no visitors, no friendly male neighbors who might have dropped in for a drink.

The blond man smiled to himself. Even in her mid-forties, his sister drew men as the proverbial flame drew moths: they, scorched into satiety by the heat, saved from themselves by their inability to reach the flame itself. For Gretchen did not fulfill the promise of her sexuality unless told to do so. It was a weapon to be used, as all potentially lethal weapons were to be used—with discretion.

Tennyson did not relish what he had to do, but he knew he had no choice. All threads that led to Geneva had to be cut, and his sister was one of them. As

Anthony Beaumont had been one. Gretchen simply knew too much; Wolfs-schanze's enemies could break her—and they would.

There were three items of information the Nachrichtendienst did not have: the timetable, the methods of dispersing the millions, and the lists. Gretchen knew the timetable; she was familiar with the methods of dispersal; and, as the methods were tied to the names of recipients all over the world, she was all too aware of the lists.

His sister had to die.

As the Welshman had to make the sacrifice he spoke of so nobly. Once the airtight carton and the master list were delivered, the Welshman's contributions were finished. He remained only a liability; for, except for the sons of Erich Kessler and Wilhelm von Tiebolt, no one else alive would ever see those lists. Thousands of names, in every country, who were the true inheritors of Wolfs-schanze, the perfect race, the *Sonnenkinder.*

PORTSEA—15 M

The blond man pressed the accelerator; the Jaguar shot forward.

"So, at last it's here," said Gretchen Beaumont, sitting next to Tennyson on the soft leather couch, her hand caressing his face, her fingers darting in and out between his lips, arousing him as she was always able to do since they were children. "And you're so beautiful. There's no other man like you; there never will be."

She leaned forward, her unbuttoned blouse exposing her breasts, inviting his caress. She opened her mouth and covered his, groaning in that throaty way that drove him wild.

But he could not succumb. When he did, it would be the last act of a secret ritual that had kept him pure and unentangled . . . since he was a child. He held her shoulders and gently pushed her back on the couch.

"It's here," he said. "I must learn everything that's happened while my mind's clear. We have lots of time. I'll leave about six in the morning for Heathrow, for the first plane to Paris. But now, is there anything you forgot to tell me about the American? Are you sure he never made the connection between you and New York?"

"Never. The dead woman across from his apartment was known to be a heavy smoker. I don't smoke, and made a point of it when he was here. I also made it clear that I hadn't been anywhere in weeks. If he questioned that, I could have proved it, of course. And, obviously, I was very much alive."

"So when he left, he had no idea that the highly erotic, straying wife he went to bed with was the woman in New York."

"Of course not. And he didn't leave," said Gretchen, laughing. "He fled. Bewildered and panicked, convinced I was unbalanced—as we had planned—thus making you next in line for Geneva." She stopped laughing. "He also fled with Tony's photograph, which we had not planned. You're getting it back, I assume."

Tennyson nodded. "Yes."

"What will you tell Holcroft?"

"He believes Beaumont was an ODESSA agent; that I was somehow embroiled with Graff and had to escape from Brazil or be shot. That's what he told Kessler. The truth is, he's not at all sure what happened in Rio except that I killed someone; he's worried about it." Tennyson smiled. "I'll play on his assumptions. I'll think of something startling, something that will stun him, convince him I'm holier than John the Baptist. And, of course, I'll be grateful that our partner has caused the removal of the terrible Beaumont from our concerns."

Gretchen took his hand, pressing it between her legs, rubbing her stockings up and down against his flesh. "You are not only beautiful; you're brilliant."

"Then I'll turn the tables, make him feel he must convince me *he's* worthy of Geneva. He will be the one who must justify his part of the covenant. It's psychologically vital that he be put in that position; his dependency on me must grow."

Gretchen locked her legs against his hand and held his wrist; the grip was abrupt and sexual. "You can excite me with words, but you know that, don't you?"

"In a while, my love . . . my only love. We've got to talk." Tennyson dug his fingers into his sister's leg; she moaned. "Of course, I'll know more what to say after I've spoken to Helden."

"You'll see her before you meet with Holcroft, then?"

"Yes. I'll call her and tell her I've got to see her right away. For the first time in her life, she'll observe me in the throes of self-doubt, desperately needing to be convinced my actions are right."

"Brilliant again." She took his hand from between her legs and placed it under her breast. "And does our little sister still run with the flotsam and jetsam? The self-imposed *Verwünschten Kinder,* with their beards and bad teeth?"

"Of course. She has to feel needed; it was always her weakness."

"She wasn't born in the Reich."

Tennyson laughed derisively. "To compound her striving for adequacy, she's become a nursemaid. She lives in Herr Oberst's house and cares for the crippled bastard. Two changes of cars each evening, so as not to lead the assassins of the Rache and the ODESSA to him."

"One or the other may kill her one day," mused Gretchen. "That's something to think about. Soon after the bank frees the account, she'll have to go. She's not stupid, Johann. One more murder laid at the foot of the Rache. Or the ODESSA."

"It's crossed my mind. . . . Speaking of murder, tell me: While Holcroft was here, did he mention Peter Baldwin?"

"Not a word. I never thought he would, not if I was playing my part right. I was an unbalanced, resentful wife. He didn't want to frighten me; nor did he wish to give me information dangerous to Geneva."

Tennyson nodded; they had projected accurately. "What was his reaction when you talked about me?"

"I gave him very little time to react," said Gretchen. "I simply told him you spoke for the Von Tiebolts. Why did Baldwin try to intercept him in New York. Do you know?"

"I've pieced it together. Baldwin operated out of Prague, an MI Sixer whose allegiance, many said, was to the highest bidder. He sold information to anyone, until his own people began to suspect him. They fired him, but didn't prosecute, because they couldn't be sure; he'd operated as a double agent in the past and claimed it as his cover. He swore he was developing a two-way network. He also knew the name of every British contact in Central Europe, and obviously let his superiors know that those names would surface if anything happened to him. He maintained his innocence, said he was being punished for doing his job too well."

"What's that got to do with Holcroft?"

"To understand, you have to see Baldwin for what he was. He was good; his sources, the best. In addition to which he was a courier specialist; he could track anything. While in Prague, he heard rumors of a great fortune being held in Geneva. Nazi spoils. The rumor wasn't unusual; such stories have been around since Berlin fell. The difference with this rumor was that Clausen's name was mentioned. Again, not completely startling; Clausen was the financial genius of the Reich. But Baldwin checked out everything to the finest point; it was the way he worked."

"He went back to the courier archives," interrupted Gretchen.

"Yes. Concentrating on the Finanzministerium. Hundreds of runs were made, Manfredi the recipient in dozens. Once he had Manfredi's name, the rest was patient observation—and money spread cautiously within the bank. His break came when he heard that Manfredi was setting up contact with a heretofore-unheard-of American named Holcroft. *Why?* He studied Holcroft and found the mother."

"She was Manfredi's strategy," Gretchen broke in again.

"From the beginning," agreed Tennyson, nodding. "He convinced Clausen she had to leave Germany. She had money of her own and moved in monied circles; she could be of great use to us in America. With Clausen's help, she came to accept that, but she was essentially Manfredi's creation."

"Underneath that gnome's benign appearance," said Gretchen, "was a Machiavelli."

"Without that kindly innocence of his, I doubt he'd ever have got away with it. But Machiavelli isn't the parallel. Manfredi's interest was solely the money; it was the only power he wanted. He was a sworn companion of the gold quota. It was his intention to control the agency in Zürich; it's why we killed him."

"How much did Baldwin learn?"

"We'll never know, exactly; but whatever it was, it was to be his vindication with British Intelligence. You see, he wasn't a double agent; he was exactly what he claimed to be: MI Six's very effective man in Prague."

"He reached Manfredi?"

"Oh, yes. He implied that much by his knowledge of the Geneva meeting. He was just a little late, that's all." The blond man smiled. "I can picture the confrontation: two specialists circling each other, both wanting something desperately; one to pry out information, the other to retain it at all costs, knowing he was dealing with a potentially catastrophic situation. Certain agreements must have been made; and, true to form, Manfredi broke his word, moved up the meeting with Holcroft, and then alerted us about Baldwin. He covered everything. If your husband were to be caught killing Peter Baldwin, there would be no connection with Ernst Manfredi. He was a man to be respected. He might have won."

"But not against Johann von Tiebolt," said Gretchen, squeezing his hand beneath her breast, moving it up. "Incidentally, I received another code from Graff, from Rio. He's upset again. He says he's not being kept informed."

"His senility is showing. He, too, has served his purpose. Age makes him careless; it's no time for him to be sending messages to England. I'm afraid the moment has arrived for *unser Freund* in Brazil."

"You'll send the order out?"

"In the morning. One more arm of the hated ODESSA severed. He trained me too well." Tennyson leaned forward, his hand cupping his sister's breast. "I think we are finished talking. As always, talking with you clears my mind. I can't think of anything more to say, anything more to ask you."

"Then make demands instead. It's been so long for you; you must be bursting inside. I'll take care of you, as I always have."

"Since we were children," said Tennyson, his mouth covering hers, her hand groping for his trousers. Both of them were trembling.

Gretchen lay naked beside him, her breathing steady, her body drained and satisfied. The blond man raised his hand and looked at the radium dial of his watch. It was two-thirty in the morning. Time to do the terrible thing demanded of him by the covenant of Wolfsschanze. All traces to Geneva had to be removed.

He reached over the side of the bed for his shoes. He lifted one up, feeling the heel with his fingers in the darkness. There was a small metal disk in the center. He pressed it, turning it to the left until a spring was released. He placed the disk on the bedside table, then tilted the shoe back and removed a steel needle ten inches long, concealed in a tiny bore drilled from heel to sole. The needle was flexible but unbreakable. Inserted properly between the fourth and fifth ribs, it punctured the heart, leaving a mark more often missed than found, even during an autopsy.

He held it delicately between the thumb and index finger of his right hand, reaching for his sister with his left. He touched her right breast and then her naked shoulder. She opened her eyes.

"You are insatiable," she whispered, smiling.

"Only with you." He drew her up to him until their flesh touched. "You are my only love," he said, his right arm sliding behind her, extended a foot beyond her spine. He turned his wrist inward; the needle was positioned. He thrust it forward.

The back-country roads were confusing, but Tennyson had memorized the route. He knew the way to the hidden cottage that housed the enigmatic Herr Oberst, that betrayer of the Reich. Even the title, "Oberst," was an ironic commentary. The traitor had been no colonel; he had been general in the Wehrmacht, General Klaus Falkenheim, at one time fourth-in-command of all Germany. Praise had been lavished on him by his military peers, and even by the Führer himself. And all the while a jackal had lived in that shiny, hollow shell.

God, how Johann von Tiebolt loathed the misfit liar that was Herr Oberst! But John Tennyson would not show that loathing. On the contrary, Tennyson would fawn on the old man, proclaiming awe and respect. For if there was one certain way to get his younger sister's total cooperation, it was by showing such deference.

He had called Helden at Gallimard, telling her that he had to see where she lived. Yes, he knew she lived in Herr Oberst's small house; and again, yes, he knew where it was.

"I'm a newspaperman now. I wouldn't be a very good one if I didn't have sources."

She had been stunned. He insisted on seeing her in the late morning, before meeting Holcroft in the afternoon. He would *not* meet with the American unless and until he saw her. Perhaps Herr Oberst could help clarify the situation. Perhaps the old gentleman might allay sudden fears that had arisen.

He reached the dirt road that led through the overgrown grass into the untamed glen that protected Herr Oberst's house from prying eyes. Three minutes later he stopped in front of the path that led to the cottage. The door opened; Helden came out to greet him. How lovely she looked, so like Gretchen.

They exchanged a brother-and-sister embrace, both anxious to begin the meeting with Herr Oberst. Helden's eyes conveyed her bewilderment. She led him inside the small, spartan house. Herr Oberst stood by the fireplace. Helden introduced the two men.

"This is a moment I shall treasure throughout my life," said Tennyson. "You've earned the gratitude of Germans everywhere. If I can ever be of service to you, tell Helden, and I'll do whatever you ask."

"You're too kind, Herr von Tiebolt," replied the old man. "But according to your sister, it's you who seek something from me, and I can't imagine what it is. How can I help you?"

"My problem is the American. This Holcroft."

"What about him?" asked Helden.

"Thirty years ago a magnificent thing was done, an incredible feat engineered by three extraordinary men who wished to make restitution for the anguish inflicted by butchers and maniacs. Through circumstances that seemed right at the time, Holcroft was projected to be a key factor in the distribution of millions throughout the world. I'm now asked to meet with him, cooperate with him. . . ." Tennyson stopped, as if the words eluded him.

"And?" Herr Oberst moved forward.

"I don't trust him," said the blond man. "He's met with Nazis. Men who would kill us, Helden. Men like Maurice Graff, in Brazil."

"What are you saying?"

"The bloodiness reemerge. Holcroft is a Nazi."

Helden's face was stretched in shock, her eyes a mixture of anger and disbelief. "That's absurd! Johann, that's insane!"

"Is it? I don't think so."

Noel waited until Helden left for work before placing the phone call to Miles, in New York. Their night had been filled with love and comfort. He knew he had to convince her they would go on; there was no predetermined ending to their being together. He would not accept that now.

The telephone rang. "Yes, operator, this is the Mr. Fresca calling Lieutenant Miles."

"I thought it had to be you," said the man whose voice had no matching face for Noel. "Interpol reach you?"

"*Reach* me? There are men following me, if that's what you mean. I think it's called a 'trace.' Put out by *you?*"

"That's right."

"You gave me two weeks! What the hell are you doing?"

"Trying to find you. Trying to get you information I think you should have. It concerns your mother."

Noel felt a sharp pain in his chest. "What about my mother?"

"She ran." Miles paused. "I'll give her credit; she's damned good. It was a very professional skip. She went the Mexican route, and before you could say 'Althene Holcroft,' she was a little old lady on her way to Lisbon with a new name and a new passport courtesy of dealers in Tulancingo. Unfortunately, those tactics are outdated. We know them all."

"Maybe she thought you were harassing her," said Noel, with little conviction. "Maybe she just wanted to get away from you."

"There's no harassment. And whatever her reasons, she'd better realize that someone else is aware of them. Someone very serious."

"What are you telling me?"

"She was being followed by a man we couldn't place in any file anywhere. His papers were as counterfeit as hers. We had him picked up at the airport in Mexico City. Before anyone could question him, he slipped a cyanide capsule in his mouth."

29

A meeting ground was chosen. There was a vacant flat in Montmartre, on the top floor of an old building, its owner an artist now in Italy. Helden telephoned, gave Noel the address and the time. She would be there to introduce her brother, but would not stay.

Noel climbed the last step and knocked on the door. He heard hurrying footsteps; the door opened; Helden was in the narrow foyer. "Hello, my darling," she said.

"Hello," he answered awkwardly as he met her lips, his eyes glancing behind her.

"Johann's on the terrace," she said, laughing. "A kiss is permitted, in any event. I told him . . . how fond I am of you."

"Was that necessary?"

"Strangely enough, it was. I'm glad I did. It made me feel good." She closed the door, holding his arm. "I can't explain this," she said. "I haven't seen my brother in over a year. But he's changed. The situation in Geneva has affected him; he's profoundly committed to its success. I've never seen him so . . . oh, I don't know . . . so thoughtful."

"I still have questions, Helden."

"So does he. About you."

"Really?"

"At one point this morning, he didn't want to meet with you. He didn't trust you. He believed you'd been reached, paid to betray Geneva."

"*Me?*"

"Think about it. He learned from people in Rio that you'd met with Maurice Graff. From Graff you went straight to London, to Anthony Beaumont. You were right about him: He's ODESSA." Helden stopped briefly. "He said you . . . spent the night with Gretchen, went to bed with her."

"Wait a minute," interrupted Noel.

"No, darling, it's not important. I told you, I know my sister. But there's a pattern, don't you see? To the ODESSA, women are only conveniences. You were a friend of ODESSA; you'd had a long, exhausting trip. It was perfectly natural that your needs should be fulfilled."

"That's barbaric!"

"It's the way Johann saw it."

"He's wrong."

"He knows that now. At least, I think he does. I told him about the things that had happened to you—to us—and how you'd nearly been killed. He was amazed. He may still have questions to ask you, but I think he's convinced."

Holcroft shook his head in bewilderment. *Nothing is as it was for you . . . nothing can ever be the same.* Not only was nothing the same, it wasn't even what it appeared *not* to be. There was no straight line from point A to point B.

"Let's get this over with," he said. "Can we meet later?"

"Of course."

"Are you going back to work?"

"I haven't been to work."

"I forgot. You were with your brother. You said you were going to work, but you were with him."

"It was a necessary lie."

"They're all necessary, aren't they?"

"Please, Noel. Shall I come back for you? Say, in two hours?"

Holcroft considered. Part of his mind was still on the startling news Miles had given him. He had tried to reach Sam Buonoventura in Curaçao, but Sam had been in the field. "You could do me a favor instead," he said to Helden. "I've told you about Buonoventura, in the Caribbean. I put in a call to him from the hotel; he hasn't returned it. If you're free, would you wait in the room in case he does call? I wouldn't ask you, but it's urgent. Something happened; I'll tell you about it later. Will you?"

"Certainly. What shall I say to him?"

"Tell him to stay put for a few hours. Or to give you a number where I can call him later. Six to eight, Paris time. Tell him it's important." Noel reached in his pocket. "Here's the key. Remember, my name's Fresca."

Helden took the key and then his arm, leading him into the studio. "And you remember, my brother's name is Tennyson. John Tennyson."

Holcroft saw Tennyson through thick panes of leaded glass windows that looked out on the terrace. He wore a dark pinstriped suit, no overcoat or hat; his hands were on the railing as he peered out at the Paris skyline. He was tall and slender, the body tapered almost too perfectly; it was the body of an athlete, a series of coiled springs, taut and contained. He turned slightly to his right, revealing his face. It was a face like no other Noel had seen. It was an artist's rendering, the features too idealized for actual flesh and blood. And because it did not accept blemish, the face was cold. It was a face cast in marble, topped by glistening light-blond hair, perfectly groomed, matching the stone.

Then Von Tiebolt-Tennyson saw him through the window; their eyes met, and the image of marble collapsed. The blond man's eyes were alive and penetrating. He pushed himself away from the railing and walked toward the terrace door.

Stepping inside, he extended his hand. "I am the son of Wilhelm von Tiebolt."

"I'm . . . Noel Holcroft. My . . . father was Heinrich Clausen."

"I know. Helden has told me a great deal about you. You've been through a lot."

"We both have," agreed Holcroft. "I mean, your sister and I. I gather you've had your share, too."

"Our legacy, unfortunately." Tennyson smiled. "It's awkward meeting like this, isn't it?"

"I've been more comfortable."

"And I've not said a word," interjected Helden. "You were both quite capable of introducing yourselves. I'll leave now."

"You certainly don't have to," said Tennyson. "What we have to say to each other concerns you, I think."

"I'm not sure it does. Not for the moment. Besides, I have something to do," replied Helden. She started toward the foyer. "I think it's terribly important—for a great many people—that you trust each other. I hope you can." She opened the door and left.

Neither man spoke for several moments; each looked toward the spot where Helden had stood.

"She's remarkable," said Tennyson. "I love her very much."

Noel turned his head. "So do I."

Tennyson acknowledged the look as well as the statement. "I hope it's not a complication for you."

"It isn't, although it may be for her."

"I see." Tennyson walked to the window and gazed outside. "I'm not in a position to give you my blessing—Helden and I live very separate lives—and even if I could, I'm not sure I would."

"Thanks for your frankness."

The blond man turned. "Yes, I'm frank. I don't know you. I know only what Helden has told me about you, and what I've learned for myself. What she tells me is basically what you've told her, colored by her feelings, of course. What I've learned is not so clear-cut. Nor does the composite fit my sister's rather enthusiastic picture."

"We both have questions. Do you want to go first?"

"It doesn't really matter, does it? Mine are very few and very direct." Tennyson's voice was suddenly harsh. "What was your business with Maurice Graff?"

"I thought Helden told you."

"Again it was what you told *her*. Now, tell *me*. I'm somewhat more experienced than my sister. I don't accept things simply because you say them. Over the years, I've learned not to do that. Why did you go to see Graff?"

"I was looking for you."

"For *me?*"

"Not you, specifically. For the Von Tiebolts. For information about any of you."

"Why Graff?"

"His name was given to me."

"By whom?"

"I don't remember. . . ."

"You don't *remember?* Of thousands and thousands of men in Rio de Janeiro, the name of Maurice Graff just *happens* to be the one casually given to you."

"It's the truth."

"It's ludicrous."

"Wait a minute." Noel tried to reconstruct the sequence of events that led him to Graff. "It started in New York. . . ."

"*What* started? Grass was in New York?"

"No, the consulate. I went to the Brazilian consulate and spoke to an attaché. I wanted to find out how I'd go about locating a family that had immigrated to Brazil in the forties. The attaché put the facts together and figured out I was looking for Germans. He gave me a lecture about . . . well, there's a Spanish phrase for it. *La otra cara de los almanes.* It means the other side of the German; what's beneath his thinking."

"I'm aware of that. Go on."

"He told me there was a strong, close-knit German community in Rio run by a few powerful men. He warned me about looking for a German family that had disappeared; he said it could be dangerous. Maybe he exaggerated because I wouldn't give him your name."

"Thank God you didn't."

"When I got to Rio, I couldn't find out anything. Even the immigration records were doctored."

"At great cost to a great many people," said Tennyson bitterly. "It was our only protection."

"I was stuck. Then I remembered what the attaché had said about the German community being run by a few powerful men. I went to a German bookstore and asked a clerk about the houses. Large ones, mansions with a lot of acreage. I called them 'Bavarian,' but he knew what I meant. I'm an architect and I figured—"

"I understand." Tennyson nodded. "Large German estates, the most influential leaders in the German community."

"That's right. The clerk gave me a couple of names. One was Jewish, the other was Graff. He said Graff's estate was among the most impressive in Brazil."

"It is."

"And that's it. That's how I came to go to Graff."

Tennyson stood motionless, his expression noncommittal. "It's not unreasonable."

"I'm glad you think so," said Noel.

"I said it was reasonable; I didn't say I believed you."

"I've no reason to lie."

"Even if you do, I'm not sure you have the talent. I'm very good at seeing through liars."

Noel was struck by the statement. "That's practically what Helden said the night I met her."

"I've trained her well. Lying is a craft; it must be developed. You're out of your depth."

"What the hell are you trying to say?"

"I'm saying you're a very convincing amateur. You built your story well, but it is not sufficiently professional. Your keystone is missing. As an architect, I'm sure you understand."

"I'll be goddamned if I do. Tell me."

"With pleasure. You left Brazil knowing the name Von Tiebolt. You arrive in England and within twelve hours you're in a suburb of Portsmouth with my sister, *sleeping* with my sister. You didn't even have the name of Tennyson. How could you possibly have known about Beaumont?"

"But I *did* have the name of Tennyson."

"How? How did you get it?"

"I told Helden. This couple, a brother and sister named Cararra, came to see me at the hotel."

"Oh, yes. Cararra. A very common name in Brazil. Did it mean anything to you?"

"Of course not."

"So these Cararras come to see you, out of nowhere, claiming to be dear friends of ours. But as Helden told *you,* we've never heard of them. Come, Mr. Holcroft, you'll have to do better than that." Tennyson raised his voice. "Graff gave you Beaumont's name, didn't he? ODESSA to ODESSA."

"No! Graff didn't know. He thinks you're still hiding somewhere in Brazil."

"He said that?"

"He implied it. The Cararras confirmed it. They mentioned some colonies in the south—'Catarinas,' or something. A mountain region settled by Germans."

"You've done your homework well. The Santa Catarinas are German settlements. But again, we're back to the elusive Cararras."

Noel remembered clearly the fear in the faces of the young brother and sister in Rio. "Maybe they're elusive to you, but not to me. You've either got a lousy memory or you're a lousy friend. They said they barely knew Helden, but knew you very well. They risked a hell of a lot to come and see me. Portuguese Jews who—"

"Portuguese . . ." interrupted Tennyson, suddenly alarmed. "Oh, my God! And they used the name Cararra. . . . Describe them!"

Holcroft did. When he had finished, Tennyson said, in a whisper, "Out of the past. . . . Out of the past, Mr. Holcroft. It all fits. The use of the name Cararra. Portuguese Jews. Santa Catarina. . . . They came back to Rio."

"Who came back?"

"The Montealegres—that's their real name. Ten, twelve years ago. . . . What they told you was a cover, so you'd never be able to reveal their identities, even unconsciously."

"What happened twelve years ago?"

"The details aren't important, but we had to get them out of Rio, so we sent them to the Catarinas. Their parents helped the Israelis; they were killed for it.

The two children were hunted; they would have been shot, too. They had to be taken south."

"Then there are people in the Catarinas who know about you?"

"Yes, a few. Our base of operations was in Santa Catarina. Rio was too dangerous."

"What operations? Who's 'we'?"

"Those of us in Brazil who fought the ODESSA." Tennyson shook his head. "I have an apology to make. Helden was right: I did you an injustice. You've told the truth."

Noel had the sensation of having been vindicated when vindication had not been sought. He felt awkward questioning a man who had fought the ODESSA; who had rescued children from death as surely as if he'd taken them out of Auschwitz, or Belsen; who had trained the woman he loved to survive. But he *had* questions; it was no time to forget them.

"It's my turn now," said Noel. "You're very quick, and you know about things I've never heard of, but I'm not sure you've said a hell of a lot."

"If one of your questions concerns the Tinamou," said Tennyson, "I'm sorry, but I won't answer you. I won't even discuss it."

Holcroft was stunned. "You won't *what?*"

"You heard me. The Tinamou is a subject I won't discuss. It's not your business."

"I think it is! For starters, let's put it this way: If you won't discuss the Tinamou, we haven't *anything* to discuss."

Tennyson paused, startled. "You mean that, don't you?"

"Absolutely."

"Then try to understand me. Nothing can be left to chance now, to the offhand possibility—no matter how remote—that the wrong word might be dropped to the wrong person. If I'm right, and I think I am, you'll have your answer in a matter of days."

"That's not good enough!"

"Then I'll go one step further. The Tinamou was trained in Brazil. By the ODESSA. I've studied him as thoroughly as any man on earth. I've been tracking him for six years."

It took several seconds for Noel to find his voice. "You've been . . . for six years?"

"Yes. It's time for the Tinamou to strike; there'll be another assassination. It's why the British contacted you; they know it, too."

"Why don't you work with them? For God's sake, do you know what they think!"

"I know what someone's tried to *make* them think. It's why I can't work with them. The Tinamou has sources everywhere; they don't know him, but he uses them."

"You said a matter of days."

"If I'm wrong, I'll tell you everything. I'll even go to the British with you."

"A matter of days. . . . Okay. We'll pass on the Tinamou—for a matter of days."

"Whatever else I can tell you, I will. I've nothing to hide."

"You knew Beaumont in Rio, knew he was part of the ODESSA. You even accused me of having gotten his name from Graff. Yet in spite of all this, he married your sister. ODESSA to ODESSA? Are you one of them?"

Tennyson did not waver. "A question of priorities. Put simply, it was planned. My sister Gretchen is not the woman she once was, but she's never lost her hatred of the Nazis. She's made a sacrifice greater than any of us. We know every move that Beaumont makes."

"But he knows you're Von Tiebolt! Why doesn't he tell Graff?"

"Ask him, if you like. He may tell you."

"*You* tell me."

"He's afraid to," replied Tennyson. "Beaumont is a pig. Even his commitments lack cleanliness. He works less and less for the ODESSA, and only then when they threaten him."

"I don't understand."

"Gretchen has her own . . . shall we say, persuasive powers; I think you're aware of them. Beyond these, a large sum of untraceable money found its way into Beaumont's account. In addition to these circumstances, he fears exposure from Graff on one side . . . and from me on the other. He's useful to us both, more so to me than to Graff, of course. He's checkmated."

"If you knew every move he made, you had to know he was on that plane to Rio. You had to know he was following me."

"How could I? I didn't know *you.*"

"He was there. Someone sent him!"

"When Helden told me, I tried to find out who. What I learned was very little, but enough to alarm me. In my judgment, our checkmated pig was reached by a third party. Someone who had unearthed his ODESSA connection and was using him—as Graff used him. As I used him."

"Who?"

"I wish to heaven I knew! He was granted an emergency leave from his ship in the Mediterranean. He went to Geneva."

"Geneva?" Noel's memory raced back. To a fragment of time obscured by swift movement, and rushing crowds, and screams . . . on a station platform. On a *concrete station platform.* A fight had broken out; a man had arched backward with blood on his shirt, another had gone after a third. . . . A man in panic had raced by, his eyes wide in fright, beneath . . . thick eyebrows of black and white hair. "That was it," said Holcroft, astonished. "Beaumont was in Geneva."

"I just told you that."

"That's where I saw him! I couldn't remember where before. He followed me from Geneva."

"I'm afraid I don't know what you're talking about."

"Where's Beaumont now?" asked Noel.

"Back on board ship. Gretchen left several days ago to join him. In Saint-Tropez, I think."

Tomorrow I go to the Mediterranean. To a man I loathe. . . . Everything made so much more sense now. Perhaps Tennyson was not the only man in that room who had been unfair in his judgments.

"We've got to find out who sent Beaumont after me," said Noel, picturing the man in a black leather jacket. Tennyson was right; their conclusions were the same. There *was* someone else.

"I agree," said the blond man. "Shall we go together?"

Holcroft was tempted. But he had not finished. There could be no unanswered questions later. Not once the commitment had been made between them.

"Maybe," he replied. "There are two other things I want to ask you about. And I warn you, I want the answers now, not in a 'matter of days.'"

"All right."

"You killed someone in Rio."

Tennyson's eyes narrowed. "Helden told you."

"I had to know; she understood that. There are conditions in Geneva that won't allow surprises. If you can be blackmailed, I can't let you go on."

Tennyson nodded. "I see."

"Who was it? Whom did you kill?"

"You mistake my reticence," replied the blond man. "I've no compunction whatsoever about telling you who it was. I'm trying to think how you can check up on what I say. There's no blackmail involved. There couldn't be; but how can you be sure?"

"Let's start with a name."

"Manuel Cararra."

"Cararra? . . ."

"Yes. It's why those two young people used it. They knew I'd see the political connection. Cararra was a leader in the Chamber of Deputies, one of the most powerful men in the country. But his allegiance was not to Brazil; it was to Graff. To the Odessa. I killed him seven years ago, and I'd kill him tomorrow."

Noel studied Tennyson's face. "Who knew?"

"A few old men. Only one's still alive. I'll give you his name, if you like. He'd never say anything about the killing."

"Why not?"

"The shoe, as they say, was on the other foot. Before I left Rio de Janeiro, I met with them. My threat was clear. If ever they pursued me, I would make public what I knew about Cararra. The long-revered image of a conservative martyr would be shattered. The conservative cause in Brazil can't tolerate that."

"I want the name."

"I'll write it out for you." Tennyson did. "I'm sure you can reach him by transatlantic telephone. It won't take much; my name coupled with Cararra's should be enough."

"I may do that."

"By all means," said Tennyson. "He'll confirm what I've told you."

The two men faced each other, only feet apart. "There was a subway accident in London," Noel went on. "A number of people were killed, including a man who worked for the *Guardian*. He was the man whose signature was on your employment records. The man who interviewed you, the only one who could shed any light on how or why you were hired."

Tennyson's eyes were suddenly cold again. "It was a shock. I'll never get over it. What is your question?"

"There was another accident. In New York. Only days ago. A number of innocent people were killed then, too, but one of them was the target. Someone I loved very much."

"I repeat! What's your *point*, Holcroft?"

"There's a certain similarity, wouldn't you say? MI Five doesn't know anything about the accident in New York, but it has very specific ideas about the one in London. I've put them together and come up with a disturbing connection. What do you know about that accident five years ago in London?"

Tennyson's body was rigid. "Watch out," he said. "The British go too far. What do you want of me? How far will you go to discredit me?"

"Cut the bullshit!" said Noel. "What happened in that subway?"

"I was *there!*" The blond man thrust his hand up to his collar beneath the pinstriped suit. He yanked furiously, ripping his shirt half off his chest, exposing a scar that extended from the base of his throat to his breast. "I don't know anything about New York, but the experience in Charing Cross five years ago is one I'll live with for the rest of my life! Here it is; there's not a day when I'm not reminded of it. Forty-seven stitches, neck to thorax. I thought for a few moments—five years ago in London—that my head had been half cut off from the rest of me. And that man you speak of so enigmatically was my dearest friend in England! He helped get us out of Brazil. If someone killed him, they tried to kill me, too! I was with him."

"I didn't know. . . . The British didn't say anything. They didn't know you were there."

"Then I suggest someone look. There's a hospital record around somewhere. It shouldn't be hard to find." Tennyson shook his head in disgust. "I'm sorry, I shouldn't be angry at you. It's the British; they'll use anything."

"It's possible they really didn't know."

"I suppose so. Hundreds of people were taken off that train. A dozen clinics in London were filled that night; no one paid much attention to names. But you'd think they would have found mine. I was in the hospital for several days." Tennyson stopped abruptly. "You said someone you loved was killed in New York only a few days ago? What happened?"

Noel told him how Richard Holcroft had been run down in the streets, and of the theory conceived by David Miles. It was pointless to withhold anything from this man he had come close to misjudging so completely.

In the telling was the conclusion both men had arrived at.

In my judgment, our checkmated pig was reached by a third party.
Who?
I wish to heaven I knew. . . .
Someone else.
A man in a black leather jacket. Defiant in a dark alley in Berlin. Willing to die . . . asking to be shot. Refusing to say who he was or where he came from. Someone or something more powerful, more knowledgeable, than the Rache or the ODESSA.
Someone else.

Noel told Tennyson everything, relieved that he could say it all. The relief was heightened by the way the blond man listened. His speckled gray eyes never wavered from Holcroft's face; they were riveted, totally absorbed. When he had finished, Noel felt exhausted. "That's all I know."

Tennyson nodded. "We've finally met, haven't we? We both had to say what was on our minds. We both thought the other was the enemy, and we were both wrong. Now, we have work to do."

"How long have you known about Geneva?" asked Holcroft. "Gretchen told me that you said a man would come one day and speak of a strange arrangement."

"Since I was a child. My mother told me there was an extraordinary sum of money that was to be used for great works, to make amends for the terrible things done in Germany's name, but not by true Germans. But only that fact, no specifics."

"You don't know Erich Kessler, then."

"I remember the name, but only vaguely. I was very young."

"You'll like him."

"As you describe him, I'm sure I will. You say he's bringing his brother to Geneva? Is that allowed?"

"Yes. I said I'd telephone him in Berlin and give him dates."

"Why not wait until tomorrow or the day after? Call him from Saint-Tropez?"

"Beaumont?"

"Beaumont," said Tennyson, his mouth set. "I think we should meet with our checkmated pig. He has something to tell us. Specifically, who was his latest employer? Who sent him to that train station in Geneva? Who paid him for—or blackmailed him into—following you to New York and then to Rio de Janeiro? When we find this out, we'll know where your man in the black leather jacket came from."

Someone else.

Noel looked at his watch. It was nearly six o'clock; he and Tennyson had talked for more than two hours, yet there was still a great deal more to say. "Do you want to have dinner with your sister and me?" he asked.

Tennyson smiled. "No, my friend. We'll talk on our way south. I've calls to make and copy to file. I mustn't forget I'm a newspaperman. Where are you staying?"

"At the George Cinq. Under the name of Fresca."

"I'll phone you later this evening." Tennyson extended his hand. "Until tomorrow."

"Tomorrow."

"Incidentally, if my fraternal blessings mean anything, you have them."

Johann von Tiebolt stood at the railing of the terrace in the cold air of the early evening. Below, on the street, he could see Holcroft emerge from the building and walk east on the sidewalk.

It had all been so easy. The orchestration of lies had been studiously thought out and arranged, the rendering underpinned with outraged conviction and sudden revelation that led to acceptance. An old man would be alerted in Rio; he knew what to say. A medical record would be placed in a London hospital, the dates and information corresponding to a tragic accident on the Charing Cross underground five years ago. And if all went according to schedule, a news item would be carried in the evening papers reporting another tragedy. A naval officer and his wife had disappeared in a small pleasure boat off the Mediterranean coast.

Von Tiebolt smiled. Everything was going as it had been projected thirty years ago. Even the Nachrichtendienst could not stop them now. In a matter of days the Nachrichtendienst would be castrated.

It was time for the Tinamou.

30

Noel hurried through the lobby of the George V, eager to get to his room, to Helden. Geneva was closer now; it would be closer still when they met Anthony Beaumont in Saint-Tropez and forced the truth from him.

Too, he was anxious to learn whether Buonoventura had returned his call. His mother had said she would let Sam know her plans. All Miles knew in New York was that Althene had left Mexico City for Lisbon. Why Lisbon? And who had followed her?

The image of the man in the black leather jacket came back to Holcroft. The steady look in his eyes, the acceptance of death . . . *kill me and another will take my place. Kill him, another his.*

The elevator was empty, the ascent swift. The door opened; Noel caught his breath at the sight of the man standing in the corridor facing him. It was the

Verwünschtes Kind from Sacré-Coeur, the fashion plate who had searched him in front of the candles.

"Good evening, monsieur."

"What are you doing here? Is Helden all right?"

"She can answer your questions."

"So can you." Holcroft grabbed the man's arm and turned him forcefully toward the door of the room.

"Take your hands off me!"

"When she tells me to let you go, I'll let you go. Come on." Noel propelled the man down the corridor to the door, and knocked.

In seconds the door opened. Helden stood there, startled at the sight of the two of them. In her hand was a folded newspaper; in her eyes was something beyond her astonishment: sadness.

"What's the matter?" she asked.

"That's what I wanted to know, but he wouldn't tell me." Holcroft pushed the man through the door.

"Noel, *please.* He's one of us."

"I want to know why he's here."

"I called him; he had to know where I was. He told me he had to see me. I'm afraid he's brought us dreadful news."

"What?"

"Read the papers," said the man. "There are both French and English."

Holcroft picked up a copy of the *Herald Tribune* from the coffee table.

"Page two," said the man. "Top left."

Noel turned the page, snapping it flat. He read the words, a sense of anger . . . and fear . . . sweeping over him.

NAVAL OFFICER AND WIFE
LOST IN MEDITERRANEAN

St.-Tropez—Commander Anthony Beaumont, captain of the patrol ship *Argo* and a highly decorated officer of Her Majesty's Royal Navy, along with his wife, who had joined him in this resort town for the weekend, were feared drowned when their small boat foundered in an angry squall several miles south along this rockbound coast. A capsized craft fitting the description of the small boat was sighted by low-flying coastal search planes. The commander and his wife had not been heard from in over forty-eight hours, prompting second-in-command of the *Argo*, Lt. Morgan Llewellen, to issue search directives. The Admiralty has concluded that Commander and Mrs. Beaumont lost their lives in the tragic accident. The couple had no children.

"Oh, *God,*" whispered Holcroft. "Did your brother tell you?"

"About Gretchen?" Helden asked. "Yes. She suffered so much, gave so much. It's why she wouldn't see me or talk to me. She never wanted me to know what she did, why she married him. She was afraid I might sense the truth."

"If what you *say* is true," said the well-dressed man, "that Beaumont was ODESSA, we don't believe that newspaper story for a minute."

"He means your friend in Berlin," interrupted Helden. "I told him that you had a friend in Berlin who said he would transmit your suspicions to London."

Noel understood. She was telling him she had said nothing about Geneva. Noel turned to the man. "What do you think happened?"

"If the British discovered an ODESSA agent in the upper ranks of the navy, especially one commanding a coastal-patrol vessel—a euphemism for an espionage ship—it would mean they had been duped again. There's just so much they can take; there'd be no inquiries. A swift execution is preferable."

"That's a pretty rough indictment," said Holcroft.

"It's an embarrassing situation."

"They'd kill an innocent woman?"

"Without thinking twice—on the possibility that she might not be innocent. The message would be clear, at any rate. The ODESSA network would have its warning."

Noel turned away in disgust and put his arms around Helden. "I'm sorry," he said. "I know how you must feel, and I wish there was something I could do. Outside of reaching your brother, I'm not sure there is."

Helden turned and looked at him, her eyes searching. "You trust each other?"

"Very much. We're working together now."

"Then there's no time for mourning, is there? I'm going to stay here tonight," she told the well-dressed man. "Is it all right? Can I be covered?"

"Of course," said the man. "I'll arrange it."

"Thank you. You're a good friend."

He smiled. "I don't think Mr. Holcroft believes that. But then, he's got a great deal to learn." The man nodded and went to the door; he stopped, his hand on the knob, and turned to Noel. "I apologize if that appears cryptic to you, but be tolerant, monsieur. What's between you and Helden also seems cryptic to me, but I don't inquire. I trust. But, if that trust is found to be misplaced, we'll kill you. I just thought you ought to know."

The *Verwünschtes Kind* left quickly. Noel took an angry step after him, but Helden touched his arm. "Please, darling. He, too, has a lot to learn, and we can't tell him. He *is* a friend."

"He's an insufferable little bastard." Holcroft paused. "I'm sorry. You've got enough on your mind; you don't need foolishness from me."

"A man threatened your life."

"Someone took your sister's. Under the circumstances, I was foolish."

"We've no time for such thoughts. Your friend Buonoventura returned your call. I wrote down the number where you can reach him. It's by the telephone."

Noel walked to the bedside table and picked up the paper. "Your brother and I were going to Saint-Tropez tomorrow. To make Beaumont tell us what he knew. The news'll be shattering to him. On both counts."

"You said you were going to call him. I think it's best that I do. He and Gretchen were very close. When they were younger, they were inseparable. Where is he?"

"Actually, I don't know; he didn't say. He just told me he'd reach me later

this evening. That's what I meant." Holcroft lifted the phone and gave Buonoventura's number to the operator.

"I'll speak to Johann when he calls," said Helden, going to the window.

The transatlantic lines were light; the link to Curaçao was made in less than
a minute.

"You're a pistol, Noley! I'm glad I don't have to pay your phone bills. You're
seeing the goddamn world; I'll say that for you."

"I'm seeing a lot more than that, Sam. Did my mother call you?"

"She did. She said to tell you she'll see you in Geneva in about a week. You're
to stay at the Hôtel d'Accord, but you're not to say anything to anyone."

"Geneva? She's going to Geneva? Why the hell did she even leave the country?"

"She said it was an emergency. You were to keep your mouth shut, and not
do anything until you see her. She was one upset lady."

"I've got to get hold of her. Did she give you a telephone number—an
address—where I could reach her?"

"Not a thing, pal. She didn't have much time to talk, and the connection was
rotten. It was out of Mexico. Anybody mind telling me what's going on?"

Holcroft shook his head as if Buonoventura were in the room facing him.
"Sorry, Sam. Perhaps someday. I owe you."

"I think maybe you do. We'll cut a deck for it. Take care of yourself. You got
a real nice mother. Be good to her."

Holcroft hung up. Buonoventura was a good friend to have. As good a friend
as the well-dressed man was to Helden, he thought. He wondered what she meant
when she asked the *Verwünschtes Kind* if she were covered. Covered for what?
By whom?

"My mother's on her way to Geneva," he said.

Helden turned. "I heard you. You sounded upset."

"I am. A man followed her to Mexico. Miles had him picked up at the airport;
he took a cyanide capsule before they could find out who he was or where he came
from."

" 'Kill me, another will take my place. Kill him, another his.' Weren't those
the words?"

"Yes. I was thinking about them on the way up."

"Does Johann know?"

"I told him everything."

"What does he think?"

"He doesn't know what to think. The key was Beaumont. I don't know where
we go now, except to Geneva, with the hope that no one stops us."

Helden came toward him. "Tell me something. What can they—whoever they
are—really do? Once the three of you present yourselves to the bank in Geneva,
each of you in agreement, all reasonable men, it's over. So what can they actually
do?"

"You said it last night."

"What?"

"They can kill us."

The telephone rang. Holcroft reached for it. "Yes?"

"It's John Tennyson." The voice was strained.

"Your sister wants to talk to you," said Holcroft.

"In a moment," replied Tennyson. "We must speak first. Does she know?"

"Yes. Obviously you do, too."

"My paper called me with the news. The night editor knew how close Gretchen and I were. It's horrible."

"I wish there was something I could say."

"I couldn't help you when you told me about your stepfather. We have to live with these things by ourselves. There's nothing anyone can do or say when they happen. Helden understands."

"Then you don't believe the story that was given out? About the boat and the storm?"

"That they went out in a boat and never came back? Yes, I believe it. That he was responsible? Of course not. It's not even plausible. Whatever else he was, Beaumont was a superb sailor. He could smell a storm twenty miles away. If he was in a small craft, he'd have it in shore before any weather struck."

"Who then?"

"Come, my friend, we both know the answer. That someone else who hired him also killed him. They made him follow you to Rio. You spotted him; his usefulness had come to an end." Tennyson paused. "It was as if they'd known we were to leave for Saint-Tropez. The unpardonable act was to kill Gretchen as well. For appearances."

"I'm sorry. *God*, I feel responsible."

"It was totally out of your control."

"Could it have been the British?" asked Holcroft. "I told Kessler about Beaumont. He said he was going to work through channels. Bonn to London. Maybe an ODESSA agent commanding one of those reconnaissance ships was too much of an embarrassment."

"The temptation might be there, but no one in authority would grant permission. The English would put him into isolation and break him on a rack if they had to get information, but they wouldn't kill him. They *had* him. He and Gretchen were killed by someone who could be damaged by what he knew, not by anyone who could benefit."

Tennyson's reasoning was persuasive. "You're right. The British wouldn't gain anything. They'd keep him under wraps."

"Exactly. And there's another factor, a moral one. I think MI Six is riddled with self-seekers, but I don't believe they kill to avoid embarrassment. It's not in their nature. But they'll go to extraordinary lengths to maintain a reputation. Or revive it. And I pray to God I'm right about that."

"What do you mean?"

"I'm flying to London tonight. In the morning I'll contact Payton-Jones at MI

Five. I've an exchange to offer him, one I think he'll find difficult to resist. I may be able to give him a ground-dwelling bird that moves rapidly from one place to another, its feathers blending in with the environment."

Holcroft was as surprised as he was bewildered. "I thought you said you couldn't work with them."

"*Him.* Only Payton-Jones, no one else. He must give me his assurance of that, or we go no farther."

"Do you think he will?"

"He really has no choice. That ground-dwelling bird has become an MI obsession."

"Suppose you do? What do you get in return?"

"Access to classified material. The British have thousands of secret files. They concern the last years of the war and are embarrassing to a lot of people. But somewhere in those files is our answer. A man, a group of men, a band of fanatics—I don't know who or what, but it's there. Someone who had a connection with the Finanzministerium thirty years ago, or with our fathers; someone they trusted and to whom they gave responsibility. It could even be a Loch Torridon infiltration."

"A what?"

"Loch Torridon. It was an espionage and sabotage operation mounted by the British from 'forty-one to 'forty-four. Hundreds of former nationals were sent back to Germany and Italy to work in factories and railroads and government offices everywhere. It's common knowledge there were Loch Torridon personnel in the Finanzministerium. . . . The answer is in the archives."

"From those thousands of files, you expect to find one identity? Even if it's there, it could take months."

"Not really. I know precisely what to look for: people who may have been associated with our fathers."

Tennyson spoke so rapidly, with such assurance, that Noel found it difficult to keep up with him. "Why are you so convinced the information is there to begin with?"

"Because it has to be. You made that clear to me this afternoon. The man who called you in New York, the one who was killed—"

"Peter Baldwin?"

"Yes. MI Six. He knew about Geneva. We start with him; he's our key now."

"Then go to the file called 'Wolfsschanze,' " said Holcroft. " 'Code Wolfsschanze.' That may be it!"

Tennyson did not reply at first. He was either thinking or startled; Noel could not tell which. "Where did you hear that?" he asked. "You never mentioned it. Neither did Helden."

"Then we both forgot," Holcroft told him.

"We should be careful," said Tennyson, when Noel had finished. "If the name 'Wolfsschanze' is tied to Geneva, we must be *extremely* careful. The British can't learn about Geneva. It would be disastrous."

"I agree. But what reason will you give Payton-Jones for wanting access to the archives?"

"Part of the truth," answered Tennyson. "I want Gretchen's killer."

"And for that you're willing to give up the . . . ground-dwelling bird you've been tracking for six years?"

"For that and for Geneva. With all my heart."

Noel was touched. "Do you want me to talk to Payton-Jones?"

"*No!*" Tennyson shouted; then he lowered his voice. "I mean, it would be far too dangerous. Trust me. Do as I ask you, please. You and Helden must stay out of sight. Completely. Until I contact you, Helden must not return to work. She must stay with you, and you both must remain invisible."

Holcroft looked at Heldon. "I don't know if she'll agree to that."

"I'll convince her. Let me speak with her. You and I have finished our talk."

"You'll call me?"

"In a few days. If you change hotels, leave word where Mr. Fresca can be reached. Helden has my message-service number. Let me talk with her now. In spite of our differences, we need each other now, perhaps as we've never needed each other before. And . . . Noel?"

"Yes?"

"Be kind to her. Love her. She needs you, too."

Holcroft stood up and handed the phone to Helden.

"Mein Bruder. . . ."

31

Code Wolfsschanze!

Von Tiebolt-Tennyson slammed his fist on the desk in the small out-of-the-way office he used in Paris.

Code Wolfsschanze. That sacrosanct phrase had been given to Peter Baldwin by Ernst Manfredi! The banker had played a dangerous but ingenious game. He knew that Baldwin's mere use of the phrase was enough to guarantee his death. But Manfredi would never have given the Englishman more than that; it would not have been in the banker's interests. Still, Baldwin had possessed one of the best minds in Europe. Had he pieced together more than Manfredi had considered possible? How much had he really learned? What was contained in Baldwin's file at MI Five?

Or did it matter? The British had rejected whatever it was Baldwin had to offer. One file folder among thousands upon thousands. Buried in the archives, lost because it was one more entry of rejected information.

Code Wolfsschanze. It meant nothing to those who knew nothing, and the few hundred who did—those district leaders in every country—knew only that it was a signal. They were to make themselves ready; enormous funds would soon be sent to them, to be used for the cause.

Die Sonnenkinder. All over the world, prepared to rise and assert their birthright.

Baldwin's file could not contain that information; it was not possible. But those who held that file would be used. Above all else, the British wanted the Tinamou. His capture by MI Five would reassert English supremacy in intelligence operations—a supremacy lost through years of blunders and defections.

MI Five would be handed the Tinamou, and with that gift would come an obligation to the giver. That was the splendid irony: The hated British Intelligence, that quiet, serpentine monster that had wreaked such havoc on the Third Reich, would help create the Fourth.

For MI Five would be told that the Nachrichtendienst was involved in an extraordinary conspiracy. The British would believe the man who told them; that man was giving them the Tinamou.

Tennyson walked through the London offices of the *Guardian,* receiving the compliments of his colleagues and their subordinates. As always, he accepted the compliments modestly.

He studied the women casually. The secretaries and the receptionists invited this most beautiful of men to acknowledge them, invited him, actually, to take whatever he wished. It struck him that he might have to select one of these women. His beloved Gretchen was gone, but his appetites were not. Yes, thought Tennyson as he walked toward the door of the senior editor's office, he would select a woman. The excitement was mounting, the intensity of Wolfsschanze growing with every passing hour. He would need sexual release. It was always this way; Gretchen had understood.

"John, it's good to see you," said the senior editor, getting up from behind the desk and extending his hand. "We're running the Bonn article tomorrow. Fine job."

Tennyson sat down in a chair in front of the desk. "Something has come up," he said. "If my sources are accurate, and I'm sure they are, a killing—killings—will be attempted that could provoke a world crisis."

"Good heavens. Have you written it up?"

"No. We can't write about it. I don't think any responsible newspaper should."

The editor leaned forward. "What is it, John?"

"There's an economic summit conference called for next Tuesday. . . ."

"Of course. Right here in London. Leaders from the East and West."

"That's the point. East and West. They're flying in from Moscow and Washington, from Peking and Paris. The most powerful men on earth." Tennyson paused.

"And?"

"Two are to be assassinated."

"*What?*"

"Two are to be killed; which two is irrelevant as long as they are from opposing sides; the president of the United States and the chairman of the People's Republic; or the prime minister and the premier of the Soviet Union."

"Impossible! Security measures will be airtight."

"Not really. There'll be crowds, processions, banquets, motorcades. Where's the absolute guarantee found?"

"It has to be!"

"Not against the Tinamou."

"The *Tinamou?*"

"He's accepted the highest fee in history."

"Good God, from *whom?*"

"An organization known as the Nachrichtendienst."

Harold Payton-Jones stared across the table at Tennyson in the dimly lit room that had no other furniture but the table and two chairs. The location had been selected by MI Five; it was a deserted boardinghouse in east London.

"I repeat," said the gray-haired agent curtly. "You expect me to accept the things you say merely because you're willing to go on record? Preposterous!"

"It's my only proof," replied Tennyson. "Everything I've told you is true. We haven't time to fight each other any longer. Every hour is vital."

"Nor have I the inclination to be hoodwinked by an opportunistic journalist who may be much more than a correspondent! You're very clever. And quite possibly an outrageous liar."

"For God's sake, if that's true, why am I *here?* Listen to me! I'll say it for the last time: The Tinamou was trained by the ODESSA. In the hills of Rio de Janeiro! I've fought the ODESSA all my life; that's on my record, if anyone cares to examine it. The ODESSA forced us out of Brazil, cut us off from everything we'd built there. I want the Tinamou!"

Payton-Jones studied the blond man. The argument had been vicious, lasting nearly a half hour. The agent had been relentless, pounding Tennyson with a barrage of questions, lashing out at him with insults. It was a studied technique of MI Five's, designed to separate truth from falsehood. It was apparent that the Englishman was now satisfied. He lowered his voice.

"All right, Mr. Tennyson. We can stop fighting each other. I gather we owe you an apology."

"The apologies are not one-sided. It's just that I knew I could work better alone. I had to pretend to be so many things. If ever anyone had seen me with a member of your service, my effectiveness would have been destroyed."

"Then I'm sorry for the times we called you in."

"They were dangerous moments for me. I could feel the Tinamou slipping away."

"We haven't caught him yet."

"We're close. It's only a matter of days now. We'll succeed if we're painstaking in every decision we make, every street the delegations travel—the locations of every meeting, every ceremony, every banquet. There's an advantage that's never existed before: We know he's there."

"You're absolutely convinced of your source?"

"Never more so in my life. That man in the Berlin pub was the courier. Every courier used to reach the Tinamou has been killed. His last words were 'London . . . next week . . . the summit . . . one from each side . . . a man with a tattoo of a rose on the back of his hand . . . Nachrichtendienst.' "

Payton-Jones nodded. "We'll put out inquiries to Berlin as to the man's identity."

"I doubt you'll find anything. From what little I know about the Nachrichtendienst, it was extremely thorough."

"But it was neutral," Payton-Jones said. "And its information was always accurate. It spared no one. The prosecutors of Nuremberg were continuously fed data by the Nachrichtendienst."

"I suggest," said Tennyson, "that the prosecutors were given only what the Nachrichtendienst wanted to give them. You can't know what was withheld."

The Britisher nodded again. "It's possible. That's something we'll never know. The question is, why? What's the motive?"

"If I may," replied the blond man. ". . . A few old men about to die, taking their final vengeance. The Third Reich had two specific philosophical enemies who allied themselves in spite of their antagonisms: the communists and the democracies. Now each vies for supremacy. What better revenge than for each to accuse the other of assassination? For each to destroy the other?"

"If we could establish that," interrupted Payton-Jones, "it could be the motive behind a number of assassinations during the past years."

"How does one establish it beyond doubt?" asked Tennyson. "Did British Intelligence ever have a direct connection with the Nachrichtendienst?"

"Oh, yes. We insisted on identities—to be kept locked in the vaults, of course. We couldn't act on such information blindly."

"Are any alive today?"

"It's possible. It's been years since anyone has mentioned the Nachrichtendienst. I'll check, of course."

"Will you give me their names?"

The MI-Five man leaned back in the chair. "Is this one of the conditions you spoke of, Mr. Tennyson?"

"Spoke of, but made clear that under the circumstances I could never insist upon."

"No civilized man would. If we catch the Tinamou, you'll have the gratitude of world governments; the names are minor. If we have them, so will you. Do you have other requests? Should I have brought a notebook?"

"They're limited," answered Tennyson, overlooking the insult, "and may surprise you. Out of gratitude to my employers, I should like a five-hour advance exclusive for the *Guardian.*"

"It's yours," said Payton-Jones. "What else?"

"Insofar as MI Five has approached various people, implying that I was the subject of inquiries, I should like a letter from British Intelligence making it clear not only that my personal dossier is without blemish but that I've made an active contribution to your efforts to maintain—shall we say—'international stability.' "

"Quite unnecessary," said the Englishman. "Should the Tinamou be caught through the information you bring us, governments everywhere no doubt will decorate you with highest honors. A letter from us would be gratuitous. You won't need it."

"But, you see, I will," said Tennyson. "For my next-to-last request is that my name never be mentioned."

"Never be—" Payton-Jones was stunned. "That's hardly in character, is it?"

"Please don't confuse my professional endeavors with my private way of life. I seek no credit. The Von Tiebolts owe a debt; call this part payment."

The MI-Five operative was silent for a moment. "I *have* misjudged you. I apologize again. Of course you'll have your letter."

"Frankly, there's another reason for wanting anonymity. I realize that the Royal Navy and the French authorities are satisfied that my sister and her husband died accidentally while on holiday, and they're probably right. But I think you'll agree the timing was unfortunate. I have one sister left; she and I are the last of the Von Tiebolts. If anything happened to her, I'd never forgive myself."

"I understand."

"I'd like to offer you whatever assistance I can. I believe I know as much about the Tinamou as anyone alive. I've studied him for years. Every killing, every projected move he made before and after the acts. I think I can help. I'd like to be a part of your team."

"I'd be a damn fool to turn you down. What's your last request?"

"We'll get to it." Tennyson stood up. "The thing to realize about the Tinamou is that his technique is instant variation, practiced improvisation. He doesn't have a single strategy, but ten or twelve—each methodically conceived and rehearsed so that it can be adapted to the moment."

"I'm not sure I know what you mean."

"Let me explain. That killing in Madrid seven months ago, during the riots— do you remember?"

"Of course. The rifle was fired from a fourth-floor window, above the crowds."

"Exactly. A government building in a government square where the demonstrations were scheduled to take place. A *government* building. That bothered me. Suppose the guards were more alert, security measures more effective, people checked thoroughly for weapons? Suppose he could *not* have gotten to that window? It was an ideal spot, incidentally, for getting the target in his gun sight; but suppose there'd been people in that room?"

"He would have moved to another location."

"Naturally. But no matter how well concealed the weapon—whether part of a crutch, or strapped to his leg, or sewn in sections into his clothing—it would have been awkward. He had to move quickly; timing was important; the demonstration wasn't going to last that long. The Tinamou had to have more than one location, more than one option. And he did."

"How do you know?" asked the MI-Five man, fascinated.

"I spent two days in Madrid, going over every building, every window, every rooftop in that square. I found four weapons intact, and three other locations where floorboards had been ripped out, window sashes removed, and moldings torn apart. Additional weapons had been concealed in those places. I even found two pounds of plastic explosives in a garbage can on the sidewalk. Fifty feet from the center of the demonstration. *Eight* positions from which to kill. Alternate selections for him to choose, each designed to fit a projected moment during a specific time span."

Payton-Jones sat forward, his hands on the table. "That complicates things. Standard protective measures concentrate on a single location. Which of half a hundred possibilities is the most likely? The assumption is that the killer will have stationed himself in one location. The strategy you describe adds another dimension: instant mobility. Not a single preset hiding place, but several, selected at any given moment."

"Within a given time span," finished the blond-haired man. "But as I mentioned, we have an advantage. We know he's there. There's also a second advantage, and it's one we should use immediately." Tennyson stopped.

"What is it?"

"I'll qualify that statement. We should use it only if we agree that the capture of the Tinamou is almost as vital as the ultimate safety of his targets."

The Englishman frowned. "That's a rather dangerous thing to say. There can be no risks—calculated or otherwise—where those men are concerned. Not on British soil."

"Hear me out, please. He's killed political leaders before, spreading suspicion, arousing hostilities between governments. And always steadier heads have prevailed; they've cooled things off. But the Tinamou must be stopped, on the outside chance that one day the steadier heads will not be swift enough. I think we can stop him now, if all consent."

"Consent to what?"

"To adhering to published schedules. Bring the leaders of the delegations together; tell them what you know. Tell them that extraordinary precautions will be mounted, but by keeping to schedules, there's a good chance that the Tinamou will at last be caught." Tennyson paused and leaned over the chair, his hands on the rim. "I think if you're honest, no one will disagree. After all, it's not much more than what political leaders face every day."

The frown on the MI-Five man's face disappeared. "And no one will want to be called a coward. Now, what's this second advantage?"

"The Tinamou's technique requires him to preset concealed weapons in a number of locations. To do that, he must begin days, perhaps weeks, before the designated assassination. He's no doubt begun already here in London. I suggest we start a very quiet but thorough search, staking out those areas that conform to the published reports of the summit's schedule."

Payton-Jones brought his hands together in a gesture of agreement. "Of course. We need only find one and we have not only the general location but the time span."

"Exactly. We'll know that within a given number of minutes, during a specific event at a precise area, the assassination will be attempted." Again the blond man paused. "I'd like to help in that search. I know what to look for, and, perhaps more important, where not to look. We haven't much time."

"Your offer's appreciated, sir," said the Englishman. "MI Five is grateful. Shall we begin tonight?"

"Let's give him one more day to set his guns. It'll increase our chances of finding something. Also, I'll need an innocuous sort of uniform and a permit that identifies me as 'building inspector,' or some such title."

"Very good," said Payton-Jones. "I'm embarrassed to say we have a photograph of you on file; we'll use it for the permit. I'd guess you are a size forty-four, trousers long, waist thirty-three or -four."

"Close enough. A civil-service uniform should hardly be tailored."

"Quite so. We'll take care of both items in the morning." Payton-Jones got up. "You said you had one more request."

"I do. Since I left Brazil, I've not owned a weapon. I'm not even sure it's permitted, but I should like to have one now. Only for the duration of the summit, of course."

"I'll have one issued to you."

"That would need my signature, wouldn't it?"

"Yes."

"Forgive me, but I meant what I said before. As I want no credit for what I've brought you, I feel equally strongly about having my name listed anywhere as an associate of MI Five. I wouldn't want anyone to know the nature of my contributions. My name on a weapon's file card could lead a curious person to the truth. Someone, perhaps, connected to the Nachrichtendienst."

"I see." The Englishman unbuttoned the jacket of his suit coat and reached inside. "This is highly irregular, but so are the circumstances." He withdrew a small, short-barreled revolver and handed it to Tennyson. "Since we both know the source, take mine. I'll list it out for overhaul and have it replaced."

"Thank you," said the blond man, holding the weapon as if it were an unfamiliar object.

Tennyson entered a crowded pub off Soho Square. He scanned the room through the heavy layers of smoke and saw what he was looking for: a hand raised by a man at a table in the far corner. The man, as always, wore a brown raincoat made specifically for him. It looked like any other raincoat; the difference was found in the additional pockets and straps that often contained various handguns, silencers, and explosives. He had been trained by the Tinamou, trained so well that he often performed services contracted by the assassin when the Tinamou was unavailable.

His last assignment had been at Kennedy Airport during a rainswept night when a cordon of police surrounded the glistening fuselage of a British Airways 747. He had found his quarry in a fuel truck. He had done his job.

John Tennyson carried his pint to the table and joined the man in the brown raincoat. The table was round and small; the chairs were so close together that their heads were only inches apart, allowing both men to keep their voices low.

"Is everything placed?" asked the blond man.

"Yes," replied his companion. "The motorcade goes west on the Strand, around Trafalgar Square, through the gates of Admiralty Arch, and into the Mall toward the palace. There are seven locations."

"Give me the sequence."

"From east to west, in order of progression, we start at the Strand Palace Hotel, opposite Savoy Court. Third floor, room three-zero-six. Automatic repeating rifle and scope are sewn into the mattress of the bed nearest the window. A block west, east side, fourth floor, the men's room of an accounting firm. The weapon is in the ceiling, above the tile to the left of the fluorescent light. Directly across the street, again on the fourth floor—there's a penny arcade on the first—the offices of a typing service. Rifle and scope are strapped to the undercarriage of a photocopier. Moving on toward Trafalgar . . ."

The man in the brown raincoat went through the locations of the remaining caches of weapons. They were within a stretch of approximately half a mile, from Savoy Court to Admiralty Arch.

"Excellent choices," said Tennyson, pushing the untouched pint of beer away. "You understand your moves fully?"

"I know what they are; I can't say I understand them."

"That's not really necessary, is it?" asked the blond man.

"Of course not; but I'm thinking of you. If you're hemmed in, or blocked, I could do the job. From any of the locations. Why not give me one?"

"Even you're not qualified for this. There can be no room whatsoever for the slightest error. A single misplaced bullet would be disastrous."

"May I remind you, I was trained by the best there is."

Tennyson smiled. "You're right. Very well. Make the moves I gave you and position yourself in an eighth location. Choose a room in the Government Building, beyond Admiralty Arch, and let me know which. Can you do that?"

"Ducks in a gallery," replied the man, lifting his pint of beer to his lips. Tennyson could see the tattoo of a red rose on the back of his right hand.

"May I make a suggestion?" asked John Tennyson.

"Of course, what is it?"

"Wear gloves," said the Tinamou.

32

The blond man opened the door and reached for the light switch on the wall; two table lamps went on in the hotel room marked 306. He motioned for his middle-aged companion to follow him inside.

"It's all right," said Tennyson. "Even if the room is being watched, the curtains are drawn, and the hour corresponds to the time the maids turn down the beds. Over here."

Payton-Jones kept pace as Tennyson took a miniature metal-detector from his overcoat pocket. He touched the button, holding the device over the bed. The tiny hum grew louder; the needle on the dial jumped to the right.

Carefully, he folded back the covers and undid the sheets. "It's there. You can feel the outlines," he said, pressing his fingers into the mattress.

"Remarkable," said Payton-Jones. "And the room has been leased for ten days?"

"By telegraph and postal money order, originating in Paris. The name is Le Fèvre, a meaningless pseudonym. No one's been here."

"It's there all right." Payton-Jones removed his hands from the bed.

"I can make out the rifle," said Tennyson, "but what's the other object?"

"A telescopic sight," replied the Englishman. "We'll leave everything intact and post men in the corridor."

"The next location is down the street, in the lavatory of an accounting firm on the fourth floor. The gun's in the ceiling, wired to a suspension rod above a fluorescent light."

"Let's go," said Payton-Jones.

An hour and forty-five minutes later, the two men were on the roof of a building overlooking Trafalgar Square. Both knelt by the short wall that bordered the edge. Below was the route the summit motorcade would take on its way through Admiralty Arch and into the Mall.

"The fact that the Tinamou would put a weapon here," said Tennyson, his hand on the tar paper that bulged slightly next to the wall, "makes me think he'll be wearing a police uniform."

"I see what you mean," said Payton-Jones. "A policeman walking onto a roof where we've stationed a man wouldn't cause any great alarm."

"Exactly. He could kill your man and take up his position."

"But then he isolates himself. He has no way out."

"I'm not sure the Tinamou needs one, in the conventional sense. A taut rope into a back alley, hysterical crowds below, stairwells jammed, general pandemonium. He's escaped under less dramatic conditions. Remember, he has more identities than a telephone directory. In Madrid I'm convinced he was one of the interrogators on the scene."

"We'll have two men up here, one out of sight. And four sharpshooters on adjacent rooftops." Payton-Jones crawled away from the wall; the blond man followed. "You've done extraordinary work, Tennyson," said the MI-Five agent. "You've unearthed five locations in something over thirty-six hours. Are you satisfied these are all?"

"Not yet. However, I'm satisfied that we've established the parameters. From the Savoy Court to the end of Trafalgar—somewhere in those half-dozen blocks he'll make his move. Once the motorcade's through the arch and into the Mall, we can breathe again. Until that moment, I'm not sure I will. Have the delegations been told?"

"Yes. Each head of state will be outfitted with chest, groin, and leg plate, as well as crowns of bulletproof plastic in their hats. The president of the United States, naturally, objected to any hat at all, and the Russian wants the plastic fitted into his fur, but otherwise we're in good shape. The risk is minimal."

Tennyson looked at Payton-Jones. "Do you really believe that?"

"Yes. Why?"

"I think you're wrong. The Tinamou is no mere marksman. He's capable of rapid-fire accuracy that would spin a shilling into figure eights at five hundred yards. An expanse of flesh beneath a hat brim is no challenge for him. He'd go for the eyes, and he wouldn't miss."

The Englishman glanced briefly at Tennyson. "I said the risk was minimal, not nonexistent. At the first sign of disturbance, each head of state will be covered by human shields. You've found five locations, so far; say there's another five. If you find no others, we've still reduced his efficiency by fifty percent, and it's a good chance—at least fifty percent—that he'll show up at one of those uncovered. The odds are decidedly against the Tinamou. We'll catch him. We've *got* to."

"His capture means a great deal to you, doesn't it?"

"As much as it does to you, Mr. Tennyson. More than any single objective in more than thirty years of service."

The blond man nodded. "I understand. I owe this country a great deal, and I'll do whatever I can to help. But I'll also be profoundly relieved when that motorcade reaches Admiralty Arch."

By three in the morning on Tuesday, Tennyson had "uncovered" two additional weapons. There were now seven in all, forming a straight line down the Strand from the Savoy Court to the rooftop at the corner of Whitehall and Trafalgar. Every location was covered by a minimum of five agents, hidden in corridors and on rooftops, rifles and handguns poised, prepared to fire at anyone who even approached the hidden weapons.

Still, Tennyson was not satisfied. "There's something *wrong,*" he kept repeating to Payton-Jones. "I don't know what it is, but something doesn't fit."

"You're overworked," said the agent in the room at the Savoy that was their base of operations. "And overwrought. You've done a splendid job."

"Not splendid enough. There's *something,* and I can't put my finger on it!"

"Calm down. Look at what you *have* put your finger on: seven weapons. In all likelihood, that's all there are. He's bound to get near one of those guns, bound to betray the fact that he knows it's there. He's ours. Relax. We've got scores of men out there."

"But something's *wrong.*"

The crowds lined the Strand, the sidewalks jammed from curb to storefronts. Stanchions were placed on both sides of the street, linked by thick steel cables. The London police stood in opposing rows in front of the cables, their eyes darting continuously in every direction, their clubs unsheathed at their sides.

Beyond the police and intermingling with the crowds were over a hundred operatives of British Intelligence, many flown back from posts overseas. They were the experts Payton-Jones had insisted upon, his insurance against the master assassin who could spin a shilling into figure eights at five hundred yards. They were linked by miniature radios on an ultrahigh frequency that could neither be interfered with nor intercepted.

The operations room at the Savoy was tense, each man there an expert. Computer screens showed every yard of the gauntlet, graphs and grid marks signifying blocks and sidewalks. The screens were connected to radios outside; they showed as tiny moving dots that lit up when activated. The time was near. The motorcade was in progress.

"I'm going back down on the street," said Tennyson, pulling out the small radio from his pocket. "I set the green arrow on the receiving position, is that correct?"

"Yes, but don't send any messages unless you feel they're vital," said Payton-Jones. "Once the motorcade reaches Waterloo Bridge, everything is on five-second report intervals each fifty yards—except for emergencies, of course. Keep the channels clear."

An agent sitting by a computer panel spoke in a loud voice. "Within five hundred feet of Waterloo, sir. Spread holding at eight MPH."

The blond man hurried from the room. It was time to put into motion the swift moves that would destroy the Nachrichtendienst once and for all and cement the Wolfsschanze covenant.

He walked out into the Strand and looked at his watch. Within thirty seconds the man in the brown raincoat would appear in a window on the second floor of the Strand Palace Hotel. The room was 206, directly beneath the room with the weapon concealed in the mattress. It was the first move.

Tennyson glanced around for one of Payton-Jones's specialists. They were not difficult to spot; they carried small radios identical to his. He approached an agent trying to keep his position by a storefront against the jostling crowds, a man he had purposely spoken with; he had spoken to a number of them.

"Hello, there. How are things going?"

"I beg your pardon? Oh, it's you, sir." The agent was watching the people within the borders of his station. He had no time for idle conversation.

An eruption of noise came from the Strand, near Waterloo Bridge. The motorcade was approaching. The crowds pushed nearer the curb, waving miniature flags. The two lines of police in the street beyond the stanchions seemed to close ranks, as if anticipating a stampede.

"Over there!" yelled Tennyson, grabbing the agent's arm. "Up *there!*"

"What? *Where?*"

"That window! It was closed a few seconds ago!"

They could not see the man in the brown raincoat clearly, but it was obvious that a figure stood in the shadows of the room.

The agent raised his radio. "Suspect possibility. Sector One, Strand Palace Hotel, second floor, third window from south corner."

Static preceded the reply. "That's beneath three-zero-six. Security check immediately."

The man in the window disappeared.

"He's gone," said the agent quickly.

Five seconds later another voice came over the radio. "There's no one here. Room's empty."

"Sorry," said the blond man.

"Better safe than that, sir," said the agent.

Tennyson moved away, walking south through the crowds. He checked his watch again: twenty seconds to go. He approached another man holding a radio in his hand; he produced his own to establish the relationship.

"I'm one of you," he said, half-shouting to be heard. "Things all right?"

The agent faced him. "What?" He saw the radio in Tennyson's hand. "Oh, yes, you were at the morning's briefing. Things are fine, sir."

"That *doorway!*" Tennyson put his hand on the agent's shoulder. "Across the street. The open doorway. You can see the staircase above the heads of the crowd. That *doorway.*"

"What about it? The man on the steps? The one running?"

"Yes! It's the same man."

"Who? What are you talking about?"

"In the hotel room. A few moments ago. It's the same man; I *know* it! He was carrying a briefcase."

The agent spoke into his radio. "Security check requested. Sector Four, west flank. Doorway adjacent to jewelry shop. Man with briefcase. Up the stairs."

"In progress," came the reply.

Across the Strand, Tennyson could see two men racing through the open door and up the dark steps. He looked to the left; the man in the brown raincoat was walking out of the jewelry shop into the crowd. There was a door on the first landing, normally locked—as it was locked now—that connected the two buildings.

A voice came over the radio. "No one with a briefcase on second to fifth floors. Will check roof."

"Don't bother," ordered another voice. "We're up here, and there's no sign of anyone."

Tennyson shrugged apologetically and moved away. He had three more alarms to raise as the motorcade made its stately way down the Strand. The last of these would cause the lead vehicle to stop, clearance required before it continued toward Trafalgar. This final alarm would be raised by him. It would precede the chaos.

The first two happened rapidly, within three minutes of each other. The man in the brown raincoat was adhering to his tight schedule with precision and subtle execution. Not once as he maneuvered his way swiftly into Trafalgar Square was he stopped by a member of British Intelligence. Across his chest were strapped two cameras and a light meter, all dangling precariously as this "tourist" tried to find the best vantage points from which to record his moment in history.

Alarm One. An arm was grabbed; an arm whose hand held a radio.

"That scaffold! Up there!"

"*Where?*"

The entire side of a building opposite Charing Cross Station was in the middle of reconstruction. People had scaled the pipes; they were cheering and whistling as the international motorcade came into view.

"Up on the right. He went behind the plywood!"

"*Who,* sir?"

"The man in the hotel, on those steps in the doorway! The briefcase!"

"Security check. Sector Seven. Man on construction scaffold. With a briefcase."

Static. An eruption of voices.

"We're all *over* the scaffolds, mate."

"No one here with a briefcase!"

"Dozens of cameras. No briefcases, or luggage of any sort."

"The plywood on the second level!"

"Man was changing film, mate. He's climbing down. No bird."

"I'm sorry."

"You gave us a start, sir."

"My apologies."

Alarm Two. Tennyson showed a policeman his temporary MI-Five identification and rushed across the intersection into a packed Trafalgar Square.

"The lions! My *God,* the lions!"

The agent—one of those Tennyson had spoken to during the morning's briefing—stared at the base of the Lord Nelson monument. Scores of onlookers were perched on the lions surrounding the towering symbol of Nelson's victory at Trafalgar.

"What, sir?"

"He's there again! The man on the scaffold!"

"I heard that report just moments ago," said the agent. "Where is he?"

"He went behind the lion on the right. It's not a briefcase. It's a leather bag, but it's too large for a camera! Can't you *see?* It's too large for a camera!"

The agent did not hesitate; the radio was at his lips. "Security check. Sector Nine. North cat. Man with large leather bag."

The static crackled; two voices rode over each other.

"Man with two cameras, larger one at his feet. . . ."

"Man checking light meter, corresponds. . . . See no danger; no bird here."

"Man descending, setting camera focus. No bird."

The MI-Five agent glanced at Tennyson, then looked away, his eyes scanning the crowds.

The moment had come. The start of the final alarm, the beginning of the end of the Nachrichtendienst.

"You're *wrong!*" shouted Tennyson furiously. "You're *all* wrong! Every one of you!"

"What?"

The blond man ran as best he could, threading his way through the packed square toward the curbside, the radio next to his ear. He could hear excited voices commenting upon his outburst.

"He's mad as hell!"

"He says we're wrong."

"About what?"

"Have no idea."

"He ran."

"Where?"

"I don't know. I can't see him."

Tennyson reached the iron fence that bordered the monument. He could see his colleague—the Tinamou's apprentice—dashing across the street, toward the arch. The man in the raincoat held a small black plastic case in his hand. The identification card inside was an exact replica of the one in Tennyson's pocket, except that the photograph was different.

Now!

The blond man pressed the button and shouted into the radio.

"It's him! I know it!"

"Who's that?"

"Respond."

"It's from Sector Ten."

"I understand now! I see what it was that didn't fit."

"Is that you, Tennyson?" Payton-Jones's voice.

"Yes!"

"Where are you?"

"That's it! Now I see it."

"See what? Tennyson, is that you? What's the matter! Respond."

"It's so clear now! That's where we made our mistake! It's not going to happen when we thought it would—*where* we thought it would."

"What are you talking about? Where are you?"

"We were wrong; don't you see? The weapons. The seven locations. They were *meant* to be found! That's what didn't fit!"

"What? . . . Push the red button, Tennyson. Clear all channels. . . . What didn't fit?"

"The hiding of the weapons. It wasn't good enough. We found them too easily."

"For God's sake, what are you trying to say?"

"I'm not sure yet," replied Tennyson, walking toward an opening in the gate. "I just know those weapons were meant to be found. It's in the progression!"

"What progression? Push the red button. Where are you?"

"Somewhere between Sector Ten and back toward Nine," intruded another voice. "West flank. In Trafalgar."

"The progression from one weapon to another!" shouted Tennyson. "Going from east to west! As each position is passed, we eliminate it. We shouldn't! They're open limousines!"

"What do you mean?"

"Stop the motorcade! In the name of all that's holy, stop it!"

"Stop the motorcade! . . . The command's been relayed. Now, where are you?"

The blond man crouched; two MI-Five men passed within feet of him. "I think I've spotted him! The man on the scaffold! In the doorway. In the hotel window. It's him! He's doubling back; he's running now!"

"Describe him. For God's sake, describe the man."

"He's wearing a jacket. A brown checked jacket."

"All operatives alert. Pick up man in brown checked jacket. Running north past Sector Nine, Eight, and Seven. West flank."

"It has to be another weapon! A weapon we never found. He's going to fire from behind! Distance is nothing to him. He'll hit the back of a neck from a thousand yards! Start the motorcade up again! Quickly!"

"Vehicle One, proceed. Operatives mount trunks of all cars. Protect targets from rear fire."

"He's stopped!"

"Tennyson, where are you? Give us your location."

"Still between Sectors Nine and Ten, sir," a voice intruded.

"He's not wearing the jacket now, but it's the same man! He's running across the Strand!"

"Where?"

"There's no one crossing in Sector Eight."

"Sector Nine?"

"No one, sir."

"Back farther! Behind the motorcade!"

"Sector Five reporting. Police have relaxed the lines. . . ."

"Tighten them. Get everyone out of the street. Tennyson, what's he wearing? Describe him."

The blond man was silent; he walked through the square for a distance of twenty yards, then brought the radio to his lips again. "He's in a brown raincoat. He's heading back toward Trafalgar Square."

"*Sector Eight, sir. Transmission in Sector Eight.*"

Tennyson switched off the radio, shoved it into his pocket, and ran back to the iron fence. The motorcade had reached Charing Cross, perhaps four hundred yards away. The timing was perfect. The Tinamou's timing was always perfect.

The man in the brown raincoat positioned himself in a deserted office of the Government Building beyond Admiralty Park, a room commandeered by the bogus MI-Five identification card. The card was a license; no one argued with it, not today. The line of fire from that room to the motorcade was difficult, but it was no problem for one trained by the Tinamou.

Tennyson leaped over the iron fence and raced diagonally across Trafalgar Square toward Admiralty Arch. Two police officers stopped him, their clubs raised in unison; the motorcade was three hundred yards away.

"This is an emergency!" shouted the blond man, showing his identification. "Check your radios! MI-Five frequency, Savoy operations. I've got to get to the Government Building!"

The police were confused. "Sorry, sir. We don't have radios."

"Then get them!" yelled Tennyson, rushing past.

At the Arch, he activated his radio. "It's the Mall! Once the motorcade's through the Arch, stop all vehicles. He's in the trees!"

"*Tennyson, where are you?*"

"*Sector Twelve, sir. He's in Sector Twelve. East flank.*"

"*Relay his instructions. Quickly, for God's sake.*"

Tennyson switched off the radio, put it in his pocket, and continued through the crowds. He entered the Mall and turned left, racing across the path to the first doorway of the Government Building. Two uniformed guards blocked him; he produced the MI-Five card.

"Oh yes, sir," said the guard on the left. "Your team's on the second floor. I'm not sure which office."

"I am," said the blond man as he ran toward the staircase. The cheers in Trafalgar Square mounted; the motorcade approached Admiralty Arch.

He took the steps three at a time, crashing the corridor door open on the second floor, pausing in the hallway to shift his gun from his pocket to his belt. He walked swiftly to the second door on the left. There was no point in trying to open it; it was locked. Yet to break it down without warning was to ask for a bullet in his head.

"*Es ist Von Tiebolt!*" he shouted. "*Bleib beim Fenster!*"

"*Herein!*" was the reply.

Tennyson angled his shoulder, rushed forward, and slammed his body against the fragile door; the door flew open, revealing the man in the raincoat, crouched in front of the window, a long-barreled rifle in his hands. His hands were encased in sheer, flesh-colored gloves.

"Johann?"

"They found *everything,*" said the blond man. "Every weapon, every location!"

"Impossible!" yelled the man in the raincoat. "One or two, perhaps. Not all!"

"Every one," said Tennyson, kneeling behind the man in front of the window. The advance-security car had passed through Admiralty Arch; they would see the first limousine in seconds. The cheers from the crowds lining the Mall swelled like a mammoth chorus. "Give me the rifle!" Tennyson said. "Is the sight calibrated?"

"Of course," said the man, handing over the weapon.

Tennyson thrust his left hand through the strap, lashing it taut, then raised the rifle to his shoulder, the telescopic sight to his eye. The first limousine moved into the light-green circle, the prime minister of Great Britain in the cross hairs. Tennyson moved the rifle slightly; the smiling face of the president of the United States was now in the gunsight, the cross hairs bisecting the American's left temple. Tennyson shifted the weapon back and forth. It was important for him to know that with two squeezes of the trigger he could eliminate them both.

A third limousine came slowly into the green circle. The chairman of the People's Republic of China was in the gunsight, the cross hairs centered below the visor of his peasant's cap. A slight pressure against the trigger would blow the man's head apart.

"What are you *waiting* for?" asked the Tinamou's apprentice.

"I'm making my decision," replied Tennyson. "Time is relative. Half seconds become half hours." The fourth limousine was there now, the premier of the Soviet Union in the lethal green circle.

The exercise was over. In his mind he had done it. The transition between desire and the reality was minor. It would have been so simple to pull the trigger.

But this was not the way to destroy the Nachrichtendienst. The killing would come later; it would commence in a matter of weeks and continue for a matter of weeks. It was part of the Wolfsschanze covenant, an intrinsic part. So many of the leaders would die. But not now, not this afternoon.

The motorcade stopped; Payton-Jones had relayed Tennyson's instructions. No limousine entered the Mall. Dozens of agents began fanning out over the grass, guns drawn but held unobtrusively as they raced through the foliage, their eyes on the trees.

Tennyson held the rifle in the grip of his left hand, the strap taut from barrel to shoulder. He removed his finger from the trigger housing and lowered his right hand to his wrist, pulling the revolver from his belt.

"*Now,* Johann! They've stopped," whispered the apprentice. "Now, or they'll start up again. You'll lose them!"

"Yes, now," said Tennyson softly, turning to the man crouched beside him. "And I lose nothing."

He fired the gun, the explosion echoing through the deserted office. The man spun wildly off his feet, blood erupting from his forehead. He fell to the floor, his eyes wide and staring.

It was doubtful that the gunshot was heard for any distance over the noise of the outside crowds, but it didn't really matter. In seconds there'd be gunfire no one would miss. Tennyson sprang to his feet, removed the rifle from his arm, and took a folded slip of paper from his pocket. He knelt beside the dead man and shoved the paper into the bloodied, lifeless mouth, pushing it as far as he could down the throat.

Strapping the weapon back on its owner's arm, he dragged the body over to the window. Pulling out a handkerchief, he wiped the rifle clean and forced the dead fingers into the trigger housing, tearing the fabric of the right-hand glove so he could see the tattoo.

Now.

He took out the radio and leaned out the window.

"I think I've spotted him! It's the same as Madrid. That's it! Madrid!"

"Madrid? Tennyson, where—"

"Sector Thirteen, sir. East flank."

"Thirteen? Specify. Madrid? . . ."

Tennyson pushed himself off the sill and back into the deserted office. It would be only seconds now. Seconds until the connection was made by Payton-Jones.

Tennyson placed the radio on the floor and knelt by the dead man. He edged the dead arm and weapon up into the open window. He listened to the excited voices over the radio.

"Sector Thirteen. East flank. Beyond the Arch to the left, heading south."

"All agents concentrate on Sector Thirteen. East flank. Converge."

"All personnel converging, sir. Sector—"

"Madrid! . . . The Government Building. It's the Government Building."

Now.

The blond man yanked at the dead finger four times, firing indiscriminately into the crowds near the motorcade. He could hear the screams, see the bodies fall.

"Get out. All vehicles move out. Alert One. Move out."

The engines of the limousines roared; the cars lurched forward. The sounds of sirens filled Saint James's Park.

Tennyson let the dead man fall back to the floor and sprang toward the doorway, the pistol in his hand. He pulled the trigger repeatedly until there were no more shells left in the chamber. The body of the dead man jerked as each new bullet hit.

The voices on the radio were now indistinguishable. He could hear the sounds of racing footsteps in the corridor.

Johann von Tiebolt walked to the wall and sank to the floor, his face drawn in exhaustion. It was the end of his performance. The Tinamou had been caught.

By the Tinamou.

33

Their final meeting took place twenty-seven and a half hours after the death of the unknown man presumed to be the Tinamou.

Since the first account of the momentous event—initially reported by the *Guardian* and subsequently confirmed by Downing Street—the news had electrified the world. And British Intelligence, which refused all comment on the operation other than to express gratitude to sources it would not reveal, regained the supremacy it had lost through years of defections and ineptitude.

Payton-Jones took two envelopes from his pocket and handed them to Tennyson. "These seem such inadequate compensation. The British government owes you a debt it can never repay."

"I never sought payment," said Tennyson, accepting the envelopes. "It's enough that the Tinamou is gone. I assume one of these is the letter from MI Five, and the other the names pulled from the Nachrichtendienst file?"

"They are."

"And my name has been removed from the operation?"

"It was never there. In the reports you are referred to as 'Source Able.' The letter, a copy of which remains in the files, states that your dossier is unblemished."

"What about those who heard my name used over the radios?"

"Indictable under the Official Secrets Act should they reveal it. Not that it makes much difference; they heard only the name 'Tennyson.' There must be a dozen Tennysons under deep cover in British Intelligence, any one of which can be mocked up in the event it's necessary."

"Then I'd say our business is concluded."

"I imagine so," agreed Payton-Jones. "What will you do now?"

"Do? My job, of course. I'm a newspaperman. I might request a short leave of absence, however. My older sister's effects, sadly, must be taken care of, and then I'd like a brief holiday. Switzerland, perhaps. I like to ski."

"It's the season for it."

"Yes." Tennyson paused. "I hope it won't be necessary to have me followed any longer."

"Of course not. Only if you request it."

"Request it?"

"For protection." Payton-Jones gave Tennyson a photocopy of a note. "The Tinamou was professional to the end; he tried to get rid of this, tried to swallow it. And you were right. It's the Nachrichtendienst."

Tennyson picked up the copy. The words were blurred but legible: NACH-RICHT. 1360.78K. AU 23°.22°.

"What does it mean?" he asked.

"Actually, it's rather simple," replied the agent. "The Nachricht is obviously the Nachrichtendienst. The figure '1360.78K' is the metric equivalent of three thousand pounds, or one and a half tons. 'Au' is the chemical symbol for gold. The '23°.22°' we believe are the map coordinates of Johannesburg. The Tinamou was being paid out of Johannesburg in gold for his work yesterday. Something in the neighborhood of three million, six hundred thousand pounds sterling, or more than seven million American dollars."

"It's frightening to think the Nachrichtendienst has that kind of money."

"More frightening when one considers how it was being used."

"You're not going to release the information? Or the note?"

"We'd rather not. However, we realize we have no right to prevent you—especially you—from revealing it. In your *Guardian* story, you alluded to an unknown group of men who might have been responsible for the assassination attempt."

"I speculated on the possibility," corrected Tennyson, "insofar as it was the Tinamou's pattern. He was a hired assassin, not an avenger. Did you learn anything about the man himself?"

"Virtually nothing. The only identification on him, unfortunately, was an excellent forgery of an MI-Five authorization card. His fingerprints aren't in any files anywhere—from Washington to Moscow. His suit was off a rack; we doubt it's English. There were no laundry marks on his underclothing, and even his raincoat, which we traced to a shop in Old Bond Street, was paid for in cash."

"But he traveled continuously. He must have had papers."

"We don't know where to look. We don't even know his nationality. The laboratories have worked around the clock for something to go on: dental work, evidence of surgery, physical marks that a computer might pick up somewhere. *Anything.* So far, nothing."

"Then maybe he wasn't the Tinamou. The only evidence is the tattoo on the back of his hand and a similar caliber of weapons. Will it be enough?"

"It is now; you can add it to your story tomorrow. The ballistics tests are irrefutable. Two of the concealed rifles that were removed, plus the one on his person, match three guns used in previous assassinations."

Tennyson nodded. "There's a certain comfort in that, isn't there?"

"There certainly is." Payton-Jones gestured at the copy of the note. "What's your answer?"

"About what? The note?"

"The Nachrichtendienst. You brought it to us, and now it's confirmed. It's an extraordinary story. You unearthed it; you have every right to print it."

"But you don't want me to."

"We can't stop you."

"On the other hand," said the blond man, "there's nothing to prevent you from including my name in your reports, and that's one thing I don't want."

The MI-Five man cleared his throat. "Well, actually, there is something. I gave you my word, Mr. Tennyson. I'd like to think it's good."

"I'm sure it is, but I'm equally sure your giving it could be reappraised should the situation warrant it. If not by you, then by someone else."

"I see no likelihood of that. You've dealt only with me; that was our understanding."

"So 'Source Able' is anonymous. He has no identity."

"Right. Nor is it unusual at the levels in which I negotiate. I've spent my life in the service. My word's not questioned when it's given."

"I see." Tennyson stood. "Why don't you want the Nachrichtendienst identified?"

"I want time. A month or two. Time to get closer without alarming it."

"Do you think you'll be able to?" Tennyson pointed to one of the envelopes on the table. "Will those names help?"

"I'm not sure. I've just begun. There are only eight men listed; we're not even certain they're all alive. There's been no time to check them out."

"*Someone's* alive. Someone very wealthy and powerful."

"Obviously."

"So the compulsion to catch the Tinamou is replaced by an obsession with the Nachrichtendienst."

"A logical transfer, I'd say," agreed Payton-Jones. "And I should add, there's another reason—quite professional, but also part personal. I'm convinced the Nachrichtendienst killed a young man I trained."

"Who was he?"

"My assistant. As committed as any man I've ever met in service. His body was found in a small village called Montereau some sixty miles south of Paris. He went to France initially to track Holcroft, but found that Holcroft was a dead end."

"What do you think happened?"

"I *know* what happened. Remember, he was after the Tinamou. When Holcroft proved to be only what he said he was—a man looking for you because of a minor inheritance—"

"Very minor," interrupted Tennyson.

". . . our young man went underground. He was a first-rate professional; he made progress. More than that, he made a connection. He *had* to have made a connection. The Tinamou, the Nachrichtendienst . . . Paris. Everything fits."

"Why does it fit?"

"There's a name on that list. A man living near Paris—we don't know where— who was a general in the German High Command. Klaus Falkenheim. But he was more than that. We believe he was a prime mover of the Nachrichtendienst, one of the original members. He's known as Herr Oberst."

John Tennyson stood rigidly by the chair. "You have my word," he said. "I'll print nothing."

Holcroft sat forward on the couch, the newspaper in his hand. The headline reached from border to border. It said it all.

ASSASSIN TRAPPED, KILLED IN LONDON

Nearly every article on the page was related to the dramatic capture and subsequent death of the Tinamou. There were stories reaching back fifteen years, linking the Tinamou to both Kennedys and to Martin Luther King, as well as to Oswald and Ruby; more recent speculations touched on killings in Madrid and Beirut, Paris and Lisbon, Prague and even Moscow itself.

The unknown man with the rose tattoo on his hand was an instant legend. Tattoo parlors from cities everywhere reported a surge in business.

"My God, he did it," said Noel.

"Yet his name isn't mentioned anywhere," Helden said. "It's unlike Johann to give up credit in something as extraordinary as this."

"You said he'd changed, that Geneva had affected him. I believe that. The man I talked to wasn't concerned with himself. I told him that the bank in Geneva didn't want complications. The directors would be looking for anything that might disqualify one of us, that would put the money in potentially compromising circumstances. A man who's placed himself in a dangerous situation, who's had to deal with the kind of people your brother's had to deal with in tracking the Tinamou, could scare the hell out of the bankers."

"But you and my brother say there's someone more powerful than the Rache or the ODESSA—or Wolfsschanze—who's trying to stop you. How do you think the men in Geneva will accept all that?"

"They'll be told only what they have to be told," said Holcroft. "Which may be nothing, if your brother and I find out who it is."

"Can you?"

"Maybe. Johann thinks so, and God knows he's had more experience in these matters than I've had. It's been a crazy process of elimination. First we're convinced it's one thing—one group—then another; then it turns out to be neither."

"You mean the ODESSA and the Rache?"

"Yes. They're eliminated. Now we're looking for someone else. All we need is a name, an identity."

"What will you do when you find it?"

"I don't know," Holcroft said. "I hope your brother will tell me. I just know that whatever we do, we've got to do it quickly. Miles will get to me in a few days. He's going to connect me publicly to homicides ranging from Kennedy Airport to the Plaza Hotel. He'll ask for extradition, and he'll get it. If that happens, Geneva's finished, and for all intents and purposes, so am I."

"If they can find you," said Helden. "We have ways . . ."

Noel stared at her. "No," he replied. "I'm not going to live with three changes of clothing and rubber-soled shoes and guns with silencers. I want you to be a part of my life, but I won't be a part of yours."

"You may not have a choice."

The telephone rang, startling them both. Holcroft picked it up.

"Good afternoon, Mr. Fresca."

It was Tennyson.

"Can you talk?" asked Noel.

"Yes. This telephone is fine, and I doubt the George Cinq switchboard is interested in a routine call from London. Still, we should be careful."

"I understand. Congratulations. You did what you said you would."

"I had a great deal of help."

"You worked with the British?"

"Yes. You were right. I should have done so a long time ago. They were splendid."

"I'm glad to hear it. It's nice to know we have friends."

"More than that. We have the identity of Geneva's enemy."

"*What?*"

"We have the names. We can move against them now. We *must* move against them; the killing must stop."

"How? . . ."

"I'll explain when I see you. Your friend Kessler was close to the truth."

"A splinter faction of ODESSA?"

"Be careful," interrupted Tennyson. "Let's say a group of tired old men with too much money and a vendetta that goes back to the end of the war."

"What do we do?"

"Perhaps very little. The British may do it for us."

"They know about Geneva?"

"No. They simply understand a debt."

"It's more than we could ask for."

"No more than we deserve," said Tennyson. "If I may say so."

"You may. These . . . old men. They were responsible for *everything?* Including New York?"

"Yes."

"Then I'm clear."

"You will be shortly."

"Thank Christ!" Noel looked at Helden across the room and smiled. "What do you want me to do?"

"It's Wednesday. Be in Geneva Friday night. I'll see you then. I'll take the late flight from Heathrow and get there by eleven-thirty or midnight. Call Kessler in Berlin; tell him to join us."

"Why not today, or tomorrow?"

"I've got things to do. They'll be helpful to us. Make it Friday. Do you have a hotel?"

"Yes. The d'Accord. My mother's flying to Geneva. She got word to me to stay there."

There was a silence on the line from London. Finally, Tennyson spoke, his voice a whisper. "What did you say?"

"My mother's flying to Geneva."

"We'll talk later," said Helden's brother, barely audibly. "I've got to go."

Tennyson replaced the phone on the small table in his Kensington flat. As always, he detested the instrument when it was the carrier of unexpected news. News in this case that could be as dangerous as the emergence of the Nachrichtendienst.

What insanity had made Althene Clausen decide to fly to Geneva? It was never part of the plan—as she understood the plan. Did the old woman think she could travel to Switzerland without arousing suspicions, especially *now?* Or perhaps the years had made her careless. In that event she would not live long enough to regret her indiscretion. Perhaps, again, she had divided loyalties—as she understood those loyalties. If so, she would be reminded of her priorities before she took leave of a life in which she had abused so many.

So be it. He had his own priorities; she would take her place among them. The covenant of Wolfsschanze was about to be fulfilled. Everything was timing now.

First the lists. There were two, and they were the key to Wolfsschanze. One was eleven pages in length, with the names of nearly sixteen hundred men and women—powerful men and women in every country in the world. These were the elite of the *Sonnenkinder,* the leaders waiting for the signal from Geneva, waiting to receive the millions that would purchase influence, buy elections, shape policies. This was the primary list, and with it would emerge the outlines of the Fourth Reich.

But outlines required substance, depth. Leaders needed followers. These would come with the second list, this one in the form of a hundred spools of film. The master list. Microdot records of their people in every part of the globe. By now, thousands upon thousands, begat and recruited by the children sent out of the Reich by ship and plane and submarine.

Operation *Sonnenkinder.*

The lists, the names. One copy only, never to be duplicated, guarded as closely as any holy grail. For years they had been kept and updated by Maurice Graff in Brazil, then presented to Johann von Tiebolt on his twenty-fifth birthday. The ceremony signified the transfer of power; the chosen new absolute leader had exceeded all expectations.

John Tennyson had brought the lists to England, knowing it was imperative to find a repository safer than any bank, more removed from potential scrutiny than any vault in London. He had found his secret place in an obscure mining town in Wales, with a *Sonnenkind* who would gladly give his life to protect the precious documents.

Ian Llewellen: brother of Morgan, second-in-command of Beaumont's *Argo.*

And it was nearly time for the Welshman to arrive. After he had delivered his cargo, the loyal *Sonnenkind* would make the sacrifice he had pleaded to make only days ago when they drove down the highway from Heathrow. His death was mandatory; no one could be aware of those lists, those names. When that sacrifice was made, only two men on earth would have the key to Wolfsschanze. One a quiet professor of history in Berlin, the other a man revered by British Intelligence—above suspicion.

Nachrichtendienst. The next priority.

Tennyson stared at the sheet of paper next to the telephone; it had been there for several hours. It was another list—light years away from the *Sonnenkinder*—given him by Payton-Jones. It was the Nachrichtendienst.

Eight names, eight men. And what the British had not learned in two days he had learned in less than two hours. Five of those men were dead. Three remained, one of them now close to death in a sanatorium outside of Stuttgart. That left two: the traitor, Klaus Falkenheim, known as Herr Oberst, and a former diplomat of eighty-three named Werner Gerhardt, who lived quietly in a Swiss village on Lake Neuchâtel.

But old men did not travel in transatlantic aircraft and put strychnine in glasses of whiskey. They did not beat a man unconscious for a photograph. They did not fire guns at that same man in a French village or assault that man in a back alley in Berlin.

The Nachrichtendienst had indoctrinated younger, very capable disciples. Indoctrinated them to the point of absolute commitment . . . as the disciples of Wolfsschanze were committed.

Nachrichtendienst! Falkenheim, Gerhardt. How long had they known about Wolfsschanze?

Tomorrow he would find out. In the morning he would take a plane to Paris, and call on Falkenheim, on the hated Herr Oberst. Consummate actor, consummate garbage. Betrayer of the Reich.

Tomorrow he would call on Falkenheim and break him. Then kill him.

A car horn sounded from outside. Tennyson looked at his watch as he walked to the window. Eight o'clock precisely. Down in the street was the Welshman's automobile, and inside, sealed in a steel carton, were the lists.

Tennyson took a gun from a drawer and shoved it into the holster strapped to his shoulder.

He wished the events of the night were over and he was on the plane to Paris. He could hardly wait to confront Klaus Falkenheim.

Holcroft sat silently on the couch in the semidarkness, the glow of an unseen moon filling the windows. It was four in the morning. He smoked a cigarette. He had opened his eyes fifteen minutes ago and had not been able to go back to sleep, his thoughts on the girl beside him.

Helden. She was the woman he wanted to be with for the rest of his life, yet she would not tell him where she lived or whom she lived with. It was past flippancy now; he was not interested in games any longer.

"Noel?" Helden's voice floated across the shadows.

"Yes?"

"What's the matter, darling?"

"Nothing. Just thinking."

"I've been thinking, too."

"I thought you were asleep."

"I felt you get out of bed. What are you thinking about?"

"A lot of things," he said. "Mostly Geneva. It'll be over soon. You're going to be able to stop running; so am I."

"That's what I've been thinking about." She smiled at him. "I want to tell you my secret."

"Secret?"

"It's not much of one, but I want to see your face when I tell you. Come here."

She held out both her hands and he took them, sitting naked in front of her. "What's your secret?"

"It's your competition. The man I live with. Are you ready?"

"I'm ready."

"It's Herr Oberst. I love him."

"The old man?" Noel breathed again.

"Yes. Are you furious?"

"Beside myself. I'll have to challenge him to a duel." Holcroft took her in his arms.

Helden laughed and kissed him. "I've got to see him today."

"I'll go with you. I've got your brother's blessing. I'll see if I can get his."

"No. I must go alone. I'll only be an hour or so."

"Two hours. That's the limit."

"Two hours. I'll stand in front of his wheelchair and say, 'Herr Oberst. I'm leaving you for another man.' Do you think he'll be crushed?"

"It'll kill him," whispered Noel. He pulled her gently down on the bed.

34

Tennyson walked into the parking lot at Orly Airport and saw the gray Renault. The driver of the car was the second-highest-ranking official of the Sûreté. He had been born in Düsseldorf, but grew up a Frenchman, sent out of Germany on a plane from a remote airfield north of Essen. He was six years old at the time—March 10, 1945—and he had no memories of the Fatherland. But he did have a commitment: He was a *Sonnenkind*.

Tennyson reached the door, opened it, and climbed inside

"Bonjour, monsieur," he said.

"Bonjour," replied the Frenchman. "You look tired."

"It's been a long night. Did you bring everything I asked for? I have very little time."

"Everything." The Sûreté official reached for a file folder on the ledge under the dashboard and handed it to the blond man. "I think you'll find this complete."

"Give me a summary; I'll read it later. I want to know quickly where we stand."

"Very well." The Frenchman put the folder on his lap. "First things first. The man named Werner Gerhardt in Neuchâtel cannot possibly be a functioning member of the Nachrichtendienst."

"Why not? Von Papen had his enemies in the diplomatic corps. Why couldn't this Gerhardt have been one of them?"

"He may very well have been. But I use the present tense; he is no longer. He's not only senile; he's feebleminded. He's been this way for years; he's a joke in the village where he lives. The old man who mumbles to himself and sings songs and feeds pigeons in the square."

"Senility can be faked," said Tennyson. "And 'feeble' is hardly a pathological term."

"There's proof. He's an outpatient at the local clinic, with a bona fide medical record. He has the mentality of a child and is barely able to care for himself."

Tennyson nodded, smiling. "So much for Werner Gerhardt. Speaking of patients, what's the status of the traitor in Stuttgart?"

"Cerebral cancer, final stages. He won't last a week."

"So the Nachrichtendienst has but one functioning leader left," said Tennyson. "Klaus Falkenheim."

"It would appear so. However, he may have delegated authority to a younger man. He has soldiers available to him."

"Merely available? From the children he protects? The *Verwünschte Kinder?*"

"Hardly. They're sprinkled with a few idealists, but there's no essential strength in their ranks. Falkenheim has sympathy for them, but he keeps those interests separate from the Nachrichtendienst."

"Then where do the Nachrichtendienst soldiers come from?"

"They're Jews."

"Jews!"

The Frenchman nodded. "As near as we can determine, they're recruited as they're needed, one assignment at a time. There's no organization, no structured group. Beyond being Jews, they have only one thing in common: where they come from."

"Which is?"

"The kibbutz Har Sha'alav. In the Negev."

"Har Sha'alav? . . . My God, how perfect," said Tennyson with cold, professional respect. "Har Sha'alav. The kibbutz in Israel with but one requirement for residency: The applicant has to be the sole survivor of a family destroyed in the camps."

"Right," said the Frenchman. "The kibbutz has more than two hundred men—men, now—who can be recruited."

Tennyson looked out the window. " 'Kill me, another will take my place. Kill him, another his.' The implication was an unseen army willing to accept a collective death sentence. The commitment is understandable, but this is no army. It is a series of patrols, selected at random." Tennyson turned back to the driver. "Are you sure of your information?"

"Yes. The breakthrough came with the two unknown men killed in Montereau. Our laboratories traced a number of things: clothing, sediment in shoes and in skin pores, the alloys used in dental work, and especially surgical history. Both men had been wounded; one had shell fragments in his shoulder. The Yom Kippur war. We narrowed the evidence to the southwest Negev and found the kibbutz. The rest was simple."

"You sent a man to Har Sha'alav?"

The Frenchman nodded again. "One of us. His report is in here. No one talks freely at Har Sha'alav, but what's going on is clear. Someone sends a cablegram; a few men are chosen and given orders."

"Potential suicide squads committed to the destruction of anything related to the swastika."

"Exactly. And to confirm our findings, we've established the fact that Falkenheim traveled to Israel three months ago. The computers picked up his name."

"Three months ago. . . . At the time Manfredi first reached Holcroft to set up the meeting in Geneva. So Falkenheim not only knew about Wolfsschanze, he projected the schedule. He recruited and prepared his army three months in advance. It's time he and I met each other in our proper roles: two sons of the Reich. One true, one false."

"To what should I attribute his death?"

"To the ODESSA, of course. And call a strike on Har Sha'alav. I want every leader killed; prepare it carefully. Blame it on Rache terrorists. Let's go."

For the next minutes, the blond man walking down the winding dirt road would not be John Tennyson. Instead, he would be called by his rightful name, Johann von Tiebolt, son of Wilhelm, leader of the new Reich.

The cottage was in sight; the death of a traitor approached. Von Tiebolt turned and looked back up the hill. The man from the Sûreté waved. He would remain there, blocking the road until the job was done. Von Tiebolt continued walking until he was within ten yards of the stone path that led to the small house. He stopped, concealed by the foliage, and shifted his gun from the shoulder holster to his overcoat pocket. Crouching, he stepped through the overgrown grass, toward the door and beyond it, then stood up, his face at the edge of the single front window.

Though the morning was bright with sunlight, a table lamp was turned on in the dark interior of the room. Beyond the lamp Klaus Falkenheim sat in his wheelchair, his back to the window.

Von Tiebolt walked silently back to the door and considered for a moment whether or not to break it down, as a killer from the ODESSA undoubtedly would do. He decided against it. Herr Oberst was old and decrepit, but he was no fool. Somewhere on his person, or in that wheelchair, was a weapon. At the first sound of a crash it would be leveled at the intruder.

Johann smiled at himself. There was no harm in a little game. One consummate actor onstage with another. Who would be applauded most enthusiastically? The answer was obvious: he who was there for the curtain call. It would not be Klaus Falkenheim.

He rapped on the door. "Mein Herr. Forgive me, it's Johann von Tiebolt. I'm afraid my car couldn't negotiate the hill."

At first there was only silence. If it continued beyond five seconds, Von Tiebolt realized he would have to take sterner measures; there could be no sudden telephone calls. Then he heard the old man's words.

"Von Tiebolt?"

"Yes. Helden's brother. I've come to speak with her. She's not at work, so I assume she's here."

"She's not." The old man was silent again.

"Then I shan't disturb you, Mein Herr, but if I may, is it possible to use your telephone and call for a taxi?"

"The telephone?"

The blond man smiled. Falkenheim's confusion carried through the barrier between them. "I'll only be a moment. I really must find Helden by noon. I leave for Switzerland at two o'clock."

Again silence, but it was short-lived. He heard a bolt slide back, and the door opened. Herr Oberst was there in the chair, wheeling backward, a blanket on his lap. There had been no blanket moments ago.

"Danke, mein Herr," said Von Tiebolt, holding out his hand. "It's good to see you again."

Bewildered, the old man raised his hand in greeting. Johann wrapped his fingers swiftly around the bony hand, twisting it to the left. With his free hand, he reached down and yanked the blanket from Falkenheim's lap. He saw what he expected: a Luger across the emaciated legs. He removed it, kicking the door shut as he did.

"Heil Hitler! General Falkenheim," he said. *"Who ist der Nachrichtendienst?"*

The old man remained motionless, staring up at his captor, no fear in his eyes. "I wondered when you would find out. I didn't think it would be so quickly. I commend you, *Sohn Wilhelm von Tiebolts.*"

"Yes, son of Wilhelm, and something else as well."

"Oh, yes. The new Führer. That's your objective, but it won't happen. We'll stop you. If you've come to kill me, do so. I'm prepared."

"Why should I? Such a valuable hostage."

"I doubt you'd get much ransom."

Von Tiebolt spun the old man's chair toward the center of the room. "I imagine that's true," he replied, abruptly stopping the chair. "I assume you have certain funds available, perhaps solicited by the wandering children you think so much of. However, Pfennigs and francs are immaterial to me."

"I was sure of that. So fire the gun."

"And," said Von Tiebolt, "it's doubtful that a man dying of cerebral cancer in a Stuttgart sanatorium could offer much. Wouldn't you say that, too, is true?"

Falkenheim controlled his surprise. "He was a very brave man," he said.

"I'm sure. You're all brave men. Successful traitors must be imbued with a certain warped courage. Werner Gerhardt, for instance."

"Gerhardt? . . . " This time the old man could not conceal his shock. "Where did you hear that name?"

"You wonder how I could know? How I even found out about you, perhaps?"

"Not about me. The risk I took was quite apparent. I arranged for a Von Tiebolt to be near me. I considered that risk necessary."

"Yes, the beautiful Helden. But then, I'm told we're all beautiful. It has its advantages."

"She's no part of you; she never was."

"She's part of your wandering garbage, *die Verwünschten Kinder*. A weak whore. She whores now with the American."

"Your judgments don't interest me. How did you find out about Gerhardt?"

"Why should I tell you?"

"I'm going to die. What difference does it make?"

"I'll strike a bargain. Where did you learn of Wolfsschanze?"

"Agreed. Gerhardt first."

"Why not. He's of no value. A senile, feebleminded old man."

"Don't harm him!" shouted Falkenheim suddenly. "He's been through so much . . . so much *pain.*"

"Your concern is touching."

"They broke him. Four months of torture; his mind snapped. Leave him in peace."

"Who broke him? The Allies? The British?"

"ODESSA."

"For once they served a useful purpose."

"Where did you hear his name? How did you find him?"

Von Tiebolt smiled. "The British. They have a file on the Nachrichtendienst. You see, they're very interested in the Nachrichtendienst right now. Their objective is to find you and destroy you."

"Destroy? There's no *reason.* . . ."

"Oh, but there is. They have proof you hired the Tinamou."

"The Tinamou? Absurd!"

"Not at all. It was your final vengeance, the revenge of tired old men against their enemies. Take my word for it: The proof is irrefutable. I gave it to them."

The old man looked at Johann, his expression filled with revulsion. "You're obscene."

"About Wolfsschanze!" Von Tiebolt raised his voice. "Where? How? I'll know if you lie."

Falkenheim sank back in the wheelchair. "It doesn't matter now. For either of us. I'll die, and you'll be stopped."

"Now it is I who am not interested in *your* judgments. Wolfsschanze!"

Falkenheim glanced up listlessly. "Althene Clausen," he said quietly. "Heinrich Clausen's nearly perfect strategy."

Von Tiebolt's face was frozen in astonishment. "Clausen's wife? . . ." He trailed off the words. "You found out about her?"

The old man turned back to Johann. "It wasn't difficult; we had informers everywhere. In New York as well as Berlin. We knew who Mrs. Richard Holcroft was, and because we knew, we sent out orders to protect her. That was the irony: to *protect* her. Then word came: At the height of the war, while her American husband is at sea, she flies in a private plane to Mexico. From Mexico she goes secretly on to Buenos Aires, where the German embassy takes over and she's flown under diplomatic cover to Lisbon. To *Lisbon.* Why?"

"Berlin gave you the answer?" asked Von Tiebolt.

"Yes. Our people in the Finanzministerium. We'd learned that extraordinary sums of money were being siphoned out of Germany; it was in our interest not to interfere. Whatever helped cripple the Nazi machine, we sanctioned; peace and sanity would return sooner. But five days after Mrs. Holcroft left New York for Lisbon, by way of Mexico and Buenos Aires, Heinrich Clausen, the genius of the Finanzministerium, flew covertly out of Berlin. He stopped first in Geneva to meet with a banker named Manfredi, then he too went on to Lisbon. We knew he was no defector; above all men, he was a true believer in German—Aryan—supremacy. So much so that he couldn't stomach the flaws in Hitler's ranks of gangsters." Herr Oberst paused. "We made the simple addition. Clausen and his supposedly treasonous former wife in Lisbon together; millions upon millions banked in Switzerland . . . and the defeat of Germany now assured. We looked for the deeper meaning and found it in Geneva."

"You read the documents?"

"We read everything from La Grande Banque de Genève. The price was five hundred thousand Swiss francs."

"To Manfredi?"

"Naturally. He knew who we were; he thought we'd believe—and honor—the objectives espoused in those papers. We let him think so. Wolfsschanze! *Whose* Wolfsschanze? 'Amends must be made.' " Falkenheim spoke the words scathingly. "The thought furthest from any of their minds. That money was to be used to revive the Reich."

"What did you do then?"

The old soldier looked directly at Von Tiebolt. "Returned to Berlin and executed your father, Kessler, and Heinrich Clausen. They never intended to take their own lives; they expected to find sanctuary in South America, oversee their plan, watch it come to fruition. We gave them their pact with death that Clausen wrote so movingly about to his son."

Von Tiebolt fingered the Luger in his hand. "So you learned the secret of Althene Clausen?"

"You spoke of whores. She's the whore of the world."

"I'm surprised you let her live."

"A second irony: We had no choice. With Clausen gone we realized she was the key to Wolfsschanze. *Your* Wolfsschanze. We knew that she and Clausen had refined every move that was to be made during the coming years. We had to learn; she'd never tell us, so we had to watch. When were the millions to be taken from Geneva? How specifically were they to be used? And by whom?"

"The *Sonnenkinder*," said Von Tiebolt.

The old man's eyes were blank. "What did you say?"

"Never mind. So it was a question of waiting for Althene Clausen to make her move, whatever it might be?"

"Yes, but we learned nothing from her. Ever. As the years went by, we realized she had absorbed her husband's genius. In thirty years she never once betrayed the cause by word or action. One had to admire the sheer discipline. Our first signal came when Manfredi made contact with the son." Falkenheim winced. "The despicable thing is that she consented to the rape of her own child. Holcroft knows nothing."

The blond man laughed. "You're so out of touch. The renowned Nachrichtendienst is a collection of fools."

"You think so?"

"I *know* so. You watched the *wrong* horse in the *wrong* stable!"

"What?"

"For thirty years your eyes were focused on the one person who knew absolutely *nothing*. The whore of the world, as you call her, is secure in the knowledge that she and her son are truly part of a great apology. She's never thought otherwise!" Von Tiebolt's laughter echoed off the walls of the room. "That trip to Lisbon," he continued, "was Heinrich Clausen's most brilliant manipulation. The contrite sinner turned holy man with a holy cause. It must have been the performance of his life. Even down to his final instructions that she was not to give her instant approval. The son was to see for himself the justness of his martyred father's cause, and, being convinced, become committed beyond anything in his life." Von Tiebolt leaned against the table, his arms folded, the Luger in his hand. "Don't you see? None of *us* could do it. The document in Geneva was utterly correct about that. The fortunes stolen by the Third Reich are legendary. There could not be a single connection between that account in Geneva and a true son of Germany."

Falkenheim stared at Johann. "She never *knew?* . . ."

"Never! She was the ideal puppet. Even psychologically. The fact that Heinrich Clausen was revealed to be that holy man reaffirmed her confidence in her own judgments. She had married *that* man, not the Nazi."

"Incredible," whispered Herr Oberst.

"At least that," agreed Von Tiebolt. "She followed his instructions to the letter. Every contingency was considered, including a death certificate for an infant male in a London hospital. All traces to Clausen were obliterated." The blond man laughed again, the sound unnerving. "So you see, you're no match for Wolfsschanze."

"Your Wolfsschanze, not mine." Falkenheim glanced away. "You are to be commended."

Suddenly Von Tiebolt stopped laughing. Something was wrong. It was in the old man's eyes—flashed briefly, clouded, deep within that emaciated skull. "Look at me!" he shouted. "*Look* at me!"

Falkenheim turned. "What is it?"

"I said something just now . . . something you knew about. You *knew.*"

"What are you talking about?"

Von Tiebolt grabbed the old man by the throat. "I spoke of contingencies, of a death certificate! In a London hospital! You've heard it before!"

"I don't know what you mean." Falkenheim's trembling fingers were wrapped around the blond man's wrists, his voice rasping under the pressure of Johann's grip.

"I think you do. Everything I've just told you shocked you. Or did it? You pretended shock, but you're *not* shocked. The hospital. The death certificate. You didn't react at all! You've heard it before!"

"I've heard nothing," gasped Falkenheim.

"Don't lie to me!" Von Tiebolt whipped the Luger across Herr Oberst's face, lacerating the cheek. "You're not that good anymore. You're too *old.* You have lapses! Your brain is atrophied. You pause at the wrong instant, *Herr General.*"

"You're a maniac. . . ."

"You're a *liar!* A poor liar at that. *Traitor.*" Again he struck Herr Oberst in the face with the barrel of the weapon. Blood poured from the open wounds. "You *lied* about her! . . . My God, you *knew!*"

"Nothing . . . *nothing.*"

"Yes! *Everything!* That's why she's flying to Geneva. I asked myself why." Von Tiebolt struck furiously again; the old man's lip was torn half off his face. "You! In your last desperate attempt to stop us, you reached her! You threatened her . . . and in those threats you told her what she never *knew!*"

"You're wrong. *Wrong.*"

"No," said Von Tiebolt, suddenly lowering his voice. "There's no other reason for her to fly to Geneva. . . . So that's how you think you'll stop us. The mother reaches the child and tells him to turn back. Her covenant is a *lie.*"

Falkenheim shook his bloodied head. "No. . . . Nothing you say is true."

"It's all true, and it answers a last question. If you so dearly wanted to destroy Geneva, all you had to do was let the word go out. Nazi treasure. Claims would be made against it from the Black Sea to the northern Elbe, from Moscow to Paris. But you don't do that. Again, *why?*" Von Tiebolt bent over farther, inches from the battered face beneath him. "You think you can control Geneva, use the millions as *you* want them used. 'Amends must be made.' Holcroft learns the truth and becomes *your* soldier, his anger complete, his commitment tripled."

"He *will* find out," whispered Falkenheim. "He's better than you; we've both learned that, haven't we? You should find satisfaction in that. After all, in his own way, he's a *Sonnenkind.*"

"*Sonnen—*" Von Tiebolt swung the barrel of his pistol again across Herr Oberst's face. "You're filled with lies. I said the name; you showed nothing."

"Why should I lie now? *Operation Sonnenkinder,*" said Falkenheim. "By ship, and plane, and submarine. Everywhere the children. We never got the lists, but we don't need them. They'll be stopped when you're stopped. When Geneva's stopped."

"For that to happen, Althene Clausen must reach her son. She won't expose Geneva for what it is until she's tried everything else. To do so would destroy her son, let the world know who he is. She'll do anything before she lets that happen. She'll try to reach him quietly. We'll stop her."

"*You'll* be stopped!" said Falkenheim, choking on the blood that flowed over his lips. "There'll be no vast sums dispensed to your *Sonnenkinder.* We, too, have an army, one you'll never know about. Each man will gladly give his life to stop you, expose you."

"Of course, *Herr General.*" The blond man nodded. "The Jews of Har Sha'a-lav."

The words were spoken softly, but they had the effect of a lash on the old man's wounds. "*No! . . .*"

"Yes," said Von Tiebolt. " 'Kill me, another will take my place. Kill him, another his.' The Jews of Har Sha'alav. Indoctrinated by the Nachrichtendienst so thoroughly they became the Nachrichtendienst. The living remains of Auschwitz."

"You're an *animal. . . .*" Falkenheim's body trembled in a spasm of pain.

"I am Wolfsschanze, the true Wolfsschanze," said the blond man, raising the Luger. "Until you knew the truth, the Jews tried to kill the American, and now the Jews will die. Within the week Har Sha'alav will be destroyed, and with it the Nachrichtendienst. Wolfsschanze will triumph."

Von Tiebolt held the gun in front of the old man's head. He fired.

35

Tears streaked down Helden's cheeks. She cradled the body of Klaus Falkenheim, but could not bring herself to look at the head. Finally, she let go of the corpse and crawled away; filled with horror . . . and guilt. She lay curled on the floor, her sobbing uncontrollable. In pain, she pushed herself to the wall, her forehead pressed against the molding, and let the tears pour out. Gradually it became clear to her that her screams and sobs had not been heard. She had come upon the horrible scene alone, and had found signs of the hated ODESSA everywhere: swastikas scratched into wood, scrawled with soap on the window, painted with Falkenheim's blood on the floor. Beyond the despicable symbols, the room had been torn apart. Books ripped, shelves broken, furniture slashed; the house had been searched by maniacs. There was nothing left but ruins.

Yet there was something . . . not in the house. Outside. In the forest. Helden pressed her hands on the floor and raised herself against the wall, trying desperately to remember the words spoken by Herr Oberst only five mornings ago: *If anything should happen to me, you must not panic. . . . Go alone into the woods where you took me for my brief walk the other day. Do you remember? I asked you to pick up a cluster of wildflowers, as I remained by a tree. I pointed out to you that there was a perfect V formed by the limbs. Go to that tree. Wedged into the branches is a small canister. Inside, there is a message to be read only by you. . . .*

Helden pried the small tubular receptacle from its recess and tore open the rubber top. Inside there was a rolled-up piece of paper; attached to it were several bills, each worth ten thousand francs. She removed the money and read the message.

My dearest HELDEN—
   Time and danger to your person will not permit me to write here what you must know. Three months ago I arranged for you to come to me because I believed you were an arm of an enemy I have waited thirty years to confront. I have come to know you—to love you—and with great relief to understand that you are not part of the horror that might once again be visited upon the world.
   Should I be killed, it will mean I have been found out. Further, it will signify that the time is near for the catastrophes to begin. Orders must be relayed to those courageous men who will stand at the final barricade.
   You must go alone—I repeat, alone—to Lake Neuchâtel, in Switzerland. Don't let anyone follow you. I know you can do this. You have been taught. In the village of Près-du-Lac there is a man named Werner Gerhardt. Find him. Give him the following message: "The coin of Wolfsschanze has two sides." He will know what to do.
   You must go quickly. There is very little time. Again, say nothing to anyone. Raise no alarms. Tell your employers and your friends that you have personal matters in England, a logical statement considering the fact that you lived there for more than five years.
   Quickly now, my dearest Helden. To Neuchâtel. To Près-du-Lac. To Werner Gerhardt. Memorize the name and burn this paper.

Godspeed,
HERR OBERST

Helden leaned against the tree and looked up at the sky. Wisps of thin clouds moved swiftly in an easterly course; the winds were strong. She wished she could be carried by them, and that she did not have to run from point to point, every move a risk, every person she looked at a potential enemy.

Noel had said it would be over soon and she would be able to stop running. He was wrong.

Holcroft pleaded over the telephone, trying to convince her not to go—at least for another day—but Helden would not be dissuaded. Word had reached her through Gallimard that her sister's personal effects were awaiting her inspection; decisions had to be considered, arrangements made.

"I'll call you in Geneva, my darling. You'll be staying at the d'Accord?"

"Yes." What was wrong with her? She'd been so happy, so elated, barely two hours ago. She sounded tense now; her words were clear, but her voice was strained.

"I'll phone you in a day or so. Under the name of Fresca."

"Do you want me to go with you? I don't have to be in Geneva until late tomorrow night. The Kesslers won't get there till ten, your brother even later."

"No, darling. It's a sad trip. I'd rather make it alone. Johann's in London now. . . . I'll try to reach him."

"You've got some clothes here."

"A dress, a pair of slacks, shoes. Its quicker for me to stop at . . . Herr Oberst's . . . and pick up others more appropriate for Portsmouth."

"Quicker?"

"On the way to the airport. I have to go there, at any rate. My passport, money. . . ."

"I have money," interrupted Noel. "I thought you'd been to his place by now."

"*Please,* darling. Don't be difficult." Helden's voice cracked. "I told you, I stopped at the office."

"No, you didn't. You didn't say that. You said you got word." Holcroft was alarmed; she wasn't making sense. Herr Oberst's hidden cottage was *not* on the way to Orly. "Helden, what's the matter?"

"I love you, Noel. I'll call you tomorrow night. Hotel d'Accord, Geneva." She hung up.

Holcroft replaced the phone, the sound of her voice echoing in his ears. It was possible she was going to London, but he doubted it. Where *was* she going? Why did she lie? God damn it! What was *wrong* with her? What had happened?

There was no point in staying in Paris. Since he had to reach Geneva on his own, he might as well get started.

He could not chance the airlines or the trains. Unseen men would be watching; he had to elude them. The assistant manager of the George V could hire him a car under the name of Fresca. The route would be mapped for him. He would drive through the night to Geneva.

Althene Holcroft looked out the window of the TAP airliner at the lights of Lisbon below; they would be on the ground in minutes. She had a great deal to accomplish during the next twelve hours, and she hoped to God she was capable of doing it. A man had followed her in Mexico; she knew that. But then he had disappeared at the airport, which meant that another had taken his place.

She had failed in Mexico. She had not dropped out of sight. Once in Lisbon, she would have to vanish; she could not fail again.

Lisbon.

Oh, *God,* Lisbon!

It had been in Lisbon where it all began. The lie of a lifetime, conceived in diabolical brilliance. What an imbecile she had been; what a performance Heinrich had given.

She had at first refused to meet with Heinrich in Lisbon, so total was her loathing, but she had gone because the threat was clear: Her son would be branded by his father. Noel *Holcroft* would never be left in peace, for the name Noel *Clausen*—only son of the infamous Nazi—would trail him throughout his life.

How relieved she'd been! How grateful that the threat had been only a device to bring her to Lisbon. And how stunned and awestruck when Heinrich calmly outlined the extraordinary plan that would take years to bring to pass, but when it did, would make the world a far better place. She listened, was convinced, and did everything he asked her to do. For amends *would* be made.

She had loved him again—during those brief few days in Lisbon—and in a rush of emotion had offered herself to him.

With tears in his eyes, he had refused. He was not worthy, he said.

It was the consummate deception! The ultimate irony!

For now, at this moment, the very threat that brought her to Lisbon thirty years ago was the threat that brought her here again. Noel Holcroft would be destroyed; he would become Noel Clausen, son of Heinrich, instrument of the new Reich.

A man had come to her in the middle of the night in Bedford Hills. A man who had gained entrance by invoking the name "Manfredi" behind the closed door; she had admitted him thinking perhaps her son had sent him. He had said he was a Jew from a place called Har Sha'alav, and that he was going to kill her. And then he would kill her son. There'd be no specter of Wolfsschanze—the *false* Wolfsschanze—spreading from Zürich out of Geneva.

Althene had been furious. Did the man know to whom he was speaking? What she had *done?* What she *stood for?*

The man knew only about Geneva and Zürich . . . and Lisbon thirty years ago. It was all he had to know, to know what she stood for, and that stance was an abomination to him and all men like him throughout the world.

Althene had seen the pain and the anger in the dark eyes that held her at bay as surely as if a weapon had been leveled at her. In desperation, she had demanded that he tell her what he thought he knew.

He had told her that extraordinary sums were to be funneled to committees and causes throughout all nations. To men and women who had been waiting for thirty years for the signal.

There would be killing and disruption and conflagrations in the streets; governments would be bewildered, their agencies crippled. The cries for stability and order would be heard across the lands. Strong men and women with massive sums at their disposal would then assert themselves. Within months control would be theirs.

They were everywhere. In all countries, awaiting only the signal from Geneva.

Who were they?

The *Sonnenkinder.* The children of fanatics, sent out of Germany more than thirty years ago by plane and ship and submarine. Sent out by men who knew their cause was lost—but believed that cause could live again.

They were everywhere. They could not be fought by ordinary men in ordinary ways through ordinary channels of authority. In too many instances the *Sonnenkinder* controlled those channels. But the Jews of Har Sha'alav were not ordinary men; nor did they fight in ordinary ways. They understood that to stop the false Wolfsschanze, they had to fight secretly, violently, never allowing the *Sonnenkinder* to know where they were—or where they would strike next. And the first order of business was to stop the massive infusion of funds.

Expose them now!

Who? Where? What are their identities? How will proof be furnished? Who can say this general or that admiral, this chief of police or that corporation president, this justice or that senator, Congressman, or governor is a Sonnenkind? Men run for office espousing clichés wrapped in code words, appealing to hatreds, and still they are not suspect. Instead, crowds cheer them and wave flags and put emblems in their lapels.

They are everywhere. The Nazi is among us and we don't see him. He is cloaked in respectability and a pressed suit of clothes.

The Jew of Har Sha'alav had spoken passionately. "Even you, old woman. You and your son, instruments of the new Reich. Even you do not know who they are."

I know nothing. I swear on my life I know nothing. I'm not what you think I am. Kill me. For God's sake, kill me. Now! Take your vengeance out on me. You deserve that and so do I if what you say is true. But I implore you, reach my son. Take him. Explain to him. Stop him! Don't kill him; don't brand him. He's not what you think he is. Give him his life. Take mine, but give him his!

The Jew of Har Sha'alav had spoken. "Richard Holcroft was killed. It was no accident."

She had nearly collapsed, but she would not allow herself to fall. She could not permit the momentary oblivion that would have been so welcome.

Oh, my God. . . .

"Wolfsschanze killed him. The false Wolfsschanze. As surely as if they had marched him into a chamber at Auschwitz."

What is Wolfsschanze? Why do you call it false?

"Learn for yourself. We'll talk again. If you've lied, we'll kill you. Your son will live—for as long as the world lets him—but he will live with a swastika across his face."

Reach him. Tell him.

The man from Har Sha'alav left. Althene sat in a chair by the window, staring out at the snow-covered grounds throughout the night. Her beloved Richard, the husband who had given her and her son their lives again. . . . What had she done?

But she knew what to do now.

The plane touched ground, the impact pushing Althene's reveries out of her mind, bringing her back to the moment at hand. To Lisbon.

She stood at the railing of the ferry, the waters of the Tagus River slapping against the hull as the old ship made its way across the bay. In her left hand was a lace handkerchief, fluttering in the wind.

She thought she saw him but, as instructed, made no move until he approached her. She had never seen him before, of course, but that was not important. He was an old man in rumpled clothes, with heavy gray sideburns that met the stubble of a white beard. His eyes searched the passengers as if he were afraid one of them might yell for the police. He was the man; he stood behind her.

"The river looks cold today," he said.

The lace handkerchief flew away in the wind. "Oh, dear, I've lost it." Althene watched it plummet into the water.

"You've found it," said the man.

"Thank you."

"Please do not look at me. Look at the skyline across the lagoon."

"Very well."

"You spread money too generously, senhora," the man said.

"I'm in a great hurry."

"You bring up names so long in the past there are no faces. Requests that have not been made in years."

"I can't believe times have changed that much."

"Oh, but they have, senhora. Men and women still travel secretly, but not with such simple devices as doctored passports. It's the age of the computer. False papers are not what they once were. We go back to the war. To the escape routes."

"I have to get to Geneva as quickly as possible. No one must know I'm there."

"You'll get to Geneva, senhora, and only those you inform will know you're there. But it will not be as quickly as you wish; it will not be a matter of a single flight on an airline."

"How long?"

"Two or three days. Otherwise there are no guarantees. You'll be picked up, either by the authorities or by those you care to avoid."

"How do I get there?"

"Across borders that are unpatrolled, or where the guards can be bribed. The northern route. Sierra de Gata, across to Zaragoza, on the eastern Pyrénées. From there to Montpellier and Avignon. At Avignon a small plane will take you to Grenoble, another to Chambéry and to Genève. It will cost."

"I can pay. When do we start?"

"Tonight."

The blond man signed the Hôtel d'Accord registration card and handed it to the desk clerk.

"Thank you, Mr. Tennyson. You'll be staying fourteen days?"

"Perhaps longer, certainly no less. I appreciate your making a suite available."

The clerk smiled. "We received a call from your friend, the first deputy of canton Genève. We assured him we would do everything to make your stay pleasant."

"I'll inform him of my complete satisfaction."

"You're most kind."

"Incidentally, I'm expecting to meet an old friend here during the next few days. A Mrs. Holcroft. Could you tell me when she's expected?"

The clerk took up a ledger and thumbed through the pages. "Did you say the name was Holcroft?"

"Yes. Althene Holcroft. An American. You might also have a reservation for her son, Mr. N. Holcroft."

"I'm afraid we have no reservations in that name, sir. And I know there's no one named Holcroft presently a guest."

The muscles of the blond man's jaw tensed. "Surely an error has been made. My information is accurate. She's expected at this hotel. Perhaps not this evening, but certainly tomorrow or the day after. Please check again. Is there a confidential listing?"

"No, sir."

"If there were, I'm quite certain my friend, the first deputy, would ask you to let me see it."

"If there were, that wouldn't be necessary, Mr. Tennyson. We understood fully that we are to cooperate with you in all requests."

"Perhaps she's traveling incognito. She's been known to be eccentric that way."

The clerk turned the ledger around. "Please, look for yourself, sir. It's possible you'll recognize a name."

Tennyson did not. It was infuriating. "This is the complete list?" he asked again.

"Yes, sir. We are a small and, if I may say, rather exclusive hotel. Most of our guests have been here previously. I'm familiar with nearly every one of those names."

"Which ones aren't you familiar with?" pressed the blond man.

The clerk placed his finger on two. "These are the only names I don't know," he said. "The gentlemen from Germany, two brothers named Kessler, and a Sir William Ellis, from London. The last was made only hours ago."

Tennyson looked pointedly at the desk clerk. "I'm going to my rooms, but I need to ask you for an example of that cooperation the first deputy spoke of. It's most urgent that I find out where Mrs. Holcroft is staying in Geneva. I'd appreciate your calling the various hotels, but under no circumstances should my name be mentioned." He took out a one-hundred-franc note. "Locate her for me," he said.

By midnight Noel reached Châtillon-sur-Seine, where he made the phone call to an astonished Ellis in London.

"You'll do *what?*" Ellis said.

"You heard me, Willie. I'll pay you five hundred dollars and your expenses for one, maybe two days in Geneva. All I want you to do is take my mother back to London."

"I'm a dreadful nanny. And from what you've told me about your mother, she's the last person in the world who needs a traveling companion."

"She does now. Someone was following her. I'll tell you about it when I see you in Geneva. How about it, Willie? Will you do it?"

"Of course. But stuff your five hundred. I'm sure your mother and I will have far more in common than we ever did. You may, however, pick up the tabs. I travel well, as you know."

"While we're on the subject, travel with a little cool, will you, please? I want you to call the Hôtel d'Accord in Geneva and make a reservation for late this morning. The first plane should get you there by nine-thirty."

"I'll be on my best behavior, befitting Louis Vuitton luggage. Perhaps a minor title. . . ."

"Willie!"

"I know the Swiss better than you. They adore titles; they reek of money, and money's their mistress."

"I'll phone you around ten, ten-thirty. I want to use your room until I know what's going on."

"That's extra," said Willie Ellis. "See you in Geneva."

Holcroft had decided to call on Willie because there was no one else he could think of who would not ask questions. Ellis was not the outrageous fool he pretended to be. Althene could do far worse for an escort out of Switzerland.

And she had to get out. The covenant's enemy had killed her husband; it would kill her, too. Because Geneva was where it was going to happen. In two or three days a meeting would take place, and papers would be signed, and money would be transferred to Zürich. The covenant's enemy would try everything to abort those negotiations. His mother could not stay in Geneva. There would be violence in Geneva; he could feel it.

He drove south to Dijon, arriving well after midnight. The small city was asleep, and as he passed through the dark streets, he knew he needed sleep, too;

tomorrow he had to be alert. More alert than he had ever been in his life. He continued driving until he was back in the countryside and stopped the rented car on the side of a road. He smoked a cigarette, then crushed it out and put his feet on the seat, his head against the window, cushioned by his raincoat.

In a few hours he'd be at the border, crossing into Switzerland with the first wave of morning traffic. Once in Switzerland . . . He couldn't think anymore. The mist was closing in on him; his breathing was low and heavy. And then the face appeared, strong, angular, so unfamiliar yet so recognizable to him now.

It was the face of Heinrich Clausen, and he was calling to him, telling him to hurry. The agony would be over soon; amends would be made.

He slept.

Erich Kessler watched as his younger brother, Hans, showed the airline security officer his medical bag. Since the Olympics of '72, when the Palestinians were presumed to have flown into Munich with dismantled rifles and submachine guns, the airport's security measures had tripled.

It was a wasted effort, mused Erich. The Palestinians' weapons had been brought to Munich by Wolfsschanze—*their* Wolfsschanze.

Hans laughed with the airline official, sharing a joke. But, thought Erich, there would be no such jokes in Geneva, for there would be no inspection by the airlines or by customs or by anyone else. The first deputy of canton Genève would see to it. One of Munich's most highly regarded doctors, a specialist in internal medicine, was arriving as his guest.

Hans was all that and more, thought Erich, as his brother approached him at the gate. Hans was a medium-sized bull with enormous charm. A superb soccer player who captained his district team and later ministered to the opponents he had injured.

It was odd, thought Erich, but Hans was far better equipped than he to be the elder son. Save for the accident of time, it would have been Hans who worked with Johann von Tiebolt, and Erich, the quiet scholar, would have been the subordinate. Once, in a moment of self-doubt, he had said as much to Johann.

Von Tiebolt would not hear of it. A pure intellectual was demanded. A man who lived a bloodless life—someone never swayed by reasons of the heart, by intemperance. Had that not been proved by those infrequent but vital moments when he—the quiet scholar—had stood up to the Tinamou and stated his reservations? Reservations that resulted in a change of strategy?

Yes, it was true, but it was not the essential truth. That truth was something Johann did not care to face: Hans was nearly Von Tiebolt's equal. If they clashed, Johann might die.

That was the opinion of the quiet, bloodless intellectual.

"Everything proceeds," said Hans, as they walked through the gate to the plane. "The American is as good as dead, and no laboratory will trace the cause."

Helden got off the train at Neuchâtel. She stood on the platform, adjusting her eyes to the shafts of sunlight that shot down from the roof of the railroad station.

She knew she should mingle with the crowds that scrambled off the train, but for a moment she had to stand still and breathe the air. She had spent the past three hours in the darkness of a freight car, crouched behind crates of machinery. A door had been opened electronically for precisely sixty seconds at Besançon, and she had gone inside. At exactly five minutes to noon the door was opened again; she had reached Neuchâtel unseen. Her legs ached and her head pounded, but she made it. It had cost a great deal of money.

The air filled her lungs. She picked up her suitcase and started for the doors of the Neuchâtel station. The village of Près-du-Lac was on the west side of the lake, no more than twenty miles south. She found a taxi driver willing to make the trip.

The ride was jarring and filled with turns, but it was like a calm, floating glide for her. She looked out the window at the rolling hills and the blue waters of the lake. The rich scenery had the effect of suspending everything. It gave her the precious moments she needed to try to understand. What had Herr Oberst meant when he wrote that he had arranged for her to be near him because he had believed she was "an arm of an enemy"? An enemy he had "waited thirty years to confront." What enemy was that? And why had he chosen her?

What had she done? Or not done? Was it again the terrible dilemma? Damned for what she was and damned for what she wasn't? When in God's name would it *stop?*

Herr Oberst knew he was going to die. He had prepared her for his death as surely as if he had announced it, making sure she had the money to buy secret passage to Switzerland, to a man named Werner Gerhardt in Neuchâtel. Who was he? What was he to Klaus Falkenheim that he was to be contacted only upon the latter's death?

The coin of Wolfsschanze has two sides.

The taxi driver interrupted her thoughts. "The inn's down by the shoreline," he said. "It's not much of a hotel."

"It will do, I'm sure."

The room overlooked the waters of Lake Neuchâtel. It was so peaceful that Helden was tempted to sit at the window and do nothing but think about Noel, because when she thought about him, she felt . . . comfortable. But there was a Werner Gerhardt to find. The telephone directory of Près-du-Lac had no such listing; God knew when it was last updated. But it was not a large village; she would begin casually with the concierge. Perhaps the name was familiar to him.

It was, but not in a way that gave her any confidence.

"Mad Gerhardt?" said the obese man, sitting in a wicker chair behind the counter. "You bring him greetings from old friends? You should bring him instead a potion to unscramble his doddering brains. He won't understand a thing you say."

"I didn't know," replied Helden, overwhelmed by a feeling of despair.

"See for yourself. It is midafternoon and the day is cool, but the sun is out. He'll no doubt be in the square, singing his little songs and feeding the pigeons. They soil his clothes and he doesn't notice."

She saw him sitting on the stone ledge of the circular fountain in the village square. He was oblivious of the passersby who intermittently glanced down at him, more often in revulsion than in tolerance. His clothes were frayed, the tattered overcoat soiled with droppings, as the concierge had predicted. He was as old and as sickly as Herr Oberst, but much shorter and puffier in face and body. His skin was pallid and drawn, marred by spider veins, and he wore thick steel-rimmed glasses that moved from side to side in rhythm with his trembling head. His hands shook as he reached into a paper bag, taking out bread crumbs and scattering them, attracting scores of pigeons that cooed in counterpoint to the high-pitched, singsong words that came from the old man's lips.

Helden felt sick. He was only a remnant of a man. He was beyond senility; no other state could produce what she saw before her on the fountain's edge.

The coin of Wolfsschanze has two sides. The time is near for the catastrophe to begin. . . . It seemed pointless to repeat the words. Still, she'd come this far, knowing only that a great man had been butchered because his warning was real.

She approached the old man and sat beside him, aware that several people in the square looked at her as if she, too, were feeble-minded. She spoke quietly, in German.

"Herr Gerhardt? I've traveled a long way to see you."

"Such a pretty lady . . . a pretty, pretty lady."

"I come from Herr Falkenheim. Do you remember him?"

"A falcon's home? Falcons don't like my pigeons. They hurt my pigeons. My friends and I don't like them, do we, sweet feathers?" Gerhardt bent over and pursed his lips, kissing the air above the rapacious birds on the ground.

"You'd like this man, if you remembered him," said Helden.

"How can I like what I don't know? Would *you* like some bread? You can eat it, if you wish, but my friends might be hurt." The old man sat up with difficulty and dropped crumbs at Helden's feet.

" 'The coin of Wolfsschanze has two sides,' " whispered Helden.

And then she heard the words. There was no break in the rhythm; the quiet, high-pitched singsong was the same, but there was meaning now. "He's dead, isn't he? . . . Don't answer me; just nod your head or shake it. You're talking to a foolish old man who makes very little sense. Remember that."

Helden was too stunned to move. And by her immobility, she gave the old man his answer. He continued in his singsong cadence. "Klaus is dead. So, finally, they found him and killed him."

"It was the ODESSA," she said. "The ODESSA killed him. There were swastikas everywhere."

"Wolfsschanze wanted us to believe that." Gerhardt threw crumbs in the air; the pigeons fought among themselves. "Here, sweet feathers! It's teatime for you." He turned to Helden, his eyes distant. "The ODESSA, as always, is the scapegoat. Such an obvious one."

"You say Wolfsschanze," whispered Helden. "A letter was given to a man named Holcroft, threatening him. It was written thirty years ago, signed by men who called themselves the survivors of Wolfsschanze."

For an instant, Gerhardt's trembling stopped. "There were no survivors of Wolfsschanze, save one! Klaus Falkenheim. Others were there, and they lived, but they were not the eagles; they were filth. And now they think their time has come."

"I don't understand."

"I'll explain it to you, but not here. After dark, come to my house on the lake. South on the waterfront road, precisely three kilometers beyond the fork, is a path. . . ." He gave her the directions as though they were words written to accompany a childish tune. When he had finished, he stood up painfully, tossing the last crumbs to the birds. "I don't think you'll be followed," he said with a senile smile, "but make sure of it. We have work to do, and it must be done quickly. . . . Here, my sweet feathers! The last of your meal, my fluttering ones."

37

A small single-engine plane circled in the night sky above the flat pasture in Chambéry. Its pilot waited for the dual line of flares to be ignited: his signal to land. On the ground was another aircraft, a seaplane with wheels encased in its pontoons, prepared for departure. It would be airborne minutes after the first plane came to the end of the primitive runway, and would carry its valuable cargo north along the eastern leg of the Rhone River, crossing the Swiss border at Versoix, and landing on Lake Geneva, twelve miles north of the city. The cargo had no name, but that did not matter to the pilots. She had paid as well as the highest-priced narcotics courier.

Only once had she shown any emotion, and that was four minutes out of Avignon, toward Saint-Vallier, when the small plane had run into an unexpected and dangerous hailstorm.

"The weather may be too much for this light aircraft," the pilot said. "It would be wiser to turn back."

"Fly above it."

"We haven't the power, and we have no idea how extensive the front is."

"Then go through it. I'm paying for a schedule as well as transportation. I must get to Geneva tonight."

"If we're forced down on the river, we could be picked up by the patrols. We have no flight registration."

"If we're forced down on the river, I'll buy the patrols. They were bought at the border in Port-Bou; they can be bought again. Keep going."

"And if we crash, madame?"

"Don't."

Below them in the darkness, the Chambéry flares were ignited successively, one row at a time. The pilot dipped his wing to the left and circled downward for his final approach. Seconds later they touched ground.

"You're good," said the valuable cargo, reaching for the buckle of her seat belt. "Is my next pilot your equal?"

"As good, madame, and with an advantage I don't have. He knows the radar points within a tenth of an air mile in the darkness. One pays for such expertness."

"Gladly," replied Althene.

The seaplane lifted off against the night wind at exactly ten-fifty-seven. The flight across the border at Versoix would be made at very low altitude and would take very little time, no more than twenty minutes to a half hour. It was the specialist's leg of the journey, and the specialist in the cockpit was a stocky man with a red beard and thinning red hair. He chewed a half-smoked cigar and spoke English in the harsh accent associated with Alsace-Lorraine. He said nothing for the first few minutes of the flight, but when he spoke, Althene was stunned.

"I don't know what the merchandise is that you carry, madame, but there is an alert for your whereabouts throughout Europe."

"*What?* Who put out this alert, and how would you know? My name hasn't been mentioned; I was guaranteed that!"

"An all-Europe bulletin circulated by Interpol is most descriptive. It's rare that the international police look for a woman of—shall we say—your age and appearance. I presume your name is Holcroft."

"Presume nothing." Althene gripped her seat belt, trying to control her reaction. She did not know why it startled her—the man of Har Sha'alav had said they were everywhere—but the fact that this Wolfsschanze had sufficient influence with Interpol to use its apparatus was unnerving. She had to elude not only the Nazis of Wolfsschanze but also the network of legitimate law enforcement. It was a well-executed trap; her crimes were undeniable: traveling under a false passport, and then with none. And she could give no explanation for those crimes. To do so would link her son—the son of Heinrich Clausen—to a conspiracy so massive he'd be destroyed. That extremity had to be faced; her son might have to be sacrificed. But the irony was found in the very real possibility that Wolfsschanze itself had reached deep within the legitimate authorities. . . . *They were everywhere.* Once taken, Wolfsschanze would kill her before she could say what she knew.

Death was acceptable; stilling her voice was not. She turned to the bearded pilot. "How do you know about this bulletin?"

The man shrugged. "How do I know about the radar vectors? You pay me; I pay others. There's no such thing as a clear profit these days."

"Does the bulletin say why this . . . old woman . . . is wanted?"

"It's a strange alert, madame. It states clearly that she is traveling with false papers, but she is not to be picked up. Her whereabouts are to be reported to Interpol-Paris, where they will be relayed to New York."

"New York?"

"That's where the request originated. The police in New York, a detective-lieutenant named Miles."

"Miles?" Althene frowned. "I've never heard of him."

"Perhaps this woman has," said the pilot, shifting the cigar in his mouth.

Althene closed her eyes. "How would you like to make a very clear profit?"

"I'm no communist; the word doesn't offend me. How?"

"Hide me in Geneva. Help me reach someone."

The pilot checked his panel, then banked to the right. "It will cost you."

"I'll pay," she said.

Johann von Tiebolt paced the hotel suite, a graceful, angry animal, consumed. His audience was composed of the brothers Kessler; the first deputy of canton Genève had left minutes ago. The three were alone; the tension was apparent.

"She's somewhere in Geneva," said Von Tiebolt. "She *has* to be."

"Obviously under an assumed name," added Hans Kessler, his medical bag at his feet. "We'll find her. It's merely a question of fanning men out, after giving them a description. Our deputy has assured us it's no problem."

Von Tiebolt stopped his pacing. "No problem? I trust you and he have examined this 'no problem.' According to our deputy, the Geneva police report an Interpol bulletin on her. Quite simply, that means she's traveled a minimum of four thousand miles without being found. Four thousand miles through banks of computers, on aircraft crossing borders and landing with manifests, through at least two immigration points. And there's nothing. Don't fool yourself, Hans. She's better than we thought she was."

"Tomorrow's Friday," said Erich. "Holcroft is due tomorrow, and he'll get in touch with us. When we have him, we have her."

"He said he was staying at the d'Accord, but he has changed his mind. There is no reservation, and Mr. Fresca has checked out of the George Cinq." Von Tiebolt stood by the window. "I don't like it. Something's wrong."

Hans reached for his drink. "I think you're overlooking the obvious."

"What?"

"By Holcroft's lights, a great deal is wrong. He thinks people are after him; he'll be cautious, and he'll travel cautiously. I'd be surprised if he did make a reservation in his own name."

"I assumed the name would be Fresca, or a derivation I'd recognize," said Von Tiebolt, dismissing the younger Kessler's observation. "There's nothing like it in any hotel in Geneva."

"Is there a Tennyson," asked Erich softly, "or anything like *it?*"

"Helden?" Johann turned.

"Helden." The older Kessler nodded. "She was with him in Paris. It's to be assumed she's helping him; you even suggested it."

Von Tiebolt stood motionless. "Helden and her filthy, wandering outcasts are preoccupied at the moment. They're scouring the ODESSA for the killers of Herr Oberst."

"*Falkenheim?*" Hans sat forward. "Falkenheim's *dead?*"

"Falkenheim was the leader of the Nachrichtendienst—the last functioning member, to be precise. With his death, Wolfsschanze is unopposed. His army of Jews will be headless; what little they know, buried with *their* leaders."

"Jews? With Nachrichtendienst?" Erich was exasperated. "What in God's name are you *talking* about?"

"A strike has been called on the kibbutz Har Sha'alav; Rache terrorists will be held responsible. I'm sure the name 'Har Sha'alav' has meaning for you. At the last, the Nachrichtendienst turned to the Jews of Har Sha'alav. Garbage to garbage."

"I should like a more specific explanation!" said Erich.

"Later. We must concentrate on the Holcrofts. We must . . ." Von Tiebolt stopped, a thought striking him. "Priorities. Always look to priorities," he added, as if talking to himself. "And the first priority is the document at La Grande Banque de Genève, which means the son takes precedence. Find *him;* isolate *him;* keep him in absolute quarantine. For our purposes, it need only be for thirty-odd hours."

"I don't follow you," interrupted Hans. "What happens in thirty hours?"

"The three of us will have met with the bank's directors," Erich said. "Everything will have been signed, executed in the presence of the Grand Banque's attorney, all the laws of Switzerland observed. The money will be released to Zürich, and we assume control Monday morning."

"But thirty hours from Friday morning is—"

"Saturday noon," completed Von Tiebolt. "We meet with the directors Saturday morning at nine o'clock. There was never any question of our acceptance—except in Holcroft's mind. Manfredi took care of that months ago. We're not only acceptable; we're damn near holy men. My letter from MI Five is merely a final crown. By Saturday noon it will have been accomplished."

"They're so anxious to lose seven hundred and eighty million dollars they will open the bank on a Saturday?"

The blond man smiled. "I made the request in Holcroft's name, for reasons of speed and confidentiality. The directors didn't object—they look for crumbs—and neither will Holcroft when we tell him. He has his own reasons for wanting everything over with. He's stretched to the limits of his capacities." Von Tiebolt glanced at Erich, his smile broader. "He looks upon us both as friends, as pillars of strength, as two men he desperately needs. The programming has exceeded our hopes."

Kessler nodded. "By noon Saturday he'll have signed the final condition."

"What final condition?" asked Hans, alarmed. "What does that mean? What does he sign?"

"We each will have signed it," answered Von Tiebolt, pausing for emphasis. "It's a *requirement* of Swiss law for the release of such accounts. We've met, and fully understand our responsibilities; we've come to know each other and to trust each other. Therefore, in the event one of us predeceases the others, each assigns all rights and privileges to his coinheritors. Except, of course, the stipend of two million, which is to be distributed to the individual's heirs. That two million—legally assigned and prohibited from being given to the other executors—removes any motive for double-cross."

The younger Kessler whistled softly. "Utterly brilliant. So this final condition—this death clause wherein you each assign to the others your responsibility—never had to be made part of the document . . . because it's the law. If it had been included, Holcroft might have been suspicious from the beginning." The doctor shook his head in respect, his eyes bright. "But it never was because it's the *law.*"

"Precisely. And every legality must be observed. A month—six weeks—from now, it'll be irrelevant, but until we've made substantive progress, there can be no alarms."

"I understand that," said Hans. "But actually, by Saturday noon, Holcroft's expendable, isn't he?"

Erich held up his hand. "Best put him under your drugs for a period of time, available for display, as it were. A functioning mental cripple . . . until a great portion of the funds is dispersed. By then it won't matter; the world will be too preoccupied to care about an accident in Zürich. Right now we must do as Johann says. We must find Holcroft before his mother does."

"And under one pretext or another," added Von Tiebolt, "keep him isolated until our meeting the day after tomorrow. She will undoubtedly try to reach him, and then we will know where she is. We have men in Geneva who can take care of the rest." He hesitated. "As always, Hans, your brother addresses himself to what is optimum. But the answer to your question is yes. By noon Saturday, Holcroft is expendable. When I think about it, I'm not sure the additional weeks are even desirable."

"You annoy me again," said the scholar. "I defer to your exotic mind in many things, but a deviation in strategy at this juncture is hardly welcome. Holcroft *must* be available. In your words, until 'substantive progress' is made, there can be no alarms."

"I don't think there will be," replied Von Tiebolt. "The change I'm implementing would be approved by our fathers. I've moved up the timetable."

"You've *what?*"

"When I used the word 'alarms,' I referred to legalities, not Holcroft. Legalities are constant; life spans, never."

"What timetable? Why?"

"Second question first, and you may answer it." Johann stood in front of the older Kessler's chair. "What was the single most effective weapon of war the Fatherland employed? What strategy would have brought England to her knees had there been no hesitation? What were the lightning bolts that shook the world?"

"*Blitzkrieg,*" said the doctor, answering for his brother.

"Yes. Swift, sharp onslaughts, out of nowhere. Men and weapons and machinery, sweeping across borders with extraordinary speed, leaving in their wake confusion and devastation. Whole peoples divided, unable to reform ranks, incapable of making decisions. The *Blitzkrieg,* Erich. We must adapt it now; we can't hesitate."

"Abstractions, Johann! Give me specifics!"

"Very well. Specific one: John Tennyson has written an article that will be picked up by the wire services and flashed everywhere tomorrow. The Tinamou kept records, and there is talk that they've been found. Names of those powerful men who've hired him, dates, sources of payments. It will have the effect of massive electric shocks throughout the world's power centers. Specific two: Saturday, the Geneva document is executed, the funds transferred to Zürich. Sunday, we move to our headquarters there; they've been prepared; all communications are functioning. If Holcroft is with us, Hans has him narcotized; if not, he's dead. Specific three: Monday, the assets are deemed liquid and in our control. Using the Greenwich time zones, we begin cabling funds to our people, concentrating on the primary targets. We start right here in Geneva. Then to Berlin, Paris, Madrid, Lisbon, London, Washington, New York, Chicago, Houston, Los Angeles, and San Francisco. By five, Zürich time, we move into the Pacific. Honolulu, the Marshalls, and the Gilberts. By eight we go into New Zealand, Auckland, and Wellington. By ten, it's Australia—Brisbane, Sydney, Adelaide— then to Perth and across to Singapore, into the Far East. The first phase stops in New Delhi; on paper we're financed over three quarters of the globe. Specific four: At the end of another twenty-four hours—Tuesday—we receive confirmations that the funds have been received and converted into cash, ready for use. Specific five: I will make twenty-three telephone calls from Zürich. They will be made to twenty-three men in various capitals who have employed the services of the Tinamou. They will be told that certain demands will be made of them during the next few weeks; they are expected to comply. Specific six: On Wednesday, it begins. The first killing will be symbolic. The Chancellor in Berlin, the leader of the Bundestag. We sweep westward in a *Blitzkrieg.*" Von Tiebolt paused for a moment. "On Wednesday, Code Wolfsschanze is activated."

The telephone rang; at first no one seemed to hear it. Then Von Tiebolt answered it.

"Yes?"

He stared at the wall as he listened in silence. Finally he spoke. "Use the words I gave you," he said softly. "Kill them." He hung up.

"What is it?" asked the doctor.

Von Tiebolt, his hand still on the telephone, replied in a monotone. "It was only a guess—a possibility—but I sent a man to Neuchâtel. To observe someone.

And that someone met with another. It's no matter; they will soon be dead. My beautiful sister and a traitor named Werner Gerhardt."

It did not make sense, thought Holcroft, as he listened to Willie Ellis's words over the phone. He had reached Willie at the d'Accord from a booth in Geneva's crowded Place Neuve, fully expecting the designer to have made contact with Althene by now. He hadn't; she wasn't there. But his mother had said the Hôtel d'Accord. She would meet him at the *Hôtel d'Accord.*

"Did you describe her? An American, around seventy, tall for a woman?"

"Naturally. Everything you mentioned a half hour ago. There's no one here by the name of Holcroft, or any woman fitting the description. There are no Americans at all."

"It's crazy." Noel tried to think. Tennyson and the Kesslers weren't due until evening; he had no one to turn to. Was his mother doing the same thing he was doing? Trying to reach *him* from outside the hotel, expecting *he'd* be there? "Willie, call up the front desk and say you just heard from me. Use my name. Tell them I asked you if there were any messages for me."

"I don't think you understand the rules in Geneva," Willie said. "Messages between two people aren't given to unknown third parties, and the d'Accord is no exception. Frankly, when I asked about your mother, I was given some very odd looks. Despite my Louis Vuitton, the little bastard couldn't wait for me to stop talking."

"Try it anyway."

"There's a better way. I think if I—" Willie stopped; from somewhere in the distance there was a tapping. "Just a minute; there's someone at the door. I'll get rid of whoever it is and be right back."

Noel could hear the sound of a door opening. There were voices, indistinct, questioning; a brief exchange took place, and then there were footsteps. Holcroft waited for Willie to get back on the line.

There was the sound of a cough, but more than a cough. What was it? The start of a cry? Was it the start of a *cry?*

"Willie?"

Silence. Then footsteps again.

"Willie?" Suddenly, Noel felt cold. And pain came back to his stomach as he remembered the words. *The same words!*

. . . *There's someone at the door. I'll get rid of whoever it is and be right back.* . . .

Another Englishman. Four thousand miles away in New York. And a match flaring up in the window across the courtyard.

Peter Baldwin.

"Willie! Willie, where *are* you?! *Willie!"*

There was a click. The line went dead.

Oh, Christ! What had he *done?* Willie!

Beads of sweat broke out on his forehead; his hands trembled.

He had to get to the d'Accord! He had to get there as fast as he could and find Willie, help Willie. Oh, Christ! He wished the hammering pain would get out of his eyes!

He ran out of the phone booth and down the street to his car. He started the engine, unsure for a moment where he was or where he was going. The d'Accord. Hôtel d'Accord! It was on the rue des Granges, near the Puits-Saint-Pierre; a street lined with enormous old houses—mansions. The d'Accord was the largest. On the hill . . . *what* hill? He had no idea how to get there!

He sped down to the corner; the traffic was stopped. He yelled through his window at a startled woman driving the car next to his.

"Please! The rue des Granges—which way?"

The woman refused to acknowledge his shouts; she pulled her eyes away and looked straight ahead.

"Please, someone's been hurt! I think hurt badly. Please, lady! I can't speak French very well. Or German, or . . . *please!*"

The woman turned back to him, studying him for a moment. Then she leaned over and rolled down the window.

"Rue des Granges?"

"Yes, please!"

She gave him rapid instructions. Five streets down, turn right toward the bottom of the hill, then left. . . .

The traffic started up. Perspiring, Noel tried to memorize every word, every number, every turn. He shouted his thanks and pressed the accelerator.

He would never know how he found the old street, but it was suddenly there. He drove up the steep incline toward the top and saw the flat gold lettering: HÔTEL D'ACCORD.

His hands shaking, he parked the car and got out. He had to lock it; twice he tried to insert the key but could not hold his hand steady enough. So he held his breath and pressed his fingers against the metal until they stopped trembling. He had to control himself now; he had to *think*. Above all, he had to be careful. He had seen the enemy before, and he had fought that enemy. He could do so again.

He looked up at the d'Accord's ornate entrance. Beyond the glass doors, he could see the doorman talking with someone in the lobby. He could not go through that entrance and into that lobby; if the enemy had trapped Willie Ellis, that enemy was waiting for him.

There was a narrow alley that sloped downward at the side of the building. On the stone wall was a sign: LIVRAISONS.

Somewhere in that alley was a delivery entrance. He pulled the collar of his raincoat up around his neck and walked across the pavement, putting his hands in his pockets, feeling the steel of the revolver in his right, the perforated cylinder of the silencer in his left. He thought briefly of the giver, of Helden. Where was she? What had happened?

Nothing is as it was for you. . . .

Nothing at all.

He reached the door as a tradesman in a white smock coat was leaving. He held up his hand and smiled at the man.

"Excuse me. Do you speak English?"

"But of course, monsieur. This is Geneva."

It was a harmless joke—that's all—but the foolish American with the broad smile would pay fifty francs for the cheap coat, twice its value new. The exchange was made swiftly; this was Geneva. Holcroft removed his raincoat and folded it over his left arm. He put on the smock and went inside.

Willie had reserved a suite on the third floor; its entrance was the last door in the corridor toward the street. Noel walked through a dark hallway that led to a darker staircase. At the landing, there was a cart against the wall, three small, unopened cases of hotel soap beneath one that was half empty. He removed the top carton, picked up the remaining three, and proceeded up the marble steps, hoping he looked even vaguely like someone who might belong there.

"Jacques? C'est vous?" The caller spoke from below, his voice pleasant.

Holcroft turned and shrugged.

"Pardon. Je croyais que c'était Jacques qui travaille chez la fleuriste."

"Non," said Noel quickly, continuing up the stairs.

He reached the third floor, put the cartons of soap on the staircase, and removed the smock. He put on his raincoat, felt the revolver, and opened the door slowly; there was no one in the corridor.

He walked to the last door on the right, listening for sounds; there were none. He remembered listening at another door in another hallway light-years away from this ivoried, ornamental corridor in which he now stood. In a place called Montereau. . . . There had been gunfire then. And death.

Oh, God, had anything happened to Willie? Willie, who had not refused him, who had been a friend when others could not be found. Holcroft took out the gun and reached for the knob. He stepped back as far as he could.

In one motion he twisted the knob and threw his full weight against the door, his shoulder a battering ram. The door sprang open unimpeded, crashing into the wall behind it; it had not been locked.

Noel crouched, the weapon leveled in front of him. There was no one in the room, but a window was open, the cold winter air billowing the curtains. He walked to it bewildered; why would a window be open in this weather?

Then he saw them: circles of blood on the sill. Someone had bled profusely. Outside the window was a fire escape. He could see streaks of red on the steps. Whoever had run down them had been severely wounded.

Willie?

"Willie? Willie, are you here?"

Silence.

Holcroft ran into the bedroom.

No one.

"Willie?"

He was about to turn around when he saw strange markings on the paneling of a closed door. The paneling was profuse with gold fluting and ornate fleurs-de-lis, pink and white and light blue. But what he saw was not part of the rococo design.

They were blurred handprints outlined in blood.

He raced to the door, kicking it in with such force that the paneling cracked and splintered.

What he saw was the horror of a lifetime. Arched over the rim of the empty bathtub was the mutilated body of Willie Ellis, soaked in blood. There were huge punctures in his chest and stomach, intestines protruding over his red-drenched shirt, his throat slashed so deeply that his head was barely attached to his neck, his eyes wide open, glaring upward in agony.

Noel collapsed, trying to swallow the air that would not fill his lungs.

And then he saw the word, scrawled in blood on the tiles above the mutilated corpse.

NACHRICHTENDIENST

38

Helden found the path three kilometers beyond the fork in the road leading out of Près-du-Lac. She had borrowed a flashlight from the concierge, and now she angled the beam of light in front of her as she began the trek through the woods to Werner Gerhardt's house.

It was not so much a house, thought Helden as she reached the strange-looking structure, as a miniature stone fortress. It was very small—smaller than Herr Oberst's cottage—but from where she stood the walls appeared to be extremely thick. The beam of the flashlight caught bulging rocks that had been cemented together along the two sides she could see; and the roof, too, was heavy. The few windows were high off the ground and narrow. She had never seen a house like it before. It seemed to belong in a children's fairy tale, subject to magic incantations.

It answered a question provoked by the concierge's remarks when she had returned from the village square several hours ago.

"Did you find Mad Gerhardt? They say he was once a great diplomat before the marbles rattled in his head. It's rumored old friends still care for him, although none come to see him anymore. They cared once, though. They built him a strong cottage on the lake. No Christmas wind will ever knock it down."

No wind, no storm, no winter snows, could have any effect on this house. Someone had cared deeply.

She heard the sound of a door opening. It startled Helden, because there was no door at the side or rear walls. Then the beam of light caught the short figure of Werner Gerhardt; he stood on the edge of the lakeside porch and raised his hand.

How could the old man possibly have heard her?

"You've come, I see," said Gerhardt, no madness in his voice. "Quickly now, these woods are cold. Get inside, in front of the fire. We'll have tea."

The room seemed larger than the outside structure would indicate. The heavy furniture was old but comfortable, a profusion of leather and wood. Helden sat on an ottoman, warmed by the fire and the tea. She had not realized how cold she'd been.

They had talked for a few minutes, Gerhardt answering the first question before she'd had a chance to ask it.

"I came here from Berlin five years ago, by way of München, where my cover was established. I was a 'victim' of ODESSA, a broken man living out his years in senility and solitude. I am a figure of ridicule; a doctor at the clinic keeps my records. His name is Litvak, should you ever need him. He's the only one who knows I'm perfectly sane."

"But why was your cover necessary?"

"You'll understand as we talk. Incidentally, you were surprised that I knew you were outside." Gerhardt smiled. "This primitive lakeside cottage is very sophisticated. No one approaches without my knowing it. A hum is heard." The old man's smile vanished. "Now, what happened to Klaus?"

She told him. Gerhardt was silent for a while, pain in his eyes.

"*Animals,*" he said. "They can't even execute a man with any semblance of decency; they must mutilate. May God *damn* them!"

"Who?"

"The false Wolfsschanze. The animals. Not the eagles."

"Eagles? I don't understand."

"The plot to kill Hitler in July of 'forty-four was a conspiracy of the generals. Military men—by and large, decent men—who came to see the horrors committed by the Führer and his madmen. It was not the Germany they cared to fight for. Their objective was to assassinate Hitler, sue for a just peace, and expose the killers and sadists who'd functioned in the name of the Reich. Rommel called these men 'the true eagles of Germany.'"

"The eagles. . . ." Helden repeated. "'You won't stop the eagles . . .'"

"I beg your pardon?" asked the old man.

"Nothing. Go on, please."

"Of course, the generals failed, and a bloodbath followed. Two hundred and twelve officers, many only vaguely suspect, were tortured and put to death. Then, suddenly, Wolfsschanze became the excuse to still all dissent within the Reich. Thousands who had voiced even the most minor political or military criticisms were arrested on fabricated evidence and executed. The vast majority had never heard of a staff headquarters called Wolfsschanze, much less any attempt on Hitler's life. Rommel was ordered to kill himself, the penalty for refusal to carry out an additional five thousand *indiscriminate* executions. The worst fears of the generals were borne out: the maniacs were in total control of Germany. It was what they had hoped to stop at Wolfsschanze. *Their* Wolfsschanze: the true Wolfsschanze."

"*Their* . . . Wolfsschanze?" asked Helden. " 'The coin of Wolfsschanze has two sides.' "

"Yes," said Gerhardt. "There was another Wolfsschanze, another group of men who also wanted Hitler killed. But for an entirely different reason. These men thought he had failed. They saw his weaknesses, his diminished capacities. They wanted to supplant the madness that *was* with another madness, far more efficient. There were no appeals for peace in their plans, only the fullest prosecution of the war. Their strategies included tactics unheard of since the Mongol armies swept through Asia centuries ago. Whole peoples held as hostages, mass executions for the slightest infractions, a reign of abuse so terrible the world would seek a truce, if only in the name of humanity." Gerhardt paused; when he continued, his voice was filled with loathing. "This was the false Wolfsschanze, the Wolfsschanze that was never meant to be. They—the men of *that* Wolfsschanze—are committed still."

"Yet these same men were part of the conspiracy to kill Hitler," Helden said. "How did they escape?"

"By becoming the fiercest of Hitler's loyalists. They regrouped quickly, feigned revulsion at the treachery, and turned on the others. As always, zealousness and ferocity impressed the Führer; he was essentially a physical coward, you see. He put some of them in charge of the executions and delighted in their devotion."

Helden moved to the edge of the seat. "You say these men—this other Wolfsschanze—are still committed. Surely most of them are dead by now."

The old man sighed. "You really don't know, do you? Klaus said you didn't."

"You know who I am?" asked Helden.

"Of course. You yourself mailed the letters."

"I mailed a lot of letters for Herr Oberst. But none to Neuchâtel."

"Those that were meant for me, I received."

"He wrote you about me?"

"Often. He loved you very much." Gerhardt's smile was warm. It faded as he spoke. "You asked me how the men of the false Wolfsschanze could still be committed after so many years. You're right, of course. Most of them are dead. So it's not they; it's the children."

"The *children?*"

"Yes. They're everywhere—in every city, province, and country. In every profession, every political group. Their function is to apply pressure constantly, convincing people that their lives could be so much better if strong men protested weakness. Angry voices are being substituted for genuine remedies; rancor supplants reason. It's happening everywhere, and only a few of us know what it is: a massive preparation. The children have grown up."

"Where did they come from?"

"Now we come to the heart of the matter. It will answer other questions for you." The old man leaned forward. "It was called 'Operation Sonnenkinder,' and it took place in 1945. Thousands of children between the ages of six months and sixteen years were sent out of Germany. To all parts of the world. . . ."

As Gerhardt told the story, Helden felt ill, physically ill.

"A plan was devised," continued Gerhardt, "whereby millions upon millions of dollars would be available to the *Sonnenkinder* after a given period of time. The time was calculated by projections of the normal economic cycles; it was thirty years."

Helden's sharp intake of breath interrupted him, but only briefly.

"It was a plan conceived by three men. . . ."

A cry emerged from Helden's throat.

". . . These three men had access to funds beyond calculation, and one of them was perhaps the most brilliant financial manipulator of our time. It was he and he alone who brought the international economic forces together that insured the rise of Adolf Hitler. And when his Reich failed him, he set about creating another."

"Heinrich Clausen. . . ." whispered Helden. "Oh, *God,* no! . . . Noel! Oh, God, Noel!"

"He was never more than a device, a conduit for money. He knows nothing."

"Then . . ." Helden's eyes grew wide; the pain in her temples sharpened.

"Yes," said Gerhardt, reaching for her hand. "A young boy was chosen, another of the sons. An extraordinary child, a fanatically devoted member of the Hitler Youth. Brilliant, beautiful. He was watched, developed, trained for his mission in life."

"Johann. . . . Oh, God in heaven, it's *Johann."*

"Yes. Johann von Tiebolt. It is he who expects to lead the *Sonnenkinder* into power all over the world."

The sound of an echoing drum inside her temples grew louder, the percussive beats jarring and thunderous. Images went out of focus; the room spun and darkness descended. Helden fell into a void.

She opened her eyes, not knowing how long she had been unconscious. Gerhardt had managed to prop her up against the ottoman and was holding a glass of brandy beneath her nostrils. She gripped the glass and swallowed, the alcohol spreading quickly, bringing her back to the terrible moment.

"Johann," she whispered, the name itself a cry of pain. "That's why Herr Oberst—"

"Yes," said the old man, anticipating her. "It's why Klaus had you brought to him. The rebellious Von Tiebolt daughter, born in Rio, estranged from her brother and sister. Was that estrangement real, or were you being used to infiltrate the ranks of wandering, disaffected German youth? We had to know."

"Used, then killed," added Helden, shuddering. "They tried to kill me in Montereau. Oh, God, my *brother.*"

The old man stood up with difficulty. "I'm afraid you're wrong," he said. "It was a tragic afternoon, filled with errors. The two men who came after you were from us. Their instructions were clear: Learn everything there was to learn about Holcroft. He was still an unknown factor then. Was he part of Wolfsschanze— their Wolfsschanze? If an unknowing conduit, he was to live, and we would convince him to come with us. If part of Wolfsschanze, he was to be killed. If that was the case, you were to be taken away before you were harmed, before you were implicated. For reasons we don't know, our men decided to kill him."

Helden lowered her eyes. "Johann sent a man to follow us that afternoon. To find out who was so interested in Noel."

Gerhardt sat down. "So our people saw that man and thought it was a rendez-vous with Von Tiebolt, with an emissary of the *Sonnenkinder.* For them it meant Holcroft *was* part of Wolfsschanze. They needed nothing else."

"It was my fault," said Helden. "When that man took my arm in the crowd, I was frightened. He told me I had to go with him. He spoke German. I thought he was Odessa."

"He was the furthest thing from it. He was a Jew from a place called Har Sha'alav."

"A Jew?"

Gerhardt told her briefly of the strange kibbutz in the Negev desert. "They are our small army. A cable is sent; men are dispatched. It's as simple as that."

Orders must be relayed . . . to the courageous men who will stand at the final barricade. Helden understood Herr Oberst's words. "You'll send that cable now?"

"*You* will send it. Awhile ago, I mentioned a Dr. Litvak at the clinic. He keeps my medical records for any who may be curious. He's one of us; he has long-range-radio equipment and checks with me every day. It's too dangerous to have a telephone here. Go to him tonight. He knows the codes and will reach Har Sha'alav. A team must be sent to Geneva; you must tell them what to do. Johann, Kessler, even Noel Holcroft, if he's beyond pulling out, must be killed. Those funds must not be dispersed."

"I'll convince Noel."

"For your sake, I hope you can. It may not be as simple as you think. He's been manipulated brilliantly. He believes deeply, even to the point of vindicating a father he never knew."

"How did you learn?"

"From his mother. For years we believed she was part of Clausen's plan, and for years we waited. Then we confronted her and learned she was never part of it. She was the bridge to—as well as the source of—the perfect conduit. Who else but a Noel Clausen-Holcroft, whose origins had been obliterated from every record but his own mind, would accept the conditions of secrecy demanded by the Geneva document? A normal man would have asked for legal and financial advice. But Holcroft, believing in his covenant, kept everything to himself."

"But he had to be *convinced,*" said Helden. "He's a strong man, a very moral man. How could they do it?"

"How is anyone convinced his cause is just?" asked the old man rhetorically. "By seeing that there are those who desperately wish to stop him. We've read the reports out of Rio. Holcroft's experience with Maurice Graff, the charges he registered with the embassy. It was all a charade; no one tried to kill him in Rio, but Graff wanted him to think so."

"He's ODESSA."

"Never. He's one of the leaders of the false Wolfsschanze . . . the only Wolfsschanze now. I should say he was; he's dead."

"What?"

"Shot yesterday by a man who left a note claiming vengeance from Portuguese Jews. Your brother's work, of course. Graff was too old, too cantankerous. He'd served his purpose."

Helden placed the glass of brandy on the floor. The question had to be asked. "Herr Gerhardt, why haven't you ever exposed Geneva for what it was?"

The old man returned her inquisitive stare. "Because exposing Geneva would be only half the story. As soon as we did, we'd be killed; but that's inconsequential. It's the rest."

"The rest?"

"The second half. Who are the *Sonnenkinder?* What are their names? Where are they? A master list was made thirty years ago; your brother must have it. It's huge—hundreds of pages—and has to be hidden somewhere. Von Tiebolt would die in fire before revealing its whereabouts. But there *has* to be another list! A short one—a few pages, perhaps. It's either on his person or near him. The identities of all those receiving funds. These will be the trusted manipulators of Wolfsschanze. This is the list that can and must be found. You must tell the soldiers of Har Sha'alav to find it. Stop the money and find the list. It's our only hope."

"I'll tell them," said Helden. "They'll find it." She looked away, lost in another thought. "Wolfsschanze. Even the letter written to Noel Holcroft more than thirty years ago—pleading with him, threatening him—was part of it."

"They appealed and threatened in the name of eagles, but their commitment was to animals."

"He couldn't know that."

"No, he couldn't. The name 'Wolfsschanze' is awesome, a symbol of bravery. That was the only Wolfsschanze Holcroft could relate to. He had no knowledge of the other Wolfsschanze, the filth. No one did. Save one."

"Herr Oberst?"

"Falkenheim, yes."

"How did he escape?"

"By the most basic of coincidences. A confusion of identities." Gerhardt walked to the fireplace and prodded the logs with a poker. "Among the giants of Wolfsschanze was the commander of the Belgian sector, Alexander von Falkenhausen. Falken*hausen*, Falken*heim*. Klaus Falkenheim had left East Prussia for a meeting in Berlin. When the assassination attempt failed, Falkenhausen somehow managed to reach Falkenheim by radio to tell him of the disaster. He begged Klaus to stay away. He would be the 'falcon' who was caught. The other 'falcon' was loyal to Hitler; he would make that clear. Klaus objected, but understood. He had work to do. Someone had to survive."

"Where is Noel's mother?" Helden asked. "What has she learned?"

"She knows everything now. Let's hope she hasn't panicked. We lost her in Mexico; we think she's trying to reach her son in Geneva. She'll fail. The instant she's spotted, she's a dead woman."

"We've got to find her."

"Not at the expense of the other priorities," said the old man. "Remember, there is only one Wolfsschanze now. Crippling it is all that matters." Gerhardt put the poker down. "You'll see Dr. Litvak tonight. His house is near the clinic, above it, on a hill two kilometers north. The hill is quite steep; the radio functions well there. I'll give you—"

A sharp humming sound filled the room. It echoed off the walls so loudly that Helden felt the vibrations going through her and jumped to her feet. Gerhardt turned from the fireplace and stared up at a narrow window high in the left wall. He seemed to be studying the panes of glass that were too far above him to see through.

"There's a night mirror that picks up images in the black light," he said, watching intently. "It's a man. I recognize him, but I don't know him." He walked to the desk, took out a small pistol, and handed it to Helden.

"What should I do?" she asked.

"Hide it under your skirt."

"You don't know who it is?" Helden lifted her skirt and sat down in a chair facing the door, the weapon hidden.

"No. He arrived yesterday; I saw him in the square. He may be one of us; he may not. I don't know."

Helden could hear footsteps outside the door. They stopped; there was a moment of silence, then rapid knocking.

"Herr Gerhardt?"

The old man answered, his voice now high pitched and in the singsong cadence he had used in the square. "Good heavens, who is it? It's very late; I'm in the middle of my prayers."

"I bring you news from Har Sha'alav."

The old man exhaled in relief, and nodded to Helden. "He's one of us," he said, unlatching the bolt. "No one but us knows about Har Sha'alav."

The door opened. For the briefest instant Helden froze, then spun out of the chair and lunged for the floor. The figure in the doorway held a large-barreled gun in his hand; its explosion was thunderous. Gerhardt arched backward, blown off his feet, his body a contorted bloody mass, suspended in the air before it fell into the desk.

Helden lurched behind the leather armchair, reaching for the pistol under her skirt.

There was another gunshot as thunderous as the first. The leather back of the chair exploded out of its shell. *Another,* and she felt an icelike pain in her leg. Blood spread over her stocking.

She raised the pistol and squeezed the trigger repeatedly, aiming—and not aiming—at the huge figure in shadows by the door.

She heard the man scream. In panic, she crashed into the wall, a cornered insect, trapped, about to lose its insignificant life. Tears streamed down her face as she aimed again and pulled the trigger until the firing stopped, replaced by the sickening clicks of the empty gun. She screamed in terror; there were no bullets left. She hoped to God her death would come quickly.

She heard her screams—she *heard* them—as if she were floating in the sky, looking below at chaos and smoke.

There *was* smoke. Everywhere. It filled the room, the acrid fumes stinging her eyes, blinding her. She did not understand; nothing happened.

Then she heard faint, whispered words.

"My child. . . ."

It was Gerhardt! Sobbing, she pressed her hand against the wall and pushed herself away. Dragging her bloodied leg, she crawled toward the source of the whisper.

The smoke was beginning to clear. She could see the figure of the killer. He was lying on his back, small red circles in his throat and forehead. He was dead.

Gerhardt was dying. She crept to him and put her face on his face, her tears falling on his flesh.

"My child . . . get to Litvak. Cable Har Sha'alav. Stay away from Geneva."

"Stay *away?* . . ."

"You, child. They know you came to me. Wolfsschanze has seen you. . . . You're all that's left. Nachricht—"

"What?"

"You are . . . Nachrichtendienst."

Gerhardt's head slipped away from her face. He was gone.

39

The red-bearded pilot walked rapidly down the rue des Granges toward the parked car. Inside, Althene saw him approaching. She was alarmed. Why hadn't the pilot brought her son with him? And why was he hurrying so?

The pilot climbed in behind the wheel, pausing for a moment to catch his breath.

"There's great confusion at the d'Accord, madame. A killing."

Althene gasped. *"Noel?* Is it my *son?"*

"No. An Englishman."

"Who was it?"

"A man named Ellis. A William Ellis."

"Dear God!" Althene gripped her purse. "Noel had a friend in London named Ellis. He talked about him frequently. I've got to reach my son!"

"Not in there, madame. Not if there's a connection between your son and the Englishman. The police are everywhere, and there's an alert out for you."

"Get to a telephone."

"I'll make the call. It may be the last thing I do for you, madame. I have no wish to be associated with killing; that's not part of any agreement between us."

They drove for nearly fifteen minutes before the pilot was satisfied no one had followed them.

"Why should anyone follow us?" Althene asked. "Nobody saw me; you didn't mention my name. Or Noel's."

"Not you, madame. Me. I don't make it a point to fraternize with the Geneva police. I have run into a few now and then, off and on. We don't get along very well."

They entered the lakefront district, the pilot scanning the streets for an out-of-the-way telephone. He found one, swerved the car to the curb, and dashed outside to the booth. Althene watched him make the call. Then he returned, got behind the wheel more slowly than he had left it, and sat for a moment, scowling.

"For heaven's sake, what happened?"

"I don't like it," he said. "They expected a call from you."

"Of course. My son arranged it."

"But it was not you on the phone. It was me."

"What difference does it make? I had someone call for me. What did they say?"

"Not they. He. And what he said was far too specific. In this city, one is not that free with information. Specifics are exchanged when ears recognize voices, or when certain words are used that mean the caller has a right to know."

"What *was* the information?" asked Althene, irritated.

"A rendezvous. As soon as possible. Ten kilometers north, on the road to Vésenaz. It's on the east side of the lake. He said your son would be there."

"Then we'll go."

" 'We,' madame?"

"I'd like to negotiate further with you."

She offered him five hundred American dollars. "You're crazy," he said.

"We have an agreement, then?"

"On the condition that until you and your son are together, you do exactly as I say," he replied. "I don't accept such money for failure. However, if he's not there, that's no concern of mine. I get paid."

"You'll be paid. Let's go."

"Very well." The pilot started the car.

"Why are you suspicious? It all seems quite logical to me," said Althene.

"I told you. This city has its own code of behavior. In Geneva, the telephone is the courier. A second number should have been given, so that you yourself could talk with your son. When I suggested it, I was told there wasn't time."

"All quite possible."

"Perhaps, but I don't like it. The switchboard said they were connecting me to the front desk, but the man I talked with was no clerk."

"How do you know that?"

"Desk clerks can be arrogant and often are, but they aren't demanding. The man I spoke with was. And he wasn't from Geneva. He had an accent I couldn't place. You'll do exactly as I say, madame."

Von Tiebolt replaced the phone and smiled in satisfaction. "We have her," he said simply, walking to the couch where Hans Kessler lay holding an ice pack to his right cheek, his face bruised where it had not been stitched by the first deputy's personal physician.

"I'll go with you," said Hans, his voice strained in anger and pain.

"I don't think so," interjected his brother from a nearby armchair.

"You can't be seen," added Von Tiebolt. "We'll tell Holcroft you were delayed."

"No!" roared the doctor, slamming his fist on the coffee table. "Tell Holcroft anything you like, but I'm going with you tonight. That bitch is responsible for this!"

"I'd say *you* were," said Von Tiebolt. "There was a job to do and you wanted to do it. You were most anxious. You always are in such matters; you're a very physical man."

"He wouldn't die! That faggot wouldn't *die!*" Hans yelled. "He had the strength of five lions. Look at my stomach!" He ripped the shirt below his face, revealing a curving pattern of crisscrossed black threads. "He tore it with his hands! With his *hands!*"

Erich Kessler turned his eyes from his brother's wound. "You were lucky to get away without being seen. And now we must get you out of this hotel. The police are questioning everyone."

"They won't come here," countered Hans angrily. "Our deputy's taken care of that."

"Nevertheless, one curious policeman walking through the door could lead to complications," Von Tiebolt said, looking at Erich. "Hans must go. Dark glasses, a muffler, his hat. The deputy's in the lobby." The blond man shifted his gaze to the wounded brother. "If you can move, you'll have your chance at the Holcroft woman. That may make you feel better."

"I can move," said Hans, his face contorted in pain.

Johann turned back to the older Kessler. "You'll stay here, Erich. Holcroft will start calling soon, but he won't identify himself until he recognizes your voice. Be solicitous; be concerned. Say I reached you in Berlin and asked you to get here early, that I tried to call *him* in Paris, but he'd gone. Then tell him that we're both shocked at what happened here this afternoon. The man who was killed had been asking about him; we're both concerned for his safety. He must *not* be seen at the d'Accord."

"I could say that someone fitting his description was seen leaving by the service entrance," added the scholar. "He was in a state of shock; he'll accept that. It will add to his panic."

"Excellent. Meet him and take him to the Excelsior. Register under the name of"—the blond man thought for a moment—"under the name of Fresca. If he has any lingering doubts, that will convince him. He never used the name with you; he'll know we've met and talked."

"Fine," said Erich. "And at the Excelsior, I'll explain that because of everything that's happened, you reached the bank's directors and set up the conference for tomorrow morning. The quicker it's over, the quicker we can get to Zürich and set up proper security measures."

"Excellent again, Herr Professor. Come, Hans," Von Tiebolt said, "I'll help you."

"It's not necessary," said the bull of Munich's district soccer, his expression belying his words. "Just get my bag."

"Of course." Von Tiebolt picked up the physician's leather case. "I'm fascinated. You must tell me what you intend to inject. Remember, we want a death, but not a killing."

"Don't worry," Hans said. "Everything's clearly coded. There'll be no mistakes."

"After our meeting with the Holcroft woman," said Von Tiebolt, draping an overcoat over Hans's shoulders, "we'll decide where Hans should stay tonight. Perhaps at the deputy's house."

"Good idea," agreed the scholar. "The doctor would be available."

"I don't *need* him," argued Hans, his breath escaping between clenched teeth, his walk hesitant and painful. "I could have sewn myself up; he's not very good. *Auf wiedersehen,* Erich."

"Auf wiedersehen."

Von Tiebolt opened the door, looked back at Erich, and escorted the wounded Hans out into the corridor. "You say each vial is coded?"

"Yes. For the woman, the serum will accelerate her heart to the point . . ."

The door closed. The older Kessler shifted his bulk in the chair. It was the way of Wolfsschanze; there was no other decision. The physician who had tended Hans made it clear that there was internal bleeding; the organs had been severely damaged, as if torn by claws possessing extraordinary strength. Unless Hans were taken to the hospital, he could easily die. But his brother could not be admitted to a hospital; questions would be asked. A man had been killed that afternoon at the d'Accord; the wounded patient had been at the d'Accord. Too many questions. Besides, Hans's contributions were in the black leather case Johann carried. The Tinamou would learn everything they had to know. Hans Kessler, *Sonnenkind,* was no longer needed; he was a liability.

The telephone rang. Kessler picked it up.

"Erich?"

It was Holcroft.

"Yes?"

"I'm in Geneva. You got here early; I thought I'd try."

"Yes, Von Tiebolt called me this morning in Berlin; he tried to reach you in Paris. He suggested—"

"Has he arrived?" interrupted the American.

"Yes. He's out making the final arrangements for tomorrow. We've got a great deal to tell you."

"And I've got a great deal to tell *you,* " said Holcroft. "Do you know what's happened?"

"Yes, it's horrible." Where was the panic? Where was the anxiety of a man stretched to the limit of his capacities? The voice on the phone was not that of someone drowning, grasping for a lifeline. "He was a friend of yours. They say he asked for you."

There was a pause. "He asked for my mother."

"I didn't understand. We know only that he used the name Holcroft."

"What does *Nach . . . Nach-rich . . .* I can't pronounce it."

" 'Nachrichtendienst'?"

"Yes. What does it mean?"

Kessler was startled. The American was in control of himself; it was not to be expected. "What can I tell you? It's Geneva's enemy."

"That's what Von Tiebolt found out in London?"

"Yes. Where are you, Noel? I must see you, but you can't come here."

"I know that. Listen to me. Do you have money?"

"Some."

"A thousand Swiss francs?"

"A thousand? . . . Yes, I imagine so."

"Go downstairs to the front desk and talk to the desk clerk privately. Get his name and give him the money. Tell him it's for me and that I'll be calling him in a few minutes."

"But how—"

"Let me finish. After you pay and get his name, go to the pay telephones near the elevators. Stand by the one on the left toward the entrance. When it rings, pick it up. It'll be me."

"How do you know the number?"

"I paid someone to go inside and get it."

This was not a man in panic. It was a rational man with a deadly purpose. . . . It was what Erich Kessler had feared. But for the arrangement of genes—and a headstrong woman—the man on the phone might be one of them. A *Sonnenkind.*

"What will you say to the clerk?"

"I'll tell you later; there's no time now. How long will it take you?"

"I don't know. Not long."

"Ten minutes?"

"Yes, I think so. But Noel, perhaps we should wait until Johann returns."

"When's that?"

"No more than an hour or two."

"Can't do it. I'll call you in the lobby in ten minutes. My watch says eight-forty-five. How about yours?"

"The same." Kessler did not bother to look at his watch; his mind was racing. Holcroft's spine was too dangerously firm. "I really think we should wait."

"I can't. They killed him. God! *How* they killed him! They want her, but they won't find her."

"Her? Your mother? . . . Von Tiebolt told me."

"They won't find her," repeated Holcroft. "They'll find *me;* I'm who they really want. And I want *them.* I'm going to trap them, Erich."

"Control yourself. You don't know what you're doing."

"I know exactly."

"The Geneva police are in the hotel. If you speak to the desk clerk, he may say something. They'll be looking for you."

"They can have me in a few hours. In fact, I'll be looking for them."

"*What?* Noel, I *must* see you!"

"Ten minutes, Erich. It's eight-forty-six." Holcroft went off the line.

Kessler replaced the phone, knowing that he had no choice but to follow instructions. To do anything else would be suspect. But what did Holcroft expect to accomplish? What would he say to the desk clerk? It probably did not matter. With the mother gone, it was necessary only to keep Holcroft functioning until tomorrow morning. By noon, he would be expendable.

Noel waited on the dark street corner at the base of the rue des Granges. He was not proud of what he was about to do, but the rage inside him had numbed any feelings of morality. The sight of Willie Ellis had caused something to snap in his head. That sight gave rise to other images: Richard Holcroft, crushed into a stone building by a car gone wild by design. Strychnine poisoning in an airplane, and death in a French village, and murder in Berlin. And a man who had followed his mother. . . . He would not let them near her! It was *over;* he would bring it to a close himself.

It was a question now of using every available resource, every bit of strength he had, every fact he could recall, that would work for him. And it was the murder in Berlin that provided him with the single fact that could work for him now. In Berlin he had led killers to Erich Kessler. Stupidly, carelessly—to a pub on the Kurfürstendamm. Kessler and Holcroft; Holcroft and Kessler. If those killers were looking for Holcroft, they would keep Kessler in their sights. And if Kessler left the hotel, they would follow him.

Holcroft looked at his watch. It was time to call; he started across the pavement toward the booth.

He hoped Erich would answer.

And later understand.

Kessler stood in the hotel lobby, in front of the pay phone, a slip of paper in his hand. On it the astonished desk clerk had written his name; the man's hand had shaken when he had taken the money. Professor Kessler would appreciate knowing the gist of Mr. Holcroft's message to the clerk. For Mr. Holcroft's benefit. And for the clerk's insofar as an additional five hundred francs would be his.

The telephone rang; Erich had it off the hook before the ring was finished. "Noel?"

"What's the desk clerk's name?"

Kessler gave it.

"Fine."

"Now, I insist we meet," said Erich. "There's a great deal you should know. Tomorrow's a very important day."

"Only if we get through tonight. If I find her tonight."

"Where are you? We *must* meet."

"We will. Listen carefully. Wait by that phone for five minutes. I may have to call you again. If I don't—after five minutes—go outside and begin walking down the hill. Just keep walking. When you get to the bottom, turn left and keep going. I'll join you in the street."

"Good! Five minutes, then." Kessler smiled. Whatever games the amateur indulged in were worthless. He would doubtless ask the desk clerk to relay a message or a telephone number to his mother if and when she called him—the unregistered guest; so much for that. Perhaps Johann was right: Perhaps Holcroft had reached the limits of his capacity. Perhaps the American was not a potential *Sonnenkind* after all.

Police were still in the d'Accord's lobby, as well as several journalists who sensed a story behind the clouded report of robbery the police had given out. This was Geneva. And there were the curious—guests milling about, talking with one another; reassuring one another, some afraid, some seeking sensation.

Erich stayed off to the side, avoiding the crowd, remaining as inconspicuous as possible. He did not like being in the lobby at all; he preferred the anonymity of the hotel room upstairs.

He looked at his watch; four minutes had passed since Holcroft's call. If the American did not call again during the next minute, he would find the desk clerk and . . .

The desk clerk approached, walking on his own hot fragments of glass. "Professor?"

"Yes, my friend." Kessler put his hand in his pocket.

The message Holcroft left was not what Erich had expected. Noel's mother was to remain hidden and to leave a telephone number where her son could reach *her*. The clerk had sworn not to reveal that number, of course; but then, prior commitments always took precedence. When and if the lady called, the number would be left on a piece of paper in Herr Kessler's box.

"Paging Mr. Kessler? Professor Erich Kessler."

A bellboy was walking through the lobby, shouting his name. *Shouting* it! It was *impossible.* No one knew he was here!

"Yes? Yes, I'm Professor Kessler," said Erich. "What *is* it?" He tried to keep his voice low, to remain inconspicuous. People were looking at him.

"The message is to be delivered orally, sir," said the bellboy. "The caller said there was no time for a note. It's from Mr. H. He says you're to start out now, sir."

"What?"

"That's all he said, sir. I spoke to him myself. To Mr. H. You're to start out now. That's what he told me to tell you."

Kessler held his breath. It was suddenly, unexpectedly clear. Holcroft was using *him* as the bait.

From the American's point of view, whoever killed the man in the black leather jacket in Berlin knew that Noel Holcroft had been with Erich Kessler.

The strategy was simple but ingenious: Expose Erich Kessler, have Erich Kessler receive a message from Mr. H., and leave the hotel for the dark streets of Geneva.

And if no one followed, the disparity between cause and effect might be difficult to explain. So difficult that Holcroft might reexamine his bait. Questions might surface that could blow Geneva apart.

Noel Holcroft was a potential *Sonnenkind,* after all.

40

Helden crawled through Gerhardt's house, over the smashed furniture and the blood on the floor, opening drawers and panels until she found a small tin box of first-aid supplies. Trying desperately not to think of anything but becoming mobile, rejecting the pain as an unwanted state of mind, she strapped her wound as tightly as she could and struggled to her feet. Using Gerhardt's cane for support, she managed to walk up the path and north, three kilometers, to the fork.

A farmer driving a vintage automobile picked her up. Could he drive her to a Doctor Litvak on the hill near the clinic?

He could. It was not far out of his way.

Would he please *hurry?*

Walther Litvak was in his late forties, with a balding head and clear eyes and a penchant for short, precise sentences. Being slender, he moved quickly, wasting as few motions as he did words; being highly intelligent, he made observations before replies; and being a Jew hidden by Dutch Catholics as a child and brought up by sympathetic Lutherans, he had no tolerance for intolerance.

He had one bias, and it was understandable. His father and mother, two sisters, and a brother, had been gassed at Auschwitz. Save for an appeal of a Swiss doctor who spoke of a district in the hills of Neuchâtel that had no medical care, Walther Litvak would be living in Kibbutz Har Sha'alav, in the Negev desert.

He had intended to spend three years at the clinic; that was five years ago. And then, after several months in Neuchâtel, he was told who his recruiter was: one of a group of men who fought the resurgence of Nazism. They knew things other men did not know: about thousands of grown-up children—everywhere; and about untold millions that could reach those unknown people—everywhere. There was much nonmedical work to be done. His contact was a man named Werner Gerhardt, and the group was called Nachrichtendienst.

Walther Litvak stayed in Neuchâtel.

"Come inside, quickly," he said to Helden. "Let me help you, I have an office here."

He removed her coat and half carried her into a room with an examination table.

"I was shot." It was all Helden could think of to say.

Litvak placed her on the table and removed her skirt and half slip. "Don't waste your strength trying to talk." He scissored the bandage and studied the wound, then took a hypodermic needle from a sterilizer. "I'm going to let you sleep for a few minutes."

"You *can't*. There isn't time! I have to tell you. . . ."

"I said a few minutes," interrupted the doctor, inserting the needle into Helden's arm.

She opened her eyes, the shapes around her out of focus, a numb sensation in her leg. As her vision cleared, she saw the doctor across the room. She tried to sit up; Litvak heard her and turned.

"These are antibiotics," he said. He was holding a bottle of pills. "Every two hours for a day, then every four. What happened? Tell me quickly. I'll go down to the cottage and take care of things."

"The cottage? You knew?"

"While you were under, you talked; people generally do after trauma. You repeated 'Nachrichtendienst' several times. Then 'Johann.' I assume that's Von Tiebolt, and you're his sister—the one who's been with Falkenheim. It's happening, isn't it? The inheritors are closing ranks in Geneva."

"Yes."

"I thought as much this morning. The news bulletins from the Negev are horrible. They found out, God knows how."

"What bulletins?"

"Har Sha'alav." The doctor gripped the bottle; veins swelled on his forearm. "A raid. Houses bombed, people massacred, fields burnt to the ground. The death count isn't complete yet, but the estimates exceed one hundred and seventy. Men mostly, but women and children too."

Helden closed her eyes; there were no words. Litvak went on.

"To a man, the elders were killed, butchered in the gardens. They say it was the work of terrorists, of the Rache. But that's not true. It's Wolfsschanze. Rache fighters would never attack Har Sha'alav; they know what would happen. Jews from every kibbutz, every commando unit, would go after them."

"Gerhardt said you were supposed to cable Har Sha'alav," whispered Helden.

Litvak's eyes clouded. "There's nothing to cable now. There's no one left. Now, tell me what happened down at the lake."

She did. When she had finished, the doctor helped her off the table and carried her into the large Alpine living room. He lowered her to the couch and summarized.

"Geneva's the battleground, and there's not an hour to be lost. Even if Har Sha'alav could be reached, it would be useless. But there is a man from Har Sha'alav in London; he's been ordered to stay there. He followed Holcroft to Portsmouth. He was the one who took the photograph from Holcroft's pocket."

"It was a picture of Beaumont," said Helden. "ODESSA."

"Wolfsschanze," corrected Litvak. "A *Sonnenkind*. One of thousands, but also one of the few to work with Von Tiebolt."

Helden raised herself, frowning. "The records. Beaumont's *records*. They didn't make sense."

"What records?"

She told the angry doctor about the obscure and contradictory information found in Beaumont's naval records. And of the similar dossier belonging to Beaumont's second-in-command, Ian Llewellen.

Litvak wrote down the name on a note pad. "How convenient. Two men of Wolfsschanze commanding an electronic-espionage vessel. How many more are there like them? In how many places?"

"Llewellen was quoted in the papers the other day. When Beaumont and Gretchen—" She could not finish.

"Don't dwell on it," said the doctor. "The *Sonnenkinder* have their own rules. Llewellen is a name to add to the list that must be found in Geneva. Gerhardt was right: Above all, that list must be found. It's as vital as stopping the money. In some ways, more vital."

"Why?"

"The funds are a means to the Fourth Reich, but the people *are* that Reich; they'll be there whether or not the funds are dispersed. We've got to find out who they are."

Helden leaned back. "My . . . Johann von Tiebolt can be killed. So, too, can Kessler and . . . if it's necessary . . . even Noel. The money can be stopped. But how can we be sure the list will be found?"

"The man from Har Sha'alav in London will have ideas. He has many talents." Litvak glanced briefly away. "You should know, because you'll have to work with him. He's called a killer and a terrorist. He doesn't consider himself either, but the laws he's broken and the crimes he's committed would tend to dispute that judgment." The doctor glanced at his watch. "It's three minutes of nine; he lives less than a mile from Heathrow. If I can contact him, he can be in Geneva by midnight. Do you know where Holcroft is staying?"

"Yes. At the d'Accord. You understand, he knows nothing. He believes deeply in what he's doing. He thinks it's right."

"I understand. Unfortunately, that may be irrelevant in terms of his life. The first thing, however, is to reach him."

"I said I'd call him tonight."

"Good. Let me help you to the telephone. Be careful what you say. He'll be watched; his line will be tapped." Litvak helped her to the table where the phone was.

"Hôtel d'Accord. *Bonsoir,*" said the operator.

"Good evening. Mr. Noel Holcroft, please?"

"Monsieur Holcroft? . . ." The operator hesitated. "Just one minute, madame."

There was a silence, a click, and a man spoke. "Mrs. Holcroft?"

"What?"

"This is Mrs. Holcroft, is it not?"

Helden was surprised. Something was wrong; the switchboard had not even tried to ring Noel's room. "You were expecting me, then?" she asked.

"But of course, madame," replied the desk clerk with confidentiality. "Your son was most generous. He said to tell you it's imperative you remain out of sight, but you are to leave a telephone number where he can reach you."

"I see. Just one minute, please." Helden cupped the phone and turned to Litvak. "They think I'm Mrs. Holcroft. He's paid them to take a number where he can reach her."

The doctor nodded and walked quickly to a desk. "Keep talking. Say you want to make sure this number will not be given to anyone else. Offer money. Anything to stall them." Litvak took out a worn address book.

"Before I give you a number, I'd like to be certain . . ." Helden paused; the desk clerk swore on his mother's grave he would give the number only to Holcroft. The doctor rushed back to the table, a number written on a slip of paper. Helden repeated it to the desk clerk and hung up. "Where is this?" she asked Litvak.

"It reaches an empty apartment on the avenue de la Paix, but the apartment is not at the address listed with the telephone exchange. Here it is." Litvak wrote the address beneath the number. "Memorize them both."

"I will."

"Now, I'll try our man in London," said the doctor, heading for the staircase. "I have radio equipment here. It links me with a routine-mobile-telephone service." He stopped on the bottom step. "I'll get you to Geneva. You won't be able to move around much, but the wound isn't deep; your stitches will hold under the pressure of the bandage, and you'll have the chance to reach Holcroft. I hope you do, and I hope you're successful. Noel Holcroft must walk away from Von Tiebolt and Kessler. If he fights you, if he even hesitates, he must be killed."

"I know."

"Knowing it may not be enough. I'm afraid the decision will not be yours to make."

"Whose, then? Yours?"

"I can't leave Neuchâtel. It will be up to the man in London."

"The terrorist? The killer who has only to hear the word 'Nazi' and he fires a gun?"

"He'll be objective," said Litvak, continuing up the staircase. "He won't have other pressures on him. You'll meet him at the apartment."

"How will I get to Geneva? I—" Helden stopped.

"What?"

"I asked how I would get to Geneva. Are there trains?"

"There's no time for trains. You'll fly."

"Fine. It will be quicker."

"Much quicker."

And far better, thought Helden. For the one thing she had not relayed to the doctor was Werner Gerhardt's final warning. To her.

My child. Stay away from Geneva. . . . Wolfsschanze has seen you.

"Who will take me?"

"There are pilots who fly the lakes at night," said Litvak.

Althene was irritated, but she had agreed to the condition. The pilot had asked her a single question.

"Do you know by sight the people who are looking for you?"

She had replied that she did not.

"You may before the night is over."

Which was why she was standing now beside a tree in the dark woods above the road in sight of the car. It was a sloping forest of pine that rose above the lakeside highway. She had been guided to her watch post by the pilot.

"If your son is there, I'll send him to you," he had said.

"Of course he'll be there. Why wouldn't he?"

"We'll see."

For a moment his doubts had disturbed her. "If he's not, what then?"

"Then you'll know who it is who's looking for you." He had started back toward the road.

"What about you?" she had called after him. "If my son isn't there?"

"Me?" The pilot had laughed. "I've been through many such negotiations. If your son isn't there, it will mean they are desperate to find you, won't it? Without me, they can't have you."

She waited now by the tree, no more than forty yards away, the line of sight reasonably clear considering the profusion of limbs and branches. The car was off the side of the road, pointing north, its parking lights on. The pilot had told the man at the d'Accord to be there in one hour, not before, and to approach from the south, blinking his lights repeatedly within a quarter of a mile of the rendezvous.

"Can you hear me, madame?" The pilot stood by the car and spoke in a normal tone of voice.

"Yes."

"Good. They're coming. Lights are flashing on and off down the road. Stay where you are; watch and listen, but don't show yourself. If your son steps out, say nothing until I send him to you." The pilot paused. "If they force me to go with them, get to the landing on the west side of the lake, where we flew in. It's called Atterrisage Médoc. I'll reach you there. . . . I don't like this."

"Why? What is it?"

"There are two men in the car. The one next to the driver holds up a weapon; he checks it, perhaps."

"How would I get there?" asked Althene.

"There's a second set of keys in a small magnet box under the hood." The bearded man raised one hand to his mouth, speaking loudly above the roar of the approaching automobile. "On the right side. Be still!"

A long black car came to a stop ten yards in front of the pilot. A man on the passenger side got out, but it was not her son. He was stocky, wearing an overcoat with the lapels pulled up, a heavy muffler around his throat. Large-framed dark glasses covered his eyes, giving him the appearance of a huge insect. He limped as he walked into the spill of the headlights.

The driver remained behind the wheel. Althene stared at him, hoping to recognize Noel. It was not he; she could not see the man's face clearly, but the hair was blond.

"Mrs. Holcroft is in the car, I presume," said the man with the dark glasses to the pilot. The language was English but the accent unmistakably German.

"Her son is in yours, then? replied the pilot.

"Please ask Mrs. Holcroft to step out."

"Please ask her son to do the same."

"Don't be difficult. We have a schedule to keep."

"So do we. There's only one other person in your automobile, monsieur. He doesn't fit the description of her son."

"We'll take Mrs. Holcroft to him."

"We'll take *him* to Mrs. Holcroft."

"Stop it!"

"Stop what, monsieur? I am paid, as I'm sure you are paid. We both do our jobs, do we not?"

"I've no time for you!" the German shouted, limping past the pilot, toward the car.

The pilot nodded. "May I suggest you find the time. For you won't find Mrs. Holcroft."

"Du Sauhund! Wo ist die Frau?"

"May I further suggest, monsieur, that you don't call me names. I come from Châlons-sur-Marne. Twice you won there, and I was brought up with a certain distaste for your name-calling."

"Where is the *woman?*"

"Where is the son?"

The German took his right hand from his overcoat pocket. He was holding a gun. "You're not paid so much that it's worth your life. Where is she?"

"And you, monsieur? Perhaps you're paid too much to shoot me and not find out."

The gunshot was deafening. Dirt exploded at the pilot's feet. Althene gripped the tree in shock.

"Now, Frenchman, perhaps *you* see that payment is not so important to me as the woman. Where is she?"

"Les Boches!" said the pilot in disgust. "Give you a gun and you go mad. You never change. If you want the woman, you'll produce the son and I will take him to her."

"You'll tell me where she is now!" The German raised his gun, leveling it at the pilot's head. "Now!"

Althene could see the car door open. A gunshot exploded, then another. The pilot lunged to the dirt. The German screamed, his eyes bulging. "Johann? *Johann!"*

There was a third explosion. The German collapsed on the road; the pilot scrambled to his feet.

"He was going to *kill* you," yelled the driver, his voice incredulous. "We knew he was sick, but not insane. What can I say?"

"He would have killed me? . . ." The pilot asked the question no less incredulously. "It doesn't make sense!"

"Of course it didn't," said the blond man. "Your *request* made sense. First, help me pull him into the woods and remove his identification. Then come with me."

"Who are you?"

"A friend of Holcroft's."

"I'd like to believe that."

"You will."

It was all Althene could do to hold her place. Her legs were weak, her throat was dry, and the ache in her eyes caused her to shut them repeatedly.

The blond man and the pilot dragged the body into the woods not twenty feet below her. The pilot's instructions meant a great deal to her now. He had been right.

"Shall I take my car, monsieur?"

"No. Shut off the lights and come with me. We'll pick it up in the morning."

The pilot did as he was told, then hesitated. "I don't like to leave it so near a corpse."

"We will get it before daybreak. Have you your keys?"

"Yes."

"Hurry!" said the blond man.

The pilot's relief was in his silence; he made no further protest. In seconds, they had sped away.

Althene pushed herself away from the tree. She tried to recall the pilot's exact words. *There's a second set of keys . . . a small magnet box . . . under the hood . . . get to the landing . . . where we flew in. Atterrisage Médoc.*

Atterrisage Médoc. On the west side of the lake.

Five minutes later, her hands covered with grease, she was traveling south on the lakeside highway, toward Geneva. As the moments passed, her foot became firmer on the gas pedal, her grip on the steering wheel more relaxed. She began to think again.

Atterrisage Médoc. On the west side of the lake . . . ten or twelve miles north of the city. If she thought only of that, of the small, obscure stretch of lakefront with the gas pumps on the single dock, she might slow her heartbeat and breathe again.

Atterrisage Médoc. Please, God, let me find it! Let me live to find it and reach my son! Dear God! What have I done? A lie of thirty years . . . . a betrayal so horrible, a stigma so terrifying. . . . I must find him!

Helden sat directly behind the pilot in the small seaplane. She felt the bandage beneath her skirt; it was tight, but did not cut off circulation. The wound throbbed now and then, but the pills reduced the pain; she could walk adequately. Even if she could not, she would force herself to.

The pilot leaned back toward her. "A half hour after landing you'll be driven to a restaurant on the lake where you can get a taxi into the city," he said. "Should you require our services within the next two weeks, our base for this period is a private marina called Atterrisage Médoc. It's been a pleasure having you on board."

41

Erich Kessler was not a physical man, yet he approved of physical violence when that violence brought about practical objectives. He approved of it as observer and theoretician, not as participant. However, there was no alternative now, and no time to seek one. He would have to become a part of the violence.

Holcroft had left him no choice. The amateur had sorted out his own priorities and acted on them with alarming perception. The chromosomes of Heinrich Clausen were in the son. He had to be controlled again, remaneuvered again.

Erich chose the person he needed from among the clusters of people in the lobby: a newspaperman, and, from the ease of his manner and his expertness with notebook and pencil, probably a good one.

Kessler approached the man, keeping his voice low. "You're the journalist from . . . what paper is it?"

"Genève Soir," said the reporter.

"Dreadful, what happened. That poor man. A tragedy. I've been standing here for quite a while trying to decide whether to say anything. But I simply can't get involved."

"You're staying at the hotel?"

"Yes. I'm from Berlin. I come to Geneva often. My conscience tells me to go right over to the police and tell them what I know. But my attorney says it could be misconstrued. I'm here on business; it could be detrimental. Still, they should have it."

"What kind of information?"

Erich looked at the journalist sadly. "Let's say I knew the man who was killed very well."

"And?"

"Not here. My attorney says I should stay out of it."

"Are you telling me you *were* involved?"

"Oh, good heavens, *no*. Not like that, not at all. It's just that I have . . . information. Perhaps even a name or two. There are . . . reasons."

"If you're not involved, I'll protect you as a source."

"That's all I ask. Give me two or three minutes to go upstairs and get my coat. I'll come down and head outside. Follow me down the hill. I'll find a secluded spot where we can talk. Don't approach me until I call for you."

The journalist nodded. Kessler turned toward the elevators. He would get his overcoat and two revolvers, both untraceable. The minor delay would heighten Holcroft's anxieties, and that was fine.

Noel waited in the doorway across the street from the Hôtel d'Accord. Kessler should have received the message five minutes ago. What was holding him up?

There he was! The corpulent figure walking slowly down the short steps of the d'Accord's entrance could be no one else's. The bulk, the deliberate pace, the heavy overcoat. That was it; Kessler had gone back to his room for the coat.

Holcroft watched as Erich made his stately way down the hill, nodding pleasantly to the passersby. Kessler was a gentle person, thought Noel, and probably would not understand why he was being used as the lure; it wasn't in his nature to think that way. Nor had it ever been in Holcroft's to use a man this way, but *nothing* is as it was. It was natural for him now.

And it was successful. God damn it, it worked! A man in his mid-thirties, perhaps, reached the bottom step of the d'Accord and looked directly at Kessler's receding figure. He began walking slowly—too slowly for someone going somewhere—and took up his position far enough behind Erich not to be seen.

Now, if only Kessler would do as he was told. The intersecting avenue at the bottom of the rue des Granges was made up of old three-story office buildings, manicured and expensive, but, after five o'clock in the evening, essentially deserted. Noel had done his homework; on it depended his trapping a killer from the Nachrichtendienst. Just one killer was enough; he'd lead him to others. It was not out of the question to break that man's neck to get the information. Or to fire bullets across that man's eyes.

Noel felt the gun in his pocket and took up slow pursuit, staying on his side of the street.

Four minutes later Kessler reached the bottom of the hill and turned left. The man behind him did the same. Holcroft waited until the traffic passed and both men were out of sight. Then he crossed the intersection, still keeping on the opposite side, his view clear.

Suddenly he stopped. Kessler was nowhere in sight.

Neither was the man who had followed him.

Noel began running.

Kessler turned left into a dimly lit street, walked about a hundred and fifty feet, and held up a small mirror. The journalist was behind him; Holcroft was not. It was the moment to move quickly.

On the left was a cul-de-sac, designed to accommodate two or three parked automobiles, a chain across the front denoting its private ownership. There were no cars, and it was dark. Very dark. Ideal. With difficulty, he stepped over the chain and walked rapidly to the wall at the rear. He put his hand into his right pocket and took out the first gun—the first gun he would use. He had to tug at it; the silencer was caught momentarily in the cloth.

"In here!" he said, loud enough to be heard by the newspaperman. "We can talk here and no one will see us."

The journalist climbed over the chain, his eyes squinting into the shadows. "Where are you?"

"Over here." Erich raised the gun as the journalist approached. When he was within several feet, Kessler fired into the dim silhouette of the man's neck. The spit had a hollow sound; the expulsion of air from the punctured throat echoed between the two buildings. The newspaperman collapsed. Erich pulled the trigger once again, shooting him in the head.

He unscrewed the silencer from the pistol, rummaged through the dead man's clothes, extracting a billfold and the notebook, throwing them into the shadows. He took out the second gun from his left pocket and pressed the weapon into the reporter's hand, the index finger around the trigger.

Still kneeling, Kessler tore the front of his shirt and ripped two buttons off his overcoat. He rubbed the flat of his hand harshly over the oil and dirt of the parking lot and soiled his face with the residue.

He was ready. He rose to his feet and lurched toward the chain. At first he could not see Holcroft, but then he did. The American was running in the street; he stopped briefly in front of a streetlight.

Now.

Kessler walked back to the dead man, leaned over, and grabbed the hand with the gun, holding it up toward the sky and pressing the dead finger against the trigger.

The small-caliber gunshot was amplified by the surrounding stone. Erich yanked at the frozen finger twice more, let it drop, and swiftly removed the gun from his own pocket.

"Noel! *Noel!*" he screamed, throwing himself against the wall, his heavy body sinking to the concrete. "Noel, where *are* you?"

"Erich?! For God's sake . . . *Erich?*" Holcroft's voice was not far off; in seconds it was closer.

Kessler aimed his unsilenced gun toward the clump of dead flesh in the shadows. It was the last shot he would have to fire . . . and he did so the instant he saw the silhouette of Noel Holcroft in the dim spill of the light.

"Erich!"

"*Here.* He tried to *kill* me! Noel, he tried to kill me!"

Holcroft felt the chain, jumped over it, and raced to Kessler. He knelt down in the darkness. "Who? Where?"

"Over there! Johann made me carry a gun. . . . I had to shoot it. I had no choice!"

"Are you all right?"

"I think so. He came *after* me. He knew about you. 'Where is he?' he kept saying. 'Where is *H?* Where's Holcroft?' He threw me to the ground. . . ."

"Oh, *Christ!"* Noel leaped up and lunged toward the body in the shadows. He pulled his lighter from his pocket and snapped it on; the flame spread light over the corpse. Noel searched the pockets of the outer clothes, then rolled the body over to check the trousers. "Goddammit, there's *nothing!"*

"Nothing? What do you mean, nothing? Noel, we have to get out of here. Think of tomorrow!"

"There's no wallet, no license, nothing!"

"Tomorrow. We must think about tomorrow!"

"Tonight!" roared Holcroft. "I wanted them tonight!"

Kessler was silent for several seconds, then spoke softly, incredulity in his voice. "You planned this. . . ."

Holcroft got up angrily, the anger lessened by Erich's words. "I'm sorry," he said. "I didn't want you to get hurt. I thought I had everything under control."

"Why did you do it?"

"Because they'll kill her if they find her. Just as they killed Willie Ellis and . . . Richard Holcroft. So many others."

"Who?"

"Geneva's enemy. This Nachrichtendienst. I wanted just one of them! Alive, *goddammit!"*

"Help me up," said Kessler.

"Can you understand?" Holcroft found Erich's hand and lifted him up.

"Yes, of course. But I don't think you should have acted alone."

"I was going to trap him, get the names of others from him if I had to blind him for them. Then turn him over to the police, ask them to help me find my mother, protect her."

"We can't do that now. He's dead; there'd be too many questions we can't answer. But Johann can help."

"Von Tiebolt?"

"Yes. He told me he had an influential friend here in Geneva. A first deputy. He said when I found you to take you to the Excelsior. Register under the name of Fresca. I don't know why that name."

"It's one we're used to," said Noel. "He'll reach us there?"

"Yes. He's making the final arrangements for tomorrow. At the bank."

"The *bank?"*

"It'll be over tomorrow; that's what I tried to tell you. Come, we must hurry. We can't stay here; someone may pass by. Johann told me to tell you that if your mother was in Geneva, *we'll* find her. She'll be protected."

Holcroft helped Kessler toward the chain. The scholar looked back into the dark recesses of the walled enclosure and shuddered.

"Don't think about it," said Noel.

"It was horrible."

"It was necessary."

Yes, it was, thought Kessler.

Helden saw the old woman sitting on a bench at the base of the dock, looking out at the water, oblivious of the few mechanics and passengers who walked to and from the seaplanes.

As Helden drew near, she noticed the woman's face in the moonlight, the angular features and the high cheekbones that set off the wide eyes. The woman was lost in thought, strong and distant, she was so alone, so out of place, so . . .

Helden limped in front of the bench and stared at the face below. My God! She was looking down at a face that but for years and gender could belong to Noel Holcroft. It was his mother!

What was she doing *here?* Of all the places in the world, why *here?* The answer was obvious: Noel's mother was flying into Geneva secretly!

The old woman looked up, then looked away, uninterested, and Helden hurried as best she could across the path that led to a small building that was both waiting room and radio base. She went inside and approached a man standing behind a makeshift counter beyond which were telephones and radio equipment. "The woman outside. Who is she?"

The man looked up briefly from a clipboard, studying her. "No names are mentioned here," he said. "You should know that."

"But it's terribly important! If she's who I think she is, she's in great danger. I say this to you because I know you know Dr. Litvak."

At the name, the man looked up again. It was apparent that at Atterrisage Médoc, they lived with risk and danger but avoided both where possible. And Dr. Litvak was obviously a trusted customer. "She's waiting for a phone call."

"From whom?"

The man studied her again. "From one of our pilots: *'Le Chat rouge.'* Has she trouble with the police?"

"No."

"The Corsicans? Mafia?"

Helden shook her head. "Worse."

"You're a friend of Dr. Litvak?"

"Yes. He booked the flight from Neuchâtel for me. Check if you like."

"I don't have to. We don't want trouble here. Get her out."

"How? A car's supposed to drive me to a restaurant on the lake where I'm to wait for a taxi. It'll be a half hour, I'm told."

"Not now." The man looked past her. "Henri, come here." He took a set of car keys from under the counter. "Go talk to the old woman. Tell her she must leave. Henri will drive you."

"She may not listen."

"She has to. You'll have your transportation."

Helden went back outside as quickly as her wound permitted. Mrs. Holcroft was not on the bench, and for an instant Helden panicked. Then she saw her, out on the now-deserted dock, standing motionless in the moonlight. Helden started toward her.

The old woman turned at the sound of Helden's footsteps. She held her place and offered no greeting.

"You're Mrs. Holcroft," said Helden. "Noel's mother."

At the mention of her son's name, Althene Holcroft brought her hands together; she seemed to stop breathing. "Who are you?"

"A friend. Please believe that. More than you know."

"Since I know nothing, it can be neither more nor less."

"My name is Von Tiebolt."

"Then get out of my sight!" The old woman's words were lashes in the night air. "Men here have been paid. They'll not let you interfere with me. They'll kill you first. Go join your wolfpack!"

"I'm no part of Wolfsschanze, Mrs. Holcroft."

"You're a Von Tiebolt!"

"If I were part of Wolfsschanze, I wouldn't come near you. Surely you understand that."

"I understand the filth you represent. . . ."

"I've lived with that judgment in one form or another all my life, but you're wrong! You must believe me. You can't stay here; it's not safe for you. I can hide you; I can help you. . . ."

"*You?* How? Through the barrel of a gun? Under the wheels of a car?"

"*Please!* I know why you've come to Geneva. I'm here for the same reason. We've got to reach him, tell him before it's too late. The funds must be stopped!"

The old woman seemed stunned by Helden's words. Then she frowned, as if the words were a trap.

"Must they? Or must *I?* Well, I won't be. I'm going to call out, and when I do, men will come. If they kill you, it means nothing to me. You're thirty years of a lie! All of you! You won't reach *anyone.*"

"Mrs. Holcroft! I love your son. I love him so much . . . and if we don't reach him, he'll be killed. By either side! Neither can let him live! You've got to *understand.*"

"Liar!" said Althene. "You're all liars!"

"Damn you!" cried Helden. "No one will come to help you. They want you out of here! And I'm not a cripple. This is a *bullet* in my leg! It's there because I'm trying to reach Noel! You don't know what we've been through! You have no right to—"

There was a loud commotion from the small building on the waterfront. The two women could hear the words . . . as they were meant to hear them.

"You're not welcome here, monsieur! There's no such woman as you describe! Please leave."

"Don't give me orders! She's here!"

Helden gasped. It was a voice she'd heard all her life.

"This is a private marina. I ask you again to leave!"

"Open that door!"

"What? What door?"

"Behind you!"

Helden turned to Althene Holcroft. "I've no time to explain. I can only tell you I'm your friend. Get into the water! Out of sight. Now!"

"Why should I believe you?" The old woman stared beyond Helden, to the base of the dock and the building; she was alarmed, indecisive. "You're young and strong. You could easily kill me."

"That man wants to kill you," whispered Helden. "He tried to kill me."

"Who is he?"

"My brother. In the name of God, be quiet!"

Helden grabbed Althene around the waist and forced the old woman down to the wood of the dock. As gently as possible, she rolled both of them over the edge and into the water. Althene trembled, her mouth full of water; she coughed and thrashed her hands. Helden kept her arm around the old woman's waist, holding her up, scissoring the water below.

"Don't cough! We can't make noise. Put the strap of your purse around your neck. I'll help you."

"Dear God, what are you *doing?*"

"Be quiet."

There was a small outboard motorboat moored thirty feet from the dock. Helden pulled Althene toward the protective shadows of its hull. They were halfway there when they heard the crash of a door and saw the beam of a powerful flashlight. It danced in ominous figures as the blond man ran toward the pier, then stopped and shot the light out at the water. Helden struggled, her leg an agony now, trying to reach the boat.

She could not do it; she had no strength in the leg, and the weight of the wet clothes was too much.

"Try to get to the boat," she whispered. "I'll head back . . . he'll see me and—"

"Be still!" said the old woman, her arms now spreading out in quick, floating motions, easing the burden on Helden. "It's the same man. Your brother. He has a gun. *Hurry.*"

"I can't."

"You will."

Together, each supporting the other, they propelled themselves toward the boat.

The blond man was on the dock, the beam of the flashlight crisscrossing the water's surface in methodical patterns. In seconds the light would hit them; it was moving out like a deadly laser beam. The instant it centered on them, a fusillade of bullets would come and it would all be over.

Johann von Tiebolt was a superb marksman, and his sister knew it.

The blinding beam came; the hull was above them. Instinctively, both women put their faces in the water and surged underneath. The beam passed; they were behind the boat, the chain tangled in their clothes. They held on to it, a lifeline, filling their exhausted lungs with air.

Silence. Footsteps, at first slow and deliberate, then suddenly gathering momentum as Johann von Tiebolt left the dock. And then the crash of a door again, and voices again.

"Where did she go?"

"You're mad!"

"You're dead!"

A gunshot echoed through the waterfront. It was followed by a scream of pain, then a second gunshot. And then silence.

Minutes passed; the two women in the water looked at each other under the wash of moonlight. Tears filled the eyes of Helden von Tiebolt. The old woman touched the girl's face and said nothing.

The roar of an engine broke the terror of the silence. Then spinning tires and the sound of erupting gravel from an unseen drive came from the shore. The two women nodded at each other, and, once more, each holding the other, started for the dock.

They crawled up a ladder and knelt in the darkness, breathing deeply.

"Isn't it odd," said Althene. "At one point I thought about my shoes. I didn't want to lose them."

"Did you?"

"No. That's even stranger, I imagine."

"Mine are gone," said Helden aimlessly. She stood up. "We must leave. He may come back." She looked toward the building. "I don't want to go in there, but I think we have to. There was a set of car keys. . . ." She reached down to help the old woman up.

Helden opened the door and instantly closed her eyes. The man was slumped over the counter, his face blown off. For a moment the image of the mutilated head of Klaus Falkenheim flashed across her mind, and she wanted to scream. Instead, she whispered.

"Mein Bruder. . . ."

"Come, child. Quickly now!" Unbelievably, it was the old woman who spoke, giving the order with authority. She had spotted a ring of keys. "It's better to take their car. I have one, but it's been seen."

And then Helden saw the word, printed clearly in a heavy crayon on the floor beneath the dead man.

"No! It's a lie!"

"What is it?" The old woman grabbed the keys and rushed over to the girl.

"There. It's a lie!"

The word on the floor was written hastily, the letters large.

NACHRICHTENDIENST

Helden limped toward it, sank to her knees, and tried to rub the letters away, her hands moving furiously, the tears streaming down her face. "A lie! A *lie!* They were great men!"

Althene touched the hysterical girl's shoulder, then took her arm and pulled her off the floor. "There's no time for this! You said it yourself. We must leave here."

Gently but firmly, the older woman led the younger out to the drive. A single light was on above the door, creating as much shadow as illumination. There were two cars—the one Althene had driven and a gray automobile with a license plate wired to the bumper. She guided Helden toward the latter.

And then stopped. Whatever control she had managed to summon was shattered.

The body of her red-haired pilot lay in the gravel. He was dead, his hands tied behind his back. All over his face—around his eyes and mouth—were slashes made by the blade of a knife.

He had been tortured and shot.

They drove in silence, each with her own agonizing thoughts. "There's an apartment," said Helden finally. "I've been given directions. We'll be safe there. A man has flown in from London to help us. He should be there by now."

"Who is he?"

"A Jew from a place called Har Sha'alav."

Althene looked at the girl through the racing shadows. "A Jew from Har Sha'alav came to see me. It's why I'm here."

"I know."

The door of the apartment was opened by a slender man with dark skin and very dark eyes. He was neither tall nor short, but he emanated raw physical power. This was conveyed by his enormous shoulders, accentuated by the stretched cloth of his white shirt, open at the neck, with the sleeves rolled up, displaying a pair of muscular arms. His black hair was trimmed, his face striking, as much for its rigid solemnity as for its features.

He studied the two women, then nodded, gesturing them inside. He watched Helden's limp without comment; observed their drenched clothing in the same manner.

"I am Yakov Ben-Gadíz," he said. "So that we understand one another, it is I who will make the decisions."

"On what basis?" asked Althene.

Ben-Gadíz looked at her. "You are the mother?"

"Yes."

"I didn't expect you."

"I didn't expect to be here. I'd be dead if it weren't for this girl."

"Then you have a further obligation, in addition to your overwhelming one."

"I asked you a question. On whose authority do you make decisions for me? No one does."

"I've been in contact with Neuchâtel. There's work to be done tonight."

"There's only one thing *I* must do. That's reach my son."

"Later," said Yakov Ben-Gadíz. "There's something else first. A list must be found. We think it is in the Hôtel d'Accord."

"It's vital," interrupted Helden, her hand on Althene's arm.

"As vital as reaching your son," continued Yakov, staring at the Holcroft woman. "And I need a decoy."

42

Von Tiebolt spoke into the telephone, Kessler's note in his free hand. On the other end of the line was the first deputy of canton Genève. "I tell you, the address is wrong! It's an old deserted building, no telephone wires going through it. I'd say the Nachrichtendienst rather successfully invaded your state telephone service. Now, find me the right one!"

The blond man listened for several moments and then exploded. "You idiot, I *can't* call the number! The clerk swore he'd give it to no one but Holcroft. No matter what I might say, she'd be alarmed. Now, find me that address! I don't care if you have to wake up the president of the Federal Council to do it. I expect you to call me back within the hour." He slammed down the phone and looked again at Kessler's note.

Erich had gone to meet Holcroft. Undoubtedly they were at the Excelsior by now, registered under the name of Fresca. He could phone to make sure, but calling might lead to complications. The American had to be pushed to the edge of sanity. His friend from London murdered, his mother nowhere to be found; it was even possible he'd heard of Helden's death in Neuchâtel. Holcroft would be close to breaking; he might demand a meeting.

Johann was not prepared to agree to one yet. It was shortly past three o'clock in the morning, and the mother had not been located. He had to find her, kill her. There were six hours to go before the conference at the bank. At any moment—from out of a crowd, from a taxi in traffic, on a staircase or in a corner—she might confront her son and scream the warning: *Betrayal! Stop! Abandon Geneva!*

That could not happen! Her voice had to be stilled, the programming of her son carried out. Quite simply, she had to die tonight, all risks eliminated with her death. And then another death would follow quickly, quietly. The son of Heinrich Clausen would have fulfilled his function.

But first, his mother. Before daybreak. What was infuriating was that she was out there. At the end of a telephone line whose accurate address was buried in some bureaucrat's file!

The blond man sat down and took a long, double-edged knife from a scabbard sewn into his coat. He'd have to wash it. The red-bearded pilot had soiled it.

Noel opened his suitcase on the luggage rack and looked at the rumpled mass of clothes inside. Then his eyes scanned the white walls with the flock paper and the French doors and the small, overly ornate chandelier in the ceiling. Hotel rooms were all beginning to look alike; he remembered the seedy exception in Berlin with a certain fondness. That he even remembered it under the circumstances was a little startling. He had settled into his unsettling new world with his faculties intact. He was not sure whether that was good or bad, only that it was so.

Erich was on the phone, trying to reach Von Tiebolt at the d'Accord. Where the hell was Johann? It was three-thirty in the morning. Kessler hung up and turned to Noel. "He left a message saying we weren't to be alarmed. He's with the first deputy. They're doing everything they can to find your mother."

"No call from her, then?"

"No."

"It doesn't make sense. Is the desk clerk still there?"

"Yes. You paid him two weeks' wages. The least he could do is to stay through the night." Kessler's expression grew pensive. "You know, it's quite possible she's simply delayed. Missed connections, a fog-bound airport, difficulties with immigration somewhere."

"Anything's possible, but it still doesn't make sense. I know her; she'd get word to me."

"Perhaps she's being detained."

"I thought about that; it's the best thing that could happen. She's traveling under a false passport. Let's hope she's arrested and thrown into a cell for a couple of days. No call from Helden, either?"

"No calls at all," replied the German, his eyes suddenly riveted on Noel.

Holcroft stretched, shaving kit in hand. "It's the waiting without knowing that drives me crazy." He gestured at the bathroom door. "I'm going to wash up."

"Good idea. Then why don't you rest for a while? You must be exhausted. We have less than five hours to go, and I do believe Johann's a very capable man."

"I'm banking on it," said Noel.

He took off his shirt and ran the hot water at full force, generating steam. The vapor rose, clouding the mirror and fogging the area above the sink. He put his face into the moist heat, supporting himself on the edge of the basin, and stayed there until sweat poured down his forehead. The practice was one he had learned from Sam Buonoventura several years ago. It was no substitute for a steam bath, but it helped.

Sam? Sam! For Christ's sake, why hadn't he *thought* of him? If his mother had changed her plans, or something had happened, it was entirely possible she'd call Sam. Especially if there was no one at the d'Accord named Noel Holcroft.

He looked at his watch; it was three-thirty-five, Geneva time, ten-thirty-five, Caribbean. If Sam had something to tell him, he'd stay by the telephone.

Noel turned off the faucet. He could hear Kessler's voice from the bedroom, but there was no one else there. Whom was he talking to, and why was he keeping his voice so low?

Holcroft turned to the door and opened it less than an inch. Kessler was across the room, his back to the bathroom door, speaking into the telephone. Noel heard the words and stepped out.

"I tell you, that's our answer. She's traveling with a false passport. Check immigration records for—"

"*Erich!*"

Yakov Ben-Gadíz closed the first-aid kit, stood up beside the bed, and surveyed his handiwork. Helden's wound was inflamed, but there was no infection. He had replaced the soiled bandage with a clean one.

"There," he said, "that will do for a while. The swelling will go down in an hour or so, but you must stay off your feet. Keep the leg elevated."

"Don't tell me you're a doctor," said Helden.

"One doesn't have to be a doctor to treat bullet wounds. You just have to get used to them." The Israeli crossed to the door. "Stay here. I want to talk to Mrs. Holcroft."

"No!"

Ben-Gadíz stopped. "What did you say?"

"Don't send her out alone. She's beside herself with guilt and frightened for her son. She can't think clearly; she won't have a chance. Don't do it."

"And if I do, you'll stop me?"

"There's a better way. You want my brother. Use *me.*"

"I want the *Sonnenkinder* list first. We've got three days to kill Von Tiebolt."

"Three days?"

"Banks are closed tomorrow and Sunday. Monday would be the earliest they could meet with the Grande Banque's directors. The list comes first. I agree with Litvak; *it* is the priority."

"If it's so important, he's surely got it *with* him."

"I doubt it. Men like your brother don't take chances like that. An accident, a robbery in the streets . . . someone like me. No, he wouldn't carry that list around. Nor would he put it in a hotel vault. It's in his room. In a better vault. I want to get in that room, get him out of there for a while."

"Then all the more reason to use me!" said Helden. "He thinks I'm *dead.* He didn't see me at the seaplane base; he was looking for her, not me. The shock will stun him; he'll be confused. He'll go anywhere I say to find me. All I have to do is say the word 'Nachrichtendienst.' I'm *sure* of it."

"And I'm counting on it," replied Yakov. "But for tomorrow. Not tonight. You're not the one he wants tonight. Holcroft's mother is."

"I'll tell him she's *with* me! It's perfect!"

"He'd never believe you. You, who went to Neuchâtel to meet Werner Gerhardt? Who escaped? You're synonymous with a trap."

"Then at least let me go with her," pleaded Helden. "Set up a meeting and I'll stay out of sight. Give her *some* protection. I have a gun."

Ben-Gadíz thought a moment before answering. "I know what you're offering, and I admire you for it. But I can't risk the two of you. You see, I need her tonight, and I'll need you tomorrow. She'll draw him away tonight; you'll draw him out tomorrow. It has to be that way."

"You can accomplish *both* tonight!" pressed Helden. "Get your *list.* I'll *kill* him. I swear it!"

"I believe you, but you're missing a point. I give your brother more credit than you do. No matter how we plan, he'll control the meeting with Mrs. Holcroft tonight. He has the numbers, the methods. We don't."

Helden stared at the Israeli. "You're not only using her; you're sacrificing her."

"I'll use *each* of us, sacrifice each of us, to do what has to be done. If you interfere, I'll kill you." Yakov walked to the bedroom door and let himself out.

Althene was sitting at a desk at the far end of the room, its small lamp the only source of light. She wore a deep-red bathrobe that she'd found in a closet, and it fit her loosely. The drenched clothes she and Helden had worn were draped over radiators, drying out. She was writing on a sheet of stationery. At the sound of Yakov's footsteps, she turned.

"I borrowed some paper from your desk," she said.

"It's not my paper, not my desk," answered the Israeli. "Are you writing a letter?"

"Yes. To my son."

"Why? With any luck we'll reach him. You'll talk."

Althene leaned back in the chair, her gaze steady on Ben-Gadíz. "I think we both know that there's little chance I'll see him again."

"Do we?"

"Of course. There's no point in my deceiving myself . . . or in your trying to deceive me. Von Tiebolt has to meet with me. When he does, he won't let me go. Not alive. Why would he?"

"We'll take precautions as best we can."

"I'll take a gun, thank you. I've no intention of standing there, telling him to fire away."

"It would be better if you were sitting."

They smiled at each other. "We're both practical, aren't we? Survivors."

Yakov shrugged. "It's easier that way."

"Tell me. This list you want so badly. The *Sonnenkinder.* It must be enormous. Volumes. Names of people and families everywhere."

"That's not the list we're after; that's the master list. I doubt we'll ever see it. The list we *can* find—we've *got* to find—is the practical one. The names of the leaders who'll receive the funds, who'll distribute them in strategic areas. That list has to be where Von Tiebolt can get it readily."

"And with it, you'll have the identity of Wolfsschanze's leaders."

"Everywhere."

"Why are you so sure it's at the d'Accord?"

"It's the only place it could be. Von Tiebolt trusts no one. He lets others deal in fragments; he controls the whole. He wouldn't leave the list in a vault; nor would he carry it on him. It will be in his hotel room, the room itself filled with traps. And he would leave it only under the direst of circumstances."

"We agree I'm that circumstance."

"Yes. He fears you as he fears no one else, for no one else could convince your son to walk away from Geneva. They need him; they always have. The laws must be observed for the funds to be released. There was never any other way."

"There's irony in that. The law is used to perpetrate the greatest illegality imaginable."

"It is not a new device, Mrs. Holcroft."

"What about my son? Will you kill him?"

"I don't want to."

"I'd like something more concrete."

"There'll be no reason to, if he comes with us. If he can be convinced of the truth and not think he's being tricked, there's good reason to keep him alive. Wolfsschanze won't end with the collapse of the funds. The *Sonnenkinder* are out there. They'll be crippled, but not exposed. Or destroyed. We'll need every voice that can be raised against them. Your son will have a vital story to tell. Together we'll reach the right people."

"How will you convince him . . . if I don't come back from my meeting with Von Tiebolt?"

The Israeli saw the hint of a smile on Althene's lips and understood her pause. His assumption had been clear: She would not come back.

"As the contact in Neuchâtel and I see it, we have today and tomorrow; the moves at La Grande Banque will no doubt begin Monday. They'll keep him isolated, out of reach. It's my job to break that isolation, get him away."

"And when you do, what will you say?"

"I'll tell him the truth, explain everything we learned at Har Sha'alav. Helden can be extremely helpful—if she's alive, frankly. And then there's the list. If I find it, I'll show it to him."

"Show him this letter," interrupted Althene, turning back to the paper on the desk.

"It, too, would be helpful," said the Israeli.

"Erich!"

Kessler whipped around, his obese body rigid. He started to lower the phone, but Holcroft stopped him.

"Hold it! Who are you talking to?" Noel grabbed the telephone; he spoke into it. "Who is this?"

Silence.

"Who is this?"

"Please," said Kessler, regaining his composure. "We're trying to *protect* you. You can't be seen on the streets; you know that. They'll kill you. You're the key to Geneva."

"You weren't talking about me!"

"We're trying to find your mother! You said she was traveling on a false passport, out of Lisbon. We didn't understand that. Johann knows people who provide such papers; we were discussing it now."

Holcroft spoke again into the phone. "Von Tiebolt? Is that you?"

"Yes, Noel," came the calm reply. "Erich's right. I have friends here who are trying to help us. Your mother could be in danger. You can't be a part of the search. You must stay out of sight."

" 'Can't'?" Holcroft said the word sharply. " 'Must'? Let's get something straight—both of you." Noel spoke into the phone, his eyes on Kessler. "I'll decide what I do and what I don't do. Is that clear?"

The scholar nodded. Von Tiebolt said nothing. Holcroft raised his voice. "I asked you if that was *clear!*"

"Yes, of course," said Johann finally. "As Erich has told you, we only want to help. This information about your mother's traveling on a passport that's not her own could be helpful. I know men who deal in such matters. I'll make calls and keep you informed."

"Please."

"If I don't see you before morning, we'll meet at the bank. I assume Erich's explained."

"Yes, he has. And, Johann . . . I'm sorry I blew; I know you're trying to help. The people we're after are called the Nachrichtendienst, aren't they? That's what you found out in London."

There was a pause on the line. Then, "How did you know?"

"They left a calling card. I want those bastards."

"So do we."

"Thanks. Call me the minute you hear anything." Noel hung up. "Don't ever do that again," he told Kessler.

"I apologize. I thought I was doing the right thing. Just as I think you believed you were doing the right thing to have me followed from the d'Accord."

"It's a lousy world these days," Noel said, reaching for the phone.

"What are you doing?"

"There's a man in Curaçao I want to talk to. He may know something."

"Oh, yes. The engineer who's been relaying your messages."

"I owe him."

Noel reached the overseas operator and gave her the number in Curaçao. "Shall I stay on the line, or will you call me back?"

"The cables are not crowded at this hour, sir."

"I'll stay on." He sat on the bed and waited. Before ninety seconds had passed, he heard the ring of Buonoventura's phone.

A male voice answered. But it was not Sam's voice.

"Yeah?"

"Sam Buonoventura, please."

"Who wants him?"

"A personal friend. I'm calling from Europe."

"He ain't gonna come runnin', mister. He ain't takin' no more phone calls."

"What are you talking about?"

"Sam bought it, mister. Some fuckin' nigger native put a wire through his throat. We're beating the high grass and the beaches for that son of a bitch."

Holcroft lowered his head, his eyes closed, his breath suspended. His moves had been traced to Sam, and Sam's help could not be tolerated. Buonoventura was his information center; he had to be killed, no more messages relayed. The Nachrichtendienst was trying to isolate him. He had owed Sam a debt, and that debt had been paid with death. Everything he touched was touched with death; he was its carrier.

"Don't bother with the high grass," he said, barely aware he was talking. "I killed him."

43

"Did your son ever mention the name 'Tennyson'?" asked Ben-Gadíz.

"No."

"Damn it! When was the last time you talked with him?"

"After my husband's death. He was in Paris."

Yakov unfolded his arms; he had heard something he wanted to hear. "Was it the first time you'd spoken since your husband's death?"

"His murder," corrected Althene. "Although I didn't know it then."

"Answer my question. Was it the first time you'd talked since your husband died?"

"Yes."

"It was a sad conversation, then."

"Obviously. I had to tell him."

"Good. Such times cloud the mind; things are said that are rarely recalled with clarity. *That's* when he mentioned the name 'Tennyson.' He told you he was on his way to Geneva, probably with a man named Tennyson. Can you convey that to Von Tiebolt?"

"Certainly. But will he accept it?"

"He has no choice. He wants you."

"I want him."

"Make the call. And remember, you're close to hysterics; a panicked woman is unmanageable. Throw him off balance with your voice. Shout, whisper, stutter. Tell him you were to call your pilot at the seaplane base. There's been a killing; it was swarming with police, and you're frightened out of your mind. Can you do it?"

"Just listen," said Althene, reaching for the phone.

The d'Accord switchboard connected her to the room of its very important guest Mr. John Tennyson.

And Yakov listened in admiration as Althene performed.

"You must get hold of yourself, Mrs. Holcroft," said the stranger at the d'Accord.

"Then you *are* the Tennyson my son referred to?"

"Yes. I'm a friend. We met in Paris."

"For the love of God, can you help me?"

"Of course. It would be a privilege."

"Where's Noel?"

"I'm afraid I don't know. . . . He has business in Geneva with which I'm not involved."

"You're not?" A statement made in relief.

"Oh, no. We had dinner earlier—last night, actually—and he left to see his associates."

"Did he say where he was going?"

"I'm afraid he didn't. You see, I'm on my way to Milan. . . . In Paris, I told Noel I'd stop over with him in Geneva and show him the city. He's never been here, of course."

"Can you meet with me, Mr. Tennyson?"

"Certainly. Where are you?"

"We must be careful. I can't let you take risks."

"There's no risk for me, Mrs. Holcroft. I move freely in Geneva."

"I don't. That dreadful business at Médoc."

"Come now, you're overwrought. Whatever it was, I'm sure it doesn't concern you. Where are you? Where can we meet?"

"The train station. The north entrance waiting room. In forty-five minutes. God bless you."

She hung up abruptly. Yakov Ben-Gadíz smiled in approval.

"He'll be very careful," said the Israeli. "He'll mount his defenses, and that will give us more time. I'll head for the d'Accord. I'll need every minute."

Von Tiebolt replaced the receiver slowly. The possibilities of a trap were greater rather than fewer, he thought, but the evidence was not conclusive. He had purposely made the statement that Holcroft had never been to Geneva; it was a lie, and the old woman knew it. On the other hand, she sounded genuinely panicked, and a woman of her age in panic did not so much listen as wish to be listened to. It was conceivable that she had not heard the remark, or, if she had, that she considered it subordinate to her own concerns.

Holcroft's using the name "Tennyson"—if he had—was not out of character for the American. He was subject to quick emotional outbursts, often speaking without thinking. The news of Richard Holcroft's death in New York could easily have put him in such an emotional state that the name "Tennyson" slipped out without his realizing it.

On the other hand, the American had displayed strengths where strengths had not been thought to exist. Giving the name to his mother contradicted the discipline he had developed. And further, Johann knew that he was dealing with a woman who was capable of obtaining false papers, who had disappeared in Lisbon. He would take extraordinary precautions. He would not be trapped by an old woman in panic—or by one who pretended to be in panic.

The telephone rang, breaking his concentration.

"Yes?"

It was the first deputy. They were still trying to locate the accurate address of the telephone number given the d'Accord by Mrs. Holcroft. A bureaucrat was on his way to the state telephone office to open a file. Von Tiebolt replied icily.

"By the time he finds it, it will be of no use to us. I've made contact with the woman. Send a policeman driving an official car to the d'Accord immediately. Tell him I'm a visitor of state who requires a personal courtesy. Have him in the lobby in fifteen minutes." Von Tiebolt did not wait for a reply. He replaced the phone and went back to the table where there were two handguns. They had been broken down for cleaning; he would reassemble them quickly. They were two of the Tinamou's favorite weapons.

If Althene Holcroft had the audacity to bait a trap, she would learn she was no match for the leader of Wolfsschanze. Her trap would snap back, crushing her in its teeth.

The Israeli stayed out of sight in an alleyway across from the d'Accord. On the hotel steps, Von Tiebolt was talking quietly with a police officer, giving him instructions.

When they had finished talking, the officer ran to his car. The blond man walked to a black limousine at the curb and climbed in behind the wheel. Von Tiebolt wanted no chauffeur for the trip he was about to make.

Both cars drove off down the rue des Granges. Yakov waited until he could see neither, then, briefcase in hand, walked across the street to the d'Accord.

He approached the front desk, the picture of weary officialdom. He sighed as he spoke to the clerk. "Police examiners. I've been rousted from my bed to take additional scrapings from the dead man's room. That Ellis fellow. The inspectors never have ideas until everyone they need is asleep. What's the number?"

"Third floor. Room thirty-one," said the clerk, grinning sympathetically. "There's an officer on duty outside."

"Thanks." Ben-Gadíz walked to the elevator, pressing the button for the fifth floor. John Tennyson was registered in room 512. There was no time to indulge in games with a policeman on guard duty. He needed every minute—every second—he could get.

The man in the uniform of the Geneva police walked through the north entrance of the railroad station, his leather heels clicking against the stone. He approached the old woman seated at the far end of the first row of benches.

"Mrs. Althene Holcroft?"

"Yes?"

"Please come with me, madame."

"May I ask why?"

"I'm to escort you to Mr. Tennyson."

"Is that necessary?"

"It is a courtesy of the city of Geneva."

The old woman got to her feet and accompanied the man in uniform. As they walked toward the double doors of the north entrance, four additional policemen emerged from the outside and took up positions in front of the doors. No one would pass by them until permission was granted.

Outside, on the platform, flanking a police car at the curb, were two more uniformed men. The one near the hood opened the door for the woman. She climbed in; her escort addressed his subordinates.

"As instructed, no private automobiles or taxis are to leave the terminal for a period of twenty minutes. Should any attempt to do so, get the identifications and have the information radioed to my car."

"Yes, sir."

"If there are no incidents, the men may go back to their posts in twenty minutes." The police officer got inside the car and started the engine.

"Where are we going?" asked Althene.

"To a guest house on the estate of the first deputy of Geneva. This Mr. Tennyson must be a very important man."

"In many ways," she replied.

Von Tiebolt waited behind the wheel of the black limousine. He was parked fifty yards from the ramp that led out of the station's north entrance, the limousine's motor idling. He watched as the police car drove out into the street and turned right, then waited until he saw the two police officers take up their positions.

He pulled out into the street. As planned, he would follow the police car at a discreet distance, keeping alert for signs of other automobiles showing interest in that vehicle. All contingencies had to be considered, including the possibility that somewhere on her person the old woman had concealed an electronic homing device that would send out signals attracting the carrion she employed.

The last obstacle to Code Wolfsschanze would be eliminated within the hour.

Yakov Ben-Gadíz stood in front of Von Tiebolt's door. The "do not disturb" sign was posted. The Israeli knelt down and opened his briefcase. He took out an odd-shaped flashlight and snapped it on; the glow was a barely perceptible light green. He pointed the light at the bottom left of the door, worked across, and up, and over the top. He was looking for strands of thread or of human hair—tiny alarms that if removed told the occupant his room had been entered. The light identified two threads stretched below, then three vertically, and one above. Yakov removed a tiny pin recessed in the handle of the flashlight. Delicately, he touched the wood beside each thread; the pin markings were infinitesimal— unseen by the naked eye but picked up by the green light. He then knelt again and took a small metal cylinder from his briefcase. It was a highly sophisticated electronic lock-picking instrument developed in the counterterrorist laboratories at Tel Aviv.

He placed the mouth of the cylinder over the lock and activated the tumbler probes. The lock sprung, and Yakov carefully slid the fingers of his left hand along the borders of the door, removing the threads. Slowly, he pushed the door open. He reached for his briefcase, stepped inside, and closed the door. There was a small table by the wall; he put the threads down carefully on it, weighting them with the cylinder, and again snapped on the flashlight.

He looked at his watch. Conservatively, he had no more than thirty minutes to deactivate whatever alarms Von Tiebolt had set and to find the *Sonnenkinder* list. The fact that threads had been planted in the door was a good sign. They were there for a reason.

He angled the beam of green light around the sitting room. There were two closets and the bedroom door, all closed. He eliminated the closets first. No threads, no bolted locks, nothing.

He approached the door to the bedroom and threw the beam along the edges. There were no threads, but there was something else. The wash of green light picked up the reflection of a tiny yellow light recessed between the door and the frame, approximately two feet above the floor. Ben-Gadíz knew immediately what he was looking at: a miniature photoelectric cell, making contact with another drilled into the wood of the door's edging.

If the door was opened, the contact would be broken and the alarm triggered. It was as foolproof as modern technology allowed; there was no way to immobilize the device. Yakov had seen them before, tiny cells with built-in timers. Once implanted, they were there for the specific durations called for, rarely less than five hours. No one, including the person who set them, could neutralize them before the timers ran down.

Which meant that Johann von Tiebolt expected to break the contact if he wanted to enter the room. Emergencies might arise that required his tripping the alarm.

What kind of alarm was it? Sound had to be ruled out; any loud noise would draw attention to the room. Radio signals were a possibility, but signals had too limited a range.

No, the alarm itself had to release a deterrent within the immediate vicinity of the protected area. A deterrent that would immobilize an intruder but could be defused by Von Tiebolt himself.

Electric shock was not dependable. Acid was uncontrollable; Von Tiebolt might sustain permanent injury and disfigurement. Was it a gas? A vapor? . . .

Toxin. A vaporized poison. Toxic *fumes.* Powerful enough to render a trespasser unconscious. An oxygen mask would be protection against the vapor. If Von Tiebolt used one, he could enter the room at will.

Tear gas and Mace were not unknown in Yakov's line of work. He returned to his briefcase, knelt down, and pulled out a gas mask with a small canister of oxygen. He put it on, inserted the mouthpiece, and went back to the door. He pushed the door open quickly, and stepped back.

A burst of vapor filled the door frame. It was suspended for several seconds and then evaporated rapidly, leaving the space as clear as if it had never appeared. Ben-Gadíz felt a minor stinging around his eyes. It was an irritant, not blinding, but Yakov knew that if inhaled, the chemicals that produced that stinging would inflame the lungs and cause his instant collapse. It was the proof he was looking for. The *Sonnenkinder* list was somewhere in that room.

He stepped through the doorway, past a tripod with a cylinder of gas attached to the top. To remove whatever traces might remain of the fumes, he opened a window; cold winter air rushed in, billowing the curtains.

Ben-Gadíz went back into the sitting room, picked up his briefcase, and returned to the bedroom to begin the search. Assuming that the list would be protected by a fire-resistant steel container of some sort, he took out a small metal scanner with a luminous dial. He started at the bed area and began working his way around the room.

The needle of the detector leaped forward in front of the clothes closet. The green light picked up the familiar tiny yellow dots in the door frame.

He had found the vault.

He opened the door; vapor burst forth, filling the closet as it had filled the space of the bedroom door. Only now it remained longer than before, the cloud denser. If the first alarm had malfunctioned, this one contained enough toxin to kill a man. On the floor of the closet was an overnight suitcase, its dark-brown leather soft and expensive, but Yakov knew it was not an ordinary piece of luggage. There were no wrinkles on the front or back, as there were across the top and down the sides. The leather was reinforced with steel.

He checked for threads and markings with the green light; there were none. He lifted the suitcase to the bed, then pushed a second button on the flashlight. The green light was replaced with a sharp beam of yellowish white. He studied the two locks. They were different; doubtless each triggered a different alarm.

He removed a thin pick from his pocket and inserted it in the lock on the right, careful to keep his hand as far back as possible.

There was a rush of air; a long needle shot out from the left of the lock. Fluid oozed from the point, globules dripping to the carpet. Yakov took out a handkerchief, wiped the needle clean, and slowly, cautiously, pushed it back into its recess, using his pick to press it through the tiny orifice.

He turned his attention to the lock on the left. Standing to the side he repeated the manipulations with the pick; the latch snapped up; there was a second rush of air. Instead of a needle, something shot out, embedding itself in the fabric of an armchair across the room. Ben-Gadíz rushed over, shining the light on the point of entry. There was a circle of dampness where the object had entered the cloth. With the pick, he dug it out.

It was a gelatinous capsule, its tip made of steel. It would enter flesh as easily as it had broken the threads of fabric. The fluid was a powerful narcotic of some sort.

Satisfied, Ben-Gadíz put the capsule in his pocket, returned to the suitcase, and opened it. Inside was a flat metal envelope attached to the steel reinforcement. He had reached the safety box beyond the alarms, within the successive deadly vaults, and it was his.

He looked at his watch; the operation had taken eighteen minutes.

He lifted the flap of the metal envelope and took out the papers. There were eleven pages, each page containing six columns—names, cable addresses, and cities—perhaps one hundred fifty entries per page. Approximately sixteen hundred and fifty identities.

The elite of the *Sonnenkinder.* The manipulators of Wolfsschanze.

Yakov Ben-Gadíz knelt down over his open briefcase and removed a camera.

"Vous êtes très aimable. Nous vous téléphonons dans une demiheure. Merci." Kessler hung up the telephone, shaking his head at Noel, who stood by the window of the Excelsior suite. "Nothing. Your mother didn't call the d'Accord."

"They're certain?"

"There've been no calls at all for a Mr. Holcroft. I even checked the switchboard, in case the desk clerk had stepped out for a moment or two. You heard me."

"I don't understand her. Where *is* she? She should have called hours ago. And Helden. She said she'd phone me Friday night; goddammit, it's Saturday morning!"

"Nearly four o'clock," said Erich. "You really should get some rest. Johann's doing everything he can to find your mother. He's got the best people in Geneva working for us."

"I can't rest," said Noel. "You forget: I just killed a man in Curaçao. His crime was helping me, and I killed him."

"You didn't. The Nachrichtendienst did."

"Then let's *do* something!" cried Holcroft. "Von Tiebolt has friends in high places. Tell them about it! British Intelligence owes him one hell of a debt; he gave them the Tinamou! Call in that debt! Now! Let the whole goddamn world know about those bastards! What are we waiting for?"

Kessler took several steps toward Noel, his eyes level and compassionate. "We're waiting for the most important thing of all. The meeting at the bank. The covenant. Once that's over with, there's nothing we can't do. And when we do it, the 'whole goddamn world,' as you put it, will have to listen. Look to our covenant, Noel. It's the answer to so much. For you, your mother, Helden . . . so much. I think you know that."

Holcroft nodded slowly, his voice tired, his mind exhausted. "I do. It's the not knowing, not hearing, that drives me crazy."

"I know it's been difficult for you. But it will be over soon; everything will be fine." Erich smiled. "I'm going to wash up."

Noel went to the window. Geneva was asleep—as Paris had been asleep, and Berlin and London and Rio. Through how many windows had he looked out at the sleeping cities at night? Too many. *Nothing is as it was for you. . . .*

Nothing.

Holcroft frowned. *Nothing.* Not even his name. His *name.* He was registered as Fresca. Not Holcroft, but Fresca! That was the name Helden was to call! *Fresca.*

He spun around toward the telephone. There was no point in having Erich make the call; the d'Accord operator spoke English, and he knew the number. He dialed.

"Hôtel d'Accord. *Bonsoir.*"

"Operator, this is Mr. Holcroft. Dr. Kessler spoke to you a few minutes ago about the messages I was expecting."

"I beg your pardon, monsieur. Dr. Kessler? You wish Dr. Kessler?"

"No, you don't understand. Dr. Kessler spoke to you just a few minutes ago about my messages. There's another name I want to ask you about. 'Fresca.' 'N. Fresca.' Have there been any messages for N. Fresca?"

The operator paused. "There's no Fresca at the d'Accord, monsieur. Do you wish me to ring Dr. Kessler's room?"

"No, he's *here.* He just spoke to you!" Goddammit, thought Noel, the woman could speak English, but she couldn't seem to understand it. Then he remembered the name of the desk clerk; he gave it to the operator. "May I speak with him, please?"

"I'm sorry, monsieur. He left over three hours ago. He's off duty at midnight."

Holcroft held his breath, his eyes on the bathroom door. He could hear water running; Erich could not hear him. And the operator understood English perfectly. "Wait a minute, miss. Let me get this straight. You didn't talk with Dr. Kessler a few minutes ago?"

"No, monsieur."

"Is there another operator on the switchboard?"

"No. There are very few calls during these hours."

"And the desk clerk left at midnight?"

"Yes, I just told you."

"And there've been no calls for Mr. Holcroft?"

Again the operator paused. When she spoke, she was hesitant, as if remembering. "I think there was, monsieur. Shortly after I came on duty. A woman called. I was instructed to give the call to the head clerk."

"Thank you," said Noel softly, hanging up.

The water in the bathroom stopped running. Kessler stepped out. He saw Holcroft's hand on the telephone. The scholar's eyes were no longer gentle.

"What the hell's going on?" asked Noel. "You didn't talk to the clerk. *Or* the switchboard. My mother called hours ago. You never told me. You *lied.*"

"You must not get upset, Noel."

"You lied to me!" roared Holcroft, grabbing his jacket off the chair and going to the bed where he had thrown his raincoat—the raincoat with the gun in the pocket. "She *called* me, you son of a bitch!"

Kessler ran to the foyer and placed himself in front of the door. "She wasn't where she said she would be! We are worried. We are trying to find her, *protect* her. Protect you! Von Tiebolt understands these things; he's lived with them. Let *him* make the decisions."

"Decisions? What goddamn decisions? He doesn't make decisions for me! Neither do you! Get out of my way!"

Kessler did not move, so Noel grabbed him by the shoulders and threw him across the room.

Holcroft raced into the hallway, toward the staircase.

44

The gates of the estate parted; the official vehicle drove through. The policeman nodded to the guard and glanced warily through the window at the Doberman, straining on its leash, prepared to attack. He turned to Mrs. Holcroft.

"The guest house is four kilometers from the gate. We take the road that veers to the right, off the main drive."

"I'll take your word for it," said Althene.

"I tell you because I've never been here before, madame. I trust I'll find my way in the dark."

"I'm sure you will."

"I'm to leave you there and return to my official duties," he said. "There's no one at the guest house, but the front entrance, I'm told, will be open."

"I see. Mr. Tennyson is waiting for me?"

The police officer seemed to hesitate. "He'll be along shortly. He'll drive you back, of course."

"Of course. Tell me, do your orders come from Mr. Tennyson?"

"My present instructions, yes. Not the orders. They come from the first deputy, through the prefect of police."

"The first deputy? The prefect? They're friends of Mr. Tennyson's?"

"I imagine so, madame. As I mentioned, Mr. Tennyson must be a very important man. Yes, I'd say they are friends."

"But you're not?"

The man laughed. "Me? Oh, no, madame. I only met the gentleman briefly. As I said to you, this is merely a municipal courtesy."

"I see. Do you think you might extend a courtesy to me?" asked Althene, pointedly opening her purse. "On a confidential basis."

"That would depend, madame. . . ."

"It's only a telephone call to a friend who may be worried about me. I forgot to call her from the railroad station."

"Gladly," said the officer. "As a friend of Mr. Tennyson, I assume you're also an important visitor to Genève."

"I'll write out the number. A young lady will answer. Tell her exactly where you've taken me."

The guest house was high ceilinged, with tapestries on the walls and French-provincial furniture. It belonged in the Loire Valley, an adjunct to a great château.

Althene sat in a large chair, the pistol belonging to Yakov Ben-Gadíz wedged between the pillow and the base of the arm. The police officer had left five minutes ago; she waited now for Johann von Tiebolt.

The almost overpowering temptation to shoot the instant Von Tiebolt walked through the door had to be controlled. If there were things she could learn, she had to learn them. If only on the possibility she could relay them to the Israeli, or to the girl. Somehow . . .

He had arrived; the low, vibrating sound of a car motor outside was proof. She had heard that powerful engine hours before as it came to a stop on a deserted stretch of highway above Lake Geneva. She had watched through the trees as the blond man killed. As he had killed ruthlessly hours later at Atterrisage Médoc. To bring about his death would be a privilege. She touched the handle of the gun, secure in her purpose.

The door opened, and the tall man with the shining blond hair and the sculptured features walked inside. He closed the door; his movements in the soft, indirect lighting were supple.

"Mrs. Holcroft, how good of you to come."

"It was I who asked for the meeting. How good of you to arrange it. Your precautions were commendable."

"You seemed to feel they were called for."

"No automobile could have followed us from the station."

"None did. We're alone."

"This is a pleasant house. My son would find it interesting. As an architect, he'd call it an example of something or other, and point out the various influences."

"I'm sure he would; his mind works that way."

"Yes," said Althene, smiling. "He'll be walking down a street and suddenly stop and stare up at a window or a cornice, seeing a detail others don't see. He's quite devoted to his work. I never knew where he got it from. I have no talents in that direction, and his late father was a banker."

The blond man stood motionless. "Then both fathers were associated with money."

"You know, then?" Althene asked.

"Of course. Heinrich Clausen's son. I think we can stop lying to each other, Mrs. Holcroft."

"I understood it was a lie on your part, Herr von Tiebolt. I wasn't sure you knew it was one on mine."

"To be frank, until this moment I didn't. If your objective was to set a trap, I'm sorry to have spoiled it for you. But then, I'm sure you knew the risk."

"Yes, I did."

"Why did you take it? You must have considered the consequences."

"I considered them. But I felt it was only fair to let you know the consequences of a previous action on my part. Knowing it, perhaps an accommodation can be reached between us."

"Really? And what would this accommodation entail?"

"Abandoning Geneva. Dismantling Wolfsschanze."

"Is that all?" The blond man smiled. "You're mad."

"Suppose I told you that I had written a very long letter detailing a lie I have lived with for over thirty years. A letter in which I identify the participants and their strategy by name and family and bank."

"And destroyed your son in so doing."

"He'd be the first to agree with what I did, if he knew."

Von Tiebolt folded his arms. "You said, 'Suppose I told you' . . . about this letter of yours. Well, you've told me. And I'm afraid I'd have to say that you wrote about something you know nothing about. All the laws have been observed, and the pitifully few facts you claim to have would be called the ramblings of a crazy old woman who's been the object of official surveillance for a very long time. But this is irrelevant. You never wrote such a letter."

"You don't know that."

"Please," said Von Tiebolt. "We have copies of every bit of correspondence, every will, every legal document you've written . . . as well as the substance of every phone call you've made during the past five years."

"You've *what?*"

"There's a file at your Federal Bureau of Investigation with the code name 'Mother Goddamn.' It's one that will never be released under the Freedom of Information Act, because it deals with national security. No one's quite sure why, but it does, and certain latitudes are permitted. That file is also at the Central Intelligence Agency and the Defense Intelligence Agency and in the computer banks of Army G-Two." Von Tiebolt smiled again. "We are *everywhere*, Mrs.

Holcroft. Can't you understand that? You should know it before you leave this world; your remaining here would change nothing. You can't stop us. No one can."

"You'll be stopped because you offer lies! You always did. And when the lies fail, you kill. It was your way then; it's your way now."

"Lies are palliatives; death is often the answer for irritating problems that interfere with progress."

"The problems being people."

"Always."

"You are the most contemptible man on earth. You're *insane!*"

The blond killer put his hand in his jacket pocket. "You make my work pleasant," he said, withdrawing a pistol. "Another woman said those words to me. She was no less headstrong than you. I put a bullet in her head—through a car window. At night. In Rio de Janeiro. She was my mother, and she called me insane, called our work contemptible. She never grasped the necessity—the beauty—of our cause. She tried to interfere." The blond man raised the gun. "A few old men—devoted lovers of the whore—suspected me of killing her and in their feeble way tried to have me charged. Can you imagine? Have me *charged.* It sounds so official. What they didn't realize was that we controlled the courts. No *one* can stop us."

"Noel will stop you!" cried Althene, her hand edging toward the concealed weapon at her side.

"Your son will be dead in a day or two. But even if we don't kill him, others will. He's left a trail of murder from which he can never extricate himself. A former member of British Intelligence was garroted in New York. His last conversation was with your son. A man named Graff was killed in Rio; your son threatened him. A construction engineer in the Caribbean died tonight, also garroted. He relayed confidential messages to Noel Holcroft from Rio to Paris and stops in between. Tomorrow morning a New York detective named Miles will be slain in the streets. The current case file that obsesses him has been altered somewhat, but not its subject—Noel Holcroft. In fact, for Noel's own peace of mind it would probably be better if we killed him after all. He has no life now." Von Tiebolt raised his weapon higher, then stretched out his arm slowly, his target the woman's head. "So you see, Mrs. Holcroft, you can't possibly stop us. We are *everywhere.*"

Althene suddenly twisted in her chair, thrusting her hand toward the gun. Johann von Tiebolt fired. Then he fired again. And again.

Yakov Ben-Gadíz rearranged Von Tiebolt's suite, leaving it exactly as he had found it, airing out the rooms so that there was no evidence of entry.

Were he alive, Klaus Falkenheim would be appalled at what Yakov was doing. *Get the list. The identities. Once the names are yours, expose the account for what it is. Cause the distribution of the millions to be abandoned. Cripple the Sonnenkinder.* Those had been Falkenheim's instructions.

But there was another way. It had been discussed quietly among the elders at Har Sha'alav. They'd never had time to bring it to Falkenheim's attention, but it was their intention to do so. They called it the option of Har Sha'alav.

It was dangerous, but it could be done.

Get the list and control the millions. Don't expose the account; steal it. Use the great fortune to fight the Sonnenkinder. Everywhere.

The strategy had not been perfected, because not enough was known. But Yakov knew enough now. Of the three sons who would present themselves to the bank, one was not what the others were.

In the beginning, Noel Holcroft was the key to fulfilling the Wolfsschanze covenant. At the end, he would be its undoing.

Falkenheim was dead, Yakov reflected. The elders of Har Sha'alav were dead; there was no one else. The decision was his alone.

The option of Har Sha'alav.

Could it be done?

He would know within the next twenty-four hours.

His eyes fell on every object in the room. Everything was in place, everything as it had been. Except that in his briefcase now were eleven photographs that could signify the beginning of the end of Wolfsschanze. Eleven pages of names, the identities of the most trusted, most powerful *Sonnenkinder* across the world. Men and women who had lived the Nazi lie in deep cover for thirty years.

Never again.

Yakov picked up his briefcase. He would rethread the outer door and . . .

He stopped all movement, all thought, and concentrated on the sudden intrusion from beyond the door. He could hear footsteps, racing footsteps, muffled by the carpet but distinguishable, running up the hotel corridor. They drew near, then came to an abrupt stop. Silence, followed by the sound of a key in the lock and the frantic turning of both knob and key. The inside latch held firm. A fist pounded against the door inches from Ben-Gadíz.

"Von Tiebolt! Let me in!"

It was the American. In seconds he would break down the door.

Kessler crawled to the bed, held on to the post, and pulled his large frame off the floor. His glasses had flown off his face under the force of Holcroft's attack. He would find them in a few minutes, but right now he had to think, to analyze his immediate course of action.

Holcroft would go to the d'Accord to confront Johann; there was nothing else he *could* do. But Johann was not there, and it was no time for the American to create a scene.

Nor *would* he, thought Kessler, smiling in spite of his anxiety. Holcroft had only to gain admittance to Von Tiebolt's suite. A simple hotel key was the answer. Once inside, the American would open the bedroom door. The instant he did, he would collapse, no longer an immediate problem.

An antidote and several ice packs would revive him sufficiently for the conference at the bank; a dozen explanations would be given to him. It was only a matter of getting Johann's room key to him.

The clerks at the d'Accord would not give him one on the strength of another guest's request, but they would if the first deputy told them to. Von Tiebolt was his personal friend; accommodations were to be granted in all things.

Kessler picked up the phone.

Helden limped about the apartment, forcing her leg to get used to the pain, angry that she had been left behind, but knowing it was the sensible thing to do—the only thing. The Israeli did not think Noel would call, but it was a contingency that had to be considered. Yakov was convinced Noel was being isolated, all messages intercepted; but there was a remote chance . . .

The telephone rang; Helden thought the blood would burst from her throat. She swallowed, and limped across the room to pick it up. *Oh, God! Let it be Noel!*

It was an unfamiliar voice belonging to someone who would not identify himself.

"Mrs. Holcroft was driven to a guest house on an estate thirteen kilometers south of the city. I'll give you directions."

He did. Helden wrote them down. When he had finished, the stranger added, "There is a guard at the main gate. He has an attack dog."

Yakov could not let the pounding continue, nor Holcroft's shouted demands. The disturbance would draw attention.

The Israeli twisted the latch and pressed himself against the wall. The door crashed open, the figure of the tall American filling the frame. He lunged into the room, his arms in front of him as if prepared to repel an assault.

"Von Tiebolt! Where *are* you?"

Holcroft was obviously startled by the darkness. Ben-Gadíz stepped silently to the side, the flashlight in his hand. He spoke rapidly, completing two sentences in a single breath.

"Von Tiebolt's not here and I mean you no harm. We are not on opposite sides."

Holcroft spun around, his hands extended. "Who are you? What the hell are you doing here? Turn on the light!"

"No lights! Just listen."

The American stepped forward angrily. Yakov pressed the button on his flashlight; the wash of green spread over Holcroft, causing him to cover his eyes. "Turn that off!"

"No. Listen to me first."

Holcroft lashed his right foot out, catching Ben-Gadíz in the knee; at contact, Noel sprang forward, his eyes shut, his hands clutching for the Israeli's body.

Yakov crouched and threw his shoulder up into the American's chest; Holcroft would not be stopped. He brought his knee into Ben-Gadíz's temple; his fist smashed into Yakov's face.

There could be no lacerations! No traces of blood on the floor! Yakov dropped the light and held on to the American's arms; he was amazed at Holcroft's strength. He spoke as loudly as he dared to.

"You must *listen!* I'm not your enemy. I've got news of your mother. I have a letter. She's been with *me.*"

The American struggled; he was breaking the grip. "Who *are* you?"

"Nachrichtendienst," whispered Ben-Gadíz.

At the sound of the name, Holcroft went wild. He roared, his arms and legs battering rams that would not, could not, be repulsed.

"I'll *kill you.* . . ."

Yakov had no choice. He surged through the hammering attack, his fingers centering in on the American's neck, his thumbs grinding into the pronounced veins of the stiffened throat. By touch, he found a nerve and pressed with all his strength. Holcroft collapsed.

Noel opened his eyes in the darkness, but the darkness was not complete. Angled against the wall was a wash of green light—the same green light that had blinded him earlier—and at the sight of it his outrage returned.

He was being pressed against the floor, a knee sunk into his shoulder, the barrel of a gun against his head. His throat was in agony but still he twisted, trying to rise from the carpet, away from the weapon. His neck could not take the strain. He fell back, and heard the intense whisper of the man above him.

"Be very clear in this. If I were your enemy, I would have killed you. Can you understand that?"

"You *are* my enemy!" answered Noel, barely able to speak through the bruised muscles about his throat. "You said you were Nachrichtendienst. Geneva's enemy . . . *my* enemy!"

"The first, absolutely; but not the second. Not yours."

"You're lying!"

"Think! Why haven't I pulled this trigger? Geneva is stopped; you are stopped; no funds are transferred. If I'm your enemy, what prevents me from blowing your head off? I can't use you as a hostage; there's no point. You have to *be* there. So I gain nothing by letting you live . . . if I am your enemy."

Holcroft tried to grasp the words, tried to find the meaning behind them, but he could not. He wanted only to strike out at the man holding him captive. "What do you want? Where have you got my mother? You said you had a letter."

"We'll take all things in order. What I want first is to leave here. With *you.* Together we can do what Wolfsschanze never believed possible."

"Wolfsschanze? . . . Do what?"

"Make the laws work for us. Make amends."

"Make—Whoever you are, you're out of your mind!"

"It's the option of Har Sha'alav. Control the millions. Fight them. *Everywhere.* I'm prepared to offer you the only proof I have." Yakov Ben-Gadíz took the pistol away from Noel's head. "Here's my gun." He offered it to Holcroft.

Noel studied the stranger's face in the odd shadows produced by the macabre green light. The eyes above him belonged to a man who was speaking the truth.

"Help me up," he said. "There's a back staircase. I know the way."

"First we have to straighten up anything that's out of place. Everything must be as it was."

Nothing is as it was. . . .

"Where are we going?"

"To an apartment in rue de la Paix. The letter's there. So is the girl."

"The girl?"

"Von Tiebolt's sister. He thinks she's dead. He ordered her killed."

"Helden?"

"Later."

45

They raced out of the alley and down the rue des Granges to the Israeli's car. They climbed in, Ben-Gadíz behind the wheel. Holcroft held his throat; he thought the veins were ruptured, so intense was the pain.

"You left me no choice," said Yakov, seeing Holcroft's agony.

"You left me one," replied Noel. "You gave me the gun. What's your name?"

"Yakov."

"What kind of name is that?"

"Hebrew. . . . Jacob, to you. Ben-Gadíz."

"Ben who?"

"Gadíz."

"Spanish?"

"Sephardic," said Yakov, speeding down the street, across the intersection, toward the lake. "My family immigrated to Krakow in the early nineteen hundreds." Yakov swung the car to the right in a small, unfamiliar square.

"I thought you were Kessler's brother," said Holcroft. "The doctor from Munich."

"I know nothing about a doctor from Munich."

"He's here somewhere. When I got to the d'Accord, the front desk gave me Von Tiebolt's key, then asked if I wanted Hans Kessler."

"What's that got to do with me?"

"The clerk knew that the Kesslers and Von Tiebolt had dinner together in Johann's suite. He thought Kessler's brother was still there."

"Wait a minute!" broke in Yakov. "The brother is a stocky man? Short? Strong?"

"I've no idea. Could be; Kessler said he was a soccer player."

"He's dead. Your mother told us. Von Tiebolt killed him. I think he was injured by your friend Ellis; they couldn't carry him any longer."

Noel stared at the Israeli. "Are you saying he was the one who did that to Willie? Killed him and knifed him like that?"

"It's only a guess."

"Oh, Christ! . . . Tell me about my mother. Where is she?"

"Later."

"Now."

"There's a telephone. I have to call the apartment. Helden's there." Ben-Gadíz swung the car to the curb.

"I said *now!*" Holcroft leveled the gun at Yakov.

"If you decide to kill me now," said Yakov, "I deserve to die, and so do you. I'd ask you to make the call yourself, but we haven't time for emotion."

"We've all the time we need," answered Noel. "The bank can be postponed."

"The bank? La Grande Banque de Genève?"

"Nine o'clock this morning."

"My God!" Ben-Gadíz gripped Holcroft's shoulder and lowered his voice; it was the voice of a man pleading for more than his life. "Give the option of Har Sha'alav a chance. It will never come again. Trust me. I've killed too many people not to have killed you twenty minutes ago. We must know every moment where we stand. Helden may have learned something."

Again Noel studied the face. "Make the call. Tell her I'm here and I want explanations from both of you."

They sped down the country road past the gates of the estate, driver and passenger oblivious to the sounds of an angry dog suddenly disturbed from its sleep by the racing car. The road curved to the left. Gradually, Yakov coasted to a stop off the shoulder, into the underbrush.

"Dogs' ears pick up engines that stop quickly. A diminuendo is much more difficult for them."

"Are you a musician?"

"I was a violinist."

"Any good?"

"Tel Aviv Symphony."

"What made you—"

"I found more suitable work," interrupted Ben-Gadíz. "Get out quickly. Remove your overcoat; take your weapon. Press the door closed; make no sound. The guest house will be back quite a way, but we'll find it."

There was a thick brick wall bordering the grounds, a string of coiled barbed wire on the top of it. Yakov scaled a tree to study the wire and the wall. "There are no alarms," he said. "Small animals would trigger them too frequently. But it's messy; the coil's nearly two feet wide. We'll have to jump."

The Israeli came down, crouched next to the wall, and cupped his hands. "Step up," he ordered Noel.

The ring of wire barbs on the top of the wall was impossible to avoid; there was no space on the ledge untouched by it.

Straining, Holcroft managed to get his left toe on the edge, then sprang up, vaulting the ominous coil and plummeting to the ground. His jacket had been caught, his ankles badly scraped, but he had made it. He stood up, only vaguely aware that he was breathing heavily, the pain in his throat and shins merely irritations. If the stranger had given Helden the right information on the phone, he was within a few hundred yards of Althene.

On top of the wall, the silhouette of the Israeli loomed like a large bird in the night sky; he vaulted over the coiled wire and spun down to the ground. He rolled once, as a tumbler might roll to break a fall, and sprang up next to Noel, raising his wrist in front of him to look at his watch.

"It's nearly six. It'll be light soon. Hurry."

They sliced through the forest, sidestepping branches, leaping over the tangled foliage, until they found the dirt road that led toward the guest house. In the distance they could see a dim glow of lights that shone from small cathedral windows.

"Stop!" Ben-Gadíz said.

"What?" Yakov's hand gripped Noel's shoulder. The Israeli fell on him, dragging Holcroft to the ground. "What are you doing?"

"Be still! There's activity in the house. People."

Noel peered through the grass at the house no more than a hundred yards away. He could see no movement, no figures in the windows. "I don't see anyone."

"Look at the lights. They're not steady. People are moving in front of lamps."

Holcroft saw instantly what Ben-Gadíz had seen. There *were* subtle changes of shading. The normal eye—especially the normal eye of an anxious runner—would not notice them, but they were there. "You're right," he whispered.

"Come," said Yakov. "We'll cut through the woods and approach from the side."

They went back into the forest and emerged at the edge of a small croquet course, grass and wickets cold and rigid in the winter night. Beyond the flat ground were the windows of the house.

"I'll run across and signal you to follow," Yakov whispered. "Remember, no noise."

The Israeli dashed across the lawn and crouched at the side of a window. Slowly he stood up and peered inside. Noel got to his knees, prepared to race out from the foliage.

The signal did not come. Ben-Gadíz stood motionless at the side of the window, but made no move to raise his hand. What was wrong? Why didn't the signal come?

Holcroft could wait no longer. He sprang up and ran over the stretch of grass. The Israeli turned, his eyes glaring. "Get away!" he whispered.

"What are you talking about? She's in there!"

Ben-Gadíz grabbed Holcroft by the shoulders, pushing him backward. "I said go *back!* We must get out of here. . . ."

"The hell we will!" Noel swung both arms up violently, breaking the Israeli's grip. He leaped to the window and looked inside.

The universe went up in fire. His mind burst open. He tried to scream, but no scream would come, only pure, raw horror, beyond sound, beyond sanity.

Inside the dimly lit room he saw the body of his mother arched diagonally in death across the back of a chair. The graceful, wondrous head was streaked with blood, scores of red rivers over wrinkled flesh.

Noel raised his hands, his arms, his whole being in the process of exploding. He could feel the air. His first plunged toward the panes of glass.

The impact never came. Instead, an arm was around his neck, a hand clasped over his mouth; both were giant tentacles pulling his head back viciously, lifting him off his feet, his spine arching, his legs crumbling beneath him as he was forced to the ground. His face was being pushed into dirt until there was no air. And then a sharp agonizing pain shot through his throat, and the fire returned.

He knew he was moving, but he did not know how or why. Branches kept slapping his face, hands hammered at his back, propelling him forward into the darkness. He could not know how long he was in the suspended state of chaos, but finally there was a stone wall. Harsh commands barked into his ear.

"Get up! Over the wire!"

Cognizance began to return. He felt the sharp metal points stabbing him, scraping his skin, ripping his clothes. Then he was being dragged across a hard surface and slammed against the door of an automobile.

The next thing he knew he was in the seat of a car, staring through the glass of a windshield. Dawn was coming up.

He sat in the chair, drained, numb, and read the letter from Althene.

Dearest NOEL—

It is unlikely that we shall see each other, but I beg you, do not mourn me. Later, perhaps, but not now. There is no time.

I do what I have to do for the simple reason that it must be done and I am the most logical person to do it. Even if there were another, I'm not at all sure I would allow him to do what has been reserved for me.

I'll not dwell on the lie I have lived for over thirty years. My new friend, Mr. Ben-Gadíz, will explain it fully to you. Suffice it to say I was never aware of the lie, nor—God in heaven—the terrible role you would be called upon to play.

I come from another era, one in which debts were called by their rightful name, and honor was not held to be an anachronism. I willingly pay my debt in hopes that a vestige of honor may be restored.

If we do not meet again, know that you have brought great joy to my life. If ever man needed proof that we are better than our sources, you are that proof.

I add a word about your friend Helden. I think she is the lovely daughter I might have had. It's in her eyes, in her strength. I've known her but a few hours, during which time she saved my life, prepared to sacrifice her own in doing so. It is true that we often perceive a lifetime in a moment of clarity. The moment was there for me, and she has my deep affection.

God speed you, my Noel.

My love,
ALTHENE

Holcroft looked up at Yakov, who was standing by the apartment window looking out at the gray light of the early winter morning.

"What was it she wouldn't let anyone else do?" he asked.

"Meet with my brother," answered Helden from across the room.

Noel clenched his fist and closed his eyes. "Ben-Gadíz said he ordered you killed."

"Yes. He's had many people killed."

Holcroft turned to the Israeli. "My mother wrote that you would explain the lie."

"I defer to Helden. I know a great deal of the story, but she knows it all."

"This is what you went to London for?" asked Noel.

"It's why I left Paris," she replied. "But it wasn't to London; it was to a small village on Lake Neuchâtel."

She told him the story of Werner Gerhardt, of Wolfsschanze, of the coin that had two sides. She tried to remember every detail given her by the last of the Nachrichtendienst.

When she had finished, Holcroft got out of the chair. "So all along I've been the figurehead for the lie. For the other side of Wolfsschanze."

"You are the code numbers that open the *Sonnenkinder* vaults," said Ben-Gadíz. "You were the one who made all the laws work for them. Such massive funds cannot spring from the earth without a structure. The chain of legalities must be met, or they are challenged. Wolfsschanze could not afford that. It was a brilliant deception."

Noel stared at the wall by the bedroom door. He stood facing it, facing the dimly lit wallpaper, the obscure figures in the pattern of a series of concentric circles engulfing themselves. The muted light—or his own unbalanced sight—made them spin with dizzying speed, black dots disappearing, only to become large circles again. *Circles. Circles of deception.* There were no straight lines of truth in those circles, only deceit. Only lies!

He heard the scream come out of his throat and felt the impact of his hands upon the wall, pounding furiously, wanting only to destroy the terrible circles.

Other hands touched him. Gentle hands.

A man in agony had cried out to him. And that man was false!

Where was he? What had he done?

He felt tears in his eyes and knew they were there because the circles became blurs, meaningless designs. And Helden was holding him, pulling his face to hers, her gentle fingers brushing away the tears.

"My darling. My only darling. . . ."

"*I . . . will . . . kill!*" Again, he heard the sound of his own scream, the horrible conviction of his own words.

"You *will,*" a voice answered, echoing in the chambers of his mind. It was loud and resonant, and it belonged to Yakov Ben-Gadíz, who had pushed Helden aside and had spun him around, pinning his shoulders to the wall. "You *will!*"

Noel tried to focus his burning eyes, tried to control his trembling. "You tried to stop me from seeing her!"

"I knew I couldn't," said Yakov quietly. "I knew it when you lunged. I've been trained as few others on this earth, but you have something extraordinary inside you. I'm not sure I care to speculate, but I'm grateful you're not my enemy."

"I don't understand you."

"I give you the option of Har Sha'alav. It will demand the most extraordinary discipline of which you are capable. I'll be frank: I couldn't do it, but perhaps you can."

"What is it?"

"Go through with the meeting at the bank. With the killers of your mother, with the man who ordered Helden's death, Richard Holcroft's death. Face him; face them. Sign the papers."

"You're out of your mind! Out of your fucking *mind!*"

"I'm not! We've studied the laws. You'll be required to sign a release. In it, in the event of your death, you assign all rights and privileges to the coinheritors. When you do, you'll sign a death warrant. Sign it! It won't be your death warrant, but theirs!"

Noel looked into Yakov's dark, imploring eyes. There it was again: the straight line of truth. Neither spoke for a while, and slowly Holcroft began to find the control he had lost. Ben-Gadíz released his shoulders; balance returned.

"They'll be looking for me," said Noel. "They think I went to Von Tiebolt's rooms."

"You did; the door wasn't rethreaded. You saw that no one was there, so you left."

"Where did I go? They'll want to know."

"Are you familiar with the city?"

"Not really."

"Then you took taxis; you traveled along the waterfront, stopping at a dozen piers and marinas, looking for anyone who might have seen your mother. It's plausible; they think you were in panic."

"It's almost seven-thirty," Noel said. "An hour and a half left. I'll go back to the hotel. We'll meet after the conference at the bank."

"Where?" asked Yakov.

"Take a room at the Excelsior in the name of a married couple. Get there after nine-thirty, but long before noon. I'm in four-eleven."

He stood outside the hotel door; it was three minutes past eight. He could hear angry voices from inside. Von Tiebolt dominated whatever conversation was taking place, his tone incisive, on the edge of violence.

Violence. Holcroft took a deep breath and forced himself to reject the instincts that seared through him. He would face the man who killed his mother and his father and look that man in the eyes and not betray his rage.

He knocked on the door, grateful that his hand did not tremble.

The door opened, and he stared into the eyes of the blond-haired killer of loved ones.

"Noel! Where have you been? We've been looking everywhere!"

"So have I," said Holcroft, the weariness not difficult to feign, the control of outrage nearly impossible. "I've spent the night looking for her. I couldn't find her. I don't think she ever got here."

"We'll keep trying," said Von Tiebolt. "Have some coffee. We'll be off to the bank soon, and it will all be over."

"Yes, it will, won't it?" said Noel.

The three of them sat on one side of the long conference table, Holcroft in the center, Kessler on his left, Von Tiebolt on his right. Facing them were the two directors of La Grande Banque de Genève.

In front of each man was a neat pile of legal papers, all identical and arranged in sequence. Eyes followed the typed words, pages were turned, and more than an hour passed before the precious document had been read aloud in its entirety.

There were two remaining articles of record, their cover pages bordered in dark blue. The director on the left spoke.

"As I'm sure you're aware, with an account of this magnitude and the objectives contained therein, La Grande Banque de Genève cannot legally assume responsibility for disbursements once the funds are released and are no longer under our control. The document is specific as to the burden of that responsibility. It is equally divided among the three participants. Therefore, the law requires that each of you assign all rights and privileges to your coinheritors-in-trust in the event you predecease them. These rights and privileges, however, do not affect the individual bequests; they are to be distributed to your estates in the event of your death." The director put on his spectacles. "Please read the pages in front of you to see that they conform to what I've represented, and sign above your names in the presence of one another. Exchange papers so that all signatures appear on each."

The reading was rapid; the signatures followed, and the pages were exchanged. As Noel handed his signed paper to Kessler, he spoke casually.

"You know, I forgot to ask you, Erich. Where's your brother? I thought he was going to be here in Geneva."

"With all the excitement, I forgot to tell you," Kessler said, smiling. "Hans was delayed in München. I'm sure we'll see him in Zürich."

"Zürich?"

The scholar looked past Holcroft toward Von Tiebolt. "Well, yes. Zürich. I thought we planned to be there Monday morning."

Noel turned to the blond man. "You didn't mention it."

"We've had no time to talk. Is Monday inconvenient for you?"

"Not at all. Maybe I'll have heard from her by then."

"What?"

"My mother. Or even Helden. She should be calling."

"Yes, of course. I'm sure they'll both reach you."

The last article of record was the formal release of the account. A computer had been preset. Upon the signatures of everyone in the room, the codes would be punched, the funds made liquid and transferred to a bank in Zürich.

All signed. The director on the right picked up a telephone. "Enter the following numbers on computer bank eleven. Are you ready? . . . Six, one, four, four, two. Break four. Eight, one, zero, zero. Break zero. . . . Repeat, please." The director listened, then nodded. "Correct. Thank you."

"Is it complete, then?" asked his colleague.

"It is," answered the director. "Gentlemen, as of this moment, the sum of seven hundred and eighty million American dollars is in your collective names at La Banque du Livre, Zürich. May you have the wisdom of prophets, and may your decisions be guided by God."

Outside, on the street, Von Tiebolt turned to Holcroft. "What are your plans, Noel? We must still be careful, you know. The Nachrichtendienst won't take this easily."

"I know. . . . Plans? I'm going to keep trying to find my mother. She's somewhere; she's got to be."

"I've arranged through my friend, the first deputy, for the three of us to receive police protection. Your detail will pick you up at the Excelsior, ours at the d'Accord. Unless, of course, you'd prefer to move in with us."

"That's too much work," said Holcroft. "I'm half settled now. I'll stay at the Excelsior."

"Shall we go to Zürich in the morning?" asked Kessler, deferring the decision to Von Tiebolt.

"It might be a good idea for us to travel separately," said Holcroft. "If the police have no objections, I'd just as soon go by car."

"Very good thinking, my friend," said Von Tiebolt. "The police won't object, and traveling separately makes sense. You take the train, Erich; I'll fly; and Noel will drive. I'll make us reservations at the Columbine."

Holcroft nodded. "If I don't hear from my mother or Helden by tomorrow, I'll leave word for them to reach me there," he said. "I'll grab a cab." He walked rapidly to the corner. Another minute and the rage within him would have exploded. He would have killed Von Tiebolt with his bare hands.

Johann spoke quietly. "He knows. How much, I'm not certain. But he knows."

"How can you be sure?" Kessler asked.

"At first I merely sensed it; then I knew. He asked about Hans and accepted your answer that he was still in München. He knows that's not true. A clerk at the d'Accord offered to ring Hans's room for him last night."

"Oh, my God. . . ."

"Don't be upset. Our American colleague will die on the road to Zürich."

46

The attempt on Noel's life—if it was going to be made—would take place on the roads north of Fribourg, south of Köniz. That was the judgment of Yakov Ben-Gadíz. The distance was something more than twenty kilometers, with stretches in the hills that rarely had traffic this time of year. It was winter, and although the climate was not Alpine, light snows were frequent, the roads not the best; drivers were discouraged from them. But Holcroft had mapped out a route that avoided the highways, concentrating on rural towns with architecture he claimed he wanted to see.

That was to say, Yakov mapped it out, and Noel had delivered it to police who were under orders from the first deputy to act as his escort north. The fact that no one discouraged Holcroft from this chosen route lent substance to the Israeli's judgment.

Yakov further speculated on the method of killing. Neither Von Tiebolt nor Kessler would be near the area. Each would be very much in evidence somewhere else. And if there was to be an execution, it would be carried out by as few men as possible—paid killers in no way associated with Wolfsschanze. No chances would be taken so soon after the meeting at La Grande Banque de Genève. The killer, or killers, would in turn be murdered by *Sonnenkinder;* all traces to Wolfsschanze would be obliterated.

That was the stragegy as Ben-Gadíz saw it, and a counterstrategy had to be mounted. One that got Noel to Zürich; that was all that mattered. Once in Zürich, it would be *their* strategy. There were a dozen ways to kill in a large city, and Yakov was an expert in all of them.

The trip began, the counterstrategy put into play. Holcroft drove a heavy car rented from Bonfils, Geneva, the most expensive leasing firm in Switzerland, specializing in the unusual automobile for the unusual client. It was a Rolls-Royce, outfitted with armor plate, bulletproof glass, and tires that could withstand successive punctures.

Helden was a mile in front of Noel, driving a nondescript but maneuverable Renault; Ben-Gadíz was behind, never more than half a mile, and his car was a

Maserati, common among the wealthy of Geneva and capable of very high speeds. Between Yakov and Holcroft was the two-man police car assigned to the American as protection. The police knew nothing.

"They'll be immobilized en route," the Israeli had said while the three of them studied maps in Noel's hotel room. "They won't be sacrificed; there'd be too many questions. They're legitimate police. I got the numbers off their helmets and called Litvak. We checked. They're first-year men from the central headquarters' barracks. As such, not very experienced."

"Will they be the same men tomorrow?"

"Yes. Their orders read that they're to stay with you until the Zürich police take over. Which I think means that they'll find themselves with a malfunctioning vehicle, call their superiors, and be told to return to Geneva. The order for your protection will evaporate."

"Then they're just window dressing."

"Exactly. Actually, they'll serve a purpose. As long as you can see them, you're safe. No one will try anything."

They were in sight now, thought Noel, glancing at the rearview mirror, applying the brakes of the Rolls-Royce for the long curving descent at the side of the hill. Far below, he could see Helden's car come out of a turn. In two more minutes she would slow down and wait until they were in plain sight of each other before resuming speed; that, too, was part of the plan. She had done so three minutes ago. Every five minutes they were to be in eye contact. He wished he could *speak* with her. Just talk . . . simple talk, quiet talk . . . having nothing to do with death or the contemplation of death, or the strategies demanded to avoid it.

But that talk could only come after Zürich. There would be death in Zürich, but not like any death Holcroft had ever thought about. Because he would be the killer; no one else. *No one.* He demanded the right. He would look into the eyes of Johann von Tiebolt and tell him he was about to die.

He was going too fast; his anger had caused him to press too hard on the accelerator. He slowed down; it was no time to do Von Tiebolt's work for him. It had started to snow, and the downhill road was slippery.

Yakov cursed the light snowfall, not because it made the driving difficult but because it reduced visibility. They relied on sight; radio communication was out of the question, the signals too easily intercepted.

The Israeli's hand touched several items on the seat beside him; similar items were in Holcroft's Rolls. They were part of the counter-strategy—the most effective part.

Explosives. Eight in all. Four charges, wrapped in plastic, timed to detonate precisely three seconds after impact; and four antitank grenades. In addition there were two weapons: a U.S. Army Colt automatic and a carbine rifle, each loaded, safeties off, prepared for firing. All had been purchased through Litvak's contacts in Geneva. Peaceful Geneva, where such arsenals were available in quantities smaller than terrorists believed but greater than the Swiss authorities thought conceivable.

Ben-Gadíz peered through the windshield. If it happened, it would happen shortly. The police car several hundred yards in front would be immobilized, the result, probably, of cleats coated with acid, timed to eat through tires; or a defective radiator filled with a coagulant that would clog the hoses. . . . There were so many ways. But the police car would suddenly not be there, and Holcroft would be isolated.

Yakov hoped Noel remembered precisely what he was to do if a strange car approached. He was to start zigzagging over the road while Yakov accelerated, braking his Maserati within feet of the unknown automobile, hurling the plastic charges at it, waiting the precious seconds for the explosions to take place as Holcroft got out of firing range. If there were problems—defective charges, no explosives—the grenades were a backup.

It would be enough. Von Tiebolt would not risk more than one execution car. The possibility of stray drivers, unwitting observers, would be considerable; the killers would be few and professional. The leader of the *Sonnenkinder* was no idiot; if Holcroft's death did not take place on the road to Köniz, it would take place in Zürich.

That was the *Sonnenkinder*'s mistake, thought the Israeli, filled with a sense of satisfaction. Von Tiebolt did not know about Yakov Ben-Gadíz. Also no idiot, also professional. The American *would* get to Zürich, and once in Zürich, Johann von Tiebolt was a dead man, as Erich Kessler was a dead man, killed by a man filled with rage.

Yakov cursed again. The snow was heavier and the flakes were larger. The latter meant the snowfall would not last long, but for the time being it was an interruption he did not like.

He could not see the police car! Where was it? The road was filled with sharp curves and offshoots. The police car was nowhere to be seen. He had lost it! How in God's name *could* he have?

And then it was there, and he breathed again, pressing his foot on the accelerator to get closer. He could not allow his mind to wander so; he was not in the Symphony Hall in Tel Aviv. The police car was the key; he could not let it out of his sight for a moment.

He was going faster than he thought; the speedometer read seventy-three kilometers, much too fast for this road. Why?

Then he knew why. He was closing the gap between himself and the Geneva police car, but the police car was accelerating. It was going faster than it had before; it was racing into the curves, speeding through the snowfall . . . closing in on Holcroft!

Was the driver *insane?*

Ben-Gadíz stared through the windshield, trying to understand. Something bothered him, and he was not sure what it was. What were they *doing?*

Then he saw it; it had not been there before.

A dent in the trunk of the police car. A dent! There'd been no dent in the trunk of the car he had followed for the past three hours!

It was a different police car!

From one of the offshoots on the maze of curves a radio command had been given ordering the original car off the road. Another had taken its place. Which meant the men in that car now were aware of the Maserati, and, infinitely more dangerous, Holcroft was not aware of *them*.

The police car swung into a long curve; Yakov could hear continuous blasts of its horn through the snow and the wind. It was *signaling* Holcroft. It was pulling alongside.

"No! Don't do it!" screamed Yakov at the glass, holding his thumbs on the horn, gripping the wheel as his tires skidded over the surface of the curve. He hurled the Maserati toward the police car, fifty yards away. "Holcroft! Don't!"

Suddenly, his windshield shattered. Tiny circles of death appeared everywhere; he could feel glass slice his cheeks, his fingers. He was hit. A submachine gun had fired at him from the smashed rear window of the police car.

There was a billow of smoke from the hood; the radiator exploded. An instant later the tires were pierced, strips of rubber blown off. The Maserati lurched to the right, crashing into an embankment.

Ben-Gadíz roared to the heavens, hammering his shoulder against a door that would not open. Behind him, the gasoline fires started.

Holcroft saw the police car in the rearview mirror. It was suddenly coming closer, its headlights flickering on and off. For some reason the police were signaling him.

There was no place to stop on the curve; there had to be a straightaway several hundred yards down the road. He slowed the Rolls as the police car came alongside, the figure of the young officer blurred by the snow.

He heard the blasts of the horn and saw the continuous rapid flashing of the lights. He rolled down the window.

"I'll pull over as soon as—"

He saw the face. And the expression on that face. It was not one of the young policemen from Geneva! It was a face he had never seen before. Then the barrel of a rifle was there.

Desperately, he tried to roll up the window. It was too late. He heard the gunfire, saw the blinding flashes of light, could feel a hundred razors slashing his skin. He saw his own blood splattered against glass and sensed his own screams echoing through a car gone wild.

Metal crunched against metal, groaning under the force of a thousand impacts. The dashboard was upside down; the pedals were where the roof should be; and he was against that roof; and then he was not; now plummeted over the back of the seat, now hurled against glass and away from glass, now impaled on the steering wheel, then lifted in space and thrown into more space.

There was peace in that space. The pain of the razors went away, and he walked through the mists of his mind into a void.

Yakov smashed the glass of the remaining windshield with his pistol. The carbine had been jarred to the floor; the plastic explosives remained strapped in their box; the grenades were nowhere to be seen.

All the weapons were useless save one, because it was available, and in his hand, and he would use it until the ammunition was gone—and until his life was gone.

There were three men in the false police car, the third, the marksman, once again crouched in back. Ben-Gadíz could see his head in the rear window! Now! He took careful aim through the blankets of steam and squeezed the trigger. The face whipped diagonally up and then fell back into the jagged glass of the window.

Yakov crashed his shoulder once more against the door; it loosened. He had to get out fast: The fires behind guaranteed the explosion of the fuel tank. Up ahead, the driver of the police car was slamming it into the Rolls; the second man was on the road, reaching into Holcroft's window, yanking at the steering wheel. They were trying to send the car over the embankment.

Ben-Gadíz hammered his whole upper body against the door; it swung open. The Israeli lunged out on the snow-covered surface of the road, his wounds producing a hundred red streaks on the white powder. He raised his pistol and fired one shot after another, his eyes blurred, his aim imperfect.

And then two terrible things happened at the same moment.

The Rolls went over the embankment, and a roar of gunfire filled the snow-laden air. A line of bullets kicked up the road and cut across Yakov's legs. He was beyond pain.

There was no feeling left, but he twisted and turned and rolled wherever he could. His hands touched the slashed rubber of the tires, then steel and more steel, and cold patches of glass and snow.

The explosion came; the fuel tank of the Maserati burst into flames. And Ben-Gadíz heard the words, shouted in the distance. "They're dead! Turn around! Get out of here!"

The attackers fled.

Helden had slowed the car well over a minute ago. Noel should have been in sight by now. Where was he? She stopped at the side of the road and waited. Another two minutes went by; she could not wait any longer.

She swung the car into a U-turn and started back up the hill. Pushing the accelerator to the floor, she passed the half-mile mark; still there was no sign of him. Her hands began to tremble.

Something had happened. She knew it; she could feel it!

She saw the Maserati! It was demolished! On fire!

Oh, *God!* Where was Noel's car? Where was Noel? Yakov?

She slammed on the brakes and ran out, screaming. She fell on the slippery road, unaware that her own wounded leg had caused the fall, and pushed herself up, and screamed again, and ran again.

"Noel! *Noel!*"

Tears streaked down her face in the cold air; her screams tore the raw nerves of her throat. She could not cope with her own hysteria.

She heard the command out of nowhere.

"*Helden!* Stop it. Here. . . ."

A voice. Yakov's voice! From where? Where was it *coming* from? She heard it again.

"Helden! Down here!"

The embankment. She raced to the embankment and her world collapsed. Below was the Rolls-Royce—overturned and smoking, crushed metal everywhere. In horror she saw the figure of Yakov Ben-Gadíz on the ground next to the Rolls. And then she saw the streaks of red on the snow that formed a path across the road and down the embankment to where Yakov lay.

Helden lunged over the embankment, rolling in the snow and over the rocks, screaming at the death she knew awaited her. She fell by Ben-Gadíz and stared through the open window at her love. He was sprawled out, immobile, his face drenched with blood.

"No! . . . *No!*"

Yakov grabbed her arm and pulled her to him. He could barely speak, but his commands were clear. "Get back to your car. There's a small village south of Treyvaux, no more than five kilometers from here. Call Litvak. Près-du-Lac's not so far away . . . twenty, twenty-two kilometers. He can hire pilots, fast cars. Reach him; tell him."

Helden could not take her eyes off Noel. "He's dead. . . . He's *dead!*"

"He may not be. Hurry!"

"I can't. I can't *leave* him!"

Ben-Gadíz raised his pistol. "Unless you do, I'll kill him now."

Litvak walked into the room where Ben-Gadíz lay on the bed, his lower body encased in bandages. Yakov was staring out the window at the snow-covered fields and the mountains beyond; he continued to stare, taking no notice of the doctor's entrance.

"Do you want the truth?"

The Israeli turned his head slowly. "There's no point in avoiding it, is there? At any rate, I can see it in your face."

"I could bring you worse news. You'll not walk very well ever again; the damage is too extensive. But, in time, you'll get around. At first with the help of crutches; later, perhaps, with a cane."

"Not exactly the physical prognosis needed for my work, is it?"

"No, but your mind's intact and your hands will heal. It won't affect your music."

Yakov smiled sadly. "I was never that good. My mind wandered too frequently. I was not as fine a professional as I was in my other life."

"That mind can be put to other uses."

The Israeli frowned, looking again out the window. "We'll see when we know what's left out there."

"It's changing out there, Yakov. It's happening quickly," said the doctor.

"What about Holcroft?"

"I don't know what to say. He should have died. But he's still alive. Not that it makes much difference in terms of his life. He can't go back to who he was. He's wanted in half a dozen countries for murder. The death penalty's been restored everywhere, for all manner of crimes, the laws of defense a travesty. Everywhere. He'd be shot on sight."

"They've won," said Yakov, his eyes filling with tears. "The *Sonnenkinder* have won."

"We'll see," said Litvak, "when we know what's left out there."

EPILOGUE

Images. Shapeless, unfocused, without meaning or definition. Outlines etched in vapor. There was only awareness. Not thought, nor any memory of experience, just awareness. Then the shapeless images began to take form; the mists cleared, turning awareness into recognition. Thought would come later; it was enough to be able to see and to remember.

Noel saw her face above him, framed by the cascading blond hair that touched his face. There were tears in her eyes; they ran down her cheeks. He tried to wipe away the tears, but he could not reach the lovely, tired face above. His hand fell, and she took it in hers.

"My darling. . . ."

He heard her. He was able to hear. Sight and sound had meaning. He closed his eyes, knowing that somehow thought would come soon, too.

Litvak stood in the doorway, watching Helden sponge Noel's chest and neck. There was a newspaper under his arm. He examined Holcroft's face, the face that had taken such punishment from the fusillade of bullets. There were scars on his left cheek and across his forehead and all over his neck. But the healing process had begun. From somewhere inside the house came the sounds of a violin being played by a very professional musician.

"I'd like to recommend a raise for your nurse," said Noel weakly.

"For which duties?" Litvak laughed.

"Physician, heal thyself." Helden joined the laughter.

"I wish I could. I wish I could heal a lot of things," replied the doctor, dropping the newspaper at Holcroft's side. It was the Paris edition of the *Herald Tribune*. "I picked this up for you in Neuchâtel. I'm not sure you want to read it."

"What's the lesson for today?"

" 'The Consequences of Dissent' would be a fair title, I imagine. The editorial staff of the New York *Times* have been enjoined by your Supreme Court from any further coverage of the Pentagon. The issue, of course, is national security. Said Supreme Court also upheld the legality of the multiple executions in your state of Michigan. The Court's opinion expresses the profound thought that when minorities threaten the well-being of the general public, swift and visible examples are to be made in the cause of deterrence."

"Today John Smith is a minority," said Noel weakly, his head resting back on the pillow. "Boom, he's dead."

This is the world news, reported by BBC of London. Since the wave of assassinations that took the lives of political figures across the globe, security measures of unparalleled severity have been mounted in the nations' capitals. It is to the military and police authorities everywhere that the greatest responsibility falls, and so that international cooperation at the highest levels may be achieved, an agency has been formed in Zürich, Switzerland. This agency, to be called Anvil, will facilitate the swift, accurate, and confidential exchange of information between member military and police forces. . . .

Yakov Ben-Gadíz was halfway through the scherzo of Mendelssohn's Violin Concerto when he found his mind wandering again. Noel Holcroft was stretched out on the couch across the room, Helden sitting on the floor beside him.

The plastic surgeon who had flown from Los Angeles to operate on his unidentified patient had done a remarkable job. The face was still Holcroft's, yet not entirely. The scars that had resulted from the facial wounds were gone, in their place slight indentations that lent a chiseled look to the features. The lines on his forehead were deeper, the wrinkles about his eyes more pronounced. There was no innocence in the slightly altered, restored face; instead there was a touch of cruelty. Perhaps more than a touch.

In addition to the changes, Noel had grown older, the aging process swift and painful. It had been four months since they had taken him from the embankment on the road north of Fribourg, but, looking at him, one might judge the time elapsed to be nearer ten years.

Still, he had his life, and his body had sprung back under the care of Helden and the rigor of the never-ending exercises ordered by Litvak, supervised by a once-formidable commando from Har Sha'alav.

Yakov took pleasure in these sessions. He demanded excellence, and Holcroft met the demands; full health was required in the physical instrument before the real training could begin.

It would begin tomorrow. High in the spring hills and mountains, beyond the scrutiny of prying eyes, but under the harshest scrutiny of Yakov Ben-Gadíz. The pupil would do what the master could do no longer; the pupil would be put through the rigors of hell until he excelled the master.

Tomorrow it would begin.

DEUTSCHE ZEITUNG

Berlin, July 4—The Bundestag today gave its formal consent to the establishment of rehabilitation centers patterned after those in America in the states of Arizona and Texas.

These centers will be, as their U.S. counterparts, primarily educational in nature and will be under the supervision of the military.

Those sentenced for rehabilitation terms will have been judged by the courts to be guilty of crimes against the German people. . . .

"Wire! Rope! Chain!"

"Use your fingers! They're weapons; never forget it. . . ."

"Scale that tree again, you were too slow. . . ."

"Climb the hill and get back down without my seeing you. . . ."

"I *saw* you. Your head was blown off!"

"Press the *nerve*, not the vein! There are five nerve points. Find them. With the blindfold on. *Feel* them. . . ."

"*Roll* out of a fall; don't crouch. . . ."

"Every action must have two alternate, split-second options. Train yourself to think in those terms. *Instinctively.* . . ."

"Accuracy is a question of zero-sighting, immobility, and breathing. Fire again, seven shots; they *must* be within a two-inch diameter. . . ."

"Escape, escape, *escape! Use* your surroundings; *melt* into them! Don't be afraid to stay still. A man standing motionless is often the last person seen. . . ."

The summer months passed, and Yakov Ben-Gadíz was pleased. The pupil was now better than the master. He was ready.

As was his colleague; she was ready, too. Together they would form the team.

The *Sonnenkinder* were marked. The list was taken out and studied.

THE HERALD TRIBUNE

Paris, Oct. 10—The international agency in Zürich known as Anvil today announced the formation of an independent Board of Chancellors selected by secret ballot from member nations. The first Anvil Congress will be held on the 25th of the month. . . .

The couple walked down the street in Zürich's Lindenhof district, on the left bank of the Limmat River. The man was fairly tall, but stooped, a pronounced limp impeding his progress through the crowds, the shabby suitcase in his hand a further hindrance. The woman held his arm, more as though guiding an irritable responsibility than with affection. Neither spoke: They were a couple grown to an indeterminable age together in mutual loathing.

They reached an office building and went inside, the man limping after the woman toward the bank of elevators. They stopped in front of the starter; the woman asked in decidedly middle-class German the office number of a small accounting firm.

She was given a number on the twelfth floor, the top floor, but as it was the lunch hour, the starter doubted anyone was there. It did not matter; the couple would wait.

They stepped out of the elevator on the twelfth floor; the hallway was deserted. The moment the elevator door closed, the couple ran to the staircase at the right end of the corridor. Gone was the limp; gone were the somber faces. They raced up the steps to the door of the roof and stopped on the landing. The man set down the suitcase, knelt, and opened it. Inside were the barrel and stock of a rifle, a telescopic sight clamped to the former, a strap to the latter.

He took the parts out and attached them. Then he removed his hat with the wig sewn into the crown and threw it into the suitcase. He stood up and helped the woman take off her coat, pulling the sleeves through, reversing the cloth. It was now a well-cut, expensive beige topcoat, purchased at one of the better shops in Paris.

The woman then helped the man reverse his overcoat. It was transformed into a fashionable gentleman's fall coat, trimmed in suede. The woman took off her kerchief, removed several pins, and let her blond hair fall down over her shoulders. She opened her purse and took out a revolver.

"I'll be here," said Helden. "Good hunting."

"Thanks," said Noel, opening the door to the roof.

He crouched against the wall by an out-of-use chimney, inserted his arm through the sling, and pulled the strap taut. He reached into his pocket and took out three shells; he pressed them into the chamber and slapped the bolt into firing position. *Every action must have two alternate, split-second options.*

He would not need them. He would not miss.

He turned and knelt by the wall. He edged the rifle over the top and put his eye to the telescopic sight.

Twelve stories below, across the street, crowds were cheering various men coming out of the huge glass doors of the Lindenhof Hôtel. They walked into the sunlight under banners hailing the first Anvil Congress.

There he was. In the gunsight, the cross hairs centered on the sculptured face beneath the shining blond hair.

Holcroft squeezed the trigger. Twelve stories below, the sculptured face erupted into a mass of blood and shattered flesh.

The Tinamou was killed at last.

By the Tinamou.

They were everywhere. It had only begun.

THE
MATARESE
CIRCLE

For Jonathan

With much love and deep respect

PART
ONE

We three Kings of Orient are,
Bearing gifts we traverse afar. . . .

The band of carolers huddled at the corner, stamping their feet and swinging their arms, their young voices penetrating the cold night air between the harsh sounds of automobile horns and police whistles and the metallic strains of Christmas music blaring from storefront speakers. The snowfall was dense, snarling traffic, causing the hordes of last-minute shoppers to shield their eyes. Nevertheless, they managed to sidestep each other, as well as the lurching automobiles, and the mounds of slush. Tires spun on the wet streets; buses inched in maddening starts and stops, and the bells of uniformed Santas kept up their incessant if futile clanging.

Field and fountain,
Moor and mow-an-ten. . . .

A dark Cadillac sedan turned the corner and crept past the carolers. The lead singer, dressed in a costume that was somebody's idea of Dickens' Bob Cratchit, approached the right rear window, his gloved hand outstretched, his face contorted in song next to the glass.

Following ya-hon-der star. . . .

The angry driver blew his horn and waved the begging caroler away, but the middle-aged passenger in the backseat reached into his overcoat pocket and pulled out several bills. He pressed a button; the rear window glided down and the gray-haired man thrust the money into the outstretched hand.

"God bless you, sir," shouted the caroler. "The Boys Club of East Fiftieth Street thanks you. Merry Christmas, sir!"

The words would have been more effective had there not been a stench of whisky emanating from the mouth that yelled them.

"Merry Christmas," said the passenger, pressing the window button to shut off further communication.

There was a momentary break in the traffic. The Cadillac shot forward only to be forced to an abrupt, sliding stop thirty feet down the street. The driver gripped the steering wheel; it was a gesture that took the place of cursing out loud.

"Take it easy, Major," said the gray-haired passenger, his tone of voice at once sympathetic and commanding. "Getting upset won't solve anything; it won't get us where we're going any faster."

"You're right, General," answered the driver with a respect he did not feel.

Normally, the respect was there, but not tonight, not on this particular trip. The general's self-indulgence aside, he had one hell of a nerve requesting his aide to be available for duty on Christmas Eve. For driving a rented, *civilian* car to New York so the general could play games. The major could think of a dozen acceptable reasons for being on duty tonight, but this was not one of them.

A whorehouse. Stripped of its verbal frills, that's what it was. The Chairman of the Joint Chiefs of Staff was going to a *whorehouse* on Christmas Eve! And because games were played, the general's most confidential aide had to be there to pick up the mess when the games were over. Pick it up, put it together, nurse it through the next morning at some obscure motel, and make goddamn sure no one found out what the games were or who the mess was. And by noon tomorrow, the Chairman would resume his ramrod bearing, issue his orders, and the evening and the mess would be forgotten.

The major had made these trips many times during the past three years—since the day after the general had assumed his awesome position—but the trips always followed periods of intense activity at the Pentagon, or moments of national crisis, when the general had shown his professional mettle. But never on such a night as this. Never on Christmas Eve, for Christ's sake! If the general were anyone but Anthony Blackburn, the major might have objected on the grounds that even a subordinate officer's family had certain holiday priorities.

But the major would never offer the slightest objection about anything where the general was concerned. "Mad Anthony" Blackburn had carried a broken young lieutenant out of a North Vietnamese prison camp, away from torture and starvation, and brought him through the jungles back to American lines. That was years ago; the lieutenant was a major now, the senior aide to the Chairman of the Joint Chiefs of Staff.

Military men often spoke bromidically of certain officers they'd follow to hell and back. Well, the major had been to hell with Mad Anthony Blackburn and he'd return to hell in a shot with a snap of the general's fingers.

They reached Park Avenue and turned north. The traffic was less snarled than on the crosstown route, as befitted the better section of the city. Fifteen more blocks to go; the brownstone was on Seventy-first Street between Park and Madison.

The senior aide to the Chairman of the Joint Chiefs of Staff would park the Cadillac in a prearranged space in front of the building and watch the general get out of the car and walk up the steps to the bolted entrance door. He would not say anything, but a feeling of sadness would sweep over the major as he waited.

Until a slender woman—dressed in a red silk gown with a diamond choker at her throat—reopened the door in three and a half or four hours and flicked the front lights. It would be the major's signal to come up and collect his passenger.

"Hello, Tony!" The woman swept across the dimly lit hallway and kissed the general's cheek. "How are you, darling?" she said, fingering her choker as she leaned toward him.

"Tense," replied Blackburn, slipping his arms out of his civilian overcoat, held by a uniformed maid. He looked at the girl; she was new and lovely.

The woman saw his glance. "She's not ready for you, darling," she commented, taking his arm. "Perhaps in a month or two. Come along now, we'll see what we can do about that tension. We've got everything you need. The best hashish from Ankara, absinthe from the finest still in Marseilles, and precisely what the doctor ordered from our own special catalogue. Incidentally, how's your wife?"

"Tense," said the general quietly. "She sends you her best."

"Do give her my love, darling."

They walked through an archway into a large room with soft, multi-colored lights that came from unseen sources; circles of blue and magenta and amber revolving slowly across the ceiling and the walls. The woman spoke again.

"There's a girl I want to have join you and your regular. Her background is simply tailor-made, darling. I couldn't believe it when I interviewed her; it's incredible. I just got her from Athens. You'll adore her."

Anthony Blackburn lay naked on the king-sized bed, tiny spotlights shooting down from the mirrored ceiling of blue glass. Aromatic layers of hashish smoke were suspended in the still air of the dark room; three glasses of clear absinthe stood on the bedside table. The general's body was covered with streaks and circles of waterpaint, fingermarks everywhere, phallic arrows pointing to his groin, his testicles and erect penis coated in red, his breasts black, matching the matted hair of his chest, the nipples blue and joined by a straight fingerline of flesh-white. He moaned and whipped his head back and forth in sexual oblivion as his companions did their work.

The two naked women alternately massaged and spread thick globules of paint on his writhing body. As one revolved her breasts about his moaning, moving face, the other cupped his genitalia, groaning sensually with each stroke, uttering false, muted screams of climax as the general approached orgasm—halted by the professional who knew her business.

The auburn-haired girl by his face kept whispering breathless, incomprehensible phrases in Greek. She removed herself briefly to reach for a glass on the table; she held Blackburn's head and poured the thick liquid onto his lips. She smiled at her companion, who winked back, Blackburn's red-coated organ in her hand.

Then the Greek girl slid off the bed, gesturing toward the bathroom door. Her associate nodded, extending her left hand up toward the general's head, inserting her fingers into his lips to cover for her companion's brief indisposition. The auburn-haired woman walked across the black carpet and went into the bathroom. The room resounded with the groans of the general's writhing euphoria.

Thirty seconds later, the Greek girl emerged, but she was no longer naked. She was dressed now in a dark tweed coat with a hood that covered her hair. She stood momentarily in the shadows, then stepped to the nearest window and gently pulled back the heavy drapes.

The sound of shattering glass filled the room as a rush of wind billowed the curtains. The figure of a broad-shouldered, stocky man loomed in the window; he had kicked in the panes, and now leaped through the frame, his head encased in a ski mask, a gun in his hand.

The girl on the bed swung around and screamed in terror as the killer leveled his weapon and pulled the trigger. The explosion was muted by a silencer; the girl slumped over the obscenely painted body of Anthony Blackburn. The man approached the bed; the general raised his head, trying to focus through the mists of narcotics, his eyes floating, guttural sounds coming from his throat. The killer fired again. And again, and again, the bullets entering Blackburn's neck and chest and groin, the eruptions of blood mingling with the glistening colors of the paint.

The man nodded to the girl from Athens; she rushed to the door, opened it and said in Greek, "She'll be downstairs in the room with revolving lights. She's in a long red dress, with diamonds around her neck."

The man nodded again and they rushed out into the corridor.

The major's thoughts were interrupted by the unexpected sounds that seemed to come from somewhere inside the brownstone. He listened, his breath suspended.

They were shrieks of some kind . . . yelling . . . *screams*. People were screaming!

He looked up at the house; the heavy door flew open as two figures ran outside and down the steps, a man and a woman. Then he saw it and a massive pain shot through his stomach: the man was shoving a gun into his belt.

Oh, my God!

The major thrust his hand under the seat for his Army automatic, pulled it out, and leaped from the car. He raced up the steps and inside the hallway. Beyond, through the arch, the screams mounted; people were running, several up the staircase, others down.

He ran into the large room with the insanely revolving colored lights. On the floor he could see the figure of the slender woman with the diamonds around her neck. Her forehead was a mass of blood; she'd been shot.

Oh, Christ!

"*Where is he?*" he shouted.

"Upstairs!" came the scream from a girl huddled in the corner.

The major turned in panic and raced back to the ornate staircase, taking the steps three at a time, passing a telephone on a small table on the landing; its image stuck in his mind. He knew the room; it was always the same room. He turned in the narrow corridor, reached the door and lunged through it.

Oh, Jesus! It was beyond anything in his imagination, beyond any mess he had seen before. The naked Blackburn covered with blood and painted obscenities, the dead girl slumped over him, her face on his genitals. It was a sight from hell, if hell could be so terrible.

The major would never know where he found the self-control, but find it he did. He slammed the door shut and stood in the corridor, his automatic raised. He grabbed a woman who raced by toward the staircase, and shouted:

"Do as I say, or I'll kill you! There's a telephone over there. Dial the number I give you! Say the words I tell you, the *exact words!*" He shoved the girl viciously toward the hallway phone.

The President of the United States walked grimly through the doorway of the Oval Office and over to his desk. Already there, and standing together, were the Secretary of State and the Director of the Central Intelligence Agency.

"I know the facts," said the President harshly in his familiar drawl, "and they turn my stomach. Now tell me what you're doing about them."

The Director of the CIA stepped forward. "New York Homicide is cooperating. We're fortunate insofar as the general's aide remained by the door and threatened to kill anyone who tried to get past him. Our people arrived, and were at the scene first. They cleaned up as best they could."

"That's cosmetics, goddamn it," said the President. "I suppose they're necessary, but that's not what I'm interested in. What are your ideas? Was it one of those weird, kinky New York murders, or was it something else?"

"In my judgment," answered the Director, "it was something else. I said as much to Paul here last night. It was a thoroughly analyzed, pre-arranged assassination. Brilliantly executed. Even to the killing of the establishment's owner, who was the only one who could shed any light."

"Who's responsible?"

"I'd say KGB. The bullets fired were from a Russian Graz-Burya automatic, a favorite weapon of theirs."

"I *must* object, Mr. President," said the Secretary of State. "I can't subscribe to Jim's conclusion; that gun may be unusual, but it *can* be purchased in Europe. I was with the Soviet Ambassador for an hour this morning. He was as shaken as we were. He not only disclaimed any *possible* Russian involvement, but correctly pointed out that General Blackburn was far more acceptable to the Soviets than any who might immediately succeed him."

"The KGB," interrupted the Director, "is often at odds with the Kremlin's diplomatic corps."

"As the Company is with ours?" asked the Secretary.

"No more than your own Consular Operations, Paul," replied the Director.

"Goddamn it," said the President, "I don't need that crap from you two. Give me facts. You first, Jim. Since you're so sure of yourself, what have you come up with?"

"A great deal." The Director opened the file folder in his hand, took out a sheet of paper, and placed it in front of the President. "We went back fifteen years and put everything we learned about last night into the computers. We cross-checked the concepts of method, location, egress, timing and teamwork. We matched it all with every known KGB assassination during the period. We've come up with three profiles. Three of the most elusive and successful killers in Soviet intelligence. In each case, of course, the man operates under normal covert procedures, but they're all assassins. We've listed them in order of expertise."

The President studied the three names.

Taleniekov, Vasili. Last reported post; Southwest Soviet Sectors.
Krylovich, Nikolai. Last reported post: Moscow, VKR.
Zhukovski, Georgi. Last reported post: East Berlin, Embassy Attaché.

The Secretary of State was agitated; he could not remain silent. "Mr. President, this kind of speculation—based at best on the widest variables—can only lead to confrontation. It's not the time for it."

"Now, wait a minute, Paul," said the President. "I asked for facts, and I don't give a damn whether the time's right or not for a confrontation. The Chairman of the Joint Chiefs of Staff has been killed. He may have been a sick son of a bitch in private life, but he was a hell of a good soldier. If it was a Soviet assassination, I want to know it." The Chief Executive put the paper down on the desk, his eyes still on the Secretary. "Besides," he added, "until more is known, there won't be any confrontations. I'm certain Jim has kept this at the highest level of secrecy."

"Of course," said the Director of the CIA.

There was a rapid knock on the Oval Office door. The President's senior communications aide entered without waiting for a response.

"Sir, the Premier of Soviet Russia is on the Red Telephone. We've confirmed the transmission."

"Thank you," said the President, reaching for a phone behind his chair. "Mr. Premier? This is the President."

The Russian's words were spoken rapidly, briskly, and at the first pause, an interpreter translated. As was customary, the Soviet interpreter stopped and another voice—that of the interpreter's American counterpart—said simply, "Correct, Mr. President."

The four-way conversation continued.

"Mr. President," said the Premier, "I mourn the death—the murder—of General Anthony Blackburn. He was a fine soldier who loathed war, as you and I loathe war. He was respected here, his strength and perception of global problems a beneficial influence on our own military leaders. He will be sorely missed."

"Thank you, Mr. Premier. We, too, mourn his death. His murder. We are at a loss to explain it."

"That is the reason for my call, Mr. President. You must know beyond doubt that General Blackburn's death—his murder—would never be desired by the responsible leadership of the Soviet Socialist Republics. If I may, the contemplation of it would be anathema. I trust I make myself clear, Mr. President."

"I think so, Mr. Premier, and I thank you again. But if I may, are you alluding to the outside possibility of *irresponsible* leadership?"

"No more than those in your Senate who would bomb the Ukraine. Such idiots are dismissed, as they should be."

"Then I'm not sure I grasp the subtlety of your phrasing, Mr. Premier."

"I shall be clearer. Your Central Intelligence Agency has produced three names it believes may be involved with the death of General Blackburn. They are not, Mr. President. You have my solemn word. They are *responsible* men, held in absolute control by their superiors. In point of fact, one man, Zhukovski, was hospitalized a week ago. Another, Krylovich, has been stationed at the Manchurian border for the past eleven months. And the respected Taleniekov is, for all intents and purposes, retired. He is currently in Moscow."

The President paused and stared at the Director of the CIA. "Thank you for the clarification, Mr. Premier, and for the accuracy of your information. I realize it wasn't easy for you to make this call. Soviet intelligence is to be commended."

"As is your own. There are fewer secrets these days; some say that is good. I weighed the values, and had to reach you. We were not involved, Mr. President."

"I believe you. I wonder who it was."

"I'm troubled, Mr. President. I think we should both know the answer to that."

2

"Dimitri Yuri Yurievich!" roared the buxom woman good-naturedly as she approached the bed, a breakfast tray in her hand. "It's the first morning of your holiday. The snow is on the ground, the sun is melting it, and before you shake the vodka from your head, the forests will be green again!"

The man buried his face in the pillow, then rolled over and opened his eyes, blinking at the sheer whiteness of the room. Outside the large windows of the *dacha*, the branches of the trees were sagging under the weight of the snow.

Yurievich smiled at his wife, his fingers touching the hairs of his chin beard, grown more gray than brown. "I think I burned myself last night," he said.

"You would have!" laughed the woman. "Fortunately, my peasant instincts were inherited by our son. He sees fire and doesn't waste time analyzing the components, but puts it out!"

"I remember him leaping at me."

"He certainly did." Yurievich's wife put the tray on the bed, pushing her husband's legs away to make room for herself. She sat down and reached for his forehead. "You're warm, but you'll survive, my cossack."

"Give me a cigarette."

"Not before fruit juice. You're a very important man; the cupboards are filled with cans of fruit juice. Our lieutenant says they're probably there to put out the cigarettes that burn your beard."

"The mentality of soldiers will never improve. We scientists understand that. The cans of juice are there to be mixed with vodka." Dimitri Yurievich smiled again, not a little forlornly. "A cigarette, my love? I'll even let you light it."

"You're impossible!" She picked up a pack of cigarettes from the bedside table, shook one out and put it between her husband's lips. "Be careful not to breathe when I strike the match. We'd both explode, and I'll be buried in dishonor as the killer of the Soviet's most prominent nuclear physicist."

"My work lives after me; let me be interred with smoke." Yurievich inhaled as his wife held the match. "How's our son this morning?"

"He's fine. He was up early oiling the rifles. His guests will be here in an hour or so. The hunt begins around noon."

"Oh Lord, I forgot about that," said Yurievich, pushing himself up on the pillow into a sitting position. "Do I really have to go?"

"You and he are teamed together. Don't you remember telling everyone at dinner that father and son would bring home the prize game?"

Dimitri winced. "It was my conscience speaking. All those years in the laboratories while he grew up somehow behind my back."

His wife smiled. "It will be good for you to get out in the air. Now finish your cigarette, eat your breakfast, and get dressed."

"You know something?" said Yurievich, taking his wife's hand. "I'm just beginning to grasp it. This *is* a holiday. I can't remember our last one."

"I'm not sure there ever was one. You work harder than any man I've ever known."

Yurievich shrugged. "It was good of the army to grant our son leave."

"He requested it. He wanted to be with you."

"That was good of him, too. I love him, but I hardly know him."

"He's a fine officer, everyone says. You can be proud."

"Oh I am, indeed. It's just that I don't know what to say to him. We have so little in common. The vodka made things easier last night."

"You haven't seen each other in nearly two years."

"I've had my work, everyone knows that."

"You're a scientist." His wife squeezed Dimitri's hand. "But not today. Not for the next three weeks! No laboratories, no blackboards, no all-night sessions with eager young professors and students who want to tell everybody they've worked with the great Yurievich." She took the cigarette from between his lips and crushed it out. "Now, eat your breakfast and get dressed. A winter hunt will do you a world of good."

"My dear woman," protested Dimitri, laughing, "it will probably be the death of me. I haven't fired a rifle in over twenty years!"

Lieutenant Nikolai Yurievich trudged through the deep snow toward the old building that was once the *dacha*'s stables. He turned and looked back at the huge three-story main house. It glistened in the morning sunlight, a small alabaster palace set in an alabaster glen carved out of snow-laden forest.

Moscow thought a great deal of his father. Everyone wanted to know about the great Yurievich, this brilliant, irascible man whose mere name frightened the leaders of the Western world. It was said that Dimitri Yuri Yurievich carried the formulae for a dozen nuclear tactical weapons in his head; that left alone in a munitions depot with an adjacent laboratory he could fashion a bomb that could destroy greater London, all of Washington, and most of Peking.

That was the great Yurievich, a man immune to criticism or discipline, in spite of words and actions which were at times intemperate. Not in terms of his devotion to the state; that was never in question. Dimitri Yurievich was the fifth child of impoverished peasants from Kourov. Without the state he would be behind a mule on some aristocrat's land. No, he was a Communist to his boots, but like all brilliant men he had no patience with bureaucracies. He had been outspoken about interference and he had never been taken to task for it.

Which was why so many wanted to know him. On the assumption, Nikolai suspected, that even knowing the great Yurievich would somehow transfer a touch of his immunity to them.

The lieutenant knew that was the case today and it was an uncomfortable feeling. The "guests" who were now on their way to his father's *dacha* had practically invited themselves. One was the commander of Nikolai's battalion in Vilnius, the other a man Nikolai did not even know. A friend of the commander from Moscow, someone the commander said could do a young lieutenant a good turn when it came to assignments. Nikolai did not care for such enticements; he was his own man first, his father's son second. He would make his own way; it was very important to him that he do so. But he could not refuse this particular commander, for if there was any man in the Soviet Army who deserved a touch of "immunity," it was Colonel Janek Drigorin.

Drigorin had spoken out against the corruption that was rife in the Select Officer Corps. The resort clubs on the Black Sea paid for with misappropriated funds, the stockhouses filled with contraband, the women brought in on military aircraft against all regulations.

He was cut off by Moscow, sent to Vilnius to rot in mediocrity. Whereas Nikolai Yurievich was a twenty-one-year-old lieutenant exercising major responsibility in a minor post, Drigorin was a major military talent relegated to oblivion in a minor command. If such a man wished to spend a day with his father, Nikolai could not protest. And, after all, the colonel was a delightful person; he wondered what the other man was like.

Nikolai reached the stables and opened the large door that led to the corridor of stalls. The hinges had been oiled; the old entrance swung back without a sound. He walked down past the immaculately kept enclosures that once had held the best of breeds and tried to imagine what that Russia had been like. He could almost hear the whinnies of fiery-eyed stallions, the impatient scruffing of hooves, the snorting of hunters eager to break out for the fields.

That Russia must have been something. If you weren't behind a mule.

He came to the end of the long corridor where there was another wide door. He opened it and walked out into the snow again. In the distance, something caught his eye; it seemed out of place. *They* seemed out of place.

Veering from the corner of a grain bin toward the edge of the forest, there were tracks in the snow. Footprints, perhaps. Yet the two servants assigned by Moscow to the *dacha* had not left the main house. And the groundskeepers were in their barracks down the road.

On the other hand, thought Nikolai, the warmth of the morning sun could have melted the rims of any impressions in the snow; and the blinding light played tricks on the eyes. They were no doubt the tracks of some foraging animal. The lieutenant smiled to himself at the thought of an animal from the forest looking for grain here, at this cared-for relic that was the grand *dacha*'s stables. The animals had not changed, but Russia had.

Nikolai looked at his watch; it was time to go back to the house. The guests would be arriving shortly.

Everything was going so well, Nikolai could hardly believe it. There was nothing uncomfortable at all, thanks in large measure to his father and the man from Moscow. Colonel Drigorin at first seemed ill-at-ease—the commander who had imposed himself on the well-known, or well-connected, subordinate—but Yuri Yurievich would have none of it. He welcomed his son's superior as an anxious—if celebrated—father, interested only in furthering his son's position. Nikolai could not help but be amused; his father was so obvious. Vodka was delivered with the fruit juice and coffee, and Nikolai kept a sharp eye out for dangling cigarettes.

The surprise and delight was the colonel's friend from Moscow, a man named Brunov, a high-ranking party functionary in Military-Industrial Planning. Not only did Brunov and Nikolai's father have mutual friends, it was soon apparent that they shared an irreverent attitude toward much of Moscow's bureaucracy—which encompassed, naturally, many of those mutual friends. The laughter was not long coming, each rebel trying to outdo the other with biting comments about this commissar-with-an-echo-chamber-for-a-head and that economist-who-could-not-keep-a-ruble-in-his-pocket.

"We are wicked, Brunov!" roared Nikolai's father, his eyes alive with laughter.

"Too true, Yurievich!" agreed the man from Moscow. "It's a pity we're so accurate."

"But be careful, we're with soldiers. They'll report us!"

"Then I shall withhold their payrolls and you'll design a backfiring bomb."

Dimitri Yurievich's laughter subsided for a brief moment. "I wish there were no need for the functioning kind."

"And I that such large payrolls were not demanded."

"Enough," said Yurievich. "The groundskeepers say the hunting here is superb. My son has promised to look out for me, and I promised to shoot the biggest game. Come now, whatever you lack we have here. Boots, furs . . . vodka."

"Not while firing, father."

"By God, you *have* taught him something," said Yurievich, smiling at the colonel. "Incidentally, gentlemen, I won't hear of you leaving today. You'll stay the night, of course. Moscow is generous; there are roasts and fresh vegetables from Lenin-knows-where. . . ."

"And flasks of vodka, I trust."

"Not flasks, Brunov. *Casks!* I see it in your eyes. We'll both be on holiday. You'll stay."

"I'll stay," said the man from Moscow.

Gunshots rang through the forest, vibrating in the ears. Nor were they lost on the winter birds; screeches and the snapping of wings formed a rolling coda to the echoes. Nikolai could hear excited voices as well, but they were too far away to be understandable. He turned to his father.

"We should hear the whistle within sixty seconds if they hit something," he said, his rifle angled down at the snow.

"It's an outrage!" replied Yurievich in mock anger. "The groundskeepers swore to me—on the side, mind you—that all the game was in this section of the woods. Near the lake. There was *nothing* over there! It's why I insisted they go there. . . ."

"You're an old scoundrel," said the son, studying his father's weapon. "Your safety's released. Why?"

"I thought I heard a rustle back there. I wanted to be ready."

"With respect, my father, please put it back on. Wait until your sight matches the sound you hear before you release it."

"With respect, my soldier, then there'd be too much to do at once." Yurievich saw the concern in his son's eyes. "On second thought, you're probably right. I'd fall and cause a detonation. That's something I know about."

"Thank you," said the lieutenant, suddenly turning. His father was right; there was something rustling behind them. A crack of a limb, the snap of a branch. He released the safety on his weapon.

"What is it?" asked Dimitri Yurievich, excitement in his eyes.

"*Shh,*" whispered Nikolai, peering into the shaggy corridors of white surrounding them.

He saw nothing. He snapped the safety into its locked position.

"You heard it, too, then?" asked Dimitri. "It wasn't just this pair of fifty-five-year-old ears."

"The snow's heavy," suggested his son. "Branches break under its weight. That's what we heard."

"Well, one thing we *didn't* hear," said Yurievich, "was a whistle. They didn't hit a damn thing!"

Three more distant gunshots rang out.

"They've seen *something,*" said the lieutenant. "Perhaps now we'll hear their whistle. . . ."

Suddenly they heard it. A sound. But it was not a whistle. It was, instead, a panicked, elongated scream, faint but distinct. Distinctly a terrible scream. It was followed by another, more hysterical.

"My *God*, what *happened?*" Yurievich grabbed his son's arm.

"I don't—"

The reply was cut off by a third scream, searing and terrible.

"Stay *here!*" yelled the lieutenant to his father. "I'll go to them."

"I'll follow," said Yurievich. "Go quickly, but be careful!"

Nikolai raced through the snow toward the source of the screams. They filled the woods now, less shrill, but more painful for the loss of power. The soldier used his rifle to crash his path through the heavy branches, kicking up sprays of snow. His legs ached, the cold air swelled in his lungs; his sight was obscured by tears of fatigue.

He heard the roars first, and then he saw what he most feared, what no hunter ever wanted to see.

An enormous, wild black bear, his terrifying face a mass of blood, was wreaking his vengeance on those who'd caused his wounds, clawing, ripping, slashing at his enemy.

Nikolai raised his rifle and fired until there were no more shells in the chamber.

The giant bear fell. The soldier raced to the two men; he lost what breath he had as he looked at them.

The man from Moscow was dead, his throat torn, his bloodied head barely attached to his body. Drigorin was only just alive, and if he did not die in seconds, Nikolai knew he would reload his weapon and finish what the animal had not done. The colonel had no face; it was not there. In its place a sight that burned itself into the soldier's mind.

How? How could it have happened?

And then the lieutenant's eyes strayed to Drigorin's right arm and the shock was beyond anything he could imagine.

It was half severed from his elbow, the method of surgery clear: Heavy caliber bullets.

The colonel's firing arm had been shot off!

Nikolai ran to Brunov's corpse; he reached down and rolled it over.

Brunov's arm was intact, but his left hand had blown apart, only the gnarled, bloody outline of a palm left, the fingers strips of bone. His *left* hand. Nikolai Yurievich remembered the morning; the coffee and fruit juice and vodka and cigarettes.

The man from Moscow was left-handed.

Brunov and Drigorin had been rendered defenseless by someone with a gun, someone who knew what was in their path.

Nikolai stood up cautiously, the soldier in him primed, seeking an unseen enemy. And this was an enemy he wanted to find and kill with all his heart. His mind raced back to the footprints he had seen behind the stables. They were not those of a scavenging animal—though an animal's they were—they were the tracks of an obscene killer.

Who *was* it? Above all, *why?*

The lieutenant saw a flash of light. Sunlight on a weapon.

He made a move to his right, then abruptly spun to his left and lunged to the ground, rolling behind the trunk of an oak tree. He removed the empty magazine from his weapon, replacing it with a fresh one. He squinted up at the source of the light. It came from high in a pine tree.

A figure was straddling two limbs fifty feet above the ground, a rifle with a telescopic sight in his hands. The killer wore a white snow parka with a white fur hood, his face obscured behind wide, black sunglasses.

Nikolai thought he would vomit in rage and revulsion. The man was smiling, and the lieutenant knew he was smiling down at him.

Furiously, he raised his rifle. An explosion of snow blinded him, accompanied by the loud report of a high-powered rifle. A second gunshot followed; the bullet thumped into the wood above his head. He pulled back into the protection of the trunk.

Another gunshot, this one in the near distance, not from the killer in the pine tree.

"Nikolai!"

His mind burst. There was nothing left but rage. The voice that screamed his name was his father's.

"Nikolai!"

Another shot. The soldier sprang up from the ground, firing his rifle into the tree and raced across the snow.

An icelike incision was made in his chest. He heard nothing and felt nothing until he knew his face was cold.

The Premier of Soviet Russia placed his hands on the long table beneath the window that looked out over the Kremlin. He leaned down and studied the photographs, the flesh of his large peasant face sagging with exhaustion, his eyes filled with anger and shock.

"Horrible," he whispered. "That men should die like this is horrible. At least, Yurievich was spared—not his life, but such an end as this."

Across the room, seated around another table, were two men and a woman, their faces stern, watching the Premier. In front of each was a brown file folder, and it was apparent that each was anxious to proceed with the conference. But with the Premier one did not push or intrude on his thoughts; his temper could be unleashed by such displays of impatience. The Premier was a man whose mind raced faster than anyone's in that room, but his deliberations were nevertheless slow, the complexities considered. He was a survivor in a world where only the most astute—and subtle—survived.

Fear was a weapon he used with extraordinary skill.

He stood up, pushing the photographs away in disgust, and strode back to the conference table.

"All nuclear stations are on alert, our submarines approaching firing positions," he said. "I want this information transmitted to all embassies. Use codes Washington has broken."

One of the men at the table leaned forward. He was a diplomat, older than the Premier, and obviously an associate of long standing, an ally who could speak somewhat more freely than the other two. "You take a risk I'm not sure is wise. We're not that certain of the reaction. The American Ambassador was profoundly shocked. I know him; he wasn't lying."

"Then he wasn't informed," said the second man curtly. "Speaking for the VKR, we *are* certain. The bullets and shell casings were identified: seven millimeter—grooved for implosion. Bore markings, unmistakable. They were fired from a Browning Magnum, Grade Four. What more do you need?"

"A great deal more than that. Such a weapon is not so difficult to obtain, and I doubt an American assassin would leave his business card."

"He might if it was the weapon he was most familiar with. We've found a pattern." The VKR man turned to the middle-aged woman, whose face was chiseled granite. "Explain, if you will, Comrade Director."

The woman opened her file folder and scanned the top page before speaking. She turned to the second page and addressed the Premier, her eyes avoiding the diplomat. "As you know, there were two assassins, presumably both male. One had to be a marksman of extreme skill and coordination, the other someone who undoubtedly possessed the same qualifications, but who was also an expert in electronic surveillance. There was evidence in the stables—bracket scrapings, suction imprints, footprints indicating unobstructed vantage points—that lead us to believe all conversations in the *dacha* were intercepted."

"You describe CIA expertise, comrade," interrupted the Premier.

"Or Consular Operations, sir," replied the woman. "It's important to bear that in mind."

"Oh, yes," agreed the Premier. "The State Department's small band of 'negotiators.'"

"Why not the Chinese Tao-pans?" offered the diplomat earnestly. "They're among the most effective killers on earth. The Chinese had more to fear from Yurievich than anyone else."

"Physiognomy rules them out," countered the man from VKR. "If one was caught, even after cyanide, Peking knows it would be destroyed."

"Get back to this pattern you've found," interrupted the Premier.

The woman continued. "We fed everything through KGB computers, concentrating on American intelligence personnel we know have penetrated Russia, who speak the language fluently, and are known killers. We have arrived at four names. Here they are, Mr. Premier. Three from the Central Intelligence Agency, one from the Department of State's Consular Operations." She handed the page to the VKR man, who in turn rose and gave it to the Premier.

He looked at the names.

Scofield, Brandon Alan. State Department, Consular Operations. Known to have been responsible for assassinations in Prague, Athens, Paris, Munich. Suspected of having operated in Moscow itself. Involved in over twenty defections.

Randolph, David. Central Intelligence Agency. Cover is Import Traffic Manager, Dynamax Corporation, West Berlin Branch. All phases of sabotage. Known to have been instrumental in hydroelectrical explosions in Kazan and Tagil.

Saltzman, George Robert. Central Intelligence Agency. Operated as pouch courier and assassin in Vientiane under AID cover for six years. Oriental expert. Currently—as of five weeks ago—in the Tashkent sectors. Cover: Australian immigrant, sales manager: Perth Radar Corporation.

Bergstrom, Edward. Central Intelligence Agency—

"Mr. Premier," interrupted the man from VKR. "My associate meant to explain that the names are in order of priority. In our opinion, the entrapment and execution of Dimitri Yurievich bears all the earmarks of the first man on that list."

"This Scofield?"

"Yes, Mr. Premier. He disappeared a month ago in Marseilles. He's done more damage, compromised more operations, than any agent the United States has fielded since the war."

"Really?"

"Yes, sir." The VKR man paused, then spoke hesitantly, as if he did not want to go on, but knew he must. "His wife was killed ten years ago. In East Berlin. He's been a maniac ever since."

"*East* Berlin?"

"It was a trap. KGB."

The telephone rang on the Premier's desk; he crossed rapidly and picked it up.

It was the President of the United States. The interpreters were on the line; they went to work.

"We grieve the death—the terrible murder—of a very great scientist, Mr. Premier. As well as the horror that befell his friends."

"Your words are appreciated, Mr. President, but as you know, those deaths and that horror were premeditated. I'm grateful for your sympathies, but I can't help but wonder if perhaps you are not somewhat relieved that the Soviet Union has lost its foremost nuclear physicist."

"I am not, sir. His brilliance transcended our borders and differences. He was a man for all peoples."

"Yet he chose to be a part of *one* people, did he not? I tell you frankly, my concerns do not transcend our differences. Rather, they force me to look to my flanks."

"Then, if you'll forgive me, Mr. Premier, you're looking for phantoms."

"Perhaps we've found them, Mr. President. We have evidence that is extremely disturbing to me. So much so that I have—"

"Forgive me once again," interrupted the President of the United States. "Your evidence has prompted my calling you, in spite of my natural reluctance to do so. The KGB has made a great error. Four errors, to be precise."

"*Four?*"

"Yes, Mr. Premier. Specifically the names Scofield, Randolph, Saltzman and Bergstrom. None was involved, Mr. Premier."

"You astonish me, Mr. President."

"No more than you astonished me the other week. There are fewer secrets these days, remember?"

"Words are inexpensive; the evidence is strong."

"Then it's been so calculated. Let me clarify. Two of the three men from Central Intelligence are no longer in sanction. Randolph and Bergstrom are currently at their desks in Washington. Mr. Saltzman was hospitalized in Tashkent; the diagnosis is cancer." The President paused.

"That leaves one name, doesn't it?" said the Premier. "Your man from the infamous Consular Operations. So bland in diplomatic circles, but infamous to us."

"This is the most painful aspect of my clarification. It's inconceivable that Mr. Scofield could have been involved. There was less chance of his involvement than any of the others, frankly. I tell you this because it no longer matters."

"Words cost little—"

"I must be explicit. For the past several years a covert, in-depth dossier has been maintained on Dr. Yurievich, information added almost daily, certainly every month. In certain judgments, it was time to reach Dimitri Yurievich with viable options."

"*What?*"

"Yes, Mr. Premier. Defection. The two men who traveled to the *dacha* to make contact with Dr. Yurievich did so in our interests. Their source-control was Scofield. It was his operation."

The Premier of Soviet Russia stared across the room at the pile of photographs on the table. He spoke softly. "Thank you for your frankness."

"Look to other flanks."

"I shall."

"We both must."

3

The late afternoon sun was a fireball, its rays bouncing off the waters of the canal in blinding oscillation. The crowds walking west on Amsterdam's Kalverstraat squinted as they hurried along the pavement, grateful for the February sun and gusts of wind that came off the myriad waterways that stemmed from the Amstel River. Too often February brought the mists and rain, dampness everywhere; it was not the case today and the citizens of the North Sea's most vital port city seemed exhilarated by the clear, biting air warmed from above.

One man, however, was not exhilarated. Neither was he a citizen nor on the streets. His name was Brandon Alan Scofield, attaché-at-large, Consular Operations, United States Department of State. He stood at a window four stories above the canal and the Kalverstraat, peering through binoculars down at the crowds, specifically at the area of the pavement where a glass telephone booth reflected the harsh flashes of sunlight. The light made him squint, but there was no energy evident on Scofield's pallid face, a face whose sharp features were drawn and taut beneath a vaguely combed cover of light-brown hair, fringed at the edge with strands of gray.

He kept refocusing the binoculars, cursing the light and the swift movements below. His eyes were tired, the hollows beneath dark and stretched, the results of too little sleep for too many reasons Scofield did not care to think about. There was a job to do and he was a professional; his concentration could not waver.

There were two other men in the room. A balding technician sat at a table with a dismantled telephone, wires connecting it to a tape machine, the receiver off the hook. Somewhere under the streets in a telephone complex, arrangements had been made; they were the only cooperation that would be given by the Amsterdam police, a debt called in by the attaché-at-large from the American State Department. The third person in the room was younger than the other two, in his early thirties and with no lack of energy on his face, no exhaustion in his eyes. If his features were taut, it was the tautness of enthrallment; he was a young man eager for the kill. His weapon was a fast-film motion picture camera mounted on a tripod, a telescopic lens attached. He would have preferred a different weapon.

Down in the street, a figure appeared in the tinted circles of Scofield's binoculars. The figure hesitated by the telephone booth and in that brief moment was jostled by the crowds off to the side of the pavement, in front of the flashing glass, blocking the glare with his body, a target surrounded by a halo of sunlight. It would be more comfortable for everyone concerned if the target could be zeroed where he was standing now. A high-powered rifle calibrated for seventy yards could do it; the man in the window could squeeze the trigger. He had done so often before. But comfort was not the issue. A lesson had to be taught, another lesson learned, and such instruction depended on the confluence of vital factors. Those teaching and those being taught had to understand their respective roles. Otherwise an execution was meaningless.

The figure below was an elderly man, in his middle to late sixties. He was dressed in rumpled clothing, a thick overcoat pulled up around his neck to ward off the chill, a battered hat pulled down over his forehead. There was a stubble of a beard on his frightened face; he was a man on the run and for the American watching him through the binoculars, there was nothing so terrible, or haunting, as an old man on the run. Except, perhaps, an old woman. He had seen both. Far more often than he cared to think about.

Scofield glanced at his watch. "Go ahead," he said to the technician at the table. Then he turned to the younger man who stood beside him. "You ready?"

"Yes," was the curt reply. "I've got the son of a bitch centered. Washington was right; you proved it."

"I'm not sure what I've proved yet. I wish I was. When he's in the booth, get his lips."

"Right."

The technician dialed the pre-arranged numbers and punched the buttons of the tape machine. He rose quickly from his chair and handed Scofield a semicircular headset with a mouthpiece and single earphone. "It's ringing," he said.

"I know. He's staring through the glass. He's not sure he wants to hear it. That bothers me."

"Move, you son of a bitch!" said the young man with the camera.

"He will," said Scofield, the binoculars and headset held firmly in his hands. "He's frightened. Each half-second is a long time for him and I don't know why. . . . There he goes; he's opening the door. Everybody quiet." Scofield continued to stare through the binoculars, listened, and then spoke quietly into the mouthpiece. *"Dobri dyen, priyatyel. . . ."*

The conversation, spoken entirely in Russian, lasted for eighteen seconds.

"Dosvidaniya," said Scofield, adding, *"zavtra nochyn. Na mostye."* He continued to hold the headset to his ear and watched the frightened man below. The target disappeared into the crowds; the camera's motor stopped, and the attaché-at-large put down the binoculars, handing the headset to the technician. "Were you able to get it all?" he asked.

"Clear enough for a voice print," said the balding operator, checking his dials.

"You?" Scofield turned to the young man by the camera.

"If I understood the language better, even I could read his lips."

"Good. Others will; they'll understand it very well." Scofield reached into his pocket, took out a small leather notebook, and began writing. "I want you to take the tape and the film to the embassy. Get the film developed right away and have duplicates made of both. I want miniatures; here are the specifications."

"Sorry, Bray," said the technician, glancing at Scofield as he wound a coil of telephone wire. "I'm not allowed within five blocks of the territory; you know that."

"I'm talking to Harry," replied Scofield, angling his head toward the younger man. He tore out the page from his notebook. "When the reductions are made, have them inserted in a single watertight flatcase. I want it coated, good enough for a week in the water."

"Bray," said the young man, taking the page of paper. "I picked up about every third word you said on the phone."

"You're improving," interrupted Scofield, walking back to the window and the binoculars. "When you get to every other one, we'll recommend an upgrade."

"That man wanted to meet tonight," continued Harry. "You turned him down."

"That's right," said Scofield, raising the binoculars to his eyes, focusing out the window.

"Our instructions were to take him as soon as we could. The cipher plaintext was clear about that. No time lost."

"Time's relative, isn't it? When that old man heard the telephone ring, every second was an agonizing minute for him. For us, an hour can be a day. In Washington, for Christ's sake, a day is normally measured by a calendar year."

"That's no answer," pressed Harry, looking at the note. "We can get this stuff reduced and packed in forty-five minutes. We could make the contact tonight. Why don't we?"

"The weather's rotten," said Scofield, the binoculars at his eyes.

"The weather's perfect. Not a cloud in the sky."

"That's what I mean. It's rotten. A clear night means a lot of people strolling around the canals; in bad weather, they don't. Tomorrow's forecast is for rain."

"That doesn't make sense. In ten seconds we block a bridge, he's over the side and dead in the water."

"Tell that clown to shut up, Bray!" shouted the technician at the table.

"You heard the man," said Scofield, focusing on the spires of the buildings outside. "You just lost the upgrade. Your outrageous statement that we intend to commit bodily harm tarnishes our friends in the Company."

The younger man grimaced. The rebuke was deserved. "Sorry. It still doesn't make sense. That cipher was a priority alert; we should take him tonight."

Scofield lowered the binoculars and looked at Harry. "I'll tell you what *does* make sense," he said. "Somewhat more than those silly goddamned phrases someone found on the back of a cereal box. That man down there was terrified. He hasn't slept in days. He's strung out to the breaking point, and I want to know why."

"There could be a dozen reasons," countered the younger man. "He's old. Inexperienced. Maybe he thinks we're on to him, that he's about to be caught. What difference does it make?"

"A man's life, that's all."

"Come on, Bray, not from *you*. He's Soviet poison; a double-agent."

"I want to be sure."

"And I want to get out of here," broke in the technician, handing Scofield a reel of tape and picking up his machine. "Tell the clown we never met."

"Thanks, Mr. No-name. I owe you."

The CIA man left, nodding at Bray, avoiding any contact with his associate.

"There was no one here but us chickens, Harry," said Scofield after the door was shut. "You do understand that."

"He's a nasty bastard—"

"Who could tap the White House toilets, if he hasn't already," said Bray, tossing the reel of tape to Harry. "Get our unsolicited indictments over to the embassy. Take out the film and leave the camera here."

Harry would not be put off; he caught the reel of tape, but made no move toward the camera. "I'm in this, too. That cipher applied to me as well as you. I want to have answers in case I'm asked questions; in case something happens between tonight and tomorrow."

"If Washington's right, nothing will happen. I told you. I want to be sure."

"What more do you *need?* The target thinks he just made contact with KGB-Amsterdam! You engineered it. You proved it!"

Scofield studied his associate for a moment, then turned away and walked back to the window. "You know something, Harry? All the training you get, all the words you hear, all the experiences you go through, never take the place of the first rule." Bray picked up the binoculars, and focused on a faraway point above the skyline. "Teach yourself to think like the enemy thinks. Not how you'd like him to think, but how he *really* thinks. It's not easy; you can kid yourself because that *is* easy."

Exasperated, the younger man spoke angrily. "For God's sake, what's that got to do with anything? We've got our proof!"

"Do we? As you say, our defector's made contact with his own. He's a pigeon who's found his own particular route to Mother Russia. He's safe; he's out of the cold."

"That's what he thinks, yes!"

"Then why isn't he a happy man?" asked Bray Scofield, angling the binoculars down at the canal.

The mist and the rain fulfilled Amsterdam's promise of winter. The night sky was an impenetrable blanket, the edges mottled by the shimmering lights of the city. There were no strollers on the bridge, no boats on the canal below; pockets of fog swirled overhead—evidence that the North Sea winds traveled south unencumbered. It was three o'clock in the morning.

Scofield leaned against the iron railing at the west entrance of the ancient stone bridge. In his left hand was a small transistorized radio—not for verbal communication, only for receiving signals. His right hand was in his raincoat pocket, his extended fingers touching the barrel of a .22 caliber automatic, not much larger than a starter's pistol, with a report nowhere near as loud. At close range it was a very feasible weapon. It fired rapidly, with an accuracy sufficient for a distance measured in inches, and could barely be heard above the noises of the night.

Two hundred yards away, Bray's young associate was concealed in a doorway on the Sarphatistraat. The target would pass him on the way to the bridge; there was no other route. When the old Russian did so, Harry would press a button on his transmitter: the signal. The execution was in progress; the victim was walking his last hundred yards—to the midpoint of the bridge, where his own personal hangman would greet him, insert a watertight packet in the victim's overcoat, and carry out the appointed task.

In a day or so that packet would find its way to KGB Amsterdam. A tape would be listened to, a film observed closely. And another lesson would be taught.

And, naturally, go unheeded, as all lessons went unheeded—as they always went unheeded. Therein lay the futility, thought Scofield. The never-ending futility that numbed the senses with each repetition.

What difference does it make? A perceptive question asked by an eager if not very perceptive young colleague.

None, Harry. None at all. Not any longer.

But on this particular night, the needles of doubt kept pricking Bray's conscience. Not his morality; long ago morality had been replaced by the practical. If it worked, it was moral; if it did not, it wasn't practical, and *thus* was immoral. What bothered him tonight had its basis in that utilitarian philosophy. Was the execution practical? Was the lesson about to be taught the best lesson, the most feasible option? Was it worth the risks and the fallout that came with the death of an old man who'd spent his adult life in space engineering?

On the surface the answer would appear to be yes. Six years ago the Soviet engineer had defected in Paris during an international space exposition. He had sought and been granted asylum; he had been welcomed by the space fraternity in Houston, given a job, a house, and protection. However, he was not considered an outstanding prize. The Russians had actually joked about his ideological deviation, implying that his talents might be more appreciated by the less-demanding capitalistic laboratories than by theirs. He rapidly became a forgotten man.

Until eight months ago when it was discovered that Soviet tracking stations were gridding into American satellites with alarming frequency, reducing the value of photographic checks through sophisticated ground camouflage. It was as if the Russians knew in advance the great majority of orbital trajectories.

They did. And a trace was made; it led to the forgotten man in Houston. What followed was relatively simple: A technical conference that dealt exclusively with one forgotten man's small area of expertise was called in Amsterdam; he was flown over on a government aircraft and the rest was up to a specialist in these matters. Brandon Scofield, attaché-at-large, Consular Operations.

Scofield had long since broken KGB-Amsterdam's codes and methods of contact. He put them in motion and was mildly surprised at the target's reaction; it was the basis of his profound concern now. The old man showed no relief at the summons. After six years of a balancing act, the target had every right to expect termination with honors, the gratitude of his government, and the last years of his life spent in comfort. Expect, hell. Bray had indicated as much in their ciphered conversations.

But the old Russian was not a happy man. And there were no overriding personal relationships evident in Houston. Scofield had requested the Four-Zero dossier on the target, a file so complete it detailed the projected hours of bowel movements. There was nothing in Houston; the man was a mole—apparently, in both senses of the word. And that, too, bothered Bray. A mole in espionage did not assume the characteristics of the social equivalent.

Something was wrong. Yet the evidence was there, the proof of duplicity confirmed. The lesson had to be taught.

A short, sharp whine came from the transmitter in his hand. It was repeated three seconds later; Scofield acknowledged receipt with the press of a button. He put the radio in his pocket and waited.

Less than a minute passed; he saw the figure of the old man coming through the blanket of fog and rain, a streetlight beyond creating an eerie silhouette. The target's gait was hesitant but somehow painfully determined, as if he were about to keep a rendezvous both desired and loathed. It did *not* make sense.

Bray glanced to his right. As he expected, there was no one in the street, no one anywhere to be seen in this deserted section of the city at this hour. He turned to his left and started up the ramp toward the midpoint of the bridge, the old Russian on the opposite side. He kept in the shadows; it was easy to do as the first three lights above the left railing had been shorted out.

Rain pounded the ancient cobblestones. Across the bridge proper, the old man stood facing the water below, his hands on the railing. Scofield stepped off the walkway and approached from behind, the sound of the downpour obscuring his footsteps. In his left raincoat pocket, his hand now gripped a round, flat case, two inches in diameter and less than an inch thick. It was coated in waterproof plastic, the sides possessing a chemical that when immersed in liquid for thirty seconds became an instant adhesive; under such conditions it would remain where it was placed until cut free. In the case was the evidence: a reel of film and a reel of magnetic tape. Both could be studied by KGB-Amsterdam.

"*Plakhaya noch, stary priyatyel,*" said Bray to the Russian's back, while taking the automatic from his pocket.

The old man turned, startled. "Why did you contact me?" he asked in Russian. "Has anything happened? . . ." He saw the gun and stopped. Then he went on, an odd calm in his voice suddenly replacing the fear. "I see it has, and I'm no longer of value. Go ahead, comrade. You'll do me an enormous favor."

Scofield stared at the old man; at the penetrating eyes that were no longer frightened. He had seen that look before. Bray answered in English.

"You've spent an active six years. Unfortunately, you haven't done us any favors at all. You weren't as grateful as we thought you might be."

The Russian nodded. "American," he said, "I wondered. A hastily called conference in Amsterdam over problems as easily analyzed in Houston. My being allowed out of the country, albeit covertly, and guarded—that protection something less than complete once here. But you had all the codes, you said all the right words. And your Russian is flawless, *priyatyel.*"

"That's my job. What was yours?"

"You know the answer. It's why you're here—"

"I want to know why."

The old man smiled grimly. "Oh, no. You'll get nothing but what you've learned. You see, I meant what I said. You'll do me a favor. You're my *listok.*"

"Solution to what?"

"Sorry."

Bray raised the automatic; its small barrel glistened in the rain. The Russian looked at it and breathed deeply. The fear returned to his eyes, but he did not waver or say a word. Suddenly, deliberately, Scofield thrust the gun up beneath the old man's left eye, steel and flesh making contact. The Russian trembled but remained silent.

Bray felt sick.

What difference does it make?

None, Harry. Not at all. Not any longer.

A lesson had to be taught. . . .

Scofield lowered the gun. "Get out of here," he said.

"What? . . ."

"You heard me. Get out of here. The KGB operates out of the diamond exchange on the Tolstraat. Its cover is a firm of Hasidim, *Diamant Bruusteen.* Beat it."

"I don't understand," said the Russian, his voice barely audible. "Is this another trick?"

"Goddamn it!" yelled Bray, now trembling. "Get out of here!"

Momentarily, the old man staggered, then grabbed the railing to steady himself. He backed away awkwardly, then started running through the rain.

"Scofield!" The shout came from Harry. He was at the west entrance of the bridge, directly in the path of the Russian. "Scofield, for God's *sake!"*

"Let him go!" screamed Bray.

He was either too late or his words were lost in the pounding rain; he did not know which. He heard three muted, sharp reports and watched in disgust as the old man held his head and fell against the railing.

Harry was a professional. He supported the body, fired a last shot into the neck, and with an upward motion, edged the corpse over the railing into the canal below.

What difference does it make?

None at all. Not any longer.

Scofield turned away and walked toward the east side of the bridge. He put the automatic in his pocket; it seemed heavy.

He could hear racing footsteps drawing nearer through the rain. He was terribly tired and did not want to hear them. Any more than he wanted to hear Harry's abrasive voice.

"Bray, what the hell *happened* back there? He nearly got away!"

"But he didn't," said Scofield, walking faster. "You made sure of that."

"You're damn right I did! For Christ's sake, what's *wrong* with you?" The younger man was on Bray's left; his eyes dropped to Scofield's hand. He could see the edge of the watertight case. *"Jesus!* You never planted it!"

"What?" Then Bray realized what Harry was talking about. He raised his head, looked at the small round receptacle, then threw it past the younger man over the railing.

"What are you *doing?"*

"Go to hell," said Scofield quietly.

Harry stopped, Bray did not. In seconds, Harry caught up and grabbed the edge of Scofield's raincoat. "Christ Almighty! You *let* him get away!"

"Take your hands off me."

"*No,* damn it! You can't—"

It was as far as Harry got. Bray shot his right hand up, his fingers clasping the younger man's exposed thumb, and yanked it counterclockwise.

Harry screamed; his thumb was broken.

"Go to hell," repeated Scofield. He continued walking off the bridge.

The safe-house was near the Rosengracht, the meeting to take place on the second floor. The sitting room was warmed by a fire, which also served to destroy any notes that might be taken. A State Department official had flown in from Washington; he wanted to question Scofield at the scene, as it were, in the event there were circumstances that only the scene could provide. It was important to understand what had happened, especially with someone like Brandon Scofield. He was the best there was, the coldest they had; he was an extraordinary asset to the American intelligence community, a veteran of twenty-two years of the most complicated "negotiations" one could imagine. He had to be handled with care . . . at the source. Not ordered back on the strength of a departmental complaint filed by a subordinate. He was a specialist, and something had happened.

Bray understood this and the arrangements amused him. Harry was taken out of Amsterdam the next morning in such a way that there was no chance of Scofield seeing him. Among the few at the embassy who had to be aware of the incident, Bray was treated as though nothing had taken place. He was told to take a few days off; a man was flying in from Washington to discuss a problem in Prague. That's what the cipher said. Wasn't Prague an old hunting ground of his?

Cover, of course. And not a very good one. Scofield knew that his every move in Amsterdam was now being watched, probably by teams of Company men. And if he had walked to the diamond exchange on the Tolstraat, he undoubtedly would have been shot.

He was admitted into the safe-house by a nondescript maid of indeterminate age, a servant convinced that the old house belonged to the retired couple who lived there and paid her. He said he had an appointment with the owner and his attorney. The maid nodded and showed him up the stairs to the second-floor sitting room.

The old gentleman was there but not the man from State. When the maid closed the door, the owner spoke.

"I'll wait a few minutes and then go back up to my apartment. If you need anything, press the button on the telephone; it rings upstairs."

"Thanks," said Scofield, looking at the Dutchman, reminded of another old man on a bridge. "My associate should be along shortly. We won't need anything."

The man nodded and left. Bray wandered about the room, absently fingering the books on the shelves. It occurred to him that he wasn't even trying to read the titles; actually he didn't see them. And then it struck him that he didn't feel anything, neither cold nor heat, not even anger or resignation. He didn't feel *anything*. He was somewhere in a cloud of vapor, numbed, all senses dormant. He wondered what he would say to the man who had flown thirty-five hundred miles to see him.

He did not care.

He heard footsteps on the stairs beyond the door. The maid had obviously been dismissed by a man who knew his way in this house. The door opened and the man from State walked in.

Scofield knew him. He was from Planning and Development, a strategist for covert operations. He was around Bray's age, but thinner, a bit shorter, and given to old-school-tie exuberance which he did not feel, but which he hoped concealed his ambition. It did not.

"Bray, how *are* you, old buddy?" he said in a half-shout, extending an exuberant hand for a more exuberant grip. "My God, it must be damn near two years. Have I got a couple of stories to tell *you!*"

"Really?"

"Have I!" An exuberant statement, no question implied. "I went up to Cambridge for my twentieth, and naturally ran into friends of yours right and left. Well, old buddy, I got pissed and couldn't remember what lies I told *who* about you! Christ Almighty, I had you an import analyst in Malaya, a language expert in New Guinea, an undersecretary in Canberra. It was hysterical. I mean, I couldn't *remember* I was so pissed."

"Why would anyone ask you about me, Charlie?"

"Well, they knew we were both at State; we were friends, everybody knew that."

"Cut it out. We were never friends. I suspect you dislike me almost as much as I dislike you. And I've never seen you drunk in my life."

The man from State stood motionless; the exuberant smile slowly disappeared from his lips. "You want to play it rough?"

"I want to play it as it is."

"What happened?"

"Where? When? At Harvard?"

"You know what I'm talking about. The other night. What happened the other night?"

"You tell me. You set it in motion, you spun the first wheels."

"We uncovered a dangerous security leak. A pattern of active espionage going back years that reduced the effectiveness of space surveillance to the point where we now know it's been a mockery. We wanted it confirmed; you confirmed it. You knew what had to be done and you walked away."

"I walked away," agreed Scofield.

"And when confronted with the fact by an associate, you did bodily injury to him. To your *own man!*"

"I certainly did. If I were you I'd get rid of him. Transfer him to Chile; you can't fuck up a hell of a lot more down there."

"*What?*"

"On the other hand, you won't do that. He's too much like you, Charlie. He'll never learn. Watch out. He'll take your job one day."

"Are you drunk?"

"No, I'm sorry to say. I thought about it, but I've got a little acidity in my stomach. Of course, if I'd known they were sending you, I might have fought the good fight and tried. For old time's sake, naturally."

"If you're not drunk, you're off your trolley."

"The track veered; those wheels you spun couldn't take the curve."

"Cut the horseshit!"

"What a dated phrase, Charlie. These days we say bullshit, although I prefer lizardshit—"

"That's enough! Your action—or should I say *in*action—compromised a vital aspect of counterespionage."

"Now, *you* cut the horseshit!" roared Bray, taking an ominous step toward the man from State. "I've heard all I want to hear from you! I didn't compromise anything. *You* did! You and the rest of those bastards back there. You found an ersatz leak in your goddamned sieve and so you had to plug it up with a corpse. Then you could go to the Forty Committee and tell *those* bastards how efficient you were!"

"What are you talking about?"

"The old man *was* a defector. He was reached, but he *was* a *defector.*"

"What do you mean 'reached'?"

"I'm not sure; I wish I was. Somewhere in that Four-Zero dossier something was left out. Maybe a wife that never died, but was in hiding. Or grandchildren no one bothered to list. I don't know, but it's there. Hostages, Charlie! That's why he did what he did. And I was his *listok.*"

"What's that mean?"

"For Christ's sake, learn the language. You're supposed to be an expert."

"Don't pull that language crap on me, I *am* an expert. There's no evidence to support an extortion theory, no family reported or referred to by the target at any time. He was a dedicated agent for Soviet intelligence."

"*Evidence?* Oh, come on, Charlie, even you know better than that. If he was good enough to pull off a defection, he was smart enough to bury what had to be buried. My guess is that the key was timing, and the timing blew up. His secret—or secrets—were found out. He was reached; it's all through his dossier. He lived abnormally, even for an abnormal existence."

"We rejected that approach," said Charlie emphatically. "He was an eccentric."

Scofield stopped and stared. "You rejected? . . . An eccentric? Goddamn you, you *did* know. You could have *used* that, fed him anything you liked. But no, you wanted a quick solution so the men upstairs would see how good you were. You could have *used* him, not killed him! But you didn't know how, so you kept quiet and called out the hangmen."

"That's preposterous. There's no way you could prove he'd been reached."

"Prove it? I don't have to prove it, I know it."

"How?"

"I saw it in his eyes, you son of a bitch."

The man from State paused, then spoke softly. "You're tired, Bray. You need a rest."

"With a pension," asked Scofield, "or with a casket?"

4

Taleniekov walked out of the restaurant into a cold blast of wind that disturbed the snow, swirling it up from the sidewalk with such force that it became a momentary haze, diffusing the light of the streetlamp above. It was going to be another freezing night. The weather report on Radio Moscow had the temperature dropping to minus eight Celsius.

Yet it had stopped snowing early that morning; the runways at Sheremetyevo Airport were cleared and that was all that concerned Vasili Taleniekov at the moment. Air France, Flight 85, had left for Paris ten minutes ago. Aboard that plane was a Jew who was meant to leave two hours later on Aeroflot for Athens.

He would not have left for Athens if he had shown up at the Aeroflot terminal. Instead, he would have been asked to step into a room. Greeting him would have been a team from the Vodennaya Kontra Rozvedka, and the absurdity would have begun.

It was stupid, thought Taleniekov, as he turned right, pulling the lapels of his overcoat up around his neck and the brim of his *addyel* lower on his head. Stupid in the sense that the VKR would have accomplished nothing but provide a wealth of embarrassment. It would have fooled no one, least of all those it was trying to impress.

A dissident recanting his dissidency! What comic literature did the young fanatics in the VKR read? Where were the older and wiser heads when fools came up with such schemes?

When Vasili had heard of the plan, he had laughed, actually *laughed*. The objective was to mount a brief but strong campaign against Zionist accusations, to show people in the West that not all Jews thought alike in Soviet Russia.

The Jewish writer had become something of a minor cause in the American press—the New York press, to be specific. He had been among those who had spoken to a visiting senator in search of votes 8,000 miles away from a constituency. But race notwithstanding, he simply was not a good writer, and, in fact, something of an embarrassment to his co-religionists.

Not only was the writer the wrong choice for such an exercise, but for reasons intrinsic to another operation it was imperative that he be permitted to leave Russia. He was a blind trade-off for the senator in New York. The senator had been led to believe it was his acquaintanceship with an attaché at the consulate that had caused Soviet immigration to issue a visa; the senator would make capital out of the incident and a small hook would exist where one had not existed before. Enough hooks and an awkward relationship would suddenly exist between the senator and "acquaintances" within the Soviet power structure; it could be useful. The Jew had to leave Moscow tonight. In three days the senator had scheduled a welcoming news conference at Kennedy Airport.

But the young aggressive thinkers at the VKR were adamant. The writer would be detained, brought to the Lubyanka, and the process of transformation would commence. No one outside the VKR was to be told of the operation; success depended upon sudden disappearance, total secrecy. Chemicals were to have been administered until the subject was ready for a different sort of news conference. One in which he revealed that Israeli terrorists had threatened him with reprisals against relatives in Tel Aviv if he did not follow their instructions and cry publicly to be able to leave Russia.

The scheme was preposterous and Vasili had said as much to his contact at the VKR, but was told confidentially that not even the extraordinary Taleniekov could interfere with Group Nine, Vodennaya Kontra Rozvedka. And what in the name of all the discredited Tzars was Group Nine?

It was the *new* Group Nine, his friend had explained. It was the successor to the infamous Section Nine, KGB. Smert Shpiononam. That division of Soviet intelligence devoted exclusively to the breaking of men's minds and wills through extortion, torture and that most terrible of methods—killing loved ones in front of loved ones.

Killing was nothing strange to Vasili Taleniekov, but that kind of killing turned his stomach. The *threat* of such killing was often useful, but not the act itself. The State did not require it, and only sadists demanded it. If there was truly a successor to Smert Shpiononam, then he would let it know with whom it had to contend within the larger sphere of KGB. Specifically, one "extraordinary Taleniekov." They would learn not to contradict a man who had spent twenty-five years roaming all of Europe in the cause of the State.

Twenty-five years. It had been a quarter of a century since a twenty-one-year-old student with a gift for languages had been taken out of his classes at the Leningrad University and sent to Moscow for three years of intensive training. It was training the likes of which the son of introspective Socialist teachers could barely believe. He had been plucked out of a quiet home where books and music were the staples, and set down in a world of conspiracy and violence, where ciphers, codes, and physical abuse were the main ingredients. Where all forms of surveillance and sabotage, espionage and the taking of life—not murder; murder was a term that had no application—were the subjects studied.

He might have failed had it not been for an incident that changed his life and gave him the motive to excel. It had been provided by animals—American animals.

He had been sent to East Berlin on a training exercise, an observer of undercover tactics at the height of the Cold War. He had formed a relationship with a young woman, a German girl who fervently believed in the cause of the Marxist state, and who had been recruited by the KGB. Her position was so minor her name was not even on a payroll; she was an unimportant organizer of demonstrations, paid with loose Reichsmarks from an expense drawer. She was quite simply a university student far more passionate in her beliefs than knowledgeable, a wild-eyed radical who considered herself a kind of Joan of Arc. But Vasili had loved her.

They had lived together for several weeks and they were glorious weeks, filled with the excitement and anticipation of young love. And then one day she was sent across Checkpoint Kasimir. It was such an unimportant thing, a street corner protest on the Kurfürstendamm. A child leading other children, mouthing words they barely understood, espousing commitments they were ill-prepared to accept. An unimportant ritual. Insignificant.

But not to the animals of the American Army of Occupation, G2 Branch, who set other animals upon her.

Her body was sent back in a hearse, her face bruised almost beyond recognition, the rest of her clawed to the point where the flesh was torn, the blood splotches of dried red dust. And the doctors had confirmed the worst. She had been repeatedly raped and sodomized.

Attached to the body—the note held in place by a nail driven into her arm—were the words: *Up your commie ass. Just like hers.*

Animals!

American animals who bought their way to victory without a shell having fallen on their soil, whose might was measured by unfettered industry that made enormous profits from the carnage of foreign lands, whose soldiers peddled cans of food to hungry children so as to gratify other appetites. All armies had animals, but the Americans were most offensive; they proclaimed such righteousness. The sanctimonious were always the most offensive.

Taleniekov had returned to Moscow, the memory of the girl's obscene death burned into his mind. Whatever he had been, he became something else. According to many, he became the best there was, and by his own lights none could possibly wish to be better than he was. He had seen the enemy and he was filth. But that enemy had resources beyond imagination, wealth beyond belief; so it was necessary to be better than the enemy in things that could not be purchased. One had to learn to think as he did. Then outthink him. Vasili had understood this; he became the master of strategy and counterstrategy, the springer of unexpected traps, the deliverer of unanticipated shock—death in the morning sunlight on a crowded street corner.

Death in the Unter den Linden at five o'clock in the afternoon. At that hour when the traffic was maximum.

He had brought that about, too. He had avenged the murder of a child-woman years later, when as the director of KGB operations, East Berlin, he had drawn the wife of an American killer across the checkpoint. She had been run down cleanly, professionally, with a minimum of pain; it was a far more merciful death than that delivered by the animals four years earlier.

He had nodded in appreciation at the news of that death, yet there was no joy. He knew what that man was going through, and as deserved as it was, there was no elation. For Taleniekov also knew that that man would not rest until he found his own vengeance.

He did. Three years later in Prague.

A brother.

Where was the hated Scofield these days? wondered Vasili. It was close to a quarter of a century for him, too. They each had served their causes well, that much could be said for both of them. But Scofield was more fortunate; things were less complicated in Washington, one's enemies within more defined. The despised Scofield did not have to put up with such amateurish maniacs as Group Nine, VKR. The American State Department had its share of madmen, but sterner controls were exercised, Vasili had to admit that. In a few years, if Scofield survived in Europe, he would retire to some remote place and grow chickens or oranges or drink himself into oblivion. He did not have to be concerned about surviving in Washington, just in Europe.

Taleniekov had to worry about surviving in Moscow.

Things . . . *things* had changed in a quarter of a century. And he had changed; tonight was an example, but not the first. He had covertly thwarted the objectives of a fellow intelligence unit. He would not have done so five years ago—perhaps not even two years ago. He would have confronted the strategists of that unit, and strenuously objected on professional grounds. He was an expert, and in his expert judgment, the operation was not only miscalculated, but less vital than another with which it interfered.

He did not take such action these days. He had not done so during the past two years as director of the Southwest Sectors. He had made his own decisions, caring little for the reactions of damn fools who knew far less than he did. Increasingly, those reactions caused minor furors back in Moscow; still he did what he believed was right. Ultimately, those minor furors became major grievances and he was recalled to the Kremlin and a desk where strategies were remote, dealing with progressive abstractions such as getting shadowy hooks into an American politician.

Taleniekov had fallen, he knew that. It was only a question of time. How much time had he left? Would he be given a small *fverma* north of Grasnov and told to grow his crops and keep his own counsel? Or would the maniacs interfere with that course of action, too? Would they claim the "extraordinary Taleniekov" was, indeed, too dangerous?

As he made his way along the street, Vasili felt tired. Even the loathing he felt for the American killer who had murdered his brother was muted in the twilight of his feelings. He had little feeling left.

The sudden snowstorm reached blizzard proportions, the winds gale force, causing eruptions of huge white sprays through the expanse of Red Square. Lenin's Tomb would be covered by morning. Taleniekov let the freezing particles massage his face as he trudged against the wind toward his flat. KGB had been considerate; his rooms were ten minutes from his office in Dzerzhinsky Square, three blocks away from the Kremlin. It was either consideration, or something less benevolent but infinitely more practical: his flat was ten minutes from the centers of crisis, three minutes in a fast automobile.

He walked into the entranceway of his building, stamping his feet as he pulled the heavy door shut, cutting off the harsh sound of the wind. As he always did, he checked his mail slot in the wall and as always, there was nothing. It was a futile ritual that had become a meaningless habit for so many years, in so many mail slots, in so many different buildings.

The only personal mail he ever received was in foreign countries—under strange names—when he was in deep cover. And then, the correspondence was in code and cipher, its meaning in no way related to the words on the paper. Yet sometimes those words were warm and friendly, and he would pretend for a few minutes that they meant what they said. But only for a few minutes; it did no good to pretend. Unless one was analyzing an enemy.

He started up the narrow staircase, annoyed by the dim light of the low-wattage bulbs. He was quite sure the planners in Moscow's Iliktrichiskaya did not live in such buildings.

Then he heard the creak. It was not the result of structural stress; it had nothing to do with the subfreezing cold or the winds outside. It was the sound of a human being shifting his weight on a floorboard. His ears were the ears of a trained craftsman, distances judged quickly. The sound did not come from the landing above, but from higher up the staircase. His flat was on the next floor; someone was waiting for him to approach. Someone wanted him inside his rooms perhaps, egress awkward, a trap being set.

Vasili continued his climb, the rhythm of his footsteps unbroken. The years had trained him to keep such items as keys and coins in his left-hand pockets, freeing his right to reach quickly for a weapon, or to be used as a weapon itself. He came to the landing and turned; his door was only feet away.

There was the creak again, faint, barely heard, mixed with the sound of the distant wind outside. Whoever was on the staircase had moved back, and that told him two things: the intruder would wait until he was definitely inside his flat, and whoever it was was either careless or inexperienced or both. One did not move when this close to a quarry; the air was a conductor of motion.

In his left hand was his key; his right had unfastened the buttons of his overcoat and was now gripped around the handle of his automatic, strapped in an open holster across his chest. He inserted the key, opened the door, then yanked it shut, stepping back rapidly, silently into the shadows of the staircase. He stayed against the wall, his gun leveled in front of him over the railing.

The sound of footsteps preceded the rushing figure as it raced to the door. In the figure's left hand was an object; he could not see it now, it was hidden by the heavily clothed body. Nor were there seconds to wait. If the object was an explosive, it would be on a timer-release. The figure had raised his right hand to knock on the door.

"Press yourself into the door! Your *left hand in front* of you! Between your stomach and the wood! *Now!*"

"Please!" The figure spun halfway around; Taleniekov was on him, throwing him against the panel. He was a young man, a boy really, barely in his teens, thought Vasili. He was tall for his age, but his age was obvious from his face; it was callow, the eyes wide and clear and frightened.

"Move back slowly," said Taleniekov harshly. "Raise your left hand. *Slowly.*"

The young man moved back, his left hand exposed; it was clenched into a fist.

"I didn't do anything wrong, sir. I swear it!" The young man's whisper cracked in fear.

"Who are you?"

"Andreev Danilovich, sir. I live in the Cheremushki."

"You're a long way from home," said Vasili. The housing development referred to by the youth was nearly forty-five minutes south of Red Square. "The weather's terrible and someone your age could be picked up by the *militsianyer.*"

"I had to come here, sir," answered Andreev. "A man's been shot; he's hurt very badly. I think he's going to die. I am to give this to you." He opened his left hand; in it was a brass emblem, an army insignia denoting the rank of general. Its design had not been used in more than thirty years. "The old man said to say the name Krupskaya, Aleksie Krupskaya. He made me say it several times so I wouldn't forget it. It's not the name he uses down at the Cheremushki, but it's the one he said to give you. He said I must bring you to him. He's dying, sir!"

At the sound of the name, Taleniekov's mind raced back in time. Aleksie Krupskaya! It was a name he had not heard in years, a name few people in Moscow wanted to hear. Krupskaya was once the greatest teacher in the KGB, a man of infinite talent for killing and survival—as well he might be. He was the last of the notorious Istrebiteli, that highly specialized group of exterminators that had been an élite outgrowth of the old NKVD, its roots in the barely remembered OGPU.

But Aleksie Krupskaya had disappeared—as so many had disappeared—at least a dozen years ago. There had been rumors linking him to the deaths of Beria and Zhurkov, some even mentioning Stalin himself. Once in a fit of rage—or fear—Khrushchev had stood up in the Presidium and called Krupskaya and his associates a band of maniacal killers. That was not true; there was never any mania in the work of the Istrebiteli, it was too methodical. Regardless, suddenly one day Aleksie Krupskaya was no longer seen at the Lubyanka.

Yet there were other rumors. Those that spoke of documents prepared by Krupskaya, hidden in some remote place, that were his guarantees to a personal old age. It was said these documents incriminated various leaders of the Kremlin in scores of killings—reported, unreported, and disguised. So it was presumed that Aleksie Krupskaya was living out his life somewhere north of Grasnov, on a *fverma*, perhaps, growing crops and keeping his mouth shut.

He had been the finest teacher Vasili had ever had; without the old master's patient instructions, Taleniekov would have been killed years ago. "Where is he?" asked Vasili.

"We brought him down to our flat. He kept pounding on the floor—our ceiling. We ran up and found him."

"We?"

"My sister and I. He's a good old man. He's been good to my sister and me. Our parents are dead. And I think he will soon be dead, too. Please, hurry, sir!"

The old man on the bed was not the Aleksie Krupskaya Taleniekov remembered. The close-cropped hair and the clean-shaven face that once displayed such strength were no more. The skin was pale and stretched, wrinkled beneath the white beard, and his long white hair was a bird's nest of tiny thin strings, matted, separated, revealing splotches of grayish flesh that was Krupskaya's gaunt skull. The man was dying and could barely speak. He lowered the covers briefly and lifted a blood-soaked cloth away from the perforated flesh of a bullet wound.

Virtually no time was spent on greetings; the respect and affection in each man's eyes were sufficient.

"I widened my pupils into the death-stare," said Krupskaya, smiling weakly. "He thought I was dead. He had done his job and ran."

"Who was it?"

"An assassin. Sent by the Corsicans."

"The Corsicans? What Corsicans?"

The old man took a long, painful breath, gesturing for Vasili to lean closer. "I will be dead before the hour is gone, and there are things you must be told. No one else will tell you; you are the best we have and you *must* be told. Above all men, you have the skills to match their skills. You and another, one from each side. You may be all that's left."

"What are you talking about?"

"The Matarese."

"The *what?*"

"The Matarese. They know I know . . . what they are doing, what they are about to do. I am the only one left who would recognize them, who would dare speak of them. I stopped the contacts once, but I had neither the courage nor the ambition to expose them."

"I can't understand you."

"I will try to explain." Krupskaya paused, gathering strength. "A short while ago, a general named Blackburn was killed in America."

"Yes, I know. The Chairman of the Joint Chiefs. We were not involved, Aleksie."

"Are you aware that *you* were the one the Americans believed the most likely assassin?"

"No one told me. It's ridiculous."

"No one tells you much anymore, do they?"

"I don't fool myself, old friend. I've given. I don't know how much more I have to give. Grasnov is not far distant, perhaps."

"If it is permitted," interrupted Krupskaya.

"I think it will be."

"No matter. . . . Last month, the scientist, Yurievich. He was murdered while on holiday up in a Provasoto *dacha*, along with Colonel Drigorin and the man, Brunov, from Industrial Planning."

"I heard about it," said Taleniekov. "I gather it was horrible."

"Did you read the report?"

"What report?"

"The one compiled by VKR—"

"Madmen and fools," interjected Taleniekov.

"Not always," corrected Krupskaya. "In this case they have specific facts, accurate as far as they go."

"What are these supposedly accurate facts?"

Krupskaya, breathing with difficulty, swallowed and continued. "Shell casings, seven millimeter, American. Bore markings from a Browning Magnum, Grade Four."

"A brutal gun," said Taleniekov, nodding. "Very reliable. And the last weapon that would be used by someone sent from Washington."

The old man did not seem to hear. "The gun used to kill General Blackburn was a Graz-Burya."

Vasili raised his eyebrows. "A prized weapon when obtainable." He paused and added quietly, "I favor mine."

"Exactly. As the Magnum, Grade Four, is a favored weapon of another."

Taleniekov stiffened. "Oh?"

"Yes, Vasili. VKR came up with several names it thinks could be responsible for Yurievich's death. The leading contender was a man you despise: 'Beowulf Agate.' "

Taleniekov spoke in a monotone. "Brandon Scofield, Consular Operations. Code name, Prague—Beowulf Agate."

"Yes."

"Was he?"

"No." The old man struggled to raise his head on the pillow. "No more than you were involved with Blackburn's death. Don't you see? They know everything; even of operatives whose skills are proven, but whose minds are tired. Who, perhaps, need a significant kill. They are testing the highest levels of power before they make their move."

"Who? Who are *they?*"

"The Matarese. The Corsican fever—"

"What does that *mean?*"

"It spreads. It has changed, far more deadly in its new form." The old Istrebiteli fell back on the pillow.

"You must be clearer, Aleksie. I can see nothing. What is this Corsican fever, this . . . Matarese?"

Krupskaya's eyes were wide, now staring at the ceiling; he whispered. "No one speaks; no one dares to speak. Our own Presidium; England's Foreign Office, its MI-Six boardroom; the French Société Diable d'État. And the Americans. Oh, never forget the Americans! . . . No one speaks. We all used it! We are stained by the Matarese."

"*Stained?* How? What are you trying to say? What in heaven's name *is* the Matarese?"

The old man turned his head slowly; his lips trembled. "Some say it goes back as far as Sarajevo. Others swear it claims Dollfuss, Bernadotte . . . even Trotsky on its list. We know about Stalin; we contracted for his death."

"Stalin? It's true then what was said?"

"Oh, yes. Beria, too; we paid." The Istrebiteli's eyes seemed now to float out of focus. "In forty-five . . . the world thought Roosevelt succumbed to a massive stroke." Krupskaya shook his head slowly, saliva at the corners of his mouth. "There were financial interests who believed his policies with the Soviets were economically disastrous. They could not permit any further decisions on his part. They paid, and an injection was administered."

Taleniekov was stunned. "Are you telling me that Roosevelt was *killed?* By this *Matarese?*"

"Assassinated, Vasili Vasilivich Taleniekov. That is the word, and that is one of the truths no one will speak of. So many . . . for so many years. None dare talk of the contracts, the payments. The admissions would be catastrophic . . . for governments everywhere."

"But *why?* Why was it used, this Matarese?"

"Because it was available. And it removed the client from the scene."

"It's preposterous! Assassins have been *caught*. There's been no such name ever mentioned!"

"You should know better than that, Vasili Vasilivich. You've used the same tactics yourself; no different from the Matarese."

"What do you mean?"

"You both kill . . . and program killers." The old man acknowledged Taleniekov's nod. "The Matarese was dormant for years. Then it came back, but it was not the same. Killings took place without clients, without payments. Senseless butchery without a pattern. Men of value kidnapped and slain; aircraft stolen or blown up in mid-air, governments paralyzed—payments demanded or wholesale slaughter the result. The incidents have become more refined, more professional."

"You're describing the work of terrorists, Aleksie. Terrorism has no central apparatus."

Once again the old Istrebiteli struggled to raise his head. "It does *now*. It has for the past several years. Baader-Meinhoff, the Red Brigades, the Palestinians, the African maniacs—they all gravitate to the Matarese. It kills with impunity. And now it is throwing the two superpowers into chaos before it makes its boldest move. And that is to assume control of one or the other. Ultimately, both."

"How can you be certain?"

"A man was caught, a blemish on his chest, a soldier of the Matarese. Chemicals were administered, everyone ordered from the room but my source. I had warned him."

"*You?*"

"Hear me out. There is a timetable, but to speak of it would be to acknowledge the past; none dare do that! Moscow by assassination, Washington by political maneuver, murder if necessary. Two months, three at the outside; everything is in motion now. Action and reaction has been tested at the highest levels, unknown men positioned at the centers of power. Soon it will happen, and when it does, we are consumed. We are destroyed, subjects of the Matarese."

"Where is this man?"

"Dead. The chemicals wore off; there was a cyanide pellet sewn into his skin. He tore his own flesh and reached it."

"Assassination? Political maneuver, murder? You must be more specific."

Krupskaya's breath came shorter as he again fell back on the pillow. But strangely, his voice grew firmer. "There is no time—I do not *have* the time. My source is the most reliable in Moscow—in all the Soviet."

"Forgive me, dear Aleksie, you were the best, but you do not exist anymore. Everyone knows that."

"You must reach Beowulf Agate," said the old Istrebiteli, as though Vasili had not spoken. "You and he must find them. Stop them. Before one of us is taken, the other's destruction guaranteed. You and the man Scofield. You are best now, and the best are needed."

Taleniekov looked impassively at the dying Krupskaya. "That is something no one can ask me to do. If Beowulf Agate were in my sight, I would kill him. As he would kill me, if he were capable."

"You are *insignificant!*" The old man had to breathe slowly, in desperation, to get the air back in his lungs. "You have no time for yourselves, can't you understand that? They are in our clandestine services, in the most powerful circles of both governments. They used the two of you once; they will use you again, and *again.* They use only the best and they will kill only the best! You are their diversions, you and men like you!"

"Where is the proof?"

"In the pattern," whispered Krupskaya. "I've studied it. I know it well."

"What pattern?"

"The Graz-Burya shells in New York; the seven-millimeter casings of a Browning Magnum in Provasoto. Within hours Moscow and Washington were at each other's throats. This is the way of the Matarese. It never kills without leaving evidence—often the killers themselves—but it is never the right evidence, never the true killers."

"Men have been caught who pulled triggers, Aleksie."

"For the wrong reasons. For reasons provided by the Matarese. . . . Now, it takes us to the edge of chaos and overthrow."

"But *why?*"

Krupskaya turned his head, his eyes in focus, pleading. "I don't *know.* The pattern is there but not the *reasons* for it. That is what frightens me. One must go back to understand. The roots of the Matarese are in Corsica. The madman of Corsica; it started with him. The Corsican fever. Guillaume de Matarese. He was the high priest."

"When?" asked Taleniekov. "How long ago?"

"During the early years of the century. Guillaume de Matarese and his council. The high priest and his ministers. They've come back. They must be stopped. You and the man Scofield!"

"Who are they?" asked Vasili. "Where are they?"

"No one knows." The old man's voice was failing now. He was failing. "The Corsican fever. It spreads."

"Aleksie, *listen* to me," said Taleniekov, disturbed by a possibility that could not be overlooked: the fantasies of a dying man could not be taken seriously. "Who is this reliable source of yours? Who is the man so knowledgeable in Moscow—in all the Soviet? How did you get the information you've given me? About the killing of Blackburn, the VKR report on Yurievich? Above all, this unknown man who speaks of timetables?"

Through the personal haze of his approaching death, Krupskaya understood. A faint smile appeared on his thin, pale lips. "Every few days," he said, struggling to be heard, "a driver comes to see me, perhaps take me for a ride in the countryside. Sometimes to meet quietly with another. It's the State's kindness to a pensioned old soldier whose name was appropriated. I am kept informed."

"I don't understand, Aleksie."

"The Premier of Soviet Russia is my source."

"The Premier! But why you?"

"He is my son."

Taleniekov felt a wave of cold rush through him. The revelation explained so much. Krupskaya had to be taken seriously; the old Istrebiteli had possessed the information—the ammunition—to eliminate all who stood in the way of his son's march to premiership of Soviet Russia.

"Would he see me?"

"Never. At the first mention of the Matarese, he would have you shot. Try to understand, he would have no choice. But he knows I am right. He agrees, but will never acknowledge it; he cannot afford to. He simply wonders whether it is he or the American President who will be in the gunsight."

"I understand."

"Leave me now," said the dying Krupskaya. "Do what you must do, Talenie-kov. I have no more breath. Reach Beowulf Agate, find the Matarese. It must be stopped. The Corsican fever can spread no further."

"The Corsican fever? . . . In *Corsica?*"

"The answer may be there. It is the only place to start. Names. The first council! Many years ago."

5

A coronary inefficiency had made it necessary for Robert Winthrop to use a wheelchair, but in no way did it impair the alertness of his mind, nor did he dwell on the infirmity. He had spent his life in the service of his government; there was never any lack of problems he considered more important than himself.

Guests at his Georgetown home soon forgot the wheelchair. The slender figure with the graceful gestures and the intensely interested face reminded them of the man he was: an energetic aristocrat who had used his private fortune to free himself from the marketplace and pursue a life of public advocacy. Instead of an infirm elder statesman with thinning gray hair and the still perfectly clipped moustache, one thought of Yalta and Potsdam and an aggressive younger man from the State Department forever leaning over Roosevelt's chair or Truman's shoulder to clarify this point or suggest that objection.

There were many in Washington—and in London and Moscow as well—who thought the world would be a better place had Robert Winthrop been made Secretary of State by Eisenhower, but the political winds had shifted and he was not a feasible choice. And later, Winthrop could not be considered; he had become involved in another area of government that required his full concentration. He had been quietly retained as Senior Consultant, Diplomatic Relations, Department of State.

Twenty-six years ago Robert Winthrop had organized a select division within State called Consular Operations. And after sixteen years of commitment he had resigned—some said because he was appalled at what his creation had become, while others claimed he was only too aware of the necessary directions it had taken, but could not bring himself to make certain decisions. Nevertheless, during the ten years since his departure, he had been consistently sought out for advice and counsel. As he was tonight.

Consular Operations had a new director. A career intelligence officer named Daniel Congdon had been shifted from a ranking position at the National Security Agency to the clandestine chair at State. He had replaced Winthrop's successor and was finely attuned to the harsh decisions required by *Cons Op*. But he was new; he had questions. He also had a problem with a man named Scofield and was not sure how to handle it. He knew only that he wanted Brandon Alan Scofield terminated, removed from the State Department for good. His actions in Amsterdam could not be tolerated; they revealed a dangerous and unstable man. How much more dangerous would he be removed from the controls of Consular Operations? It was a serious question; the man with the code name, Beowulf Agate knew more about the State Department's clandestine networks than any other man alive. And since Scofield had initially been brought to Washington years ago by Ambassador Robert Winthrop, Congdon went to the source.

Winthrop had readily agreed to make himself available to Congdon but not in an impersonal office or an operations room. Over the years, the Ambassador had learned that men involved with covert operations too instinctively reflected their surroundings. Short, cryptic sentences took the place of freer, rambling conversations wherein a great deal more could be revealed and learned. Therefore, he had invited the new director over for dinner.

The meal was finished, nothing of substance discussed. Congdon understood: the Ambassador was probing the surface before delving deeper. But now the moment had come.

"Let's go into the library, shall we?" said Winthrop, wheeling himself away from the table.

Once inside the book-lined room, the Ambassador wasted no time. "So you want to talk about Brandon."

"Very much so," replied the new director of *Cons Op*.

"How do we thank such men for what they've done?" asked Winthrop. "For what they've lost? The field extracts a terrible price."

"They wouldn't be there if they didn't want to be," said Congdon. "If, for some reason, they didn't need it. But once having been out there and survived, there's another question. What do we do with them? They're walking explosives."

"What are you trying to say?"

"I'm not sure, Mr. Winthrop. I want to know more about him. Who is he? What is he? Where did he come from?"

"The child being the father of the man?"

"Something like that. I've read his file—a number of times, in fact—but I've yet to speak to anyone who really knows him."

"I'm not sure you'll find such a person. Brandon. . . ." The elder statesman paused briefly and smiled. "Incidentally, he's called Bray, for reasons I've never understood. It's the last thing he does. Bray, I mean."

"That's one of the things I've learned," interrupted the director, returning Winthrop's smile as he sat down in a leather armchair. "When he was a child he had a younger sister who couldn't say Brandon; she called him Bray. The name just stuck with him."

"That must have been added to his file after I left. Indeed, I imagine a great deal has been added to that file. But as for his friends, or lack of them, he's simply a private person, quite a bit more so since his wife died."

Congdon spoke quietly. "She was killed, wasn't she?"

"Yes."

"In fact, she was killed in East Berlin ten years ago next month. Isn't that right?"

"Yes."

"And ten years ago next month you resigned the directorship of Consular Operations. The highly specialized unit you built."

Winthrop turned, his eyes leveled at the new director. "What I conceived and what finally emerged were two quite different entities. Consular Operations was designed as a humanitarian instrument, to facilitate the defection of thousands from a political system they found intolerable. As time went on—and circumstances seemed to warrant—the objectives were narrowed. The thousands became hundreds—and as other voices were heard, the hundreds were reduced to dozens. We were no longer interested in the scores of men and women who daily appealed to us, but only in those select few whose talents and information were considered far more important than those of ordinary people. The unit concentrated on a handful of scientists and soldiers and intelligence specialists. As it does today. That's not what we began with."

"But as you pointed out, sir," said Congdon, "the circumstances warranted the change."

Winthrop nodded. "Don't mistake me, I'm not naive. I dealt with the Russians at Yalta, Potsdam, Casablanca. I witnessed their brutality in Hungary in '56, and I saw the horrors of Czechoslovakia and Greece. I think I know what the Soviets are capable of as well as any strategist in covert services. And for years I permitted those more aggressive voices to speak with authority. I understood the necessity. Did you think I didn't?"

"Of course not. I simply meant . . ." Congdon hesitated.

"You simply made a connection between the murder of Scofield's wife and my resignation," said the statesman kindly.

"Yes, sir, I did. I'm sorry, I didn't mean to pry. It's just that the circumstances. . . ."

" 'Warranted a change,' " completed Winthrop. "That's what happened, you know. I recruited Scofield; I'm sure that's in his file. I suspect that's why you're here tonight."

"Then the connection? . . ." Congdon's words trailed off.

"Accurate. I felt responsible."

"But surely there were other incidents, other men . . . and women."

"Not the same, Mr. Congdon. Do you know why Scofield's wife was selected to be the target that afternoon in East Berlin?"

"I assume it was a trap meant for Scofield himself. Only she showed up and he didn't. It happens."

"A trap meant for Scofield? In *East* Berlin?"

"He had contacts in the Soviet sector. He made frequent penetrations, set up his own cells. I imagine they wanted to catch him with his contact sheets. Her body was searched, her purse taken. It's not unusual."

"Your assumption being that he'd use his wife in the operation?" asked Winthrop.

Congdon nodded. "Again, not unusual, sir."

"Not unusual? I'm afraid in Scofield's case it was impossible. She was part of his cover at the embassy, but never remotely connected to his covert activities. No, Mr. Congdon, you're wrong. The Russians knew they could never spring a trap on Bray Scofield in East Berlin. He was too good, too efficient . . . too elusive. So they tricked his wife into crossing the checkpoint and killed her for another purpose."

"I beg your pardon?"

"An enraged man is a careless man. That's what the Soviets wanted to accomplish. But they, as you, misunderstood their subject. With his rage came a new determination to sting the enemy in every way he could. If he was brutally professional before his wife's death, he was viciously so afterwards."

"I'm still not sure I understand."

"Try, Mr. Congdon," said Winthrop. "Twenty-two years ago I ran across a government major at Harvard University. A young man with a talent for languages and a certain authority about him that indicated a bright future. He was recruited through my office, sent to the Maxwell School in Syracuse, then brought to Washington to become part of Consular Operations. It was a fine beginning for a possibly brilliant career in the State Department." Winthrop paused, his eyes straying as if lost in a personal reverie. "I never expected him to stay in *Cons Op;* strangely enough I thought of it as a springboard for him. To the diplomatic corps, to the ambassadorial level, perhaps. His gifts cried out to be used at international conference tables. . . .

"But something happened," continued the statesman, glancing absently back at the new director. "As *Cons Op* was changing, so was Brandon Scofield. The more vital those highly specialized defections were considered, the quicker the violence escalated. On both sides. Very early, Scofield requested commando training; he spent five months in Central America going through the most rigorous survival techniques—offensive and defensive. He mastered scores of codes and ciphers; he was as proficient as any cryptographer in NSA. Then he returned to Europe and became *the* expert."

"He understood the requirements of his work," said Congdon, impressed. "Very commendable, I'd say."

"Oh yes, very," agreed Winthrop. "Because, you see, it had happened: he'd reached his plateau. There was no turning back, no changing. He could never be accepted around a conference table; his presence would be rejected in the strongest diplomatic terms because his reputation was established. The bright young government major I'd recruited for the State Department was now a killer. No matter the justification, he was a professional killer."

Congdon shifted his position in the chair. "Many would say he was a soldier in the field, the battleground extensive, dangerous . . . never ending. He had to survive, Mr. Winthrop."

"He had to and he did," concurred the old gentleman. "Scofield was able to change, to adapt to the new rules. But I wasn't. When his wife was killed, I knew I didn't belong. I saw what I had done: taken a gifted student for one purpose and seen that purpose warped. Just as the benign concept of Consular Operations had been warped—by circumstances that warranted those changes we spoke of. I had to face my own limitations. I couldn't continue any longer."

"But you did ask to be kept informed of Scofield's activities for several years. That's in the file, sir. May I ask why?"

Winthrop frowned, as if wondering himself. "I'm not sure. An understandable interest in him—even fascination, I suppose. Or punishment, perhaps; that's not out of the question. Sometimes the reports would stay in my safe for days before I read them. And, of course, after Prague I no longer wanted them sent to me. I'm sure that's in the file."

"Yes, it is. By Prague, I assume you refer to the courier incident."

"Yes," answered Winthrop softly. " 'Incident' is such an impersonal word, isn't it? It fit the Scofield in that report. The professional killer, motivated by the need to survive—as a soldier survives, turned into a cold-blooded killer, driven solely by vengeance. The change was complete."

Again the new director of *Cons Op* shifted his position, crossing his legs uncomfortably. "It was established that the courier in Prague was the brother of the KGB agent who ordered the death of Scofield's wife."

"He was the brother, not the man who issued that order. He was a youngster, no more than a low-level messenger."

"He might have become something else."

"Then where does it end?"

"I can't answer that. But I can understand Scofield's doing what he did. I'm not sure I wouldn't have done the same."

"With no sense of righteousness," said the aging statesman. "I'm not sure I would have. Nor am I convinced that that young man in Cambridge twenty-two years ago would have done so. Am I getting through to you, as is so often asked these days?"

"Painfully, sir. But in my defense—and in defense of the current Scofield— we didn't create the world we operate in. I think that's a fair thing to say."

"Painfully fair, Mr. Congdon. But you perpetuate it." Winthrop wheeled his chair to his desk and reached for a box of cigars. He offered the box to the director, who shook his head. "I don't like them, either, but ever since Jack Kennedy we're all expected to keep our supply of Havanas. Do you disapprove?"

"No. As I recall, the Canadian supplier was one of President Kennedy's more accurate sources of information about Cuba."

"Have you been around that long?"

"I joined the National Security Agency when he was a senator. . . . Did you know that Scofield has recently begun to drink?"

"I know nothing about the current Scofield, as you called him."

"His file indicates previous use of alcohol, but no evidence of excess."

"I would think not; it would interfere with his work."

"It may be interfering now."

"*May* be? It either is or it isn't. I don't think that's such a difficult thing to establish. If he's drinking a great deal, that's excess; it would have to interfere. I'm sorry to hear it, but I can't say I'm surprised."

"Oh?" Congdon leaned forward in the chair. It was apparent that he thought he was about to be given the information he was seeking. "When you knew him as well as you did, were there signs of potential instability?"

"None at all."

"But you just said you weren't surprised."

"I'm not. I wouldn't be surprised at any thinking man turning to alcohol after so many years of living so unnaturally. Scofield is—or was—a thinking man, and God knows he's lived unnaturally. If I'm surprised, it's only that it's taken so long to reach him, affect him. What got him through the nights?"

"Men condition themselves. As you put it, he adapted. Extremely successfully."

"But still unnaturally," maintained Winthrop. "What are you going to do with him?"

"He's being recalled. I want him out of the field."

"Good. Give him a desk and an attractive secretary and have him analyze theoretical problems. Isn't that the usual way?"

Congdon hesitated before replying. "Mr. Winthrop, I think I want him separated from the State Department."

The creator of *Cons Op* arched his eyebrows. "Really? Twenty-two years is insufficient for an adequate pension."

"That's not a problem; generous settlements are made. It's common practice these days."

"Then what does he do with his life? What is he? Forty-five . . . six?"

"Forty-six."

"Hardly ready for one of these, is he?" said the statesman, fingering the wheel of his chair. "May I ask why you've come to that conclusion?"

"I don't want him around personnel involved with covert activities. According to our latest information, he's displayed hostile reactions to basic policy. He could be a negative influence."

Winthrop smiled. "Someone must have pulled a beaut. Bray never did have much patience with fools."

"I said *basic* policy, sir. Personalities are not the issue."

"Personalities, Mr. Congdon, unfortunately are *intrinsic* to basic policy. They form it. But that's probably beside the point . . . at this point. Why come to me? You've obviously made your decision. What can I add?"

"Your judgment. How will he take it? Can he be trusted? He knows more about our operations, our contacts, our tactics, than any man in Europe."

Winthrop's eyes became suddenly cold. "And what is your alternative, Mr. Congdon?" he asked icily.

The new director flushed; he understood the implication. "Surveillance. Controls. Telephone and mail intercepts. I'm being honest with you."

"Are you?" Winthrop now glared at the man in front of him. "Or are you looking for a word from me—or a question—that you can use for another solution?"

"I don't know what you mean."

"I think you do. I've heard how it's done, incidentally, and it appalls me. Word is sent to Prague, or Berlin, or Marseilles that a man's no longer in sanction. He's finished, out. But he's restless, drinks a lot. Contacts' names might be revealed by this man, whole networks exposed. In essence, the word spreads: your lives are threatened. So it's agreed that another man, or perhaps two or three, get on planes from Prague or Berlin or Marseilles. They converge on Washington with but one objective: the silencing of that man who's finished. Everyone's more relaxed, and the American intelligence community—which has remained outside the *incident*—breathes easier. Yes, Mr. Congdon, it appalls me."

The director of *Cons Op* remained motionless in the chair. His reply was delivered in a quiet monotone. "To the best of my knowledge, Mr. Winthrop, that solution has been exaggerated far out of proportion to its practice. Again, I'll be completely honest with you. In fifteen years I've heard of it being exercised only twice, and in both . . . incidents . . . the agents out of sanction were beyond salvage. They had sold out to the Soviets; they *were* delivering names."

"Is Scofield 'beyond salvage'? That's the correct phrase, isn't it?"

"If you mean do I think he's sold out, of course not. It's the last thing he'd do. I really came here to learn more about him, I'm sincere about that. How is he going to react when I tell him he's terminated?"

Winthrop paused, his relief conveyed, then frowned again. "I don't know because I don't know the current Scofield. It's drastic; what's he going to do? Isn't there a halfway measure?"

"If I thought there was one acceptable to us both, I'd leap at it."

"If I were you I'd try to find one."

"It can't be on the premises," said Congdon firmly. "I'm convinced of that."

"Then may I suggest something?"

"Please do."

"Send him as far away as you can. Someplace where he'll find a peaceful oblivion. Suggest it yourself; he'll understand."

"He will?"

"Yes. Bray doesn't fool himself, at least he never did. It was one of his finer gifts. He'll understand because I think *I* do. I think you've described a dying man."

"There's no medical evidence to support that."

"Oh, for God's sake," said Robert Winthrop.

Scofield turned off the television set. He had not seen an American news broad-cast in several years—since he was last brought back for an interoperations briefing—and he was not sure he wanted to see one again for the next several years. It wasn't that he thought all news should be delivered in the ponderous tones of a funeral, but the giggles and leers that accompanied descriptions of fire and rape struck him as intolerable.

He looked at his watch; it was twenty past seven. He knew it because his watch read twenty past midnight; he was still on Amsterdam time. His appointment at the State Department was for eight o'clock.

P.M. That was standard for specialists of his rank, but what was not standard was the State Department location itself. Attachés-at-large for Consular Opera-tions invariably held strategy conferences in safe-houses, usually in the Maryland countryside, or perhaps in hotel suites in downtown Washington.

Never at the State Department. Not for specialists expected to return to the field. But then Bray knew he was not scheduled to return to the field. He had been brought back for only one purpose. Termination.

Twenty-two years and he was out. An infinitesimal speck of time into which was compressed everything he knew—everything learned, absorbed and taught. He kept waiting for his own reaction, but there was none. It was as though he were a spectator, watching the images of someone else on a white wall, the inevitable conclusion drawing near, but not drawing him into the events as they took place. He was only mildly curious. How would it be done?

The walls of Undersecretary of State Daniel Congdon's office were white. There was a certain comfort in that, thought Scofield, as he half-listened to Congdon's droning narrative. He could see the images. Face after face, dozens of them, coming into focus and fading rapidly. Faces of people remembered and un-remembered, staring, thinking, weeping, laughing, dying . . . death.

His wife. Five o'clock in the afternoon. Unter den Linden.

Men and women running, stopping. In sunlight, in shadows.

But where was he? He was not there.

He was a spectator.

Then suddenly he wasn't. He could not be sure he heard the words correctly. What had this coldly efficient undersecretary said? *Bern, Switzerland?*

"I beg your pardon?"

"The funds will be deposited in your name, proportionate allocations made annually."

"In addition to whatever pension I'm entitled to?"

"Yes, Mr. Scofield. And regarding that, your service record's been predated. You'll get the maximum."

"That's very generous." It *was*. Calculating rapidly, Bray estimated that his income would be over $50,000 a year.

"Merely practical. These funds are to take the place of any profits you might realize from the sale of books or articles based on your activities in Consular Operations."

"I see," said Bray slowly. "There's been a lot of that recently, hasn't there? Marchetti, Agee, Snepp."

"Exactly."

Scofield could not help himself; the bastards *never* learned. "Are you saying that if you'd banked funds for them they wouldn't have written what they did?"

"Motives vary, but we don't rule out the possibility."

"Rule it out," said Bray curtly. "I know two of those men."

"Are you rejecting the money?"

"Hell, no. I'll take it. When I decide to write a book, you'll be the first to know."

"I wouldn't advise it, Mr. Scofield. Such breaches of security are prohibited. You'd be prosecuted, years in prison inevitable."

"And if you lost in the courts, there just *might* follow certain extralegal penalties. A shot in the head while driving in traffic, for example."

"The laws are clear," said the undersecretary. "I can't imagine that."

"I can. Look in my Four-Zero file. I trained with a man in Honduras. I killed him in Madrid. He was from Indianapolis and his name was—"

"I'm *not interested* in past activities," interrupted Congdon harshly. "I just want us to understand each other."

"We do. You can relax, I'm not . . . breaching any security. I haven't the stomach for it. Also, I'm not that brave."

"Look, Scofield," said the undersecretary, leaning back in his chair, his expression pleasant. "I know it sounds trite, but there comes a time for all of us to leave the more active areas of our work. I want to be honest with you."

Bray smiled, a touch grimly. "I'm always nervous when someone says that."

"What?"

"That he wants to be honest with you. As if honesty was the last thing you should expect."

"I *am* being honest."

"So am I. If you're looking for an argument, you won't get it from me. I'll quietly fade away."

"But we don't want you to do that," said Congdon, leaning forward, his elbows on the desk.

"Oh?"

"Of course not. A man with your background is extraordinarily valuable to us. Crises will continue to arise; we'd like to be able to call upon your expertise."

Scofield studied the man. "But not in-territory." A statement. "Not in-strategy."

"No. Not officially. Naturally, we'll want to know where you're living, what trips you make."

"I'll bet you will," said Bray softly. "But for the record, I'm terminated."

"Yes. However, we'd like it kept out of the record. A Four-Zero entry."

Scofield did not move. He had the feeling that he was in the field, arranging a very sensitive exchange. "Wait a minute, let me understand you. You want me officially terminated, but no one's supposed to know it. And although I'm officially finished, you want to maintain contact on a permanent basis."

"Your knowledge is invaluable to us, you know that. And I think we're paying for it."

"Why the Four-Zero then?"

"I'd have thought you'd appreciate it. Without official responsibilities you retain a certain status. You're still part of us."

"I'd like to know why this way."

"I'll be . . ." Congdon stopped, a slightly embarrassed smile on his face. "We really *don't* want to lose you."

"Then why terminate me?"

The smile left the undersecretary's face. "I'll call it as I see it. You can confirm it with an old friend of yours if you like. Robert Winthrop. I told him the same thing."

"Winthrop? What did you tell him?"

"That I don't want you around here. And I'm willing to pay out of budget and predate records to get you out. I listened to your words; you were taped by Charles Englehart in Amsterdam."

Bray whistled softly. "Old Crimson Charlie. I should have known it."

"I thought you did. I thought you were sending us a personal message. Nevertheless, we got it. We have a lot to do here and your kind of obstinacy, your cynicism, isn't needed."

"Now, we're getting somewhere."

"But everything else is true. We *do* need your expertise. We have to be able to reach you anytime. You have to be able to reach *us.*"

Bray nodded. "And the Four-Zero means that my separation is top secret. The field doesn't know I'm terminated."

"Precisely."

"All right," said Scofield, reaching into his pocket for a cigarette. "I think you're going to a lot of unnecessary trouble to keep a string on me, but, as you said, you're paying for it. A simple field directive could accomplish the same thing: issue clearance until rescinded. Special category."

"Too many questions would be asked. It's easier this way."

"Really?" Bray lit the cigarette, his eyes amused. "All right."

"Good." Congdon shifted his weight in the chair. "I'm glad we understand each other. You've earned everything we've given you and I'm sure you'll continue to earn it. . . . I was looking at your file this morning; you enjoy the water. God knows your record's filled with hundreds of contacts made in boats at night. Why not try it in the daylight? You've got the money. Why not go to someplace like the Caribbean and enjoy your life? I envy you."

Bray got up from his chair; the meeting was over. "Thanks, I may do that. I like warm climates." He extended his hand; Congdon rose and took it. While they shook hands, Scofield continued. "You know that Four-Zero business would make me nervous if you hadn't called me in here."

"What do you mean?" Their hands were clasped, but the movement stopped.

"Well, our own field personnel won't know I'm terminated, but the Soviets will. They won't bother me now. When someone like me is taken out-of-strategy, everything changes. Contacts, codes, ciphers, sterile locations; nothing remains the same. They know the rules; they'll leave me alone. Thanks very much."

"I'm not sure I understand you," said the undersecretary.

"Oh, come on, I said I'm grateful. We both know that the KGB operations in Washington keep their cameras trained on this place twenty-four hours a day. No specialist who's to remain in sanction is *ever* brought here. As of an hour ago they know I'm out. Thanks again, Mr. Congdon. It was considerate of you."

The Undersecretary of State, Consular Operations, watched as Scofield walked across the office and let himself out the door.

It was over. Everything. He would never have to hurry back to an antiseptic hotel room to see what covert message had arrived. No longer would it be necessary to arrange for three changes of vehicle to get from point *A* to point *B*. The lie to Congdon notwithstanding, the Soviets probably did know by now he had been terminated. If they didn't, they would soon. After a few months of inactivity, the KGB would accept the fact that he was no longer of value. That rule was constant; tactics and codes *were* altered. The Soviets would leave him alone; they would not kill him.

But the lie to Congdon had been necessary, if only to see the expression on his face. *We'd like it kept out of the record. Four-Zero entry.* The man was so transparent! He really believed he had created the climate for the execution of his own man, a man he considered dangerous. That a supposedly active agent would be killed by the Soviets for the sake of a kill. Then—pointing to official separation—the Department of State would disclaim any responsibility, no doubt insisting that the dead man refused safeguards.

The bastards *never* changed, but they knew so little. An execution for its own sake was pointless, the fallout often too hazardous. One killed for a purpose; to learn something by removing a vital link in a chain, or to stop something from happening. Or to teach a specific lesson. But always for a reason.

Except in instances like Prague, and even that could be considered a lesson. *A brother for a wife.*

But it was over. There were no strategies to create, no decisions to make that resulted in a defection or a turnback, of someone living or not living. It was *over.*

Perhaps now even the hotel rooms would come to an end. And the stinking beds in rundown rooming houses in the worst sections of a hundred cities. He was so sick of them; he despised them all. With the exception of a single brief period—too brief, too *terribly* brief—he had not lived in a place he could call his own for twenty-two years.

But that pitifully brief period, twenty-seven months in a lifetime, was enough to see him through the agonies of a thousand nightmares. The memories never left him; they would sustain him until the day he died.

It had been only a small flat in West Berlin, but it was the home of dreams and love and laughter he had never thought he'd be capable of knowing. His beautiful Karine, his adorable Karine. She of the wide, curious eyes and the laughter that came from deep inside her, and moments of quiet when she touched him. He was hers and she was his and . . .

Death in the Unter den Linden.

Oh, *God!* A telephone call and a password. Her husband needed her. *Desperately.* See a guard, cross the checkpoint. *Hurry!*

And a KGB pig had no doubt laughed. Until Prague. There was no laughter in that man after Prague.

Scofield could feel the sting in his eyes. The few sudden tears had made contact with the night wind. He brushed them aside with his glove and crossed the street.

On the other side was the lighted front of a travel agency, the posters in the window displaying idealized, unreal bodies soaking up the sun. The Washington amateur, Congdon, had a point; the Caribbean was a good idea. No self-respecting intelligence service sent agents to the islands in the Caribbean—for fear of winning. Down in the islands, the Soviets would *know* he was out-of-strategy. He had wanted to spend some time in the Grenadines; why not now? In the morning he would. . . .

The figure was reflected in the glass—tiny, obscure, in the background across the wide avenue, barely noticeable. In fact, Bray would *not* have noticed had the man not walked around the spill of a streetlamp. Whoever it was wanted the protection of the shadows in the street; whoever it was was following him. And he was good. There were no abrupt movements, no sudden jumping away from the light. The walk was casual, unobtrusive. He wondered if it was anyone he had trained.

Scofield appreciated professionalism; he would commend the man and wish him a lesser subject for surveillance next time. The State Department was not wasting a moment. Congdon wanted the reports to begin at once. Bray smiled; he would give the undersecretary his initial report. Not the one he wanted, but one he should have.

The amusement began, a short-lived pavane between professionals. Scofield walked away from the storefront window, gathering speed until he reached the corner, where the circles of light from the four opposing streetlamps overlapped each other. He turned abruptly left, as if to head back to the other side of the street, then halfway through the intersection stopped. He paused in the middle of the traffic lane and looked up at the street sign—a man confused, not sure of where he was. Then he turned and walked rapidly back to the corner, his pace quickening until he was practically running when he reached the curb. He continued down the pavement to the first unlighted storefront, then he spun into the darkness of the doorway and waited.

Through the right-angled glass he had a clear view of the corner. The man following him would have to come into the overlapping circles of light now; they could not be avoided. A quarry was getting away; there was no time to look for shadows.

It happened. The overcoated figure came dashing across the avenue. His face came into the light.

His face came into the light.

Scofield froze. His eyes ached; blood rushed to his head. His whole body trembled, and what remained of his mind tried desperately to control the rage and the anguish that welled up and swept through him. The man at the corner was not from the State Department, the face under the light did not belong to anyone remotely connected to American intelligence.

It belonged to the KGB. To KGB-East Berlin!

It was a face on one of the half-dozen photographs he had studied—studied until he knew every blemish, every strand of hair—in Berlin ten years ago.

Death on the Unter den Linden. His beautiful Karine, his adorable Karine. Trapped by a team across the checkpoint, a unit set up by the filthiest killer in the Soviet. V. Taleniekov. Animal.

This was one of those men. That unit. One of Taleniekov's hangmen.

Here! In Washington! Within minutes after his termination from State!

So KGB had found out. And someone in Moscow had decided to bring a stunning conclusion to the finish of Beowulf Agate. Only one man could think with such dramatic precision. V. Taleniekov. Animal.

As Bray stared through the glass, he knew what he was going to do, what he had to do. He would send a last message to Moscow; it would be a fitting capstone, a final gesture to mark the end of one life and the beginning of another—whatever it might be.

He would trap the killer from KGB. He would kill him.

Scofield stepped out of the doorway and ran down the sidewalk, racing in a zigzag pattern across the deserted street. He could hear running footsteps behind him.

6

Aeroflot's night flight from Moscow approached the sea of Azov northeast of Crimea. It would arrive in Sevastopol by one o'clock in the morning, something over an hour. The aircraft was crowded, the passengers by and large jubilant, on winter holiday leaves from their offices and factories. A scattering of military personnel—soldiers and sailors—were less exuberant; for them the Black Sea signified not a vacation, but a return to work at the naval and air bases. They'd had their leaves in Moscow.

In one of the rear seats sat a man with a dark leather violin case held firmly between his knees. His clothes were rumpled, undistinguished, somehow in conflict with the strong face and the sharp, clear eyes that seemed to belong above other apparel. His papers identified him as Pietre Rydukov, musician. His flight pass explained curtly that he was on his way to join the Sevastopol Symphony as third-chair violinist.

Both items were false. The man was Vasili Taleniekov, master strategist, Soviet Intelligence.

Former master strategist. Former director of KGB operations—East Berlin, Warsaw, Prague, Riga and the Southwest Sectors, which consisted of Sevastopol, the Bosporus, the Sea of Marmara and the Dardanelles. It was this last post that dictated the papers that put him on board the Sevastopol plane. It was the beginning of his flight from Russia.

There were scores of escape routes out of the Soviet Union, and in his professional capacity he had exposed them as he had found them. Ruthlessly, more often than not killing the agents of the West who kept them open, enticing malcontents to betray Russia with lies and promises of money. Always money. He had never wavered in his opposition to the liars and the proselytizers of greed; no escape route was too insignificant to warrant his attention.

Except one. A minor network-route through the Bosporus and the Sea of Marmara into the Dardanelles. He had uncovered it several months ago, during his last weeks as director, KGB-Southwest Soviet Sectors. During the days when he found himself in continuous confrontation with hot-headed fools at the military bases and asinine edicts from Moscow itself.

At the time, he was not sure why he held back exposure; for a while he had convinced himself that by leaving it open and watching it closely, it could lead to a larger network. Yet in the back of his mind, he knew that was not true.

His time was coming; he was making too many enemies in too many places. There could be those who felt that a quiet retirement north of Grasnov was not for a man who held the secrets of the KGB in his head. Now he possessed another secret, more frightening than anything conceived of by Soviet intelligence. The Matarese. And that secret was driving him out of Russia.

It had happened so fast, thought Taleniekov, sipping the hot tea provided by the steward. *Everything* had happened so fast. The bedside—deathbed—talk with old Aleksie Krupskaya and the astonishing things the dying man had said. Assassins sent forth to kill the élite of the nation—both nations. Pitting the Soviet and the United States against one another, until it controlled one or the other. A Premier and a President, one or both to be in a gunsight. Who were they? What *was* it, this fever that had begun in the first decades of the century in Corsica? The Corsican fever. The Matarese.

But it existed; it was functioning—alive and deadly. He knew that now. He had spoken its name and for speaking it, a plan had been put in motion that called for his arrest; the sentence of execution would follow shortly.

Krupskaya had told him that going to the Premier was out of the question, so he had sought out four once-powerful leaders of the Kremlin, now generously retired, which meant that none dared touch them. With each he had spoken of the strange phenomenon called the Matarese, repeated the words whispered by the dying Istrebiteli.

One man obviously knew nothing; he was as stunned as Taleniekov had been. Two *said* nothing, but the acknowledgment was in their eyes, and in their frightened voices when they protested. Neither would be a party to the spreading of such insanity; each had ordered Vasili from his house.

The last man, a Georgian, was the oldest—older than the dead Krupskaya—and in spite of an upright posture had little time left to enjoy a straight spine. He was ninety-six, his mind alert but given swiftly to an old man's fear. At the mention of the name Matarese, his thin, veined hands had trembled, then tiny muscular spasms seemed to spread across his ancient, withered face. His throat became suddenly dry; his voice cracked, his words barely audible.

It was a name from long ago in the past, the old Georgian had whispered, a name no one should hear. He had survived the early purges, survived the mad Stalin, the insidious Beria, but no one could survive the Matarese. In the name of all things sacred to Russia, the terrified man pleaded, walk *away* from the Matarese!

"We were fools, but we were not the only ones. Powerful men everywhere were seduced by the sweet convenience of having enemies and obstacles eliminated. The guarantee was absolute: the eliminations would never be traced to those who required them. Agreements were made through parties four and five times removed, dealing in fictitious purchases, unaware of what they were buying. Krupskaya saw the danger; he knew. He warned us in 'forty-eight never to make contact again."

"Why did he do that?" Vasili had asked. "If the guarantee was proven true. I speak professionally."

"Because the Matarese added a condition: the council of the Matarese demanded the right of approval. That's what I was told."

"The prerogative of killers-for-hire, I'd think," Taleniekov had interjected. "Some targets simply aren't feasible."

"Such approval was never sought in the past. Krupskaya did not think it was based on feasibility."

"On what, then?"

"Ultimate extortion."

"How were the contacts made with this council?"

"I never knew. Neither did Aleksie."

"*Someone* had to make them."

"If they are alive, they will not speak. Krupskaya was right about that."

"He called it the Corsican fever. He said the answers might be in Corsica."

"It's possible. It's where it began, with the maniac of Corsica. Guillaume de Matarese."

"You still have influence with the party leaders, sir. Will you help me? Krupskaya told me this Matarese must be—"

"*No!*" the old man had screamed. "Leave me in peace! I've said more than I should, admitted more than I had a right to. But only to warn you, to *stop* you! The Matarese can do no good for Russia! Turn your back on it!"

"You've misunderstood me. It is *I* who want to stop *it. Them.* This Matarese council. I gave my word to Aleksie that—"

"But you've had no words with *me!*" the withered, once-powerful leader had shouted, his voice childlike in its panic. "I will deny you ever came here, deny anything you say! You are a stranger, and I do not know you!"

Vasili had left, disturbed, perplexed. He had returned to his flat expecting to spend the night analyzing the enigma that was the Matarese, trying to decide what to do next. As usual he had glanced at the mailslot in the wall; he had actually taken a step away before he realized there *was* something inside.

It was a note from his contact at the VKR, written in one of the elliptical codes they had arranged between them. The words were innocuous: an agreement to have a late dinner at 11:30 and signed with a girl's first name. The very blandness of the note concealed its meaning. There was a problem of magnitude; the use of *eleven* meant emergency. No time was to be lost making contact; his friend would be waiting for him at the usual place.

He had been there. At a *piva kafe* near the Lomonosov State University. It was a raucous drinking establishment in tune with the new student permissiveness. They had moved to the rear of the hall; his contact had wasted no seconds getting to the point.

"Make plans, Vasili, you're on their list. I don't understand it but that's the word."

"Because of the Jew?"

"Yes, and it doesn't make sense! When that idiotic news conference was held in New York, we division men laughed. We called it 'Taleniekov's surprise.' Even a section chief from Group Nine said he admired what you did; that you taught a lesson to impetuous potato-heads. Then yesterday everything changed. What you did was no longer a joke, but rather a serious interference with basic policy."

"Yesterday?" Vasili had asked his friend.

"Late afternoon. Past four o'clock. That bitch director marched through the offices like a gorilla in heat. She smelled a gang rape and she loved it. She told each division man to be at her office at five o'clock. When we got there and listened, it was unbelievable. It was as if you were personally responsible for every setback we've sustained for the past two years. Those maniacs from Group Nine were there, but not the section chief."

"How long have I got?"

"Three or four days at the outside. Incriminating evidence against you is being compiled. But silently, no one is to say anything."

"Yesterday? . . ."

"What happened, Vasili? This isn't a VKR operation. It's something else."

It *was* something else and Taleniekov had recognized it instantly. The yesterday in question had been the day he had seen the two former Kremlin officials who had ordered him from their homes. The something else was the Matarese.

"One day I'll tell you, my friend," Vasili had answered. "Trust me."

"Of course. You're the best we have. The best we've ever had."

"Right now I need thirty-six, perhaps forty-eight hours. Do I have them?"

"I think so. They want your head, but they'll be careful. They'll document as much as they can."

"I'm sure they will. One needs words to read over the corpse. Thank you. You'll hear from me."

Vasili had not returned to his flat, but instead to his office. He had sat in the darkness for hours, arriving at his extraordinary decision. Hours before it would have been unthinkable, but not now. If the Matarese could corrupt the highest levels of the KGB it could do the same in Washington. If the mere mention of its name called for the death of a master strategist of his rank—and there was no mistaking it: death was the objective—then the power it possessed was unthinkable. If, in truth, it was responsible for the murders of Blackburn and Yurievich, then Krupskaya was right. There was a timetable. The Matarese were closing in, the Premier or the President moving into the gunsight.

He had to reach a man he loathed. He had to reach Brandon Alan Scofield, American killer.

In the morning, Taleniekov had put several wheels in motion, one after the other. With his customary—if curtailed—freedom of decision, he let it be known quietly that he was traveling under cover to the Baltic Sea for a conference. He then scoured the rolls of the Musicians Protective and found the name of a violinist who had retired five years ago to the Ural Mountains; he would do. Lastly, he had put the computers to work looking for a clue to the whereabouts of Brandon Scofield. The American had disappeared in Marseilles, but an incident had taken place in Amsterdam that bore the unmistakable mark of Scofield's expertise. Vasili had sent a cipher to an agent in Brussels, a man he could trust, for he had saved his life on more than one occasion.

Approach Scofield, white status. Amsterdam. Contact must be made. Imperative. Stay with him. Apprise situation Southwest Sector codes.

Everything had happened rapidly, and Taleniekov was grateful for the years that made it possible for him to arrive at swift decisions. Sevastopol was less than an hour away. In Sevastopol—and beyond—those years of hard experience would be put to the test.

He took a room at a small hotel on the boulevard Chersonesus and called a number at the KGB headquarters that was not attached to a recorder; he had installed it himself.

VKR-Moscow had not as yet put out an alarm for him, that much could be ascertained from headquarters' warm greeting. An old friend had returned; it gave Vasili the latitude he needed.

"To be frank," he said to the night duty officer, a former associate, "we have our ongoing problem with VKR. They've interfered again. You may get a teletype inquiry. You haven't heard from me, all right?"

"That's no problem as long as you don't show up here; you called on the right telephone. Are you staying in cover?"

"Yes. I won't burden you with my whereabouts. We're involved with a courier probe, convoys of trucks heading for Odessa, then south to the mountains. It's a CIA network."

"That's easier than fishing boats through the Bosporus. By the way, does Amsterdam fit into your blueprints?"

Taleniekov was startled. He had not expected so quick a reply from his man there. "It could. What have you got?"

"It came in two hours ago; it took that long to break. Our cryptographer—the man you brought from Riga—recognized an old code of yours. We were going to send it on to Moscow with the morning's dispatches."

"Don't do that," said Vasili. "Read it to me."

"Wait a minute." Papers were shuffled. "Here it is. 'Beowulf removed from orbit. Storm clouds Washington. On strength of imperative will pursue and deliver white contact. Cable instructions capitol depot.' That's it."

"It's enough," said Taleniekov.

"Sounds impressive, Vasili. A white contact? You've struck a high-level defection, I gather. Good for you. Is it tied in with your probe?"

"I think so," lied Taleniekov. "But don't say anything. Keep VKR out."

"With pleasure. You want us to cable for you?"

"No," replied Vasili, "I can do it. It's routine. I'll call you this evening. Say nine-thirty; that should be time enough. Tell my old friend from Riga I said hello. No one else, however. And thank you."

"When your probe's over, let's have dinner. It's good to have you back in Sevastopol."

"It's good to be back. We'll talk." Taleniekov hung up, concentrating on the message from Amsterdam. Scofield had been recalled to Washington, but the circumstances were abnormal. Beowulf Agate had run into a severe State Department storm. That fact alone was enough to propel an agent from Brussels into a transatlantic pursuit, debts notwithstanding. A white status contact was a momentary truce; a truce generally meant that someone was about to do something drastic. And if there existed even the remote possibility that the legendary Scofield might defect, any risk was worth the candle. The man who brought in Beowulf Agate would have all of Soviet Intelligence at his feet.

But defection was not possible for Scofield . . . any more than it was for him. The enemy was the enemy; that would never change.

Vasili picked up the phone again. There was an all-night number in the Lazarev district of the waterfront used by Greek and Iranian businessmen to send out cables to their home offices. By saying the right words, priority would be given over the existing traffic; within several hours his cable would reach "capitol depot." It was a hotel on Nebraska Avenue in Washington, D.C.

He would meet with Scofield on neutral ground, some place where neither could take advantage of the location. Within the departure gates of an airline where the security measures were the harshest—West Berlin or Tel Aviv, it did not matter; distance was inconsequential. But they had to meet, and Scofield had to be convinced of the necessity of that meeting. The cipher to Washington instructed the agent from Brussels to convey the following to Beowulf Agate.

We have traded in blood very dear to both of us. In truth, I more than you but you could not know it. Now there is another who would hold us responsible for international slaughter on a scale to which neither of us can subscribe. I operate outside of authority and alone. We must exchange views—as loathsome as it may be to both of us. Choose a neutral location, within an airport security compound. Suggest El Al, Tel Aviv or German domestic carrier, West Berlin. This courier will know how to reply.

My name is known to you.

It was nearly four o'clock in the morning before he closed his eyes. He had not slept in nearly three days, and when sleep came, it was deep and long. He had gone to bed before there was any evidence of the sun in the eastern sky; he awoke an hour after it had descended in the west. That was good. His mind and his body had needed the rest, and one traveled at night to the place he was going in Sevastopol.

There were three hours before the duty officer arrived at KGB; it was simpler not to involve anyone else at headquarters. The fewer who knew he was in the city, the better. Of course, the cryptographer knew, he had deduced the connection from the cipher out of Amsterdam, but the man would say nothing. Taleniekov had trained him, taken a bright young man from the austerity of Riga to the freer life in Sevastopol.

The time could be well spent, thought Vasili. He would eat, then make arrangements for passage in the hold of a Greek freighter that would cut straight across the sea, then follow the southern coast through the Bosporus, and on to the Dardanelles. If any of the Greek or Iranian units in the pay of the CIA or SAVAK recognized him—and it was possible—he would be entirely professional. As the previous director of the KGB sector, he had not exposed the escape route for personal reasons. However, if a musician named Pietre Rydukov did not make a telephone call to Sevastopol within two days after departure, exposure was guaranteed, KGB reprisals to follow. It would be a shame; other privileged men might wish to use the route later, their talents and information worth having.

Taleniekov put on the undistinguished, ill-fitting overcoat and his battered hat. A slouch and a pair of steel-rimmed spectacles were added. He checked his appearance in the mirror; it was satisfactory. He picked up the leather violin case; it completed his disguise, for no musician left his instrument in a strange hotel room. He went out the door, down the staircase—never an elevator—and out into the Sevastopol streets. He would walk to the waterfront; he knew where to go and what to say.

Fog rolled in from the sea, curling through the beams of the floodlights on the pier. There was activity everywhere as the hold of the freighter was loaded. Giant cranes swung cables cradling enormous boxcars of merchandise over the side of the ship. The loading crews were Russian, supervised by Greeks. Soldiers milled about, weapons slung casually over their shoulders, ineffectual patrols more interested in watching the machinery than in looking for irregularities.

If they wanted to know, mused Vasili as he approached the officer at the entrance gate, he could tell them. The irregularities were in the huge containers being lifted over the hull of the ship. Men and women packed in shredded cardboard, tubes from mouths to airspaces where necessary, instructions having been given to empty bladders and bowels several hours ago; there would be no relief until well past midnight when they were at sea.

The officer at the gate was a young lieutenant, bored with his work, irritation in his face. He scowled at the slouching, bespectacled old man before him.

"What do you want? The pier is off limits unless you have a pass." He pointed to the violin case. "What's that?"

"My livelihood, Lieutenant. I'm with the Sevastopol Symphony."

"I wasn't aware of any concerts scheduled for the docks."

"Your name, please?" said Vasili casually.

"What?"

Taleniekov stood up to his full height, the slouch gradually but clearly disappearing. "I asked you your name, Lieutenant."

"What for?" The officer was somewhat less hostile. Vasili removed the spectacles and looked sternly into his bewildered eyes.

"For a commendation or a reprimand."

"What are you talking about? Who are you?"

"KGB-Sevastopol. This is part of our waterfront inspection program."

The young lieutenant was politely hesitant; he was not a fool. "I'm afraid I wasn't told, sir. I'll have to ask you for identification."

"If you didn't, it would be the first reprimand," said Taleniekov, reaching into his pocket for his KGB card. "The second would come if you speak of my appearance here tonight. The name, please."

The lieutenant told him, then added, "Do you people suspect trouble down here?" He studied the plastic card and returned it.

"Trouble?" Taleniekov smiled, his eyes humorous and conspiratorial. "The only trouble, Lieutenant, is that I'm being deprived of a warm dinner in the company of a lady. I think the new directors in Sevastopol feel compelled to earn their rubles. You men are doing a good job; they know that but don't care to admit it."

Relieved, the young officer smiled back. "Thank you, sir. We do our best in a monotonous job."

"But don't say anything about my being here, they're serious about that. Two officers-of-the-guard were reported last week." Vasili smiled again. "In the directors' secrecy lies their true security. Their jobs."

The lieutenant grinned. "I understand. Have you a weapon in that case?"

"No. Actually it's a very good violin. I wish I could play it."

Both men nodded knowingly. Taleniekov continued onto the pier, into the melee of machinery, dock workers and supervisors. He was looking for a specific supervisor, a Greek from Kavalla named Zaimis. Which was to say he was looking for a man whose heritage was Greek and whose mother's name was Zaimis, but whose citizenship was American.

Karras Zaimis was a CIA agent, formerly station chief in Salonika, now field expediter of the escape route. Vasili knew the agent's face from several photographs he had removed from the KGB files. He peered through the bodies and the fog and the floodlights; he could not spot the man.

Taleniekov threaded his way past rushing fork-lifts and crews of complaining laborers toward the huge cargo warehouse. Inside the enormous enclosure, the light was dim, the wire-meshed floods too high in the ceiling to do much good. Beams of flashlights crisscrossed the containers; men were checking numbers. Vasili wondered briefly how much talent was in those boxcars. How much information was being taken out of Russia. Actually, not a great deal of either, he reminded himself. This was a minor escape route; more comfortable accommodations were provided for serious talent and significant bearers of intelligence data.

His slouch controlling his walk and his spectacles awkwardly in place, he excused himself past a Greek supervisor arguing with a Russian laborer. He wandered toward the rear of the warehouse, past stacks of cartons and aisles blocked with freight dollies, studying the faces of those holding flashlights. He was becoming annoyed; he did not have the time to waste. Where was Zaimis? There had been *no* change of status; the freighter *was* the carrier, the agent *still* the conduit. He had read every report sent from Sevastopol; there had been no mention of the escape route whatsoever. Where *was* he?

Suddenly Taleniekov felt a shock of pain as the barrel of a gun was shoved viciously into his right kidney. Strong fingers gripped the loose cloth of his overcoat, crunching the flesh of his lower rib cage; he was propelled into a deserted aisle. Words were whispered harshly in English.

"I won't bother speaking Greek, or trying to get through to you in Russian. I'm told your English is as good as anyone's in Washington."

"Conceivably better than most," said Vasili through his teeth. "Zaimis?"

"Never heard of him. We thought you were out of Sevastopol."

"I am. Where is Zaimis? I must speak with Zaimis."

The American disregarded the question. "You've got balls, I'll say that for you. There's no one from KGB within ten blocks of here."

"Are you sure about that?"

"Very. We've got a flock of night owls out there. They see in the dark. They saw you. A violin case, Christ!"

"Do they look to the water?"

"Seagulls do that."

"You're very well organized, all you birds."

"And you're less bright than everyone says. What did you think you were doing? A little personal reconnaissance?"

Vasili felt the grip lessen on his ribs, then heard the muted sound of an object pulled out of rubber. A vial of serum. A *needle.* "Don't!" he said firmly. "Don't do that! Why do you think I'm here alone? I want to get out."

"That's just where you're going. My guess would be an interrogation hospital somewhere in Virginia for about three years."

"*No.* You don't understand. I have to make contact with someone. But not *that* way."

"Tell it to the nice doctors. They'll listen to everything you say."

"There's no time!" There *was* no time. Taleniekov could feel the man's weight shift; in seconds a needle would puncture his clothes and enter his flesh. It could not happen this way! He could not deal with Scofield officially!

None dare talk. The admissions would be catastrophic . . . for governments everywhere. The Matarese.

If he could be destroyed in Moscow, the Americans would not think twice about silencing him.

Vasili raised his right shoulder—a gesture of pain from the gun barrel in his kidney. The gun was abruptly pressed further into his back—a reaction to the gesture. In that split instant, the pressure point of the hand holding the gun was on the heel of the palm, not the index finger. Taleniekov's movement was timed for it.

He spun to his left, his arm arcing up, crashing down over the American's elbow, vicing it into his hip until the forearm cracked. He jabbed the fingers of his right hand into the man's throat, bruising the windpipe. The gun fell to the floor, its clatter obscured by the din of the warehouse. Vasili picked it up and shoved the CIA agent against a boxcar container. In his pain, the American held the hypodermic needle limply in his left hand; it, too, dropped to the floor. His eyes were glazed, but not beyond cognizance.

"Now, you *listen* to me," said Taleniekov, his face against Zaimis' face. "I've known about 'Operation Dardanelles' for nearly seven months. I know you're Zaimis. You deal in mediocre traffic; you're not significant. But that's not the reason I didn't blow you apart. I thought one day you might be of use to me. That time has come. You can accept it or not."

"Taleniekov defect?" said Zaimis, holding his throat. "No way. You're Soviet poison. A double entry, but no defector."

"You're right. I do not defect. And if that unthinkable option ever entered my mind, I'd contact the British or the French before you. I said I wanted to get out of Russia, not betray it."

"You're lying," said the American, his hand slipping down to the lapel of his heavy cloth jacket. "You can go anywhere you want."

"Not at the moment, I'm afraid. There are complications."

"What did you do, turn capitalist? Make off with a couple of pouches?"

"Come on, Zaimis. Which of us doesn't have his small box of resources? Often legitimate; funneled monies can be delayed. Where's yours? I doubt Athens, and Rome is too unstable. I'd guess Berlin or London. Mine's quite ordinary: certificates of deposit. Chase Manhattan, New York City."

The CIA man's expression remained passive, his thumb curled beneath his jacket's lapel. "So you got caught," he said absently.

"We're wasting time!" Vasili barked. "Get me to the Dardanelles. I'll make my own way from there. If you don't, if a telephone call is not received here in Sevastopol when expected, your operation is finished. You'll be—"

Zaimis' hand shot up toward his mouth; Taleniekov grabbed the agent's fingers and twisted them violently outward. Stuck to the American's thumb was a small tablet.

"You damn *fool!* What do you think you're doing?!"

Zaimis winced, the pain excruciating. "I'd rather go this way than in the Lubyanka."

"You *ass!* If anyone goes to the Lubyanka, it will be *me!* Because there are maniacs just like you sitting at their desks in Moscow. And *fools*—just like *you*—who would prefer a tablet rather than listen to the truth! You want to die, I'll accommodate you. But first get me to the Dardanelles!"

The agent, breathing with difficulty, stared at Taleniekov. Vasili released his hand, removing the tablet from Zaimis' thumb.

"You're for real, aren't you?" Zaimis said.

"I'm for real. Will you help me?"

"I haven't got anything to lose," said the agent. "You'll be on our carrier."

"Don't forget. Word must get back here from the Dardanelles. If it doesn't, you're finished."

Zaimis paused, then nodded. "Check. We trade off."

"We trade off," agreed Taleniekov. "Now, can you get me to a telephone?"

The cinderblock cubicle in the warehouse had two phones—installed by Russians and no doubt electronically monitored by SAVAK and CIA for intercepts, thought Vasili. They would be sterile; he could talk. The American agent picked up his when Taleniekov finished dialing. The instant the call was answered, Vasili spoke.

"Is this you, my old comrade?"

It was and it was not. It was not the station chief he had spoken with earlier; instead, it was the cryptographer Taleniekov had trained years ago in Riga and brought to Sevastopol. The man's voice was low, anxious.

"Our mutual friend was called to the code room; it was arranged. I said I'd wait for your call. I have to see you right away. Where are you?"

Zaimis reached over, his bruised fingers gripping the mouthpiece of Vasili's phone. Taleniekov shook his head; in spite of the fact that he trusted the cryptographer, he had no intention of answering the question.

"That's of no consequence. Did the cable come from 'depot'?"

"A great deal more than that, old friend."

"But it *came?*" pressed Vasili.

"Yes. But it's not in any cipher I've ever heard of. Nothing you and I ever used before. Neither during our years in Riga nor here."

"Read it to me."

"There's something *else,*" insisted the code man, his tone now intense. "They're after you *openly.* I recycled the teletype to Moscow for in-house confirmation and burnt the original. It will be back in less than two hours. I can't *believe* it. I *won't* believe it!"

"Calm down. What was it?"

"There's an alert out for you from the Baltic to the Manchurian borders."

"VKR?" asked Vasili, alarmed but controlled; he expected Group Nine to act swiftly but not quite this swiftly.

"*Not* just VKR. *KGB*—and every intelligence station we *have!* As well as all military units. *Everywhere.* This isn't *you* they speak of; it couldn't be. I will not believe it!"

"What do they say?"

"That you've betrayed the State. You're to be taken, but there's to be no *detention,* no interrogation *at all.* You're to be . . . executed . . . without delay."

"I see," said Taleniekov. And he did see; he expected it. It was not the VKR. It was powerful men who'd heard he had spoken a name that no one should hear. *Matarese.* "I've betrayed no one. Believe that."

"I do. I know you."

"Read me the cable from 'depot.' "

"Very well. Have you a pencil? It makes no sense."

Vasili reached into his pocket for his pen; there was paper on the table. "Go ahead."

The man spoke slowly, clearly. "As follows: 'Invitation Kasimir. Schrankenwarten five goals. . . .'" The cryptographer stopped; Taleniekov could hear voices in the distance over the line. "I can't go on. People are coming," he said.

"I *must* have the rest of that cable!"

"Thirty minutes. The *Amar Magazin.* I'll be there." The line went dead.

Vasili slammed his fist on the table, then replaced the phone. "I *must have* it," he repeated in English.

"What's the *Amar Magazin*—the Lobster Shop?" asked the CIA man.

"A fish restaurant on Kerenski Street, about seven blocks from headquarters. No one who knows Sevastopol goes there; the food is terrible. But it fits what he was trying to tell me."

"What's that?"

"Whenever the cryptographer wanted me to screen certain incoming material before others saw it, he would suggest we meet at the *Amar.*"

"He didn't just come to your office and talk?"

Taleniekov glanced over at the American. "You know better than that."

The agent looked hard at Vasili. "They want you very dead, don't they?"

"It's a gargantuan error."

"It always is," said Zaimis, frowning. "You trust him?"

"You heard him. When do you sail?"

"Eleven-thirty. Two hours. Roughly the same time that confirmation's due back from Moscow."

"I'll be here."

"I know you will," said the agent. "Because I'm going with you."

"You *what?*"

"I've got protection out there in the city. Of course, I'll want my gun back. *And* yours. We'll see how much you want to get through the Bosporus."

"Why would you do this?"

"I have an idea you may reconsider that unthinkable option of yours. I want to bring you in."

Vasili shook his head slowly. "Nothing ever changes. It will not happen. I can still expose you and you don't know how. And by exposing you, I blow apart your Black Sea network. It would take years to re-establish. Time is always the issue, isn't it?"

"We'll see. You want to get to the Dardanelles?"

"Of course."

"Give me the gun," said the American.

The restaurant was filled, the waiters' aprons as dirty as the sawdust on the floor. Taleniekov sat alone by the right rear wall, Zaimis two tables away in the company of a Greek merchant seaman in the pay of the CIA. The Greek's face was creased with loathing for his surroundings. Vasili sipped iced vodka which helped disguise the taste of the fifth-rate caviar.

The cryptographer came through the door, spotted Taleniekov, and weaved his way awkwardly between waiters and patrons to the table. His eyes behind the thick lenses of his glasses conveyed at once joy and fear and a hundred unspoken questions.

"It's all so incredible," he said, sitting down. "What have they *done* to you?"

"It's what they're doing to themselves," replied Vasili. "They don't want to listen, they don't want to hear what has to be said, what has to be stopped. It's all I can tell you."

"But to call for your *execution.* It's inconceivable!"

"Don't worry, old friend. I'll be back—and, as they say—rehabilitated with honors." Taleniekov smiled and touched the man's arm. "Never forget. There are good and decent men in Moscow, more committed to their country than to their own fears and ambitions. They'll always be there, and those are the men who I will reach. They'll welcome me and thank me for what I've done. Believe that. . . . Now, we're dealing in minutes. Where is the cable?"

The cryptographer opened his hand. The paper was neatly folded, creased into his palm. "I wanted to be able to throw it away, if I had to. I know the words." He handed the cipher to Vasili.

A dread came over Taleniekov as he read the message from Washington.

Invitation Kasimir. Schrankenwarten five goals. Unter den Linden. Przseslvac zero. Prague. Repeat text. Zero. Repeat again at will. Zero.

Beowulf Agate.

When he had finished reading, the former master strategist of KGB whispered, "Nothing ever changes."

"What is it?" asked the cryptographer. "I didn't understand it. It's no code we've ever used."

"There's no way that you could understand," answered Vasili, anger and sadness in his voice. "It's a combination of two codes. Ours and theirs. Ours from the days in East Berlin, theirs from Prague. This cable was not sent by our man from Brussels. It was sent by a killer who won't stop killing."

It happened so fast there were only seconds to react, and the Greek seaman moved first. His weathered face had been turned toward the incoming customers. He spat out the words.

"Watch it! The goats are filthy!"

Taleniekov looked up; the cryptographer spun in his chair. Twenty feet away, in an aisle peopled by waiters, were two men who had not come in for a meal; their expressions were set, their eyes darting about the room. They were scanning the tables, but not for friends.

"Oh, my God," whispered the cryptographer turning back to Vasili. "They found the phone and tapped it. I was afraid of that."

"Followed you, yes," said Taleniekov, glancing over at Zaimis, who was half out of his chair, the *idiot.* "They know we're friends; you're being watched. But they didn't find the phone. If they were certain that I was here, they'd break in with a dozen soldiers. They're district VKR. I know them. Calmly now, take off your hat and slide out of your chair. Head toward the back hallway, to the men's room. There's a rear exit, remember?"

"Yes, yes, I remember," sputtered the man. He got up, his shoulders hunched, and started for the narrow corridor several tables away.

But he was an academic, not a field man, and Vasili cursed himself for trying to instruct him. One of the two VKR men spotted him and came forward, pushing aside the waiters in the aisle.

Then he saw Taleniekov and his hand whipped into the open space of his jacket and toward an unseen weapon. As he did so, the Greek seaman lurched up from his chair, weaving unsteadily, waving his arms like a man with too much vodka in him. He slammed against the VKR man, who tried to push him away. The Greek feigned drunken indignation and pushed back with such force that the Russian went sprawling over a table, sending dishes and food crashing to the floor.

Vasili sprang up and raced past his old friend from Riga, pulling him toward the narrow hallway; then he saw the American. Zaimis was on his feet, his gun in his hand. *Idiot!*

"Put that *away!*" shouted Taleniekov. "Don't expose—"

It was too late. A gunshot exploded through the sounds of chaos, escalating it instantly into pandemonium. The CIA man brought both his hands to his chest as he fell, the shirt beneath his jacket suddenly drenched with blood.

Vasili grabbed the cryptographer by the shoulder, yanking him through the narrow archway. There was a second gunshot; the code man arched spastically, his legs together, an eruption of flesh at his throat. He had been shot through the back of the neck.

Taleniekov lunged to the floor of the hallway, stunned at what followed. He heard a third gunshot, a shrill scream after it, penetrating the cacophony of screams surrounding it. And then the Greek seaman crashed through the archway, an automatic in his hand.

"Is there a way out back here?" he roared in broken English. "We have to run. The first goat got away. Others will come!"

Taleniekov scrambled to his feet and gestured for the Greek to follow him. Together they raced through a door into a kitchen filled with terrified cooks and waiters, and out into an alley. They turned left and ran through a maze of dark connecting pavements between the old buildings until they reached the back streets of Sevastopol.

They kept running for more than a mile. Vasili knew every inch of the city, but it was the Greek who kept shouting the turns they must make. As they entered a dimly lit side street, the seaman grabbed Taleniekov's arm; the man was out of breath.

"We can rest here for a minute," he said, gasping. "They won't find us."

"It's not a place we think of first in a search," agreed Vasili, looking at the row of neat apartment buildings.

"Always hide out in a well-kept neighborhood," said the seaman. "The residents veer from controversy; they'd inform on you in a minute. Everybody knows it so they don't look in such places."

"You say we can stay 'for a minute,' " said Taleniekov. "I'm not sure where we'll go after that. I need time to think."

"You rule out the ship then?" asked the Greek. "I thought so."

"Yes. Zaimis had papers on him. Worse, he had one of my guns. The VKR will be swarming over the piers within the hour."

The Greek studied Vasili in the dim light. "So the great Taleniekov flees Russia. He can remain only as a corpse."

"Not from Russia, only from frightened men. But I do have to leave—for a while. I've got to figure out how."

"There is a way," said the merchant seaman simply. "We'll head over the northwest coast, then south into the mountains. You'll be in Greece in three days."

"How?"

"There's a convoy of trucks that go first to Odessa. . . ."

Taleniekov sat on the hard bench in the back of the truck, the light of dawn seeping through the billowing canvas flaps that covered the sides. In a while, he and the others would have to crawl beneath the floorboards, remaining motionless and silent on a concealed ledge between the axles, while they passed through the next checkpoint. But for an hour or so they could stretch and breathe air that did not reek of oil and grease.

He reached into his pocket and took out the cipher from Washington, the cable that had already cost three lives.

Invitation Kasimir. Schrankenwarten five goals. Unter den Linden. Przseslvac zero. Prague. Repeat text. Zero. Repeat again at will. Zero.

Beowulf Agate.

Two codes. One meaning.

With his pen, Vasili wrote out that meaning beneath the cipher.

Come and take me, as you took someone else across a checkpoint at five o'clock on the Unter den Linden. I've broken and killed your courier, as another courier was killed in Prague. Repeat: Come to me. I'll kill you.

Scofield

Beyond the American killer's brutal decision, the most electrifying aspect of Scofield's cable was the fact that he was no longer in the service of his country. He had been separated from the intelligence community. And considering what he had done and the pathological forces that drove him to do it, the separation was undoubtedly savage. For no government professional would murder a courier under the circumstances of this extraordinary Soviet contact. And if Scofield was nothing else, he was a professional.

The storm clouds over Washington had been catastrophic for Beowulf Agate. They had destroyed him.

As the storm over Moscow had destroyed a master strategist named Taleniekov.

It was strange, bordering on the macabre. Two enemies who loathed each other had been chosen by the Matarese as the first of its lethal decoys—ploys and diversions as old Krupskaya had called them. Yet only one of those enemies knew it; the other did not. He was concerned solely with ripping scars open, letting the blood between them flow again.

Vasili put the paper back into his pocket, and breathed deeply. The coming days would be filled with move and countermove, two experts stalking each other until the inevitable confrontation.

My name is Taleniekov. We will kill each other or we will talk.

7

Undersecretary of State Daniel Congdon shot up from the chair, the telephone in his hand. Since his early days at NSA he had learned that one way of controlling an outburst was to physically move during a moment of crisis. And control was the key to everything in his profession; at least, the appearance of it. He listened as this particular crisis was defined by an angry Secretary of State.

Goddamn it, *he* was controlled.

"I've just met privately with the Soviet Ambassador and we both agree the incident must not be made public. The important thing now is to bring Scofield in."

"Are you *certain* it was Scofield, sir? I can't *believe* it!"

"Let's say that until he denies it with irrefutable proof that he was a thousand miles away during the past forty-eight hours we must assume it *had* to be Scofield. No one else in clandestine operations would have committed such an act. It's unthinkable."

Unthinkable? *Incredible.* The body of a dead Russian delivered through the gates of the Soviet Embassy in the backseat of a Yellow Cab at 8:30 in the morning at the height of Washington's rush-hour traffic. And a driver who knew absolutely nothing except that he had picked up *two* drunks, not one—although one was in worse shape than the other. What the hell had happened to the other guy? The one who sounded like a Ruskie and wore a hat and dark glasses and said the sunlight was too bright after a whole night of *Wodka.* Where was he? And was the fellow in the backseat all right? He looked like a mess.

"Who was the man, Mr. Secretary?"

"He was a Soviet intelligence officer stationed in Brussels. The Ambassador was frank; the KGB had no knowledge he was in Washington."

"A possible defection?"

"There's no evidence whatsoever to support that."

"Then what ties him to Scofield? Beyond the method of dispatch and delivery."

The Secretary of State paused, then replied carefully. "You must understand, Mr. Congdon, the Ambassador and I have a unique relationship that goes back several decades. We are often more candid with each other than diplomatic. Always with the understanding that neither speaks for the record."

"I understand, sir," said Congdon, realizing that the answer about to be given could never be referred to officially.

"The intelligence officer in question was a member of a KGB unit in East Berlin roughly ten years ago. I assume in light of your recent decisions that you're familiar with Scofield's file."

"His wife?" Congdon sat down. "The man was one of those who killed Scofield's *wife?*"

"The Ambassador made no reference to Scofield's wife; he merely mentioned the fact that the dead man had been part of a relatively autonomous section of the KGB in East Berlin ten years ago."

"That section was controlled by a strategist named Taleniekov. He gave the orders."

"Yes," said the Secretary of State. "We discussed Mr. Taleniekov and the subsequent incident several years later in Prague at some length. We looked for the connection you've just considered. It may exist."

"How is that, sir?"

"Vasili Taleniekov disappeared two days ago."

"Disappeared?"

"Yes, Mr. Congdon. Think about it. Taleniekov learned that he was to be officially retired, mounted a simple but effective cover, and disappeared."

"Scofield's been terminated. . . ." Congdon spoke softly, as much to himself as into the telephone.

"Exactly," agreed the Secretary of State. "The parallel is our immediate concern. Two retired specialists now bent on doing what they could not do—or pursue—officially. Kill each other. They have contacts everywhere, men who are loyal to them for any number of reasons. Their personal vendetta could create untold problems for both governments during these precious months of conciliation. This cannot happen."

The director of *Cons Op* frowned; there was something wrong in the secretary's conclusions. "I spoke with Scofield myself three nights ago. He didn't appear consumed with anger or revenge or anything like that. He was a tired field agent who'd lived . . . abnormally . . . for a long time. For years. He told me he just wanted to fade away, and I believed him. I discussed Scofield with Robert Winthrop, by the way, and he felt the same way about him. He said—"

"Winthrop knows *nothing,*" interrupted the Secretary of State with unexpected harshness. "Robert Winthrop is a brilliant man, but he's never understood the meaning of confrontation except in its most rarefied forms. Bear in mind, Mr. Congdon, Scofield killed that intelligence officer from Brussels."

"Perhaps there were circumstances we're not aware of."

"Really?" Again the Secretary of State paused, and when he spoke, the meaning behind his words was unmistakable. "If there *are* such circumstances, I submit we have a far more potentially dangerous situation than any personal feud might engender. Scofield and Taleniekov know more about the field operations of both intelligence services than any two men alive. They must not be permitted to make contact. Either as enemies intent on killing one another, or for those circumstances we know nothing about. Do I make myself clear, Mr. Congdon? As director of Consular Operations, it is your responsibility. How you *execute* that responsibility is no concern of mine. You may have a man beyond salvage. That's for you to decide."

Daniel Congdon remained motionless as he heard the click on the other end of the line. In all his years of service he had never received such an ill-disguised if oblique order. The language could be debated, not the command. He replaced the phone in its cradle and reached for another on the left side of his desk. He pressed a button and dialed three digits.

"Internal Security," said a male voice.

"This is Undersecretary Congdon. Pick up Brandon Scofield. You have the information. Bring him in at once."

"One minute, sir," replied the man politely. "I think a level-two surveillance entry on Scofield came in a couple of days ago. Let me check the computer. All the data's there."

"A couple of days ago?"

"Yes, sir. It's on the screen now. Scofield checked out of his hotel at approximately eleven P.M. on the sixteenth."

"The sixteenth? Today's the nineteenth."

"Yes, sir. There was no time lapse as far as the entry was concerned. The management informed us within the hour."

"Where is he?"

"He left two forwarding addresses, but no dates. A sister's residence in Minneapolis and a hotel in Charlotte Amalie, St. Thomas, U.S. Virgin Islands."

"Have they been verified?"

"As to accuracy, yes sir. A sister does live in Minneapolis and the hotel in St. Thomas is holding a prepaid reservation for Scofield effective the seventeenth. The money was wired from Washington."

"Then he's there."

"Not as of noon today, sir. A routine call was made; he hasn't arrived."

"What about the sister?" interrupted Congdon.

"Again a routine call. She confirmed the fact that Scofield called her and said he'd stop by, but he didn't say when. She added that it wasn't unusual; it was normal for him to be casual about visits. She expected him sometime during the week."

The director of *Cons Op* felt the urge to get up again, but he suppressed it. "Are you telling me you don't really know where he is?"

"Well, Mr. Congdon, an S-level-two operates on reports received, not continuous visual contact. We'll shift to level-one right away. Minneapolis won't be any problem; the Virgin Islands could be, though."

"Why?"

"We have no reliable sources there, sir. Nobody does."

Daniel Congdon got up from his chair. "Let me try to understand you. You say Scofield's on a level-two surveillance, yet my instructions were clear; his whereabouts were to be known at all times. Why wasn't a level-one put on him? Why *wasn't* continuous visual contact maintained?"

The man from Internal Security answered haltingly. "That wouldn't be my decision, sir, but I think I can understand it. If a level-one was put on Scofield, he'd spot it and . . . well, sheer perversity would make him mislead us."

"What the hell do you think he's just *done?* Find him! Report your progress hourly to this office!" Congdon sat down angrily, replacing the phone with such force that it jarred the bell. He stared at the instrument, picked it up, and dialed again.

"Overseas Communications, Miss Andros," said the woman's voice.

"Miss Andros, this is Undersecretary Congdon. Please send a cipher specialist to my office immediately. Classification Code *A* maximum security and priority."

"An emergency, sir?"

"Yes, Miss Andros, an emergency. The cable will be sent in thirty minutes. Clear all traffic to Amsterdam, Marseilles . . . and Prague."

Scofield heard the footsteps in the hallway and got out of the chair. He walked to the door and peered through the tiny disk in the center. The figure of a man passed by; he did not stop at the door across the way, the entrance to the suite of rooms used by Taleniekov's courier. Bray went back to the chair and sat down. He leaned his head against the rim, staring at the ceiling.

It had been three days since the race in the streets, three nights since he'd taken the messenger from Taleniekov—messenger three nights ago, killer on the Unter den Linden ten years before. It had been a strange night, an odd race, a finish that might have been otherwise.

The man could have lived; the decision to kill him had gradually lost its urgency for Bray, as so much had lost urgency. The courier had brought it upon himself. The Soviet had gone into panic and pulled out a four-inch, razor-sharp blade from the recesses of the hotel chair and attacked. His death was due to Scofield's reaction; it was not the premeditated murder planned in the street.

Nothing ever changed much. The KGB courier had been used by Taleniekov. The man was convinced that Beowulf Agate was coming over, and the Russian who brought him in would be given the brassiest medal in Moscow.

"You've been tricked," Bray had told the courier.

"Impossible!" the Soviet had yelled. "It's Taleniekov!"

"It certainly is. And he chooses a man from the Unter den Linden to make contact, a man whose face he knows I'll never forget. The odds were that I'd lose control and kill you. In *Washington.* I'm exposed, vulnerable. . . . And you've been taken."

"You're wrong! It's a white contact!"

"So was East Berlin, you son of a bitch."

"What are you going to do?"

"Earn some of my severance pay. You're coming in."

"No!"

"Yes."

The man had lunged at Scofield.

Three days had passed since that moment of violence, three mornings since Scofield had deposited the package at the embassy and sent the cipher to Sevastopol. Still no one had come to the door across the hall; and that was not normal. The suite was leased by a brokerage house in Bern, Switzerland, to be available for its "executives." Standard procedure for international businessmen, and also a transparent cover for a Soviet drop.

Bray had forced the issue. The cipher and the courier's dead body *had* to provoke *someone* into checking the suite of rooms. Yet no one had; it did not make sense.

Unless part of Taleniekov's cable was true: he *was* acting alone. If that were the case, there was only one explanation: the Soviet killer had been terminated, and before retiring to an isolated life somewhere in the vicinity of Grasnov, he had decided to settle an outstanding debt.

He had sworn to do so after Prague; the message had been clear: *You're mine, Beowulf Agate. Someday, somewhere. I'll see you take your last breath.*

A brother for a wife. The husband for the brother. It was vengeance rooted in loathing and that loathing never left. There'd be no peace for either of them until the end came for one. It was better to know that now, thought Bray, rather than find out on a crowded street or a deserted stretch of beach, with a knife in the side or a bullet in the head.

The courier's death was an accident, Taleniekov's would not be. There *would* be no peace until they met, and then death would come—one way or the other. It was a question now of drawing the Russian out; he had made the first move. He was the stalker, the role established.

The strategy was classic: tracks clearly defined for the stalker to follow, and at the chosen moment—least expected—the tracks would not be there, the stalker bewildered, exposed—the trap sprung.

Like Bray, Taleniekov could travel anywhere he wished, with or without official sanction. Over the years, both had learned too many methods; a plethora of false papers were out there for purchase, hundreds of men everywhere ready to provide concealment or transportation, cover or weapons—any and all. There were only two basic requirements: identities and money.

Neither he nor Taleniekov lacked either. Both came with the profession, the identities quite naturally, the money less so—more often than not the result of having been hung by bureaucratic delays in the forwarding of payments demanded. Every specialist worth his rank had his own personal sources of funds. Payments exaggerated, monies diverted and deposited in stable territories. The objective was neither theft nor wealth, merely survival. A man in the field had only to be burned once or twice to learn the necessity of economic backups.

Bray had accounts under various names in Paris, Munich, London, Geneva and Lisbon. One avoided Rome and the Communist bloc; the Italian Treasury was madness, and banking in the Eastern satellites too corrupt.

Scofield rarely thought about the money that was his for the spending; in the back of his mind he supposed he would give it back one day. Had the predatory Congdon not flirted with his own temptations and made the official termination so complicated, Bray might have walked in the next morning and handed him the bankbooks.

Not now. The undersecretary's actions ruled it out. One did not hand over several hundred thousand dollars to a man who tried to orchestrate one's elimination while remaining outside the act itself. It was a very professional concept. Scofield recalled that years ago it had been brought to its zenith by the killers of the Matarese. But they were assassins for hire; there'd been no one like them in centuries, since the days of Hasan ibn-al-Sabbah. There would be no one like them ever again, and someone like Daniel Congdon was a pale joke in comparison.

Congdon. Scofield laughed and reached into his pocket for his cigarettes. The new director of Consular Operations was not a fool and only a fool would underestimate him, but he had the upper-Washington mentality so prevalent in the management of clandestine services. He did not really understand what being in the field did to a man; he might mouth the phrases, but he did not see the simple line of action and reaction. Few did, or wanted to, because to recognize it meant admitting knowledge of abnormality in a subordinate whose function the department—or the Company—could not do without. Quite simply, pathological behavior was a perfectly normal way of life for a field man, and no particular attention was paid to it. The man in the field accepted the fact that he was a criminal before any crimes had been committed. Therefore, at the first hint of activity he took measures to protect himself before anything happened; it was second nature.

Bray had done just that. While the messenger from Taleniekov had been seated across the room in the hotel on Nebraska Avenue, Scofield had made several calls. The first was to his sister in Minneapolis: he was flying out to the Midwest in a couple of hours and would see her in a day or so. The second was to a friend in Maryland who was a deep-sea fisherman with a roomful of stuffed victims and trophies on the walls: where was a good, small place in the Caribbean that would take him on short notice? The friend had a friend in Charlotte Amalie; he owned a hotel and always kept two or three rooms open for just such emergencies. The fisherman from Maryland would call him for Bray.

So, for all intents and purposes, as of the night of the sixteenth, he was en route to the Midwest . . . or the Caribbean. Both more than fifteen hundred miles from Washington—where he remained unobserved, never leaving the hotel room across the hall from the Soviet drop.

How often had he hammered the lesson into younger, less experienced field agents? Too many times to count. A man standing motionless in a crowd was difficult to spot.

But every hour escalated the complexity. All possible explanations had to be examined. The most obvious was that the Russian had activated a dormant drop known to him and his messenger; instructions could be sent quietly to Bern, the suite of rooms leased by cable. It would take weeks before the information was filtered back to Moscow—one drop among thousands around the world.

If so—and it was perhaps the *only* explanation—Taleniekov was not merely acting alone, he was acting in conflict with KGB interests. His vendetta superseded his allegiance to his government, if the term had meaning any longer; it had little for Scofield. It *was* the only explanation. Otherwise the suite of rooms across the hall would be swarming with Soviets. They might wait twenty-four or thirty-six hours to check out FBI observation, but no more than that; there were too many ways to elude the bureau's surveillance.

Bray had the gut instinct that he was right, an instinct developed over the years to the point where he trusted it implicitly. Now he had to put himself into Taleniekov's place, think as Vasili Taleniekov would think. It was his protection against a knife in the side or a bullet from a high-powered rifle. It was the way to bring it all to an end, and not have to go through each day wondering what the shadows held. Or the crowds.

The KGB man had no choice: it was his move and it had to be in Washington. One started with the physical connection and it was the dormant drop across the hall. In a matter of days—perhaps hours now—Taleniekov would fly into Dulles Airport and the hunt would begin.

But the Russian was no idiot; he would not walk into a trap. Instead, another would come, someone who knew nothing, who had been paid to be an unknowing decoy. An unsuspecting passenger whose friendship was carefully cultivated on a transatlantic flight; or one of dozens of blind contacts Taleniekov had used in Washington. Men and women who had no idea that the European they did well-paid favors for was a strategist for the KGB. Among them would be the decoy, or decoys, and the birds. Decoys knew nothing; they were bait. Birds watched, sending out alarms when the bait was being taken. Birds and decoys; they would be Taleniekov's weapons.

Someone would come to the hotel on Nebraska Avenue. Whoever it was would have no instructions beyond getting into those rooms; no telephone number, no name that meant anything. And nearby, the birds would be waiting for the quarry to go after the bait.

When the quarry was spotted the birds would reach the hunter. Which meant that the hunter was also nearby.

This would be Taleniekov's strategy, for no other was available; it was also the strategy that Scofield would use. Three or four—five at the outside—persons readily available for such employment. Simply mounted: phone calls placed at the airport, a meeting at a downtown restaurant. An inexpensive exercise considering the personal value of the quarry.

Sounds came from beyond the door. Voices. Bray got out of the chair and walked quickly to the tiny glass circle in the panel.

Across the hall a well-dressed woman was talking with the bell captain who carried her overnight bag. Not a suitcase, not luggage from a transatlantic flight, but a small overnight case. The decoy had arrived, the birds not far away. Taleniekov had landed; it had started.

The woman and the bell captain disappeared into the suite of rooms.

Scofield walked to the telephone. It was the moment to begin the counterexercise. He needed time; two or three days were not out of the question.

He called the deep-sea fisherman on the Maryland shore, making sure to dial direct. He capped the mouthpiece with his right hand, filtering his voice through his barely separated fingers. The greeting was swift, the caller in a hurry. "I'm in the Keys and can't reach that damned hotel in Charlotte Amalie. Call it for me, will you? Tell them I'm on a charter out of Tavernier and will be there in a couple of days."

"Sure, Bray. On a real vacation, aren't you?"

"More than you know. And thanks."

The next call needed no such artifice. It was to a Frenchwoman he had lived with briefly in Paris several years ago. She had been one of the most effective undercover personnel at Interpol until her cover was blown; she worked now for a CIA proprietary based in Washington. There was no sexual attraction between them any longer but they were friends. She asked no questions.

He gave her the name of the hotel on Nebraska Avenue. "Call in fifteen minutes and ring suite two-eleven. A woman will answer. Ask for me."

"Will she be furious, darling?"

"She won't know who I am. But someone else will."

Taleniekov leaned against the brick of the dark alleyway across from the hotel. For several moments he let his body sag and rolled his neck back and forth, trying to ease the tension, reduce the exhaustion. He had been traveling for nearly three days, flying for more than eighteen hours, driving into cities and villages finding those men who would provide him with false documents that would get him through three immigration stations. From Salonika to Athens, Athens to London, London to New York. Finally a late afternoon shuttle flight to Washington after visits to three banks in lower Manhattan.

He had made it; his people were in place. An expensive whore he'd brought from New York and three others from Washington, two men and an older woman. All but one were well-spoken *nichivo*, what the Americans called hustlers. Each had performed services in the past for the generous "businessman" from The Hague, who had a proclivity for checking up on his associates and a penchant for confidence, both of which he paid for in large sums.

They were primed for their evening's employment. The whore was in the suite of rooms that was the Bern-Washington depot; within minutes Scofield would know it. But Beowulf Agate was no amateur; he would receive the news—from a desk clerk or switchboard operator—and send another to question the girl.

Whoever it was would be seen by one or all of Taleniekov's birds. The two men and the older woman. He had provided each with a miniaturized walkie-talkie no larger than a hand-held recorder; he had purchased four at the Mitsubi complex on Fifth Avenue. They could reach him instantly, unobtrusively. Except the whore. No risk could be taken that such a device would be found on her. She was expendable.

One of the two men sat in a booth in the dimly lit cocktail lounge with small candle lanterns on each table. Beside him was an open attaché case, papers pulled out and placed under candlelight; a salesman summarizing the events of a business trip. The other man was in the dining room, the table set for two, the reservation made by a highly placed aide at the White House. The host was delayed; several apologetic calls were received by the maitre d'. The guest would be treated as befitted one receiving such apologies from 1600 Pennsylvania Avenue.

But it was the older woman Taleniekov counted on most; she was paid well above the others and with good reason. She was not a *nichivo* at all. She was a killer.

His unexpected weapon. A gracious, articulate woman who had no compunction about firing a weapon into a target across the room, or plunging a knife into the stomach of a dinner companion. Who could, on a moment's notice, change her appearance from the dignified to the harridan—and all shades in between. Vasili had paid her thousands over the past half-dozen years, several times having flown her to Europe for chores that suited her extraordinary talents. She had not failed him; she would not fail him tonight. He had reached her soon after landing at Kennedy Airport; she had had a full day to prepare for the evening. It was sufficient.

Taleniekov pushed himself away from the brick wall, shaking his fingers, breathing deeply, forcing thoughts of sleep from his mind. He had covered his flanks; now he could only wait. *If* Scofield wanted to keep the appointment—in the American's judgment, fatal to one of them. And why wouldn't he? It was better to get it over with rather than be obsessed with every patch of darkness or each crowded street in sunlight, wondering who might be concealed . . . taking aim, unsheathing a knife. No, it was far more desirable to conclude the hunt; that would be Beowulf Agate's opinion. And yet, how *wrong* he was! If there was only some way to reach him, *tell* him! There was the *Matarese!* There were people to see, to appeal to, to convince! Together they could do it; there were decent men in Moscow *and* Washington, men who would *not* be afraid.

But there was no way to reach Brandon Scofield on neutral ground, for no ground would be neutral to Beowulf Agate. At the first sight of his enemy, the American would instantly use every weapon he had mustered to blow that enemy away. Vasili understood, for if he were Scofield, he would do the same. So it was a question of waiting, circling, knowing that each thought the other was the quarry who would expose himself first; each maneuvering to cause his adversary to make that mistake.

The terrible irony was that the only significant mistake would come about if

Scofield won. Taleniekov could not let that happen. Wherever Scofield was, he had to be taken, immobilized, *forced to listen.*

Which was why the waiting was so important now. And the master strategist of East Berlin and Riga and Sevastopol was an expert in patience.

"The waiting paid off, Mr. Congdon," said the excited voice over the phone. "Scofield's on a charter out of Tavernier in the Florida Keys. We estimate he'll arrive in the Virgin Islands the day after tomorrow."

"What's the source of your information?" asked the Director of Consular Operations apprehensively, clearing the sleep from his throat, squinting at the clock on his bedside table. It was three in the morning.

"The hotel in Charlotte Amalie."

"What's the source of *their* information?"

"They received an overseas call asking that the reservation be held. That he'd be there in two days."

"Who made the call? Where did it come from?"

There was a pause on the other end of the State Department line. "We assume Scofield. From the Keys."

"Don't assume. Find out."

"We're confirming everything, of course. Our man in Key West is on his way to Tavernier now. He'll check out all the charter logs."

"Check out that phone call. Let me know." Congdon hung up and raised himself on the pillow. He looked over at his wife on the twin bed next to him. She had pulled the sheet over her head. The years had taught her to sleep through the all-night calls. He thought about the one he had just received. It was too simple, too believable. Scofield was covering himself in the haze of casual, spur-of-the-moment traveling; an exhausted man getting away for a while. But there was the contradiction: Scofield was not a man ever exhausted to the point of being casual about anything. He had deliberately obscured his movements . . . which meant he *had* killed the intelligence officer from Brussels.

KGB. Brussels. Taleniekov.

East Berlin.

Taleniekov and the man from Brussels had worked together in East Berlin. In a "relatively autonomous section of KGB"—which means East Berlin . . . and beyond.

In Washington? Had that "relatively autonomous" unit from East Berlin sent men to Washington? It was not unreasonable. The word "autonomous" had two meanings. Not only was it designed to absolve superiors from certain acts of their subordinates but it signified freedom of movement. A CIA agent in Lisbon might track a man to Athens. Why not? He was familiar with an operation. Conversely, a KGB agent in London would follow an espionage suspect to New York. Given general clearance, it was in his line of duty. Taleniekov had operated in Washington; there was speculation that he had made a dozen trips or more to the United States within the past decade.

Taleniekov and the man from Brussels; *that* was the connection they had to examine. Congdon sat forward and reached for the telephone, then stopped. Timing was everything now. The cables had been received in Amsterdam, Marseilles and Prague nearly twelve hours ago. According to reliable informants, they had stunned the recipients. Covert sources in all three cities had reacted to the news of Scofield's "unsalvageable" behavior with some panic. Names could be revealed, men and women tortured, killed, whole networks exposed; no time was to be lost in eliminating Beowulf Agate. Word had been relayed by early evening that two men had already been chosen as the killers. In Prague and Marseilles; they were in the air now, on their way to Washington, no delays anticipated regarding passports or immigration procedures. A third would be leaving Amsterdam before morning; it was morning now in Amsterdam.

By noon, an execution team totally disassociated from the United States government would be in Washington. Each man had the same telephone number to call, an untraceable phone in the Baltimore ghetto. Whatever information had been gathered on Scofield would be relayed by the person at that number. And only one man could give that information to Baltimore. The man responsible: the Director of Consular Operations. No one else in the United States government had the number.

Could one final connection be made? wondered Congdon. There was so little time and it would take extraordinary cooperation. Could that cooperation be requested, even approached? Nothing like it had ever happened. But if it *could* be made, a location might be uncovered, a dual execution guaranteed.

He had been about to call the Secretary of State to suggest a very unusual, early morning meeting with the Soviet Ambassador. But too much time would be consumed with diplomatic complications, neither side wishing to acknowledge the objective of violence. There was a better way; it was dangerous but infinitely more direct.

Congdon got out of bed quietly, went downstairs, and entered the small study that was his office at home. He went to his desk, which was bolted into the floor, the lower right-hand drawers concealing a safe with a combination lock. He turned on the lamp, opened the panel and twisted the dial. The lock clicked; the steel plate sprung open. He reached inside and took out an index card with a telephone number written on it.

The number was one he never thought he would call. The area code was 902—Nova Scotia—and it never went unanswered; it was the number for a computer complex, the central clearing station for all Soviet intelligence operations in North America. By calling it, he exposed information that should not be revealed; the complex in Nova Scotia was not supposedly known by U.S. intelligence, but time and the extraordinary circumstances overrode security. There was a man in Nova Scotia who would understand; he would not be concerned about appearances. He had called for too many sentences of death. He was the highest ranking KGB officer outside of Russia.

Congdon reached for the telephone.

"Cabot Strait Exporters," said the male voice in Nova Scotia. "Night dispatcher."

"This is Daniel Congdon, Undersecretary of State, Consular Operations, United States Government. I request that you put a trace on this call to verify that I'm telephoning from a private residence in Herndon Falls, Virginia. While you're doing that, please activate electronic scanners for evidence of taps on the line. You won't find any. I'll wait as long as you wish, but I must speak with Voltage One, *Vol't Adin,* I think you call him."

His words were greeted by silence from Nova Scotia. It did not take much imagination to visualize a stunned operator pushing emergency buttons. Finally, the voice replied.

"There seems to be interference. Please repeat your message."

Congdon did so.

Again, silence. Then, "If you'll hold on, the supervisor will speak with you. However, we think you've reached the wrong party here in Cape Breton."

"You're not in Cape Breton. You're in Saint Peter's Bay, Prince Edward Island."

"Hold on, please."

The wait took nearly three minutes. Congdon sat down; it was working.

Voltage One got on the line. "Please wait for a moment or two," said the Russian. There followed the hollow sound of a connection still intact but suspended; electronic devices were in operation. The Soviet returned. "This call, indeed, originates from a residential telephone in the town of Herndon Falls, Virginia. The scanners pick up no evidence of interference but, of course, that could be meaningless."

"I don't know what other proof to give you. . . ."

"You mistake me, Mr. Undersecretary. The fact that you possess this number is not in itself earthshaking; the fact that you have the audacity to use it and ask for me by my code name, perhaps is. I have the proof I need. What is this business between us?"

Congdon told him in as few words as possible. "You want Taleniekov. We want Scofield. The contact ground is Washington, I'm convinced of it. The key to the location is your man from Brussels."

"If I recall, his body was delivered to the embassy several days ago."

"Yes."

"You've connected it with Scofield?"

"Your own Ambassador did. He pointed out that the man was part of a KGB section in East Berlin in 1968. Taleniekov's unit. There was an incident involving Scofield's wife."

"I see," said the Russian. "So Beowulf Agate still kills for revenge."

"That's a bit much, isn't it? May I remind you that it would appear Taleniekov is coming after Scofield, not the other way around."

"Be specific, Mr. Undersecretary. Since we agree in principle, what do you want from us?"

"It's in your computers, or in a file somewhere. It probably goes back a number of years, but it's there; it would be in ours. We believe that at one time or another the man from Brussels and Taleniekov operated in Washington. We need to know the address of the hole. It's the only connection we have between Scofield and Taleniekov. We think that's where they'll meet."

"I see," repeated the Soviet. "And presuming there is such an address, or addresses, what would be the position of your government?"

Congdon was prepared for the question. "No position at all," he replied in a monotone. "The information will be relayed to others, men very much concerned about Beowulf Agate's recent behavior. Outside of myself, no one in my government will be involved."

"A ciphered cable, identical in substance, was sent to three counter-revolutionary cells in Europe. To Prague, Marseilles, and Amsterdam. Such cables can produce killers."

"I commend you on your interception," said the Director of *Cons Op*.

"You do the same with us every day. No compliments are called for."

"You made no move to interfere?"

"Of course not, Mr. Undersecretary. Would you?"

"No."

"It's eleven o'clock in Moscow. I'll call you back within the hour."

Congdon hung up and leaned back in the chair. He desperately wanted a drink, but would not give in to the need. For the first time in a long career he was dealing directly with faceless enemies in Moscow. There could be no hint of irresponsibility; he was alone and in that solitary contact was his protection. He closed his eyes and pictured blank walls of white concrete in his mind's eye.

Twenty-two minutes later the phone rang. He sprang forward and picked it up.

"There's a small, exclusive hotel on Nebraska Avenue. . . ."

8

Scofield let the cold water run in the basin, leaned against the sink, and looked into the mirror. His eyes were bloodshot from lack of sleep, the stubble of his beard pronounced. He had not shaved in nearly three days, the periods of rest cumulatively not much more than three hours. It was shortly past four in the morning and no time to consider sleeping or shaving.

Across the hall, Taleniekov's well-dressed decoy was getting no more sleep than he was; the telephone calls were coming every fifteen minutes now.

Mr. Brandon Scofield, please.
I don't know any Scofield! Stop calling me! Who are you?
A friend of Mr. Scofield's. It's urgent that I speak with him.
He's not here! I don't know him. Stop it! You're driving me crazy. I'll tell the hotel not to ring this phone anymore!
I wouldn't do that, if I were you. Your friend would not approve. You wouldn't be paid. Stop it!

Bray's former lover from Paris was doing her job well. She had asked only one question when he had made the request that she keep up the calls.

"Are you in trouble, darling?"

"Yes."

"Then I'll do as you ask. Tell me what you can, so I'll know what to say."

"Don't talk over twenty seconds. I don't know who controls the switchboard."

"You *are* in trouble."

Within an hour, or less, the woman across the hall would go into panic and flee the hotel. Whatever she had been promised was not worth the macabre phone calls, the escalating sense of danger. The decoy would be removed, the hunter stymied.

Taleniekov would then be forced to send in his birds and the process would start over again. Only the phone calls would come less frequently, perhaps every hour, just when sleep was settling in. Eventually, the birds would fly away, there being limits as to how long they could stay in the air. The hunter's resources were extensive, but not *that* extensive. He was operating in foreign territory; how many decoys and birds were available to him? He could not go on indefinitely calling blind contacts, setting up hastily summoned meetings, issuing instructions and money.

No, he could not do that. Frustration and exhaustion would converge and the hunter would be alone, at the end of his resources. Finally, he would show himself. He had no choice; he could not leave the drop unattended. It was the only trap he had, the only connection between himself and the quarry.

Sooner or later Taleniekov would walk down the hotel corridor and stop at the door of suite 211. When he did, it would be the last sight he'd see.

The Soviet killer was good, but he was going to lose his life to the man he called Beowulf Agate, thought Scofield. He turned off the faucet and plunged his face into the cold water.

He pulled up his head; there were sounds of movement in the corridor. He walked to the tiny circular peephole. Across the way, a matronly looking hotel maid was unlocking the door. Draped over her right forearm were several towels and sheets. A maid at four o'clock in the morning? Bray silently acknowledged Taleniekov's imagination; he had hired an all-night maid to be his late-night eyes inside. It was an able move, but flawed. Such an individual was too limited, too easily removed; she could be called away by the front desk. A guest had had an accident, a burning cigarette, an overturned pitcher of water. Too limited. And with a greater flaw.

In the morning she would go off duty. And when she did, she would be summoned by a guest across the hall.

Scofield was about to go back to his basin when he heard the commotion; he looked once more through the glass circle.

The well-dressed woman had walked out of the room, her overnight case in her hand. The maid stood in the doorway. Scofield could hear the decoy's words.

"Tell him to go to hell!" shouted the woman. "He's a fucking nut, dear. This whole goddamn place is filled with nuts!"

The maid watched in silence as the woman walked rapidly down the corridor. Then she closed the door, remaining inside.

The matronly looking maid had been paid well; she would be paid better in the morning by a guest across the hall. The negotiations would begin quickly the second she stepped out of the suite.

The string was drawing tighter, everything was patience now. And staying awake.

Taleniekov walked the streets, aware that his legs were close to buckling, struggling to stay alert and avoid colliding with the crowds on the sidewalk. He played mental games to keep his concentration alive, counting footsteps and cracks in the pavement and blocks between telephone booths. The radios could not be used any longer; the citizen-bands were filled with babble. He cursed the fact that there had not been time to purchase more sophisticated equipment. But he never thought it could possibly go on so *long!* Madness!

It was twenty minutes past eleven in the morning, the city of Washington vibrating, people rushing, automobiles and buses clogging the streets . . . and still the insane telephone calls kept coming to the suite at the hotel on Nebraska Avenue.

Brandon Scofield, please. It's urgent that I speak with him. . . .

Insanity!

What was Scofield *doing?* Where *was* he? Where were his intermediaries?

Only the old woman remained in the hotel. The whore had revolted, the two men long since exhausted, their presence merely embarrassing, accomplishing nothing. The woman stayed in the suite, getting what rest she could between the maddening telephone calls, relaying every word spoken by the caller. A female with a pronounced "foreign" accent, probably French, never staying on the line more than fifteen seconds, unable to be drawn out and very abrupt. She was either a professional, or being instructed by a professional; there could be no tracing the number or the location of the calls.

Vasili approached the phone booth fifty yards north of the hotel's entrance on the opposite side of the street. It was the fourth call he had made from this particular booth, and he had memorized the graffiti and the odd numbers scratched on the gray metal of the edge. He walked in, pulled the glass door shut, and inserted a coin; the tone hummed in his ear and he reached for the dial.

Prague!

His eyes were playing tricks on him! Across Nebraska Avenue a man got out of a taxi and stood on the pavement looking down the street toward the hotel. He knew that *man!*

At least, he knew the face. And it *was* Prague!

The man had a history of violence, both political and nonpolitical. His police record was filled with assaults, thefts, and unproven homicides, his years in prison nearer ten than five. He had worked against the state more for profit than for ideology; he had been well paid by the Americans. His firing arm was good, his knife better.

That he was in Washington and less than fifty yards from this particular hotel could only mean he had a connection with Scofield. Yet there was no sense in the connection! Beowulf Agate had scores of men and women he could call upon for help in dozens of cities, but he would not call on someone from Europe *now*, and he certainly would not call on *this* man; the streak of sadism was conceivably unmanageable. Why was he here? Who had summoned him?

Who had *sent* him? And were there others?

But it was the *why* that burned into Taleniekov's brain. It was profoundly disturbing. Beyond the fact that the Bern-Washington depot had been revealed—undoubtedly, unwittingly by Scofield himself—someone knowing it had reached Prague for a walking gun known to have performed extensively for the Americans.

Why? Who was the target?

Beowulf Agate?

Oh, God! There *was* a method; it had been used before by Washington . . . and strangely enough there was a vague similarity to the ways of the Matarese. *Storm clouds over Washington. . . .* Scofield had run into a storm so severe that he had not only been terminated, but conceivably his execution had been ordered. Vasili had to be sure; the man from Prague might himself be a ploy, a brilliant ploy, designed to trap a Russian, not kill an American.

His hand was still suspended in front of the dial. He pressed down on the coin return lever and thought for a moment, wondering if he could take the risk. Then he saw the man across the street check his watch and turn toward the entrance of a coffee shop; he was going to meet someone. There *were* others, and Vasili knew that he could not afford *not* to take the risk. He had to find out; there was no way to know how much time was left. It might only be minutes.

There was a *pradavyet* at the embassy, a diplomatic assistant whose left foot had been blown off during a counterinsurgency operation in Riga a number of years ago. He was a KGB veteran, and he and Taleniekov had once been friends. It perhaps was not the moment to test that former friendship, but Vasili had no choice. He knew the number of the embassy; it had not changed in years. He reinserted the coin and dialed.

"It's been a long time since that terrible night in Riga, old friend," said Taleniekov after having been connected to the *pradavyet*'s office.

"Would you remain on the line, please," was the reply. "I have another call."

Vasili stared at the telephone. If the wait was more than thirty seconds, he'd have his answer; the former friendship would not serve. There were ways for even the Soviets to trace a call in the national capital of the United States. He turned his wrist and kept his eyes on the thin, jumping hand of his watch. *Twenty-eight, twenty-nine, thirty, thirty-one . . . thirty-two.* He reached up to break the connection when he heard the voice.

"Taleniekov? It is you?"

Vasili recognized the echoing sound of an activated jamming device placed over the mouthpiece of a telephone. It operated on the principle of electronic spillage; any intercepts would be clogged with static. "Yes, old friend. I nearly hung up on you."

"Riga was not that long ago. What *happened?* The stories we get are crazy."

"I'm no traitor."

"No one over here thinks you are. We assume you stepped on some large Muscovite feet. But can you return?"

"Someday, yes."

"I can't believe the charges. Yet you're *here!*"

"Because I must be. For Russia's sake, for all our sakes. *Trust* me. I need information, quickly. If anyone at the embassy has it, you would."

"What is it?"

"I've just seen a man from Prague, someone the Americans used for his more violent talents. We kept an extensive file on him; I assume we still keep it. Do you know anything—"

"Beowulf Agate," interrupted the diplomat quietly. "It's Scofield, isn't it? That's what drives you still."

"Tell me what you know!"

"Leave it alone, Taleniekov. Leave *him* alone. Leave him to his own people; he's finished."

"My God, I'm *right,*" said Vasili, his eyes on the coffee shop across Nebraska Avenue.

"I don't know what you think you're right about, but I know three cables were intercepted. To Prague, Marseilles and Amsterdam."

"They've sent a team," broke in Taleniekov.

"Stay away. You have your revenge, the sweetest imaginable. After a lifetime, he's taken by his own."

"It can't happen! There are things you *don't know.*"

"It can happen regardless of what I know. We can't stop it."

Suddenly, Vasili's attention was drawn to a pedestrian about to cross the intersection not ten yards from the telephone booth. There was something about the man, the set expression of his face, the eyes that darted from side to side behind the lightly tinted glasses—bewildered, perhaps, but not lost, studying his surroundings. And the man's clothes, loose-fitting, inexpensive tweeds, thick and made to last . . . they were French. The glasses were *French,* the man's face itself *Gallic.* He looked across the street toward the marquee of the hotel, and hastened his step.

Marseilles had arrived.

"Come in to us." The diplomat was speaking. "Whatever happened cannot be irreparable in light of your extraordinary contributions." The former comrade from Riga was being persuasive. Too persuasive. It was not in character between professionals. "The fact that you came in voluntarily will be in your favor. Heaven knows, you'll have our support. We'll ascribe your flight to a temporary aberration, a highly emotional state. After all, Scofield killed your brother."

"I killed his wife."

"A wife is not blood. These things are understandable. Do the right thing. Come in, Taleniekov."

The excessive persuasion was now illogical. One did not voluntarily turn himself in until the evidence of exoneration was more concrete. Not with an order for summary execution on one's head. Perhaps, after all, the former friendship could not stand the strain. "You'll protect me?" he asked the *pradavyet.*

"Of course."

A lie. No such protection could be promised. Something *was* wrong.

Across the street, the man wearing tinted glasses approached the coffee shop. He slowed his pace, then stopped and went up to the window as if studying a menu affixed to the glass. He lit a cigarette. From inside, barely seen in the sunlight, there was a flicker of a match. The Frenchman went inside. Prague and Marseilles had made contact.

"Thank you for your advice," said Vasili into the phone. "I'll think it over and call you back."

"It would be best if you didn't delay," answered the diplomat, urgency replacing sympathetic persuasion. "Your situation would not be improved by any involvement with Scofield. You should not be seen down there."

Seen down there? Taleniekov reacted to the words as though a gun had been fired in front of his face. In his old friend's knowledge was the betrayal! Seen down *where?* His colleague from Riga knew! The hotel on Nebraska Avenue. Scofield had not exposed the Bern depot—unwittingly or otherwise. *KGB had!* Soviet intelligence was a participant in Beowulf Agate's execution. *Why?*

The Matarese? There was no time to think, only act. . . . The hotel! Scofield was not sitting alone by a phone in some out-of-the-way place, waiting to hear from intermediaries. He was in the *hotel.* No one would have to leave the premises to report to Beowulf Agate, no bird could be followed to the target. The target had executed a brilliant maneuver: he was in the direct range of fire, but unseen, observing but unobservable.

"You really *must* listen to me, Vasili." The *pradavyet's* words came faster now; he obviously sensed indecision. If his former colleague from Riga had to be killed, it could be done any number of ways within the embassy. That was infinitely preferable to a comrade's corpse being found in an American hotel, somehow tied to the murder of an American intelligence officer by foreign agents. Which meant the KGB had revealed the location of the depot to the Americans, but had not known the precise schedule of the execution at the time.

They knew it *now*. Someone in the State Department had told them, the message clear. His countrymen had to stay away from the hotel—as did the Americans. None could be involved. Vasili had to buy minutes, for minutes might be all he had left. Diversion.

"I'm listening." Taleniekov's voice was choked with sincerity, an exhausted man coming to his senses. "You're right. I've nothing to gain now, only everything to lose. I put myself in your hands. If I can find a taxi in this insane traffic, I'll be at the embassy in thirty minutes. Watch for me. I need you."

Vasili broke the connection, and inserted another coin. He dialed the hotel's number; no second could be wasted.

"He's *here?*" said the old woman incredulously, in response to Taleniekov's statement.

"My guess would be nearby. It would explain the timing, the phone calls, his knowing when someone was in the suite. He could hear sounds through the walls, open a door when he heard someone in the corridor. Are you still in your uniform?"

"Yes. I'm too tired to take it off."

"Check the surrounding rooms."

"Good heavens, do you know what you're asking? What if he . . ."

"I know what I'm paying; there's more if you do it. Do it! There's not a moment to be lost! I'll call you back in five minutes."

"How will I *know* him?"

"He won't let you into the room."

Bray sat shirtless between the open window and the door, and let the cold air send shivers through his body. He had brought the temperature of the room down to fifty degrees, the chill was necessary to keep him awake. A cold tired man was far more alert than a warm one.

There was the tiny, blunt sound of metal slapping against metal, then the twisting of a knob. Outside in the hallway a door was being opened. Scofield went to the window and closed it, then walked quickly to another window, his minute lookout on a narrow world that soon would be the site of his reverse trap. It *had* to be soon; he was not sure how much longer he could go on.

Across the way, the pleasant-looking elderly maid had come out of the suite, towels and sheets still draped over her arm. From the expression on her face, she was perplexed but resigned. Undoubtedly, from her point of view, an unheard-of sum of money had been offered by a foreigner who only wished her to remain in a grand suite of rooms and stay awake to receive a series of very strange telephone calls.

And someone else had stayed awake to make those calls. Someone Bray owed a great deal to; he would repay her one day. But right now he concentrated on Taleniekov's bird. She was leaving; she was not capable of staying in the air any longer.

She had abandoned the drop. It was only a question of time now and very little time at that. The hunter would be forced to examine his trap. And be caught in it.

Scofield walked over to his open suitcase on the luggage rack and took out a fresh shirt. Starched, not soft; a crisp, starched shirt was like a cold room, a benign irritant; it kept one alert.

He put it on, and crossed to the bedside table where he had placed his gun, a Browning Magnum, Grade 4, with a custom-made silencer drilled to his specifications.

Bray spun around at an unexpected sound. There was a hesitant tapping at his door. Why? He had paid for total isolation. The front desk had made it clear to those few employees who might have reason to enter room 213 that the sign on the knob was to be respected.

Do Not Disturb.

Yet someone was now disregarding that order, bypassing a guest's request that had been re-enforced with several hundred dollars. Whoever it was was either deaf or illiterate or . . .

It was the maid. Taleniekov's bird, still in the air. Scofield peered through the tiny circle of glass that magnified the aged features of the face only inches away. The tired eyes, encased in wrinkled flesh swollen by lack of sleep, looked to the left, then the right, then dropped to the lower part of the door. The old woman had to be aware of the *Do Not Disturb* sign, but it had no meaning for her. Beyond the contradictory behavior, there was something odd about the face . . . but Bray had no time to study it further. Under these new circumstances, the negotiations had to begin quickly. He shoved the gun into his shirt, the stiff cloth keeping the bulge to a minimum.

"Yes?" he asked.

"Maid service, sir," was the reply, spoken in an indeterminate brogue, more guttural than definable. "The management has asked that all rooms be checked for supplies, sir."

It was a poor lie, the bird too flawed to think of a better one.

"Come in," said Scofield, reaching for the latch.

"There's no answer in suite two-eleven," said the switchboard operator, annoyed by the persistence of the caller.

"Try it *again*," replied Taleniekov, his eyes on the entrance of the coffee shop across the street. "They may have stepped out for a moment, but they'll be right back. I *know* it. Keep ringing, I'll stay on the line."

"As you wish, sir," snapped the operator.

Madness! Nine minutes had passed since the old woman had begun the search, nine minutes to check four doors in the hallway. Even assuming all the rooms were occupied, and a maid had to give explanations to the occupants, nine minutes was far longer than she needed. A fourth conversation would be brief and blunt. *Go away. I am not to be disturbed.* Unless . . .

A match flared in the sunlight, its reflection sharp in the dark glass of the coffee shop window. Vasili blinked and stared; from one of the unseen tables inside there was a corresponding signal, extinguished quickly.

Amsterdam had arrived; the execution team was complete. Taleniekov studied the figure walking toward the small restaurant. He was tall and dressed in a black overcoat, a gray silk muffler around his throat. His hat, too, was gray, and obscured his profile.

The ringing on the telephone was now abrasive. Long sudden bursts resulting from a furious operator punching a switchboard button. There was no answer and Vasili began to think the unthinkable: Beowulf Agate had intercepted his bait. If so, the American was in greater danger than he could imagine. Three men had flown in from Europe to be his executioners, and—no less lethal—a gentle-appearing old woman whom he might try to compromise would kill him the instant she felt cornered. He would never know where the shot came from, nor that she even had a weapon.

"I'm sorry, sir!" said the operator angrily. "There's still no pickup in suite two-eleven. I suggest you call again." She did not wait for a reply; the switchboard line was disconnected.

The *switchboard?* The *operator?*

It was a desperate tactic, one he would never condone except as a last-extremity measure; the risk of exposure was too great. But it *was* the last extremity and if there were alternatives he was too exhausted to think of them. Again, he knew only that he had to act, each decision an instinctive reflex, the shaping of those instincts trusted. He reached into his pocket for his money and removed five one-hundred dollar bills. Then he took out his passport case, and extracted a letter he had written on an English-language typewriter five days ago in Moscow. The letterhead was that of a brokerage house in Bern; it identified the bearer as one of the firm's partners. One never knew. . . .

He walked out of the telephone booth and entered the flow of pedestrians until he was directly opposite the entrance of the hotel. He waited for a break in the traffic, then walked rapidly across Nebraska Avenue.

Two minutes later a solicitous day manager introduced a Monsieur Blanchard to the operator of the hotel switchboard. This same manager—as impressed with Monsieur Blanchard's credentials as he was with the two hundred dollars the Swiss financier had casually insisted he take for his troubles—dutifully provided a relief operator while the woman talked alone with the generous Monsieur Blanchard.

"I ask you to forgive a worried man's rudeness over the telephone," said Taleniekov, as he pressed three one-hundred-dollar bills into her nervous hand. "The ways of international finance can be appalling in these times. It is a bloodless war, a constant struggle to prevent unscrupulous men from taking advantage of honest brokers and legitimate institutions. My company has just such a problem. There's someone in this hotel. . . ."

A minute later, Vasili was reading a master list of telephone charges, recorded by a mindless computer. He concentrated on the calls made from the second floor; there were two corridors, suites 211 and 212 opposite three double rooms in the west wing, four single rooms on the other side. He studied all charges billed to telephones 211 through 215. Names would mean nothing; local calls were not identified by number; long distance charges were the only items that might provide information. Beowulf Agate had to build a cover and it would not be in Washington. He had killed a man in Washington.

The hotel was, as Taleniekov knew, an expensive one. This was further confirmed by the range of calls made by guests who thought nothing of picking up a telephone and calling London as easily as a nearby restaurant. He scanned the sheets, concentrating on the *O.O.T.* areas listed.

212 . . . London, U.K. chgs: $26.50
214 . . . Des Moines, Ia. chgs: $4.75
214 . . . Cedar Rapids, Ia. chgs: $6.20
213 . . . Minneapolis, Minn. chgs: $7.10
215 . . . New Orleans, La. chgs: $11.55
214 . . . Denver, Col. chgs: $6.75
213 . . . Easton, Md. chgs: $8.05
215 . . . Atlanta, Ga. chgs: $3.15
212 . . . Munich, Germ. chgs: $41.10
213 . . . Easton, Md. chgs: $4.30
212 . . . Stockholm, Swed. chgs: $38.25

Where was the pattern? Suite 212 had made frequent calls to Europe, but that was too obvious, too dangerous. Scofield would not place such traceable calls. Room 214 was centered in the Midwest, Room 215 in the south. There *was* something but he could not pinpoint it. *Something* that triggered a memory.

Then he saw it and the memory was activated, clarified. The one room without a pattern. Room 213. Two calls to Easton, Maryland, one to Minneapolis, Minnesota. Vasili could see the words in the dossier as if he were reading them. Brandon Scofield had a sister in Minneapolis, Minnesota.

Taleniekov memorized both numbers in case it was necessary to use them, if there was *time* to use them, to confirm them. He turned to the operator. "I don't know what to say. You've been most helpful but I don't think there's anything here that will help."

The switchboard operator had entered into the minor conspiracy, and was enjoying her prominence with the impressive Swiss. "If you'll note, Monsieur Blanchard, suite two-twelve placed a number of overseas calls."

"Yes, I see that. Unfortunately, no one in those cities would have anything to do with the present crisis. Strange, though. Room two-thirteen telephoned Easton and Minneapolis. An odd coincidence, but I have friends in both places. However, nothing relevant. . . ." Vasili let his words drift off, inviting comment.

"Just between the two of us, Monsieur Blanchard, I don't think the gentleman in room two-thirteen is all there, if you know what I mean."

"Oh?"

The woman explained. The *DND* on 213 was a standing order; no one was to disturb the man's privacy. Even room service was instructed to leave the tray tables in the hallway, and maid service was to be suspended until specifically requested. To the best of the operator's knowledge, there had been no such request in three days. Who could live like that?

"Of course, we get people like him all the time. Men who reserve a room so they can stay drunk for hours on end, or get away from their wives or meet other women. But three days without maid service, I think is *sick.*"

"It's hardly fastidious."

"You see it more and more," said the woman confidentially. "Especially in the government; everyone's so harried. But when you think our taxes are *paying* for it—I don't mean *yours,* Monsieur. . . ."

"He's in the government?" interrupted Taleniekov.

"Oh, we think so. The night manager wasn't supposed to say anything to *anybody,* but we've been here for years, if you know what I mean."

"Old friends, of course. What happened?"

"Well, a man came by last evening—actually it was this morning, around five A.M.—and showed the manager a photograph."

"A picture of the man in two-thirteen?"

The operator glanced around briefly; the door of the office was open, but she could not be overheard. "Yes. Apparently he's *really* sick. An alcoholic or something, a psychiatric case. No one's to say anything; they don't want to alarm him. A doctor will be coming for him sometime today."

"Sometime today? And, of course, the man who showed the photograph identified himself as someone from the government, didn't he? I mean, that's how you learned the guest upstairs was *in* the government?"

"When you've spent as many years in Washington as we have, Monsieur Blanchard, you don't have to ask for identification. It's all over their faces."

"Yes, I imagine it is. Thank you so much. You've been a great help."

Vasili left the room quickly and rushed out into the lobby. He had his confirmation. He had found Beowulf Agate.

But others had found him, too. Scofield's executioners were only a few hundred feet away, preparing to close in on the condemned man.

To break into the American's room to warn him would be to invite an exchange of gunfire; one or both would die. To reach him on the telephone would provoke only disbelief; where was the credibility in such an alarm delivered by an enemy one loathed about a *new* enemy one did not know existed?

There had to be a way and it had to be found quickly. If there was only time to send another, with something on his person that would explain the truth to Scofield. Something Beowulf Agate would accept. . . .

There was no time. Vasili saw the man in the black overcoat walk through the entrance of the hotel.

9

Scofield knew the instant the maid walked through the door what disturbed him about the elderly face. It was the eyes. There was an intelligence behind them beyond that of a plain-spoken domestic who spent her nights cleaning up the soils of pampered hotel guests. She was frightened—or perhaps merely curious—but whichever, neither was born of a blunt mind.

An actress, perhaps?

"Forgive my disturbin' you, sir," said the woman, noticing his unshaven face and the cold room and heading for the open bathroom door. "I'll not be a minute."

An actress. The brogue was an affectation, no roots in Ireland. Too, the walk was light; she did not have the leg muscles of an old woman used to the drudgery of carrying linens and bending over beds. And the hands were white and soft, not those of someone used to abrasive cleansers.

Bray found himself pitying her even while faulting Taleniekov's choice again. A real maid would have made a better bird.

"You've a fresh supply of towels, sir," said the old woman coming out of the bathroom and heading for the door. "I'll be on my way. Sorry for disturbin' you."

Scofield stopped her with a gesture.

"Sir?" asked the woman, her eyes alert.

"Tell me, what part of Ireland do you come from? I can't place the dialect. County Wicklow, I think."

"Yes, sir."

"The south country?"

"Yes, sir; very good, sir," she said rapidly, her left hand on the doorknob.

"Would you mind leaving me an extra towel? Just put it on the bed."

"Oh?" The old woman turned, the perplexed expression again on her face. "Yes, sir, of course." She started toward the bed.

Bray went to the door and pushed the bolt into place. He spoke as he did so, but gently; there was nothing to be gained by alarming Taleniekov's frightened bird. "I'd like to talk to you. You see, I watched you last night, at four o'clock this morning to be precise—"

A rush of air, the scratching of fabric. Sounds he was familiar with. *Behind him in the room.*

He spun, but not in time. He heard the muted spit and felt a razorlike cut across the skin of his neck. An eruption of blood, spread over his left shoulder. He lunged to his right; a second shot followed, the bullet embedding itself in the wall above him. He swung his arm in a violent arc, sending a lamp off a table toward the *impossible* sight six feet away, in the center of the room.

The old woman had dropped the towels and in her hand was a gun. Gone was her soft, gentle bewilderment; in its place, the calm, determined face of an experienced killer. *He should have known!*

He dove to the floor, his fingers gripping the base of the table; he spun again to his right, then twisted to his left, lifting the table by its legs like a small battering ram. He rose, crashing forward; two more shots were fired, splintering the wood inches above his head.

He rammed the woman, hammering her back into the wall with such force that a stream of saliva accompanied the expulsion of breath from the snarling lips.

"Bastard!" The scream was swallowed as the gun clattered to the floor. Scofield dropped the table, slamming it down on her feet as he reached for the weapon.

He held it, stood up, and grabbed the bent-over woman by the hair, yanking her away from the wall. The red wig beneath the ruffled maid's cap came off in his hand, throwing him off balance. From somewhere beneath the uniform, the gray-haired killer had pulled a knife—a thin stiletto. Bray had seen such weapons before; they were as deadly as any gun, the blades coated with succinyl choline. Paralysis began in seconds, death seconds later. A scrape or a superficial puncture was all the attacker needed to inflict.

She was on him, the thin knife plunging straight forward, the most difficult thrust to parry, used by the most experienced. He leaped backwards, crashing the gun down on the woman's forearm. She withdrew it quickly in pain, but no suspension of purpose.

"Don't *do* it!" he shouted, leveling the gun directly at her head. "Four shots were fired; two shells are left! I'll kill you!"

The old woman stopped and lowered the knife. She stood motionless, speechless, breathing heavily, staring at him in a kind of ethereal disbelief. It occurred to Scofield that she had never been in this position before; she had always won.

Taleniekov's bird was a vicious hawk in the guise of a small, gray dove. That protective coloration was her insurance. It had never failed her.

"Who are you? KGB?" asked Bray, reaching for the towel on the bed, and holding it against the wound on his neck.

"What?" she whispered, her eyes barely in focus.

"You work for Taleniekov. Where is he?"

"I'm paid by a man who uses many names," she replied, the lethal knife still held limply in her hand. Her fury was gone, replaced by fear and exhaustion. "I don't know who he is. I don't know where he is."

"He knew where to find you. You're something. Where did you learn? When?"

"When?" she repeated in her bloodless whisper. "When you were a child. Where? Out of Belsen and Dachau . . . to other camps, other fronts. All of us."

"Christ. . . ." uttered Scofield softly. *All of us.* They were legion. Girls taken from the camps, sent to the war fronts, to barracks everywhere, to airfields. Surviving as whores, dishonored by their own, unwanted, ostracized. They became the scavengers of Europe. Taleniekov *did* know where to find his flocks.

"Why do you work for him? He's no better than those who sent you to the camps."

"I have to. He'll kill me. Now you say you will."

"Thirty seconds ago, I would have. You didn't give me a choice; you can now. I'll take care of you. You stay in contact with this man. How?"

"He calls. In the suite across the hall."

"How often?"

"Every ten or fifteen minutes. He'll call again soon."

"Let's go," said Bray cautiously. "Move to your right and drop the knife on the bed."

"Then you'll *shoot,*" whispered the old woman.

"If I was going to, I'd do it now," said Scofield. He *needed* her, needed her confidence. "There'd be no reason to wait, would there? Let's get over to that phone. Whatever he was paying, I'll double."

"I don't think I can walk. I think you broke my foot."

"I'll help you." Bray lowered the towel and took a step toward her. He held out his hand. "Take my arm."

The old woman placed her left foot in front of her painfully. Then suddenly, like an enraged lioness, she lunged forward, her face again contorted, her eyes wild.

The blade came rushing toward Scofield's stomach.

Taleniekov followed the man from Amsterdam into the elevator. There was one other couple in the car. Young, rich, pampered Americans; fashionably dressed lovers or newlyweds, aware only of themselves and their hungers. They had been drinking.

The Hollander in the black overcoat removed his gray homburg, as Vasili, his face briefly turned away, stood next to him against the paneled wall of the small enclosure. The doors closed. The girl laughed softly; her companion pressed the button for the fifth floor. The man from Amsterdam stepped forward and touched number 2.

As he moved back, he glanced to his left, his eyes making contact with Taleniekov's. The man froze, the shock total, the recognition absolute. And in that shock, that recognition, Vasili saw another truth: the execution trap was meant for him as well. The team had a priority, and it was Beowulf Agate, but if a KGB agent known as Taleniekov appeared on the scene he was to be taken out as ruthlessly as Scofield.

The man from Amsterdam swung his hat in front of his chest, plunging his right hand into his pocket. Vasili rushed him, pinning him against the wall, his left hand gripping the wrist in the pocket, slipping down, separating hand from weapon, groping for the thumb, twisting it back until the bone cracked and the man bleated. He sank to his knees.

The girl screamed. Taleniekov spoke in a loud voice. He addressed the couple. "You will not be harmed. I repeat, you will not be harmed if you do as I say. Make no noise, and take us to your room."

The Hollander lurched to the right; Vasili slammed his knee into the man's face, vicing the head against the wall. He took his gun from his pocket and held it up, pointing at the ceiling.

"I will not use this. I *will not* use this unless you disobey. You're no part of our dispute and I don't want you harmed. But you must do as I say."

"*Jesus. Jesus Christ!* . . ." The young man's lips trembled.

"Take out your key," ordered Taleniekov almost amiably. "When the doors open walk casually in front of us to your room. You will be perfectly safe if you do as I say. If you don't, if you cry out, or try to raise an alarm, I shall have to shoot. I won't kill you; instead, I'll fire into your spines. You'll be paralyzed for life."

"Oh, *Christ, please!* . . ." The young man's trembling spread throughout his head, neck, and shoulders.

"*Please,* mister! We'll do whatever you say!" The girl at least was lucid; she took the key from her lover's vest.

"Get up!" said Vasili to the man from Amsterdam. He reached into the killer's overcoat pocket and removed the Hollander's weapon.

The elevator door opened. The couple walked out stiffly, passing an elderly man reading a newspaper, and turned right down the corridor. Taleniekov, his Graz-Burya concealed at his side, gripped the cloth of Amsterdam's overcoat, propelling him forward.

"One sound, Dutchman," he whispered, "and you'll not make another. I'll blow your back away; you won't have time to scream."

Inside the double room, Vasili shoved the Hollander into a chair, held his gun on him, and issued orders once again to the frightened couple. "Get inside that clothes closet. *Quickly!*"

Tears were streaming down the young man's pampered face; the girl pushed him into their dark, temporary cell. Taleniekov propped a chair underneath the knob and kicked it until it was wedged firmly between the metal and the rug. He turned to the Hollander.

"You have exactly five seconds to explain how it's to be done," he said, raising the automatic diagonally across the executioner's face.

"You'll have to be clearer," came the professional reply.

"By all means." Vasili slammed the barrel of the Graz-Burya downward, ripping the flesh of the assassin's face. Blood spread; the man raised his hands. Taleniekov bent over the chair and cracked both wrists in rapid succession. "Don't touch! We've just begun. Drink it! Soon you'll have no lips. Then no teeth, no chin, no cheekbones! Finally, I'll take your eyes! Have you ever seen a man like that? The face is a terrible source of pain, puncturing the eyes unendurable." Vasili struck again, now arcing upwards, catching the man's nostrils in the swing.

"No. . . . *No!* I followed *orders!*"

"Where have I heard that before?" Taleniekov raised the weapon; again the hands were raised and again they were repulsed with blows. "What *are* those orders, Dutchman? There are three of you and the five seconds have passed! We must be serious now." He tapped the barrel of the Graz-Burya harshly over the Hollander's left eye, then the right. "No more time!" He pulled the weapon back, then shoved it knifelike into Amsterdam's throat.

"*Stop!*" screamed the man, his air cut off, the word garbled. "I'll tell you. . . . He betrays us, he takes money for our names. He's sold out to our enemies!"

"No judgments. The *orders!*"

"He's never seen me. I'm to draw him out."

"*How?*"

"*You.* I've come to warn him. You're on your way."

"He'd reject you. Kill you! A transparent device. How did you know the room?"

"We have a photograph."

"Of *him.* Not of me."

"Both of you, actually. But I show him only his. The night manager identified him."

"Who gave you this photograph?"

"Friends from Prague, operating in Washington, with ties to the Soviets. Former friends of Beowulf Agate who know what he's done."

Taleniekov stared at the man from Amsterdam. He was telling the truth, because the explanation was based on partial truth. Scofield would look for flaws, but would not reject Amsterdam's words; he could not afford that luxury. He would take the Dutchman as hostage, and then position himself. Waiting, watching, unseen. Vasili pressed the barrel of the Graz-Burya into the Hollander's right eye.

"Marseilles and Prague. Where are they? Where will they be?"

"Besides the main elevators there are only two exits from the floors. The staircase and the service lift. One will be stationed in each."

"Which are where?"

"Prague on the staircase, Marseilles on the service lift."

"What's the schedule? By minutes."

"It's floating. I approach the door at ten past twelve."

Taleniekov glanced at the antique clock on the hotel room's desk. It was eleven minutes past twelve. "They're in position now."

"I don't know. I can't see my watch, the blood's in my eyes."

"What's the termination? If you lie, I'll know it. You'll die in a way you've never dreamed of. Describe it!"

"Zero-lock is five minutes past the half hour. If Beowulf has not appeared in either location, the room is to be stormed. Frankly, I don't trust Prague. I think he'd throw Marseilles and myself in first to take the initial fire. He's a maniac."

Vasili stood up. "Your judgment exceeds your talents."

"I've told you everything! Don't strike me again. For God's sake, let me wipe my eyes. I can't *see.*"

"Wipe them. I want you to see clearly. Get up!" The Hollander rose, his hands covering his face, brushing away the rivulets of blood, the Graz-Burya jammed into his neck.

Taleniekov stood motionless for a moment, looking at the telephone across the room. He was about to speak with an enemy he had hated for a decade, about to hear his voice.

He would try to save that enemy's life.

Scofield spun away as the lethal blade sliced into his shirt, blunted by the steel of his gun concealed under the starched cloth only minutes ago. The old woman was insane, suicidal! He would have to kill her and he did not *want* to kill her!

The *gun.*

He said four shells had been fired, two were left. *She* knew differently!

She was coming at him again, the knife crisscrossing in slashing diagonals; anything in its path would have to be touched, scraped—under normal circumstances a meaningless scratch, but not with this blade. He aimed the gun at her head and squeezed the trigger; there was nothing but the click of the firing pin.

He lashed his right foot out catching her between her breast and her armpit, staggering her for an instant, but only an instant. She was wild, clutching the knife as if it were her passport to life; if she touched him, she was free. She crouched, swinging her left arm in front of her, covering the blade that worked furiously in her right. He jumped back, looking for something, *anything* he could use to parry her lunges.

Why had she delayed before? Why had she suddenly stopped and spoken with him, telling him *things* that would make him think? Then he knew. The old hawk was not only vicious, but wise; she knew when she had to restore dissipated strength, knew she could do it only by engaging her enemy, lulling him, waiting for the unguarded instant . . . one *touch* of the coated blade.

She lunged again, the knife arcing up from the floor toward his legs. He kicked; she whipped the blade back, then slashed laterally, missing the kneecap by centimeters. As her arm swung left with the slash, he caught her shoulder with his right foot and hammered her backwards.

She fell; he grabbed the nearest upright object—a floor lamp with a heavy brass base—hurling it down at her as he kicked again at the hand that held the stiletto.

Her wrist was bent; the point of the blade pierced the fabric of her maid's uniform, entering the flesh above her left breast.

What followed was a sight he did not care to remember. The old woman's eyes grew wide and thyroid, her lips stretched into a macabre, horrible grin that was no smile. She began to writhe on the floor, her body convulsed and trembling.

She rolled into a fetal position, pulling her thin legs into her stomach, the agony complete. Prolonged, muffled screams came from her throat as she rolled again, clawing the rug; mucus disgorged from her convoluted mouth, a swollen tongue blocking passage.

Suddenly there was a horrible gasp and a final expulsion of breath. Her body jerked off the floor spastically; it became rigid. Her eyes were open wide, staring at nothing, her lips parted in death. The process had taken less than sixty seconds.

Bray leaned over and lifted the hand, separating the bony fingers. He removed the knife, stood up, and walked to the bureau where there was a book of matches. He struck one and held it under the blade. There was an eruption of flame spitting so high that it singed his hair, the heat so intense it burned his face. He dropped the stiletto, stamping the fire out under his foot.

The phone rang.

"This is Taleniekov," said the Russian into the silence of the telephone. It had been picked up but there was no voice on the line. "I submit that your position is not lessened by acknowledging our contact."

"Acknowledged," was the one-word reply.

"You reject my cable, my white flag, and were I you, I would do the same. But you're wrong and I would be wrong. I swore I'd kill you, Beowulf Agate, and perhaps one day I will, but not now and not *this* way."

"You read my cipher," was the answer, delivered in a monotone. "You killed my wife. Come and get me. I'm ready for you."

"*Stop it!* We both killed. You took a *brother* . . . and before that, an innocent young girl who was no threat to the animals who raped her and killed her!"

"What?"

"There's no time! There are men who want to kill you, but I'm not one of them! I've caught one, however; he's with me now—"

"You sent another," interrupted Scofield. "She's dead. The knife went into her, not me. The cut didn't have to be very deep."

"You had to have provoked her; it *was not* planned! But we waste seconds and you don't have them. Listen to the man I put on the phone. He's from Amsterdam. His face is damaged and he can't see very well, but he can speak." Vasili pressed the telephone against the Hollander's bloody lips and shoved the Graz-Burya into his neck. "Tell him, Dutchman!"

"Cables were sent. . . ." The injured man whispered, choking on fear and blood. "Amsterdam, Marseilles, Prague. Beowulf Agate was beyond salvage. We could all be killed if he lived. The cables made the usual statements: they were alerts, urging us to take precautions, but we knew what they meant. Don't take precautions, take out the problem, eliminate Beowulf ourselves. . . . None of this is new to you, Herr Scofield. You have given such orders; you know they must be carried out."

Taleniekov yanked the phone away while keeping the barrel of his weapon pressed against Amsterdam's neck. "You heard it. The trap you set for me is being used to ambush *you*. By your own people."

Silence. Beowulf Agate said nothing. Vasili's patience was running out. "Don't you *understand?* They've exchanged information, it's the only way they could have found the depot—what you call a 'drop.' Moscow *provided* it, can't you *see* that? Each of us is being used as the reason to execute the other, to kill us *both*. My people are more direct than yours. The order for my death has been sent to every Soviet station, civilian and military. Your State Department does it somewhat differently; the analysts take no responsibility for such unconstitutional decisions. They simply send warnings to those who care little for abstractions, but deeply for their lives."

Silence. Taleniekov exploded.

"What more do you *want?* Amsterdam was to draw you out; you would have had no choice. You would have tried to position yourself in one of two exits: the service area or the staircase. At this moment, Marseilles is by the service elevator, Prague on the staircase. The man from Prague is one you know well, Beowulf. You've employed his gun and his knife on many occasions. He's waiting for you. In less than fifteen minutes, if you do not appear in either place, they will take you in your room. What more *do* you want?"

Scofield answered at last. "I want to know why you're telling me this."

"Reread my cipher to you! This isn't the first time you and I have been used. An incredible thing is happening and it goes beyond you and me. A few men know about it. In Washington *and* Moscow. But they say nothing; no one can say anything. The admissions are catastrophic."

"What admissions?"

"The hiring of assassins. On both sides. It goes back years, *decades.*"

"How does it concern me? I don't care about you."

"Dimitri Yurievich."

"What about him?"

"They said you killed him."

"You're lying, Taleniekov. I thought you'd be better at it. Yurievich was leaning, he was a probable. The civilian killed was my contact, under *my* source-control. It was a KGB operation. Better a dead physicist than a defected one. I repeat, come and get me."

"You're *wrong!* . . . Later! There's no time to argue. You want proof? Then listen! I trust your ear is more skilled than your mind!" The Russian quickly shoved the Graz-Burya into his belt and held the mouthpiece up in the air. With his left hand he gripped the throat of the man from Amsterdam, his thumb centering on the rings of trachea cartilage. He pressed; his hand was a vise, his fingers talons crushing fiber and bone as the vise closed. The Hollander twisted violently, his arms and hands thrashing, trying to break Vasili's grip, the effort useless. His cry of pain was an unbroken scream that diminished into a wail of agony. The man from Amsterdam fell to the floor unconscious. Taleniekov spoke again into the telephone. "Is there human bait alive who would permit what I've just done?"

"Was he given an alternative?"

"You're a *fool,* Scofield! Get yourself killed!" Vasili shook his head in desperation; it was a reaction to his own loss of control. *"No. . . .* No, you mustn't. You can't understand, and I must try to grasp that, so you must try to understand me. I loathe everything you are, everything you stand for. But right now, we can do what few others can do. Make men listen, make them speak out. If for no other reason than they fear us, fear what we know. The fear is on *both* sides—"

"I don't know what you're talking about," interrupted Scofield. "You're mounting a nice KGB strategy; they'll probably give you a large *dacha* in Grasnov, but no sale. I repeat, come and get me."

"Enough!" shouted Taleniekov, looking at the clock on the desk. "You have eleven minutes! You know where your final proof is. You can find it in a service lift or on the staircase. Unless you care to learn it as you die in your room. If you create a disturbance, you'll draw a crowd. That's more to their liking, but I don't have to tell you that; you may recognize Prague, you won't Marseilles. You can't call the police, or risk the chance that the management will; we both know that. Go find your proof, Scofield! See if this enemy is lying. You'll get as far as your first turn in the corridor! If you live—which is unlikely—I'm on the fifth floor. Room five-zero-five. I've done what I can!" Vasili slammed down the phone, the gesture equal parts artifice and anger. Anything to jar the American, anything to make him think.

Taleniekov needed every second now. He had told Beowulf Agate that he had done all he could, but it was not true. He knelt down and tore off the black overcoat from Amsterdam's unconscious body.

Bray replaced the phone, his mind was churning. If he'd only had sleep, or if he had not gone through the totally unexpected violence of the old woman's attack, or if Taleniekov had not told him so much of the truth, things would be clearer. But it had all happened and, as he had done so often in the past, he had to shift into a state of blind acceptance and think in terms of immediate purpose.

It was not the first time he had been the target of factions distinct from each other. One got used to it when dealing with opposing partisans from the same broad-based camps, although killing was rarely the objective. What was unusual was the timing, the converging of separate assaults. Yet it was so understandable, so *clear.*

Undersecretary of State Daniel Congdon had really done it! The seemingly bloodless deskman had found the courage of his own convictions. More specifically, he had found Taleniekov and Taleniekov's moves toward Beowulf Agate. What better reasoning existed for breaking the rules and eliminating a terminated specialist he considered dangerous? What better motive for reaching the Soviets, who could only favor the dispatch of both men.

So clear. So well orchestrated he or Taleniekov might have conceived of the strategy. Denials and astonishment would go hand in hand, statesmen in Washington and Moscow decrying the violence of *former* intelligence officers—from another era. An era when personal animosities often superseded national inter-

ests. *Christ,* he could hear the pronouncements, couched in sanctimonious platitudes made by men like Congdon who concealed filthy decisions under respectable titles.

The infuriating thing was that the reality supported the platitudes, the words
validated by Taleniekov's hunt for revenge. *I swore I'd kill you, Beowulf Agate,
and perhaps one day I will.*

That day was today, the *perhaps* without meaning for the Russian. Taleniekov
wanted Beowulf Agate for himself; he would brook no interference from killers
recruited and programmed by deskmen in Washington and Moscow. *I will see
you take your last breath. . . .* Those were Taleniekov's words six years ago; he
meant them then and he meant them now.

Certainly he would save his enemy from the guns of Marseilles and Prague.
His enemy was worthy of a better gun, *his* gun. And no ploy was too unreasonable, no words too extreme, to bring his enemy into that gunsight.

He was tired of it all, thought Scofield, taking his hand away from the phone.
Tired of the tension of move and countermove. In the final analysis, who cared?
Who gave a goddamn for two aging *specialists,* dedicated to the proposition that
each's counterpart should die?

Bray closed his eyes, pressing his lids together, aware that there was moisture
in his sockets. Tears of fatigue, mind and body spent; it was no time to acknowledge exhaustion. Because he *cared.* If he had to die—and it was always an
around-the-corner possibility—he was not going to be taken by guns from Marseilles, Prague *or* Moscow. He was better than that; he had always *been* better.

According to Taleniekov he had eleven minutes; two had passed since the
Russian had made the statement. The trap was his room and if the man from
Prague was the one Taleniekov had described, the attack would be made quickly,
with a minimum of risk. Gas-filled pellets would precede any use of weapons, the
fumes immobilizing anyone in the room. It was a tactic favored by the killer from
Prague; he took few gambles.

The immediate objective, therefore, was to get out of the trap. Walking in the
corridor was not feasible, perhaps not even opening the door. Since it was
Amsterdam's function to draw him out, and he had not been drawn, Prague and
Marseilles would close in. If there was no one in the hallway—as the absence of
sound indicated—they had nothing to lose. Their schedule would not be postponed, but it could be accelerated.

No one in the hallway . . . *someone* in the hallway. People milling around,
excited, creating a diversion. Most of the time a crowd was to the killers' advantage, not the target's, especially if the target was identifiable and one or more of
the killers were not. On the other hand, a target who knew precisely when and
where the attack was to be made could use a crowd to cover his run from
ground-zero. An escape based on confusion, and a change of appearance. The
change did not have to be much, just enough to cause indecision; indiscriminate
gunfire during an execution had to be avoided.

Eight minutes. Or less. Everything was preparation. He would take his essential belongings, for when he began running, he'd have to keep running; how long

and how far there was no way to tell, nor could he think about that now. He had to get out of the trap and elude four men who wanted him dead, one more dangerous than the other three, for he was not sent by Washington or Moscow. He had come himself.

Bray crossed rapidly to the dead woman on the floor, dragged her to the bathroom, rolled the corpse inside, and closed the door. He picked up the heavy-based lamp and smashed it down on the knob; the lock was jammed, the door could be opened only by breaking it down.

His clothes could be left behind. There were no laundry marks or overt evidence connecting them immediately to Brandon Scofield; fingerprints would do that, but lifting and processing them would take time. He would be far away by then—if he got out of the hotel alive. His attaché case was something else; it contained too many tools of his profession. He closed it, spun the combination lock, and threw it on the bed. He put on his jacket and went back to the telephone. He picked it up and dialed the operator.

"This is room two-thirteen," he said in a whisper, effortlessly made to sound weak. "I don't want to alarm you, but I know the symptoms. I've had a stroke. I need help. . . ."

He let the phone crash against the table and drop to the floor.

10

Taleniekov put on the black overcoat, and reached down for the gray scarf, still draped around Amsterdam's throat. He yanked it off, wound it around his throat, and picked up the gray hat which had fallen beside the chair. It was too large; he creased the crown so it covered his head less awkwardly, and started for the door, passing the closet. He spoke firmly to the couple within.

"Remain where you are and make no sound! I shall be outside in the corridor. If I hear noise, I'll come back and you'll be the worse for it."

In the hall, he ran toward the main elevators, and then beyond them, to the plain dark elevator at the end of the corridor. Against the wall was a tray table used by room service. He removed his Graz-Burya from his belt, shoved it in his overcoat pocket, and pushed the button with his left hand. The red light went on above the door; the elevator was on the second floor. Marseilles was in position, waiting for Beowulf Agate.

The light went off and seconds later the number 3 shone brightly, then number 4. Vasili turned around, his back to the sliding panel.

The door opened, but there were no words of recognition, no surprise expressed at the sight of the black overcoat or the gray hat. Taleniekov spun around, his finger on the trigger of his gun.

There was no one inside the elevator. He stepped in and pressed the button for the second floor.

"Sir? Sir? My God, it's the crazy one in two-thirteen!" The excited voice of the operator floated up piercingly from the telephone on the rug. "Send up a couple of boys! See what they can do! I'll call an ambulance. He's had an attack or something. . . ."

The words were cut off; the chaos had begun.

Scofield stood by the door, unlatched it and waited. No more than forty seconds had passed when he heard racing footsteps and shouts in the corridor. The door burst open; the bell captain ran in, followed by a younger, larger man, a bellboy.

"Thank Christ it wasn't locked! *Where?* . . ."

Bray kicked the door shut, revealing himself to the two men. In his hand was his automatic. "No one's going to get hurt," he said calmly. "Just do exactly as I tell you. You," Bray ordered the younger man. "Take off your jacket and your cap. And you," he continued, speaking to the bell captain, "get on the phone and tell the operator to send up the manager. You're scared; you don't want to touch anything, there may have been trouble up here. You think I'm dead."

The older man stuttered, his eyes riveted on the gun, then ran to the phone. The performance was convincing, he was frightened out of his wits.

Bray took the maroon and gold-striped jacket held out for him by the large subordinate. He removed his coat and put it on, bunching his own under his arm. "The *cap,*" demanded Scofield. It was given.

The bell captain finished, his eyes staring wildly at Bray, his last plea screamed! "For Christ's sake, *hurry!* Get someone up here!"

Scofield gestured with his weapon. "Stand by the door next to me," he said to the frantic man, then addressed the younger. "There's a closet over there beyond the bed. Get inside. *Now!*"

The large, dense bellboy hesitated, looked at Bray's face, and retreated quickly into the closet. Scofield, his weapon pointed at the bell captain, took the necessary steps toward the closet and kicked the door shut. He picked up the lamp by its stem. "Get over to your right! Do you understand? Answer me!"

"Yeah," came the muffled reply from inside.

"Knock on the door!"

The tap came from the extreme left, the young man's right. Bray crashed the base of the lamp down on the knob; it broke off. Then he raised his gun, its silencer attached, and fired one shot into the right side of the door. "That was a bullet!" he said. "No matter what you hear, keep your mouth shut or there'll be another. I'm right outside this door!"

"Oh, my *God.* . . ."

The man would stay silent through an earthquake. Scofield went back to the bell captain, picking up his attaché case on the way. "Where's the staircase?"

"Down the hall to the elevators, turn right. It's at the end of the corridor."

"The service elevator?"

"Same thing, the other way, the other end. Turn left at—"

"Listen to me," interrupted Bray, "and remember what I tell you. In a few seconds we'll hear the manager and probably others coming down the hall. When I open the door, you step outside and shout—and I mean scream your fucking head off—then start running down the corridor with me."

"*Christ!* What am I supposed to *say?*"

"That you want to get out of here," answered Bray. "Say it anyway you like. I don't think it'll be difficult for you."

"Where are we *going?* I got a wife and four kids!"

"That's nice. Why don't you go home?"

"*What?*"

"What's the quickest way to the lobby?"

"Christ, I don't know!"

"Elevators can take a long time."

"The staircase? The *staircase!*" The panicked bell captain found triumph in his deduction.

"Use the staircase," said Scofield, his ear at the door.

The voices were muffled, but intense. He could hear the words *police* and *ambulance,* and then *emergency.* There were three or four people.

Bray yanked the door back and pushed the bell captain out into the corridor. "*Now,*" he said.

Taleniekov turned away as the service elevator opened on the second floor. Again the black overcoat and the distinctive gray hat evoked no sounds of recognition, and again he spun, his hand gripping the Graz-Burya in his pocket. There were tray tables of half-eaten food and the odor of coffee—remnants of late breakfasts piling up outside the elevator door—but no Marseilles.

A pair of hinged metal doors opened into the second-floor corridor, round windows in the center of each panel. Vasili approached and peered through the right circle.

There he was. The figure in the heavy tweed suit was edging his way along the wall toward the corner of the intersecting hallway that led to room 213. Taleniekov looked at his watch; it was 12:31. Four minutes until the attack; a lifetime if Scofield kept his head about him. A diversion was needed; fire was the surest. A telephone call, a flaming pillowcase stuffed with cloth and paper thrown into the hallway. He wondered if Beowulf Agate had thought of it.

Scofield had thought of *something.* Down the hall the light above one of the two main elevators went on; the door opened, and three men rushed out talking frantically. One was the manager, now close to panic; another carried a black bag: a doctor. The third was burly, his face set, the hair close-cropped . . . the hotel's private police officer.

They raced past the startled Marseilles—who turned abruptly away—and proceeded down the long corridor that led to Scofield's room. The Frenchman took out a gun.

At the other end of the hallway, below a red *Exit* sign, a heavy door with a crash bar was pulled back. The figure of Prague stepped out, nodding at Marseilles. In his right hand was a long-barreled, heavy-caliber automatic; in his left, what looked like . . . it *was* . . . a *grenade*. The thumb was curved, pressing on the lever; the firing pin was out!

And if he had one grenade he had more than one. Prague was an arsenal. He would take whoever was in the area, as long as he took Beowulf Agate. A grenade hurled into a dead-end corridor, a swift race into the carnage before the smoke had cleared to put bullets into the heads of those surviving, making sure Scofield was the first. No matter what the American had thought of, he was cornered. There was no way out through the gauntlet.

Unless Prague could be stopped where he was, the grenade exploding beneath him. Vasili pulled the Graz-Burya from his pocket and pushed the swinging door in front of him.

He was about to shoot when he heard the scream . . . screams from a man in panic.

"Get out of here! For Christ's sake, I've got to get *out of here!"*

What followed was madness. Two men in hotel uniforms came running out of the corridor, one turning right, crashing into Prague, who propelled him away, beating him with the barrel of his gun. Prague shouted at Marseilles, ordering him down the corridor.

Marseilles was no fool—any more than Amsterdam was; he saw the grenade in Prague's hand. The two men screamed at each other.

The elevator door closed.

It *closed.* The light went *off.* It had been on *Hold!*

Beowulf Agate had made his escape.

Taleniekov spun back behind the metal doors; in the confusion he had not been spotted. But Prague and Marseilles had seen the elevator; it obviously prodded the immediate recollection of a second man in a dark red jacket, running straight ahead, without panic, knowing what he was doing . . . and *carrying something under his left arm.* Like Vasili, the two executioners watched the lighted numbers above the elevator door, expecting, as Taleniekov expected, the letter *L* to light up. It did not.

The light reached *3.* It stopped.

What was Scofield *doing?* He could be running in the streets in seconds, finding safety in the crowds, heading for any of a hundred sanctuaries. He was staying at the killing ground! Again, *madness!*

Then Vasili understood. Beowulf Agate was coming after *him.*

He looked through the circular service window. Prague was talking wildly. Marseilles nodded, holding his finger on the left elevator button, as Prague ran back toward the staircase and disappeared beyond the door.

Taleniekov had to know what had been said. It could save seconds—if he could learn in seconds. He put the Graz-Burya in his pocket, burst through the swinging door, the gray silk scarf bunched high around his neck, the gray hat firmly down on his head, his face obscured. He shouted.

"Alors—vous avez découvert quelque chose par hazard?"

In Marseilles' excitement, the swiftness and the deception had their effect. The black overcoat, the gray blur of silk and fur and the French spoken with a Dutchman's guttural inflections; they were enough to confuse the image of a man he had met only once, briefly in a coffee shop. He was stunned; he ran toward Taleniekov, shouting in his native tongue, the words so rushed they were barely clear.

"What are you doing *here?* All hell has broken loose! Men are yelling in Beowulf's room; they break down doors! He got *away.* Prague has . . ."

Marseilles stopped. He saw the face in front of him and his stunned expression turned into one of shock. Vasili's hand shot out, gripping the weapon in the Frenchman's hand, twisting it with such force that Marseilles screamed aloud. The gun was pried out of his fingers. Taleniekov slammed the man against the wall, hammering his knee into the Frenchman's groin, his left hand tearing at Marseilles' right ear.

"Prague has *what?* You have one second to tell me!" He crashed his knee up into the Frenchman's testicles. *"Now!"*

"We work our way to the roof. . . ." Marseilles choked the answer, spitting it out between clenched teeth, his head thrown back in pain. "Floor by floor . . . to the roof."

"Why?" My God! thought Vasili. There was a metal airduct connecting the hotel to the adjacent building. Did they know? He rammed his knee again and repeated, *"Why?"*

"Prague believes Scofield thinks you have men in the streets . . . at the hotel doors. He'll wait until the police come . . . the confusion. He did something in the room! In the name of God, *stop!"*

Vasili smashed the handle of the Frenchman's gun into Marseilles' skull behind his left temple. The assassin collapsed, as the wound spat blood. Taleniekov propelled the unconscious body along the wall, letting it drop so that it fell across the intersecting corridor. Whoever came out of room 213 would be greeted by another unexpected sight. The panic would mount, precious minutes obtained.

The elevator on the left had responded to the Frenchman's call. Vasili raced inside and pressed the button for the third floor. The doors closed, as far down the hallway two excited men ran out of room 213. One was the hotel manager; he saw the fallen Frenchman in the center of a blood-soaked carpet. He screamed.

Scofield took off the jacket and the cap, bunching them in a corner, and put on his coat. The elevator stopped at the third floor; he tensed at the sight of a portly maid who walked in carrying towels over her arm. She nodded; he stared at her. The doors closed and they proceeded to the fourth, where the maid got off. Bray reached over quickly and again pressed the button for the sixth floor; there were none above it.

If it were possible, one part of the insanity was going to be over with! He was not going to run away only to start running again, wondering where the next trap would be sprung. Taleniekov was in the hotel and that was all he had to know.

Room five-zero five. Taleniekov had given the number over the phone; he had said he would be waiting. Bray tried to think back, tried to recall a cipher or a code that matched the digits, but there were none he could remember, and he doubted the KGB man would pinpoint his location.

Five—Zero—Five.

Five—*Death*—Five?

I'm waiting for you on the fifth floor. One of us will die.

Was it as simple as that? Was Taleniekov reduced to a challenge? Was his ego so inflamed or his exhaustion so complete, that there was nothing left but spelling out the dueling ground?

For Christ's sake, let's get it over with! I'm coming, Taleniekov! You may be good, but you're no match for the man you call Beowulf Agate!

Ego. So necessary. So tiring.

The elevator reached the sixth floor. Bray held his breath as two well-dressed men entered. They were talking business, last-year's figures the bothersome topic. Both glanced briefly, disapprovingly at him; he understood. The beard, his blood-shot eyes. He clutched his attaché case and avoided their looks. The door started to close and Bray stepped forward, his hand inside his jacket.

"Sorry," he muttered. "My floor."

There was no one in the long corridor directly ahead, four stories above 211 and 213. Far down on the right were two doors with circular windows. The service elevator. One panel had just swung shut; it still trembled. Scofield pulled his automatic partially out of his belt, then held it in place when he heard the rattle of dishes beyond the swinging doors. A service tray was being taken away; a man concealing himself with intent to kill did not make noise.

Down on the left, toward the staircase, a cleaning woman had finished a room. She pulled the door shut and wearily began to roll her cart toward the next.

Five-zero-five.

Five-death-five.

If there was a meeting ground, he was above it, on the high ground. But it was a high ground from which he could not see and time was running out. He thought briefly of approaching the cleaning woman, using her as a point some-how, but his appearance ruled it out. His appearance ruled out a great many things; shaving had been a luxury he could not afford; relieving himself meant precious moments given up, away from the sounds of the trap. The little things became so ominous, so all-important during the waiting. And he was so tired.

Using the service elevator had to be ruled out; it was an enclosure too easily immobilized, isolated. The staircase was not much better, but he had an advantage; except for a roof—if there was an exit from the roof—it did not go higher.

The sightlines favored the one above. Birds of prey swooped, they rarely attacked from below.

Sharks did, however.

Diversion. Any kind of diversion. Sharks were known to lunge up at inanimate objects, floating debris.

Bray walked rapidly toward the heavy door to the staircase, stopping briefly at the cleaning woman's cart. He removed four glass ashtrays, stuffing them into his pockets, and wedged the attaché case between his arm and chest.

As quietly as he could, he pressed on the crash bar; the heavy steel door opened. He started down the steps, staying close to the wall, listening for the sound of his enemy.

It was there. Several stories below he could hear rapid footsteps slapping against the concrete stairs. They stopped and Scofield stood motionless. What followed confused him. There was a slicing sound, a series of quick movements—abrasive, metallic. What was it?

He looked back up the steps at the metal door he had just walked through, and he knew. The staircase was essentially a fire exit; the crash-bar doors opened from the inside, not from the staircase, thus inhibiting thieves. The person below was using a thin sheet of metal, or plastic, stabbing the crack around the lock, pulling up and down to catch the rounded latch and open the door. The method was universal; most fire exits could be manipulated this way, if they were functional. They would be functional in this hotel.

The abrasive slicing stopped; the door had been opened.

Silence.

The door slammed shut. Scofield moved to the edge of the steps and looked below; he saw nothing but angled railings, squared at the corners, descending into darkness. Silently, he lowered one foot at a time and reached the next landing. He was on the fifth floor.

Five-zero-five. A meaningless number, a meaningless verbal complication.

Taleniekov's strategy was clear now. And logical. Bray would have used it himself. Once the chaos had begun, the Russian waited in the lobby, watching the elevators for a sign of his enemy, and when he did not appear, the assumption had to be that Beowulf was cut off, roving, probing for a way out. Only after Taleniekov was certain that his enemy had not run into the streets, could he begin the final hunt from the staircase, lurching into the hallways, his weapon leveled for his moving target.

But the Russian could not start the kill from the top, he had to begin from the staircase in the lobby. He was forced to give up the high-ground, as deadly a disadvantage on the staircase as it was in the hill country. Scofield put down his attaché case and took out two of the glass ashtrays from his pocket. The waiting was about over; it would happen any second now.

The door below crashed open. Bray hurled the first ashtray down between the railing; the smashing of glass echoed throughout the descending walls of concrete and steel.

Footsteps lurching. The thud of a heavy body making contact with a wall. Scofield sprang toward the open space; he threw down the second ashtray. The glass shattered directly beneath; the figure below darted past the edge of the railing. Bray fired his gun; his enemy screamed, twisting in the air, hurling himself out of the sightline.

Scofield took three steps down, pressing himself against the wall. He saw a thrashing leg and fired again. There was the singing sound of a bullet ricocheting off steel, embedding itself in cement. He had missed; he had wounded the Russian, but not lamed him.

There was suddenly another sound. Sirens. Distant. Outside. Drawing closer. And shouting, muted by the heavy exit doors; orders screamed in corridors and hallways.

Options were being cut off, the chance of escape diminishing with each new sound. It had to end *now*. There was nothing left but a final exchange. A hundred lessons from the past were summarized in one: *Draw fire first, make the gun expose itself—which means exposing part of you. A superficial wound means nothing if it saves your life.*

The seconds ticked off; there was no alternative.

Bray took out the two remaining ashtrays from his pocket and hurled them over the open space above the railing. He stepped down, and at the first sound of shattering glass, swung out his left arm and shoulder, jabbing the air, arcing in a half-circle, part of him in the Russian's direct line of fire. But not his weapon; it was ready for his own attack.

Two deafening explosions filled the vertical tunnel. . . .

The gun was blown out of his hand! Out of his *right hand!* He watched helplessly as the weapon sprang out of his fingers, specks of blood spreading over his palm, the high-pitched ring of a still-ricocheting bullet bouncing from steel to steel.

He had been disarmed by a misplaced shot. Killed by an echo.

The Browning automatic clattered down the staircase. He dove for it, yet even as he did so he knew it was too late. The killer below came into view, struggling to his feet, the large barrel of his gun rising, directed at Scofield's head.

It was not Taleniekov, not the face in a thousand photographs, the face he had hated for a decade! It was the man from Prague, a man he had used so often in the cause of free-thinking people. That man was going to kill him now.

Two thoughts came rapidly, one upon the other. Final summations, as it were. His death would come quickly; he was grateful for that. And, at the last, he had deprived Taleniekov of his trophy.

"We all do our jobs," said the man from Prague, his three fingers tightening on the handle of the gun. "You taught me that, Beowulf."

"You'll never get out of here."

"You forget your own lessons. 'Drop your weapons, leave with the crowds.' I'll get out. But you won't. If you did, too many would die."

"Padazdit!" The voice thundered from above, no crash of a door preceding

it, the man who roared having intruded swiftly, silently. The executioner from Prague spun to his left, ducking, swinging his powerful gun up the stairs at Vasili Taleniekov.

The Russian fired one shot, drilling a hole in Prague's forehead. The Czech fell across Scofield as Bray lunged for his gun, grabbing it off the step, rolling furiously down around the bend in the staircase. He fired wildly up at the KGB man; he would not permit Taleniekov to save him from Prague only to preserve his trophy.

I'll see you take your last breath. . . .

Not here! Not now! Not while I can move!

And then he could not move. The impact came and Scofield only knew that his head seemed to have split wide open. His eyes were filled with blinding streaks of jagged white light, somehow mingling with sounds of chaos. Sirens, screams, voices yelling from distant chasms far below.

In his rolling dive to get out of Taleniekov's line of fire, he had crashed his skull into the sharp steel edge of the corner railing post. A misplaced bullet, an echo, an inanimate shaft of structural steel. They would lead him to death.

The image was blurred but unmistakable. The figure of the powerfully built Russian came running down the staircase. Bray tried to raise the gun still in his hand; he could not. It was being crushed under a heavy boot; the weapon was being pried out of his hand.

"Do it," whispered Scofield. "For Christ's sake, do it now! You've won by an accident. It's the only way you could."

"I've won *nothing!* I want no such victory. Come! *Move!* The police are here; they'll be swarming up the staircase any moment."

Bray could feel the strong arms lifting him up, pulling his arm around a thick neck, a shoulder shoved into his side for support. "What the hell are you *doing?*" He was not sure the words were his; he could not think through the pain.

"You're hurt. The wound in your neck has opened; it's not bad. But your head is cut, I don't know how severely."

"What?"

"There is a way out. This was my depot for two years. I know every inch of the building. Come! *Help* me. Move your legs! The *roof.*"

"My case. . . ."

"I've *got* it."

They were in a large, pitch-black metal enclosure, steady blasts of cold air causing the corrugated sides to rattle, the near-freezing temperature producing audible vibrations. They crawled along the ribbed floor in darkness.

"This is the main air duct," explained Taleniekov, his voice low, aware of the magnified echo. "The unit serves the hotel and the adjacent office building. Both are comparatively small structures, owned by the same company."

Scofield had begun to find his mind again, the sheer movement forcing him to send impulses to his arms and legs. The Russian had torn a silk scarf apart, wrapping one half around Bray's head, the other around his throat. The bleeding had not stopped, but it was contained. He had found part of his mind, but there was still no clarity in what was happening.

"You saved my life. I want to know *why!*"

"Keep your voice down!" whispered the KGB man. "And keep moving."

"I want an answer."

"I gave it to you."

"You weren't convincing."

"You and I, we live only with lies. We see nothing else."

"From you I expect nothing else."

"In a few minutes you can make your determination. I give you that."

"What do you mean?"

"We'll reach the end of the duct; there is a transom ten or twelve feet from the floor. In a rooftop storage area. Once down I can get us out on the street, but every second counts. If there are people in the vicinity of the transom, they must be frightened away. Gunshots will do it; fire above their heads."

"*What?*"

"Yes. I'll give you your gun back."

"You killed my wife."

"You killed my brother. Before that your Army of Occupation returned the corpse of a young girl—a child—I loved very much."

"I don't know anything about that."

"Now you do. Make your determination."

The metal-webbed transom was perhaps four feet wide. Below was a huge, dimly lit room that served as a miniature warehouse filled with crates and boxes of supplies. There was no one in sight. Taleniekov handed Scofield the automatic, and began forcing the metal screen from its brackets with his shoulder. It sprang loose and fell crashing to the cement floor. The Russian waited several moments for a response to the noise; there was none.

He turned his body around and, legs first, began sliding out of the duct. His shoulders and head passed over the rim, his fingers gripping the edge; he was finding his balance, prepared for the drop to the floor.

The strange sound came faintly at first, then louder. *Step . . . scrape. Step . . . scrape. Step . . . scrape. Step.* Taleniekov froze, his body suspended between transom and floor.

"Good morning, comrade," said the voice softly in Russian. "My walk has improved since Riga, no? They gave me a new foot."

Bray pulled back into the shadows of the duct. Below, beside a large crate was a man with a cane. A cripple whose right leg was no leg at all, but instead a limb of stiff, straight wood beneath the trousers. The man continued as he took a gun from his pocket.

"I knew you too well, old friend. You were a great teacher. You gave me an hour to study your depot. There were several means of escape, but this is the one you would choose. I'm sorry, my teacher. We cannot afford you any longer." He raised his gun.

Scofield fired.

They raced into the alley across the street from the hotel on Nebraska Avenue. Both leaned against the brick wall, breathing heavily, their eyes on the activity beyond. Three patrol cars, their lights revolving on their roofs, blocked the entrance of the hotel, hemming in an ambulance. Two stretchers were carried out, the bodies covered with canvas; another emerged and Taleniekov could see the bloodied head of Prague. Uniformed police held back curious pedestrians, as their superiors rushed back and forth, barking into handheld radios, issuing orders.

A net was being formed around the hotel, all exits covered, all windows observed, weapons drawn against the unexpected.

"When you feel strong enough," said Taleniekov, speaking between swallows of air, "we'll slip into the crowds and walk several blocks away where it will be safer to find a taxi. However, I'll be honest with you. I don't know where to go."

"I do," said Scofield, pushing himself away from the wall. "We'd better get going while there's confusion out there. Pretty soon they'll start an area search. They'll look for anyone wounded; there was a lot of gunfire."

"One moment." The Russian faced Bray. "Three days ago I was on a truck in the hills outside of Sevastopol. I knew then what I would say to you if we met. I say it now. We will either kill each other, Beowulf Agate, or we will talk."

Scofield stared at Taleniekov. "We may do both," he said. "Let's go."

11

The cabin was in the backwoods of Maryland, on the banks of the Patuxent River, fields on three sides, water below. It was isolated, no other houses within a mile in any direction, accessible only by a primitive dirt road over which no taxi would venture. None was asked to do so.

Instead, Bray telephoned a man at the Iranian Embassy, an unregistered SAVAK agent into hard drugs and exchange students whose exposure would be embarrassing to a benevolent Shah. A rented car was left for them in a metered parking lot on K Street, the keys under the floor mat.

The cabin belonged to a professor of Political Science at Georgetown, a closet homosexual Scofield had befriended years ago when he had torn up a fragment of a dossier that had nothing to do with the man's ability to evaluate classified data for the State Department. Bray had used the cabin a number of times during his recalls to Washington, always when he wished to be beyond reach of the deskmen, usually with a woman. A phone call to the professor was all that it took; no questions were asked, the location of the house key given. This afternoon it was nailed beneath the second shingle from the right on the front roof. Bray got it by using a ladder propped against a nearby tree.

Inside, the decor was properly rustic; heavy beams and Spartan furniture relieved by a profusion of quilted cushions, white walls and red-checked curtains. Flanking the stone fireplace were floor-to-ceiling bookcases, filled to capacity, the varied bindings lending additional color and warmth.

"He is an educated man," said Taleniekov, his eyes scanning the titles.

"Very," replied Bray, lighting a gas-fed Franklin stove. "There are matches on the mantel, the kindling stacked and ready to light."

"How convenient," said the KGB man, taking a wooden match from a small glass on the mantel, kneeling down and striking it.

"It's part of the rent. Whoever uses the cabin cleans the fireplace and stacks it."

"Part of the rent? What are the other arrangements?"

"There's only one. Say nothing. About the place or the owner."

"Again, convenient." Taleniekov pulled his hand back as the fire leapt up from the dry wood.

"Very," repeated Scofield, adjusting the heater, satisfied it was functioning. He stood up and faced the Russian. "I don't want to discuss anything until I've had some sleep. You may not agree, but that's the way it's going to be."

"I have no objection. I'm not sure I'm capable of being lucid right now, and I must be when we talk. If it's possible, I've had less sleep than you."

"Two hours ago we could have killed each other," said Bray, standing motionless. "Neither of us did."

"Quite the reverse," agreed the KGB man. "We prevented others from doing so."

"Which cancels any obligation between us."

"No such obligations exist, of course. However, I submit you may find a larger one when we talk."

"You could be right, but I doubt it. You may have to live with Moscow, but I don't have to live with what happened here in Washington today. I can do something about it. Maybe that's the difference between us."

"For both our sakes—for all our sakes—I fervently hope you're right."

"I am. I'm also going to get some sleep." Scofield pointed to a couch against the wall. "That pulls out into a bed; there are blankets in the closet over there. I'll use the bedroom." He started for the door, then stopped and turned to the Russian. "Incidentally, the room will be locked, and I'm a very light sleeper."

"A condition that afflicts us both, I'm sure," said Taleniekov. "You have nothing to fear from me."

"I never did," Bray said.

Scofield heard faint, sharp crackling sounds and spun under the sheets, his hand gripping the Browning automatic by his knees. He raised it beneath the covers as his feet shot out over the side of the bed; he was prepared to crouch and fire.

There was no one in the room. Moonlight streamed through the north window, shafts of colorless white light separated by the thick panes into single streaks of suspended, eerie illumination. For a moment he was not sure where he was, so complete had been his exhaustion, so deep his sleep. He knew by the time his feet touched the floor; his enemy was in the next room. A very strange enemy who had saved his life, and whose life he had saved minutes later.

Bray looked at the luminous dial of his watch. It was quarter past four in the morning. He had slept nearly thirteen hours, the heavy weight of his arms and legs, the adhesive moisture in his eyes, and the dryness of his throat evidence of his having moved very little during that time. He sat for a while on the side of the bed, breathing the cold air deeply, putting the gun down and shaking his hands, slapping his fingers together. He looked over at the locked door of the bedroom.

Taleniekov was up and had started a fire, the sharp crackling now the unmistakable sound of burning wood. Scofield decided to put off seeing the Russian for a few more minutes. His face itched, the growth of his beard so uncomfortable it had caused the beginning of a rash on his neck. There was always shaving equipment in the bathroom; he would afford himself the luxury of a shave and change the bandages he had placed on his neck and skull fourteen hours ago. It would postpone for a bit longer his talk with the former—defected?—KGB man. Whatever it concerned, Bray wanted no part of it, yet the unexpected events and decisions of the past twenty-four hours told him he was already involved.

It was 4:37 when he unlocked the door and opened it. Taleniekov was standing in front of the fire, sipping from a cup in his hand.

"I apologize if the fire awakened you," the Russian said. "Or the sound of the front door—if you heard it."

"The heater went out," said Scofield, looking down at the flameless Franklin.

"I think the propane tank is empty."

"Is that why you went outside?"

"No. I went outside to relieve myself; there's no toilet here."

"I forgot."

"Did you hear me leave? Or return?"

"Is that coffee?"

"Yes," answered Taleniekov. "A bad habit I picked up from the West. Your tea has no character. The pot's on the burner." The KGB man gestured beyond a room divider where stove, sink and refrigerator were lined up against the wall. "I'm surprised you did not smell it boiling."

"I thought I did," lied Scofield, crossing to the stove and the pot. "But it was weak."

"And now we've both made our childish points."

"Childishly," added Bray, pouring coffee. "You keep saying you have something to tell me. Go ahead."

"First, I shall ask you a question. Have you ever heard of an organization called the Matarese?"

Scofield paused, remembering; he nodded. "Political killers for hire, run by a council in Corsica. It started well over a half-century ago and died out in the middle forties, after the war. What about it?"

"It never died out. It went further underground—became dormant, if you like—but it returned in a far more dangerous form. It's been operating since the early fifties. It operates now. It has infiltrated the most sensitive and powerful areas of both our governments. Its objective is the control over both our countries. The Matarese was responsible for the murders of General Blackburn here and Dimitri Yurievich in my country."

Bray sipped his coffee, studying the Russian's face over the rim of the cup. "How do you know that? Why do you believe it?"

"An old man who saw more in his lifetime than you and I combined made the identification. He was not wrong; he was one of the few who admitted—or will ever admit—having dealt with the Matarese."

"Saw? Was? Past tenses."

"He died. He called for me while he was dying; he wanted me to know. He had access to information neither you nor I would be given under any circumstances."

"Who was he?"

"Aleksie Krupskaya. The name is meaningless, I realize, so I'll explain."

"Meaningless?" interrupted Scofield, crossing to an armchair in front of the fire, and sitting down. "Not entirely. Krupskaya, the white cat of Krivoi Rog. Istrebiteli. The last of the exterminators from Section Nine, KGB. The original Nine, of course."

"You do your schoolwork well, but then, as they say, you're a Harvard man."

"That kind of schoolwork can be helpful. Krupskaya was banished twenty years ago. He became a nonperson. If he were alive, I figured he was vegetating in Grasnov, not a consultant being fed information by people in the Kremlin. I don't believe your story."

"Believe it now," said Taleniekov, sitting down opposite Bray. "Because it was not 'people' in the Kremlin, just one man. His son. For thirty years one of the highest-ranking survivors of the Politburo. For the past six, Premier of Soviet Russia."

Scofield put his cup down on the floor and again studied the KGB man's face. It was the face of a practiced liar, a professional liar, but not a liar by nature. He was not lying now. "Krupskaya's son the Premier? That's . . . a shock."

"As it was to me, but not so shocking when you think about it. Guided at every turn, protected by his father's extensive collection of . . . shall we say memorabilia. Hypothetically, it could have happened here. Suppose your late John Edgar Hoover had a politically ambitious son. Who could have stood in his way? Hoover's secret files would have paved any road, even the one leading to the Oval Office. The landscape is different, but the trees are the same genus. They haven't varied much since the senators gave Rome to Caligula."

"What did Krupskaya tell you?"

"The past first. There were things I could not believe, until I spoke of them to several retired leaders of the Politburo. One frightened old man confirmed them, the others caused a plan to be mounted that called for my execution."

"Your . . . ?"

"Yes. Vasili Vasilivich Taleniekov, master strategist, KGB. An irascible man who may have seen his best years, but whose knowledge could be called upon for several decades perhaps—from a farm in Grasnov. We are a practical people; that would have been the practical solution. In spite of the minor doubts we all have, I believe that, I knew it was my future. But not after I mentioned the Matarese. Abruptly, everything changed. I, who have served my country well, was suddenly the enemy."

"What specifically did Krupskaya say? What—in your judgment—was confirmed?"

Taleniekov recounted the dying Istrebiteli's words, missions that traced scores of assassinations to the Matarese, including Stalin, Beria and Roosevelt. How the Corsican organization had been used by all the major governments, both within their borders and outside of them. None were exempt from the stain. Soviet Russia, England, France, Germany, Italy . . . the United States; the leaders of each, at one time or another, had made contracts with the Matarese.

"That's all been speculated upon before," said Bray. "Quietly, I grant you, but nothing concrete ever came of the investigations."

"Because no one of substance ever dared testify. In Krupskaya's words, the revelations would be catastrophic for governments everywhere. Now, there are new tactics being employed, all for the purpose of creating instability in the power centers."

"What are they?"

"Acts of terrorism. Bombings, kidnappings, the hijackings of aircraft; ultimatums issued by bands of fanatics, wholesale slaughter promised if they are not met. They grow in numbers every month and the vast majority are funded by the Matarese."

"How?"

"I can only surmise. The Matarese council studies the objectives of the parties involved, sends in the experts, and provides covert financing. Fanatics do not labor over the sources of funds, only their availability. I submit that you and I have used such men and women more often than we can count."

"For distinctly accountable purposes," said Bray, picking up his cup from the floor. "What about Blackburn and Yurievich? What did the Matarese accomplish by killing them?"

"Krupskaya believed it was to test the leaders, to see if their own men could control each government's reactions. I'm not so sure now. I think perhaps there was something else. Frankly, because of what you've told me."

"What's that?"

"Yurievich. You said he was your operation. Is that true?"

Bray frowned. "True, but not that simple. Yurievich was gray; he wasn't going to defect in any normal sense. He was a scientist, convinced both sides had gone too far. He didn't trust the maniacs. It was a probe; we weren't sure where we were going."

"Are you aware that General Blackburn, who was nearly destroyed by the war in Vietnam, did what no Chairman of the Joint Chiefs has ever done in your history? He met secretly with your potential enemies. In Sweden, in the city of Skelleftea on the Gulf of Bothnia, traveling undercover as a tourist. It was our judgment that he would go to any lengths to avoid the repetition of pointless slaughter. He abhorred conventional warfare, and he did not believe nuclear weapons would ever be used." The Russian stopped and leaned forward. "Two men who believed deeply, passionately, in the rejection of human sacrifice, who sought accommodation—both killed by the Matarese. So perhaps testing was only a part of the exercise. There could well have been another: eliminate powerful men who believed in stability."

At first Scofield did not reply; the information about Blackburn was astonishing. "In the testing then, they pointed at me with Yurievich . . ."

"And at me with Blackburn," completed Taleniekov. "A Browning Magnum, Grade Four, was used to kill Yurievich; a Graz-Burya for Blackburn."

"And both of us set up for execution."

"Exactly," said the Soviet. "Because above all men in either country's intelligence service, we cannot be permitted to live. That will never change because we cannot change. Krupskaya was right: we are diversions; we will be used and killed. We are too dangerous."

"Why do they think so?"

"They've studied us. They know we could no more accept the Matarese than we do the maniacs within our own branches. We are dead men, Scofield."

"Speak for yourself!" Bray was suddenly angry. "I'm out, terminated, *finished!* I don't give a goddamn what happens out there! Don't you make judgments about me!"

"They've already been made. By others."

"Because *you* say so?" Scofield got up, putting the coffee down, his hand not far from the Browning in his belt.

"Because I *believed* the man who told me. It's why I'm *here,* why I *saved* your life and did not take it myself."

"I have to wonder about that, don't I?"

"What?"

"Everything timed, even to your knowing where Prague was on the staircase."

"I killed a man who had you under his gun!"

"*Prague?* A minor sacrifice. I'm a terminated encyclopedia. I have no proof my government reached Moscow, only possible conclusions based on what *you* told me. Maybe I'm missing the obvious, maybe the great Taleniekov is eating a little temporary crow to bring in Beowulf Agate."

"*Damn* you, Scofield!" roared the KGB man, springing up from the chair. "I should have let you die! Hear me clearly. What you suggest is unthinkable and the KGB knows it. My feelings run too deep. I'd never bring you in. I'd kill you first."

Bray stared at the Russian, the honesty of Taleniekov's statement obvious. "I believe you," said Scofield, nodding, his anger diminishing in weariness. "But it doesn't change anything. I don't care. I really don't give a goddamn. . . . I'm not even sure I want to kill you anymore. I just want to be left alone." Bray turned away. "Take the keys to the car and get out of here. Consider yourself . . . alive."

"Thank you for your generosity, Beowulf, but I'm afraid it's too late."

"What?" Scofield turned back to the Soviet.

"I did not finish. A man was caught, chemicals administered. There is a timetable, two months, three at the outside. The words were: 'Moscow by assassination; Washington by political maneuver—murder, if necessary.' When it happens, neither you nor I will survive. They'll track us to the ends of the earth."

"Wait a minute," said Bray, furious. "Are you telling me that your people *have* a man?"

"Had," corrected Taleniekov. "Cyanide was implanted under his skin; he reached it."

"But he was *heard.* He was taped, recorded. His words were there!"

"Heard. Not taped, not recorded. And only by one man—who was warned by his father not to permit anyone else to listen."

"The *Premier?*"

"Yes."

"Then he knows!"

"Yes, he knows. And all he can do is try to protect himself—nothing particularly new in his position—but he can't speak of it. For to speak of it, as Krupskaya said, is to acknowledge the past. This is the age of conspiracy, Scofield. Who cares to bring up past contracts? In my country there are a number of unexplained corpses; you're not so different over here. The Kennedys, Martin Luther King; perhaps most stunning, Franklin Roosevelt. We could all be at each others' throats—more precisely on the nuclear buttons—if our combined pasts were revealed. What would you do, if you were the Premier?"

"Protect myself," said Bray softly. "Oh, my God. . . ."

"Now do you see?"

"I don't want to. I *really* don't *want* to. I'm out!"

"I submit that you cannot be. Nor I. The proof was yesterday on Nebraska

Avenue. We're marked; they want us. They convinced others to have us killed—for the wrong reasons—but they were behind the strategy. Can you doubt it?"

"I wish I could. The manipulators are always easiest to manipulate, con-men the biggest suckers. *Jesus.*" Scofield walked to the stove to pour himself more coffee. Suddenly, he was struck by something not said, unclear. "I don't understand. From what little's known about the Matarese, it started as a cult and evolved into a business. It accepted contracts—or *supposedly* accepted contracts—on the basis of feasibility and price. It killed for money; it was never interested in power, *per se.* Why is it interested now?"

"I don't know," said the KGB man. "Neither did Krupskaya. He was dying and not very lucid, but he said the answer might be in Corsica."

"Corsica? Why?"

"It's where it all began."

"Not where it *is. If* it is. The word was that the Matarese moved out of Corsica in the mid-thirties. Contracts were negotiated as far away as London, New York . . . even Berlin. Centers of international traffic."

"Then perhaps clues to an answer is more appropriate. The council of the Matarese was formed in Corsica, only one name ever revealed. Guillaume de Matarese. Who were the others? Where did they go? Who are they *now?*"

"There's a quicker way of finding out than going to Corsica. If the Matarese is even a whisper in Washington, there's one person who can track it down. He's the one I was going to call anyway. I wanted my life straightened out."

"Who is he?"

"Robert Winthrop," said Bray.

"The creator of Consular Operations." The Russian nodded. "A good man who had no stomach for what he built."

"The *Cons Op* you're referring to isn't the one he began. He's still the only man I've heard of who can call up to the White House and see the President in twenty minutes. Very little goes on that he doesn't know about. Or can't find out about." Scofield glanced over at the fire, remembering. "It's strange. In a way, he's responsible for everything I am, and he doesn't approve of me. But I think he'll listen."

The nearest telephone booth was three miles down the highway beyond the dirt road to the cabin. It was ten past eight when Bray stepped in, shielding his eyes from the glare of the morning sun, and pulled the glass door shut. He had found Winthrop's private number in his attaché case; he had not called it in years. He dialed, hoping it was still the same.

It was. The cultivated voice on the line brought back many memories. Possibilities missed, many others taken.

"Scofield! Where *are* you?"

"I'm afraid I can't tell you that. Please try to understand."

"I understand you're in a great deal of trouble, and nothing will be served by running *away.* Congdon called. The man killed in the hotel was shot with a Russian gun. . . ."

"I know. The Russian who killed him saved my life. That man was *sent* by Congdon; so were the other two. They were my execution team. From Prague, Marseilles and Amsterdam."

"Oh, my *God*. . . ." The elder statesman was silent for a moment and Bray did not interrupt that silence. "Do you know what you're saying?" asked Winthrop.

"Yes, sir. You know me well enough to know I *wouldn't* say it unless I were sure. I'm not mistaken. I spoke to the man from Prague before he died."

"He *confirmed* it?"

"In oblique words, yes. But then, that's how those cables are sent; the words are always oblique."

Again there was a moment of silence before the old man spoke. "I can't believe it, Bray. For a reason you couldn't know. Congdon came to see me a week ago. He was concerned how you'd take retirement. He had the usual worries: a highly knowledgeable agent terminated against his will with too much time on his hands, perhaps too much to drink. He's a cold fellow, that Congdon, and I'm afraid he angered me. After all you've been through to have so little trust. . . . I rather sardonically mentioned what you've just described—not that I ever dreamed he would consider such a thing, just that I was appalled at his attitude. So I *can't* believe it. Don't you see? He'd know I'd recognize it. He wouldn't take that risk."

"Then someone gave him the order, sir. That's what we have to talk about. Those three men knew where to find me, and there was only one way they could've learned. It was a KGB drop and they were *Cons Op* personnel. Moscow gave it to Congdon; he relayed it."

"Congdon reached the *Soviets?* That's not plausible. Even if he tried, why would they cooperate? Why would they reveal a drop?"

"Their own man was part of the negotiation; they wanted him killed. He was trying to contact me. We'd exchanged cables."

"Taleniekov?"

It was Scofield's moment to pause. He answered quietly. "Yes, sir."

"A *white* contact?"

"Yes. I misread it, but that's what it was. I'm convinced now."

"*You* . . . and Taleniekov? *Extraordinary*. . . ."

"The circumstances are extraordinary. Do you remember an organization from the forties that went by the name of the Matarese? . . ."

They agreed to meet at nine o'clock that evening, a mile north of the Missouri Avenue exit of Rock Creek Park on the eastern side. There was an indented stretch of pavement off the road where automobiles could park and strollers could enter the various paths that overlooked a scenic ravine. Winthrop intended to cancel the day's appointments and concentrate on learning whatever there was to learn about Bray's astonishing—if fragmentary—information.

"He'll convene the Forty Committee, if he has to," said Scofield to Taleniekov on the way back to the cabin.

"Can he do that?" asked the Russian.

"The President can," answered Bray.

The two men talked little during the day, the strain of proximity uncomfortable for each. Taleniekov read from the extensive bookshelves, glancing at Scofield now and then, the look in his eyes a mixture of remembered fury and curiosity.

Bray felt the glances; he refused to acknowledge them. He listened to the radio for news reports about the carnage at the hotel on Nebraska Avenue, and the death of a Russian attaché in the adjacent building. They were played down, de-emphasized, no mention made of the dead embassy official. The hotel killings were theorized to be foreign in origin—that much was allowed—and no doubt criminally oriented, probably related to upper-level narcotics. The suppressants had been applied; the Department of State had moved swiftly, with sure-footed censorship.

And with each progressively fading report Scofield felt progressively trapped. He was becoming intrinsic to something he wanted no part of; his new life was not around the corner any longer. He began to wonder where it was, or if it would be. He was being inexorably drawn into an enigma called the Matarese.

At four o'clock he went for a walk in the fields and along the banks of the Patuxent. As he left the cabin, he made sure the Russian saw him slip the Browning automatic into his holster. The KGB man did see; he placed his Graz-Burya on the table next to the chair.

At five o'clock, Taleniekov made an observation. "I think we should position ourselves a good hour before the appointment."

"I trust Winthrop," replied Bray.

"With good reason, I'm sure. But can you trust those he'll be contacting?"

"He won't tell anyone he's meeting us. He wants to talk to you at length. He'll have questions. Names, past positions, military ranks."

"I'll try to provide answers where they are relative to the Matarese. I will not be compromised in other areas."

"Bully for you."

"Nevertheless, I still think—"

"We'll leave in fifteen minutes," interrupted Scofield. "There's a diner on the way; we'll eat separately."

At 7:35, Bray drove the rented car into the south end of the parking area on the border of Rock Creek Park. He and the KGB man made four penetrations into the woods, sweeping in arcs off the paths, checking the trees and the rocks and the ravine below for signs of intruders. The night was bitterly cold; there were no strollers, no one anywhere. They met at a pre-arranged spot on the edge of the small gorge. Taleniekov spoke first.

"I saw nothing; the area is secure."

Scofield looked at his watch in the darkness. "It's nearly eight-thirty. I'll wait by the car; you stay up here at this end. I'll meet with him first and then signal you."

"How? It's several hundred yards."

"I'll strike a match."

"Very appropriate."

"What?"

"Nothing. It's unimportant."

At two minutes to nine, Winthrop's limousine came out of the Rock Creek exit, drove into the parking area, and stopped within twenty feet of the rented car. The sight of the chauffeur disturbed Bray, but only momentarily. Scofield recognized the huge man almost instantly; he had been with Robert Winthrop for more than two decades. Rumors about a checkered Marine Corps career cut short by several courts-martial followed the chauffeur, but Winthrop never discussed him other than to call him "my friend Stanley." No one ever pressed.

Bray walked out of the shadows toward the limousine. Stanley opened the door and was on the pavement in one motion, his right hand in his pocket, in his left a flashlight. He turned it on. Scofield shut his eyes. It went off in seconds.

"Hello, Stanley," said Bray.

"It's been a long time, Mr. Scofield," replied the chauffeur. "Nice to see you."

"Thanks. Good to see you."

"The Ambassador's waiting," continued the driver, reaching down and snapping the lock release. "The door's open now."

"Fine. By the way, in a couple of minutes I'm going to get out of the car and strike a match. It's the signal for a man to come and join us. He's up at the other end; he'll walk out of one of the paths."

"I gotcha'. The Ambassador said there'd be two of you. Okay."

"What I'm trying to say is, if you still smoke those thin cigars of yours, wait till I get out before you light up. I'd like a few moments alone with Mr. Winthrop."

"You've got a hell of a memory," said Stanley, tapping his jacket pocket with the flashlight. "I was about to have one."

Bray got into the backseat of the car and faced the man who was responsible for his life. Winthrop had grown old, but in the dim light his eyes were still electric, still filled with concern. They shook hands, the elder statesman prolonging the grip.

"I've thought about you often," he said softly, his eyes searching Scofield's, then noting the bandages and wincing. "I have mixed feelings, but I don't think I have to tell you that."

"No, sir, you don't."

"So many things changed, didn't they, Bray? The ideals, the opportunities to do so much for so many. We were crusaders, really. At the beginning." The old man released Scofield's hand and smiled. "Do you remember? You came up with a processing plan that was to be crosscollateralized with lend-lease. Debts in occupied territories for multiple immigration. A brilliant concept in economic diplomacy, I've always said that. Human lives for monies that were never going to be repaid anyway."

"It would have been rejected."

"Probably, but in the arena of world opinion it would have pushed the Soviets to the wall. I recall your words. You said 'if we're supposed to be a capitalistic government, don't walk away from it. Use it, define it. American citizens paid for half the Russian Army. Stress the psychological obligation. Get something, get *people.*' Those were your words."

"That was a graduate student expounding on naive theoretical geopolitics."

"There's often a great deal of truth in such naiveté. You know, I can still see that graduate student. I wonder about him—"

"There's no time now, sir," interrupted Scofield. "Taleniekov's waiting. Incidentally, we checked the area; it's clear."

The old man's eyes blinked. "Did you think it would be otherwise?"

"I was worried about a tap on your phone."

"No need for that," said Winthrop. "Such devices have to be listed somewhere, recorded somewhere. I wouldn't care to be the person who did such a thing. Too many private conversations take place on my telephone. It's my best protection."

"Did you learn anything?"

"About the Matarese? No . . . and *yes.* No, in the sense that even the most rarefied intelligence data contained no mention of it whatsoever, hasn't for the past forty-three years. The President assured me of this and I trust him. He was appalled; he leapt at the possibility and put men on the alert. He was furious, and frightened, I think."

"What's the 'yes'?"

The old man chose his words carefully. "It's obscure but it's there. Before I decided to call the President, I reached five men who for years—decades—have been involved in the most sensitive areas of intelligence and diplomacy. Of the five, three remembered the Matarese and were shocked. They offered to do whatever they could to help, the spectre of the Matarese's return was quite terrifying to them. . . . Yet the other two—men, who if anything, are far more knowledgeable than their colleagues—claimed *never* to have heard of it. Their reactions made no sense; they *had* to have heard of it. Just as I had—my information minimal but certainly not forgotten. When I said as much, when I pressed them, both behaved rather strangely, and considering our past associations, not without insult. Each treated me as though I were some kind of senile patrician, given to senile fantasies. Really, it was astonishing."

"Who were they?"

"Again, odd. . . ."

A flash of light in the distance; Scofield's eyes were drawn to it. And another . . . and *another.* Matches were being struck in rapid succession.

Taleniekov.

The KGB man was cupping matches and lighting one after another furiously. It was a warning. Taleniekov was warning him that something had happened— *was happening.* Suddenly the distant flame was constant, but broken by a hand held in front of the flame—in rapid sequences, more light, less light. Basic Morse. Dots and dashes.

Three dots repeated twice. *S.* A long spill, repeated once. A single dash. *T. S. T.*

"What's the matter?" asked Winthrop.

"Just a second," replied Scofield.

Three dots, broken, then followed by a dash. The letters *S* and *T* were being repeated. *S. T.*

Surveillance. Terminal.

The flame moved to the left, toward the road bordering the woods of the parking area, and was extinguished. The Soviet agent was repositioning himself. Bray turned back to the old man.

"How certain are you about your telephone?"

"Very. It's never been tapped. I have ways of knowing."

"They may not be extensive enough." Scofield touched the window button; the glass rolled down and he called to the chauffeur standing in front of the limousine. "Stan, come here!" The driver did so. "When you drove through the park, did you check to see if anyone followed you?"

"Sure did and no way. I keep one eye on the rearview mirror. I always do, especially when we're meeting someone at night. . . . Did you see the light up there? Was it your man?"

"Yes. He was telling me someone else was here."

"Impossible," said Winthrop emphatically. "If there is, it's no concern of ours. This is, after all, a public park."

"I don't want to alarm you, sir, but Taleniekov's experienced. There are no headlights, no cars in the road. Whoever's out there doesn't want us to know it, and it's not a night for a casual walk. I'm afraid it does concern us." Bray opened the door. "Stan, I'm going to grab my briefcase from my car. When I get back, drive out of here. Stop briefly at the north end of the lot by the road."

"What about the Russian?" asked Winthrop.

"That's why we're stopping. He'll know enough to jump in. He'd better."

"*Wait* a minute," said Stanley, no deference in his voice. "If there's any trouble, I'm not stopping for anyone. I've only got one job. To get *him* out of here. Not you or anybody else."

"We don't have time to argue. Start the engine." Bray ran to the rented car, the keys in his hand. He unlocked the door, removed his attaché case from the front seat, and started back toward the limousine.

He never reached it. A beam of powerful light pierced through the darkness, aimed at Robert Winthrop's huge automobile. Stanley was behind the wheel, gunning the motor, prepared to bolt out of the area. Whoever held the light was not going to allow that to happen. He wanted that car . . . and whoever was in that car.

The limousine's wheels spun, screeching on the pavement, as the huge car surged forward. A staccato spray of gunfire erupted; windows shattered, bullets crunched into metal. The limousine weaved back and forth in abrupt half-circles, seemingly out of control.

Two loud reports came from the woods beyond; the searchlight exploded, a scream of pain followed. Winthrop's car straightened out briefly, then lurched into a sharp left turn. Caught in the headlights were two men, weapons drawn, a third on the ground.

Bray's gun was in his hand; he dropped to the pavement and fired. One of the two men fell. The limousine completed the turn and roared out of the parking lot into the southbound road.

Scofield rolled to his right; two shots were fired, the bullets singing off the pavement where he had been seconds ago. Bray got to his feet and ran in the darkness toward the railing that fronted the ravine.

He lunged over the top rail, his attaché case slamming into the wood post, the sound distinct. The next gunshot was expected; it came as he hugged the earth and the rocks.

Lights. Headlights! Two beams shooting overhead, accompanied by the sound of a racing car. The smashing of glass came hard upon tires screeching to a sudden stop. A shout—unclear, hysterical . . . cut off by a loud explosion—preceded silence.

The engine had stalled, the headlights still on, revealing curls of smoke and two immobile bodies on the ground, a third on his knees, looking around in panic. The man heard something; he spun and raised his gun.

A weapon was fired from the woods. It was final; the would-be killer fell.

"Scofield!" Taleniekov shouted.

"Over here!" Bray lunged up over the railing and ran toward the source of the Russian's voice. Taleniekov walked out of the woods; he was no more than ten feet from the stalled automobile. Both men approached the car warily; the driver's window had been shattered, blown apart by a single shot from the KGB man's automatic. The head beyond the fragmented glass was bloodied but recognizable. The right hand was wrapped in a tight bandage—still wrapped from an injured thumb broken on a bridge in Amsterdam at three o'clock in the morning by an angry, tired older man.

It was the aggressive young agent, Harry, who had killed so needlessly in the rain that night.

"I don't believe it," said Scofield.

"You know him?" asked Taleniekov, a curious note in his voice.

"His name was Harry. He worked for me in Amsterdam."

The Russian was silent for a moment, then spoke. "He was *with* you in Amsterdam, but he did not work for you, and his name was not 'Harry.' That young man is a Soviet intelligence officer, trained since the age of nine at the American Compound in Novgorod. He was a VKR agent."

Bray studied Taleniekov's face, then looked back through the shattered window at Harry. "Congratulations. Things fall into place more clearly now."

"They don't for me, I'm afraid," said the KGB man. "Believe me when I tell you that it is most unlikely that any order out of Moscow would include a direct attack on Robert Winthrop. We're not fools. He's above reprisals—a voice and a skill to be preserved, not struck down. And certainly not for such—personnel— as you and me."

"What do you mean?"

"This was an execution team, as surely as those men at the hotel. You and I were not to be isolated, not to be taken separately. The kill was inclusive. Winthrop was to be executed as well, and for all we know he may have been. I submit that the order did not come from Moscow."

"It didn't come from the State Department, I'm damn sure of that."

"Agreed. Neither Washington nor Moscow, but a source capable of issuing orders in the name of one, or the other, or both."

"The Matarese?" said Scofield.

The Russian nodded. "The Matarese."

Bray held his breath, trying to think, to absorb it all. "If Winthrop's still alive, he'll be caged, trapped, held under a microscope. I won't be able to get near him. They'd kill me on sight."

"Again, I agree. Are there others you trust that can be reached?"

"It's crazy," said Scofield, shivering in the cold—and at the thought that now struck him. "There should be, but I don't know who they are. Whoever I went to would have to turn me over, the laws are clear about that. Police warrants aside, there's a little matter of national security. The case against me will be built quickly, legally. Suspected of treason, internal espionage, delivering information to the enemy. No one will touch me."

"Surely there are people who will *listen* to you."

"Listen to what? What do I tell them? What have I got? *You?* You'd be thrown into a maximum security hospital before you could say your name. The words of a dying Istrebiteli? A Communist killer? Where's the verification, even the logic? Goddamn it, we're cut off. All we've got are shadows!"

Taleniekov took a step forward, his conviction in his voice. "Perhaps old Krupskaya was right; perhaps the answer is in Corsica, after all."

"Oh, Christ. . . ."

"Hear me out. You say we have only shadows. If so we need a great deal more. If we *had* more, traced even a few names, constructed a fabric of probability— built our own case, if you will. Then could you go to someone, force him to listen to you?"

"From a distance," answered Bray slowly. "Only from a distance. Beyond reach."

"Naturally."

"The case would have to be more than probable, it'd have to be damned conclusive."

"I could move men in Moscow if I had such proof. It was my hope that over here an inquiry might be made with less evidence. You're notorious for your never-ending Senate inquiries. I merely assumed it could be done, that you could bring it about."

"Not now. Not me."

"Corsica, then?"

"I don't know. I'd have to think about it. There's still Winthrop."

"You said yourself you could not reach him. If you tried to get near him, they'd kill you."

"People have tried before. I'll protect myself. I've got to find out what happened. He saw it for himself; if he's alive and I can talk to him, he'll know what to do."

"And if he's *not* alive, or you cannot reach him?"

Scofield looked at the dead men on the pavement. "Maybe the only thing that's left. Corsica."

The KGB man shook his head. "I look at odds more thoroughly than you, Beowulf. I won't wait. I won't risk that 'hospital' you speak of. I'll go to Corsica now."

"If you do, start on the southeast coast, north of Porto Vecchio."

"Why?"

"It's where it all began. It's Matarese country."

Taleniekov nodded. "Again, the schoolwork. Thank you. Perhaps we'll meet in Corsica."

"Can you get out of the country?" asked Bray.

"Getting in, getting out . . . easily managed. These are not obstacles. What about yourself? If you decide to join me."

"I can buy my way to London, to Paris. I've got accounts there. If I do, count on three days, four at the outside. There are small inns up in the hills. I'll find you. . . ."

Scofield stopped. Both men turned swiftly at the sound of an approaching automobile. A sedan swung casually off the road into the parking area. In the front seat was a couple, the man's arm draped over the woman's shoulder. The headlights shone directly on the immobile bodies on the pavement, the spill illuminating the shattered window of the stalled car and the bloody head inside.

The driver whipped his arm off the woman's shoulder, pushing her down on the seat, and gripped the steering wheel with both hands. He spun it violently to the right and sped back into the road, the roar of the motor echoing throughout the woods and the open space.

"They'll reach the police," said Bray. "Let's get out of here."

"I submit it would be best not to use that car," replied the KGB man.

"Why not?"

"Winthrop's chauffeur. You may trust him. I'm not sure I do."

"That's crazy! He was damn near killed!"

Taleniekov gestured at the dead men on the pavement. "These were marksmen, Russian or American, it makes no difference, they were experts—the Matarese would employ no less. The windshield of that limousine was at least five feet wide, the driver behind it an easy target for a novice. Why wasn't he shot? Why wasn't that car stopped? We look for traps, Beowulf. We were led into one and we didn't see it. Perhaps even by Winthrop himself."

Bray felt sick; he had no answer. "We'll separate. It's better for both of us."

"Corsica, perhaps?"

"Maybe. You'll know if I get there."

"Very well."

"Taleniekov?"

"Yes?"

"Thanks for using the matches."

"Under the circumstances, I believe you would have done the same for me."

"Under the circumstances . . . yes, I would."

"Has it struck you? We did not kill each other, Beowulf Agate. We talked."

"We talked."

A lone siren was carried on the cold night wind. Others would be heard soon; patrol cars would converge on the killing ground. Both men turned away from each other and ran, Scofield down the dark path into the woods beyond the rented car, Taleniekov toward the railing that fronted the ravine in Rock Creek Park.

PART
TWO

PART
TWO

12

The thick-beamed fishing boat plowed through the chopping swells like a heavy awkward animal dimly aware that the waters were unfriendly. Waves slapped against the bow and the sides sending cascading sprays over the gunnels, the tails of salt whipped by the early morning winds into the faces of men handling the nets.

One man, however, was not involved with the drudgery of the catch. He pulled at no rope and manipulated no hook, nor did he join in the cursing and laughter that were byproducts of making a living from the sea. Instead, he sat alone on the deck, a thermos of coffee in one hand, a cupped cigarette in the other. It was understood that should French or Italian patrol boats approach, he would become a fisherman, but if none did he was to be left by himself. No one objected to this strange man without a name, for each member of the crew was 100,000 *lire* richer for his presence. The boat had picked him up on a pier in San Vincenzo. The vessel's schedule had called for a dawn departure from the Italian coast, but the stranger had suggested that if the coast of Corsica were seen by dawn, captain and crew would have a far better catch for their labors. Rank had its privileges; the captain received 150,000 *lire*. They had sailed out of San Vincenzo before midnight.

Scofield twisted the top back onto the thermos and threw his cigarette over the side. He stood up and stretched, peering through the mists at the coastline. They had made good time. According to the captain they would be in sight of Solenzara within minutes; and within an hour they would drop off their esteemed passenger between Sainte-Lucie and Porto Vecchio. No problems were anticipated; there were scores of deserted inlets on the rocky shoreline for a temporarily disabled fishing boat.

Bray yanked on the cord looped around the handle of his attaché case and strapped it to his wrist; it was firm—and wet. The string burn on his wrist was irritated by the saltwater, but it would heal quickly, actually aided by the salt. The precaution might seem unwarranted, but the appearance of it was as valuable as the attachment. One could doze, and *Corsos* were known to be quick to relieve travelers of valuables—especially travelers who journeyed without identification, but with money.

"*Signore!*" The captain approached, his wide smile revealing an absence of key teeth. "*Ecco Solenzara! Ci arriveremo subito—trenta minuti. E nord di* Porto Vecchio!"

"*Benissimo, grazie.*"

"*Prego!*"

In a half-hour he'd be on land, in Corsica, in the hills where the Matarese was born. That it had been born was not disputed, that it had provided assassins-for-hire until the mid-thirties was accepted as a firm probability. But so little was known about it that no one really knew how much of its story was myth and how much based in reality. The legend was both encouraged and scorned at the same time; it was basically an enigma because no one understood its origins. Only that a madman named Guillaume de Matarese had summoned a council—from where was never recorded—and given birth to a band of assassins, based, some said, on the killer-society of Hasan ibn-al-Sabbah in the eleventh century.

Yet this smacked of cult-orientation, thus feeding the myth and diminishing the reality. No court testimony was ever given, no assassin ever caught who could be traced to an organization called the Matarese; if there were confessions, none were ever made public. Still the rumors persisted. Stories were circulated in high places; articles appeared in responsible newspapers, only to be denied editorial substance in later editions. Several independent studies were begun; if any were completed, no one knew about them. And through it all governments made no comment. Ever. They were silent.

And for a young intelligence officer studying the history of assassination years ago, it was this silence that lent a certain credibility to the Matarese.

Just as another silence, suddenly imposed three days ago, convinced him that the rendezvous in Corsica was no proposal made in the heat of violence, but the only thing that *was* left. The Matarese remained an enigma, but it was no myth. It was a reality. A powerful man had gone to other powerful men and spoken the name in alarm; it was not to be tolerated.

Robert Winthrop had disappeared.

Bray had run from Rock Creek Park three nights ago and made his way to a motel on the outskirts of Fredericksburg. For six hours he had traveled up and down the highway calling Winthrop from a series of telephone booths, never the same one twice, hitching rides on the pretext of a disabled car to put distance between them. He had talked to Winthrop's wife, alarming her he was sure, but saying nothing of substance, only that he had to speak with the Ambassador. Until it was dawn, and there was no answer on the phone, just interminable rings spaced farther and farther apart—or so it seemed—and no one at all on the line.

There had been nowhere to turn, no one to go to; the networks were spreading out for him. If they found him, his termination would be complete; he understood that. If he was permitted to live, it would be within the four walls of a cell, or worse, as a vegetable. But he did not think he would be permitted to live. Taleniekov was right: they were both marked.

If there was an answer, it was four thousand miles away in the Mediterranean. In his attaché case were a dozen false passports, five bank books under assumed names, and a list of men and women who could find him all manner of transportation. He had left Fredericksburg at dawn two days ago, had stopped at banks in London and Paris, and late last night had reached a fishing pier in San Vincenzo.

And now he was within minutes of setting foot on Corsica. The long stretches of immobility in the air and over the water had given him time to think or at least the time to organize his thoughts. He had to start with the incontrovertible; there were two established facts:

Guillaume de Matarese had existed and there'd been a group of men who had called themselves the Council of the Matarese, dedicated to the insane theories of its sponsor. The world moved forward by constant, violent changes of power. Shock and sudden death were intrinsic to the evolution of history. Someone had to provide the means. Governments everywhere would pay for political murder. Assassination—carried out under the most controlled methods untraceable to those contracting for it—could become a global resource with riches and influence beyond imagination. This was the theory of Guillaume de Matarese.

Among the international intelligence community, a minority maintained that the Matarese had been responsible for scores of political killings from the second decade of the century through the mid-thirties, from Sarajevo to Mexico City, from Tokyo to Berlin. In their view, the collapse of the Matarese was attributed to the explosion of World War II with its growth of covert services where such murders were legitimized, or the council's absorption by the Sicilian Mafia, now entrenched everywhere, but centralized in the United States.

But this positive judgment was decidedly a minority viewpoint. The vast majority of professionals held with Interpol, Britain's MI-Six, and the American Central Intelligence Agency who claimed that the power of the Matarese was exaggerated. It undoubtedly had killed a number of minor political figures in the maze of passionately ineffective French and Italian politics, but there was no hard evidence of anything beyond this. It was essentially a collection of paranoiacs led by a wealthy eccentric who was as misinformed about philosophy as he was about governments accepting his outrageous contracts. If it were anything else, these professionals claimed further, why had not *they* ever been contacted?

Because, Bray had believed years ago, as he believed now, *you were—we were—the last people on earth the Matarese wanted to do business with. From the beginning we were the competition—in one form or another.*

"*Ancora quindici minuti,*" bellowed the captain from the open wheelhouse— "*la costa è molto vicina.*"

"*Grazie tante, capitano.*"

"*Prego.*"

The Matarese. *Was* it possible? A group of men selecting and controlling global assassinations, providing structure to terrorism, spawning chaos everywhere?

For Bray the answer was yes. The words of a dying Istrebiteli, the sentence of death imposed by the Soviets on Vasili Taleniekov, his own execution team recruited from Marseilles, Amsterdam and Prague . . . all were a prelude to the disappearance of Robert Winthrop. All were tied to this modern Council of the Matarese. It was the unseen, unknown mover.

Who were they, these hidden men who had the resources to reach into the highest places of governments as readily as they financed wild-eyed terrorists and selected celebrated men for murder? The larger question was why. *Why?* For what purpose or purposes did they exist?

The *who* was the riddle that had to be unraveled first . . . and whoever they were, there had to be a connection between them and those fanatics initially summoned by Guillaume de Matarese; where else could they have come from, how else could they have known? Those early men had come to the hills of Porto Vecchio; they had names. The past was the only point of departure he had.

There'd been another, he reflected, but the flare of a match in the woods of Rock Creek Park had erased it. Robert Winthrop had been about to name two powerful men in Washington who had vehemently denied any knowledge of the Matarese. In their denials was their complicity; they *had* to have heard of the Matarese—one way or the other. But Winthrop had not said those names; the violence had interfered. Now he might never say them.

Names past could lead to names present; in this case, they had to. Men left their works, their imprints on their times . . . their money. All could be traced and lead somewhere. If there were keys to unlock the vaults that held the answers to the Matarese, they would be found in the hills of Porto Vecchio. He had to find them . . . as his enemy, Vasili Taleniekov, had to find them. Neither would survive unless they did. There'd be no farm in Grasnov for the Russian, no new life for Beowulf Agate, until they found the answers.

"*La costa si avvicina!*" roared the captain, spinning the wheel. He turned, grinning at his passenger through the wind-blown spray. "*Ancora cinque minuti, signore, e poi la Corsica.*"

"*Grazie, capitano.*"

"*Prego.*"

Corsica.

Taleniekov raced up the rocky hill in the moonlight, ducking into the patches of tall grass to obscure his movements, but not the path he was breaking. He did not want those following him to give up the hunt, merely to be slowed down, separated if possible; if he could trap one, that would be ideal.

Old Krupskaya had been right about Corsica, Scofield accurate about the hills north of Porto Vecchio. There were secrets here; it had taken him less than two days to learn that. Men now chased him through the hills in the darkness to prevent him from learning anything further.

Four nights ago Corsica had been a wildly speculative source, an alternative to capture, Porto Vecchio merely a town on the southeast coast of the island, the hills beyond unknown.

The hills were still unknown; the people who lived in them were distant, strange, and uncommunicative, their Oltramontan dialect difficult to understand, but the speculation had been removed. The mere mention of the Matarese was enough to further cloud eyes that were hostile to begin with; pressing for even the most innocuous information was enough to end conversations barely begun. It was as if the name itself were part of a tribal rite of which no one spoke outside the enclaves in the hills, and never in the presence of strangers. Vasili had begun to understand within hours after he had entered the rock-dotted countryside; it had been dramatically confirmed the first night.

Four days ago he would not have believed it; now he knew it was so. The Matarese was more than legend, more than a mystic symbol to primitive hill people; it was a form of religion. It *had* to be; men were prepared to die to keep its secret.

Four days and the world had changed for him. He was no longer dealing with knowledgeable men, sophisticated equipment at their disposal. There were no computer tapes whirling inside glass panels at the touch of a button, no green letters *rat-a-tat-tatting* across black screens, delivering immediate information necessary for the next decision. He was probing the past among people of the past.

Which was why he wanted so desperately to trap one of the men following him up the hill in the darkness. He judged there were three of them; the crest of the hill was long and wide and profuse with ragged trees and jagged rocks. They would have to separate in order to cover the various descents that led to further hills and the flatlands that preceded the mountain forests. If he could take one man and have several hours to work on his mind and body he could learn a great deal. He had no compunction about doing so. The night before a wooden bed had been blown apart in the darkness as a Corsican stood silhouetted in the doorframe, a Lupo shotgun in his hand. Taleniekov was presumed to have been in that bed. . . . Just one man—*that* man—thought Vasili, suppressing his anger, as he ran into a small cluster of wild fir trees just beneath the crown of the hill. He could rest for a few moments.

Far below he could see the weak beams of flashlights. *One, two . . . three.* Three men and they *were* separating. The one on the extreme left was covering his area; it would take that man ten minutes of climbing to reach the cluster of wild fir. Taleniekov hoped it was the man with the Lupo. He leaned against a tree, breathing heavily, and let his body go limp.

It had happened so fast, the excursion into this primitive world. Yet there was a symmetry of a kind. He had begun running at night along the wooded banks of a ravine in Washington's Rock Creek Park and here he was in an isolated, tree-lined sanctuary high in the hills of Corsica. At night. The journey had been swift; he had known precisely what to do and when to do it.

Five o'clock yesterday afternoon, he had been in Rome's Leonardo da Vinci Airport where he had negotiated for a private flight to Bonifacio, due west, on the southern tip of Corsica. He had reached Bonifacio by seven, and a taxi had driven him north along the coast to Porto Vecchio and to an inn up in the hill country. He had sat down to a heavy Corsican meal, engaging the curious owner in offhand conversation.

"I am a scholar of sorts," he had said. "I seek information about a *padrone* of many years ago. A Guillaume de Matarese."

"I do not understand," the innkeeper had replied. "You say a scholar of sorts.

It would seem to me that one either is or is not, signore. Are you with some great university?"

"A private foundation, actually. But universities have access to our studies."

"Un' fondazione?"

"Un' organizzazione accademica. My section deals with little-known history in Sardinia and Corsica during the late nineteenth and early twentieth centuries. Apparently there was this *padrone* . . . Guillaume de Matarese . . . who controlled much of the land in these hills north of Porto Vecchio."

"He owned most of it, signore. He was good to the people who lived on his lands."

"Naturally. And we would like to grant him a place in Corsica's history. I'm not sure I know where to begin."

"Perhaps . . ." The innkeeper had leaned back in the chair, his eyes leveled, his voice strangely noncommittal. "The ruins of the Villa Matarese. It is a clear night, signore. They are quite beautiful in the moonlight. I could find someone to take you. Unless, of course, you are too exhausted from your journey."

"Not at all. It was a quick flight."

He had been taken further up into the hills, to the skeletal remains of a once-sprawling estate, the remnants of the great house itself covering nearly an acre of land. Jagged walls and broken chimneys were the only structures still intact. On the ground, the brick borders of an enormous circular drive could be discerned beneath the overgrowth. On both sides of the great house, stone paths sliced through the tall grass, dotted by broken trellises; remembrances of lushly cultivated gardens long since destroyed.

The entire ruins stood eerily on the hill in silhouette, heightened by the backwash of moonlight. Guillaume de Matarese had built a monument to himself and the power of the edifice had lost nothing in its destruction by time and the elements. Instead, the skeleton had a force of its own.

Vasili had heard the voices behind him, the young boy who'd escorted him nowhere to be seen. There had been two men and those opening words of dubious greeting had been the beginning of an interrogation that had lasted more than an hour. It would have been a simple matter to subdue both Corsicans, but Taleniekov knew he could learn more through passive resistance; unschooled interrogators imparted more than they dragged forth when they dealt with trained subjects. He had stayed with his story of the *organizzazione accademica;* at the end, he had been given expected advice.

"Go back where you came from, signore. There is no knowledge here that would serve you, we know nothing. Disease swept through these mountains years ago; none are left who might help you."

"There must be older people in the hills. Perhaps if I wandered about and made a few inquiries."

"We are older people, signore, and we cannot answer your inquiries. Go back. We are ignorant men in these parts, shepherds. We are not comfortable when strangers intrude on our simple ways. Go back."

"I shall take your advice under consideration—"

"Do not take such trouble, signore. Just leave us. Please."

In the morning, Vasili had walked back up into the hills, to the Villa Matarese and beyond, stopping at numerous thatched farmhouses, asking his questions, noting the glaring dark Corsican eyes as the nonanswers had been delivered, aware that he was being followed.

He had been told nothing, of course, but in the progressively hardened reactions to his presence he had learned something of consequence. Men were not only following him, they had been preceding him, alerting families in the hills that a stranger was coming. He was to be sent away, told nothing.

That night—last night, thought Taleniekov, as he watched the waving beam of the flashlight on the left slowly ascend the hill—the innkeeper had approached his table.

"I am afraid, signore, that I cannot permit you to stay here any longer. I have rented the room."

Vasili had glanced up, no hesitation now in his speech. "A pity. I need only an armchair or a cot, if you could spare one. I shall be leaving first thing in the morning. I've found what I came for."

"And what is that, signore?"

"You'll know soon enough. Others will come after me, with the proper equipment and land records. There'll be a very thorough, very scholarly investigation. What happened here is fascinating. I speak academically, of course."

"Of course. . . . Perhaps one more night."

Six hours later a man had burst into his room and fired two shots from the thick barrels of a deadly sawed-off shotgun called the Lupo—the "wolf." Taleniekov had been waiting; he had watched from behind a partially open closet door as the wooden bed exploded, the firm stuffing beneath the covers blown into the dark wall.

The sound had been shattering, an explosion echoing throughout the small country inn, yet no one had come running to see what had happened. Instead, the man with the Lupo had stood in the doorframe and had spoken quietly in Oltramontan, as if uttering an oath.

"*Per nostro circolo,*" he had said; then he had raced away.

It had meant nothing, yet Vasili knew then that it meant everything. Words delivered as an incantation after taking a life. . . . *For our circle.*

Taleniekov had gathered his things together and fled from the inn. He had made his way toward the single dirt road that led up from Porto Vecchio and had positioned himself in the underbrush twenty feet from the edge. Several hundred yards below, he had seen the glow of a cigarette. The road was being guarded; he had waited. He had to.

If Scofield was coming he would use that road; it had been the dawn of the fourth day. The American had said that if Corsica was all that was left, he'd be there in three or four days.

By three in the afternoon there had been no sign of him, and an hour later

Vasili knew he could wait no longer. Men had sped down the road toward the burgeoning port resort. Their mission had been clear: the intruder had eluded the roadblock. Find him, kill him.

Search parties had begun fanning through the woods; two Corsicans slashing the overgrowth with mountain machetes had come within thirty feet of him; soon the patrols would become more concentrated, the search more thorough. He could not wait for Scofield; there was no guarantee that Beowulf Agate had even escaped from the net being spread for him in his own country, much less on his way to Corsica.

Vasili had spent the hours until sundown creating his own assaults on those who would trap him. Like a swamp fox, his trail appeared one moment heading in *this* direction, his appearance sighted over *there;* broken limbs and trampled reeds were proof that he was cornered in a stretch of marshland that fronted an unclimbable wall of schist, and as men closed in, his figure could be seen racing through a field a mile to the west. He was a yellow jacket on the wind, visually stinging in a dozen different places at once.

When darkness had come, Taleniekov had begun the strategy that led him to where he was at the moment, hidden in a cluster of fir trees below the crown of a high hill, waiting for a man carrying a flashlight to approach. The plan was simple, carried out in three stages, each phase logically evolved from the previous one. First came the diversion, drawing off the largest number of the attack pack as possible; then the exposure to the few left behind, pulling them farther away from the many; finally the separation of those few and the trapping of one. The third phase was about to be concluded as the fires raged a mile and a half below to the east.

He had made his way through the woods, descending in the direction of Porto Vecchio, traveling on the right side of the dirt road. He had gathered together dried branches and leaves, breaking several Graz-Burya shells, sprinkling the powder inside the pile of debris. He had ignited his pyre in the forest, waited until it had erupted and he had heard the shouts of the converging Corsicans. He had raced northward, across the road, into a denser, drier section of the wooded hill and repeated the action, lighting a larger pile of dried foliage next to a dead chestnut tree. It had spread like a fire bomb, the flames leaping upward through the tree, promising to leap again, laterally into the surrounding forest. He had run once more to the north and had set his last and largest fire, choosing a beech tree long since destroyed by insects. Within a half-hour the hills were blazing in three distinct areas, the hunters racing from one to another, containment and the search vying for priority. Fire. Always fire.

He had crossed diagonally back to the southwest, climbing through the woods to the road that fronted the inn. He had emerged within sight of the window through which he had escaped the night before. He had walked out on the road, seeing several men with rifles standing, talking anxiously among themselves. The rear guard, confused by the chaos below, unsure whether they should remain where they were, as instructed by superiors, or go to the aid of their island brothers.

The irony of coincidence had not been lost on Vasili as he had struck the match. The striking of a match had started it all so many days ago on Washington's Nebraska Avenue; it was the sign of a trap. It signified another in the hills of Corsica.

"*Ecco!*"

"*Il fiammifero.*"

"*E lui!*"

The chase had begun; it was now coming to an end. The man with the flashlight was within a stone's lob from him; he would climb up into the cluster of wild fir before the next thirty seconds elapsed. Below, on the slope of the hill, the flashlight in the center was several hundred yards to the south, its beam crisscrossing the ground in front of the Corsican holding it. Far down to the right, the third flashlight, which only seconds ago had been sweeping frantically back and forth in semicircles, was now oddly stationary, its beam angled down to a single spot. The position of the light and its abrupt immobility bothered Taleniekov, but there was no time to evaluate either fact. The approaching Corsican had reached the first tree in Vasili's natural sanctuary.

The man swung the beam of light into the cluster of trunks and hanging limbs. Taleniekov had broken a number of branches, stripping more than a few so that any light would catch the white wood. The Corsican stepped forward, following the trail; Vasili stepped to his left, concealed by a tree. The hunter passed within eighteen inches, his rifle at the ready. Taleniekov watched the Corsican's feet in the wash of light; when the left foot moved forward, a beat would be lost for a right-handed marksman, the brief imbalance impossible to recover.

The foot left the ground and Vasili lunged, lashing his arm around the man's neck, his fingers surging in for the trigger enclosure, ripping the rifle out of the Corsican's hand. The beam of the flashlight shot up into the trees. Taleniekov crashed his right knee into his victim's kidney, dragging him backward, down onto the ground. He scissored the man's waist with his legs, forcing the Corsican's neck into a painful arch, the man's ear next to his lips.

"You and I will spend the next hour together!" he whispered in Italian. "When the time's up, you'll have told me what I want to know, or you won't speak again. I'll use your own knife. Your face will be so disfigured no one will recognize you. Now get up slowly. If you raise your voice, you're dead!"

Gradually, Vasili released the pressure on the man's waist and neck. Both men started to rise, Taleniekov's fingers gripped around the man's throat.

There was a sudden *crack* from above, the sound echoing throughout the trees. A foot had stepped on a fallen branch. Vasili spun around, peering up into the dense foliage. What he saw caused him to lose his breath.

A man was silhouetted between two trees, the silhouette familiar, last seen in the doorframe of a country inn. And as that last time, the thick barrels of a Lupo were leveled straight ahead. But now they were leveled at him.

In the rush of thought, Taleniekov understood that not all professionals were trained in Moscow and Washington. The frenetically waving beam of light at the base of the hill, suddenly still, motionless. A flashlight strapped to a sapling or a resilient limb, pulled back and set in motion to give the illusion of movement, its owner racing in darkness up a familiar incline.

"You were very clever last night, signore," said the man with the Lupo. "But there is nowhere to hide here."

"The *Matarese!*" screamed Vasili at the top of his lungs. *"Per nostro circolo!"* he roared. He lunged to his left. The double-barreled explosion of the Lupo filled the hills.

13

Scofield jumped over the side of the skiff and waded through the waves toward the shoreline. There was no beach, only boulders joined together, forming a three-dimensional wall of jagged stone. He reached a promontory of flat, slippery rock and braced himself against the waters, balancing the attaché case in his left hand, his canvas duffel bag in his right.

He rolled onto the sandy, vine-covered ground until the surface was level enough to stand. Then he ran into the tangled brush that concealed him from any wandering patrols above on the broken cliffs. The captain had warned him that the police were inconsistent; some could be bought, others could not.

He knelt down, took a penknife from his pocket, and cut the webbed strap off his wrist, freeing the case. Then he opened the duffel bag and took out dry corduroy trousers, a pair of ankle boots, a dark sweater, a cap, and a coarse woolen jacket, all bought in Paris, all labels torn off. They were sufficiently rough in appearance to be accepted as native garb.

He changed, rolled up the wet clothes, and stuffed them into the duffel bag along with the attaché case, then started the long, winding climb to the road above. He had been to Corsica twice before—Porto Vecchio once—both trips basically concerned with an obnoxious, constantly sweating owner of fishing boats in Bastia on State's payroll as one more "observer" of Soviet Ligurian Sea operations. The brief visit south to Porto Vecchio had been in connection with the feasibility of covertly financing resort projects in the Tyrrhenian; he never knew what happened. While in Porto Vecchio he had rented a car and driven up into the hills. He had seen the ruins of Villa Matarese in the broiling afternoon sun and had stopped for a glass of beer at a roadside *taverna,* but the excursion had faded quickly from his mind. It never occurred to him that he would ever return. The legend of the Matarese was no more alive than the ruins of the villa. Not then.

He reached the road and pulled the cap down, the cloth covering the bruise on his upper forehead where he had collided with an iron post in a stairwell.

Taleniekov. Had he reached Corsica? Was he somewhere in the hills of Porto Vecchio? It would not take long to find out. A stranger asking questions about a legend would be easily tracked down. On the other hand, the Russian would be cautious; if it had occurred to them to go back to the source of the legend, it might well occur to others to do the same.

Bray looked at his watch; it was nearly 11:30. He took out a map estimating his position as two and a half miles south of Sainte Lucie; the most direct line to the hills—to the Matarese hills, he reflected—was due west. But there was something to find before he entered those hills. A base of operations. A place where he could conceal his things with the reasonable expectation that they would be there when he came back. That ruled out any normal stop a traveler might make. He could not master the Oltramontan dialect in a few hours; he'd be marked as a stranger and strangers were marks. He would have to make camp in the woods, near water if possible, and preferably within walking distance of a store or inn where he could get food.

He had to assume he would be in Porto Vecchio for several days. No other assumption was feasible; anything could happen once he found Taleniekov—*if* he found him—but for the moment the necessities had to be considered before any plan was formulated. All the little things.

There was a path—too narrow for any car to travel, a shepherd's route per-haps—that veered off the road into a gently rising series of fields; it headed west. He shifted the canvas duffel bag to his left hand and entered the path, pushing aside low-hanging branches until he was in the tall grass.

By 12:45 he had walked no more than five or six miles inland, but he had purposely traveled in a zigzag pattern that afforded him the widest views of the area. He found what he was looking for, a section of forest that rose abruptly above a stream, thick branches of Corsican pine sweeping down to the ground on the banks. A man and his belongings would be safe behind those walls of green. A mile or so to the southwest there was a road that led further up into the hills. From what he could remember he was fairly certain this was the road he had taken to the ruins of Villa Matarese; there had been only one. Again, if memory served, he recalled driving past a number of isolated farmhouses on the way to the ruins on the hill and the inn where he had stopped for native beer during that hot afternoon. Only the inn came first, near that road on the hill, where a narrower road swung off it. To the *right* on the way up, on the *left* returning to Porto Vecchio. Bray checked his map again; it showed the hill road, and the branch to the right. He knew where he was.

He waded across the stream, and climbed the opposite bank to the cascading pines. He crawled underneath, opened his duffel bag and took out a small shovel, amused that two packets of toilet paper fell out with the instrument. The little things, he thought, as he started to dig into the soft earth.

It was nearly four o'clock. He had set up his camp beneath the screen of green branches, his duffel bag buried, the bandage on his neck changed, his face and hands washed in the stream. Too, he had rested, staring up at the filtered sunlight strained through the webbing of pine needles. His mind wandered, an indulgence he tried to reject but could not. Sleep would not come; thoughts did.

He was under a tree on the banks of a stream in Corsica, a journey that had begun on a bridge at night in Amsterdam. And now he could never go back unless he and Taleniekov found what they were looking for in the hills of Porto Vecchio.

It would not be so difficult to disappear. He had arranged many such disappearances in the past with less money and less expertise than he had now. There were so many places—Melanesia, the Fijis, New Zealand, across to Tasmania, the vast expanses of Australia, Malaysia, or any of a dozen Sunda islands—he had sent men to such places, stayed cautiously in touch with a few over the years. Lives had been rebuilt, past histories beyond the reach of present associates, new friends, new occupations, even families.

He could do the same, thought Bray. Maybe he would; he had the papers and the money. He could pay his way to Polynesia or the Cook Islands, buy a boat for charters, probably make a decent living. It could be a good life, an anonymous existence, an end.

Then he saw the face of Robert Winthrop, the electric eyes searching his, and heard the anxiety in the old man's voice as he spoke of the Matarese.

He heard something else, too. Less distant, immediate, above in the sky. Birds were swooping down in frantic circles, their screeches echoing harshly, angrily over the fields and throughout the woods. Intruders had disturbed their fiefdom. He could hear men running, hear their shouts.

Had he been *spotted?* He rose quickly to his knees, taking his Browning from his jacket pocket, and peered through a spray of pine needles.

Below, a hundred yards to the left, two men had hacked their way with machetes down the overgrown bank to the edge of the stream. They stood for a moment, pistols in their belts, glancing swiftly in every direction, as if unsure of their next moves. Slowly Bray let out his breath; they were not after him; he had not been seen. Instead, the two men had been hunting—an animal that had attacked their goats, perhaps, or a wild dog. Not him. Not a stranger wandering in the hills.

Then he heard the words and knew he was only partially right. The shout did not come from either Corsican holding a machete; it came from over the bank of the stream, from the field beyond.

"Ecco la—nel campo!"

It was no animal being pursued, but a man. A man was running from other men, and to judge from the fury of his pursuers, that man was running for his life.

Taleniekov? Was it Taleniekov? And if it was, why? Had the Russian learned something so quickly? Something that the Corsicans in Porto Vecchio would kill for?

Scofield watched as the two men below took the guns from their belts and ran up the bank out of sight into the bordering field. He crawled back to the trunk of the tree and tried to gather his thoughts. Instinct convinced him that *il uomo* was Taleniekov. If so, there were several options. He could head for the road and walk up into the hills, an Italian crewman with a fishing boat in for repairs and time on his hands; he could stay where he was until nightfall, then thread his way under cover of darkness, hoping to get near enough to hear men's conversations; or he could leave now and follow the hunt.

The last was the least attractive—but likely to be the most productive. He chose it.

It was 5:35 when Bray first saw him, running along the crest of a hill, shots fired at his weaving, racing figure in the glare of the setting sun. Taleniekov, as expected, was doing the unexpected. He was not trying to escape; rather, he was using the chase to sow confusion and through that confusion learn something. The tactic was sound; the best way to uncover vital information was to make the enemy protect it.

But what had he so far learned that would justify the risk? How long would he—or could he—keep up the pace and the concentration to elude his enemy? . . . The answers were as clear as the questions: isolate, trap, and break. Within the territory.

Scofield studied the terrain as best he could from his prone position in the field. The early evening breezes made his task easier; the grass bent with each gentle sweep of wind, his view clearer for it. He tried to analyze the choices open to Taleniekov, where best to intercept him. The KGB man was running due north; another mile or so and he would reach the base of the mountains where he would stop. Nothing could be achieved by going up into them. He would double back, heading southwest to avoid being hemmed in by the roads. And somewhere he would create a diversion, one significant enough to escalate the confusion into a moment of chaos, the trap to follow shortly.

Intercepting Taleniekov might have to wait until that moment, thought Bray, but he preferred that it did not; there would be too much activity compressed into a short period of time. Mistakes were made that way. It would be better to reach the Russian beforehand. That way, they could develop the strategy together. Crouching, Scofield made his way southwest through the tall grass.

The sun fell behind the distant mountains; the shadows lengthened until they became long shafts of ink, spilling over the hills, enveloping whole fields that moments ago had been drenched in orange sunlight. Darkness came and still there was no sign, no sound of Taleniekov. Bray moved swiftly within the perimeters of the Russian's logical area of movement, his eyes adjusting to the darkness, his ears picking up every noise foreign to the fields and the woods. *Still no Taleniekov.*

Had the KGB man taken the risk of using either dirt road for faster mobility? If he had, it was foolhardy, unless he had conceived of a tactic better employed in the lower hills. The entire countryside was now alive with search parties ranging in size from two to six men, all armed; knives, guns and mountain machetes hanging from their clothing, their flashlight beams crisscrossing each other like intersecting lasers. Scofield raced further west to higher ground, the myriad beams of light his protection against the roving, angry Corsicans; he knew when to stop, when to run.

He ran, cutting between two teams of converging men, halting abruptly at the sight of a whining animal, its fur thick, its eyes wide and staring. He was about to use his knife when he realized it was a shepherd's dog, its nostrils uninterested in human scent. The realization did not prevent him from losing his breath; he stroked the dog, reassuring it, then ducked beneath a flashlight beam that shot out of the woods, and scrambled further up the sloping field.

He reached a boulder half buried in the ground and threw himself behind it. He got up slowly, his hands on the rock, prepared to spring away and run again. He looked over the top, down at the scene below, the flashlight beams breaking up the darkness, defining the whereabouts of the search parties. He was able to make out the crude wooden structure that was the inn he had stopped at years ago. In front of it was the primitive dirt road he had crossed several hours before to reach the higher ground. A hundred yards to the right of the inn was the wider, winding road that descended out of the hills down into Porto Vecchio.

The Corsicans were spread over the fields. Here and there Bray could hear the barking of dogs amid angry human shouts and the slashing of machetes. It was an eerie sight, no figures seen, just beams of light, shooting in all directions; invisible puppets dancing on illuminated strings in the darkness.

Suddenly, there was another light, yellow not white. *Fire.* An abrupt explosion of flames in the distance, to the right of the road that led to Porto Vecchio.

Taleniekov's diversion. It had its effect.

Men ran, shouting, the beams of light converging on the road, racing toward the spreading fire. Scofield held his place, wondering—clinically, professionally— how the KGB man would use his diversion. What would he do next? What method would he use to spring his trap on one man?

The beginning of the answer came three minutes later. A second, larger eruption of flames surged skyward about a quarter of a mile to the *left* of the road to Porto Vecchio. A single diversion was now two, dividing the Corsicans, confusing the search; fire was lethal in the hills.

He could see the puppets now, their strings of light fusing with the glow of the spreading flames. Another fire appeared, this one massive, an entire tree bursting into a ball of yellowish white as though engulfed by napalm. It was three or four hundred yards *farther* left, a third diversion greater than the previous two. Chaos spread as rapidly as the flames, both in danger of leaping out of control. Taleniekov was covering all his bases; if a trap was not feasible he could escape in the confusion.

But if the Russian's mind was working as his might, thought Bray, the trap would be sprung in moments. He crawled around the boulder and started down the expanse of descending field, keeping his shoulders close to the ground, propelling himself like an animal, hands and feet working in concert.

There was a sudden flash far below on the road. It lasted no more than a second, a tiny eruption of light. A match had been struck. It appeared senseless until Bray saw a flashlight beam shoot out from the right, followed instantly by two others. The three beams converged in the direction of the briefly held match; seconds later they separated at the base of the hill that bordered the road below.

Scofield knew what the tactic was now. Four nights ago a match had been struck in Rock Creek Park to expose a trap; it was struck now to execute one. By the same man. Taleniekov had succeeded in throwing the Corsicans' search into chaotic paralysis; he was now drawing off the few left behind. The final chase had started; the Russian would take one of those men.

Bray took the automatic from the holster strapped beneath his jacket and reached into his pocket for his silencer. Snapping it into place, he unlatched the safety and began running diagonally to his left, below the crest of the hill. Somewhere within those acres of grassland and forest the trap would be sprung. It was a question of finding out precisely where, if possible immobilizing one of the pursuers, thus favoring the odds for the trap's success. Better still, taking one of the Corsicans; two sources of information were better than one.

He ran in spurts, staying close to the ground, his eyes on the three flashlight beams below. Each was covering a section of the hill and in the spills, he could see weapons clearly; at the first sign of the hunted, shots would be fired. . . .

Scofield stopped. Something was wrong; it was the beam of light on the right, the one perhaps two hundred yards directly beneath him. It was waving back and forth too rapidly, without focus. And there was no reflection—not even a dull reflection—of light bouncing off metal—even dull metal. There was no weapon.

There was no hand holding that flashlight! It had been secured to a thick branch or a limb; a feint, a false placement given false motion to cover another movement. Bray lay on the ground, concealed by the grass and the darkness, watching, listening for signs of a man running.

It happened so fast, so unexpectedly, that Scofield nearly fired his gun in instinctive defense. The figure of a large Corsican was suddenly beside him, above him, the crunch of a racing foot not eighteen inches from his head. He rolled to his left, out of the running man's path.

He inhaled deeply, trying to throw off the shock and the fear, then rose cautiously and followed as best he could the trail of the racing Corsican. The man was heading directly north along the hill, below the ridge, as Bray had intended doing, relying on beams of light and sound—or the sudden absence of both—to find Taleniekov. The Corsican was familiar with the terrain. Scofield quickened his pace, passing the center beam of light still far below, and by passing it knowing that Taleniekov had fixed on the third man. The flashlight—barely seen—on the extreme north side of the hill.

Bray hurried faster; instinct told him to keep the Corsican in his sight. But the man was nowhere to be seen. All was silent, too silent. Scofield dropped to the ground and joined that silence, peering about in the darkness, his finger around the trigger of his automatic. It would happen any second But how? *Where?*

About a hundred and fifty yards ahead, diagonally down to the right, the third beam of light appeared to go off and on in a series of short, irregular flashes. No. . . . It was not being turned off and on rapidly; the light was being *blocked. Trees.*

Whoever held the flashlight was walking into a cluster of trees growing on the side of the hill.

Suddenly, the beam of light shot upward, dancing briefly in the higher regions of the thinning trunks, then plummeted down, the glow stationary, dulled by the foliage on the ground. That was it! The trap had been sprung, but Taleniekov did not know a Corsican was waiting for a sign of that trap.

Bray got to his feet and ran as fast as he could, his boots making harsh contact with the profusion of rocks on the hillside. He had only seconds, there was so much ground to cover, and too much darkness; he could not tell where the trees began. If there was only an outline to fire at, the sound of a voice. . . . *Voice.* He was about to shout, to warn the Russian, when he heard a voice. The words were in that strange Italian spoken by the southern Corsicans; the sound floated up in the night breezes.

Thirty feet below him! He saw the man standing between two trees, his body outlined in the spill of the muted, immobile beam of light that glowed up from the ground; the Corsican held a shotgun in his hands. Scofield pivoted to his right and sprang toward the armed man, his automatic leveled.

"The *Matarese!*" The name was screamed by Taleniekov, as was the enigmatic phrase that followed. *"Per nostro circolo!"*

Bray fired into the back of the Corsican, the three rapid spits overwhelmed by an explosion from the shotgun. The man fell forward. Scofield dug his feet into the body, crouching, expecting an attack. What he saw next had prevented it; the Corsican trapped by Taleniekov had been blown apart by his would-be rescuer.

"Taleniekov?"

"You! Is it *you,* Scofield?"

"Put that light out!" cried Bray. The Russian lunged for the flashlight on the ground, snapping it off. "There's a man on the hill; he's not moving. He's waiting to be called."

"If he comes, we must kill him. If we don't, he'll go for help. He'll bring others back with him."

"I'm not sure his friends can spare the time," replied Scofield, watching the beam of light in the darkness. "You've got them pretty well tied up. . . . There he goes! He's running down the hill."

"Come!" said the Russian, getting up, approaching Bray. "I know a dozen places to hide. I've got a great deal to tell you."

"You must have."

"I do. It's here!"

"What is?"

"I'm not sure . . . the answer, perhaps. Part of it anyway. You've seen for yourself. They're hunting me; they'd kill me on sight. I've intruded—"

"Fermate!" The sudden command was shouted from beyond Scofield on the hill. Bray spun on the ground; the Russian raised his gun. *"Basta!"* The second command was accompanied by the snarling of an animal, a dog straining on a leash. "I have a two-barreled rifle in my hands, signori," continued the voice

. . . the unmistakable voice of a woman, speaking now in English. "As the one fired moments ago, it is a Lupo, and I know how to use it better than the man at your feet. But I do not wish to. Hold your guns to your sides, signori. Do not drop them; you may need them."

"Who are you?" asked Scofield, squinting his eyes at the woman above. From what he could barely see in the night light, she was dressed in trousers and a field jacket. The dog snarled again.

"I look for the scholar."

"The *what?*"

"I am he," said Taleniekov. "From the *organizzazione accademica.* This man is my associate."

"What the hell are you . . . ?"

"Basta," said the Russian quietly. "Why do you look for me, yet do not kill me?"

"Word goes everywhere. You ask questions about the *padrone* of *padrones."*

"I do. Guillaume de Matarese. No one wants to give me answers."

"One does," replied the girl. "An old woman in the mountains. She wants to speak with the scholar. She has things to tell him."

"But you know what's happened here," said Taleniekov, probing. "Men are hunting me; they would kill me. You're willing to risk your own life to bring me—bring us—to her?"

"Yes. It is a long journey, and a hard one. Five or six hours up into the mountains."

"Please answer me. Why are you taking this risk?"

"She is my grandmother. Everyone in the hills despises her; she cannot live down here. But I love her."

"Who is she?"

"She is called the whore of Villa Matarese."

14

They traveled swiftly through the hills to the base of the mountains and up into winding trails cut out of the mountain forests. The dog had sniffed both men when the woman had first come up to them; it was set free and preceded them along the overgrown paths, sure in its knowledge of the way.

Scofield thought it was the same dog he had come across so suddenly, so frighteningly, in the fields. He said as much to the woman.

"Probably, signore. We were there for many hours. I was looking for you and I let him roam, but he was always near in case I needed him."

"Would he have attacked me?"

"Only if you raised your hand to him. Or to me."

It was past midnight when they reached a flat stretch of grassland that fronted what appeared to be a series of imposing, wooded hills. The low-flying clouds had thinned out; moonlight washed over the field, highlighting the peaks in the distance, lending grandeur to this section of the mountain range. Bray could see that Taleniekov's shirt beneath the open jacket was as drenched with sweat as his own; and the night was cool.

"We can rest for a while now," said the woman, pointing to a dark area several hundred feet ahead, in the direction the dog had raced. "Over there is a cave of stone in the hill. It is not very deep, but it is shelter."

"Your dog knows it," added the KGB man.

"He expects me to build a fire," laughed the girl. "When it is raining, he takes sticks in his mouth and brings them inside to me. He is fond of the fire."

The cave was dug out of dark rock, no more than ten feet deep, but at least six in height. They entered.

"Shall I light a fire?" Taleniekov asked.

"If you wish. Uccello will like you for it. I am too tired."

" 'Uccello'?" asked Scofield. " 'Bird'?"

"He flies over the ground, signore."

"You speak English very well," said Bray, as the Russian piled sticks together within a circle of stones obviously used for previous fires. "Where did you learn?"

"I went to the convent school in Vescovato. Those of us who wished to enter the government programs studied French and English."

Taleniekov struck a match beneath the kindling; the fire caught instantly, the flames crackling the wood, throwing warmth and light through the cave. "You're very good at that sort of thing," said Scofield to the KGB man.

"Thank you. It's a minor talent."

"It wasn't minor a few hours ago." Bray turned back to the woman, who had removed her cap and was shaking free her long dark hair. For an instant he stopped breathing and stared at her. Was it the hair? Or the wide, clear brown eyes that were the color of a deer's eyes, or the high cheekbones or the chiseled nose above the generous lips that seemed so ready to laugh? Was it any of these things, or was he simply tired and grateful for the sight of an attractive, capable woman? He did not know; he knew only that this Corsican girl of the hills reminded him of Karine, his wife whose death was ordered by the man three feet away from him in that Corsican cave. He suppressed his thoughts and breathed again. "And did you," he asked, "enter the government programs?"

"As far as they would take me."

"Where was that?"

"To the *scuola media* in Bonifacio. The rest I managed with the help of others. Monies supplied by the *fondos.*"

"I don't understand."

"I am a graduate of the University of Bologna, signore. I am a *Comunista*. I say it proudly."

"Bravo . . . ," said Taleniekov softly.

"One day we shall set things right throughout all Italy," continued the girl, her eyes bright. "We shall end the chaos, the Christian stupidity."

"I'm sure you will," agreed the Russian.

"But never as Moscow's puppets; that we will never be. We are *independente*. We do not listen to vicious bears who would devour us and create a worldwide fascist state. Never!"

"Bravo," said Bray.

The conversation trailed off, the young woman reluctant to answer further questions about herself. She told them her name was Antonia, but beyond that said little. When Taleniekov asked why she, a political activist from Bologna, had returned to this isolated region of Corsica, she replied only that it was to be with her grandmother for a while.

"Tell us about her," said Scofield.

"She will tell you what she wants you to know," said the girl, getting up. "I have told you what she instructed me to say."

" 'The whore of Villa Matarese,' " repeated Bray.

"Yes. They are not words I would choose. Or ever use. Come, we have another two hours to walk."

They reached a flat crown of a mountain and looked down a gentle slope to a valley below. It was no more than a hundred and fifty yards from mountain crest to valley floor, perhaps a mile of acreage covering the basin. The moon had grown progressively brighter; they could see a small farmhouse in the center of the pasture, a barn at the end of a short roadway. They could hear the sound of rushing water; a stream flowed out of the mountain near where they stood, tumbling down the slope between a row of rocks, passing within fifty feet of the small house.

"It's very beautiful," said Taleniekov.

"It is the only world she has known for over half a century," replied Antonia.

"Were you brought up here?" asked Scofield. "Was this your home?"

"No," said the girl, without elaborating. "Come, we will see her. She has been waiting."

"At this hour of the night?" Taleniekov was surprised.

"There is no day or night for my grandmother. She said to bring you to her as soon as we arrived. We have arrived."

There *was* no day or night for the old woman sitting in the chair by the wood-burning stove, not in the accepted sense of sunlight and darkness. She was blind, her eyes two vacant orbs of pastel blue, staring at sounds and at the images of remembered memories. Her features were sharp and angular beneath the covering of wrinkled flesh; the face had once been that of an extraordinarily beautiful woman.

Her voice was soft, with a hollow whispering quality that forced the listener to watch her thin white lips. If there was no essential brilliance about her, neither was there hesitancy nor indecision. She spoke rapidly, a simple mind secure in its own knowledge. She had things to say and death was in her house, a reality that seemed to quicken her thoughts and perceptions. She spoke in Italian, but it was an idiom from an earlier era.

She began by asking both Taleniekov and Scofield to answer—each in his own words—why he was so interested in Guillaume de Matarese. Vasili replied first, repeating his story of an academic foundation in Milan, his department concentrating on Corsican history. He kept it simple, thus allowing Scofield to elaborate in any way he wished. It was standard procedure when two or more intelligence officers were detained and questioned together. Neither had to be primed for the exercise; the fluid lie was second nature to them both.

Bray listened to the Russian and corroborated the basic information, adding details on dates and finances he believed pertinent to Guillaume de Matarese. When he finished, he felt not only confident about his response, but superior to the KGB man; he had done his "schoolwork" better than Taleniekov.

Yet the old woman just sat there, nodding her head in silence, brushing away a lock of white hair that had fallen to the side of her gaunt face. Finally, she spoke.

"You're both lying. The second gentleman is less convincing. He tries to impress me with facts any child in the hills of Porto Vecchio might learn."

"Perhaps in Porto Vecchio," protested Scofield gently, "but not necessarily in Milan."

"Yes. I see what you mean. But then neither of you is from Milan."

"Quite true," interrupted Vasili. "We merely work in Milan. I myself was born in Poland . . . northern Poland. I'm sure you detect my imperfect speech."

"I detect nothing of the sort. Only your lies. However, don't be concerned, it doesn't matter."

Taleniekov and Scofield looked at each other, then over at Antonia, who sat curled up in exhaustion on a pillow in front of the window.

"What doesn't matter?" Bray asked. "We *are* concerned. We want you to speak freely."

"I will," said the blind woman. "For your lies are not those of self-seeking men. Dangerous men, perhaps, but not men moved by profit. You do not look for the *padrone* for your own personal gain."

Scofield could not help himself; he leaned forward. "How do you know?"

The old woman's vacant yet powerful pale blue eyes held his; it was hard to accept the fact that she could not see. "It is in your voices," she said. "You are afraid."

"Have we reason to be?" asked Taleniekov.

"That would depend on what you believe, wouldn't it?"

"We believe a terrible thing has happened," said Bray. "But we know very little. That's as honestly as I can put it."

"What *do* you know, signori?"

Again Scofield and Taleniekov exchanged glances; the Russian nodded first. Bray realized that Antonia was watching them closely. He spoke as obviously to her as to the old woman. "Before we answer you, I think it would be better if your granddaughter left us alone."

"No!" said the girl so harshly that Uccello snapped up his head.

"Listen to me," continued Scofield. "It's one thing to bring us here, two strangers your grandmother wanted to meet. It's something else again to be involved with us. My . . . associate . . . and I have experience in these matters. It's for your own good."

"Leave us, Antonia." The blind woman turned in the chair. "I have nothing to fear from these men and you must be tired. Take Uccello with you; rest in the barn."

"All right," said the girl, getting up, "but Uccello will remain here." Suddenly, from beneath the pillow, she took out the Lupo and leveled it in front of her. "You both have guns. Throw them on the floor. I don't think you would leave here without them."

"That's ridiculous!" cried Bray, as the dog got to its feet growling.

"Do as the lady says," snapped Taleniekov, shoving his Graz-Burya across the floor.

Scofield took out his Browning, checked the safety, and threw the weapon on the rug in front of Antonia. She bent down and picked up both automatics, the Lupo held firmly in her hand. "When you've finished, open the door and call out to me. I will summon Uccello. If he does not come, you won't see your guns again. Except looking down the barrels." She let herself out quickly; the dog emitted a growl and returned to the floor.

"My granddaughter is high-spirited," said the old woman, settling back in her chair. "The blood of Guillaume, though several times removed, is still apparent."

"She's *his* granddaughter?" asked Taleniekov.

"His great-grandchild, born to my daughter's child quite late in *her* life. But that first daughter was the result of the *padrone* bedding his young whore."

" 'The whore of Villa Matarese,' " said Bray. "You told her to tell us that was what you were called."

The old woman smiled, brushing aside a lock of white hair. For an instant she was in that other world, and vanity had not deserted her. "Many years ago. We will go back to those days, but before we do, your answers, please. What *do* you know? What brings you here?"

"My associate will speak first," said Taleniekov. "He is more learned in these matters than I am, although I came to him with what I believed to be startling new information."

"Your name, please," interrupted the blind woman. "Your true name and where you come from."

The Russian glanced at the American; in the look between them was the understanding that no purpose would be served by further lies. On the contrary, that purpose might be thwarted by them. This simple but strangely eloquent old woman had listened to the voices of liars for the better part of a century—in darkness; she was not to be fooled.

"My name is Vasili Vasilovich Taleniekov. Formerly external affairs strategist, KGB, Soviet Intelligence."

"And you?" The woman shifted her blind eyes to Scofield.

"Brandon Scofield. Retired intelligence officer, Euro-Mediterranean sectors, Consular Operations, United States Department of State."

"I see." The old courtesan brought her thin hands and delicate fingers up to her face, a gesture of quiet reflection. "I am not a learned woman, and live an isolated life, but I am not without news of the outside world. I often listen to my radio for hours at a time. The broadcasts from Rome come in quite clearly, as do those from Genoa, and frequently Nice. I pretend no knowledge, for I have none, but your coming to Corsica together would appear strange."

"It is, madame," said Taleniekov.

"Very," agreed Scofield.

"It signifies the gravity of the situation."

"Then let your associate begin, signore."

Bray sat forward in the chair, his arms on his knees, his eyes on the blind eyes in front of him. "At some point between the years 1909 and 1913, Guillaume de Matarese summoned a group of men to his estate in Porto Vecchio. Who they were and where they came from has never been established. But they gave themselves a name—"

"The date was April 4, 1911," interrupted the old woman. "They did not give themselves a name, the *padrone* chose it. They were to be known as the Council of the Matarese. . . . Go on, please."

"You were *there?*"

"Please continue."

The moment was unsettling; they were talking about an event that had been the object of speculation for decades, with no records of dates or identities, no witnesses. Now—delivered in a brief few seconds—they were told the correct year, the exact month, the precise day.

"Signore? . . ."

"Sorry. During the next thirty years or so, this Matarese and his 'council' were the subject of controversy. . . ." Scofield told the story rapidly, without embellishment, keeping his words in the simplest Italian he knew so there'd be no misunderstanding. He admitted that the majority of experts who had studied the Matarese legend had concluded it was more myth than reality.

"What do *you* believe, signore? That is what I asked you at the start."

"I'm not sure what I believe, but I know a very great man disappeared four days ago. I think he was killed because he spoke to other powerful men about the Matarese."

"I see." The old woman nodded. "Four days ago. Yet I thought you said thirty years . . . from that first meeting in 1911. What happened then, signore? There are many years to be accounted for."

"According to what we know—or what we think we know—after Matarese died the council continued to operate out of Corsica for a number of years, then moved away, negotiating contracts in Berlin, London, Paris, New York and God knows where else. Its activities began to fade at the start of the Second World War. After the war it disappeared; nothing was heard from it again."

A trace of a smile was on the old woman's lips. "So from nowhere it comes back, is that what you are saying?"

"Yes. My associate can tell you why we believe it." Bray looked at Taleniekov.

"Within recent weeks," said the Russian, "two men of peace from both our countries were brutally assassinated, each government led to believe the other was responsible. Confrontation was avoided by a swift exchange between our leaders, but they were dangerous moments. A dear friend sent for me; he was dying and there were things he wanted me to know. He had very little time and his mind wandered, but what he told me compelled me to seek out others for help, for guidance."

"What did he tell you?"

"That the Council of the Matarese was very much with us. That, in fact, it never disappeared but instead went underground, where it continued to grow silently and spread its influence. That it was responsible for hundreds of acts of terrorism and scores of assassinations during recent years for which the world condemned others. Among them the two men I just mentioned. But the Matarese no longer killed for money; instead, it killed for its own purposes."

"Which were?" asked the old woman in that strange, echoing voice.

"He did not know. He knew only that the Matarese was a spreading disease that had to be stamped out, but he could not tell me how, or whom to go to. No one who ever had dealings with the council will speak of it."

"He offered you nothing, then?"

"The last thing he said to me before I left him was that the answer might be in Corsica. Naturally, I was not convinced of that until subsequent events left no alternative. For either me or my associate, agent Scofield."

"I understand your associate's reason: a great man disappeared four days ago because he spoke of the Matarese. What was yours, signore?"

"I, too, spoke of the Matarese. To those men from whom I sought guidance, and I was a man of credentials in my country. The order was put out for my execution."

The old woman was silent and, again, there was that slight smile on her wrinkled lips. "The *padrone* returns," she whispered.

"I think you must explain that," said Taleniekov. "We've been frank with you."

"Did your dear friend die?" she asked instead.

"The next day. He was given a soldier's funeral and he was entitled to it. He lived a life of violence without fear. Yet at the end, the Matarese frightened him profoundly."

"The *padrone* frightened him," said the old woman.

"My friend did not know Guillaume de Matarese."

"He knew his disciples. It was enough; they were him. He was their Christ, and as Christ, he died for them."

"The *padrone* was their god?" asked Bray.

"And their prophet, signore. They believed him."

"Believed what?"

"That they would inherit the earth. That was his vengeance."

15

The old woman's vacant eyes stared at the wall as she spoke in her half-whisper.

He found me in the convent at Bonifacio and negotiated a favorable price with the Mother Superior. "Render unto Caesar," he said, and she complied, for she agreed that I was not given to God. I was frivolous and did not take to my lessons and looked at myself in dark windows for they showed me my face and my body. I was to be given to man, and the padrone *was the man of all men.*

I was ten and seven years of age and a world beyond my imagination was revealed to me. Carriages with silver wheels and golden horses with flowing manes took me above the great cliffs and into the villages and the fine shops where I could purchase whatever struck me. There was nothing I could not have, and I wanted everything, for I came from a poor shepherd's family—a God-fearing father and mother who praised Christ when I was taken into the convent and never seen again.

And always at my side was the padrone. *He was the lion and I was his cherished cub. He would take me around the countryside, to all the great houses and introduce me as his* protetta, *laughing when he used the word. Everyone understood and joined in the laughter. His wife had died, you see, and he had passed his seventieth year. He wanted people to know—his two sons above all, I think— that he had the body and the strength of youth, that he could lie with a young woman and satisfy her as few men could.*

Tutors were hired to teach me the graces of his court: music and proper speech, even history and mathematics, as well as the French language which was the fashion of the time for ladies of bearing. It was a wondrous life. We sailed often across the sea, on to Rome, then we would train north to Switzerland and across into France and to Paris. The padrone *made these trips every five or six months. His business holdings were in those places, you see. His two sons were his directors, reporting to him everything they did.*

For three years I was the happiest girl in the world for the world was given me by the padrone. *And then that world fell apart. In a single week it came crashing down and Guillaume de Matarese went mad.*

Men traveled from Zürich and Paris, from as far away as the great exchange in London, to tell him. It was a time of great banking investments and speculation. They said that during the four months that had passed, his sons had done terrible things, made unwise decisions, and most terrible of all had entered into dishonest agreements, committing vast sums of money to dishonorable men who operated outside the laws of banking and the courts. The governments of France and England had seized the companies and stopped all trade, all access to funds. Except for the accounts he held in Genoa and Rome, Guillaume de Matarese had nothing.

He summoned his two sons by wireless, ordering them home to Porto Vecchio to give him an accounting of what they had done. The news that came back to him, however, was like a thunderbolt striking him down in a great storm; he was never the same again.

Word was sent through the authorities in Paris and London that both the sons were dead, one by his own hand, the other killed—it was said—by a man he had ruined. There was nothing left for the padrone; *his world had crumbled around him. He locked himself in his library for days on end, never coming out, taking trays of food behind the closed door, speaking to no one. He did not lie with me for he had no interest in matters of the flesh. He was destroying himself, dying by his own hand as surely as if he had taken a knife to his stomach.*

Then one day a man came from Paris and insisted on breaking into the padrone's *privacy. He was a journalist who had studied the fall of the Matarese companies, and he brought with him an incredible story. If the* padrone *was driving himself into madness before he heard it, afterward he was beyond hope.*

The destruction of his world was deliberately brought about by bankers working with their governments. His two sons had been tricked into signing illegal documents, and blackmailed—held up to ruin—over matters of the flesh. Finally, they had been murdered, the false stories of their deaths acceptable, for the "official" evidence of their terrible crimes was complete.

It was beyond reason. Why had these things been done to the great padrone? *His companies stolen from him and destroyed; his sons killed. Who would want such things to be done?*

The man from Paris gave part of the answer. "One mad Corsican was enough for Europe for five hundred years," was the phrase he had heard. The padrone *understood. In England, Edward was dead but he had brought about the French and English treaties of finance, opening the way for the great companies to come together, fortunes made in India and Africa and the Suez. The* padrone, *however, was Corsican. Beyond making profit from them, he had no use for the French, less so for the English. He not only refused to join the companies and the banks but he opposed them at every turn, instructing his sons to out-maneuver their competitors. The Matarese fortune blocked powerful men from carrying out their designs.*

For the padrone *it was all a great game. For the French and English companies, his playing was a great crime to be answered with greater crimes. The companies and their banks controlled their governments. Courts of law and the police, politicians and statesmen, even kings and presidents—all were lackeys and servants to the men who possessed vast sums of money. It would never change. This was the beginning of his final madness. He would find a way to destroy the corruptors and the corrupted. He would throw governments everywhere into chaos, for it was the political leaders who were the betrayers of trust. Without the cooperation of government officials his sons would be alive, his world as it was. And with governments in chaos, the companies and the banks would lose their protectors.*

"They look for a mad Corsican," he screamed. "They will not find him, yet he will be there."

We made a last trip to Rome—not as before, in finery and in carriages with silver wheels, but as a humble man and woman staying in cheap lodgings in the Via Due Maccelli. The padrone *spent days prowling the Borsa Valori, reading the histories of the great families who had come to ruin.*

We returned to Corsica. He composed five letters to five men known to be alive in five countries, inviting them to journey in secrecy to Porto Vecchio on matters of the utmost urgency, matters pertaining to their own personal histories.

He was the once-great Guillaume de Matarese. None refused.

The preparations were magnificent, Villa Matarese made more beautiful than it had ever been. The gardens were sculptured and bursting with color, the lawns greener than a brown cat's eyes, the great house and the stables washed in white, the horses curried until they glistened. It was a fairyland again, the padrone *running everywhere at once, checking all things, demanding perfection. His great vitality had returned, but it was not the vitality we had known before. There was a cruelty in him now. "Make them remember, my child," he roared at me in the bedroom. "Make them remember what once was theirs!"*

For he came back to my bed, but his spirit was not the same. There was only brute strength in the performance of his manhood; there was no joy.

If all of us—in the house and the stables and in the fields—knew then what we soon would learn, we would have killed him in the forest. I, who had been given everything by the great padrone, *who worshiped him as both father and lover, would have plunged in the knife myself.*

The great day came, the ships sailed in at dawn from Lido di Ostia, and the carriages were sent down to Porto Vecchio to bring up the honored guests to Villa Matarese. It was a glorious day, music in the gardens, enormous tables heaped with delicacies, and much wine. The finest wines from all Europe, stored for decades in the padrone's *cellars.*

The honored guests were given their own suites, each with a balcony and a magnificent view, and—not the least—each guest was provided with his own young whore for an afternoon's pleasure. Like the wines they were the finest, not of Europe, but of southern Corsica. Five of the most beautiful virgins to be found in the hills.

Night came and the grandest banquet ever seen at Villa Matarese was held in the great hall. When it was over, the servants placed bottles of brandy in front of the guests and were told to remain in the kitchens. The musicians were ordered to take their instruments into the gardens and continue playing. We girls were asked to go to the upper house to await our masters.

We were flushed with wine, the girls and I, but there was a difference between myself and them. I was the protetta *of Guillaume de Matarese and I knew a great event was taking place. He was my* padrone, *my lover, and I wished to be a part of it. In addition to which I'd spent three years with tutors, and although hardly a learned woman, I was given to better things than the giddy talk of ignorant girls from the hills.*

I crept away from the others and concealed myself behind a railing on the balcony above the great hall. I watched and listened for hours, it seems, under-standing very little then of what my padrone *was saying, only that he was most persuasive, his voice at times barely heard, at others shouting as though he were possessed by the fever.*

He spoke of generations past when men ruled empires given them by God and by their own endeavors. How they ruled them with iron might because they were able to protect themselves from those who would steal their kingdoms, and the fruits of their labors. However, those days were gone and the great families, the great empire builders—such as those in that room—were now being stripped by thieves and corrupt governments that harbored thieves. They—those in that room—had to look to other methods to regain what was rightfully theirs.

They had to kill—cautiously, judiciously, with skill and daring—and divide the thieves and their corrupt protectors. They were never to kill by themselves, for they were the decision-makers, the men who selected victims—wherever possible victims chosen by others among the corrupted. Those in that room were to be known as the Council of the Matarese, and word was to go forth in the circles of power that there was a group of unknown, silent men who understood the necessity of sudden change and violence, who were unafraid to provide the means, and who would guarantee beyond living doubt that those performing the acts could never be traced to those purchasing them.

He went on to speak of things I could not understand; of killers trained by great pharaohs and Arabian princes centuries ago. How men could be trained to do terrible things beyond their wills, even beyond their knowledge. How others needed only the proper encouragement for they sought the assassin's martyrdom. These were to be the methods of the Matarese, but in the beginning there would be disbelief in the circles of power, so examples had to be made.

During the next few years selected men were to be assassinated. They would be chosen carefully, killed in ways that would breed mistrust, pitting political faction against political faction, corrupt government against corrupt government. There would be chaos and bloodshed and the message would be clear: the Matarese existed.

The padrone *distributed to each guest pages on which he had written down his thoughts. These writings were to be the council's source of strength and direction, but they were never to be shown to eyes other than their own. These pages were the Last Will and Testament of Guillaume de Matarese . . . and those in that room were his inheritors.*

Inheritors? asked the guests. They were compassionate, but direct. In spite of the villa's beauty and the servants and the musicians and the feast they had enjoyed, they knew he had been ruined—as each of them had been ruined. Who among them had anything left but his wine cellars and his lands and rents from tenants to keep but a semblance of his former life intact? A grand banquet once in a great while, but little else.

The padrone *did not answer them at first. Instead, he demanded to know from each guest whether that man accepted the things he had said, if that man was prepared to become a* consigliere *of the Matarese.*

They replied yes, each more vehement than the last, pledging himself to the padrone's *goals, for great evil had been done to each of them and they wanted revenge. It was apparent that Guillaume de Matarese appeared to each at that moment a saint.*

Each, except one, a deeply religious Spaniard who spoke of the word of God and of His commandments. He accused the padrone *of madness, called him an abomination in the eyes of God.*

"Am I an abomination in your eyes, sir?" asked the padrone.

"You are, sir," replied the man.

Whereupon the first of the most terrible things happened. The padrone *took a pistol from his belt, aimed it at the man, and fired. The guests sprang up from their chairs and stared in silence at the dead Spaniard.*

"He could not be permitted to leave this room alive," said the padrone.

As if nothing had happened, the guests returned to their chairs, all eyes on this mightiest of men who could kill with such deliberateness, perhaps afraid for their own lives, it was difficult to tell. The padrone *went on.*

"All in this room are my inheritors," he said. "For you are the Council of the Matarese and you and yours will do what I can no longer do. I am too old and death is near—nearer than you believe. You will carry out what I tell you, you will divide the corruptors and the corrupted, you will spread chaos and through the strength of your achievements, you will inherit far more than I leave you. You will inherit the earth. You will have your own again."

"What do you—can you—leave us?" asked a guest.

"A fortune in Genoa and a fortune in Rome. The accounts have been transferred in the manner described in a document, one copy of which has been placed in each of your rooms. There also will you find the conditions under which you will receive the monies. These accounts were never known to exist; they will provide millions for you to begin your work."

The guests were stunned until one had a question.

" 'Your' work? Is it not 'our' work?"

"It will always be ours, but I shall not be here. For I leave you something more precious than all the gold in the Transvaal. The complete secrecy of your identities.

I speak to each of you. Your presence here this day will never be revealed to anyone on earth. No name, no description, no likeness of your face, no pattern of your speech can ever be traced to you. Neither will it ever be forced from the senile wanderings of an old man's mind."

Several of the guests protested—mildly to be sure—but with reason. There were many people at Villa Matarese that day. The servants, the grooms, the musicians, the girls. . . .

The padrone *held up his hand. It was as steady as his eyes were glaring. "I will show you the way. You must never step back from violence. You must accept it as surely as the air you breathe, for it is necessary to life. Necessary to your lives, to the work you must do."*

He dropped his hand and the peaceful, elegant world of Villa Matarese erupted in gunfire and screams of death everywhere. It came first from the kitchen. Deafening blasts of shotguns, glass shattering, metal crashing, servants slain as they tried to escape through the doors into the great hall, their faces and chests covered with blood. Then from the gardens; the music abruptly stopped, replaced by supplications to God, all answered by the thunder of the guns. And then—most horribly—the high-pitched screams of terror from the upper house where the young ignorant girls from the hills were being slaughtered. Children who only hours ago had been virgins, defiled by men they had never seen before on the orders of Guillaume de Matarese, now butchered by new commands.

I pressed myself back into the wall in the darkness of the balcony, not knowing what to do, trembling, frightened beyond any fear I could imagine. And then the gunfire stopped, the silence that followed more terrible than the screams, for it was the evidence of death.

Suddenly I could hear running—three or four men, I could not tell—but I knew they were the killers. They were rushing down staircases and through doors, and I thought, Oh God in heaven, they are looking for me. But they were not. They were racing to a place where all would gather together; it seemed to be the north veranda, I could not be sure, all was happening so fast. Below in the great hall, the four guests were in shock, frozen to their chairs, the padrone *holding them in their places by the strength of his glaring eyes.*

There came what I thought would be the final sounds of gunfire until my own death. Three shots—only three—between terrible screams. And then I understood. The killers had themselves been killed by a lone man given those orders.

The silence came back. Death was everywhere—in the shadows and dancing on the walls in the flickering candlelight of the great hall. The padrone *spoke to his guests.*

"It is over," he said. "Or nearly over. All but you at this table are dead save one man you will never see again. It is he who will drive you in a shrouded carriage to Bonifacio where you may mingle with the night revelers and take the crowded morning steamer to Naples. You have fifteen minutes to gather your things and meet on the front steps. There are none to carry your luggage, I'm afraid."

A guest found his voice, or part of it. "And you, padrone?" *he whispered.*

"At the last, I give you my life as your final lesson. Remember me! I am the way. Go forth and become my disciples! Rip out the corruptors and the corrupted!" He was raving mad, his shouts echoing throughout the great house of death. *"Entrare!"* he roared.

A small child, a shepherd boy from the hills, walked through the large doors of the north veranda. He held a pistol in his two hands; it was heavy and he was slight. He approached the master.

The *padrone* raised his eyes to the heavens, his voice to God. *"Do as you were told!"* he shouted. *"For an innocent child shall light your path!"*

The shepherd boy raised the heavy pistol and fired it into the head of Guillaume de Matarese.

The old woman had finished, her unblinking eyes filled with tears.

"I must rest," she said.

Taleniekov, rigid in his chair, spoke softly. "We have questions, madame. Surely you know that."

"Later," said Scofield.

16

Light broke over the surrounding mountains as pockets of mist floated up from the fields outside the farmhouse. Taleniekov found tea, and with the old woman's permission, boiled water on the wood-burning stove.

Scofield sipped from his cup, watching the rippling stream from the window. It was time to talk again; there were too many discrepancies between what the blind woman had told them and the facts as they were assumed to be. But there was a primary question: why had she told them at all? The answer to that might make clear whether any part of her narrative should be believed.

Bray turned from the window and looked at the old woman in the chair by the stove. Taleniekov had given her tea and she drank it delicately, as though remembering those lessons in the social graces given a girl of "ten and seven years of age" decades ago. The Russian was kneeling by the dog, stroking its fur again, reminding it they were friends. He glanced up, as Scofield walked toward the old woman.

"We've told you our names, signora," said Bray, speaking in Italian. "What is yours?"

"Sophia Pastorine. If one goes back to look, I'm sure it can be found in the records of the convent at Bonifacio. That is why you ask, is it not? To be able to check?"

"Yes," answered Scofield. "If we think it's necessary, and have the opportunity."

"You will find my name. The *padrone* may even be listed as my benefactor, to whom I was ward—as an intended bride for one of his sons, perhaps. I never knew."

"Then we must believe you," said Taleniekov, getting to his feet. "You would not be so foolish as to direct us to such a source if it were not true. Records that have been meddled with are easily detected these days."

The old woman smiled, a smile with its roots in sadness. "I have no understanding of such matters, but I can understand if you have doubts." She put down her cup of tea on the ledge of the stove. "There are none in my memories. I have spoken the truth."

"Then my first question is as important as any we may ask you," said Bray, sitting down. "Why did you tell us this story?"

"Because it had to be told and no one else could do so. Only I survived."

"There was a man," interrupted Scofield. "And a shepherd boy."

"They were not in the great hall to hear what I heard."

"Have you told it before?" asked Taleniekov.

"Never," replied the blind woman.

"Why not?"

"Who was I to tell it to? I have few visitors, and those that come are from down in the hills, bringing me the few supplies I need. To tell them would be to bring them death, for surely they would tell others."

"Then the story *is* known," pressed the KGB man.

"Not what I've told you."

"But there's a secret down there! They tried to send me away, and when I would not go they tried to kill me."

"My granddaughter did not tell me that." She seemed truly surprised.

"I don't think she had time to," said Bray.

The old woman did not seem to be listening, her focus still on the Russian. "What did you say to the people in the hills?"

"I asked questions."

"You had to have done more than that."

Taleniekov frowned, remembering. "I tried to provoke the innkeeper. I told him I would bring back others, scholars with historical records to study further the question of Guillaume de Matarese."

The woman nodded. "When you leave here, do not go back the way you came. Nor can you take my child's granddaughter with you. You must promise me that. If they find you, they will not let you live."

"We know that," said Bray. "We want to know why."

"All the lands of Guillaume de Matarese were willed to the people of the hills. The tenants became the heirs of a thousand fields and pastures, streams and forests. It was so recorded in the courts of Bonifacio and great celebrations were held everywhere. But there was a price, and there were other courts that would take away the lands if that price were known." The blind Sophia stopped, as if weighing another price, perhaps one of betrayal.

"*Please*, Signora Pastorine," said Taleniekov, leaning forward in the chair.

"Yes," she answered quietly. "It must be told. . . ."

Everything was to be done quickly for fear of unwanted intruders happening upon the great house of Villa Matarese and the death that was everywhere. The guests gathered their papers and fled to their rooms. I remained in the shadows of the balcony, my body filled with pain, the silent vomit of fear all around me. How long I stayed there, I could not tell, but soon I heard the running feet of the guests racing down the staircase to their appointed meeting place. Then there was the sound of carriage wheels and the neighing of horses; minutes later the carriage sped away, hooves clattering on the hard stone along with the rapid cracking of a whip, all fading away quickly.

I started to crawl toward the balcony door, not able to think, my eyes filled with bolts of lightning, my head trembling so I could barely find my way. I pressed my hands on the wall, wishing there were brackets I could hold onto when I heard a shout and threw myself to the floor again. It was a terrible shout for it came from a child, and yet it was cold and demanding.

"Vieni subito!"

The shepherd boy was screaming at someone from the north veranda. If all was senseless up to that moment, the child's shouts intensified the madness beyond any understanding. For he was a child . . . and a killer.

Somehow I rose to my feet and ran through the door to the top of the staircase. I was about to run down, wanting only to get away, into the air and the fields and the protection of darkness, when I heard other shouts and saw the figures of running men through the windows. They were carrying torches, and in seconds crashed through the doors.

I could not run down for I would be seen, so I ran above to the upper house, my panic such that I no longer knew what I was doing. Only running . . . running. And, as if guided by an unseen hand that wanted me to live, I burst into the sewing room and saw the dead. There they were, sprawled everywhere in blood, mouths stretched in such terror that I could still hear their screams.

The screams I heard were not real, but the shouts of men on the staircase were; it was the end for me. There was nothing left, I was to be caught. I would be killed. . . .

And then, as surely as an unseen hand had led me to that room, it forced me to do a most terrible thing—I joined the dead.

I put my hands in the blood of my sisters, and rubbed it over my face and clothes. I fell on top of my sisters and waited.

The men came into the sewing room, some crossing themselves, others whispering prayers, but none deterred from the work they had to do. The next hours were a nightmare only the devil could conceive of.

The bodies of my sisters and I were carried down the staircase and hurled through the doors, beyond the marble steps into the drive. Wagons had been brought from the stables, and by now many were filled with bodies. Again, my sisters and I were thrown into the back of a cart, crowded with dead, like so much refuse.

The stench of waste and blood was so overpowering I had to sink my teeth into my own flesh to keep from screaming. Through the corpses above me and over the railings, I could hear men shouting orders. Nothing could be stolen from the Villa Matarese; anyone found doing so would join the bodies inside. For there were to be many bodies left inside, charred flesh and bones to be found at a later time.

The wagons began to move, smoothly at first, then we reached the fields, and the horses were whipped unmercifully. The wagons raced through the grass and over the rocks at immense speeds, as if every second was a second our living guards wished to leave behind in hell. There was death below me, death above me, and I prayed to Almighty God to take me also. But I could not cry out, for although I wanted to die, I was afraid of the pain of dying. The unseen hand held me by the throat. But mercy was granted me. I fell into unconsciousness; how long I do not know, but I think it was a very long time.

I awakened; the wagons had come to a stop and I peered through the bodies and the slats in the side. There was moonlight and we were far up in the wooded hills, but not in the mountains. Nothing was familiar to me. We were far, far away from Villa Matarese, but where I could not tell you then and cannot tell you now.

The last of the nightmare began. Our bodies were pulled off the wagons and thrown into a common grave, each corpse held by two men so that they could hurl it into the deepest part. I fell in pain, my teeth sinking into my fingers to keep my mind from crossing into madness. I opened my eyes and the vomit came again at what I saw. All around me dead faces, limp arms, gaping mouths. Stabbed, bleeding carcasses that only hours ago had been human beings.

The grave was enormous, wide and deep—and strangely, it seemed to me in my silent hysteria, shaped in the form of a circle.

Beyond the edge I would hear the voices of our gravediggers. Some were weeping, while others cried out to Christ for mercy. Several were demanding that the blessed sacraments be given to the dead, that for the sake of all their souls, a priest be brought to the place of death and intercede with God. But other men said no, they were not the killers, merely those chosen to put the slain to rest. God would understand.

"Basta!" they said. It could not be done. It was the price they paid for the good of generations yet to be born. The hills were theirs; the fields and streams and forests belonged to them! There was no turning back now. They had made their pact with the padrone, *and he had made it clear to the elders: Only the government's knowledge of a* cospirazione *could take the lands away from them. The* padrone *was the most learned of men, he knew the courts and the laws; his ignorant tenants did not. They were to do exactly as he had instructed the elders or the high courts would take the lands from them.*

There could be no priests from Porto Vecchio or Sainte Lucie or anywhere else.

No chance taken that word would go out of the hills. Those who had other thoughts could join the dead; their secret was never to leave the hills. The lands were theirs!

It was enough. The men fell silent, picked up their shovels, and began throwing dirt over the bodies. I thought then that surely I would die, my mouth and nostrils smothered under the earth. Yet I think all of us trapped with death find ways to elude its touch, ways we could never dream of before we are caught. It happened for me.

As each layer of earth filled the circular grave and was trampled upon, I moved my hand in the darkness, clawing the dirt above me so that I could breathe. At the very end I had nothing but the smallest passage of air but it was enough; there was space around my head, enough for God's air to invade. The unseen hand had guided mine and I lived.

It was hours later, I believe, when I began to burrow my way to the surface, a . . . blind . . . unknowing animal seeking life. When my hand reached through to nothing but cold moist air, I wept without control, and a part of my brain went into panic, frightened that my weeping would be heard.

God was merciful; everyone had left. I crawled out of the earth, and I walked out of that forest of death into a field and saw the early sunlight rising over the mountains. I was alive, but there was no life for me. I could not go back to the hills for surely I would be killed, yet to go elsewhere, to arrive at some strange place and simply be, was not possible for a young woman in this island country. There was no one I could turn to, having spent three years a willing captive of my padrone. Yet I could not simply die in that field with God's sunlight spreading over the sky. It told me to live, you see.

I tried to think what I might do, where I might go. Beyond the hills, on the ocean's coasts, were other great houses that belonged to other padrones, friends of Guillaume. I wondered what would happen were I to appear at one of them and plead for shelter and mercy. Then I saw the error of such thinking. Those men were not my padrone; they were men with wives and families, and I was the whore of Villa Matarese. While Guillaume was alive, my presence was to be tolerated, even enjoyed, for the great man would have it no other way. But with him dead, I was dead.

Then I remembered. There was a man who tended the stables of an estate in Zonza. He had been kind to me during those times we visited and I rode his employer's mounts. He had smiled often and guided me as to my proper deportment in the saddle, for he saw that I was not born to the hunt. Indeed, I admitted it and we had laughed together. And each time I had seen the look in his eyes. I was used to glances of desire, but his eyes held more than that. There was gentleness and understanding, perhaps even respect—not for what I was, but for what I did not pretend to be.

I looked at the early sun and knew that Zonza was on my left, probably beyond the mountains. I set out for those stables and that man.

He became my husband and although I bore the child of Guillaume de Mata-rese, he accepted her as his own, giving us both love and protection through the

*days of his life. Those years and our lives during those years are no concern of yours;
they do not pertain to the* padrone. *It is enough to say that no harm came to us.
For years we lived far north in Vescovato, away from the danger of the hill people,
never daring to mention their secret. The dead could not be brought back, you see,
and the killer and his killer son—the man and the shepherd boy—had fled Corsica.*

*I have told you the truth, all of it. If you still have doubts, I cannot put them
to rest.*

Again she had finished.

Taleniekov got up and walked slowly to the stove and the pot of tea. *"Per nostro
circolo,"* he said, looking at Scofield. "Seventy years have passed and still they
would kill for their grave."

"Perdona?" The old woman did not understand English, so the KGB man
repeated his statement in Italian. Sophia nodded. "The secret goes from father
to son. These are the two generations that have been born since the land was
theirs. It is not so long. They are still afraid."

"There aren't any laws that could take it from them," said Bray. "I doubt there
ever were. Men might have been sent to prison for withholding information
about the massacre, but in those days, who would prosecute? They buried the
dead, that was their conspiracy."

"There was a greater conspiracy. They did not permit the blessed sacraments."

"That's another court. I don't know anything about it." Scofield glanced at
the Russian, then brought his eyes back to the blind eyes in front of him. "Why
did you come back?"

"I was able to. And I was old when we found this valley."

"That's not an answer."

"The people of the hills believe a lie. They think the *padrone* spared me, sent
me away before the guns began. To others I am a source of fear and hatred. It
is whispered that I was spared by God to be a remembrance of their sin, yet
blinded by God so never to reveal their grave in the forests. I am the blind whore
of Villa Matarese, permitted to live because they are afraid to take the life of
God's reminder."

Taleniekov spoke from the other side of the stove. "But you said a while ago
that they would not hesitate to kill you if you told the story. Perhaps if they were
even aware that you *knew* it. Yet now you tell it to us, and imply that you want
us to bring it out of Corsica. Why?"

"Did not a man in your own country call for you and tell you things he wanted
you to know?" The Russian began to reply; Sophia Pastorine interrupted. "Yes,
signore. As that man, the end of my life draws near; with each breath I know
it. Death, it seems, invites those of us who know some part of the Matarese to
speak of it. I'm not sure I can tell you why, but for me, there was a sign. My
granddaughter traveled down to the hills and came back with news of a scholar

seeking information about the *padrone*. You were my sign. I sent her back to find you."

"Does she know?" asked Bray. "Have you ever told her? She could have brought the story out."

"Never! She is known in the hills, but she is not *of* the hills! She would be hunted down wherever she went. She would be killed. I asked for your word, signori, and you must give it to me. You must have nothing further to do with her!"

"You have it," agreed Taleniekov. "She's not in this room because of us."

"What did you hope to accomplish by speaking to my associate?" asked Bray.

"What his friend hoped for, I think. To make men look beneath the waves, to the dark waters below. It is there that the power to move the sea is found."

"The Council of the Matarese," said the KGB man, staring at the blind eyes.

"Yes. . . . I told you. I listen to the broadcasts from Rome and Genoa and Nice. It is happening everywhere. The prophecies of Guillaume de Matarese are coming true. It does not take an educated person to see that. For years I listened to the broadcasts and wondered. Could it be so? Was it possible they survive still? Then one night many days ago I heard the words and it was as though time had no meaning. I was suddenly back in the shadows of the balcony in the great hall, the gunfire and the screams of horror echoing in my ears. I was *there*, with my eyes before God took them from me, watching the terrible scene below. And I was remembering what the *padrone* had said moments before: 'You and *yours* will do what I can no longer do.' " The old woman stopped, her blind eyes swimming, then began again, her sentences rushed in fear.

"It *was* true! They *had* survived—not the council as it was then, but as it is today. 'You and yours.' The *yours* had survived! Led by the one man whose voice was crueler than the wind." Sophia Pastorine abruptly stopped again, her frail, delicate hands grasping for the wooden arm of her chair. She stood up and with her left hand reached for her cane by the edge of the stove.

"The list. You must have it, signori! I took it out of a blood-soaked gown seventy years ago after crawling out of the grave in the mountains. It had stayed next to my body through the terror. I had carried it with me so I would not forget their names and their titles, to make my *padrone* proud of me." The old woman tapped the cane in front of her as she walked across the room to a primitive shelf on the wall. Her right hand felt the edge, her fingers hesitantly dancing among the various jars until she found the one she wanted. She removed the clay top, reached inside, and pulled out a scrap of soiled paper, yellow with age. She turned. "It is yours. Names from the past. This is the list of honored guests who journeyed in secrecy to Villa Matarese on the fourth of April, in the year nineteen hundred and eleven. If by giving it to you I do a terrible thing, may God have mercy on my soul."

Scofield and Taleniekov were on their feet. "You haven't," said Bray. "You've done the right thing."

"The only thing," added Vasili. He touched her hand. "May I?" She released the faded scrap of paper; the Russian studied it. "It's the key," he said to Scofield. "It's also quite beyond anything we might have expected."

"Why?" asked Bray.

"The Spaniard—the man Matarese killed—has been crossed out, but two of these names will startle you. To say the least, they are prominent. Here." Taleniekov crossed to Scofield, holding the paper delicately between two fingers so as not to damage it further. Bray took it in the palm of his hand.

"I don't believe it," said Scofield, reading the names. "I'd like to get this analyzed to make sure it wasn't written five days ago."

"It wasn't," said the KGB man.

"I know. And that scares the hell out of me."

"Perdona?" Sophia Pastorine stood by the shelf. Bray answered her in Italian. "We recognize two of these names. They are well-known men—"

"But they are *not* the men!" broke in the old woman, stabbing her cane on the floor. "None of them! They are only the inheritors! They are controlled by *another. He* is the man!"

"What are you talking about? Who?"

The dog growled. Neither Scofield nor Taleniekov paid any attention: an angry voice had been raised. The animal got to its feet, now snarling, the two men— their concentration on Sophia—still ignoring it. But the old woman did not. She held up her hand, a gesture for silence. She spoke, her anger replaced by alarm.

"Open the door. Call out for my granddaughter. *Quickly!*"

"What is it?" asked the Russian.

"Men are coming. They're passing through the thickets. Uccello hears them."

Bray walked rapidly to the door. "How far away are they?"

"On the other side of the ridge. Nearly here. Hurry!"

Scofield opened the door and called out. "You! Antonia. Come here. Quickly!"

The dog's snarls came through bared teeth. Its head was thrust forward, its legs stretched and taut, prepared to defend or attack. Leaving the door open, Bray crossed to a counter and picked up a lettuce leaf. He tore it in half and placed the yellow scrap of paper between the two sections, and folded them together. "I'll put this in my pocket," he said to the KGB man.

"I've memorized the names and the countries," replied Taleniekov. "But then, I'm sure you have, too."

The girl ran through the door, breathless, her field jacket only partially buttoned, the Lupo in her hand, the bulges of the automatics in her side pockets. "What's the matter?"

Scofield turned from the counter. "Your . . . grandmother said men were coming. The dog heard them."

"On the other side of the hill," interrupted the old woman. "Nine hundred paces perhaps, no more."

"Why would they *do* that?" asked the girl. "Why would they come?"

"Did they see you, my child? Did they see Uccello?"

"They must have. But I said nothing. I did not interfere with them. They had no reason to think—"

"But they saw you the day before," said Sophia Pastorine interrupting again.

"Yes. I bought the things you wanted."

"Then why would you come back?" The old woman spoke rhetorically. "That is what they tried to understand, and they did. They are men of the hills; they look down at the grass and the dirt and see that three people traveled over the ground, not one. You must leave. All of you!"

"I will not do that, grandmother!" cried Antonia. "They won't harm us. I'll say I may have been followed, but I know nothing."

The old woman stared straight ahead. "You have what you came for, signori. Take it. Take her. Leave!"

Bray turned to the girl. "We owe her that," he said. He grabbed the shotgun out of her hands. She tried to fight back but Taleniekov pinned her arms and removed the Browning and the Graz-Burya automatics from her pockets. "You saw what happened down there," continued Scofield. "Do as she says."

The dog raced to the open door and barked viciously. Far in the distance, voices were carried on the morning breezes; men were shouting to others behind them.

"Go!" said Sophia Pastorine.

"Come on." Bray propelled Antonia in front of him. "We'll be back after they've left. We haven't finished."

"A moment, signori!" shouted the blind woman. "I think we have finished. The names you possess may be helpful to you, but they are only the inheritors. Look for the one whose voice is crueler than the wind. I heard it! Find him. The shepherd boy. It is he!"

17

They ran along the edge of the pasture on the border of the woods and climbed to the top of the ridge. The shadows of the eastern slope kept them from being seen. There had been only a few seconds when they might have been spotted; they were prepared for that but it did not happen. The men on the opposite ridge were distracted by a barking dog, deciding whether or not to use their rifles on it. They did not, for the dog was retrieved by a whistle before such a decision could be made. Uccello was beside Antonia now in the grass, his breath coming as rapidly as hers.

There were four men on the opposite ridge—as there were four remaining names on the scrap of yellow paper in his pocket, thought Scofield. He wished finding them, trapping *them*, were as easy as trapping and picking off the four men who now descended into the valley. But the four men on the list were just the beginning.

There was a shepherd boy to find. "A voice crueler than the wind" . . . a *child's* voice recognized decades later as one and the same . . . coming from the throat of what had to be a very, very old man.

I heard the words and it was as though time had no meaning. . . .

What were those *words?* Who was that *man?* The true descendant of Guillaume de Matarese . . . an old man who uttered a phrase that peeled away seventy years from the memory of a blind woman in the mountains of Corsica. In what *language?* It had to be French or Italian; she understood no other.

They had to speak with her again; they had to understand far more. They had *not* finished with Sophia Pastorine.

Bray watched as the four Corsicans approached the farmhouse, two covering the sides, two walking up to the door, all with weapons drawn. The men by the door paused for an instant; then the one on the left raised his boot and rammed it into the wood, crashing the door inward.

Silence.

Two shouts were heard, questions asked harshly. The men outside ran around opposite corners of the farmhouse and went inside. There was more shouting . . . and the unmistakable sound of flesh striking flesh.

Antonia started to get up, fury on her face. Taleniekov pulled her down by the shoulder of her field jacket. The muscles in her throat were contorted; she was about to scream. Scofield had no choice. He clamped his hand over her mouth, forcing his fingers into her cheeks; the scream was reduced to a series of coughs.

"Be quiet!" whispered Bray. "If they hear you, they'll use her to get you down there!"

"It would be far worse for her," said Vasili, "and for you. You would hear her pain, and they would take you."

Antonia's eyes blinked; she nodded. Scofield relieved his grip, but did not release it. She whispered through his hand. "They *hit* her! A blind woman and they *hit* her!"

"They're frightened," said Taleniekov. "More than you can imagine. Without their land, they have nothing."

The girl's fingers gripped Bray's wrist. "What do you mean?"

"Not now!" commanded Scofield. "There's something wrong. They're staying in there too long."

"They've found something, perhaps," agreed the KGB man.

"Or she's telling them something. Oh, *Christ,* she *can't!*"

"What are you thinking?" asked Taleniekov.

"She said we'd finished. We *haven't.* But she's going to make sure of it! They'll see our footprints on the floor; we walked over wet ground; she can't deny we were there. With her hearing, she knows which way we went. She'll send them in another direction."

"That's fine," said the Russian.

"Goddamn it, they'll *kill* her!"

Taleniekov snapped his head back toward the farmhouse below. "You're right," he said. "If they believe her—and they will—they can't let her live. She's the source; she'll tell them that, too, if only to convince them. Her life for the shepherd boy. So we can find the shepherd boy!"

"But we don't *know* enough! Come on, let's go!" Scofield got to his feet, yanking the automatic from his belt. The dog snarled; the girl rose and Taleniekov pushed her down to the ground again.

They were not in time. Three gunshots followed one upon the other.

Antonia screamed; Bray lunged, holding her, cradling her. *"Please,* please!" he whispered. He saw the Russian pull a knife from somewhere inside his coat. *"No!* It's all right!"

Taleniekov palmed the knife and knelt down, his eyes on the farmhouse below. "They're running outside. You were right; they're heading for the south slope."

"Kill them!" The girl's words were muffled by Scofield's hand.

"To what purpose now?" said the KGB man. "She did what she wished to do, what she felt she had to do."

The dog would not follow them; commands from Antonia had no effect. It raced down into the farmhouse and would not come out; its whimpering carried up to the ridge.

"Goodbye, Uccello," said the girl sobbing. "I will come back for you. Before *God,* I will come back!"

They walked out of the mountains, circling northwest beyond the hills of Porto Vecchio, then south to Sainte Lucie, following the stream until they reached the massive pine under which Bray had buried his attaché case and duffel bag. They traveled cautiously, using the woods as much as possible, separating and walking in sequence across open stretches so no one would see them together.

Scofield pulled the shovel from beneath a pile of branches, dug up his belongings, and they started out again, retracing the stream north toward Sainte Lucie. Conversation was kept to a minimum; they wasted no time putting distance between themselves and the hills.

The long silences and brief separations served a practical purpose, thought Bray, watching the girl as she pressed forward, bewildered, following their commands without thinking, tears intermittently appearing in her eyes. The constant movement occupied her mind; she had to come to some sort of acceptance of her "grandmother's" death. No words from relative strangers could help her; she needed the loneliness of her own thoughts. Scofield suspected that in spite of her handling of the Lupo, Antonia was not a child of violence. She was no child to begin with; in the daylight he could see that she would not see thirty again, but beyond that, she came from a world of radical academics, not revolution. He doubted she would know what to do at the barricades.

"We must stop *running!*" she cried suddenly. "You may do what you like, but I am returning to Porto Vecchio. I'll see them *hanged!*"

"There's a great deal you don't know," said Taleniekov.

"She was killed! That is all I *have* to know!"

"It's not that simple," said Bray. "The truth is she killed herself."

"*They* killed her!"

"She forced them to." Scofield took her hand, gripping it firmly. "Try to understand me. We can't let you go back; your grandmother knew that. What happened during the past forty-eight hours has got to fade away just as fast as possible. There'll be a certain amount of panic up in those hills; they'll send men trying to find us, but in several weeks when nothing happens, they'll cool off. They'll live with their own fears but they'll be quiet. It's the only thing they can do. Your grandmother understood that. She counted on it."

"But *why?*"

"Because we have other things to do," said the Russian. "She understood that, too. It's why she sent you back to find us."

"What are these things?" asked Antonia, then answered for herself. "She said you had names. She spoke of a shepherd boy."

"But you must speak of neither," ordered Taleniekov. "Not if you wish her death to mean anything. We cannot let you interfere."

Scofield caught the sound in the KGB man's voice and for an instant found himself reaching for his gun. In that split second the memory of Berlin ten years ago was prodded to the surface. Taleniekov had already made a decision: if the Russian had the slightest doubt, he would kill this girl.

"She won't interfere," said Bray without knowing why he gave such a guarantee, but delivering it firmly. "Let's go. We'll make one stop; I'll see a man in Murato. Then if we can reach Bastia. I can get us out."

"To *where,* signore? You cannot order me—"

"Be quiet," said Bray. "Don't press your luck."

"No, don't," added the KGB man, glancing at Scofield. "We must talk. As before, we should travel separately, divide our work, set up schedules and points of contact. We have much to discuss."

"By my guess, there are ninety miles between here and Bastia. There'll be plenty of time to talk." Scofield reached down for his attaché case; the girl snapped her hand out of his, angrily moving away. The Russian leaned over for the duffel bag.

"I suggest we talk alone," he said to Bray. "She's not an asset, Beowulf."

"You disappoint me." Scofield took the duffel bag from the KGB man. "Hasn't anyone ever taught you to convert a liability into an asset?"

Antonia had lived in Vescovato, on the Golo River, twenty-odd miles south of Bastia. Her immediate contribution was to get them there without being seen. It was important that she make decisions, if only to take her mind off the fact that she was following orders she disagreed with. She did so rapidly, choosing primitive back roads and mountain trails she had known as a child growing up in the province.

"The nuns brought us here for a picnic," she said, looking down at a dammed-up stream. "We built fires and ate sausage, and took turns going into the woods to smoke cigarettes."

They went on. "This hill has a fine wind in the morning," she said. "My father made marvelous kites and we would fly them here on Sundays. After Mass, of course."

"We?" asked Bray. "Do you have brothers and sisters?"

"One of each. They're older than I am and still live in Vescovato. They have families and I do not see them often; there's not much to talk about between us."

"They didn't go to the upper schools then?" said Taleniekov.

"They thought such pursuits were foolish. They're good people but prefer a simple life. If we need help, they will offer it."

"It would be better not to seek it," said the Russian. "Or them."

"They are my family, signore. Why should I avoid them?"

"Because it may be necessary."

"That's no answer. You kept me from Porto Vecchio and the justice that should be done; you can't give me orders any longer."

The KGB man looked at Scofield, his intent in his eyes. Bray expected the Russian to draw his weapon. He wondered briefly what his own reaction would be; he could not tell. But the moment passed, and Scofield understood something he had not fully understood before. Vasili Taleniekov did not wish to kill, but the professional in him was in strong conflict with the man. The Russian was pleading with him. He wanted to know how to convert a liability into an asset. Scofield wished he knew.

"Take it easy," said Bray. "Nobody wants to tell you what to do except where your own safety's concerned. We said that before and it's ten times more valid now."

"I think it is something else. You wish me to stay silent. *Silent* over the killing of a blind, old woman!"

"Your safety depends on it, we told you that. She understood."

"She's dead!"

"But you want to *live,*" insisted Scofield calmly. "If the hill people find you, you won't. And if it's known that you've talked to others, they'll be in danger, too. Can't you see that?"

"Then what am I to *do?*"

"Just what we're doing. Disappear. Get out of Corsica." The girl started to object; Bray cut her off. "And *trust* us. You *must* trust us. Your grandmother did. She died so we could live and find some people who are involved in terrible things that go beyond Corsica."

"You're not talking to a child. What do you mean, 'terrible things'?"

Bray glanced at Taleniekov, accepting his disapproval, but by nodding, overriding it. "There are men—we don't know how many—whose lives are committed to killing other men, who spread mistrust and suspicion by choosing victims and financing murder. There's no pattern except violence, *political* violence, pitting faction against faction, government against government . . . people against people." Scofield paused, seeing the concentration in Antonia's face. "You said you were a political activist, a Communist. Fine. Good. So's my associate here; he was trained in Moscow. I'm an American, trained in Washington. We're enemies; we've fought each other a long time. The details aren't important, but the fact that we're working together now is. The men we're trying to find are much more dangerous than any differences between us, between our governments. Because these men can escalate those differences into something nobody wants; they can blow up the globe."

"Thank you for telling me," said Antonia pensively. Then she frowned. "But how could *she* know of such things?"

"She was there when it all began," answered Bray. "Nearly seventy years ago at Villa Matarese."

The words emerged slowly as Antonia whispered. " 'The whore of Villa Matarese.' . . . The *padrone*, Guillaume?"

"He was as powerful as any man in England or France, an obstacle to the cartels and the combines. He stood in their way and won too often, so they destroyed him. They used their governments to bring about his collapse; they killed his sons. He went crazy . . . but in his madness—and with the resources he had left—he put in motion a long-range plan to get revenge. He called together other men who'd been destroyed the same way he had; they became the Council of the Matarese. For years their specialty was assassination; years later they were presumed to have died. Now they've come back, more deadly than they ever were." Scofield paused; he had told her enough. "That's as plainly as I can explain it and I hope you understand. You want the men who killed your grandmother to pay for it. I'd like to think that one day they will, but I've also got to tell you that they don't much matter."

Antonia was silent for a few moments, her intelligent brown eyes riveted on Bray. "You're quite clear, Signor Scofield. If they don't matter, then I don't matter, either. Is that what you're saying?"

"I guess I am."

"And my Socialist comrade," she added, glancing at Taleniekov, "would as soon remove my insignificant presence as not."

"I look at an objective," answered Vasili, "and I do my best to analyze the problems inherent in reaching it."

"Yes, of course. Then do I turn around and walk into the woods, expecting the gunshot that will end my life?"

"That's your decision," said Taleniekov.

"I have a choice then? You would take my word that I'll say nothing?"

"No," replied the KGB man. "I would not."

Bray studied Taleniekov's face, his right hand inches from the Browning automatic in his belt. The Russian was leading up to something, testing the girl as he did so.

"Then what is the choice?" continued Antonia. "To let one or the other of your governments put me away, until you have found the men you seek?"

"I'm afraid that's not possible," said Taleniekov. "We're acting outside our governments; we do not have their approvals. To put it frankly, they seek us as intensely as we seek the men we spoke of."

The girl reacted to the Russian's startling information as though struck. "You're hunted by your own people?" she asked.

Taleniekov nodded.

"I see. I understand clearly now. You will not accept my word and you cannot imprison me. Therefore I am a threat to you—far more than I imagined. So I have *no* choice, do I?"

"You may have," replied the KGB man. "My associate mentioned it."

"What was that?"

"Trust us. Help us get to Bastia and trust us. Something may come of it." Taleniekov turned to Scofield and spoke one word. "Conduit."

"We'll see," said Bray, removing his hand from his belt. They were thinking along the same lines.

The State Department contact in Murato was not happy; he did not want the complication he was faced with. As an owner of fishing boats in Bastia he wrote reports on Soviet naval maneuvers for the Americans. Washington paid him well and Washington had cabled *alerts* to stations everywhere that Brandon Alan Scofield, former specialist in Consular Operations, was to be considered a defector. Under such a classification the rules were clear: Take into custody, if possible, but if custody was out of the question, employ all feasible measures for dispatch.

Silvio Montefiori wondered briefly if such a course of action was worth a try. But he was a practical man and in spite of the temptation he rejected the idea. Scofield had the proverbial knife to Montefiori's mouth, yet there was some honey on the blade. If Silvio refused the American's request, his activities would be exposed to the *Soviets.* Yet if Silvio acceded to Scofield's wishes, the defector promised him ten thousand dollars. And ten thousand dollars—even with the poor rate of exchange—was probably more than any bonus he might receive for Scofield's death.

Also, he would be alive to spend the money.

Montefiori reached the warehouse, opened the door and walked through the dark, deserted cavern until he stood next to the rear wall, as instructed. He could not see the American—there was too little light—but he knew Scofield was there. It was a matter of waiting while birds circled and signals were somehow relayed.

He took a thin, crooked cigar from his handkerchief pocket, fumbled through his trousers for a box of matches, extracted one, and struck it. As he held the flame to the tip of the cigar, he was annoyed to see that his hand trembled.

"You're sweating, Montefiori." The voice came from the shadows on the left.

"The match shows up the sweat all over your face. The last time I saw you, you were sweating. I was in charge of the pouch then, and asked you certain questions."

"Brandon!" exclaimed Silvio, his greeting effusive. "My dear good friend! How fine it is to see you again . . . if I could see you."

The tall American walked out of the shadows into the dim light. Montefiori expected to see a gun in his hand, but, of course, it was not there. Scofield never did the expected.

"How are you, Silvio?" said the "defector."

"Well, my dear good friend!" Montefiori knew better than to reach for a handshake. "Everything's arranged. I take a great risk, pay my crew ten times their wages, but nothing is too much for a friend I admire so. You and the *provocateur* need only to go to the end of Pier Seven in Bastia at one o'clock this morning. My best trawler will get you to Livorno by daybreak."

"Is that its usual run?"

"Naturally not. The usual port is Piombino. I pay for the extra fuel gladly, with no thought of my loss."

"That's generous of you."

"And why not? You have always been fair with me."

"And why not? You've always delivered." Scofield reached into his pocket and took out a roll of bills. "But I'm afraid there'll be some changes. To begin with, I need two boats; one is to sail out of Bastia to the south, the other north, both staying within a thousand yards of the coastline. Each will be met by a speedboat which will be scuttled. I'll be in one, the Russian in the other; I'll give you the signals. Once on board, he and I will both head for open water, where the two courses will be charted, the destinations known only to the captains and ourselves."

"So many complications, my friend! They are not necessary, you have my word!"

"And I'll treasure it, Silvio, but while it's locked in my heart, do as I say."

"Naturally!" said Montefiori, swallowing. "But you must realize how this will add to my costs."

"Then they should be covered, shouldn't they?"

"It gladdens me you understand."

"Oh, I do, Silvio." The American peeled off a number of very large bills. "For starters, I want you to know that your activities on behalf of Washington will never be revealed by me; that in itself is a considerable payment, if you place any value on your life. And I want you to have this. It's five thousand dollars." Scofield held out the money.

"My dearest fellow, you said *ten* thousand! It was on your *word* that I predicated my very expensive arrangements!" Perspiration oozed from Montefiori's pores. Not only was his relationship with the Department of State in untenable jeopardy, but this pig of a traitor was about to rob him blind!

"I haven't finished, Silvio. You're much too anxious. I know I said ten thousand

and you'll have it. That leaves five thousand due you, without figuring in your additional expenses. Is that right?"

"Quite right," said the Corsican. "The expenses are murderous."

"So much is these days," agreed Bray. "Let's say . . . fifteen percent above the original price, is that satisfactory?"

"With others I might argue, but never with you."

"Then we'll settle for an additional fifteen hundred, okay? That leaves a total of six thousand, five hundred coming to you."

"That is a troublesome phrase. It implies a future delivery and my expenses are current. They cannot be put off."

"Come on, old friend. Certainly someone of your reputation can be trusted for a few days."

"A few days, Brandon? Again, so vague. A 'few days' and you could be in Singapore. Or Moscow. Can you be more specific?"

"Sure. The money will be in one of your trawlers, I haven't decided which yet. It'll be under the forward bulkhead, to the right of the center strut, and hidden in a hollow piece of stained wood attached to the ribbing. You'll find it easily."

"Mother of God, so will others!"

"Why? No one will be looking unless you make an announcement."

"It's far too risky! There's not a crewman on board who would hesitate to kill his mother in front of his priest for such an amount! Really, my dear friend, come to your senses!"

"Don't worry, Silvio. Meet your boats in the harbor. If you don't find the wood, look for a man with his hand blown off; he'll have the money."

"It will be *trapped?*" asked Montefiori incredulously, the sweat drenching his shirt collar.

"A set screw on the side; you've done it before. Just remove it and the charge is deactivated."

"I'll hire my brother. . . ." Silvio was depressed; the American was not a nice person. It was as if Scofield had been reading his thoughts. Since the money was on board, it would be counterproductive to have either boat sunk; the State Department might not pay in full. And by the time both were back in Bastia, the despicable Scofield could be sailing down the Volga. Or the Nile. "You won't reconsider my dear good friend?"

"I'm afraid I can't. And I won't tell anybody how much Washington thinks of you, either. Don't fret, Silvio, the money will be there. You see, we may be in touch again. Very soon."

"Do not hurry, Brandon. And please, say nothing further. I do not care to know anything. Such burdens! What are the signals for tonight?"

"Simple. Two flashes of light, repeated several times, or until the trawlers stop."

"Two flashes, repeated. . . . Distressed speedboats seeking help. I cannot be responsible for accidents at sea. *Ciao,* my old *friend.*" Montefiori blotted his neck with his handkerchief, turned in the dim light of the warehouse, and started across the concrete floor.

"Silvio?"

Montefiori stopped. "Yes?"

"Change your shirt."

They had watched her closely for nearly two days now, both men silently acknowledging that a judgment had to be made. She would either be their conduit or she would have to die. There was no middle ground, no security prison or isolated compound to which she could be sent. She would be their conduit or an act of sheer, cold necessity would take place.

They needed someone to relay messages between them. They could not communicate directly; it was too dangerous. There had to be a third party, stationed in one spot, undercover, familiar with whatever basic codes they mounted—above all, secretive and accurate. Was Antonia capable of being that person? And if she was, would she accept the risks that went with the job? So they studied her as if thrown into a crash-analysis of an impending exchange between enemies on neutral ground.

She was quick and had surface courage, qualities they had seen in the hills. She was also alert, conscious of danger. Yet she remained an enigma; her core eluded them. She was defensive, guarded, quiet for long periods, her eyes darting in all directions at once as though she expected a whip to crack across her back, or a hand to grab her throat from the shadows behind. But there were no whips, no shadows in the sunlight.

Antonia was a strange woman and it occurred to both professionals that she was hiding something. Whatever it was—if it was—she was not about to reveal it. The moments of rest provided nothing; she kept to herself—intensely to herself—and refused to be drawn out.

But she did what they had asked her to do. She got them to Bastia without incident, even to the point of knowing where to flag down a broken-down bus that carried laborers from the outskirts into the port city. Taleniekov sat with Antonia in the front while Scofield remained at the rear, watching the other passengers.

They emerged on the crowded streets, Bray still behind them, still watching, still alert for a break in the pattern of surrounding indifference. A face suddenly rigid, a pair of eyes zeroing in on the erect, middle-aged man walking with the dark-haired woman thirty paces ahead. There was only indifference.

He had told the girl to head for a bar on the waterfront, a rundown hole where no one dared intrude on a fellow drinker. Even most Corsos avoided the place; it served the dregs of the piers.

Once inside, they separated again, Taleniekov joining Bray at a table in the corner, Antonia ten feet away at another table, the chair next to her angled against the edge, reserved. It did nothing to inhibit the drunken advances of the customers. These, too, were part of her testing; it was important to know how she handled herself.

"What do you think?" asked Taleniekov.

"I'm not sure," said Scofield. "She's elusive. I can't find her."

"Perhaps you're looking too hard. She's been through an emotional upheaval; you can't expect her to act with even the semblance of normalcy. I think she can do the job. We'd know soon enough if she can't; we can protect ourselves with prearranged cipher. And quite frankly, who else do we turn to? Is there a man at any station anywhere you could trust? Or I could trust? Even what you call drones outside the stations; who would not be curious? Who could resist the pressures of Washington or Moscow?"

"It's the emotional upheaval that bothers me," Bray said. "I think it happened long before we found her. She said she was down in Porto Vecchio to get away for a while. Get away from what?"

"There could be a dozen explanations. Unemployment is rampant throughout Italy. She could be without work. Or an unfaithful lover, an affair gone sour. Such things are not relevant to what we would be asking her to do."

"Those aren't the things I saw. Besides, why should we trust her, and even if we took the chance, why would she accept?"

"She was there when that old woman was killed," said the Russian. "It may be enough."

Scofield nodded. "It's a start, but only if she's convinced there's a specific connection between what we're doing and what she saw."

"We made that clear. She heard the old woman's words; she repeated them."

"While she was still confused, still in shock. She's got to be convinced."

"Then convince her."

"Me?"

"She trusts you more than she does her 'Socialist comrade,' that's obvious." Scofield lifted his glass. "Were you going to kill her?"

"No. That decision would have had to come from you. It still does. I was uncomfortable seeing your hand so close to your belt."

"So was I." Bray put down the glass and glanced over at the girl. Berlin was never far away—Taleniekov understood that—but Scofield's mind and his eyes were not playing tricks with his memories now; he was not in a cave on the side of a hill watching a woman toss her hair free in the light of a fire. There was no similarity between his wife and Antonia any longer. He could kill her if he had to. "She'll go with me, then," he said to the Russian. "I'll know in forty-eight hours. Our first communication will be direct; the next two through her in prearranged code so we can check the accuracy. . . . If we want her and she says she'll do it."

"And if we do not, or she does not?"

"That'll be my decision, won't it." Bray made a statement; he did not ask a question. Then he took out the leaf of lettuce from his jacket pocket and opened it. The yellowed scrap of paper was intact, the names blurred but legible. Without looking down, Taleniekov repeated them.

"Count Alberto Scozzi, Rome. Sir John Waverly, London. Prince Andrei Voroshin, St. Petersburg—the name Russia is added, and, of course, the city is now Leningrad. Señor Manuel Ortiz Ortega, Madrid; he's crossed out. Josua—

which is presumed to be Joshua—Appleton, State of Massachusetts, America. The Spaniard was killed by the *padrone* at Villa Matarese, so he was never part of the council. The remaining four have long since died, but two of their descendants are very prominent, very available. David Waverly and Joshua Appleton the fourth. Britain's Foreign Secretary and the senator from Massachusetts. I say we go for immediate confrontation."

"I don't," said Bray, looking down at the paper and the childlike writing of the letters. "Because we do know who they are, and we don't know anything about the others. Who are their descendants? Where are they? If there're more surprises, let's try to find them first. The Matarese isn't restricted to two men, and these two in particular may have nothing to do with it."

"Why do you say that?"

"Everything I know about both of them would seem to deny anything like the Matarese. Waverly had what they call in England a 'good war'; a young commando, highly decorated. Then a hell of a record in the Foreign Office. He's always been a tactical compromiser, not an inciter; it doesn't fit. . . . Appleton's a Boston Brahmin who bolted the class lines and became a liberal reformer for three terms in the Senate. Protector of the working man as well as the intellectual community. He's a shining knight on a solid, political horse that most of America thinks will take him to the White House next year."

"What better residence for a *consigliere* of the Matarese?"

"It's too jarring, too pat. I think he's genuine."

"The art of conviction—in both instances, perhaps. But you're right: they won't vanish. So we start in Leningrad and Rome, trace what we can."

" 'You and *yours* will do what I can no longer do. . . .' Those were the words Matarese used seventy years ago. I wonder if it's that simple."

"Meaning the 'yours' could be selected, not born?" asked Taleniekov. "Not direct descendants?"

"Yes."

"It's possible, but these were all once-powerful families. The Waverlys and the Appletons still are. There are certain traditions in such families, the blood is always uppermost. Start with the families. They were to inherit the earth; those were his words, too. The old woman said it was his vengeance."

Scofield nodded. "I know. She also said they were only the survivors, that they were controlled by another . . . that we should look for someone else."

" 'With a voice crueler than the wind,' " added the Russian. " 'It is he,' she said."

"The shepherd boy," said Bray, staring at the scrap of yellow paper. "After all these years, who is he? What is he?"

"Start with the families," repeated Taleniekov. "If he's to be found, it is through them."

"Can you get back into Russia? To Leningrad?"

"Easily. Through Helsinki. It will be a strange return for me. I spent three years at the university in Leningrad. It's where they found me."

"I don't think anyone'll throw you a welcome-home party." Scofield folded the scrap of yellow paper into the leaf of lettuce and put it in his pocket. He took out a small notebook. "When you're in Helsinki, stay at the Tavastian Hotel until you hear from me. I'll tell you who to see there. Give me a name."

"Rydukov, Pietri," replied the KGB man without hesitating.

"Who's that?"

"A third-chair violinist for the Sevastopol Symphony. I'll have his papers somewhat altered."

"I hope no one asks you to play."

"Severe arthritis has caused indisposition."

"Let's work out our codes," said Bray, glancing at Antonia, who was smoking a cigarette and talking to a young Bastian sailor standing next to her. She was handling herself well; she laughed politely but coolly, putting a gentle distance between herself and the importunate young man. In truth, there was more than a hint of elegance in her behavior, out of place in the waterfront café, but welcome to the eyes. His eyes, reflected Scofield, without thinking further.

"What do you think will happen?" asked Taleniekov, watching Bray.

"I'll know in forty-eight hours," Scofield said.

18

The trawler approached the Italian coastline. The winter seas had been turbulent, the crosscurrents angry and the boat slow; it had taken them nearly seventeen hours to make the trip from Bastia. It would be dark soon, and a small lifeboat would be lowered over the side to take Scofield and Antonia ashore.

Besides getting them to Italy where the hunt for the family of Count Alberto Scozzi would begin, the tediously slow journey served another purpose for Bray. He had the time and the seclusion to learn more about Antonia Gravet—for that unexpectedly was her last name, her father having been a French artillery sergeant stationed in Corsica during the Second World War.

"So you see," she had told him, the curve of a smile on her lips, "my French lessons were very inexpensive. It was only necessary to anger pa*pa*, who was never comfortable with my mother's Italian."

Except for those moments when her mind wandered back to Porto Vecchio, a change had come over her. She began to laugh, her brown eyes reflecting the laughter, bright, infectious, at times nearly manic, as if the act of laughing itself were a release she needed. It was almost impossible for Scofield to realize that the girl sitting next to him, dressed in khaki trousers and a torn field jacket, was the same woman who had been so sullen and unresponsive. Or who had shouted orders in the hills and handled the Lupo so efficiently. They had several minutes left before going into the lifeboat, so he asked her about the Lupo.

"I went through a phase; we all do, I think. A time when drastic social change seems possible only through violence. Those maniacs from the Brigate Rosse knew how to play us."

"The Brigades? You were with the *Red Brigades?* Good *Lord!*"

She nodded. "I spent several weeks at a Brigatisti camp in Medicina, learning how to fire weapons, and scale walls and hide contraband—none of which I did particularly well, incidentally—until one morning when a young student, a boy, really, was killed in what the leaders called a 'training accident.' A *training accident*, such a *military* sound, but they were not soldiers. Only brutes and bullies, let loose with knives and guns. He died in my arms, the blood flowing from his wound . . . his eyes so frightened and bewildered. I hardly knew him but when he died, I couldn't stand it. Guns and knives and clubs were not the way; that night I left and returned to Bologna.

"So what you saw in Porto Vecchio was an act. It was dark, and you did not see the fear in my eyes."

He had been right. She was not for the barricades; there would be no merry month of May for her.

"You know," he said slowly, "we're going to be together for a while."

There was no fear in her eyes now. "We have not settled that question, have we?"

"What question?"

"Where I'm going. You and the Russian said I was to trust you, do as you were doing, leave Corsica and say nothing. Well, signore, we've left Corsica and I've trusted you. I didn't run away."

"Why didn't you?"

Antonia paused briefly. "Fear, and you know it. You're not normal men. You speak courteously, but move too quickly for courteous men. The two don't go together. I think underneath you are what the crazy people in the Brigate Rosse would like to be. You frighten me."

"That stopped you?"

"The Russian wanted to kill me. He watched me closely; he would have shot me the instant he thought I was running."

"Actually, he didn't want to kill you and he wouldn't have. He was just sending a message."

"I don't understand."

"You don't have to, you were perfectly safe."

"Am I safe now? Will you take my word that I will say nothing and let me go?"

"Where to?"

"Bologna. I can always get work there."

"Doing what?"

"Nothing very impressive. I'm hired as a researcher at the university. I look up boring statistics for the *professori* who write their boring books and articles."

"A researcher?" Bray smiled to himself. "You must be very accurate."

"What is it to be accurate? Facts are facts. Will you let me go back to Bologna?"

"Your work isn't steady then?"

"It is work I *like*," replied Antonia. "I work when I wish to, leaving me time for other things."

"You're actually a self-employed freelancer with your own business," said Scofield, enjoying himself. "That's the essence of capitalism, isn't it?"

"And you're maddening! You ask questions but you don't answer mine!"

"Sorry. Occupational characteristic. What was your question?"

"Will you let me go? Will you accept my word; will you trust me? Or must I wait for that moment when you cannot be watching and run?"

"I wouldn't do that, if I were you," replied Bray courteously. "Look, you're an honest person. I don't meet many. A minute ago you said you didn't run away before because you were afraid to, not because you trusted us. That's being honest. You brought us up to Bastia. Be honest with me now. Knowing what you know—seeing what you saw in Porto Vecchio—how good is your word?"

At midships, the lifeboat was being hoisted over the railing by four crewmen; Antonia watched it as she spoke. "You're being unfair. You know what I saw, and you know what you told me. When I think about it, I want to cry out and . . ." She did not finish; instead she turned back to him, her voice weary. "How good is my word? I don't know. So what's left for me? Will it be you and not the Russian who fires the bullet?"

"I may offer you a job."

"I don't want work from you."

"We'll see," said Bray.

"*Venite subito, signori. La lancia va partire.*"

The lifeboat was in the water. Scofield reached for the duffel bag at his side and got to his feet. He held out his hand for Antonia. "Come on. I've had easier people to deal with."

The statement was true. He could kill this woman if he had to. Still, he would try not to have to.

Where was the new life for Beowulf Agate now?

God, he hated this one.

Bray hired a taxi in Fiumicino, the driver at first reluctant to accept a fare to Rome, changing his mind instantly at the sight of the money in Scofield's hand. They stopped for a quick meal and still reached the inner city before eight o'clock. The streets were crowded, the shops doing a brisk evening's business.

"Pull up in that parking space," said Bray to the driver. They were in front of a clothing store. "Wait here," he added, including Antonia in the command. "I'll guess your size." He opened the door.

"What are you doing?" asked the girl.

"A transition," replied Scofield in English. "You can't walk into a decent shop dressed like that."

Five minutes later he returned carrying a box containing denim slacks, a white blouse, and a woolen sweater. "Put these on," he said.

"You're mad!"

"Modesty becomes you, but we're in a hurry. The stores'll close in an hour. I've got things to wear; you don't." He turned to the driver, whose eyes were riveted on the rearview mirror. "You understand English better than I thought," he said in Italian. "Drive around. I'll tell you where to go." He opened his duffel bag, and pulled out a tweed jacket.

Antonia changed in the backseat of the taxi, glancing frequently at Scofield. As she slipped the khakis off and the denims on, her long legs caught the light of the streets. Bray looked out the window, conscious of being affected by what he saw in the corner of his eye. He had not had a woman in a long time; he would not have this one. It was entirely possible that he might have to kill her.

She pulled the sweater over her blouse; the loose-fitting wool did not conceal the swell of her breasts and Scofield made it a point to focus his eyes on hers. "That's better. Phase one complete."

"You're very generous, but these would not have been my choices."

"You can throw them away in an hour. If anyone asks you, you're off a charter boat in Ladispoli." He addressed the driver again. "Go to the Via Condotti. I'll pay you there; we won't need you any longer."

The shop on the Via Condotti was expensive, catering to the idle and the rich, and it was obvious that Antonia Gravet had never been in one like it. Obvious to Bray; he doubted it was so to anyone else. For she had innate taste—born, not cultivated. She might have been bursting at the sight of the wealth of garments displayed, but she was the essence of control. It was the elegance Bray had seen in the filthy waterfront café in Bastia.

"Do you like it?" she asked, coming out of a fitting room in a subdued, dark silk dress, a wide-brimmed white hat, and a pair of high-heeled white shoes.

"Very nice," said Scofield, meaning it, and her, and everything he saw.

"I feel like a traitor to all the things I've believed for so long," she added, whispering. "These prices could feed ten families for a month! Let's go somewhere else."

"We don't have time. Take them and get some kind of coat and anything else you need."

"You *are* mad."

"I'm in a hurry."

From a booth on the Via Sistina, he called a *pensione* in the Piazza Navona where he stayed frequently when in Rome. The landlord and his wife knew nothing at all about Scofield—they were not curious about any of their transient tenants—except that Bray tipped generously whenever they accommodated him. The owner was happy to do so tonight.

The Piazza Navona was crowded; it was always crowded, thus making it an ideal location for a man in his profession. The Bernini fountains were magnets for citizens and tourists alike, the profusion of outdoor cafés places of assignation, planned and spontaneous; Scofield's had always been planned. A table in a crowded square was a good vantage point for spotting surveillance. It was not necessary to be concerned about such things now.

Now it was only necessary to get some sleep, let the mind clear itself. Tomorrow a decision would have to be made. The life or the death of the woman at his side whom he guided through the Piazza to an old stone building and the door of the *pensione.*

The ceiling of their room was high, the windows enormous, opening onto the square three stories below. Bray pushed the overstuffed sofa against the door and pointed to the bed across the room.

"Neither of us slept very much on that damned boat. Get some rest."

Antonia opened one of the boxes from the shop in the Via Condotti and took out the dark silk dress. "Why did you buy me these expensive clothes?"

"Tomorrow we're going to a couple of places where you'll need them."

"Why are we going to these places? They must surely be extravagant."

"Not really. There are some people I have to see, and I want you with me."

"I wanted to thank you. I've never had such beautiful clothes."

"You're welcome." Bray went over to the bed and removed the spread; he returned to the sofa. "Why did you leave Bologna and go to Corsica?"

"More questions?" she said quietly.

"I'm just curious, that's all."

"I told you. I wanted to get away for a while. Is that not a good enough reason?"

"It's not much of an explanation."

"It's the one I prefer to give." She studied the dress in her hands.

Scofield slapped the spread over the sofa. "Why Corsica?"

"You saw that valley. It is remote, peaceful. A good place to think."

"It's certainly remote; that makes it a good place to hide out. Were you hiding from someone—or something?"

"Why do you say things like that?"

"I have to know. Were you hiding?"

"Not from anything you would understand."

"Try me."

"*Stop* it!" Antonia held the dress out for him. "Take your clothes. Take anything you want from me, I can't stop you! But leave me *alone.*"

Bray approached her. For the first time, he saw fear in her eyes. "I think you'd better tell me. All that talk about Bologna . . . it was a lie. You wouldn't go back there even if you could. Why?"

She stared at him for a moment, her brown eyes glistening. When she began, she turned away, and walked to the window overlooking the Piazza Navona. "You might as well know, it doesn't matter any longer. . . . You're wrong. I can go back;

they expect me back. And if I do not return, one day they will come looking for me."

"Who?"

"The leaders of the Red Brigades. I told you on the boat how I had run away from the camp in Medicina. That was over a year ago and for over a year I have lived a lie far greater than the one I told you. They found me, and I was put on trial in the Red Court—they call it the Red Court of Revolutionary Justice. Sentences of death are not mere phrases, they are very real executions, as the world knows now.

"I had not been indoctrinated, yet I knew the location of the camp and had witnessed the death of the boy. Most damaging, I had run away. I couldn't be trusted. Of course, I didn't matter compared to the objectives of the revolution; they said I had proved myself less than insignificant. A traitor.

"I saw what was coming, so I pleaded for my life. I claimed that I had been the student's lover, and that my reaction—although perhaps not admirable—was understandable. I stressed that I had said nothing to *anyone*, let alone the police. I was as committed as any in that court to the revolution—more so than most, for I came from a truly poor family.

"In my own way, I was persuasive, but there was something else working for me. To understand, you must know how such groups are organized. There is always a cadre of strong men, and one or two among these who vie for leadership, like male wolves in a pack—snarling, dominating, choosing their various mates at will, for that is part of the domination. A man such as this wanted me. He was probably the most vicious of the pack; the others were frightened of him— and so was I.

"But he could save my life, and I made my choice. I lived with him for over a year, hating every day, despising the nights he took me, loathing myself as much as I loathed him.

"Still, I could do nothing. I lived in fear; in such a terrible fear that my slightest move would be mistaken, and my head blown away . . . their favorite method of execution." Antonia turned from the window. "You asked me why I did not run from you and the Russian. Perhaps you understand better now; the conditions of my survival were not new to me. To run away meant death; to run away from you means death now. I was a captive in Bologna, I became a captive in Porto Vecchio . . . and I am a captive now in Rome." She paused, then spoke again. "I am tired of you all. I can't stand it much longer. The moment will come, and I will run . . . and you will shoot." She held out the dress again. "Take your clothes, Signore Scofield. I am faster in a pair of trousers."

Bray did not move, nor did he object by gesture or voice. He almost smiled, but he could not do that, either. "I'm glad to hear that your sense of fatalism doesn't include intentional suicide. I mean, you *do* expect to give us a 'run.' "

"You may count on it." She dropped the dress on the floor.

"I won't kill you, Antonia."

She laughed quietly, derisively. "Oh, yes, you will. You and the Russian are the worst kind. In Bologna, they kill with fire in their eyes, shouting slogans. You kill without anger . . . you need no inner urging."

I once did. You get over it. There's no compulsion, only necessity. Please don't talk about these things. The way you've lived is your stay of execution; that's all you need to know.

"I won't argue with you. I didn't say I couldn't—or wouldn't—I simply said I won't. I'm trying to tell you, you don't have to run."

The girl frowned. "Why?"

"Because I need you." Scofield knelt down and picked up the dress, and gave it back to her. "All I've got to do is convince you that you need me."

"To save my life?"

"To give it back to you, at any rate. In what form, I'm not sure, but better than before. Without the fear, eventually."

" 'Eventually' is a long time. Why should I believe you?"

"I don't think you have a choice. I can't give you any other answer until I know more, but let's start with the fact that the Brigatisti aren't confined to Bologna. You said if you didn't go back, they'd come looking for you. Their . . . packs . . . roam all over Italy. How long can you keep hiding until they find you—if they want to find you badly enough?"

"I could have hidden for years in Corsica. In Porto Vecchio. They would *never* find me."

"That's not possible now, and even if it were, is that the kind of existence you want? To spend your life as a recluse in those goddamn hills? Those men who killed that old woman are no different from the Brigades. One wants to keep its world—and its filthy little secret—and it will kill to do it. The other wants to change the world—with terror—and it kills every day to do *that*. Believe me they're connected to each other. That's the connection Taleniekov and I are looking for. We'd better find it before the maniacs blow us all up. Your grandmother said it: It's happening *everywhere*. Stop hiding. Help us. Help *me*."

"There's no way I can help you."

"You don't know what I'm going to ask."

"Yes, I do. You want me to go back!"

"Later, perhaps. Not now."

"I won't! They're pigs. He's the pig of the world!"

"Then remove him from the world. Remove *them*. Don't let them grow, don't let them make you a prisoner—whether you're in Corsica or here or anywhere else. Don't you understand? They *will* find you if they think you're a threat to them. Do you want to go back that way? To an execution?"

Antonia broke away, stopped by the overstuffed sofa Bray had placed in front of the door. "How will they find me? Will you help them?"

"No," said Scofield, remaining motionless. "I won't have to."

"There are a hundred places I can go. . . ."

"And there are a thousand ways they have of tracing you."

"That's a lie!" She turned and faced him. "They have no such methods."

"I think they do. Groups like the Brigades everywhere are being fed information, financed, given access to sophisticated equipment, and most of the time they don't know how or why. They're all foot soldiers and that's the irony, but they'll find you."

"Soldiers for what?"

"The Matarese."

"Madness!"

"I wish it were but I'm afraid it isn't. Too much has happened to be coincidence any longer. Men who believed in peace have been killed; a statesman respected by both sides went to others and spoke of it. He disappeared. It's in Washington, Moscow . . . in Italy and Corsica and God knows where. It's *there,* but we can't *see* it. I only know we've got to find it, and that old woman in the hills gave us the first concrete information to go on. She gave up what was left of her life to give it to us. She was blind but she saw it . . . because she was there when it began."

"Words!"

"Facts. Names."

A sound. Not part of the hum from the square below, but beyond the door. All sounds were part of a pattern, or distinctly their own; this was its own. A footstep, a shifting of weight, a scratch of leather against stone. Bray brought his index finger to his lips, then gestured for Antonia to move to the left end of the sofa while he walked quickly to the right. She was bewildered; she had heard nothing. He motioned for her to help him lift the sofa away from the door. Smoothly, silently.

It was done.

Scofield waved her back into the corner, took out his Browning and resumed a normal conversational tone. He inched his way to the door, his face turned away from it.

"It's not too crowded in the restaurants. Let's go down to Tre Scalini for some food. God knows I could use . . . ."

He pulled the door open; there was no one in the hallway. Yet he had not been mistaken; he knew what he had heard; the years had taught him not to *make* mistakes about such things. And the years had also taught him when to be furious with himself over his own carelessness. Since Fiumicino he had been very careless, disregarding the probability of surveillance. Rome was a low-priority station; since the heavy traffic four years ago, CIA, *Cons Op,* and KGB activity had been held to a minimum. It had been more than eleven months since he had been in the city, and the scanner sheets then had shown no agents of status in operation there. If anything Rome had lessened in intelligence potential during the past year; who could be around?

Someone was and he had been spotted. Someone moments ago had been close to the door, listening, trying to confirm a sighting. The sudden break in conversation had served to warn whomever it was, but he was there, somewhere in the shadows of the squared-off hallway or on the staircase.

Goddamn it, thought Bray angrily as he walked silently around the landing, had he forgotten that alerts had been sent to every station in the world by now? He was a *fugitive* and he had been careless. Where had he been picked up? In the Via Condotti? Crossing the Piazza?

He heard a rush of air, and even as he heard it, his instinct told him he was too late to react. He stiffened his body as he spun to his right, lunging downward to lessen the impact of the blow.

A door behind him had suddenly been yanked open and a figure that was only a blur above his back rushed out, an arm held high, but only for an instant. It came crashing down, the sickening bolt of pain spreading from the base of his skull throughout his chest, surging downward into his kneecaps where it settled, bringing on the wind of collapse and darkness.

He blinked his eyes, tears of pain filling them, disorienting him, but somehow providing a measure of relief. How many minutes had he been lying on the hallway floor? He could not tell, yet he sensed it was not long.

He rose slowly and looked at his watch. He had been out for roughly fifteen minutes; had he not twisted the instant before impact, the elapsed time would have been closer to an hour.

Why was he *there?* Alone? Where was his captor? It did not make sense! He had been taken, then left by himself. What was his capture *for?*

He heard a muted cry, quickly cut off, and turned toward the source, bewildered. Then bewilderment left him. *He* was not the target; he never had been. It was *she.* Antonia. *She* was the one who had been spotted, not he.

Scofield got to his feet, braced himself against the railing and peered down at the floor around him. His Browning was gone, naturally, and he had no other weapon. But he had something else. Consciousness. His assailant would not expect that—the man had known precisely where to hammer the butt of his gun; in his mind his victim would be unconscious far longer than the few minutes involved. Drawing that man out was not a significant problem.

Bray walked noiselessly to the door of the single room and put his ear to the wood. The moans were more pronounced now. Sharp cries of pain, abruptly stilled. A strong hand clasped over a mouth, fingers pressed into flesh, choking off all but throated protests. And there were words, spoken harshly in Italian.

"Whore! Pig! It was to be *Marseilles!* Nine hundred thousand *lire!* Two or three weeks at most! We sent our people; you were not *there. He* was not there. No courier of drugs had ever heard of you! *Liar! Whore!* Where were you? What have you *done?! Traitor!"*

A scream was suddenly formed, more suddenly cut off, the guttural cry that followed searing in its torment. What in the name of God was *happening?* Scofield slammed his hand against the door, shouting as though only half-conscious, incoherent, his words slurred and barely comprehensible.

"Stop it! *Stop* it! What *is* this? I can't . . . can't . . . *Wait!* I'll run downstairs! There are police in the square. I'll bring the *police!"*

He pounded his feet on the stone floor as if running, his shouts trailing off until there was silence. He pressed his back into the wall and waited, listening to the commotion within. He heard slaps and gasps of pain.

There was a sudden, loud thud. A body—her body—was slammed into the door, and then the door was pulled open, Antonia propelled through it with such force she sprawled forward falling to her knees. What Bray saw of her caused him to suppress all reaction. There was no emotion, only movement . . . and the inevitable: he would inflict punishment.

The man rushed through the door, weapon first. Scofield shot out his right hand, catching the gun, pivoting as he did so, his left foot arching up viciously into the attacker's groin. The man grimaced in shock and sudden agony; the gun fell to the floor, metal clattering against stone. Bray grabbed the man's throat, smashing his head into the wall, and twisting him by the neck into the open doorframe. He held the Italian upright, and hammered his fist into the man's lower rib cage; he could hear the bone crack. He plunged his knee into the small of the man's back and with both hands acting as a battering ram, sent him plummeting through the door into the room. The Italian collapsed over the obstructing sofa and fell senseless to the floor beyond it. Scofield turned and ran to Antonia.

Reaction was allowed now; he felt sick. Her face was bruised; spidery veins of red had spread from the swellings caused by repeated blows to the head. The corner of her left eye was so battered the skin had broken; a two-pronged rivulet of blood flowed down her cheek. The loose-fitting sweater had been removed by force, the white blouse torn to shreds, nothing left but ragged patches of fabric. Beneath, her brassiere had been pulled from its hasps, yanked off her breasts, hanging from a single shoulder strap.

It was the flesh of this exposed part of her body that made him swallow in revulsion. There were cigarette burns, ugly little circles of charred skin, progressing from her pelvic area across the flat of her stomach over the swell of her right breast toward the small red nipple.

The man who had done this to her was no interrogator seeking information; that role was secondary. He was a sadist, indulging his sickness as brutally and as rapidly as possible. And Bray had not finished with that man.

Antonia moaned, shaking her head back and forth, pleading not to be hurt again. He picked her up and carried her back into the room, kicking the door shut, edging his way around the sofa, past the unconscious man on the floor, to the bed. He placed her gently down, sat beside her and drew her to him.

"It's all right. It's over, he can't touch you anymore." He felt her tears against his face, and then was aware that she had put her arms around him. She was suddenly holding him fiercely, her body trembling, the cries from her throat more than pleas for release from immediate pain. She was begging to be set free from a torment that had been deep within her for a very long time. But it was not the time now to probe; the extent of her wounds had to be examined and treated.

There was a doctor on the Viale Regina, and a man on the floor that had to be dealt with. Getting Antonia to the doctor might be difficult unless he could calm her down; disposing of the sadist on the floor would be simple. It might even accomplish something.

He would call the police from a booth somewhere in the city and direct them to the *pensione*. They would find a man and his weapon and a crude sign over his unconscious body.

Brigatisti.

19

The doctor closed the door of the examining room and spoke in English. He had been schooled in London and recruited by British intelligence. Scofield had found him during an operation involving *Cons Op* and MI-Six. The man was safe. He thought all clandestine services were slightly mad, but since the British had paid for his last two years in medical school, he accepted his part of the bargain. He was simply on-call to treat unbalanced people in a very foolish business. Bray liked him.

"She's sedated and my wife is with her. She'll come out of it in a few minutes and you can go."

"How is she?"

"In pain, but it won't last. I've treated the burns with an ointment that acts as a local anesthetic. I've given her a jar." The doctor lit a cigarette; he had not finished. "An ice pack or two should be applied to the facial contusions; the swellings will go down overnight. The cuts are minor, no stitches required."

"Then she's all right," said Scofield, relieved.

"No, she's not, Bray." The doctor exhaled smoke. "Oh, medically she's sound and with a little makeup and dark glasses she'll no doubt be up and about by noon tomorrow. But she is not all right."

"What do you mean?"

"How well do you know her?"

"Barely. I found her several days ago, it doesn't matter where—"

"I'm not interested," interrupted the doctor. "I never am. I just want you to know that tonight was not the first time this has happened to her. There is evidence of previous beatings, some quite severe."

"Good Lord. . . ." Scofield thought immediately of the cries of anguish he had heard less than an hour ago. "What kind of evidence?"

"Scars from multiple lacerations and burns. All small and precisely placed to cause maximum pain."

"Recent?"

"Within the last year or so, I'd say. Some of the tissue is still soft, relatively new."

"Any ideas?"

"Yes. During severe trauma, people speak of things." The doctor stopped, inhaling on his cigarette. "I don't have to tell you that; you count on it."

"Go on," said Bray.

"I think she was systematically, psychologically broken. She kept repeating catchwords. Allegiances to this and that; loyalty beyond death and torture of self and comrades. That sort of garbage."

"The Brigatisti were busy little pricks," Bray said.

"What?"

"Forget it."

"Forgotten. She has a mass of confusion in that lovely head of hers."

"Not as much as you think. She got away."

"Intact and functioning?" asked the doctor.

"Mostly."

"Then she's remarkable."

"More to the point, she's exactly what I need," said Scofield.

"Is that, too, a required response?" The medical man's ire was apparent. "You people never cease to disappoint me. That woman's scars aren't only on her skin, Bray. She's been brutalized."

"She's alive. I'd like to be there when she comes out of sedation. May I?"

"So you can catch her while her mind is only *half* alive, extract your *own* responses?" The doctor paused again. "I'm sorry, it's not my business."

"I'd like her to be your business if she needs help. If you don't mind."

The doctor studied him. "My services are limited to medicine, you know that."

"I understand. She has no one else, she's not from Rome. Can she come to you . . . if any of those scars get torn away?"

The Italian nodded. "Tell her to come and see me if she needs medical attention. Or a friend."

"Thank you very much. And thanks for something else. You've fit several pieces into a puzzle I couldn't figure out. I'll go in now, if it's all right."

"Go ahead. Send my wife out here."

Scofield touched Antonia's cheek. She lay still on the bed, but at the touch rolled her head to the side, her lips parted, a moan of protest escaping her throat. Things *were* clearer now, the puzzle that was Antonia Gravet coming more into focus. For it was the focus that had been lacking; he had not been able to see through the opaque glass wall she had erected between herself and the outside world. The commanding woman in the hills who displayed courage without essential strength; yet who could face a man she believed wanted her dead and tell him to fire away. And the childlike woman on the trawler drenched by the sea, given to sudden moments of infectious laughter. The laughter had confused him; it did not confuse him now. It was her way of grasping for small periods of relief and normality. The boat was her temporary sanctuary; she would not be hurt while at sea, and so she had made the most of it. An abused child—or a prisoner—allowed an hour of fresh air and sunshine. Take the moments and find joy in them. If only to forget. For those brief moments.

A scarred mind worked that way. Scofield had seen too many scarred minds not to recognize the syndrome once he understood the scars. The doctor had used the phrase "a mass of confusion in her lovely head." What could anyone expect? Antonia Gravet had spent her own eternity in a maze of pain. That she had survived above a vegetable was not only remarkable . . . it was the sign of a professional.

Strange, thought Bray, but that conclusion was the highest compliment he could pay. In a way, it made him sick.

She opened her eyes, blinking in fear, her lips trembling. Then she seemed to recognize him; the fear receded and the trembling stopped. He touched her cheek again and her eyes reflected the comfort she felt at the touch.

"*Grazie*," she whispered. "Thank you, thank you, thank you. . . ."

He bent over her. "I know most of it," he said quietly. "The doctor told me what they did to you. Now tell me the rest. What happened in Marseilles?"

Tears welled up in her eyes and the trembling began again. "No! No, you must not ask me!"

"*Please.* I have to know. They can't touch you; they'll never touch you again."

"You saw what they *do!* Oh, God, the *pain.* . . ."

"It's *over.*" He brushed away the tears with his fingers. "Listen to me. I understand now. I said stupid things to you because I didn't know. Of course you wanted to get away, stay away, isolate yourself—resign from the human race, for Christ's sake—I *understand* that. But don't you see? You *can't.* Help us stop them, help *me* stop them. They've put you through so much . . . make them pay for it, Antonia. Goddamn it, get *angry.* I look at you and I'm angry as hell!"

He was not sure what it was; perhaps the fact that he cared, for he did, and he did not try to conceal that care. It was in his eyes, in his words; he knew it. Whatever it was, the tears stopped, her brown eyes glistened, as they had glistened on the trawler. Anger and purpose were surfacing. She told the rest of her story.

"I was to be the drug whore," she said. "The woman who traveled with the courier, keeping her eyes open and her body available at all times. I was to sleep with men—or women, it made no difference—performing whatever services they wished." Antonia winced, the memories sickening to her. "The drug whore is valuable to the courier. She can do things he cannot do, being bribe and decoy and unsuspected watchdog. I was . . . trained. I let them think I had no resistance left. My courier was chosen, a foul-mouthed animal who could not wait to have me, for I had been the favorite of the strongest; it gave him status. I was sick to my stomach at what was before me, but I counted the hours, knowing that each one brought me closer to what I had dreamed of for months. My filthy courier and I were taken to La Spezia where we were smuggled aboard a freighter, our destination Marseilles and the contact who would set up the drug runs.

"The courier could not wait, and I was ready for him. We were put into a storage room below deck. The ship was not scheduled to sail for over an hour, so I said to the pig that perhaps we should wait and not risk being intruded upon. But he would not and I knew he would not; if he had I would have provoked him. For each minute was precious to me. I knew I could not go out to sea; once at sea what remained of my life was over. I had made a promise to myself. I would leap into water at night and drown in peace rather than face Marseilles where the horror would begin again. But I did not have to. . . ."

Antonia stopped, the pain of the memory choking her. Bray took her hand and held it in his. "Go on," he said. She had to say it. It was the final moment she had to somehow face and exorcize; he felt it as surely as if it were his own.

"The pig pulled off my coat and tore the blouse from my chest. It did not matter that I was willing to remove them, he had to show his bull strength; he had to rape, for he was taking—not being given. He ripped the skirt off my waist until I stood naked before him. Like a maniac, he removed his own clothes and placed himself under the light, I suppose so that I might stand in awe of his nakedness.

"He grabbed me by the hair and forced me to my knees . . . to his waist . . . and I was sick beyond sickness. But I knew the time was coming, and so I shut my eyes and played my part and thought about the beautiful hills in Porto Vecchio, where my grandmother lived . . . where I would live for the rest of my life.

"It happened. The courier threw himself upon me.

"I moved us both closer to the coil of rope, shouting the things my rapist wanted to hear, as I inched my hand toward the middle of the coil. My moment had come. I had carried a knife—a plain dinner knife I had sharpened on stone—and had shoved it into the coil of rope. I touched the handle and thought again about the beautiful hills in Porto Vecchio.

"And as that scum lay naked on top of me, I raised the knife behind him and plunged it into his back. He screamed and tried to raise himself, but the wound was too deep. I pulled it out and brought it down again, and again, and again . . . and, *oh mother of Christ,* again and *again!* I could not *stop killing!*"

She had said it, and now she cried uncontrollably. Scofield held her, stroking her hair, saying nothing for there was nothing he could say that would ease the pain. Finally, the terrible control she forced upon herself returned.

"It had to be done. You understand that, don't you?" Bray said.

She nodded, "Yes."

"He didn't deserve to live, that's clear to you, isn't it?"

"Yes."

"That's the first step, Antonia. You've got to accept it. We're not in a court of law where lawyers can argue philosophies. For us, it's cut and dried. It's a war and you kill because if you don't, someone will kill you."

She breathed deeply, her eyes roaming over his face, her hand still in his. "You are an odd man. You say the right words, but I have the feeling you don't like saying them."

I don't. I do not like what I am. I did not choose my life, it fell down upon me.

I am in a tunnel deep in the earth and I cannot get out. The right words are a comfort. And most of the time I need them for my sanity.

Bray squeezed her hand. "What happened after? . . ."

"After I killed the courier?"

"After you killed the animal who raped you—who would have killed you."

"Grazie ancora," said Antonia. "I dressed in his clothes, rolled up the trousers, pushing my hair into the cap, and filling out the large jacket with what was left of my dress. I made my way up to the deck. The sky was dark, but there was light on the pier. Dock workers who were walking up and down the gangplank carried boxes like an army of ants. It was simple. I got in line and walked off the ship."

"Very good," said Scofield, meaning it.

"It was not difficult. Except when I first put my foot on the ground."

"Why? What happened?"

"I wanted to scream. I wanted to shout and laugh and run off the pier yelling to everyone that I was free. *Free!* The rest was very easy. The courier had been given money; it was in his trouser's pocket. It was more than enough to get me to Genoa, where I bought clothes and a ticket on the plane to Corsica. I was in Bastia by noon the next day."

"And from there to Porto Vecchio?"

"Yes. Free!"

"Not exactly. God knows the prison was different, but you were still a prisoner. Those hills were your cell."

Antonia looked away. "I would have been happy there for the rest of my life. Since I was a child I loved the valley and the mountains."

"Keep the memories," said Bray. "Don't try to go back."

She turned her head toward him. "You said one day I could! Those men must pay for what they did! You, yourself, agreed to that!"

"I said I hoped they would. Maybe they will, but let others do the work, not you. Someone would blow your head off if you stepped foot in those hills." Scofield released her hand and brushed away the strands of dark hair that had fallen over her cheek when she turned so abruptly to him. Something disturbed him; he was not sure what it was. Something was missing, a quantum jump had been made, a step omitted. "I know it's not fair to ask you to talk about it, but I'm confused. These drug runs . . . how are they mounted? You say a courier is chosen, a woman assigned to travel with him, both to meet a contact at some given location?"

"Yes. A specific article of clothing is worn by the woman and the contact approaches her first. He pays for an hour of her time and they go off together, the courier following. If anything happens, anything like police interception, the courier claims he is the girl's *mezzano* . . . pimp."

"So the contact and the courier rendezvous through the woman. Is the narcotics delivery made then?"

"I don't think so. Remember, I never actually made a run, but I believe the contact only sets up the distribution schedules. Where the drugs are to be taken and who is to receive them. After that, he sends the courier to a source, again using the whore as his protection."

"So if there are any arrests, the . . . whore . . . takes the fall?"

"Yes. Drug authorities do not pay much attention to such women; they're let out quickly."

"But the source is now known, the schedules in hand and the courier protected. . . ." What *was* it? Bray stared at the wall, trying to sort out the facts, trying to spot the omission that bothered him so. Was it in the pattern?

"Most of the risks are reduced to the minimum," said Antonia. "Even the delivery runs are made in such a way that the merchandise can be abandoned at a moment's notice. At least, that's what I gathered from the other girls."

" 'Most of the risks . . . ,' " repeated Scofield. " 'Reduced to a minimum?' "

"Not all, of course, but a great many. It is very well organized. Each step has a means to escape built in."

"Organized? Escape? . . ." *Organized!* That was *it.* Minimum risks, maximum returns! It *was* the pattern, the *entire* pattern. It went back to the beginning . . . to the concept *itself.* "Antonia, tell me, where did the contacts come from? How did they reach the Brigades in the first place?"

"The Brigades make a great deal of money from narcotics. The drug market is its main source of income."

"But how did it start? When?"

"A few years ago, when the Brigades began to expand."

"It didn't just *happen. How* did it happen?"

"I can only tell you what I heard. A man came to the leaders—several were in jail. He told them to find him when they got out on the streets again. He could lead them to large sources of money that could be made without the heavy risks involved in robbery and kidnapping."

"In other words," said Scofield, thinking rapidly as he spoke, "he offered to finance them in a major way with minor effort. Teams of two people going out for three or four weeks—and returning with something like nine million lire. Seventy thousand dollars for a month's work. Minimum risk, maximum return. Very few personnel involved."

"Yes. In the beginning, the contacts came from him, that man. They in turn led to others. As you say, it does not take many people and they bring in large amounts of money."

"So the Brigades can concentrate on their true calling," completed Bray sardonically. "The disruption of the social order. In a single word, terrorism." He got up from the bed. "That man who came to see the leaders in jail. Did he stay in touch with them?"

She frowned. "Again, I can only tell you what I heard. He was never seen after the second meeting."

"I'll bet he wasn't. Every negotiation always five times removed from the course. . . . A geometric progression, no single line to retrace. That's how they do it."

"Who?"

"The Matarese."

Antonia stared at him. "Why do you say that?"

"Because it's the only explanation. Serious dealers in narcotics wouldn't *touch* maniacs like the Brigades. It's a controlled situation, a charade mounted to finance terrorism, so the Matarese can continue to finance the guns and the killing. In Italy it's the Red Brigades; in Germany, Baader-Meinhof; in Lebanon, the PLO; in my country, the Minutemen and the Weathermen, the Ku Klux Klan and the JDL and all the goddamn fools who blew up banks and laboratories and embassies. Each financed differently, secretly. All pawns for the Matarese— maniacal pawns, and that's the scary thing. The longer they're fed the bigger they grow, and the bigger they grow the more damage they do." He reached for her hand, aware that he had done so only after they had touched.

"You are convinced, aren't you? That it's happening."

"Now more than ever. You just showed me how one small part of the whole is manipulated. I knew—or thought I knew—it was *being* manipulated but I didn't know how. Now I do and it doesn't take much imagination to think of variations. It's a guerrilla war with a thousand battlegrounds, none of them defined."

Antonia lifted his hand, as though reassuring herself it was there, freely given; and then her dark brown eyes shifted to his, suddenly questioning. "You talk as if it were new to you, this war. Surely that's not so. You're an intelligence officer. . . ."

"I was," corrected Bray. "Not anymore."

"That doesn't change what you know. You said to me only a moment ago that certain things must be accepted, that courts and *avvocati* had no place, that one killed in order not to be killed oneself. Is this war so different now?"

"More than I can explain," answered Scofield, glancing up at the white wall. "We were professionals and there were rules—most of them our own, most harsh, but there *were* rules and we abided by them. We knew what we were doing, nothing was pointless. I guess you could say we knew when to stop." He turned back to her. "These are wild animals, let loose in the streets. They have no rules. They don't know when to stop, and those who are financing them never want them to learn. Don't fool yourself, they're capable of paralyzing governments. . . ."

Bray caught himself, his voice trailing off. He heard his own words and they astonished him. *He had said it.* In a single phrase he had said it! It was there all the time and neither he nor Taleniekov had seen it! They had approached it, circled it, used words that came close to defining it, but they had never clearly faced it.

. . . *they're capable of paralyzing governments.* . . .

When paralysis spreads, control is lost, all functions stop. A vacuum is created for a force *not* paralyzed to move into the host and assume control.

You will inherit the earth. You will have your own again. Other words, spoken by a madman seventy years ago. Yet those words were not political; they were, in fact, *apolitical.* Nor did they apply to given borders, no single nation rising to ascendency. Instead, they were directed to a council, a group of men bound together by a common bond.

But those men were dead; who were they now? And what bound them together? *Now. Today.*

"What is it?" asked Antonia, seeing the strained expression on his face.

"There *is* a timetable," said Bray, his voice barely above a whisper. "It's being orchestrated. The terrorism escalates every month, as if on schedule. Blackburn, Yurievich . . . they *were* tests, probes for reaction at the highest levels. Winthrop raised alarms in those circles; he had to be silenced. It all fits."

"And you're talking to yourself. You hold my hand, but you're talking to yourself."

Scofield looked at her, struck by another thought. He had heard two remarkable stories from two remarkable women, both tales rooted in violence as both women were tied to the violent world of Guillaume de Matarese. The dying Istrebiteli had said in Moscow that the answer might lie in Corsica. The answer did not, but the first clues to that answer did. Without Sophia Pastorine and Antonia Gravet, mistress and descendant, there was nothing; each in her own way had provided startling revelations. The enigma that was the Matarese remained still an enigma, but it was no longer inexplicable. It had form; it had purpose. Men bound together by some common cause, whose objective was to paralyze governments and assume control . . . *to inherit the earth.*

Therein lay the possibility of catastrophe: that same earth could be blown up in the process of being inherited.

"I'm talking to myself," agreed Bray, "because I've changed my mind. I said I wanted you to help me, but you've gone through enough. There are others, I'll find them."

"I see." Antonia pressed her elbows into the bed, raising herself. "Just like that, I'm no longer needed?"

"No."

"Why was I considered at all?"

Scofield paused before replying; he wondered how she would accept the truth. "You were right before; it *was* one or the other. Enlisting you or killing you."

Antonia winced. "But that is no longer true? It's not necessary to kill me?"

"No. It'd be pointless. You won't say anything. You weren't lying; I know what you've lived through. You don't want to go back; you were going to kill yourself rather than land in Marseilles. I believe you would have."

"Then what's to become of me?"

"I found you in hiding, I'll send you back in hiding. I'll give you money, and in the morning get you papers and a flight out of Rome to someplace very far away. I'll write a couple of letters; you'll give them to the people I tell you to. You'll be fine." Bray stopped for a moment. He could not help himself; he touched her swollen cheek and brushed aside a strand of hair. "You may even find another valley in a mountain, Antonia. As beautiful as the one you left, but with a difference. You won't be a prisoner there. No one from this life will ever bother you again."

"Including you, Brandon Scofield?"

"Yes."

"Then I think you had better kill me."

"What?"

"I will *not* leave! You cannot force me to, you cannot send me away because it is convenient . . . or *worse,* because you pity me!" Antonia's dark Corsican eyes glistened again. "What *right* have you? Where were you when the terrible things were done? To *me,* not to *you.* Don't make such decisions for me! Kill me first!"

"I don't want to kill you—I don't *have* to. You wanted to be free, Antonia. Take it. Don't be a damn fool."

"*You're* the fool! I can help you in ways no one else could!"

"How? The courier's whore?"

"If need be, *yes!* Why not?"

"For Christ's sake, *why?*"

The girl was rigid; her answer was spoken quietly. "Because of things you said—"

"I know," interrupted Scofield. "I told you to get angry."

"There's something else. You said that all around the world, people who believe in causes—many not wisely, many with anger and defiance—are being manipulated by others, encouraged to violence and murder. Well, I've seen something of causes. Not all are unwise, and not all believers are animals. There are those of us who want to change this unfair world, and it is our right to try! And no one has the right to turn us into whores and killers. You call these manipulators the Matarese. I say they are richer, more powerful, but no better than the Brigades, who kill children and make liars and murderers out of people like me! I *will* help you. I will *not* be sent away!"

Bray studied her face. "You're all alike," he said. "You can't stop making speeches."

Antonia smiled; it was a wry smile, engaging yet shy. "Most of the time, they're all we have." The smile disappeared, replaced by a sadness Scofield was not sure he understood. "There's another thing."

"What's that?"

"You. I've watched you. You are a man with so much sorrow. It's as clear on your face as the marks on my body. But I can remember when I was happy. Can you?"

"The question's not relevant."

"It is to me."

"Why?"

"I could say you saved my life and that would be enough, but that life wasn't worth much. You've given me something else: a reason to leave the hills. I never thought anyone could ever do that for me. You offered me freedom just now but you're too late. I already have it, you gave it to me. I am breathing again. So you're important to me. I would like you to remember when you were happy."

"Is this the courier's . . . woman speaking?"

"She is not a whore. She never was."

"I'm sorry."

"Don't be. It is permitted. And if that is the gift you want, take it. I would like to think there are others."

Bray suddenly ached. The ingenuousness of her offer moved him, pained him. She was hurt and he had hurt her again and he knew why. He was afraid; he preferred whores; he did not want to go to bed with anyone he cared about—it was better not to remember a face or recall a voice. It was far better to remain deep within the earth; he had been there so long. And now this woman wanted to pull him out and he was afraid.

"You learn the things I teach you, that'll be gift enough."

"Then you'll let me stay?"

"You just said there wasn't anything I could do about it."

"I meant that."

"I know you did. If I thought otherwise I'd be on the telephone to one of the best counterfeiters in Rome."

"Why *are* we in Rome? Will you tell me now?"

Bray did not answer for a moment; then he nodded. "Why not? To find what's left of a family named Scozzi."

"Is it one of the names my grandmother gave you?"

"The first. They were from Rome."

"They're still from Rome," said Antonia, as if commenting on the weather. "At least a branch of the family, and not far outside of Rome."

Amazed, Scofield looked at her. "How do you know?"

"The Red Brigades. They kidnapped a nephew of the Scozzi-Paravacinis from an estate near Tivoli. His index finger was cut off and sent to the family along with the ransom demand."

Scofield remembered the newspaper stories; the young man had been released, but Bray did not recall the name Scozzi, only Paravacini. However, he recalled something else: no ransom had ever been paid. The negotiations had been intense, a young life in balance. But there'd been a breakdown, a defection, a nephew released by a frightened kidnapper, several Brigatisti subsequently killed, led into an ambush by the defector.

Had the Red Brigades been taught a lesson by one of their unseen sponsors?

"Were you involved?" he asked. "In *any* way?"

"No. I was at the camp in Medicina."

"Did you overhear anything?"

"A great deal. The talk was mainly about traitors and how to kill them in brutal ways to make examples of them. The leaders always talked like that. With the Scozzi-Paravacini kidnapping it was very important to them. The traitor had been bribed by the Fascists."

"What do you mean by 'Fascists'?"

"A banker who represented the Scozzis years ago. The Paravacini interests authorized payment."

"How did he reach him?"

"With a large sum of money there are ways. Nobody really knows."

Bray got up from the bed. "I won't ask you how you're feeling, but are you up to getting out of here?"

"Of course," she replied, wincing as she swung her long legs over the side of the bed. The pain struck her; a sharp intake of breath followed. She remained still for a moment; Scofield held her shoulders.

Again he could not help himself; he touched her face. "The forty-eight hours are over," he said softly. "I'll cable Taleniekov in Helsinki."

"What does that mean?"

"It means you're alive and well and living in Rome. Come on, I'll help you dress."

She brought her fingers up to his hand. "If you had suggested that yesterday I am not sure what I'd have said."

"What do you say now?"

"Help me."

20

There was an expensive restaurant on the Via Frascati owned by the three Crispi brothers, the oldest of whom ran the establishment with the perceptions of an accomplished thief and the eyes of a hungry jackal, both masked by a cherubic face, and a sweeping ebullience. Most who inhabited the velvet lairs of Rome's *dolce vita* adored Crispi, for he was always understanding and discreet, the discretion more valuable than the sympathy. Messages left with him were passed between men and their mistresses, wives and their lovers, the makers and the made. He was a rock in the sea of frivolity, and the frivolous children of all ages loved him.

Scofield used him. Five years ago when NATO's problems had reached into Italy, Bray had put his clamp on Crispi. The restaurateur had been a willing drone.

Crispi was one of the men Bray had wanted to see before Antonia had told him about the Scozzi-Paravacinis; now it was imperative. If anyone in Rome could shed light on an aristocratic family like the Scozzi-Paravacinis, it was the effusive crown prince of foolishness that was Crispi. They would have lunch at the restaurant on the Via Frascati.

An early lunch for Rome, considered Scofield, putting down his coffee and looking at his watch. It was barely noon, the sun outside the window warming the sitting room of the hotel suite, the sounds of traffic floating up from the Via Veneto below. The doctor had called the Excelsior and made the arrangements shortly past midnight, explaining confidentially to the manager that a wealthy patient was in sudden need of quarters—confidentially. Bray and Antonia had been met at the delivery entrance and taken up the service elevator to a suite on the eighth floor.

He had ordered a bottle of brandy and poured three successive drinks for Antonia. The cumulative effects of the alcohol, the medication, the pain, and the tension had brought about the state he knew was best: sleep. He had carried her into the bedroom, undressed her, and put her to bed, covering her, touching her face, resisting the ache that would have placed him beside her.

On his way back to the couch in the sitting room he had remembered the clothes from the Via Condotti; he had stuffed them in his duffel bag before leaving the *pensione.* The white hat was the worse for the packing, but the silk dress was less wrinkled than he had thought it would be. He had hung them up before sleeping himself.

He had gotten up at ten and gone down to the shops in the lobby to buy a flesh-colored makeup base that would cover Antonia's bruises, and a pair of Gucci sunglasses that looked remarkably like the eyes of a grasshopper. He had left them along with the clothes on the chair next to the bed.

She had found them an hour ago, the dress the first thing she had seen when she opened her eyes.

"You are my personal *fanciulla!*" she had called out to him. "I am a princess in a fairy tale and my handmaidens wait upon me! What will my Socialist comrades think?"

"That you know something they don't know," Bray had replied. "They'd hang Marx in effigy to change places with you. Have some coffee and then get dressed. We're having lunch with a disciple of the Medicis. You'll love his politics."

She was dressing now, humming fragments of an unfamiliar tune that sounded like a Corsican sea chanty. She had found part of her mind again and a semblance of freedom; he hoped she could keep both. There were no guarantees. The hunt would accelerate at the restaurant in the Via Frascati and she was part of it now.

The humming stopped, replaced by the sound of high-heeled shoes crossing a marble floor. She stood in the door and the ache returned to Scofield's chest. The sight of her moved him and he felt oddly helpless. Stranger still, for a moment he wanted only to hear her speak, listen to her voice, as if hearing it would somehow confirm her immediate presence. Yet she did not speak. She stood there, lovely and vulnerable, a grown-up child seeking approval, resentful that she felt the need to seek it. The silk dress was tinged with deep red, complimenting her skin, bronzed by the Corsican sun; the large wide hat framed half her face in white, the other half bordered by her long dark-brown hair. The strains of France and Italy had merged in Antonia Gravet; the results were striking.

"You look fine," said Bray, getting up from the chair.

"Does the makeup cover the marks on my face?"

"I forgot about them so I guess it does." In the ache he *had* forgotten. "How are you feeling?"

"I'm not sure. I think the brandy did as much damage as the Brigatisti."

"There's a remedy. A few glasses of wine."

"I think not, thank you."

"Whatever you say. I'll get your coat; it's in the closet." He started across the room, then stopped, seeing her wince. "You're not all right, are you? It hurts."

"No, please, really, I'm fine. The salve your doctor friend gave me is very good, very soothing. He's a nice man."

"I want you to go back and see him anytime you need help," he said. "Whenever anything bothers you."

"You sound as though you won't be with me," she replied. "I thought we settled that. I accepted your offer of employment, remember?"

Bray smiled. "It'd be hard to forget, but we haven't defined the job. We'll be together for a while in Rome, then depending on what we find, I'll be moving on. Your job will be to stay here and relay messages between Taleniekov and me."

"I am to be a *telegraph* service?" asked Antonia. "What kind of job is that?"

"A vital one. I'll explain as we go along. Come on, I'll get your coat." He saw her close her eyes again. Pain had jolted her. "Antonia, listen to me. When you hurt, don't try to hide it, that doesn't help anybody. How bad is it?"

"Not so bad. It will pass, I know. I've been through this before."

"Do you want to go back to the doctor?"

"No. But thank you for your concern."

The ache was still there, but Scofield resisted it. "My only concern is that a person can't function well when he's hurt. Mistakes are made when he's in pain. You won't be allowed any mistakes."

"I may have that glass of wine after all."

"Please do," he said.

They stood in the foyer of the restaurant, Bray aware of the glances Antonia attracted. Beyond the delicate lattice work that was the entrance to the dining room, the oldest Crispi was all teeth and obsequiousness. When he saw Bray he was obviously startled; for a split second his eyes became clouded, serious, then he recovered and approached them.

"Benvenuto, amico mio!" he cried.

"It's been over a year," said Scofield, returning the firm grip. "I'm here on business for only a day or so, and wanted my friend to try your *fettucini.*"

These were the words that meant Bray wished to speak privately with Crispi at the table when the opportunity arose.

"It is the best in Rome, signorina!" Crispi snapped his fingers for an inferior brother to show the couple to their table. "I shall hear you say it yourself momentarily. But first, have some wine, in case the sauce is not perfect!" He winked broadly, giving Scofield's hand an additional clasp to signify he understood. Crispi never came to Bray's table unless summoned.

A waiter brought them a chilled bottle of Pouilly Fumé, compliments of the *fratelli,* but it was not until the *fettucini* had come and gone that Crispi came to the table. He sat in the third chair; introductions and the small talk that accompanied them were brief.

"Antonia's working with me," Scofield explained, "but she's never to be mentioned. To anyone, do you understand?"

"Of course."

"And neither am I. If anyone from the embassy—or anywhere else—asks about me, you haven't seen me. Is that clear?"

"Clear, but unusual."

"In fact, no one's to know I'm here. Or *was* here."

"Even your own people?"

"Especially my own people. My orders supersede embassy interests. That's as plainly as I can put it."

Crispi arched his brows, nodding slowly. "Defectors?"

"That'll do."

Crispi's eyes became serious. "Very well, I have not seen you, Brandon. Then why are you here? Will you be sending people to me?"

"Only Antonia. Whenever she needs help getting cables off to me . . . and to someone else."

"Why should she need my help to send cables?"

"I want them rerouted, different points of origin. Can you do it?"

"If the idiot *Communisti* do not strike the telephone service again, it is no problem. I call a cousin in Firenze, he sends one; an exporter in Athens or Tunis or Tel Aviv, they do the same. Everybody does what Crispi wants and no one asks a single question. But you know that."

"What about your own phones? Are they clean?"

Crispi laughed. "With what is known to be said on my telephone, there is not an official in Rome who could permit such impertinence."

Scofield remembered Robert Winthrop in Washington. "Someone else said that to me not so long ago. He was wrong."

"No doubt he was," agreed Crispi, his eyes amused. "Forgive me, Brandon, but you people deal merely in matters of state. We on the Via Frascati deal in matters of the heart. Ours take precedence where confidentiality is concerned. They always have."

Bray returned the Italian's smile. "You know, you may be right." He lifted the glass of wine to his lips. "Let me throw a name at you. Scozzi-Paravacini." He drank.

Crispi nodded reflectively. "Blood seeks money, and money seeks blood. What else is there to say?"

"Say it plainly."

"The Scozzis are one of the noblest families in Rome. The venerable contessa to this day is chauffeured in her restored Bugatti up the Veneto, her children pretenders to thrones long since abandoned. Unfortunately, all they had were their pretensions, not a thousand lire between them. The Paravacinis had money, a great deal of money, but not a drop of decent blood in their veins. It was a marriage made in the heavenly courts of mutual convenience."

"Whose marriage?"

"The contessa's daughter to Signor Bernardo Paravacini. It was a long time ago, the dowry a number of millions and gainful employment for her son, the count. He assumed his father's title."

"What's his name?"

"Guillamo. Count Guillamo Scozzi."

"Where does he live?"

"Wherever his interests—financial and otherwise—take him. He has an estate near his sister's in Tivoli, but I don't think he's there very often. Why do you ask? Is he connected with defectors? It's hardly likely."

"He may not be aware of it. It could be he's being used by people who work for him."

"Even more unlikely. Beneath his charming personality, there's the mind of a Borgia. Take my word for it."

"How do you know that?"

"I know *him,*" said Crispi, smiling. "He and I are not so different."

Bray leaned forward. "I want to meet him. Not as Scofield, of course. As someone else. Can you arrange it?"

"Perhaps. If he's in Italy, and I think he is. I read somewhere that his wife is a patron of the Festa Villa d'Este, being held tomorrow night. It is a charity affair for the gardens. He would not miss it; as they say, everyone in Rome will be there."

"Your Rome, I trust," said Scofield. "Not mine."

He watched her across the hotel room as she lifted the skirt out of the box and folded it on her lap as though checking for imperfections. He understood that the pleasure he derived from buying her things was out of place. Clothes were a necessity; it was as simple as that, but his knowing it did not erase the warmth that spread through him watching her.

The prisoner was free, the decisions restored, and although she had commented about the exorbitant prices at the Excelsior, she had not refused to let him buy clothes for her at the shops. It had been a game. She would look over at Bray; if he nodded, she would frown, feigning disapproval—invariably glancing at the price tag—then slowly re-evaluate, ultimately acknowledging his taste.

His wife used to do that in West Berlin. In West Berlin it had been one of *their* games. His Karine was always worried about money. They were going to have children one day, money was important, and the government was not a generous corporation. No Grade Twelve foreign service officer was about to open a Swiss bank account.

Of course, by then Scofield had. In Bern. And in Paris and London and, naturally, Berlin. He had not told her; his true professional life had never touched her. Until it touched her with finality. Had things been different, he might have given her one of those accounts. After he had transferred out of Consular Operations into a civilized branch of the State Department.

Goddamn it! He was *going* to! It had only been a matter of *weeks!*

"You are so far away."

"What?" Bray brought the glass to his lips; it was a reflex gesture for he had finished the drink. It occurred to him that he was drinking too much.

"You're looking at me, but I don't think you see me."

"I certainly do. I miss the hat. I liked the white hat."

She smiled. "You don't wear a hat inside. The waiter who brought us dinner would have thought me silly."

"You wore it at Crispi's place. That waiter didn't."

"A restaurant is different."

"Both inside." He got up and poured himself a drink.

"Thank you again for these." Antonia glanced at the boxes and shopping bags beside the chair. "It is like Christmas Eve, I don't know which to open next." She laughed. "But there was never a Christmas in Corsica like this! Pa*pa* would scowl for a month at the sight of such things. Yes, I *do* thank you."

"No need to." Scofield remained by the table, adding more whisky to his glass. "They're equipment. Like an office typewriter or an adding machine or file cabinets. They go with the job."

"I see." She replaced the skirt and the blouse into the box. "But you don't," she said.

"I beg your pardon?"

"*Niente.* Does the whisky help you relax?"

"You could say that. Would you like one?"

"No, thank you. I'm more relaxed than I have been in a long time. It would be wasted."

"To each according to his needs. Or wants," said Scofield, lowering himself into a chair. "You can go to bed, if you like. Tomorrow's going to be a long day."

"Does my company bother you?"

"No, of course not."

"But you prefer to be alone."

"I hadn't thought about it."

She used to say that. In West Berlin, when there were problems and I would sit by myself trying to think as others might think. She would be talking and I would not hear her. She used to get angry—not angry, hurt—and say, "You'd rather be alone, wouldn't you?" And I would, but I could not explain. Perhaps if I had explained. . . . Perhaps an explanation would have served as a warning.

"If something's troubling you, why not talk about it?"

Oh, God, her words. In West Berlin.

"Stop trying to be *somebody else!*" He heard the statement shouted in his own voice. It was the whisky, the goddamn *whisky!* "I'm sorry, I didn't mean that," he added quickly, putting the glass down. "I'm tired and I've had too much to drink. I didn't mean it."

"Of course you did," said Antonia, getting up. "I think I understand now. But you should understand also. I am not somebody else. I have had to pretend to be someone who was not me and that is the surest way to know who you are. I am myself, and you helped me—find that person again." She turned and walked rapidly into the bedroom, closing the door behind her.

"Toni, I'm *sorry.* . . ." Bray stood up, furious with himself. In an outburst, he had revealed far more than he cared to. He hated the loss of control.

There was a knock on the door, the hallway door; Scofield spun around. Instinctively he felt the holster strapped to his chest under his jacket. He went to the side of the door and spoke.

"*Si? Chi è?*"

"*Un messaggio, Signor Pastorine. Da vostro amico, Crispi. Di Via Frascati.*"

Bray put his hand inside his jacket, checked the chain on the door, and opened it. In the hallway stood the waiter from Crispi's who had served their table. He held up an envelope and handed it to Scofield through the open space. Crispi had taken no risks; his own man was the messenger.

"*Grazie. Un momento,*" said Bray, reaching into his pocket for a lire note.

"*Prego,*" replied the waiter, accepting the tip.

Scofield closed the door, and tore open the envelope. Two gold-embossed tickets were attached to a note. He removed them and read Crispi's message, the handwriting as florid as the language.

Word has reached Count Scozzi from the undersigned that an American named Pastor will introduce himself at Villa d'Este. The count understands that this Pastor has extensive connections in the OPEC countries, acting frequently as a purchasing agent for oil-soaked sheiks. These are endeavors such men never discuss, so just smile and learn where the Arabian Gulf is located. The count understands too that Pastor is merely on holiday and seeks pleasant diversions. All things considered, the count may offer them.

I kiss the hand of the bella signorina.

Ciao,
Crispi

Bray smiled. Crispi was right; no one who performed middleman services for the sheiks ever discussed those services. Profiles were kept excessively low because the stakes were excessively high. He would talk of other things with Count Guillamo Scozzi.

He heard the latch turn on the bedroom door. There was a moment of hesitation before Antonia opened it. When she did, Bray realized why. She stood in the doorframe in a black slip he had bought her downstairs. She had removed her brassiere, her breasts swelling against the sheer silk, her long legs outlined below in opaque darkness. She was barefoot, the bronzed skin of her calves and ankles in perfect concert with her arms and face. Her lovely face, striking yet gentle, with the dark eyes that held his without wavering, without judgment.

"You must have loved her very much," she said.

"I did. It was a long time ago."

"Not long enough, apparently. You called me Toni. Was that her name?"

"No."

"I'm glad. I would not wish to be mistaken for someone else."

"You made that clear. It won't happen again."

Antonia was silent, remaining motionless in the doorway, her eyes still without judgment. When she spoke, it was a question. "Why do you refuse yourself?"

"I'm not an animal in the hold of a freighter."

"We both know that. I've seen you look at me, then look away as though it were not permitted. You're tense, but you seek no release."

"If I want that kind of . . . release . . . I know where to find it."

"I offer it to you."

"The offer will be taken under consideration."

"*Stop it!*" cried Antonia, stepping forward. "You want a whore? Then think of me as a courier's *whore!*"

"I can't do that."

"Then don't look at me the way you do! A part of you with me, another far away. What do you *want?*"

Please don't do this. Leave me where I was, deep in the earth, comfort in the darkness. Don't touch me, for if you do, you die. Can't you understand that? Men will call you across a barrier and they will kill you. Leave me with whores, professionals—as I am a professional. We know the rules. You don't.

She stood in front of him; he had not seen her come to him, she was simply there. He looked down at her, her face tilted up to his, her eyes close, her tears near, her lips parted.

Her whole body was trembling; she was gripped by fear. The scars had been torn away; he had ripped them because she had seen the ache in his eyes.

She could not erase *his* pain. What made her think he could erase hers?

And then, as if she were reading his thoughts, she whispered again.

"If you loved her so much, love me a little. It may help."

She reached up to him, her hands cupping his face, her lips inches from his, the trembling no less for the nearness. He put his arms around her; their lips touched and the ache was released. He was drawn into a wind; he felt his own tears well up in his eyes and roll down his cheeks, mingling with hers. He let his hands fall down her back, caressing her, pulling her to him, holding her, *holding* her. Please, *closer,* the moisture of her mouth arousing him, replacing the ache of pain with the ache of wanting her beside him. He swept his hand around to her breast; she pulled her own hand down and pressed it over his, pushing herself against him, revolving her body to the rhythm that infused them both.

She pulled her mouth away. "Take me to bed. In the name of God, *take me*. And love me. Please love me a little."

"I tried to warn you," he said. "I tried to warn us both."

He was coming out of the earth and there was sunlight above. Yet in the distance there was the darkness still. And fear; he felt it sharply. But for the moment, he chose to remain in the sunlight—if only for a while. With her.

21

The magnificence of the Villa d'Este was not lost in the chill of the evening. The floodlights had been turned on and the banks of fountains illuminated—thousands of cascading streams caught in the light as they arced in serrated ranks down the steep inclines. In the centers of the vast pools, the geysers surged up into the night, umbrella sprays sprinkling in the floodlights like diadems. And at each formation of rock constructed into a waterfall, screens of rushing silver fell in front of ancient statuary; saints and centaurs were drenched in splendor.

The gardens were officially closed to the public; only Rome's most beautiful people were invited to the Festa Villa d'Este. The purpose was ostensibly to raise funds for its maintenance, augmenting the dwindling government subsidies, but Scofield had the distinct impression that there was a secondary, no less desirable motive: to provide an evening where Villa d'Este could be enjoyed by its true inheritors, unencumbered by the tourist world. Crispi was right. Everyone in Rome was there.

Not his Rome, thought Bray, feeling the velvet lapels of his tuxedo. Their Rome.

The huge rooms of the villa itself had been transformed into palace courtyards, complete with banquet tables and gilded chairs lining the walls—resting spots for the courtiers and courtesans at play. Russian sable and mink, chinchilla and golden fox draped shoulders dressed by Givenchy and Pucci; webs of diamonds and strings of pearls fell from elongated throats, and all too often from too many chins. Slender *cavalieri*, dashing in their scarlet cummerbunds and graying temples, coexisted with squat, bald men who held cigars and more power than their appearances might signify. Music was provided by no fewer than four orchestras ranging in size from six to twenty instruments, playing everything from the stately strains of Monteverdi to the frenzied beat of the disco. Villa d'Este belonged to the *belli Romani*.

Of all the beautiful people, one of the most striking was Antonia—Toni. (It was Toni now by dual decree, arrived at in the comfort of the bed.) No jewels adorned her neck or wrists; somehow they would have detracted from the smooth, bronzed skin set off by the simple gown of white and gold. The facial swellings had receded, as the doctor had said they would. She wore no sunglasses now, her wide brown eyes reflecting the light. She was as lovely as any part of her surroundings, lovelier than most of her would-be equals for her beauty was understated, and grew with each second of observation in the beholder's eyes.

For convenience, Toni was introduced quite simply as the rather mysterious Mr. Pastor's friend from Lake Como. Certain parts of the lake were known to be retreats for the expensive children of the Mediterranean. Crispi had done his job well; he had provided just enough information to intrigue a number of guests. Those who might wish to learn the most about the quiet Mr. Pastor were told the least while others too imbued with themselves to care about Pastor were told more, so they could relate what they had learned as gossip, which was their major industry.

Those men whose concerns were more directly—even exclusively—financial, were prone to take his elbow and inquire softly about the projected status of the dollar or the stability of investments in London, San Francisco and Buenos Aires. With such inquisitors, Scofield inclined his head briefly at some suggestions and shook it with a single motion at others. Eyebrows were raised—unobtrusively. Information had been imparted, although Bray had no idea what it was.

After one such encounter with a particularly insistent questioner he took Toni's arm and they walked through a massive archway into the next crowded "courtyard." Accepting two glasses of champagne from a waiter's tray, Bray handed one to Toni and looked around over the crystal rim as he drank.

Without having seen him before Scofield knew he had just found Count Guillamo Scozzi. The Italian was in a corner chatting with two long-legged young women, his eyes roaming from their attentive stares, glancing about the room with feigned casualness. He was a tall, slender man, a *cavaliere* complete with tails and graying hair that spread in streaks from his temples throughout his perfectly groomed head. In his lapel were tiny colorful ribbons, around his waist a thin gold sash, bordered in dark red and knotted off-center. If any missed the significance of the ribbons, they could not overlook the mark of distinction inherent in the sash; Scozzi wore his escutcheons prominently. In his late fifties the count was the embodiment of the *bello Romano;* no *Siciliano* had ever crept into the bed of his ancestors and *per Dio* the world had better know it.

"How will you find him?" asked Antonia, sipping the wine.

"I think I just have."

"Him? Over there?" she asked. Bray nodded. "You're right. I've seen his picture in the newspapers. He's a favorite subject of the *paparazzi.* Are you going to introduce yourself?"

"I don't think I'll have to. Unless I'm mistaken, he's looking for me." Scofield gestured toward a buffet table. "Let's walk over to the end table, by the pastries. He'll see us."

"But how would he know you?"

"Crispi. Our benevolent intermediary may not have bothered to describe me, but he sure as hell wouldn't overlook describing you. Not with someone like Scozzi."

"But I had those huge sunglasses on."

"You're very funny," said Bray.

It took less than a minute before they heard a mellifluous voice behind them at the buffet table. "Signore Pastor, I believe."

They turned. "I beg your pardon? Have we met?" Scofield asked.

"We were about to, I think," said the count, extending his hand. "Scozzi.

Guillamo Scozzi. It is a pleasure to make your acquaintance." The title was emphasized by its absence.

"Oh, of *course*. Count Scozzi. I told that delightful fellow Crispi I'd look you up. We arrived here less than an hour ago and it's been a little hectic. I would have recognized you, naturally, but I'm surprised you knew me."

Scozzi laughed, displaying teeth so white and so perfectly formed they could not possibly have come with the original machine. "Crispi is, indeed, delightful, but I'm afraid a bit of a rascal. He was rapturous over *la bella signorina.*" The count inclined his head to Antonia. "I see her, I find you. As always, Crispi's taste is impeccable."

"Excuse me." Scofield touched Toni's forearm. "Count Scozzi, my friend, Antonia . . . from Lake Como." The first name and the lake said it all; the count took her hand and raised it to his lips.

"An adorable creature. Rome must see more of you."

"You're too kind, Excellency," said Antonia, as if born to attend the Festa Villa d'Este.

"Truthfully, Mister Pastor," continued Scozzi. "I've been told that many of my more brothersome friends have been annoying you with questions. I apologize for them."

"No need to. I'm afraid Crispi's descriptions included more mundane matters." Bray smiled with disarming humility. "When people learn what I do, they ask questions. I'm used to it."

"You're very understanding."

"It's not hard to be. I just wish I were as knowledgeable as so many think I am. Usually I simply try to implement decisions made before I got there."

"But in those decisions," said the count, "there is knowledge, is there not?"

"I hope so. Otherwise an awful lot of money's being thrown away."

"Blown away with the desert winds, as it were," clarified Scozzi. "Why do I think we actually *have* met before, Mister Pastor?"

The sudden question had been considered by Scofield; it was always a possibility and he was prepared for it. "If we had I think I'd remember, but it might have been the American Embassy. Those parties were never as grand as this, but just as crowded."

"Then you are a fixture on Embassy Row?"

"Hardly a fixture, but sometimes a last-minute guest." Bray smiled self-deprecatingly. "It seems there are times when my countrymen are as interested in asking me questions as your friends here in Tivoli."

Scozzi chuckled. "Information is often the road to heroic national stature, Mister Pastor. You are a reluctant hero."

"Not really. I have to make a living, that's all."

"I would not care to negotiate with you," said Scozzi. "I detect the mind of an experienced bargainer."

"That's too bad," replied Scofield, altering the tone of his voice just enough to signal the Italian's inner antenna. "I thought we might talk for a bit."

"Oh?" The count glanced at Antonia. "But we bore the *bella signorina.*"

"Not at all," said Toni. "I've learned more about my friend during the last several minutes than for the past week. But I *am* famished—"

"Say no more," interrupted Scozzi, as if her hunger were a matter of corporate survival. He raised his hand. In seconds a young, dark-haired man dressed in tails appeared beside him. "My aide will see to your needs, signorina. His name is Paolo and, incidentally, he is a charming dancer. I believe my wife taught him."

Paolo bowed, avoiding the count's eyes, and offered his arm to Antonia. She accepted it, stepping forward, her face turned to Scozzi and Bray.

"*Ciao,*" she said, her eyes wishing Scofield good hunting.

"You are to be envied, Mister Pastor," remarked Count Guillamo Scozzi, watching the receding figure in white. "She *is* adorable. You bought her in Como?"

Bray glanced at the Italian. Scozzi meant exactly what he said. "To be honest with you, I'm not even sure she's ever been there," he answered, knowing the double lie was mandatory; the count could make inquiries too easily. "Actually, a friend in Ar-Riyād gave me a number to call at the lake. She joined me in Nice. From where I've never asked."

"Would you consider, however, asking her about her calendar? Tell her for me the sooner the better. She may reach me through the Paravacini offices in Torino."

"Turin?"

"Yes, our plants in the north. Agnelli's Fiat gets far more attention, but I can assure you, Scozzi-Paravacini runs Turin—as well as a great deal of Europe."

"I never realized that."

"You didn't? I thought it was perhaps the basis for your wishing to . . . 'talk for a bit,' I believe you said."

Scofield drank the last of his champagne, speaking as he took the glass from his lips. "Do you think we might go outside for a minute or two? I have a confidential message for you from a client on—let's say, the Arabian Gulf. It's why I'm here tonight."

Scozzi's eyes clouded. "A message for me? Naturally, as most of Rome and Torino, I've met casually with a number of gentlemen from the area, but none I can recall by name. But, of course, we'll take a stroll. You intrigue me." The count started forward, but Bray stopped him with a gesture.

"I'd rather we weren't seen going out together. Tell me where you'll be and I'll show up in twenty minutes."

"How extraordinary. Very well." The Italian paused. "Ippolito's Fountain. Do you know it?"

"I'll find it."

"It's quite a distance. There shouldn't be anyone around."

"That's fine. Twenty minutes." Scofield nodded. Both turned and walked away in opposite directions through the crowd.

There were no floodlights at the fountain or sounds of disturbance as a man crawled around the rocks and walked silently through the foliage. Bray was taking no chances that Scozzi had stationed aides in the vicinity. If he had, Scofield would have sent a message to the Italian, naming a second, immediate rendez-vous.

They were alone—or would be in a matter of minutes. The count was strolling down the path toward the fountain. Bray doubled back through a weed-filled garden, emerging on the path fifty feet behind Scozzi. He cleared his throat the moment Scozzi reached the waist-high wall of the fountain's pool. The count turned; there was just enough light from the terraces above for each to see the other. Scofield was bothered by the darkness. Scozzi could have chosen any number of places more convenient, less filled with shadows. Bray did not like shadows.

"Was it necessary to come down this far?" he asked. "I wanted to see you alone, but I hadn't figured on walking halfway back to Rome."

"Nor had I, Mr. Pastor, until you made the statement that you did not care to have us seen leaving together. It brought to my mind the obvious. It is, perhaps, not to my advantage to be seen talking in private with you. You are a broker for the sheiks."

"Why should that bother you?"

"Why did you wish to leave separately?"

Scozzi had a quick mind, bearing out Crispi's allusion to a Borgia mentality. "A matter of being *too* obvious, I'd say. But if someone wandered down here and saw us, that would also be too obvious. There's a middle ground, a casual encoun-ter in the gardens, for example."

"You have the encounter and no one will see us," said the count. "There is only one entrance to the fountain of Ippolito; it is forty meters behind us. I have an aide standing there. Guillamo Scozzi has been known to stroll with a compan-ion of his choice down—if you will—a primrose path. At such times he does not care to be disturbed."

"Does my doing what I do call for those precautions?"

The count raised his hand. "Remember, Mr. Pastor. Scozzi-Paravacini deals throughout all Europe and both Americas. We look constantly for new markets, but we do not look for Arab capital. It is highly suspect; barriers are being erected everywhere to prevent its excessive infusion. We would not come to be so scrutinized. Jewish interests in Paris and New York alone could cost us dearly."

"What I have to say to you has nothing to do with Scozzi-Paravacini," said Scofield. "It concerns the Scozzi part, not the Paravacini."

"You allude to a sensitive area, Mr. Pastor. Please be specific."

"You are the son of Count Alberto Scozzi, aren't you?"

"It is well known. As are my contributions to the growth of Paravacini Indus-tries. The significance of the corporate conversion to the name of *Scozzi-*Paravacini is, I trust, not lost on you."

"It isn't, but even if it were, it doesn't matter. I'm only a go-between, sup-posedly the first of several contacts, each further removed from the next. As far as I'm concerned, I ran into you casually at a charity affair in Tivoli. We never had this talk."

"Your message must, indeed, be dramatic. Who sends it?"

It was Bray's turn to raise his hand. "Please. As we understand the rules, identities are never specific at the first conference. Only a geographical area and a political equation that involves hypothetical antagonists."

Scozzi's eyes narrowed; the lids fell in concentration. "Go on," he said.

"You're a count, so I'll bend the rules a bit. Let's say there's a prince living in a sizeable country, a sheikdom, really, on the Gulf. His uncle, the king, is from another era; he's old and senile but his word is law, just as it was when he led a Bedouin tribe in the desert. He's squandering millions with bad investments, depleting the sheikdom's resources, taking too much out of the ground too quickly. This hypothetical prince would like him removed. For everyone's good. He appeals to the council through the son of Alberto Scozzi, named for the Corsican *padrone*, Guillaume. . . . That's the message. Now I'd like to speak for myself."

"Who *are* you?" asked the Italian, his eyes now wide. "Who *sent* you?"

"Let me finish," said Bray quickly. He had to get past the initial jolt, jump to a second plateau. "As an observer of this . . . hypothetical equation, I can tell you it's reached a crisis. There isn't a day to lose. The prince needs an answer and, frankly, if I bring it to him, I'll be a much richer man for it. You, of course, can name the council's price. And I can tell you that . . . fifty million, American, is not out of the question."

"Fifty *million.*"

It worked; the second plateau was reached. Even for a man like Guillamo Scozzi, the amount was staggering. His arrogant lips were parted in amazement. It was the moment to complicate, to stun again.

"The sum is conditional, of course. It's a maximum figure that presumes an immediate answer, eliminating subsequent contacts, and delivery of the package within seven days. It won't be easy. The old man is guarded day and night by *sabathi*—they're a collection of mad dogs who . . ." Scofield paused. "But then, I don't have to tell you about anything related to Hasan ibn-al-Sabbah, do I? From what I gather, the Corsican drew on him pretty extensively. At any rate, the prince suggests a programmed suicide—"

"*Enough!*" whispered Scozzi. "Who *are* you, Pastor? Is the name to mean something to me? Pastor? *Priest?* Are you a high priest sent to *test* me?" The Italian's voice rose stridently. "You talk of things buried in the past. How *dare you!*"

"I'm talking about fifty million American dollars. And don't tell me—or my client—about things buried. His father was buried with his throat slit from chin to collarbone by a maniac sent by the council. Check your records, if you keep them; you'll find it. My client wants his own back again and he's willing to pay roughly fifty times what his father's brother paid." Bray stopped for a moment and shook his head in disapproval and sudden frustration. "This is crazy! I told him for less than half the amount I could buy him a legitimate revolution, sanctioned by the United Nations. But he wants it *this* way. With you. And I think I know why. He said something to me; I don't know if it's part of his message but I'll deliver it anyway. He said, 'The way of the Matarese is the only way. They'll see my faith.' He wants to join you."

Guillamo Scozzi recoiled; his legs were pressed against the wall of the fountain, his arms rigidly at his side. "What right have you to say these things to me? You're insane, a madman! I don't know what you're talking about."

"Really? Then we've got the wrong man. We'll find the right one; I'll find him. We were given the words; we know the response."

"What words?"

"*Per nostro . . .*" Scofield let his voice trail off, his eyes riveted on Scozzi's lips in the dim light.

Involuntarily, the lips parted. The Italian was about to utter the third word, complete the phrase that had lived for seventy years in the remote hills of the Porto Vecchio. . . .

No word came. Instead, Scozzi whispered again, shock replaced by a concern so deeply felt he could barely be heard. "My *God.* You cannot . . . you *must* not. Where have you *come* from? What have you been *told?*"

"Just enough to know I've found the right man. One of them, at any rate. Do we deal?"

"Do not presume, Mr. Pastor! Or whatever your name is." There was fury now in the Italian's voice.

"Pastor'll do. All right, I've got my answer. You pass. I'll tell my client." Bray turned.

"*Alto!*"

"*Perchè? Che cosa?*" Scofield spoke over his shoulder without moving.

"Your Italian is very quick, very fluent."

"So are several other languages. It helps when you travel a lot. I travel a lot. What do you want?"

"You will stay here until I say you may leave."

"Really?" said Scofield, turning to face Scozzi again. "What's the point? I've got my answer."

"You'll do as I tell you. I have only to raise my voice and an aide will be beside you, blocking any departure you may consider."

Bray tried to understand. This powerful *consigliere* could deny everything—he had, after all, said nothing—and have a strange American followed. Or he could call for help; or he might simply walk away himself and send armed men to find him. He could do any of these things—he *was* part of the Matarese; the admission was in his eyes—but he chose to do none of them.

Then Scofield thought he did understand. Guillamo Scozzi, the quick thinking industrial pirate with the Borgia mentality, was not sure what he should do. He was caught in a dilemma that suddenly had overwhelmed him. It had all happened too fast, he was not prepared to make a decision. So he made none.

Which meant that there was someone else—someone nearby, accessible—who *could.*

Someone at Villa d'Este that night.

"Does this mean that you're reconsidering?" asked Bray.

"It means *nothing!*"

"Then why should I stay? I don't think you should give orders to me, I'm not one of your Praetorians. We don't deal; it's as simple as that."

"It is *not* that simple!" Scozzi's voice rose again, fear more pronounced than anger now.

"I say it is, and I say the hell with it," said Scofield, turning again. It was important that the Italian summon his unseen guard. Very important.

Scozzi did so. *"Veni! Presto!"*

Bray heard racing feet on the dark path; in seconds a broad-shouldered, stocky man in evening clothes came running out of the shadows.

"Sorveglia quest'uomo!"

The guard did not hesitate. He pulled out a short-barreled revolver, leveling it at Bray. Scozzi spoke, as if superimposing a control on himself, explaining the unnecessary.

"These are troubled times, Signore Pastore. All of us travel with these Praetorians you just mentioned. Terrorists are everywhere."

The moment was irresistible. It was the instant to insert the final, verbal blade. "That's something you people should know about. Terrorists, I mean. Like the Brigades. Do the orders come from the shepherd boy?"

It was as though Scozzi had been struck by an unseen hammer. His upper body convulsed, fending off the blow, feeling its impact, trying to recover but not sure it was possible. In the dim light, Scofield could see perspiration forming at the Italian's hairline, matting the perfectly groomed gray temples. His eyes were the eyes of a terrified animal.

"Rimanere," he whispered to the guard, then rushed away up the dark path.

Scofield turned to the man, looking afraid and speaking in Italian. "I don't know what this is all about any more than you do! I offered your boss a lot of money from someone and he goes crazy. Christ, I'm just a salesman!" The guard said nothing, but Bray's obvious fear relieved him. "Do you mind if I have a cigarette? Guns scare the hell out of me."

"Go ahead," said the broad-shouldered man.

It was the last thing he would say for several hours. Scofield reached into his pocket with his left hand, his right at his side—in shadow, under the guard's elbow. As he pulled out a pack of cigarettes, he shot his right hand up, clasping his fingers around the barrel of the guard's revolver, twisting hand and weapon violently in a counterclockwise motion. Dropping the cigarettes, he gripped the man's throat with his left hand, choking off all sound, propelling the guard off the path, over the bordering rocks into the dense foliage beyond. As the man fell, Bray ripped the gun away from the twisted wrist, and brought the handle down sharply on the man's skull. The guard went limp; Scofield pulled him farther into the weeds.

No second could be wasted. Guillamo Scozzi had raced away seeking council; it was the only explanation. Somewhere alone, on a terrace or in a room, the *consigliere* was bringing his shocking information to another. Or others.

Bray ran up the path, keeping in the shadows as much as possible, slowing down to a rapid walk as he emerged on the plateau of terraces that fronted the final incline of steps into the villa itself. Somewhere just above, *somewhere* was the panicked Scozzi. To whom was he running? Who could make the decision this powerful, frightened man was incapable of making?

Scofield took the steps rapidly, the guard's revolver in his trouser pocket, his Browning strapped to his chest beneath his tuxedo. He walked through the French doors into a crowded room; it was the "courtyard" devoted anachronistically to the crashing sounds of the disco beat. Revolving, mirrored globes of colored lights hung from the ceiling, spinning crazily, as dancers weaved together, their faces set in rigid expressions, lost in the beat and grass and alcohol.

This was the nearest room to the most direct set of steps from the closest terrace to the path from Ippolito's Fountain. In Scozzi's state of mind it *had* to be the one he entered first; there were two entrances. Which had he taken?

There was a break in the movement on the dance floor, and Bray had his answer. There was a heavy door in the wall behind a long buffet table. Two men were rushing toward it; they had been summoned; an alarm had been raised.

Scofield made his way to the door, excusing himself around the rim of frenzied bodies, and slowly pushed it open, his hand on the Browning under his jacket. Beyond was a narrow winding staircase of thick reddish stone; he could hear footsteps above.

There were other sounds as well. Men were shouting, two voices raised in counterpoint, one stronger, calmer; the other on the verge of hysteria. The latter voice was Count Guillamo Scozzi's.

Bray started up the steps, pressing his back against the wall, the Browning held at his side. Around the first curve was a door, but the voices did not come from within it; they were farther up, beyond a second door, diagonally above on a third landing. Scozzi was screaming now. Scofield was close enough to hear the words clearly.

"He spoke of the *Brigades*, and—oh my *God*—of the *shepherd!* Of the *Corsicans!* He *knows!* Mother of Christ, he *knows!*"

"*Silence!* He probes, he does not know. We were told he might do so; the old man called for him, and *he* had certain facts. More than we presumed, and that is troublesome, I grant you."

"*Troublesome?* It's *chaos!* A word, a hint, a breath, and I could be *ruined!* Everywhere!"

"You?" said the stronger voice contemptuously. "You are nothing, Guillamo! You are only what we tell you, you are. Remember that. . . . You walked away, of course. You gave him no inkling that there was a shred of credibility to what he said."

There was a pause. "I called my guard, told the American to remain where he was. He is under the gun, still by the fountain."

"You *what?* You left him with a *guard?* An *American?* Are you *mad?* That is impossible. He is no such thing!"

"He's American, of course he is! His English is American—*completely* American. He uses the name Pastor, I told you that!"

Another pause, this one ominous, the tension electric. "You were always the weakest link, Guillamo; we know that. But now you've caved in too far. You've left an open question where there can be *none!* That man is Vasili Taleniekov! He changes languages as a chameleon alters its colors, and he will kill a guard with no more effort than stepping on a maggot. We cannot afford you, Guillamo. There can be no link at all. None whatsoever."

Silence . . . brief, cut short by a gunshot and a guttural explosion of breath. Guillamo Scozzi was dead.

"Leave him!" commanded the unknown *consigliere* of the Matarese. "He'll be found in the morning, his car at the bottom of the gorge of Hadrian. Go find this 'Pastor,' this elusive Taleniekov! He won't be taken alive, don't try. Find him. Kill him. . . . And the girl in white. She, also. Kill them both."

Scofield lunged down the narrow staircase, around the curve. The last words he heard from beyond the door above, however, were so strange, so arresting, he nearly stopped, tempted to fire at the emerging killers and go back up to face the unknown man, who spoke them.

". . . *Scozzi!* Mother of Christ! Reach Turin. Tell them to cable the eagles, the cat. The burials must be absolute. . . ."

There was no time to think, he had to reach Antonia; he had to get them out of Villa d'Este. He pulled back the door and rushed out into the pounding madness. Suddenly, he was aware of the row of chairs lined up against the wall, most were empty, some draped with discarded capes and furs and stoles.

If he could eliminate one pursuer the advantage would be several fold. One man sending out an alarm would be far less effective than two. And there was something else. A trapped man convinced he was about to lose his life would more than likely reveal an identity to save it. He turned into the wall, his hands on the rim of a chair, a *cavaliere* with too much wine in him.

The heavy door burst open and the first of the two killers raced out, his companion close behind. The first man headed for the French doors and the steps to the terrace below; the second started around the edge of the dance floor toward the far archway.

Scofield leaped forward, twisting his body in a series of contortions as though he were a lone dancer gone wild with the percussive sounds of the rock music; he was not the only picture of drunkenness; there were more than a few on the crowded dance floor. He reached the second man and threw his arm over a shoulder, clamping his hand on the holster beneath the jacket, immobilizing the weapon inside it by gripping the handle through the cloth, forcing the barrel into the man's chest. The Italian struggled; it was useless and in seconds he knew it. Bray surged his right hand along the edge of the man's waist and dug his fingers into the base of the rib cage, yanking back with such force that the man screamed.

The scream went unnoticed for there were screams everywhere, and deafening music and revolving lights that blinded one moment, leaving residues of white the next. Scofield pulled the man back to the row of chairs against the wall and spun him around, forcing him down into the one at the end nearest the heavy door. He plunged his fingers into the Italian's throat, his left hand now under the jacket, his fingers inching toward the trigger, the barrel still jammed into the man's flesh. He put his lips next to the killer's ear.

"The man upstairs! Who *is* he? Tell me, or your own gun will blow your lungs out! The shot won't even be heard in here! Who *is* he?"

"No!" The man tried to arch out of the chair; Bray sunk his kneecap into the rising groin, his fingers choking the windpipe. He pressed both; pain without release or relief.

"I warn you and it's final! *Who is he?"*

Saliva poured out of the man's mouth, his eyes two circles of red webs, his chest heaving in surrender. He abandoned his cause, and he expelled the name in a strained whisper.

"Paravacini."

Bray viced a last clamp on the killer's windpipe; the air to the lungs and the head was suspended for slightly more than two seconds; the man fell limp. Scofield angled him down over the adjacent chair; one more drunken *bello Romano.*

He turned and threaded his way through the narrow path between the row of chairs and the jagged line of fever-pitched dancers. The first man had gone outside; Bray could roam freely for a minute or two, but no longer. He pressed his way through the crowd in the entranceway and walked into a less-frenzied gathering in the next room.

He saw her in the corner, the dark-haired Paolo standing next to her, two other *cavalieri* in front, all vying for her attention. Paolo, however, seemed less insistent; he knew future possessions when he saw them, where his count was concerned. The first thought that came to Bray's mind was that Toni's dress had to be covered.

. . . the girl in white. She, also. Kill them both. . . .

He walked rapidly up to the foursome, knowing precisely what he would do. A diversion was needed, the more hysterical the better. He touched Paolo's arm, his eyes on Antonia, his look telling her to stay quiet.

"You *are* Paolo, aren't you?" he asked the dark-haired man in Italian.

"Yes, sir."

"Count Guillamo wants to see you right away. It's some kind of emergency, I think."

"Of course! Where is he, sir?"

"Go through the arch over there and turn right, past a row of chairs, to a door. There's a staircase. . . ." The young Italian rushed away; Bray excused Toni and himself from the remaining two men. He held her arm and propelled her toward the arch that led into the disco.

"What's happening?" she asked.

"We're leaving," he answered. "Inside here, there are some coats and things on the chairs. Grab the darkest and the largest one you can find. Quickly, we haven't much time."

She found a long black cape, as Bray stood between her and the contortionists on the dance floor. She bunched it under her arm and they elbowed their way to the French doors and the steps outside.

"Here, put it on," ordered Scofield, draping it over her shoulders. "Let's go," he said, starting down the steps. "We'll cut through the terraces to the right and back inside through the hall to the parking . . ."

Screams erupted from inside. Men shouted, women shrieked, and within seconds figures in various stages of drunkenness surged out of doors, colliding with each other. There was sudden chaos inside and the panicked words were clear.

E stato ucciso!

Terroristi!

Fuggiamo!

The body of Count Guillamo Scozzi had been found.

Bray and Antonia raced down to the first level of terrace, and began running by a wall filled with ornate planter boxes. At the end of the enclosure there was a narrow opening into the next. Scofield held her hand and pulled her through.

"Alto! You stay!"

The shout came from above; the first man who had rushed out of the door only minutes before stood on the stone steps, a weapon in his hand. Bray slammed his shoulder into Antonia, sending her crashing into the wall. He dove to his right on the concrete, rolled to his left, and yanked the Browning from his holster. The man's shots exploded the ancient stone above Scofield; Bray aimed from his back, his shoulders off the pavement, his right hand steadied by his left. He fired twice; the killer fell forward, tumbling down the steps.

The gunshots accelerated the chaos; screams of terror filled the elegant terraces of the Villa d'Este. Bray reached Antonia; she was crouching by the wall.

"Are you all right?"

"I'm alive."

"Come on!"

They found a break in the wall where a trough carried a rushing stream of water to a pool below. They stepped through and ran down the side of the manmade rivulet to the first path, an alleyway, bordered on both sides by what appeared to be hundreds of stone statues spewing arcs of water in unison. The floodlights filtered through the trees; the scene was eerily peaceful, juxtaposed to but not affected by the stampeding chaos from the terraces above.

"Straight through!" said Scofield. "At the end there's a waterfall and another staircase. It'll get us back up there."

They started running through the tunnel of foliage, mist from the arcs of water joining the sweat on their faces.

"*Dannazione!*" Antonia fell, the long black cape torn from her shoulders by a branch of sapling. Bray stopped and pulled her up.

"*Ecco la!*"

"*La donna!*"

Shouts came from behind them; gunshots followed. Two men came running through the water-filled alleyway; they were targets, silhouetted by the light from the fountain beyond. Scofield fired three rounds. One man fell, holding his thigh; the second grabbed his shoulder, his gun flying out of his hand as he dove for the protection of the nearest statue.

Bray and Antonia reached the staircase at the end of the path. An entrance of the villa. They ran up, taking the steps two at a time, until they joined the panicked crowds rushing out through the enclosed courtyard into the huge parking lot.

Chauffeurs were everywhere, standing by elegant automobiles, protecting them, waiting for sight of their employers—and as with all chauffeurs in Italy in these times, their guns were drawn; protection was everything. They had been schooled; they were prepared.

One, however, was not prepared enough. Bray approached him. "Is this Count Scozzi's car?" he asked breathlessly.

"No, it is not, signore! Stand back!"

"Sorry." Scofield took a step away from the man, sufficiently to allay his fears, then lunged forward, hammering the barrel of his automatic into the side of the chauffeur's skull. The man collapsed. "Get in!" he yelled to Antonia. "Lock the doors and stay on the floor until we're out of here."

It took them nearly a quarter of an hour before they reached the highway out of Tivoli. They sped down the road for six miles, then took an offshoot to the right that was free of traffic. Bray pulled over to the side of the road, stopped, and for several minutes let his head fall back against the seat and closed his eyes. The pounding lessened; he sat up, reached into his pocket for his cigarettes, and offered one to Antonia.

"Normally, I do not," she said. "But right now I will. What happened?"

He lighted both their cigarettes and told her, ending with the murder of Guillamo Scozzi, the enigmatic words he had heard on the staircase, and the identity of the man who spoke them. Paravacini. The specifics were clear, the conclusions less so. He could only speculate.

"They thought I was Taleniekov; they'd been warned about him. But they knew nothing about *me*, my name was never mentioned. It doesn't make sense; Scozzi described an American. They should have known."

"Why?"

"Because Washington and Moscow both knew Taleniekov was coming after me. They tried to trap us; they failed, and so they had to presume we made contact. . . ." Or did they? wondered Scofield. The only one who actually *knew* he and the Russian had made contact was Robert Winthrop, and if he was alive, his silence could be counted upon. The rest of the intelligence community had only hearsay evidence to go on; no one had actually seen them together. Still, the presumption had to be made, unless "They think I'm dead," he said out loud, staring through the cigarette smoke to the windshield. "It's the only explanation. Someone told them I was dead. That's what 'impossible' meant."

"Why would anyone do that?"

"I wish I knew. If it were purely an intelligence maneuver, it could be for a reason as basic as buying time, throwing the opposition off, your own trap to follow. But this isn't that kind of thing, it couldn't be. The Matarese has lines into Soviet and U.S. operations—I don't doubt it for a minute—but not the other way around. I don't understand."

"Could whoever it was think you *are* dead?"

Bray looked at her, his mind racing. "I don't see how. Or why. It's a damn good idea but I didn't think of it. To pull off a burial without a corpse takes a lot of doing."

Burial. . . . The burials must be absolute.

Reach Turin. . . . Tell them to cable the eagles, the cat.

Turin. Paravacini.

"Have you thought of something?" asked Antonia.

"Something else," he replied. "This Paravacini. He runs the Scozzi-Paravacini companies in Turin?"

"He did once. And in Rome and Milan, New York and Paris, as well. All over. He married the Scozzi daughter and as time went on her brother, the count, assumed more and more control. The count's the one who ran the companies. At least, that's what the newspapers said."

"It's what Paravacini wanted them to say. It wasn't true. Scozzi was a well-put-together figurehead."

"Then he wasn't part of the Matarese?"

"Oh, he was part of it all right, in some ways the most important part. Unless I'm wrong, he brought it with him. He and his mother, the contessa, presented it to Paravacini along with his blueblooded new wife. But now we come to the real question. Why would a man like Paravacini even listen? Men like Paravacini need, above all things . . . political stability. They pour fortunes into governments that have it and candidates who promise it—because they lose fortunes when it isn't there. They look for strong authoritarian regimes, capable of stamping out a Red Brigades or a Baader-Meinhof no matter how indiscriminate the process, or how much legitimate dissent goes down with them."

"That government does not exist in Italy," interrupted Antonia.

"And in not many other places, either. That's what doesn't make sense. The Paravacinis of this world thrive on law and order. They have nothing to gain by, or nothing to substitute *for*, its breakdown. Yet the Matarese is against all that.

It wants to *paralyze* governments; it feeds the terrorists, funnels money to them, spreads the paralysis as quickly as possible." Scofield drew on his cigarette. The clearer some things became, the more obscure did others.

"You're contradicting yourself, Bray." Antonia touched his arm; it had become a perfectly natural gesture during the past twenty-four hours. "You say Paravacini *is* the Matarese. Or part of it."

"He is. That's what's missing. The reason."

"Where do you look for it?"

"Not here any longer. I'll ask the doctor to pick up our things at the Excelsior. We're getting out."

"We?"

Scofield took her hand. "Tonight changed a lot of things. *La bella signorina* can't stay in Rome now."

"Then I can go with *you.*"

"As far as Paris," said Bray hesitantly, the hesitation not born of doubt, only of how to arrange the avenues of communication in Paris. "You'll stay there. I'll work out the procedures and get you a place to stay."

"Where will you go?"

"London. We know about Paravacini now; he's the Scozzi factor. London's next."

"Why there?"

"Paravacini said Turin was to cable 'the eagles, the cat.' With what your grandmother told us in Corsica, that code isn't hard to figure out. One eagle is my country, the other Taleniekov's."

"It doesn't follow," disagreed Antonia. "Russia is the bear."

"Not in this case. The Russian bear is Bolshevik, the Russian eagle, Tzarist. The third guest at Villa Matarese in April of nineteen eleven was a man named Voroshin. Prince Andrei Voroshin. From St. Petersburg. That's Leningrad now. Taleniekov's on his way there."

"And the 'cat'?"

"The British lion. The second guest, Sir John Waverly. A descendant, David Waverly, is England's Foreign Secretary."

"A very high position."

"Too high, too visible. It doesn't make sense for him to be involved, either. Any more than the man in Washington, a senator who will probably be President next year. And because it doesn't make sense, it scares the hell out of me." Scofield released her hand, and reached for the ignition. "We're getting closer. Whatever there is to be found under the two eagles and the cat may be harder to dig out, but it's there. Paravacini made that clear. He said the 'burials' had to be 'absolute.' He meant that all the connections had to be re-examined, put farther out of reach."

"You'll be in a great deal of danger." She touched his arm again.

"Nowhere near as much as Taleniekov. As far as the Matarese is concerned, I'm dead, remember? He's not. Which is why we're going to send our first cable. To Helsinki. We've got to warn him."

"About what?"

"That anyone prowling around Leningrad looking for information about an illustrious old St. Petersburg family named Voroshin will probably get his head blown off." Bray started the car. "It's wild," he said. "We're going after the inheritors—or we think we are—because we've got their names. But there's someone else, and I don't think any of them mean much without him."

"Who is that?"

"A shepherd boy. He's the one we've really got to find, and I don't have the vaguest idea of how to do it."

22

Taleniekov walked to the middle of the block on Helsinki's Itä Kaivopuisto, noting the lights of the American Embassy down the street. The sight of the building was appropriate; he had been thinking of Beowulf Agate off and on for most of the day.

It had taken him most of the day to absorb the news in Scofield's cable. The words themselves were innocuous, a salesman's report to an executive of a home office regarding Italian imports of Finnish crystal, but the new information was startling and complex. Scofield had made extraordinary progress in a very short time.

He had found the first connection; it *was* a Scozzi—the first name on the guest list of Guillaume de Matarese—and the man was dead, killed by those who controlled him. Therefore, the American's assumption in Corsica that the members of the Matarese council were not born, but selected, proved accurate. The Matarese had been taken over, a mixture of descendants and usurpers. It was consistent with the dying words of Aleksie Krupskaya in Moscow.

The Matarese was dormant for years. No one could make contact. Then it came back, but it was not the same. Killings . . . without clients, senseless butchery without a pattern . . . governments paralyzed.

This was, indeed, a new Matarese and infinitely more deadly than a cult of fanatics dedicated to paid political assassination. And Beowulf had added a warning in his cable. The Matarese now assumed that the guest list had been found; the stalking of the Voroshin family in Leningrad was infinitely more complicated than it might have been only days ago.

Men were waiting in Leningrad for someone to ask questions about the Voroshins. But not the men—or man—he would reach, thought Taleniekov, stamping his feet against the cold, looking for a sign of the automobile and the man who was to meet him and drive him east along the coast past Hamina toward the Soviet border.

Scofield was on his way to Paris with the girl, the American to continue on to England after setting up procedures in France. The Corsican woman had passed whatever tests Beowulf Agate had created; she would live and be their conduit. But, as Vasili was beginning to learn, Scofield rarely operated on a simple line; there was a third party, the manager of the Tavastian Hotel in Helsinki.

Once in Leningrad, Taleniekov was to cable the manager with whatever particulars he could put into ciphers and the man, in turn, would wait for direct telephone calls from Paris and relate the codes received from Leningrad. It was then up to the woman to reach Scofield in England. Vasili knew that monitoring cable traffic was a particular talent of the KGB; the only sure way to eliminate it was to use KGB equipment. Somehow, he would find a way to do that.

An automobile pulled up to the curb, the headlights dimming once, the driver wearing a red muffler, one end draped over a dark leather jacket. Taleniekov crossed the pavement and got in the front seat beside the driver. He was on his way back to Russia.

The town of Vainikala was on the northwest shore of the lake; across the water was the Soviet Union, the southeast banks patroled by teams of soldiers and dogs plagued more often by ennui than by threats of penetration or escape. When the KGB first knew about it, prolonged exposure to the freezing winds during winter months made it simply too dangerous to use as an escape route; and in summer the interminable flow of tourist visas in and out of Tallin and Riga, to say nothing of Leningrad itself, made those cities the easiest avenues to freedom. As a result the northwest garrisons along the Finnish border were staffed by the least motivated Russian military personnel, often a collection of misfits and drunks commanded by men being punished for errors of judgment. Checkpoint Vainikala was a logical place to cross into Russia; even the dogs were third rate.

The Finns, however, were not, nor had they ever lost their hatred of the Soviet invaders who had lunged into their country in '39. As they had been masters of the lakes and the forests then, repulsing whole divisions with brilliantly executed traps, so they were masters forty years later, avoiding others. It was not until Taleniekov had been escorted across an inlet of ice and brought up beyond the patrols above the snow-clogged banks that he realized Checkpoint Vainikala had become an escape route of considerable magnitude. It was no longer minor.

"If ever," said the Finn who had taken him on his last leg of the journey, "any of you men from Washington want to get beyond these Bolshevik bastards, remember us. Because we do not forget."

The irony was not lost on Vasili Vasilovich Taleniekov, former master strategist for the KGB. "You should be careful with such offers," he replied. "How do you know I'm not a Soviet plant?"

The Finn smiled. "We traced you to the Tavastian and made our own inquiries. You were sent by the best there is. He has used us in a dozen different Baltic operations. Give the quiet one our regards." The man extended his hand. "Arrangements have been made to drive you south through Vyborg into Zelenogorsk," continued the escort.

"*What?*" Taleniekov had made no such request; he had made it clear that once inside the Soviet Union, he preferred to be on his own. "I didn't ask you to do that. I didn't pay for it."

The Finn smiled condescendingly. "We thought it best; it will be quicker for you. Walk two kilometers down this road. You'll find a car parked by the snowbank. Ask the man inside for the time, saying your car has broken down—but speak Russian; they say you can do so passably well. If the man answers, then begins winding his watch, that's your ride."

"I really don't think this is necessary," objected Vasili. "I expected to make my own arrangements—for both our sakes."

"Whatever you might arrange, this is better; it will be daybreak soon and the roads are watched. You have nothing to worry about. The man you're meeting has been on Washington's payroll for a long time." The Finn smiled again. "He is second-in-command, KGB-Vyborg."

Taleniekov returned the smile. Whatever annoyance he had felt evaporated. In one sentence his escort had provided the answers to several problems. If stealing from a thief was the safest form of larceny, a "defector" compromising a traitor was even safer.

"You're a remarkable people," he said to the Finn. "I'm sure we'll do business again."

"Why not? Geography keeps us occupied. We have scores to settle."

Taleniekov had to ask. "Still? After so many years?"

"It never ends. You are fortunate, my friend, you don't live with a wild, unpredictable bear in your backyard. Try it sometime, it's depressing. Haven't you heard? We drink too much."

Vasili saw the car in the distance, a black shadow among other shadows surrounded by the snow on the road. It was dawn; in an hour the sun would throw its yellow shafts across the Arctic mists and the mists would disappear. As a child, he had been warmed by that sun.

He was home. It had been many years, but there was no sense of return, no joy at the prospect of seeing familiar sights, perhaps a familiar face . . . grown much older, as he had grown older.

There was no elation at all, only purpose. Too much had happened; he was cold and the winter sun would bring no warmth on this trip. There was only a family named Voroshin. He approached the car, staying as far to the right as possible, in the blind spot, his Graz-Burya in his gloved right hand. He stepped through the shoulder of snow, keeping his body low, until he was parallel with the front window. He raised his head and looked at the man inside.

The glow of a cigarette partially illuminated the vaguely familiar face. Taleniekov had seen it before, in a dossier photograph, or perhaps during a brief interview in Riga too insignificant to be remembered. He even remembered the man's name, and that name triggered his memory of the facts.

Maletkin. Pietre Maletkin. From Grodro, just north of the Polish border. He was in his early fifties—the face confirmed that—considered a sound if uninspired professional, someone who did his work quietly, by rote-efficiency, but with little else. Through seniority he had risen in the KGB, but his lack of initiative had relegated him to a post in Vyborg.

The Americans had made a perceptive choice in his recruitment. Here was a man doomed to insignificance by his own insignificance, yet privy to ciphers and schedules because of accumulated rank. A second-in-command at Vyborg knew the end of a rather inglorious road had been reached. Resentments could be played upon; promises of a richer life were powerful inducements. He could always be shot crossing the ice on a final trip to Vainikala. No one would miss him, a minor success for the Americans, a minor embarrassment to the KGB. But all that was changed now. Pietre Maletkin was about to become a very important person. He himself would know it the instant Vasili walked up to the window, for if the traitor's face was vaguely familiar to Taleniekov, the "defector's" would be completely known to Maletkin. Every KGB station in the world was after Vasili Vasilovich Taleniekov.

Sheltered by the bank of snow, he crept back some twenty meters behind the automobile, then walked out on the road. Maletkin was either deep in thought or half asleep; he gave no indication that he saw anyone, no turn of the head, no crushing out of the cigarette. It was not until Vasili was within ten feet of the window that the traitor jerked his shoulders around, his face turned to the glass. Taleniekov angled his head away as if checking the road behind him as he walked; he did not want his face seen until the window was rolled down. He stood directly by the door, his head hidden above the roof.

He heard the cranking of the handle, felt the brief swell of heat from inside the car. As he expected, the beam of a flashlight shot out from the seat; he bent over and showed his face, the Graz-Burya shoved through the open window.

"Good morning, Comrade Maletkin. It is Maletkin, isn't it?"

"My *God! You!*"

With his left hand, Taleniekov reached in and held the flashlight, turning it slowly away, no urgency in the act. "Don't upset yourself," he said. "We have something in common now, haven't we? Why don't you give me the keys?"

"What . . . *what?*" Maletkin was paralyzed; he could not speak.

"Let me have the keys, please," continued Vasili. "I'll give them back to you as soon as I'm inside. You're nervous, comrade, and nervous people do nervous things. I don't want you driving away without me. The keys, please."

The ominous barrel of the Graz-Burya was inches from Maletkin's face, his eyes shifting rapidly between the gun and Taleniekov as he fumbled for the ignition switch and removed the keys. "Here," he whispered.

"Thank you, comrade. And we are comrades, you know that, don't you? There'd be no point in either of us trying to take advantage of the other's predicament. We'd both lose."

Taleniekov walked around the hood of the car, stepped through the snowbank, and climbed in the front seat beside the morose traitor.

"Come now, Colonel Maletkin—it is colonel by now, isn't it?—there's no reason for this hostility. I want to hear all the news."

"I'm a temporary colonel; the rank has not been made permanent."

"A shame. We never did appreciate you, did we? Well, we were certainly mistaken. Look what you've accomplished right under our noses. You must tell me how you did it. In Leningrad."

"*Leningrad?*"

"A few hour's ride from Zelenogorsk. It's not so much, and I'm sure Vyborg's second-in-command can come up with a reasonable explanation for the trip. I'll help you. I'm very good at that sort of thing."

Maletkin swallowed, his eyes apprehensively on Vasili. "I am to be back in Vyborg tomorrow morning. To hold a briefing with the patrols."

"Delegate it, Colonel! Everyone loves to have responsibility delegated to them. It shows they're appreciated."

"It was delegated to me," said Maletkin.

"See what I mean? By the way, where are *your* bank accounts? Norway? Sweden? New York? Certainly not in Finland; that would be foolish."

"In the city of Atlanta. A bank owned by Arabs."

"Good thinking." Taleniekov handed him the keys. "Shall we get started, comrade?"

"This is *crazy*," said Maletkin. "We're dead men."

"Not for a while. We have business in Leningrad."

It was noon when they drove over the Kirov Bridge, past the summer gardens wrapped in burlap, and south to the enormous boulevard that was the Nevsky Prospeckt. Taleniekov fell silent as he looked out the window at the monuments of Leningrad. The blood of millions had been sacrificed to turn the freezing mud and marshland of the Neva River into Peter's window-on-Europe.

They reached the end of the Prospeckt under the gleaming spire of the Admiralty Building and turned right into the Quay. There along the banks of the river stood the Winter Palace; its effect on Vasili was the same as it had always been. It made him think about the Russia that once had been and ended here.

There was no time for such reflections, nor was this the Leningrad he would roam for the next several days—although ironically, it was *this* Leningrad, *that* Russia, that brought him here. Prince Andrei Voroshin had been part of both.

"Drive over the Anichov Bridge and turn left," he said. "Head into the old housing development district. I'll tell you where to stop."

"What's down there?" asked Maletkin, his apprehension growing with each block they traveled, each bridge they crossed, into the heart of the city.

"I'm surprised you don't know; you should. A string of illegal boarding houses, and equally illegal cheap hotels that seem to have a collectively revisionist attitude regarding official papers."

"In *Leningrad?*"

"You *don't* know, do you?" said Taleniekov. "And no one ever told you. You *were* overlooked, comrade. When I was stationed in Riga, those of us who were area leaders frequently came up here and used the district for conferences we wished to keep secret, the ones that concerned our own people throughout the sector. It's where I first heard your name, I believe."

"*Me?* I was brought up?"

"Don't worry, I threw them off and protected you. You and the other man in Vyborg."

"*Vyborg?*" Maletkin lost his grip on the wheel; the car swerved, narrowly avoiding an oncoming truck.

"Control yourself!" Vasili shouted. "An accident would send us both to the black rooms of Lubyanka!"

"But Vyborg!" repeated the astonished traitor. "KGB-*Vyborg?* Do you know what you're *saying?*"

"Precisely," replied Taleniekov. "Two informers from the same source, neither aware of the other. It's the most accurate way to verify information. But if one does learn about the other . . . well, he has the best of both worlds, wouldn't you say? In your case, the advantages would be incalculable."

"Who *is* he?!"

"Later, my friend, later. You cooperate fully with everything I ask and you'll have his name when I leave."

"Agreed," said Maletkin, his composure returning.

Taleniekov leaned back in the seat as they progressed down the traffic-laden Sadovaya into the crowded streets of the old housing district, the *dom vashen.* The patina of clean pavements and sandblasted buildings concealed the mounting tensions rampant within the area. Two and three families living in a single flat, four and five people sleeping in a room; it would all explode one day.

Vasili glanced at the traitor beside him; he despised the man. Maletkin thought he was going to be given an advantage undreamed of only minutes before: the name of a high-ranking KGB intelligence officer from his own station, a traitor like himself, who could be manipulated unmercifully. He would do almost anything to get that name. It would be given to him—in three words, no other identification necessary. And, of course, it would be false. Pietre Maletkin would not be shot by the Americans crossing the ice to Vainikala, but instead in a barracks courtyard in Vyborg. So much for the politics of the insignificant man, thought Vasili, as he recognized the building he was looking for down the street.

"Stop at the next corner, comrade," he said. "Wait for me. If the person I want to see isn't there, I'll be right back. If he's home, I'll be an hour or so." Maletkin pulled to the right behind a cluster of bicycles chained to a post on the curb. "Do remember," Taleniekov continued, "that you have two alternatives. You can race away to KGB headquarters—it's on the Ligovsky Prospeckt, incidentally—and turn me in; that will lead to a chain of revelations which will result in your execution. Or you can wait for me, do as I ask you to do, and you will have bought yourself the identity of someone who can bring you present and future rewards. You'll have your hook in a very important man."

"Then I don't really have a choice, do I?" said Maletkin. "I'll be here." The traitor grinned; he perspired on his chin and his teeth were yellow.

Taleniekov approached the stone steps of the building; it was a four-story structure with twenty to thirty flats, many crowded, but not hers. Lodzia Kronescha had her own apartment; that decision had been made by the KGB five years ago.

With the exception of a brief weekend conference fourteen months ago in Moscow, he had not seen her since Riga. During the conference they had spent one night together—the first night—but had decided not to meet subsequently, for professional reasons. The "brilliant Taleniekov" had been showing signs of strain, his oddly intemperate behavior annoying too many people—and too many people had been talking about it, whispering about it. Him. It was best they sever all associations outside the conference rooms. For in spite of total clearance, she was still being watched. He was not the sort of man she should be seen with; he had told her that, insisted upon it.

Five years ago Lodzia Kronescha had been in trouble; some said it was serious enough to remove her from her post in Leningrad. Others disagreed, claiming her lapses of judgment were due to a temporary siege of depression brought on by family problems. Besides, she was extremely effective in her work; whom would they get to replace her during those times of crisis? Lodzia was a ranking mathematician, a doctoral graduate from Moscow University, and trained in the Lenin Institute. She was among the most knowledgeable computer programmers in the field.

So she was kept on and given the proper warnings regarding her responsibility to the state—which had made her education possible. She was relegated to Night Operations, Computer Division, KGB-Leningrad, Ligovsky Prospeckt. That was five years ago; she would remain there for at least another two.

Lodzia's "crimes" might have been dismissed as professional errors—a series of minor mathematical variations—had it not been for a disturbing occurrence thirteen hundred miles away in Vienna. Her brother had been a senior air defense officer and he had committed suicide, the reasons for the act unexplained. Nevertheless the air defense plans for the entire southwest German border had been altered. And Lodzia Kronescha had been called in for questioning.

Taleniekov had been present, intrigued by the quiet, academic woman brought in under the KGB lamps. He had been fascinated by her slow, thoughtful responses that were as convincing as they were lacking in panic. She had readily admitted that she adored her brother and was distressed to the point of a breakdown over his death and the manner of it. No, she had known of nothing irregular about his life; yes, he had been a devoted member of the party; no, she had not kept his correspondence—it had never occurred to her to do so.

Taleniekov had kept silent, knowing what he knew by instinct and a thousand encounters with concealed truth. She had been lying. From the beginning. But her lies were not rooted in treason, or even for her own survival. It was something else. When the daily KGB surveillance was called off, he had flown frequently to Leningrad from nearby Riga to institute his own.

Vasili's trailing of Lodzia had revealed what he then knew he would find. Extremely artful contacts in the parks of the Petrodvorets with an American agent out of Helsinki. The meetings were not sought, they had been forced upon her.

He had followed her to her flat one evening and had confronted her with his evidence. Instinct had told him to hold back official action. There was far less than treason in her activities.

"What I have done is *insignificant!*" she had cried, tears of exhaustion filling her eyes. "It is *nothing* compared to what they want! But they have proof of my doing *something;* they will not do what they threaten to do!"

The American had shown her photographs, dozens of them, mostly of her brother, but also of other high-ranking Soviet officials in the Vienna sectors. They depicted the grossest obscenities, extremes of sexual behavior—male with female, and male with male—all taken while the subjects were drunk, all showing a Vienna of excessive debauchery in which responsible Soviet figures were willingly corrupted by any who cared to corrupt them.

The threat was simple: these photographs would be spread across the world. Her brother—as well as those superior to him in rank and stature—would be held up to universal ridicule. As would the Soviet Union.

"What did you hope to gain by doing what you did?" he had asked.

"Wear them out!" she had replied. "They will keep me on a string, never knowing what I will do, can do . . . have *done*. Every now and then they get word of computer errors. They are minor, but it is enough. They will not carry out their threats."

"There is a better way," he had suggested. "I think you should leave it to me. There's a man in Washington who spent his fire in Southeast Asia, a general named Blackburn. Anthony Blackburn."

Vasili had returned to Riga and sent out word through his network in London. Washington got the information within hours: whatever exploitation American intelligence cared to make out of Vienna would be matched by equally devastating exposure—and photographs—of one of the most respected men in the American military establishment.

No one from Helsinki ever bothered Lodzia Kronescha again. And she and Taleniekov became lovers.

As Vasili climbed the dark staircase to the second floor, memories came back to him. Theirs had been an affair of mutual need, without any feverish emotional attachment. They had been two insular people, dedicated to their professions almost to the exclusion of everything else; they had both required the release of mind and body. Neither had demanded more than that release from the other, and when he had been transferred to Sevastopol, their goodbyes were the painless parting of good friends who liked each other a great deal but who felt no dependency, grateful in fact for its absence. He wondered what she would say when she saw him, what she would feel . . . what he would feel.

He looked at his watch: ten minutes to one. If her schedule had not been altered, she would have been relieved from duty at eight in the morning, arrived home by nine, read the papers for a half-hour and fallen asleep. Then a thought struck him. Suppose she had a lover? If so, he would not put her in danger; he would leave quickly before any identification was made. But he hoped it was not the case; he needed Lodzia. The man he had to reach in Leningrad could not be approached directly; she could help him—if she would.

He knocked on her door. Within seconds he heard the footsteps beyond, the sound of leather heels against hard wood. Oddly, she had not been in bed. The door opened halfway and Lodzia Kronescha stood there fully clothed—strangely clothed—in a bright-colored cotton dress, a *summer* dress, her light-brown hair falling over her shoulders, her sharp aquiline face set in a rigid expression, her hazel-green eyes staring at him—*staring* at him—as if his sudden appearance after so long were not so much unexpected as it was an intrusion.

"How nice of you to drop by, old friend," she said without a trace of an inflection.

She was telling him something. There was someone inside with her. Someone waiting for him.

"It's good to see you again, old friend," said Taleniekov, nodding in acknowledgment, studying the crack between the door and the frame. He could see the cloth of a jacket, the brown fabric of a pair of trousers. There was only one man, she was telling him that, too. He pulled out his Graz-Burya, holding up his left hand, three fingers extended, gesturing to his left. On the third nod of his head, she was to drive to her right; her eyes told him she understood. "It's been many months," he continued casually. "I was in the district, so I thought I would . . ."

He gave the third nod; she lunged to her right. Vasili crashed his shoulder into the door—into the left panel, so the arc would be clean, the impact total—then battered it again, crushing the figure behind it into the wall.

He plunged inside, pivoting to the right, his shoulder smashing the door again. He ripped a gun out of the man's hand, peeling the body away from the wall, hammering his knee into the exposed neck, propelling his would-be assailant off his feet into a nearby armchair where he collapsed on the floor.

"You *understood,*" cried Lodzia, crouching against the wall. "I was so worried that you wouldn't!"

Taleniekov shut the door. "It's not yet one o'clock," he said, reaching for her hand. "I thought you'd be asleep."

"I was hoping you'd realize that."

"Also it's freezing outside, hardly the season for a summer dress."

"I knew you'd notice that. Most men don't, but you would."

He held her shoulders, speaking rapidly. "I've brought you terrible trouble. I'm sorry. I'll leave immediately. Tear your clothes, say you tried to stop me. I'll break into a flat upstairs and—"

"Vasili, *listen* to me! That man's not one of us. He's *not* KGB."

Taleniekov turned toward the man on the floor. He was regaining consciousness slowly, trying to rise and orient himself at the same time. "Are you sure?"

"Very. To begin with he's an Englishman, his Russian shouts with it. When he mentioned your name I pretended to be shocked, angry that our people would think me capable of harboring a fugitive. . . . I said I wanted to telephone my superior. He refused to let me. He said, 'We have all we want from you.' Those were his exact words."

Vasili looked at her. "Would you have called your superior?"

"I'm not sure," replied Lodzia, her hazel-green eyes steady on his. "I suppose it would have depended on what he said. It's very difficult for me to believe you're what they say you are."

"I'm not. On the other hand, you must protect yourself."

"I was hoping it wouldn't come to that."

"Thank you . . . old friend." Taleniekov turned back to the man on the floor and started toward him.

He saw it. He was too late!

Vasili lunged, diving at the figure by the chair, his hands ripping at the man's mouth, pulling it apart, his knee hammering the stomach, jamming it up into the rib cage, trying to induce vomit.

The acrid odor of almonds. Potassium cyanide. A massive dose. Oblivion in seconds, death in minutes.

The cold blue English eyes beneath him were wide and clear with satisfaction. The Matarese had escaped.

23

"We have to go over it *again*," insisted Taleniekov, looking up from the naked corpse. They had stripped the body; Lodzia was sitting in a chair checking the articles of clothing meticulously for the second time. "Everything he said."

"I've left out nothing. He wasn't that talkative."

"You're a mathematician; we must fill in the missing numbers. The sums are clear."

"Sums?"

"Yes, sums," repeated Vasili, turning the corpse over. "He wanted me, but was willing to kill himself if the trap failed. That warrants two conclusions: first, he could not risk being taken alive because of what he knew. And second, he expected no assistance. If I thought otherwise, you and I would not be here now."

"But why did he think you would come here to begin with?"

"Not would," corrected Taleniekov. "*Might.* I'm sure it's in a file somewhere in Moscow that you and I saw a lot of each other. And the men who want me have access to those files, I know that. But they'll cover only the people here in Leningrad they think I *might* contact. They won't bother with the sector leaders or the Ligovsky staff. If any of them got wind of me they'd send out alarms heard in Siberia; those who want me would step in then. No, they'll only concern themselves with people they can't trust to turn me in. You're one of them."

"Are there others? Here in Leningrad?"

"Three or four, perhaps. A Jew at the university, a good friend I'd drink and argue with all night; he'll be watched. Another at the Zhdanov, a political theorist who teaches Marx but is more at home with Adam Smith. One or two others, I suppose. I never really worried about whom I was seen with."

"You didn't have to."

"I know. My post had its advantages; there were a dozen explanations for any single thing I did, any person I saw." He paused. "How extensive *is* their coverage?"

"I don't understand."

"There's one man I do want to reach. They'd have to go back a great many years to find him, but they may have." Vasili paused again, his finger on the base of the spine of the naked body beneath him. He looked up at the strong yet curiously gentle face of the woman he had known so well. "What were the words again? 'We have all we want from you.' "

"Yes. At which point he grabbed the telephone away from my hand."

"He was convinced you were going to call headquarters?"

"I was convincing. Had he told me to go ahead, I might have changed tactics, I don't know. Remember, I knew he was English. I didn't think he would let me call. But he did not deny being KGB."

"And later, when you put on the dress. He didn't object?"

"On the contrary. It convinced him you were actually coming here, that I was cooperating."

"What were his words, then? The precise words. You said he smiled and said something about women being all alike; you didn't recall what else."

"It was trivial."

"Nothing is. Try to remember. Something about 'whiling away the hours,' that's what you mentioned."

"Yes. The language was ours but the phrase was very English, I remember that. He said he'd 'while away the hours pleasantly' . . . more so than the others. That there were . . . 'no such sights on the Quay.' I told you, he insisted I change clothes in front of him."

"The 'Quay.' The Hermitage, Malachite Hall. There's a woman there," said Taleniekov, frowning. "They were thorough. One more missing number."

"My lover was unfaithful?"

"Frequently, but not with her. She was an unreconstructed Tzarist put in charge of the architectural tours and perfectly delightful. She's also closer to seventy than sixty, although neither seems so far away to me now. I took her to tea quite often."

"That's touching."

"I enjoyed her company. She was a fine instructor in things I knew little about. Why would anyone have put her on a list in a file?"

"Speaking for Leningrad," said Lodzia, amused, "if we saw our competition from Riga meeting with such a person, we'd insert it."

"It's probably as stupid as that. What else did he say?"

"Nothing memorable. While I was in my underwear, he made a foolish remark to the effect that mathematicians had the advantage over academics and librarians. We studied figures. . . ."

Taleniekov got to his feet. "That's it," he said. "The missing number. They've found him."

"What are you talking about?"

"Our Englishman either couldn't resist the bad pun, or he was probing. The Quay—the Hermitage Museum. The academics—my drinking companions at the Zhdanov. The reference to a librarian—the Saltykov-Shchedrin Library. The man I want to reach is there."

"Who is he?"

Vasili hesitated. "An old man who years ago befriended a young university student and opened his eyes to things he knew nothing about."

"Who is he? Who is he?"

"I was a very confused young man," Taleniekov said. "How was it possible for over three-quarters of the world to reject the teachings of the revolution? I could not accept the fact that so many millions were unenlightened. But that's what the textbooks said, what our professors told us. But *why?* I had to understand how our enemies thought the way they did."

"And this man was able to tell you?"

"He *showed* me. He let me find out for myself. I was sufficiently fluent in English and French then, reasonably so in Spanish. He opened the doors, literally *opened* the steel doors, of the forbidden books—thousands of volumes Moscow disapproved of—and let me free with them. I spent weeks, months poring over them, trying to understand. It was there that the . . . 'great Taleniekov' . . . learned the most valuable lesson of all: how to see things as the enemy sees them, how to be able to *think* like him. That is the keystone of every success I've ever had. My old friend made it possible."

"And you must reach him now?"

"Yes. He's lived all his life here. He's seen it all happen and he's survived. If anyone can help me, he can."

"What are you looking for? I think I have a right to know."

"Of course you do, but it's a name you must forget. At least, never mention it. I need information about a family named Voroshin."

"A family? From Leningrad?"

"Yes."

Lodzia shook her head in exasperation. "Sometimes I think the great Talenie-kov is a great fool! I can run the name through our computers!"

"The minute you did, you'd be marked—for all purposes, dead. That man on the floor has accomplices everywhere." He turned and walked back to the body, kneeling down to continue his examination of the corpse. "Besides, you'd find nothing; it's too many years ago, too many changes of regimes and emphases. If any entry, or entries, had ever been made, I doubt they'd be there now. The irony is that if there was something in the data banks, it would probably mean the Voroshin family is no longer involved."

"Involved with *what*, Vasili?"

He did not answer immediately, for he had turned the nude body over. There was a small discoloration of the skin on the lower midsection of the chest, around the area of the heart, barely visible through the matted hair. It was tiny, no more than a half-inch in diameter—the bluish-purple mark was a circle. At first glance it appeared to be a birthmark, a perfectly natural phenomenon, in no way superimposed on the flesh. But it was not natural; it was placed there by a very experienced needle. Old Krupskaya had said the words as he lay dying: *a man was caught, a bluish circle on his chest, a soldier of the Matarese.*

"With this." Taleniekov separated the black hair on the dead man's chest so the jagged circle could be seen clearly. "Come here."

Lodzia got up, walked to the corpse, and knelt down. "What? The birthmark?"

"*Per nostro circolo,*" he said. "It wasn't there when our Englishman was born. It had to be earned."

"I don't understand."

"You will. I'm going to tell you everything I know. I wasn't sure that I wanted to, but I don't think there's a choice now. They might easily kill me. If they do, there's someone you must reach, I'll tell you how. Describe this mark, fourth rib, border of the cage, near the heart. It was not meant to be found."

Lodzia was silent as she looked at the bluish mark on the flesh, and finally at Taleniekov. "Who is 'they'?"

"They go by the name of the Matarese. . . ."

He told her. Everything. When he was finished, Lodzia did not speak for a long time, nor did he intrude on her thoughts. For she had heard shocking things, not the least of which was the incredible alliance between Vasili Vasilovich Taleniekov and a man known throughout the KGB world as Beowulf Agate. She walked to the window overlooking the dreary street. She spoke, her face to the glass.

"I imagine you've asked this question of yourself a thousand times; I ask it again. Was it necessary to contact Scofield?"

"Yes," he said.

"Moscow wouldn't *listen* to you?"

"Moscow ordered my execution. Washington ordered his."

"Yes, but you say that neither Moscow nor Washington knows about this Matarese. The trap set for you and Beowulf was based on keeping you apart. I can understand that."

"*Official* Washington and *official* Moscow are blind to the Matarese. Otherwise, someone would have stepped forward in our behalf; we would have been summoned to present what we know—what I brought Scofield. Instead, we're branded traitors, ordered to be shot on sight, no provisions made to give us a hearing. The Matarese orchestrated it, using the clandestine apparatuses of both countries."

"Then this Matarese *is* in Moscow, in Washington."

"Absolutely. In, but not of. Capable of manipulating, but unseen."

"Not unseen, Vasili," objected Lodzia. "The men you spoke to in Moscow—"

"Panicked *old* men," interrupted Taleniekov. "Dying war horses put out to pasture. Impotent."

"Then the man Scofield approached. The statesman, Winthrop. What of him?"

"Undoubtedly dead by now."

Lodzia walked away from the window and stood in front of him. "Then where do you go? You're cornered."

Vasili shook his head. "On the contrary, we're making progress. The first name on the list, Scozzi, was accurate. Now, we have our dead Englishman here. No papers, no proof of who he is or where he came from, but with a mark more telling than a billfold filled with false documents. He was part of their army, which means there's another soldier here in Leningrad watching an old man who's curator of literary archives at the Shchedrin Library. I want him almost as much as I want to reach my old friend; I want to break him, get answers. The Matarese are in Leningrad to protect the Voroshins, to conceal the truth. We're getting closer to that truth."

"But suppose you *find* it. Whom can you take it to? You cannot protect yourselves because you don't know who they are."

"We know who they are not, and that's enough. The Premier and the President to begin with."

"You won't get near them."

"We will if we have our proof. Beowulf was right about that; we need incontrovertible proof. Will you help us? Help *me?*"

Lodzia Kronescha looked into his eyes, her own softening. She reached up with both her hands and cupped his face. "Vasili Vasilovich. My life had become so uncomplicated, and now you return."

"I didn't know where else to go. I couldn't approach that old man directly. I testified on his behalf at a security hearing in 1954. I'm terribly sorry, Lodzia."

"Don't be. I've missed you. And, of course, I'll help you. Were it not for you, I might be teaching primary grades in our Tashkent sectors."

He touched her face, returning her gesture. "That must not be the reason for your help."

"It isn't. What you've told me frightens me."

Under no condition was the traitor, Maletkin, to be aware of Lodzia. The Vyborg officer had remained in the automobile at the corner, but when more than an hour had passed Taleniekov could see him pacing nervously on the pavement below.

"He's not sure whether it's this building or the one next door," said Vasili, stepping back from the window. "The cellars still connect, don't they?"

"They did when I was last there."

"I'll go down and come out on the street several doors away. I'll meet him and tell him the man I'm with wants another half hour. That should give us enough time. Finish dressing the Englishman, will you?"

Lodzia was right, nothing had changed in the old buildings. Each cellar connected with the one next door, the filthy, damp underground alleyway extending most of the block. Taleniekov emerged on the street four buildings away from Lodzia's flat. He walked up to the unsuspecting Maletkin, startling him.

"I thought you went in there!" said the traitor from Vyborg, nodding his head at the staircase on his left.

"There?"

"Yes, I was sure of it."

"You're still too excited, comrade, it interferes with your observation. I don't know anyone in that building. I came down to tell you that the man I'm meeting with needs more time. I suggest you wait in the car; it's not only extremely cold, but you'll draw less attention to yourself."

"You won't be much longer, will you?" asked Maletkin anxiously. "Are you going somewhere? Without me?"

"No, no, of course not. I have to go to the toilet."

"Discipline your bladder," said Taleniekov, hurrying away.

Twenty minutes later he and Lodzia had worked out the details of his contact with the curator of archives at the Saltykov-Shchedrin Library on the Maiorov Prospeckt. She would tell him that a student from many years ago, a man who had risen high in government office and who had testified for the old gentleman in 1954—wanted to meet with him privately. That student, this friend, could not be seen in public; he was in trouble and needed help.

There was to be no doubt as to the identity of that student, or of the danger in which he found himself. The old man had to be jolted, frightened, concern for a once-dear young friend forced to the surface. He had to communicate his alarms to anyone who might be watching him. The arrangements for the meeting just complicated enough to confuse an old man's mind. For the scholar's confusion and fear would lead to tentative movements, bewildered starts and stops, sudden turns and abrupt reversals, decisions made and instantly rejected. Under these circumstances, whoever followed the old man would be revealed; for whatever moves the scholar made, the one following would have to make.

Lodzia would instruct the old man to leave the enormous library complex by the southwest exit at ten minutes to six that evening; the streets would be dark and no snow was expected. He would be told to walk a given number of blocks one way, then another. If no contact was made, he was to return to the library, and wait; if it were at all possible, his friend from long ago could try to get there. However, there were no guarantees.

Placed in this situation of stress, the numbers alone would serve to confuse the scholar, for Lodzia was to abruptly terminate the telephone call without repeating them. Vasili would take care of the rest, a traitor named Maletkin serving as an unknowing accomplice.

"What will you do after you see the old man?" asked Lodzia.

"That depends on what he tells me, or what I can learn from the man who follows him."

"Where will you stay? Will I see you?"

Vasili stood up. "It could be dangerous for you if I come back here."

"I'm willing to risk that."

"I'm not willing to let you. Besides, you work until morning."

"I can go in early and get off at midnight. Things are much more relaxed than when you were last in Leningrad. We trade hours frequently, and I am completely rehabilitated."

"Someone will ask you why."

"I'll tell him the truth. An old friend has arrived from Moscow."

"I don't think that's such a good idea."

"A party secretary from the Presidium with a wife and several children. He wishes to remain anonymous."

"As I said, a splendid idea." Taleniekov smiled. "I'll be careful and go through the cellars."

"What will you do with him?" Lodzia nodded at the dead Englishman.

"Leave him in the farthest cellar I can find. Do you have a bottle of vodka?"

"Are you thirsty?"

"He is. One more unknown suicide in paradise. We don't publicize them. I'll need a razor blade."

Pietre Maletkin stood next to Vasili in the shadows of an archway across from the southeast entrance to the Saltykov-Shchedrin Library. The floodlights in the rear courtyard of the complex shone down in wide circles from the high walls, giving the illusion of an enormous prison compound. But the arches that led to the street beyond were placed symmetrically every hundred feet in the wall; the prisoners could come and go at will. It was a busy evening at the library; streams of prisoners came and went.

"You say this old man is one of us?" asked Maletkin.

"Get your new enemies straight, comrade. The old fellow's KGB, the man following him—about to make contact—is one of us. We've got to reach him before he's trapped. The scholar is one of the most effective weapons Moscow's developed for counterintelligence. His name is known to no more than five people in KGB; to be aware of him marks a person as an American informer. For God's sake, don't ever mention him."

"I've never heard of him," said Maletkin. "But the Americans think he's *theirs?*"

"Yes. He's a plant. He reports everything directly to Moscow on a private line."

"Incredible," muttered the traitor. "An old man. Ingenious."

"My former associates are not fools," said Taleniekov, checking his watch. "Neither are your present ones. Forget you've ever heard of Comrade Mikovsky."

"That's his name?"

"Even I would rather not repeat it. . . . There he is."

An old man bundled up in an overcoat and a black fur hat walked out of the entrance, his breath vaporizing in the cold air. He stood for a moment on the steps, looking around as if trying to decide which archway to take into the street. His short beard was white; what could be seen of his face was filled with wrinkles and tired, pale flesh. He started down the stairs cautiously, holding on to the railing. He reached the courtyard and walked toward the nearest arch on his right.

Taleniekov studied the stream of people that came out through the glass doors after the old curator. They seemed to be in groups of twos and threes; he looked for a single man whose eyes strayed to the courtyard below. None did and Vasili was disturbed. Had he been wrong? It did not seem likely, yet there was no single man Taleniekov could pick out of the crowds whose focus was on Mikovsky, now halfway across the courtyard. When the scholar reached the street, there was no point in waiting any longer; he *had* been wrong. The Matarese had not found his friend.

A woman. He was *not* wrong. It was a *woman.* A lone woman broke away from the crowd and hurried down the steps, her eyes on the old man. How plausible, thought Vasili. A single woman remaining for hours alone in a library would draw far less attention than a man. Among its élite soldiers, the Matarese trained women.

He was not sure why it surprised him—some of the best agents in the Soviet KGB and the American Consular Operations were women, but their duties rarely included violence. *That's* what startled him now. The woman following old Mikovsky was trailing the curator only to find *him.* Violence was intrinsic to that assignment.

"That woman," he said to Maletkin. "The one in the brown overcoat and the visored cap. She's the informer. We've got to stop her from making contact."

"A *woman?*"

"She is capable of a variety of things which you are not, comrade. Come along now, we must be careful. She won't approach him right away; she'll wait for the most opportune moment and so must we. We've got to separate her, take her when she's far enough away from him so he can't identify her if there's any noise."

"Noise?" echoed the perplexed Maletkin. "Why would she make any noise?"

"Women are unpredictable; it's common knowledge. Let's go."

The next eighteen minutes were as disorganized and as painful to watch as

Taleniekov had anticipated. Painful in that a concerned old man grew progressively bewildered as the moments passed, his agitation turning into panic when there was no sign of his young friend. He crossed the bitterly cold streets, his walk slow, his legs unsteady. He kept checking his watch, the light too dim for his eyes; he was jostled by pedestrians whenever he stopped. And he stopped incessantly, breath and strength diminishing. Twice he started for an omnibus shelter in the block beyond where he stood, momentarily convinced that he had made the wrong count of the streets; at the intersection where the Kirov Theatre stood, there were three shelters and his confusion mounted. He visited all three, more and more bewildered.

The strategy had the expected effect on the woman following Mikovsky. She interpreted the old man's actions as those of a subject aware that he might be under surveillance, a subject unschooled in methods of evasion but also old and frightened and capable of creating an uncontrollable situation. So the woman in the brown overcoat and visored cap kept her distance, staying in shadows, going from darkened storefront to dimly lit alleyways, propelled into agitation herself by the unpredictability of her subject.

The old scholar started on his return pattern to the library. Vasili and Maletkin watched from a vantage point seventy-five meters away. Taleniekov studied the route directly across the wide avenue; there were two alleyways, both of which would be used by the woman as Mikovsky passed her on the way back.

"Come along," ordered Vasili, grabbing Maletkin's arm, pushing him forward. "We'll get behind him in the crowd on the other side. She'll turn away as he goes by, and when he passes that second alleyway, she'll use it."

"Why are you so sure?"

"Because she used it before; it's the natural thing to do. I'd use it. *We* will use it now."

"How?"

"I'll tell you when we're in position."

The moment was drawing near and Taleniekov could feel the drumlike beat in his chest. He had orchestrated the events of the past sixteen minutes, the next few would determine whether the orchestration had merit. He knew two indisputable facts: one, the woman would recognize him instantly; she would have been provided with photographs and a detailed physical description. Two, should the violence go against her, she would take her own life as quickly and as efficiently as the Englishman had done in Lodzia's flat.

Timing and shock were the only tools at his immediate disposal. He would provide the first, the traitor from Vyborg the second.

They crossed the square with a group of pedestrians and walked into the crowds in front of the Kirov Theatre. Vasili glanced over his shoulder and saw Mikovsky weave his way awkwardly through the line forming for tickets, breathing with difficulty.

"Listen to me and do exactly as I say," said Taleniekov, holding Maletkin's arm. "Repeat the words I say to you. . . ."

They entered the flow of pedestrians walking up the pavement, remaining behind a quartet of soldiers, their bulky overcoats serving as a wall Vasili could see beyond at will. The scholar up ahead approached the first alleyway; the woman briefly disappeared into it, then re-emerged as he passed.

Moments now. Only moments.

The second alleyway. Mikovsky was in front of it, the woman within.

"Now!" Vasili ordered, rushing with Maletkin toward the entrance.

He heard the words Maletkin shouted so they would be unmistakable above the noise of the streets.

"Comrade, wait. Stop! *Circolo! Nostro circolo!*"

Silence. The shock was almost total.

"Who *are* you?" The question was asked in a cold, tense voice.

"Stop everything! I have news from the shepherd!"

"What?"

The shock was now complete.

Taleniekov spun around the corner of the alley, rushing toward the woman, his hands two springs uncoiling as he lunged. He grabbed her arms, his fingers sliding instantly down to her wrists, immobilizing her hands, one of which was in her overcoat pocket, gripped around a gun. She recoiled, spinning to her left, her weight dead, pulling him forward, then sprang to her right, her left foot lashing up into him, close to her body like an enraged cat's claw repelling another animal.

He countered, attacking directly, lifting her off her feet, crashing her writhing body into the alleyway wall, pummeling her with his shoulder, crushing her into the brick.

It happened so fast he was only vaguely aware of what she was doing until he felt her teeth sinking into the flesh of his neck. She had thrust her face into his—a move so unexpected he could only twist away in pain. Her mouth was wide, her red lips parted grotesquely. The bite was vicious, her jaws two clamps vicing into the side of his neck. He could feel blood drenching his collar; she *would not let go!* The pain was excruciating; the harder he battered her into the wall, the deeper her teeth went into his flesh. He *could not stand it.* He released her arms, his hands clawing at her face, pulling her from him.

The explosion was loud, distinct, yet muffled by the heavy cloth of her overcoat, the echo carried on the wind throughout the alley; she fell away from him, limp against the stone.

He looked at her face; her eyes were wide and dead; she sank slowly to the pavement. She had done precisely what she had been programmed to do: she had appraised the odds—two men against herself—and fired the weapon in her pocket, blowing away her chest.

"She's *dead!* My God, she *killed* herself!" screamed Maletkin. "The *shot,* people will have heard it! We've got to run! The police!"

Several curious passersby stood motionless at the alley's entrance, peering in.

"Be quiet!" commanded Taleniekov. "If anyone comes in use your KGB card. This is official business; no one's permitted here. I want thirty seconds."

Vasili pulled a handkerchief from his pocket and pressed it against his neck, reducing the flow of blood. He knelt over the body of the dead woman. With his right hand, he ripped the coat away, exposing a blouse stained everywhere with red. He tore the drenched fabric away from the skin; the hole below her left breast was massive, tissue and intestines clogging the opening. He probed the flesh around the wound; the light was too dim. He took out his cigarette lighter.

He snapped it, stretching the bloody skin beneath the breast, holding the light inches above it; the flame danced in the wind.

"For God's sake, *hurry!*" Maletkin stood several feet away, his voice a panicked whisper. "What are you *doing?*"

Taleniekov did not reply. Instead, he moved his fingers around the flesh, wiping away the blood to see more clearly.

He found it. In the crease beneath the left breast, angled toward the center of the chest. A jagged circle of blue surrounded by white skin streaked with red. A blemish that was no blemish at all, but the mark of an incredible army.

The Matarese circle.

24

They walked rapidly out of the far end of the alley, melting into the crowds heading north. Maletkin was trembling, his face ashen. Vasili's right hand gripped the traitor's elbow, controlling the panic that might easily cause Maletkin to burst into a run, riveting attention on both of them. Taleniekov needed the man from Vyborg; a cable had to be sent that would elude KGB interception and Maletkin could send it. He realized that he had very little time to work out the cipher for Scofield. It would take old Mikovsky another ten minutes before he reached his office, but soon after that Vasili knew he should be there. A frightened old man could say the wrong things to the wrong people.

Taleniekov held the handkerchief against the wound on his neck. The bleeding had ebbed to a trickle in the cold, it would stop sufficiently for a bandage soon; it occurred to Vasili to buy a high-necked sweater to conceal it.

"Slow down!" he ordered, yanking Maletkin's elbow. "There's a café up ahead. We'll go inside for a few minutes, get a drink."

"I could *use* one," whispered Maletkin. "My God, she *killed* herself! Who *was* she?"

"Someone who made a mistake. Don't you make another."

The café was crowded; they shared a table with two middle-aged women, who objected to the intrusion and morosely kept to themselves; it was a splendid arrangement.

"Go up to the manager by the door," said Taleniekov. "Tell him your friend had too much to drink and cut himself. Ask for a bandage and some adhesive." Maletkin started to object; Vasili reached for his forearm. "Just do it. It's nothing unusual in a place like this."

The traitor got up and made his way to the man at the door. Taleniekov refolded the handkerchief, pressing the cleaner side against the torn skin, and dug into his pocket for a pencil. He moved the coarse paper napkin in front of him and began selecting the cipher for Beowulf Agate.

His mind closed out all noise as he concentrated on an alphabet and a progression of numbers. Even as Maletkin returned with a cotton bandage and a small roll of tape, Vasili wrote crossing out errors as rapidly as he made them. Their drinks arrived; the traitor had ordered three apiece. Taleniekov kept writing.

Eight minutes later he was finished. He tore the napkin in two and copied the wording in large unmistakable letters. He handed it to Maletkin. "I want this cable sent to Helsinki, to the name and hotel listed on top. I want it routed on a white line, commercial traffic, not subject to duplicate interception."

The traitor's eyes grew wide. "How do you expect *me* to do that?"

"The same way you get information to our friends in Washington. You know the unmonitored schedules; we all protect ourselves from ourselves. It's one of our more finely honed talents."

"That's through *Stockholm*. We bypass Helsinki!" Maletkin flushed; his state of agitation and the rapid infusion of alcohol had made him careless. He had not meant to reveal the Swedish connection. It wasn't done, even among fellow defectors.

Nor could Vasili use Stockholm. The cable would then be under American scrutiny. There was another way.

"How often do you come down here to the Ligovski headquarters for sector conferences?"

The traitor pursed his lips in embarrassment. "Not often. Perhaps three or four times during the past year."

"You're going over there now," said Taleniekov.

"I'm *what?* You've lost your head!"

"You'll lose yours if you don't. Don't worry, Colonel. Rank still has its privileges and its effect. You are sending an urgent cable to a Vyborg man in Helsinki. White line, nonduplicated traffic. However, you must bring me a verifying copy."

"Suppose they *check* with Vyborg?"

"Who on duty up there now would interfere with the second-in-command?"

Maletkin frowned nervously. "There will be questions later."

Vasili smiled, the promise of untold riches in his voice. "Take my word for it, Colonel. When you return to Vyborg there won't be anything you cannot have . . . or command."

The traitor grinned, the sweat on his chin glistening. "Where do I bring the verifying copy? Where will we meet? When?"

Taleniekov held the bandage in place over the wound on his neck and unrolled a strip of tape, the end in his teeth. "Tear it," he said to Maletkin. It was done and Vasili applied it, ripping off another strip as he spoke. "Stay the night at the Evropeiskaya Hotel on Brodsky Street. I'll contact you there."

"They'll demand identification."

"By all means, give it to them. A colonel of the KGB will no doubt get a better room. A better woman, too, if you go down to the lounge."

"Both cost money."

"My treat," Taleniekov said.

It was the dinner hour. The huge reading rooms of the Saltykov-Shchedrin Library with their tapestried walls and the enormously high ceilings were nowhere near as crowded as usual. A scattering of students sat at the long tables, a few groups of tourists strolled about studying the tapestries and the oil paintings, speaking in hushed whispers, awed by the grandeur that was the Shchedrin.

As Vasili walked through the marble hallways toward the complex of offices in the west wing he remembered the months he had spent in these rooms—that room—awakening his mind to a world he had known so little about. He had not exaggerated to Lodzia; it was here, through the enlightened courage of one man, that he had learned more about the enemy than in all the training he had later received in Moscow and Novgorod.

The Saltykov-Shchedrin was his finest school, the man he was about to see after so many years his most accomplished teacher. He wondered whether the school or the teacher could help him now. If the Voroshin family was bound to the new Matarese there would be no revealing information in the intelligence data banks, of that he was certain. But was it here? Somewhere in the thousands of volumes that detailed the events of the revolution, of families and vast estates banished and carved up, all documented by historians of the time because they knew the time would never be seen again, the explosive beginnings of a new world. It had happened here in Leningrad—St. Petersburg—and Prince Andrei Voroshin was a part of the cataclysm. The revolutionary archives at the Saltykov-Shchedrin were the most extensive in all Russia; if there was a repository for any information about the Voroshins, it would be here. But being here was one thing, finding it something else again. Would his old teacher know where to look?

He turned left into the corridor lined with glass-paneled office doors, all dark except one at the end of the hallway. There was a dim light on inside, intermittently blocked by the silhouette of a figure passing back and forth in front of a desk lamp. It was Mikovsky's office, the same room he had occupied for more than a quarter of a century, the slow-moving figure beyond the rippled glass unmistakably that of the scholar.

He walked up to the door and knocked softly; the dark figure loomed almost instantly behind the glass.

The door opened and Yanov Mikovsky stood there, his wrinkled face still flushed from the cold outside, his eyes behind the thick lenses of his spectacles wide, questioning and afraid. He gestured for Vasili to come in quickly, shutting the door the instant Taleniekov was inside.

"Vasili Vasilovich!" The old man's voice was part whisper, part cry. He held out his arms, embracing his younger friend. "I never thought I'd see you again." He stepped back, his hands still on Taleniekov's overcoat, peering up at him, his wrinkled mouth tentatively forming words that did not emerge. The events of the past half-hour were more than he could accept. Halting sounds emerged, but no meaning.

"Don't upset yourself," said Vasili as reassuringly as he could. "Everything's fine."

"But *why?* Why this secrecy? This running from place to place? Can it be called for? Of all men in the Soviet . . . *you.* The years you were in Riga you never came to see me, but I heard from others how respected you were, how you were in charge of so many things."

"It was better that we did not meet during those days. I told you that over the telephone."

"I never understood."

"They were merely precautions that seemed reasonable at the time." They had been more than reasonable, thought Taleniekov. He had learned that the scholar was drinking heavily, depressed over the death of his wife. If the head of KGB-Riga had been seen with the old man, people might have looked for other things. And found them.

"No matter now," said Mikovsky. "It was a difficult period for me, as I'm sure you were told. There are times when some men should be left to themselves, even by old friends. But this is now! What's *happened* to you?"

"It's a long story; I'll tell you everything I can. I must, for I need your help." Taleniekov glanced beyond the scholar; there was a kettle of water on the coils of an electric plate on the right side of the desk. Vasili could not be sure but he thought it was the same kettle, the same electric burner he remembered from so many years ago. "Your tea was always the best in Leningrad. Will you make some for us?"

The better part of a half-hour passed as Taleniekov spoke, the old scholar sitting in his chair, listening in silence. When Vasili first mentioned the name, Prince Andrei Voroshin, he made no comment. But he did when his student was finished.

"The Voroshin estates were confiscated by the new revolutionary government. The family's wealth had been vastly reduced by the Romanovs and their industrial partners. Nicholas and his brother, Michael, loathed the Voroshins, claiming they were the thieves of all northern Russia and the sea routes. And, of course, the prince was marked by the Bolsheviks for execution. His only hope was Kerenski, who was too indecisive or corrupt to cut off the illustrious families so completely. That hope vanished with the collapse of the Winter Palace."

"What happened to Voroshin?"

"He was sentenced to death. I'm not positive, but I think his name was announced on the execution lists. Those who escaped were generally heard from during the succeeding years; I would have remembered had Voroshin been among them."

"Why would you? There were hundreds here in Leningrad alone. Why the Voroshins?"

"They were not easily forgotten for many reasons. It was not often that the tzars of Russia called their own kind thieves and pirates and sought to destroy them. The Voroshin family was notorious. The prince's father and grandfather dealt in the Chinese and African slave trades, from the Indian Ocean to the American South; they manipulated the Imperial banks, forcing merchant fleets and companies into bankruptcies, and absorbing them. It is said that when Nicholas secretly ordered Prince Andrei Voroshin from the palace court, he proclaimed: 'Should our Russia fall prey to maniacs, it will be because of men like you. You drive them to our throats.' That was a number of years before the revolution."

"You say 'secretly ordered' him. Why secretly?"

"It was not a time to expose dissent among the aristocrats. Their enemies would have used it to justify the cries of national crisis. The revolution was in foment decades before the event. Nicholas understood, he knew it was happening."

"Did Voroshin have sons?"

"I don't know but I would presume so—one way or the other. He had many mistresses."

"What about the family itself?"

"Again I have no specific knowledge, but I assume they perished. As you're aware, the tribunals were usually lenient where women and children were concerned. Thousands were allowed to flee; only the most fanatic wanted that blood on their hands. But I don't believe the Voroshins were allowed to. Actually, I'm quite sure of it, but I don't know specifically."

"I need specific knowledge."

"I understand that, and in my judgment you have it. At least enough to refute any theory involving Voroshin and this incredible Matarese society."

"Why do you say that?"

"Because had the prince escaped, it would not have been to his advantage to keep silent. The Whites in exile were organizing everywhere. Those with legitimate titles were welcomed with open arms and excessive remuneration by the great companies and the international banks; it was good business. It was not in Voroshin's nature to reject such largess and notoriety. No, Vasili. He was killed."

Taleniekov listened to the scholar's words, looking for an inconsistency. He got up from the chair and went to the pot of tea; he filled his cup and stared absently at the brown liquid. "Unless he was offered something of greater value to keep silent, to remain anonymous."

"This Matarese?" asked Mikovsky.

"Yes. Money had been made available. In Rome and in Genoa. It was their initial funding."

"But it was earmarked for just that, wasn't it?" Mikovsky leaned forward. "From what you've told me, it was to be used for the hiring of assassins, spreading the gospel of vengeance according to this Guillaume de Matarese, is that not so?"

"That's what the old woman implied," agreed Taleniekov.

"Then it was not to be spent recouping individual fortunes or financing new ones. You see, that's what I can't accept where Voroshin is concerned. If he had escaped he would not have turned his back on the opportunities offered him. Not to join an organization bent on political vengeance; he was far too pragmatic a man."

Vasili had started back to his chair; he stopped and turned, the cup suspended, motionless in his hand. "What did you just say?"

"That Voroshin was too pragmatic to reject—"

"No," interrupted Taleniekov. "Before that. The money was not to be used recouping fortunes or . . . ?"

"Financing new ones. You see, Vasili, large sums of capital *were* made available to the exiles."

Taleniekov held up his hand. " 'Financing new ones,' " he repeated. "There are many ways to spread a gospel. Beggars and lunatics do it in the streets, priests from pulpits, politicians from rostrums. But how can you spread a gospel that cannot stand scrutiny? How do you *pay* for it?" Vasili put the cup down on the small table next to his chair. "You do both anonymously, using the complicated methods and procedures of an existing structure. One in which whole areas operate as separate entities, distinct from one another yet held together by a common identity. Where enormous sums of capital are transferred daily." Taleniekov walked back to the desk and leaned over, his hands on the edge. "You make the necessary *purchase!* You buy the seat of decision! The structure is yours for the using!"

"If I follow you," the scholar said, "the money left by Matarese was to be divided, and used to buy participation in giant, established enterprises."

"Exactly. I'm looking in the wrong *place*—sorry, the *right* place, but the wrong *country*. Voroshin *did* escape. He got out of Russia probably a long time before he had to because the Romanovs crippled him, stripped him, watched his every financial move. He was hamstrung here . . . and later the sort of investments Guillaume de Matarese envisioned were prohibited in the Soviet. Don't you see, he had no reason to stay in Russia. His decision was made long *before* the revolution; it's why you never heard of him in exile. He became someone *else*."

"You're wrong, Vasili. His name was among those sentenced to death. I remember seeing it myself."

"But you're not sure you saw it later, in the announcements of those actually executed."

"There were so many."

"That's my point."

"There were his communications with the Kerenski provisional government, they're a matter of record."

"Easily dispatched and recorded." Taleniekov pushed himself away from the desk, his every instinct telling him he was near the truth. "What better way for a man like Voroshin to lose his identity but in the chaos of a revolution? The mobs out of control; the discipline did not come for weeks, and it was a miracle it came then. Absolute chaos. How easily it could be done."

"You're oversimplifying," said Mikovsky. "Although there was a period of rampage, teams of observers traveled throughout the cities and countryside writing down everything they saw and heard. Not only facts but impressions, opinions, interpretations of what they witnessed. The academicians insisted upon it, for it was a moment in history that would never be repeated and they wanted no instant lost, none unaccounted for. Everything was written down, no matter how harsh the observation. *That* was a form of discipline, Vasili."

Taleniekov nodded. "Why do you think I'm here?"

The old man sat forward. "The archives of the revolution?"

"I must see them."

"An easy request to make but most difficult to grant. The authority must come from Moscow."

"How is it relayed?"

"Through the Ministry of Cultural Affairs. A man is sent over from the Leningrad office with the key to the rooms below. There is no key here."

Vasili's eyes strayed to the mounds of papers on Mikovsky's desk. "Is that man an archivist? A scholar such as yourself?"

"No. He is merely a man with a key."

"How often are the authorizations granted?"

Mikovsky frowned. "Not very frequently. Perhaps twice a month."

"When was the last time?"

"About three weeks ago. An historian from the Zhdanov doing research."

"Where did he do his reading?"

"In the archive rooms. Nothing is permitted to be taken from them."

Taleniekov held up his hand. "Something was. It was sent to you and for everyone's sake it should be returned to the archives immediately. Your telephone call to the Leningrad office should be rather excited."

The man arrived in twenty-one minutes, his face burnt from the cold.

"The night duty officer said it was urgent, sir," said the young man breathlessly, opening his briefcase and removing a key so intricately ridged it would take a precision-tooled instrument to duplicate it.

"Also highly irregular and without question a criminal offense," replied Mikovsky, getting up from his chair. "But no harm done now that you're here." The scholar walked around the desk, a large envelope in his hand. "Shall we go below?"

"Is that the material?" asked the man with the key.

"Yes." The scholar lowered the envelope.

"*What* material?" Taleniekov's voice was sharp, the question an accusation.

The man was caught. He dropped the key and reached for his belt. Vasili lunged, grabbing the young man's hand, pulling it downward, throwing his shoulder into the man's chest, hurling him to the floor. "You said the wrong thing!" shouted Vasili. "No duty officer tells a messenger the particulars of an emergency. *Per nostro circolo!* There'll be no pills this time! No guns. I've got you, *soldier!* And by your Corsican christ, you'll tell me what I want to know!"

"*Ich sterbe für unseren Verein. Für unser Heiligtum,*" whispered the young man, his mouth stretched, his lips bulging, his tongue . . . his *tongue.* His *teeth.* The bite came, the jaw clamped, the results irreversible.

Taleniekov watched in furious astonishment as the capsule's liquid entered the throat, paralyzing the muscles. In seconds it happened; an expulsion of air, a final breath.

"Call the ministry!" he said to the shocked Mikovsky. "Tell the night duty officer that it will take several hours to re-insert the material."

"I don't *understand. Anything!*"

"They tapped the ministry's phone. This one intercepted the man with the key. He would have left it and fled after he had killed us both." Vasili ripped the dead man's overcoat apart and then the shirt beneath.

It was there. The blemish that was no blemish, the jagged blue circle of the Matarese.

The old scholar reached for the two ledgers on the top shelf of the metal racks and handed them to Taleniekov. They were the seventeenth and eighteenth volumes they had each gone through, searching for the name Voroshin.

"It would be far easier if we were in Moscow," said Mikovsky, descending the ladder cautiously, heading for the table. "All this material has been transcribed and indexed. One volume would tell us exactly where to look."

"There'll be something; there *has* to be." Taleniekov handed one book to the scholar and opened the second for himself. He began to scan the handwritten entries of ink, cautiously turning the brittle pages.

Twelve minutes later Yanov Mikovsky spoke. "It's here."

"What?"

"The crimes of Prince Andrei Voroshin."

"His execution?"

"Not yet. His life, and the lives and criminal acts of his father and grandfather."

"Let me see."

It was all there, meticulously if superficially recorded by a steady, precise hand. The fathers Voroshin were described as enemies-of-the-masses, replete with the crimes of wanton murder of serfs and tenants, and the more rarefied manipulations of the Imperial banks causing thousands to be unemployed, casting thousands more into the ranks of the starving. The prince had been sent to Southern Europe for his higher education, a grand tour that lasted five years, solidifying his pursuance of imperialistic dominance and the suppression of the people.

"*Where?*" Taleniekov spoke out loud.

"Referring to what?" asked the scholar, reading the same page.

"Where was he *sent?*"

Mikovsky turned the page. "Krefeld. The University of Krefeld. Here it is."

"That bastard spoke *German. Ich sterbe für unseren Verein! Für unser Heiligtum!* It's in Germany!"

"*What* is?"

"Voroshin's new identity. It's *here.* Read further."

They read. The prince had spent three years at Krefeld, two in graduate studies at Düsseldorf, returning frequently in his adult years when he developed close personal ties with such German industrialists as Gustav von Bohlen-Holbach, Friedrich Schotte, and Wilhelm Habernicht.

"Essen," said Vasili. "Düsseldorf led to Essen. It was territory Voroshin knew, a language he spoke. The timing was perfect; war in Europe, revolution in Russia, the world in chaos. The armaments companies in Essen, that's what he became a part of."

"*Krupp?*"

"Or Verachten. Krupp's competitor."

"You think he bought himself into one of them?"

"Through a rear door and a new identity. German industrial expansion then was as chaotic as the Kaiser's war, management personnel raided and shifted about like small armies. The circumstances were ideal for Voroshin."

"Here is the execution," interrupted Mikovsky, who had turned the pages. "The description starts here at the top. Your theory loses credibility, I'm afraid."

Taleniekov leaned over, scanning the words. The entry detailed the deaths of Prince Andrei Voroshin, his wife, two sons and their wives, and one daughter, on the afternoon of October 21, 1917, at his estate in Tsarskoye Selo on the banks of the Slovyanka River. It described in bloody particulars the final minutes of fighting, the Voroshins trapped in the great house with their servants, repelling the attacking mob, firing weapons from the windows, hurling cans of flaming petrol from the sloping roofs—at the end, releasing their servants and in a pact of death—using their own gunpowder to blow up themselves and the great house in a final conflagration. Nothing was left but the burning skeleton of a tzarist estate, the remains of the Voroshins consumed in the flames.

Images came back to Vasili, memories from the hills at night above Porto Vecchio. The ruins of Villa Matarese. There, too, was a final conflagration.

"I must disagree," he said softly to Mikovsky. "This was no execution at all."

"The tribunals' courts may have been absent," countered the scholar, "but I daresay the results were the same."

"There were no results, no evidence, no proof of death. There were only charred ruins. This entry is false."

"Vasili Vasilovich! These are the *archives,* every document was scrutinized and approved by the academicians! At the *time.*"

"One was bought. I grant you a great estate was burned to the ground, but that is the limit of existing proof." Taleniekov turned several pages back. "Look. This report is very descriptive. Figures with guns at windows, men on roofs, servants streaming out, explosions starting in the kitchens, everything seemingly accounted for."

"Agreed," said Mikovsky, impressed with the minute details he read.

"Wrong. There's something missing. In every entry of this nature that we've seen—the storming of palaces and estates, the stopping of trains, the demonstrations—there are always such phrases as 'the advance column was led by Comrade So-and-So, the retreat under fire from the tzarist guards commanded by provisional Captain Such-and-Such, the execution carried out under the authority of Comrade Blank. As you said before, these entries are all bulging with identities, everything recorded for future confirmation. Well, read this again." Vasili flipped the pages back and forth. "The detail *is* extraordinary, even to the temperature of the day and the color of the afternoon sky and the fur overcoats worn by the men on the roof. But there's not one identity. Only the Voroshins are mentioned by name, no one else."

The scholar put his fingers on a yellowed page, his old eyes racing down the lines, his lips parted in astonishment. "You're right. The excessive detail obscures the absence of specific information."

"It always does," said Taleniekov. "The 'execution' of the Voroshin family was a hoax. It never happened."

25

"That young man of yours was quite impossible," said Mikovsky into the telephone, words and tone harshly critical of the night duty officer at the Ministry of Cultural Affairs. "I made it quite clear—as I assume *you* made it clear—that he was to remain in the archives until the material was returned. *Now,* what do I find? The man gone and the key shoved under my door! Really, it's most irregular. I suggest you send someone over to pick it up."

The old scholar hung up quickly, ending any chance for the duty officer to speak further. He glanced up at Taleniekov, his eyes filled with relief.

"That performance would have merited you a certificate from Stanislavsky," Vasili smiled, wiping his hands with paper towels taken from the nearby washroom. "We're covered—*you're* covered. Just remember, a body without papers will be found behind the furnaces. If you're questioned, you know nothing, you've never seen him before, your only reaction is one of shock and astonishment."

"But Cultural Affairs, surely *they'll* know him!"

"Surely they won't. He wasn't the man sent over with the key. The ministry will have its own problem, quite a serious one. It will have the key back in its possession, but it will have lost a messenger. If that phone is still tapped, the one listening will assume his man was successful. We've bought time."

"For what?"

"I've got to get to Essen."

"Essen. On an assumption, Vasili? On speculation?"

"It's more than speculation. Two of the names mentioned in the Voroshin report were significant. Schotte and Bohlen-Holbach. Friedrich Schotte was convicted by the German courts soon after the First World War for transferring money out of the country; he was killed in prison the night he arrived. It was a highly publicized murder, the killers never found. I think he made a mistake and the Matarese called for his silence. Gustav Bohlen-Holbach married the sole survivor of the Krupp family and assumed control of the Krupp Works. If these were Voroshin's friends a half-century ago, they could have been extraordinarily helpful to him. It all fits."

Mikovsky shook his head. "You're looking for fifty-year-old ghosts."

"Only in the hope that they will lead to present substances. God knows they exist. Do you need further proof?"

"No. It's their existence that frightens me for you. An Englishman waits for you at someone's flat, a woman follows me, a young man arrives here with a key to the archives he steals from another . . . all from this Matarese. It seems they have you trapped."

"From their point of view, they do. They've studied my files and sent out their soldiers to cover my every conceivable course of action, the assumption being that if one fails another will not."

The scholar removed his spectacles. "Where do they find such . . . soldiers, as you call them? Where are to be found these motivated men and women who give up their lives so readily?"

"The answer to that may be more frightening than either of us can imagine. Its roots go back centuries, to an Islamic prince named Hasan ibn-al-Sabbah. He formed cadres of political killers to keep him in power. They were called the *Fida'is*."

Mikovsky dropped his glasses on the desk; the sound was sharp. "The *Fida'is*? The assassins? I'm familiar with what you're talking about, but the concept is preposterous. The *Fida'is*—the assassins of Sabbah—were based on the prohibitions of a stoic religion. They exchanged their souls, their minds, their bodies for the pleasures of a Valhalla while on this earth. Such incentives are not credible in these times."

"In these times?" asked Vasili. "These *are* the times. The larger house, the fattened bank account, or the use of a *dacha* for a longer period of time, supplied more luxuriously than one's comrades; a greater fleet of aircraft or a more powerful battleship, the ear of a superior or an invitation to an event others cannot attend. These are very much the times, Yanov. The world you and I live in—personally, professionally, even vicariously—is a global society bursting with greed, nine out of ten inhabitants a Faust. I think it was something Karl Marx never understood."

"A deliberate transitional omission, my friend. He understood fully; there were other issues to be attacked first."

Taleniekov smiled. "That sounds dangerously like an apology."

"Would you prefer words to the effect that the governing of a nation is too important to be left to the people?"

"A monarchist statement. Hardly applicable. It could have been made by the Tzar."

"But it wasn't. It was made by America's Thomas Jefferson. Again, exercising a transitional omission. Both countries, you see, had just gone through their revolutions: each was a new, emerging nation. Words and decisions had to be practical."

"Your erudition does not change my judgment. I've seen too much, used too much."

"I don't want to change anything, least of all your talents of observation. I would only like you to keep things in perspective. Perhaps we're all in a state of transition."

"To what?"

Mikovsky put on his spectacles. "To heaven or hell, Vasili. I haven't the vaguest idea which. My only consolation is that I will not be here to find out. How will you get to Essen?"

"Back through Helsinki."

"Will it be difficult?"

"No. There's a man from Vyborg who'll help."

"When will you leave?"

"In the morning."

"You're welcome to stay the night with me."

"No, it could be dangerous for you."

The scholar raised his head in surprise. "But I thought you said that my performance on the phone removed such concerns."

"I believe it. I don't think anything will be said for days. Eventually, of course, the police will be called; but by then the incident—as far as you're concerned—will have faded into an unpleasant lapse of procedures."

"Then where's the problem?"

"That I'm wrong. In which case I will have killed us both."

Mikovsky smiled. "There's a certain finality in that."

"I had to do what I did. There was no one else. I'm sorry."

"Don't be." The scholar rose and walked unsteadily around the desk. "You must go then, and I will not see you again. Embrace me, Vasili Vasilovich. Heaven or hell, which will it be? I think you know. It is the latter and you have reached it."

"I got there a long time ago," said Taleniekov, holding the gentle old man he would never see again.

"Colonel Maletkin?" asked Vasili, knowing that the hesitant voice on the other end of the line indeed belonged to the traitor from Vyborg.

"Where are you?"

"At a telephone in the street, not far away. Do you have something for me?"

"Yes."

"Good. And I have something for you."

"Also good," Maletkin said. "When?"

"Now. Walk out the front entrance of the hotel and turn right. Keep walking, I'll catch up with you."

There was a moment of silence. "It's almost midnight."

"I'm glad your watch is accurate. It must be expensive. Is it one of those Swiss chronometers so popular with the Americans?"

"There's a woman here."

"Tell her to wait. *Order* her, Colonel. You're an officer of the KGB."

Seven minutes later Maletkin emerged ferret-like on the pavement in front of the entrance, looking smaller-than-life and glancing in several directions at once without seemingly turning his head. Although it was cold and dark, Vasili could almost see the sweat on the traitor's chin; in a day or so there would be no chin. It would be blown off in a courtyard in Vyborg.

Maletkin began walking north. There were not many pedestrians on Brodsky Street, a few couples linked arm in arm, the inevitable trio of young soldiers looking for warmth somewhere, anywhere, before returning to the sterility of their barracks. Taleniekov waited, watching the scene in the street, looking for someone who did not belong.

There was no one. The traitor had not considered a double-cross nor had any soldier of the Matarese picked him up. Vasili left the shadows of the doorway and hastened up the block; in sixty seconds he was directly across from Maletkin. He began whistling "Yankee Doodle Dandy."

"There's your cable!" said the traitor, spitting out the words in the darkness of a recessed storefront. "This is the only duplicate. Now tell me. Who is the informer in Vyborg?"

"The *other* informer, don't you mean?" Taleniekov snapped his cigarette lighter and looked at the copy of the coded message to Helsinki. It was accurate. "You'll have the name in a matter of hours."

"I want it *now!* For all I know someone's already checked with Vyborg. I want my protection, you guaranteed it! I'm leaving first thing in the morning."

"*We're* leaving," interrupted Vasili. "Before morning, actually."

"No!"

"Yes. You'll make that roster after all."

"I don't want anything to *do* with you. Your photograph's on every KGB bulletin board; there were *two* of them down at the Ligovsky headquarters! I found myself sweating."

"I wouldn't have thought it. But, you see, you must drive me back to the lake and put me in contact with the Finns. My business here in Leningrad is finished."

"Why *me?* I've done enough!"

"Because if you don't, I will not be able to remember a name you should know in Vyborg." Taleniekov patted the traitor's cheek; Maletkin flinched. "Go back to your woman, comrade, and perform well. But finish with her before too long. I want you checked out of the hotel by three-thirty."

"Three-*thirty?*"

"Yes. Drive your car to the Anichkov Bridge; be there no later than four o'clock. Make two trips over the bridge and back. I'll meet you on one side or the other."

"The *militsianyera.* They stop suspicious vehicles, and a car traveling back and forth over the Anichkov at four in the morning is not a normal sight."

"Exactly. If there are *militsianyera* around, I want to know it."

"Suppose they stop me?"

"Must I keep reminding you that you are a colonel of the KGB? You're on official business. Very official and very secret." Vasili started to leave, then turned back. "It just struck me," he said. "It may have occurred to you to borrow a weapon and shoot me down at an opportune moment. On the one hand, you could take credit for bringing me in and on the other, you could swear you tried to prevent my being killed at great risk to yourself. As long as you were willing to forgo the name of the man in Vyborg, such a strategy would appear to be sound. Very little risk, rewards from both camps. But you should know that every step I take in your presence here in Leningrad is being watched by another now."

Maletkin spoke with mounting intensity. "I *swear* to you such a thing never occurred to me!"

You really are a damn fool, thought Taleniekov. "Four o'clock then, comrade."

Vasili approached the staircase of the building four doors down the block from Lodzia's flat. He had glanced up at her windows; her lights were on. She was home.

He climbed the steps slowly, as a tired man might, returning to an uninviting home after putting in unwanted, unpaid-for overtime behind a never-ending conveyor belt in the cause of some new economic plan no one understood. He opened the glass door and went inside the small vestibule.

Instantly, he straightened up, the brief performance over; there was no hesitation now. He opened the inner door, walked to the basement staircase, and descended into the filthy environs of the connecting cellars. He passed the door in which he had placed the dead Englishman, vodka poured down the throat, wrists slashed with a razor. He pulled out his lighter, ignited it, and pushed the door back.

The Englishman was gone. Not only was he gone but there were no signs of blood; everything had been scrubbed clean.

Taleniekov's body went rigid, his thoughts suspended in shock. *Something terrible had happened. He had been wrong.*

So wrong!

Yet he had been *sure.* The soldiers of the Matarese were expendable, but the last thing they would do would be to return to a scene of violence. The possibilities of a trap were too great; the Matarese would not, *could* not, take that risk!

But they had, the target worth the gamble. What had he *done?*

Lodzia!

He left the door ajar and started walking rapidly, through the connecting cellars, the Graz-Burya in his hand, his steps silent, his eyes and ears primed.

He reached Lodzia's building and started up the steps to the ground-level foyer. He pulled the door back slowly and listened; there was a burst of laughter from the staircase above. A high-pitched female voice, joined seconds later by the laughter of a man.

Vasili put the Graz-Burya in his pocket, stepped inside around the railing, and walked unsteadily up the steps after the couple. They approached the second-floor landing, diagonally across from Lodzia's door. Taleniekov spoke, a foolish grin on his face.

"Would you young people do a middle-aged lover a favor? I'm afraid I had that one vodka too many."

The couple turned, smiling as one. "What's the problem, friend?" the young man asked.

"My friend is the problem," said Taleniekov, gesturing at Lodzia's door. "I was to meet her after the performance at the Kirov. I'm afraid I was delayed by an old army comrade. I think she's angry as hell. Please knock for me; if she hears my voice she probably won't let me in." Vasili grinned again, his thoughts in opposition to his smile. The conceivable sacrifice of the young and the attractive grew more painful as one got older.

"It's the least we can do for a soldier," said the girl, laughing brightly. "Go on, husband-mine, do your bit for the military."

"Why not?" The young man shrugged and walked to Lodzia's door. Taleniekov crossed beyond it, his back to the wall, his right hand again in his pocket. The husband knocked.

There was no sound from within. He glanced over at Vasili, who nodded, indicating another try. The young man knocked again, now louder, more insistent. Again there was only silence from inside.

"Perhaps she's still waiting for you at the Kirov," said the girl.

"Then again," added the young man, smiling, "perhaps she found your old army comrade and they're both avoiding you."

Taleniekov tried to smile back but could not. He knew only too well what he might find behind the door. "I'll wait here," he said. "Thank you very much."

The husband seemed to realize he had been facetious at the wrong moment. "I'm sorry," he mumbled, taking his wife's arm.

"Good luck," said the girl awkwardly. They both walked rapidly up the staircase.

Vasili waited until he heard the sound of a door closing two stories above. He took his automatic from his pocket and reached for the knob in front of him, afraid to find out that it was not locked.

It was not and his fear mounted. He pushed the door open, stepped inside, and closed it. What he saw sent pain through his chest; he knew a greater pain would follow shortly. The room was a shambles, chairs, tables, and lamps overturned; books and cushions were strewn on the floor, articles of clothing lying in disarray. The scene was created to depict a violent struggle, but it was false, overdone—as such constructed scenes were usually overdone. There had been no struggle, but there had been something else. There had been an interrogation based in torture.

The bedroom door was open; he walked toward it, knowing the greater pain would come in seconds, sharp bolts of anguish. He went inside and looked at her. She was on the bed, her clothes torn from her body, the positioning of her legs indicating rape, the act if it was done, done only for the purposes of an autopsy, undoubtedly performed after she had died. Her face was battered, lips and eyes swollen, teeth broken. Streaks of blood had flowed down her cheeks leaving abstract patterns of deep red on her light skin.

Taleniekov turned away, a terrible passivity sweeping over him. He had felt it many times before; he wanted only to kill. He would kill.

And then he was touched, so deeply that his eyes filled suddenly with tears and he could not breathe. Lodzia Kronescha had not broken; she had not revealed to the animal who had operated on her that her lover from the days of Riga was due after midnight. She had done more than keep the secret, far more. She had sent the animal off in another direction. What she must have *gone* through!

He had not loved in more than half a lifetime; he loved now and it was too late.

Too late? Oh, God!

. . . where is the problem?

. . . that I'm wrong. In which case I will have killed us both.

Yanov Mikovsky.

If a follow-up soldier had been sent by the Matarese to Lodzia Kronescha, another surely would have been sent to seek out the scholar.

Vasili raced into the sitting room, to the telephone that had carefully not been disturbed. It did not matter whether or not the line was tapped; he would learn what he had to learn in seconds, be away seconds later before anyone intercepting him could send men to the *dom vashen*.

He dialed Mikovsky's number. The phone was picked up immediately . . . too quickly for an old man.

"Yes?" The voice was muffled, unclear.

"Dr. Mikovsky, please."

"Yes?" repeated the male voice. It was not the scholar's.

"I'm an associate of Comrade Mikovsky and it's urgent that I speak with him. I know he wasn't feeling well earlier; does he need medical attention? We'll send it right away, of course."

"*No.*" The man spoke too swiftly. "Who is calling please?"

Taleniekov forced a casual laugh. "It's only his office neighbor. Comrade Rydukov. Tell him I've found the book he was looking for . . . no, let me tell him myself."

Silence.

"Yes?" It was Mikovsky; they had let him get on the line.

"Are you all right? Are those men friends?"

"Run, Vasili! Get away! They are—"

A deafening explosion burst over the line. Taleniekov held the telephone in his hand, staring at it. He stood for a moment, allowing sharp bolts of pain to sear through his chest. He loved two people in Leningrad and he had killed them both.

No, that was not true. The Matarese had killed them. And now he would kill in return. Kill . . . and kill . . . and *kill.*

He went into a telephone booth on the Nevesky Prospeckt and dialed the Europeiskaya Hotel. There would be no small talk; there was no time to waste on insignificant men. He had to get across Lake Vainikala, into Helsinki, reach the Corsican woman in Paris, and send the word to Scofield. He was on his way to Essen, for the secret of the Voroshins was there and animals were loose, killing to prevent that secret from being revealed. He wanted them now . . . so badly . . . these élite soldiers of the Matarese. They were all dead men in his hands.

"Yes, yes, what is it?" were the rushed, breathless words of the traitor from Vyborg.

"Get out of there at once," commanded Taleniekov. "Drive to the Moskva Station. I'll meet you at the curb in front of the first entrance."

"Now? It is barely two o'clock! You said—"

"Forget what I said, do as I *say.* Did you make the arrangements with the Finns?"

"A simple telephone call."

"Did you *make* it?"

"It can be done in a minute."

"Do it. Be at the Moskva in fifteen."

The drive north was made in silence, broken only by Maletkin's intermittent whining over the events of the past twenty-four hours. He was a man dealing in things so far beyond his depth that even his treachery had a rancid, shallow quality about it.

They drove through Vyborg, past Selzneva, toward the border. Vasili recognized the snowbanked road he had walked down from the edge of the frozen lake; soon they would reach the fork in the road where he had first observed the traitor beside him. It had been dawn then; soon it would be dawn again. And so much had happened, so much learned.

He was exhausted. He had had no sleep, and he needed it badly. He knew better than to try to function while his mind resisted thought; he would get to Helsinki and sleep for as long as his body and his faculties would permit, then make his arrangements. To Essen.

But there was a final arrangement to be made now, before he left his beloved Russia, *for* his Russia.

"In less than a minute we'll reach the rendezvous at the lake," Maletkin said. "You'll be met by a Finn along the path to the water's edge. Everything's

THE MATARESE CIRCLE   619

arranged. Now, *comrade,* I've carried out my end of the bargain, you deliver yours. Who is the other informer at Vyborg?"

"You don't need his name. You just need his rank. He's the only man in your sector who can give you orders, your sole superior. First in command at Vyborg."

"What? He's a tyrant, a fanatic!"

"What better cover? Drop in to see him . . . privately. You'll know what to say."

"Yes," agreed Maletkin, his eyes on fire, slowing the car down as they approached a break in the snowbank. "Yes, I think I will know what to say. . . . Here's the path."

"And here is your gun," said Taleniekov, handing the traitor his weapon, minus its firing pin.

"Oh? Yes, thank you," replied Maletkin, not listening, his thoughts on power unimagined only seconds ago.

Vasili got out of the car. "Goodbye," he said, closing the door.

As he rounded the trunk of the automobile toward the path, he heard the sound of Maletkin's window being rolled down.

"It's *incredible,"* said the traitor, gratitude in his voice. *"Thank* you."

"You're welcome."

The window was rolled up. The roar of the engine joined the screaming whine of the tires as they spun on the snow. The car sped forward; Maletkin would waste no time getting back to Vyborg.

To his execution.

Taleniekov entered the path that would take him to an escort, to Helsinki, to Essen. He began whistling softly; the tune was "Yankee Doodle Dandy."

26

The gentle-looking man in the rumpled clothes and the high-necked cotton sweater clamped a violin case between his knees and thanked the Finn Air stewardess for the container of tea. If anyone on board were inclined to guess the musician's age, he'd probably say somewhere between fifty-five and sixty, possibly a little older. Those sitting farther away would start at sixty-plus and add that he was probably older than that.

Yet with the exception of streaks of white brushed into his hair he had used no cosmetics. Taleniekov had learned years ago that the muscles of the face and body conveyed age and infirmity far better than powders and liquid plastics. The trick was to set the muscles in the desired position of abnormal stress, then go about one's business as normally as possible, overcoming the discomfort by fighting it, as older people fight the strain of age and cripples do the best they can with their deformities.

Essen. He had been to the black jewel of the Ruhr twice, neither trip recorded for they were sensitive assignments involving industrial espionage—operations Moscow did not care to have noted anywhere. Therefore, the Matarese had no information that could help it in Essen. No contacts to keep under surveillance, no friends to seek out and trap, nothing. No Yanov Mikovsky, no . . . Lodzia Kronescha.

Essen. Where could he begin? The scholar had been right: he was looking for a fifty-year-old ghost, a hidden absorption of one man and his family into a vast industrial complex during a period of world chaos. Legal documents going back more than half a century would be out of reach—if they had ever existed in the first place. And even if they had, and were available, they would be so obscured that it could take weeks to trace money and identities—in the tracing, his own exposure guaranteed.

Too, the court records in Essen had to be among the most gargantuan and complicated anywhere. Where was the man who could make his way through such a maze? Where was the time to do it?

There *was* a man, a patent attorney, who would no doubt throw up his hands at the thought of trying to find the name of a single Russian entering Essen fifty years ago. But he *was* a lawyer; he was a place to start. If he was alive, and if he was willing to talk with a long-ago embarrassment. Vasili had not thought of the man in years. Heinrich Kassel had been a thirty-five-year-old junior partner in a firm that did legal work for many of Essen's prominent companies. The KGB dossier on him had depicted a man often at odds with his superiors, a man who championed extremely liberal causes—some so objectionable to his employers they had threatened to fire him. But he was too good; no superior cared to be responsible for his dismissal.

The conspiratorial asses in Moscow had decreed in their wisdom that Kassel was prime material for patent-design espionage. In their better wisdom, the asses had sent their most persuasive negotiator, one Vasili Taleniekov, to enlist the attorney for a better world.

It had taken Vasili less than an hour over a trumped-up dinner to realize how absurd the assignment was. The realization had come when Heinrich Kassel had leaned back in his chair and exclaimed:

"Are you out of your *mind?* I do what I do to keep you bastards out!"

There had been nothing for it. The persuasive negotiator and the misguided attorney had gotten drunk, ending the evening at dawn, watching the sun come up over the gardens in Gruga Park. They had made a drunken pact: the lawyer would not report Moscow's attempt to the Bonn government if Taleniekov would guarantee that the KGB dossier was substantially altered. The lawyer had kept silent, and Vasili had returned to Moscow, amending the German's file with the judgment that the "radical" attorney was probably a provocateur in the pay of the Americans. Kassel might help him, at least tell him where he could start.

If he was able to reach Heinrich Kassel. So many things might have happened to prevent it. Disease, death, relocation, accidents of living and livelihood; it had been twelve years since the abortive assignment in Essen.

There was something else he had to do in Essen, he mused. He had no gun; he would have to purchase one. The West German airport security was such these days that he could not chance the dismantling of his Graz-Burya and packing it in his carry-on travel bag.

There was so much to do, so little time. But a pattern was coming into focus. It was obscure, elusive, contradictory . . . but it was there. The Corsican fever was spreading, the infectors using massive sums of money and ingenious financing methods to create pockets of chaos everywhere, recruiting an army of élite soldiers who would give up their lives instantly to protect the cause. But again, *what* cause? To what purpose? What were the violent philosophical descendants of Guillaume de Matarese trying to achieve? Assassination, terrorism, indiscriminate bombings and riots, kidnapping and murder . . . all the things that men of wealth had to detest, for in the breakdown of order was their undoing. This was the giant contradiction. *Why?*

He felt the plane dip, the pilot was starting his descent into Essen.

Essen. Prince Andrei Voroshin. Whom had he become?

"I don't believe it!" exclaimed Heinrich Kassel over the telephone, his voice conveying the same good-natured incredulity Taleniekov remembered from twelve years ago. "Everytime I pass the gardens in the Gruga, I pause for a moment and laugh. My wife thinks it must be the memory of an old girlfriend."

"I trust you cleared that up."

"Oh, yes. I tell her it was where I nearly became an international spy and she's *convinced* it's an old girlfriend."

"Meet me at the Gruga, please. It's urgent and has nothing to do with my former business."

"Are you sure? It wouldn't do for one of Essen's more prominent attorneys to have a Russian connection. These are odd times. Rumors abound that the Baader-Meinhof are financed by Moscow, that our neighbors to the far north are up to some nasty old tricks."

Taleniekov paused for a moment, wincing at the coincidence. "You have the word of an old conspirator. I'm unemployed."

"Really? How interesting. Gruga Park, then. It's almost noon. Shall we say one o'clock? Same place in the gardens, although there'll be no flowers this time of year."

The ice on the pond glistened in the sunlight, the shrubbery curled for the cold of winter yet briefly alive in the noonday's warmth from the sky. Vasili sat on the bench; it was fifteen minutes past one and he felt the stirrings of concern.

Without thinking, he touched the bulge in his right-hand pocket that was the small automatic he had purchased in Kopstadt Square, then took his hand away when he saw the hatless figure walking rapidly up the garden path.

Kassel had grown portly, and nearly bald. In his large overcoat with the black fur lapels he was the image of a successful burgomaster, his obviously expensive attire at odds with Taleniekov's memory of the fiery young lawyer who had wanted to *keep you bastards out!* As he drew nearer, Taleniekov saw that the face was cherubic—a great deal of *Schlagsahne* had gone down that throat, but the eyes were alive, still humorous . . . and sharp.

"I'm so sorry, my dear fellow," said the German as Taleniekov got up and accepted the outstretched hand. "A last-minute problem with an American contract."

"That has a certain symmetry to it," replied Vasili. "When I returned to Moscow twelve years ago, I wrote in your file that I thought you were on Washington's payroll."

"How perceptive. Actually, I'm paid out of New York, Detroit, and Los Angeles, but why quibble over cities?"

"You look well, Heinrich. Quite prosperous. What happened to that very vocal champion of the underdog?"

"They made him an overdog." The lawyer chuckled. "It would never have happened if you people controlled the Bundestag. I'm an unprincipled capitalist who assuages his guilt with sizable contributions to charity. My deutshmarks do far more than my vocal cords ever did."

"A reasonable statement."

"I'm a reasonable man. And what appears somewhat unreasonable to me now is why you would look me up. Not that I don't enjoy your company, for I do. But why now? You say you're not employed in your former profession; what could I possibly have that you'd be interested in?"

"Advice."

"You have legal problems in *Essen*? Don't tell me a dedicated Communist has private investments in the Ruhr."

"Only of time, and I have very little of that. I'm trying to trace a man, a family from Leningrad who came to Germany—to Essen, I'm convinced—between sixty and seventy years ago. I'm also convinced they entered illegally, and secretly bought into Ruhr industry."

Kassel frowned. "My dear fellow, you're mad. I'm trying to tick off the decades—I was never very good at figures—but if I'm not mistaken, you're referring to the period between 1910 and 1920. Is that correct?"

"Yes. They were turbulent times."

"You don't say? There was merely the great war to the south, the bloodiest revolution in history in the north, mass confusion in the eastern Slavic states, the Atlantic ports in chaos, and the ocean a graveyard. In essence, all Europe was—if I may be permitted—in flames and Essen itself experiencing an industrial expansion unseen before or since, including the Hitler years. Everything, naturally, was secret, fortunes made every day. Into this insanity comes one White Russian selling his jewels—as hundreds did—to buy himself a piece of the pie in any of a dozen companies, and you expect to *find* him?"

"I thought that might be your reaction."

"What other could I possibly have?" Kassel laughed again. "What is the name of this man?"

"For your own good, I'd rather not tell you."

"Then how can I help you?"

"By telling me where you would look first if you were me."

"In Russia."

"I did. The Revolutionary archives. In Leningrad."

"You found nothing?"

"On the contrary. I found a detailed description of a mass family suicide so patently at odds with reality that it had to be false."

"How was this suicide described? Not the particulars, just in general."

"The family's estate was stormed by the mobs; they fought all day, but in the end used the remaining explosives and blew themselves up with the main house."

"One family holding off a rioting mob of Bolsheviks for an entire day? Hardly likely."

"Precisely. Yet the account was as detailed as a von Clauswitz exercise, even to the climate and the brightness of the sky. Every inch of the vast estate was described, but outside of the name of the family itself, not one other identity was entered. There were no witnesses listed to confirm the event."

The attorney frowned again. "Why did you just say that 'every inch of the vast estate was described'?"

"It was."

"But why?"

"To lend credibility to the false account, I assume. A profusion of detail."

"Too profuse, perhaps. Tell me, were the actions of this family on that day described in your usual enemies-of-the-people vitriol?"

Taleniekov thought back. "No, they weren't actually. They could almost be termed individual acts of courage." Then he remembered specifically. "They released their servants before they took their own lives . . . . they *released* them. That *wasn't* a normal thing."

"And the inclusion of such a generous act in a revolutionary's account would not really be all that acceptable, would it?"

"What are you driving at?"

"That account may have been written by the man himself, or a literate member of the family and then passed on through corrupt channels to the archives."

"Entirely possible, but I still don't understand your point."

"The odds are long, I grant you, but bear with me. Over the years I've learned that when a client is asked to outline a deposition, he always shows himself in the best light; that's understandable. But he also invariably includes trivial particulars about things that mean a great deal to him. They slip out unconsciously: a lovely wife or a beautiful child, a profitable business or a . . . beautiful home. 'Every inch of the vast estate.' That was this family's passion, wasn't it? Land. Property."

"Yes." Vasili recalled Mikovsky's descriptions of the Voroshin estates. How the patriarchs were absolute rulers over the land, even to holding their own courts of law. "You could say they were excessively addicted to property."

"Might they have brought this addiction to Germany?"

"They might have. Why?"

The attorney's eyes turned cold. "Before I answer that, I must ask the old conspirator a very serious question. Is this search a Soviet reprisal of some sort? You say you're unemployed, that you're not working at your former occupation, but what proof do I have?"

Taleniekov breathed deeply. "I could say the word of a KGB strategist who altered an enemy's file twelve years ago, but I'll go farther than that. If you have connections with Bonn intelligence and can inquire discreetly, ask them about me. Moscow has sentenced me to death."

The coldness thawed in Kassel's eyes. "You wouldn't say such a thing if it weren't true. An attorney who deals every day with international business could check too easily. But you were a dedicated Communist."

"I still am."

"Then surely an enormous mistake has been made."

"A manipulated mistake," said Vasili.

"So this is not a Moscow operation, not in the Soviet interest?"

"No. It's in the interests of both sides, all sides, and that is all I'll say. Now, I've answered your serious question very seriously. Answer mine. What was your point regarding this family's preoccupation with the land?"

The lawyer pursed his thick lips. "Tell me the name. I may be able to help you."

"How?"

"The Records of Property that are filed in the State House. There were rumors that several of the great estates in Rellinghausen and Stadtwald—those on the northern shores of Lake Baldeney—were bought by Russians decades ago."

"They would not have bought in their own name, I'm certain of that."

"Probably not. I said the odds were long, but the covert acquisition of property is not unlike depositions. Things slip out. Possession of land is very close to a man's view of himself; in some cultures he is the land."

"Why can't I look for myself? If the records are available, tell me where to find them."

"It wouldn't do you any good. Only certified attorneys are permitted to search the titles. Tell me the name."

"It could be dangerous for anyone who looks," said Taleniekov.

"Oh, *come* now." Kassel laughed, his eyes amused again. "A seventy-year-old purchase of land."

"I believe there's a direct connection between that purchase and the extreme acts of violence that are occurring everywhere today."

"Extreme acts of . . ." The lawyer trailed off the phrase, his expression solemn. "An hour ago I mentioned Baader-Meinhof on the phone. Your silence was quite loud. Are you suggesting . . . ?"

"I'd rather not suggest anything," interrupted Vasili. "You're a prominent man, a resourceful man. Give me a letter of certification and get me into the Records of Property."

The German shook his head. "No, I won't do that. You wouldn't know what to look for. But you may accompany me."

"You'd do this yourself? Why?"

"I despise extremists who deal in violence. I remember too vividly the screams and diatribes of the Third Reich. I shall, indeed, look for myself, and if we get lucky you can tell me what you wish." Kassel lightened his voice, but sadness was there. "Besides, anyone sentenced to death by Moscow cannot be all bad. Now, tell me the name."

Taleniekov stared at the attorney, seeing another sentence of death. "Voroshin," he said.

The uniformed clerk in the Essen Hall of Records treated the prominent Heinrich Kassel with extreme deference. Herr Kassel's firm was one of the most important in the city. He made it plain that the coarse-looking receptionist behind the desk would be delighted to make copies of anything Herr Kassel wished to have duplicated. The woman stared up unpleasantly, her expression disapproving.

The steel file cabinets in the enormous room that housed the Records of Property were like gray robots stacked one on top of the other, circling the room, staring down at the open cubicles where the certified lawyers did their research.

"Everything is recorded by date," said Kassel. "Year, month, day. Be as specific as you can. What was the earliest Voroshin might have reasonably bought property in the Essen districts?"

"Allowing for the slow methods of travel at the time, say late May or early June of 1911. But I told you, he wouldn't have bought under his own name."

"We won't be looking for his name, or even an assumed name. Not to begin with."

"Why not an assumed name? Why couldn't he buy what was available under another name if he had the funds?"

"Because of the times, and they haven't changed that much. A man does not simply enter a community with his family and proceed to assume ownership of a large estate without arousing curiosity. This Voroshin, as you've described him, would hardly have wanted that. He would establish a false identity very slowly, very carefully."

"Then what do we look for?"

"A purchase made by attorneys for owners *in absentia*. Or by a trust legation from a bank for an estate investment; or by officers of a company or a limited partnership for acquisition purposes. There are any number of ways to set up concealed ownership, but eventually the calendar runs out; the owners want to move in. It's always the pattern, whether you talk about a candy store or a conglomerate or a large estate. No legal maneuver is a match for human nature." Kassel paused, looking at the gray cabinets. "Come. We'll start with the month of May, 1911. If there's anything here it may not be that difficult to find. There were no more than thirty or forty such estates in the whole of the Ruhr, perhaps ten to fifteen in the Rellinghausen-Stadtwald districts."

Taleniekov felt the same anticipation he had experienced with Yanov Mikovsky in the archives in Leningrad. The same feeling of peeling away layers of time, looking for a clue in documents recorded with precision decades ago. But now he was awed by the seeming irrelevancies that Heinrich Kassel spotted and extracted from the thick pages of legalese. The attorney was like a child in that candy store he had referred to; a young expert whose eyes roamed over the jellybeans and the sour balls, picking out the flawed items for sale.

"Here. Learn something, my international spy. This tract of land in Bredeney, thirty-seven acres in the Baldeney valley—ideal for someone like Voroshin. It was purchased by the Staatsbank of Duisburg for the minors of the family in Remscheid. Ridiculous!"

"What's the name?"

"It's irrelevant. A device. We find out who moved in a year or so after, *that's* the name we want."

"You think it may be Voroshin. Under his new identity?"

"Don't jump. There are others like this." Kassel laughed. "I had no idea my predecessors were so full of legal caprice; it's positively shocking. Look," he said, pulling out another sheaf of papers, his eyes automatically riveted on an indented clause on the first page, "here's another. A cousin of the Krupps is transferring ownership of property in Rellinghausen to a woman in Düsseldorf in gratitude for her many years of service. Really!"

"It's possible, isn't it?"

"Of course not; the family would never permit it. A relative found a way to turn a handsome profit by selling to someone who did not want his peers—or his creditors—to know he had the money. Someone who controlled the woman in Düsseldorf, if she ever existed. The Krupps probably congratulated their cousin."

And so it went. 1911, 1912, 1913, 1914 . . . 1915.

August 20, 1915.

The name was there. It meant nothing to Heinrich Kassel, but it did to Taleniekov. It brought to mind another document 2,000 miles away in the archives in Leningrad. The crimes of the Voroshin family, the intimate associates of Prince Andrei.

Friedrich Schotte.

"Wait a minute!" Vasili placed his hand over the pages. "Where's this?"

"Stadtwald. There's nothing irregular here. As a matter of fact, it's absolutely legal, very clean."

"Perhaps too legal, too clean. Just as the Voroshin massacre was too profuse with detail."

"What in God's name are you talking about?"

"What do you know of this Friedrich Schotte?"

The attorney grimaced in thought, trying to recall irrelevant history; this was not what he was looking for. "He worked for the Krupps, I think, in a very high position. It would have had to be for him to buy this. He got in trouble after the First World War. I don't remember the circumstances—a prison sentence or something—but I can't see why it's relevant."

"I can," said Taleniekov. "He was convicted of manipulating money out of Germany. He was killed on the first night of that prison sentence in 1919. Was the estate sold then?"

"I would think so. It would appear by the map survey to be a rather expensive property for a prison widow to maintain."

"How can we find out?"

"Look through the year 1919. We'll get there—"

"Let's get there now. *Please.*"

Kassel sighed. He got up and headed for the cabinets, returning a minute later with a bulging folder. "When a brief is interrupted continuity is lost," he muttered.

"Whatever we lose can be restored; we may gain time."

It took nearly thirty minutes before Kassel extracted a file within a file and placed it on the table. "I'm afraid we've just wasted a half-hour."

"Why?"

"The estate was purchased by the Verachten family on November 12, 1919."

"The Verachten Works? Krupp's competitor?"

"Not then. More so now, perhaps. The Verachtens came to Essen from Munich soon after the turn of the century, sometime around nineteen six or seven. It's common knowledge, the Verachtens were Munichers, and they couldn't be more respectable. You have a V, but no Voroshin."

Vasili's mind raced back over the information already known. Guillaume de Matarese had summoned the heads of once-powerful families, stripped—nearly but not entirely—of their past riches and influence. According to old Mikovsky, the Romanovs had waged a long battle against the Voroshins, labeling them the thieves of Russia, provokers of revolution. . . . It was clear! The *padrone* from the hills of Porto Vecchio had summoned a man—and by extension, his family— *already* in the *process* of a covert immigration, taking with them everything they could out of Russia!

"The imperial V, that's what we've found," said Taleniekov. "My God, what a strategy! Even to the prolonged use of truckloads of gold and silver sent out of Leningrad with the imperial *V!*" Vasili picked up the pages in front of the attorney. "You said it yourself, Heinrich. Voroshin would build a false identity very slowly, very carefully. That's exactly what he did; he simply began five or six years before I thought he had. I'm sure if such records were kept or memories could be activated, we'd find that Herr Verachten came first to Essen alone, until he was established. A man of wealth, testing new waters for investments and a future, bringing with him a carefully constructed history from faraway Munich, money flowing through the Austrian banks. So simple, and the times were so right!"

Suddenly Kassel frowned. "His wife," said the lawyer quietly.

"What about his wife?"

"She was not a Municher. She was Hungarian, from a wealthy family in Debrecen, it was said. Her German was never very good."

"Translated, she was from Leningrad and a poor linguist. What was Verachten's full name?"

"Ansel Verachten," said the attorney, his eyes now on Taleniekov. "*Ansel.*"

"*Andrei.*" Vasili let the pages fall. "It's incredible how the ego strives to be sublime, isn't it? Meet Prince Andrei Voroshin."

27

They strolled across the Gildenplatz, the Kaffee Hag building blazing with light, the Bosch insignia subdued but prominent below the enormous clock. It was eight in the evening now, the sky dark, the air cold. It was not a good night for walking, but Taleniekov and Kassel had spent nearly six hours in the Records of Property; the wind that blew across the square was refreshing.

"Nothing should shock a German from the Ruhr," said the lawyer, shaking his head. "After all, we are the Zürich of the north. But this is incredible. And I know only a *part* of the story. You won't reconsider and tell me the rest?"

"One day I may."

"That's too cryptic. Say what you mean."

"If I'm alive." Vasili looked at Kassel. "Tell me everything you can about the Verachtens."

"There isn't that much. The wife died in the mid-thirties, I think. One son and a daughter-in-law were killed in a bombing raid during the war, I remember that. The bodies weren't found for several days, buried under the rubble as so many were. Ansel lived to a ripe old age, somehow avoiding the war crimes penalties that caught the Krupps. He died in style, heart seizure while on horseback sometime in the fifties."

"Who's left?"

"Walther Verachten, his wife and their daughter; she never married, but it didn't prevent her from enjoying connubial pleasures."

"What do you mean?"

"She cut a bold figure, as they say, and when she was younger, had one to match her reputation. The Americans have a term that fits: she was—in some ways, still is—a 'man-eater.' " The attorney paused. "Strange how things turn out. It's Odile who really runs the companies now. Walther and his wife are in their late seventies and are rarely seen in public these days."

"Where do they live?"

"They're still in Stadtwald, but not at the original estate, of course. As we saw, it was one of those sold to postwar developers; it's why I didn't recognize it. They have a house further out in the countryside now."

"What about the daughter, this Odile?"

"*That,*" replied Kassel, chuckling, "depends on the lady's whims. She keeps a penthouse on the Werdenstrasse, and through those portals pass many a business adversary who wakes up the next morning too exhausted to best her at the conference table. When she's not in the city I understand she maintains a cottage on her parents' grounds."

"She sounds like quite a woman."

"In the forty-five-plus sweepstakes, few outclass her on the track." Kassel paused again, again not finished. "She has a flaw, however, and I'm told it's maddening. Although she runs Verachten firmly, when things aren't going well and swift decisions are called for, she often announces that she must confer with her father, thus postponing actions sometimes for days. At heart she's a woman, forced by circumstances to wear a man's hat, but the power still resides with old Walther."

"Do you know him?"

"We're acquaintances, that's all."

"What do you think of him?"

"Not much, never did. He always struck me as a rather pretentious autocrat without a great deal of talent."

"The Verachten Works thrive, however," said Vasili.

"I know, I know. That's what I'm told whenever I voice that opinion. My weak rejoinder is that it might do so much better without him; and it *is* weak. If Verachten did any better, it would own Europe. So, I assume it's a personal dislike on my part and I'm wrong."

Not necessarily, thought Taleniekov. *The Matarese make strange and effective arrangements. They need only the apparatus.*

"I want to meet him," said Vasili. "Alone. Have you ever been to his house?"

"Once, several years ago," replied Kassel. "The Verachten lawyers called us in on a patent problem. Odile was out of the country. I needed a Verachten signature on the affidavit of complaint—wouldn't proceed without it, as a matter of fact—and so I called old Walther and drove out to get it. The dam broke when Odile got back to Essen. She shouted at me over the telephone, 'My father should not have been disturbed! You will never serve Verachten again!' Oh, she was impossible. I told her as courteously as I could that we never would have served her in the first place had *I* received the initial request."

Taleniekov watched the attorney's face as he spoke; the German was genuinely angry. "Why did you say that?"

"Because it's true. I don't like the company—companies. There is a meanness over there." Kassel laughed at himself. "My feeling's probably a hangover from that radical young lawyer you tried to recruit twelve years ago."

It is the perceptive instincts of a decent man, thought Vasili. *You sense the Matarese, yet you know nothing.*

"I have a last request to make of you, my old friendly enemy," said Taleniekov. "Two actually. The first is not to say anything to anyone about our meeting today, or what we found. The second is to describe the location of the Verachten house and whatever you can remember about it."

The corner of a brick wall loomed into view in the glare of the headlights. Vasili pressed down on the accelerator of the rented Mercedes, his eyes glancing at the odometer, judging the distance between the start of the wall and the iron gate. Five-eighths of a kilometer, nearly 1,800 feet. The tall gate was closed; it was electronically operated, electronically protected.

He came to the end of the wall; it was somewhat shorter in length than its counterpart on the other side of the gate. Beyond there was only the extension of the forest, in the middle of which had been built the Verachten compound. He depressed the pedal and looked for an opening off the road, somewhere he could conceal the Mercedes.

He found it between two trees, the shrubbery dampened down by previous snows. He angled the coupe into the natural cave of greenery, plunging in as far off the road as possible. He turned off the engine, got out, and retraced the car's path, pulling up the shrubbery until he reached the road fifteen feet away. He stood on the shoulder and examined the camouflage; in the darkness, it was sufficient. He started back toward the Verachten wall.

If he could get over it without setting off any alarms, he knew he could reach the house. There was no way to electronically scan a forest; wires and cells were too easily tripped by animals and birds. It was the wall itself that had to be negotiated. He reached it and studied the brick in the flame of his cigarette lighter. There were no devices of any sort. It was an ordinary brick wall, its very ordinariness misleading, and Vasili knew it. There was a tall oak on his right, limbs curling up above the top of the wall, but not extending over it.

He leaped, his hands clawing the bark, his knees vicing the trunk; he scaled up to the first limb, swinging his leg over it, pulling himself up into a sitting position, his back against the tree. He leaned forward and downward, his hands balancing his body on the limb until he was prone, and studied the top of the wall in the dim light. He found what he knew had to be there.

Grooved into the flat surface of the concrete was a crisscrossing network of wire-coated plastic tubing through which air and current flowed. The electricity was of sufficient voltage to inhibit animals from gnawing at the plastic, and the air pressure was calibrated to set off alarms the instant a given amount of weight fell on the tubes. The alarms were undoubtedly received in a scanning room in the compound, where instruments pinpointed the place of penetration. Taleniekov knew the system was practically fail-safe; if one strand was shorted out, there were five or six others to back it up, and the pressure of a knife across the wire coating would be enough to set off the alarm.

But practically fail-safe was not totally fail-safe. Fire. Melting the plastic and releasing the air without the pressure of a blade. The only alarm set off in this way was that of malfunction; the trace would begin where the system originated, which had to be much nearer the house.

He estimated the distance between the edge of the tree limb and the top of the wall. If he could loop his leg as close to the end of the limb as possible, swing underneath, and brace himself with one hand against the ridge of the wall, his free hand could hold his lighter against the plastic tubes.

He pulled out his cigarette lighter—his American lighter, he reflected with a certain chagrin—and pushed the tiny butane lever to its maximum. He tested it; the flame shot out and held steady; he lowered it slightly for the light was too bright. He took a deep breath, firmed the muscles of his right leg, and dropped to his left, his left hand making contact with the edge of the wall as he arched downward. He steadied himself and began breathing slowly, orienting his vision to the upside-down view. Blood raced to his head; he revolved his neck briefly to lessen the pressure, then snapped on the lighter, holding the flame against the first tube.

There was a crackling of electricity, then an expulsion of air as the tube turned black and melted. He reached the second in the immediate series; this one exploded like a small, wet firecracker, the sound no more than that of a low-gauge air gun. The third grew into a thin, outsized bubble. A *bubble*. Pressure! Weight! He pushed the flame into it and it burst; he held his breath, waiting for the sound of an alarm. It did not come; he had punctured the tube in time, before the heat and the expansion had reached the weight tolerance. It taught him something: hold the flame closer at first contact. He did so with the following two strands, each bursting on touch. There was a final tube.

Suddenly the flame receded, sinking back into its invisible source. He was out of fuel. He closed his eyes for a moment in frustration, and sheer anger. His leg ached furiously; the blood in his head made him dizzy. Then he thought of the obvious, annoyed with himself that he had not considered it immediately. The one remaining tube might well prevent a full-malfunction alarm; he was far better off leaving it intact. There were at least fifteen free inches on the surface of the concrete, more than enough to place a foot on and plunge over the wall to the other side.

He struggled back up to the limb and rested for a while, letting his head clear. Then slowly, carefully, he lowered his left foot to the wall, setting it securely on top of the burnt-out tubes. With equal caution he raised his right leg over the limb, sliding down until the limb was in the small of his back. He took a deep breath, tensed his muscles, and leaped forward, pressing his left foot into the stone, propelling himself over the wall. He fell to the ground, rolling to break his fall. He was inside the Verachten compound.

He got to his knees, listening for any sounds of an alert. There were none, so he rose to his feet and started threading his way through the dense woods toward what he presumed to be the central area of the property. The fact that he was half-walking, half-crawling in the right direction was confirmed in less than a minute. He could see the lights of the main house filtered through the trees, the beginning of a large expanse of lawn clearer with each step.

A glow of a cigarette! He dropped to the ground. Directly ahead, perhaps fifty feet, stood a man at the edge of the lawn. Instantly, Taleniekov was aware of the forest breezes; he listened for the sounds of an animal.

Nothing. There were no dogs. Walther Verachten had confidence in his electronic gates and sophisticated alarm system; he needed only human patrols to make the darkness of his compound secure.

Vasili inched forward, his eyes on the guard ahead. The man was in uniform, a visored hat and a heavy winter jacket pinched at the waist by a thick belt that held a holstered gun. The guard checked his watch and stripped his cigarette, shaking the tobacco to the grass; he had been in the army. He walked several paces to his left, stretched, yawned, proceeded another twenty feet, then strolled aimlessly back toward where he had been standing. That short stretch of ground was his post, other guards no doubt stationed every several hundred feet, ringing the main house like Caesar's Praetorian Guard. But these were neither Caesar's times nor Caesar's dangers; the duty was boring, the guard given to openly smoked cigarettes, yawns and aimless wandering. The man would not be a problem.

But getting across the stretch of lawn to the shadows of the drive on the right side of the house might well be. He would have to walk briefly in the glare of the floodlights that shot down from the roof.

A hatless man in a dark sweater and trousers doing such a thing would be ordered to stop. But a guard dressed in a visored cap and a heavy jacket with a holster at his side would not cause so much concern. And if reprimanded, that guard could always return to his post; it was important to bear that in mind.

Taleniekov crawled through the underbrush, elbows and knees working on the hard ground, pausing with every snap of a branch, blending what noise he made into the sounds of the night forest. He was within five feet, a spray of juniper between himself and the guard. The bored man reached into his jacket pocket and took out his pack of cigarettes.

It was the moment to move. *Now.*

Vasili sprang up, his left hand clutching the guard's throat, his left heel dug into the earth to provide backward leverage. In one motion, he pulled the man off his feet, arching him down into the juniper bush, crashing the guard's skull into the ground, his fingers clawing the windpipe, tightening around it. The shock of the assault, combined with the blow to the head and the choking of air, rendered the man unconscious. There was a time when Taleniekov would have finished the job, killing the guard because it was the most practical thing to do; that time was past. This was no soldier of the Matarese; there was no point in his death. He removed the man's jacket and visored hat, put them on quickly and buckled the holster around his waist. He dragged the guard further into the woods, angled the head into the dirt, removed his own small weapon and smashed the handle down above the man's right ear. He would remain unconscious for hours.

Vasili crept back to the edge of the lawn, stood up, breathed deeply, and started across the grass. He had watched the guard walk—a slight casual swagger, the neck settled, the head angled back, and he imitated the memory. With each step he expected a rebuke or an order or an inquiry; if any were shouted he would shrug and return to the man's post. None came.

He reached the drive and the shadows. Fifty yards down the pavement there was a light streaming out of an open door and the figure of a woman opening a garbage can, two paper bags at her feet. Vasili walked faster, his decision made. He approached the woman; she was in the white uniform of a maid.

"Excuse me, the captain ordered me to bring a message to Herr Verachten."

"Who the hell are you?" asked the stocky woman.

"I'm new. Here, let me help you." Taleniekov picked up the bags.

"You *are* new. It's Helga this, Helga that. What do they care? What's the message? I'll bring it to him."

"I wish I could give it to you. I've never met the old man and I don't want to, but that's what I was told to do."

"They're all farts down there. *Kommandos!* A bunch of beer-soaked ruffians, I say. But you're better looking than most of them."

"Herr Verachten, please? I was told to hurry."

"Everything's hurry this and hurry that. It's ten o'clock. The old fool's wife is in her rooms and he's in his chapel, of course."

"Where? . . ."

"Oh, all right. Come on in, I'll show you. . . . You *are* better looking, more polite, too. Stay that way."

Helga led him through a corridor that ended at a door opening into a large entrance hall. Here the walls were covered with numerous Renaissance oil paintings, the colors vivid and dramatic under pinpoint spotlights. They extended up a wide circular staircase, the steps of Italian marble. Branching off the hall were several larger rooms, and the brief glimpses Taleniekov had of them confirmed Heinrich Kassel's description of a house filled with priceless antiques. But the glimpses were brief; the maid turned the corner beyond the staircase and they approached a thick mahogany door filled with ornate biblical carvings. She opened it and they descended steps carpeted in scarlet until they reached some kind of anteroom, the floor marble like the staircase in the great hall. The walls were covered with tapestries depicting early Christian scenes. An ancient church pew was on the left, the bas-relief examples of an art long forgotten; it was a place of meditation, for the tapestry facing it was of the Stations of the Cross. At the end of the small room was an arched door, beyond it obviously Walther Ver-achten's chapel.

"You can interrupt, if you want to," said Helga without enthusiasm. "The head *Kommando* will be blamed for it, not you. But I'd wait a few minutes; the priest will be finished with his claptrap by then."

"A *priest?*" The word slipped out of Vasili's throat; the presence of such a man was the furthest thing from his mind. A *consigliere* of the Matarese with a priest?

"His fart-filled holiness, that's what I say." Helga turned and started back. "Do as you wish," she said, shrugging. "I don't tell anybody what to do."

Taleniekov waited for the heavy mahogany door above to open and close. Then he walked quietly to the door of the chapel, his ear against the wood, trying to pick up meaning from the sing-song chant he could hear from within.

Russian. The language being chanted was Russian!

He was not sure why he was so startled. After all, the congregation inside consisted of the sole surviving son of Prince Andrei Voroshin. It was the fact of the service itself that was so astonishing.

Vasili placed his hand on the knob, turned it silently, and opened the door several inches. Two things struck him instantly: the sweet-sour odor of incense and the shimmering flames of outsized candles, which caused him to blink his eyes, adjusting to the chiaroscuro effect of bright fires against the moving black shadows on the gray concrete walls. Recessed in those walls everywhere were icons of the Russian Orthodox Church, those nearest the altar raising their saintly arms, reaching for the cross of gold in the center.

In front of the cross was the priest, dressed in his cassock of white silk, trimmed with silver and gold. He had his eyes closed, his hands folded across his chest, and out of his barely moving mouth came words of a chant fashioned more than a thousand years ago.

Then Taleniekov saw Walther Verachten—an old man with thinning white hair, strands of which fell over the back of a long, gaunt neck. He was prostrate on the three marble steps of the altar, at the feet of the high priest, his arms stretched out in supplication, his forehead pressed against the marble in absolute submission. The priest raised his voice, signifying the finish of the Orthodox *Kyrie Eleison*. The Litany of Forgiveness commenced; priestly statement followed by sinner's response, a choral exercise in self-indulgence and self-delusion. Vasili thought of the pain inflicted, demanded by the Matarese, and was revolted. He opened the door, stepped inside.

The priest opened his eyes, startled, his hands surging down from his chest in indignation. Verachten spun on the steps, his skeletal body trembling. Awk-wardly, painfully, he struggled to his knees.

"How dare you interfere?" he shouted in German. "Who gave you permission to come in here?"

"An historian from Petrograd, Voroshin," said Taleniekov in Russian. "That's as good an answer as any, isn't it?"

Verachten fell back on the steps, gripping the edge of the stone with his hands.

Steadying himself, he brought them up to his face, covering his eyes as if they had been clawed or burned. The priest dropped to his knees, grabbing the old man by the shoulders, embracing him. The cleric turned to Vasili, his voice harsh.

"Who *are* you? What *right* have you?"

"Don't talk to me of rights! You turn my stomach. Parasite!"

The priest held his place, cradling Verachten. "I was summoned years ago and I came. As my predecessors in this house I ask for nothing and I receive nothing."

The old man lowered his hands from his face, struggling to compose himself, nodding his trembling head; the priest released him. "So you've come at last," he said. "They always said you would. Vengeance is the Lord's, but then you people do not accept that, do you? You've taken God from the people and given so little in return. I have no quarrel with you on this earth. Take my life, Bolshevik. Carry out your orders, but let this good priest go. He's no Voroshin."

"You *are*, however."

"It is my burden." Verachten's voice grew firmer. "And our secret. I've borne both well, as God has given me the vision to do so."

"One talks of rights, the other of God!" spat out Taleniekov. "Hypocrites! *Per nostro circolo!*"

The old man blinked, no reaction in his eyes. "I beg your pardon?"

"You heard me! *Per nostro circolo!*"

"I hear you, but I don't understand you."

"Corsica! Porto Vecchio! *Guillaume de Matarese!*"

Verachten looked up at the priest. "Am I senile, father? What's he talking about?"

"Explain," said the priest. "Who are you? What do you want? What's the meaning of these words?"

"*He* knows!"

"I know *what?*" Verachten leaned forward. "We Voroshins have blood on our souls, I accept that. But I cannot accept what I don't know."

"The *shepherd boy,*" said Taleniekov. "With a voice crueler than the wind. Do you need more than that? The shepherd boy!"

"The Lord is my shepherd—"

"Stop it, you sanctimonious *liar!*"

The priest stood up. "*You* stop it, whoever you are! This good and decent man has lived his life in atonement for sins that were never *his!* Since a child he wanted to be a man of God, but it was not permitted. Instead, he has become a man *with* God. Yes, *with God.*"

"He is a Matarese!"

"I don't know what that is, but I know what *he* is. Millions dispensed every year to the starving, to the deprived. All he asks in return is our presence to see him through his devotions. It is all he has *ever* asked."

"You're a *fool!* Those funds are Matarese funds! They buy death!"

"They buy *hope. You're* the liar!"

The door of the chapel burst open. Vasili spun around. A man in a dark business suit stood inside the frame, legs apart, arms outstretched, a gun in his right hand, steadied by his left. "Don't move!" The language was German.

Through the door came two women. One was tall and slender, dressed in an ankle-length blue velvet gown, a fur stole around her shoulders, her face white, angular, beautiful. The coarse-looking woman at her side was short, in a cloth overcoat, her face puffy, her narrow eyes wary. He had seen her only hours ago; a guard had said she would be accommodating, should Heinrich Kassel need duplicates.

"That's the man," said the receptionist who had sat behind the desk at the Records of Property.

"Thank you," replied Odile Verachten. "You may go now, the chauffeur will drive you back into the city."

"Thank *you*, ma'am. Thank you *very* much."

"You're most welcome. The chauffeur's in the hallway. Good night."

"Good night, ma'am." The woman left.

"*Odile!*" cried her father, struggling to his feet. "This man came in—"

"I'm *sorry*, father," interrupted his daughter. "Putting off unpleasantries only compounds them; it's something you never understood. I'm sure this . . . *man* . . . said things you shouldn't have heard."

With those few words, Odile Verachten nodded at her escort. He shifted the weapon to his left and fired. The explosion was deafening; the old man fell. The killer raised his gun and fired again; the priest spun, the top of his head a sudden mass of dark red.

Silence.

"That was one of the most brutal acts I've ever seen," said Taleniekov. *He would kill . . . somehow.*

"From Vasili Vasilovich Taleniekov, that's quite a statement," said the Verachten woman, taking a step forward. "Did you really believe that this ineffectual old man—this would-be priest—could be a part of *us?*"

"My error was in the man, not in the name. Voroshin is Matarese."

"Correction. Verachten. We are not merely born, we are chosen." Odile gestured at her dead father. "He never was. When his brother was killed during the war, Ansel chose me!" She glared at him. "We wondered what you had learned in Leningrad."

"Would you really like to know?"

"A name," answered the woman. "A name from a chaotic period in recent history. Voroshin. But it hardly matters that you know. There is nothing you could say, no accusation you could make, that the Verachtens could not deny."

"You don't *know* that."

"We know enough, don't we?" said Odile, glancing at the man with the gun.

"We know enough," repeated the killer. "I missed you in Leningrad. But I did not miss the woman, Kronescha, did I? If you know what I mean."

"*You!*" Taleniekov started forward; the man clicked the gun's hammer back with his thumb.

Vasili held his place, body and mind aching. He *would* kill; to do so control had to be found. And shock. *Lodzia, my Lodzia! Help me.*

He stared at Odile Verachten, and spoke softly, slowly, giving each word equal emphasis. *"Per . . . nostro . . . circolo!"*

The smile faded from her lips, her white skin grew paler. "Again from the past. From a primitive people who don't know what they're saying. We should have known you might learn it."

"You believe that? You think they don't know what they're saying?"

"Yes."

It was now, or it was not, thought Taleniekov. He took a deliberate step toward the woman. The killer's gun inched out, only feet away, aimed directly at his skull. "Then why do they talk of the shepherd boy?"

He took another step; the killer breathed abruptly, audibly through his nostrils—prelude to fire—the trigger was being squeezed.

"Stop!" screamed the Verachten woman.

The explosion came as Vasili dropped to a crouch. Odile Verachten had thrust her arm out in a sudden command to prevent the gunshot, and in that instant, Taleniekov sprang, eye and mind and body on a single object. The gun, the *barrel* of the gun.

He reached it, his fingers gripping the warm steel, hand and wrist twisting counter-clockwise, pulling downward to inflict the greatest pain. He threw his right hand—fingers curled and rigid—into the man's stomach, tearing at the muscles, feeling the protrusion of the rib cage. He yanked up with all his strength; the killer screamed, and fell.

Vasili spun and lunged at Odile. In the brief moment of violence, she had hesitated; now she reacted with precision, her hand underneath her fur stole pulling out a gun. Taleniekov tore at that hand, that gun, throwing her to the chapel floor, his knee hammering into her chest. The handle of her own gun pressed across her throat.

"There'll be no mistake this time!" he said. "No capsules in the mouth."

"You'll be killed!" she whispered.

"Probably," agreed Vasili. "But you'll go with me, and you don't want that. I was wrong. You're not one of your soldiers; the chosen don't take their own lives."

"I'm the only one who can save yours." She choked under the pressure of the steel, but went on. "The *shepherd.* . . . Where? *How?*"

"You want information. Good! So do I." Taleniekov removed the gun from her throat, clamping his left hand where it had been, the fingers of his right hand entering her mouth, depressing the tongue, digging through the soft tissue downward. She coughed again, only mucus and spit rolling down her chin; there were no lethal pills in her mouth. He had been right; the chosen did not commit suicide. He then spread the stole and ran his hand over her body, pulling her off the floor, and reaching around her back, pushing her down again and plunging his hand between her legs, ankles to pelvis, feeling for a gun or a knife. There was nothing. "Get up!" he ordered.

She rose only partially, her knees pulled up under her, holding her neck. "You *must tell* me!" she whispered. "You know you can't get out. Don't be a fool, Russian! Save your life! What do you *know of the shepherd?*"

"What am I offered to tell you?"

"What do you *want?*"

"What does the *Matarese* want?!"

The woman paused. "Order."

"Through *chaos?*"

"Yes! The shepherd? In the name of God, tell me!"

"I'll tell you when we're out of the compound."

"No! *Now.*"

"Do you think I'd trade that off?" He pulled her to her feet. "We're leaving now. Your friend here will wake up before too long, and a part of me would give my life to take his. Slowly, in great pain as he took another's. But I will not do that; he must report to faceless men and they must make their moves—and we must watch. For Verachten is suddenly headless; you'll be far away from Essen."

"No!"

"Then you'll die," said Taleniekov simply. "I got in, I'll get out."

"I gave orders! No one's to leave!"

"Who's leaving? A uniformed guard returns to his post. Those aren't Matarese out there. They're exactly what they're supposed to be: former *Kommandos* hired to protect wealthy executives." Vasili jammed the gun into her throat. "Your choice? It doesn't matter to me."

She flinched; he grabbed her neck, pulling it into the barrel. She nodded. "We will talk in my father's car," she whispered. "We're both civilized people. You have information I need, and I have a revelation for you. You have nowhere to turn but to us now. It could be far worse for you."

He sat next to her in the front seat of Walther Verachten's limousine. He had taken off the uniform, and was now no more than another stud in Odile Verachten's stable. She was behind the wheel, his arm around her shoulders, his automatic again jammed into her, out of sight. As the guard at the gatehouse nodded and turned to press the release button, he leaned into her; one uncalled for move, one gesture, and she was dead. She knew it; none came.

She sped through the open gate, turning the wheel to the left. He grabbed it, his foot reaching across hers to the brake, and spun the wheel to the right. The car skidded into a half spin; he steadied it and slammed his foot over hers on the accelerator.

"What are you *doing?*" she cried.

"Avoiding any prearranged rendezvous."

It was in her eyes; another car had been waiting on the road to Essen. For the third time, Odile Verachten was genuinely frightened.

They sped down the country road; several hundred yards ahead he could see a fork clearly in the headlights. He waited; instinctively she bore to the right. The fork was reached, the turn began; he moved his hand swiftly to the rim of the wheel and pushed it up, sending them into the left road.

"You'll *kill* us!" screamed the Verachten woman.

"Then both of us will go," said Taleniekov. The surrounding woods diminished; there were open spaces ahead. "That field on the right. Pull over."

"*What?*"

He raised the gun and put it against her temple. "Stop the car," he repeated.

They got out. Vasili took the keys from the ignition and put them in his pocket. He pushed her forward, into the grass, and they walked toward the middle of the field. In the distance was a farmhouse, beyond it a barn. There were no lights; the farmers of Stadtwald were asleep. But the winter moon was brighter now than it was in the Gildenplatz.

"What are you going to do?" asked Odile.

"Find out if you have the courage you demand of your soldiers."

"Taleniekov, *listen* to me! No matter what you do to me, you won't change anything. We're too far along. The world needs us too desperately!"

"This world needs killers?"

"To *save* it from killers! You talk of the shepherd. *He* knows. Can you *doubt* it? Join us. Come with us."

"Perhaps I will. But I have to know where you're going."

"Do we trade?"

"Again, perhaps."

"Where did you hear of the shepherd?"

Vasili shook his head. "Sorry, you first. Who are the Matarese? *What* are they? What are they doing?"

"Your first answer," said Odile, parting her stole, her hands on the neckline of her gown. She ripped it downward, the white buttons breaking from the threads, exposing her breasts. "It's one we know you've found," she added.

In the moonlight Taleniekov saw it. Larger than he had seen before, a jagged circle that was part of the breast, part of the body. The mark of the Matarese. "The grave in the hills of Corsica," he said. "*Per nostro circolo.*"

"It can be *yours,*" said Odile, reaching out to him. "How many lovers have lain across these breasts and admired my very distinctive birthmark. You are the *best,* Taleniekov. *Join* the best! Let me bring you over!"

"A little while ago, you said I had no choice. That you would reveal something to me, force me to turn to you. What is it?"

Odile pulled the top of her gown together. "The American is dead. You are alone."

"*What?*"

"Scofield was killed."

"*Where?*"

"In Washington. . . ."

The sound of an engine interrupted her words. Headlights pierced the darkness of the road that wound out of the woods from the south; a car came into view. Then suddenly, as if suspended in a black void, it stopped on the shoulder behind the limousine. Before the headlights could be extinguished, he could see three men leaping out, the driver following. All were armed; two carried rifles. All were predators.

"They've found me," cried Odile Verachten. "Your answer, Taleniekov! You really have no choice, you see that, don't you? Give me the gun. An order from me can change your life. Without it, you're dead."

Stunned, Vasili looked behind him; the fields stretched into pastures, the pastures into darkness. Escape was not a problem—perhaps not even the right decision. Scofield *dead?* In *Washington?* He had been on his way to England; what had sent him prematurely to Washington? But Odile was not lying; he would bank his life on it! She had spoken the truth as she knew the truth—just as her offer was made in truth. The Matarese would make good use of one Vasili Taleniekov.

Was it the *way?* The *only* way?

"Your *answer!*" Odile stood motionless, her hand outstretched.

"Before I give it, tell me. When was Scofield killed? How?"

"He was shot two weeks ago in a place called Rock Creek Park."

A lie. A calculated lie! She had been lied to! Did they have an ally deep within the Matarese? If so, he had to reach that man. Vasili spun the automatic in his hand, offering it to Odile. "There's nowhere else to turn. I'm with you. Give your order."

She turned from him and shouted. "You men! Put up your guns! Hold your fire!"

A single flashlight beam shot out and Taleniekov saw what she did not see—and knew instantly what she did not know. The light was held by one man to free the other three; and although he was in the spill, the beam was not directed at him. It was directed at *her.* He dove to his left into the grass. A fusillade of bullets erupted from the rifles across the field.

Another order had been given. Odile Verachten screamed. She was blown off her feet, her body caved forward, then arched backward in midair under the force of the shells.

Other gunshots followed, digging up the earth to the right of Taleniekov as he lurched, scrambling through the grass away from the target ground. The shouts grew louder as the men attacked, converging on the site on which only seconds ago a living member of the Matarese council had stood—issuing an order that was not hers to give.

Vasili reached the relative safety of the woods. He rose and started running into the darkness, knowing that soon he would stop, and turn, and kill a man on his way back to the limousine. In other darkness.

But now he kept running.

The aging musician sat in the last row of the plane, a shabby violin case between his knees. Absently, he thanked the stewardess for the cup of hot tea; his thoughts consumed him.

He would be in Paris in an hour, meet with the Corsican girl, and set up direct communications with Scofield. It was imperative they work in concert now; things were happening too rapidly. He had to join Beowulf Agate in England.

Two of the names on the guest list of Guillaume de Matarese seventy years ago were accounted for.

Scozzi. Dead.

Voroshin-Verachten. Dead.

Sacrificed.

The direct descendants were expendable, which meant they were not the true inheritors of the Corsican *padrone*. They had been merely messengers, bearing gifts for others far more powerful, far more capable of spreading the Corsican fever.

This world needs killers?

To save it from killers! Odile Verachten had said.

Enigma.

David Waverly, Foreign Secretary, Great Britain.

Joshua Appleton, IV, Senator, United States Congress.

Were they, too, expendable messengers? Or were they something else? Did each carry the mark of the jagged blue circle on his chest? Had Scozzi? And if either did, or Scozzi had, was that unnatural blemish the mark of mystical distinction Odile Verachten had thought it was, or was it, too, something else? A symbol of expendability, perhaps. For it occurred to Vasili that wherever that mark appeared, death was a partner.

Scofield was searching in England now. The same Beowulf Agate that someone within the Matarese had reported killed in Rock Creek Park. Who was that someone, and why had the false report gone out? It was as though that person—or persons—wanted Scofield spared, beyond reach of the Matarese killers. But why?

You talk of the shepherd. He knows! Can you doubt it?

The shepherd. A shepherd boy.

Enigma.

Taleniekov put the tea down on the tray in front of him, his elbow jarred by his seat companion. The businessman from Essen had fallen asleep, his arm protruding over the divider. Vasili was about to remove it when his eyes fell on the folded newspaper spread out on the German's lap.

The photograph stared up at him and he stopped breathing, sharp bolts of pain returning to his chest.

The smiling, gentle face was that of Heinrich Kassel. The bold print above the photograph screamed the information.

ADVOKAT MORD

Taleniekov reached over and picked up the paper, the pain accelerating as he read.

Heinrich Kassel, one of Essen's most prominent attorneys, was found murdered in his car outside his residence last evening. The authorities have called the killing bizarre and brutal.

Kassel was found garroted, with multiple head injuries and lacerations of the face and body. An odd aspect of the killing was the tearing of the victim's upper clothing, exposing the chest area on which was a circle of dark blue. The paint was still wet when the body was discovered shortly past midnight. . . .

Per nostro circolo.

Vasili closed his eyes. He had pronounced Kassel's sentence of death with the name *Voroshin.*

It had been carried out.

PART THREE

28

"Scofield?" The gray-faced man was astonished, the name uttered in shock.

Bray broke into a run through the crowds in the London underground, toward the Charing Cross exit. It had happened; it was bound to happen sooner or later. No brim of a hat could conceal a face if trained eyes saw that face, and no unusual clothing dissuaded a professional once the face had been marked.

He had just been marked, the man making the identification—and without question now racing to a phone—was a veteran agent for the Central Intelligence Agency stationed at the American Embassy on Grosvenor Square. Scofield knew him slightly; one or two lunches at The Guinea; two or three conferences, inevitably held prior to Consular Operations invading areas the Company considered possessively sacrosanct. Nothing close, only cold; the man was a fighter for CIA prerogatives and Beowulf Agate had transgressed too frequently.

Goddamn it! Within minutes the U.S. network in London would be put on alert, within hours every available man, woman, and paid informer would spread throughout the city looking for him. It was conceivable that even the British would be called in, but it was not likely. Those in Washington who wanted Brandon Alan Scofield wanted him dead, not questioned, and this was not the English style. No, the British would be avoided.

Bray counted on it. There was a man he had helped several years ago, under circumstances that had little to do with their allied professions, that had made it possible for the Englishman to remain in British Intelligence. Not only remain but advance to a position of considerable responsibility.

Roger Symonds had dropped £2,000 of MI-Six funds at the tables of Les Ambassadeurs. Bray had replaced the sum from one of his accounts. The money had never been repaid—not by default, only because Scofield had not crossed Symonds' path. In their work, one did not leave a forwarding address.

A form of repayment would be asked for now. That it would be offered, Scofield did not question, but whether it could be delivered was something else again. Yet it would be neither if Roger Symonds learned that he was on Washington's terminal list. Debts aside, the Englishman took his work seriously; there'd be no Fuchs or Philbys on his conscience. Much less a former killer from Consular Operations conceivably turned paid assassin.

Bray wanted Symonds to arrange a private, isolated meeting between himself and England's Foreign Secretary, David Waverly. The meeting, however, had to be negotiated without Scofield's name being used—the British agent would balk at that, refuse entirely if he learned of Washington's hunt for him. Scofield knew he had to come up with a credible motive; he had not thought of one yet.

He ran out of Charing Cross station and walked into the flow of pedestrians heading south on the Strand. At Trafalgar Square, he crossed the wide intersection, joining the early evening crowds. He looked at his watch. It was 6:15, 7:15 in Paris. In thirty minutes he was to start calling Toni at her flat in the rue de Bac; there was a telephone center a few blocks away on Haymarket. He would make his way there slowly, stopping to buy a new hat and jacket. The CIA man would give a precise description of his clothing; changing it was imperative.

He was wearing the same windbreaker he had worn in Corsica, the same visored fishing cap. He left them in a curtained dressing room at a branch of Dunns, buying a dark tweed Mackinaw jacket and an Irish walking hat, the soft brim falling around his head, a circle of narrow fabric throwing shadows downward across his face. He walked south again, more rapidly now, and cut through the winding back streets into Haymarket.

He paid one of the operators at the telephone center counter, was assigned a booth, went inside, and closed the glass door, wishing it were solid. It was ten minutes to seven. Antonia would be waiting by the phone. They always allowed a variable of a half-hour for channel telephone traffic; if he did not reach her by 8:15, Paris time, she could expect his next call between 11:45 and 12:15. The one condition Toni had insisted upon was for them to talk to each other every day. Bray had not objected; he had come out of the earth and found something very precious to him, something he had thought he had lost permanently. He could love again; the excitement of anticipation had come back. The sound of a voice stirred him, the touch of a hand was meaningful. He had found Antonia Gravet at the most inopportune time of his life, yet finding her gave a significance to his life he had not felt for a number of years. He wanted to live and grow old with her, it was as simple as that. And remarkable. He had never thought about growing old before; it was time he did.

If the Matarese allowed it.

The *Matarese.* An international power without a profile, its leaders faceless men trying to achieve *what?*

Chaos? *Why?*

Chaos. Scofield was suddenly struck by the root meaning of the word. The state of formless matter, of clashing bodies in space, before the creation. Before order was imposed on the universe.

The telephone rang; Bray picked it up quickly.

"Vasili's here," said Antonia.

"In *Paris?* When did he get in?"

"This afternoon. He's hurt."

"How badly?"

"His neck. He should have stitches."

There was a brief pause as the phone was being passed. Or taken.

"He should have sleep," said Taleniekov in English. "But I have things to tell you first, several warnings."

"What about Voroshin?"

"He kept the *V* for practical if foolish purposes. He became Essen's Verachten. Ansel Verachten."

"The *Verachten* Works?"

"Yes"

"Good Christ!"

"His son believed that."

"What?"

"It's irrelevant; there's too much to tell you. His granddaughter was the chosen one. She's dead, killed on Matarese orders."

"As Scozzi was," said Scofield.

"Exactly," agreed the Soviet. "They were vessels; they carried the plans but were commandeered by others. It will be interesting to see what happens to the Verachten companies. They have no leadership now. We must watch and note who assumes control."

"We've reached the same conclusion then," said Bray. "The Matarese work through large corporations."

"It would appear so, but to what end I haven't the faintest idea. It's extremely contradictory."

"Chaos. . . ." Scofield spoke the word softly.

"I beg your pardon."

"Nothing. You said you wanted to warn me."

"Yes. They've studied our files under microscopes. It seems they know every drone we've ever used, every past friend, every contact, every . . . teacher and lover. Be careful."

"They can't know what was never entered; they can't cover everyone."

"Don't bank on that. You received my cable about the body marks?"

"It's crazy! Squads of killers identifying themselves? I'm not sure I believe it."

"Believe it," said Taleniekov. "But there's something I wasn't able to explain. They're suicidal; they won't be taken. Which leads me to believe they're not as extensive in numbers as the leaders would like us to think. They're some kind of élite soldiers sent out to the troubled areas, not to be confused with hired guns employed by second and third parties."

Bray paused, remembering. "You know what you're describing, don't you?"

"All too well," replied the Russian. "Hasan ibn-al-Sabbah. The *Fida'is.*"

"Cadres of assassins . . . 'til death do us part from our pleasures. How is it modernized?"

"I have a theory; it may be worthless. We'll discuss it when I see you."

"When will that be?"

"Tomorrow night—early the next morning probably. I can hire a pilot and a plane in the Cap Gris district; I've done it before. There's a private airfield between Hyth and Ashford. I should be in London by one o'clock, two or three at the latest. I know where you're staying, the girl told me."

"Taleniekov."

"Yes?"

"Her name's Antonia."

"I know that."

"Let me speak to her."

"Of course. Here she is."

He found the name in the London directory: *R. Symonds, Brdbry Ln, Chelsea.* He memorized the number and placed the first call at 7:30 from a booth in Piccadilly Circus. The woman who answered told him politely that Mr. Symonds was on his way home from the office.

"He should be here any mo' now. Shall I tell him who called?"

"The name wouldn't mean anything. I'll call back in a while, thank you."

"He's got a marvelous memory. You're sure you don't care to leave your name?"

"I'm sure, thank you."

"He's coming directly from the office."

"Yes, I understand that."

Scofield hung up, disturbed. He left the booth and walked down Piccadilly past Fortnum and Mason to St. James Street and beyond. There was another booth at the entrance to Green Park; slightly more than ten minutes had passed. He wanted to hear the woman's voice again.

"Has your husband arrived?" he asked.

"He *just* called from the local, wouldn't you know! The Brace and Bit on Old Church. He's quite irritable, if I do say. Must have had a *dreadful* day."

Bray hung up. He knew the number of MI-Six–London; it was one a member of the fraternity kept in mind. He dialed.

"Mr. Symonds, please. Priority."

"Right away, sir."

Roger Symonds was not on his way home, nor was he in a pub called The Brace and Bit. Was he playing a domestic game?

"Symonds here," said the familiar English voice.

"Your wife just told me you were on your way home, but got detained at The Brace and Bit. Is that the best you could come up with?"

"I what? . . . Who's this?"

"An old friend."

"Not much of a one, I'm afraid. I'm not married. My friends know that."

Bray paused, then spoke urgently. "Quickly. Give me a sterile number, or one on a scrambler. *Quickly!*"

"Who *is* this?"

"Two thousand pounds."

It took Symonds less than a second to understand and adjust; he reeled off a number, repeated it once, then added, "The cellars. Forty-five stories high."

There was a click; the line went dead. Forty-five stories high to the cellars meant halving the figure, minus one. He was to call the number in exactly twenty-two minutes—within the one-minute span—during which scrambling and jamming devices would be activated. He left the booth to find another as far away as time and rapid walking permitted. Telephone intercepts were potentially two-way traces; the booth at Green Park could be under observation in a matter of minutes.

He went up Old Bond Street into New until he reached Oxford, where he turned right and began running toward Wardour Street. At Wardour he slowed down, turned right again, and melted into the crowds of Soho.

Elapsed time: nineteen and a half minutes.

There was a booth at the corner of Shaftsbury Avenue; inside a callow young man wearing an electric-blue suit was screaming into the phone. Scofield waited by the door, looking at his watch.

Twenty-one minutes.

He could not take the chance. He took out a five-pound note and tapped on the glass. The young man turned; he saw the bill and held up his middle finger in a gesture that was not cooperative.

Bray opened the door, put his left hand on the electric-blue shoulder, tightened his grip, and as the offensive young man began screeching, pulled him out of the booth, tripping him with his left foot, dropping the fiver on top of him. It floated; the youth grabbed it and ran.

Twenty-one minutes, thirty seconds.

Scofield took several deep breaths, trying to slow the rapid pounding in his chest. Twenty-two minutes. He dialed.

"Don't go home," said Bray the instant Symonds was on the line.

"Don't *you* stay in London!" was the reply. "Grosvenor Square has an alert out for you."

"You *know?* Washington called you *in?*"

"Hardly. They won't say a word about you. You're terminated personnel, an off-limits subject. We probed several weeks ago when we first got word."

"Word from *where?*"

"Our sources in the Soviet. In KGB. They're after you, too, but then they always have been."

"What did Washington say when you probed?"

"Played it down. Failure to report whereabouts, something like that. They're too embarrassed to put an official stamp on the nonsense. Are you authoring something? There's a lot of that over there—"

"How did you know about the alert?" interrupted Scofield. "The one out for me now?"

"Oh, come now, we do keep tabs, you know. A number of people Grosvenor has on its payroll quite rightly have first loyalties to us."

Bray paused briefly, bewildered. "Roger, why are you telling me this? I can't believe two thousand pounds would make you do it."

"That misappropriated sum has been sitting in a Chelsea bank drawing interest for you since the morning after you bailed me out."

"Then why?"

Symonds cleared his throat, a proper Englishman facing the necessity of showing emotion. "I have no idea what your quarrel is over there and I'm not sure I care to—you have such puritanical outbursts—but I was appalled to learn that our prime source in Washington confirmed that the State Department subscribes to the Soviet ploy. As I said, it's not only nonsense, I find it patently offensive."

"A ploy? What ploy?"

"That you joined forces with the Serpent."

"The 'Serpent'?"

"It's what we call Vasili Taleniekov, a name I'm sure you'll recall. To repeat, I don't know what your trouble is, but I *do* know a goddamned lie, a macabre lie at that, when I hear one." Symonds cleared his throat again. "Some of us remember East Berlin. And I was here when you came back from Prague. How dare they . . . after what you've *done?* Churlish bastards!"

Scofield took a long, deep breath. "Roger, don't go home."

"Yes, you said that before." Symonds was relieved they were back to practicality; it was his voice. "You say someone's there, claiming to be my wife?"

"Probably not inside, but nearby, with a clear view. They've tapped into your phone and the equipment's good. No echoes, no static."

"*My* phone? They're trailing *me?* In *London?*"

"They're covering you; they're after me. They knew we were friends and thought I might try to reach you."

"Goddamned *cheek!* That embassy will get a bolt that'll char the gold feathers off that fucking ridiculous eagle! They go too *far!*"

"It's not the Americans."

"*Not* the . . . ? Bray, what in God's name are you talking about?"

"That's just it. We have to talk. But it's got to be a very complicated route. Two networks are looking for me, and one of them has you under a glass. They're good."

"We'll see about that," snapped Symonds, annoyed, challenged and curious. "I daresay several vehicles, one or two decoys, and a healthy bit of official lying can do the trick. Where are you?"

"Soho. Wardour and Shaftsbury."

"Good. Head over to Tottenham Court. In about twenty minutes, a gray Mini—rear license plate askew—will enter south from Oxford and stall at the curb. The driver's black, a West Indian chap; he's your contact. Get in with him; the engine will make a remarkable recovery."

"Thank you, Roger."

"Not at all. But don't expect me to have the two thousand quid. The banks are closed, you know."

Scofield got in the front seat of the Mini, the black driver looking at him closely, courteously, his right hand out of sight. The man had obviously been given a photograph to study. Bray removed the Irish hat.

"Thank you," said the driver, his hand moving swiftly to his jacket pocket, then to the wheel. The engine caught instantly and they sped out of Tottenham Court.

"My name is Israel. You are Brandon Scofield—obviously. Good to make your acquaintance."

"Israel?" he asked.

"That's it, mon," replied the driver, smiling, a pronounced West Indian lilt to his voice. "I don't think my parents had in mind the cohesiveness of minorities when they gave it to me, but they were avid readers of the Bible. Israel Isles."

"It's a nice name."

"My wife thinks they blew it, as you Americans say. She keeps telling me that if they had only used Ishmael instead, all my introductions would be memorable."

" 'Call me Ishmael.' . . ." Bray laughed. "It's close enough."

"This banter covers a slight nervousness on my part, if I may say so," said Isles.

"Why?"

"We studied a number of your accomplishments in training; it wasn't that long ago. I'm chauffeuring a man we'd all like to emulate."

The trace of laughter vanished from Scofield's face. "That's very flattering. I'm sure you will if you want to." *And when you get to be my age, I hope you think it's been worth it.*

They drove south out of London on the road toward Heathrow, branching off the highway at Redhill, heading west into the countryside. Israel Isles was sufficiently perceptive to curtail the banter. He apparently understood that he was driving either a very preoccupied or exhausted American. Bray was grateful for the silence; he had to reach a difficult decision. The risks were enormous no matter what he decided.

Yet part of that decision had already been forced upon him, which meant he had to tell Symonds that Washington wasn't the immediate issue. He could not permit Roger to vent his misplaced outrage on the American Embassy; it was not the embassy that had placed the intercept on his telephone. It was the Matarese.

Yet to tell the whole truth meant involving Symonds, who would not remain silent. He would go to others and those others to their superiors. It was not the time to speak of conspiracy so massive and contradictory that it would be branded no more than the product of two terminated intelligence officers—both wanted for treason in their respective countries. The time *would* come, but it was not now. For the truth of the matter was that they did not possess a shred of hard evidence. Everything they knew to be true was so easily denied as the paranoid ramblings of lunatics and traitors. On the surface, the logic was their enemies'. Why would the leaders of mammoth corporations, conglomerates that depended on stability, finance chaos?

Chaos. Formless matter, clashing bodies in space. . . .

"Another few minutes, we'll reach our first destination," said Israel Isles.

"First destination?"

"Yes, our trip's in two stages. We change vehicles up ahead; this one is driven back to London—the driver black, his passenger white—and we proceed in another, quite different car. The next leg is less than a quarter of an hour. Mr. Symonds may be a little late, however. He had to make four changes of vehicles in city garages."

"I see," said Scofield, relieved. The West Indian had just provided Bray with his answer. As the rendezvous with Symonds was in stages, so, too, would be the explanation *to* Symonds. He would tell him part of the truth, but nothing that would implicate the Foreign Secretary, David Waverly. However, Waverly had to be given information on a most confidential basis; decisions of foreign policy could be affected by the news of massive shifts of capital being manipulated secretly. *This* was the information Scofield had come across and was tracing: massive shifts of capital. And although all clandestine economic maneuvers were subjects for intelligence scrutiny, these went beyond MI-Five and -Six, just as they superseded the interests of the FBI and the CIA.

In Washington, there were those who wanted to prevent him from disclosing what he knew, but could not prove. The surest way of doing so was to discredit him, kill him, if it came to that. Symonds would understand. Men killed facilely for money; no one knew it better than intelligence officers. So often it was the spine of their . . . accomplishments.

Isles slowed the Mini down and pulled to the side of the road. He made a U-turn, pointing the car in the direction from which they came.

Within thirty seconds another, larger automobile approached; it had picked them up along the way and had followed at a discreet distance. Bray knew what was expected; he got out, as did the West Indian. The Bentley came to a stop. A white driver opened the rear door for a black companion. No one spoke as the exchange was made, both cars now driven by blacks.

"May I ask you a question?" said Israel Isles hesitantly.

"Sure."

"I've gone through all the training, but I've never had to kill a man. I worry about that sometimes. What's it like?"

Scofield looked out the window at the shadows rushing past. *It's like walking through a door into a place you've never been before. I hope you do not have to go there, for it's filled with a thousand eyes—a few angry, more frightened, most pleasing . . . all wondering. Why me now?* "There's not very much of that," said Bray. "You never take a life unless it's absolutely necessary, knowing that if you have to, you're saving many more. That's the justification, the only one there should ever be. You put it out of your mind, lock it away behind a door somewhere in your head."

"Yes, I think I understand. The justification is in the necessity. One has to accept that, doesn't one?"

"That's right. Necessity." *Until you grow older and the door opens more and more frequently. Finally it will not close and you stand there, staring inside.*

They drove into the deserted parking area of a picnic grounds in the Guildford countryside. Beyond the post-and-rail fence were swings and slides and seesaws, all silhouetted in the bright moonlight. Not too many weeks hence, spring would come and the playground would be filled with the shouts and laughter of children; now it echoed the roar of powerful engines and the quiet sounds of men talking.

A car was waiting for them, but Roger Symonds was not in it; he was expected momentarily. Two men had arrived early to make certain there was no one else in the picnic grounds, no intercepts placed on phones considered sterile.

"Hello, Brandon," said a short, stocky man in a bulky overcoat, extending his hand.

"Hi, how are you?" Scofield did not recall the agent's name, but remembered the face, the red hair; he was one of the best men fielded by MI-Six. *Cons Op* had called him in—with British permission—when the Moscow-Paris-Cuba espionage ring was operating inside the Chamber of Deputies. Bray was impressed at seeing him now. Symonds was using a first team.

"It's been eight or ten years, hasn't it?"

"At least," agreed Scofield. "How've you been?"

"Still here. I'll be pensioned off before too long. Looking forward to that."

"Enjoy it."

The Englishman hesitated, then spoke with embarrassment. "Never did see you after that awful business in East Berlin. Not that we were such friends, but you know what I mean. Delayed condolences, chap. Rotten thing. Fucking animals, I say."

"Thanks. It was a long time ago."

"Never that long," said the MI-Six man. "It was my source in Moscow that brought us that garbage about you and the Serpent. Beowulf and the Serpent! My God, how could those pricks in D.C. swallow such rot?"

"It's complicated."

He saw the headlights first, then heard the engine. A London taxi drove into the picnic grounds. The driver, however, was no London cabbie; it was Roger Symonds.

The middle-aged MI-Six officer climbed out and for a second or two blinked and stretched, as if to get his bearings. Bray watched him, noting that Roger had not changed during the years since they had known each other. The Englishman was still given to an excess pound or two, and his thatch of rumpled brown hair was still unmanageable. There was an air of disorientation about the veteran operative that masked a first-rate analytical mind. He was not an easy man to fool—with part of the truth or none of it.

"Bray, how *are* you?" said Symonds, hand held out. "For God's sake, don't answer that, we'll get to it. Let me tell you, those are *not* easy cars to drive. I feel as though I've just limped through the worst rugger match in Liverpool. I shall be far more generous with cabbies in the future." Roger looked around, nodding to his men, then spotting the opening in the fence which led into the playground. "Let's take a stroll. If you're a good lad, I may even give you a push or two in one of the swings."

The Englishman listened in silence, leaning against the iron leg of the swing, as Bray sat on the seat and told his story of the massive shifting of funds. When Scofield had finished, Symonds pushed himself away from the pole, walked behind Bray and shoved him between the shoulder blades.

"There's the push I promised you, although you don't deserve it. You haven't been a good lad."

"Why not?"

"You're not telling me what you should and your tactics are disturbing."

"I see. You don't understand why I'm asking you not to use my name with Waverly?"

"Oh, no, that's perfectly all right. He has to deal with Washington every day. Granting an *unofficial* meeting with a retired American intelligence officer is not something he'd care to have on the Foreign Office's record. I mean we don't actually defect to one another, you know. I'll take that responsibility, if it's to be taken."

"Then what's bothering you?"

"The people after you. Not Grosvenor, of course, but the others. You haven't been candid; you said they were good, but you didn't tell me *how* good. Or the depth of their resources."

"What do you mean?"

"We pulled your dossier and selected three names known to you, calling each, telling each that the man on the line was an intermediary from you, instructing each to go to a specific location. All three messages were intercepted; those called were followed."

"Why does that surprise you? I told you as much."

"What surprises me is that one of those names was known only to us. Not MI-Five, not Secret Service, not even the Admiralty. Only us."

"Who was it?"

"Grimes."

"Never heard of him," said Bray.

"You only met him once. In Prague. Under the name of Brazuk."

"KGB" said Scofield, astonished. "He defected in '72. I gave him to you. He wouldn't have anything to do with us and there was no point in wasting him."

"But only you knew that. You said nothing to your people and, frankly, we at Six took credit for the purchase."

"You've got a leak, then."

"Quite impossible," replied Symonds. "At least regarding the present circumstances as you've described them to me."

"Why?"

"You say you ran across this global financial juggling act only a short while ago. Let's be generous and say several months, would you agree?"

"Yes."

"And since then, those who want to silence you have been active against you, also correct?" Bray nodded. The MI-Six man leaned forward, his hand on the chain above Scofield's head. "From the day I took office two and a half years ago, Beowulf Agate's file has been in my private vault. It is removed only on dual signatures, one of which must be mine. It has not been removed, and it's the only file in England that contains any connection between you and the Grimes-Brazuk defection."

"What are you trying to say?"

"There's only one other place where that information might be found."

"Spell it out."

"Moscow." Symonds drew out the word softly.

Bray shook his head. "That assumes Moscow knows Grimes' identity."

"Entirely possible. Like a few you've purchased, Brazuk was a bust. We don't really want him, but we can't give him back. He's a chronic alcoholic, has been for years. His job at KGB was ornamental, a debt paid to a once-brave soldier. We suspect he blew his cover quite a while ago. Nobody cared, until you came along. Who are these people after you?"

"It seems I didn't do you any favors when I handed over Brazuk," said Scofield, avoiding the MI-Six man's eyes.

"You didn't know that and neither did we. Who are these people, Bray?"

"Men who have contacts in Moscow. Obviously. Just as we do."

"Then I must ask you a question," continued Symonds. "One that would have been inconceivable several hours ago. Is it true what Washington thinks? Are you working with the Serpent?"

Scofield looked at the Englishman. "Yes."

Calmly, Symonds released the chain and rose to his full height. "I think I could kill you for that," he said. "For God's sake, *why?*"

"If it's a question of either your killing me or my telling you, I don't have a choice, do I?"

"There's a middle ground. I take you in and turn you over to Grosvenor Square."

"Don't do it, Roger. And don't ask me to tell you anything now. Later, yes. Not now."

"Why should I agree?"

"Because you know me. I can't think of any other reason."

Symonds turned away. Neither spoke for several moments. Finally, the Englishman turned again, facing Bray. "Such a simple phrase. 'You know me.' Do I?"

"I wouldn't have reached you if I didn't think you did. I don't ask strangers to risk their lives for me. I meant what I said before. Don't go home. You're marked . . . just as I'm marked. If you covered yourself, you'll be all right. If they find out you met with me, you're dead."

"I am at this moment logged in at an emergency meeting at the Admiralty. Phone calls were placed to my office and my flat demanding my presence."

"Good. I expected as much."

"*Goddamn you,* Scofield! It was always your gift. You pull a man in until he can't stand it! Yes, I *do* know you, and I'll do as you ask—for a little while. But not because of your melodramatics; they don't impress me. Something else does, however. I said I could kill you for working with Taleniekov. I think I could, but I suspect you kill yourself a little every time you look at him. That's reason enough for me."

29

Bray walked down the steps of the rooming house into the morning sunlight and the crowds of shoppers in Knightsbridge. It was an area of London compatible with staying out of sight; from nine A.M. on, the streets were jammed with traffic. He stopped at a newsstand, shifted his attaché case to his left hand, picked up *The Times,* and went into a small restaurant where he slipped into a chair, satisfied that it provided a clear view of the entrance, more satisfied still that the pay telephone on the wall was only feet away. It was quarter to ten; he was to call Roger Symonds at precisely 10:15 on the sterile number that could not be tapped.

He ordered breakfast from a laconic Cockney waitress and unfolded the newspaper. He found what he was looking for in a single column on the upper left section of the front page.

VERACHTEN HEIRESS DEAD

Essen. Odile Verachten, daughter of Walther, granddaughter of Ansel Verachten, founder of the Verachten Works, was found dead in her Werdenstrasse penthouse last evening, an apparent victim of a massive coronary stroke. For nearly a decade, Fraulein Verachten had assumed the managerial reins of the diversified companies under the guidance of her father, who has receded from active participation during the past years. Both parents were in seclusion at their estate in Stadtwald, and were not available for comment. A private family burial will take place on the residential grounds. A corporate statement is expected shortly, but none from Walther Verachten who is reported to be seriously ill.

Odile Verachten was a dramatically attractive addition to the boardrooms of this city of coldly efficient executives. She was mercurial, and when younger, given to displays of exhibitionism often at odds with the behaviour of Essen's business leaders. But no one doubted her ability to run the vast Verachten Works. . . .

Scofield's eyes quickly scanned the biographical hyperbole that was an obituary editor's way of describing a spoiled, headstrong bitch who undoubtedly slept around with the frequency if not the delicacy of a Soho whore.

There was a follow-up story directly beneath. Bray began reading and knew instantly, instinctively that another fragment of the elusive truth was being revealed.

VERACHTEN DEATH CONCERNS TRANS-COMM

New York, N.Y. In a move that took Wall Street by surprise, it was learned today that a team of management consultants from Trans-Communications, Incorporated, was flying to Essen, Germany, for conferences with executives of the Verachten Works. The untimely death of Fraulein Odile Verachten, 47, and the virtual seclusion of her father,

Walther, 76, has left the Verachten companies without an authoritative voice at the top. What astonished supposedly well-informed sources here was the extent of Trans-Comm's holdings in Verachten. In the legal labyrinths of Essen, American investments are often beyond scrutiny, but rarely when those holdings exceed twenty percent. Rumors persist that Trans-Comm's are in excess of fifty percent, although denials labelling such figures as ridiculous have been issued by the Boston headquarters of the conglomerate. . . .

The words sprang up from the page at Scofield. *The Boston headquarters.* . . .

Were *two* fragments of their elusive truth being revealed? Joshua Appleton, IV, was the Senator from Massachusetts, the Appleton family the most powerful political entity in the state. They were the Episcopal Kennedys, far more restrained in self-evocation, but every bit as influential on the national scene. Which was intrinsic to the international financial scene.

Would a retrospective of the Appletons include connections—covert or otherwise—with Trans-Communications? It was something that would have to be learned.

The telephone on the wall behind him rang; he checked his watch. It was eight minutes past ten; another seven and he would call Symonds at MI-Six headquarters. He glanced at the phone, annoyed to see the Cockney waitress wincing into the mouthpiece, a groan or an expletive forming at her lips. He hoped her conversation would not last long.

"Mister *Hagate?* Is there a Mister B. *Hagate* 'ere?" The question was shouted angrily.

Bray froze. *B. Hagate 'ere?*

Agate, B.

Beowulf Agate.

Was Symonds playing some insane game of one-upmanship? Had the Englishman decided to prove the superior quality of British Intelligence's tracking techniques? Was the damn fool so egotistical he could not leave well enough alone?

God, what a fool!

Scofield rose as unobtrusively as possible, holding his attaché case. He went to the phone and spoke.

"What is it?"

"Good morning, Beowulf Agate," said a male voice with vowels so full and consonants so sharp they could have been formed at Oxford. "We trust you've rested since your arduous journey from Rome."

"Who's this?"

"My name's irrelevant; you don't know me. We merely wanted you to understand. We found you; we'll always be able to find you. But it's all so tedious. We feel that it would be far better for everyone concerned if we sat down and thrashed out the differences between us. You may discover they're not so great after all."

"I don't feel comfortable with people who've tried to kill me."

"I must correct you. *Some* have tried to kill you. Others have tried to save you."

"For what? A session of chemical therapy? To find out what I've learned, what I've done?"

"What you've learned is meaningless, and you can't *do* anything. If your own people take you, you know what you can expect. There'll be no trial, no public hearing; you're far too dangerous to too many people. You've collaborated with the enemy, killed a young man your superiors believe was a fellow intelligence officer in Rock Creek Park, and fled the country. You're a traitor; you'll be executed at the first opportune moment. Can you doubt it after the events on Nebraska Avenue? *We* can execute you the instant you walk out of that restaurant. Or before you leave."

Bray looked around, studying the faces at the tables, looking for the inevitable pair of eyes, a glance behind a folded newspaper, or above the rim of a coffee cup. There were several candidates; he could not be sure. And without question, there were unseen killers in the crowds outside. He was trapped; his watch read eleven minutes past ten. Another four and he could dial Symonds on the sterile line. But he was dealing with professionals. If he hung up and dialed was there a man now at one of these tables—innocuously raising a fork to his mouth or sipping from a cup—who would pull out a weapon powerful enough to blow him into the wall? Or were those inside merely hired guns, unwilling to make the sacrifice the Matarese demanded of its élite? He had to buy time and take the risk, watching the tables every second as he did so, preparing himself for that instant when escape came with sudden movement and the conceivable—unfortunate—sacrifice of innocent people.

"You want to meet, I want a guarantee I'll get out of here."

"You've got it."

"Your saying it isn't enough. Identify one of your employees in here."

"Let's put it this way, Beowulf. We can hold you there, call the American Embassy, and before you could blink, they'd have you cornered. Even should you get past them, we'd be waiting on the outer circle, as it were."

His watch read twelve past ten. *Three minutes.*

"Then obviously you're not that anxious to meet with me." Scofield listened, his concentration total. He was almost certain the man on the line was a messenger; someone above wanted Beowulf Agate taken, not killed.

"I said we felt it would be better for everyone concerned—"

"Give me a face!" interrupted Bray. The voice *was* a messenger. "Otherwise call the goddamned embassy. I'll take my chances. *Now.*"

"Very well," came the reply, spoken rapidly. "There's a man with rather sunken cheeks, wearing a gray overcoat. . . ."

"I see him." Bray did, five tables away.

"Leave the restaurant; he'll get up and follow you. He's your guarantee."

Thirteen past ten. Two minutes.

"What guarantee does he have? How do I know you won't take him out with me?"

"Oh, come now, Scofield. . . ."

"I'm glad to hear you've got another name for me. What's *your* name?"

"I told you, it's irrelevant."

"Nothing's irrelevant." Bray paused. "I want to know your name."

"Smith. Accept it."

Ten-fourteen. One minute. Time to start.

"I'll have to think about it. I also want to finish my breakfast." Abruptly hanging up, he shifted his attaché case to his right hand and walked over to the plain-looking man five tables away.

The man stiffened as Scofield approached; his hand reached under his overcoat.

"The alert's off," said Scofield, touching the concealed hand under the cloth of the coat. "I was told to tell you that; you're to take me out of here. But first, I'm to make a telephone call. He gave me the number; I hope I can remember it."

The hollow-cheeked killer remained immobile, speechless. Scofield walked back to the telephone on the wall.

Ten-fourteen and fifty-one seconds. Nine seconds to go. He frowned, as if trying to recall a number, picked up the phone, and dialed. Three seconds past 10:15 he heard the echoing sound that followed the interruption of the bell; the electronic devices were activated. He inserted his coin.

"We have to talk fast," he said to Roger Symonds. "They found me. I've got a problem."

"Where are you? We'll help."

Scofield told him. "Just send in two sirens, regular police will do. Say it's an Irish incident, possible subjects inside. That's all I'll need."

"I'm writing it down. They're on their way."

"What about Waverly?"

"Tomorrow night. His house in Belgravia. I'm to escort you, of course."

"Not before then?"

"*Before* then? Good God, man, the only reason it's so soon is that I managed an open-end memorandum from the Admiralty. From that same mythical conference I was logged into last night." Bray was about to speak, but Symonds rushed on. "Incidentally, you were right. An inquiry was made to see if I was there."

"Were you covered?"

"The caller was told the conference could not be interrupted, that I would be given the message when it was over."

"Did you return the call?"

"Yes. From the Admiralty's cellars an hour and ten minutes after I left you. I woke up some poor chap in Kensington. An intercept, of course."

"Then if you got back there, they saw you leave the Admiralty building?"

"From the well-lighted front entrance."

"Good. You didn't use my name with Waverly, did you?"

"I used *a* name, not yours. Unless your talk is extremely fruitful, I expect I'll take a lot of gaff for that."

An obvious fact struck Bray. Roger Symonds' strategy had been successful. The Matarese had him trapped inside the Knightsbridge restaurant, yet Waverly had granted him a confidential interview thirty-six hours away. Therefore, no connection had been made between the interview in Belgravia and Beowulf Agate.

"Roger, what time tomorrow night?"

"Eightish. I'm to ring him first. I'll pick you up around seven. Have you any idea where you'll be?"

Scofield avoided the question. "I'll call you at this number at four-thirty. Is that convenient?"

"So far as I know. If I'm not here, leave an address two blocks north of where you'll be. I'll find you."

"You'll bring the photographs of all those following your decoys yesterday?"

"They should be on my desk by noon."

"Good. And one last thing. Think up a very good, very official reason why you can't bring me to Belgravia Square tomorrow night."

"*What?*"

"That's what you'll tell Waverly when you call him just before our meeting. It's an intelligence decision; you'll pick him up personally and drive back to MI-Six."

"*MI-Six?*"

"But you won't take him there; you'll bring him to the Connaught. I'll give you the room number at four-thirty. If you're not there, I'll leave a message. Subtract twenty-two from the number I give."

"See here, Brandon, you're asking *too* much!"

"You don't know that. I may be asking to save his life. And yours." In the distance, from somewhere outside, Bray could hear the piercing, two-note sound of a London siren; an instant later it was joined by a second. "Your help's arrived," said Scofield. "Thanks." He hung up and started back to the hollow-cheeked Matarese killer.

"Who were you talking to?" asked the man, his accent American. The sirens were drawing nearer; they were not lost on him.

"He didn't give me his name," replied Bray. "But he did give me instructions. We're to get out of here fast."

"Why?"

"Something happened. The police spotted a rifle in one of your cars; it's being held. There's been a lot of I.R.A. activity in the stores around here. Let's go!"

The man got out of his chair, nodding to his right. Across the crowded restaurant, Scofield saw a stern-faced, middle-aged woman get up, acknowledge the command by slipping the wide strap of a large purse over her shoulder, and start for the door of the restaurant.

Bray reached the cashier's cage, timing his movements, fumbling his money and his check, watching the scene beyond the glass window. Two police cars converged, screeching simultaneously to a stop at the curb. A crowd of curious pedestrians gathered, then dispersed, curiosity replaced by fear as four helmeted London police jumped out of the vehicles and headed for the restaurant.

Bray judged the distance, then moved quickly. He reached the glass door and yanked it open several seconds before the police had it blocked. The hollow-cheeked man and the middle-aged woman were at his heels, at the last moment side-stepping around him to avoid confronting the police.

Scofield turned suddenly and lurched to his right, clutching his attaché case under his arm, grabbing his would-be escorts by the shoulders and pulling them down.

"These are the ones!" he shouted. "Check them for guns! I heard them say they were going to bomb Scotch House!"

The police fell on the two Matarese, arms and hands and clubs thrashing the air. Bray dropped to his knees, releasing his double-grip, and dove to his left out of the way. He scrambled to his feet, raced through the crowds to the corner and ran into the street, threading his way between the traffic. He kept up the frantic race for three blocks, stopping briefly, under canopies and in storefronts to see if anyone followed him. None did, and two minutes later he slowed down and entered the enormous bronze-bordered portals of Harrods.

Once inside, he accelerated his pace as rapidly and as unobtrusively as possible, looking for a telephone. He had to reach Taleniekov at the flat in the rue de Bac before the Russian left for Cap Gris. He *had* to, for once Taleniekov reached England, he would head for London and a cheap rooming house in Knights-bridge. If the KGB man did that, he would be taken by the Matarese.

"Through the chemists toward the south entry," said an imperturbable clerk. "There's a bank of phones against the wall."

The late morning telephone traffic was light; the call went through without delay.

"I was leaving in a few minutes," said Taleniekov, his voice oddly hesitant.

"Thank Christ you didn't. What's the matter with you?"

"Nothing. Why?"

"You sound strange. Where's Antonia? Why didn't she answer the phone?"

"She stepped out to the grocer's. She'll be back shortly. If I sounded strange, it's because I don't like answering this telephone." The Russian's voice was normal now, his explanation logical. "What is the matter with *you?* Why this unscheduled call?"

"I'll tell you when you get here, but forget Knightsbridge."

"Where will you be?"

Scofield was about to mention the Connaught, when Taleniekov interrupted.

"On second thought, when I get to London I'll phone Tower-Central. You recall that exchange, don't you?"

Tower Central? Bray hadn't heard the name in years, but he remembered. It was a code name for a KGB drop on the Victoria Embankment, abandoned when

Consular Operations discovered it sometime back in the late sixties. The tourist boats that traveled up and down the Thames, that was it. "I remember," said Scofield, bewildered. "I'll respond."

"Then I'll be going—"

"Wait a minute," interrupted Bray. "Tell Antonia I'll call in a while."

There was a brief silence before Taleniekov replied. "Actually, she said she might take in the Louvre; it's so close by. I can get to the Cap Gris district in an hour or so. There's nothing—I repeat—nothing to worry about." There was a click and the line to Paris went dead. The Russian had hung up.

There's nothing—I repeat—nothing to worry about. The words cracked with the explosive sounds of nearby thunder; his eyes were blinded by bolts of lightning that carried the message into his brain. There *was* something to worry about and it concerned Antonia Gravet.

Actually, she said she might take in the Louvre . . . I can get to the Cap Gris district in an hour or so. . . . Nothing to worry about.

Three disconnected statements, preceded by an interruption that prohibited disclosure of the contact point in London. Scofield tried to analyze the sequence; if there was meaning it was in the progression. The *Louvre* was only blocks away from the rue de Bac—across the Seine, but nearby. The *Cap Gris district* could not be reached in an hour or so; two and a half or three were more logical. *Nothing—I repeat—nothing to worry about;* then why the interruption? Why the necessity of avoiding any mention of the Victoria Embankment?

Sequence. Progression. Further *back?*

I do not like answering this telephone. Words spoken firmly, almost angrily. That was *it.* Suddenly, Bray understood and the relief he felt was like cool water sprayed over a sweat-drenched body. Taleniekov had seen something wrong—a face in the street, a chance meeting with a former colleague, a car that remained too long on the rue de Bac—any number of unstabling incidents or observations. The Russian had decided to move Toni out of the Rive Gauche, across the river into another flat. *She* would be settled in an *hour or so* and he would not leave until she was; that was why there was nothing to worry about. Still, on the assumption that there could be substance to a disturbing incident or observation, the KGB man had operated with extreme caution—always caution, it was their truest shield—and the telephone was an instrument of revelation. Nothing revealing was to be said.

Sequence, progression . . . meaning. Or was it? The Serpent had killed his wife. Was Bray finding comfort where none existed? The Russian had been the first to suggest eliminating the girl from the hills of Porto Vecchio—the love that had come into his life at the most inopportune time of his life. *Could* he? . . .

No! Things were different now! There was no Beowulf Agate to stretch to the breaking point, because that breaking point guaranteed the death of the Serpent, the end of the hunt for the Matarese. The best of professionals did not kill unnecessarily.

Still, he wondered as he picked up the phone in Harrods' south entranceway, what was necessity but a man convinced of the need? He put the question out of his mind; he had to find sanctuary.

London's staid Connaught Hotel not only possessed one of the best kitchens in London but was an ideal choice for quick concealment, as long as one stayed out of the lobby and tested the kitchen from room service. Quite simply, it was impossible to get a room at the Connaught unless a reservation was made weeks in advance. The elegant hotel on Carlos Place was one of the last bastions of the Empire, catering in large measure to those who mourned its passing and had the wealth to do so gracefully. There were enough to keep it perpetually full; the Connaught rarely had an available room.

Scofield knew this, and years ago had decided that occasions might arise when the Connaught's particular exclusivity could be useful. He had reached and cultivated a director of the financial group that owned the hotel and made his appeal. As all theaters have "house seats," and most restaurants keep constantly "reserved" tables for those exalted patrons who have to be accommodated, so do hotels retain empty rooms for like purposes. Bray was convincing; his work was on the side of the angels, the Tory side. A room would be at his disposal whenever he needed it.

"Room six-twenty-six," were the director's first words when Scofield placed his second, confirming call. "Just go right up on the lift as usual. You can sign the registration in your room—as usual."

Bray thanked him and turned his thoughts to another problem, an irritating one. He could not return to the rooming house several blocks away, and all his clothes except those on his back were there. In a duffel bag on the unmade bed. There was nothing else of consequence; his money as well as several dozen useful letterheads, identification cards, passports, and bank books, were all in his attaché case. But outside of the rumpled trousers, the cheap Mackinaw jacket, and the Irish hat, he didn't have a damn thing to wear. And clothes were not merely coverings for the body, they were intrinsic to the work and had to match the work; they were tools, consistently more effective than weapons and the spoken word. He left the bank of telephones and walked back into the aisles of Harrods. The selections would take an hour; that was fine. It would take his mind off Paris. And the inopportune love of his life.

It was shortly past midnight when Scofield left his room at the Connaught, dressed in a dark raincoat and a narrow-brimmed black hat. He took the service elevator to the basement of the hotel and emerged on the street through the employees' entrance. He found a taxi and told the driver to take him to Waterloo Bridge. He settled back in the seat and smoked a cigarette, trying to control his swelling sense of concern. He wondered if Taleniekov understood the change that had taken place, a change so unreasonable, so illogical that he was not sure how he would react were he the Russian. The core of his excellence, his longevity in his work, had always been his ability to think as the enemy thought; he was incapable of doing so now.

I'm not your enemy!

Taleniekov had shouted that unreasonable, illogical statement over the telephone in Washington. Perhaps—illogically—he was right. The Russian was no friend, but he was not *the* enemy. That enemy was the Matarese

And crazily, *so* unreasonably, through the Matarese he had found Antonia Gravet. The love . . .

What had *happened?*

He forced the question out of his mind. He would learn soon enough, and what he learned would no doubt bring back the relief he had felt at Harrods, diminished by too much time on his hands and too little to do. The telephone call to Roger Symonds, made precisely at 4:30, had been routine. Roger was out of the office so he had given information to the security room operator. The unexplained number that was to be relayed was six-four-three . . . minus twenty-two . . . Room 621, Connaught.

The taxi swung out of Trafalgar Square, up the Strand, past Savoy Court, toward the entrance of Waterloo Bridge. Bray leaned forward; there was no point walking any farther than he had to. He would cut through side streets down to the Thames and the Victoria Embankment.

"This'll be fine," he said to the driver, holding out payment, annoyed to see that his hand shook.

He went down the cobbled lane by the Savoy Hotel, and reached the bottom of the hill. Across the wide, well-lighted boulevard was the concrete walk and the high brick wall that fronted the river Thames. Moored permanently as a pub was a huge refurbished barge named *Caledonia,* closed by the eleven o'clock curfew imposed on all England's drinking halls, the few lights beyond the thick windows signifying the labors of clean-up crews removing the stains and odors of the day. A quarter of a mile south on the tree-lined Embankment were the sturdy, wide-beamed, full-decked riverboats that plowed the Thames most of the year round, ferrying tourists up to the Tower of London and back to Lambeth Bridge before returning to the waters of Cleopatra's Needle.

Years ago these boats were known as Tower Central, drops for Soviet couriers and KGB agents making contact with informers and deep-cover espionage personnel. Consular Operations had uncovered the drop; in time, the Russians knew it. Tower Central was taken out; a known drop was eliminated for some other that would take months to find.

Scofield cut through the garden paths of the park behind the Savoy; music from the ballroom floated down from above. He reached a small band amphitheater with its rows of slatted benches. A few couples were scattered around, talking quietly. Bray looked for a single man, for he was within the vicinity of Tower Central. The Russian would be somewhere in the area.

He was not; Scofield walked out of the amphitheater into the widest path that led to the boulevard. He emerged on the pavement; the traffic in the street was constant, bright headlights flashing by in both directions, mottled by the winter mists that rolled off the water. It occurred to Bray that Taleniekov must have hired an automobile. He looked up and down the avenue to see if any were parked on either side; none were. Across the boulevard, in front of the Embankment wall, strollers walked casually in couples, threesomes and several larger groups; there was no man by himself. Scofield looked at his watch; it was five minutes to one. The Russian had said he might be as late as two or three o'clock in the morning. Bray swore at his impatience, at the anxiety in his chest whenever he thought about Paris. About Toni.

There was the sudden flare of a cigarette lighter, the flame steady, then extinguished, only to be relighted, a second later. Diagonally across the wide avenue, to the right of the closed, chained gates of the pier that led to the tourist boats, a white-haired man was holding the flame under a blond woman's cigarette; both leaned against the wall, looking at the water.. Scofield studied the figure, what he could see of the face, and had to stop himself from breaking into a run. Taleniekov had arrived.

Bray turned right and walked until he was parallel with the Russian and the blond decoy. He knew Taleniekov had seen him and wondered why the KGB man did not dismiss the woman, paying her whatever price they had agreed upon to get her out of the way. It was foolish—conceivably dangerous— for a decoy to observe both parties at a contact point. Scofield waited at the curb, seeing now that Taleniekov's head was fully turned, the Russian staring at him, his arm around the woman's waist. Bray gestured first to his left, then to his right, his meaning clear. Get her out! Walk south; we'll meet shortly.

Taleniekov did not move. What was the Soviet *doing?* It was no time for whores!

Whores? The *courier's whore?* Oh, my *God!*

Scofield stepped off the curb, an automobile horn bellowed, as a car swerved toward the center of the boulevard to avoid hitting him. Bray barely heard the sound, was barely aware of the sight; he could only stare at the woman beside Taleniekov.

The arm around the waist was no gesture of feigned affection, the Russian was holding her up. Taleniekov spoke in the woman's ear; she tried to spin around; her head fell back on her neck, her mouth open, a scream or a plea about to emerge, but nothing was heard.

The strained face was the face of his love. Under the blond wig, it was *Toni.* All control left him; he raced across the wide avenue, speeding cars braking, spinning wheels, blowing horns. His thoughts converged like staccato shots of gunfire, one thought, one observation, more painful than all others.

Antonia looked more dead than alive.

30

"She's been *drugged,*" said Taleniekov.

"Why the hell did you bring her *here?*" asked Bray. "There are hundreds of places in France, dozens in Paris, where she'd be safe! Where she'd be cared for! You know them as well as *I* do!"

"If I could have been certain, I would have left her," replied Vasili, his voice calm. "Don't probe. I considered other alternatives."

Bray understood, his brief silence an expression of gratitude. Taleniekov could easily have killed Toni, probably would have killed her had it not been for East Berlin. "A doctor?"

"Helpful in terms of time, but not essentially necessary."

"What was the chemical?"

"Scopolamine."

"When?"

"Early yesterday morning. Over eighteen hours."

"*Eighteen? . . .*" It was no time for explanations. "Do you have a car?"

"I couldn't take the chance. A lone man with a woman who could not stand up under her own power; the trail would have been obvious. The pilot drove us up from Ashford."

"Can you trust him?"

"No, but he stopped for petrol ten minutes outside of London and went inside to relieve himself. I added a quart of oil to his fuel tank; it should be taking effect on the road back to Ashford."

"Find a taxi." Scofield's look conveyed the compliment he would not say.

"We have much to discuss," added Taleniekov, moving away from the wall.

"Then hurry," said Bray.

Antonia's breathing was steady, the muscles of her face relaxed in sleep. When she awoke she would be nauseated, but it would pass with the day. Scofield pulled the covers over her shoulders, leaned down and kissed her on her pale white lips, and got up from the bed.

He walked out of the bedroom, leaving the door ajar. Should Toni stir he wanted to hear her; hysterics were a byproduct of scopolamine. They had to be controlled; it was why Taleniekov could not risk leaving her alone, even for the few minutes it would have taken to lease a car.

"What happened?" he asked the Russian, who sat in a chair, a glass of whisky in his hand.

"This morning—yesterday morning," said Taleniekov, correcting himself, his white-haired head angled back against the rim of the chair, his eyes closed; the man was clearly exhausted. "They say you're dead, did you know that?"

"Yes. What's that got to do with it?"

"It's how I got her back." The Russian opened his eyes and looked at Bray. "There's very little about Beowulf Agate I don't know."

"And?"

"I said I was you. There were several basic questions to answer; they were not difficult. I offered myself in exchange for her. They agreed."

"Start from the beginning."

"I wish I could, I wish I knew what it was. The Matarese, or someone within the Matarese, wants you alive. It's why certain people were told that you are not. They don't look for the American, only the Russian. I wish I understood." Taleniekov drank.

"What *happened?*"

"They found her. Don't ask me how, I don't know. Perhaps Helsinki, perhaps you were picked up out of Rome, perhaps anything or anyone, I don't know."

"But they found her," said Scofield, sitting down. "Then what?"

"Early yesterday morning, four or five hours before you called, she went down to a bakery; it was only a few doors away. An hour later she had not returned. I knew then I had two choices. I could go out after her—but where to start, where to look? Or I could wait for someone to come to the flat. You see, *they* had no choice, I knew that. The telephone rang a number of times but I did not answer, knowing that each time I didn't, it brought someone closer."

"You answered my call," interrupted Bray.

"That was later. By then we were negotiating."

"Then?"

"Finally two men came. It was one of the more testing moments of my life not to kill them both, especially one. He had that small, ugly little mark on his chest. When I ripped his clothes off and saw it, I nearly went mad."

"Why?"

"They killed in Leningrad. In Essen. Later you'll understand. It's part of what we must discuss."

"Go on." Scofield poured himself a drink.

"I'll tell it briefly, fill in the spaces yourself; you've been there. I kept the soldier and his hired gun bound and unconscious for over an hour. The phone rang and this time I answered, using the most pronounced American accent I could manage. You'd have thought the sky over Paris had fallen, so hysterical was the caller. 'An imposter in London!' he squeaked. Something about 'a gross error having been made by the embassy, the information they received completely erroneous.'"

"I think you skipped something," interrupted Bray again. "I assume that was when you said you were me."

"Let's say I answered in the affirmative when the hysterical question was posed. It was a temptation I could not resist, since I had heard less than forty-eight hours previously that you had been killed." The Russian paused, then added, "Two weeks ago in Washington."

Scofield walked back to the chair, frowning. "But the man on the phone knew I was alive, just as those here in London knew I was alive. So you were right. Only certain people inside the Matarese were told I was dead."

"Does that tell you something?"

"The same thing it tells you. They make distinctions."

"Exactly. When either of us ever wanted a subordinate to do nothing, we told him the problem was solved. For such people you're no longer alive, no longer hunted."

"But why? I *am* hunted. They trapped me."

"One question with two answers, I think," said the Russian. "As any diverse organization, the Matarese is imperfect. Among its ranks are the undisciplined, the violence-prone, men who kill for the score alone or because of fanatic beliefs. These were the people who were told you were dead. If they did not hunt you, they would not kill you."

"That's your first answer; what's the second? Why does someone want to keep me alive?"

"To make you a *consigliere* of the Matarese."

"*What?*"

"Think about it. Consider what you'd bring to such an organization."

Bray stared at the KGB man. "No more than you would."

"Oh, much more. There are no great shocks to come out of Moscow, I accept that. But there are astonishing revelations to be found in Washington. You could provide them; you'd be an enormous asset. The sanctimonious are always far more vulnerable."

"I accept that."

"Before Odile Verachten was killed, she made an offer to me. It was not an offer she was entitled to make; they don't want the Russian. They want you. If they can't have you, they'll kill you, but someone's giving you the option."

It would be far better for all concerned if we sat down and thrashed out the differences between us. You may discover they're not so great after all. Words from a faceless messenger.

"Let's get back to Paris," said Bray. "How did you get her?"

"It wasn't so difficult. The man on the phone was too anxious; he saw a generalship in his future, or his own execution. I discussed what might happen to the soldier with the ugly little mark on his chest; the fact that I knew about it was nearly enough in itself. I set up a series of moves, offering the soldier and Beowulf Agate for the girl. Beowulf was tired of running and was perfectly willing to listen to whatever anyone had to say. He—I—knew I was cornered, but professionalism demanded that he—you—extract certain guarantees. The girl had to go free. Were my reactions consistent with your well-known obstinacy?"

"Very plausible," replied Scofield. "Let's see if I can fill in a few spaces. You answered the questions: What was my mother's middle name? or When did my father change jobs?"

"Nothing so ordinary," broke in the Russian. " 'Who was your fourth kill. Where?' "

"Lisbon," said Bray quietly. "An American beyond salvage. Yes, you'd know that. . . . Then your moves were made by a sequence of telephone calls to the flat—my call from London was the intrusion—and with each call you gave new instructions, any deviation and the exchange was canceled. The exchange ground itself was in traffic, preferably one-way traffic, with one vehicle, one man and Antonia. Everything to take place within a time span of sixty to a hundred seconds."

The Russian nodded. "Noon on the Champs Elysées, south of the Arch. Vehicle and girl taken, man and soldier bound at the elbows, thrown out at the intersection of the Place de la Concorde, and a swift, if roundabout, drive out of Paris."

Bray put the whisky down, and walked to the hotel window overlooking Carlos Place. "A little while ago you said you had two choices. To go out after her, or wait in the rue de Bac. It seems to me there was a third but you didn't take it. You could have gotten out of Paris yourself right away."

Taleniekov closed his eyes. "That was the one choice I didn't have. It was in her voice, in every reference she made to you. I thought I saw it in Corsica, that first night in the cave above Porto Vecchio when you looked at her. I thought then, how *insane*, how perfectly . . ." The Russian shook his head.

"Unreasonable?" asked Bray.

Taleniekov opened his eyes. "Yes. Unreasonable . . . as in unnecessary, uncalled for." The KGB man raised his glass and drank the remaining whisky in one swallow. "The slate from East Berlin is as clean as it will ever be; there'll be no more cleansing."

"None will be asked for. Or expected."

"Good. I presume you've seen the newspapers."

"Trans-Communications? Its holdings in Verachten?"

"Ownership would be more like it. I trust you noted the location of the corporate headquarters. Boston, Massachusetts. A city quite familiar to you, I think."

"What's more to the point, it's the city—and state—of Joshua Appleton, the Fourth, patrician and Senator, whose grandfather was the guest of Guillaume de Matarese. It'll be interesting to see what—if any—his connections are to Trans-Comm."

"Can you doubt they exist?"

"At this point I doubt everything," said Scofield. "Maybe I'll think differently after we've put together those facts you say we now have. Let's start with when we left Corsica."

Taleniekov nodded. "Rome came first. Tell me about Scozzi."

Bray did, taking the time to explain the role Antonia had been forced to play in the Red Brigades.

"That's why she was in Corsica, then?" asked Vasili. "Running from the Brigades?"

"Yes. Everything she told me about their financing spells Matarese. . . ." Scofield clarified his theories, moving swiftly on to the events at Villa d'Este and the murder of Guillamo Scozzi, ordered by a man named Paravacini. "It was the first time I heard that I was dead. They thought I was you. . . . Now Leningrad. What happened there?"

Taleniekov breathed deeply before answering. "They killed in Leningrad, in Essen," he said, his voice barely audible. "Oh, how they kill, these twentieth-century *Fida'is*, these contemporary mutants of Hasan ibn-al-Sabbah. I should tell you, the soldier I pushed from the car in the Place de la Concorde had more than a blemish on his chest. His clothes were stained by a gunshot that left another mark. I told his associate it was for Leningrad, for Essen."

The Russian told his story quietly, the depth of his feelings apparent when he spoke of Lodzia Kronescha, the scholar Mikovsky, and Heinrich Kassel. Especially Lodzia; it was necessary for him to stop for a while and pour more whisky in his glass. Scofield remained silent; there was nothing he could say. The Russian finished with the field at night in Stadtwald and the death of Odile Verachten.

"Prince Andrei Voroshin became Ansel Verachten, founder of the Verachten Works, next to Krupp the largest company in Germany, now one of the most sprawling in all Europe. The granddaughter was his chosen successor in the Matarese."

"And Scozzi," said Bray, "joined Paravacini through a marriage of convenience. Bloodlines, a certain talent, and charm in exchange for a seat in the board room. But the chair was a prop; it's all it ever was. The count was expendable, killed because he made a mistake."

"As was Odile Verachten. Also expendable."

"And the name Scozzi-Paravacini is misleading. The control lies with Paravacini."

"Add to that Trans-Communication's ownership of Verachten. So two descendants of the *padrone's* guest list are accounted for, both a part of Matarese, yet neither significant. What do we have?"

"What we suspected, what old Krupskaya told you in Moscow. The Matarese was taken over, obviously in part, possibly in whole. Scozzi and Voroshin were useful for what they brought or what they knew or what they owned. They were tolerated—even made to feel important—as long as they *were* useful, eliminated the moment they were not."

"But useful for *what?* That's the question!" Taleniekov banged his glass down in frustration. "What does the Matarese want? They finance intimidation and murder through huge corporate structures; they spread panic, but *why?* This world is going mad with terror, bought and paid for by men who lose the most by it. Their investment is in total *disorder!* It makes no sense!"

Scofield heard the sound—the moan—and sprang out of the chair. He walked quickly to the bedroom door; Toni had changed her position, twisting to her left, the covers bunched around her shoulders. But she was still asleep; the cry had come from her unconscious. He went back to the chair and stood behind it.

"Total disorder," he said softly. "Chaos. The clashing of bodies in space. Creation."

"What are you talking about?" asked Taleniekov.

"I'm not sure," replied Scofield. "I keep going back to the word 'chaos' but I'm not sure why."

"We're not sure of *anything*. We have four names—but two didn't amount to much—and they're dead. We see an alignment of companies who are the superstructure—the *essential superstructure*—behind terrorism everywhere, but we cannot prove the alignment and don't know why they're sponsoring it. Scozzi-Paravacini finances the Red Brigades, Verachten no doubt Baader-Meinhof, God only knows what Trans-Communications pays for—and these may be only a few of the many involved. We have *found* the Matarese, but still we don't see them! Whatever charges we leveled against such conglomerates would be called the ravings of madmen, or worse."

"Much worse," said Bray, remembering the voice over the restaurant's telephone. "Traitors. We'd be shot."

"Your words have the ring of prophecy. I don't like them."

"Neither do I, but I like being executed less."

"A *non sequitur*."

"Not when coupled with what you just said. 'We've found the Matarese, but still we don't see them,' wasn't that it?"

"Yes."

"Suppose we not only found one, but had him. In our hands."

"A *hostage?*"

"That's right."

"That's insane."

"Why? You had the Verachten woman."

"In a car. In a farmer's field. At night. I had no delusions of taking her into Essen and setting up a base of operations."

Scofield sat down. "The Red Brigades held Aldo Moro eight blocks away from a police headquarters in Rome. Although that's not exactly what I had in mind."

Taleniekov leaned forward. "Waverly?"

"Yes."

"*How?* The American network is after you, the Matarese nearly trapped you; what did *you* have in mind? Dropping into the Foreign Office and proffering an invitation for tea?"

"Waverly's to be brought here—to this room—at eight o'clock tonight."

The Russian whistled. "May I ask how you managed it?"

Bray told him about Symonds. "He's doing it because he thinks whatever convinced me to work with you must be strong enough to get me an interview with Waverly."

"They have a name for me. Did he tell you?"

"Yes. The Serpent."

"I suppose I should be flattered, but I'm not. I find it ugly. Does Symonds have any idea that this meeting has a hostile basis? That you suspect Waverly of being something more than England's Foreign Secretary?"

"No, the reverse, in fact. When he objected, the last thing I said to him was that I might be trying to save Waverly's life."

"Very good," said Taleniekov. "Very frightening. Assassination, like acts of terror, is a spreading commodity. They'll be alone then?"

"Yes, I made a point of it. A room at the Connaught; there'd be no reason for Roger to think anything's wrong. And we know the Matarese haven't made the connection between me and the man Waverly is supposedly meeting at the MI-Six offices."

"You're certain of that? It strikes me as the weakest part of the strategy. They've got you in London, they know you have the four names from Corsica. Suddenly, from nowhere, Waverly, the *consigliere,* is asked to meet secretly with a man at the office of a British intelligence agent known to have been a friend of Beowulf Agate. The equation seems obvious to me; why would it elude the Matarese?"

"A very specific reason. They don't think I ever made contact with Symonds."

"They can't be sure you didn't."

"The odds are against it. Roger's an experienced field man; he covered himself. He was logged in at the Admiralty and later returned a blind inquiry. I wasn't picked up in the streets and we used a sterile phone. We met an hour outside of London, two changes of vehicle for me, at least four for him. No one followed."

"Impressive. Not conclusive."

"It's the best I can do. Except for a final qualification."

"Qualification?"

"Yes. There isn't going to be a meeting tonight. They'll never reach this room."

"No *meeting?* Then what's the purpose of their coming here?"

"So we can grab Waverly downstairs before Symonds knows what's happened. Roger'll be driving; when he gets here, he won't go through the lobby, he'll use a side entrance, I'll find out which one. In the event—and I agree it's possible— that Waverly is followed, you'll be down in the street. You'll know it; you'll see them. Take them out. I'll be right inside that entrance."

"Where they least expect you," broke in the Russian.

"That's right. I'm counting on it. I can take Roger by surprise, hammer lock him and force a pill down his throat. He won't wake up for hours."

"It's not enough," said Taleniekov, lowering his voice. "You'll have to kill him. Sacrifices inevitably must be made. Churchill understood that with Coventry and the Ultra; this is no less, Scofield. British Intelligence will mount the most extensive manhunt in England's history. We've got to get Waverly out of the country. If the death of one man can buy us time—a day perhaps—I submit it's worth it."

Bray looked at the Russian, studying him. "You submit too goddamn much."

"You know I'm right."

Silence. Suddenly Scofield hurled his glass across the room. It shattered against the wall. "God*damn* it!"

Taleniekov bolted forward, his right hand under his coat. "What is it?"

"You're right and I *do* know it. He trusts me and I've got to kill him. It'll be days before the British will know where to start. Neither MI-Six nor the Foreign Office know anything about the Connaught."

The KGB man removed his hand, sliding it onto the arm of the chair. "We need the time. I don't think there's any other way."

"If there is, I hope to God it comes to me." Bray shook his head. "I'm sick to death of necessity." He looked over at the bedroom door. "But then she told me that."

"The rest is detail," continued Taleniekov, rushing the moment. "I'll have an automobile on the street outside the entrance. The moment I'm finished—if, indeed, there's anything for me to do—I'll come inside and help you. It will be necessary, of course, to take the dead man along with Waverly. Remove him."

"The dead man has no name," said Scofield quietly. He got out of the chair and walked to the window. "Has it occurred to you that the closer we get, the more like them we become?"

"What occurs to me," replied the Russian, "is that your strategy is nothing short of extraordinary. Not only will we have a *consigliere* of the Matarese, but *what a consigliere!* The Foreign Secretary of England! Have you any idea what that means? We'll break that man wide open, and the world will listen. It will be *forced* to listen!" Taleniekov paused, then added softly, "What you've done lives up to the stories of Beowulf Agate."

"Bullshit," said Bray. "I hate that name."

The moan was sudden, bursting into a prolonged sob, followed by a cry of pain, muffled, uncertain, desperate. Scofield raced into the bedroom. Toni was writhing on the bed, her hands clawing her face, her legs kicking viciously at imaginary demons that surrounded her. Bray sat down and pulled her hands from her face, gently, firmly, bending each finger so that the nails would not puncture her skin. He pinned her arms and held her, cradling her as he had cradled her in Rome. Her cries subsided, replaced once more by sobs; she shivered, her breathing erratic, slowly returning to normal as her rigid body went limp. The first hysterics brought about by the dissipation of scopolamine had passed. Scofield heard footsteps in the doorway; he angled his head to signify that he was listening.

"It will keep up until morning, you know," said the KGB man. "It leaves the body slowly, with a great deal of pain. As much from the images in the mind as anything else. There's nothing you can do. Just hold her."

"I know. I will."

There was a moment of silence; Bray could feel the Russian's eyes on him, on Antonia. "I'll leave now," Taleniekov said. "I'll call you here at noon, come up later in the day. We can refine the details then, coordinate signals, that kind of thing."

"Sure. That kind of thing. Where'll you go? You can stay here, if you like."

"I think not. As in Paris, there are dozens of places here. I know them as well as you do. Besides, I must find a car, study the streets. Nothing takes the place of preparation, does it?"

"No, it doesn't."

"Good night. Take care of her."

"I'll try." Footsteps again; the Russian walked out of the room. Scofield spoke. "Taleniekov."

"Yes?"

"I'm sorry about Leningrad."

"Yes." Again there was silence; then the words were spoken quietly. "Thank you."

The outside door closed; he was alone with his love. He lowered her to the pillow and touched her face. So illogical, so unreasonable. *Why did I find you? Why did you find me? You should have left me where I was—deep in the earth. It isn't the time for either of us, can't you understand that? It's all so . . . uncalled for.*

It was as if his thoughts had been spoken out loud. Toni opened her eyes, the focus imperfect, the recognition slight, but she knew him. Her lips formed his name, the sound a whisper.

"Bray?"

"You'll be all right. They didn't hurt you. The pain you feel is from chemicals; it will pass, believe that."

"You came back."

"Yes."

"Don't go away again, *please*. Not without me."

"I won't."

Her eyes suddenly widened, the stare glazed, her white teeth bared like a young animal's caught in a snare that was breaking its back. A heartbreaking whimper came from deep inside her.

She collapsed in his arms.

Tomorrow, my love, my only love. Tomorrow comes with the sunlight, everyone knows that. And then the pain will pass, I promise you. And I promise you something else, my inopportune love so late in my life. Tomorrow, today, tonight . . . I will take the man who will bring this nightmare to a close. Taleniekov is right. We will break him—as no man has ever been broken—and the world will listen to us. When it does, my love, my only adorable love, you and I are free. We will go far away where the night brings sleep and love, not death, not fear and loathing of the darkness. We will be free because Beowulf Agate will be gone. He will disappear—for he hasn't done much good. But he has one more thing to do. Tonight.

Scofield touched Antonia's cheek. She held his hand briefly, moving it to her lips, smiling, reassuring him with her eyes.

"How's the head?" asked Bray.

"The ache is barely a numbness now," she said. "I'm fine, really."

Scofield released her hand and walked across the room where Taleniekov was bent over a table, studying a road map. Without having discussed it, both men were dressed nearly alike for their work. Sweaters and trousers of dark material, tightly strapped shoulder holsters with black leather belts laterally across the chest. Their shoes were also dark in color, but light in weight, with thick rubber soles that had been scraped with knives until they were coarse.

Taleniekov now glanced up as Bray approached the table. "Out of Great Dunmow, we'll head east toward Coggeshall on our way to Nayland. Incidentally, there's an airfield capable of handling small jets south of Hadleigh. Such a field might be of value to us in a few days."

"You may be right."

"Too," added the KGB man with obvious reluctance, "this route passes the Blackwater River; the forests are dense in that area. It would be a . . . good place to drop off the package."

"The dead man still hasn't got a name," said Scofield. "Give him his due. He's Roger Symonds, honorable man, and I hate this fucking world."

"At the risk of appearing fatuous, may I submit—forgive me, suggest—that what you do tonight will benefit that sad world we both have abused too well for too long."

"I'd just as soon you didn't submit or suggest anything." Bray looked at his watch. "He'll be calling soon. When he does, Toni will go down to the lobby and pay Mr. Edmonton's bill—that's me. She'll come back up with a steward and take our bags and briefcases down to the car we've rented in Edmonton's name and drive directly to Colchester. She'll wait at a restaurant called Bonner's until 11:30. If there are any changes of plans or we need her, we'll reach her there. If she doesn't hear from us, she'll go on to Nayland, to the Double Crown Inn where she has a room reserved in the name of Vickery."

Taleniekov pushed himself up from the table. "My briefcase is not to be opened," he said. "It's tripped."

"So's mine," replied Scofield. "Any more questions?"

The telephone rang; all three looked at it—a moment suspended in time, for the bell meant the time had come. Bray walked over to the desk, let the phone ring a second time, then picked it up.

Whatever the words he might have expected, whatever greetings, information, instructions or revelations that might have come, nothing on this earth could have prepared him for what he heard. Symonds' voice was a cry from some inner space of torment, a pain of such extreme that was beyond belief.

"They're all *dead*. It's a *massacre!* Waverly, his wife, children, three servants . . . *dead*. What in *hell have you done?*"

"Oh, my *God!*" Scofield's mind raced, thoughts swiftly translated into carefully selected words. "Roger, listen to me. It's what I tried to *prevent!*" He cupped the phone, his eyes on Taleniekov. "Waverly's dead, everyone in the house killed."

"Method?" shouted the Russian. "Marks on the bodies. Weapons. Get it all!"

Bray shook his head. "We'll get it later." He took his hand from the mouthpiece; Symonds was talking rapidly, close to hysterics.

"It's *horrible.* Oh, God, the most terrible thing! They've been slaughtered . . . like animals!"

"Roger! Get hold of yourself! Now listen to me. It's part of a pattern. Waverly knew about it. He knew too much; it's why he was killed. I couldn't reach him in time."

"You couldn't? . . . For the love of God . . . why *didn't* you, *couldn't* you . . . *tell me?* He was the Foreign Secretary, England's *Foreign Secretary!* Have you any idea the repercussions, the . . . oh, my *God,* a tragedy! A *catastrophe! Butchered!"* Symonds paused. When he spoke again it was obvious that the professional in him was struggling for control. "I want you down in my office as soon as you can get there. Consider yourself under detention by the British government."

"I can't do that. Don't ask me."

"I'm not asking, Scofield! I'm giving you a direct order backed up by the highest authorities in England. You will *not* leave that hotel! By the time you reached the lift, all the current would be shut off, every staircase, every exit under armed guard."

"All right, all right. I'll get to MI-Six," lied Bray.

"You'll be *escorted.* Remain in your room."

"Forget the room, Roger," said Scofield, grasping for whatever words he could find that might fit the crisis. "I've got to see you, but not at MI-Six."

"I don't think you *heard* me!"

"Put the guards on the doors, shut off the goddamned elevators, do anything you like, but I've got to see you *here.* I'm going to walk out of this room and go down to the bar, to the darkest booth I can find. Meet me there."

"I *repeat*—"

"Repeat all you want to, but if you don't come over here and listen to me, there'll be other assassinations—*that's* what they are, Roger! *Assassinations.* And they won't stop at a Foreign Secretary, or a Secretary of State . . . or a President or a Prime Minister."

"Oh, my . . . *God,*" whispered Symonds.

"It's what I couldn't tell you last night. It's the reason you looked for when we talked. But I won't put it on-record, I can't work in-sanction. And that should tell you enough. Get over here, Roger." Bray closed his eyes, held his breath; it was now or it was not.

"I'll be there in ten minutes," said Symonds, his voice cracking.

Scofield hung up the phone, looking first at Antonia, then Taleniekov. "He's on his way."

"He'll take you in!" exclaimed the Russian.

"I don't think so. He knows me well enough to know I won't go on-record if

I say I won't. And he doesn't want the rest of it on his head." Bray crossed to the chair where he had thrown his raincoat and travel bag. "I'm sure of one thing. He'll meet me downstairs, and give me a chance. If he accepts, I'll be back in an hour. If he doesn't . . . I'll kill him." Scofield unzipped his bag, reached into it, and pulled out a sheathed, long-bladed hunting knife. It still had the Harrods price tag on it. He looked at Toni; her eyes told him she understood. Both the necessity and his loathing of it.

Symonds sat across from Bray in the booth of the Connaught lounge. The subdued lighting could not conceal the pallor of the Englishman's face; he was a man forced to make decisions of such magnitude that the mere thought of them made him ill. Physically ill, mentally exhausted.

They had talked for nearly forty minutes. Scofield, as planned, had told him part of the truth—a great deal more of it than he cared to—but it was necessary. He was now about to make his final request of Roger and both men knew it. Symonds felt the terrible weight of his decision; it was in his eyes. Bray felt the knife in his belt; his appalling decision to use it if necessary made it difficult for him to breathe.

"We don't know how extensive it is, or how many people in the various governments are involved, but we know it's being financed through large corporations," Scofield explained. "What happened in Belgravia Square tonight can be compared to what happened to Anthony Blackburn in New York, to the physicist Yurievich in Russia. We're closing in; we have names, covert alliances, knowledge that intelligence branches in Washington, Moscow, and Bonn have been manipulated. But we have no proof; we'll get it, but we don't have it now. If you take me in, we'll never get it. The case against me is beyond salvage; I don't have to tell you what that means. I'll be executed at the first . . . opportune moment. For the wrong reason, by the wrong people, but the result will be the same. Give me *time*, Roger."

"What will you give me?"

"What more do you want?"

"Those names, the alliances."

"They're *meaningless* now. Worse than that, if they're recorded, they'll either go further underground, cutting off all traces, or the killing, the terrorism, will accelerate. There'll be a series of bloodbaths . . . and you'll be dead."

"That's my condition. The names, the alliances. Or you will not leave here."

Bray stared at the MI-Six man. "Will you stop me, Roger? I mean here, now, at this moment, will you? *Can* you?"

"Perhaps not. But those two men over there will." Symonds nodded to his left.

Scofield shifted his eyes. Across the room, at a table in the center of the lounge, were two British agents, one of them the red-haired, stocky man he had spoken with last night at the moonlit playground in Guildford. There was no sympathy now, only hostility in his look. "You covered yourself," said Scofield.

"Did you think I wouldn't? They're armed and have their instructions. The names, please." Symonds took out a notebook and a ballpoint pen; he placed them in front of Bray. "Don't write nonsense, I beg you. Be practical. If you and the Russian are killed, there's no one else. I may not be in a class with Beowulf Agate and the Serpent, but I'm not without certain talents."

"How much time will you give me?"

"One week. Not a day more."

Scofield picked up the pen, opened the small notebook and began to write.

April 4th, 1911
Porto Vecchio, Corsica
Scozzi
Voroshin
Waverly
Appleton

Current:
Guillamo Scozzi—Dead
Odile Verachten—Dead
David Waverly—Dead
Joshua Appleton—?

Scozzi-*Paravacini*. Milan
Verachten Works. (Voroshin). Essen
Trans-Communications. Boston

Below the names and the companies, he then wrote one word: *Matarese*.

Bray walked out of the elevator, his mind on air routes, accessibilities, and cover. Hours now took on the significance of days; there was so much to learn, so much to find, and so little time to do it all.

They had thought it might end in London with the breaking of David Waverly. They should have known better; the descendants were expendable.

Three were dead, three names removed from the guest list of Guillaume de Matarese for the date of April 4, 1911. Yet one was left. The golden politician of Boston, the man few doubted would win the summer primaries and without question the election in the fall. He would be President of the United States. Many had cried out during the violent sixties and seventies that he could bind the country together; Appleton was never so presumptuous as to make the statement, but most of America thought he was perhaps the only man who could.

But bind it for what? For whom? That was the most frightening prospect of all. Was he the one descendant not expendable? Chosen by the council, by the shepherd boy, to do what the others could not do?

They would reach Appleton, thought Bray as he rounded the corner of the Connaught hallway toward his room, but not where Appleton expected to be reached—*if* he expected to be reached. They would not be drawn to Washington where chance encounters with State, FBI and Company personnel were ten times greater than any other place in the hemisphere. There was no point in taking on two enemies simultaneously. Instead, they would go to Boston, to the conglomerate so aptly named Trans-Communications.

Somewhere, somehow, within the upper ranks of that vast company, they would find one man—one man with a blue circle on his chest or connections to Scozzi-Paravacini or Verachten, and that man would whisper an alarm summoning Joshua Appleton, IV. They would trap him, take him in Boston. And when they were finished with him the secret of the Matarese would be exposed, told by a man whose impeccable credentials were matched only by his incredible deceit. It *had* to be Appleton; there was no one else. If they . . .

Scofield reached for the weapon in his holster. The door of his room twenty feet down the corridor was open. There were no circumstances imaginable that allowed it to be *conceivably* left open by choice! There had been an intruder—intruders.

He stopped, shook the paralysis from his mind, and ran to the side of the door, pressing his back into the wall by the molding. He lunged inside, crouching, leveling his gun in front of him, prepared to fire.

There was no one, no one at all. Nothing but silence and a very neat room. Too neat; the road map had been removed from the table, the glasses washed, returned to the silver tray on the bureau, the ashtrays wiped clean. There was no evidence that the room had been occupied. Then he saw it—them—and the paralysis returned.

On the floor by the table were his attaché case and travel bag, positioned—neatly—beside each other the way a steward or a bellboy might position them. And folded—neatly—over the travel bag was his dark blue raincoat. A guest was prepared for departure.

Two visitors had already departed. Antonia was gone, Taleniekov gone.

The bedroom door was open, the bed fully made up, the bedside table devoid of the water pitcher and the ashtray which an hour ago had been filled with half-smoked cigarettes—testimony to an anxious, pain-stricken night and day.

Silence. Nothing.

His eyes were suddenly drawn to the one thing—again on the floor—that was not in keeping with the neatness of the room, and he felt sick. On the rug by the left side of the table was a circle of blood—a jagged circle, still moist, still glistening. And then he looked up. A small pane of glass had been blown out of the window.

"*Toni!*" The scream was his; it broke the silence, but he could not help himself. He could not think, he could not move.

The glass shattered; a second windowpane blew out of its wooden frame and he heard the whine of a bullet as it embedded itself in the wall behind him. He dropped to the floor.

The telephone rang, its jangling bell somehow proof of insanity! He crawled to the desk below the sightline of the window.

"Toni? . . . *Toni!*" He was screaming, crying, yet he had not reached the desk, had not touched the phone.

He raised his hand and pulled the instrument to the floor beside him. He picked up the receiver and held it to his ear.

"We can always find you, Beowulf," said the precise English voice on the other end of the line. "I told you that when we spoke before."

"What have you *done with her?*" shouted Bray. "Where *is she?*"

"Yes, we thought that might be your reaction. Rather strange coming from you, isn't it? You don't even inquire about the Serpent."

"*Stop* it! Tell me!"

"I intend to. Incidentally, you had a grave lapse of judgment—again strange for one so experienced. We merely had to follow your friend Symonds from Belgravia. A quick perusal of the hotel registry—as well as the time and the method of registering—gave us your room."

"What have you *done* with her? . . . *Them?*"

"The Russian's wounded, but he may survive. At least sufficiently long for our purposes."

"The *girl!*"

"She's on her way to an airfield, as is the Serpent."

"Where are you taking her?"

"We think you know. It was the last thing you wrote down before you named the Corsican. A city in the state of Massachusetts."

"Oh, God. . . . *Symonds?*"

"Dead, Beowulf. We have the notebook. It was in his car. For all intents and purposes, Roger Symonds, MI-Six, has disappeared. In light of his schedule, he may even be tied in with the terrorists who massacred the Foreign Secretary of England and his family."

"You . . . *bastards.*"

"No. Merely professionals. I'd think you'd appreciate that. If you want the girl back you'll follow us. You see, there's someone who wants to meet with you."

"Who?"

"Don't be a fool," said the faceless messenger curtly.

"In Boston?"

"I'm afraid we can't help you get there, but we have every confidence in you. Register at the Ritz Carlton Hotel under the name of . . . Vickery. Yes, that's a good name, such a benign sound."

"Boston," said Bray, exhausted.

Again there was the sudden shattering of glass; a third windowpane blew out of its frame.

"That shot," said the voice on the phone, "is a symbol of our good faith. We could have killed you with the first."

31

He reached the coast of France, the same way he had left it four days ago; by motor launch at night. The trip to Paris took longer than anticipated; the drone he had expected to use wanted no part of him. The word was out, the price for his dead body too high, the punishment for helping Beowulf Agate too severe. The man owed Bray; he preferred to walk away.

Scofield found an off-duty *gendarme* in a bar in Boulogne-sur-Mer; the negotiations were swift. He needed a fast ride to Paris, to Orly Airport. To the *gendarme*, the payment was staggering; Bray reached Orly by daybreak. By 9:00 A.M., a Mr. Edmonton was on the first Air Canada flight to Montreal. The plane left the ground and he turned his thoughts to Antonia.

They would use her to trap him, but there was no way they would permit her to stay alive once the trap had closed. Any more than they would let Taleniekov live once they had learned everything he knew. Even the Serpent could not withstand injections of scopolamine or sodium amytal; no man could block his memory or prohibit the flow of information once the gates of recall were chemically pried open.

These were the things he had to accept, and having accepted them, base his moves on their reality. He would not grow old with Antonia Gravet; there would be no years of peace. Once he understood this, there was nothing left but to try to reverse the conclusion, knowing that the chances of doing so were remote. Simply put, since there was absolutely nothing to lose, conversely there was no risk not worth taking, no strategy too outlandish or outrageous to consider.

The key was Joshua Appleton, that remained constant. Was it possible that the Senator was such a consummate actor that he had been able to deceive so many so well for so long? Apparently it was so; one trained from birth to achieve a single goal, with unlimited money and talent available to him, could probably conceal anything. But the gap that needed filling was found in the stories of Josh Appleton, Marine combat officer, Korea. They were well known, publicized by campaign managers, emphasized by the candidate's reluctance to discuss them, other than to praise the men who had served with him.

Captain Joshua Appleton had been decorated for bravery under fire on five separate occasions, but the medals were only symbols, the tributes of his men paeans of genuine devotion. Josh Appleton was an officer dedicated to the proposition that no soldier should take a risk he would not take himself; and no infantryman, regardless of how badly he was wounded or how seemingly hopeless the situation, was to be left to the enemy if there was any chance at all to get him back. With such tenets, he was not always the best of officers, but he was the best of men. He continuously exposed himself to the severest punishment to save a private's life, or draw fire away from a corporal's squad. He had been wounded twice dragging men out of the hills of Panmunjom, and nearly lost his life at Chosan when he had crawled through enemy lines to direct a helicopter rescue.

After the war, when he was home, Appleton had faced another struggle as dangerous as any he had experienced in Korea. A near fatal accident on the Massachusetts Turnpike. His car had swerved over the divider, crashing into an onrushing truck, the injuries sustained from head to legs so punishing the doctors at Massachusetts General had about given him up for dead. When bulletins were issued about this decorated son of a prominent family, men came from all over the country. Mechanics, bus drivers, farmhands, and clerks; the soldiers who had served under "Captain Josh."

For two days and nights they had kept vigil, the more demonstrative praying openly, others simply sitting with their thoughts or reminiscing quietly with their former comrades. And when the crisis had passed and Appleton had been taken off the critical list, these men went home. They had come because they had wanted to come; they had left not knowing whether they had made any difference, but hoping that they had. Captain Joshua Appleton, IV, USMCR, was deserving of that hope.

This was the gap that Bray could neither fill nor understand. The captain who had risked his life so frequently, so openly for the sake of other men; how could those risks be reconciled with a man programmed since birth to become the President of the United States? How could repeated exposure to death be justified to the Matarese?

Somehow they had been, for there was no longer any doubt where Senator Joshua Appleton stood. The man who would be elected President of the United States before the year was over was inextricably tied to a conspiracy as dangerous as any in American history.

At Orly, Scofield picked up the Paris edition of the *Herald-Tribune* to see if the news of the Waverly massacre had broken; it had not. But there was something else, on the second page. It was another follow-up story concerning Trans-Communications' holdings in Verachten, including a partial list of the Boston conglomerate's board of directors. The third name on the roster was the Senator from Massachusetts.

Joshua Appleton was not only a *consigliere* of the Matarese, he was the sole descendant of that guest list seventy years ago in Porto Vecchio to become a true inheritor.

"*Mesdames et messieurs, s'il vous plaît. À votre gauche, Les Illes de la Manche. . . .*" The voice of the pilot droned from the aircraft's speaker. They were passing the Channel Islands; in six hours they would reach the coast of Nova Scotia, an hour later Montreal. And four hours after that, Bray would cross the U.S. border south of Lacolle on the Richelieu River, into the waters of Lake Champlain.

In hours the final madness would begin. He would live or he would die. And if he could not live in peace with Toni, without the shadow of Beowulf Agate in front of him or behind him, he did not care to live any longer. He was filled with . . . emptiness. If the awful void could be erased, replaced with the simple delight of being with another human being, then whatever years he had left were most welcome.

If not, to hell with them.

Boston.

There's someone who wants to meet with you.

Who? Why?

To make you a consigliere *of the Matarese. . . . Consider what you bring to such an organization.*

It was not hard to define. Taleniekov was right. There were no shocks out of Moscow, but there were astounding revelations to be found in Washington. Beowulf Agate knew where the bodies were, and how and why they no longer breathed. He could be invaluable.

They want you. If they can't have you, they'll kill you. So be it; he would be no prize for the Matarese.

Bray closed his eyes; he needed sleep. There would be little in the days ahead.

Rain splattered against the windshield in continuous sheets, streaking to the right under the force of the wind that blew off the Atlantic over the coastal highway. Scofield had rented the car in Portland, Maine, with a driver's license and credit card he had never used before. Soon he would be in Boston but not in the way the Matarese expected. He would not race halfway across the world and announce his arrival by registering at the Ritz Carlton as Vickery, only to wait for the Matarese's next move. A man in panic would, a man who felt the only way to save the life of someone he deeply loved would—but he was beyond panic, he had accepted total loss, therefore he could hold back and conceive of his own strategy.

He would be in Boston, in his enemy's den, but his enemy would not know it. The Ritz Carlton would receive two telegrams spaced a day apart. The first would arrive tomorrow requesting a suite for Mr. B. A. Vickery of Montreal, arriving the following day. The second would be sent the next afternoon, stating that Mr. Vickery had been delayed, his arrival now anticipated two days later. There would be no address for Vickery, only telegraph offices on Montreal's King and Market streets, and no request for confirmations, the assumption here being that someone in Boston would make sure rooms were available.

Only the two telegrams, sent from Montreal; the Matarese had little choice but to believe he was still in Canada. What they could not know—suspect surely, but not be certain—was that he had used a drone to send them. He had. He had contacted a man, a felony-prone *séparatiste* he had known before, and met him at the airport, giving him the two handwritten messages on telegraph forms along with a sum of money and instructions when and from where to send them. Should the Matarese phone Montreal for immediate confirmations of origin, they would find the forms written in Bray's handwriting.

He had three days and one night to operate within Matarese territory, to learn everything he could about Trans-Communications and its hierarchy. To find another flaw, one significant enough to summon Senator Joshua Appleton, IV, to Boston—on *his* terms. In panic.

So much to learn, so little time.

Scofield let his mind wander back to everyone he had ever known in Boston and Cambridge—both as student and professional. Among that crowd of fits and misfits there had to be someone who could help him.

He passed a road sign telling him he had left the town of Marblehead; he'd be in Boston in less than thirty minutes.

It was 5:35, the horns of impatient drivers blaring on all sides as the taxi inched its way down Boylston Street's crowded shopping district. He had parked the rented car in the farthest reaches of the Prudential underground lot, available should he need it, but not subject to the vagaries of weather or vandalism. He was on his way to Cambridge; a name had come into focus. A man who had spent twenty-five years teaching corporate law at the Harvard School of Business. Bray had never met him; there was no way the Matarese could make him a target.

It was strange, thought Bray, as the cab clamored over the ribs of the Longfellow Bridge, that both he and Taleniekov had been brought back—however briefly—to those places where it had begun for each of them.

Two students, one in Leningrad, one in Cambridge, with a certain, not dissimilar talent for foreign languages.

Was Taleniekov still alive? Or was he dead or dying somewhere in Boston? Toni was alive; they'd keep her alive . . . for a while.

Don't think about them. Don't think about her now! There is no hope. Not really. Accept it, live with it. Then do the best you can. . . .

The traffic congealed again at Harvard Square, the downpour causing havoc in the streets. People were crowded in storefronts, students in ponchos and jeans racing from curb to curb, jumping over the flooded gutters, crouching under the awning of the huge newspaper stand. . . .

The newspaper stand. NEWSPAPERS FROM ALL OVER THE WORLD was the legend printed across the white sign above the canopy. Bray peered out the window, through the rain and the collection of bodies. One name, one man, dominated the observable headlines.

Waverly! David Waverly! England's Foreign Secretary!

"Let me off here," he said to the driver, reaching for the travel bag and briefcase at his feet.

He pushed his way through the crowd, grabbed two domestic papers off the row of twenty-odd different editions, left a dollar, and ran across the street at the first break in traffic. A half a block down Massachusetts Avenue was a German-style restaurant he vaguely remembered from his student days. The entrance was jammed; Scofield excused his way to the door, using his travel bag for interference, and went inside.

There was a line waiting for tables; he went to the bar, and ordered Scotch. The drink arrived; he unfolded the first newspaper. It was the Boston *Globe;* he started reading, his eyes racing over the words, picking out the salient points of the article. He finished and picked up the Los Angeles *Times,* the story identical to the *Globe*'s, a wire service report, and almost surely, the official version put out by Whitehall, which was what Bray wanted to know.

The massacre of David Waverly, his wife, children, and servants in Belgravia Square was held to be the work of terrorists, most likely a splinter group of fanatic Palestinians. It was pointed out, however, that no group had as yet come forth to claim responsibility, and the P.L.O. vehemently denied participation. Messages of shock and condolence were being sent by political leaders across the world; parliaments and presidiums, congresses and royal courts, all interrupted their businesses at hand to express their fury and grief.

Bray reread both articles and the related stories in each paper looking for Roger Symonds' name. It was not to be found; it would not come for days, if ever. The speculations were too wild, the possibilities too improbable. A senior officer of British Intelligence somehow connected to the slaughter of Britain's Foreign Secretary. The Foreign Office would put a clamp on Symonds' death for any number of reasons. It was no time to . . .

Scofield's thoughts were interrupted. In the dim light of the bar he had missed the insert; it was a late bulletin in the *Globe.*

London, March 3—An odd and brutal aspect of the Waverly killings was revealed by the police only hours ago. After receiving a gunshot in the head, David Waverly received an apparently grotesque *coup de grâce* in the form of a shotgun blast fired directly into his chest, literally removing the left side of his upper abdomen and rib cage. The medical examiner was at a loss to explain the method of killing, for the administering of such a wound—considering the caliber and the proximity of the weapon—is considered extremely dangerous to the one firing the gun. The London police speculate that the weapon used might have been a primitive short-barrelled, hand-held shotgun once favored by roaming gangs of bandits in the Mediterranean. The 1934 *Encyclopedia of Weaponry* refers to the gun as the Lupo, the Italian word for "wolf."

The medical examiner in London might have trouble finding a reason for the "method of killing," but Scofield did not. If England's Foreign Secretary had a jagged blue circle affixed to his chest in the form of a birthmark, it was gone.

And there was a message in the use of the Lupo. The Matarese wanted Beowulf Agate to understand clearly how far and how wide the Corsican fever had spread, into what rarefied circles of power it had reached.

He finished his drink, left his money on the bar with the two newspapers, and looked around for a telephone. The name that had come into focus, the man he wanted to see, was Dr. Theodore Goldman, a dean of the Harvard School of Business and a thorn in the side of the Justice Department. For he was an outspoken critic of the Anti-Trust Division, incessantly claiming that Justice prosecuted the minnows and let the sharks roam free. He was a middle-aged *enfant terrible* who enjoyed taking on the giants, for he was a giant himself, cloaking his genius behind a facade of good-humored innocence that fooled no one.

If anyone could shed light on the conglomerate called Trans-Communications, it was Goldman.

Bray did not know the man, but he had met Goldman's son a year ago in The Hague—under circumstances that were potentially disastrous for a young pilot in the Air Force. Aaron Goldman had gotten drunk with the wrong people near the Groote Kerk, men known to be involved in a KGB infiltration of NATO. The son of a prominent American Jew was prime material for the Soviets.

An unknown intelligence officer had gotten the pilot away from the scene, slapped him into sobriety and told him to go back to his base. And after countless cups of coffee, Aaron Goldman had expressed his thanks.

"If you've got a kid who wants to go to Harvard, let me know, whoever you are. I'll talk to my dad, I swear it. What the hell's your name anyway?"

"Never mind," Scofield had said. "Just get out of here, and don't buy typing paper at the Coop. It's cheaper down the block."

"What the . . ."

"Get out of here."

Bray saw the pay phone on the wall; he grabbed his luggage and walked over to it.

32

He picked up a small wet piece of newspaper on the rain-soaked sidewalk and walked to the MPTA subway station in Harvard Square. He went downstairs and checked his soft leather suitcase in a locker. If it was stolen that would tell him something, and there was nothing in it he could not replace. He slid the wet scrap of paper carefully under the far right corner of the bag. Later, if the fragile scrap was curled or the surface broken, that would tell him something else: the bag had been searched and he was in the Matarese' sights.

Ten minutes later he rang the bell of Theodore Goldman's house on Brattle Street. It was opened by a slender, middle-aged woman, her face pleasant, her eyes curious.

"Mrs. Goldman?"

"Yes?"

"I telephoned your husband a few minutes ago—"

"Oh, yes, of course," she interrupted. "Well, for heaven's sake, get out of the rain! It's coming down like the forty-day flood. Come in, come in. I'm Anne Goldman."

She took his coat and hat; he held his attaché case.

"I apologize for disturbing you."

"Don't be foolish. Aaron told us all about that night in . . . The Hague. You know, I've never been able to figure out where that place *is*. Why would a city be called *the* anything?"

"It's confusing."

"I gather our son was very confused *that* night; which is a mother's way of saying he was plastered." She gestured toward a squared-off, double doorway so common to old New England houses. "Theo's on the telephone and trying to mix his stinger at the same time; it's making him frantic. He hates the telephone and loves his evening drink."

Theodore Goldman was not much taller than his wife, but there was an expansiveness about him that made him appear much larger than he was. His intellect could not be concealed, so he took refuge in humor, putting guests— and, no doubt, associates—at ease.

They sat in three leather armchairs that faced the fire, the Goldmans with their stingers, Bray drinking Scotch. The rain outside was heavy, drumming on the windows. The recapping of their son's escapade in The Hague was over quickly, Scofield dismissing it as a minor night out on the town.

"With major consequences, I suspect," said Goldman, "if an unknown intelligence officer hadn't been in the vicinity."

"Your son's a good pilot."

"He'd better be; he's not much of a drinker." Goldman sat back in his chair. "But now, since we've met this unknown gentleman who's been kind enough to give us his name, what can we do for him?"

"To begin with, please don't tell anyone I came to see you."

"That sounds ominous, Mr. Vickery. I'm not sure I approve of Washington's tactics in these areas."

"I'm no longer attached to the government; the request is personal. Frankly, the government doesn't approve of me any longer, because in my former capacity, I think I uncovered information Washington—especially the Department of Justice—doesn't want exposed. I believe it should be; that's as plain as I can put it."

Goldman rose to the occasion. "That's plain enough."

"In all honesty, I used my brief meeting with your son as an excuse to talk to you. It's not admirable, but it's the truth."

"I admire the truth. Why did you want to see me?"

Scofield put his glass down. "There's a company here in Boston, at least the corporate headquarters are here. It's a conglomerate called Trans-Communications."

"It certainly is." Goldman chuckled. "The Alabaster Bride of Boston. The Queen of Congress Street."

"I don't understand," said Bray.

"The Trans-Comm Tower," explained Anne Goldman. "It's a white stone building thirty or forty stories high, with rows of tinted blue glass on every floor."

"The ivory tower with a thousand eyes staring down at you," added Goldman, still amused. "Depending on the angle of the sun, some seem to be open, some closed, while others appear to be winking."

"Winking? Closed?"

"Eyes," pressed Anne, blinking her own. "The horizontal lines of tinted glass are huge windows, rows and rows of large bluish circles."

Scofield caught his breath. *Per nostro circolo.* "It sounds strange," he said without emphasis.

"Actually, it's quite imposing," replied Goldman. "A bit *outre* for my taste, but I gather that's the point. There's a kind of outraged purity about it, a white shaft set down in the middle of the dark concrete jungle of a financial district."

"That's interesting." Bray could not help himself; he found an obscure analogy in Goldman's words. The white shaft became a beam of light; the jungle was chaos.

"So much for the Alabaster Bride," said the lawyer-professor. "What did you want to know about Trans-Comm?"

"Everything you can tell me," answered Scofield.

Goldman was mildly startled. "Everything? . . . I'm not sure I know that much. It's your classic multinational conglomerate, I can tell you that. Extraordinarily diversified, brilliantly managed."

"I read the other day that a lot of financial people were stunned by the extent of its holdings in Verachten."

"Yes," agreed Goldman, nodding his head in that exaggerated way a man does when he hears a foolish point being repeated. "A lot of people *were* stunned, but I wasn't. Of course, Trans-Comm owns a great deal of Verachten. I daresay I could name four or five other countries where its holdings would stun these same people. The philosophy of a conglomerate is to buy as far and as wide as possible and diversify its markets. It both uses and refutes the Malthusian laws of economics. It creates aggressive competition within its own ranks, but does its best to remove all outside competitors. *That's* what multinationals are all about, and Trans-Comm's one of the most successful anywhere in the world."

Bray watched the lawyer as he spoke. Goldman was a born teacher—infectious in delivery, his voice rising with enthusiasm. "I understand what you're saying, but you lost me with one statement. You said you could name four or five other countries where Trans-Comm has heavy investments. How can you do that?"

"Not just me," objected Goldman. "Anybody can. All he has to do is read and use a little imagination. The laws, Mr. Vickery. The laws of the host country."

"The laws?"

"They're the only things that can't be avoided, the only protection buyers and sellers have. In the international financial community they take the place of armies. Every conglomerate must adhere to the laws of the country in which its divisions operate. Now, these same laws often ensure confidentiality; they're the frameworks within which the multinationals have to function—corrupting and altering them when they can, of course. And since they do, they must seek intermediaries to represent them. *Legally.* A Boston attorney practicing before the Massachusetts bar would be of little value in Hong Kong. Or Essen."

"What are you driving at?" Bray asked.

"You study the *law firms.*" Goldman leaned forward again. "You match the firms and their locations with the general level of their clients and the services for which they're most recognized. When you find one that's known for negotiating stock purchases and exchanges, you look around to see what companies in the area might be ripe for invading." The legal academician was enjoying himself. "It's really quite simple," he continued, "and a hell of an amusing game to play. I've scared the bejesus out of more than one corporate flunkie in those summer seminars by telling him where I thought his company's money men were heading. I've got a little index file—three by five cards—where I jot down my goodies."

Scofield spoke; he had to know. "What about Trans-Comm? Did you ever do a file card on it?"

"Oh, sure. That's what I meant about the other countries."

"What are they?"

Goldman stood up in front of the fire, frowning in recollection. "Let's start with the Verachten Works. Trans-Comm's overseas reports included sizeable payments to the Gehmeinhoff-Salenger firm in Essen. Gehmeinhoff's a direct legal liaison to Verachten. And they're not interested in nickel-and-dime transactions; Trans-Comm had to be going after a big chunk of the complex. Although I admit; even I didn't think it was as much as the rumors indicate. Probably isn't."

"What about the others?"

"Let's see. . . . Japan. Kyoto. T-C uses the firm of Aikawa-Onmura-and-something. My guess would be Yakashubi Electronics."

"That's pretty substantial, isn't it?"

"Panasonic can't compare."

"What about Europe?"

"Well, we know about Verachten." Goldman pursed his lips. "Then, of course, there's Amsterdam; the law firm there is Hainaut and Sons, which leads me to think that Trans-Comm's bought into Netherlands Textiles, which is an umbrella for a score of companies ranging from Scandinavia to Lisbon. From here we can head over to Lyon. . . ." The lawyer stopped, and shook his head. "No, that's probably tied in with Turin."

"Turin?" Bray sat forward.

"Yes, they're so close together, the interests so compatible, there's no doubt prior ownership buried in Turin."

"Who in Turin?"

"The law firm's Palladino-e-LaTona, which can only mean one company—or companies. Scozzi-Paravacini."

Scofield went rigid. "They're a cartel, aren't they?"

"My God, yes. They—*it*—certainly is. Agnelli and Fiat get all the publicity, but Scozzi-Paravacini runs the Colosseum and all the lions. When you combine it with Verachten and Netherlands Textiles, throw in Yakashubi, add Singapore, and Perth, and a dozen other names in England, Spain, and South Africa I haven't mentioned, the Alabaster Bride of Boston has put together a global federation."

"You sound as if you approve."

"No, actually I don't. I don't think anyone can when so much economic power is so centralized. It's a corruption of the Malthusian law; the competition is false. But I respect the reality of genius when its accomplishments are so obviously staggering. Trans-Communications was an idea born and developed in the mind of one man. Nicholas Guiderone."

"I've heard of him. A modern-day Carnegie or Rockefeller, isn't he?"

"More. Much more. The Geneens, the Lucases, the Bluedhorns, the wonder-boys of Detroit and Wall Street, none of them can touch Guiderone. He's the last of the vanishing giants, a really benign monarch of industry and finance. He's been honored by most of the major governments of the West, and not a few in the Eastern bloc, including Moscow."

"Moscow?"

"Certainly," said Goldman, nodding thanks to his wife, who was pouring a second stinger into his glass. "No one's done more to open up East-West trade than Nicholas Guiderone. As a matter of fact I can't think of anyone who's done more for world trade in general. He's over eighty now, but I understand he's still filled with as much pee and vinegar as he was the day he walked out of Boston Latin."

"He's from Boston?"

"Yes, a remarkable story. He came to this country as a boy. An immigrant boy of ten or eleven, without a mother, traveling with a barely literate father in the hold of a ship. I suppose you could call it the definitive story of the American dream."

Involuntarily, Scofield gripped the arm of the chair. He could feel the pressure on his chest, the tightening in his throat. "Where did that ship come from?"

"Italy," said Goldman, sipping his drink. "Southern part. Sicily, or one of the islands."

Bray was almost afraid to ask the question. "Would you by any chance know whether Nicholas Guiderone ever knew a member of the Appleton family?"

Goldman looked over the rim of his glass. "I know it, and so does most everyone in Boston. Guiderone's father worked for the Appletons. For the Senator's grandfather at Appleton Hall. It was old Appleton who spotted the boy's promise, gave him the backing, and persuaded the schools to take him. It wasn't so easy in those days, the early nineteen hundreds. The two-toilet Irish had barely gotten their second john, and there weren't too many of them. An Italian kid—excuse me, *Eye*talian—was nowhere. Gutter meat."

Bray's words floated; he could hardly hear them himself. "That was Joshua Appleton, the second, wasn't it?"

"Yes."

"He did all that for this . . . child."

"Hell of a thing, wasn't it? And the Appletons had enough troubles then. They'd lost damn near everything in the market fluctuations. They were hanging on by the skin of their teeth. It was almost as if old Joshua had seen a message on some mystical wall."

"What do you mean?"

"Guiderone paid everything back several thousand fold. Before Appleton was in his grave he saw his companies back on top, making money in areas he'd never dreamed of, the capital flowing out of the banks owned by the Italian kid he'd found in his carriage house."

"Oh, my *God*. . . ."

"I told you," said Goldman. "It's one hell of a story. It's all there to be read."

"If you know where to look. And why."

"I beg your pardon?"

"Guiderone. . . ." Scofield felt as though he were walking through swirling circles of mist toward some eerie light. He put his head back and stared at the ceiling, at the dancing shadows thrown up by the fire. "*Guiderone*. It's a derivative of the Italian 'guida.' A guide."

"Or shepherd," said Goldman.

Bray snapped his head down, his eyes wide, riveted on the lawyer. "What did you say?"

Goldman was puzzled. "I didn't say it, he did. About seven or eight months ago at the U.N."

"The United Nations?"

"Yes. Guiderone was invited to address the General Assembly; the invitation was unanimous, incidentally. Didn't you hear it? It was broadcast all over the world. He even taped it in French and Italian for Radio-International."

"I didn't hear it."

"The U.N.'s perennial problem. Nobody listens."

"What did he say?"

"Pretty much what you just said. That his name had its roots in the word 'guida,' or guide. And that was the way he'd always thought of himself. As a simple shepherd, guiding his flocks, aware of the rocky slopes and uncrossable streams . . . that sort of thing. His plea was for international relationships based on the mutuality of material need, which he claimed would lead to the higher morality. It was a little strange philosophically, but it was damned effective. So effective, in fact, that there's a resolution on this session's agenda that'll make him a full-fledged member of the U.N.'s Economic Council. That's not just a title, by the way. With his expertise and resources, there's not a government in the world which won't listen very hard when he talks. He'll be one damned powerful *amicus curiae.*"

"Did you hear him give that speech?"

"Sure," laughed the lawyer. "It was mandatory in Boston; you were cut off the *Globe*'s subscription list if you missed it. We saw the whole thing on Public Television."

"What did he sound like?"

Goldman looked at his wife. "Well, he's a very old man. Still vigorous, but nevertheless old. How would you describe him, darling?"

"Just as you do," said Anne. "An old man. Not large, but quite striking, with that look of a man who's so used to being listened to. I do remember one thing, though—about the voice. It was high-pitched and maybe a little breathless, but he spoke extremely clearly, every phrase very precise, very penetrating. Quite cold, in fact. You couldn't miss a word he said."

Scofield closed his eyes and thought of a blind woman in the mountains above Corsica's Porto Vecchio, twisting the dials of a radio and hearing *a voice crueler than the wind.*

He had found the shepherd boy.

33

He had found him!

Toni, I've found him! Stay alive! Don't let them destroy you. They won't kill your body; instead, they'll try to kill your mind. Don't let them do it. They will go after your thoughts and the way you think. They will try to change you, alter the processes that make you what you are. They have no choice, my darling. A hostage must be programmed even after the trap is closed; professionals understand that. No extremity is beyond consideration. Find something within yourself—for my sake. You see, my dearest love, I've found something. I've found him. The shepherd boy! It is a weapon. I need time to use it. Stay alive. Keep your mind!

Taleniekov, the enemy I can't bring myself to hate anymore. If you're dead there's nothing I can do but turn away, knowing that I'm alone. If you're alive, keep breathing. I promise nothing; there is no hope, not really. But we have something we never had before. We have him. We know who the shepherd boy is. The web is defined now and it circles the world. Scozzi-Paravacini, Verachten, Trans-Communications . . . and a hundred different companies between each one. All put together by the shepherd boy, all run from an alabaster tower that looks over the city with a thousand eyes. . . . And yet there's something else. I know it, I feel it! Something else that's in the middle of the web. We who've 'abused this world so well for so long' develop instincts, don't we? Mine is strong. It's out there. I just need time. Keep breathing . . . my friend.

I can't think about them any longer. I've got to put them out of my mind; they intrude, they interfere, they are barriers. They do not exist; she does not exist and I have lost her. We will not grow old together; there is no hope. . . . Now, move. For Christ's sake, move!

He had left the Goldmans quickly, thanking them, bewildering them by his abrupt departure. He had asked only a few more questions—about the Appleton family—questions any knowledgeable person in Boston could answer. Having the information was all he needed; there was no point in staying longer. He walked now in the rain, smoking a cigarette, his thoughts on the missing fragment his instinct told him was a greater weapon than the shepherd boy, yet somehow part of the shepherd boy, intrinsic to the deceits of Nicholas Guiderone. What *was* it? Where was the false note he heard so clearly?

He knew one thing, however, and it was more than instinct. He had enough to panic Senator Joshua Appleton, IV. He would telephone the Senator in Washington and quietly recite a bill-of-particulars that began seventy years ago, on the date of April 4, 1911, in the hills of Porto Vecchio. Did the Senator have anything to say? Could he shed any light on an organization known as the Matarese which began its activities in the second decade of the century—at Sarajevo, perhaps—by selling political murder? An organization the Appleton family had never left, for it could be traced to a white skyscraper in Boston, a company honored by the Senator's presence on its board of directors. The age of Aquarius had turned into the age of conspiracy. A man on his march to the White House would have to panic, and in panic mistakes were made.

But panic could be controlled. The Matarese would mount the Senator's defenses swiftly, the presidency was too great a prize to lose. And charges leveled by a traitor were no charges at all; they were merely words spoken by a man who had betrayed his country.

Instinct. Look at the man—the *man*—more closely.

Joshua Appleton was *not* as he was perceived to be by the nation. The paternal figure whose appeal ran across the spectrum. Then what about the day-to-day individual? Was it possible that the everyday man had weaknesses he'd find infinitely more difficult to deny than a grand conspiracy leveled by a traitor? Was it conceivable—and the more Bray thought about it, the more logical it seemed—that the entire Korean experience had been a hoax? Had commanders been bought and medals paid for, a hundred men convinced by money to keep a vigil none gave a damn about? It would not have been the first time war had been used as a springboard for a celebrated civilian life. It was a natural, the perfect ploy, if the scenario could be executed with precision—and what scenario could not be with the resources controlled by the Matarese?

Look at the man. The *man*.

Goldman had brought the Appleton family up to date for Bray. The Senator's official residence was a house in Concord where he and his family stayed only during the summer months. His father had died several years ago; Nicholas Guiderone had paid his last respects to the son of his mentor by purchasing the outsized Appleton Hall from the widow at a price far above the market, promising to keep the name in perpetuity. Old Mrs. Appleton currently lived on Beacon Hill, in a brownstone on Louisburg Square.

The mother. What kind of woman was she? In her middle seventies, Goldman had estimated. Could she tell him anything? Involuntarily perhaps a great deal. Mothers were much better sources of information than was generally believed, not for what they said, but for what they did not say, for subjects that were changed abruptly.

It was twenty minutes past nine. Bray wondered if he could reach Appleton's mother and talk with her. The house might be watched, but not on a priority basis. A car parked in the Square with a view of the brownstone, one man, possibly two. If there were such men and he took them out, the Matarese would know he was in Boston; he was not ready for that. Still, the mother might provide a short cut, a name, an incident, something he could trace quickly; there was so little time. Mr. B. A. Vickery was expected at the Ritz Carlton Hotel, but when he got there he had to bring leverage with him. At the optimum, he had to have his own hostage; he had to have Joshua Appleton, IV.

There was no hope. There was nothing not worth trying. There was instinct.

The steep climb up Chestnut Street toward Louisburg Square was marked by progressively quieter blocks. It was as if one were leaving a profane world to enter a sacred one; garish neons were replaced by the muted flickering of gas lamps, the cobblestone streets washed clean. He reached the Square, staying in the shadows of a brick building on the corner.

He took out a pair of small binoculars from his attaché case and raised them to his eyes, focusing the powerful Zeiss-Icon lenses on each stationary car in the streets around the fenced-in park that was the center of Louisburg Square.

There was no one.

Bray put the binoculars back in his attaché case, left the shadows of the brick building, and walked down the peaceful street toward the Appleton brownstone. The stately houses surrounding the small park with the wrought-iron fence and gate were quiet. The night air was bitterly cold now, the gas lamps flickering more rapidly with the intermittent gusts of winter wind; windows were closed, fires burning in the hearths of Louisburg Square. It *was* a different world, remote, almost isolated, certainly at peace with itself.

He climbed the white stone steps and rang the bell. The carriage lamps on either side of the door threw more light than he cared for.

He heard the sound of footsteps; a nurse opened the door and he knew instantly that the woman recognized him; it was in the short, involuntary gasp that escaped her lips, in the brief widening of her eyelids. It explained why no one was on the street, the guard was *inside* the house.

"Mrs. Appleton, please?"

"I'm afraid she's retired."

The nurse started to close the door. Scofield jammed his left foot into the base, his shoulder against the heavy black panel, and forced it open.

"I'm afraid you know who I am," he said, stepping inside, dropping his attaché case.

The woman pivoted, her right hand plunging into the pocket of her uniform. Bray countered, pushing her farther into her own pivot, gripping her wrist, twisting it downward and away from her body. She screamed. Scofield yanked her to the floor, his knee crashing up into the base of her spine. With his left arm, he viced her neck from behind, forearm across her shoulder blades, and pulled up violently as she fell; ten more pounds of pressure and he would have broken her neck. But he did not want to do that. He wanted this woman alive; she collapsed unconscious to the floor.

He crouched in silence, removing the short-barreled revolver from the nurse's pocket, waiting for sounds or signs of people. The scream had to have been heard by anyone inside the house.

There was nothing—there was *something*, but it was so faint he could not fathom what it was—he saw a telephone next to the staircase and crept over to pick it up. There was only the hum of a dial tone; no one was using the phone. Perhaps the woman had told the truth; it was entirely possible that Mrs. Appleton had retired. He'd know shortly.

First, he had to know something else. He went back to the nurse, pulled her across the floor under the hallway light, and ripped apart the front of her uniform. He tore the slip and brassiere beneath, pushed up her left breast, and studied the flesh.

There it was. The small, jagged blue circle as Taleniekov had described it. The birthmark that was no birthmark at all, but instead, the mark of the Matarese.

Suddenly, from above, there was the whirring sound of a motor, the vibration constant, bass-toned. Bray lunged across the unconscious body of the nurse, into the shadows of the stairs, and raised the revolver.

From around the curve of the first landing an old woman came into view. She was sitting in the ornate chair of an automatic lift, her frail hands holding the sculptured pole that shot up from the guard rail. She was encased in a high-collared dressing gown of dark gray, and her once-delicate face was ravaged, her voice strained.

"I imagine that's one way to leash the bitch-hound, or corner the wolf-in-season, but if your objective is sexual, young man, I question your taste."

Mrs. Joshua Appleton, III, was drunk. From the looks of her, she had been drunk for years.

"My only objective, Mrs. Appleton, is to see *you*. This woman tried to stop me; this is her gun, not mine. I'm an experienced intelligence officer employed by the

United States government and fully prepared to show you my identification. In light of what happened I am checking for concealed weapons. I would do the same under like circumstances anywhere, anytime." With those words, he had begun, and with an equanimity born of prolonged alcohol-saturation, the old woman accepted his presence.

Scofield carried the nurse into a small drawing room, bound her hands and feet in slipknots made from the torn nylon of her hose, saving the elastic waistband for a gagging brace, pulled between her teeth, tied firmly to the back of her neck. He closed the door and returned to Mrs. Appleton in the living room. She had poured herself a brandy; Bray looked at the odd-shaped glass and at the decanters that were placed on tables about the room. The glass was so thick that it could not be broken easily, and the crystal decanters were positioned so that a new drink was accessible every seven to ten feet in all directions. It was strange therapy for one so obviously an alcoholic.

"I'm afraid," said Scofield, pausing at the door, "that when your nurse regains consciousness I'm going to give her a lecture about the indiscriminate display of firearms. She has an odd way of protecting you, Mrs. Appleton."

"Very odd, young man." The old woman raised her glass and cautiously sat down in an antimacassared armchair. "But since she tried and failed so miserably, why don't you tell me what she was protecting me from? Why did you come to see me?"

"May I sit down?"

"By all means."

Bray began his ploy. "As I mentioned, I'm an intelligence officer attached to the Department of State. A few days ago we received a report that implicates your son—through his father—with an organization in Europe known for years to be involved in international crime."

"In *what?*" Mrs. Appleton giggled. "Really, you're very amusing."

"Forgive me, but there's nothing amusing about it."

"What are you talking about?"

Scofield described a group of men not unlike the Matarese council, watching the old woman closely for signs that she had made a connection. He was not even sure he had penetrated her clouded mind; he had to appeal to the mother, not the woman. "The information from Europe was sent and received under the highest security classification. To the best of my knowledge, I'm the only one in Washington that's read it, and further, I'm convinced I can contain it. You see, Mrs. Appleton, I think it's very important for this country, that none of this touch the Senator."

"Young *man,*" interrupted the old woman. "Nothing can touch the Senator, don't you know that? My son will be the President of the United States. He'll be elected in the fall. Everybody says so. Everybody wants him."

"Then I haven't been clear, Mrs. Appleton. The report from Europe is devastating and I need information. Before your son ran for office, how closely did he work with his father in the Appleton business ventures? Did he travel frequently to Europe with your husband? Who were his closest friends here in Boston? That's terribly important. People that only you might know, men and women who came to see him at Appleton Hall."

" 'Appleton Hall . . . way up on Appleton Hill,' " broke in the old woman in a strained, whispered sing-song of no discernible tune. " 'With the grandest view of Boston . . . and ever will be still.' Joshua the First wrote that over a hundred years ago. It's not very good, but they say he picked out the notes on a harpsichord. So like the Joshuas, a harpsichord. So like us all, really."

"Mrs. Appleton? After your son came back from the Korean War—"

"We *never* discuss that war!" For an instant the old woman's eyes became focused, hostile. Then the clouds returned. "Of course, when my son is President they won't wheel me out like Rose or Miss Lillian. I'm kept for very special occasions." She paused and laughed a soft, eerie laugh that was self-mocking. "After very *special* sessions with the doctor." She paused again and raised her left forefinger to her lips. "You see, young man, sobriety isn't my strongest suit."

Scofield watched her closely, saddened by what he saw. Beneath the ravaged face there had been a lovely face, the eyes once clear and alive, not floating in dead sockets as they were now. "I'm sorry. It must be painful to know that."

"On the contrary," she replied whimsically. It was her turn to study him. "Do you think you're clever?"

"I've never thought about it one way or the other." *Instinct.* "How long have you been . . . ill, Mrs. Appleton?"

"As long as I care to remember and that is quite long enough, thank you."

Bray looked again at the decanters. "Has the Senator been here recently?"

"Why do you ask?" She seemed amused. Or was she on guard?

"Nothing, really," said Scofield casually; he could not alarm her. Not now. He was not sure why—or what—but something was happening. "I indicated to the nurse that the Senator might have sent me here, that he might be on his way himself."

"Well, there you *are!*" cried the old woman, triumph in her strained, alcoholic voice. "No wonder she tried to stop you!"

"Because of all these?" asked Bray quietly, gesturing at the decanters. "Bottles filled—obviously every day—with booze. Perhaps your son might object."

"Oh, don't be a damn fool! She tried to stop you because you *lied.*"

"Lied?"

"Of course! The Senator and I meet only on special occasions—after those *very* special treatments—when I'm trotted out so his adoring public can see his adoring mother. My son has never been to this house and he would never come here. The last time we were alone was over eight years ago. Even at his father's funeral, although we stood together, we barely spoke."

"May I ask why?"

"You may not. But I can tell you it has nothing to do with that gibberish— what I could make of it—you talked about."

"Why did you say you never discussed the Korean War?"

"Don't presume, young man!" Mrs. Appleton raised the glass to her lips; her hand trembled and the glass fell, brandy spilling on her gown. *"Damn!"* Scofield started out of his chair. "Leave it alone," she commanded.

"I'll pick it up," he said, kneeling down in front of her. "No point stumbling over it."

"Then pick it up. And get me another, if you please."

"Certainly." He crossed to a nearby table and poured her a brandy in a fresh glass. "You say you don't like to discuss the war in Korea—"

"I said," interrupted the old woman, "I *never* discussed it."

"You're very fortunate. I mean just to be able to say it and let it go at that. Some of us aren't so lucky." He remained in front of her, his shadow falling over her, the lie calculated. "I can't. I was there. So was your son."

The old woman drank several swallows without stopping. "Wars kill so much more than the bodies they take. Terrible things happen. Did they happen to you, young man?"

"They've happened to me."

"Did they do those awful things to you?"

"What awful things, Mrs. Appleton?"

"Starve you, beat you, bury you alive, your nostrils filled with dirt and mud, unable to breathe? Dying slowly, consciously, wide awake and dying?"

The old woman was describing tortures documented by men held captive in North Korean camps. What was the relevance? "No, those things didn't happen to me."

"They happened to him, you know. The doctors told me. It's what made him change. Inside. Change so much. But we must never talk about it."

"Talk about . . . ?" What was *she* talking about? "You mean the Senator?"

"Shhh!" The old woman drank the remainder of the brandy. "We must never, *never* talk about it."

"I see," said Bray, but he did *not* see. Senator Joshua Appleton, IV, had never been held captive by the North Koreans. Captain Josh Appleton had *eluded* capture on numerous occasions, the very acts of doing so behind enemy lines a part of his commendations. Scofield remained in front of her chair and spoke again. "But I can't say I ever noticed any great changes in him, other than getting older. Of course, I didn't know him that well twenty years ago, but to me he's still one of the finest men I've ever known."

"Inside!" The old woman whispered harshly. "It's all inside! He's a *mask* . . . and people adore him so." Suddenly tears were in her clouded eyes, and the words that followed a cry from deep within her memory. "They *should* adore him! He was such a beautiful boy, such a beautiful young man. There was no one ever like my Josh, no one more loving, more filled with kindness! . . . Until they did those terrible things to him." She wept. "And I was such a dreadful person. I was his mother and I couldn't understand! I wanted my Joshua back! I wanted him back so badly!"

Bray knelt down and took the glass from her. "What do you mean you wanted him back?"

"I couldn't understand! He was so cold, so distant. They'd taken the joy out of him. There was no *joy* in him! He came out of the hospital . . . and the pain had been too much and I *couldn't understand.* He looked at me and there was no joy, no love. Not inside!"

"The hospital? The accident after the war—just after the war?"

"He suffered so much . . . and I was drinking so much . . . so much. Every week he was in that awful war I drank more and more. I couldn't stand it! He was all I *had.* My husband was . . . in name only—as much my fault as his, I suppose. He was disgusted with me. But I loved my Josh so." The old woman reached for the glass. He got to it first and poured her a drink. She looked at him through her tears, her floating eyes filled with the sadness of knowing what she was. "I thank you very much," she said with simple dignity.

"You're welcome," he answered, feeling helpless.

"In a way," she whispered, "I still have him but he doesn't know it. No one does."

"How is that?"

"When I moved out of Appleton Hall . . . on Appleton Hill . . . I kept his room just the way it was, the way it had been. You see, he never came back, not really. Only for an hour one night to pick up some things. So I took a room here and made it his. It will always be his, but he doesn't know it."

Bray knelt down in front of her again. "Mrs. Appleton, may I see that room? *Please,* may I see it?"

"Oh, no, that wouldn't be right," she said. "It's very private. It's his, and I'm the only one he lets in. He lives there still, you see. My beautiful Joshua."

"I've got to see that room, Mrs. Appleton. Where is it?" *Instinct.*

"Why do you have to see it?"

"I can help you. I can help your son. I know it."

She squinted, studying him from some inner place. "You're a kind man, aren't you? And you're not as young as I thought. Your face has lines, and there is gray at your temples. You have a strong mouth, did anyone ever tell you that?"

"No, I don't think anyone ever did. Please, Mrs. Appleton, I *must* see that room. Allow me to."

"It's nice that you ask. People rarely ask me for anything anymore; they just tell me. Very well, help me to my lift, and we'll go upstairs. You understand, of course, we'll have to knock first. If he says you can't come in, you'll have to stay outside."

Scofield guided her through the living room arch to the chair lift. He walked beside her up the staircase to the second floor landing where he helped her to her feet.

"This way," she said, gesturing toward a narrow, darkened corridor. "It's the last door on the right."

They reached it, stood in front of it for a moment, and then the old woman rapped lightly on the wood. "We'll know in a minute," she continued, bending her head as if listening for a command from within. "It's all right," she said, smiling. "He said you could come in, but you mustn't touch anything. He has everything arranged the way he likes it." She opened the door, and flipped a switch on the wall. Three separate lamps went on; still the light was dim. Shadows were thrown across the floor and up on the walls.

The room was a young man's room, mementos of an expensive youth on display everywhere. The banners above the bed and the desk were those of Andover and Princeton, the trophies on the shelves for such sports as sailing, skiing, tennis, and lacrosse. The room had been preserved—eerily preserved—as if it had once belonged to a Renaissance prince. A microscope sat alongside a chemistry set, a volume of *Britannica* lay open, most of the page underlined, handwritten notes in the margins. On the bedside table were novels of Dos Passos and Koestler, beside them the typewritten title page of an essay authored by the celebrated inhabitant of that room. It was called: *The Pleasures and Responsibilities of Sailing in Deep Waters. Submitted by Joshua Appleton, Senior. Andover Academy. March, 1945.* Protruding from below the bed were three pairs of shoes: loafers, sneakers, and black patent leathers worn with formal clothes. A life was somehow covered in the display.

Bray winced in the dim light. He was in the tomb of a man very much alive, the artifacts of a life preserved, somehow meant to transport the dead safely on its journey through the darkness. It was a macabre experience when one thought of Joshua Appleton, the electric, mesmerizing Senator from Massachusetts. Scofield glanced at the old woman. She was staring impassively at a cluster of photographs on the wall. Bray took a step forward and looked at them.

They were pictures of a younger Joshua Appleton and several friends—the same friends, apparently the crew of a sailboat—the occasion identified by the center photograph. It showed a long banner being held by four men standing on the deck of a sloop. *Marblehead Regatta Championship—Summer, 1949.*

Only the center photograph and the three above it showed all four crew members. The three lower photographs were shots of only two of the four. Appleton and another young man, both stripped to the waist—slender, muscular, shaking hands above a tiller; smiling at the camera as they stood on either side of the mast, and sitting on the gunnels, drinks held forward in a salute.

Scofield looked closely at the two men, then compared them to their associates. Appleton and his obviously closer friend had a strength about them absent in the other two, a sense of assurance, of conviction somehow. They were not alike except perhaps in height and breadth—athletic men comfortable in the company of each's peer—yet neither were they dissimilar. Both had sharp if distinctly different features—strong jaws, wide foreheads, large eyes, and thatches of straight, dark hair—the kind of faces seen in scores of Ivy League yearbooks.

There was something disturbing about the photographs. Bray did not know what it was—but it was there. *Instinct.*

"They look as if they could be cousins," he said.

"For years they acted as though they were *brothers,*" replied the old woman. "In peace, they would be *partners,* in war, *soldiers* together! But he was a coward, he betrayed my son. My beautiful Joshua went to war alone and terrible things were done to him. He ran away to Europe, to the safety of a château. But justice is odd; he died in Gstaad, from injuries on a slope. To the best of my knowledge, my son has never mentioned his name since."

"Since? . . . When was that?"

"Twenty-five years ago."

"Who was he?"

She told him.

Scofield could not breathe; there was no air in the room, only shadows in a vacuum. He had found the shepherd boy, but instinct told him to look for something else, a fragment as awesome as anything he had learned. He had found it. The most devastating piece of the puzzle was in place, the quantum jump explained. He needed only proof, for the truth was so extraordinary.

He *was* in a tomb; the dead had journeyed in darkness for twenty-five years.

34

He guided the old woman to her bedroom, poured her a final brandy, and left her. As he closed the door she was sitting on the bed chanting that unsingable tune. *Appleton Hall . . . way up on Appleton Hill.*

Notes picked out on a harpsichord more than a hundred years ago. Notes lost, as she was lost without ever knowing why.

He returned to the dimly lit room that was the resting place of memories and went to the cluster of photographs on the wall. He removed one and pulled the small picture hook out of the plaster, smoothing the wallpaper around the hole; it might delay discovery, certainly not prevent it. He turned off the lights, closed the door, and went downstairs to the front hall.

The guard-nurse was still unconscious; he left her where she was. There was nothing gained by moving her or killing her. He turned off every light, including the carriage lamps above the front steps, opened the door, and slipped out into Louisburg Square. On the pavement, he turned right and began walking rapidly to the corner where he would turn right again, descending Beacon Hill into Charles Street to find a taxi. He had to pick up his luggage in the subway locker in Cambridge. The walk down the hill would give him time to think, time to remove the photograph from its glass frame, folding it carefully into his pocket so that neither face was damaged.

He needed a place to stay. A place to sit and fill up pages of paper with facts, conjectures and probabilities, his bill-of-particulars. In the morning, he had several things to do, among which were visits to the Massachusetts General Hospital and the Boston Public Library.

The room was no different from any other room in a very cheap hotel in a very large city. The bed sagged, and the single window looked out on a filthy stone wall not ten feet from the cracked panes of glass. The advantage, however, was the same as it was everywhere in such places; nobody asked questions. Cheap hotels had a place in this world, usually for those who did not care to join it. Loneliness was a basic human right, not to be tampered with lightly.

Scofield was safe; he could concentrate on his bill-of-particulars.

By 4:35 in the morning, he had filled seventeen pages. Facts, conjectures, probabilities. He had written the words carefully, legibly, so they could be clearly reproduced. There was no room for interpretation; the indictment was specific even where the motives were not. He was gathering his weapons, storing his bandoliers of ammunition; they were all he had. He fell back on the sagging bed and closed his eyes. Two or three hours sleep would be enough.

He heard his own whisper float up to the cracked ceiling.

"Taleniekov . . . keep breathing. Toni, my love, my dearest love. Stay alive . . . keep your mind."

The portly female clerk in the hospital's Department of Records and Billing seemed bewildered but she was not about to refuse Bray's request. It wasn't as if the medical information held there was that confidential, and a man who produced government identification certainly had to be given cooperation.

"Now, let me get this *cleah*," she said in a strong Boston accent, reading the labels on the front of the cabinets. "The Senator wants the names of the doctors and the nurses who attended him during his stay here in 'fifty-three and 'fifty-four. From around November through March?"

"That's right. As I told you, next month's sort of an anniversary for him. It'll be twenty-five years since he was given his 'reprieve,' as he calls it. Confidentially, he's sending each of them a small medallion in the shape of the medical shield with their names and his thanks inscribed on them."

The clerk stopped. "Isn't that just like him, though? To *remembah*? Most people go through an experience like that and just want to forget the whole thing. They figure they beat the *reapah* so the hell with everybody. Until the next time, of course. But not him; he's so . . . well, concerned, if you know what I mean."

"Yes, I do."

"The *votahs* know it, too, let me tell you. The Bay State's going to have its first President since J.F.K. And there won't be any of that religious nonsense about the Pope and the *cahdnells* running the White House, neither."

"No, there won't," agreed Bray. "I'd like to stress again the confidential nature of my being here. The Senator doesn't want any publicity about his little gesture. . . ." Scofield paused and smiled at the woman. "And as of now you're the only person in Boston who knows."

"Oh, don't you worry about that. As we used to say when we were kids, my lips are sealed. And I'd really treasure a note from Senator Appleton with his signature and everything, I mean." The woman stopped and tapped a file cabinet. *"Heah* we are," she said, opening the drawer. "Now, *remembah,* all that's *heah* are the names of the *doctahs*—surgeons, anesthesiologists, consultants—listed by floor and O.R. desks; the staff nurses assigned, and a schedule of the equipment used. There are no psychiatric evaluations or disease-related information; they can only be obtained directly through the physician. But then you're not interested in any of that; you'd think I was *tahkin'* to one of those damned insurance sneaks." She gave him the file. "There's a table at the end of the aisle. When you're finished, just leave the *foldah* on my desk."

"That's okay," said Bray, knowing better. "I'll put it back; no sense bothering you. Thanks again."

"Thank *you."*

Scofield read through the pages rapidly to get a general impression. Medically, most of what he read was beyond his comprehension, but the conclusion was inescapable. Joshua Appleton had been more dead than alive when the ambulance had brought him to the hospital from the collision on the turnpike. Lacerations, contusions, convulsions, fractures, along with severe head and neck wounds painted the bloody picture of a mutilated human face and body. There were lists of drugs and serums used to prolong the life that was ebbing, detailed descriptions of the sophisticated machinery employed to stop deterioration. And ultimately, weeks later, the reversal began to take place. The incredibly more sophisticated machine that was the human body started to heal itself.

Bray wrote down the names of the doctors and the attending nurses listed in the floor and O.R. schedules. Two surgeons, one a skin-graft specialist, and a rotating team of eight nurses appeared consistently during the first weeks, then abruptly their names were no longer there, replaced by two different physicians and three private nurses assigned to eight-hour shifts.

He had what he needed, a total of fifteen names, five primary, ten secondary. He would concentrate on the former, the last two physicians and the three nurses; the earlier names were removed from the time in question.

He replaced the folder and went back out to the clerk's desk. "All done," he said, then added as if the thought had just struck him. "Say, you could do me—the Senator—one more favor, if you would."

"If I can, sure."

"I've got the names here, but I need a little updating. After all, it was twenty-five years ago. Some of them may not be around any longer. It would help if I got some current addresses."

"I can't help," said the clerk, reaching for the phone on her desk, "but I can send you upstairs. This is patient territory; they've got the personnel records. Lucky *bahstaads,* they're computerized."

"I'm still very concerned about keeping this confidential."

"Hey, don't you worry, you've got Peg Flannagan's word for it. My girlfriend runs that place."

Scofield sat next to a bearded black college student in front of a computer keyboard. The young man had been assigned to help by Peg Flannagan's girlfriend. He was annoyed that his office-temp job had suddenly required him to put down his textbooks.

"I'm sorry to bother you," said Bray, wanting a temporary friend.

"It's nothin', man," answered the student, punching the keys. "It's just that I got an exam tomorrow and any piss ant can run this barbarian hardware."

"What's the exam?"

"Tertiary kinetics."

Scofield looked at the student. "Someone once used the word 'tertiary' with me when I was in school around here. I didn't know what he meant."

"You probably went to Harvard, man. That's turkey-time. I'm at Tech."

Bray was glad the old school spirit was still alive in Cambridge. "What have you got?" he asked, looking at the screen above the keyboard. The black had keyed in the name of the first doctor.

"I've got an omniscient tape, and you've got nothin'."

"What do you mean?"

"The good doctor doesn't exist. Not as far as this institution is concerned. He's never so much as dispensed an aspirin in this joint."

"That's crazy. He was listed in the Appleton records."

"Speak to the lord-of-the-*phi's*, man. I punched the letters and up comes *No Rec.*"

"I know something about these machines. They're easily programmed."

The black nodded. "Which means they're easily deprogrammed. Rectified, as it were. Your doctor was *dee*-leted. Maybe he stole from Medicare."

"Maybe. Let's try the next."

The student keyed in the name. "Well, we know what happened to this boy. *Ceb. Hem.* He died right here on the third floor. Cerebral hemorrhage. Never even got a chance to get his tuition back."

"What do you mean?"

"Med school, man. He was only thirty-two. Hell of a way to go at thirty-two."

"Also unusual. What's the date?"

"March 21, 1954."

"Appleton was discharged on the thirtieth," said Scofield as much to himself as to the student. "These three names are nurses. Try them, please."

Katherine Connally. Deceased 3-26-54.

Alice Bonelli. Deceased 3-26-54.

Janet Drummond. Deceased 3-26-54.

The student sat back; he was not a fool. "Seems there was a real epidemic back then, wasn't there? March was a rough month, and the twenty-sixth was a *baad* day for three little girls in white."

"Any cause of death?"

"Nothin' listed. Which only means they didn't die on the premises."

"But all three on the same *day?* It's . . ."

"I dig," said the young man. "Crazy." He held up his hand. "Hey, there's an old cat who's been here for about six thousand years. He runs the supply room on the first floor. He might remember something; let me get him on the horn." The black wheeled his chair around and reached for a telephone on the counter. "Get on line two," he said to Bray, pointing to another phone on a nearby table.

"Furst floor supply," said the voice in a loud Irish brogue.

"Hey, Methusala, this is Amos—as in Amos and Andy."

"You're a nutty boy-yo, you are."

"Hey, Jimmy, I got this honkey friend on the horn here. He's looking for information that goes back to when you were the terror of the angels' dorm. As a matter of fact, it concerns three of them. Jimmy, you recall a time in the middle fifties when three nurses all died on the same day?"

"T'ree. . . . Oh, indeed I do. 'Twas a terrible thing. Little Katie Connally was one of 'em."

"What happened?" asked Bray.

"They drowned, sir. All three of the girls drowned. They was in a boat and the damn thing pitched over, throwin' 'em into a bad sea."

"In a boat? In *March?*"

"One of those crazy things, sir. You know how rich kids prowl around the nurses' dormitories. They figure the girls see naked bodies all the time, so maybe they wouldn't mind lookin' at theirs. Well, one night these punk-swells were throwin' a party at this fancy yacht club and asked the girls up. There was drinkin' and all kinds of nonsense, and some jackass got the bright idea to take out a boat. Damn fool thing, of course. As you say, it was in March."

"It happened at night?"

"Yes, indeed, sir. The bodies didn't wash up for a week, I believe."

"Was anyone else killed?"

"Of course not. It's never that way, is it? I mean, rich kids are always such good swimmers, aren't they now?"

"Where did it happen?" asked Scofield. "Can you remember?"

"Sure, I can, sir. It was up the coast. Marblehead."

Bray closed his eyes. "Thank you," he said quietly, replacing the phone.

"Thanks, Methusala." The student hung up, his eyes on Scofield. "You got trouble, don't you?"

"I got trouble," agreed Bray, walking back to the keyboard. "I've also got ten more names. Two doctors and eight nurses. Can you run them through for me just as fast as you can?"

Of the eight nurses, half were still alive. One had moved to San Francisco—address unknown; another lived with a daughter in Dallas, and the remaining two were in the St. Agnes Retirement Home in Worcester. One of the doctors was still alive. The skin-graft specialist had died eighteen months ago at the age of seventy-three. The first surgeon of record, Dr. Nathaniel Crawford, had retired and was living in Quincy.

"May I use your phone?" asked Scofield. "I'll pay whatever charges there are."

"Last time I looked, none of these horns was in my name. Be my guest."

Bray had written down the number on the screen; he went to the telephone and dialed.

"Crawford here." The voice from Quincy was brusque but not discourteous.

"My name is Scofield, sir. We've never met and I'm not a physician, but I'm very interested in a case you were involved with a number of years ago at Massachusetts General. I'd like to discuss it briefly with you, if you wouldn't mind."

"Who was the patient? I had a few thousand."

"Senator Joshua Appleton, sir."

There was a slight pause on the line; when Crawford spoke, his brusque voice took on an added tone of weariness. "Those goddamned incidents have a way of following a man to his grave, don't they? Well, I haven't practiced for over two years now, so whatever *you* say or *I* say, it won't make any goddamned difference. . . . Let's say I made a mistake."

"Mistake?"

"I didn't make many, I was head of surgery for damn near twelve years. My summary's in the Appleton medical file; the only reasonable conclusion is that the X-rays got fouled up, or the scanning equipment gave us the wrong data."

There was no summary from Dr. Nathaniel Crawford in the Appleton medical file.

"Are you referring to the fact that you were replaced as surgeon of record?"

"Replaced, hell! Tommy Belford and I got our asses kicked four-square out of there by the family."

"Belford? Is that Dr. Belford, the skin-graft specialist?"

"A *surgeon*. A plastic surgeon and a goddamned artist. Tommy put the man's face back on like he was Almighty God Himself. That whiz-kid they brought in messed up Tommy's work, in my opinion. Sorry about him, though. The kid hardly finished when his head blew."

"Do you mean a cerebral hemorrhage, sir?"

"That's right. The Swiss was right there when it happened. He operated but it was too late."

"When you say 'the Swiss,' do you mean the surgeon who replaced you?"

"You got it. The great *Herr Doktor* from Zürich. That bastard treated me like a retarded med school dropout."

"Do you know what happened to him?"

"Went back to Switzerland, I guess. Never was interested in looking him up, myself."

"Doctor, you say you made a mistake. Or the X-rays did or the equipment. What kind of a mistake?"

"Simple. I gave up. We had him on total support systems, and that's exactly what I figured they were. Total support; without them he wouldn't have lasted a day. And if he had, I thought it would be a waste; he'd live like a vegetable."

"You saw no hope of recovery?"

Crawford lowered his voice, strength in his humility. "I was a surgeon, I wasn't God. I was fallible. It was my opinion then that Appleton was not only beyond recovery, he was dying a little more with each minute. . . . I was wrong."

"Thank you for talking to me, Doctor Crawford."

"As I said before, it can't make any difference now, and I don't mind. I had a hell of a lot of years with a knife in my hand; I didn't make many mistakes."

"I'm sure you didn't, sir. Goodbye." Scofield walked back to the keyboard; the black student was reading his textbook. "X-rays? . . ." said Bray softly.

"What?" The black looked up. "What about X-rays?"

Bray sat down next to the young man. If he ever needed a temporary friend it was now; he hoped he had one. "How well do you know the hospital staff?"

"It's a big place, man."

"You knew enough to call Methusala."

"Well, I've been working here off and on for three years. I get around."

"Is there a repository for X-rays going back a number of years?"

"Like maybe twenty-five?"

"Yes."

"There is. It's no big deal."

"Can you get me one?"

The student raised an eyebrow. "That's another matter, isn't it?"

"I'm willing to pay. Generously."

The black grimaced. "Oh, man! It's not that I look askance at bread, believe me. But I don't steal and I don't push and God knows I didn't inherit."

"What I'm asking you to do is the most legitimate—even moral, if you like—thing I could ask anyone to do. I'm not a liar."

The student looked into Bray's eyes. "If you are, you're a damned convincing one. And you've got troubles, I've seen that. What do you want?"

"An X-ray of Joshua Appleton's mouth."

"Mouth? His *mouth?*"

"His head injuries were extensive, dozens of pictures had to be taken. There had to be a lot of projected dental work. Can you do it?"

The young man nodded. "I think so."

"One more thing. I know it'll sound . . . outrageous to you, but take my word for it, nothing's outrageous. How much do you make a month here?"

"I average eighty, ninety a week. About three-fifty a month. It's not bad for a graduate student. Some of these interns make less. Course, they get room and board. Why?"

"Suppose I told you that I'd pay you ten thousand dollars to take a plane to Washington and bring me back another X-ray. Just an envelope with an X-ray in it."

The black tugged at his short beard, his eyes on Scofield as though he were observing a lunatic. *"Suppose?* I'd say 'feets, do your stuff.' Ten thousand *dollars?"*

"There'd be more time for those tertiary kinetics."

"And there's nothin' illegal? It's straight—I mean really straight?"

"For it to be considered remotely illegal as far as you're concerned, you'd have to know far more than anyone would tell you. That's straight."

"I'm just a messenger? I fly to Washington and bring back an envelope . . . with an X-ray in it?"

"Probably a number of small ones. That's all."

"What are they of?"

"Joshua Appleton's mouth."

It was 1:30 in the afternoon when Bray reached the library on Boylston Street. His new friend, Amos Lafollet, was taking the two o'clock shuttle to Washington and would return on the eight o'clock flight. Scofield would meet him at the airport.

Obtaining the X-rays had not been difficult; anyone who knew the bureaucratic ways of Washington could have gotten them. Bray made two calls, the first to the Congressional Liaison Office and the second to the dentist in question. The first call was made by a harried aide of a well-known Representative suffering from an abscessed tooth. Could Liaison please get this aide the name of Senator Appleton's dentist? The Senator had mentioned the man's superior work to the congressman. Liaison gave out the dentist's name.

The call to the dentist was a routine spot check by the General Accounting Office, all bureaucratic form, no substance, forgotten tomorrow. GAO was collecting backup evidence for dental work done on senators and some idiot on K Street had come up with X-rays. Would the receptionist please pull Appleton's and leave it at the front desk for a GAO messenger? It would be returned in twenty-four hours.

Washington operated at full speed; there simply was not enough time to do the work that had to be done and GAO spot checks were not legitimate work. They were irritants and complied with in irritation, but nevertheless obeyed. Appleton's X-rays would be left at the desk.

Scofield checked the library directory, took the elevator to the second floor, and walked down the hallway to the *Journalism Division—Current and Past Publications. Microfilm.* He went to the counter at the far end of the room and spoke to the clerk behind it.

"March and April, 1954, please. The *Globe* or the *Examiner,* whatever's available."

He was given eight boxes of film, and assigned a cubicle. He found it, sat down and inserted the first roll of film.

By March of '54 the bulletins detailing the condition of Joshua Appleton— "Captain Josh"—had been relegated to the back pages; he had been in the hospital more than twenty weeks by then. But he was not ignored. The famous vigil was covered in detail. Bray wrote down the names of several of those interviewed; he would know by tomorrow whether there'd be any reason to get in touch with them.

MARCH 21, 1954

YOUNG DOCTOR DIES OF CEREBRAL HEMORRHAGE

The brief story was on page sixteen. No mention that the surgeon was attending Joshua Appleton.

MARCH 26, 1954

THREE MASS. GEN'L NURSES
KILLED IN FREAK BOATING ACCIDENT

The story had made the lower left corner of the front page, but again, there was no mention of Joshua Appleton. Indeed, it would have been strange if there had been; the three were on a rotating twenty-four-hour schedule. If they were all in Marblehead that night, who was at the Appleton bedside?

APRIL 10, 1954

BOSTONIAN DIES IN GSTAAD SKIING TRAGEDY

He had found it.
It was—naturally—on the front page, the headlines prominent, the copy written as much to evoke sympathy as to report the tragic death of a young man. Scofield studied the story, positive that he would come to certain lines.
He did.

Because of the victim's deep love of the Alps—and to spare family and friends further anguish—the family has announced that the burial will take place in Switzerland, in the village of Col du Pillon.

Bray wondered who was in that coffin in Col du Pillon. Or was it merely empty?

He returned to the cheap hotel, gathered his things together, and took a cab to the Prudential Center Parking Lot, Gate A. He drove the rented car out of Boston, along Jamaica Way into Brookline. He found Appleton Hill, driving past the gates of Appleton Hall, absorbing every detail he could within the short space of time.
The huge estate was spread like a fortress across the crest of the hill, a high stone wall surrounding the inner structure, tall roofs that gave the illusion of parapets seen above the distant wall. The roadway beyond the main gate wound up the hill around a huge brick carriage house, covered with ivy, housing no fewer

than eight to ten complete apartments, five garages fronting an enormous concrete parking area below.

He drove around the hill. The ten-foot-high wrought-iron fence was continuous; every several hundred yards, small lean-to shelters were built into the earth of the hill like miniature bunkers, and within a number of them he could see uniformed men sitting and standing, smoking cigarettes and talking on telephones.

It was the seat of the Matarese, the home of the Shepherd Boy.

At 9:30 he drove out to Logan Airport. He had told Amos Lafollet to get off the plane and head directly to the dimly lit bar across from the main newsstand. The booths were so dark it was nearly impossible to see a face five feet in front of one, the only light a series of flashes from an enormous television screen on the wall.

Bray slid into the black plastic booth, adjusting his eyes to the lack of light. For an instant he thought of another booth in another dimly lit room and another man. London, the Connaught Hotel, Roger Symonds. He pushed the memory from his mind; it was an obstacle. He could not handle obstacles right now.

He saw the student walk through the bar's entrance. Scofield stood up briefly; Amos saw him and came over. There was a manila envelope in his hand and Bray felt a quick acceleration in his chest.

"I gather everything went all right," he said.

"I had to sign for it."

"You *what?*" Bray was sick; it was such a little thing, an obvious thing, and he had not thought of it.

"Take it easy. I wasn't brought up on 135th Street and Lenox Avenue for nothing."

"What name did you use?" asked Scofield, his pulse receding.

"R. M. Nixon. The receptionist was real nice. She thanked me."

"You'll go far, Amos."

"I intend to."

"I hope this'll help." Bray handed his envelope across the table.

The student held it between his fingers. "Hey, man, you know you don't really have to do this."

"Of course I do. We had an agreement."

"I know that. But I've got an idea you've gone through a lot of sweat for a lot of people you don't know."

"And a number that I know very well. The money's incidental. Use it." Bray opened his attaché case and slipped the X-ray envelope inside—right above a file folder containing Joshua Appleton's X-ray from twenty-five years ago. "Remember, you never knew my name and you never went to Washington. If you're *ever* asked, you merely ran some forgotten names through a computer for a man who never identified himself. *Please.* Remember that."

"That's going to be tough."

"Why?" Scofield was alarmed.

"How am I going to dedicate my first textbook to you?"

Bray smiled. "You'll think of something. Goodbye," he said, getting out of the booth. "I've got an hour's drive and several more of sleep to catch up on."

"Stay well, man."

"Thanks, professor."

Scofield stood in the dentist's waiting room on Main Street in Andover, Massachusetts. The name of the dentist had been supplied—happily, even enthusiastically—by the Nurse's Office of Andover Academy. Anything for Andover's illustrious—and generous—alumnus, and by extension the Senator's aide, of course. Naturally, the dentist was not the same man who had tended Senator Appleton when he was a student; the practice had been taken over by a nephew a number of years ago, but there was no question that the present doctor would cooperate. The Nurse's Office would call him and let him know the Senator's aide was on the way over.

Bray had counted on a psychology as old as the dentist's drill. Two young boys who were close friends and away at prep school might not see eye-to-eye on every issue, but they would share the same dentist.

Yes, both boys had gone to the very same man in Andover.

The dentist came out of the door that led to a storeroom, half-glasses perched on the edge of his nose. In his hand were two sheets of cardboard, small negatives embedded in each. X-rays of two Andover students taken over thirty years ago.

"Here you are, Mr. Vickery," said the dentist, holding out the X-rays. "*Damn*, will you look at the primitive way they used to mount these things! One of these days I've got to clean out that mess back there, but then you never know. Last year I had to identify an old patient of my uncle's who was burned to death in that fire over in Boxford."

"Thank you very much," said Scofield, accepting the X-ray sheets. "By the way, doctor, I know you're rushed but I wonder if you'd mind one more favor. I've got two newer sets here of both men and I've got to match them with the ones you're lending us. Of course, I can get someone to do it, but if you've got a minute."

"Sure. Won't even take a minute. Let me have them." Bray removed the two sets of X-rays from their envelopes; one stolen from the Massachusetts General Hospital, the other obtained in Washington. He had placed white tape over the names. He gave them to the dentist who carried them to a lamp and held them in sequence against the glare of the light bulb above the shade. "There you are," he said, holding the matching X-rays separately in each hand.

Scofield put each set in a different envelope. "Thanks again, doctor."

"Anytime." The dentist walked rapidly back into his office. He was a man in a hurry.

Bray sat in the front seat of the car, his breathing erratic, perspiration on his forehead. He opened the envelopes and took out the X-ray sheets.

He pulled off the small strips of tape that covered the names.

He had been right. The awesome fragment was irrevocably in place, the proof in his hand.

The man who sat in the Senate, the man who unquestionably would be the next President of the United States, was not Joshua Appleton, IV.

He was Julian Guiderone, son of the Shepherd Boy.

35

Scofield drove southeast to Salem. Delay was irrelevant now, previous schedules to be thrown away. He had everything to gain by moving as fast as he could, as long as every move was the right move, every decision the perceptive decision. He had his cannons and his nuclear bomb—his bill-of-particulars and the X-rays. It was a question now of mounting his weapons properly, *using* them, not only to blow the Matarese out of existence but first—above all, *first*—to find Antonia and force them to release her. And Taleniekov, if he was still alive.

Which meant he had to create a deception of his own. All deceptions were based on illusion, and the illusion he had to convey was that Beowulf Agate could be had, his cannons and his bomb defused, his assault stopped, the man himself destroyed. To do this he had to take the initial position of strength . . . the weakness to follow.

The hostage strategy would not wash any longer; he would not be able to get near Appleton. The Shepherd Boy would not permit it, the prize of the White House too great to place in jeopardy. Without the man there was no prize. So his position of strength lay in the X-rays. It was imperative he establish the fact that only a single set of X-rays existed, that duplicates were out of the question. Spectro analysis would reveal any such duplicating process and Beowulf Agate was not a fool; he would expect an analysis to be made. He wanted the girl, he wanted the Russian; the X-rays could be had for them.

There would be a subtle omission in the mechanics of the exchange, a seeming weakness the enemy would pounce on; but it would be calculated, no weakness at all. The Matarese would be forced to go through with the exchange. A Corsican girl and a Soviet intelligence officer for X-rays that showed incontrovertibly that the man sitting in the Senate, on his way to the presidency, was not Joshua Appleton, IV—legend of Korea, politician extraordinaire—but instead, a man supposedly buried in 1954 in the Swiss village of Col du Pillon.

He drove down toward Salem harbor, drawn as he was always drawn, toward the water, not precisely sure what he was looking for until he saw it: a shield-shaped sign on the lawn of a small hotel. *Efficiency Suites.* It made sense. Rooms with a refrigerator and cooking facilities. There'd be no stranger eating in restaurants; it was not the tourist season in Salem.

He parked the car in a lot covered with white gravel and bordered by a white picket fence, the gray water of the harbor across the way. He carried his attaché case and travel bag inside, registered under an innocuous name, and asked for a suite.

"Will payment be made by credit card, sir?" asked the young woman behind the counter.

"I beg your pardon?"

"You didn't check off the method of payment. If it's a credit card, our policy is to run the card through the machine."

"I see. No, actually, I'm one of those strange people who use real money. One man's fight against plastic. Why don't I pay you for a week in advance, I doubt I'll stay any longer." He gave her the money. "I assume there's a grocery store nearby."

"Yes, sir. Just up the street."

"What about other stores? I've a number of things to get."

"There's the Shopping Plaza about ten blocks west. I'm sure you'll find everything you need there."

Bray hoped so; he was counting on it.

He was taken to his "suite," which was in effect one large room with a pull-out bed and divider that concealed the smallest stove this side of a hot plate and a refrigerator. But the room looked out over the harbor; it was fine. He opened his attaché case, took out the photograph he had removed from the wall in Mrs. Appleton's tomb for her son, and stared at it. Two young men, tall, muscular, neither to be mistaken for the other but enough alike for an unknown surgeon somewhere in Switzerland to sculpt one into the other. A young American doctor paid to sign the medical authorization of discharge, then killed for security. A mother maintained as an alcoholic, kept at a distance, but paraded whenever it was convenient and fruitful to do so. Who knew a son better than his mother? Who in America would argue with, much less confront, Mrs. Joshua Appleton, III?

Scofield sat down and added a page to the seventeen in his bill-of-particulars. Doctors: *Nathaniel Crawford and Thomas Belford. A Swiss physician deprogrammed from a computer; a young plastic surgeon dead suddenly of a cerebral hemorrhage. Three nurses drowned off Marblehead. Gstaad; a coffin in Col du Pillon; X-rays—one set from Boston, one set from Washington, two from Main Street, Andover, Massachusetts. Two different men merged into one, and the one was a lie. A fraud was about to become President of the United States.*

Bray finished writing, and walked to the window that looked out on the still, cold waters of Salem Harbor. The dilemma was clearer than it had ever been: they had traced the Matarese from its roots in Corsica through a federation of multinational corporations that encircled the globe; they knew it financed terror the world over, encouraged the chaos that resulted from assassinations and kidnappings, killing in the streets and aircraft blown out of the skies. They understood all this but they did not know why.

Why?

The reason would have to wait. Nothing mattered but the deception that was Senator Joshua Appleton, IV. For once the son of the Shepherd Boy reached the presidency, the White House belonged to the Matarese.

What better residence for a *consigliere. . . .*

Keep breathing, my old enemy.

Toni, my love. Stay alive. Keep your mind.

Scofield went back to his attaché case on the table, opened a side flap and took out a single-edge razor blade that was wedged down between the leather. He then held the two matted sheets of cardboard with the embedded X-ray slides of two Andover students thirty-five years ago and placed them on the table, one on top of the other. There were four rows of negatives, each with four slides, a total of sixteen on each card. Small red-bordered labels identifying the patients and the dates of the X-rays were affixed to the upper left-hand corners. He checked carefully to see that the borders of the cardboard sheets matched; they did. He pressed a manila envelope down on the top sheets between the first and second rows of X-rays, took the razor blade and began to cut, slicing so that the blade went through both sheets of X-rays. The top row fell clean, two strips of four X-ray negatives.

The names of the patients and dates of entry—typed on the small red-bordered labels more than thirty-five years ago—were on the strips; the simplest chemical analysis would confirm their authenticity.

Bray doubted that any such analysis would be made on the new labels he would purchase and stick on the remaining two sheets with twelve X-rays each; it would be a waste of time. The X-rays themselves would be compared with new X-rays of the man who called himself Joshua Appleton, IV. Julian Guiderone. That was all the proof the Matarese would need.

He took the strips and the larger sheets of negatives, knelt down and carefully buffed the edges of the cuts across the rug. Within five minutes each of the edges was rubbed smooth, soiled just enough to match the age of the original borders.

He got up and put everything back in his attaché case. It was time to return to Andover, to put the plan in motion.

"Mr. Vickery, is something wrong?" asked the dentist, coming out of his office, still harried, three afternoon patients reading magazines, glancing up in mild irritation.

"I'm afraid I forgot something. May I speak with you for a second?"

"Come on in here," said the dentist, ushering Scofield into a small workroom, the shelves lined with impressions of teeth mounted on moveable clamps. He lit a cigarette from a pack on the counter. "I don't mind telling you it's been one hell of a day. What's the matter?"

"The laws, actually." Bray smiled, opening his attaché case and taking out the two envelopes. "HR Seven-Four-Eight-Five."

"What the hell is that?"

"A new congressional regulation, part of the post-Watergate morality. Whenever a government employee borrows property from any source, for whatever purpose, a full description of said property must be accompanied by a signed authorization."

"Oh, for Christ's sake."

"I'm sorry, doctor. The Senator's a stickler for these things." Scofield took the X-rays from the envelopes. "If you'll re-examine these, call in your nurse and give her a description, she can type the authorization on your letterhead and I'll get out of here."

"I suppose anything for the next President of the United States," said the dentist, taking the shortened X-ray sheets and reaching for his telephone. "Tell Appleton to lower my taxes." He pressed the intercom button. "Bring in your pad, please."

"Do you mind?" Bray took out his cigarettes.

"Are you nuts? Carcinoma loves company." The nurse came through the door, steno pad and pencil in hand. "How do I start this?" asked the doctor, looking at Scofield.

" 'To Whom It May Concern' is fine."

"Okay." The dentist glanced at his nurse. "We're keeping the government honest." He snapped on a scanning lamp and held both X-ray sheets against the glass. " 'To Whom It May Concern. Mister' . . ." The doctor stopped, looking at Bray again. "What's your first name?"

"B.A. will do."

" 'Mister B. A. Vickery of Senator Appleton's office in Washington, D.C., had requested and received from me two sets of X-rays dated November 11, 1943, for patients identified as Joshua Appleton and . . . Julian Guiderone.' " The dentist paused. "Anything else?"

"A description, doctor. That's what HR Seven-Four-Eight-Five calls for."

The dentist sighed, the cigarette protruding from his lips. " 'Said identical sets include' . . . one, two, three, four across . . . 'twelve negatives.' " The doctor stopped, squinting through his half-glasses. "You know," he interjected. "My uncle wasn't only primitive, he was downright careless."

"What do you mean?" asked Scofield, watching the dentist closely.

"The right and left bicuspids are missing in both of these. I was so rushed I didn't notice before."

"They're the cards you gave me this morning."

"I'm sure they are; there are the labels. I think I matched the upper and lower incisors. He held out the X-rays for Scofield and turned to the nurse. "Put what I said into English and type it up, will you? I'll sign it outside." He crushed out his cigarette and extended his hand. "Nice to meet you, Mr. Vickery. I've really got to get back in there."

"Just one more thing, doctor. Would you mind initialing these sheets and dating them?" Bray separated the X-rays and placed them on the counter.

"Not at all," said the dentist.

Scofield drove back to Salem. A great deal was still to be clarified, new decisions to be made as events shaped them, but he had his overall plan; he had a place to begin. It was almost time for Mr. B. A. Vickery to arrive at the Ritz Carlton, but not yet.

He had stopped earlier at the Shopping Plaza in Salem where he had found small red-bordered labels almost identical to those used more than thirty-five years ago, and a store selling typewriters where he had typed in the names and the dates, rubbing them lightly to give the labels an appearance of age. And while walking to his car he had looked briefly around at the shops, again seeing what he had hoped to see.

COPIES MADE WHILE YOU WAIT

EQUIPMENT BOUGHT, SOLD, LEASED

EXPERT SERVICE

It was conveniently two doors away from a liquor store, three from a supermarket. He would stop there now and have copies made of his bill-of-particulars, and afterward pick up something to drink and eat. He would be in his room for a long time; he had phone calls to make. They would take five to seven hours to complete. They had to be routed on a very precise schedule through Lisbon.

Bray watched as the manager of the Plaza Duplicating Service extracted the collated sheets of his indictment from the levels of gray trays that protruded from the machine. He had chatted briefly with the balding man, remarking that he was doing a favor for a nephew; the young fellow was taking one of those creative writing courses at Emerson and had entered some sort of college competition.

"That kid's got some imagination," said the manager, clipping the stacks of copies together.

"Oh, did you read it?"

"Just parts. You stand over that machine with nothing to do but make sure there's no jamming; you look. But when people come in with personal things— like letters and wills, you know what I mean—I always try to keep my eyes on the dials. Sometimes it's hard."

Bray laughed. "I told my nephew he'd better win or he'd be put in jail."

"Not anymore. These kids today, they're great. They say anything. I know a lot of people don't like 'em for it, but I do."

"I think I do, too." Bray looked at the bill placed in front of him and took his money from his pocket. "Say, you wouldn't by any chance have an Alpha Twelve machine here, would you?"

"Alpha *Twelve?* That's an eighty-thousand-dollar piece of equipment. I do a good business, but I'm not in that class."

"I suppose I could find one in Boston."

"That insurance company over on Lafayette Street has one; you can bet your life the home office paid for it. It's the only one I know of *north* of Boston, and I mean right up to Montreal."

"An insurance company?"

"West Hartford Casualty. I trained the two girls who run the Alpha Twelve. Isn't that just like an insurance company? They buy a machine like that but they won't pay for a service contract."

Scofield leaned on the counter, a weary man confiding. "Listen, I've been traveling for five days and I've got to get a report into the mails by tonight. I need an Alpha Twelve. Now, I can drive into Boston and probably find one. But it's damn near four o'clock and I'd rather not do that. My company's a little crazy; it thinks my time is valuable and lets me have enough money to save it where I can. What do you say? Can you help me?" Bray removed a hundred-dollar bill from his clip.

"You work for one hell of a company."

"That I do."

"I'll make a call."

It was 5:45 when Bray returned to the hotel on Salem harbor. The Alpha Twelve had performed the service he had needed, and he had found a stationery store where he had purchased a stapler, six manila envelopes, two rolls of packaging tape, and a Park-Sherman scale that measured weight in ounces and grams. At the Salem Post Office he had bought fifty dollars worth of stamps.

A porterhouse steak and a bottle of Scotch completed his shopping list. He spread his purchases on the bed, removing some to the table, others to the Formica counter between the Lilliputian stove and refrigerator. He poured a drink and sat in the chair in front of the window overlooking the harbor. It was growing dark, he could barely see the water except where it reflected the lights of the piers.

He drank the whisky in short swallows, letting the alcohol spread, suspending all thought. He had no more than ten minutes before the telephone calls would begin. His cannons were in place, his nuclear bomb in its rack. It was vital now that everything take place in sequence—always sequence—and that meant choosing the right words at the right time; there was no room for error. To avoid error, his mind had to be free, loose, unencumbered—capable of listening closely, picking up nuances.

Toni? . . .

No!

He closed his eyes. The gulls in the distance were foraging the waters for their last meal before darkness was complete. He listened to their screeches, the dissonance somehow comforting; there was a kind of energy in every struggle to survive. He hoped he would have it.

He dozed, awakening with a start. He looked at his watch, annoyed. It was six minutes past six; his ten minutes had stretched nearer to fifteen. It was time for the first telephone call, the one he considered least likely to bring results. It would not have to be routed through Lisbon, the chances of a tap so remote as to be practically nonexistent. But practically was not totally; therefore, his conversation would last no longer than twenty seconds, the minimum amount of time needed for even the most sophisticated tracing equipment to function.

The twenty-second limit was the one he had instructed the Frenchwoman to use weeks ago when she had placed calls for him all through the night to a suite of rooms at the hotel on Nebraska Avenue.

He rose from the chair and went to his attaché case, taking out notes he had written to himself. Notes with names and telephone numbers. He walked over to the bedside telephone, pulled the armchair next to the phone, and sat down. He thought for a moment, composing a verbal shorthand French for what he wanted to say, doubting, however, that it would make any difference. Ambassador Robert Winthrop had disappeared more than a month ago; there was no reason to think he had survived. Winthrop had raised the names of the Matarese with the wrong men—or man—in Washington.

He picked up the phone and dialed; three rings followed before an operator got on the line and asked for his room number. He gave it and more distant rings continued.

"Hello?"

"Listen! There's no time. Do you understand?"

"Yes. Go ahead."

She knew him; she was with him. He spoke rapidly in French, his eyes on the sweep hand of his watch. "Ambassador Robert Winthrop. Georgetown. Take two Company men with you, no explanations. If Winthrop's there ask to see him alone, but say nothing out loud. Give him a note with the words 'Beowulf wants to reach you.' Let him advise in writing. The contact must be sterile. I'll call you back."

Seventeen seconds.

"We *must* talk," was the strong, quick reply. "Call back."

He hung up; she'd be safe. It was not only unlikely that the Matarese had found her and tapped her, but even if they had, they would not kill her. There was nothing to gain, more to learn by keeping the intermediary alive, and too much of a mess killing the Company men with her. Besides, there were limits to his liability under the circumstances; he was sorry, but there were.

It was time for Lisbon. He had known since Rome that he would use Lisbon when the moment came. A series of telephone calls could be placed through Lisbon only once. For once those receiving the calls were listed in the overnight data banks, red cards would fly out of computers into alarm slots, the coded source traced through other computers in Langley, and no further calls permitted by that source, all transmissions terminated. Access to Lisbon was restricted to those who dealt solely with high-level defections, men in the field who in times of emergency had to go directly to their superiors in Washington who in turn were authorized to make immediate decisions. No more than twenty intelligence officers in the country had the codes for Lisbon, and no man in Washington ever refused a call from Lisbon. One never knew whether a general, or a nuclear physicist, or a ranking member of the presidium or the KGB might be the prize.

It was also understood that any abuse of the Lisbon access would result in the severest consequences for the abuser. Bray was amused—grimly—at the concept; the abuse he was about to inflict was beyond anything conceived by the men who made the rules. He looked at the five names and titles he was about to call. The names in themselves were not that unusual; they could probably be found in any telephone book. Their positions, however, could not.

The Secretary of State
The Chairman of the National Security Council
The Director of the Central Intelligence Agency
The Chief Foreign Policy Advisor to the President
The Chairman of the Joint Chiefs of Staff

The probability that one, possibly two of these men were *consiglieri* of the Matarese convinced Bray not to try to send his indictment directly to the President. Taleniekov and he had believed that once the proof was in their hands the two leaders of both their countries could be reached and convinced. It was not true; Presidents and Premiers were too closely guarded, too protected; messages were filtered, words interpreted. The charges of "traitors" would be dismissed. Others had to reach Presidents and Premiers. Men whose positions of trust and responsibility were beyond reproach; such men had to bring them the news, not "traitors."

The majority if not all of those he was about to call were committed to the well-being of the nation; any one of them could get the ear of the President. It was all he asked for, and none would refuse a call from Lisbon. He picked up the telephone and dialed the overseas operator.

Twenty minutes later the operator called back. Lisbon had, as always, cleared the traffic to Washington quickly; the Secretary of State was on the line.

"This is State One," said the Secretary. "Your codes are cleared, Lisbon. What is it?"

"Mr. Secretary, within forty-eight hours you'll receive a manila envelope in the mail; the name Agate will be printed in the upper left corner—"

"Agate? *Beowulf Agate?*"

"Please, listen to me, sir. Have the envelope brought directly to you unopened. Inside there's a detailed report describing a series of events which have taken place—and are taking place right now—that amount to a conspiracy to assume control of the government—"

"Conspiracy? Please be specific. Communist?"

"I don't think so."

"You *must* be specific, Mr. Scofield! You're a wanted man, and you're abusing the Lisbon connection! Self-seeking cries of alarm from you are not in your interest. Or in the interest of the country."

"You'll find all the specifics you need in my report. Among them is proof—I repeat, *proof*, Mr. Secretary—that there's been a deception in the Senate that goes back twenty years. It's of such magnitude that I'm not at all sure the country can absorb the shock. It may not even be in its interest to expose it."

"Explain yourself!"

"The explanation's in the envelope. But not a recommendation; I haven't got any recommendations. That's your business. And the President's. Bring the information to him as soon as you get it."

"I order you to report to me immediately!"

"I'll come out in forty-eight hours, if I'm alive. When I do I want two things: vindication for me and asylum for a Soviet intelligence officer—if he's alive."

"Scofield, where *are* you?"

Bray hung up.

He waited ten minutes and placed his second call to Lisbon. Thirty-five minutes later the Chairman of the National Security Council was on the line.

"Mr. Chairman, within forty-eight hours you'll receive a manila envelope in the mail; the name Agate will be printed in the upper left corner. . . ."

It was exactly fourteen minutes past midnight when he completed the final call. Among the men he had reached were honorable men. Their voices would be heard by the President.

He had forty-eight hours. A lifetime.

It was time for a drink. Twice during the placement of calls he had looked at the bottle of Scotch, close to rationalizing the necessity of calming his anxieties, but both times rejected the method. Under pressure, he was the coldest man he knew; he might not always feel that way, but it was the way he functioned. He deserved a drink now; it would be a fitting salute to the call he was about to make to Senator Joshua Appleton, IV, born Julian Guiderone, son of the Shepherd Boy.

The telephone rang, the shock of its sound causing Bray to grip the bottle in his hand, oblivious to the whisky he was pouring. Liquor spilled over the glass onto the counter. *It was impossible!* There was no way the calls to Lisbon could be retraced so rapidly. The magnetic trunklines fluctuated hourly, ensuring blind origins; the entire system would have to be shut down for a minimum of eight hours in order to trace a single call. Lisbon was an absolute; place a call through it and a man was safe, his location buried until it no longer mattered.

The phone rang again. Not to answer was not to know, the lack of knowledge infinitely more dangerous than any tracing. No matter what, he still had cards to play; or at least the conviction that those cards were playable. He would convey that. He lifted up the phone. "Yes?"

"Room Two-twelve?"

"What is it?"

"The manager, sir. It's nothing really, but the outside operator has—quite naturally—kept our switchboard informed of your overseas telephone calls. We noticed that you've chosen not to use a credit card, but rather have billed the calls to your room. We thought you'd appreciate knowing that the charges are currently in excess of three hundred dollars."

Scofield looked over at the depleted bottle of Scotch. Yankee skepticism would not change until the planet blew up; and then the New England bookkeepers would sue the universe.

"Why don't you come up personally and I'll give you the money for the calls. It'll be in cash."

"Oh, not necessary, not necessary at all, sir. Actually, I'm not at the hotel, I'm at home." There was the slightest, slightly embarrassed pause. "In Beverly. We'll just attach—"

"Thank you for your concern," interrupted Bray, hanging up and heading back to the counter and the bottle of Scotch.

Five minutes later he was ready, icelike calm spreading through him as he sat down next to the telephone. The words would be there because the outrage was there; he did not have to think about them, they would come easily. What he had thought about was the sequence. Extortion, compromise, weakness, exchange. Someone within the Matarese wanted to talk with him, recruit him for the most logical reasons in the world; he'd give that man—whoever he was—the chance to do both. It was part of the exchange, prelude to escape. But the first step on the tightrope would not be made by Beowulf Agate; it would be made by the son of the Shepherd Boy.

He picked up the phone; thirty seconds later he heard the famous voice laced with the pronounced Boston accent that reminded so many so often of a young President cut down in Dallas.

"Hello? *Hello?*" The Senator had been roused from his sleep; it was in the clearing of his throat. "Who's there, for God's sake?"

"There is a grave in the Swiss village of Col du Pillon. If there's a body in the coffin below it's not the man whose name is on the stone."

The gasp on the line was electrifying, the silence that followed a scream suspended in the grip of fear. "Who? . . ." The man was in shock, unable to form the question.

"There's no reason for you to say anything, Julian—"

"*Stop it!*" The scream was released.

"All right, no names. You know who I am—if you don't, the Shepherd Boy hasn't kept his son informed."

"I won't *listen!*"

"Yes you will, Senator. Right now that phone is part of your hand; you won't let it go. You can't. So just listen. On November 11, 1943, you and a close friend of yours went to the same dentist on Main Street in Andover, Massachusetts. You had X-rays taken that day." Scofield paused for precisely one second. "I have them, Senator. Your office can confirm it in the morning. Your office also can confirm the fact that yesterday a messenger from the General Accounting Office picked up a set of more recent X-rays from your current dentist in Washington. And finally, if you're so inclined, your office might check the X-ray Depository of the Massachusetts General Hospital in Boston. They'll find that a single plate, frontal X-ray taken twenty-five years ago is missing from the Appleton file. As of an hour ago all are in my possession."

There was a quiet, plaintive cry on the line, a moan without words.

"Keep listening, Senator," continued Bray. "You've got a chance. If the girl's alive you've got a chance, if she's not you don't. Regarding the Russian, if he's going to die, I'll be the one who kills him. I think you know why. You see, accommodations can be made. What I know I don't *want* to know. What you do is no concern of mine, not any longer. What you want, you've already won, and men like me simply end up working for people like you, that's all that ever happens. Ultimately, there's not much difference between any of you. Anywhere." Scofield paused again, the bait was glaring; would he take it?

He did, the whisper hoarse, the statement tentative. "There are . . . people who want to talk with you."

"I'll listen. But only after the girl is free, the Russian turned over to me."

"The X-rays? . . ." The words were rushed, cut off; a man was drowning.

"That's the exchange."

"How?"

"We'll negotiate it. You've got to understand, Senator, the only thing that matters to me now is me. The girl and I, we just want to get away."

"What . . . ?" Again the man was incapable of forming the question.

"Do I want?" completed Scofield. "Proof that she's alive, that she can still walk."

"I don't understand."

"You don't know much about exchanges, either. A package that's immobile isn't any package at all; it voids the exchange. I want proof and I've got a very powerful pair of binoculars."

"Binoculars?"

"Your people will understand. I want a telephone number and a sighting. Obviously, I'm in the Boston vicinity. I'll call you in the morning. At this number."

"There's a debate on the Senate floor, a quorum—"

"You'll miss it," said Bray, hanging up.

The first move had been made; telephones would be in use all night between Washington and Boston. Move and countermove, thrust and parry, press and check; the negotiations had begun. He looked at the manila envelopes on the table. Between calls he had sealed all of them, weighed and stamped them; they were ready to go.

Except one, and there was no reason to believe he would mail it, the tragedy found in the disappearance of the man and what he might have done. It was time to call back his old friend from Paris. He picked up the phone and dialed.

"Bray, thank God! We've been waiting for hours!"

"We?"

"Ambassador Winthrop."

"He's *there?*"

"It's all right. It was handled extremely well. His man, Stanley, assured me that no one could possibly have followed them and for all purposes, the ambassador is in Alexandria."

"Stanley's good!" Scofield felt like yelling to the skies in sheer relief, sheer *joy.*

Winthrop was alive! The flanks were covered, the Matarese destroyed. He was free to negotiate as he had never negotiated in his life before, and he was the best there was. "Let me talk to Winthrop."

"Brandon, I'm on the line. I'm afraid I took the phone from your friend quite rudely. Forgive me, my dear."

"What *happened?* I tried calling you—"

"I was hurt—not seriously—but enough to require treatment. I went to a doctor I knew in Fredericksburg; he has a private clinic. It wouldn't do for the eldest of so-called statesmen to show up at a Washington hospital with a bullet in his arm. I mean, can you imagine Harriman turning up in a Harlem emergency ward with a gunshot wound? . . . I couldn't involve you any further, Brandon."

"*Jesus.* I should have considered that."

"You had enough to consider. Where are you?"

"Outside of Boston. There's so much to tell you, but not on the phone. It's all in an envelope, along with four strips of X-rays. I've got to get it to you right away, and you've got to get it to the President."

"The Matarese?"

"More than either of us could imagine. I have the proof."

"Take the first plane to Washington. I'll reach the President now and get you full protection, a military escort, if need be. The search will be called off."

"I can't do that, sir."

"Why *not?*" The Ambassador was incredulous.

"There are . . . hostages involved. I need time. They'll be killed unless I negotiate."

"Negotiate? You don't have to negotiate. If you have what you say you have, let the government do it."

"It takes roughly one pound of pressure and less than a fifth of a second to pull a trigger," said Scofield. "I've got to negotiate. . . . But you see, I *can* now. I'll stay in touch, pinpoint the exchange ground. You can cover me."

"Those words again," said Winthrop. "They never leave your vocabulary, do they?"

"I've never been so grateful for them."

"How much time?"

"It depends; it's delicate. Twenty-four, possibly thirty hours. It has to be less than forty-eight; that's the deadline."

"Get the proof to me, Brandon. There's an attorney, his firm's in Boston but he lives in Waltham. He's a good friend. Do you have a car?"

"Yes. I can get to Waltham in about forty minutes."

"Good. I'll call him; he'll be on the first plane to Washington in the morning. His name is Paul Bergeron; you'll have to get his address from the phone book."

"No problem."

It was 1:45 A.M. when Bray rang the bell of the fieldstone house in Waltham. The door was opened by Paul Bergeron, dressed in a bathrobe, creases of concern on his aging, intelligent face.

"I know I'm not to ask your name, but would you care to come in? From what I gather, I'm sure you can use a drink."

"Thanks just the same, but I still have work to do. Here's the envelope, and thanks again."

"Another time, perhaps." The attorney looked at the thick manila envelope in his hand. "You know, I feel the way Jim St. Clair must have felt when he got that last call from Al Haig. Is this some kind of smoking-gun?"

"It's on fire, Mr. Bergeron."

"I called the airline an hour ago; I'm on the 7:55 to Washington. Winthrop will have this by ten in the morning."

"Thanks. Good night."

Scofield drove back toward Salem, scanning the roads instinctively for signs of anyone following him: there were none, nor did he expect to see any. He was also looking for an all-night supermarket. Their wares were rarely, if ever, restricted to foodstuffs.

He found one on the outskirts of Medford, set back from the highway. He parked in front, walked inside, and saw what he was looking for in the second aisle. A display of inexpensive Big Ben alarm clocks. He bought ten of them.

It was 3:18 when he walked into his room. He took the alarm clocks from their boxes, lined them up on the table, and opened his attaché case, taking out a small leather case containing miniature hand tools. He would buy bell wire and batteries first thing in the morning, the explosives later in the day. The charges might be a problem, but it was not insurmountable; he needed more show than power— and in all likelihood he would need nothing at all. The years, however, had taught him caution; an exchange was like the workings of a giant aircraft. Each system had a backup system, each backup an alternative.

He had six hours to prepare his alternatives. It was good he had something to do; sleep now was out of the question.

36

The shift from dawn to daybreak was barely discernible; winter rain was promised again. By eight o'clock it had arrived. Bray stood, his hands on the windowsill, looking out at the ocean, thinking about calmer, warmer seas, wondering if he and Toni would ever sail them. Yesterday there was no hope; today there was and he was primed to function as he had never functioned before. All that was Beowulf Agate would be seen and heard from this day. He had spent his life preparing for the few brief hours that would prolong it the only way that was acceptable to him. He would bring her out or he would die; that had not changed. The fact that he had effectively destroyed the Matarese was almost incidental now. That was a professional objective and he was the best . . . he and the Russian were the best.

He turned from the window and went to the table, surveying his work of the last few hours. It had taken less time than he had projected, so total was his concentration. Each clock was dismantled, every main wheel spring drilled at the spindle, new pinion screws inserted in the ratchet mechanisms, the miniature bolts balanced. Each was now prepared to accept the insertion of bell wires leading to battery terminals that would throw thirty seconds of sparks into exposed powder. These sparks would, in turn, burn and ignite explosives over a span of fifteen minutes. Each alarm had been set and reset a dozen times, infinitesimal grooves filed across the gears, ensuring sequence; all worked a dozen times in sequence. Professional tools, no particular significance attached to his knowing them. The designer was also a mechanic, the architect a builder, the critic a practitioner of the craft. It was essential.

Powder could be obtained at any gunsmith's with the purchase of shells. As for explosives, a simple visit to a demolition or excavation site, armed with the proper government identification, was all that it took for an on-the-spot inventory. The rest was a matter of having large pockets in a raincoat. He had done it all before: lay mentality was the same everywhere. Beware the man bearing a black plastic ID case who spoke softly. He was dangerous. Cooperate; do not allow your name to get on a list.

He placed the clock mechanisms in a box given him by the supermarket clerk five hours ago, sealed the top, and carried it outside to his car. He opened the trunk, wedged the box into the corner, and returned to the hotel lobby.

"I find that I'll be leaving shortly," he said to the young man behind the front desk. "I paid for a week, but my plans have changed."

"You also had a lot of phone calls billed to your room."

"True," agreed Scofield, wondering how many people in Salem were also aware of it. Did witches still burn in Salem? "If you'd have the balance ready for me, I'll be down in about a half-hour. Add these papers to my bill, please." He took two newspapers from the stacks on the counter, the morning *Examiner* and a local weekly. He walked back up the staircase to his room.

He made instant coffee, carried the cup to the table, and sat down with the newspapers and the Salem telephone book. It was 8:25. Paul Bergeron had been in the air thirty minutes, weather at Logan Airport permitting. It was something he would check when he started his calls.

He opened the *Examiner,* turning to the classified section. There were two openings for construction workers, the first in Newton, the second in Braintree. He wrote down the addresses hoping to find a third or a fourth nearer by.

He did. In the Salem weekly, there was a photograph taken five days ago showing Senator Joshua Appleton at a groundbreaking ceremony in Swampscott.

It was a federal project coordinated with the state of Massachusetts, a middle-income housing development being built on the rocky land north of Phillips Beach. The caption read BLASTING AND EXCAVATION TO COMMENCE. . . .

The irony was splendid.

He opened the telephone book, and found a gunsmith in Salem; he had no reason to look further. He wrote down the address.

It was 8:37. Time to call the lie that went under the name of Joshua Appleton. He got up and went to the bed, deciding impulsively to phone Logan Airport first. He did, and the words he heard were the words he wanted to hear.

"Seven-fifty-five to Washington? That would be Eastern Flight Six-two. Let me check, sir. . . . There was a twelve-minute delay, but the plane's airborne. No change in the E.T.A."

Paul Bergeron was on his way to Washington and Robert Winthrop. There would be no delays now, no crisis-conferences, no hastily summoned meetings between arrogant men trying to decide how and when to proceed. Winthrop would call the Oval Office; an immediate audience would be granted and the full might of government would be pitted against the Matarese. And tomorrow morning—Winthrop had agreed to that—the Senator would be picked up by Secret Service and taken directly to Walter Reed Hospital where he would be subjected to intensive examinations. A twenty-five-year fraud would be exposed, the son destroyed with the Shepherd Boy.

Bray lit a cigarette, sipped his coffee, and picked up the phone. He was in full command; he would concentrate totally on his negotiations on the exchange that would be meaningless to the Matarese.

The Senator's voice was tense, exhaustion in his tight delivery. "Nicholas Guiderone wants to see you."

"The Shepherd Boy himself," said Scofield. "You know my conditions. Does he? Is he prepared to meet them?"

"Yes," whispered the son. "A telephone number he agrees to. He's not sure what you mean by a 'sighting.' "

"Then there's nothing further to talk about. I'll hang up."

"*Wait!*"

"Why? It's a simple word; I told you I had binoculars. What else is there to say? He's refused. Goodbye, Senator."

"*No!*" Appleton's breathing was audible. "All right, all right. You'll be told a time and a location when you call the number I give you."

"I'll be *what?* You're a dead man, Senator. If they want to sacrifice you, that's their business—and yours, I suppose, but not mine."

"What the hell are you talking about? What's wrong?"

"It's unacceptable. I'm not *told* a time and a location, I tell *you* and you tell them. Specifically I give you a location and a time *span,* Senator. Between three and five o'clock this afternoon, at the north windows of Appleton Hall, the ones looking out over Jamaica Pond. Have you got that? Appleton Hall."

"That *is* the telephone number!"

"You don't say. Have the windows lighted, the woman in one room, the

Russian in another. I want mobility, conversation; I want to see them walking, talking, reacting. Is that clear?"

"Yes. Walking . . . reacting."

"And, Senator, tell your people not to bother looking for me. I won't have the X-rays on me; they'll be with someone else who's been told where to send them if I'm not back at a specific bus stop by five-thirty."

"A *bus* stop?"

"The north road below Appleton Hall is a public bus route. Those buses are always crowded and the long curve around Jamaica Pond makes them slow down. If the rain keeps up they'll be slower than usual, won't they? I'll have plenty of time to see what I want to see."

"Will you *see* Nicholas *Guiderone?*" The question was rushed, on the edge of hysteria.

"If I'm satisfied," said Scofield coldly. "I'll call you from a phone booth around five-thirty."

"He wants to talk with you *now!*"

"Mr. Vickery doesn't talk to anyone until he checks into the Ritz Carlton Hotel. I thought that was clear."

"He's concerned you may have duplicates made; he's very concerned about that."

"These are twenty-five and thirty-eight-year-old negatives. Any exposure to photographic light would show up on a spectrograph instantly. I won't get killed for that."

"He insists you reach him *now!* He says it's vital!"

"Everything's vital."

"He says to tell you you're wrong. *Very* wrong."

"If I'm satisfied this afternoon he'll have a chance to prove it later. And you'll have the presidency. Or will he?" Bray hung up and crushed out his cigarette. As he had thought, Appleton Hall was the most logical place for Guiderone to hold his hostages. He had tried *not* to think about it when he had driven around the massive estate—the nearness of Toni was an obstruction he could barely surmount—but instinctively he had known it. And because he knew it, his eyes had reacted like the rapid shutters of a dozen cameras clicking off a hundred images. The grounds had space; acres filled with dense trees and thick shrubbery and guards in lean-to shelters positioned around the hill. Such a fortress was a likely target for an invasion—indeed the possibility was obviously never far from Guiderone's mind—and Scofield intended to capitalize on that fear. He would mount an imaginary invasion, its roots in the sort of army the Shepherd Boy understood as well as anyone on earth.

He made a last call before leaving Salem; to Robert Winthrop in Washington. The Ambassador might well be tied up for hours at the White House—his advice intrinsic to any decision made by the President—and Scofield wanted his first line of protection. It was his only protection, really; imaginary invasions had no invaders.

"Brandon? I haven't slept all night."

"Neither did a lot of other people, sir. Is this line sterile?"

"I had it electronically checked early this morning. What's happening? Did you see Bergeron?"

"He's on his way. Eastern Flight Six-two. He's got the envelope and will be in Washington by ten."

"I'll send Stanley to meet him at the airport. I spoke to the President fifteen minutes ago. He's clearing his calendar and will see me at two o'clock this afternoon. I expect it will be a very long meeting. I'm sure he'll want to bring in others."

"That's why I'm calling now; I thought as much. I've got the exchange ground. Have you a pencil?"

"Yes, go ahead."

"It's a place called Appleton Hall in Brookline."

"Appleton? *Senator* Appleton?"

"You'll understand when you get the envelope from Bergeron."

"My *God!*"

"The estate's above Jamaica Pond, on a hill called Appleton Hill; it's well known. I'll set the meeting for eleven-thirty tonight; I'll time my arrival exactly. Tell whoever's in charge to start surrounding the hill at eleven-forty-five. Block off the roads a half-mile in all directions, using detour signs, and approach carefully. There are guards inside the fence every two or three hundred feet. Station the command post on the dirt road across from the front gate; there's a large white house there, if I remember correctly. Take it and sever the telephone wires; it may belong to the Matarese."

"Just a minute, Brandon," interrupted Winthrop. "I'm writing all this and my hands and eyes aren't what they once were."

"I'm sorry, I'll slow down."

"It's all right. 'Sever telephone wires.' Go on."

"My strategy's right out of the book. They may expect it, but they can't stop it. I'll say my deadline's fifteen minutes past midnight. That's when I'm to go out the front door with the hostages to my car and strike two matches one after the other; they'll recognize a pattern. I'll tell them a drone is outside the gate with an envelope containing the X-rays."

"Drone? *X-rays?*"

"The first is only a name for someone I hire. The second is the proof they expect me to deliver."

"But you *can't* deliver it!"

"It wouldn't make any difference if I did. You'll have enough in the envelope Bergeron's bringing you."

"Of course. What else?"

"When I strike the second match, tell the C.P. to give me corresponding signals."

"Corresponding? . . ."

"Strike two matches."

"Of course. Sorry. Then?"

"Wait for me to drive down to the gate. I'll time everything as close to twelve-twenty as I can. As soon as the gate's opened, the troops move in. They'll be covered by diversionary static—tell them it's just that. Static."

"What? I don't understand."

"They will. I've got to leave now, Mr. Ambassador. There's still a lot to do."

"Brandon!"

"Yes, sir?"

"There's one thing you do *not* have to do."

"What's that?"

"Worry about vindication. I promise you. You were always the best there was."

"Thank you, sir. Thank you for everything. I just want to be free."

The gunsmith on Salem's Hawthorne Boulevard was both amused and pleased that the stranger purchased two grosses of *Ought-Four* shotgun shells during off-season. Tourists were damn fools anyway, but this one compounded the damn-foolery of paying good money not only for the shells, but for ten plastic display tubes that the manufacturers supplied for nothing. He spoke with one of those smooth, kinda' oily voices. Probably a New York lawyer who never had a gun in his hand. Damn fools.

The rain hammered down, forming pools in the mud as disgruntled crews of construction workers sat in cars waiting for a break in the weather so they could sign in; four hours meant a day's pay, but without signing in there was nothing.

Scofield approached the door of a prefabricated shack, stepping on a plank sinking into the mud in front of the rain-splashed window. Inside he could see the foreman sitting behind a table talking into a telephone. Ten yards to the left was a concrete bunker, a heavy padlock on the steel door, the red-lettered sign stenciled across it explicit.

DANGER

AUTHORIZED PERSONNEL ONLY

SWAMPSCOTT DEV. CORP.

Bray rapped first on the window, distracting the man on the phone inside the shack, then stepped off the plank and opened the door.

"Yeah, what is it?" yelled the foreman.

"I'll wait till you're finished," said Scofield, closing the door. A sign on the table gave the man's name. *A. Patelli.*

"That could be a while, pal! I got a thief on the phone. A fucking thief who says his fucking pansy drivers can't roll because it's wet out!"

"Don't make it too long, please." Bray removed his ID case. He flipped it open. "You are Mr. Patelli, aren't you?"

The foreman stared at the identification card. "Yeah." He turned back to the phone. "I'll call you back, thief!" He got out of the chair. "You government?"

"Yes."

"What the hell's the matter *now?*"

"Something we don't think you're aware of, Mr. Patelli. My unit's working with the Federal Bureau of Investigation—"

"The FBI?"

"That's right. You've had several shipments of explosive materials delivered to the site here."

"Locked up tight and accounted for," interrupted the foreman. "Every fucking stick."

"We don't think so. That's why I'm here."

"*What?*"

"There was a bombing two days ago in New York, maybe you read about it. A bank in Wall Street. Oxidation raised several numbers on the serial imprint that blew with the detonating cap; we think it may be traced to one of your shipments."

"That's fuckin'-a-nuts!"

"Why don't we check?"

The explosives inside the concrete bunker were not sticks, they were solid blocks roughly five inches long, three high and two thick, packaged in cartons of twenty-four.

"Prepare a statement of consignment, please," said Scofield, studying the surface of a brick. "We were right. These are the ones."

"A statement?"

"I'm taking a carton for evidenciary analysis."

"*What?*"

"Look, Mr. Patelli, your ass may be in a very tight sling. You signed for these shipments and I don't think you counted. I'd advise you to cooperate fully. Any indication of resistance could be misinterpreted; after all, it's your responsibility. Frankly, I don't think you're involved, but I'm only the field investigator. On the other hand, my word counts."

"I'll sign any fucking thing you want. What do I write?"

At a hardware store, Bray bought ten dry-cell batteries, ten five-quart plastic containers, a roll of bell wire and a can of black spray paint. He asked for a very large box to carry everything in through the rain.

He sat in the backseat of his rented car, placed the last of the clocks into its plastic container, pressing the explosive brick down beside the battery. He listened for the steady tick of the mechanism; it was there. Then he snapped the edges of the cover in place and sealed it with tape.

It was forty-two minutes past noon, the alarms set in sequence, the grooves in the gears locked by the teeth of the pinions, the sequence to begin in precisely eleven hours and twenty-six minutes.

As he had done with the previous nine, he sprayed the container with black paint. A great deal of it soiled the rear seat cushion; he would leave a hundred-dollar bill in the crease.

He inserted the coin in the pay phone; he was in West Roxbury, two minutes from the border of Brookline. He dialed, waited for the line to be answered, and roared into the mouthpiece.

"Sanitation?"

"Yes, sir. What can we do for you?"

"Appleton Drive! Brookline! The sewer's backed up! It's all over my *gohdahm* front lawn."

"Where is that, sir?"

"I just told you. Appleton Drive and Beachnut Terrace. It's terrible!"

"We'll dispatch a truck right away, sir."

"Please hurry!"

The Sanitation Department van made its way haltingly up Beachnut Terrace toward the intersection of Appleton Drive, its driver obviously checking the sewer drains in the street. When he reached the corner, a man in a dark-blue raincoat flagged him down. It was impossible to go around the man; he moved back and forth in the middle of the street, waving his arms frantically. The driver opened his door and shouted through the rain.

"What's the *mattah?*"

It was the last thing he would say for several hours.

Within the Appleton Hall compound, a guard in a cedar lean-to picked up his wall telephone and told the operator on the switchboard to give him an outside line. He was calling the Sanitation Department in Brookline. One of their vans was on Appleton Drive, stopping every hundred feet or so.

"There are reports of a blockage in the vicinity of Beachnut and Appleton, sir. We have a truck checking it out."

"Thank you," said the guard, pushing a button that was the intercom for all stations. He relayed the information and returned to his chair.

What kind of idiot would check out sewers for a living?

Scofield wore the black rain slicker with the stenciled white letters across the back. *Sanitation Dept. Brookline.* It was 3:05. The sighting had started, Antonia and Taleniekov standing behind windows on the other side of the estate; the concentration in Appleton Hall would be on the road below. He drove the sanitation van slowly up Appleton Drive, staying close to the curb, stopping at every sewer drain in the street. As the road was long, there were roughly twenty to thirty such drains. At each stop he got out carrying a six-foot extension snake and whatever other tools he could find in the van that seemed to fit a hastily imagined problem. This was at every stop; at ten, however, he added one other item. A five-quart plastic container that had been sprayed black. With seven he was able to wedge them between the spikes of the wrought-iron fence beyond the sightlines of the lean-tos, pushing them into the foliage with the snake. With three he used what was left of the bell wire and suspended them beneath the grates of the sewers.

At 4:22 he was finished and drove back to Beachnut Terrace where he began the embarrassing process of reviving the sanitation employee in the rear of the van. There was no time to be solicitous; he removed the rain slicker and slapped the man into consciousness.

"What the hell *happened?*" The man was frightened, recoiling at the sight of Bray above him.

"I made a mistake," said Scofield simply. "You can accept that or not, but nothing's missing, no harm's been done, and there is no problem with the sewers."

"You're crazy!"

Bray took out his money clip. "I'm sure it appears that way, so I'd like to pay you for the use of your truck. No one has to know about it. Here's five hundred dollars."

"*Five?* . . ."

"For the past hour you've been checking the drains along Beachnut and Appleton, that's all anyone has to know. You were dispatched and did your job. That is, if you want the five hundred."

"You're *crazy!*"

"I haven't got time to argue with you. Do you want the money or not?"

The man's eyes bulged. He took the money.

It did not matter whether they saw him now; only what he saw mattered. His watch read 4:57, three minutes remained before the sighting was terminated. He stopped his car directly below the midpoint of Appleton Hall, rolled down his window, and raised the binoculars, focusing through the rain on the lighted windows three hundred yards above.

The first figure to come into view was Taleniekov, but it was not the Taleniekov he had last seen in London. The Russian stood motionless behind the window, the side of his head encased in a bandage, a bulge beneath the open collar of his shirt further evidence of wounds wrapped tightly with gauze. Standing beside the Soviet was a dark-haired muscular man, his hand hidden behind Taleniekov's back. Scofield had the distinct impression that without that man's support Taleniekov would collapse. But he was alive, his eyes staring straight ahead, blinking every other second or so; the Russian was telling him he *was* alive.

Bray moved the glasses to the right, his breathing stopped, the pounding in his chest like a rapidly accelerating drum in an echo chamber. It was almost more than he could bear; the rain blurred the lenses; he was going out of his mind.

There she *was!* Standing erect behind the window, her head held up, angled first to her left, then to her right, her eyes leveled, responding to voices. *Responding.*

And then Scofield saw what he dared not hope to see. Relief swept over him and he wanted to shout through the rain in sheer exuberance. There was fear in Antonia's eyes, to be sure, but there was also something else. *Anger.*

The eyes of his love were filled with anger, and there was nothing on earth that took its place! An angry mind was a mind intact.

He put the binoculars down, rolled up the windows, and started the engine. He had several telephone calls and a final arrangement to make. When these were done, it was time for Mr. B. A. Vickery to arrive at the Ritz Carlton Hotel.

37

"Were you satisfied?" The Senator's voice was more controlled than it had been that morning. The anxiety was still there but it was farther below the surface.

"How badly is the Russian hurt?"

"He's lost blood; he's weak."

"I could see that. Is he ambulatory?"

"Enough to put him into a car, if that's what you want to do."

"It's what I want to do. Both he and the woman in my car with me at the exact moment I say. I'll drive the car down to the gate and on my signal, the gate will be opened. That's when you get the X-rays and we get out."

"I thought you wanted to kill him."

"I want something else first. He has information that can make the rest of my life very pleasant, no matter who runs what."

"I see."

"I'm sure you do."

"You said you'd meet with Nicholas Guiderone, listen to what he has to say."

"I will. I'd be a liar if I didn't admit I had questions."

"He'll know when I check into the Ritz Carlton. Tell him to call me there. And let's get one thing clear, Senator. A telephone call, no troops. The X-rays won't be in the hotel."

"Where will they be?"

"That's my business." Scofield hung up and left the phone booth. He'd place his next call from a booth in the center of Boston, to check in with Robert Winthrop, as much to get the Ambassador's reaction to the material in the envelope as anything else. And to make sure his protection was being mounted. If there were hitches he wanted to know about them.

"It's Stanley, Mr. Scofield." As always, Winthrop's chauffeur spoke gruffly, not unpleasantly. "The Ambassador's still at the White House; he asked me to come back here and wait for any calls from you. He told me to tell you that everything you asked for is being taken care of. He said I should repeat the times. Eleven-thirty, eleven forty-five, and twelve-fifteen."

"That's what I wanted to hear. Thanks very much." Bray opened the door of the drugstore telephone booth and walked over to a counter where construction paper and felt markers in varying colors were sold. He chose bright yellow paper and a dark-blue marker.

He went back to his car and, using his attaché case for a desk, wrote his message in large, clear letters on the yellow paper. Satisfied, he opened the case, removed the five sealed manila envelopes, stamped and addressed to five of the nation's most powerful men, and placed them on the seat next to him. It was time to mail them. Then he took out a sixth envelope and inserted the yellow page; he sealed it with tape and wrote on the front.

FOR THE BOSTON POLICE

He drove slowly up Newbury Street looking for the address he had found in the telephone booth. It was on the left side, four doors from the corner, a large painted sign in the window.

PHOENIX MESSENGER SERVICE
24-HOUR DELIVERY—
MEDICAL, ACADEMIC, INDUSTRIAL

A thin, prim-looking woman with an expression of serious efficiency rose from her desk and came to the counter.

"May I help you?"

"I hope so," said Scofield, efficiency in his voice as he opened his identification. "I'm with the BPD, attached to Interdepartmental Examinations."

"The police? Good heavens. . . ."

"Nothing to be concerned about. We're running an exercise, checking up on precinct response to outside emergencies. We want this envelope delivered to the station on Boylston tonight. Can you handle it?"

"We certainly can."

"Fine. What's the charge?"

"Oh, I don't think that will be necessary, officer. We're all in this together."

"I couldn't accept that, thank you. Besides, we need the outside record. And your name, of course."

"Of course. The charge for night deliveries is usually ten dollars."

"If you'll let me have a receipt, please." Scofield took the money from his pocket. "And if you wouldn't mind, please specify that delivery is to be made between eleven and eleven-fifteen; that's very important to us. You will make sure of it, won't you?"

"I'll do better than that, officer. I'll deliver it myself. I'm on till midnight, so I'll just leave one of the boys in charge and go right over there myself. I really admire the sort of thing you're doing. Crime is simply astronomical these days; we've all got to pitch in, I say."

"You're very kind, ma'am."

"You know, there're a lot of very strange people around the apartment house where I live. *Very* strange."

"What's the address? I'll have the patrol cars look a little more closely from here on."

"Why *thank* you."

"Thank *you*, ma'am."

It was 9:20 when he walked into the lobby of the Ritz Carlton. He had driven down to the piers and eaten a fish dinner, his time spent thinking about what he and Toni would do after the night was over. Where would they go? How would they live? Finances did not concern him; Winthrop had promised vindication and the calculating head of Consular Operations, the would-be executioner named Daniel Congdon, had been generous in pension and unrecorded benefits that would come his way as long as his silence was maintained. Beowulf Agate was about to disappear from this world; where would Bray Scofield go? As long as Antonia was with him, it did not matter.

"There's a message for you, Mr. Vickery," said the desk clerk, holding out a small envelope.

"Thank you," said Scofield, wondering if beneath the man's white shirt there was a small blue circle inked into his flesh.

The message was only a telephone number. He crumpled it in his hand and dropped it on the counter.

"Is something wrong?" asked the clerk.

Bray smiled. "Tell that son of a bitch I don't make calls to numbers. Only to names."

He let the telephone ring three times before he picked it up. "Yes?"

"You're an arrogant man, Beowulf." The voice was high-pitched, crueler than the wind. It was the Shepherd Boy, Nicholas Guiderone.

"I was right, then," said Scofield. "That man downstairs doesn't work full time for the Ritz Carlton. And when he showers, he can't wash off a small blue circle on his chest."

"It's worn with enormous pride, sir. They are extraordinary men and women who have enlisted in our extraordinary cause."

"Where do you find them? People who'll blow themselves away and bite into cyanide?"

"Quite simply, in our companies. Men have been willing to make the ultimate sacrifice for causes since the dawn of time. It does not always have to be on a battlefield, or in a wartime underground, or even in the world of international espionage. There are many causes; I don't have to tell you that."

"Such as themselves? The *Fida'is*, Guiderone? Hasan ibn-al-Sabbah's cadre of assassins?"

"You've studied the *padrone*, I see."

"Very closely."

"There are certain practical and philosophical similarities, I will not deny it. These men and women have everything they want on this earth, and when they leave it, their families—wives, children, husbands—will have more than they ever need. Isn't that the dream? With over five hundred companies, computers can select a handful of people willing and capable of entering into the arrangement. A simple extension of the dream, Mr. Scofield."

"Pretty damned extended."

"Not really. Far more executives collapse from heart seizure than from violence. Read the daily obituaries. But I'm sure this is only one of many questions. May I send a car for you?"

"You may not."

"There's no cause for hostility."

"I'm not hostile, I'm cautious. Basically I'm a coward. I've set a schedule and I intend to stick with it. I'll get there at exactly eleven-thirty; you talk, I'll listen. At precisely twelve-fifteen, I'll walk out with the girl and the Russian. A signal will be given, we'll get into the car and drive to your main gate. That's when you'll get the X-rays and we get away. If there's the slightest deviation, the X-rays will disappear. They'll show up somewhere else."

"We have a right to examine them," protested Guiderone. "For accuracy and spectroanalysis; we want to make sure no duplicates were made. We *must* have time for that."

The Shepherd Boy bit; the omission of the examination was the weakness Guiderone quite naturally pounced upon. The huge electronic iron gate had to be opened and stay open. If it remained shut, all the troops and all the diversions that could be mounted would not prevent a man firing a rifle into the car. Bray hesitated. "Fair enough. Have equipment and a technician down at the gatehouse. Verification will take two or three minutes, but the gate has to remain open while it's being done."

"Very well."

"By the way," added Scofield, "I meant what I said to your son—"

"You mean Senator Appleton, I believe."

"Believe it. You'll find the X-rays intact, no light-marks of duplication. I won't get killed for that."

"I'm convinced. But I find a weakness in these arrangements."

"A weakness? . . ." Bray felt cold.

"Yes. Eleven-thirty to twelve-fifteen is only forty-five minutes. That's not much time for us to talk. For me to talk and you to listen."

Scofield breathed again. "If you're convincing, I'll know where to find you in the morning, won't I?"

Guiderone laughed softly in his eerily high-pitched voice. "Of course. So simple. You're a logical man."

"I try to be. Eleven-thirty then." Bray hung up.

He had *done* it! Every system had a backup system, every backup an alternative. The exchange was covered on all flanks.

It was 11:29 when he drove through the gates of Appleton Hall and entered the drive that curved up past the carriage house to the walled estate on the crest of the hill. As he drove by the cavernous garage of the carriage house, he was surprised to see a number of limousines. Between ten and twelve uniformed chauffeurs were talking; they were men who knew each other. They had been here before together.

The wall surrounding the enormous main house was more for effect than protection; it was barely eight feet high, designed to look far higher from below. Joshua Appleton, the first, had erected an expensive plaything. One-third castle, one-third fortress, one-third functional estate with an incredible view of Boston. The lights of the city flickered in the distance; the rain had stopped, leaving a chilly translucent mist in the air.

Bray saw two men in the glare of his headlights; the one on the right signaled him to stop in front of a separation in the wall. He did so; the path beyond the wall was bordered by two heavy chains suspended from thick iron posts, the door at the end set in an archway. All that was missing was a portcullis, deadly spikes to come crashing down with the severing of a rope.

Bray got out of the car and was immediately shoved over the hood, every pocket, every area of his body searched for weapons. Flanked by the guards, he was escorted to the door in the archway and admitted.

At first full glance, Scofield understood why Nicholas Guiderone had to possess the Appleton estate. The staircase, the tapestries, the chandeliers . . . the sheer magnificence of the great hall was breathtaking. The nearest thing to it Bray could imagine was the burned-out skeleton in Porto Vecchio that once had been the Villa Matarese.

"Come this way, please," said the guard on his right, opening a door. "You have three minutes with the guests."

Antonia ran across the room into his arms, her tears moistening his cheeks, the strength of her embrace desperate. "My darling! You've come for us!"

"*Shhh.* . . ." He held her. *Oh, God, he held her!* "We haven't time," he said softly. "In a little while we're going to walk out of here. Everything's going to be all right. We're going to be free."

"He wants to talk to you," she whispered. "Quickly."

"What?" Scofield opened his eyes and looked beyond Toni. Across the room Taleniekov sat rigidly in an armchair. The Russian's face was pale, so pale it was like chalk, the left side of his head taped; his ear and half his cheek had been blown away. His neck and shoulder blade were also bandaged, encased in a T-squared metal brace; he could barely move them. Bray held Antonia's hand and approached. Taleniekov was dying. "We're getting out of here," said Scofield. "We'll take you to a hospital. It'll be all right."

The Russian shook his head slowly, painfully, deliberately.

"He can't talk, darling." Toni touched Vasili's right cheek. "He has no voice."

"*Jesus*. What did they . . . ? Never mind, in forty-five minutes we're driving out of here."

Again Taleniekov shook his head; the Russian was trying to tell him something.

"When the guards were helping him down the staircase, he had a convulsion," said Antonia. "It was terrible; they were pulled down with him and were furious. They kept hitting him—and he's in such pain."

"They were pulled down . . . ?" asked Bray, wondering, looking at Taleniekov.

The Russian nodded, reaching under his shirt to the belt beneath. He pulled out a gun and shoved it across his legs toward Scofield.

"He fell all right," whispered Bray, smiling, kneeling down and taking the weapon. "You can't trust these Commie bastards." Then he shifted the Russian, putting his lips close to Taleniekov's right ear. "Everything's clean. We've got men outside. I've set explosive charges all around the hill. They want the proof I've got; we'll get out."

The KGB man once more shook his head. Then he stopped, his eyes wide, gesturing for Scofield to watch his lips.

The words were formed; *Pazhar . . . sigda pazhar.*

Bray translated. "Fire, always fire?"

Taleniekov nodded, then formed other words, a barely audible whisper now emerging. "*Zazhiganiye . . . pazhar.*"

"Explosions? After the explosions, fire? Is that what you're saying?"

Again Taleniekov nodded, his eyes beseeching.

"You don't understand," said Bray. "We're covered."

The Russian once more shook his head, now violently. Then he raised his hand, two fingers across his lips.

"A cigarette?" asked Scofield. Vasili nodded. Bray took the pack out of his pocket along with a book of matches. Taleniekov waved away the cigarettes and grabbed the matches.

The door opened; the guard spoke sharply. "That's it. Mr. Guiderone's waiting for you. They'll be here when you're finished."

"They'd better be." Scofield rose to his feet, hiding the gun in his belt beneath his raincoat. He gripped Antonia's hand and walked with her to the door. "I'll be back in a while. No one's going to stop us."

Nicholas Guiderone sat behind the desk in his library, his large head with the fringe of white hair supporting an old man's face, the pale skin taut, receding into the temples and stretched, sinking into the hollows that held his dark, shining eyes. There was a gnomelike quality about him; it was not hard to think of him as the Shepherd Boy.

"Would you care to reconsider your schedule, Mr. Scofield?" asked Guiderone in his high, somewhat breathless voice, not looking at Bray, but instead studying papers. "Forty minutes is really very little time, and I've got a great deal to tell you."

"You can tell me some other time, perhaps. Tonight the schedule stands."

"I see." The old man looked up, now staring at Scofield. "You think we've done terrible things, don't you?"

"I don't know what you've done."

"Certainly you do. We've had nearly four full days with the Russian. His monologues were not voluntary, but with chemical assistance, the words were there. You've uncovered the pattern of huge companies linked across the world; you've perceived that through these companies we have funneled sums of money to terrorist groups everywhere. Incidentally, you're quite right. I doubt there's an effective group of fanatics anywhere that has not benefited from us. You perceive all this but you can't understand why. It's at your fingertips, but it eludes you."

"At my fingertips?"

"The words are yours. The Russian used them, but they were yours. Under chemical inducement, multilingual subjects speak the language of their sources. . . . *Paralysis,* Mr. Scofield. Governments must be paralyzed. Nothing achieves this more rapidly or more completely than the rampant global chaos of what we call terrorism."

"Chaos. . . ." Bray whispered; *that* was the word he kept coming back to, never sure why. *Chaos.* Clashing bodies in space. . . .

"Yes. Chaos!" repeated Guiderone, his startling eyes two shining black stones reflecting the light of the desk lamp. "When the chaos is complete, when civilian and military authorities are impotent, admitting they cannot destroy a thousand vanishing wolf packs with tanks and warheads and tactical weapons, then men of reason will move in. The period of violence will at last be over and this world can go about the business of living productively."

"In a nuclear ashheap?"

"There'll be no such consequences. We've tested the controls; we have men at them."

"What the hell are you talking about?"

"Governments, Mr. Scofield!" shouted Guiderone, his eyes on fire. "Governments are obsolete! They can no longer be permitted to function as they have functioned throughout history. If they do, this planet will not see the next century. Governments as we have known them are no longer viable entities. They must be replaced."

"By whom? With what?"

The old man softened his voice; it became hollow, hypnotic. "By a new breed of philosopher-kings, if you like. Men who understand this world as it has truly emerged, who measure its potential in terms of resources, technology and productivity, who care not one whit about the color of a man's skin, or the heritage of his ancestors, or what idols he may pray to. Who care only about his full productive potential as a human being. And his contribution to the marketplace."

"My God," said Bray. "You're talking about the conglomerates."

"Does it offend you?"

"Not if I owned one."

"Very good." Guiderone broke into a short jackal-like laugh; it disappeared instantly. "But that's a limited point of view. There are those among us who thought you of all people would understand. You've seen the other futility; you've lived it."

"By choice."

"Very, very good. But that presumes there is no choice in our structure. Untrue. A man is free to develop his full potential; the greater his productivity, the greater his freedom and rewards."

"Suppose he doesn't want to be productive? As you define it?"

"Then obviously there's a lesser reward for the lesser contribution."

"Who *does* define it?"

"Trained units of management personnel, using all the technology developed in modern industry."

"I guess it'd be a good idea to get to know them."

"Don't waste time with sarcasm. Such teams operate daily all over the world. The international companies are not in business to lose money or forfeit profits. The system *works.* We prove it every day. The new society will function within a competitive, non-violent structure. Governments can no longer guarantee that; they're on nuclear collision courses everywhere. But the Chrysler Corporation does not make war on Volkswagen; no planes fill the skies to wipe out factories and whole towns centered on one or the other company. The new world will be committed to the marketplace, to the developing of resources and technology that ensure the productive survival of mankind. There's no other way. The multinational community is proof; it is aggressive, highly competitive, but it is non-violent. It bears no arms."

"Chaos," said Bray. "The clashing of bodies in space . . . destruction before the creation of order."

"Yes, Mr. Scofield. The period of violence before the permanent era of tranquility. But governments and their leaders do not relinquish their responsibilities easily. Alternatives must be given men whose backs are to the wall."

"Alternatives?"

"In Italy, we control nearly twenty percent of the Parliament. In Bonn, twelve percent of the Bundestag; in Japan, almost thirty-one percent of the Diet. Could we have done this without the Brigate Rosse or Baader-Meinhof or the Red Army of Japan? We grow in authority every month. With each act of terrorism we are closer to our objective: the total absence of violence."

"That wasn't what Guillaume de Matarese had in mind seventy years ago."

"It's much closer than you think. The *padrone* wanted to destroy the corruptors in governments, which all too frequently meant entire governments themselves. He gave us the structure, the methods—hired assassins to pit political factions against adversaries everywhere. He provided the initial fortune to put it all in motion; he showed us the way to chaos. All that remained was to put something in its place. We have found it. We'll save this world from itself. There can be no greater cause."

"You're convincing," said Scofield. "I think we may have a basis for talking further."

"I'm glad you think so," answered Guiderone, his voice suddenly cold again. "It's gratifying to know one is convincing, but much more interesting to watch the reactions of a liar."

"Liar?"

"You could have been part of this!" Once more the old man shouted. "After that night in Rock Creek Park, I myself convened the council. I told it to reassess, re-evaluate! Beowulf Agate could be of incalculable value! The Russian was useless, but not *you*. The information you possessed could make a mockery of Washington's moral positions. I myself would have made you director of all security! On my instructions, we tried for weeks to reach you, bring you in, make you one of us. It is, of course, no longer possible. You're *relentless* in your *deceptions!* In short words, you cannot be trusted. You can *never* be trusted!"

Bray sat forward. The Shepherd Boy was a maniac; it was in the maniacal eyes set in the hollows of his pale, gaunt skull. He was a man capable of quiet, seemingly logical discourse, but irrationality ruled him. He was a bomb; a bomb had to be controlled. "I wouldn't forget the purpose of my coming here, if I were you."

"Your *purpose?* By all means it will be achieved. You want the woman? You want Taleniekov? They're yours! You'll be together, I assure you. You will be taken from this house and driven far away, never to be heard from again."

"Let's deal, Guiderone. Don't make any foolish mistakes. You have a son who can be the next President of the United States—as long as he's Joshua Appleton. But he's not, and I have the X-rays to prove it."

"The *X-rays!*" roared Guiderone. "You *ass!*" He pressed a button on his desk console and spoke. "Bring him in," he said. "Bring in our esteemed guest." The Shepherd Boy sat back in his chair. The door behind Scofield opened.

Bray turned, mind and body suspended in pain at what he saw.

Seated in a wheelchair, his eyes glazed, his gentle face bruised, Robert Winthrop was brought through the door by his chauffeur of twenty years. Stanley smiled, his expression arrogant. Scofield sprang up; the chauffeur raised his hand from behind the wheelchair. In it was a gun.

"Years ago," said Guiderone, "a marine combat sergeant was sentenced to spend the greater part of his life in prison. We found more productive work for a man of his skills. It was necessary that the benign elder statesman whom everyone in Washington sought out for comfort and advice be watched very thoroughly. We learned a great deal."

Bray looked away from the battered Winthrop and stared at Stanley. "Congratulations, you . . . *bastard!* What did you do? Pistol-whip him?"

"He didn't want to come," Stanley said, his smile vanishing. "He fell."

Scofield started forward; the chauffeur raised the gun higher, aiming at Bray's head. "I'm going to talk to him," said Scofield, disregarding the weapon, kneeling at Winthrop's feet. Stanley glanced at the Shepherd Boy; Bray could see Guiderone nod consent. "Mr. Ambassador?"

"Brandon. . . ." Winthrop's voice was weak, his tired eyes sad. "I'm afraid I wasn't much help. They told the President I was ill. There are no soldiers outside, no command post, no one waiting for you to strike a match and drive to the gate. I failed you."

"The envelope?"

"Bergeron thinks I have it; he knows Stanley, you see. He took the next plane back to Boston. I'm sorry, Brandon. I'm very, very sorry. About so many things." The old man glanced up at the ex-marine he had befriended for so many years, then back at Scofield. "I've heard the gospel of trash, according to Nicholas Guiderone. Do you know what they've done? My *God,* do you know what they've *done?*"

"They haven't done it yet," said Bray.

"Next January they'll have the White House! The administration will be *their* administration!"

"It won't happen."

"It *will* happen!" shouted Guiderone. "And the world will be a better place. *Everywhere!* The period of violence will stop—a thousand years of productive tranquility will take its place!"

"A *thousand years?* . . ." Scofield got to his feet. "Another maniac said that once. Is it going to be your own personal thousand-year Reich?"

"Parallels are meaningless, labels irrelevant! There's no connection." The Shepherd Boy rose behind his desk, his eyes again on fire. "In our world, nations can keep their leaders, people their identities. But governments will be controlled by the *companies. Everywhere.* The values of the marketplace will link the peoples of the world!"

Bray caught the word and it revolted him. *"Identities?* In your world there *are* no identities! We're numbers and symbols on computers! Circles and squares."

"We must forfeit degrees of self for the continuity of peace."

"Then we are *robots!"*

"But alive. Functioning!"

"How? Tell me *how?* 'You, there! you're not a person anymore; you're a *factor.* You're X or Y or Z, and whatever you do is measured and stored on wheels of tape by experts trained to evaluate *factors.* Go on, *factor!* Be productive or the experts will take your loaf of bread away . . . or the shiny new car!' " Scofield paused in a fever. "You're wrong, Guiderone. *So* wrong. Give me an imperfect place where I know who I am."

"Find it in the next world!" screamed the Shepherd Boy. "You'll be there soon enough!"

Bray felt the weight in his belt—the gun supplied by the dying Taleniekov.

The visitor to Appleton Hall had been searched thoroughly for weapons, none found, yet one provided by his old enemy. The decision to make a final gesture was clinical; there was no hope after all. But before he tried to kill and was killed, he would see Guiderone's face when he told him. "You said before that I was a liar, but you have no idea how extensive my lies were. You think you have the X-rays, don't you?"

"We know we have them."

"So do others."

"Really?"

"Yes, really. Have you ever heard of an Alpha Twelve duplicating machine? It's one of the finest pieces of equipment ever designed. It's the only copier made that can take an X-ray negative and turn out a positive print. A print so defined it's acceptable as evidence in a court of law. I separated the four top X-rays off both the master sheets from Andover, made copies, and sent them to five different men in Washington! You're finished, you're through! They'll see to it."

"And this has gone on long enough." Guiderone came around his desk. "We're in the middle of a conference and you've taken up enough time."

"I think you'd better listen!"

"And I think you should walk over to that drape, and pull the cord. You will see our conference room, but those inside will not see you. . . . I'm sure I don't have to explain the technology. You've been so anxious to meet the Council of the Matarese, do so now. Not all are in attendance tonight, and not all are equal, but there's a fair gathering. Help yourself. Please."

Bray crossed to the drapery, felt the cord, and pulled it downward. The curtains parted, showing a huge room with a long oval conference table around which were seated twenty-odd men. There were decanters of brandy in front of each place setting along with pads, pencils, and pitchers of water. The lighting came from crystal chandeliers, swelled by a yellowish glow from the far end of the room where a fire was blazing. It could have been the enormous dining hall of the Villa Matarese, described in such detail by a blind woman in the mountains above Porto Vecchio. Scofield nearly found himself looking for a balcony and a frightened girl of seventeen hiding in the shadows.

But his eyes were drawn to the forty-foot wall behind the table. Between two enormous tapestries linked at the top border was a map of the world. A man with a pointer in his hand was addressing the others from a small platform; all eyes were on him.

The man was in the uniform of the United States Army. He was the Chairman of the Joint Chiefs of Staff.

"I see you recognize the general in front of the map." The Shepherd Boy's voice once more proved the blind woman's words: crueler than the wind. "His presence I believe explains the death of Anthony Blackburn. Perhaps I should introduce you to a few of the others, in *absentia.* . . . In the center of the table, directly below the platform, is the Secretary of State, next to him the Soviet Ambassador. Across from the Ambassador is the director of the Central Intelligence Agency; he seems to be having a side conversation with the Soviet Commissar for Planning and Development. One man you might be interested in is missing. He didn't belong, you see, but he telephoned the CIA after receiving a very strange telephone call routed through Lisbon. The President's chief advisor on foreign affairs. He's had an accident; his mail is being intercepted, the last X-rays no doubt in our hands by now. . . . Need I go on?" Guiderone started to pull the cord, shutting out the window.

Scofield put up his hand; the curtain arced before closing. He was not looking at the men at the table; the message was clear. He was looking at a guard stationed at a small recessed door to the right of the fireplace. The man stood at attention, his eyes forward. In his hand was a .30 caliber, magazine-loaded submachine gun.

Taleniekov had known about these betrayals at the highest levels. He had heard the words spoken by others as they had inserted the needles that further ebbed his life away.

His former enemy had tried to give him his last chance to live. *His last chance.* What were the words?

Pazhar . . . sigda pazhar! Zizhiganiye pazhar!

When the explosions begin, fire will follow.

He was not sure what he meant, but he knew it was the path he had to follow. They were the best there were. One trusted the only professional on earth who was one's equal.

And that meant exercising the control his equal would demand. No false moves now. Stanley stood by Winthrop's wheelchair, his gun leveled at Bray. If somehow he could turn, twist, get the weapon from under his raincoat. . . . He looked down at Winthrop, his attention caught by the old man's eyes. Winthrop was trying to tell him something, just as Taleniekov had tried to tell him something. It was in the eyes; the old man kept shifting them to his right. That was it! Stanley was *by* the wheelchair now, not *behind* it. In tiny, imperceptible movements, Winthrop was edging his chair around; he was going to go after Stanley's gun! His eyes were telling him that. They were also telling him to *keep talking*.

Scofield glanced unobtrusively at his watch. There were six minutes left before the sequence of explosions began. He needed three for preparation; that left three minutes to take out Stanley and bring in another. One hundred and eighty seconds. *Keep talking!*

He turned to the monster at his side. "Do you remember when you killed him? When you pulled the trigger that night at Villa Matarese?"

Guiderone stared at him. "It was not a moment to be forgotten. It was my destiny. So the whore of Villa Matarese is alive."

"Not any longer."

"No? That was not in the pages you sent to Winthrop. She was killed then?"

"By the legend. *Per nostro circolo.*"

The old man nodded. "Words that long ago meant one thing, now something else entirely. They guard the grave still."

"They still fear it. That grave's going to kill them all one of these days."

"The warning of Guillaume de Matarese." Guiderone started back to his desk. *Keep talking. Winthrop was pressing the wheels of the chair, each press an inch.*

"Warning or prophecy?" asked Bray quickly.

"They're often interchangeable, aren't they?"

"They called you the Shepherd Boy."

Guiderone turned. "Yes, I know. It was only partially true. As a child I took my turn herding the flocks, but the occasions diminished. The priests demanded it; they had other plans for me."

"The priests?"

Winthrop moved again.

"I had astonished them. By the time I was seven years of age I knew and understood the catechism better than they did. By eight years I could read and write in Latin; before I was ten I could debate the most complex issues of theology and dogma. The priests saw me as the first Corsican to be sent to the Vatican, to achieve high office . . . perhaps the highest. I would bring great honor to their parishes. Those simple priests in the hills of Porto Vecchio perceived my genius before I did. They spoke to the *padrone,* petitioning him to sponsor my studies. . . . Guillaume de Matarese did so in ways far beyond their comprehension."

Forty seconds. Winthrop was within two feet of the gun. Keep talking!

"Matarese made his arrangements with Appleton then? Joshua Appleton, the Second."

"America's industrial expansion was extraordinary. It was the logical place for a gifted young man with a fortune at his disposal."

"You were married? You had a son."

"I bought a vessel, the most perfectly formed female through which to bear children. The design was always there."

"Including the death of young Joshua Appleton?"

"An accident of war and destiny. The decision was a result of the captain's own exploits, not part of the original design. It was, instead, an unparalleled opportunity to be seized upon. I think we've said enough."

Now! Winthrop lunged out of the chair, his hands gripping Stanley's gun, pulling it to him, every ounce of his strength clawing at the weapon, refusing to let it go.

It fired. Bray pulled out his own gun, aiming it at the chauffeur. Winthrop's body arched in the air, his throat blown away. Scofield squeezed the trigger once; it was all he needed. Stanley fell.

"Stay away from that desk!" yelled Bray.

"You were *searched!* It's not possible. *Where? . . .*"

"From a better man than any computer of yours could ever find!" said Scofield, looking briefly in anguish at the dead Winthrop. "Just as he was."

"You'll never get out!"

Bray sprang forward, grabbing Nicholas Guiderone by the throat, pushing him against the desk. "You're going to do what I tell you to do or I'll blow your eyes out!" He shoved the pistol up into the hollow of Guiderone's right eye.

"Do *not* kill me!" commanded the overlord of the Matarese. "The value of my life is too extraordinary! My work is not *finished;* it must be finished before I die!"

"You're everything in this world I hate," said Scofield, jamming the gun into the old man's skull. "I don't have to tell you the odds. Every second you go on living means you might get another. Do as I say. I'm going to press the button— the same button you pressed before. You're going to give the following order. Say it right or you won't ever say anything more. You tell whoever answers: 'Send in the guard from the conference room, the one with the submachine gun.' Have you got that?" He shoved Guiderone's head down over the console and pressed the button.

"Send the guard in from the conference room." The words were rushed, but the fear was not audible. "The one with the submachine gun."

Scofield viced his left arm around Guiderone's neck, dragged him over to the drapes, and pulled them open. Through the glass, across the conference room, a man could be seen approaching the guard. The guard nodded, angled his weapon to the floor, and walked rapidly across the room toward the archway exit.

"Per nostro circolo," whispered Bray. He yanked up with all his strength, the vise around Guiderone's throat clamping shut, crushing bone and cartilage. There was a snap, an expulsion of breath. The old man's eyes protruded from their sockets, his neck broken. The Shepherd Boy was dead.

Scofield ran across the room to the door, pressing his back against the wall by the hinges. The door opened; he saw the angled weapon first, the figure of the guard a split second later. Bray kicked the door closed, both his hands surging forward toward the man's throat.

The harassed desk sergeant at the precinct on Boylston Street looked down at the thin, prim-looking woman whose mouth was pursed, eyes narrowed in disapproval. He held the envelope in his hands.

"Okay, lady, you've delivered it and I've got it. Okay? The phones are a little busy tonight, okay? I'll get to it soon's I can, okay?"

"Not 'okay,' Sergeant . . . Witkowski," said the woman, reading the name on the desk sign. "The citizens of Boston will not stand idly by while their rights are being abridged by criminal elements. We are rising up in justifiable outrage, and our cries have not gone unheeded. You are being watched, Sergeant! There are those who understand our distress and they are testing you. I'd advise you not to be so cavalier—"

"Okay, *okay."* The sergeant tore open the envelope, and pulled out a sheet of yellow paper. He unfolded it and read the words printed in large blue letters. "Jesus Christ on a fuckin' *raft,"* he said quietly, his eyes suddenly widening in astonishment. He looked down at the disapproving woman as if he were seeing her for the first time. As he stared, he reached over to a button on the desk; he pressed it repeatedly.

"Sergeant, I strenuously object to your profanity. . . ."

Above every visible door in the precinct house, red lights began flashing on and off; from deep within, the sound of an alarm bell echoed off the walls of unseen rooms and corridors. In seconds, doors began opening and helmeted men came out, hastily donned two-inch shields of canvas and steel strapped over their chests.

"*Grab her!*" shouted the sergeant. "Pin her arms! Throw her into the bomb room!"

Seven police officers converged on the woman. A precinct lieutenant came running out of his office. "What the hell is it, Sergeant?"

"Look at this!"

The lieutenant read the words on the yellow paper. "Oh, my *Jesus!*"

To the Fascist Pigs of Boston, Protectors of the Alabaster Bride.
Death to the Economic Tyrants! Death to Appleton Hall!
As Pigs Read This Our Bombs Will Do What
Our Pleas Cannot. Our Suicide Brigades Are
Positioned To Kill All Who Flee The Righteous
Holocaust. Death to Appleton Hall!
Signed:
    The Third World Army of Liberation and Justice

The lieutenant issued his instructions. "Guiderone's got guards all around that place; reach the house! Then call Brookline, tell them what's going down, and raise every patrol car we've got in the vicinity of Jamaica Way; send them over." The officer paused, peering at the yellow page with the precise blue letters printed on it, then added harshly, "*Goddamn* it! Get Central Headquarters on the line. I want their best SWAT team dispatched to Appleton Hall." He started back to his office, pausing again to look in disgust at the woman being propelled through a door, arms pulled, stretched away from her sides, prodded by men with padded shields and helmets. "Third World Army of Liberation and Justice! Freaked-out bastards! *Book her!*" he roared.

Scofield dragged the guard's body across the room, concealing it behind Guiderone's desk. He raced over to the dead Shepherd Boy, and for the briefest of moments, just stared at the arrogant face. If it were possible to kill beyond killing, Bray would do so now. He pulled Guiderone to the far corner, throwing his body in a crumpled heap. He then stopped at Winthrop's corpse, wishing there was time to somehow say goodbye.

He grabbed the guard's submachine gun off the floor and ran over to the drapes. He pulled them open and looked at his watch. Fifty seconds to go until the explosions would begin. He checked the weapon in his hands; all clips were full. He looked through the window into the conference room, seeing what he had not seen before because the man had not been there before.

The Senator had arrived. All eyes were now on him, the magnetic presence mesmerizing the entire room; the easy grace, the worn, still-handsome face giving each man his attention, if only for an instant—telling that man he was special. And each man was seduced by the raw power of power; this was the next President of the United States and he was one of *them.*

For the first time in all the years Scofield had seen that face, he saw what a destroyed, alcoholic mother saw: it was a mask. A brilliantly conceived, ingeniously programmed mask . . . and mind.

Twelve seconds.

There was a burst of static from a speaker on the desk. A voice erupted.

"Mr. Guiderone, we must interrupt! We've had calls from the Boston and Brookline police! There are reports of an armed attack on Appleton Hall. Men calling themselves the Third World Army of Liberation and Justice. We have no such organization on any list, sir. Our patrols are alerted. The police want everyone to stay. . . ."

Two seconds.

The news had been relayed to the conference room. Men leaped up from chairs, gathering papers. Their own particular panic was breaking out: how would the presence of such men be explained? Who would explain it?

One second.

Bray heard the first explosion beyond the walls of Appleton Hall. It was in the distance, far down the hill, but unmistakable. The sound of rapid-fire weapons followed; men were shooting at the source of the first explosion.

Inside the conference room, the panic mounted. The *consiglieri* of the Matarese were rushing around, a single guard at the archway exit poised with his submachine gun leveled through the arch. Suddenly Scofield realized what the powerful men were doing: they were throwing papers and pads and maps into the fire at the end of the room.

It was his moment; the guard would be first, but merely the first.

Bray smashed the window with the barrel of his automatic weapon and opened fire. The guard spun as the bullets caught him. His submachine gun was on rapid-repeat; the death-pressure of his trigger finger caused the gun to erupt wildly, the spray of .30 caliber shells flying out of the ejector, walls and chandeliers and men bursting, exploding, collapsing under their impacts. Screams of death and shrieks of horror filled the room.

Scofield knew his targets, his eye rehearsed over a lifetime of violence. He smashed the jagged fragments of glass and raised the weapon to his shoulder. He squeezed the trigger in rapidly defined, reasonably aimed sequences. One step— one death—at a time.

The bursts of gunfire exploded through the window frame. The general fell, the pointer in his hand lacerating his face as he collapsed. The Secretary of State cowered at the side of the table; Scofield blew his head off. The director of the Central Intelligence Agency raced his counterpart from the National Security Council toward the arch, leaping over bodies in their hysteria. Bray caught them both. The director's throat was a mass of blood; the NSC chairman raised his hands to a forehead that was no longer there.

Where was he? He of all men had to be found!

There he was!

The Senator was crouched below the conference table in front of the roaring fire. Scofield took the aim of his life and squeezed the trigger. The spray of bullets exploded the wood, some *had* to penetrate. They did! The Senator fell back, then rose to his feet. Bray fired another burst; the Senator spun into the fireplace, then sprang back out, fire and blood covering his body. He raced blindly forward, then to his left, grabbing the tapestry on the wall as he fell.

The tapestry caught fire; the Senator in his collapse of death pulled it off the wall. The huge cloth arced down in flames over the conference table. The fire spread, flames leaping to every corner of the enormous room.

Fire!

After the explosions. Fire!

Taleniekov.

Scofield ran from the window. He had done what he had to do; it was the moment to do what he so desperately *wanted* to do. If it were possible; if there was any hope at *all.* He stopped in front of the door, checking the remaining ammunition; he had conserved it well. The third and fourth charges had detonated at the base of the hill. The fifth and sixth were timed to explode within seconds.

The fifth came; he yanked the door back, lunging through, weapon leveled. He heard the sixth explosion. Two guards at the cathedral-like entrance doors sprang from the outside path into view. Bray fired two bursts; the guards of the Matarese fell.

He raced to the door of the room that held Antonia and Taleniekov. It was locked.

"Stand way back! It's me!" He fired five rounds into the wood around the lock casing; it splintered. He kicked the heavy door open; it crashed back against the wall. He ran in.

Taleniekov was out of the chair kneeling by the couch at the far end of the room, Toni beside him. Both were working furiously, tearing pillows out of slipcovers. Tearing . . . *pillows?* What were they *doing?* Antonia looked up and shouted.

"Quickly! Help us!"

"What?" He raced over.

"Pazhar!" The Russian had to force the voice; it emerged now as a whispered roar.

Six pillows were free of their cases. Toni got to her feet, throwing five of the pillows around the room.

"Now!" said Taleniekov, handing her the matches he had taken from Bray earlier. She ran to the farthest pillow, struck a match and held it to the soft fabric. It caught fire instantly. The Russian held out his hand for Scofield. "Help me . . . get *up!*"

Bray pulled him off the floor; Taleniekov clutched the last pillow to his chest.

They heard the seventh explosion in the distance; staccato gunfire followed, piercing the screams from inside the house.

"Come on!" yelled Scofield, putting his arm around the Russian's waist. He looked over at Toni; she had set fire to the fourth pillow. Flames and smoke were filling the room. "Come *on!* We're getting out!"

"No!" whispered Taleniekov. "You! She! Get me to the *door!*" The Russian held the pillow and lurched forward.

The great hall of the house was dense with smoke, flames from the inner conference room surging beneath doors and through archways, as men raced up the staircase to windows, vantage points—high ground—to aim their weapons at invaders.

A guard spotted them; he raised his submachine gun.

Scofield fired first; the man arched backward, blown off his feet.

"Listen to me!" gasped Taleniekov. "Always *pazhar!* With you it is sequence, with me it is fire!" He held up the soft pillow. "Light this! I will have the race of my life!"

"Don't be a fool." Bray tried to take the pillow away; the Russian would not permit it.

"Nyet!" Taleniekov stared at Scofield; a final plea was in his eyes. "If I could, I would not care to live like this. Neither would you. Do this for me, Beowulf. I would do it for you."

Bray returned the Russian's look. "We've worked together," he said simply. "I'm proud of that."

"We were the best there were." Taleniekov smiled and raised his hand to Scofield's cheek. "Now, my friend. Do what I would do for you."

Bray nodded and turned to Antonia; there were tears in her eyes. He took the book of matches from her hand, struck one, and held it beneath the pillow.

The flames leapt up. The Russian spun in place, clutching the fire to his chest. And with the roar of a wounded animal suddenly set free from the jaws of a lethal trap, Taleniekov lunged, propelling himself into a limping run, careening off the walls and chairs, pressing the flaming pillow and himself into everything he touched—and everything he touched caught fire. Two guards raced down the staircase, seeing the three of them; before they or Scofield could fire, the Russian was on them hurling the flames and himself at them, throwing the fire into their faces.

"Skaryei!" screamed Taleniekov. "Run, Beowulf!" A burst of gunfire came upon the command, smothered by the flaming body of the Serpent; he fell, pulling both the Matarese guards with him down the staircase.

Bray grabbed Antonia by the arm and ran out to the stone path bordered by the lines of heavy, black chain. They raced through the opening in the wall into the concrete parking area; beams of floodlights shot down from the roof of Appleton Hall; men were at windows, weapons in their hands.

The eighth explosion came from below, at the base of the hill, the charge so filled with heat that the surrounding foliage burst into flames. Men at the windows smashed panes of glass and fired at the dancing light. Scofield saw that three of the other detonations had caused small brush fires. They were gifts he was grateful for; he and Taleniekov were both right. Sequence and fire, fire and sequence. Each was a diversion that could save one's life. There were no guarantees—ever—but there *was* hope.

The rented car was parked at the side of the wall about fifty yards to their right. It was in shadows, an isolated vehicle that was meant to stay there. Bray pulled Toni against the wall.

"The car over there. It's mine; it's our chance."

"They'll shoot at us!"

"The odds are better than running. There are patrols up and down the hill. On foot, they'd cut us down."

They raced along the wall. The ninth charge of dynamite lit up the sky at the northwest base of the hill. Automatic guns and single-shot weapons erupted. Suddenly, from within the growing fires of Appleton Hall a massive explosion blew out a section of the front wall. Men fell from windows, fragments of stone and steel burst into the night as half the floodlights disappeared. Scofield understood. The seat of the Matarese had its arsenals; the fires had found one.

"Let's *go!*" he yelled, pushing Antonia toward the car. She threw herself inside as he ran around the trunk toward the driver's side.

The concrete exploded all around him; from somewhere on the remaining roof a man with a submachine gun had spotted them. Bray crouched below the car, and saw the source of fire; he leveled his weapon and held the trigger steady in a prolonged burst. A scream preceded a body plummeting toward the ground. He opened the door and slid behind the wheel.

"There's no *key!*" cried Toni. "They've taken the *key!*"

"Here," said Scofield, handing her the gun, as he reached for the plastic shell of the roof light. He yanked it off; a key fell into his hand. He started the engine. "Get in the back!" he yelled. She obeyed, climbing over the seat. "Push that gun through the left window and when I spin out of here hold the trigger down! Aim high and keep firing; spray everything until I reach the first curve, but keep your head back! Can you do that?"

"I can do it!"

Bray spun the car into a U-turn, and sped across the parking area. Antonia did as she was told, the rapid explosions of the machine gun filling the car. They reached the curve of the drive, the first descent on the hill.

"Get over to the *right* window!" he ordered, careening the automobile around the curve, holding onto the wheel with such pressure that he was conscious of the ache in his arms. "In a few seconds we'll pass the carriage house; there's a garage there, men inside. If they've got guns, open fire the *same way*. Keep your head back and the trigger tight. Have you *got* that?"

"I've got that."

There *were* men; they had weapons and they were using them. The glass of the windshield shattered as a fusillade of bullets came from the open garage doors.

Antonia had rolled down the window; she now pushed the gun through the frame, held the trigger against its rim and the explosions once again vibrated through the racing automobile. Bodies lurched; screams and the shattering of glass and the screeching ricochets of bullets filled the cavernous garage of the carriage house. The last clip of ammunition was exhausted as Scofield, his face cut from the windshield fragments, came to the final two hundred yards toward the gates of Appleton Hall. There were men below, armed men, uniformed men, but they were not soldiers of the Matarese. Bray thrust his hand down to the knob of the light switch and repeatedly pushed it in and pulled it out. The headlights flickered on and off—in sequence, *always* sequence.

The gates had been forced open; he slammed his foot on the brake. The automobile skidded to a stop, tires screeching.

The police converged. Then more than police; black-suited men in paramilitary gear, men trained for a specialized warfare, the battlegrounds defined by momentary bursts of armed fanaticism. Their commander approached the car.

"Take it *easy*," he said to Bray. "You're out. Who are you?"

"Vickery. B. A. Vickery. I had business with Nicholas Guiderone. As you say . . . we got out! When that hell broke loose, I grabbed my wife and we hid in a closet. They smashed into the house, in teams, I think. Our car was outside. It was the only chance we had."

"Now calmly, Mr. Vickery, but quickly. What's happening up there?"

The tenth charge detonated from the other side of the hill, but its light was lost in the flames that were spreading across the crest of the hill.

Appleton Hall was being consumed by fire, the explosions more frequent now as more arsenals were opened, more ignited. The Shepherd Boy was fulfilling his destiny. He had found his Villa Matarese, and as his *padrone* seventy years ago, his remains would perish in its skeleton.

"What's *happening*, Mr. Vickery?"

"They're killers. They've killed everyone inside; they'll kill every one of you they can. You won't take them alive."

"Then we'll take them *dead*," said the commander, his voice filled with emotion. "They've come over here now, they've *really* come over. Italy, Germany, Mexico . . . Lebanon, Israel, Buenos Aires. Whatever made us think we were immune? . . . Pull your car out of here, Mr. Vickery. Head down the road about a quarter of a mile. There are ambulances down there. We'll get your statement later."

"Yes, sir," said Scofield, starting the engine.

They passed the ambulances at the base of Appleton Drive and turned left into the road for Boston. Soon they would cross the Longfellow Bridge into Cambridge. There was a locker on the MPTA subway platform in Harvard Square; in that locker was his attaché case.

They were free. The Serpent had died at Appleton Hall, but they were free, their freedom his gift.

Beowulf Agate had disappeared at last.

EPILOGUE

Men and women were taken into custody swiftly, quietly, no charges processed through the courts, for their crimes were beyond the sanity of the courts, beyond the tolerance of the nation. Of all nations. Each dealt with the Matarese in its own way. Where it could find them.

Heads of state across the world conferred by telephone, the normal interpreters replaced by ranking government personnel fluent in the necessary languages. The leaders professed astonishment and shock, tacitly acknowledging both the inadequacy and the infiltration of their intelligence communities. They tested one another with subtle shades of accusation, knowing the attempts were futile; they were not idiots. They probed for vulnerabilities; they all had them. Finally—tacitly—a single conclusion was agreed upon. It was the only one that made sense in these insane times.

Silence.

Each to be responsible for his own deception, none to implicate the others beyond the normal levels of suspicion and hostility. For to admit the massive global conspiracy was to admit the existence of the fundamental proposition: governments were obsolete.

They were not idiots. They were afraid.

In Washington, rapid decisions were made secretly by a handful of men.

Senator Joshua Appleton, IV, died as he had come into being. Burned to death in an automobile accident on a dark highway at night. There was a state funeral, the casket mounted in splendor in the Rotunda where another vigil took place. The words intoned befitted a man everyone knew would have occupied the White House but for the tragedy that had cut him down.

A government-owned Lockheed Tristar was sacrificed in the Colorado mountains north of Poudre Canyon, a dual engine malfunction causing the aircraft to lose altitude while crossing that dangerous range. The pilot and crew were mourned, full pensions granted their families regardless of their service longevities. But the true mourning was accompanied by a tragic lesson never to be forgotten. For it was revealed that on board the plane were three of the nation's most distinguished men, killed in the service of their country while on an inspection tour of military installations. The Chairman of the Joint Chiefs of Staff had requested his counterparts at the Central Intelligence Agency and the National Security Council to accompany him on the tour. Along with a message of presidential sorrow, an executive order was issued from the Oval Office. Never again were such ranking government personnel permitted to fly together in a single aircraft; the nation could not sustain such a grievous loss twice.

As the weeks went by, upper echelon employees of the State Department as well as numerous reporters who covered its day-to-day operations were gradually aware of an oddity. The Secretary of State had not been in evidence for a very long time. There was a growing concern as schedules were altered, trips abandoned, conferences postponed or canceled. Rumors spread throughout the capital, some quarters insisting the Secretary was involved with prolonged, secret negotiations in Peking, while others claimed he was in Moscow, close to a breakthrough on arms control. Then the rumors took on less attractive colorations; something was wrong; an explanation was required.

The President gave it on a warm afternoon in spring. He went on radio and television from a medical retreat in Moorefield, West Virginia.

"In this year of tragedy, it is my burden to bring you further sorrow. I have just said goodbye to a dear friend. A great and courageous man who understood the delicate balance required in our negotiations with our adversaries, who would not permit those adversaries to learn of his rapidly ebbing life. That extraordinary life ended only hours ago, succumbing at last to the ravages of disease. I have today ordered the flags of the Capitol . . ."

And so it went. All over the world.

The President sat back in his chair as Undersecretary Daniel Congdon walked into the Oval Office. The commander-in-chief did not like Congdon; there was a ferret-like quality about him, his overly sincere eyes concealing a dreadful ambition. But the man did his job well and that was all that mattered. Especially now, especially this job.

"What's the resolution?"

"As expected, Mr. President. Beowulf Agate rarely did the normal thing."

"He didn't lead much of a normal life, did he? I mean you people didn't expect him to, did you?"

"No, sir. He was—"

"Tell me, Congdon," interrupted the President. "Did you really try to have him killed?"

"It was a mandatory execution, sir. We considered him beyond salvage, dangerous to our men everywhere. To a degree, I still believe that."

"You'd better. He is. So that's why he insisted on negotiating with you. I'd advise you—no, I *order* you—to put such *mandatory* actions out of your mind. Is that understood?"

"Yes, Mr. President."

"I hope so. Because if it isn't, I might have to issue a mandatory sentence of my own. Now that I know how it's done."

"Understood, sir."

"Good. The resolution?"

"Beyond the initial demand, Scofield wants nothing further to do with us."

"But you know where he is."

"Yes, sir. The Caribbean. However, we don't know where the documents are."

"Don't bother to look for them; he's better than you. And leave him alone; never give him the slightest reason to think you have any interest in him. Because if you do, those documents will surface in a hundred different places at once. This government—this nation—cannot handle the repercussions. Perhaps in a few years, but not now."

"I accept that judgment, Mr. President."

"You damn well better. What did the resolution cost us and where is it buried?"

"One hundred and seventy-six thousand, four hundred and twelve dollars and eighteen cents. It was attached to a cost overrun for naval training equipment, the payment made by a CIA proprietary directly to the shipyard in Mystic, Connecticut."

The President looked out the window at the White House lawn; the blossoms on the cherry trees were dying, curling up and withering away. "He could have asked for the sky and we would have given it to him; he could have taken us for millions. Instead, all he wants is a boat and to be left alone."

March, 198—.

The fifty-eight-foot charter yawl, *Serpent*, its mainsail luffing in the island breezes, glided into its slip, the woman jumping onto the pier, rope in hand. She looped it around the forward post, securing the bow. At the stern, the bearded skipper tied off the wheel, stepped up on the gunnel and over to the dock, swinging the aft rope around the nearest post, pulling it taut, knotting it when all slack had vanished.

At midships, a pleasant-looking middle-aged couple stepped cautiously onto the pier. It was obvious they had said their goodbyes, and those goodbyes had been just a little bit painful.

"Well, vacation's over," said the man, sighing, holding his wife's arm. "We'll be back next year, Captain Vickery. You're the best charter in the islands. And thank you again, Mrs. Vickery. As always, the galley was terrific."

The couple walked up the dock.

"I'll stow the gear while you check on the supplies, okay?" said Scofield.

"All right, darling. We've got ten days before the couple from New Orleans arrive."

"Let's take a sail by ourselves," said the captain, smiling, jumping back on board the *Serpent.*

An hour and twenty minutes passed; the supplies were loaded, the weather bulletins logged and the coastal charts studied. The *Serpent* was ready for departure.

"Let's get a drink," Bray said, taking Toni's hand, walking up the sandy path into the hot St. Kitts' street. Across the way was a cafe, a shack with ancient wicker tables and chairs and a bar that had not changed in thirty years. It was a gathering place for charter boat skippers and their crews.

Antonia sat down, greeting friends, laughing with her eyes and spontaneous voice; she was liked by the rough, capable runaways of the Caribbean. She was a lady and they knew it. Scofield watched her from the bar as he ordered their drinks, remembering another waterfront café in Corsica. It was only a few years ago—another lifetime, really—but she had not changed. There was still the easy grace, the sense of presence and gentle, open humor. She was liked because she was immensely likeable; it was as simple as that.

He carried their drinks to the table and sat down. Antonia reached over to an adjacent table, borrowing a week-old Barbados newspaper. An article had caught her attention.

"Darling, look at this," she said, turning the paper and pushing it toward him, her index finger marking the column.

TRANS-COMMUNICATIONS

WINS LEGAL BATTLES OVER

CONGLOMERATE REORGANIZATION

Wash., D.C.—Combined Wire Services: After several years of ownership litigation in the federal courts, the way has been cleared for the executors of the Nicholas Guiderone estate to press ahead with reorganization plans which include significant mergers with European companies. It will be recalled that following the terrorist assault on the Guiderone mansion in Brookline, Massachusetts, when Guiderone and others holding large blocks of Trans-Comm stock were massacred, the conglomerate's line of ownership was thrown into a legal maze. It has been no secret that the Justice Department has been supportive of the executors, as, indeed, has been the Department of State. The feeling has been that while the multinational corporation has continued functioning, its lack of expansion due to unclear leadership has caused American prestige to suffer in the international marketplace.

The President, upon learning of the final legal resolutions, sent the following wire to the executors:

"It seems fitting to me that during the week that marks my first year in office, the obstructions have been removed and once again, a great American institution is in a position to export and expand American know-how and technology across the world, joining the other great companies to give us a better world. I congratulate you."

Bray shoved the paper aside. "The subtlety gets less and less, doesn't it?"

They tacked into the wind out of Bassaterre, the coast of St. Kitts receding behind them. Antonia pulled the jib taut, tied off the sheet, and climbed back to the wheel. She sat beside Scofield, running her fingers over his short, clipped beard that was more gray than dark. "Where are we going, darling?" she asked.

"I don't know," said Bray, meaning it. "With the wind for a while, if it's all right with you."

"It's all right with me." She leaned back, looking at his face, so pensive, so lost in thought. "What's going to happen?"

"It's happened. The mergers have taken over the earth," he answered, smiling. "Guiderone was right; nobody can stop it. Maybe nobody should. Let them have their day in the sun. It doesn't make any difference what I think. They'll leave me alone—leave us alone. They're still afraid."

"Of what?"

"Of people. Just people. Trim the jib, will you, please? We're spilling too much. We can make better time."

"To where?"

"Damned if I know. Only that I want to be there."

THE
BOURNE
IDENTITY

For Glynis

A very special light we all adore

With our love and deep respect

PREFACE

THE NEW YORK TIMES; FRIDAY, JULY 11, 1975; FRONT PAGE

DIPLOMATS SAID TO BE LINKED
WITH FUGITIVE TERRORIST
KNOWN AS CARLOS

PARIS, July 10—France expelled three high-ranking Cuban diplomats today in connection with the worldwide search for a man called Carlos, who is believed to be an important link in an international terrorist network.

The suspect, whose real name is thought to be Ilich Ramirez Sanchez, is being sought in the killing of two French counterintelligence agents and a Lebanese informer at a Latin Quarter apartment on June 27.

The three killings have led the police here and in Britain to what they feel is the trail of a major network of international terrorist agents. In the search for Carlos after the killings, French and British policemen discovered large arms caches that linked Carlos to major terrorism in West Germany and led them to suspect a connection between many terrorist acts throughout Europe.

Reported Seen in London

Since then Carlos has been reported seen in London and in Beirut, Lebanon. . . .

ASSOCIATED PRESS; MONDAY, JULY 7, 1975; SYNDICATED DISPATCH

A DRAGNET FOR ASSASSIN

LONDON (AP)—Guns and girls, grenades and good suits, a fat billfold, airline tickets to romantic places and nice apartments in a half dozen world capitals. This is the portrait emerging of a jet age assassin being sought in an international manhunt.

The hunt began when the man answered his doorbell in Paris and shot dead two French intelligence agents and a Lebanese informer. It has put four women into custody in two capitals, accused of offenses in his wake. The assassin himself has vanished—perhaps in Lebanon, the French police believe.

In the past few days in London, those acquainted with him have described him to reporters as good looking, courteous, well educated, wealthy and fashionably dressed.

But his associates are men and women who have been called the most dangerous in the world. He is said to be linked with the Japanese Red Army, the Organization for the Armed Arab Struggle, the West German Baader-Meinhof gang, the Quebec Liberation Front, the Turkish Popular Liberation Front, separatists in France and Spain, and the Provisional wing of the Irish Republican Army.

When the assassin traveled—to Paris, to the Hague, to West Berlin—bombs went off, guns cracked and there were kidnappings.

A breakthrough occurred in Paris when a Lebanese terrorist broke under questioning and led two intelligence men to the assassin's door in Paris on June 27. He shot all three to death and escaped. Police found his guns and notebooks containing "death lists" of prominent people.

Yesterday the London Observer said police were hunting for the son of a Venezuelan Communist lawyer for questioning in the triple slaying. Scotland Yard said, "We are not denying the report," but added there was no charge against him and he was wanted only for questioning.

The Observer identified the hunted man as Ilich Ramirez Sanchez, of Caracas. It said his name was on one of the four passports found by French police when they raided the Paris apartment where the slayings took place.

The newspaper said Ilich was named after Vladimir Ilych Lenin, founder of the Soviet state, and was educated in Moscow and speaks fluent Russian.

In Caracas, a spokesman for the Venezuelan Communist Party said Ilich is the son of a 70-year-old Marxist lawyer living 450 miles west of Caracas, but "neither father nor son belong to our party."

He told reporters he did not know where Ilich was now.

BOOK
ONE

1

The trawler plunged into the angry swells of the dark, furious sea like an awkward animal trying desperately to break out of an impenetrable swamp. The waves rose to goliathan heights, crashing into the hull with the power of raw tonnage; the white sprays caught in the night sky cascaded downward over the deck under the force of the night wind. Everywhere there were the sounds of inanimate pain, wood straining against wood, ropes twisting, stretched to the breaking point. The animal was dying.

Two abrupt explosions pierced the sounds of the sea and the wind and the vessel's pain. They came from the dimly lit cabin that rose and fell with its host body. A man lunged out of the door grasping the railing with one hand, holding his stomach with the other.

A second man followed, the pursuit cautious, his intent violent. He stood bracing himself in the cabin door; he raised a gun and fired again. And again.

The man at the railing whipped both his hands up to his head, arching backward under the impact of the fourth bullet. The trawler's bow dipped suddenly into the valley of two giant waves, lifting the wounded man off his feet; he twisted to his left unable to take his hands away from his head. The boat surged upward, bow and midships more out of the water than in it, sweeping the figure in the doorway back into the cabin, a fifth gunshot fired wildly. The wounded man screamed, his hands now lashing out at anything he could grasp, his eyes blinded by blood and the unceasing spray of the sea. There was nothing he could grab, so he grabbed at nothing; his legs buckled as his body lurched forward. The boat rolled violently leeward and the man whose skull was ripped open plunged over the side into the madness of the darkness below.

He felt rushing cold water envelop him, swallowing him, sucking him under, and twisting him in circles, then propelling him up to the surface—only to gasp a single breath of air. A gasp and he was under again.

And there was heat, a strange moist heat at his temple that seared through the freezing water that kept swallowing him, a fire where no fire should burn. There was ice, too; an icelike throbbing in his stomach and his legs and his chest, oddly warmed by the cold sea around him. He felt these things, acknowledging his own panic as he felt them. He could see his own body turning and twisting, arms and feet working frantically against the pressures of the whirlpool. He could feel, think, see, perceive panic and struggle—yet strangely there was peace. It was the calm of the observer, the uninvolved observer, separated from the events, knowing of them but not essentially involved.

Then another form of panic spread through him, surging through the heat and the ice and the uninvolved recognition. He could not submit to peace! Not yet! It would happen any second now; he was not sure what it was, but it would happen. He had to *be* there!

He kicked furiously, clawing at the heavy walls of water above, his chest burning. He broke surface, thrashing to stay on top of the black swells. Climb up! *Climb up!*

A monstrous rolling wave accommodated; he was on the crest, surrounded by pockets of foam and darkness. Nothing. Turn! *Turn!*

It happened. The explosion was massive; he could hear it through the clashing waters and the wind, the sight and the sound somehow his doorway to peace. The sky lit up like a fiery diadem and within that crown of fire, objects of all shapes and sizes were blown through the light into the outer shadows.

He had won. Whatever it was, he had won.

Suddenly he was plummeting downward again, into an abyss again. He could feel the rushing waters crash over his shoulders, cooling the white-hot heat at his temple, warming the ice-cold incisions in his stomach and his legs and. . . .

His chest. His chest was in agony! He had been struck—the blow crushing, the impact sudden and intolerable. It happened again! *Let me alone. Give me peace.*

And again!

And he clawed again, and kicked again . . . until he felt it. A thick, oily object that moved only with the movements of the sea. He could not tell what it was, but it was there and he could feel it, hold it.

Hold it! It will ride you to peace. To the silence of darkness . . . and peace.

The rays of the early sun broke through the mists of the eastern sky, lending glitter to the calm waters of the Mediterranean. The skipper of the small fishing boat, his eyes bloodshot, his hands marked with rope burns, sat on the stern gunnel smoking a Gauloise, grateful for the sight of the smooth sea. He glanced over at the open wheelhouse; his younger brother was easing the throttle forward to make better time, the single other crewman checking a net several feet away. They were laughing at something and that was good; there had been nothing to laugh about last night. Where had the storm come from? The weather reports from Marseilles had indicated nothing; if they had he would have stayed in the shelter of the coastline. He wanted to reach the fishing grounds eighty kilometers south of La Seyne-sur-Mer by daybreak, but not at the expense of costly repairs, and what repairs were not costly these days?

Or at the expense of his life, and there were moments last night when that was a distinct consideration.

"*Tu es fatigué, bein, mon frère?*" his brother shouted, grinning at him. "*Va te coucher maintenant. Laisse-moi faire.*"

"*D'accord,*" the brother answered, throwing his cigarette over the side and sliding down to the deck on top of a net. "A little sleep won't hurt."

It was good to have a brother at the wheel. A member of the family should always be the pilot on a family boat; the eyes were sharper. Even a brother who spoke with the smooth tongue of a literate man as opposed to his own coarse words. Crazy! One year at the university and his brother wished to start a *compagnie*. With a single boat that had seen better days many years ago. Crazy. What good did his books do last night? When his *compagnie* was about to capsize.

He closed his eyes, letting his hands soak in the rolling water on the deck. The salt of the sea would be good for the rope burns. Burns received while lashing equipment that did not care to stay put in the storm.

"Look! Over there!"

It was his brother; apparently sleep was to be denied by sharp family eyes.

"What is it?" he yelled.

"Port bow! There's a man in the water! He's holding on to something! A piece of debris, a plank of some sort."

The skipper took the wheel, angling the boat to the right of the figure in the water, cutting the engines to reduce the wake. The man looked as though the slightest motion would send him sliding off the fragment of wood he clung to; his hands were white, gripped around the edge like claws, but the rest of his body was limp—as limp as a man fully drowned, passed from this world.

"Loop the ropes!" yelled the skipper to his brother and the crewman. "Submerge them around his legs. Easy now! Move them up to his waist. Pull gently."

"His hands won't let go of the plank!"

"Reach down! Pry them up! It may be the death lock."

"No. He's alive . . . but barely, I think. His lips move, but there's no sound. His eyes also, though I doubt he sees us."

"The hands are free!"

"Lift him up. Grab his shoulders and pull him over. *Easy*, now!"

"Mother of God, look at his head!" yelled the crewman. "It's split open."

"He must have crashed it against the plank in the storm," said the brother.

"No," disagreed the skipper, staring at the wound. "It's a clean slice, razorlike. Caused by a bullet; he was shot."

"You can't be sure of that."

"In more than one place," added the skipper, his eyes roving over the body. "We'll head for Ile de Port Noir; it's the nearest island. There's a doctor on the waterfront."

"The Englishman?"

"He practices."

"When he can," said the skipper's brother. "When the wine lets him. He has more success with his patients' animals than with his patients."

"It won't matter. This will be a corpse by the time we get there. If by chance he lives, I'll bill him for the extra petrol and whatever catch we miss. Get the kit; we'll bind his head for all the good it will do."

"Look!" cried the crewman. "Look at his eyes."

"What about them?" asked the brother.

"A moment ago they were gray—as gray as steel cables. Now they're blue!"

"The sun's brighter," said the skipper, shrugging. "Or it's playing tricks with your own eyes. No matter, there's no color in the grave."

Intermittent whistles of fishing boats clashed with the incessant screeching of the gulls; together they formed the universal sounds of the waterfront. It was late afternoon, the sun a fireball in the west, the air still and too damp, too hot. Above the piers and facing the harbor was a cobblestone street and several blemished white houses, separated by overgrown grass shooting up from dried earth and sand. What remained of the verandas were patched latticework and crumbling stucco supported by hastily implanted pilings. The residences had seen better days a number of decades ago when the residents mistakenly believed Ile de Port Noir might become another Mediterranean playground. It never did.

All the houses had paths to the street, but the last house in the row had a path obviously more trampled than the others. It belonged to an Englishman who had come to Port Noir eight years before under circumstances no one understood or cared to; he was a doctor and the waterfront had need of a doctor. Hooks, needles and knives were at once means of livelihood as well as instruments of incapacitation. If one saw *le docteur* on a good day, the sutures were not too bad. On the other hand, if the stench of wine or whiskey was too pronounced, one took one's chances.

Tant pis! He was better than no one.

But not today; no one used the path today. It was Sunday and it was common knowledge that on any Saturday night the doctor was roaring drunk in the village, ending the evening with whatever whore was available. Of course, it was also granted that during the past few Saturdays the doctor's routine had altered; he had not been seen in the village. But nothing ever changed that much; bottles of scotch were sent to the doctor on a regular basis. He was simply staying in his house; he had been doing so since the fishing boat from La Ciotat had brought in the unknown man who was more corpse than man.

Dr. Geoffrey Washburn awoke with a start, his chin settled into his collarbone causing the odor of his mouth to invade his nostrils; it was not pleasant. He blinked, orienting himself, and glanced at the open bedroom door. Had his nap been interrupted by another incoherent monologue from his patient? No; there was no sound. Even the gulls outside were mercifully quiet; it was Ile de Port Noir's holy day, no boats coming in to taunt the birds with their catches.

Washburn looked at the empty glass and the half-empty bottle of whiskey on the table beside his chair. It was an improvement. On a normal Sunday both would be empty by now, the pain of the previous night having been spiraled out by the scotch. He smiled to himself, once again blessing an older sister in Coventry who made the scotch possible with her monthly stipend. She was a good girl, Bess was, and God knew she could afford a hell of a lot more than she sent him, but he was grateful she did what she did. And one day she would stop, the money would stop, and then the oblivions would be achieved with the cheapest wine until there was no pain at all. Ever.

He had come to accept that eventuality . . . until three weeks and five days ago when the half-dead stranger had been dragged from the sea and brought to his door by fishermen who did not care to identify themselves. Their errand was one of mercy, not involvement. God would understand; the man had been shot.

What the fishermen had not known was that far more than bullets had invaded the man's body. And mind.

The doctor pushed his gaunt frame out of the chair and walked unsteadily to the window overlooking the harbor. He lowered the blind, closing his eyes to block out the sun, then squinted between the slats to observe the activity in the street below, specifically the reason for the clatter. It was a horse-drawn cart, a fisherman's family out for a Sunday drive. Where the hell else could one see such a sight? And then he remembered the carriages and the finely groomed geldings that threaded through London's Regent Park with tourists during the summer months; he laughed out loud at the comparison. But his laughter was short-lived, replaced by something unthinkable three weeks ago. He had given up all hope of seeing England again. It was possible that might be changed now. The stranger could change it.

Unless his prognosis was wrong, it would happen any day, any hour or minute. The wounds to the legs, stomach, and chest were deep and severe, quite possibly fatal were it not for the fact the bullets had remained where they had lodged, self-cauterized and continuously cleansed by the sea. Extracting them was nowhere near as dangerous as it might have been, the tissue primed, softened, sterilized, ready for an immediate knife. The cranial wound was the real problem; not only was the penetration subcutaneous, but it appeared to have bruised the thalamus and hippocampus fibrous regions. Had the bullet entered millimeters away on either side the vital functions would have ceased; they had not been impeded, and Washburn had made a decision. He went dry for thirty-six hours, eating as much starch and drinking as much water as was humanly possible. Then he performed the most delicate piece of work he had attempted since his dismissal from Macleans Hospital in London. Millimeter by agonizing millimeter he had brush-washed the fibrous areas, then stretched and sutured the skin over the cranial wound, knowing that the slightest error with brush, needle, or clamp would cause the patient's death.

He had not wanted this unknown patient to die for any number of reasons. But especially one.

When it was over and the vital signs had remained constant, Dr. Geoffrey Washburn went back to his chemical and psychological appendage. His bottle. He had gotten drunk and he had remained drunk, but he had not gone over the edge. He knew exactly where he was and what he was doing at all times. Definitely an improvement.

Any day now, any hour perhaps, the stranger would focus his eyes and intelligible words would emerge from his lips.

Even any moment.

The words came first. They floated in the air as the early morning breeze off the sea cooled the room.

"Who's there? Who's in this room?"

Washburn sat up in the cot, moved his legs quietly over the side, and rose slowly to his feet. It was important to make no jarring note, no sudden noise or physical movement that might frighten the patient into a psychological regression. The next few minutes would be as delicate as the surgical procedures he had performed; the doctor in him was prepared for the moment.

"A friend," he said softly.

"Friend?"

"You speak English. I thought you would. American or Canadian is what I suspected. Your dental work didn't come from the UK or Paris. How do you feel?"

"I'm not sure."

"It will take awhile. Do you need to relieve your bowels?"

"What?"

"Take a crapper, old man. That's what the pan's for beside you. The white one on your left. When we make it in time, of course."

"I'm sorry."

"Don't be. Perfectly normal function. I'm a doctor, *your* doctor. My name is Geoffrey Washburn. What's yours?"

"What?"

"I asked you what your name was."

The stranger moved his head and stared at the white wall streaked with shafts of morning light. Then he turned back, his blue eyes leveled at the doctor. "I don't know."

"Oh, my God."

"I've told you over and over again. It will take time. The more you fight it, the more you crucify yourself, the worse it will be."

"You're drunk."

"Generally. It's not pertinent. But I can give you clues, if you'll listen."

"I've listened."

"No, you don't; you turn away. You lie in your cocoon and pull the cover over your mind. Hear me again."

"I'm listening."

"In your coma—your prolonged coma—you spoke in three different languages.

English, French and some goddamned twangy thing I presume is Oriental. That means you're multilingual; you're at home in various parts of the world. Think geographically. What's most comfortable for you?"

"Obviously English."

"We've agreed to that. So what's most *un*comfortable?"

"I don't know."

"Your eyes are round, not sloped. I'd say obviously the Oriental."

"Obviously."

"Then why do you speak it? Now, think in terms of association. I've written down words; listen to them. I'll say them phonetically. *Ma—kwa. Tam—kwan. Kee—sah.* Say the first thing that comes to mind."

"Nothing."

"Good show."

"What the hell do you want?"

"Something. Anything."

"You're drunk."

"We've agreed to that. Consistently. I also saved your bloody life. Drunk or not, I *am* a doctor. I was once a very good one."

"What happened?"

"The patient questions the doctor?"

"Why not?"

Washburn paused, looking out the window at the waterfront. "I was drunk," he said. "They said I killed two patients on the operating table because I was drunk. I could have gotten away with one. Not two. They see a pattern very quickly, God bless them. Don't ever give a man like me a knife and cloak it in respectability."

"Was it necessary?"

"Was what necessary?"

"The bottle."

"Yes, damn you," said Washburn softly, turning from the window. "It was and it is. And the patient is not permitted to make judgments where the physician is concerned."

"Sorry."

"You also have an annoying habit of apologizing. It's an overworked protestation and not at all natural. I don't for a minute believe you're an apologetic person."

"Then you know something I don't know."

"About you, yes. A great deal. And very little of it makes sense."

The man sat forward in the chair. His open shirt fell away from his taut frame, exposing the bandages on his chest and stomach. He folded his hands in front of him, the veins in his slender, muscular arms pronounced. "Other than the things we've talked about?"

"Yes."

"Things I said while in coma?"

"No, not really. We've discussed most of that gibberish. The languages, your knowledge of geography—cities I've never or barely heard of—your obsession for avoiding the use of names, names you want to say but won't; your propensity for confrontation—attack, recoil, hide, run—all rather violent, I might add. I frequently strapped your arms down, to protect the wounds. But we've covered all that. There are other things."

"What do you mean? What are they? Why haven't you told me?"

"Because they're physical. The outer shell, as it were. I wasn't sure you were ready to hear. I'm not sure now."

The man leaned back in the chair, dark eyebrows below the dark brown hair joined in irritation. "Now it's the physician's judgment that isn't called for. I'm ready. What are you talking about?"

"Shall we begin with that rather acceptable looking head of yours? The face, in particular."

"What about it?"

"It's not the one you were born with."

"What do you mean?"

"Under a thick glass, surgery always leaves its mark. You've been altered, old man."

"Altered?"

"You have a pronounced chin; I daresay there was a cleft in it. It's been removed. Your upper left cheekbone—your cheekbones are also pronounced, conceivably Slavic generations ago—has minute traces of a surgical scar. I would venture to say a mole was eliminated. Your nose is an English nose, at one time slightly more prominent than it is now. It was thinned ever so subtly. Your very sharp features have been softened, the character submerged. Do you understand what I'm saying?"

"No."

"You're a reasonably attractive man but your face is more distinguished by the category it falls into than by the face itself."

"Category?"

"Yes. You're the prototype of the white Anglo-Saxon people see every day on the better cricket fields, or the tennis court. Or the bar at Mirabel's. Those faces become almost indistinguishable from one another, don't they? The features properly in place, the teeth straight, the ears flat against the head—nothing out of balance, everything in position and just a little bit soft."

"Soft?"

"Well, 'spoiled' is perhaps a better word. Definitely self-assured, even arrogant, used to having your own way."

"I'm still not sure what you're trying to say."

"Try this then. Change the color of your hair, you change the face. Yes, there are traces of discoloration, brittleness, dye. Wear glasses and a mustache, you're a different man. I'd guess you were in your middle to late thirties, but you could be ten years older, or five younger." Washburn paused, watching the man's reactions, as if wondering whether or not to proceed. "And speaking of glasses, do you remember those exercises, the tests we ran a week ago?"

"Of course."

"Your eyesight's perfectly normal; you have no need of glasses."

"I didn't think I did."

"Then why is there evidence of prolonged use of contact lenses about your retinas and lids?"

"I don't know. It doesn't make sense."

"May I suggest a possible explanation?"

"I'd like to hear it."

"You may not." The doctor returned to the window and peered absently outside. "Certain types of contact lenses are designed to change the color of the eyes. And certain types of eyes lend themselves more readily than others to the device. Usually those that have a gray or bluish hue; yours are a cross. Hazel-gray in one light, blue in another. Nature favored you in this regard; no altering was either possible or required."

"Required for what?"

"For changing your appearance. Very professionally, I'd say. Visas, passport, driver's licenses—switched at will. Hair: brown, blond, auburn. Eyes—can't tamper with the eyes—green, gray, blue? The possibilities are far-ranging, wouldn't you say? All within that recognizable category in which the faces are blurred with repetition."

The man got out of the chair with difficulty, pushing himself up with his arms, holding his breath as he rose. "It's also possible that you're reaching. You could be way out of line."

"The traces are there, the markings. That's evidence."

"Interpreted by you, with a heavy dose of cynicism thrown in. Suppose I had an accident and was patched up? That would explain the surgery."

"Not the kind you had. Dyed hair and the removal of clefts and moles aren't part of a restoration process."

"You don't *know* that!" said the unknown man angrily. "There are different kinds of accidents, different procedures. You weren't there; you can't be certain."

"Good! Get furious with me. You don't do it half often enough. And while you're mad, *think*. What were you? What *are* you?"

"A salesman . . . an executive with an international company, specializing in the Far East. That could be it. Or a teacher . . . of languages. In a university somewhere. That's possible, too."

"Fine. Choose one. Now!"

"I . . . I *can't.* " The man's eyes were on the edge of helplessness.

"Because you don't believe either one."

The man shook his head. "No. Do you?"

"No," said Washburn. "For a specific reason. Those occupations are relatively sedentary and you have the body of a man who's been subjected to physical stress. Oh, I don't mean a trained athlete or anything like that; you're no jock, as they say. But your muscle tone's firm, your arms and hands used to strain and quite strong. Under other circumstances, I might judge you to be a laborer, accustomed to carrying heavy objects, or a fisherman, conditioned by hauling in nets all day long. But your range of knowledge, I daresay your intellect, rules out such things."

"Why do I get the idea that you're leading up to something? Something else."

"Because we've worked together, closely and under pressure, for several weeks now. You spot a pattern."

"I'm right then?"

"Yes. I had to see how you'd accept what I've just told you. The previous surgery, the hair, the contact lenses."

"Did I pass?"

"With infuriating equilibrium. It's time now; there's no point in putting it off any longer. Frankly, I haven't the patience. Come with me." Washburn preceded the man through the living room to the door in the rear wall that led to the dispensary. Inside, he went to the corner and picked up an antiquated projector, the shell of its thick round lens rusted and cracked. "I had this brought in with the supplies from Marseilles," he said, placing it on the small desk and inserting the plug into the wall socket. "It's hardly the best equipment, but it serves the purpose. Pull the blinds, will you?"

The man with no name or memory went to the window and lowered the blind; the room was dark. Washburn snapped on the projector's light; a bright square appeared on the white wall. He then inserted a small piece of celluloid behind the lens.

The square was abruptly filled with magnified letters.

GEMEINSCHAFT BANK
BAHNHOFSTRASSE. ZURICH.
ZERO—SEVEN—SEVENTEEN—TWELVE—ZERO—
FOURTEEN—TWENTY-SIX—ZERO

"What is it?" asked the nameless man.

"Look at it. Study it. *Think.*"

"It's a bank account of some kind."

"Exactly. The printed letterhead and address is the bank, the handwritten numbers take the place of a name, but insofar as they *are* written out, they constitute the signature of the account holder. Standard procedure."

"Where did you get it?"

"From you. This is a very small negative, my guess would be half the size of a thirty-five millimeter film. It was implanted—surgically implanted—beneath the skin above your right hip. The numbers are in your handwriting; it's your signature. With it you can open a vault in Zurich."

2

They chose the name Jean-Pierre. It neither startled nor offended anyone, a name as common to Port Noir as any other.

And books came from Marseilles, six of them in varying sizes and thicknesses, four in English, two in French. They were medical texts, volumes that dealt with injuries to the head and mind. There were cross-sections of the brain, hundreds of unfamiliar words to absorb and try to understand. *Lobus occipitalis* and *temporalis,* the *cortex* and the connecting fibers of the *corpus callosum;* the *limbic system*—specifically the *hippocampus* and *mammillary bodies* that together with the *fornix* were indispensable to memory and recall. Damaged, there was amnesia.

There were psychological studies of emotional stress that produced *stagnate hysteria* and *mental aphasia,* conditions which also resulted in partial or total loss of memory. Amnesia.

Amnesia.

"There are no rules," said the dark-haired man, rubbing his eyes in the inadequate light of the table lamp. "It's a geometric puzzle; it can happen in any combination of ways. Physically or psychologically—or a little of both. It can be permanent or temporary, all or part. No *rules!*"

"Agreed," said Washburn, sipping his whiskey in a chair across the room. "But I think we're getting closer to what happened. What I *think* happened."

"Which was?" asked the man apprehensively.

"You just said it: 'a little of both.' Although the word 'little' should be changed to 'massive.' Massive shocks."

"Massive shocks to what?"

"The physical *and* the psychological. They were related, interwoven—two strands of experience, or stimulate, that became knotted."

"How much sauce have you had?"

"Less than you think; it's irrelevant." The doctor picked up a clipboard filled with pages. "This is your history—your new history—begun the day you were brought here. Let me summarize. The physical wounds tell us that the situation in which you found yourself was packed with psychological stress, the subsequent hysteria brought on by at least nine hours in the water, which served to solidify the psychological damage. The darkness, the violent movement, the lungs barely getting air; these were the instruments of hysteria. Everything that preceded it—the hysteria—had to be erased so you could cope, survive. Are you with me?"

"I think so. The head was protecting itself."

"Not the head, the mind. Make the distinction; it's important. We'll get back to the head, but we'll give it a label. The brain."

"All right. Mind, not head . . . which is really the brain."

"Good." Washburn flipped his thumb through the pages on the clipboard. "These are filled with several hundred observations. There are the normal medicinal inserts—dosage, time, reaction, that sort of thing—but in the main they deal with *you*, the man himself. The words you use, the words you react to; the phrases you employ—when I can write them down—both rationally and when you talk in your sleep and when you were in coma. Even the way you walk, the way you talk or tense your body when startled or seeing something that interests you. You appear to be a mass of contradictions; there's a subsurface violence almost always in control, but very much alive. There's also a pensiveness that seems painful for you, yet you rarely give vent to the anger that pain must provoke."

"You're provoking it now," interrupted the man. "We've gone over the words and the phrases time and time again—"

"And we'll continue to do so," broke in Washburn, "as long as there's progress."

"I wasn't aware any progress had been made."

"Not in terms of an identity or an occupation. But we *are* finding out what's most comfortable for you, what you deal with best. It's a little frightening."

"In what way?"

"Let me give you an example." The doctor put the clipboard down and got out of the chair. He walked to a primitive cupboard against the wall, opened a drawer, and took out a large automatic handgun. The man with no memory tensed in his chair; Washburn was aware of the reaction. "I've never used this, not sure I'd know how to, but I do live on the waterfront." He smiled, then suddenly, without warning, threw it to the man. The weapon was caught in midair, the catch clean, swift, and confident. "Break it down; I believe that's the phrase."

"What?"

"Break it down. *Now.*"

The man looked at the gun. And then, in silence, his hands and fingers moved expertly over the weapon. In less than thirty seconds it was completely dismantled. He looked up at the doctor.

"See what I mean?" said Washburn. "Among your skills is an extraordinary knowledge of firearms."

"Army?" asked the man, his voice intense, once more apprehensive.

"Extremely unlikely," replied the doctor. "When you first came out of coma, I mentioned your dental work. I assure you it's not military. And, of course, the surgery, I'd say, would totally rule out any military association."

"Then what?"

"Let's not dwell on it now; let's go back to what happened. We were dealing with the mind, remember? The psychological stress, the hysteria. Not the physical brain, but the mental pressures. Am I being clear?"

"Go on."

"As the shock recedes, so do the pressures, until there's no fundamental need to protect the psyche. As this process takes place, your skills and talents will come back to you. You'll remember certain behavior patterns; you may live them out quite naturally, your surface reactions instinctive. But there's a gap and everything in those pages tell me it's irreversible." Washburn stopped and went back to his chair and his glass. He sat down and drank, closing his eyes in weariness.

"Go on," whispered the man.

The doctor opened his eyes, leveling them at his patient. "We return to the head, which we've labeled the brain. The *physical* brain with its millions upon millions of cells and interacting components. You've read the books; the fornix and the limbic system, the hippocampus fibers and the thalamus; the callosum and especially the lobotomic surgical techniques. The slightest alteration can cause dramatic changes. That's what happened to you. The damage was *physical.* It's as though blocks were rearranged, the *physical* structure no longer what it was." Again Washburn stopped.

"*And,*" pressed the man.

"The recessed psychological pressures will allow—*are* allowing—your skills and talents to come back to you. But I don't think you'll ever be able to relate them to anything in your past."

"Why? Why not?"

"Because the physical conduits that permit and transmit those memories have been altered. Physically rearranged to the point where they no longer function as they once did. For all intents and purposes, they've been destroyed."

The man sat motionless. "The answer's in Zurich," he said.

"Not yet. You're not ready; you're not strong enough."

"I will be."

"Yes, you will."

The weeks passed; the verbal exercises continued as the pages grew and the man's strength returned. It was midmorning of the nineteenth week, the day bright, the Mediterranean calm and glistening. As was the man's habit he had run for the past hour along the waterfront and up into the hills; he had stretched the distance to something over twelve miles daily, the pace increasing daily, the rests less frequent. He sat in the chair by the bedroom window, breathing heavily, sweat drenching his undershirt. He had come in through the back door, entering the bedroom from the dark hallway that passed the living room. It was simply easier; the living room served as Washburn's waiting area and there were still a few patients with cuts and gashes to be repaired. They were sitting in chairs looking frightened, wondering what *le docteur*'s condition would be that morning. Actually, it wasn't bad. Geoffrey Washburn still drank like a mad Cossack, but these days he stayed on his horse. It was as if a reserve of hope had been found in the recesses of his own destructive fatalism. And the man with no memory understood; that hope was tied to a bank in Zurich's Bahnhofstrasse. Why did the street come so easily to mind?

The bedroom door opened and the doctor burst in, grinning, his white coat stained with his patient's blood.

"I did it!" he said, more triumph in his words than clarification. "I should open my own hiring hall and live on commissions. It'd be steadier."

"What are you talking about?"

"As we agreed, it's what you need. You've *got* to function on the outside, and as of two minutes ago Monsieur Jean-Pierre No-Name is gainfully employed! At least for a week."

"How did you do that? I thought there weren't any openings."

"What was about to be opened was Claude Lamouche's infected leg. I explained that my supply of local anesthetic was very, *very* limited. We negotiated; you were the bartered coin."

"A week?"

"If you're any good, he may keep you on." Washburn paused. "Although that's not terribly important, is it?"

"I'm not sure any of this is. A month ago, maybe, but not now. I told you. I'm ready to leave. I'd think you'd want me to. I have an appointment in Zurich."

"And I'd prefer you function the very best you can at that appointment. My interests are extremely selfish, no remissions permitted."

"I'm ready."

"On the surface, yes. But take my word for it, it's vital that you spend prolonged periods of time on the water, some of it at night. Not under controlled conditions, not as a passenger, but subjected to reasonably harsh conditions—the harsher the better, in fact."

"Another test?"

"Every single one I can devise in this primitive Menningers of Port Noir. If I could conjure up a storm and a minor shipwreck for you, I would. On the other hand, Lamouche is something of a storm himself; he's a difficult man. The swelling in his leg will go down and he'll resent you. So will others; you'll have to replace someone."

"Thanks a lot."

"Don't mention it. We're combining two stresses. At least one or two nights on the water, if Lamouche keeps to schedule—that's the hostile environment which contributed to your hysteria—and exposure to resentment and suspicion from men around you—symbolic of the initial stress situation."

"Thanks again. Suppose they decide to throw me overboard? That'd be your ultimate test, I suppose, but I don't know how much good it would do if I drowned."

"Oh, there'll be nothing like that," said Washburn, scoffing.

"I'm glad you're so confident. I wish I were."

"You can be. You have the protection of my presence. I may not be Christiaan Barnard or Michael De Bakey, but I'm all these people have. They need me; they won't risk losing me."

"But you want to leave. I'm your passport out."

"In ways unfathomable, my dear patient. Come on, now. Lamouche wants you down at the dock so you can familiarize yourself with his equipment. You'll be starting out at four o'clock tomorrow morning. Consider how beneficial a week at sea will be. Think of it as a cruise."

There had never been a cruise like it. The skipper of the filthy, oil-soaked fishing boat was a foul-mouthed rendering of an insignificant Captain Bligh; the crew a quartet of misfits who were undoubtedly the only men in Port Noir willing to put up with Claude Lamouche. The regular fifth member was a brother of the chief netman, a fact impressed on the man called Jean-Pierre within minutes after leaving the harbor at four o'clock in the morning.

"You take food from my brother's table!" whispered the netman angrily between rapid puffs on an immobile cigarette. "From the stomachs of his children!"

"It's only for a week," protested Jean-Pierre. It would have been easier—far easier—to offer to reimburse the unemployed brother from Washburn's monthly stipend, but the doctor and his patient had agreed to refrain from such compromises.

"I hope you're good with the nets!"

He was not.

There were moments during the next seventy-two hours when the man called Jean-Pierre thought the alternative of financial appeasement was warranted. The harassment never stopped, even at night—especially at night. It was as though eyes were trained on him as he lay on the infested deck mattress, waiting for him to reach the brink of sleep.

"You! Take the watch! The mate is sick. You fill in."

"Get up! Philippe is writing his memoirs! He can't be disturbed."

"On your feet! You tore a net this afternoon. We won't pay for your stupidity. We've all agreed. Fix it now!"

The nets.

If two men were required for one flank, his two arms took the place of four. If he worked beside one man, there were abrupt hauls and releases that left him with the full weight, a sudden blow from an adjacent shoulder sending him crashing into the gunnel and nearly over the side.

And Lamouche. A limping maniac who measured each kilometer of water by the fish he had lost. His voice was a grating, static-prone bullhorn. He addressed no one without an obscenity preceding his name, a habit the patient found increasingly maddening. But Lamouche did not touch Washburn's patient; he was merely sending the doctor a message: *Don't ever do this to me again. Not where my boat and my fish are concerned.*

Lamouche's schedule called for a return to Port Noir at sundown on the third day, the fish to be unloaded, the crew given until four the next morning to sleep, fornicate, get drunk, or, with luck, all three. As they came within sight of land, it happened.

The nets were being doused and folded at midships by the netman and his first assistant. The unwelcomed crewman they cursed as "Jean-Pierre Sangsue" ("the Leech") scrubbed down the deck with a long-handled brush. The two remaining crew heaved buckets of sea water in front of the brush, more often than not drenching the Leech with truer aim than the deck.

A bucketful was thrown too high, momentarily blinding Washburn's patient, causing him to lose his balance. The heavy brush with its metal-like bristles flew out of his hands, its head upended, the sharp bristles making contact with the kneeling netman's thigh.

"Merde alors!"

"Désolé," said the offender casually, shaking the water from his eyes.

"The hell you say!" shouted the netman.

"I said I was sorry," replied the man called Jean-Pierre. "Tell your friends to wet the deck, not me."

"My friends don't make me the object of their stupidity!"

"They were the cause of mine just now."

The netman grabbed the handle of the brush, got to his feet, and held it out like a bayonet. "You want to play, Leech?"

"Come on, give it to me."

"With pleasure, Leech. Here!" The netman shoved the brush forward, downward, the bristles scraping the patient's chest and stomach, penetrating the cloth of his shirt.

Whether it was the contact with the scars that covered his previous wounds, or the frustration and anger resulting from three days of harassment, the man would never know. He only knew he had to respond. And his response was as alarming to him as anything he could imagine.

He gripped the handle with his right hand, jamming it back into the netman's stomach, pulling if forward at the instant of impact; simultaneously, he shot his left foot high off the deck, ramming it into the man's throat.

"Tao!" The guttural whisper came from his lips involuntarily; he did not know what it meant.

Before he could understand, he had pivoted, his right foot now surging forward like a battering ram, crashing into the netman's left kidney.

"Che-sah!" he whispered.

The netman recoiled, then lunged toward him in pain and fury, his hands outstretched like claws. "Pig!"

The patient crouched, shooting his right hand up to grip the netman's left forearm, yanking it downward, then rising, pushing his victim's arm up, twisting it at its highest arc clockwise, yanking again, finally releasing it while jamming his heel into the small of the netman's back. The Frenchman sprawled forward over the nets, his head smashing into the wall of the gunnel.

"*Mee-sah!*" Again he did not know the meaning of his silent cry.

A crewman grabbed his neck from the rear. The patient crashed his left fist into the pelvic area behind him, then bent forward, gripping the elbow to the right of his throat. He lurched to his left; his assailant was lifted off the ground, his legs spiraling in the air as he was thrown across the deck, his face and neck impaled between the wheels of a winch.

The two remaining men were on him, fists and knees pummeling him, as the captain of the fishing boat repeatedly screamed his warnings.

"*Le docteur! Rappelons le docteur! Va doucement!*"

The words were as misplaced as the captain's appraisal of what he saw. The patient gripped the wrist of one man, bending it downward, twisting it counterclockwise in one violent movement; the man roared in agony. The wrist was broken.

Washburn's patient viced the fingers of his hands together, swinging his arms upward like a sledgehammer, catching the crewman with the broken wrist at the midpoint of his throat. The man somersaulted off his feet and collapsed on the deck.

"*Kwa-sah!*" The whisper echoed in the patient's ears.

The fourth man backed away, staring at the maniac who simply looked at him.

It was over. Three of Lamouche's crew were unconscious, severely punished for what they had done. It was doubtful that any would be capable of coming down to the docks at four o'clock in the morning.

Lamouche's words were uttered in equal parts, astonishment and contempt. "Where you come from I don't know, but you will get off this boat."

The man with no memory understood the unintentional irony of the captain's words. *I don't know where I came from, either.*

"You can't stay here now," said Geoffrey Washburn, coming into the darkened bedroom. "I honestly believed I could prevent any serious assault on you. But I can't protect you when you've done the damage."

"It was provoked."

"To the extent it was inflicted? A broken wrist and lacerations requiring sutures on a man's throat and face, and another's skull. A severe concussion, and an undetermined injury to a kidney? To say nothing of a blow to the groin that's caused a swelling of the testicles? I believe the word is overkill."

"It would have been just plain 'kill,' and I would have been the dead man, if it'd happened any other way." The patient paused, but spoke again before the doctor could interrupt. "I think we should talk. Several things happened; other words came to me. We should talk."

"We should, but we can't. There isn't time. You've got to leave now. I've made arrangements."

"Now?"

"Yes. I told them you went into the village, probably to get drunk. The families will go looking for you. Every able-bodied brother, cousin, and in-law. They'll have knives, hooks, perhaps a gun or two. When they can't find you, they'll come back here. They won't stop until they *do* find you."

"Because of a fight I didn't start?"

"Because you've injured three men who will lose at least a month's wages between them. And something else that's infinitely more important."

"What's that?"

"The insult. An off-islander proved himself more than a match for not one, but three respected fishermen of Port Noir."

"Respected?"

"In the physical sense. Lamouche's crew is considered the roughest on the waterfront."

"That's ridiculous."

"Not to them. It's their honor. . . . Now hurry—get your things together. There's a boat in from Marseilles; the captain's agreed to stow you, and drop you a half-mile offshore north of La Ciotat."

The man with no memory held his breath. "Then it's time," he said quietly.

"It's time," replied Washburn. "I think I know what's going through your mind. A sense of helplessness, of drifting without a rudder to put you on a course. I've been your rudder, and I won't be with you; there's nothing I can do about that. But believe me when I tell you, you are *not* helpless. You *will* find your way."

"To Zurich," added the patient.

"To Zurich," agreed the doctor. "Here. I've wrapped some things together for you in this oilcloth. Strap it around your waist."

"What is it?"

"All the money I have, some two thousand francs. It's not much, but it will help you get started. And my passport, for whatever good it will do. We're about the same age and it's eight years old; people change. Don't let anyone study it. It's merely an official paper."

"What will you do?"

"I won't ever need it if I don't hear from you."

"You're a decent man."

"I think you are, too. . . . As I've known you. But then I didn't know you before. So I can't vouch for that man. I wish I could, but there's no way I can."

The man leaned against the railing, watching the lights of Ile de Port Noir recede in the distance. The fishing boat was heading into darkness, as he had plunged into darkness nearly five months ago.

As he was plunging into another darkness now.

3

There were no lights on the coast of France; only the wash of the dying moon outlined the rocky shore. They were two hundred yards from land, the fishing boat bobbing gently in the crosscurrents of the inlet. The captain pointed over the side.

"There's a small stretch of beach between those two clusters of rock. It's not much, but you'll reach it if you swim to the right. We can drift in another thirty, forty feet, no more than that. Only a minute or two."

"You're doing more than I expected. I thank you for that."

"No need to. I pay my debts."

"And I'm one?"

"Very much so. The doctor in Port Noir sewed up three of my crew after that madness five months ago. You weren't the only one brought in, you know."

"The storm? You know me?"

"You were chalk white on the table, but I don't know you and I don't want to know you. I had no money then, no catch; the doctor said I could pay when my circumstances were better. You're my payment."

"I need papers," said the man, sensing a source of help. "I need a passport altered."

"Why speak to me?" asked the captain. "I said I would put a package over the side north of La Ciotat. That's all I said."

"You wouldn't have said that if you weren't capable of other things."

"I will *not* take you into Marseilles. I will *not* risk the patrol boats. The Sûreté has squadrons all over the harbor; the narcotics teams are maniacs. You pay *them* or you pay twenty years in a cell."

"Which means I can get papers in Marseilles. And you can help me."

"I did not say that."

"Yes, you did. I need a service and that service can be found in a place where you won't take me—still the service is there. You said it."

"Said what?"

"That you'll talk to me in Marseilles—if I can get there without you. Just tell me where."

The skipper of the fishing boat studied the patient's face; the decision was not made lightly, but it was made. "There's a café on rue Sarrasin, south of Old Harbor—Le Bouc de Mer. I'll be there tonight between nine and eleven. You'll need money, some of it in advance."

"How much?"

"That's between you and the man you speak with."

"I've got to have an idea."

"It's cheaper if you have a document to work with; otherwise one has to be stolen."

"I told you. I've got one."

The captain shrugged. "Fifteen hundred, two thousand francs. Are we wasting time?"

The patient thought of the oilcloth packet strapped to his waist. Bankruptcy lay in Marseilles, but so did an altered passport, a passport to Zurich. "I'll handle it," he said, not knowing why he sounded so confident. "Tonight, then."

The captain peered at the dimly lit shoreline. "This is as far as we can drift. You're on your own now. Remember, if we don't meet in Marseilles, you've never seen me and I've never seen you. None of my crew has seen you, either."

"I'll be there. Le Bouc de Mer, rue Sarrasin, south of Old Harbor."

"In God's hands," said the skipper, signaling a crewman at the wheel; the engines rumbled beneath the boat. "By the way, the clientele at Le Bouc are not used to the Parisian dialect. I'd rough it up if I were you."

"Thanks for the advice," said the patient as he swung his legs over the gunnel and lowered himself into the water. He held his knapsack above the surface, legs scissoring to stay afloat. "See you tonight," he added in a louder voice, looking up at the black hull of the fishing boat.

There was no one there; the captain had left the railing. The only sounds were the slapping of the waves against the wood and the muffled acceleration of the engines.

You're on your own now.

He shivered and spun in the cold water, angling his body toward the shore, remembering to sidestroke to his right, to head for a cluster of rocks on the right. If the captain knew what he was talking about, the current would take him into the unseen beach.

It did; he could feel the undertow pulling his bare feet into the sand, making the last thirty yards the most difficult to cross. But the canvas knapsack was relatively dry, still held above the breaking waves.

Minutes later he was sitting on a dune of wild grass, the tall reeds bending with the offshore breezes, the first rays of morning intruding on the night sky. The sun would be up in an hour; he would have to move with it.

He opened the knapsack and took out a pair of boots and heavy socks along with rolled-up trousers and a coarse denim shirt. Somewhere in his past he had learned to pack with an economy of space; the knapsack contained far more than an observer might think. Where had he learned that? Why? The questions never stopped.

He got up and took off the British walking shorts he had accepted from Washburn. He stretched them across the reeds of grass to dry; he could discard nothing. He removed his undershirt and did the same.

Standing there naked on the dune, he felt an odd sense of exhilaration mingled with a hollow pain in the middle of his stomach. The pain was fear, he knew that. He understood the exhilaration, too.

He had passed his first test. He had trusted an instinct—perhaps a compulsion—and had known what to say and how to respond. An hour ago he was without an immediate destination, knowing only that Zurich was his objective, but knowing, too, that there were borders to cross, official eyes to satisfy. The eight-year-old passport was so obviously not his own that even the dullest immigration clerk would spot the fact. And even if he managed to cross into Switzerland with it, he had to get out; with each move the odds of his being detained were multiplied. He could not permit that. Not now; not until he knew more. The answers were in Zurich, he had to travel freely, and he had honed in on a captain of a fishing boat to make that possible.

You are not helpless. You will find your way.

Before the day was over he would make a connection to have Washburn's passport altered by a professional, transformed into a license to travel. It was the first concrete step, but before it was taken there was the consideration of money. The two thousand francs the doctor had given him were inadequate; they might not even be enough for the passport itself. What good was a license to travel without the means to do so? Money. He had to get money. He had to think about that.

He shook out the clothes he had taken from the knapsack, put them on, and shoved his feet into the boots. Then he lay down on the sand, staring at the sky, which progressively grew brighter. The day was being born, and so was he.

He walked the narrow stone streets of La Ciotat, going into the shops as much to converse with the clerks as anything else. It was an odd sensation to be part of the human traffic, not an unknown derelict, dragged from the sea. He remembered the captain's advice and gutturalized his French, allowing him to be accepted as an unremarkable stranger passing through town.

Money.

There was a section of La Ciotat that apparently catered to a wealthy clientele. The shops were cleaner and the merchandise more expensive, the fish fresher and the meat several cuts above that in the main shopping area. Even the vegetables glistened; many exotic, imported from North Africa and the Mideast. The area held a touch of Paris or Nice set down on the fringes of a routinely middle-class coastal community. A small café, its entrance at the end of a flagstone path, stood separated from the shops on either side by a manicured lawn.

Money.

He walked into a butcher shop, aware that the owner's appraisal of him was not positive, nor the glance friendly. The man was waiting on a middle-aged couple, who from their speech and manner were domestics at an outlying estate. They were precise, curt, and demanding.

"The veal last week was barely passable," said the woman. "Do better this time, or I'll be forced to order from Marseilles."

"And the other evening," added the man, "the marquis mentioned to me that the chops of lamb were much too thin. I repeat, a full inch and a quarter."

The owner sighed and shrugged, uttering obsequious phrases of apology and assurance. The woman turned to her escort, her voice no less commanding than it was to the butcher.

"Wait for the packages and put them in the car. I'll be at the grocer's; meet me there."

"Of course, my dear."

The woman left, a pigeon in search of further seeds of conflict. The moment she was out the door her husband turned to the shopowner, his demeanor entirely different. Gone was the arrogance; a grin appeared.

"Just your average day, eh, Marcel?" he said, taking a pack of cigarettes from his pocket.

"Seen better, seen worse. Were the chops really too thin?"

"My God, no. When was *he* last able to tell? But she feels better if I complain, you know that."

"Where is the Marquis of the Dungheap now?"

"Drunk next door, waiting for the whore from Toulon. I'll come down later this afternoon, pick him up, and sneak him past the marquise into the stables. He won't be able to drive his car by then. He uses Jean-Pierre's room above the kitchen, you know."

"I've heard."

At the mention of the name Jean-Pierre, Washburn's patient turned from the display case of poultry. It was an automatic reflex, but the movement only served to remind the butcher of his presence.

"What is it? What do you want?"

It was time to degutturalize his French. "You were recommended by friends in Nice," said the patient, his accent more befitting the Quai d'Orsay than Le Bouc de Mer.

"Oh?" The shopowner made an immediate reappraisal. Among his clientele, especially the younger ones, there were those who preferred to dress in opposition to their status. The common Basque shirt was even fashionable these days. "You're new here, sir?"

"My boat's in for repairs; we won't be able to reach Marseilles this afternoon."

"May I be of service?"

The patient laughed. "You may be to the chef; I wouldn't dare presume. He'll be around later and I do have some influence."

The butcher and his friend laughed. "I would think so, sir," said the shopowner.

"I'll need a dozen ducklings and, say, eighteen chateaubriands."

"Of course."

"Good. I'll send our master of the galley directly to you." The patient turned to the middle-aged man. "By the way, I couldn't help overhearing . . . no, please don't be concerned. The marquis wouldn't be that jackass d'Ambois, would he? I think someone told me he lived around here."

"Oh no, sir," replied the servant. "I don't know the Marquis d'Ambois. I was referring to the Marquis de Chamford. A fine gentleman, sir, but he has problems. A difficult marriage, sir. Very difficult; it's no secret."

"Chamford? Yes, I think we've met. Rather short fellow, isn't he?"

"No, sir. Quite tall, actually. About your size, I'd say."

"Really?"

The patient learned the various entrances and inside staircases of the two-story café quickly—a produce delivery man from Roquevaire unsure of his new route. There were two sets of steps that led to the second floor, one from the kitchen, the other just beyond the front entrance in the small foyer; this was the staircase used by patrons going to the upstairs washrooms. There was also a window through which an interested party outside could see anyone who used this particular staircase, and the patient was sure that if he waited long enough he would see two people doing so. They would undoubtedly go up separately, neither heading for a washroom but, instead, to a bedroom above the kitchen. The patient wondered which of the expensive automobiles parked on the quiet street belonged to the Marquis de Chamford. Whichever, the middle-aged manservant in the butcher shop did not have to be concerned; his employer would not be driving it.

Money.

The woman arrived shortly before one o'clock. She was a windswept blonde, her large breasts stretching the blue silk of her blouse, her long legs tanned, striding gracefully above spiked heels, thighs and fluid hips outlined beneath the tight-fitting white skirt. Chamford might have problems but he also had taste.

Twenty minutes later he could see the white skirt through the window; the girl was heading upstairs. Less than sixty seconds later another figure filled the windowframe; dark trousers and a blazer beneath a white face cautiously lurched up the staircase. The patient counted off the minutes; he hoped the Marquis de Chamford owned a watch.

Carrying his canvas knapsack as unobtrusively as possible by the straps, the patient walked down the flagstone path to the entrance of the restaurant. Inside, he turned left in the foyer, excusing himself past an elderly man trudging up the staircase, reached the second floor and turned left again down a long corridor that led toward the rear of the building, above the kitchen. He passed the washrooms and came to a closed door at the end of the narrow hallway where he stood motionless, his back pressed into the wall. He turned his head and waited for the elderly man to reach the washroom door and push it open while unzipping his trousers.

The patient—instinctively, without thinking, really—raised the soft knapsack and placed it against the center of the door panel. He held it securely in place with his outstretched arms, stepped back, and in one swift movement, crashed his left shoulder into the canvas, dropping his right hand as the door sprang open, gripping the edge before the door could smash into a wall. No one below in the restaurant could have heard the muted forced entry.

"*Nom de Dieu!*" she shrieked. "*Qui est-ce! . . .*"

"*Silence!*"

The Marquis de Chamford spun off the naked body of the blond woman, sprawling over the edge of the bed onto the floor. He was a sight from a comic opera, still wearing his starched shirt, the tie knotted in place, and on his feet black silk, knee-length socks; but that was all he wore. The woman grabbed the covers, doing her best to lessen the indelicacy of the moment.

The patient issued his commands swiftly. "Don't raise your voices. No one will be hurt if you do exactly as I say."

"My wife hired you!" cried Chamford, his words slurred, his eyes barely in focus. "I'll pay you more!"

"That's a beginning," answered Dr. Washburn's patient. "Take off your shirt and tie. Also the socks." He saw the glistening gold band around the marquis' wrist. "And the watch."

Several minutes later the transformation was complete. The marquis' clothes were not a perfect fit, but no one could deny the quality of the cloth or the original tailoring. Too, the watch was a Girard Perregaux, and Chamford's bill-fold contained over thirteen thousand francs. The car keys were also impressive; they were set in monogrammed heads of sterling silver.

"For the love of God, give me your clothes!" said the marquis, the implausibility of his predicament penetrating the haze of alcohol.

"I'm sorry, but I can't do that," replied the intruder, gathering up both his own clothes and those of the blond woman.

"You can't take *mine!*" she yelled.

"I told you to keep your voice down."

"All right, all *right,*" she continued, "but you *can't . . .*"

"Yes, I can." The patient looked around the room; there was a telephone on a desk by a window. He crossed to it and yanked the cord out of the socket. "Now no one will disturb you," he added, picking up the knapsack.

"You won't go free, you know!" snapped Chamford. "You won't get away with this! The police will find you!"

"The police?" asked the intruder. "Do you really think you should call the police? A formal report will have to be made, the circumstances described. I'm not so sure that's such a good idea. I think you'd be better off waiting for that fellow to pick you up later this afternoon. I heard him say he was going to get you past the marquise into the stables. All things considered, I honestly believe that's what you should do. I'm sure you can come up with a better story than what really happened here. I won't contradict you."

The unknown thief left the room, closing the damaged door behind him.

You are not *helpless. You* will *find your way.*

So far he had and it was a little frightening. What had Washburn said? That his skills and talents would come back . . . *but I don't think you'll ever be able to relate them to anything in your past.* The past. What kind of past was it that produced the skills he had displayed during the past twenty-four hours? Where had he learned to maim and cripple with lunging feet, and fingers entwined into hammers? How did he know precisely where to deliver the blows? Who had taught him to play upon the criminal mind, provoking and evoking a reluctant commitment? How did he zero in so quickly on mere implications, convinced beyond doubt that his instincts were right? Where had he learned to discern instant extortion in a casual conversation overheard in a butcher shop? More to the point, perhaps, was the simple decision to carry out the crime. My God, how *could* he?

The more you fight it, the more you crucify yourself, the worse it will be.

He concentrated on the road and on the mahogany dashboard of the Marquis de Chamford's Jaguar. The array of instruments was not familiar; his past did not include extensive experience with such cars. He supposed that told him something.

In less than an hour he crossed a bridge over a wide canal and knew he had reached Marseilles. Small square houses of stone, angling like blocks up from the water; narrow streets and walls everywhere—the outskirts of the old harbor. He knew it all, and yet he did not know it. High in the distance, silhouetted on one of the surrounding hills, were the outlines of a cathedral, a statue of the Virgin seen clearly atop its steeple. Notre-Dame-de-la-Garde. The name came to him; he had seen it before—and yet he had not seen it.

Oh, Christ! *Stop it!*

Within minutes he was in the pulsing center of the city, driving along the crowded Canebière, with its proliferation of expensive shops, the rays of the afternoon sun bouncing off expanses of tinted glass on either side, and on either side enormous sidewalk cafés. He turned left, toward the harbor, passing warehouses and small factories and fenced-off lots that contained automobiles prepared for transport north to the showrooms of Saint-Etienne, Lyons and Paris. And to points south across the Mediterranean.

Instinct. Follow instinct. For nothing could be disregarded. Every resource had an immediate use; there was value in a rock if it could be thrown, or a vehicle if someone wanted it. He chose a lot where the cars were both new and used, but all expensive; he parked at the curb and got out. Beyond the fence was a small cavern of a garage, mechanics in overalls laconically wandering about carrying tools. He walked casually around inside until he spotted a man in a thin, pinstriped suit whom instinct told him to approach.

It took less than ten minutes, explanations kept to a minimum, a Jaguar's disappearance to North Africa guaranteed with the filing of engine numbers.

The silver monogrammed keys were exchanged for six thousand francs, roughly one-fifth the value of Chamford's automobile. Then Dr. Washburn's patient found a taxi, and asked to be taken to a pawnbroker—but not an establishment that asked too many questions. The message was clear; this was Marseilles. And a half hour later the gold Girard Perregaux was no longer on his wrist, having been replaced by a Seiko chronograph and eight hundred francs. Everything had a value in relationship to its practicality; the chronograph was shockproof.

The next stop was a medium-sized department store in the southeast section of La Canebière. Clothes were chosen off the racks and shelves, paid for and worn out of the fitting rooms, an ill-fitting dark blazer and trousers left behind.

From a display on the floor, he selected a soft leather suitcase, additional garments placed inside with the knapsack. The patient glanced at his new watch; it was nearly five o'clock, time to find a comfortable hotel. He had not really slept for several days; he needed to rest before his appointment in the rue Sarrasin, at a café called Le Bouc de Mer, where arrangements could be made for a more important appointment in Zurich.

He lay back on the bed and stared at the ceiling, the wash of the streetlamps below causing irregular patterns of light to dance across the smooth white surface. Night had come rapidly to Marseilles, and with its arrival a certain sense of freedom came to the patient. It was as if the darkness were a gigantic blanket, blocking out the harsh glare of daylight that revealed too much too quickly. He was learning something else about himself: he was more comfortable in the night. Like a half-starved cat, he would forage better in the darkness. Yet there was a contradiction, and he recognized that, too. During the months in Ile de Port Noir, he had craved the sunlight, hungered for it, waited for it each dawn, wishing only for the darkness to go away.

Things were happening to him; he was changing.

Things *had* happened. Events that gave a certain lie to the concept of foraging more successfully at night. Twelve hours ago he was on a fishing boat in the Mediterranean, an objective in mind and two thousand francs strapped to his waist. Two thousand francs, something less than five hundred American dollars according to the daily rate of exchange posted in the hotel lobby. Now he was outfitted with several sets of acceptable clothing and lying on a bed in a reasonably expensive hotel with something over twenty-three thousand francs in a Louis Vuitton billfold belonging to the Marquis de Chamford. Twenty-three-thousand francs . . . nearly six thousand American dollars.

Where had he come from that he was able to do the things he did?

Stop it!

The rue Sarrasin was so ancient that in another city it might have been designated as a landmark thoroughfare, a wide brick alley connecting streets built centuries later. But this was Marseilles; ancient coexisted with old, both uncomfortable with the new. The rue Sarrasin was no more than two hundred feet long, frozen in time between the stone walls of waterfront buildings, devoid of streetlights, trapping the mists that rolled off the harbor. It was a back street conducive to brief meetings between men who did not care for their conferences to be observed.

The only light and sound came from Le Bouc de Mer. The café was situated roughly in the center of the wide alley, its premises once a nineteenth-century office building. A number of cubicles had been taken down to allow for a large barroom and tables; an equal number were left standing for less public appointments. These were the waterfront's answer to those private rooms found at restaurants along La Canebière, and, as befitting their status, there were curtains, but no doors.

The patient made his way between the crowded tables, cutting his way through the layers of smoke, excusing himself past lurching fishermen and drunken soldiers and red-faced whores looking for beds to rest in as well as new francs. He peered into a succession of cubicles, a crewman looking for his companions—until he found the captain of the fishing boat. There was another man at the table. Thin, pale faced, narrow eyes peering up like a curious ferret's.

"Sit down," said the dour skipper. "I thought you'd be here before this."

"You said between nine and eleven. It's quarter to eleven."

"You stretch the time, you can pay for the whiskey."

"Be glad to. Order something decent if they've got it."

The thin, pale-faced man smiled. Things were going to be all right.

They were. The passport in question was, naturally, one of the most difficult in the world to tamper with, but with great care, equipment, and artistry, it could be done.

"How much?"

"These skills—and equipment—do not come cheap. Twenty-five hundred francs."

"When can I have it?"

"The care, the artistry, they take time. Three or four days. And that's putting the artist under great pressure; he'll scream at me."

"There's an additional one thousand francs if I can have it tomorrow."

"By ten in the morning," said the pale-faced man quickly. "I'll take the abuse."

"And the thousand," interrupted the scowling captain. "What did you bring out of Port Noir? Diamonds?"

"Talent," answered the patient, meaning it but not understanding it.

"I'll need a photograph," said the connection.

"I stopped at an arcade and had this made," replied the patient, taking a small square photograph out of his shirt pocket. "With all that expensive equipment I'm sure you can sharpen it up."

"Nice clothes," said the captain, passing the print to the pale-faced man.

"Well tailored," agreed the patient.

The location of the morning rendezvous was agreed upon, the drinks paid for, and the captain slipped five hundred francs under the table. The conference was over; the buyer left the cubicle and started across the crowded, raucous, smoke-layered barroom toward the door.

It happened so rapidly, so suddenly, so completely unexpectedly, there was no time to think. Only *react.*

The collision was abrupt, casual, but the eyes that stared at him were not casual; they seemed to burst out of their sockets, widening in disbelief, on the edge of hysteria.

"No! Oh my God, no! It *cannot*—" The man spun in the crowd; the patient lurched forward, clamping his hand down on the man's shoulder.

"Wait a minute!"

The man spun again, thrusting the V of his outstretched thumb and fingers up into the patient's wrist, forcing the hand away. "*You!* You're *dead!* You could not have *lived!*"

"I lived. What do you *know?*"

The face was now contorted, a mass of twisted fury, the eyes squinting, the mouth open, sucking air, baring yellow teeth that took on the appearance of animals' teeth. Suddenly the man pulled out a knife, the snap of its recessed blade heard through the surrounding din. The arm shot forward, the blade an extension of the hand that gripped it, both surging in toward the patient's stomach. "I know I'll finish it!" whispered the man.

The patient swung his right forearm down, a pendulum sweeping aside all objects in front of it. He pivoted, lashing his left foot up, his heel plunging into his attacker's pelvic bone.

"*Che-sah.*" The echo in his ears was deafening.

The man lurched backward into a trio of drinkers as the knife fell to the floor. The weapon was seen; shouts followed, men converged, fists and hands separating the combatants.

"Get out of here!"

"Take your argument somewhere else!"

"We don't want the police in here, you drunken bastards!"

The angry coarse dialects of Marseilles rose over the cacophonous sounds of Le Bouc de Mer. The patient was hemmed in; he watched as his would-be killer threaded his way through the crowd, holding his groin, forcing a path to the entrance. The heavy door swung open; the man raced into the darkness of rue Sarrasin.

Someone who thought he was dead—wanted him dead—knew he was alive.

4

The economy class section of Air France's Caravelle to Zurich was filled to capacity, the narrow seats made more uncomfortable by the turbulence that buffeted the plane. A baby was screaming in its mother's arms; other children whimpered, swallowing cries of fear as parents smiled with tentative reassurances they did not feel. Most of the remaining passengers were silent, a few drinking their whiskey more rapidly than obviously was normal. Fewer still were forcing laughter from tight throats, false bravados that emphasized their insecurity rather than disguising it. A terrible flight was many things to many people, but none escape the essential thoughts of terror. When man encased himself in a metal tube thirty thousand feet above the ground, he was vulnerable. With one elongated, screaming dive he could be plummeting downward into the earth. And there were fundamental questions that accompanied the essential terror. What thoughts would go through one's mind at such a time? How would one react?

The patient tried to find out; it was important to him. He sat next to the window, his eyes on the aircraft's wing, watching the broad expanse of metal bend and vibrate under the brutalizing impact of the winds. The currents were clashing against one another, pounding the manmade tube into a kind of submission, warning the microscopic pretenders that they were no match for the vast infirmities of nature. One ounce of pressure beyond the flex tolerance and the wing would crack, the lift-sustaining limb torn from its tubular body, shredded into the winds; one burst of rivets and there would be an explosion, the screaming plunge to follow.

What would he do? What would he think? Other than the uncontrollable fear of dying and oblivion, would there be anything else? That's what he had to concentrate on; that was the *projection* Washburn kept emphasizing in Port Noir. The doctor's words came back to him.

Whenever you observe a stress situation—and you have the time—do your damndest to project yourself into it. Associate as freely as you can; let words and images fill your mind. In them you may find clues.

The patient continued to stare out the window, consciously trying to raise his unconscious, fixing his eyes on the natural violence beyond the glass, distilling the movement, silently doing his "damndest" to let his reactions give rise to words and images.

They came—slowly. There was the darkness again, and the sound of rushing wind, ear-shattering, continuous, growing in volume until he thought his head would burst. His head. . . . The winds were lashing the left side of his head and face, burning his skin, forcing him to raise his left shoulder for protection. . . . Left shoulder. Left *arm*. His arm was raised, the gloved fingers of his left hand gripping a straight edge of metal, his right holding a . . . a strap; he was holding on to a strap, waiting for something. A signal . . . a flashing light or a tap on the shoulder, or both. A signal. It *came.* He plunged. Into the darkness, into the void, his body tumbling, twisting, swept away into the night sky. He had . . . parachuted!

"Etes-vous malade?"

His insane reverie was broken; the nervous passenger next to him had touched his left arm—which was raised, the fingers of his hand spread, as if resisting, rigid in their locked position. Across his chest his right forearm was pressed into the cloth of his jacket, his right hand gripping the lapel, bunching the fabric. And on his forehead were rivulets of sweat; it had happened. The something-else had come briefly—insanely—into focus.

"Pardon," he said, lowering his arms. *"Un mauvais rêve,"* he added meaning-lessly.

There was a break in the weather; the Caravelle stabilized. The smiles on the harried stewardesses' faces became genuine again; full service was resumed as embarrassed passengers glanced at one another.

The patient observed his surroundings but reached no conclusions. He was consumed by the images and the sounds that had been so clearly defined in his mind's eye and ear. He had hurled himself from a plane . . . at night . . . signals and metal and straps intrinsic to his leap. He *had* parachuted. *Where? Why?*

Stop crucifying yourself!

If for no other reason than to take his thoughts away from the madness, he reached into his breast pocket, pulled out the altered passport, and opened it. As might be expected, the name *Washburn* had been retained; it was common enough and its owner had explained that there were no flags out for it. The *Geoffrey R.,* however, had been changed to *George P.,* the eliminations and spaceline blockage expertly accomplished. The photographic insertion was ex-pert, too; it no longer resembled a cheap print from a machine in an amusement arcade.

The identification numbers, of course, were entirely different, guaranteed not to cause an alarm in an immigration computer. At least, up until the moment the bearer submitted the passport for its first inspection; from that time on it was the buyer's responsibility. One paid as much for this guarantee as he did for the artistry and the equipment, for it required connections within Interpol and the immigration clearing houses. Customs officials, computer specialists, and clerks throughout the European border networks were paid on a regular basis for this vital information; they rarely made mistakes. If and when they did, the loss of an eye or an arm was not out of the question—such were the brokers of false papers.

George P. Washburn. He was not comfortable with the name; the owner of the unaltered original had instructed him too well in the basics of projection and association. *George P.* was a sidestep from *Geoffrey R.,* a man who had been eaten away by a compulsion that had its roots in escape—escape from identity. That was the last thing the patient wanted; he wanted more than his *life* to know who he was.

Or did he?

No matter. The answer was in Zurich. In Zurich there was . . .

"Mesdames et messieurs. Nous commençons notre descente pour l'aéroport de Zurich."

He knew the name of the hotel: Carillon du Lac. He had given it to the taxi driver without thinking. Had he read it somewhere? Had the name been one of those listed in the Welcome-to-Zurich folders placed in the elasticized pockets in front of his seat in the plane?

No. He knew the lobby; the heavy, dark, polished wood was familiar . . . somehow. And the huge plateglass windows that looked out over Lake Zurich.

He had been here *before;* he had stood where he was standing now—in front of the marble-topped counter—a long time ago.

It was all confirmed by the words spoken by the clerk behind the desk. They had the impact of an explosion.

"It's good to see you again, sir. It's been quite a while since your last visit."

Has it? How long? Why don't you call me by my name? For God's sake. I don't know you! I don't know me! Help me! Please, help me!

"I guess it has," he said. "Do me a favor, will you? I sprained my hand; it's difficult to write. Could you fill in the registration and I'll do my damndest to sign it?" The patient held his breath. Suppose the polite man behind the counter asked him to repeat his name, or the spelling of his name?

"Of course." The clerk turned the card around and wrote. "Would you care to see the hotel doctor?"

"Later, perhaps. Not now." The clerk continued writing, then lifted up the card, reversing it for the guest's signature.

Mr. J. Bourne. New York, N.Y. U.S.A.

He stared at it, transfixed, mesmerized by the letters. He had a name—part of a name. And a country as well as a city of residence.

J. Bourne. *John? James? Joseph?* What did the *J* stand for?

"Is something wrong, Herr Bourne?" asked the clerk.

"Wrong? No, not at all." He picked up the pen, remembering to feign discomfort. Would he be expected to write out a first name? No; he would sign exactly as the clerk had printed.

Mr. J. Bourne.

He wrote the name as naturally as he could, letting his mind fall free, allowing whatever thoughts or images that might be triggered come through. None did; he was merely signing an unfamiliar name. He felt nothing.

"You had me worried, mein Herr," said the clerk. "I thought perhaps I'd made a mistake. It's been a busy week, a busier day. But then, I was quite certain."

And if he had? Made a mistake? Mr. J. Bourne of New York City, U.S.A., did not care to think about the possibility. "It never occurred to me to question your memory . . . Herr Stossel," replied the patient, glancing up at the On-Duty sign on the left wall of the counter; the man behind the desk was the Carillon du Lac's assistant manager.

"You're most kind." The assistant manager leaned forward. "I assume you'll require the usual conditions of your stay with us?"

"Some may have changed," said J. Bourne. "How did you understand them before?"

"Whoever telephones or inquires at the desk is to be told you're out of the hotel, whereupon you're to be informed immediately. The only exception is your firm in New York. The Treadstone Seventy-One Corporation, if I remember correctly."

Another name! One he could trace with an overseas call. Fragmentary shapes were falling into place. The exhilaration began to return.

"That'll do. I won't forget your efficiency."

"This is Zurich," replied the polite man, shrugging. "You've always been exceedingly generous, Herr Bourne. *Page—hierher, bitte!*"

As the patient followed the page into the elevator, several things were clearer. He had a name and he understood why that name came so quickly to the Carillon du Lac's assistant manager. He had a country and a city and a firm that employed him—*had* employed him, at any rate. And whenever he came to Zurich, certain precautions were implemented to protect him from unexpected, or unwanted, visitors. That was what he could not understand. One either protected oneself thoroughly or one did not bother to protect oneself at all. Where was any real advantage in a screening process that was so loose, so vulnerable to penetration? It struck him as second-rate, without value, as if a small child were playing hide-and-seek. *Where am I? Try and find me. I'll say something out loud and give you a hint.*

It was not professional, and if he had learned anything about himself during the past forty-eight hours it was that he *was* a professional. Of what he had no idea, but the status was not debatable.

The voice of the New York operator faded sporadically over the line. Her conclusion, however, was irritatingly clear. And final.

"There's no listing for any such company, sir. I've checked the latest directories as well as the private telephones and there's no Treadstone Corporation—and nothing even resembling Treadstone with numbers following the name."

"Perhaps they were dropped to shorten . . ."

"There's *no* firm or company with that name, sir. I repeat, if you have a first or second name, or the type of business the firm's engaged in, I might be of further help."

"I don't. Only the name, Treadstone Seventy-One, New York City."

"It's an odd name, sir. I'm sure if there were a listing it would be a simple matter to find it. I'm sorry."

"Thanks very much for your trouble," said J. Bourne, replacing the phone. It was pointless to go on; the name was a code of some sort, words relayed by a caller that gained him access to a hotel guest not so readily accessible. And the words could be used by anyone regardless of where he had placed the call; therefore the location of New York might well be meaningless. According to an operator five thousand miles away it was.

The patient walked to the bureau where he had placed the Louis Vuitton billfold and the Seiko chronograph. He put the billfold in his pocket and the watch on his wrist; he looked in the mirror and spoke quietly.

"You are J. Bourne, citizen of the United States, resident of New York City, and it's entirely possible that the numbers 'zero-seven—seventeen-twelve—zero-fourteen—twenty-six-zero' are the most important things in your life."

The sun was bright, filtering through the trees along the elegant Bahnhofstrasse, bouncing off the windows of the shops, and creating blocks of shadows where the great banks intruded on its rays. It was a street where solidity and money, security and arrogance, determination and a touch of frivolity all coexisted; and Dr. Washburn's patient had walked along its pavements before.

He strolled into the Burkli Platz, the square that overlooked the Zurichsee, with its numerous quays along the waterfront, bordered by gardens that in the heat of summer became circles of bursting flowers. He could picture them in his mind's eye; images were coming to him. But no thoughts, no memories.

He doubled back into the Bahnhofstrasse, instinctively knowing that the Gemeinschaft Bank was a nearby building of off-white stone; it had been on the opposite side of the street on which he had just walked; he had passed it deliberately. He approached the heavy glass doors and pushed the center plate forward. The right-hand door swung open easily and he was standing on a floor of brown marble; he had stood on it before, but the image was not as strong as others. He had the uncomfortable feeling that the Gemeinschaft was to be avoided.

It was not to be avoided now.

"*Bonjour, monsieur. Vous désirez . . .?*" The man asking the question was dressed in a cutaway, the red *boutonnière* his symbol of authority. The use of French was explained by the client's clothes; even the subordinate gnomes of Zurich were observant.

"I have personal and confidential business to discuss," replied J. Bourne in English, once again mildly startled by the words he spoke so naturally. The reason for the English was twofold: he wanted to watch the gnome's expression at his error, and he wanted no possible misinterpretation of anything said during the next hour.

"Pardon, sir," said the man, his eyebrows arched slightly, studying the client's topcoat. "The elevator to your left, second floor. The receptionist will assist you."

The receptionist referred to was a middle-aged man with close-cropped hair and tortoise-shell glasses; his expression was set, his eyes rigidly curious. "Do you currently have personal and confidential business with us, sir?" he asked, repeating the new arrival's words.

"I do."

"Your signature, please," said the official, holding out a sheet of Gemeinschaft stationery with two blank lines centered in the middle of the page.

The client understood; no name was required. *The handwritten numbers take the place of a name . . . they constitute the signature of the account holder. Standard procedure.* Washburn.

The patient wrote out the numbers, relaxing his hand so the writing would be free. He handed the stationery back to the receptionist, who studied it, rose from the chair, and gestured to a row of narrow doors with frosted glass panels. "If you'll wait in the fourth room, sir, someone will be with you shortly."

"The fourth room?"

"The fourth door from the left. It will lock automatically."

"Is that necessary?"

The receptionist glanced at him, startled. "It is in line with your own request, sir," he said politely, an undertone of surprise beneath his courtesy. "This is a three-zero account. It's customary at the Gemeinschaft for holders of such accounts to telephone in advance so that a private entrance can be made available."

"I know that," lied Washburn's patient with a casualness he did not feel. "It's just that I'm in a hurry."

"I'll convey that to Verifications, sir."

"Verifications?" Mr. J. Bourne of New York City, U.S.A., could not help himself; the word had the sound of an alarm.

"Signature Verifications, sir." The man adjusted his glasses; the movement covered his taking a step nearer his desk, his lower hand inches from a console. "I suggest you wait in Room Four, sir." The suggestion was not a request; it was an order, the command in the praetorian's eyes.

"Why not? Just tell them to hurry, will you?" The patient crossed to the fourth door, opened it and walked inside. The door closed automatically; he could hear the click of the lock. J. Bourne looked at the frosted panel; it was no simple pane of glass, for there was a network of thin wires webbed beneath the surface. Undoubtedly if cracked, an alarm would be triggered; he was in a cell, waiting to be summoned.

The rest of the small room was paneled and furnished tastefully, two leather armchairs next to one another, across from a miniature couch flanked by antique tables. At the opposite end was a second door, startling in its contrast; it was made of gray steel. Up-to-date magazines and newspapers in three languages were on the tables. The patient sat down and picked up the Paris edition of the *Herald-Tribune*. He read the printed words but absorbed nothing. The summons would come any moment now; his mind was consumed by thoughts of maneuver. Maneuver without memory, only by instinct.

Finally, the steel door opened, revealing a tall, slender man with aquiline features and meticulously groomed gray hair. His face was patrician, eager to serve an equal who needed his expertise. He extended his hand, his English refined, mellifluous under his Swiss intonation.

"So very pleased to meet you. Forgive the delay; it was rather humorous, in fact."

"In what way?"

"I'm afraid you rather startled Herr Koenig. It's not often a three-zero account arrives without prior notice. He's quite set in his ways, you know; the unusual ruins his day. On the other hand, it generally makes mine more pleasant. I'm Walther Apfel. Please, come in."

The bank officer released the patient's hand and gestured toward the steel door. The room beyond was a V-shaped extension of the cell. Dark paneling, heavy comfortable furniture and a wide desk that stood in front of a wider window overlooking the Bahnhofstrasse.

"I'm sorry I upset him," said J. Bourne. "It's just that I have very little time."

"Yes, he relayed that." Apfel walked around the desk, nodding at the leather armchair in front. "Do sit down. One or two formalities and we can discuss the business at hand." Both men sat; the instant they did so the bank officer picked up a white clipboard and leaned across his desk, handing it to the Gemeinschaft client. Secured in place was another sheet of stationery, but instead of two blank lines there were ten, starting below the letterhead and extending to within an inch of the bottom border. "Your signature, please. A minimum of five will be sufficient."

"I don't understand. I just did this."

"And very successfully. Verification confirmed it."

"Then why again?"

"A signature can be practiced to the point where a single rendition is acceptable. However, successive repetitions will result in flaws if it's not authentic. A graphological scanner will pick them up instantly; but then I'm sure that's no concern of yours." Apfel smiled as he placed a pen at the edge of the desk. "Nor of mine, frankly, but Koenig insists."

"He's a cautious man," said the patient, taking the pen and starting to write. He had begun the fourth set when the banker stopped him.

"That will do; the rest really is a waste of time." Apfel held out his hand for the clipboard. "Verifications said you weren't even a borderline case. Upon receipt of this, the account will be delivered." He inserted the sheet of paper into the slot of a metal case on the right side of his desk and pressed a button; a shaft of bright light flared and then went out. "This transmits the signatures directly to the scanner," continued the banker. "Which, of course, is programmed. Again, frankly, it's all a bit foolish. No one forewarned of our precautions would consent to the additional signatures if he were an imposter."

"Why not? As long as he'd gone this far, why not chance it?"

"There is only one entrance to this office, conversely one exit. I'm sure you heard the lock snap shut in the waiting room."

"And saw the wire mesh in the glass," added the patient.

"Then you understand. A certified imposter would be trapped."

"Suppose he had a gun?"

"You don't."

"No one searched me."

"The elevator did. From four different angles. If you had been armed, the machinery would have stopped between the first and second floors."

"You're all cautious."

"We try to be of service." The telephone rang. Apfel answered. "Yes? . . . Come in." The banker glanced at his client. "Your account file's here."

"That was quick."

"Herr Koenig signed for it several minutes ago; he was merely waiting for the scanner release." Apfel opened a drawer and took out a ring of keys. "I'm sure he's disappointed. He was quite certain something was amiss."

The steel door opened and the receptionist entered carrying a black metal container, which he placed on the desk next to a tray that held a bottle of Perrier and two glasses.

"Are you enjoying your stay in Zurich?" asked the banker, obviously to fill in the silence.

"Very much so. My room overlooks the lake. It's a nice view, very peaceful, quiet."

"Splendid," said Apfel, pouring a glass of Perrier for his client. Herr Koenig left; the door was closed and the banker returned to business.

"Your account, sir," he said, selecting a key from the ring. "May I unlock the case or would you prefer doing so yourself?"

"Go ahead. Open it."

The banker looked up. "I said unlock, not open. That's not my privilege, nor would I care for the responsibility."

"Why not?"

"In the event your identity is listed, it's not my position to be aware of it."

"Suppose I wanted business transacted? Money transferred, sent to someone else?"

"It could be accomplished with your numerical signature on a withdrawal form."

"Or sent to another bank—outside of Switzerland? For me."

"Then a name would be required. Under those circumstances an identity would be both my responsibility and my privilege."

"Open it."

The bank officer did so. Dr. Washburn's patient held his breath, a sharp pain forming in the pit of his stomach. Apfel took out a sheaf of statements held together by an outsized paperclip. His banker's eyes strayed to the righthand column of the top pages, his banker's expression unchanged, but not totally. His lower lip stretched ever so slightly, creasing the corner of his mouth; he leaned forward and handed the pages to their owner.

Beneath the Gemeinschaft letterhead the typewritten words were in English, the obvious language of the client:

Account:
Zero—Seven—Seventeen—Twelve—Zero—Fourteen—Twenty-six—Zero
Name: Restricted to Legal Instructions and Owner
Access: Sealed Under Separate Cover
Current Funds on Deposit: 7,500,000 Francs

The patient exhaled slowly, staring at the figure. Whatever he *thought* he was prepared for, nothing prepared him for this. It was as frightening as anything he had experienced during the past five months. Roughly calculated the amount was over five million American dollars.

$5,000,000!

How? Why?

Controlling the start of a tremble in his hand, he leafed through the statements of entry. They were numerous, the sums extraordinary, none less than 300,000 francs, the deposits spaced every five to eight weeks apart, going back twenty-three months. He reached the bottom statement, the first. It was a transfer from a bank in Singapore and the largest single entry. Two million, seven hundred thousand Malaysian dollars converted into 5,175,000 Swiss francs.

Beneath the statement he could feel the outline of a separate envelope, far shorter than the page itself. He lifted up the paper; the envelope was rimmed with a black border, typewritten words on the front.

Identity: *Owner Access*
Legal Restrictions: *Access—Registered Officer, Treadstone Seventy-One Corporation, Bearer Will Produce Written Instructions From Owner. Subject To Verifications.*

"I'd like to check this," said the client.

"It's your property," replied Apfel. "I can assure you it has remained intact."

The patient removed the envelope and turned it over. A Gemeinschaft seal was pressed over the borders of the flap; none of the raised letters had been disturbed. He tore the flap open, took out the card, and read:

Owner: *Jason Charles Bourne*
Address: *Unlisted*
Citizenship: *U.S.A.*

Jason Charles Bourne.

Jason.

The J was for Jason! His name was *Jason Bourne.* The *Bourne* had meant nothing, the *J.* Bourne still meaningless, but in the combination Jason *and* Bourne, obscure tumblers locked into place. He could accept it; he *did* accept it. He was Jason Charles Bourne, American. Yet he could feel his chest pounding; the vibration in his ears was deafening, the pain in his stomach more acute. *What was it? Why did he have the feeling that he was plunging into the darkness again, into the black waters again?*

"Is something wrong?" asked Walther Apfel.

Is something wrong, Herr Bourne?

"No. Everything's fine. My name's Bourne. Jason Bourne."

Was he shouting? Whispering? He could not tell.

"My privilege to know you, Mr. Bourne. Your identity will remain confidential. You have the word of an officer of the Bank Gemeinschaft."

"Thank you. Now, I'm afraid I've got to transfer a great deal of this money and I'll need your help."

"Again, my privilege. Whatever assistance or advice I can render, I shall be happy to do so."

Bourne reached for the glass of Perrier.

The steel door of Apfel's office closed behind him; within seconds he would walk out of the tasteful anteroom cell, into the reception room and over to the elevators. Within minutes he would be on the Bahnhofstrasse with a name, a great deal of money, and little else but fear and confusion.

He had done it. Dr. Geoffrey Washburn had been paid far in excess of the value of the life he had saved. A teletype transfer in the amount of 1,500,000 Swiss francs had been sent to a bank in Marseilles, deposited to a coded account that would find its way to Ile de Port Noir's only doctor, without Washburn's name ever being used or revealed. All Washburn had to do was to get to Marseilles, recite the codes, and the money was his. Bourne smiled to himself, picturing the expression on Washburn's face when the account was turned over to him. The eccentric, alcoholic doctor would have been overjoyed with ten or fifteen thousand pounds; he had more than a million dollars. It would either ensure his recovery or his destruction; that was his choice, his problem.

A second transfer of 4,500,000 francs was sent to a bank in Paris on the rue Madeleine, deposited in the name of Jason C. Bourne. The transfer was expedited by the Gemeinschaft's twice-weekly pouch to Paris, signature cards in triplicate sent with the documents. Herr Koenig had assured both his superior and the client that the papers would reach Paris in three days.

The final transaction was minor by comparison. One hundred thousand francs in large bills were brought to Apfel's office, the withdrawal slip signed in the account holder's numerical signature.

Remaining on deposit in the Gemeinschaft Bank were 1,400,000 Swiss francs, a not inconsequential sum by any standard.

How? Why? From where?

The entire business had taken an hour and twenty minutes, only one discordant note intruding on the smooth proceedings. In character, it had been delivered by Koenig, his expression a mixture of solemnity and minor triumph. He had rung Apfel, was admitted, and had brought a small, black-bordered envelope to his superior.

"*Une fiche,*" he had said in French.

The banker had opened the envelope, removed a card, studied the contents, and had returned both to Koenig. "Procedures will be followed," he had said.

Koenig had left.

"Did that concern me?" Bourne had asked.

"Only in terms of releasing such large amounts. Merely house policy." The banker had smiled reassuringly.

The lock clicked. Bourne opened the frosted glass door and walked out into Herr Koenig's personal fiefdom. Two other men had arrived, seated at opposite ends of the reception room. Since they were not in separate cells behind opaque glass windows, Bourne presumed that neither had a three-zero account. He wondered if they had signed names or written out a series of numbers, but he stopped wondering the instant he reached the elevator and pressed the button.

Out of the corner of his eye he perceived movement; Koenig had shifted his head, nodding at both men. They rose as the elevator door opened. Bourne turned; the man on the right had taken a small radio out of his overcoat pocket; he spoke into it—briefly, quickly.

The man on the left had his right hand concealed beneath the cloth of his raincoat. When he pulled it out he was holding a gun, a black .38 caliber automatic pistol with a perforated cylinder attached to the barrel. A silencer.

Both men converged on Bourne as he backed into the deserted elevator.

The madness began.

5

The elevator doors started to close; the man with the hand-held radio was already inside, the shoulders of his armed companion angling between the moving panels, the weapon aimed at Bourne's head.

Jason leaned to his right—a sudden gesture of fear—then abruptly, without warning, swept his left foot off the floor, pivoting, his heel plunging into the armed man's hand, sending the gun upward, reeling the man backward out of the enclosure. Two muted gunshots preceded the closing of the doors, the bullets embedding themselves in the thick wood of the ceiling. Bourne completed his pivot, his shoulder crashing into the second man's stomach, his right hand surging into the chest, his left pinning the hand with the radio. He hurled the man into the wall. The radio flew across the elevator; as it fell, words came out of its speaker.

"Henri? Ça va? Qu'est-ce qui se passe?"

The image of another Frenchman came to Jason's mind. A man on the edge of hysteria, disbelief in his eyes; a would-be killer who had raced out of Le Bouc de Mer into the shadows of the rue Sarrasin less than twenty-four hours ago. *That* man had wasted no time sending his message to Zurich: the one they thought was dead was alive. Very much alive. *Kill him!*

Bourne grabbed the Frenchman in front of him now, his left arm around the man's throat, his right hand tearing at the man's left ear. "How *many?*" he asked in French. "How many are there down there? Where *are* they?"

"Find out, *pig!*"

The elevator was halfway to the first floor lobby.

Jason angled the man's face down, ripping the ear half out of its roots, smashing the man's head into the wall. The Frenchman screamed, sinking to the floor. Bourne rammed his knee into the man's chest; he could feel the holster. He yanked the overcoat open, reached in, and pulled out a short-barreled revolver. For an instant it occurred to him that someone had deactivated the scanning machinery in the elevator. *Koenig.* He would remember; there'd be no amnesia where Herr Koenig was concerned. He jammed the gun into the Frenchman's open mouth.

"Tell me or I'll blow the back of your skull off!" The man expunged a throated wail; the weapon was withdrawn, the barrel now pressed into his cheek.

"Two. One by the elevators, one outside on the pavement, by the car."

"What *kind* of car?"

"Peugeot."

"Color?" The elevator was slowing down, coming to a stop.

"Brown."

"The man in the lobby. What's he wearing?"

"I don't know . . ."

Jason cracked the gun across the man's temple. "You'd better remember!"

"A black coat!"

The elevator stopped; Bourne pulled the Frenchman to his feet; the doors opened. To the left, a man in a dark raincoat, and wearing an odd-looking pair of gold-rimmed spectacles, stepped forward. The eyes beyond the lenses recognized the circumstances; blood was trickling down across the Frenchman's cheek. He raised his unseen hand, concealed by the wide pocket of his raincoat, another silenced automatic leveled at the target from Marseilles.

Jason propelled the Frenchman in front of him through the doors. Three rapid *spits* were heard; the Frenchman shouted, his arms raised in a final, guttural protest. He arched his back and fell to the marble floor. A woman to the right of the man with the gold-rimmed spectacles screamed, joined by several men who called to no one and everyone for *Hilfe!* for the *Polizei!*

Bourne knew he could not use the revolver he had taken from the Frenchman. It had no silencer; the sound of a gunshot would mark him. He shoved it into his topcoat pocket, sidestepped the screaming woman and grabbed the uniformed shoulders of the elevator starter, whipping the bewildered man around, throwing him into the figure of the killer in the dark raincoat.

The panic in the lobby mounted as Jason ran toward the glass doors of the entrance. The *boutonnièred* greeter who had mistaken his language an hour and a half ago was shouting into a wall telephone, a uniformed guard at his side, weapon drawn, barricading the exit, eyes riveted on the chaos, riveted suddenly on *him.* Getting out was instantly a problem. Bourne avoided the guard's eyes, directing his words to the guard's associate on the telephone.

"The man wearing gold-rimmed glasses!" he shouted. "He's the one! I saw him!"

"What? Who are you?"

"I'm a friend of Walther Apfel! *Listen* to me! The man wearing gold-rimmed glasses, in a black raincoat. Over there!"

Bureaucratic mentality had not changed in several millenniums. At the mention of a superior officer's name, one followed orders.

"Herr Apfel!" The Gemeinschaft greeter turned to the guard. "You heard him! The man wearing glasses. Gold-rimmed glasses!"

"Yes, sir!" The guard raced forward.

Jason edged past the greeter to the glass doors. He shoved the door on the right open, glancing behind him, knowing he had to run again but not knowing if a man outside on the pavement, waiting by a brown Peugeot, would recognize him and fire a bullet into his head.

The guard had run past a man in a black raincoat, a man walking more slowly than the panicked figures around him, a man wearing no glasses at all. He accelerated his pace toward the entrance, toward Bourne.

Out on the sidewalk, the growing chaos was Jason's protection. Word had gone out of the bank; wailing sirens grew louder as police cars raced up the Bahnhofstrasse. He walked several yards to the right, flanked by pedestrians, then suddenly ran, wedging his way into a curious crowd taking refuge in a storefront, his attention on the automobiles at the curb. He saw the Peugeot, saw the man standing beside it, his hand ominously in his overcoat pocket. In less than fifteen seconds, the driver of the Peugeot was joined by the man in the black raincoat, now replacing his gold-rimmed glasses, adjusting his eyes to his restored vision. The two men conferred rapidly, their eyes scanning the Bahnhofstrasse.

Bourne understood their confusion. He had walked with an absence of panic out of the Gemeinschaft's glass doors into the crowd. He had been prepared to run, but he had *not* run, for fear of being stopped until he was reasonably clear of the entrance. No one else had been permitted to do so—and the driver of the Peugeot had not made the connection. He had *not* recognized the target identified and marked for execution in Marseilles.

The first police car reached the scene as the man in the gold-rimmed spectacles removed his raincoat, shoving it through the open window of the Peugeot. He nodded to the driver, who climbed in behind the wheel and started the engine. The killer took off his delicate glasses and did the most unexpected thing Jason could imagine. He walked rapidly back toward the glass doors of the bank, joining the police who were racing inside.

Bourne watched as the Peugeot swung away from the curb and sped off down the Bahnhofstrasse. The crowd in the storefront began to disperse, many edging their way toward the glass doors, craning their necks around one another, rising on the balls of their feet, peering inside. A police officer came out, waving the curious back, demanding that a path be cleared to the curb. As he shouted, an ambulance careened around the northwest corner, its horn joining the sharp, piercing notes from its roof, warning all to get out of its way; the driver nosed his outsized vehicle to a stop in the space created by the departed Peugeot. Jason could watch no longer. He had to get to the Carillon du Lac, gather his things, and get out of Zurich, out of Switzerland. To Paris.

Why Paris? Why had he insisted that the funds be transferred to *Paris?* It had not occurred to him before he sat in Walther Apfel's office, stunned by the extraordinary figures presented him. They had been beyond anything in his imagination—so much so that he could only react numbly, instinctively. And instinct had evoked the city of Paris. As though it were somehow vital. *Why?*

Again, no time . . . He saw the ambulance crew carry a stretcher through the doors of the bank. On it was a body, the head covered, signifying death. The significance was not lost on Bourne; save for skills he could not relate to anything he understood, he was the dead man on that stretcher.

He saw an empty taxi at the corner and ran toward it. He had to get out of Zurich; a message had been sent from Marseilles, yet the dead man was alive. Jason Bourne was alive. Kill him. Kill Jason Bourne!

God in heaven, *why?*

He was hoping to see the Carillon du Lac's assistant manager behind the front desk, but he was not there. Then he realized that a short note to the man—what was his name—Stossel? Yes, Stossel—would be sufficient. An explanation for his sudden departure was not required and five hundred francs would easily take care of the few hours he had accepted from the Carillon du Lac—and the favor he would ask of Herr Stossel.

In his room, he threw his shaving equipment into his unpacked suitcase, checked the pistol he had taken from the Frenchman, leaving it in his topcoat pocket, and sat down at the desk; he wrote out the note for Herr Stossel, Ass't. Mgr. In it he included a sentence that came easily—almost too easily.

. . . *I may be in contact with you shortly relative to messages I expect will have been sent to me. I trust it will be convenient for you to keep an eye out for them, and accept them on my behalf.*

If any communication came from the elusive Treadstone Seventy-One, he wanted to know about it. This was Zurich; he would.

He put a five hundred franc note between the folded stationery and sealed the envelope. Then he picked up his suitcase, walked out of the room, and went down the hallway to the bank of elevators. There were four; he touched a button and looked behind him, remembering the Gemeinschaft. There was no one there; a bell pinged and the red light above the third elevator flashed on. He had caught a descending machine. Fine. He had to get to the airport just as fast as he could; he had to get out of Zurich, out of Switzerland. A message had been delivered.

The elevators doors opened. Two men stood on either side of an auburn-haired woman; they interrupted their conversation, nodded at the newcomer—noting the suitcase and moving to the side—then resumed talking as the doors closed. They were in their mid-thirties and spoke French softly, rapidly, the woman glancing alternately at both men, alternately smiling and looking pensive. Decisions of no great import were being made. Laughter intermingled with semiserious interrogation.

"You'll be going home then after the summations tomorrow?" asked the man on the left.

"I'm not sure. I'm waiting for word from Ottawa," the woman replied. "I have relations in Lyon; it would be good to see them."

"It's impossible," said the man on the right, "for the steering committee to find ten people willing to summarize this Godforsaken conference in a single day. We'll all be here another week."

"Brussels will not approve," said the first man grinning. "The hotel's too expensive."

"Then by all means move to another," said the second with a leer at the woman. "We've been waiting for you to do just that, haven't we?"

"You're a lunatic," said the woman. "You're both lunatics, and that's *my* summation."

"You're not, Marie," interjected the first. "A lunatic, I mean. Your presentation yesterday was brilliant."

"It was nothing of the sort," she said. "It was routine and quite dull."

"No, no!" disagreed the second. "It was superb; it had to be. I didn't understand a word. But then I have other talents."

"Lunatic . . ."

The elevator was braking; the first man spoke again. "Let's sit in the back row of the hall. We're late anyway and Bertinelli is speaking—to little effect, I suggest. His theories of enforced cyclical fluctuations went out with the finances of the Borgias."

"Before then," said the auburn-haired woman, laughing. "Caesar's taxes." She paused, then added, "If not the Punic wars."

"The back row then," said the second man, offering his arm to the woman. "We can sleep. He uses a slide projector; it'll be dark."

"No, you two go ahead, I'll join you in a few minutes. I really must send off some cables and I don't trust the telephone operators to get them right."

The doors opened and the threesome walked out of the elevator. The two men started diagonally across the lobby together, the woman toward the front desk. Bourne fell in step behind her, absently reading a sign on a triangular stand several feet away.

WELCOME TO:
MEMBERS OF THE SIXTH WORLD ECONOMIC CONFERENCE
TODAY'S SCHEDULE:
1:00 P.M.: THE HON. JAMES FRAZIER, M.P. UNITED KINGDOM.
SUITE 12
6:00 P.M.: DR. EUGENIO BERTINELLI, UNIV. OF MILAN, ITALY.
SUITE 7
9:00 P.M.: CHAIRMAN'S FAREWELL DINNER. HOSPITALITY SUITE

"Room 507. The operator said there was a cablegram for me."

English. The auburn-haired woman now beside him at the counter spoke

English. But then she had said she was "waiting for word from Ottawa." A Canadian.

The desk clerk checked the slots and returned with the cable. "Dr. St. Jacques?" he asked, holding out the envelope.

"Yes. Thanks very much."

The woman turned away, opening the cable, as the clerk moved in front of Bourne. "Yes, sir?"

"I'd like to leave this note for Herr Stossel." He placed the Carillon du Lac envelope on the counter.

"Herr Stossel will not return until six o'clock in the morning, sir. In the afternoons, he leaves at four. Might I be of service?"

"No, thanks. Just make sure he gets it, please." Then Jason remembered: this was Zurich. "It's nothing urgent," he added, "but I need an answer. I'll check with him in the morning."

"Of course, sir."

Bourne picked up his suitcase and started across the lobby toward the hotel's entrance, a row of wide glass doors that led to a circular drive fronting the lake. He could see several taxis waiting in line under the floodlights of the canopy; the sun had gone down; it was night in Zurich. Still, there were flights to all points of Europe until well past midnight. . . .

He stopped walking, his breath suspended, a form of paralysis sweeping over him. His eyes did not believe what else he saw beyond the glass doors. A brown Peugeot pulled up in the circular drive in front of the first taxi. It's door opened and a man stepped out—a killer in a black raincoat, wearing thin, gold-rimmed spectacles. Then from the other door another figure emerged, but it was not the driver who had been at the curb on the Bahnhofstrasse, waiting for a target he did not recognize. Instead, it was another killer, in another raincoat, its wide pockets recessed for powerful weapons. It was the man who had sat in the reception room on the second floor of the Gemeinschaft Bank, the same man who had pulled a .38 caliber pistol from a holster beneath his coat. A pistol with a perforated cylinder on its barrel that silenced two bullets meant for the skull of the quarry he had followed into an elevator.

How? How could they have found him? . . . Then he remembered and felt sick. It had been so innocuous, so casual!

Are you enjoying your stay in Zurich? Walther Apfel had asked while they were waiting for a minion to leave and be alone again.

Very much. My room overlooks the lake. It's a nice view, very peaceful, quiet.

Koenig! Koenig had heard him say his room looked over the lake. How many hotels had rooms overlooking the lake? Especially hotels a man with a three-zero account might frequent. Two? Three? . . . From unremembered memory names came to him: *Carillon du Lac, Baur au Lac, Eden au Lac.* Were there others? No further names came. How easy it must have been to narrow them down! How easy it had been for him to say the words. How stupid!

No time. Too late. He could see through the row of glass doors; so, too, could the killers. The second man had spotted him. Words were exchanged over the hood of the Peugeot, gold-rimmed spectacles adjusted, hands placed in outsized pockets, unseen weapons gripped. The two men converged on the entrance, separating at the last moment, one on either end of the row of clear glass panels. The flanks were covered, the trap set; he could not race outside.

Did they think they could walk into a crowded hotel lobby and simply *kill* a man?

Of course they could, The crowds and the noise were their cover. Two, three, four muted gunshots fired at close range would be as effective as an ambush in a crowded square in daylight, escape easily found in the resulting chaos.

He could not let them get near him! He backed away, thoughts racing through his mind, outrage paramount. How *dared* they? What made them think he would not run for protection, scream for the police? And then the answer was clear, as numbing as the question itself. The killers knew with certainty that which he could only surmise: he could not seek that kind of protection—he could not seek the police. For Jason Bourne, all the authorities had to be avoided. . . . Why? Were they seeking *him?*

Jesus Christ, why?

The two opposing doors were opened by outstretched hands, other hands hidden, around steel. Bourne turned; there were elevators, doorways, corridors—a roof and cellars; there had to be a dozen ways out of the hotel.

Or were there? Did the killers now threading their way through the crowds know something else he could only surmise? Did the Carillon du Lac have only two or three exits? Easily covered by men outside, easily used as traps themselves to cut down the lone figure of a running man.

A lone man; a lone man was an obvious target. But suppose he were not alone? Suppose someone was with him? Two people were not one, but for one alone an extra person was camouflage—especially in crowds, especially at night, and it *was* night. Determined killers avoided taking the wrong life, not from compassion but for practicality; in any ensuing panic the real target might escape.

He felt the weight of the gun in his pocket, but there was not much comfort in knowing it was there. As at the bank, to use it—to even display it—was to mark him. Still, it was there. He started back toward the center of the lobby, then turned to his right where there was a greater concentration of people. It was the pre-evening hour during an international conference, a thousand tentative plans being made, rank and courtesan separated by glances of approval and rebuke, odd groupings everywhere.

There was a marble counter against the wall, a clerk behind it checking pages of yellow paper with a pencil held like a paintbrush. *Cablegrams.* In front of the counter were two people, an obese elderly man and a woman in a dark red dress, the rich color of the silk complementing her long, titian hair. . . . Auburn hair. It was the woman in the elevator who had joked about Caesar's taxes and the Punic wars, the doctor who had stood beside him at the hotel desk, asking for the cable she knew was there.

Bourne looked behind him. The killers were using the crowds well, excusing themselves politely but firmly through, one on the right, one on the left, closing in like two prongs of a pincer attack. As long as they kept him in sight, they could force him to keep running blindly, without direction, not knowing which path he took might lead to a dead end where he could run no longer. And then the muted spits would come, pockets blackened by powder burns. . . .

Kept him in sight?

The back row then. . . . We can sleep. He uses a slide projector; it'll be dark.

Jason turned again and looked at the auburn-haired woman. She had completed her cable and was thanking the clerk, removing a pair of tinted, horn-rimmed glasses from her face, placing them into her purse. She was not more than eight feet away.

Bertinelli is speaking, to little effect, I suggest.

There was no time for anything but instinctive decisions. Bourne shifted his suitcase to his left hand, walked rapidly over to the woman at the marble counter, and touched her elbow, gently, with as little alarm as possible.

"Doctor? . . ."

"I beg your pardon?"

"You *are* Doctor? . . ." He released her, a bewildered man.

"St. Jacques," she completed, using the French pronunciation of Saint. "You're the one in the elevator."

"I didn't realize it was you," he said. "I was told you'd know where this Bertinelli is speaking."

"It's right on the board. Suite Seven."

"I'm afraid I don't know where it is. Would you mind showing me? I'm late and I've got to take notes on his talk."

"On Bertinelli? Why? Are you with a Marxist newspaper?"

"A neutral pool," said Jason, wondering where the phrases came from. "I'm covering for a number of people. They don't think he's worth it."

"Perhaps not, but he should be heard. There are a few brutal truths in what he says."

"I lost, so I've got to find him. Maybe you can point him out."

"I'm afraid not. I'll show you the room, but I've a phone call to make." She snapped her purse shut.

"Please. *Hurry!*"

"What?" She looked at him, not kindly.

"Sorry, but I *am* in a hurry." He glanced to his right; the two men were no more than twenty feet away.

"You're also rude," said the St. Jacques woman coldly.

"Please." He restrained his desire to propel her forward, away from the moving trap that was closing in.

"It's this way." She started across the floor toward a wide corridor carved out of the left rear wall. The crowds were thinner, prominence less apparent in the back regions of the lobby. They reached what looked like a velvet-covered tunnel of deep red, doors on opposite sides, lighted signs above them identifying Conference Room One, Conference Room Two. At the end of the hallway were double doors, the gold letters to the right proclaiming them to be the entrance to Suite Seven.

"There you are," said Marie St. Jacques. "Be careful when you go in; it's probably dark. Bertinelli lectures with slides."

"Like a movie," commented Bourne, looking behind him at the crowds at the far end of the corridor. He was there; the man with gold-rimmed spectacles was excusing himself past an animated trio in the lobby. He was walking into the hallway, his companion right behind him.

". . . a considerable difference. He sits below the stage and pontificates." The St. Jacques woman had said something and was now leaving him.

"What did you say? A stage?"

"Well, a raised platform. For exhibits usually."

"They have to be brought in," he said.

"What does?"

"Exhibits. Is there an exit in there? Another door?"

"I have no idea, and I really must make my call. Enjoy the *professore.*" She turned away.

He dropped the suitcase and took her arm. At the touch, she glared at him. "Take your hand off me, please."

"I don't want to frighten you, but I have no choice." He spoke quietly, his eyes over her shoulder; the killers had slowed their pace, the trap sure, about to close. "You have to come with me."

"Don't be ridiculous!"

He viced the grip around her arm, moving her in front of him. Then he pulled the gun out of his pocket, making sure her body concealed it from the men thirty feet away. "I don't want to use this. I don't want to hurt you, but I'll do both if I have to."

"My God . . ."

"Be quiet. Just do as I say and you'll be fine. I have to get out of this hotel and you're going to help me. Once I'm out, I'll let you go. But not until then. Come on. We're going in there."

"You *can't* . . ."

"Yes, I can." He pushed the barrel of the gun into her stomach, into the dark silk that creased under the force of his thrust. She was terrified into silence, into submission. "Let's go."

He stepped to her left, his hand still gripping her arm, the pistol held across his chest inches from her own. Her eyes were riveted on it, her lips parted, her breath erratic. Bourne opened the door, propelling her through it in front of him. He could hear a single word shouted from the corridor.

"*Schnell!*"

They were in darkness, but it was brief; a shaft of white light shot across the room, over the rows of chairs, illuminating the heads of the audience. The projection on the faraway screen on the stage was that of a graph, the grids marked numerically, a heavy black line starting at the left, extending in a jagged pattern through the lines to the right. A heavily accented voice was speaking, amplified by a loudspeaker.

"You will note that during the years of seventy and seventy-one, when specific restraints in production were self-imposed—I repeat, *self-*imposed—by these leaders of industry, the resulting economic recession was far less severe than in—slide twelve, please—the so-called paternalistic regulation of the marketplace by government interventionists. The next slide, please."

The room went dark again. There was a problem with the projector; no second shaft of light replaced the first.

"Slide twelve, please!"

Jason pushed the woman forward, in front of the figures standing by the back wall, behind the last row of chairs. He tried to judge the size of the lecture hall, looking for a red light that could mean escape. He saw it! A faint reddish glow in the distance. On the stage, behind the screen. There were no other exits, no other doors but the entrance to Suite Seven. He had to reach it; he had to get them to that exit. On that stage.

"Marie—par ici!" The whisper came from their left, from a seat in the back row.

"Non, chérie. Reste avec moi." The second whisper was delivered by the shadowed figure of a man standing directly in front of Marie St. Jacques. He had stepped away from the wall, intercepting her. *"On nous a séparé. I'l n'y a plus de chaises."*

Bourne pressed the gun firmly into the woman's rib cage, its message unmistakable. She whispered without breathing, Jason grateful that her face could not be seen clearly. "Please, let us by," she said in French. *"Please."*

"What's this? Is he your cablegram, my dear?"

"An old friend," whispered Bourne.

A shout rose over the increasingly louder hum from the audience. "May I please have *slide twelve! Per favore!"*

"We have to see someone at the end of the row," continued Jason, looking behind him. The right-hand door of the entrance opened; in the middle of a shadowed face, a pair of gold-rimmed glasses reflected the dim light of the corridor. Bourne edged the girl past her bewildered friend, forcing him back into the wall, whispering an apology.

"Sorry, but we're in a hurry!"

"You're damned rude, too!"

"Yes, I know."

"Slide *twelve! Ma che infamia!"*

The beam of light shot out from the projector; it vibrated under the nervous hand of the operator. Another graph appeared on the screen as Jason and the woman reached the far wall, the start of the narrow aisle that led down the length of the hall to the stage. He pushed her into the corner, pressing his body against hers, his face against her face.

"I'll scream," she whispered.

"I'll shoot," he said. He peered around the figures leaning against the wall; the killers were both inside, both squinting, shifting their heads like alarmed rodents, trying to spot their target among the rows of faces.

The voice of the lecturer rose like the ringing of a cracked bell, his diatribe brief but strident. *"Ecco!* For the skeptics I address here this evening—and that is most of you—here is statistical proof! Identical in substance to a hundred other analyses I have prepared. Leave the marketplace to those who live there. Minor excesses can always be found. They are a small price to pay for the general good."

There was a scattering of applause, the approval of a definite minority. Bertinelli resumed a normal tone and droned on, his long pointer stabbing at the screen, emphasizing the obvious—his obvious. Jason leaned back again; the gold spectacles glistened in the harsh glare of the projector's side light, the killer who wore them touching his companion's arm, nodding to his left, ordering his subordinate to continue the search on the left side of the room; he would take the right. He began, the gold rims growing brighter as he sidestepped his way in front of those standing, studying each face. He would reach the corner, reach *them,* in a matter of seconds. Stopping the killer with a gunshot was all that was left; and if someone along the row of those standing moved, or if the woman he had pressed against the wall went into panic and shoved him . . . or if he missed the killer for any number of reasons, he was trapped. And even if he hit the man, there was another killer across the room, certainly a marksman.

"Slide *thirteen,* if you please."

That was *it. Now!*

The shaft of light went out. In the blackout, Bourne pulled the woman from the wall, spun her in her place, his face against hers. "If you make a sound, I'll kill you!"

"I believe you," she whispered, terrified. "You're a maniac."

"Let's go!" He pushed her down the narrow aisle that led to the stage fifty feet away. The projector's light went on again; he grabbed the girl's neck, forcing her down into a kneeling position as he, too, knelt down behind her. They were concealed from the killers by the rows of bodies sitting in the chairs. He pressed her flesh with his fingers; it was his signal to keep moving, crawling . . . slowly, keeping down, but *moving.* She understood; she started forward on her knees, trembling.

"The conclusions of this phase are irrefutable," cried the lecturer. "The profit motive is inseparable from productivity incentive, but the adversary roles can never be equal. As Socrates understood, the inequality of values is constant. Gold simply is not brass or iron; who among you can deny it? Slide fourteen, if you please!"

The darkness again. *Now.*

He yanked the woman up, pushing her forward, toward the stage. They were within three feet of the edge.

"Cosa succede?" What is the matter, please? Slide *fourteen!"*

It had happened! The projector was jammed again; the darkness was extended again. And there on the stage in front of them, above them, was the red glow of the exit sign. Jason gripped the girl's arm viciously. "Get up on that stage and run to the exit! I'm right behind you; you stop or cry out, I'll shoot."

"For God's sake, let me go!"

"Not yet." He meant it; there was another exit somewhere, men waiting outside for the target from Marseilles. "Go on! *Now.*"

The St. Jacques woman got to her feet and ran to the stage. Bourne lifted her off the floor, over the edge, leaping up as he did so, pulling her to her feet again.

The blinding light of the projector shot out, flooding the screen, washing the stage. Cries of surprise and derision came from the audience at the sight of two figures, the shouts of the indignant Bertinelli heard over the din.

"*È insoffribile! Ci sono comunisti qui!*"

And there were other sounds—three—lethal, sharp, sudden. Cracks of a muted weapon—weapons; wood splintered on the molding of the proscenium arch. Jason hammered the girl down and lunged toward the shadows of the narrow wing space, pulling her behind him.

"*Da ist er! Da oben!*"

"*Schnell! Der Projektor!*"

A scream came from the center aisle of the hall as the light of the projector swung to the right, spilling into the wings—but not completely. Its beam was intercepted by receding upright flats that masked the offstage area; *light, shadow, light, shadow.* And at the end of the flats, at the rear of the stage, was the exit. A high, wide metal door with a crashbar against it.

Glass shattered; the red light exploded, a marksman's bullet blew out the sign above the door. It did not matter; he could see the gleaming brass of the crashbar clearly.

The lecture hall had broken out in pandemonium. Bourne grabbed the woman by the cloth of her blouse, yanking her beyond the flats toward the door. For an instant she resisted; he slapped her across the face and dragged her beside him until the crashbar was above their heads.

Bullets spat into the wall to their right; the killers were racing down the aisles for accurate sightlines. They would reach them in seconds, and in seconds other bullets, or a single bullet, would find its mark. There were enough shells left, he knew that. He had no idea how or why he knew, but he *knew.* By sound he could visualize the weapons, extract the clips, count the shells.

He smashed his forearm into the crashbar of the exit door. It flew open and he lunged through the opening, dragging the kicking St. Jacques woman with him.

"Stop it!" she screamed. "I won't go any farther! You're insane! Those were gunshots!"

Jason slammed the large metal door shut with his foot. "Get up!"

"No!"

He lashed the back of his hand across her face. "Sorry, but you're coming with me. Get up! Once we're outside, you have my word. I'll let you go." But where was he going now? They were in another tunnel, but there was no carpet, no polished doors with lighted signs above them. They were in some sort of deserted loading area; the floor was concrete, and there were two pipe-framed freight dollies next to him against the wall. He had been right: exhibits used on the stage of Suite Seven had to be trucked in, the exit door high enough and wide enough to accommodate large displays.

The *door!* He had to block the door! Marie St. Jacques was on her feet; he held her as he grabbed the first dolly, pulling it by its frame in front of the exit door, slamming it with his shoulder and knee until it was lodged against the metal. He looked down; beneath the thick wooden base were footlocks on the wheels. He jammed his heel down on the front lever lock, and then the back one.

The girl spun, trying to break his grip as he stretched his leg to the end of the dolly; he slid his hand down her arm, gripped her wrist, and twisted it inward. She screamed, tears in her eyes, her lips trembling. He pulled her alongside him, forcing her to the left, breaking into a run, assuming the direction was toward the rear of the Carillon du Lac, hoping he'd find the exit. For there and only there he might need the woman; a brief few seconds when a couple emerged, not a lone man running.

There was a series of loud crashes; the killers were trying to force the stage door open, but the locked freight dolly was too heavy a barrier.

He yanked the girl along the cement floor; she tried to pull away, kicking again, twisting her body again from one side to the other; she was over the edge of hysteria. He had no choice; he gripped her elbow, his thumb on the inner flesh, and pressed as hard as he could. She gasped, the pain sudden and excruciating; she sobbed, expelling breath, allowing him to propel her forward.

They reached a cement staircase, the four steps edged in steel, leading to a pair of metal doors below. It was the loading dock; beyond the doors was the Carillon du Lac's rear parking area. He was almost there. It was only a question of appearances now.

"Listen to me," he said to the rigid, frightened woman. "Do you want me to let you go?"

"Oh God, yes! *Please!*"

"Then you do exactly as I say. We're going to walk down these steps and out that door like two perfectly normal people at the end of a normal day's work. You're going to link your arm in mine and we're going to walk slowly, talking quietly, to the cars at the far end of the parking lot. And we're both going to laugh—not loudly, just casually—as if we were remembering funny things that happened during the day. Have you got that?"

"Nothing funny at all has happened to me during the past fifteen minutes," she answered in a barely audible monotone.

"Pretend that it has. I may be trapped; if I am I don't care. Do you understand?"

"I think my wrist is broken."

"It's not."

"My left arm, my shoulder. I can't move them; they're throbbing."

"A nerve ending was depressed; it'll pass in a matter of minutes. You'll be fine."

"You're an animal."

"I want to live," he said. "Come on. Remember, when I open the door, look at me and smile, tilt your head back, laugh a little."

"It will be the most difficult thing I've ever done."

"It's easier than dying."

She put her injured hand under his arm and they walked down the short flight of steps to the platform door. He opened it and they went outside, his hand in his topcoat pocket gripping the Frenchman's pistol, his eyes scanning the loading dock. There was a single bulb encased in wire mesh above the door, its spill defining the concrete steps to the left that led to the pavement below; he led his hostage toward them.

She performed as he had ordered, the effect macabre. As they walked down the steps, her face was turned to his, her terrified features caught in the light. Her generous lips were parted, stretched over her white teeth in a false, tense smile; her wide eyes were two dark orbs, reflecting primordial fear, her tear-stained skin taut and pale, marred by the reddish splotches where he had hit her. He was looking at a face of chiseled stone, a mask framed by dark red hair that cascaded over her shoulders, swept back by the night breezes—moving, the only living thing about the mask.

Choked laughter came from her throat, the veins in her long neck pronounced. She was not far from collapsing, but he could not think about that. He had to concentrate on the space around them, at whatever movement—however slight—he might discern in the shadows of the large parking lot. It was obvious that these back, unlit regions were used by the Carillon du Lac's employees; it was nearly 6:30, the night shift well immersed in its duties. Everything was still, a smooth black field broken up by rows of silent automobiles, ranks of huge insects, the dull glass of the headlamps a hundred eyes staring at nothing.

A scratch. Metal had scraped against metal. It came from the right, from one of the cars in a nearby row. Which *row?* Which *car?* He tilted his head back as if responding to a joke made by his companion, letting his eyes roam across the windows of the cars nearest to them. Nothing.

Something? It was there but it was so small, barely seen . . . so bewildering. A tiny circle of green, an infinitesimal glow of green light. It moved . . . as they moved.

Green. Small . . . *light?* Suddenly, from somewhere in a forgotten past the image of crosshairs burst across his eyes. His eyes were looking at two thin intersecting lines! *Crosshairs!* A scope . . . an infrared scope of a rifle.

How did the killers know? Any number of answers. A hand-held radio had been used at the Gemeinschaft; one could be in use now. He wore a topcoat; his hostage wore a thin silk dress and the night was cool. No woman would go out like that.

He swung to his left, crouching, lunging into Marie St. Jacques, his shoulder crashing into her stomach, sending her reeling back toward the steps. The muffled cracks came in staccato repetition; stone and asphalt exploded all around them. He dove to his right, rolling over and over again the instant he made contact with the pavement, yanking the pistol from his topcoat pocket. Then he sprang again, now straight forward, his left hand steadying his right wrist, the gun centered, aimed at the window with the rifle. He fired three shots.

A scream came from the dark open space of the stationary car; it was drawn out into a cry, then a gasp, and then nothing. Bourne lay motionless, waiting, listening, watching, prepared to fire again. Silence. He started to get up . . . but he could not. Something had happened. He could barely move. Then the pain spread through his chest, the pounding so violent he bent over, supporting himself with both hands, shaking his head, trying to focus his eyes, trying to reject the agony. His left shoulder, his lower chest—below the ribs . . . his left thigh— above the knee, below the hip; the locations of his previous wounds, where dozens of stitches had been removed over a month ago. He had damaged the weakened areas, stretching tendons and muscles not yet fully restored. Oh, Christ! He had to get up; he had to reach the would-be killer's car, pull the killer from it, and get away.

He whipped his head up, grimacing with the pain, and looked over at Marie St. Jacques. She was getting slowly to her feet, first on one knee, then on one foot, supporting herself on the outside wall of the hotel. In a moment she would be standing, then running. Away.

He could not let her go! She would race screaming into the Carillon du Lac; men would come, some to take him . . . some to kill him. He had to stop her!

He let his body fall forward and started rolling to his left, spinning like a wildly out-of-control mannikin, until he was within four feet of the wall, four feet from her. He raised his gun, aiming at her head.

"Help me up," he said, hearing the strain in his voice.

"What?"

"You heard me! Help me *up.*"

"You said I could go! You gave me your word!"

"I have to take it back."

"No, *please.*"

"This gun is aimed directly at your face, Doctor. You come here and help me get up or I'll blow it off."

He pulled the dead man from the car and ordered her to get behind the wheel. Then he opened the rear door and crawled into the back seat out of sight.

"Drive," he said. "Drive where I tell you."

6

Whenever you're in a stress situation yourself—and there's time, of course—do exactly as you would do when you project yourself into one you're observing. Let your mind fall free, let whatever thoughts and images that surface come cleanly. Try not to exercise any mental discipline. Be a sponge; concentrate on everything and nothing. Specifics may come to you, certain repressed conduits electrically prodded into functioning.

Bourne thought of Washburn's words as he adjusted his body into the corner of the seat, trying to restore some control. He massaged his chest, gently rubbing the bruised muscles around his previous wound; the pain was still there, but not as acute as it had been minutes ago.

"You can't just tell me to drive!" cried the St. Jacques woman. "I don't know where I'm going!"

"Neither do I," said Jason. He had told her to stay on the lakeshore drive; it was dark and he had to have time to think. If only to be a sponge.

"People will be *looking* for me," she exclaimed.

"They're looking for me, too."

"You've taken me against my will. You struck me. Repeatedly." She spoke more softly now, imposing a control on herself. "That's kidnapping, assault . . . those are serious crimes. You're out of the hotel; that's what you said you wanted. Let me go and I won't say anything. I promise you!"

"You mean you'll give me your word?"

"Yes!"

"I gave you mine and took it back. So could you."

"You're different. I *won't*. No one's trying to kill me! Oh God! *Please!*"

"Keep driving."

One thing was clear to him. The killers had seen him drop his suitcase and leave it behind in his race for escape. That suitcase told them the obvious: he was getting out of Zurich, undoubtedly out of Switzerland. The airport and the train station would be watched. And the car he had taken from the man he had killed—who had tried to kill him—would be the object of a search.

He could not go to the airport or to the train station; he had to get rid of the car and find another. Yet he was not without resources. He was carrying 100,000 Swiss francs, and more than 16,000 French francs, the Swiss currency in his passport case, the French in the billfold he had stolen from the Marquis de Chamford. It was more than enough to buy him secretly to Paris.

Why Paris? It was as though the city were a magnet, pulling him to her without explanation.

You are not helpless. You will find your way. . . . Follow your instincts, reasonably, of course.

To Paris.

"Have you been to Zurich before?" he asked his hostage.

"Never."

"You wouldn't lie to me, would you?"

"I've no *reason* to! *Please.* Let me stop. Let me *go!*"

"How long have you been here?"

"A week. The conference was for a week."

"Then you've had time to get around, do some sightseeing."

"I barely left the hotel. There wasn't time."

"The schedule I saw on the board didn't seem very crowded. Only two lectures for the entire day."

"They were guest speakers; there were never more than two a day. The majority of our work was done in conference . . . small conferences. Ten to fifteen people from different countries, different interests."

"You're from Canada?"

"I work for the Canadian government Treasury Board, Department of National Revenue."

"The 'doctor's' not medical then."

"Economics. McGill University. Pembroke College, Oxford."

"I'm impressed."

Suddenly, with controlled stridency, she added, "My superiors expect me to be in contact with them. *Tonight.* If they don't hear from me, they'll be alarmed. They'll make inquiries; they'll call the Zurich police."

"I see," he said. "That's something to think about, isn't it?" It occurred to Bourne that throughout the shock and the violence of the last half hour, the St. Jacques woman had not let her purse out of her hand. He leaned forward, wincing as he did so, the pain in his chest suddenly acute again. "Give me your purse."

"What?" She moved her hand quickly from the wheel, grabbing the purse in a futile attempt to keep it from him.

He thrust his right hand over the seat, his fingers grasping the leather. "Just drive, Doctor," he said as he lifted the purse off the seat and leaned back again.

"You have no *right* . . ." She stopped, the foolishness of her remark apparent.

"I know that," he replied, opening the purse, turning on the sedan's reading lamp, moving the handbag into its spill. As befitted the owner, the purse was well organized. Passport, wallet, a change purse, keys, and assorted notes and messages in the rear pockets. He looked for a specific message; it was in a yellow envelope given her by the clerk at the Carillon du Lac's front desk. He found it, lifted the flap, and took out the folded paper. It was a cablegram from Ottawa.

DAILY REPORTS FIRST RATE. LEAVE GRANTED. WILL MEET YOU AT AIRPORT WEDNESDAY 26. CALL OR CABLE FLIGHT. IN LYON DO NOT MISS BELLE MEU-NIERE. CUISINE SUPERB. LOVE PETER

Jason put the cable back in the purse. He saw a small book of matches, the cover a glossy white, scroll writing on the front. He picked it out and read the name. Kronenhalle. A restaurant . . . A restaurant. Something bothered him; he did not know what it was, but it was there. Something about a restaurant. He kept the matches, closed the purse, and leaned forward, dropping it on the front seat. "That's all I wanted to see," he said, settling back into the corner, staring at the matches. "I seem to remember your saying something about 'word from Ottawa.' You got it; the twenty-sixth is over a week away."

"Please . . ."

The supplication was a cry for help; he heard it for what it was but could not respond. For the next hour or so he needed this woman, needed her as a lame man needed a crutch, or more aptly, as one who could not function behind a wheel needed a driver. But not in this car.

"Turn around," he ordered. "Head back to the Carillon."

"To the . . . hotel?"

"Yes," he said, his eyes on the matches, turning them over and over in his hand under the light of the reading lamp. "We need another car."

"We? No, you can't! I won't go any—" Again she stopped before the statement was made, before the thought was completed. Another thought had obviously struck her; she was abruptly silent as she swung the wheel until the sedan was facing the opposite direction on the dark lakeshore road. She pressed the accelerator down with such force that the car bolted; the tires spun under the sudden burst of speed. She depressed the pedal instantly, gripping the wheel, trying to control herself.

Bourne looked up from the matches at the back of her head, at the long dark red hair that shone in the light. He took the gun from his pocket and once more leaned forward directly behind her. He raised the weapon, moving his hand over her shoulder, turning the barrel and pressing it against her cheek.

"Understand me clearly. You're going to do exactly as I tell you. You're going to be right at my side and this gun will be in my pocket. It will be aimed at your stomach, just as it's aimed at your head right now. As you've seen, I'm running for my life, and I won't hesitate to pull the trigger. I want you to understand."

"I understand." Her reply was a whisper. She breathed through her parted lips, her terror complete. Jason removed the barrel of the gun from her cheek; he was satisfied.

Satisfied and revolted.

Let your mind fall free. . . . The matches. What was it about the matches? But it was not the matches, it was the restaurant—not the Kronenhalle, but a restaurant. Heavy beams, candlelight, black . . . triangles on the outside. White stone and black triangles. Three? . . . Three black triangles.

Someone was there . . . at a restaurant with three triangles in front. The image was so clear, so vivid . . . so disturbing. What was it? Did such a place even exist?

Specifics may come to you . . . certain repressed conduits . . . prodded into functioning.

Was it happening now? *Oh, Christ, I can't stand it!*

He could see the lights of the Carillon du Lac several hundred yards down the road. He had not fully thought out his moves, but was operating on two assumptions. The first was that the killers had not remained on the premises. On the other hand, Bourne was not about to walk into a trap of his own making. He knew two of the killers; he would not recognize others if they had been left behind.

The main parking area was beyond the circular drive, on the left side of the hotel. "Slow down," Jason ordered. "Turn into the first drive on the left."

"It's an exit," protested the woman, her voice strained. "We're going the wrong way."

"No one's coming out. Go on! Drive into the parking lot, past the lights."

The scene at the hotel's canopied entrance explained why no one paid attention to them. There were four police cars lined up in the circular drive, their roof lights revolving, conveying the aura of emergency. He could see uniformed police, tuxedoed hotel clerks at their sides, among the crowds of excited hotel guests; they were asking questions as well as answering them, checking off names of those leaving in automobiles.

Marie St. Jacques drove across the parking area beyond the floodlights and into an open space on the right. She turned off the engine and sat motionless, staring straight ahead.

"Be very careful," said Bourne, rolling down his window. "And move slowly. Open your door and get out, then stand by mine and help me. Remember, the window's open and the gun's in my hand. You're only two or three feet in front of me; there's no way I could miss if I fired."

She did as she was told, a terrified automaton. Jason supported himself on the frame of the window and pulled himself to the pavement. He shifted his weight from one foot to another; mobility was returning. He could walk. Not well, and with a limp, but he could walk.

"What are you going to do?" asked the St. Jacques woman, as if she were afraid to hear his answer.

"Wait. Sooner or later someone will drive a car back here and park it. No matter what happened in there, it's still dinnertime. Reservations were made, parties arranged, a lot of it business; those people won't change their plans."

"And when a car does come, how will you take it?" She paused, then answered her own question. "Oh, my God, you're going to kill whoever's driving it."

He gripped her arm, her frightened chalk-white face inches away. He had to control her by fear, but not to the point where she might slip into hysterics. "If I have to I will, but I don't think it'll be necessary. Parking attendants bring the cars back here. Keys are usually left on the dashboard or under the seats. It's just easier."

Headlight beams shot out from the fork in the circular drive; a small coupé entered the lot, accelerating once into it, the mark of an attendant driver. The car came directly toward them, alarming Bourne until he saw the empty space nearby. But they were in the path of the headlights; they had been seen.

Reservations for the dining room. . . . A *restaurant.* Jason made his decision; he would use the moment.

The attendant got out of the coupé and placed the keys under the seat. As he walked to the rear of the car, he nodded at them, not without curiosity. Bourne spoke in French.

"Hey, young fellow! Maybe you can help us."

"Sir?" The attendant approached them haltingly, cautiously, the events in the hotel obviously on his mind.

"I'm not feeling so well, too much of your excellent Swiss wine."

"It will happen, sir." The young man smiled, relieved.

"My wife thought it would be a good idea to get some air before we left for town."

"A good idea, sir."

"Is everything still crazy inside? I didn't think the police officer would let us out until he saw that I might be sick all over his uniform."

"Crazy, sir. They're everywhere. . . . We've been told not to discuss it."

"Of course. But we've got a problem. An associate flew in this afternoon and we agreed to meet at a restaurant, only I've forgotten the name. I've been there but I just can't remember where it is or what it's called. I do remember that on the front there were three odd shapes . . . a design of some sort, I think. Triangles, I believe."

"That's the Drei Alpenhäuser, sir. The . . . Three Chalets. It's in a sidestreet off the Falkenstrasse."

"Yes, of course, that's it! And to get there from here we . . ." Bourne trailed off the words, a man with too much wine trying to concentrate.

"Just turn left out of the exit, sir. Stay on the Uto Quai for about one hundred meters, until you reach a large pier, then turn right. It will take you into the Falkenstrasse. Once you pass Seefeld, you can't miss the street or the restaurant. There's a sign on the corner."

"Thank you. Will you be here a few hours from now, when we return?"

"I'm on duty until two this morning, sir."

"Good. I'll look for you and express my gratitude more concretely."

"Thank you, sir. May I get your car for you?"

"You've done enough, thanks. A little more walking is required." The attendant saluted and started for the front of the hotel. Jason led Marie St. Jacques toward the coupé, limping beside her. "Hurry up. The keys are under the seat."

"If they stop us, what will you do? That attendant will see the car go out; he'll know you've stolen it."

"I doubt it. Not if we leave right away, the minute he's back in that crowd."

"Suppose he *does?*"

"Then I hope you're a fast driver," said Bourne pushing her toward the door. "Get in." The attendant had turned the corner and suddenly hurried his pace. Jason took out the gun and limped rapidly around the hood of the coupé, supporting himself on it while pointing the pistol at the windshield. He opened the passenger door and climbed in beside her. "Goddamn it—I said get the *keys!*"

"All right . . . I can't *think.*"

"Try harder!"

"Oh, *God* . . ." She reached below the seat, stabbing her hand around the carpet until she found the small leather case.

"Start the motor, but wait until I tell you to back out." He watched for headlight beams to shine into the area from the circular drive; it would be a reason for the attendant to have suddenly broken into a near run; a car to be parked. They did not come; the reason could be something else. Two unknown people in the parking lot. "Go ahead. Quickly. I want to get out of here." She threw the gear into reverse; seconds later they approached the exit into the lakeshore drive. "Slow down," he commanded. A taxi was swinging into the curve in front of them.

Bourne held his breath and looked through the opposite window at the Carillon du Lac's entrance; the scene under the canopy explained the attendant's sudden decision to hurry. An argument had broken out between the police and a group of hotel guests. A line had formed, names checked off for those leaving the hotel, the resulting delays angering the innocent.

"Let's go," said Jason, wincing again, the pain shooting through his chest. "We're clear."

It was a numbing sensation, eerie and uncanny. The three triangles were as he had pictured them: thick dark wood raised in bas-relief on white stone. Three equal triangles, abstract renditions of chalet roofs in a valley of snow so deep the lower stories were obscured. Above the three points was the restaurant's name in Germanic letters: DREI ALPENHÄUSER. Below the baseline of the center triangles was the entrance, double doors that together formed a cathedral arch, the hardware massive rings of iron common to an Alpine château.

The surrounding buildings on both sides of the narrow brick street were restored structures of a Zurich and a Europe long past. It was not a street for automobiles; instead one pictured elaborate coaches drawn by horses, drivers sitting high in mufflers and top hats, and gas lamps everywhere. It was a street filled with the sights and sounds of forgotten memories, thought the man who had no memory to forget.

Yet he *had* had one, vivid and disturbing. Three dark triangles, heavy beams and candlelight. He had been right; it was a memory of Zurich. But in another life.

"We're here," said the woman.

"I know."

"Tell me what to do!" she cried. "We're going past it."

"Go to the next corner and turn left. Go around the block, then drive back through here."

"Why?"

"I wish I knew."

"What?"

"Because I said so." *Someone was there . . . at that restaurant. Why didn't other images come? Another image. A face.*

They drove down the street past the restaurant twice more. Two separate couples and a foursome went inside; a single man came out, heading for the Falkenstrasse. To judge from the cars parked on the curb, there was a medium-sized crowd at the Drei Alpenhäuser. It would grow in number as the next two hours passed, most of Zurich preferring its evening meal nearer ten-thirty than eight. There was no point in delaying any longer; nothing further came to Bourne. He could only sit and watch and hope something *would* come. *Something. thing.* For something had; a book of matches had evoked an image of reality. Within that reality there was a truth he had to discover.

"Pull over to your right, in front of the last car. We'll walk back."

Silently, without comment or protest, the St. Jacques woman did as she was told. Jason looked at her; her reaction was too docile, inconsistent with her previous behavior. He understood. A lesson had to be taught. Regardless of what might happen inside the Drei Alpenhäuser, he needed her for a final contribution. She had to drive him out of Zurich.

The car came to a stop, tires scraping the curb. She turned off the motor and began to remove the keys, her movement slow, too slow. He reached over and held her wrist; she stared at him in the shadows without breathing. He slid his fingers over her hand until he felt the key case.

"I'll take those," he said.

"Naturally," she replied, her left hand unnaturally at her side, poised by the panel of the door.

"Now get out and stand by the hood," he continued. "Don't do anything foolish."

"Why should I? You'd kill me."

"Good." He reached for the handle of the door, exaggerating the difficulty. The back of his head was to her; he snapped the handle down.

The rustle of fabric was sudden, the rush of air more sudden still; her door crashed open, the woman half out into the street. But Bourne was ready; a lesson had to be taught. He spun around, his left arm an uncoiling spring, his hand a claw, gripping the silk of her dress between her shoulder blades. He pulled her back into the seat, and, grabbing her by the hair, yanked her head toward him until her neck was stretched, her face against his.

"I won't do it again!" she cried, tears welling at her eyes. "I swear to you I won't!"

He reached across and pulled the door shut, then looked at her closely, trying to understand something in himself. Thirty minutes ago in another car he had experienced a degree of nausea when he had pressed the barrel of the gun into her cheek, threatening to take her life if she disobeyed him. There was no such revulsion now; with one overt action she had crossed over into another territory. She had become an enemy, a threat; he could kill her if he had to, kill her without emotion because it was the practical thing to do.

"*Say* something!" she whispered. Her body went into a brief spasm, her breasts pressing against the dark silk of her dress, rising and falling with the agitated movement. She gripped her own wrist in an attempt to control herself; she partially succeeded. She spoke again, the whisper replaced by a monotone. "I said I wouldn't do it again and I won't."

"You'll try," he replied quietly. "There'll come a moment when you think you can make it, and you'll try. Believe me when I tell you you can't, but if you try again I will have to kill you. I don't want to do that, there's no reason for it, no reason at all. Unless you become a threat to me, and in running away before I let you go you do just that. I can't allow it."

He had spoken the truth as he understood the truth. The simplicity of the decision was as astonishing to him as the decision itself. Killing was a practical matter, nothing else.

"You say you'll let me go," she said. "When?"

"When I'm safe," he answered. "When it doesn't make any difference what you say or do."

"When will that be?"

"An hour or so from now. When we're out of Zurich and I'm on my way to someplace else. You won't know where or how."

"Why should I believe you?"

"I don't care whether you do or not." He released her. "Pull yourself together. Dry your eyes and comb your hair. We're going inside."

"What's in there?"

"I wish I knew," he said, glancing through the rear window at the door of the Drei Alpenhäuser.

"You said that before."

He looked at her, at the wide brown eyes that were searching his. Searching in fear, in bewilderment. "I know. Hurry up."

There were thick beams running across the high Alpine ceiling, tables and chairs of heavy wood, deep booths and candlelight everywhere. An accordion player moved through the crowd, muted strains of Bavarian music coming from his instrument.

He had seen the large room before, the beams and the candlelight printed somewhere in his mind, the sounds recorded also. He had come here in another life. They stood in the shallow foyer in front of the maître d's station; the tuxedoed man greeted them.

"*Haben sie einen Tisch schon reserviert, mein Herr?*"

"If you mean reservations, I'm afraid not. But you were highly recommended. I hope you can fit us in. A booth, if possible."

"Certainly, sir. It's the early sitting; we're not yet crowded. This way, please."

They were taken to a booth in the nearest corner, a flickering candle in the center of the table. Bourne's limp and the fact that he held on to the woman, dictated the closest available location. Jason nodded to Marie St. Jacques; she sat down and he slid into the booth opposite her.

"Move against the wall," he said, after the maître d' had left. "Remember, the gun's in my pocket and all I have to do is raise my foot and you're trapped."

"I said I wouldn't try."

"I hope you don't. Order a drink; there's no time to eat."

"I couldn't eat." She gripped her wrist again, her hands visibly trembling. "Why isn't there time? What are you waiting for?"

"I don't know."

"Why do you keep *saying* that? 'I don't know.' 'I wish I knew.' Why did you come here?"

"Because I've been here before."

"That's no answer!"

"There's no reason for me to give you one."

A waiter approached. The St. Jacques woman asked for wine; Bourne ordered scotch, needing the stronger drink. He looked around the restaurant, trying to concentrate *on everything and nothing.* A sponge. But there was only nothing. No images filled his mind; no thoughts intruded on his absence of thought. *Nothing.*

And then he saw the face across the room. It was a large face set in a large head, above an obese body pressed against the wall of an end booth, next to a closed door. The fat man stayed in the shadows of his observation point as if they were his protection, the unlit section of the floor his sanctuary. His eyes were riveted on Jason, equal parts fear and disbelief in his stare. Bourne did not know the face, but the face knew him. The man brought his fingers to his lips and wiped the corners of his mouth, then shifted his eyes, taking in each diner at every table. Only then did he begin what was obviously a painful journey around the room toward their booth.

"A man's coming over here," Jason said over the flame of the candle. "A fat man, and he's afraid. Don't say anything. No matter what he says, keep your mouth shut. And don't look at him; raise your hand, rest your head on your elbow casually. Look at the wall, not him."

The woman frowned, bringing her right hand to her face; her fingers trembled. Her lips formed a question, but no words came. Jason answered the unspoken.

"For your own good," he said. "There's no point in his being able to identify you."

The fat man edged around the corner of the booth. Bourne blew out the candle, throwing the table into relative darkness. The man stared him down and spoke in a low, strained voice.

"*Du lieber Gott!* Why did you *come* here? What have I done that you should do this to me?"

"I enjoy the food, you know that."

"Have you no *feelings?* I have a family, a wife and children. I did only as I was told. I gave you the envelope; I did not look inside, I know nothing!"

"But you were paid, weren't you?" asked Jason instinctively.

"Yes, but I said nothing. We never met, I never described you. I spoke to no one!"

"Then why are you afraid? I'm just an ordinary patron about to order dinner."

"I beg you. Leave."

"Now I'm angry. You'd better tell me why."

The fat man brought his hand to his face, his fingers again wiping the moisture that had formed around his mouth. He angled his head, glancing at the door, then turned back to Bourne. "Others may have spoken, others may know who you are. I've had my share of trouble with the police, they would come directly to me."

The St. Jacques woman lost control; she looked at Jason, the words escaping. "The police. . . . They were the *police.*"

Bourne glared at her, then turned back to the nervous fat man. "Are you saying the police would harm your wife and children?"

"Not in themselves—as you well know. But their interest would lead others to me. To my family. How many are there that look for you, mein Herr? And what *are* they that do? You need no answer from me; they stop at nothing—the death of a wife or a child is nothing. *Please.* On my life. I've said nothing. *Leave.*"

"You're exaggerating." Jason brought the drink to his lips, a prelude to dismissal.

"In the name of Christ, don't *do* this!" The man leaned over, gripping the edge of the table. "You wish proof of my silence, I give it to you. Word was spread throughout the *Verbrecherwelt.* Anyone with any information whatsoever should call a number set up by the Zurich police. Everything would be kept in the strictest confidence; they would not lie in the *Verbrecherwelt* about that. Rewards were ample, the police in several countries sending funds through Interpol. Past misunderstandings might be seen in new judicial lights." The conspirator stood up, wiping his mouth again, his large bulk hovering above the wood. "A man like myself could profit from a kinder relationship with the police. Yet I did nothing. In spite of the guarantee of confidentiality, I did nothing at all!"

"Did anyone else? Tell me the truth; I'll know if you're lying."

"I know only Chernak. He's the only one I've ever spoken with who admits having even seen you. But you know that; the envelope was passed through him to me. He'd never say anything."

"Where's Chernak now?"

"Where he always is. In his flat on the Löwenstrasse."

"I've never been there. What's the number?"

"You've never been? . . ." The fat man paused, his lips pressed together, alarm in his eyes. "Are you testing me?"

"Answer the question."

"Number 37. You know it as well as I do."

"Then I'm testing you. Who gave the envelope to Chernak?"

The man stood motionless, his dubious integrity challenged. "I have no way of knowing. Nor would I ever inquire."

"You weren't even curious?"

"Of course not. A goat does not willingly enter the wolf's cave."

"Goats are surefooted; they've got an accurate sense of smell."

"And they are cautious, mein Herr. Because the wolf is faster, infinitely more aggressive. There would be only one chase. The goat's last."

"What was in the envelope?"

"I told you, I did not open it."

"But you know what was in it."

"Money, I presume."

"You *presume?*"

"Very well. Money. A great deal of money. If there was any discrepancy, it had nothing to do with me. Now *please*, I *beg* you. Get *out* of here!"

"One last question."

"*Anything.* Just leave!"

"What was the money for?"

The obese man stared down at Bourne, his breathing audible, sweat glistening on his chin. "You put me on the rack, mein Herr, but I will not turn away from you. Call it the courage of an insignificant goat who has survived. Every day I read the newspapers. In three languages. Six months ago a man was killed. His death was reported on the front page of each of those papers."

7

They circled the block, emerging on the Falkenstrasse, then turned right on the Limmat Quai toward the cathedral of Grossmünster. The Löwenstrasse was across the river, on the west side of the city. The quickest way to reach it was to cross the Münster Bridge to the Bahnhofstrasse, then to the Nüschelerstrasse; the streets intersected, according to a couple who had been about to enter the Drei Alpenhäuser.

Marie St. Jacques was silent, holding onto the wheel as she had gripped the straps of her handbag during the madness at the Carillon, somehow her connection with sanity. Bourne glanced at her and understood.

. . . *a man was killed, his death reported on the front pages of each of those papers.*

Jason Bourne had been paid to kill, and the police in several countries had sent funds through Interpol to convert reluctant informers, to broaden the base of his capture. Which meant that other men had been killed. . . .

How many are there that look for you, mein Herr? And what are they that do?
. . . They stop at nothing—the death of a wife or a child is nothing!

Not the police. Others.

The twin bell towers of the Grossmünster church rose in the night sky, floodlights creating eerie shadows. Jason stared at the ancient structure; as so much else he knew it but did not know it. He had seen it before, yet he was seeing it now for the first time.

I know only Chernak. . . . The envelope was passed through him to me. . . . Löwenstrasse. Number 37. You know it as well as I do.

Did he? Would he?

They drove over the bridge into the traffic of the newer city. The streets were crowded, automobiles and pedestrians vying for supremacy at every intersection, the red and green signals erratic and interminable. Bourne tried to concentrate on nothing . . . and everything. The outlines of the truth were being presented to him, shape by enigmatic shape, each more startling than the last. He was not at all sure he was capable—*mentally* capable—of absorbing a great deal more.

"Halt! Die Dame da! Die Scheinwerfer sind aus und sie haben links signaliziert. Das ist eine Einbahnstrasse!"

Jason looked up, a hollow pain knotting his stomach. A patrol car was beside them, a policeman shouting through his open window. Everything was suddenly clear . . . clear and infuriating. The St. Jacques woman had seen the police car in the sideview mirror; she had extinguished the headlights and slipped her hand down to the directional signal, flipping it for a left turn. A left turn into a one-way street whose arrows at the intersection clearly defined the traffic heading right. And turning left by bolting in front of the police car would result in several violations: the absence of headlights, perhaps even a premeditated collision; they would be stopped, the woman free to scream.

Bourne snapped the headlights on, then leaned across the girl, one hand disengaging the directional signal, the other gripping her arm where he had gripped it before.

"I'll kill you, Doctor," he said quietly, then shouted through the window at the police officer. "Sorry! We're a little confused! Tourists! We want the next block!"

The policeman was barely two feet away from Marie St. Jacques, his eyes on her face, evidently puzzled by her lack of reaction.

The light changed. "Ease forward. Don't do anything stupid," said Jason. He waved at the police officer through the glass. "Sorry again!" he yelled. The policeman shrugged, turning to his partner to resume a previous conversation.

"I *was* confused," said the girl, her soft voice trembling. "There's so much traffic. . . . Oh, God, you've broken my arm! . . . You *bastard.*"

Bourne released her, disturbed by her anger; he preferred fear. "You don't expect me to believe you, do you?"

"My arm?"

"Your confusion."

"You said we were going to turn left soon; that's all I was thinking about."

"Next time look at the traffic." He moved away from her but did not take his eyes off her face.

"You *are* an animal," she whispered, briefly closing her eyes, opening them in fear; it had come back.

They reached the Löwenstrasse, a wide avenue where low buildings of brick and heavy wood stood sandwiched between modern examples of smooth concrete and glass. The character of nineteenth-century flats competed against the utilitarianism of contemporary neuterness; they did not lose. Jason watched the numbers; they were descending from the middle eighties, with each block the old houses more in evidence than the high-rise apartments, until the street had returned in time to that other era. There was a row of neat four-story flats, roofs and windows framed in wood, stone steps and railings leading up to recessed doorways washed in the light of carriage lamps. Bourne recognized the unremembered; the fact that he did so was not startling, but something else was. The row of houses evoked another image, a very strong image of another row of flats, similar in outlines, but oddly different. Weathered, older, nowhere near as neat or scrubbed . . . cracked windows, broken steps, incomplete railings—jagged ends of rusted iron. Further away, in another part of . . . Zurich, yes they *were* in Zurich. In a small district rarely if ever visited by those who did not live there, a part of the city that was left behind, but not gracefully.

"Steppdeckstrasse," he said to himself, concentrating on the image in his mind. He could see a doorway, the paint a faded red, as dark as the red silk dress worn by the woman beside him. "A boardinghouse . . . in the Steppdeckstrasse."

"What?" Marie St. Jacques was startled. The words he uttered alarmed her; she had obviously related them to herself and was terrified.

"Nothing." He took his eyes off the dress and looked out the window. "There's Number 37," he said, pointing to the fifth house in the row. "Stop the car."

He got out first, ordering her to slide across the seat and follow. He tested his legs and took the keys from her.

"You can walk," she said. "If you can walk, you can *drive.*"

"I probably can."

"Then let me go! I've done everything you've wanted."

"And then some," he added.

"I won't say anything, can't you *understand* that? You're the last person on earth I ever want to see again . . . or have anything to *do* with. I don't want to be a witness, or get involved with the police, or statements, or *anything!* I don't want to be a part of what you're a part of! I'm frightened to death . . . that's your protection, don't you see? Let me go, *please.*"

"I can't."

"You don't believe me."

"That's not relevant. I need you."

"For what?"

"For something very stupid. I don't have a driver's license. You can't rent a car without a driver's license and I've got to rent a car."

"You've got *this* car."

"It's good for maybe another hour. Someone's going to walk out of the Carillon du Lac and want it. The description will be radioed to every police car in Zurich."

She looked at him, dead fear in the glaze of her eyes. "I don't want to go up there with you. I heard what that man said in the restaurant. If I hear any more you'll kill me."

"What you heard makes no more sense to me than it does to you. Perhaps less. Come on." He took her by the arm, and put his free hand on the railing so he could climb the steps with a minimum of pain.

She stared at him, bewilderment and fear converged in her look.

The name M. Chernak was under the second mail slot, a bell beneath the letters. He did not ring it, but pressed the adjacent four buttons. Within seconds a cacophony of voices sprang out of the small, dotted speakers, asking in Schweizerdeutsch who was there. But someone did not answer; he merely pressed a buzzer which released the lock. Jason opened the door, pushing Marie St. Jacques in front of him.

He moved her against the wall and waited. From above came the sounds of doors opening, footsteps walking toward the staircase.

"*Wer ist da?*"

"Johann?"

"*Wo bist du denn?*"

Silence. Followed by words of irritation. Footsteps were heard again; doors closed.

M. Chernak was on the second floor, Flat 2C. Bourne took the girl's arm, limped with her to the staircase, and started the climb. She was right, of course. It would be far better if he were alone, but there was nothing he could do about that; he did need her.

He had studied road maps during the weeks in Port Noir. Lucerne was no more than an hour away, Bern two and a half or three. He could head for either one, dropping her off in some deserted spot along the way, and then disappear. It was simply a matter of timing; he had the resources to buy a hundred connections. He needed only a conduit out of Zurich and she was it.

But before he left Zurich he had to know; he had to talk to a man named . . .

M. Chernak. The name was to the right of the doorbell. He sidestepped away from the door, pulling the woman with him.

"Do you speak German?" Jason asked.

"No."

"Don't lie."

"I'm not."

Bourne thought, glancing up and down the short hallway. Then: "Ring the bell. If the door opens just stand there. If someone answers from inside, say you have a message—an urgent message—from a friend at the Drei Alpenhäuser."

"Suppose he—or she—says to slide it under the door?"

Jason looked at her. "Very good."

"I just don't want any more violence. I don't want to *know* anything or *see* anything. I just want to—"

"I know," he interrupted. "Go back to Caesar's taxes and the Punic wars. If he—or she—says something like that, explain in a couple of words that the message is verbal and can only be delivered to the man who was described to you."

"If he asks for that description?" said Marie St. Jacques icily, analysis momentarily pre-empting fear.

"You've got a good mind, Doctor," he said.

"I'm precise. I'm frightened; I told you that. What do I do?"

"Say to hell with them, someone else can deliver it. Then start to walk away."

She moved to the door and rang the bell. There was an odd sound from within. A scratching, growing louder, constant. Then it stopped and a deep voice was heard through the wood.

"*Ja?*"

"I'm afraid I don't speak German."

"*Englisch.* What is it? Who are you?"

"I have an urgent message from a friend at the Drei Alpenhäuser."

"Shove it under the door."

"I can't do that. It isn't written down. I have to deliver it personally to the man who was described to me."

"Well, that shouldn't be difficult," said the voice. The lock clicked and the door opened.

Bourne stepped away from the wall, into the doorframe.

"You're *insane!*" cried a man with two stumps for legs, propped up in a wheelchair. Get *out!* Get away from here!"

"I'm tired of hearing that," said Jason, pulling the girl inside and closing the door.

It took no pressure to convince Marie St. Jacques to remain in a small, windowless bedroom while they talked; she did so willingly. The legless Chernak was close to panic, his ravaged face chalk white, his unkempt gray hair matted about his neck and forehead.

"What do you *want* from me?" he asked. "You swore the last transaction was our final one! I can do no more, I cannot take the risk. Messengers have been here. No matter how cautious, how many times removed from your sources, they have *been here!* If one leaves an address in the wrong surroundings, I'm a dead man!"

"You've done pretty well for the risks you've taken," said Bourne, standing in front of the wheelchair, his mind racing, wondering if there was a word or a phrase that could trigger a flow of information. Then he remembered the envelope. *If there was any discrepancy, it had nothing to do with me.* A fat man at the Drei Alpenhäuser.

"Minor compared to the magnitude of those risks." Chernak shook his head; his upper chest heaved; the stumps that fell over the chair moved obscenely back and forth. "I was content before you came into my life, mein Herr, for I *was* minor. An old soldier who made his way to Zurich—blown up, a cripple, worthless except for certain facts stored away that former comrades paid meagerly to keep suppressed. It was a decent life, not much, but enough. Then *you* found me. . . ."

"I'm touched," broke in Jason. "Let's talk about the envelope—the envelope you passed to our mutual friend at Drei Alpenhäuser. Who gave it to you?"

"A messenger. Who else?"

"Where did it come from?"

"How would *I* know? It arrived in a box, just like the others. I unpacked it and sent it on. It was *you* who wished it so. You said you could not come here any longer."

"But you opened it." A statement.

"Never!"

"Suppose I told you there was money missing."

"Then it was not paid; it was not in the envelope!" The legless man's voice rose. "However, I don't believe you. If that were so, you would not have accepted the assignment. But you did accept that assignment. So why are you here now?"

Because I have to know. Because I'm going out of my mind. I see things and I hear things I do not understand. I'm a skilled, resourceful . . . vegetable! Help me!

Bourne moved away from the chair; he walked aimlessly toward a bookcase where there were several upright photographs recessed against the wall. They explained the man behind him. Groups of German soldiers, some with shepherd dogs, posing outside of barracks and by fences . . . and in front of a high-wire gate with part of a name showing. DACH—

Dachau.

The man behind him. He was moving! Jason turned; the legless Chernak had his hand in the canvas bag strapped to his chair; his eyes were on fire, his ravaged face contorted. The hand came out swiftly, in it a short-barreled revolver, and before Bourne could reach his own, Chernak fired. The shots came rapidly, the icelike pain filling his left shoulder, then head—oh *God!* He dove to his right, spinning on the rug, shoving a heavy floor lamp toward the cripple, spinning again until he was at the far side of the wheelchair. He crouched and lunged, crashing his right shoulder into Chernak's back, sending the legless man out of the chair as he reached into his pocket for the gun.

"They'll pay for your corpse!" screamed the deformed man, writhing on the floor, trying to steady his slumped body long enough to level his weapon. "You won't put me in a coffin! I'll see you there! Carlos will pay! By Christ, he'll pay!"

Jason sprang to the left and fired. Chernak's head snapped back, his throat erupting in blood. He was dead.

A cry came from the door of the bedroom. It grew in depth, low and hollow, an elongated wail, fear and revulsion weaved into the chord. A woman's cry . . . of course it was a woman! His hostage, his conduit out of Zurich! Oh, *Jesus*, he could not focus his eyes! His temple was in agony!

He found his vision, refusing to acknowledge the pain. He saw a bathroom, the door open, towels and a sink and a . . . mirrored cabinet. He ran in, pulled the mirror back with such force that it jumped its hinges, crashing to the floor, shattered. *Shelves.* Rolls of gauze and tape and . . . they were all he could grab. He had to get out . . . *gunshots;* gunshots were alarms. He had to get out, take his hostage, and get away! The bedroom, the *bedroom.* Where *was* it?

The cry, the wail . . . follow the cry! He reached the door and kicked it open. The woman . . . his hostage—what the hell was her *name?*—was pressed against the wall, tears streaming down her face, her lips parted. He rushed in and grabbed her by the wrist, dragging her out.

"My *God*, you killed him!" she cried. "An old man with no—"

"Shut up!" He pushed her toward the door, opened it, and shoved her into the hallway. He could see blurred figures in open spaces, by railings, inside rooms. They began running, disappearing; he heard doors slam, people shout. He took the woman's arm with his left hand; the grip caused shooting pains in his shoulder. He propelled her to the staircase and forced her to descend with him, using her for support, his right hand holding the gun.

They reached the lobby and the heavy door. "Open it!" he ordered; she did. They passed the row of mailboxes to the outside entrance. He released her briefly, opening the door himself, peering out into the street, listening for sirens. There were none. "Come on!" he said, pulling her out to the stone steps and down to the pavement. He reached into his pocket, wincing, and took out the car keys. "Get in!"

Inside the car he unraveled the gauze, bunching it against the side of his head, blotting the trickle of blood. From deep inside his consciousness, there was a strange feeling of relief. The wound was a graze; the fact that it had been his head had sent him into panic, but the bullet had not entered his skull. It had *not* entered; there would be no return to the agonies of Port Noir.

"Goddamn it, start the car! Get *out* of here!"

"Where? You didn't say where." The woman was not screaming; instead she was calm. Unreasonably calm. Looking at him . . . was she looking at him?

He was feeling dizzy again, losing focus again. "Steppdeckstrasse. . . ." He heard the word as he spoke it, not sure the voice was his. But he could picture the doorway. Faded dark red paint, cracked glass . . . rusted iron. "Steppdeckstrasse," he repeated.

What was wrong? Why wasn't the motor going? Why didn't the car move forward. Didn't she *hear* him?

His eyes were closed; he opened them. The gun. It was on his lap; he had set it down to press the bandage . . . she was hitting it, *hitting* it! The weapon crashed to the floor; he reached down and she pushed him, sending his head against the window. Her door opened and she leaped out into the street and began running. She was running away! His hostage, his conduit was racing up the Löwenstrasse!

He could not stay in the car; he dared not try to drive it. It was a steel trap, marking him. He put the gun in his pocket with the roll of tape and grabbed the gauze, clutching it in his left hand, ready to press it against his temple at the first recurrence of blood. He got out and limped as fast as he could down the pavement.

Somewhere there was a corner, somewhere a taxi. *Steppdeckstrasse.*

Marie St. Jacques kept running in the middle of the wide, deserted avenue, in and out of the spills of the streetlamps, waving her arms at the automobiles in the Löwenstrasse. They sped by her. She turned in the wash of headlights behind her, holding up her hands, pleading for attention; the cars accelerated and passed her by. This was Zurich, and the Löwenstrasse at night was too wide, too dark, too near the deserted park and the river Sihl.

The men in one automobile, however, were aware of her. Its headlights were off, the driver inside having seen the woman in the distance. He spoke to his companion in Schweizerdeutsch.

"It could be her. This Chernak lives only a block or so down the street."

"Stop and let her come closer. She's supposed to be wearing a silk . . . it's *her!*"

"Let's make certain before we radio the others."

Both men got out of the car, the passenger moving discreetly around the trunk to join the driver. They wore conservative business suits, their faces pleasant, but serious, businesslike. The panicked woman approached; they walked rapidly into the middle of the street. The driver called out.

"*Was ist passiert, Fräulein?*"

"Help me!" she screamed. "I . . . I don't speak German. *Nicht sprechen.* Call the police! The . . . *Polizei!*"

The driver's companion spoke with authority, calming her with his voice. "We are with the police," he said in English. "Zurich Sicherheitpolizei." We weren't sure, miss. You *are* the woman from the Carillon du Lac?"

"*Yes!*" she cried. "He wouldn't let me go! He kept hitting me, threatening me with his gun! It was horrible!"

"Where is he now?"

"He's hurt. He was shot. I ran from the car . . . he was in the car when I ran!" She pointed down the Löwenstrasse. "Over there. Two blocks, I think—in the middle of the block. A coupé, a gray coupé! He has a gun."

"So do we, miss," said the driver. "Come along, get in the back of the car. You'll be perfectly safe; we'll be very careful. Quickly, now."

They approached the gray coupé, coasting, headlights extinguished. There was no one inside. There were, however, people talking excitedly on the pavement and up the stone steps of Number 37. The driver's associate turned and spoke to the frightened woman pressed into the corner of the rear seat.

"This is the residence of a man named Chernak. Did he mention him? Did he say anything about going in to see him?"

"He *did* go; he made me come with him! He *killed* him! He killed that crippled old man!"

"*Der Sender—schnell,*" said the associate to the driver, as he grabbed a microphone from the dashboard. "*Wir sind zwei Strassen von dort.*" The car bolted forward; the woman gripped the front seat.

"What are you doing? A man was killed back there!"

"And we must find the killer," said the driver. "As you say, he was wounded; he may still be in the area. This is an unmarked vehicle and we could spot him. We'll wait, of course, to make sure the inspection team arrives, but our duties are quite separate." The car slowed down, sliding into the curb several hundred yards from Number 37 Löwenstrasse.

The associate had spoken into the microphone while the driver had explained their official position. There was static from the dashboard speaker, then the words "*Wir kommen binnen zwanzig Minuten. Wartet.*"

"Our superior will be here shortly," the associate said. "We're to wait for him. He wishes to speak with you."

Marie St. Jacques leaned back in the seat, closing her eyes, expelling her breath. "Oh, God—I wish I had a drink!"

The driver laughed, nodded to his companion. The associate took out a pint bottle from the glove compartment and held it up, smiling at the woman. "We're not very chic, miss. We have no glasses or cups, but we do have brandy. For medical emergencies, of course. I think this is one now. Please, our compliments."

She smiled back and accepted the bottle. "You're two very nice people, and you'll never know how grateful I am. If you ever come to Canada, I'll cook you the best French meal in the province of Ontario."

"Thank you, miss," said the driver.

Bourne studied the bandage on his shoulder, squinting at the dull reflection in the dirty, streaked mirror, adjusting his eyes to the dim light of the filthy room. He had been right about the Steppdeckstrasse, the image of the faded red doorway accurate, down to the cracked windowpanes and rusted iron railings. No questions had been asked when he rented the room, in spite of the fact that he was obviously hurt. However, a statement had been made by the building manager when Bourne paid him.

"For something more substantial a doctor can be found who keeps his mouth shut."

"I'll let you know."

The wound was not that severe; the tape would hold it until he found a doctor somewhat more reliable than one who practiced surreptitiously in the Steppdeck-strasse.

If a stress situation results in injury, be aware of the fact that the damage may be as much psychological as physical. You may have a very real revulsion to pain and bodily harm. Don't take risks, but if there's time, give yourself a chance to adjust. Don't panic. . . .

He had panicked; areas of his body had frozen. Although the penetration in his shoulder and the graze at his temple were real and painful, neither was serious enough to immobilize him. He could not move as fast as he might wish or with the strength he knew he had, but he could move deliberately. Messages were sent and received, brain to muscle and limb; he could function.

He would function better after a rest. He had no conduit now; he had to be up long before daybreak and find another way out of Zurich. The building manager on the first floor liked money; he would wake up the slovenly landlord in an hour or so.

He lowered himself onto the sagging bed and lay back on the pillow, staring at the naked lightbulb in the ceiling, trying not to hear the words so he could rest. They came anyway, filling his ears like the pounding of kettledrums.

A man was killed. . . .

But you did accept that assignment. . . .

He turned to the wall, shutting his eyes, blocking out the words. Then other words came and he sat up, sweat breaking out on his forehead.

They'll pay for your corpse! . . . Carlos will pay! By Christ, he'll pay!

Carlos.

A large sedan pulled up in front of the coupé and parked at the curb. Behind them, at 37 Löwenstrasse, the patrol cars had arrived fifteen minutes ago, the ambulance less than five. Crowds from surrounding flats lined the pavement near the staircase, but the excitement was muted now. A death had occurred, a man killed at night in this quiet section of the Löwenstrasse. Anxiety was uppermost; what had happened at Number 37 could happen at 32 or 40 or 53. The world was going mad, and Zurich was going with it.

"Our superior has arrived, miss. May we take you to him, please?" The associate got out of the car and opened the door for Marie St. Jacques.

"Certainly." She stepped out on the pavement and felt the man's hand on her arm; it was so much gentler than the hard grip of the animal who had held the barrel of a gun to her cheek. She shuddered at the memory. They approached the rear of the sedan and she climbed inside. She sat back in the seat and looked at the man beside her. She gasped, suddenly paralyzed, unable to breathe, the man beside her evoking a memory of terror.

The light from the streetlamps was reflected off the thin gold rims of his spectacles.

"You! . . . You were at the hotel! You were one of them!"

The man nodded wearily; his fatigue apparent. "That's right. We're a special branch of the Zurich police. And before we speak further, I must make it clear to you that at no time during the events of the Carillon du Lac were you in any danger of being harmed by us. We're trained marksmen; no shots were fired that could have struck you. A number were withheld because you were too close to the man in our sights."

Her shock eased, the man's quiet authority reassuring. "Thank you for that."

"It's a minor talent," said the official. "Now, as I understand, you last saw him in the front seat of the car back there."

"Yes. He was wounded."

"How seriously?"

"Enough to be incoherent. He held some kind of bandage to his head, and there was blood on his shoulder—on the cloth of his coat, I mean. Who is he?"

"Names are meaningless; he goes by many. But as you've seen, he's a killer. A brutal killer, and he must be found before he kills again. We've been hunting him for several years. Many police from many countries. We have the opportunity now none of them has had. We know he's in Zurich, and he's wounded. He would not stay in this area, but how far can he go? Did he mention how he expected to get out of the city?"

"He was going to rent a car. In my name, I gather. He doesn't have a driver's license."

"He was lying. He travels with all manner of false papers. You were an expendable hostage. Now, from the beginning, tell me everything he said to you. Where you went, whom he met, whatever comes to mind."

"There's a restaurant, Drei Alpenhäuser, and a large fat man who was frightened to death. . . ." Marie St. Jacques recounted everything she could remember. From time to time the police official interrupted, questioning her about a phrase, or reaction, or a sudden decision on the part of the killer. Intermittently he removed his gold spectacles, wiping them absently, gripping the frames as if the pressure controlled his irritation. The interrogation lasted nearly twenty-five minutes; then the official made his decision. He spoke to his driver.

"Drei Alpenhäuser. *Schnell!*" He turned to Marie St. Jacques. "We'll confront that man with his own words. *His* incoherence was quite international. He knows far more than he said at the table."

"Incoherence. . . ." She said the word softly, remembering her own use of it. "Steppdeck— Steppdeck*strasse*. Cracked windows, rooms."

"What?"

" 'A boardinghouse in the Steppdeckstrasse.' That's what he said. Everything was happening so fast, but he *said* it. And just before I jumped out of the car, he said it again. *Steppdeckstrasse.*"

The driver spoke. *"Ich kenne diese Strasse. Früher gab es dort Textilfabriken."*

"I don't understand," said Marie St. Jacques.

"It's a rundown section that has not kept up with the times," replied the official. "The old fabric mills used to be there. A haven for the less fortunate . . . and others. *Los!*" he ordered.

They drove off.

8

A crack. Outside the room. Snaplike, echoing off into a sharp coda, the sound penetrating, diminishing in the distance. Bourne opened his eyes.

The staircase. The staircase in the filthy hallway outside his room. Someone had been walking up the steps and had stopped, aware of the noise his weight had caused on the warped, cracked wood. A normal boarder at the Steppdeckstrasse rooming house would have no such concerns.

Silence.

Crack. Now closer. A risk was taken, timing paramount, speed the cover. Jason spun off the bed, grabbing the gun that was by his head, and lunged to the wall by the door. He crouched, hearing the footsteps—one man—the runner, no longer concerned with sound, only with reaching his destination. Bourne had no doubt what it was; he was right.

The door crashed open; he smashed it back, then threw his full weight into the wood, pinning the intruder against the doorframe, pummeling the man's stomach, chest, and arm into the recessed edge of the wall. He pulled the door back and lashed the toe of his right foot into the throat below him, reaching down with his left hand, grabbing blond hair and yanking the figure inside. The man's hand went limp; the gun in it fell to the floor, a long-barreled revolver with a silencer attached.

Jason closed the door and listened for sounds on the staircase. There were none. He looked down at the unconscious man. Thief? Killer? What was he?

Police? Had the manager of the boardinghouse decided to overlook the code of the Steppdeckstrasse in search of a reward? Bourne rolled the intruder over and took out a billfold. Second nature made him remove the money, knowing it was ludicrous to do so; he had a small fortune on him. He looked at the various credit cards and the drivers license; he smiled, but then his smile disappeared. There was nothing funny; the names on the cards were different ones, the name on the license matching none. The unconscious man was no police officer.

He was a professional, come to kill a wounded man in the Steppdeckstrasse. Someone had hired him. Who? Who could possibly know he was there?

The woman? Had he mentioned the Steppdeckstrasse when he had seen the row of neat houses, looking for Number 37? No, it was not she; he may have said something, but she would not have understood. And if she had, there'd be no professional killer in his room; instead, the rundown boardinghouse would be surrounded by police.

The image of a large fat man perspiring above a table came to Bourne. That same man had wiped the sweat from his protruding lips and had spoken of the courage of an insignificant goat—who had survived. Was this an example of his survival technique? Had he known about the Steppdeckstrasse? Was he aware of the habits of the patron whose sight terrified him? Had he *been* to the filthy rooming house? Delivered an envelope there?

Jason pressed his hand to his forehead and shut his eyes. *Why can't I remember? When will the mists clear? Will they ever clear?*

Don't crucify yourself. . . .

Bourne opened his eyes, fixing them on the blond man. For the briefest of moments he nearly burst out laughing; he had been presented with his exit visa from Zurich, and instead of recognizing it, he was wasting time tormenting himself. He put the billfold in his pocket, wedging it behind the Marquis de Chamford's, picked up the gun and shoved it into his belt, then dragged the unconscious figure over to the bed.

A minute later the man was strapped to the sagging mattress, gagged by a torn sheet wrapped around his face. He would remain where he was for hours, and in hours Jason would be out of Zurich, compliments of a perspiring fat man.

He had slept in his clothes. There was nothing to gather up or carry except his topcoat. He put it on, and tested his leg, somewhat after the fact, he reflected. In the heat of the past few minutes he had been unaware of the pain; it was there, as the limp was there, but neither immobilized him. The shoulder was not in as good shape. A slow paralysis was spreading; he had to get to a doctor. His head . . . he did not want to think about his head.

He walked out into the dimly lit hallway, pulled the door closed, and stood motionless, listening. There was a burst of laughter from above; he pressed his back against the wall, gun poised. The laughter trailed off; it was a drunk's laughter—incoherent, pointless.

He limped to the staircase, held on to the railing, and started down. He was on the third floor of the four-story building, having insisted on the highest room when the phrase *high ground* had come to him instinctively. *Why had it come to him? What did it mean in terms of renting a filthy room for a single night? Sanctuary?*

Stop it!

He reached the second floor landing, creaks in the wooden staircase accompanying each step. If the manager came out of his flat below to satisfy his curiosity, it would be the last thing he satisfied for several hours.

A noise. A scratch. Soft fabric moving briefly across an abrasive surface. Cloth against wood. Someone was concealed in the short stretch of hallway between the end of one staircase and the beginning of another. Without breaking the rhythm of his walk, he peered into the shadows; there were three recessed doorways in the right wall, identical to the floor above. In one of them . . .

He took a step closer. Not the first; it was empty. And it would not be the last, the bordering wall forming a cul-de-sac, no room to move. It had to be the second, yes, the second doorway. From it a man could rush forward, to his left or right, or throwing a shoulder into an unsuspecting victim, send his target over the railing, plunging down the staircase.

Bourne angled to his right, shifting the gun to his left hand and reaching into his belt for the weapon with a silencer. Two feet from the recessed door, he heaved the automatic in his left hand into the shadows as he pivoted against the wall.

"*Was it?* . . ." An arm appeared; Jason fired once, blowing the hand apart. "*Ahh!*" The figure lurched out in shock, incapable of aiming his weapon. Bourne fired again, hitting the man in the thigh; he collapsed on the floor, writhing, cringing. Jason took a step forward and knelt, his knee pressing into the man's chest, his gun at the man's head. He spoke in a whisper.

"Is there anyone else down there?"

"*Nein!*" said the man, wincing in pain. "*Zwei* . . . two of us only. We were paid."

"By whom?"

"You know."

"A man named Carlos?"

"I will not answer that. Kill me first."

"How did you know I was here?"

"Chernak."

"He's dead."

"Now. Not yesterday. Word reached Zurich: you were alive. We checked everyone . . . everywhere. Chernak knew."

Bourne gambled. "You're lying!" He pushed the gun into the man's throat. "I never told Chernak about the Steppdeckstrasse."

The man winced again, his neck arched. "Perhaps you did not have to. The Nazi pig had informers everywhere. Why should the Steppdeckstrasse be any different? He could describe you. Who else could?"

"A man at the Drei Alpenhäuser."

"We never heard of any such man."

"Who's 'we?' "

The man swallowed, his lips stretched in pain. "Businessmen . . . only businessmen."

"And your service is killing."

"You're a strange one to talk. But, *nein.* You were to be taken, not killed."

"Where?"

"We would be told by radio. Car frequency."

"Terrific," said Jason flatly. "You're not only second-rate, you're accommodating. Where's your car?"

"Outside."

"Give me the keys." The radio would identify it.

The man tried to resist; he pushed Bourne's knee away and started to roll into the wall. "*Nein!*"

"You haven't got a choice." Jason brought the handle of the pistol down on the man's skull. The Swiss collapsed.

Bourne found the keys—there were three in a leather case—took the man's gun and put it into his pocket. It was a smaller weapon than the one he held in his hand and had no silencer, lending a degree of credence to the claim that he was to be taken, not killed. The blond man upstairs had been acting as the point, and therefore needed the protection of a silenced gunshot should wounding be required. But an unmuffled report could lead to complications; the Swiss on the second floor was a backup, his weapon to be used as a visible threat.

Then why was he on the second floor? Why hadn't he followed his colleague? On the staircase? Something was odd, but there was no accounting for tactics, nor the time to consider them. There was a car outside on the street and he had the keys for it.

Nothing could be disregarded. The third gun.

He got up painfully and found the revolver he had taken from the Frenchman in the elevator at the Gemeinschaft Bank. He pulled up his left trouser leg and inserted the gun under the elasticized fabric of his sock. It was secure.

He paused to get his breath and his balance, then crossed to the staircase, aware that the pain in his left shoulder was suddenly more acute, the paralysis spreading more rapidly. Messages from brain to limb were less clear. He hoped to God he could drive.

He reached the fifth step and abruptly stopped, listening as he had listened barely a minute ago for sounds of concealment. There was nothing; the wounded man may have been tactically deficient, but he had told the truth. Jason hurried down the staircase. He would drive out of Zurich—somehow—and find a doctor—somewhere.

He spotted the car easily. It was different from the other shabby automobiles on the street. An outsized, well-kept sedan, and he could see the bulge of an antenna base riveted into the trunk. He walked to the driver's side and ran his hand around the panel and left front fender; there was no alarm device.

He unlocked the door, then opened it, holding his breath in case he was wrong about the alarm; he was not. He climbed in behind the wheel, adjusting his position until he was as comfortable as he could be, grateful that the car had an automatic shift. The large weapon in his belt inhibited him. He placed it on the seat beside him, then reached for the ignition, assuming the key that had unlocked the door was the proper one.

It was not. He tried the one next to it, but it, too, would not fit. For the trunk, he assumed. It was the third key.

Or was it? He kept stabbing at the opening. The key would not enter; he tried the second again; it was blocked. Then the first. None of the keys would fit into the ignition! Or were the messages from brain to limb to fingers too garbled, his coordination too inadequate! Goddamn it! Try again!

A powerful light came from his left, burning his eyes, blinding him. He grabbed for the gun, but a second beam shot out from the right; the door was yanked open and a heavy flashlight crashed down on his hand, another hand taking the weapon from the seat.

"Get out!" The order came from his left, the barrel of a gun pressed into his neck.

He climbed out, a thousand coruscating circles of white in his eyes. As vision slowly came back to him, the first thing he saw was the outline of two circles. Gold circles; the spectacles of the killer who had hunted him throughout the night. The man spoke.

"They say in the laws of physics that every action has an equal and opposite reaction. The behavior of certain men under certain conditions is similarly predictable. For a man like you one sets up a gauntlet, each combatant told what to say if he falls. If he does not fall, you are taken. If he does, you are misled, lulled into a false sense of progress."

"It's a high degree of risk," said Jason. "For those in the gauntlet."

"They're paid well. And there's something else—no guarantee, of course, but it's there. The enigmatic Bourne does not kill indiscriminately. Not out of compassion, naturally, but for a far more practical reason. Men remember when they've been spared; he infiltrates the armies of others. Refined guerrilla tactics applied to a sophisticated battleground. I commend you."

"You're a horse's ass." It was all Jason could think to say. "But both your men are alive, if that's what you want to know."

Another figure came into view, led from the shadows of the building by a short, stocky man. It was the woman; it was Marie St. Jacques.

"That's him," she said softly, her look unwavering.

"Oh, my God. . . ." Bourne shook his head in disbelief. "How was it done, Doctor?" he asked her, raising his voice. "Was someone watching my room at the Carillon? Was the elevator timed, the others shut down? You're very convincing. And I thought you were going to crash into a police car."

"As it turned out," she replied, "it wasn't necessary. These are the police."

Jason looked at the killer in front of him; the man was adjusting his gold spectacles. "I commend you," he said.

"A minor talent," answered the killer. "The conditions were right. You provided them."

"What happens now? The man inside said I was to be taken, not killed."

"You forget. He was told what to say." The Swiss paused. "So this is what you look like. Many of us have wondered during the past two or three years. How much speculation there's been! How many contradictions! He's tall, you know; no, he's of medium height. He's blond; no, he has dark black hair. Very light blue eyes, of course; no, quite clearly they are brown. His features are sharp; no, they're really quite ordinary, can't pick him out in a crowd. But nothing was ordinary. It was all extraordinary."

Your features have been softened, the character submerged. Change your hair, you change your face. . . . Certain types of contact lenses are designed to alter the color of the eyes. . . . Wear glasses, you're a different man. Visas, passports . . . switched at will.

The design was there. Everything fit. Not all the answers, but more of the truth than he wanted to hear.

"I'd like to get this over with," said Marie St. Jacques, stepping forward.

"I'll sign whatever I have to sign—at your office, I imagine. But then I really must get back to the hotel. I don't have to tell you what I've been through tonight."

The Swiss glanced at her through his gold-rimmed glasses. The stocky man who had led her out of the shadows took her arm. She stared at both men, then down at the hand that held her.

Then at Bourne. Her breathing stopped, a terrible realization becoming clear. Her eyes grew wide.

"Let her go," said Jason. "She's on her way back to Canada. You'll never see her again."

"Be practical, Bourne. She's seen *us*. We two are professionals; there are rules." The man flicked his gun up under Jason's chin, the barrel pressed once more into Bourne's throat. He ran his left hand about his victim's clothes, felt the weapon in Jason's pocket and took it out. "I thought as much," he said, and turned to the stocky man. "Take her in the other car. The Limmat."

Bourne froze. Marie St. Jacques was to be killed, her body thrown into the Limmat River.

"Wait a minute!" Jason stepped forward; the gun was jammed into his neck, forcing him back into the hood of the car. "You're being stupid! She works for the Canadian government. They'll be all over Zurich."

"Why should that concern you? You won't be here."

"Because it's a waste!" cried Bourne. "We're professionals, remember?"

"You bore me." The killer turned to the stocky man. *"Geh! Schnell. Guisan Quai!"*

"Scream your goddamn head off!" shouted Jason. "Start yelling! Don't stop!"

She tried, the scream cut short by a paralyzing blow to her throat. She fell to the pavement as her would-be executioner dragged her toward a small nondescript black sedan.

"That was stupid," said the killer, peering through his gold-rimmed spectacles into Bourne's face. "You only hasten the inevitable. On the other hand, it will be simpler now. I can free a man to tend to our wounded. Everything's so military, isn't it? It really is a battlefield." He turned to the man with the flashlight. "Signal Johann to go inside. We'll come back for them."

The flashlight was switched on and off twice. A fourth man, who had opened the door of the small sedan for the condemned woman, nodded. Marie St. Jacques was thrown into the rear seat, the door slammed shut. The man named Johann started for the concrete steps, nodding now at the executioner.

Jason felt sick as the engine of the small sedan was gunned and the car bolted away from the curb into the Steppdeckstrasse, the twisted chrome bumper disappearing into the shadows of the street. Inside that car was a woman he had never seen in his life . . . before three hours ago. And he had killed her. "You don't lack for soldiers," he said.

"If there were a hundred men I could trust, I'd pay them willingly. As they say, your reputation precedes you."

"Suppose *I* paid you. You were at the bank; you know I've got funds."

"Probably millions, but I wouldn't touch a franc note."

"Why? Are you afraid?"

"Most assuredly. Wealth is relative to the amount of time one has to enjoy it. I wouldn't have five minutes." The killer turned to his subordinate. "Put him inside. Strip him. I want photographs taken of him naked—before and after he leaves us. You'll find a great deal of money on him; I want him holding it. I'll drive." He looked again at Bourne. "Carlos will get the first print. And I have no doubt that I'll be able to sell the others quite profitably on the open market. Magazines pay outrageous prices."

"Why should 'Carlos' believe you? Why should *anyone* believe you? You said it: no one knows what I look like."

"I'll be covered," said the Swiss. "Sufficient unto the day. Two Zurich bankers will step forward identifying you as one Jason Bourne. The same Jason Bourne who met the excessively rigid standards set by Swiss law for the release of a numbered account. It will be enough." He spoke to the gunman. *"Hurry!* I have cables to send. Debts to collect."

A powerful arm shot over Bourne's shoulder, vicing his throat in a hammerlock. The barrel of a gun was jolted into his spine, pain spreading throughout his chest as he was dragged inside the sedan. The man holding him was a professional; even without his wounds it would have been impossible to break the grip. The gunman's expertise, however, did not satisfy the bespectacled leader of the hunt. He climbed behind the wheel and issued another command.

"Break his fingers," he said.

The armlock briefly choked off Jason's air as the barrel of the gun crashed down repeatedly on his hand—*hands*. Instinctively, Bourne had swung his left hand over his right, protecting it. As the blood burst from the back of his left, he twisted his fingers, letting it flow between them until both hands were covered. He choked his screams; the grip lessened; he shouted.

"My hands! They're broken!"

"Gut."

But they were not broken; the left was damaged to the point where it was useless; not the right. He moved his fingers in the shadows; his hand was intact.

The car sped down the Steppdeckstrasse and swung into a sidestreet, heading south. Jason collapsed back in the seat, gasping. The gunman tore at his clothes, ripping his shirt, yanking at his belt. In seconds his upper body would be naked; passport, papers, cards, money no longer his, all the items intrinsic to his escape from Zurich taken from him. It was now or it was not to be. He screamed.

"My *leg!* My goddamned leg!" He lurched forward, his right hand working furiously in the dark, fumbling under the cloth of his trouser leg. He felt it. The handle of the automatic.

"Nein!" roared the professional in the front. "Watch him!" He knew; it was instinctive knowledge.

It was also too late. Bourne held the gun in the darkness of the floor; the powerful soldier pushed him back. He fell with the blow, the revolver, now at his waist, pointed directly at his attacker's chest.

He fired twice; the man arched backward. Jason fired again, his aim sure, the heart punctured; the man fell over into the recessed jump seat.

"Put it down!" yelled Bourne, swinging the revolver over the rounded edge of the front seat, pressing the barrel into the base of the driver's skull. "Drop it!"

His breathing erratic, the killer let the gun fall. "We will talk," he said, gripping the wheel. "We are professionals. We will talk." The large automobile lurched forward, gathering speed, the driver increasing pressure on the accelerator.

"Slow down!"

"What is your answer?" The car went faster. Ahead were the headlights of traffic; they were leaving the Steppdeckstrasse district, entering the busier city streets. "You want to get out of Zurich, I can get you out. Without me, you can't. All I have to do is spin the wheel, crash into the pavement. I have nothing whatsoever to lose, Herr Bourne. There are police everywhere up ahead. I don't think you want the police."

"We'll talk," lied Jason. Everything was timing, split-second timing. There were now two killers in a speeding enclosure that was in itself a trap. Neither killer was to be trusted; both knew it. One had to make use of that extra half-second the other would not take. Professionals. "Put on the brakes," said Bourne.

"Drop your gun on the seat next to mine."

Jason released the weapon. It fell on top of the killer's, the ring of heavy metal proof of contact. "Done."

The killer took his foot off the accelerator, transferring it to the brake. He applied the pressure slowly, then in short stabs so that the large automobile pitched back and forth. The jabs on the pedal would become more pronounced; Bourne understood this. It was part of the driver's strategy, balance a factor of life and death.

The arrow on the speedometer swung left: *30 kilometers, 18 kilometers, 9 kilometers.* They had nearly stopped; it was the moment for the extra half-second of effort—balance a factor, life in balance.

Jason grabbed the man by the neck, clawing at his throat, yanking him up off the seat. Then he raised his bloody left hand and thrust it forward, smearing the area of the killer's eyes. He released the throat, surging his right hand down toward the guns on the seat. Bourne gripped a handle, shoving the killer's hand away; the man screamed, his vision blurred, the gun out of reach. Jason lunged across the man's chest, pushing him down against the door, elbowing the killer's throat with his left arm, grabbing the wheel with his bloody palm. He looked up through the windshield and turned the wheel to the right, heading the car toward a pyramid of trash on the pavement.

The automobile plowed into the mound of debris—a huge, somnambulant insect crawling into garbage, its appearance belying the violence taking place inside its shell.

The man beneath him lunged up, rolling on the seat. Bourne held the automatic in his hand, his fingers jabbing for the open space of the trigger. He found it. He bent his wrist and fired.

His would-be executioner went limp, a dark red hole in his forehead.

In the street, men came running toward what must have looked like a dangerously careless accident. Jason shoved the dead body across the seat and climbed over behind the wheel. He pushed the gearshift into reverse; the sedan backed awkwardly out of the debris, over the curb and into the street. He rolled down his window, calling out to the would-be rescuers as they approached.

"Sorry! Everything's fine! Just a little too much to drink!"

The small band of concerned citizens broke up quickly, a few making gestures of admonition, others running back to their escorts and companions. Bourne breathed deeply, trying to control the involuntary trembling that seized his entire body. He pulled the gear into drive; the car started forward. He tried to picture the streets of Zurich from a memory that would not serve him.

He knew vaguely where he was—where he had been—and more important, he knew more clearly where the Guisan Quai was in relationship to the Limmat.

Geh! Schnell! Guisan Quai!

Marie St. Jacques was to be killed on the Guisan Quai, her body thrown into the river. There was only one stretch where the Guisan and the Limmat met: it was at the mouth of Lake Zurich, at the base of the western shore. Somewhere in an empty parking lot or a deserted garden overlooking the water, a short, stocky man was about to carry out an execution ordered by a dead man. Perhaps by now the gun had been fired, or a knife plunged into its mark; there was no way to know, but Jason knew he had to find out. Whoever and whatever he was, he could not walk away blindly.

The professional in him, however, demanded that he swerve into the dark wide alley ahead. There were two dead men in the car; they were a risk and a burden he could not tolerate. The precious seconds it would take to remove them could avoid the danger of a traffic policeman looking through the windows and seeing death.

Thirty-two seconds was his guess; it had taken less than a minute to pull his would-be executioners from the car. He looked at them as he limped around the hood to the door. They were curled up obscenely next to one another against a filthy brick wall. In darkness.

He climbed behind the wheel and backed out of the alley.

Geh! Schnell! Guisan Quai!

9

He reached an intersection, the traffic light red. *Lights.* On the left, several blocks east, he could see lights arching gently into the night sky. A bridge! The Limmat! The signal turned green; he swung the sedan to the left.

He was back on the Bahnhofstrasse; the start of the Guisan Quai was only minutes away. The wide avenue curved around the water's edge, riverbank and lakefront merging. Moments later, on his left was the silhouetted outline of a park, in summer a stroller's haven, now dark, devoid of tourists and Zurichers. He passed an entrance for vehicles; there was a heavy chain across the white pavement, suspended between two stone posts. He came to a second, another chain prohibiting access. But it was not the same; something was different, something odd. He stopped the car and looked closer, reaching across the seat for the flashlight he had taken from his would-be executioner. He snapped it on and shot the beam over the heavy chain. What was it? What was different?

It was not the chain. It was *beneath* the chain. On the white pavement kept spotless by maintenance crews. There were tire marks, at odds with the surrounding cleanliness. They would not be noticed during the summer months; they were now. It was as if the filth of the Steppdeckstrasse had traveled too well.

Bourne switched off the flashlight and dropped it on the seat. The pain in his battered left hand suddenly fused with the agony in his shoulder and his arm; he had to push all pain out of his mind; he had to curtail the bleeding as best he could. His shirt had been ripped; he reached inside and ripped it further, pulling out a strip of cloth which he proceeded to wrap around his left hand, knotting it with teeth and fingers. He was as ready as he would ever be.

He picked up the gun—his would-be executioner's gun—and checked the clip: full. He waited until two cars had passed him, then extinguished the headlights and made a U-turn, parking next to the chain. He got out, instinctively testing his leg on the pavement, then favoring it as he limped to the nearest post and lifted the hook off the iron circle protruding from the stone. He lowered the chain, making as little noise as possible, and returned to the car.

He pulled at the gearshift, gently pressed the accelerator, then released it. He was now coasting into the wide expanse of an unlit parking area, made darker by the abrupt end of the white entrance road and the start of a field of black asphalt. Beyond, two-hundred-odd yards in the distance, was the straight dark line of the seawall, a wall that contained no sea but, instead, the currents of the Limmat as they poured into the waters of Lake Zurich. Farther away were the lights of the boats, bobbing in stately splendor. Beyond these were the stationary lights of the Old City, the blurred floodlights of darkened piers. Jason's eyes took everything in, for the distance was his backdrop; he was looking for shapes in front of it.

To the right. The *right*. A dark outline darker than the wall, an intrusion of black on lesser black—obscure, faint, barely discernible, but there. A hundred yards away . . . now ninety, eighty-five; he cut off the engine and brought the car to a stop. He sat motionless by the open window, staring into the darkness, trying to see more clearly. He heard the wind coming off the water; it covered any sound the car had made.

Sound. A cry. Low, throated . . . delivered in fear. A harsh slap followed, then another, and another. A scream was formed, then swallowed, broken, echoing off into silence.

Bourne got out of the car silently, the gun in his right hand, the flashlight awkward in the bloody fingers of his left. He walked toward the obscure black shape, each step, each limp a study in silence.

What he saw first was what he had seen last when the small sedan had disappeared in the shadows of the Steppdeckstrasse. The shining metal of the twisted chrome bumper; it glistened now in the night light.

Four slaps in rapid succession, flesh against flesh, blows maniacally administered, received with muted screams of terror. Cries terminated, gasps permitted, thrashing movement part of it all. Inside the car!

Jason crouched as best he could, sidestepping around the trunk toward the right rear window. He rose slowly, then suddenly, using sound as a weapon of shock, shouted as he switched on the powerful flashlight.

"You move, you're dead!"

What he saw inside filled him with revulsion and fury. Marie St. Jacques' clothes were torn away, shredded into strips. Hands were poised like claws on her half-naked body, kneading her breasts, separating her legs. The executioner's organ protruded from the cloth of his trousers; he was inflicting the final indignity before he carried out the sentence of death.

"Get *out*, you *son of a bitch!*"

There was a massive shattering of glass; the man raping Marie St. Jacques saw the obvious. Bourne could not fire the gun for fear of killing the woman; he had spun off her, crashing the heel of his shoe into the window of the small car. Glass flew out, sharp fragments blanketing Jason's face. He closed his eyes, limping backward to avoid the spray.

The door swung open; a blinding spit of light accompanied the explosion. Hot, searing pain spread through Bourne's right side. The fabric of his coat was blown away, blood matting what remained of his shirt. He squeezed the trigger, only vaguely able to see the figure rolling on the ground; he fired again, the bullet detonating the surface of the asphalt. The executioner had rolled and lurched out of sight . . . into the darker blackness, unseen.

Jason knew he could not stay where he was; to do so was his own execution. He raced, dragging his leg, to the cover of the open door.

"Stay inside!" he yelled to Marie St. Jacques; the woman had started to move in panic. "Goddamn it! Stay in there!"

A gunshot; the bullet imbedded in the metal of the door. A running figure was silhouetted above the wall. Bourne fired twice, grateful for an expulsion of breath in the distance. He had wounded the man; he had not killed him. But the executioner would function less well than he had sixty seconds ago.

Lights. Dim lights . . . squared, frames. What was it? What were they? He looked to the left and saw what he could not possibly have seen before. A small brick structure, some kind of dwelling by the seawall. Lights had been turned on inside. A watchman's station; someone inside had heard the gunshots.

"*Was ist los? Wer ist da?*" The shouts came from the figure of a man—a bent-over, old man—standing in a lighted doorway. Then the beam of a flashlight pierced the blacker darkness. Bourne followed it with his eyes, hoping it would shine on the executioner.

It did. He was crouched by the wall. Jason stood up and fired; at the sound of his gun, the beam swung over to him. *He* was the target; two shots came from the darkness, a bullet ricocheting off a metal strip in the window. Steel punctured his neck; blood erupted.

Racing footsteps. The executioner was running toward the source of the light. "*Nein!*"

He had reached it; the figure in the doorway was lashed by an arm that was both his leash and his cage. The beam went out; in the light of the windows Jason could see the killer pulling the watchman away, using the old man as a shield, dragging him back into darkness.

Bourne watched until he could see no more, his gun raised helplessly over the hood. As he was helpless, his body draining.

There was a final shot, followed by a guttural cry and, once again, racing footsteps. The executioner had carried out a sentence of death, not with the condemned woman, but with an old man. He was running; he had made his escape.

Bourne could run no longer; the pain had finally immobilized him, his vision too blurred, his sense of survival exhausted. He lowered himself to the pavement. There was nothing; he simply did not care.

Whatever he was, let it be. Let it be.

The St. Jacques woman crawled out of the car, holding her clothes, every move made in shock. She stared at Jason, disbelief, horror and confusion coming together in her eyes.

"Go on," he whispered, hoping she could hear him. "There's a car back there, the keys are in it. Get out of here. He may bring others, I don't know."

"You came for me," she said, her voice echoing through a tunnel of bewilderment.

"Get out! Get in that car and go like hell, Doctor. If anyone tries to stop you, run him down. Reach the police . . . real ones, with uniforms, you damn fool." His throat was so hot, his stomach so cold. Fire and ice; he'd felt them before. Together. Where was it?

"You saved my life," she continued in that hollow tone, the words floating in the air. "You came for me. You came *back* for me, and saved . . . my . . . life."

"Don't make it what it wasn't." *You are incidental, Doctor. You are a reflex, an instinct born of forgotten memories, conduits electrically prodded by stress. You see, I know the words . . . I don't care anymore. I hurt—oh my God, I hurt.*

"You were free. You could have kept going but you didn't. You came back for me."

He heard her through mists of pain. He saw her, and what he saw was unreasonable—as unreasonable as the pain. She was kneeling beside him, touching his face, touching his head. *Stop it! Do not touch my head! Leave me.*

"Why did you do that?" It was her voice, not his.

She was asking him a question. Didn't she understand? He could not answer her.

What was she doing? She had torn a piece of cloth and was wrapping it around his neck . . . and now another, this larger, part of her dress. She had loosened his belt and was pushing the soft smooth cloth down into the boiling hot skin on his right hip.

"It wasn't *you.*" He found words and used them quickly. He wanted the peace of darkness—as he had wanted it before but could not remember when. He could find it if she left him. "That man . . . he'd seen me. He could identify me. It was him. I wanted *him.* Now get out!"

"So could half a dozen others," she replied, another note in her voice, "I don't believe you."

"Believe me!"

She was standing above him now. Then she was not there. She was gone. She had left him. The peace would come quickly now; he would be swallowed up in the dark crashing waters and the pain would be washed away. He leaned back against the car and let himself drift with the currents of his mind.

A noise intruded. A motor, rolling and disruptive. He did not care for it; it interfered with the freedom of his own particular sea. Then a hand was on his arm. Then another, gently pulling him up.

"Come on," said the voice, "help me."

"Let go of me!" The command was shouted; he had shouted it. But the command was not obeyed. He was appalled; commands should be obeyed. Yet not always; something told him that. The wind was there again, but not a wind in Zurich. In some other place, high in the night sky. And a signal came, a light flashed on, and he leaped up, whipped by furious new currents.

"All right. You're all right," said the maddening voice that would not pay attention to his commands. "Lift your foot up. *Lift* it! . . . That's right. You did it. Now, inside the car. Ease yourself back . . . slowly. That's right."

He was falling . . . falling in the pitch black sky. And then the falling stopped, everything stopped, and there was stillness; he could hear his own breathing. And footsteps, he could hear footsteps . . . and the sound of a door closing, followed by the rolling, disruptive noise beneath him, in front of him, somewhere.

Motion, swaying in circles. Balance was gone and he was falling again, only to be stopped again, another body against his body, a hand holding him, lowering him. His face felt cool; and then he felt nothing. He was drifting again, currents gentler now, darkness complete.

There were voices above him, in the distance, but not so far away. Shapes came slowly into focus, lit by the spill of table lamps. He was in a fairly large room, and on a bed, a narrow bed, blankets covering him. Across the room were two people, a man in an overcoat and a woman . . . dressed in a dark red skirt beneath a white blouse. Dark red, as the hair was. . . .

The St. Jacques woman? It *was* she, standing by a door talking to a man holding a leather bag in his left hand. They were speaking French.

"Rest, mainly," the man was saying. "If you're not accessible to me, anyone can remove the sutures. They can be taken out in a week, I'd guess."

"Thank you, Doctor."

"Thank *you*. You've been most generous. I'll go now. Perhaps I'll hear from you, perhaps not."

The doctor opened the door and let himself out. When he was gone the woman reached down and slid the bolt in place. She turned and saw Bourne looking at her. She walked slowly, cautiously, toward the bed.

"Can you hear me?" she asked.

He nodded.

"You're hurt," she said, "quite badly; but if you stay quiet, it won't be necessary for you to get to a hospital. That was a doctor . . . obviously. I paid him out of the money I found on you; quite a bit more than might seem usual, but I was told he could be trusted. It was your idea, incidentally. While we were driving, you kept saying you had to find a doctor, one you could pay to keep quiet. You were right. It wasn't difficult."

"Where are we?" He could hear his voice; it was weak, but he could hear it.

"A village called Lenzburg, about twenty miles outside of Zurich. The doctor's from Wohlen; it's a nearby town. He'll see you in a week, if you're here."

"How? . . ." He tried to raise himself but the strength wasn't there. She touched his shoulder; it was an order to lie back down.

"I'll tell you what happened, and perhaps that will answer your questions. At least I hope so, because if it doesn't, I'm not sure I can." She stood motionless, looking down at him, her tone controlled. "An animal was raping me—after which he had orders to kill me. There was no way I was going to live. In the Steppdeckstrasse, you tried to stop them, and when you couldn't, you told me to scream, to keep screaming. It was all you could do, and by shouting to me, you risked being killed at that moment yourself. Later, you somehow got free—I don't know how, but I know you were hurt very badly doing so—and you came back to find me."

"Him," interrupted Jason, "I wanted *him*."

"You told me that, and I'll say what I said before. I don't believe you. Not because you're a poor liar, but because it doesn't conform with the facts. I work with statistics, Mr. Washburn, or Mr. Bourne, or whatever your name is. I respect observable data and I can spot inaccuracies; I'm trained to do that. Two men went in that building to find you, and I heard you say they were both alive. They could identify you. And there's the owner of the Drei Alpenhäuser; he could too. Those are the facts, and you know them as well as I do. No, you came back to find me. You came back and saved my life."

"Go on," he said, his voice gaining strength. "What happened?"

"I made a decision. It was the most difficult decision I've ever made in my life. I think a person can only make a decision like that if he's nearly *lost* his life by an act of violence, his life saved by someone else. I decided to help you. Only for a while—for just a few hours, perhaps—but I would help you get away."

"Why didn't you go to the police?"

"I almost did, and I'm not sure I can tell you why I didn't. Maybe it was the rape, I don't know. I'm being honest with you. I've always been told it's the most horrible experience a woman can go through. I believe it now. And I heard the anger—the disgust—in your own voice when you shouted at him. I'll never forget that moment as long as I live, as much as I may want to."

"The police?" he repeated.

"That man at the Drei Alpenhäuser said the police were looking for you. That a telephone number had been set up in Zurich." She paused. "I couldn't give you to the police. Not then. Not after what you did."

"Knowing what I am?" he asked.

"I know only what I've heard, and what I've heard doesn't correspond with the injured man who came back for me and offered his life for mine."

"That's not very bright."

"That's the one thing I am, Mr. Bourne—I assume it's Bourne, it's what he called you. *Very* bright."

"I hit you. I threatened to kill you."

"If I'd been you, and men were trying to kill *me,* I probably would have done the same—if I were capable."

"So you drove out of Zurich?"

"Not at first, not for a half hour or so. I had to calm down, reach my decision. I'm methodical."

"I'm beginning to see that."

"I was a wreck, a mess; I needed clothes, hairbrush, makeup. I couldn't walk anywhere. I found a telephone booth down by the river, and there was no one around, so I got out of the car and called a colleague at the hotel—"

"The Frenchman? The Belgian?" interrupted Jason.

"No. They'd been at the Bertinelli lecture, and if they had recognized me up on the stage with you, I assumed they'd given my name to the police. Instead, I called a woman who's a member of our delegation; she loathes Bertinelli and was in her room. We've worked together for several years and we're friends. I told her that if she heard anything about me to disregard it, I was perfectly all right. As a matter of fact, if anyone asked about me, she was to say I was with a friend for the evening—for the night, if pressed. That I'd left the Bertinelli lecture early."

"Methodical," said Bourne.

"Yes." Marie allowed herself a tentative smile. "I asked her to go to my room—we're only two doors away from each other and the night maid knows we're friends. If no one was there she was to put some clothes and makeup in my suitcase and come back to her room. I'd call her in five minutes."

"She just accepted what you said?"

"I told you, we're friends. She knew I was all right, excited perhaps, but all right. And that I wanted her to do as I asked." Marie paused again. "She probably thought I was telling her the truth."

"Go ahead."

"I called her back and she had my things."

"Which means the two other delegates didn't give your name to the police. Your room would have been watched, sealed off."

"I don't know whether they did or not. But if they did, my friend was probably questioned quite a while ago. She'd simply say what I told her to say."

"She was at the Carillon, you were down at the river. How did you get your things?"

"It was quite simple. A little tacky, but simple. She spoke to the night maid, telling her I was avoiding one man at the hotel, seeing another outside. I needed my overnight case and could she suggest a way to get it to me. To an automobile . . . down at the river. An off-duty waiter brought it to me."

"Wasn't he surprised at the way you looked?"

"He didn't have much of a chance to see anything. I opened the trunk, stayed in the car, and told him to put it in the back. I left a ten-franc note on the spare tire."

"You're not methodical, you're remarkable."

"Methodical will do."

"How did you find the doctor?"

"Right here. The *concierge,* or whatever he's called in Switzerland. Remember, I'd wrapped you up as best I could, reduced the bleeding as much as possible. Like most people, I have a working knowledge of first aid; that meant I had to remove some of your clothing. I found the money and then I understood what you meant by finding a doctor you could pay. You have thousands and thousands of dollars on you; I know the rates of exchange."

"That's only the beginning."

"What?"

"Never mind." He tried to rise again; it was too difficult. "Aren't you afraid of me? Afraid of what you've done?"

"Of course I am. But I know what you did for me."

"You're more trusting than I'd be under the circumstances."

"Then perhaps you're not that aware of the circumstances. You're still very weak and I have the gun. Besides, you don't have any clothes."

"None?"

"Not even a pair of shorts. I've thrown everything away. You'd look a little foolish running down the street in a plastic money belt."

Bourne laughed through his pain, remembering La Ciotat and the Marquis de Chamford. "Methodical," he said.

"Very."

"What happens now?"

"I've written out the name of the doctor and paid a week's rent for the room. The *concierge* will bring you meals starting at noon today. I'll stay here until midmorning. It's nearly six o'clock; it should be light soon. Then I'll return to the hotel for the rest of my things and my airline tickets, and do my best to avoid any mention of you."

"Suppose you can't? Suppose you were identified?"

"I'll deny it. It was dark. The whole place was in panic."

"Now you're *not* being methodical. At least, not as methodical as the Zurich police would be. I've got a better way. Call your friend and tell her to pack the rest of your clothes and settle your bill. Take as much money as you want from me and grab the first plane to Canada. It's easier to deny long-distance."

She looked at him in silence, then nodded. "That's very tempting."

"It's very logical."

She continued to stare at him a moment longer, the tension inside her building, conveyed by her eyes. She turned away and walked to the window, looking out at the earliest rays of the morning sun. He watched her, feeling the intensity, knowing its roots, seeing her face in the pale orange glow of dawn. There was nothing he could do; she had done what she felt she had to do because she had been released from terror. From a kind of terrible degradation no man could really understand. From death. And in doing what she did, she had broken all the rules. She whipped her head toward him, her eyes glaring.

"Who *are* you?"

"You heard what they said."

"I know what I saw! What I *feel!*"

"Don't try to justify what you did. You simply did it, that's all. Let it be."

Let it be. Oh, God, you could have let me be. And there would have been peace. But now you have given part of my life back to me, and I've got to struggle again, face it again.

Suddenly she was standing at the foot of the bed, the gun in her hand. She pointed it at him and her voice trembled. "Should I undo it then? Should I call the police and tell them to come and take you?"

"A few hours ago I would have said go ahead. I can't bring myself to say it now."

"Then who are you?"

"They say my name is Bourne. Jason Charles Bourne."

"What does that mean? 'They say'?"

He stared at the gun, at the dark circle of its barrel. There was nothing left but the truth—as he knew the truth.

"What does it mean?" he repeated. "You know almost as much as I do, Doctor."

"What?"

"You might as well hear it. Maybe it'll make you feel better. Or worse, I don't know. But you may as well, because I don't know what else to tell you."

She lowered the gun. "Tell me what?"

"My life began five months ago on a small island in the Mediterranean called Ile de Port Noir. . . ."

The sun had risen to the midpoint of the surrounding trees, its rays filtered by windblown branches, streaming through the windows and mottling the walls with irregular shapes of light. Bourne lay back on the pillow, exhausted. He had finished; there was nothing more to say.

Marie sat across the room in a leather armchair, her legs curled up under her, cigarettes and the gun on a table to her left. She had barely moved, her gaze fixed on his face; even when she smoked, her eyes never wavered, never left his. She was a technical analyst, evaluating data, filtering facts as the trees filtered the sunlight.

"You kept saying it," she said softly, spacing out her next words. "'I don't know.' . . . 'I wish I knew.' You'd stare at something, and I was frightened. I'd ask you, what was it? What were you going to do? And you'd say it again, 'I wish I knew.' My God, what you've been through. . . . What you're *going* through."

"After what I've done to you, you can even think about what's happened to me?"

"They're two separate lines of occurrence," she said absently, frowning in thought.

"Separate—"

"Related in origin, developed independently; that's economics nonsense. . . . And then on the Löwenstrasse, just before we went up to Chernak's flat, I begged you not to make me go with you. I was convinced that if I heard any more you'd kill me. That's when you said the strangest thing of all. You said, 'What you heard makes no more sense to me than it does to you. Perhaps less. . . .' I thought you were insane."

"What I've got is a form of insanity. A sane person remembers. I don't."

"Why didn't you tell me Chernak tried to kill you?"

"There wasn't time and I didn't think it mattered."

"It didn't at that moment—to you. It did to me."

"Why?"

"Because I was holding on to an outside hope that you wouldn't fire your gun at someone who hadn't tried to kill you first."

"But he did. I was wounded."

"I didn't know the sequence; you didn't tell me."

"I don't understand."

Marie lit a cigarette. "It's hard to explain, but during all the time you kept me hostage, even when you hit me, and dragged me and pressed the gun into my stomach and held it against my head—God knows, I was terrified—but I thought I saw something in your eyes. Call it reluctance. It's the best I can come up with."

"It'll do. What's your point?"

"I'm not sure. Perhaps it goes back to something else you said in the booth at the Drei Alpenhäuser. That fat man was coming over and you told me to stay against the wall, cover my face with my hand. 'For your own good,' you said. 'There's no point in his being able to identify you.' "

"There wasn't."

" 'For your own good.' That's not the reasoning of a pathological killer. I think I held on to that—for my own sanity, maybe—that and the look in your eyes."

"I still don't get the point."

"The man with the gold-rimmed glasses who convinced me he was the police said you were a brutal killer who had to be stopped before he killed again. Had it not been for Chernak I wouldn't have believed him. On either point. The police don't behave like that; they don't use guns in dark, crowded places. And you were a man running for your life—*are* running for your life—but you're not a killer."

Bourne held up his hand. "Forgive me, but that strikes me as a judgment based on false gratitude. You say you have a respect for facts—then look at them. I repeat: you heard what they said—regardless of what you think you saw and feel—you heard the words. Boiled down, envelopes were filled with money and delivered to me to fulfill certain obligations. I'd say those obligations were pretty clear, and I accepted them. I had a numbered account at the Gemeinschaft Bank totaling about five million dollars. Where did I get it? Where does a man like me—with the obvious skills I have—get that kind of money?" Jason stared at the ceiling. The pain was returning, the sense of futility also. "Those are the facts, Dr. St. Jacques. It's time you left."

Marie rose from the chair and crushed out her cigarette. Then she picked up the gun and walked toward the bed. "You're very anxious to condemn yourself, aren't you?"

"I respect facts."

"Then if what you say is true, *I* have an obligation, too, don't I? As a law-abiding member of the social order I must call the Zurich police and tell them where you are." She raised the gun.

Bourne looked at her. "I thought—"

"Why not?" she broke in. "You're a condemned man who wants to get it over with, aren't you? You lie there talking with such finality—with, if you'll forgive me, not a little self-pity, expecting to appeal to my . . . what was it? False gratitude? Well, I think you'd better understand something. I'm not a fool; if I thought for a minute you're what they say you are, I wouldn't be here and neither would you. Facts that cannot be documented aren't facts at all. You don't have facts, you have *conclusions,* your own conclusions based on statements made by men you know are garbage."

"And an unexplained bank account with five million dollars in it. Don't forget that."

"How could I? I'm supposed to be a financial whiz. That account may not be explained in ways that you'd like, but there's a proviso attached that lends a considerable degree of legitimacy to it. It can be inspected—probably invaded— by any certified director of a corporation called something-or-other Seventy-One. That's hardly an affiliation for a hired killer."

"The corporation may be named; it isn't listed."

"In a telephone book? You *are* naive. But let's get back to you. Right now. Shall I really call the police?"

"You know my answer. I can't stop you, but I don't want you to."

Marie lowered the gun. "And I won't. For the same reason you don't want me to. I don't believe what they say you are any more than you do."

"Then what do you believe?"

"I told you, I'm not sure. All I really know is that seven hours ago I was underneath an animal, his mouth all over me, his hands clawing me . . . and I knew I was going to die. And then a man came back for me—a man who could have kept running—but who came back for me and offered to die in my place. I guess I believe in him."

"Suppose you're wrong?"

"Then I'll have made a terrible mistake."

"Thank you. Where's the money?"

"On the bureau. In your passport case and billfold. Also the name of the doctor and the receipt for the room."

"May I have the passport, please? That's the Swiss currency."

"I know." Marie brought them to him. "I gave the *concierge* three hundred francs for the room and two hundred for the name of the doctor. The doctor's services came to four hundred and fifty, to which I added another hundred and fifty for his cooperation. Altogether I paid out eleven hundred francs."

"You don't have to give me an accounting," he said.

"You should know. What are you going to do?"

"Give you money so you can get back to Canada."

"I mean afterwards."

"See how I feel later on. Probably pay the *concierge* to buy me some clothes. Ask him a few questions. I'll be all right." He took out a number of large bills and held them out for her.

"That's over fifty thousand francs."

"I've put you through a great deal."

Marie St. Jacques looked at the money, then down at the gun in her left hand. "I don't want your money," she said, placing the weapon on the bedside table.

"What do you mean?"

She turned and walked back to the armchair, turning again to look at him as she sat down. "I think I want to help you."

"Now wait a minute—"

"Please," she interrupted. "Please don't ask me any questions. Don't say anything for a while."

BOOK TWO

Neither of them knew when it happened, or, in truth, whether it had happened. Or, if it had, to what lengths either would go to preserve it, or deepen it. There was no essential drama, no conflicts to overcome or barriers to surmount. All that was required was communication, by words and looks, and, perhaps as vital as either of these, the frequent accompaniment of quiet laughter.

Their living arrangements in the room at the village inn were as clinical as they might have been in the hospital ward it replaced. During the daylight hours Marie took care of various practical matters such as clothes, meals, maps, and newspapers. On her own she had driven the stolen car ten miles south to the town of Reinach where she had abandoned it, taking a taxi back to Lenzburg. When she was out Bourne concentrated on rest and mobility. From somewhere in his forgotten past he understood that recovery depended upon both and he applied rigid discipline to both; he had been there before . . . before Port Noir.

When they were together they talked, at first awkwardly, the thrusts and parries of strangers thrown together and surviving the shock waves of cataclysm. They tried to insert normalcy where none could exist, but it was easier when they both accepted the essential abnormality: there was nothing to say not related to what had happened. And if there was, it would begin to appear only during those moments when the probing of what-had-happened was temporarily exhausted, the silences springboards to relief, to other words and thoughts.

It was during such moments that Jason learned the salient facts about the woman who had saved his life. He protested that she knew as much about him as he did, but he knew nothing about her. Where had *she* sprung from? Why was an attractive woman with dark red hair and skin obviously nurtured on a farm somewhere pretending to be a doctor of economics.

"Because she was sick of the farm," Marie replied.

"No kidding? A farm, really?"

"Well, a small ranch would be more like it. Small in comparison to the king-sized ones in Alberta. In my father's time, when a Canuck went west to buy land, there were unwritten restrictions. Don't compete in size with your betters. He often said that if he'd used the name St. James rather than St. Jacques, he'd be a far wealthier man today."

"He was a rancher?"

Marie had laughed. "No, he was an accountant who became a rancher by way of a Vickers bomber in the war. He was a pilot in the Royal Canadian Air Force. I guess once he saw all that sky, an accounting office seemed a little dull."

"That takes a lot of nerve."

"More than you know. He sold cattle he didn't own on land he didn't have before he bought the ranch. French to the core, people said."

"I think I'd like him."

"You would."

She had lived in Calgary with her parents and two brothers until she was eighteen, when she went to McGill University in Montreal and the beginnings of a life she had never contemplated. An indifferent student who preferred racing over the fields on the back of a horse to the structured boredom of a convent school in Alberta discovered the excitement of using her mind.

"It was really as simple as that," she told him. "I'd looked at books as natural enemies, and suddenly, here I was in a place surrounded by people who were caught up in them, having a marvelous time. Everything was talk. Talk all day, talk all night—in classrooms and seminars, in crowded booths over pitchers of beer; I think it was the talk that turned me on. Does that make sense to you?"

"I can't remember, but I can understand," Bourne said. "I have no memories of college or friends like that, but I'm pretty sure I was there." He smiled. "Talking over pitchers of beer is a pretty strong impression."

She smiled back. "And I was pretty impressive in that department. A strapping girl from Calgary with two older brothers to compete with could drink more beer than half the university boys in Montreal."

"You must have been resented."

"No, just envied."

A new world had been presented to Marie St. Jacques; she never returned to her old one. Except for prescribed midterm holidays, prolonged trips to Calgary grew less and less frequent. Her circles in Montreal expanded, the summers taken up with jobs in and outside the university. She gravitated first to history, then reasoned that most of history was shaped by economic forces—power and significance had to be paid for—and so she tested the theories of economics. And was consumed.

She remained at McGill for five years, receiving her masters degree and a Canadian government fellowship to Oxford.

"That was a day, I can tell you. I thought my father would have apoplexy. He left his precious cattle to my brothers long enough to fly east to talk me out of it."

"Talk you out of it? Why? He was an accountant; you were going after a doctorate in economics."

"Don't make *that* mistake," Marie exclaimed. "Accountants and economists *are* natural enemies. One views trees, the other forests, and the visions are usually at odds, as they should be. Besides, my father's not simply Canadian, he's French-Canadian. I think he saw me as a traitor to Versailles. But he was mollified when I told him that a condition of the fellowship was a commitment to work for the government for a minimum of three years. He said I could 'serve the cause better from within.' *Vive Québec libre—vive la France!*"

They both laughed.

The three-year commitment to Ottawa was extended for all the logical reasons: whenever she thought of leaving, she was promoted a grade, given a large office and an expanded staff.

"Power corrupts, of course"—she smiled—"and no one knows it better than a ranking bureaucrat whom banks and corporations pursue for a recommendation. But I think Napoleon said it better. 'Give me enough medals and I'll win you any war.' So I stayed. I enjoy my work immensely. But then it's work I'm good at and that helps."

Jason watched her as she talked. Beneath the controlled exterior there was an exuberant, childlike quality about her. She was an enthusiast, reining in her enthusiasm whenever she felt it becoming too pronounced. Of course she was good at what she did; he suspected she never did anything with less than her fullest application. "I'm sure you are—good, I mean—but it doesn't leave much time for other things, does it?"

"What other things?"

"Oh, the usual. Husband, family, house with the picket fence."

"They may come one day; I don't rule them out."

"But they haven't."

"No. There were a couple of close calls, but no brass ring. Or diamond, either."

"Who's Peter?"

The smile faded. "I'd forgotten. You read the cable."

"I'm sorry."

"Don't be. We've covered that. . . . Peter? I adore Peter. We lived together for nearly two years, but it didn't work out."

"Apparently he doesn't hold any grudges."

"He'd better not!" She laughed again. "He's director of the section, hopes for a cabinet appointment soon. If he doesn't behave himself, I'll tell the Treasury Board what he doesn't know and he'll be back as an SX-Two."

"He said he was going to pick you up at the airport on the twenty-sixth. You'd better cable him."

"Yes, I know."

Her leaving was what they had not talked about; they had avoided the subject as though it were a distant eventuality. It was not related to what-had-happened; it was something that was going to be. Marie had said she wanted to help him; he had accepted, assuming she was driven by false gratitude into staying with him for a day or so—and he was grateful for that. But anything else was unthinkable.

Which was why they did not talk about it. Words and looks had passed between them, quiet laughter evoked, comfort established. At odd moments there were tentative rushes of warmth and they both understood and backed away. Anything else *was* unthinkable.

So they kept returning to the abnormality, to what-had-happened. To *him* more than to them, for he was the irrational reason for their being together . . . together in a room at a small village inn in Switzerland. Abnormality. It was not part of the reasonable, ordered world of Marie St. Jacques, and because it was not, her orderly, analytical mind was provoked. Unreasonable things were to be examined, unraveled, explained. She became relentless in her probing, as insistent as Geoffrey Washburn had been on the Ile de Port Noir, but without the doctor's patience. For she did not have the time; she knew it and it drove her to the edges of stridency.

"When you read the newspapers, what strikes you?"

"The mess. Seems it's universal."

"Be serious. What's familiar to you?"

"Most everything, but I can't tell you why."

"Give me an example."

"This morning. There was a story about an American arms shipment to Greece and the subsequent debate in the United Nations; the Soviets protested. I understand the significance, the Mediterranean power struggle, the Mideast spillover."

"Give me another."

"There was an article about East German interference with the Bonn government's liaison office in Warsaw. Eastern bloc, Western bloc; again I understood."

"You see the relationship, don't you? You're politically—*geo*politically—receptive."

"Or I have a perfectly normal working knowledge of current events. I don't think I was ever a diplomat. The money at the Gemeinschaft would rule out any kind of government employment."

"I agree. Still, you're politically aware. What about maps? You asked me to buy you maps. What comes to mind when you look at them?"

"In some cases names trigger images, just as they did in Zurich. Buildings, hotels, streets . . . sometimes faces. But never names. The faces don't have any."

"Still you've traveled a great deal."

"I guess I have."

"You *know* you have."

"All right, I've traveled."

"How did you travel?"

"What do you mean, how?"

"Was it usually by plane, or by car—not taxis but driving yourself?"

"Both, I think. Why?"

"Planes would mean greater distances more frequently. Did people meet you? Are there faces at airports, hotels?"

"Streets," he replied involuntarily.

"Streets? Why streets?"

"I don't know. Faces met me in the streets . . . and in quiet places. Dark places."

"Restaurants? Cafés?"

"Yes. And rooms."

"Hotel rooms?"

"Yes."

"Not offices? Business offices?"

"Sometimes. Not usually."

"All right. People met you. Faces. Men? Women? Both?"

"Men mostly. Some women, but mostly men."

"What did they talk about?"

"I don't know."

"Try to remember."

"I can't. There aren't any voices; there aren't any words."

"Were there schedules? You met with people, that means you had appointments. They expected to meet with you and you expected to meet with them. Who scheduled those appointments? Someone had to."

"Cables. Telephone calls."

"From whom? From where?"

"I don't know. They would reach me."

"At hotels?"

"Mostly, I imagine."

"You told me the assistant manager at the Carillon said you *did* receive messages."

"Then they came to hotels."

"Something-or-other Seventy-One?"

"Treadstone."

"Treadstone. That's your company, isn't it?"

"It doesn't mean anything. I couldn't find it."

"Concentrate!"

"I *am*. It wasn't listed. I called New York."

"You seem to think that's so unusual. It's not."

"*Why* not?"

"It could be a separate in-house division, or a blind subsidiary—a corporation set up to make purchases for a parent company whose name would push up a negotiating price. It's done every day."

"Whom are you trying to convince?"

"You. It's entirely possible that you're a roving negotiator for American financial interests. Everything points to it: funds set up for immediate capital, confidentiality open for corporate approval, which was never exercised. These facts, plus your own antenna for political shifts, point to a trusted purchasing agent, and quite probably a large shareholder or part owner of the parent company."

"You talk awfully fast."

"I've said nothing that isn't logical."

"There's a hole or two."

"Where?"

"That account didn't show any withdrawals. Only deposits. I wasn't buying, I was selling."

"You don't know that; you can't remember. Payments can be made with shortfall deposits."

"I don't even know what that means."

"A treasurer aware of certain tax strategies would. What's the other hole?"

"Men don't try to kill someone for buying something at a lower price. They may expose him; they don't kill him."

"They do if a gargantuan error has been made. Or if that person has been mistaken for someone else. What I'm trying to tell you is that you can't be what you're not! No matter what anyone says."

"You're that convinced."

"I'm that convinced. I've spent three days with you. We've talked, I've listened. A terrible error *has* been made. Or it's some kind of conspiracy."

"Involving what? *Against* what?"

"That's what you have to find out."

"Thanks."

"Tell me something. What comes to mind when you think of money?"

Stop it! Don't do this! Can't you understand? You're wrong. When I think of money I think of killing.

"I don't know," he said. "I'm tired. I want to sleep. Send your cable in the morning. Tell Peter you're flying back."

It was well past midnight, the beginning of the fourth day, and still sleep would not come. Bourne stared at the ceiling, at the dark wood that reflected the light of the table lamp across the room. The light remained on during the nights; Marie simply left it on, no explanation sought, none offered.

In the morning she would be gone and his own plans had to crystallize. He would stay at the inn for a few more days, call the doctor in Wohlen and arrange to have the stitches removed. After that, Paris. The money was in Paris, and so was something else; he knew it, he felt it. A final answer; it was in Paris.

You are not helpless. You will find your way.

What would he find? A man named Carlos? Who was Carlos and what was he to Jason Bourne?

He heard the rustle of cloth from the couch against the wall. He glanced over, startled to see that Marie was not asleep. Instead, she was looking at him, staring at him really.

"You're wrong, you know," she said.

"About what?"

"What you're thinking."

"You don't know what I'm thinking."

"Yes, I do. I've seen that look in your eyes, seeing things you're not sure are there, afraid that they may be."

"They have been," he replied. "Explain the Steppdeckstrasse. Explain a fat man at the Drei Alpenhäuser."

"I can't, but neither can you."

"They were there. I saw them and they were there."

"Find out why. You can't be what you're not, Jason. Find out."

"Paris," he said.

"Yes, Paris." Marie got up from the couch. She was in a soft yellow nightgown, nearly white, pearl buttons at the neck; it flowed as she walked toward the bed in her bare feet. She stood beside him, looking down, then raised both her hands and began unbuttoning the top of the gown. She let it fall away, as she sat on the bed, her breasts above him. She leaned toward him, reaching for his face, cupping it, holding him gently, her eyes as so often during the past few days unwavering, fixed on his. "Thank you for my life," she whispered.

"Thank you for mine," he answered, feeling the longing he knew she felt, wondering if an ache accompanied hers, as it did his. He had no memory of a woman and, perhaps because he had none she was everything he could imagine; everything and much, much more. She repelled the darkness for him. She stopped the pain.

He had been afraid to tell her. And she was telling him now it was all right, if only for a while, for an hour or so. For the remainder of that night, she was giving him a memory because she too longed for release from the coiled springs of violence. Tension was suspended, comfort theirs for an hour or so. It was all he asked for, but God in heaven, how he *needed* her!

He reached for her breast and pulled her lips to his lips, her moisture arousing him, sweeping away the doubts.

She lifted the covers and came to him.

She lay in his arms, her head on his chest, careful to avoid the wound in his shoulder. She slid back gently, raising herself on her elbows. He looked at her; their eyes locked, and both smiled. She lifted her left hand, pressing her index finger over his lips, and spoke softly.

"I have something to say and I don't want you to interrupt. I'm not sending the cable to Peter. Not yet."

"Now, just a *minute.*" He took her hand from his face.

"Please, don't interrupt me. I said 'not yet.' That doesn't mean I won't send it, but not for a while. I'm staying with you. I'm going to Paris with you."

He forced the words. "Suppose I don't want you to."

She leaned forward brushing her lips against his cheek. "That won't wash. The computer just rejected it."

"I wouldn't be so certain, if I were you."

"But you're not me. I'm me, and I know the way you held me, and tried to say so many things you couldn't say. Things I think we both wanted to say to each other for the past several days. I can't explain what's happened. Oh, I suppose it's there in some obscure psychological theory somewhere, two reasonably intelligent people thrown into hell together and crawling out . . . together. And maybe that's all it is. But it's there right now and I can't run away from it. I can't run away from you. Because you need me, and you gave me my life."

"What makes you think I need you?"

"I can do things for you that you can't do for yourself. It's all I've thought about for the past two hours." She raised herself further, naked beside him.

"You're somehow involved with a great deal of money, but I don't think you know a debit from an asset. You may have before, but you don't now. I do. And there's something else. I have a ranking position with the Canadian government. I have clearance and access to all manner of inquiries. And protection. International finance is rotten and Canada has been raped. We've mounted our own protection and I'm part of it. It's why I was in Zurich. To observe and report alliances, not to discuss abstract theories."

"And the fact that you have this clearance, this access, can help me?"

"I think it can. And embassy protection, that may be the most important. But I give you my word that at the first sign of violence, I'll send the cable and get out. My own fears aside, I won't be a burden to you under those conditions."

"At the first sign," repeated Bourne, studying her. "And I determine when and where that is?"

"If you like. My experience is limited. I won't argue."

He continued to hold her eyes, the moment long, magnified by silence. Finally he asked, "Why are you doing this? You just said it. We're two reasonably intelligent people who crawled out of some kind of hell. That may be all we are. Is it worth it?"

She sat motionless. "I also said something else; maybe you've forgotten. Four nights ago a man who could have kept running came back for me and offered to die in my place. I believe in that man. More than he does, I think. That's really what I have to offer."

"I accept," he said, reaching for her. "I shouldn't, but I do. I need that belief very badly."

"You may interrupt now," she whispered, lowering the sheet, her body coming to his. "Make love to me, I have needs too."

Three more days and nights went by, filled by the warmth of their comfort, the excitement of discovery. They lived with the intensity of two people aware that change would come. And when it came, it would come quickly; so there were things to talk about which could not be avoided any longer.

Cigarette smoke spiraled above the table joining the steam from the hot, bitter coffee. The *concierge*, an ebullient Swiss whose eyes took in more than his lips would reveal, had left several minutes before, having delivered the *petit déjeuner* and the Zurich newspapers, in both English and French. Jason and Marie sat across from each other; both had scanned the news.

"Anything in yours?" asked Bourne.

"That old man, the watchman at the Guisan Quai, was buried the day before yesterday. The police still have nothing concrete. 'Investigation in progress,' it says."

"It's a little more extensive here," said Jason, shifting his paper awkwardly in his bandaged left hand.

"How is it?" asked Marie, looking at the hand.

"Better. I've got more play in the fingers now."

"I know."

"You've got a dirty mind." He folded the paper. "Here it is. They repeat the things they said the other day. The shells and blood scrapings are being analyzed." Bourne looked up. "But they've added something. Remnants of clothing; it wasn't mentioned before."

"Is that a problem?"

"Not for me. My clothes were bought off a rack in Marseilles. What about your dress? Was it a special design or fabric?"

"You embarrass me; it wasn't. All my clothes are made by a woman in Ottawa."

"It couldn't be traced, then?"

"I don't see how. The silk came from a bolt an FS-Three in our section brought back from Hong Kong."

"Did you buy anything at the shops in the hotel? Something you might have had on you. A kerchief, a pin, anything like that?"

"No. I'm not much of a shopper that way."

"Good. And your friend wasn't asked any questions when she checked out?"

"Not by the desk, I told you that. Only by the two men you saw me with in the elevator."

"From the French and Belgian delegations."

"Yes. Everything was fine."

"Let's go over it again."

"There's nothing to go over. Paul—the one from Brussels—didn't see anything. He was knocked off his chair to the floor and stayed there. Claude—he tried to stop us, remember?—at first thought it was me on the stage, in the light, but before he could get to the police he was hurt in the crowd and taken to the infirmary—"

"And by the time he might have said something," interrupted Jason, recalling her words, "he wasn't sure."

"Yes. But I have an idea he knew my main purpose for being at the conference; my presentation didn't fool him. If he did, it would reinforce his decision to stay out of it."

Bourne picked up his coffee. "Let me have *that* again," he said. "You were looking for . . . alliances?"

"Well, hints of them, really. No one's going to come out and say there are financial interests in his country working with interests in that country so they can buy their way into Canadian raw materials or any other market. But you see who meets for drinks, who has dinner together. Or sometimes it's as dumb as a delegate from, say, Rome—whom you know is being paid by Agnelli—coming up and asking you how serious Ottawa is about the declaration laws."

"I'm still not sure I understand."

"You should. Your own country's very touchy about the subject. Who owns what? How many American banks are controlled by OPEC money? How much industry is owned by European and Japanese consortiums? How many hundreds of thousands of acres have been acquired by capital that's fled England and Italy and France? We all worry."

"We do?"

Marie laughed. "Of course. Nothing makes a man more nationalistic than to think his country's owned by foreigners. He can adjust in time to losing a war—that only means the enemy was stronger—but to lose his economy means the enemy was smarter. The period of occupation lasts longer, and so do the scars."

"You've given these things a lot of thought, haven't you?"

For a brief moment the look in Marie's eyes lost its edge of humor; she answered him seriously. "Yes, I have. I think they're important."

"Did you learn anything in Zurich?"

"Nothing startling," she said. "Money's flying all over; syndicates are trying to find internal investments where bureaucratic machineries look the other way."

"That cablegram from Peter said your daily reports were first rate. What did he mean?"

"I found a number of odd economic bedfellows who I think may be using Canadian figureheads to buy up Canadian properties. I'm not being elusive; it's just that they wouldn't mean anything to you."

"I'm not trying to pry," countered Jason, "but I think you put *me* in one of those beds. Not with respect to Canada, but in general."

"I don't rule you out; the structure's there. You could be part of a financial combine that's looking for all manner of illegal purchases. It's one thing I can put a quiet trace on, but I want to do it over a telephone. Not words written out in a cable."

"Now I *am* prying. What do you mean and how?"

"If there's a Treadstone Seventy-One behind a multinational corporate door somewhere, there are ways to find which company, which door. I want to call Peter from one of those public telephone stations in Paris. I'll tell him that I ran across the name Treadstone Seventy-One in Zurich and it's been bothering me. I'll ask him to make a CS—a covert search—and say that I'll call him back."

"And if he finds it?"

"If it's there, he'll find it."

"Then I get in touch with whoever's listed as the 'certified directors' and surface."

"Very cautiously," added Marie. "Through intermediaries. Myself, if you like."

"Why?"

"Because of what they've done. Or *not* done, really."

"Which is?"

"They haven't tried to reach you in nearly six months."

"You don't know that—*I* don't know that."

"The bank knows it. Millions of dollars left untouched, unaccounted for, and no one has bothered to find out why. That's what I can't understand. It's as though you were being abandoned. It's where the mistake could have been made."

Bourne leaned back in the chair, looking at his bandaged left hand, remembering the sight of the weapon smashing repeatedly downward in the shadows of a racing car in the Steppdeckstrasse. He raised his eyes and looked at Marie. "What you're saying is that if I was abandoned, it's because that mistake is thought to be the truth by the directors at Treadstone."

"Possibly. They might think you've involved them in illegal transactions—with criminal elements—that could cost them millions more. Conceivably risking expropriation of entire companies by angry governments. Or that you joined forces with an international crime syndicate, probably not knowing it. Anything. It would account for their not going near the bank. They'd want no guilt by association."

"So, in a sense, no matter what your friend Peter learns, I'm still back at square one."

"*We're* back, but it's not square one, more like four-and-a-half to five on a scale of ten."

"Even if it were nine, nothing's really changed. Men want to kill me and I don't know why. Others could stop them but they won't. That man at the Drei Alpenhäuser said Interpol has its nets out for me, and if I walk into one I don't have any answers. I'm guilty as charged because I don't know what I'm guilty of. Having no memory isn't much of a defense, and it's possible that I have no defense, period."

"I refuse to believe that, and so must you."

"Thanks."

"I *mean* it, Jason. Stop it."

Stop it. How many times do I say that to myself? You are my love, the only woman I have ever known, and you believe in me. Why can't I believe in myself?

Bourne got up, as always testing his legs. Mobility was coming back to him, the wounds less severe than his imagination had permitted him to believe. He had made an appointment that night with the doctor in Wohlen to remove the stitches. Tomorrow change would come.

"Paris," said Jason. "The answer's in Paris. I know it as surely as I saw the outline of those triangles in Zurich. I just don't know where to begin. It's crazy. I'm a man waiting for an image, for a word or a phrase—or a book of matches—to tell me something. To send me somewhere else."

"Why not wait until I hear from Peter? I can call him tomorrow; we can be in Paris tomorrow."

"Because it wouldn't make any difference, don't you see? No matter what he came up with, the one thing I need to know wouldn't be there. For the same reason Treadstone hasn't gone near the bank. *Me.* I have to know why men want to kill me, why someone named Carlos will pay . . . what was it . . . a fortune for my corpse."

It was as far as he got, interrupted by the crash at the table. Marie had dropped her cup and was staring at him, her face white, as if the blood had drained from her head. "What did you just say?" she asked.

"What? I said I have to know . . ."

"The *name*. You just said the name Carlos."

"That's right."

"In all the hours we've talked, the days we've been together, you never mentioned him."

Bourne looked at her, trying to remember. It was true; he had told her everything that had come to him, yet somehow he had omitted Carlos . . . almost purposely, as if blocking it out.

"I guess I didn't," he said. "You seem to know. Who's Carlos?"

"Are you trying to be funny? If you are, the joke's not very good."

"I'm not trying to be funny. I don't think there's anything to be funny about. Who's Carlos?"

"My God—you *don't* know!" she exclaimed, studying his eyes. "It's part of what was taken from you."

"Who is Carlos?"

"An assassin. He's called the assassin of Europe. A man hunted for twenty years, believed to have killed between fifty and sixty political and military figures. No one knows what he looks like . . . but it's said he operates out of Paris."

Bourne felt a wave of cold going through him.

The taxi to Wohlen was an English Ford belonging to the *concierge*'s son-in-law. Jason and Marie sat in the back seat, the dark countryside passing swiftly outside the windows. The stitches had been removed, replaced by soft bandages held by wide strips of tape.

"Get back to Canada," said Jason softly, breaking the silence between them.

"I will, I told you that. I've a few more days left. I want to see Paris."

"I don't want you in Paris. I'll call you in Ottawa. You can make the Treadstone search yourself and give me the information over the phone."

"I thought you said it wouldn't make any difference. You had to know the *why;* the *who* was meaningless until you understood."

"I'll find a way. I just need one man; I'll find him."

"But you don't know where to begin. You're a man waiting for an image, for a phrase, or a book of matches. They may not be there."

"Something will be there."

"Something *is,* but you don't see it. I *do.* It's why you need me. I know the words, the methods. You don't."

Bourne looked at her in the rushing shadows. "I think you'd better be clearer."

"The banks, Jason. Treadstone's connections are in the banks. But not in the way that you might think."

The stooped old man in the threadbare overcoat, black beret in hand, walked down the far left aisle of the country church in the village of Arpajon, ten miles south of Paris. The bells of the evening Angelus echoed throughout the upper regions of stone and wood; the man held his place at the fifth row and waited for the ringing to stop. It was his signal; he accepted it, knowing that during the pealing of the bells another, younger man—as ruthless as any man alive—had circled the small church and studied everyone inside and outside. Had that man seen anything he did not expect to see, anyone he considered a threat to his person, there would be no questions asked, simply an execution. That was the way of Carlos, and only those who understood that their lives could be snuffed out because they themselves had been followed accepted money to act as the assassin's messenger. They were all like himself, old men from the old days, whose lives were running out, months remaining limited by age, or disease, or both.

Carlos permitted no risks whatsoever, the single consolation being that if one died in his service—or by his hand—money would find its way to old women, or the children of old women, or their children. It had to be said: there was a certain dignity to be found in working for Carlos. And there was no lack of generosity. This was what his small army of infirm old men understood; he gave a purpose to the ends of their lives.

The messenger clutched his beret and continued down the aisle to the row of confessional booths against the left wall. He walked to the fifth booth, parted the curtain, and stepped inside, adjusting his eyes to the light of a single candle that glowed from the other side of the translucent drape separating priest from sinner. He sat down on the small wooden bench and looked at the silhouette in the holy enclosure. It was as it always was, the hooded figure of a man in a monk's habit. The messenger tried not to imagine what that man looked like; it was not his place to speculate on such things.

"Angelus Domini," he said.

"Angelus Domini, child of God," whispered the hooded silhouette. "Are your days comfortable?"

"They draw to an end," replied the old man, making the proper response, "but they are made comfortable."

"Good. It's important to have a sense of security at your age," said Carlos. "But to business. Did you get the particulars from Zurich?"

"The owl is dead; so are two others, possibly a third. Another's hand was severely wounded; he cannot work. Cain disappeared. They think the woman is with him."

"An odd turn of events," said Carlos.

"There's more. The one ordered to kill her has not been heard from. He was to take her to the Guisan Quai; no one knows what happened."

"Except that a watchman was killed in her place. It's possible she was never a hostage at all, but instead, bait for a trap. A trap that snapped back on Cain. I want to think about that. In the meantime, here are my instructions. Are you ready?"

The old man reached into his pocket and took out the stub of a pencil and a scrap of paper. "Very well."

"Telephone Zurich. I want a man in Paris by tomorrow who has seen Cain, who can recognize him. Also, Zurich is to reach Koenig at the Gemeinschaft and tell him to send his tape to New York. He's to use the post office box in Village Station."

"Please," interrupted the aged messenger. "These old hands do not write as they once did."

"Forgive me," whispered Carlos. "I'm preoccupied and inconsiderate. I'm sorry."

"Not at all, not at all. Go ahead."

"Finally, I want our team to take rooms within a block of the bank on the rue Madeleine. This time the bank will be Cain's undoing. The pretender will be taken at the source of his misplaced pride. A bargain price, as despicable as he is . . . unless he's something else."

11

Bourne watched from a distance as Marie passed through customs and immigration in Bern's airport, looking for signs of interest or recognition from anyone in the crowd that stood around Air France's departure area. It was four o'clock in the afternoon, the busiest hour for flights to Paris, a time when privileged businessmen hurried back to the City of Light after dull company chores at the banks in Bern. Marie glanced over her shoulder as she walked through the gate; he nodded, waited until she had disappeared, then turned and started for the Swissair lounge. George B. Washburn had a reservation on the 4:30 plane to Orly.

They would meet later at the café Marie remembered from visits during her Oxford days. It was called Au Coin de Cluny, on the boulevard Saint-Michel, several blocks from the Sorbonne. If by any chance it was no longer there, Jason would find her around nine o'clock on the steps of the Cluny Museum.

Bourne would be late, nearby but late. The Sorbonne had one of the most extensive libraries in all Europe and somewhere in that library were back issues of newspapers. University libraries were not subject to the working hours of government employees; students used them during the evenings. So would he as soon as he reached Paris. There was something he had to learn.

Every day I read the newspapers. In three languages. Six months ago a man was killed, his death reported on the front page of each of those newspapers. So said a fat man in Zurich.

He left his suitcase at the library checkroom and walked to the second floor, turning left toward the arch that led to the huge reading room. The Salle de

Lecture was at this annex, the newspapers on spindles placed in racks, the issues going back precisely one year from the day's date.

He walked along the racks, counting back six months, lifting off the first ten weeks' worth of papers before that date a half a year ago. He carried them to the nearest vacant table and without sitting down flipped through from front page to front page, issue to issue.

Great men had died in their beds, while others had made pronouncements; the dollar had fallen, gold risen; strikes had crippled, and governments had vacillated between action and paralysis. But no man had been killed who warranted headlines; there was no such incident—no such assassination.

Jason returned to the racks and went back further. Two weeks, twelve weeks, twenty weeks. Nearly eight months. Nothing.

Then it struck him; he had gone *back* in time, not forward from that date six months ago. An error could be made in either direction; a few days or a week, even two. He returned the spindles to the racks and pulled out the papers from four and five months ago.

Airplanes had crashed and revolutions had erupted bloodily; holy men had spoken only to be rebuked by other holy men; poverty and disease had been found where everyone knew they could be found, but no man of consequence had been killed.

He started on the last spindle, the mists of doubt and guilt clearing with each turn of a page. Had a sweating fat man in Zurich lied? Was it all a lie? *All* lies? Was he somehow living a nightmare that could vanish with . . .

AMBASSADEUR LELAND ASSASSINÉ À MARSEILLE!

The thick block letters of the headline exploded off the page, hurting his eyes. It was not imagined pain, not invented pain, but a sharp ache that penetrated his sockets and seared through his head. His breathing stopped, his eyes rigid on the name LELAND. He knew it; he could picture the face, actually *picture* it. Thick brows beneath a wide forehead, a blunt nose centered between high cheekbones and above curiously thin lips topped by a perfectly groomed gray mustache. He knew the face, he knew the man. And the man had been killed by a single shot from a high-powered rifle fired from a waterfront window. Ambassador Howard Leland had walked down a Marseilles pier at five o'clock in the afternoon. His head had been blown off.

Bourne did not have to read the second paragraph to know that Howard Leland had been Admiral H. R. Leland, United States Navy, until an interim appointment as director of Naval Intelligence preceded his ambassadorship to the Quai d'Orsay in Paris. Nor did he have to reach the body of the article where motives for the assassination were speculated upon to know them; he knew them. Leland's primary function in Paris was to dissuade the French government from authorizing massive arms sales—in particular fleets of Mirage jets—to Africa and the Middle East. To an astonishing degree he had succeeded, angering interested parties at all points in the Mediterranean. It was presumed that he had been killed for his interference; a punishment which served as a warning to others. Buyers and sellers of death were not to be hindered.

And the seller of death who had killed him would have been paid a great deal of money, far from the scene, all traces buried.

Zurich. A messenger to a legless man; another to a fat man in a crowded restaurant off the Falkenstrasse.

Zurich.

Marseilles.

Jason closed his eyes, the pain now intolerable. He had been picked up at sea five months ago, his port of origin assumed to have been Marseilles. And if Marseilles, the waterfront had been his escape route, a boat hired to take him into the vast expanse of Mediterranean. Everything fitted too well, each piece of the puzzle sculpted into the next. How could he know the things he knew if he were not that seller of death from a window on the Marseilles waterfront?

He opened his eyes, pain inhibiting thought, but not all thought, one decision as clear as anything in his limited memory. There would be no rendezvous in Paris with Marie St. Jacques.

Perhaps one day he would write her a letter, saying the things he could not say now. If he was alive and could write a letter; he could not write one now. There could be no written words of thanks or love, no explanations at all; she would wait for him and he would not come to her. He had to put distance between them; she could not be involved with a seller of death. She had been wrong, his worst fears accurate.

Oh, God! He could picture Howard Leland's face, and there was no photograph on the page in front of him! The front page with the terrible headline that triggered so much, confirmed so many things. The date. *Thursday, August 26. Marseilles.* It was a day he would remember as long as he could remember for the rest of his convoluted life.

Thursday, August 26 . . .

Something was wrong. What was it? What *was* it? Thursday? . . . Thursday meant nothing to him. The twenty-sixth of August? . . . The twenty-*sixth?* It could not be the twenty-*sixth!* The twenty-sixth was wrong! He had heard it over and over again. Washburn's diary—his patient's journal. How often had Washburn gone back over every fact, every phrase, every day and point of progress? Too many times to count. Too many times not to remember!

You were brought to my door on the morning of Tuesday, August twenty-fourth, at precisely eight-twenty o'clock. Your condition was . . .

Tuesday, August 24.

August 24.

He was not in Marseilles on the twenty-sixth! He could not have fired a rifle from a window on the waterfront. He was not the seller of death in Marseilles; he had not killed Howard Leland!

Six months ago a man was killed . . . But it was not six months; it was *close* to six months but *not* six months. And he had not killed that man; he was half dead in an alcoholic's house on Ile de Port Noir.

The mists were clearing, the pain receding. A sense of elation filled him; he had found one concrete lie! If there was one there could be others!

Bourne looked at his watch; it was quarter past nine. Marie had left the café; she was waiting for him on the steps of the Cluny Museum. He replaced the spindles in their racks, then started toward the large cathedral door of the reading room, a man in a hurry.

He walked down the boulevard Saint-Michel, his pace accelerating with each stride. He had the distinct feeling that he knew what it was to have been given a reprieve from hanging and he wanted to share that rare experience. For a time he was out of the violent darkness, beyond the crashing waters; he had found a moment of sunlight—like the moments and the sunlight that had filled a room in a village inn—and he had to reach the one who had given them to him. Reach her and hold her and tell her there was hope.

He saw her on the steps, her arms folded against the icy wind that swept off the boulevard. At first she did not see him, her eyes searching the tree-lined street. She was restless, anxious, an impatient woman afraid she would not see what she wanted to see, frightened that it would not be there.

Ten minutes ago he would not have been.

She saw him. Her face became radiant, the smile emerged and it was filled with life. She rushed to him as he raced up the steps toward her. They came together and for a moment neither said anything, warm and alone on the Saint-Michel.

"I waited and *waited,*" she breathed finally. "I was so afraid, so worried. Did anything happen? Are you all right?"

"I'm fine. Better than I've been in a long time."

"What?"

He held her by the shoulders. "Six months ago a man was killed. . . .' Remember?"

The joy left her eyes. "Yes, I remember."

"I didn't kill him," said Bourne. "I couldn't have."

They found a small hotel off the crowded boulevard Montparnasse. The lobby and the rooms were threadbare, but there was a pretense to forgotten elegance that gave it an air of timelessness. It was a quiet resting place set down in the middle of a carnival, hanging on to its identity by accepting the times without joining them.

Jason closed the door, nodding to the white-haired bell captain whose indifference had turned to indulgence upon the receipt of a twenty-franc note.

"He thinks you're a provincial deacon flushed with a night's anticipation," said Marie. "I hope you noticed I went right to the bed."

"His name is Hervé, and he'll be very solicitous of our needs. He has no intention of sharing the wealth." He crossed to her and took her in his arms. "Thanks for my life," he said.

"Any time, my friend." She reached up and held his face in her hands. "But don't keep me waiting like that again. I nearly went crazy; all I could think of was that someone had recognized you . . . that something terrible had happened."

"You forget, no one knows what I look like."

"Don't count on that; it's not true. There were four men in the Steppdeck-strasse, including that bastard in the Guisan Quai. They're alive, Jason. They saw you."

"Not really. They saw a dark-haired man with bandages on his neck and head, who walked with a limp. Only two were near me: the man on the second floor and that pig in the Guisan. The first won't be leaving Zurich for a while; he can't walk and he hasn't much of a hand left. The second had the beam of the flashlight in his eyes; it wasn't in mine."

She released him, frowning, her alert mind questioning. "You can't be sure. They were there; they did see you."

Change your hair . . . you change your face. Geoffrey Washburn, Ile de Port Noir.

"I repeat, they saw a dark-haired man in shadows. How good are you with a weak solution of peroxide?"

"I've never used it."

"Then I'll find a shop in the morning. The Montparnasse is the place for it. Blonds have more fun, isn't that what they say?"

She studied his face. "I'm trying to imagine what you'll look like."

"Different. Not much, but enough."

"You may be right. I hope to God you are." She kissed his cheek, her prelude to discussion. "Now, tell me what happened. Where did you go? What did you learn about that . . . incident six months ago?"

"It wasn't six months ago, and because it wasn't, I couldn't have killed him." He told her everything, save for the few brief moments when he thought he would never see her again. He did not have to; she said it for him.

"If that date hadn't been so clear in your mind, you wouldn't have come to me, would you?"

He shook his head. "Probably not."

"I knew it. I felt it. For a minute, while I was walking from the café to the museum steps, I could hardly breathe. It was as though I were suffocating. Can you believe that?"

"I don't want to."

"Neither do I, but it happened."

They were sitting, she on the bed, he in the single armchair close by. He reached for her hand. "I'm still not sure I should be here. . . . I *knew* that man, I saw his face, I was in Marseilles forty-eight hours before he was killed!"

"But you didn't kill him."

"Then why was I there? Why do people think I did? Christ, it's insane!" He sprang up from the chair, pain back in his eyes. "But then I forgot. I'm not sane, am I? Because I've forgotten. . . . Years, a lifetime."

Marie spoke matter-of-factly, no compassion in her voice. "The answers will come to you. From one source or another, finally from yourself."

"That may not be possible. Washburn said it was like blocks rearranged, different tunnels . . . different windows." Jason walked to the window, bracing himself on the sill, looking down on the lights of Montparnasse. "The views aren't the same; they never will be. Somewhere out there are people I know, who know me. A couple of thousand miles away are other people I care about and don't care about. . . . Or, oh God, maybe a wife and children—I don't know. I keep spinning around in the wind, turning over and over and I can't get down to the ground. Every time I try I get thrown back up again."

"Into the sky?" asked Marie.

"Yes."

"You've jumped from a plane," she said, making a statement.

Bourne turned. "I never told you that."

"You talked about it in your sleep the other night. You were sweating; your face was flushed and hot and I had to wipe it with a towel."

"Why didn't you say anything?"

"I did, in a way. I asked you if you were a pilot, or if flying bothered you. Especially at night."

"I didn't know what you were talking about. Why didn't you press me?"

"I was afraid to. You were very close to hysterics, and I'm not trained in things like that. I can help you try to remember, but I can't deal with your unconscious. I don't think anyone should but a doctor."

"A doctor? I was with a doctor for damn near six months."

"From what you've said about him, I think another opinion is called for."

"I don't!" he replied, confused by his own anger.

"Why not?" Marie got up from the bed. "You need help, my darling. A psychiatrist might—"

"No!" He shouted in spite of himself, furious with himself. "I won't do that. I can't."

"Please, tell me why?" she asked calmly, standing in front of him.

"I . . . I . . . can't do it."

"Just tell me why, that's all."

Bourne stared at her, then turned and looked out the window again, his hands on the sill again. "Because I'm afraid. Someone lied, and I was grateful for that more than I can tell you. But suppose there aren't any more lies, suppose the rest is true. What do I do then?"

"Are you saying you don't want to find out?"

"Not that way." He stood up and leaned against the window frame, his eyes still on the lights below. "Try to understand me," he said. "I have to know certain things . . . enough to make a decision . . . but maybe not everything. A part of me has to be able to walk away, disappear. I have to be able to say to myself, what was isn't any longer, and there's a possibility that it *never* was because I have no memory of it. What a person can't remember didn't exist . . . for him." He turned back to her. "What I'm trying to tell you is that maybe it's better this way."

"You want evidence, but not proof, is that what you're saying?"

"I want arrows pointing in one direction or the other, telling me whether to run or not to run."

"Telling *you*. What about *us?*"

"That'll come with the arrows, won't it? You know that."

"Then let's find them," she replied.

"Be careful. You may not be able to live with what's out there. I mean that."

"I can live with you. And I mean that." She reached up and touched his face. "Come on. It's barely five o'clock in Ontario, and I can still reach Peter at the office. He can start the Treadstone search . . . and give us the name of someone here at the embassy who can help us if we need him."

"You're going to tell Peter you're in Paris?"

"He'll know it anyway from the operator, but the call won't be traceable to this hotel. And don't worry, I'll keep everything 'in-house,' even casual. I came to Paris for a few days because my relatives in Lyon are simply too dull. He'll accept that."

"Would he know someone at the embassy here?"

"Peter makes it a point to know someone everywhere. It's one of his more useful but less attractive traits."

"Sounds like he will." Bourne got their coats. "After your call we'll have dinner. I think we could both use a drink."

"Let's go past the bank on rue Madeleine. I want to see something."

"What can you see at night?"

"A telephone booth. I hope there's one nearby."

There was. Diagonally across the street from the entrance.

The tall blond man wearing tortoise-shell glasses checked his watch under the afternoon sun on the rue Madeleine. The pavements were crowded, the traffic in the street unreasonable, as most traffic was in Paris. He entered the telephone booth and untangled the telephone, which had been hanging free of its cradle, the line knotted. It was a courteous sign to the next would-be user that the phone was out of commission; it reduced the chance that the booth would be occupied. It had worked.

He glanced at his watch again; the time span had begun. Marie inside the bank. She would call within the next few minutes. He took several coins from his pocket, put them on the ledge and leaned against the glass panel, his eyes on the bank across the street. A cloud diminished the sunlight and he could see his reflection in the glass. He approved of what he saw, recalling the startled reaction of a hairdresser in Montparnasse who had sequestered him in a curtained booth while performing the blond transformation. The cloud passed, the sunlight returned, and the telephone rang.

"It's you?" asked Marie St. Jacques.

"It's me," said Bourne.

"Make sure you get the name and the location of the office. And rough up your French. Mispronounce a few words so he knows you're American. Tell him you're not used to the telephones in Paris. Then do everything in sequence. I'll call you back in exactly five minutes."

"Clock's on."

"What?"

"Nothing. I mean, let's go."

"All right. . . . The clock is on. Good luck."

"Thanks." Jason depressed the lever, released it, and dialed the number he had memorized.

"La Banque de Valois. *Bonjour.*"

"I need assistance," said Bourne, continuing with the approximate words Marie had told him to use. "I recently transferred sizable funds from Switzerland on a pouch-courier basis. I'd like to know if they've cleared."

"That would be our Foreign Services Department, sir. I'll connect you."

A click, then another female voice. "Foreign Services."

Jason repeated his request.

"May I have your name, please?"

"I'd prefer speaking with an officer of the bank before giving it."

There was a pause on the line. "Very well, sir. I'll switch you to the office of Vice President d'Amacourt."

Monsieur d'Amacourt's secretary was less accommodating, the bank officer's screening process activated, as Marie had predicted. So Bourne once more used Marie's words. "I'm referring to a transfer from Zurich, from the Gemeinschaft Bank on the Bahnhofstrasse, and I'm talking in the area of seven figures. Monsieur d'Amacourt, if you please. I have very little time."

It was not a secretary's place to be the cause of further delay. A perplexed first vice president got on the line.

"May I help you?"

"Are you d'Amacourt?" asked Jason.

"I am Antoine d'Amacourt, yes. And who, may I ask, is calling?"

"Good! I should have been given your name in Zurich. I'll make certain next time certainly," said Bourne, the redundancy intended, his accent American.

"I beg your pardon? Would you be more comfortable speaking English, monsieur?"

"Yes," replied Jason, doing so. "I'm having enough trouble with this damn phone." He looked at his watch; he had less than two minutes. "My name's Bourne, Jason Bourne, and eight days ago I transferred four and a half million francs from the Gemeinschaft Bank in Zurich. They assured me the transaction would be confidential."

"All transactions are confidential, sir."

"Fine. Good. What I want to know is, has everything cleared?"

"I should explain," continued the bank officer, "that confidentiality excludes blanket confirmations of such transactions to unknown parties over the telephone."

Marie had been right, the logic of her trap clearer to Jason.

"I would hope so, but as I told your secretary I'm in a hurry. I'm leaving Paris in a couple of hours and I have to put everything in order."

"Then I suggest you come to the bank."

"I know *that,*" said Bourne, satisfied that the conversation was going precisely the way Marie foresaw it. "I just wanted everything ready when I got there. Where's your office?"

"On the main floor, monsieur. At the rear, beyond the gate, center door. A receptionist is there."

"And I'll be dealing only with you, right?"

"If you wish, although any officer—"

"Look, mister," exclaimed the ugly American, "we're talking about over four million francs!"

"Only with me, Monsieur Bourne."

"Fine. Good." Jason put his fingers on the cradle bar. He had fifteen seconds to go. "Look, it's 2:35 now—" He pressed down twice on the lever, interrupting the line but not disconnecting it. "Hello? Hello?"

"I am here, monsieur."

"Damn phones! Listen, I'll—" He pressed down again, now three times in rapid succession. "Hello? Hello?"

"Monsieur, please—if you'll give me your telephone number."

"Operator? Operator!?"

"Monsieur Bourne, please—"

"I can't hear you!" *Four seconds, three seconds, two seconds.* "Wait a minute. I'll call you back." He held the lever down, breaking the connection. Three more seconds elapsed and the phone rang; he picked it up. "His name's d'Amacourt, office on the main floor, rear, center door."

"I've got it," said Marie, hanging up.

Bourne dialed the bank again, inserted coins again. *"Je parlais avec Monsieur d'Amacourt quand on m'a coupé . . ."*

"Je regrette, monsieur."

"Monsieur Bourne?"

"D'Amacourt?"

"Yes—I'm so terribly sorry you're having such trouble. You were saying? About the time?"

"Oh, yeah. It's a little after 2:30. I'll get there by 3:00."

"I look forward to meeting you, monsieur."

Jason reknotted the phone, letting it hang free, then left the booth and walked quickly through crowds to the shade of a storefront canopy. He turned and waited, his eyes on the bank across the way, remembering another bank in Zurich and the sound of sirens on the Bahnhofstrasse. The next twenty minutes would tell if Marie was right or not. If she was, there would be no sirens on the rue Madeleine.

The slender woman in the wide-brimmed hat that partially covered the side of her face hung up the public phone on the wall to the right of the bank's entrance. She opened her purse, removed a compact and ostensibly checked her makeup, angling the small mirror first to the left, then to the right. Satisfied, she replaced the compact, closed her purse, and walked past the tellers' cages toward the rear of the main floor. She stopped at a counter in the center, picked up a chained ballpoint pen, and began writing aimless numbers on a form that had been left on the marble surface. Less than ten feet away was a small, brass-framed gate, flanked by a low wooden railing that extended the width of the lobby. Beyond the gate and the railing were the desks of the lesser executives and behind them the desks of the major secretaries—five in all—in front of five doors in the rear wall. Marie read the name painted in gold script on the center door.

M.A.R. D'AMACOURT

VICE PRÉSIDENT

COMPTES Á L'ÉTRANGER ET DEVISES

It would happen any moment now—if it was going to happen, if she was right. And if she was, she had to know what Monsieur A.R. d'Amacourt looked like; he would be the man Jason could reach. Reach him and talk to him, but not in the bank.

It happened. There was a flurry of controlled activity. The secretary at the desk in front of d'Amacourt's office rushed inside with her notepad, emerged thirty seconds later, and picked up the phone. She dialed three digits—an inside call—and spoke, reading from her pad.

Two minutes passed; the door of d'Amacourt's office opened and the vice president stood in the frame, an anxious executive concerned over an unwarranted delay. He was a middle-aged man with a face older than his age, but striving to look younger. His thinning dark hair was singed and brushed to obscure the bald spots; his eyes were encased in small rolls of flesh, attesting to long hours with good wine. Those same eyes were cold, darting eyes, evidence of a demanding man wary of his surroundings. He barked a question to his secretary; she twisted in her chair, doing her best to maintain her composure.

D'Amacourt went back inside his office without closing the door, the cage of an angry cat left open. Another minute passed; the secretary kept glancing to her right, looking at something—for something. When she saw it, she exhaled, closing her eyes in relief.

From the far left wall, a green light suddenly appeared above two panels of dark wood; an elevator was in use. Seconds later the door opened and an elderly elegant man walked out carrying a small black case not much larger than his hand. Marie stared at it, experiencing both satisfaction and fear; she had guessed right. The black case had been removed from a confidential file inside a guarded room and signed out by a man beyond reproach or temptation—the elderly figure making his way past the ranks of desks toward d'Amacourt's office.

The secretary rose from her chair, greeted the senior executive and escorted him into d'Amacourt's office. She came out immediately, closing the door behind her.

Marie looked at her watch, her eyes on the sweep-second hand. She wanted one more fragment of evidence, and it would be hers shortly if she could get beyond the gate, with a clear view of the secretary's desk. If it was going to happen, it would happen in moments, the duration brief.

She walked to the gate, opening her purse and smiling vacuously at the receptionist, who was speaking into her phone. She mouthed the name d'Amacourt with her lips to the bewildered receptionist, reached down and opened the gate. She moved quickly inside, a determined if not very bright client of the Valois Bank.

"*Pardon, madame—*" The receptionist held her hand over the telephone, rushing her words in French, "Can I help you?"

Again Marie pronounced the name with her lips—now a courteous client late for an appointment and not wishing to be a further burden to a busy employee. "Monsieur d'Amacourt. I'm afraid I'm late. I'll just go see his secretary." She continued up the aisle toward the secretary's desk.

"*Please,* madame," called out the receptionist. "I must announce—"

The hum of electric typewriters and subdued conversations drowned out her words. Marie approached the stern-faced secretary, who looked up, as bewildered as the receptionist.

"Yes? May I help you?"

"Monsieur d'Amacourt, please."

"I'm afraid he's in conference, madame. Do you have an appointment?"

"Oh, yes, of course," said Marie, opening her purse again.

The secretary looked at the typed schedule on her desk. "I'm afraid I don't have anyone listed for this time period."

"Oh, my word!" exclaimed the confused client of the Valois Bank. "I just noticed. It's for tomorrow, not today! I'm *so* sorry!"

She turned and walked rapidly back to the gate. She had seen what she wanted to see, the last fragment of evidence. A single button was lighted on d'Amacourt's telephone; he had bypassed his secretary and was making an outside call. The account belonging to Jason Bourne had specific, confidential instructions attached to it which were not to be revealed to the account holder.

Bourne looked at his watch in the shade of the canopy; it was 2:49. Marie would be back by the telephone at the front of the bank, a pair of eyes inside. The next few minutes would give them the answer; perhaps she already knew it.

He edged his way to the left side of the store window, keeping the bank's entrance in view. A clerk inside smiled at him, reminding him that all attention should be avoided. He pulled out a pack of cigarettes, lit one, and looked at his watch again. Eight minutes to three.

And then he saw them. *Him.* Three well-dressed men walking rapidly up rue Madeleine, talking to each other, their eyes, however, directed straight ahead. They passed the slower pedestrians in front of them, excusing themselves with a courtesy that was not entirely Parisian. Jason concentrated on the man in the middle. It was *him.* A man named Johann.

Signal Johann to go inside. We'll come back for them. A tall, gaunt man wearing gold-rimmed spectacles had said the words in the Steppdeckstrasse. *Johann.* They had sent him here from Zurich; he had seen Jason Bourne. And that told him something: there were no photographs.

The three men reached the entrance. Johann and the man on his right went inside; the third man stayed by the door. Bourne started back to the telephone booth; he would wait four minutes and place his last call to Antoine d'Amacourt.

He dropped his cigarette outside the booth, crushed it under his foot and opened the door.

"*Monsieur—*" A voice came from behind.

Jason spun around, holding his breath. A nondescript man with a stubble of a beard pointed at the booth.

"*Le téléphone—il ne marche pas. Regardez la corde.*"

"*Merci bien. Je vais essayer quand même.*"

The man shrugged and left. Bourne stepped inside; the four minutes were up. He took the coins from his pocket—enough for two calls—and dialed the first.

"La Banque de Valois. *Bonjour.*"

Ten seconds later d'Amacourt was on the phone, his voice strained. "It is you, Monsieur Bourne? I thought you to say you were on your way to my office."

"A change of plans, I'm afraid. I'll have to call you tomorrow." Suddenly, through the glass panel of the booth, Jason saw a car swing into a space across the street in front of the bank. The third man who was standing by the entrance nodded to the driver.

"—I can do?" D'Amacourt had asked a question.

"I beg your pardon?"

"I asked if there was anything I can do. I have your account; everything is in readiness for you here."

I'm sure it is, Bourne thought; the ploy was worth a try. "Look, I have to get over to London this afternoon. I'm taking one of the shuttle flights, but I'll be back tomorrow. Keep everything with you, all right?"

"To London, monsieur?"

"I'll call you tomorrow. I have to find a cab to Orly." He hung up and watched the entrance of the bank. In less than half a minute, Johann and his companion came running out; they spoke to the third man, then all three climbed into the waiting automobile.

The killers' escape car was still in the hunt, on its way now to Orly Airport. Jason memorized the number on the license plate, then dialed his second call. If the pay phone in the bank was not in use, Marie would pick it up before the ring had barely started. She did.

"Yes?"

"See anything?"

"A great deal. D'Amacourt's your man."

12

They moved about the store, going from counter to counter. Marie, however, remained near the wide front window, keeping a perpetual eye on the entrance of the bank across rue Madeleine.

"I picked out two scarves for you," said Bourne.

"You shouldn't have. The prices are far too high."

"It's almost four o'clock. If he hasn't come out by now, he won't until the end of office hours."

"Probably not. If he were going to meet someone, he would have done so by now. But we had to know."

"Take my word for it, his friends are at Orly, running from shuttle to shuttle. There's no way they can tell whether I'm on one or not, because they don't know what name I'm using."

"They'll depend on the man from Zurich to recognize you."

"He's looking for a dark-haired man with a limp, not me. Come on, let's go into the bank. You can point out d'Amacourt."

"We can't do that," said Marie, shaking her head. "The cameras on the ceilings have wide-angle lenses. If they ran the tapes they could spot you."

"A blond-haired man with glasses?"

"Or me. I was there; the receptionist or his secretary could identify me."

"You're saying it's a regular cabal in there. I doubt it."

"They could think up any number of reasons to run the tapes." Marie stopped; she clutched Jason's arm, her eyes on the bank beyond the window. "There he is! The one in the overcoat with the black velvet collar—d'Amacourt."

"Pulling at his sleeves?"

"Yes."

"I've got him. I'll see you back at the hotel."

"Be careful. Be *very* careful."

"Pay for the scarves; they're at the counter in the back."

Jason left the store, wincing in the sunlight beyond the canopy, looking for a break in the traffic so he could cross the street; there was none. D'Amacourt had turned right and was strolling casually; he was not a man in a rush to meet anyone. Instead, there was the air of a slightly squashed peacock about him.

Bourne reached the corner and crossed with the light, falling behind the banker. D'Amacourt stopped at a newsstand to buy an evening paper. Jason held his place in front of a sporting goods shop, then followed as the banker continued down the block.

Ahead was a café, windows dark, entrance heavy wood, thick hardware on the door. It took no imagination to picture the inside; it was a drinking place for men, and for women brought with men other men would not discuss. It was as good a spot as any for a quiet discussion with Antoine d'Amacourt. Jason walked faster, falling in stride beside the banker. He spoke in the awkward, Anglicized French he had used on the phone.

"Bonjour, monsieur. Je . . . pense que vous . . . êtes Monsieur d'Amacourt. I'd say I was right, wouldn't you?"

The banker stopped. His cold eyes were frightened, remembering. The peacock shriveled further into his tailored overcoat. "Bourne?" he whispered.

"Your friends must be very confused by now. I expect they're racing all over Orly Airport, wondering, perhaps, if you gave them the wrong information. Perhaps on purpose."

"What?" The frightened eyes bulged.

"Let's go inside here," said Jason, taking d'Amacourt's arm, his grip firm. "I think we should have a talk."

"I know absolutely nothing! I merely followed the demands of the account. I am not involved!"

"Sorry. When I first talked to you, you said you wouldn't confirm the sort of bank account I was talking about on the phone; you wouldn't discuss business with someone you didn't know. But twenty minutes later you said you had everything ready for me. That's confirmation, isn't it? Let's go inside."

The café was in some ways a miniature version of Zurich's Drei Alpenhäuser. The booths were deep, the partitions between them high, and the light dim. From there, however, the appearances veered; the café on rue Madeleine was totally French, carafes of wine replacing steins of beer. Bourne asked for a booth in the corner; the waiter accommodated.

"Have a drink," said Jason. "You're going to need it."

"You presume," replied the banker coldly. "I'll have a whiskey."

The drinks came quickly, the brief interim taken up with d'Amacourt nervously extracting a pack of cigarettes from under his form-fitting overcoat. Bourne struck a match, holding it close to the banker's face. Very close.

"Merci." D'Amacourt inhaled, removed his cigarette, and swallowed half the small glass of whiskey. "I'm not the man you should talk with," he said.

"Who is?"

"An owner of the bank, perhaps. I don't know, but certainly not me."

"Explain that."

"Arrangements were made. A privately held bank has more flexibility than a publicly owned institution with stockholders."

"How?"

"There's greater latitude, shall we say, with regard to the demands of certain clients and sister banks. Less scrutiny than might be applied to a company listed on the Bourse. The Gemeinschaft in Zurich is also a private institution."

"The demands were made by the Gemeinschaft?"

"Requests . . . demands . . . yes."

"Who owns the Valois?"

"Who? Many—a consortium. Ten or twelve men and their families."

"Then I have to talk to you, don't I? I mean, it'd be a little foolish my running all over Paris tracking them down."

"I'm only an executive. An employee." D'Amacourt swallowed the rest of his drink, crushed out his cigarette and reached for another. And the matches.

"What are the arrangements?"

"I could lose my position, monsieur!"

"You could lose your life," said Jason, disturbed that the words came so easily to him.

"I'm not as privileged as you think."

"Nor as ignorant as you'd like me to believe," said Bourne, his eyes wandering over the banker across the table. "Your type's everywhere, d'Amacourt. It's in your clothes, the way you wear your hair, even your walk; you strut too much. A man like you doesn't get to be the vice president of the Valois Bank without asking questions; you cover yourself. You don't make a smelly move unless you can save your own ass. Now, tell me what those arrangements were. You're not important to me, am I being clear?"

D'Amacourt struck a match and held it beneath his cigarette while staring at Jason. "You don't have to threaten me, monsieur. You're a very rich man. Why not pay me?" The banker smiled nervously. "You're quite right, incidentally. I did ask a question or two. Paris is not Zurich. A man of my station must have words if not answers."

Bourne leaned back, revolving his glass, the clicking of the ice cubes obviously annoying d'Amacourt. "Name a reasonable price," he said finally, "and we'll discuss it."

"I'm a reasonable man. Let the decision be based on value, and let it be yours. Bankers the world over are compensated by grateful clients they have advised. I would like to think of you as a client."

"I'm sure you would." Bourne smiled, shaking his head at the man's sheer nerve. "So we slide from bribe to gratuity. Compensation for personal advice and service."

D'Amacourt shrugged. "I accept the definition and, if ever asked, would repeat your words."

"The arrangements?"

"Accompanying the transfer of our funds from Zurich was *une fiche confidentielle—*"

"*Une fiche?*" broke in Jason, recalling the moment in Apfel's office at the Gemeinschaft when Koenig came in saying the words. "I heard it once before. What is it?"

"A dated term, actually. It comes from the middle nineteenth century when it was a common practice for the great banking houses—primarily the Rothschilds—to keep track of the international flow of money."

"Thank you. Now what is it specifically?"

"Separate sealed instructions to be opened and followed when the account in question is called up."

" 'Called up'?"

"Funds removed or deposited."

"Suppose I'd just gone to a teller, presented a bank book, and asked for money?"

"A double asterisk would have appeared on the transaction computer. You would have been sent to me."

"I was sent to you anyway. The operator gave me your office."

"Irrelevant chance. There are two other officers in the Foreign Services Department. Had you been connected to either one, the *fiche* would have dictated that you still be sent to me. I am the senior executive."

"I see." But Bourne was not sure that he did see. There was a gap in the sequence; a space needed filling. "Wait a minute. You didn't know anything about a *fiche* when you had the account brought to your office."

"Why did I ask for it?" interrupted d'Amacourt, anticipating the question. "Be reasonable, monsieur. Put yourself in my place. A man calls and identifies himself, then says he is 'talking about over four million francs.' Four *million.* Would you not be anxious to be of service? Bend a rule here and there?"

Looking at the seedily elegant banker, Jason realized it was the most unstartling thing he had said. "The instructions. What were they?"

"To begin with a telephone number—unlisted, of course. It was to be called, all information relayed."

"Do you remember the number?"

"I make it a point to commit such things to memory."

"I'll bet you do. What is it?"

"I must protect myself, monsieur. How else could you have gotten it? I pose the question . . . how do you say it? . . . rhetorically."

"Which means you have the answer. How *did* I get it? If it ever comes up."

"In Zurich. You paid a very high price for someone to break not only the strictest regulation on the Bahnhofstrasse, but also the laws of Switzerland."

"I've got just the man," said Bourne, the face of Koenig coming into focus. "He's already committed the crime."

"At the Gemeinschaft? Are you joking?"

"Not one bit. His name is Koenig; his desk is on the second floor."

"I'll remember that."

"I'm sure you will. The number?" D'Amacourt gave it to him. Jason wrote it on a paper napkin. "How do I know this is accurate?"

"You have a reasonable guarantee. I have not been paid."

"Good enough."

"And as long as value is intrinsic to our discussion, I should tell you that it is the second telephone number; the first was canceled."

"Explain that."

D'Amacourt leaned forward. "A photostat of the original *fiche* arrived with accounts-courier. It was sealed in a black case, accepted and signed for by the senior keeper-of-records. The card inside was validated by a partner of the Gemeinschaft, countersigned by the usual Swiss notary; the instructions were simple, quite clear. In all matters pertaining to the account of Jason C. Bourne, a transatlantic call to the United States was to be placed immediately, the details relayed. . . . Here the card was altered, the number in New York deleted, one in Paris inserted and initialed."

"New York?" interrupted Bourne. "How do you know it was New York?"

"The telephone area code was parenthetically included, spaced in front of the number itself; it remained intact. It was 212. As first vice president, Foreign Services, I place such calls daily."

"The alteration was pretty sloppy."

"Possibly. It could have been made in haste, or not thoroughly understood. On the other hand, there was no way to delete the body of the instructions without renotarization. A minor risk considering the number of telephones in New York. At any rate, the substitution gave me the latitude to ask a question or two. Change is a banker's anathema." D'Amacourt sipped what remained of his drink.

"Care for another?" asked Jason.

"No, thank you. It would prolong our discussion."

"You're the one who stopped."

"I'm thinking, monsieur. Perhaps you should have in mind a vague figure before I proceed."

Bourne studied the man. "It could be five," he said.

"Five what?"

"Five figures."

"I shall proceed. I spoke to a woman—"

"A woman? How did you begin?"

"Truthfully. I was the vice president of the Valois, and was following instructions from the Gemeinschaft in Zurich. What else was there to say?"

"Go on."

"I said I had been in communication with a man claiming to be Jason Bourne. She asked me how recently, to which I replied a few minutes. She was then most anxious to know the substance of our conversation. It was at this point that I voiced my own concerns. The *fiche* specifically stated that a call should be made to New York, not Paris. Naturally, she said it was *not* my concern, and that the change was authorized by signature, and did I care for Zurich to be informed that an officer of the Valois refused to follow the Gemeinschaft instructions?"

"Hold it," interrupted Jason. "Who was she?"

"I have no idea."

"You mean you were talking all this time and she didn't tell you? You didn't ask?"

"That is the nature of the *fiche*. If a name is proffered, well and good. It if is not, one does not inquire."

"You didn't hesitate to ask about the telephone number."

"Merely a device; I wanted information. You transferred four and a half million francs, a sizable amount, and were therefore a powerful client with, perhaps, *more* powerful strings attached to him. . . . One balks, then agrees, then balks again only to agree again; that is the way one learns things. Especially if the party one is talking with displays anxiety. I can assure you, she did."

"What did you learn?"

"That you should be considered a dangerous man."

"In what way?"

"The definition was left open. But the fact that the term was used was enough for me to ask why the Sûreté was not involved. Her reply was extremely interesting. 'He is beyond the Sûreté, beyond Interpol,' she said."

"What did that tell you?"

"That it was a highly complicated matter for any number of possibilities, all best left private. Since our talk began, however, it now tells me something else."

"What's that?"

"That you really should pay me well, for I must be extremely cautious. Those who look for you are also, perhaps, beyond the Sûreté, beyond Interpol."

"We'll get to that. You told this woman I was on my way to your office?"

"Within the quarter hour. She asked me to remain on the telephone for a few moments, that she would be right back. Obviously she made another call. She returned with her final instructions. You were to be detained in my office until a man came to my secretary inquiring about a matter from Zurich. And when you left you were to be identified by a nod or a gesture; there could be no error. The man came, of course, and, of course, you never arrived, so he waited by the tellers' cages with an associate. When you phoned and said you were on your way to London, I left my office to find the man. My secretary pointed him out and I told him. The rest you know."

"Didn't it strike you as odd that I had to be identified?"

"Not so odd as intemperate. A *fiche* is one thing—telephone calls, faceless communications—but to be involved directly, in the open, as it were, is something else again. I said as much to the woman."

"What did she say to you?"

D'Amacourt cleared his throat. "She made it clear that the party she represented—whose stature was, indeed, confirmed by the *fiche* itself—would remember my cooperation. You see, I withhold nothing. . . . Apparently they don't know what you look like."

"A man was at the bank who saw me in Zurich."

"Then his associates do not trust his eyesight. Or, perhaps, what he thinks he saw."

"Why do you say that?"

"Merely an observation, monsieur; the woman was insistent. You must understand, I strenuously objected to any overt participation; that is *not* the nature of the *fiche*. She said there was no photograph of you. An obvious lie, of course."

"Is it?"

"Naturally. All passports have photographs. Where is the immigration officer who cannot be bought or duped? Ten seconds in a passport-control room, a photograph of a photograph; arrangements can be made. No, they committed a serious oversight."

"I guess they did."

"And you," continued d'Amacourt, "just told me something else. Yes, you really must pay me very well."

"What did I just tell you?"

"That your passport does not identify you as Jason Bourne. Who are you, monsieur?"

Jason did not at first answer; he revolved his glass again. "Someone who may pay you a lot of money," he said.

"Entirely sufficient. You are simply a client named Bourne. And I must be cautious."

"I want that telephone number in New York. Can you get it for me? There'd be a sizable bonus."

"I wish I could. I see no way."

"It might be raised from the *fiche* card. Under a low-power scope."

"When I said it was deleted, monsieur, I did not mean it was crossed out. It was *deleted*—it was *cut* out."

"Then someone has it in Zurich."

"Or it has been destroyed."

"Last question," said Jason, anxious now to leave. "It concerns you, incidentally. It's the only way you'll get paid."

"The question will be tolerated, of course. What is it?"

"If I showed up at the Valois without calling you, without telling you I was coming, would you be expected to make another telephone call?"

"Yes. One does not disregard the *fiche;* it emanates from powerful boardrooms. Dismissal would follow."

"Then how do *we* get *our* money?"

D'Amacourt pursed his lips. "There is a way. Withdrawal *in absentia.* Forms filled out, instructions by letter, identification confirmed and authenticated by an established firm of attorneys. I would be powerless to interfere."

"You'd still be expected to make the call, though."

"It's a matter of timing. Should an attorney with whom the Valois has had numerous dealings call me requesting that I prepare, say, a number of cashiers checks drawn upon a foreign transfer he has ascertained to have been cleared, I would do so. He would state that he was sending over the completed forms, the checks, of course, made out to 'Bearer,' not an uncommon practice in these days of excessive taxes. A messenger would arrive with the letter during the most hectic hours of activity, and my secretary—an esteemed, trusted employee of many years—would simply bring in the forms for my countersignature and the letter for my initialing."

"No doubt," interrupted Bourne, "along with a number of other papers you were to sign."

"Exactly. I would *then* place my call, probably watching the messenger leave with his briefcase as I did so."

"You wouldn't, by any remote chance, have in mind the name of a law firm in Paris, would you? Or a specific attorney?"

"As a matter of fact, one just occurred to me."

"How much will he cost?"

"Ten thousand francs."

"That's expensive."

"Not at all. He was a judge on the bench, an honored man."

"What about you? Let's refine it."

"As I said, I'm reasonable, and the decision should be yours. Since you mentioned five figures, let us be consistent with your words. Five figures, commencing with five. Fifty thousand francs."

"That's outrageous!"

"So is whatever you've done, Monsieur Bourne."

"Une fiche confidentielle," said Marie, sitting in the chair by the window, the late afternoon sun bouncing off the ornate buildings of the boulevard Montparnasse outside. "So that's the device they've used."

"I can impress you—I know where it comes from." Jason poured a drink from the bottle on the bureau and carried it to the bed; he sat down, facing her. "Do you want to hear?"

"I don't have to," she answered, gazing out the window, preoccupied. "I know exactly where it comes from and what it means. It's a shock, that's all."

"Why? I thought you expected something like this."

"The results, yes, not the machinery. A *fiche* is an archaic stab at legitimacy, almost totally restricted to private banks on the Continent. American, Canadian, and UK laws forbid its use."

Bourne recalled d'Amacourt's words; he repeated them. "It emanates from powerful boardrooms'—that's what he said."

"He was right." Marie looked over at him. "Don't you see? I knew that a flag was attached to your account. I assumed that someone had been bribed to forward information. That's not unusual; bankers aren't in the front ranks for canonization. But this is different. That account in Zurich was established—at the very beginning—with the *fiche* as part of its activity. Conceivably with your own knowledge."

"Treadstone Seventy-One," said Jason.

"Yes. The owners of the bank had to work in concert with Treadstone. And considering the latitude of your access, it's possible you were aware that they did."

"But someone *was* bribed. Koenig. He substituted one telephone number for another."

"He was well paid, I can assure you. He could face ten years in a Swiss prison."

"Ten? That's pretty stiff."

"So are the Swiss laws. He had to be paid a small fortune."

"Carlos," said Bourne. "Carlos . . . Why? What am I to him? I keep asking myself. I say the name over and over and over again! I don't *get* anything, nothing at all. Just a . . . a . . . I don't know. Nothing."

"But there's something, isn't there?" Marie sat forward. "What is it, Jason? What are you thinking of?"

"I'm not thinking . . . I don't know."

"Then you're feeling. Something. What is it?"

"I don't know. Fear, maybe . . . Anger, nerves. I don't know."

"Concentrate!"

"Goddamn it, do you think I'm *not?* Do you think I haven't? Have you any idea what it's like?" Bourne stiffened, annoyed at his own outburst. "Sorry."

"Don't be. Ever. These are the hints, the clues you have to look for—*we* have to look for. Your doctor friend in Port Noir was right; things come to you, provoked by other things. As you yourself said, a book of matches, a face, or the front of a restaurant. We've seen it happen. Now, it's a name, a name you avoided for nearly a week while you told me everything that had happened to you during the past five months, down to the smallest detail. Yet you never mentioned Carlos. You should have, but you didn't. It *does* mean something to you, can't you see that? It's stirring things inside of you; they want to come out."

"I know." Jason drank.

"Darling, there's a famous bookstore on the boulevard Saint-Germain that's run by a magazine freak. A whole floor is crammed with back issues of old magazines, thousands of them. He even catalogues subjects, indexes them like a librarian. I'd like to find out if Carlos is in that index. Will you do it?"

Bourne was aware of the sharp pain in his chest. It had nothing to do with his wounds; it was fear. She saw it and somehow understood; he felt it and could not understand. "There are back issues of newspapers at the Sorbonne," he said, glancing up at her. "One of them put me on cloud nine for a while. Until I thought about it."

"A lie was exposed. That was the important thing."

"But we're not looking for a lie now, are we?"

"No, we're looking for the truth. Don't be afraid of it, darling. I'm not."

Jason got up. "Okay. Saint-Germain's on the schedule. In the meantime, call that fellow at the embassy." Bourne reached into his pocket and took out the paper napkin with the telephone number on it; he had added the numbers of the license plate on the car that had raced away from the bank on rue Madeleine. "Here's the number d'Amacourt gave me, also the license of that car. See what he can do."

"All right." Marie took the napkin and went to the telephone. A small, spiral-hinged notebook was beside it; she flipped through the pages. "Here it is. His name is Dennis Corbelier. Peter said he'd call him by noon today, Paris time. And I could rely on him; he was as knowledgeable as any attaché in the embassy."

"Peter knows him, doesn't he? He's not just a name from a list."

"They were classmates at the University of Toronto. I can call him from here, can't I?"

"Sure. But don't say where you are."

Marie picked up the phone. "I'll tell him the same thing I told Peter. That I'm moving from one hotel to another but don't know which yet." She got an outside line, then dialed the number of the Canadian Embassy on the avenue Montaigne. Fifteen seconds later she was talking with Dennis Corbelier, attaché.

Marie got to the point of her call almost immediately. "I assume Peter told you I might need some help."

"More than that," replied Corbelier, "he explained that you were in Zurich. Can't say I understood everything he said, but I got the general idea. Seems there's a lot of maneuvering in the world of high finance these days."

"More than usual. The trouble is no one wants to say who's maneuvering whom. That's my problem."

"How can I help?"

"I have a license and a telephone number, both here in Paris. The telephone's unlisted; it could be awkward if I called."

"Give them to me." She did. *"A mari usque ad mari,"* Corbelier said, reciting the national motto of their country. "We have several friends in splendid places. We trade off favors frequently, usually in the narcotics area, but we're all flexible. Why not have lunch with me tomorrow? I'll bring what I can."

"I'd like that, but tomorrow's no good. I'm spending the day with an old friend. Perhaps another time."

"Peter said I'd be an idiot not to insist. He says you're a terrific lady."

"He's a dear, and so are you. I'll call you tomorrow afternoon."

"Fine. I'll go to work on these."

"Talk to you tomorrow, and thanks again." Marie hung up and looked at her watch. "I'm to call Peter in three hours. Don't let me forget."

"You really think he'll have something so soon?"

"He does; he started last night by calling Washington. It's what Corbelier just said; we all trade off. This piece of information here for that one there, a name from our side for one of yours."

"Sounds vaguely like betrayal."

"The opposite. We're dealing in money, not missiles. Money that's illegally moving around, outflanking laws that are good for all our interests. Unless you want the shieks of Araby owning Grumman Aircraft. *Then* we're talking about missiles . . . after they've left the launching pads."

"Strike my objection."

"We've got to see d'Amacourt's man first thing in the morning. Figure out what you want to withdraw."

"All of it."

"All?"

"That's right. If you were the directors of Treadstone, what would you do if you learned that six million francs were missing from a corporate account?"

"I see."

"D'Amacourt suggested a series of cashiers checks made out to the bearer."

"He said that? Checks?"

"Yes. Something wrong?"

"There certainly is. The numbers of those checks could be punched on a fraud tape and sent to banks everywhere. You have to *go* to a bank to redeem them; payments would be stopped."

"He's a winner, isn't he? He collects from both sides. What do we do?"

"Accept half of what he told you—the bearer part. But not checks. Bonds. Bearer bonds of various denominations. They're far more easily brokered."

"You've just earned dinner," said Jason, reaching down and touching her face.

"I tried to earn my keep, sir," she replied, holding his hand against her cheek. "First dinner, then Peter . . . and then a bookstore on Saint-Germain."

"A bookstore on Saint-Germain," repeated Bourne, the pain coming to his chest again. *What was it? Why was he so afraid?*

They left the restaurant on the boulevard Raspail and walked to the telephone complex on rue Vaugirard. There were glass booths against the walls and a huge circular counter in the center of the floor where clerks filled out slips, assigning booths to those placing calls.

"The traffic is very light, madame," said the clerk to Marie. "Your call should go through in a matter of minutes. Number twelve, please."

"Thank you. Booth twelve?"

"Yes, madame. Directly over there."

As they walked across the crowded floor to the booth, Jason held her arm. "I know why people use these places," he said. "They're a hundred and ten times quicker than a hotel phone."

"That's only one of the reasons."

They had barely reached the booth and lighted cigarettes when they heard the two short bursts of the bell inside. Marie opened the door and went in, her spiral-hinged notebook and a pencil in her hand. She picked up the receiver.

Sixty seconds later Bourne watched in astonishment as she stared at the wall, the blood draining from her face, her skin chalk white. She began shouting and dropped her purse, the contents scattering over the floor of the small booth; the notebook was caught on the ledge, the pencil broken in the grip of her hand. He rushed inside; she was close to collapse.

"This is Marie St. Jacques in Paris, Lisa. Peter's expecting my call."

"Marie? Oh, my God . . ." The secretary's voice trailed off, replaced by other voices in the background. Excited voices, muted by a cupped hand over the phone. Then there was a rustle of movement, the phone being given to or taken by another.

"Marie, this is Alan," said the first assistant director of the section. "We're all in Peter's office."

"What's the matter, Alan? I don't have much time; may I speak to him, please?"

There was a moment of silence. "I wish I could make this easier for you, but I don't know how. Peter's dead, Marie."

"He's . . . what?"

"The police called a few minutes ago; they're on their way over."

"The police? What happened? Oh God, he's *dead?* What *happened?*"

"We're trying to piece it together. We're studying his phone log, but we're not supposed to touch anything on his desk."

"His desk . . . ?"

"Notes or memos, or anything like that."

"Alan! Tell me what happened!"

"That's just it—we don't know. He didn't tell any of us what he was doing. All we know is that he got two phone calls this morning from the States—one from Washington, the other from New York. Around noon he told Lisa he was going to the airport to meet someone flying up. He didn't say who. The police found him an hour ago in one of those tunnels used for freight. It was terrible; he was shot. In the throat . . . Marie? *Marie?*"

The old man with the hollow eyes and the stubble of a white beard limped into the dark confessional booth, blinking his eyes repeatedly, trying to focus on the hooded figure beyond the opaque curtain. Sight was not easy for this eighty-year-old messenger. But his mind was clear; that was all that mattered.

"Angelus Domini," he said.

"Angelus Domini, child of God," whispered the hooded silhouette. "Are your days comfortable?"

"They draw to an end, but they are made comfortable."

"Good . . . Zurich?"

"They found the man from the Guisan Quai. He was wounded; they traced him through a doctor known to the *Verbrecherwelt.* Under severe interrogation he admitted assaulting the woman. Cain came back for her; it was Cain who shot him."

"So it was an arrangement, the woman and Cain."

"The man from the Guisan Quai does not think so. He was one of the two who picked her up on the Löwenstrasse."

"He's also a fool. He killed the watchman?"

"He admits it and defends it. He had no choice in making his escape."

"He may not have to defend it; it could be the most intelligent thing he did. Does he have his gun?"

"Your people have it."

"Good. There is a prefect on the Zurich police. That gun must be given to him. Cain is elusive, the woman far less so. She has associates in Ottawa; they'll stay in touch. We trap her, we trace him. Is your pencil ready?"

"Yes, Carlos."

13

Bourne held her in the close confines of the glass booth, gently lowering her to the seat that protruded from the narrow wall. She was shaking, breathing in swallows and gasps, her eyes glazed, coming into focus as she looked at him.

"They killed him. They *killed* him! My God, what did I *do?* Peter!"

"You didn't do it! If anyone did it, I did. Not you. Get that through your head."

"Jason, I'm frightened. He was half a world away . . . and they killed him!"

"Treadstone?"

"Who else? There were two phone calls, Washington . . . New York. He went to the airport to meet someone and he was killed."

"How?"

"Oh, Jesus Christ . . ." Tears came to Marie's eyes. "He was shot. In the throat," she whispered.

Bourne suddenly felt a dull ache; he could not localize it, but it was there, cutting off air. "Carlos," he said, not knowing why he said it.

"What?" Marie stared up at him. "What did you say?"

"Carlos," he repeated softly. "A bullet in the throat. Carlos."

"What are you trying to say?"

"I don't know." He took her arm. "Let's get out of here. Are you all right? Can you walk?"

She nodded, closing her eyes briefly, breathing deeply. "Yes."

"We'll stop for a drink; we both need it. Then we'll find it."

"Find what?"

"A bookstore on Saint-Germain."

There were three back issues of magazines under the "Carlos" index. A three-year-old copy of the international edition of *Potomac Quarterly* and two Paris issues of *Le Globe*. They did not read the articles inside the store; instead they bought all three and took a taxi back to the hotel in Montparnasse. There they began reading, Marie on the bed, Jason in the chair by the window. Several minutes passed, and Marie bolted up.

"It's here," she said, fear in both her face and voice.

"Read it."

" 'A particularly brutal form of punishment is said to be inflicted by Carlos and/or his small band of soldiers. It is death by a gunshot in the throat, often leaving the victim to die in excruciating pain. It is reserved for those who break the code of silence or loyalty demanded by the assassin, or others who have refused to divulge information. . . .' " Marie stopped, incapable of reading further. She lay back and closed her eyes. "He wouldn't tell them and he was killed for it. Oh, my *God* . . ."

"He couldn't tell them what he didn't know," said Bourne.

"But *you* knew!" Marie sat up again, her eyes open. "You knew about a gunshot in the throat! You *said* it!"

"I said it. I knew it. That's all I can tell you."

"How?"

"I wish I could answer that. I can't."

"May I have a drink?"

"Certainly." Jason got up and went to the bureau. He poured two short glasses of whiskey and looked over at her. "Do you want me to call for some ice? Hervé's on; it'll be quick."

"No. It won't be quick enough." She slammed the magazine down on the bed and turned to him—on him, perhaps. "I'm going crazy!"

"Join the party of two."

"I want to believe you; I *do* believe you. But I . . . I . . ."

"You can't be sure," completed Bourne. "Any more than I can." He brought her the glass. "What do you want me to say? What can I say? Am I one of Carlos' soldiers? Did I break the code of silence or loyalty? Is that why I knew the method of execution?"

"Stop it!"

"I say that a lot to myself. 'Stop it.' Don't think; try to remember, but somewhere along the line put the brakes on. Don't go too far, too deep. One lie can be exposed, only to raise ten other questions intrinsic to that lie. Maybe it's like waking up after a long drunk, not sure whom you fought with or slept with, or . . . goddamn it . . . killed."

"No . . ." Marie drew out the word. "You are *you*. Don't take that away from me."

"I don't want to. I don't want to take it away from myself." Jason went back to the chair and sat down, his face turned to the window. "You found . . . a method of execution. I found something else. I knew it, just as I knew about Howard Leland. I didn't even have to read it."

"Read what?"

Bourne reached down and picked up the three-year-old issue of *Potomac Quarterly*. The magazine was folded open to a page on which there was a sketch of a bearded man, the lines rough, inconclusive, as if drawn from an obscure description. He held it out for her.

"Read it," he said. "It starts with the upper left, under the heading 'Myth or Monster.' Then I want to play a game."

"A game?"

"Yes. I've read only the first two paragraphs; you'll have to take my word for that."

"All right." Marie watched him, bewildered. She lowered the magazine into the light and read.

MYTH OR MONSTER

For over a decade, the name "Carlos" has been whispered in the back streets of such diverse cities as Paris, Teheran, Beirut, London, Cairo, and Amsterdam. He is said to be the supreme terrorist in the sense that his commitment is to murder and assassination in themselves, with no apparent political ideology. Yet there is concrete evidence that he has undertaken profitable executions for such extremist radical groups as the PLO and Baader-Meinhof, both as teacher and profiteer. Indeed, it is through his infrequent gravitation to, and the internal conflicts within, such terrorist organizations that a clearer picture of "Carlos" is beginning to emerge. Informers are coming out of the bloodied spleens and they talk.

Whereas tales of his exploits give rise to images of a world filled with violence and conspiracy, high-explosives and higher intrigues, fast cars and faster women, the facts would seem to indicate at least as much Adam Smith as Ian Fleming. "Carlos" is reduced to human proportions and in the compression a truly frightening man comes into focus. The sado-romantic myth turns into a brilliant, blood-soaked monster who brokers assassination with the expertise of a market analyst, fully aware of wages, costs, distribution, and the divisions of underworld labor. It is a complicated business and "Carlos" is the master of its dollar value.

The portrait starts with a reputed name, as odd in its way as the owner's profession. Ilich Ramirez Sanchez. He is said to be a Venezuelan, the son of a fanatically devoted but not very prominent Marxist attorney (the Ilich is the father's salute to Vladimir Ilyich Lenin, and partially explains "Carlos's" forays into extremist terrorism) who sent the young boy to Russia for the major part of his education, which included espionage training at the Soviet compound in Novgorod. It is here that portrait fades briefly, rumor and speculation now the artists. According to these, one or another committee of the Kremlin that regularly monitors foreign students for future infiltration purposes saw what they had in Ilich Sanchez and wanted no part of him. He was a paranoid, who saw all solutions in terms of a well-placed bullet or bomb; the recommendation was to send the youth back to Caracas and disassociate any and all Soviet ties with the family. Thus rejected by Moscow, and deeply antithetical to western society, Sanchez went about building his own world, one in which he was the supreme leader. What better way to become the apolitical assassin whose services could be contracted for by the widest range of political and philosophical clients?

The portrait becomes clearer again. Fluent in numerous languages including his native Spanish as well as Russian, French, and English, Sanchez used his Soviet training as a springboard for refining his techniques. Months of concentrated study followed his expulsion from Moscow, some say under the tutelage of the Cubans, Che Guevera in particular. He mastered the science and handling of all manner of weaponry and explosives; there was no gun he could not break down and reassemble blindfolded, no explosive he could not analyze by smell and touch and know how to detonate in a dozen different ways. He was ready; he chose Paris as his base of operations and the word went out. A man was for hire who would kill where others dared not.

Once again the portrait dims as much for lack of birth records as anything else. Just how old is "Carlos"? How many targets can be attributed to him and how many are myth—self-proclaimed or otherwise? Correspondents based in Caracas have been unable to unearth any birth certificates anywhere in the country for an Ilich Ramirez Sanchez. On the other hand, there are thousands upon thousands of Sanchezes in Venezuela, hundreds with Ramirez attached; but none with an Ilich in front. Was it added later, or is the omission simply further proof of "Carlos's" thoroughness? The consensus is that the assassin is between thirty-five and forty years of age. No one really knows.

A GRASSY KNOLL IN DALLAS?

But one fact not disputed is that the profits from his first several kills enabled the assassin to set up an organization that might be envied by an operations analyst of General Motors. It is capitalism at its most efficient, loyalty and service extracted by equal parts fear and reward. The consequences of disloyalty are swift in coming—death—but so, too, are the benefits of service—generous bonuses and huge expense allowances. The organization seems to have hand-picked executives everywhere; and this well-founded rumor leads to the obvious question. Where did the profits initially come from? Who were the original kills?

The one most often speculated upon took place thirteen years ago in Dallas. No matter how many times the murder of John F. Kennedy is debated, no one has ever satisfactorily explained a burst of smoke from a grassy knoll three hundred yards away from the motorcade. The smoke was caught on camera; two open police radios on motorcycles recorded noise(s). Yet neither shell casings nor footprints were found. In fact, the only information about the so-called grassy knoll at that moment was considered so irrelevant that it was buried in the FBI-Dallas investigation and never included in the Warren Commission Report. It was provided by a bystander, K. M. Wright of North Dallas, who when questioned made the following statement:

"Hell, the only son of a bitch near there was old Burlap Billy, and he was a couple of hundred yards away."

The "Billy" referred to was an aged Dallas tramp seen frequently panhandling in the tourist areas; the "Burlap" defined his penchant for wrapping his shoes in coarse cloth to play upon the sympathies of his marks. According to our correspondents, Wright's statement was never made public.

Yet six weeks ago a captured Lebanese terrorist broke under questioning in Tel Aviv. Pleading to be spared execution he claimed to possess extraordinary information about the assassin "Carlos." Israeli intelligence forwarded the report to Washington; our capitol correspondents obtained excerpts.

Statement: "Carlos was in Dallas in November 1963. He pretended to be Cuban and programmed Oswald. He was the back-up. It was his operation."

Question: "What proof do you have?"

Statement: "I heard him say it. He was on a small embankment of grass beyond a ledge. His rifle had a wire shell-trap attached."

Question: "It was never reported; why wasn't he seen?"

Statement: "He may have been, but no one would have known it. He was dressed as an old man, with a shabby overcoat, and his shoes were wrapped in canvas to avoid footprints."

A terrorist's information is certainly not proof, but neither should it always be disregarded. Especially when it concerns a master assassin, known to be a scholar of deception, who has made an admission that so astonishingly corroborates an unknown unpublished statement about a moment of national crisis never investigated. That, indeed, must be taken seriously. As so many others associated—even remotely—with the tragic events in Dallas, "Burlap Billy" was found dead several days later from an overdose of drugs. He was known to be an old man drunk consistently on cheap wine; he was never known to use narcotics. He could not afford them.

Was "Carlos" the man on the grassy knoll? What an extraordinary beginning for an extraordinary career! If Dallas really was his "operation" how many millions of dollars must have been funneled to him? Certainly more than enough to establish a network of informers and soldiers that is a corporate world unto itself.

The myth has too much substance; Carlos may well be a monster of flesh and too much blood.

Marie put down the magazine. "What's the game?"

"Are you finished?" Jason turned from the window.

"Yes."

"I gather a lot of statements were made. Theory, supposition, equations."

"Equations?"

"If something happened here, and there was an effect over there, a relationship existed."

"You mean connections," said Marie.

"All right, connections. It's all there, isn't it?"

"To a degree, you could say that. It's hardly a legal brief; there's a lot of speculation, rumor, and secondhand information."

"There *are* facts, however."

"Data."

"Good. Data. That's fine."

"What's the game?" Marie repeated.

"It's got a simple title. It's called 'Trap.' "

"Trap whom?"

"Me." Bourne sat forward. "I want you to ask me questions. Anything that's in there. A phrase, the name of a city, a rumor, a fragment of . . . data. Anything. Let's hear what my responses are. My blind responses."

"Darling, that's no proof of—"

"*Do* it!" ordered Jason.

"All right." Marie raised the issue of *Potomac Quarterly*. "Beirut," she said.

"Embassy," he answered. "CIA station head posing as an attaché. Gunned down in the street. Three hundred thousand dollars."

Marie looked at him. "I remember—" she began.

"I don't!" interrupted Jason. "Go on."

She returned his gaze, then went back to the magazine. "Baader-Meinhof."

"Stuttgart. Regensburg. Munich. Two kills and a kidnapping, Baader accreditation. Fees from—" Bourne stopped, then whispered in astonishment, "U. S. sources. Detroit . . . Wilmington, Delaware."

"Jason, what are—"

"Go *on. Please.*"

"The name, Sanchez."

"The *name* is Ilich Ramirez Sanchez," he replied. "He is . . . Carlos."

"Why the Ilich?"

Bourne paused, his eyes wandering. "I don't know."

"It's Russian, not Spanish. Was his mother Russian?"

"No . . . yes. His mother. It had to be his mother . . . I think. I'm not sure."

"Novgorod."

"Espionage compound. Communications, ciphers, frequency traffic. Sanchez is a graduate."

"Jason, you read that here!"

"I did not read it! Please. Keep going."

Marie's eyes swept back to the top of the article. "Teheran."

"Eight kills. Divided accreditation—Khomeini and PLO. Fee, two million. Source: Southwest Soviet sector."

"Paris," said Marie quickly.

"All contracts will be processed through Paris."

"What contracts?"

"*The* contracts . . . Kills."

"Whose kills? Whose contracts?"

"Sanchez . . . Carlos."

"Carlos? Then they're Carlos's contracts, *his* kills. They have nothing to do with you."

"Carlos's contracts," said Bourne, as if in a daze. "Nothing to do with . . . me," he repeated, barely above a whisper.

"You just said it, Jason. None of this has anything to do with you!"

"No! That's not true!" Bourne shouted, lunging up from the chair, holding his place, staring down at her. "*Our* contracts," he added quietly.

"You don't know what you're saying!"

"I'm responding! Blindly! It's why I had to come to Paris!" He spun around and walked to the window, gripping the frame. "That's what the game is all about," he continued. "We're not looking for a lie, we're looking for the truth, remember? Maybe we've found it; maybe the game revealed it."

"This is no valid test! It's a painful exercise in incidental recollection. If a magazine like *Potomac Quarterly* printed this, it would have been picked up by half the newspapers in the world. You could have read it anywhere."

"The fact is I retained it."

"Not entirely. You didn't know where the Ilich came from, that Carlos's father was a Communist attorney in Venezuela. They're salient points, I'd think. You didn't mention a thing about the Cubans. If you had, it would have led to the most shocking speculation written here. You didn't say a word about it."

"What are you talking about?"

"Dallas," she said. "November 1963."

"Kennedy," replied Bourne.

"That's it? Kennedy?"

"It happened then." Jason stood motionless.

"It did, but that's not what I'm looking for."

"I know," said Bourne, his voice once again flat, as if speaking in a vacuum. "A grassy knoll . . . Burlap Billy."

"You read this!"

"No."

"Then you heard it before, read it before."

"That's possible, but it's not relevant, is it?"

"Stop it, Jason!"

"Those words again. I wish I could."

"What are you trying to tell me? You're Carlos?"

"God, no. Carlos wants to kill me, and I don't speak Russian, I know that."

"Then *what?*"

"What I said at the beginning. The game. The game is called Trap-the-Soldier."

"A soldier?"

"Yes. One who defected from Carlos. It's the only explanation, the only reason I know what I know. In all things."

"Why do you say defect?"

"Because he *does* want to kill me. He has to; he thinks I know as much about him as anyone alive."

Marie had been crouching on the bed; she swung her legs over the side, her hands at her sides. "That's a result of defecting. What about the cause? If it's true, then you did it, became . . . became—" She stopped.

"All things considered, it's a little late to look for a moral position," said Bourne, seeing the pain of acknowledgment on the face of the woman he loved. "I could think of several reasons, clichés. How about a falling out among thieves . . . killers."

"Meaningless!" cried Marie. "There's not a shred of evidence."

"There's buckets of it and you know it. I could have sold out to a higher bidder or stolen huge sums of money from the fees. Either would explain the account in Zurich." He stopped briefly, looking at the wall above the bed, feeling, not seeing. "Either would explain Howard Leland, Marseilles, Beirut, Stuttgart . . . Munich. Everything. All the unremembered facts that want to come out. And one especially. Why I avoided his name, why I never mentioned him. I'm frightened. I'm afraid of him."

The moment passed in silence; more was spoken of than fear. Marie nodded. "I'm sure you believe that," she said, "and in a way I wish it were true. But I don't think it is. You want to believe it because it supports what you just said. It gives you an answer . . . an identity. It may not be the identity you want, but God knows it's better than wandering blindly through that awful labyrinth you face every day. Anything would be, I guess." She paused. "And *I* wish it were true because then we wouldn't be here."

"What?"

"That's the inconsistency, darling. The number or symbol that doesn't fit in your equation. If you *were* what you say you were, and afraid of Carlos—and heaven knows you should be—Paris would be the last place on earth you'd feel compelled to go to. We'd be somewhere else; you said it yourself. You'd run away; you'd take the money from Zurich and disappear. But you're not doing that; instead, you're walking right back into Carlos's den. That's not a man who's either afraid or guilty."

"There isn't anything else. I came to Paris to find out; it's as simple as that."

"Then run away. We'll have the money in the morning; there's nothing stopping you—us. That's simple, too." Marie watched him closely.

Jason looked at her, then turned away. He walked to the bureau and poured himself a drink. "There's still Treadstone to consider," he said defensively.

"Why any more than Carlos? There's your real equation. Carlos and Tread-stone. A man I once loved very much was killed by Treadstone. All the more reason for us to run, to survive."

"I'd think you'd want the people who killed him exposed," said Bourne. "Make them pay for it."

"I do. Very much. But others can find them. I have priorities, and revenge isn't at the top of the list. *We* are. You and I. Or is that only my judgment? My feelings."

"You know better than that." He held the glass tighter in his hand and looked over at her. "I love you," he whispered.

"Then let's run!" she said, raising her voice almost mechanically, taking a step toward him. "Let's forget it all, *really* forget, and run as fast as we can, as far away as we can! Let's do it!"

"I . . . I," Jason stammered, the mists interfering, infuriating him. "There are . . . things."

"What things? We love each other, we've found each *other!* We can go anywhere, be anyone. There's nothing to stop us, is there?"

"Only you and me," he repeated softly, the mists now closing in, suffocating him. "I know. I know. But I've got to think. There's so much to learn, so much that has to come out."

"Why is it so important?"

"It . . . just is."

"Don't you know?"

"Yes . . . No, I'm not sure. Don't ask me now."

"If not now, when? When can I ask you? When will it pass? Or will it ever?!"

"Stop it!" he suddenly roared, slamming the glass down on the wooden tray. "I can't run! I won't! I've got to stay here! I've got to know!"

Marie rushed to him, putting her hands first on his shoulders, then on his face, wiping away the perspiration. "Now you've said it. Can you hear yourself, darling? You can't run because the closer you get, the more maddening it is for you. And if you did run, it would only get worse. You wouldn't have a life, you'd live a nightmare. I know that."

He reached for her face, touching it, looking at her. "Do you?"

"Of course. But you had to say it, not me." She held him, her head against his chest. "I had to force you to. The funny thing is that I *could* run. I could get on a plane with you tonight and go wherever you wanted, disappear, and not look back, happier than I've ever been in my life. But you couldn't do that. What is—or isn't—here in Paris would eat away at you until you couldn't stand it anymore. That's the crazy irony, my darling. I could live with it but you couldn't."

"You'd just disappear?" asked Jason. "What about your family, your job—all the people you know?"

"I'm neither a child nor a fool," she answered quickly. "I'd cover myself somehow, but I don't think I'd take it very seriously. I'd request an extended leave for medical and personal reasons. Emotional stress, a breakdown; I could always go back, the department would understand."

"Peter?"

"Yes." She was silent for a moment. "We went from one relationship to another, the second more important to both of us, I think. He was like an imperfect brother you want to succeed in spite of his flaws, because underneath there was such decency."

"I'm sorry. I'm truly sorry."

She looked up at him. "You have the same decency. When you do the kind of work I do decency becomes very important. It's not the meek who are inheriting the earth, Jason, it's the corrupters. And I have an idea that the distance between corruption and killing is a very short step."

"Treadstone Seventy-One?"

"Yes. We were both right. I do want them exposed, I want them to pay for what they've done. And you can't run away."

He brushed his lips against her cheek and then her hair and held her. "I should throw you out," he said. "I should tell you to get out of my life. I can't do it, but I know damned well I should."

"It wouldn't make any difference if you did. I wouldn't go, my love."

The attorney's suite of offices was on the boulevard de la Chapelle, the book-lined conference room more a stage setting than an office; everything was a prop, and in its place. Deals were made in that room, not contracts. As for the lawyer himself, a dignified white goatee and silver pince-nez above an aquiline nose could not conceal the essential graft in the man. He even insisted on conversing in poor English, for which, at a later date, he could claim to have been misunderstood.

Marie did most of the talking, Bourne deferring, client to adviser. She made her points succinctly, altering the cashiers checks to bearer bonds, payable in dollars, in denominations ranging from a maximum of twenty thousand dollars to a minimum of five. She instructed the lawyer to tell the bank that all series were to be broken up numerically in threes, the international guarantors changed with every fifth lot of certificates. Her objective was not lost on the attorney; she so complicated the issuing of the bonds that tracing them would be beyond the facilities of most banks or brokers. Nor would such banks or brokers take on the added trouble or expense; payments were guaranteed.

When the irritated, goateed lawyer had nearly concluded his telephone conversation with an equally disturbed Antoine d'Amacourt, Marie held up her hand.

"Pardon me, but Monsieur Bourne insists that Monsieur d'Amacourt also include two hundred thousand francs in cash, one hundred thousand to be included with the bonds and one hundred to be held by Monsieur d'Amacourt. He suggests that the second hundred thousand be divided as follows. Seventy-five thousand for Monsieur d'Amacourt and twenty-five thousand for yourself. He realizes that he is greatly in debt to both of you for your advice and the additional trouble he has caused you. Needless to say, no specific record of breakdown is required."

Irritation and disturbance vanished with her words, replaced by an obsequiousness not seen since the court of Versailles. The arrangements were made in accordance with the unusual—but completely understandable—demands of Monsieur Bourne and his esteemed adviser.

A leather attaché case was provided by Monsieur Bourne for the bonds and the money; it would be carried by an armed courier who would leave the bank at 2:30 in the afternoon and meet Monsieur Bourne at 3:00 on the Pont Neuf. The distinguished client would identify himself with a small piece of leather cut from the shell of the case and which, when fitted in place, would prove to be the missing fragment. Added to this would be the words: "Herr Koenig sends greetings from Zurich."

So much for the details. Except for one, which was made clear by Monsieur Bourne's adviser.

"We recognize that the demands of the *fiche* must be carried out to the letter, and fully expect Monsieur d'Amacourt to do so," said Marie St. Jacques. "However, we also recognize that the timing can be advantageous to Monsieur Bourne, and would expect no less than that advantage. Were he not to have it, I'm afraid that I, as a certified—if for the present, anonymous—member of the International Banking Commission, would feel compelled to report certain aberrations of banking and legal procedures as I have witnessed them. I'm sure that won't be necessary; we're all very well paid, *n'est-ce pas, monsieur?*

"*C'est vrai, madame!* In banking and law . . . indeed, as in life itself . . . timing is everything. You have nothing to fear."

"I know," said Marie.

Bourne examined the grooves of the silencer, satisfied that he had removed the particles of dust and lint that had gathered with nonuse. He gave it a final, wrenching turn, depressed the magazine release and checked the clip. Six shells remained; he was ready. He shoved the weapon into his belt and buttoned his jacket.

Marie had not seen him with the gun. She was sitting on the bed, her back to him, talking on the telephone with the Canadian Embassy attaché, Dennis Corbelier. Cigarette smoke curled up from an ashtray next to her notebook; she was writing down Corbelier's information. When he had finished, she thanked him and hung up the phone. She remained motionless for two or three seconds, the pencil still in her hand.

"He doesn't know about Peter," she said, turning to Jason. "That's odd."

"Very," agreed Bourne. "I thought he'd be one of the first to know. You said they looked over Peter's telephone logs; he'd placed a call to Paris, to Corbelier. You'd think someone would have followed up on it."

"I hadn't even considered that. I was thinking about the newspapers, the wire services. Peter was . . . was found eighteen hours ago, and regardless of how casual I may have sounded, he was an important man in the Canadian government. His death would be news in itself, his murder infinitely more so. . . . It wasn't reported."

"Call Ottawa tonight. Find out why."

"I will."

"What did Corbelier tell you?"

"Oh, yes." Marie shifted her eyes to the notebook. "The license in rue Madeleine was meaningless, a car rented at De Gaulle Airport to a Jean-Pierre Larousse."

"John Smith," interrupted Jason.

"Exactly. He had better luck with the telephone number d'Amacourt gave you, but he can't see what it could possibly have to do with anything. Neither can I, as a matter of fact."

"It's that strange?"

"I think so. It's a private line belonging to a fashion house on Saint-Honoré. Les Classiques."

"A fashion house? You mean a studio?"

"I'm sure it's got one, but it's essentially an elegant dress shop. Like the House of Dior, or Givenchy. *Haute couture.* In the trade, Corbelier said, it's known as the House of René. That's Bergeron."

"Who?"

"René Bergeron, a designer. He's been around for years, always on the fringes of a major success. I know about him because my little lady back home copies his designs."

"Did you get the address?"

Marie nodded. "Why didn't Corbelier know about Peter? Why doesn't everybody?"

"Maybe you'll learn when you call. It's probably as simple as time zones; too late for the morning editions here in Paris. I'll pick up the afternoon paper." Bourne went to the closet for his topcoat, conscious of the hidden weight in his belt. "I'm going back to the bank. I'll follow the courier to the Pont Neuf." He put on the coat, aware that Marie was not listening. "I meant to ask you, do these fellows wear uniforms?"

"Who?"

"Bank couriers."

"That would account for the newspapers, not the wire services."

"I beg your pardon?"

"The difference in time. The papers might not have picked it up, but the wire services would have known. And embassies have teletypes; they would have known about it. It wasn't reported, Jason."

"You'll call tonight," he said. "I'm going."

"You asked about the couriers. Do they wear uniforms?"

"I was curious."

"Most of the time, yes. They also drive armored vans, but I was specific about that. If a van was used it was to be parked a block from the bridge, the courier to proceed on foot."

"I heard you, but I wasn't sure what you meant. Why?"

"A bonded courier's bad enough, but he's necessary; bank insurance requires him. A van is simply too obvious; it could be followed too easily. You won't change your mind and let me go with you?"

"No."

"Believe me, nothing will go wrong; those two thieves wouldn't permit it."

"Then there's no reason for you to be there."

"You're maddening."

"I'm in a hurry."

"I know. And you move faster without me." Marie got up and came to him. "I do understand." She leaned into him, kissing him on the lips, suddenly aware of the weapon in his belt. She looked into his eyes. "You are worried, aren't you?"

"Just cautious." He smiled, touching her chin. "It's an awful lot of money. It may have to keep us for a long time."

"I like the sound of that."

"The money?"

"No. Us." Marie frowned. "A safety deposit box."

"You keep talking in non sequiturs."

"You can't leave negotiable certificates worth over a million dollars in a Paris hotel room. You've got to get a deposit box."

"We can do it tomorrow." He released her, turning for the door. "While I'm out, look up Les Classiques in the phone book and call the regular number. Find out how late it's open." He left quickly.

Bourne sat in the back seat of a stationary taxi, watching the front of the bank through the windshield. The driver was humming an unrecognizable tune, reading a newspaper, content with the fifty-franc note he had received in advance. The cab's motor, however, was running; the passenger had insisted upon that.

The armored van loomed in the right rear window, its radio antenna shooting up from the center of the roof like a tapered bowsprit. It parked in a space reserved for authorized vehicles directly in front of Jason's taxi. Two small red lights appeared above the circle of bulletproof glass in the rear door. The alarm system had been activated.

Bourne leaned forward, his eyes on the uniformed man who climbed out of the side door and threaded his way through the crowds on the pavement toward the entrance of the bank. He felt a sense of relief; the man was not one of the three well-dressed men who had come to the Valois yesterday.

Fifteen minutes later the courier emerged from the bank, the leather attaché case in his left hand, his right covering an unlatched holster. The jagged rip on the side of the case could be seen clearly. Jason felt the fragment of leather in his shirt pocket; if nothing else it was the primitive combination that made a life beyond Paris, beyond Carlos, possible. If there was such a life and he could accept it without the terrible labyrinth from which he could find no escape.

But it was more than that. In a manmade labyrinth one kept moving, running, careening off walls, the contact itself a form of progress, if only blind. His personal labyrinth had no walls, no defined corridors through which to race. Only space, and swirling mists in the darkness that he saw so clearly when he opened his eyes at night and felt the sweat pouring down his face. Why was it always space and darkness and high winds? Why was he always plummeting through the air at night? A parachute. Why? Then other words came to him; he had no idea where they were from, but they were there and he heard them.

What's left when your memory's gone? And your identity, Mr. Smith?
Stop it!

The armored van swung into the traffic on rue Madeleine. Bourne tapped the driver on the shoulder. "Follow that truck, but keep at least two cars between us," he said in French.

The driver turned, alarmed. "I think you have the wrong taxi, monsieur. Take back your money."

"I'm with the armored-car company, you imbecile. It's a special assignment."

"Regrets, monsieur. We will not lose it." The driver plunged diagonally forward into the combat of traffic.

The van took the quickest route to the Seine, going down sidestreets. Turning left on the Quai de la Rapée toward the Pont Neuf. Then, within what Jason judged to be three or four blocks of the bridge, it slowed down, hugging the curb as if the courier had decided he was too early for his appointment. But, if anything, Bourne thought, he was running late. It was six minutes to three, barely enough time for the man to park and walk the one prescribed block to the bridge. Then why had the van slowed down? Slowed down? No, it had stopped; it wasn't moving! Why?

The traffic? . . . Good God, of course—the traffic!

"Stop here," said Bourne to the driver. "Pull over to the curb. Quickly!"

"What is it, monsieur?"

"You're a very fortunate man," said Jason. "My company is willing to pay you an additional one hundred francs if you simply go to the front window of that van and say a few words to the driver."

"What, monsieur?"

"Frankly, we're testing him. He's new. Do you want the hundred?"

"I just go to the window and say a few words?"

"That's all. Five seconds at the most, then you can go back to your taxi and drive off."

"There's no trouble? I don't want trouble."

"My firm's among the most respectable in France. You've seen our trucks everywhere."

"I don't know . . ."

"Forget it!" Bourne reached for the door handle.

"What are the words?"

Jason held out the hundred francs. "Just these: 'Herr Koenig. Greetings from Zurich.' Can you remember those?"

" 'Koenig. Greetings from Zurich.' What's so difficult?"

"You? Behind me?"

"That's right." They walked rapidly toward the van, hugging the right side of their small alley in the traffic as cars and trucks passed them in starts and stops on their left. The van was Carlos's trap, thought Bourne. The assassin had bought his way into the ranks of the armed couriers. A single name and a rendezvous revealed over a monitored radio frequency could bring an underpaid messenger a great deal of money. *Bourne. Pont Neuf.* So simple. This particular courier was less concerned with being prompt than in making sure the soldiers of Carlos reached the Pont Neuf in time. Paris traffic was notorious; anyone could be late. Jason stopped the taxi driver, holding in his hand four additional two-hundred franc notes; the man's eyes were riveted on them.

"Monsieur?"

"My company's going to be very generous. This man must be disciplined for gross infractions."

"What, monsieur?"

"After you say 'Herr Koenig. Greetings from Zurich,' simply add, 'The schedule's changed. There's a fare in my taxi who must see you.' Have you got that?"

The driver's eyes returned to the franc notes. "What's difficult?" He took the money.

They edged their way along the side of the van, Jason's back pressed against the wall of steel, his right hand concealed beneath his topcoat, gripping the gun in his belt. The driver approached the window and reached up, tapping the glass.

"You inside! Herr Koenig! Greetings from Zurich!" he yelled.

The window was rolled down, no more than an inch or two. "What is this?" a voice yelled back. "You're supposed to be at the Pont Neuf, monsieur!"

The driver was no idiot; he was also anxious to leave as rapidly as possible. "Not me, you jackass!" he shouted through the din of the surrounding, perilously close traffic. "I'm telling you what I was told to say! The schedule's been changed. There's a man back there who says he has to see you!"

"Tell him to hurry," said Jason, holding a final fifty-franc note in his hand, beyond sight of the window.

The driver glanced at the money, then back up at the courier. "Be quick about it! If you don't see him right away you'll lose your job!"

"Now, get out of here!" said Bourne. The driver turned and ran past Jason, grabbing the franc note as he raced back to his taxi.

Bourne held his place, suddenly alarmed by what he heard through the cacophony of pounding horns and gunning engines in the crowded street. There were voices from inside the van, not one man shouting into a radio, but two shouting at each other. The courier was not alone; there was another man with him.

"Those were the words. You heard them."

"He was to come *up* to you. He was to show himself."

"Which he will *do*. And present the piece of leather, which must fit exactly! Do you expect him to do that in the middle of a street filled with traffic?"

"I don't like it!"

"You paid me to help you and your people find someone. Not to lose my job. I'm going!"

"It *must* be the Pont Neuf!"

"Kiss my ass!"

There was the sound of heavy footsteps on the metal floorboards. "I'm coming with you!"

The panel door opened; Jason spun behind it, his hand still under his coat. Below him a child's face was pressed against the glass of a car window, the eyes squinting, the young features contorted into an ugly mask, fright and insult the childish intent. The swelling sound of angry horns, blaring in counterpoint, filled the street; the traffic had come to a standstill.

The courier stepped off the metal ledge, the attaché case in his left hand. Bourne was ready; the instant the courier was on the street, he slammed the panel back into the body of the second man, crashing the heavy steel into a descending kneecap and an outstretched hand. The man screamed, reeling backward inside the van. Jason shouted at the courier, the jagged scrap of leather in his free hand.

"I'm Bourne! Here's your fragment! And you keep that gun in its holster or you won't just lose your job, you'll lose your life, you son of a bitch!"

"I meant no harm, monsieur! They wanted to find you! They have no interest in your delivery, you have my word on it!"

The door crashed open; Jason slammed it again with his shoulder, then pulled it back to see the face of Carlos's soldier, his hand on the weapon in his belt.

What he saw was the barrel of a gun, the black orifice of its opening staring him in the eyes. He spun back, aware that the split-second delay in the gunshot that followed was caused by the burst of a shrill ringing that exploded out of the armored van. The alarm had been tripped, the sound deafening, riding over the dissonance in the street; the gunshot seemed muted by comparison, the eruption of asphalt below not heard.

Once more Jason hammered the panel. He heard the impact of metal against metal; he had made contact with the gun of Carlos's soldier. He pulled his own from his belt, dropped to his knees in the street, and pulled the door open.

He saw the face from Zurich, the killer they had called Johann, the man they had brought to Paris to recognize him. Bourne fired twice; the man arched backward, blood spreading across his forehead.

The courier! The attaché case!

Jason saw the man; he had ducked below the tailgate for protection, his weapon in his hand, screaming for help. Bourne leaped to his feet and lunged for the extended gun, gripping the barrel, twisting it out of the courier's hand. He grabbed the attaché case and shouted.

"No harm, right? Give me that, you bastard!" He threw the man's gun under the van, got up and plunged into the hysterical crowds on the pavement.

He ran wildly, blindly, the bodies in front of him the movable walls of his labyrinth. But there was an essential difference between this gauntlet and one he lived in every day. There was no darkness; the afternoon sun was bright, as blinding as his race through the labyrinth.

14

"Everything is here," said Marie. She had collated the certificates by denominations, the stacks and the franc notes on the desk. "I told you it would be."

"It almost wasn't."

"What?"

"The man they called Johann, the one from Zurich. He's dead. I killed him."

"Jason, what *happened?*"

He told her. "They counted on the Pont Neuf," he said. "My guess is that the backup car got caught in traffic, broke into the courier's radio frequency, and told them to delay. I'm sure of it."

"Oh God, they're everywhere!"

"But they don't know where *I* am," said Bourne, looking into the mirror above the bureau, studying his blond hair while putting on the tortoise-shell glasses. "And the last place they'd expect to find me at this moment—if they conceivably thought I knew about it—would be a fashion house on Saint-Honoré."

"Les Classiques?" asked Marie, astonished.

"That's right. Did you call it?"

"Yes, but that's insane!"

"Why?" Jason turned from the mirror. "Think about it. Twenty minutes ago their trap fell apart; there's got to be confusion, recriminations, accusations of incompetency, or worse. Right now, at this moment, they're more concerned with each other than with me; nobody wants a bullet in his throat. It won't last long; they'll regroup quickly, Carlos will make sure of that. But during the next hour or so, while they're trying to piece together what happened, the one place they won't look for me is a relay-drop they haven't the vaguest idea I'm aware of."

"Someone will recognize you!"

"Who? They brought in a man from Zurich to do that and he's dead. They're not sure what I look like."

"The courier. They'll take him; he saw you."

"For the next few hours he'll be busy with the police."

"D'Amacourt. The lawyer!"

"I suspect they're halfway to Normandy or Marseilles or, if they're lucky, out of the country."

"Suppose they're stopped, caught?"

"Suppose they are? Do you think Carlos would expose a drop where he gets messages? Not on your life. Or his."

"Jason, I'm frightened."

"So am I. But not of being recognized." Bourne returned to the mirror. "I could give a long dissertation about facial classifications, and softened features, but I won't."

"You're talking about the evidences of surgery. Port Noir. You told me."

"Not all of it." Bourne leaned against the bureau, staring at his face. "What color are my eyes?"

"What?"

"No, don't look at me. Now, tell me, what color are my eyes? Yours are brown with speckles of green; what about mine?"

"Blue . . . bluish. Or a kind of gray, really . . ." Marie stopped. "I'm not really sure. I suppose that's dreadful of me."

"It's perfectly natural. Basically they're hazel, but not all the time. Even I've noticed it. When I wear a blue shirt or tie, they become bluer; a brown coat or jacket, they're gray. When I'm naked, they're strangely nondescript."

"That's not so strange. I'm sure millions of people are the same."

"I'm sure they are. But how many of them wear contact lenses when their eyesight is normal?"

"Contact—"

"That's what I said," interrupted Jason. "Certain types of contact lenses are worn to change the color of the eyes. They're most effective when the eyes are hazel. When Washburn first examined me there was evidence of prolonged usage. It's one of the clues, isn't it?"

"It's whatever you want to make of it," said Marie. "If it's true."

"Why wouldn't it be?"

"Because the doctor was more often drunk than sober. You've told me that. He piled conjecture on top of conjecture, heaven knows how warped by alcohol. He was never specific. He couldn't be."

"He was about one thing. I'm a chameleon, designed to fit a flexible mold. I want to find out whose; maybe I can now. Thanks to you I've got an address. Someone there may know the truth. Just one man, that's all I need. One person I can confront, break if I have to . . ."

"I can't stop you, but for God's sake be careful. If they do recognize you, they'll kill you."

"Not there they won't; it'd be rotten for business. This is Paris."

"I don't think that's funny, Jason."

"Neither do I. I'm counting on it very seriously."

"What are you going to do? I mean, how?"

"I'll know better when I get there. See if anyone's running around looking nervous or anxious or waiting for a phone call as if his life depended on it."

"Then what?"

"I'll do the same as I did with d'Amacourt. Wait outside and follow whoever it is. I'm this close; I won't miss. And I'll be careful."

"Will you call me?"

"I'll try."

"I may go crazy waiting. Not knowing."

"Don't wait. Can you deposit the bonds somewhere?"

"The banks are closed."

"Use a large hotel; hotels have vaults."

"You have to have a room."

"Take one. At the Meurice or the George Cinq. Leave the case at the desk but come back here."

Marie nodded. "It would give me something to do."

"Then call Ottawa. Find out what happened."

"I will."

Bourne crossed to the bedside table and picked up a number of five-thousand franc notes. "A bribe would be easier," he said. "I don't think it'll happen, but it could."

"It could," agreed Marie, and then in the same breath continued. "Did you hear yourself? You just rattled off the names of two hotels."

"I heard." He turned and faced her. "I've been here before. Many times. I lived here, but not in those hotels. In out-of-the-way streets, I think. Not very easily found."

The moment passed in silence, the fear electric.

"I love you, Jason."

"I love you, too," said Bourne.

"Come back to me. No matter what happens, come back to me."

The lighting was soft and dramatic, pinpoint spotlights shining down from the dark brown ceiling, bathing manikins and expensively dressed clients in pools of flattering yellows. The jewelry and accessories counters were lined with black velvet, silks of bright red and green tastefully flowing above the midnight sheen, glistening eruptions of gold and silver caught in the recessed frame lights. The aisles curved graciously in semicircles, giving an illusion of space that was not there, for Les Classiques, though hardly small, was not a large emporium. It was, however, a beautifully appointed store on one of the most costly strips of real estate in Paris. Fitting rooms with doors of tinted glass were at the rear, beneath a balcony where the offices of management were located. A carpeted staircase rose on the right beside an elevated switchboard in front of which sat an oddly out-of-place middle-aged man dressed in a conservative business suit, operating the console, speaking into a mouthpiece that was an extension of his single earphone.

The clerks were mostly women, tall, slender, gaunt of face and body, living postmortems of former fashion models whose tastes and intelligence had carried them beyond their sisters in the trade, other practices no longer feasible. The few men in evidence were also slender; reedlike figures emphasized by form-fitting clothes, gestures rapid, stances balletically defiant.

Light romantic music floated out of the dark ceiling, quiet crescendos abstractly punctuated by the beams of the miniature spotlights. Jason wandered through the aisles, studying manikins, touching the fabric, making his own appraisals. They covered his essential bewilderment. Where was the confusion, the anxiety he expected to find at the core of Carlos's message center? He glanced up at the open office doors and the single corridor that bisected the small complex. Men and women walked casually about as they did on the main floor, every now and then stopping one another, exchanging pleasantries or scraps of relevantly irrelevant information. Gossip. Nowhere was there the slightest sense of urgency, no sign at all that a vital trap had exploded in their faces, an imported killer—the only man in Paris who worked for Carlos and could identify the target—shot in the head, dead in the back of an armored van on the Quai de la Rapée.

It was incredible, if only because the whole atmosphere was the opposite of what he had anticipated. Not that he expected to find chaos, far from it; the soldiers of Carlos were too controlled for that. Still he had expected *something*. And here there were no strained faces, or darting eyes, no abrupt movements that signified alarm. Nothing whatsoever was unusual; the elegant world of *haute couture* continued to spin in its elegant orbit, unmindful of events that should have thrown its axis off balance.

Still, there was a private telephone somewhere and someone who not only spoke for Carlos but was also empowered to set in motion three killers on the hunt. A woman . . .

He saw her; it had to be her. Halfway down the carpeted staircase, a tall imperious woman with a face that age and cosmetics had rendered into a cold mask of itself. She was stopped by a reedlike male clerk who held out a salesbook for the woman's approval; she looked at it, then glanced down at the floor, at a nervous, middle-aged man by a nearby jewelry counter. The glance was brief but pointed, the message clear. *All right, mon ami, pick up your bauble but pay your bill soon. Otherwise you could be embarrassed next time. Or worse. I might call your wife.* In milliseconds the rebuke was over; a smile as false as it was broad cracked the mask, and with a nod and a flourish the woman took a pencil from the clerk and initialed the sales slip. She continued down the staircase, the clerk following, leaning forward in further conversation. It was obvious he was flattering her; she turned on the bottom step, touching her crown of streaked dark hair and tapped his wrist in a gesture of thanks.

There was little placidity in the woman's eyes. They were as aware as any pair of eyes Bourne had ever seen, except perhaps behind gold-rimmed glasses in Zurich.

Instinct. She was his objective; it remained how to reach her. The first moves of the pavane had to be subtle, neither too much nor too little, but warranting attention. She had to come to him.

The next few minutes astonished Jason—which was to say he astonished himself. The term was "role-playing," he understood that, but what shocked him was the ease with which he slid into a character far from himself—as he knew himself. Where minutes before he had made appraisals, he now made inspections, pulling garments from their individual racks, holding the fabrics up to the light. He peered closely at stitchings, examined buttons and buttonholes, brushing his fingers across collars, fluffing them up, then letting them fall. He was a judge of fine clothes, a schooled buyer who knew what he wanted and rapidly disregarded that which did not suit his tastes. The only items he did not examine were the price tags; obviously they held no interest for him.

The fact that they did not prodded the interest of the imperious woman who kept glancing over in his direction. A sales clerk, her concave body floating upright on the carpet, approached him; he smiled courteously, but said he preferred to browse by himself. Less than thirty seconds later he was behind three manikins, each dressed in the most expensive designs to be found in Les Classiques. He raised his eyebrows, his mouth set in silent approval as he squinted between the plastic figures at the woman beyond the counter. She whispered to the clerk who had spoken to him; the former model shook her head, shrugging.

Bourne stood arms akimbo, billowing his cheeks, his breath escaping slowly as his eyes shifted from one manikin to another; he was an uncertain man about to make up his mind. And a potential client in that situation, especially one who did not look at prices, needed assistance from the most knowledgeable person in the vicinity; he was irresistible. The regal woman touched her hair and gracefully negotiated the aisles toward him. The pavane had come to its first conclusion; the dancers bowed, preparing for the gavotte.

"I see you've gravitated to our better items, monsieur," said the woman in English, a presumption obviously based on the judgment of a practiced eye.

"I trust I have," replied Jason. "You've got an interesting collection here, but one does have to ferret, doesn't one?"

"The ever-present and inevitable scale of values, monsieur. However, all our designs are exclusive."

"*Cela va sans dire, madame.*"

"*Ah, vous parlez français?*"

"*Un peu.* Passably."

"You are American?"

"I'm rarely there," said Bourne. "You say these are made for you alone?"

"Oh, yes. Our designer is under exclusive contract; I'm sure you've heard of him. René Bergeron."

Jason frowned. "Yes. I have. Very respected, but he's never made a break-through, has he?"

"He will, monsieur. It's inevitable; his reputation grows each season. A number of years ago he worked for St. Laurent, then Givenchy. Some say he did far more than cut the patterns, if you know what I mean."

"It's not hard to follow."

"And how those cats try to push him in the background! It's disgraceful! Because he adores women; he flatters them and does not make them into little boys, *vous comprenez?*"

"Je vous comprends parfaitement."

"He'll emerge worldwide one day soon and they'll not be able to touch the hems of his creations. Think of these as the works of an emerging master, monsieur."

"You're very convincing. I'll take these three. I assume they're in the size twelve range."

"Fourteen, monsieur. They will be fitted, of course."

"I'm afraid not, but I'm sure there are decent tailors in Cap-Ferrat."

"Naturellement," conceded the woman quickly.

"Also . . ." Bourne hesitated, frowning again. "While I'm here, and to save time, select a few others for me along these lines. Different prints, different cuts, but related, if that makes sense."

"Very *good* sense, monsieur."

"Thanks, I appreciate it. I've had a long flight from the Bahamas and I'm exhausted."

"Would monsieur care to sit down then?"

"Frankly, monsieur would care for a drink."

"It can be arranged, of course. As to the method of payment, monsieur . . . ?"

"Je paierai cash, I think," said Jason, aware that the exchange of merchandise for hard currency would appeal to the overseer of Les Classiques. "Checks and accounts are like spoors in the forest, aren't they?"

"You are as wise as you are discriminating." The rigid smile cracked the mask again, the eyes in no way related. "About that drink, why not my office? It's quite private; you can relax and I shall bring you selections for your approval."

"Splendid."

"As to the price range, monsieur?"

"Les meilleurs, madame."

"Naturellement." A thin white hand was extended. "I am Jacqueline Lavier, managing partner of Les Classiques."

"Thank you." Bourne took the hand without offering a name. One might follow in less public surroundings, his expression said, but not at the moment. For the moment, money was his introduction. "Your office? Mine's several thousand miles from here."

"This way, monsieur." The rigid smile appeared once more, breaking the facial mask like a sheet of progressively cracked ice. Madame Lavier gestured toward the staircase. The world of *haute couture* continued, its orbit uninterrupted by failure and death on the Quai de la Rapée.

That lack of interruption was as disturbing to Jason as it was bewildering. He was convinced the woman walking beside him was the carrier of lethal commands that had been aborted by gunfire an hour ago, the orders having been issued by a faceless man who demanded obedience or death. Yet there was not the slightest indication that a strand of her perfectly groomed hair had been disturbed by nervous fingers, no pallor on the chiseled mask that might be taken for fear. Yet there was no one higher at Les Classiques, no one else who would have a private number in a very private office. Part of an equation was missing . . . but another had been disturbingly confirmed.

Himself. The chameleon. The charade had worked; he was in the enemy's camp, convinced beyond doubt that he had not been recognized. The whole episode had a *déjà vu* quality about it. He had done such things before, experienced the feelings of similar accomplishment before. He was a man running through an unfamiliar jungle, yet somehow instinctively knowing his way, sure of where the traps were and how to avoid them. The chameleon was an expert.

They reached the staircase and started up the steps. Below on the right, the conservatively dressed, middle-aged operator was speaking quietly into the extended mouthpiece, nodding his gray-haired head almost wearily, as if assuring the party on the line that *their* world was as serene as it should be.

Bourne stopped on the seventh step, the pause involuntary. The back of the man's head, the outline of the cheekbone, the sight of the thinning gray hair— the way it fell slightly over the ear; he had seen that man before! Somewhere. In the past, in the unremembered past, but remembered now in darkness . . . and with flashes of light. Explosions, mists; buffeting winds followed by silences filled with tension. What was it? Where was it? Why did the pain come to his eyes again? The gray-haired man began to turn in his swivel chair; Jason looked away before they made contact.

"I see monsieur is taken by our rather unique switchboard," said Madame Lavier. "It's a distinction we feel sets Les Classiques apart from the other shops on Saint-Honoré."

"How so?" asked Bourne, as they proceeded up the steps, the pain in his eyes causing him to blink.

"When a client calls Les Classiques, the telephone is not answered by a vacuous female, but instead by a cultured gentleman who has all our information at his fingertips."

"A nice touch."

"Other gentlemen think so," she added. "Especially when making telephone purchases they would prefer to keep confidential. There are no spoors in our forest, monsieur."

They reached Jacqueline Lavier's spacious office. It was the lair of an efficient executive, scores of papers in separate piles on the desk, an easel against the wall holding watercolor sketches, some boldly initialed, others left untouched, obviously unacceptable. The walls were filled with framed photographs of the Beautiful People, their beauty too often marred by gaping mouths and smiles as false as the one on the mask of the inhabitant of the office. There was a bitch quality in the perfumed air; these were the quarters of an aging, pacing tigress, swift to attack any who threatened her possessions or the sating of her appetites. Yet she was disciplined; all things considered, an estimable liaison to Carlos.

Who was that man on the switchboard? Where had he seen him?

He was offered a drink from a selection of bottles; he chose brandy.

"Do sit down, monsieur. I shall enlist the help of René himself, if I can find him."

"That's very kind, but I'm sure whatever you choose will be satisfactory. I have an instinct about taste; yours is all through this office. I'm comfortable with it."

"You're too generous."

"Only when it's warranted," said Jason, still standing. "Actually I'd like to look around at the photographs. I see a number of acquaintances, if not friends. A lot of these faces pass through the Bahamian banks with considerable frequency."

"I'm sure they do," agreed Lavier, in a tone that bespoke regard for such avenues of finance. "I shan't be long, monsieur."

Nor would she, thought Bourne, as Les Classiques' partner swept out of the office. Mme. Lavier was not about to allow a tired, wealthy mark too much time to think. She would return with the most expensive designs she could gather up as rapidly as possible. Therefore, if there was anything in the room that could shed light on Carlos's intermediary—or on the assassin's operation—it had to be found quickly. And, if it was there, it would be on or around the desk.

Jason circled behind the imperial chair in front of the wall, feigning amused interest in the photographs, but concentrating on the desk. There were invoices, receipts, and overdue bills, along with dunning letters of reprimand awaiting Lavier's signature. An address book lay open, four names on the page; he moved closer to see more clearly. Each was the name of a company, the individual contacts bracketed, his or her positions underlined. He wondered if he should memorize each company, each contact. He was about to do so when his eyes fell on the edge of an index card. It was only the edge; the rest was concealed under the telephone itself. And there was something else—dull, barely discernible. A strip of transparent tape, running along the edge of the card, holding it in place. The tape itself was relatively new, recently stuck over the heavy paper and the gleaming wood; it was clean, no smudges or coiled borders or signs of having been there very long.

Instinct.

Bourne picked up the telephone to move it aside. It rang, the bell vibrating through his hand, the shrill sound unnerving. He replaced it on the desk and stepped away as a man in shirtsleeves rushed through the open door from the corridor. He stopped, staring at Bourne, his eyes alarmed but noncommittal. The telephone rang a second time; the man walked rapidly to the desk and picked up the receiver.

"Allô?" There was silence as the intruder listened, head down, concentration on the caller. He was a tanned, muscular man of indeterminate age, the sun-drenched skin disguising the years. His face was taut, his lips thin, his close-cropped hair thick, dark brown, and disciplined. The sinews of his bare arms moved under the flesh as he transferred the phone from one hand to the other, speaking harshly. *"Pas ici. Sais pas. Téléphonez plus tard . . ."* He hung up and looked at Jason. *"Où est Jacqueline?"*

"A little slower, please," said Bourne, lying in English. "My French is limited."

"Sorry," replied the bronzed man. "I was looking for Madame Lavier."

"The owner?"

"The title will suffice. Where is she?"

"Depleting my funds." Jason smiled, raising his glass to his lips.

"Oh? And who are you, monsieur?"

"Who are *you?*"

The man studied Bourne. "René Bergeron."

"Oh, Lord!" exclaimed Jason. "She's looking for *you.* You're very *good,* Mr. Bergeron. She said I was to look upon your designs as the work of an emerging master." Bourne smiled again. "You're the reason I may have to wire the Bahamas for a great deal of money."

"You're most kind, monsieur. And I apologize for barging in."

"Better that you answered that phone than me. Berlitz considers me a failure."

"Buyers, suppliers, all screaming idiots. To whom, monsieur, do I have the honor of speaking?"

"Briggs," said Jason, having no idea where the name came from, astonished that it came so quickly, so naturally. "Charles Briggs."

"A pleasure to know you." Bergeron extended his hand; the grip was firm. "You say Jacqueline was looking for me?"

"On my behalf, I'm afraid."

"I shall find her." The designer left quickly.

Bourne stepped to the desk, his eyes on the door, his hand on the telephone. He moved it to the side, exposing the index card. There were two telephone numbers, the first recognizable as a Zurich exchange, the second obviously Paris.

Instinct. He had been right, a strip of transparent tape the only sign he had needed. He stared at the numbers, memorizing them, then moved the telephone back in place and stepped away.

He had barely managed to clear the desk when Madame Lavier swept back into the room, a half dozen dresses over her arm. "I met René in the steps. He approves of my selections most enthusiastically. He also tells me your name is Briggs, monsieur."

"I would have told you myself," said Bourne, smiling back, countering the pout in Lavier's voice. "But I don't think you asked."

" 'Spoors in the forest,' monsieur. Here, I bring you a feast!" She separated the dresses, placing them carefully over several chairs. "I truly believe these are among the finest creations René has brought us."

"Brought you? He doesn't work here then?"

"A figure of speech; his studio's at the end of the corridor, but it is a holy sacristy. Even I tremble when I enter."

"They're magnificent," continued Bourne, going from one to another. "But I don't want to overwhelm her, just pacify her," he added, pointing out three garments. "I'll take these."

"A fine selection, Monsieur Briggs!"

"Box them with the others, if you will."

"Of course. She is, indeed, a fortunate lady."

"A good companion, but a child. A spoiled child, I'm afraid. However, I've been away a lot and haven't paid much attention to her, so I guess I should make peace. It's one reason I sent her to Cap-Ferrat." He smiled, taking out his Louis Vuitton billfold. *"La facture, si'il vous plaît?"*

"I'll have one of the girls expedite everything." Madame Lavier pressed a button on the intercom next to the telephone. Jason watched closely, prepared to comment on the call Bergeron had answered in the event the woman's eyes settled on a slightly out-of-place phone. *"Faites venir Janine—avec les robes. La facture aussi."* She stood up. "Another brandy, Monsieur Briggs?"

"Merci bien." Bourne extended his glass; she took it and walked to the bar. Jason knew the time had not yet arrived for what he had in mind; it would come soon—as soon as he parted with money—but not now. He could, however, continue building a foundation with the managing partner of Les Classiques. "That fellow Bergeron," he said. "You say he's under exclusive contract to you?"

Madame Lavier turned, the glass in her hand. "Oh, yes. We are a closely knit family here."

Bourne accepted the brandy, nodded his thanks, and sat down in an armchair in front of the desk. "That's a constructive arrangement," he said pointlessly.

The tall, gaunt clerk he had first spoken with came into the office, a salesbook in her hand. Instructions were given rapidly, figures entered, the garments gathered and separated as the salesbook exchanged hands. Lavier held it out for Jason's perusal. *"Voici la facture, monsieur,"* she said.

Bourne shook his head, dismissing inspection. *"Combien?"* he asked.

"Vingt-mille, soixante francs, monsieur," answered the Les Classiques partner, watching his reaction with the expression of a very large, wary bird.

There was none. Jason merely removed five five-thousand-franc notes and handed them to her. She nodded and gave them in turn to the slender salesclerk, who walked cadaverously out of the office with the dresses.

"Everything will be packaged and brought up here with your change." Lavier went to her desk and sat down. "You're on your way to Ferrat, then. It should be lovely."

He had paid; the time had come. "A last night in Paris before I go back to kindergarten," said Jason, raising his glass in a toast of self-mockery.

"Yes, you mentioned that your friend is quite young."

"A child is what I said, and that's what she is. She's a good companion, but I think I prefer the company of more mature women."

"You must be very fond of her," contested Lavier, touching her perfectly coiffed hair, the flattery accepted. "You buy her such lovely—and, frankly—very expensive things."

"A minor price considering what she might try to opt for."

"Really."

"She's my wife, my third to be exact, and there are appearances to be kept up in the Bahamas. But all that's neither here nor there; my life's quite in order."

"I'm sure it is, monsieur."

"Speaking of the Bahamas, a thought occurred to me a few minutes ago. It's why I asked you about Bergeron."

"What is that?"

"You may think I'm impetuous; I assure you I'm not. But when something strikes me, I like to explore it. Since Bergeron's yours exclusively, have you ever given any thought to opening a branch in the islands?"

"The Bahamas?"

"And points south. Into the Caribbean, perhaps."

"Monsieur, Saint-Honoré by itself is often more than we can handle. Untended farmland generally goes fallow, as they say."

"It wouldn't have to be tended; not in the way that you think. A concession here, one there, the designs exclusive, local ownership on a percentage-franchise basis. Just a boutique or two, spreading, of course, cautiously."

"That takes considerable capital, Monsieur Briggs."

"Key prices, initially. What you might call entrance fees. They're high but not prohibitive. In the finer hotels and clubs it usually depends on how well you know the managements."

"And you know them?"

"Extremely well. As I say, I'm just exploring, but I think the idea has merit. Your labels would have a certain distinction—Les Classiques, Paris, Grand Bahama . . . Caneel Bay, perhaps." Bourne swallowed the rest of his brandy. "But you probably think I'm crazy. Consider it just talk. . . . Although I've made a dollar or two on risks that simply struck me on the spur of the moment."

"Risks?" Jacqueline Lavier touched her hair again.

"I don't give ideas away, madame. I generally back them."

"Yes, I understand. As you say, the idea does have merit."

"I think so. Of course, I'd like to see what kind of agreement you have with Bergeron."

"It could be produced, monsieur."

"Tell you what," said Jason. "If you're free, let's talk about it over drinks and dinner. It's my only night in Paris."

"And you prefer the company of more mature women," concluded Jacqueline Lavier, the mask cracked into a smile again, the white ice breaking beneath eyes now more in concert.

"C'est vrai, madame."

"It can be arranged," she said, reaching for the phone.

The phone. Carlos.

He would break her, thought Bourne. *Kill her if he had to. He would learn the truth.*

Marie walked through the crowd toward the booth in the telephone complex on rue Vaugirard. She had taken a room at the Meurice, left the attaché case at the front desk, and had sat alone in the room for exactly twenty-two minutes. Until she could not stand it any longer. She had sat in a chair facing a blank wall, thinking about Jason, about the madness of the last eight days that had propelled her into an insanity beyond her understanding. Jason. Considerate, frightening, bewildered Jason Bourne. A man with so much violence in him, and yet oddly, so much compassion. And too terribly capable in dealing with a world ordinary men knew nothing about. Where had he sprung from, this love of hers? Who had taught him to find his way through the dark back streets of Paris, Marseilles, and Zurich . . . as far away as the Orient, perhaps? What was the Far East to him? How did he know the languages? What *were* the languages? Or language?

Tao.

Che-sah.

Tam Quan.

Another world, and she knew nothing of it. But she knew Jason Bourne, or the man called Jason Bourne, and she held on to the decency she knew was there. Oh, God, how she loved him so!

Ilich Ramirez Sanchez. Carlos. What was he to Jason Bourne?

Stop it! she had screamed at herself while in that room alone. And then she had done what she had seen Jason do so many times: she had lunged up from the chair, as if the physical movement would clear the mists away—or allow her to break through them.

Canada. She had to reach Ottawa and find out why Peter's death—his murder—was being handled so secretly, so obscenely. It did not make sense; she objected with all her heart. For Peter, too, was a decent man, and he had been killed by indecent men. She would be told why or she would expose that death— that murder—herself. She would scream out loud to the world that she knew, and say, "Do something!"

And so she had left the Meurice, taken a cab to the rue Vaugirard, and placed the call to Ottawa. She waited now outside the booth, her anger mounting, an unlit cigarette creased between her fingers. When the bell rang, she could not take the time to crush it out.

It rang. She opened the glass door of the booth and went inside.

"Is this you, Alan?"

"Yes," was the curt reply.

"Alan, what the hell is going on? Peter was *murdered,* and there hasn't been a single word in any newspaper or on any broadcast! I don't think the embassy even knows! It's as though no one cared! What are you people *doing?*"

"What we're told to do. And so will you."

"What? That was *Peter!* He was your friend! Listen to me, Alan . . ."

"No!" The interruption was harsh. *"You* listen. Get out of Paris. Now! Take the next direct flight back here. If you have any problems, the embassy will clear them—but you're to talk only to the ambassador, is that understood?"

"No!" screamed Marie St. Jacques. "I don't understand! Peter was killed and nobody cares! All you're saying is bureaucratic bullshit! Don't get involved; for God's sake, don't *ever* get involved!"

"Stay out of it, Marie!"

"Stay out of *what?* That's what you're not telling me, isn't it? Well, you'd better . . ."

"I can't!" Alan lowered his voice. "I don't know. I'm only telling you what I was told to tell you."

"By whom?"

"You can't ask me that."

"I *am* asking!"

"Listen to me, Marie. I haven't been home for the past twenty-four hours. I've been waiting here for the last twelve for you to call. Try to understand me—I'm not *suggesting* you come back. Those are orders from your government."

"Orders? Without explanations?"

"That's the way it is. I'll say this much. They want you out of there; they want him isolated. . . . That's the way it is."

"Sorry, Alan—that's *not* the way it is. Goodbye." She slammed the receiver down, then instantly gripped her hands to stop the trembling. *Oh, my God, she loved him so . . . and they were trying to kill him. Jason, my Jason. They all want you killed. Why?*

The conservatively dressed man at the switchboard snapped the red toggle that blocked the lines, reducing all incoming calls to a busy signal. He did so once or twice an hour, if only to clear his mind and expunge the empty insanities he had been required to mouth during the past minutes. The necessity to cut off all conversation usually occurred to him after a particularly tedious one; he had just had it. The wife of a Deputy trying to conceal the outrageous price of a single purchase by breaking it up into several, thus not to be so apparent to her husband. Enough! He needed a few minutes to breathe.

The irony struck him. It was not that many years ago when others sat in front of switchboards for *him.* At his companies in Saigon and in the communications room of his vast plantation in the Mekong Delta. And here he was now in front of someone else's switchboard in the perfumed surroundings of Saint-Honoré. The English poet said it best: There were more preposterous vicissitudes in life than a single philosophy could conjure.

He heard laughter on the staircase and looked up. Jacqueline was leaving early, no doubt with one of her celebrated and fully bankrolled acquaintances. There was no question about it, Jacqueline had a talent for removing gold from a well-guarded mine, even diamonds from De Beers. He could not see the man with her; he was on the other side of Jacqueline, his head oddly turned away.

Then for an instant he did see him; their eyes made contact; it was brief and explosive. The gray-haired switchboard operator suddenly could not breathe; he was suspended in a moment of disbelief, staring at a face, a head, he had not seen in years. And then almost always in darkness, for they had worked at night . . . died at night.

Oh, my God—it was *him!* From the living—dying—nightmares thousands of miles away. It *was him!*

The gray-haired man rose from the switchboard as if in a trance. He pulled the mouthpiece-earphone off and let it drop to the floor. It clattered as the board lit up with incoming calls that made no connections, answered only with discordant hums. He stepped off the platform and sidestepped his way quickly toward the aisle to get a better look at Jacqueline Lavier and the ghost that was her escort. The ghost who was a killer—above all men he had ever known, a *killer.* They said it might happen but he had never believed them; he believed them now. It *was* the *man.*

He saw them both clearly. Saw *him.* They were walking down the center aisle toward the entrance. He had to stop them. Stop *her!* But to rush out and yell would mean death. A bullet in the head, instantaneous.

They reached the doors; *he* pulled them open, ushering her out to the pavement. The gray-haired man raced out from his hiding place, across the intersecting aisle and down to the front window. Out in the street *he* had flagged a taxi. He was opening the door, motioning for Jacqueline to get inside. Oh, God! She was going!

The middle-aged man turned and ran as fast as he could toward the staircase. He collided with two startled customers and a salesclerk, pushing all three violently out of his way. He raced up the steps, across the balcony and down the corridor, to the open studio door.

"René! René!" he shouted, bursting inside.

Bergeron looked up from his sketchboard, astonished. "What is it?"

"That man with Jacqueline! Who is he? How long has he been here?"

"Oh? Probably the American," said the designer. "His name's Briggs. A fatted calf; he's done very well by our grosses today."

"Where did they go?"

"I didn't know they went anywhere."

"She left with him!"

"Our Jacqueline retains her touch, no? And her good sense."

"Find them! Get her!"

"Why?"

"He *knows!* He'll kill her!"

"What?"

"It's him! I'd swear to it! That man is Cain!"

15

"The man is Cain," said Colonel Jack Manning bluntly, as if he expected to be contradicted by at least three of the four civilians at the Pentagon conference table. Each was older than he, and each considered himself more experienced. None was prepared to acknowledge that the army had obtained information where his own organization had failed. There was a fourth civilian but his opinion did not count. He was a member of the Congressional Oversight Committee, and as such to be treated with deference, but not seriously. "If we don't move *now*," continued Manning, "even at the risk of exposing everything we've learned, he could slip through the nets again. As of eleven days ago, he was in Zurich. We're convinced he's still there. And, gentlemen, it *is* Cain."

"That's quite a statement," said the balding, birdlike academic from the National Security Council as he read the summary page concerning Zurich given to each delegate at the table. His name was Alfred Gillette, an expert in personnel screening and evaluation, and was considered by the Pentagon to be bright, vindictive, and with friends in high places.

"I find it extraordinary," added Peter Knowlton, an associate director of the Central Intelligence Agency, a man in his middle fifties who perpetuated the dress, the appearance, and the attitude of an Ivy Leaguer of thirty years ago. "Our sources have Cain in Brussels, *not* Zurich, at the same time—eleven days ago. Our sources are rarely in error."

"That's quite a statement," said the third civilian, the only one at that table Manning really respected. He was the oldest there, a man named David Abbott, a former Olympic swimmer whose intellect had matched his physical prowess. He was in his late sixties now, but his bearing was still erect, his mind as sharp as it had ever been, his age, however, betrayed by a face lined from the tensions of a lifetime he would never reveal. He knew what he was talking about, thought the colonel. Although he was currently a member of the omnipotent Forty Committee, he had been with the CIA since its origins in the OSS. The Silent Monk of Covert Operations had been the sobriquet given him by his colleagues in the intelligence community. "In my days at the Agency," continued Abbott, chuckling, "the sources were often as not in conflict as in agreement."

"We have different methods of verification," pressed the associate director. "No disrespect, Mr. Abbott, but our transmissions equipment is literally instantaneous."

"That's equipment, not verification. But I won't argue; it seems we have a disagreement. Brussels or Zurich."

"The case for Brussels is airtight," insisted Knowlton firmly.

"Let's hear it," said the balding Gillette, adjusting his glasses. "We can return to the Zurich summary; it's right in front of us. Also, *our* sources have some input to offer, although it's not in conflict with Brussels or Zurich. It happened some six months ago."

The silver-haired Abbott glanced over at Gillette. "Six months ago? I don't recall NSC having delivered anything about Cain six months ago."

"It wasn't totally confirmed," replied Gillette. "We try not to burden the committee with unsubstantiated data."

"That's also quite a statement," said Abbott, not needing to clarify.

"Congressman Walters," interrupted the colonel, looking at the man from Oversight, "do you have any questions before we go on?"

"Hell, yes," drawled the congressional watchdog from the state of Tennessee, his intelligent eyes roaming the faces, "but since I'm new at this, you go ahead so I'll know where to begin."

"Very well, sir," said Manning, nodding at the CIA's Knowlton. "What's this about Brussels eleven days ago?"

"A man was killed in the Place Fontainas—a covert dealer in diamonds between Moscow and the West. He operated through a branch of Russolmaz, the Soviet firm in Geneva that brokers all such purchases. We know it's one way Cain converts his funds."

"What ties the killing to Cain?" asked the dubious Gillette.

"Method, first. The weapon was a long needle, implanted in a crowded square at noontime with surgical precision. Cain's used it before."

"That's quite true," agreed Abbott. "There was a Rumanian in London somewhat over a year ago; another only weeks before him. Both were narrowed to Cain."

"Narrowed but not confirmed," objected Colonel Manning. "They were high-level political defectors; they could have been taken by the KGB."

"Or by Cain with far less risk to the Soviets," argued the CIA man.

"*Or* by Carlos," added Gillette, his voice rising. "Neither Carlos nor Cain is concerned about ideology; they're both for hire. Why is it every time there's a killing of consequence, we ascribe it to Cain?"

"Whenever we do," replied Knowlton, his condescension obvious, "it's because informed sources unknown to each other have reported the same information. Since the informants have no knowledge of each other, there could hardly be collusion."

"It's all too pat," said Gillette disagreeably.

"Back to Brussels," interrupted the colonel. "If it was Cain, why would he kill a broker from Russolmaz? He used him."

"A covert broker," corrected the CIA director. "And for any number of reasons, according to our informants. The man was a thief, and why not? Most of his clients were too; they couldn't very well file charges. He might have cheated Cain, and if he did, it'd be his last transaction. Or he could have been foolish enough to speculate on Cain's identity; even a hint of that would call for the needle. Or perhaps Cain simply wanted to bury his current traces. Regardless, the circumstances plus the sources leave little doubt that it was Cain."

"There'll be a lot more when I clarify Zurich," said Manning. "May we proceed to the summary?"

"A moment, please." David Abbott spoke casually while lighting his pipe. "I believe our colleague from the Security Council mentioned the occurrence related to Cain that took place six months ago. Perhaps we should hear about it."

"Why?" asked Gillette, his eyes owl-like beyond the lenses of his rimless glasses. "The time factor removes it from having any bearing on Brussels *or* Zurich. I mentioned that, too."

"Yes, you did," agreed the once-formidable Monk of Covert Services. "I thought, however, any background might be helpful. As you also said, we can return to the summary; it's right in front of us. But if it's not relevant, let's get on with Zurich."

"Thank you, Mr. Abbott," said the colonel. "You'll note that eleven days ago, four men were killed in Zurich. One of them was a watchman in a parking area by the Limmat River; it can be presumed that he was not involved in Cain's activities, but caught in them. Two others were found in an alley on the west bank of the city, on the surface unrelated murders, except for the fourth victim. He's tied in with the dead men in the alley—all three part of the Zurich-Munich underworld—and is, without question, connected to Cain."

"That's Chernak," said Gillette, reading the summary. "At least I assume it's Chernak. I recognize the name and associate it with the Cain file somewhere."

"You should," replied Manning. "It first appeared in a G-Two report eighteen months ago and cropped up again a year later."

"Which would make it six months ago," interjected Abbott, softly, looking at Gillette.

"Yes, sir," continued the colonel. "If there was ever an example of what's called the scum-of-the-earth, it was Chernak. During the war he was a Czechoslovakian recruit at Dachau, a trilingual interrogator as brutal as any guard in the camp. He sent Poles, Slovaks and Jews to the showers after torture sessions in which he extracted—and manufactured—'incriminating' information Dachau's commandants wanted to hear. He went to any length to curry favor with his superiors, and the most sadistic cliques were hard pressed to match his exploits. What they didn't realize was that *he* was cataloguing *theirs*. After the war he escaped, got his legs blown off by an undetected land mine, and still managed to survive very nicely on his Dachau extortions. Cain found him and used him as a go-between for payments on his kills."

"Now just wait a minute!" objected Knowlton strenuously. "We've been over this Chernak business before. If you recall, it was the Agency that first uncovered him; we would have exposed him long ago if State hadn't interceded on behalf of several powerful anti-Soviet officials in the Bonn government. You assume Cain's used Chernak; you don't know it for certain any more than we do."

"We do now," said Manning. "Seven and a half months ago we received a tip about a man who ran a restaurant called the Drei Alpenhäuser; it was reported that he was an intermediary between Cain and Chernak. We kept him under surveillance for weeks, but nothing came of it; he was a minor figure in the Zurich underworld, that was all. We didn't stay with him long enough." The colonel paused, satisfied that all eyes were on him. "When we heard about Chernak's murder, we gambled. Five nights ago two of our men hid in the Drei Alpenhäuser after the restaurant closed. They cornered the owner and accused him of dealing with Chernak, working for Cain; they put on a hell of a show. You can imagine their shock when the man broke, literally fell to his knees begging to be protected. He admitted that Cain was in Zurich the night Chernak was killed; that, in fact, he had seen Cain that night and Chernak had come up in the conversation. Very negatively."

The military man paused again, the silence filled by a slow soft whistle from David Abbott, his pipe held in front of his crag-lined face. "Now, that *is* a statement," said the Monk quietly.

"Why wasn't the Agency informed of this tip you received seven months ago?" asked the CIA's Knowlton abrasively.

"It didn't prove out."

"In your hands; it might have been different in ours."

"That's possible. I admitted we didn't stay with him long enough. Manpower's limited; which of us can keep up a nonproductive surveillance indefinitely?"

"We might have shared it if we'd known."

"And we could have saved you the time it took to build the Brussels file, if we'd been told about that."

"Where did the tip come from?" asked Gillette, interrupting impatiently, his eyes on Manning.

"It was anonymous."

"You settled for that?" The birdlike expression on Gillette's face conveyed his astonishment.

"It's one reason the initial surveillance was limited."

"Yes, of course, but you mean you never dug for it?"

"Naturally we did," replied the colonel testily.

"Apparently without much enthusiasm," continued Gillette angrily. "Didn't it occur to you that someone over at Langley, or on the Council, might have helped, might have filled in a gap? I agree with Peter. We should have been informed."

"There's a reason why you weren't." Manning breathed deeply; in less military surroundings it might have been construed as a sigh. "The informant made it clear that if we brought in any other branch, he wouldn't make contact again. We felt we had to abide by that; we've done it before."

"What did you say?" Knowlton put down the page summary and stared at the Pentagon officer.

"It's nothing new, Peter. Each of us sets up his own sources, protects them."

"I'm aware of that. It's why you weren't told about Brussels. Both drones said to keep the army out."

Silence. Broken by the abrasive voice of the Security Council's Alfred Gillette. "How often is 'we've done it before,' Colonel?"

"What?" Manning looked at Gillette, but was aware that David Abbott was watching both of them closely.

"I'd like to know how many times you've been told to keep your sources to yourself. I refer to Cain, of course."

"Quite a few, I guess."

"You guess?"

"Most of the time."

"And you, Peter? What about the Agency?"

"We've been severely limited in terms of in-depth dissemination."

"For God's sake, what's *that* mean?" The interruption came from the least expected member of the conference; the congressman from Oversight. "Don't misunderstand me, I haven't begun yet. I just want to follow the language." He turned to the CIA man. "What the hell did you just say? In-depth *what?*"

"Dissemination, Congressman Walters; it's throughout Cain's file. We risked losing informants if we brought them to the attention of other intelligence units. I assure you, it's standard."

"It sounds like you were test-tubing a heifer."

"With about the same results," added Gillette. "No cross-pollinization to corrupt the strain. And, conversely, no cross-checking to look for patterns of inaccuracy."

"A nice turn of phrases," said Abbott, his craggy face wrinkled in appreciation, "but I'm not sure I understand you."

"I'd say it's pretty damned clear," replied the man from NSC, looking at Colonel Manning and Peter Knowlton. "The country's two most active intelligence branches have been fed information about Cain—for the past *three years*—and there's been no cross-pooling for origins of fraud. We've simply received all information as bona fide data, stored and accepted as valid."

"Well, I've been around a long time—perhaps too long, I concede—but there's nothing here I haven't heard before," said the Monk. "Sources are shrewd and defensive people; they guard their contacts jealously. None are in the business for charity, only for profit and survival."

"I'm afraid you're overlooking my point." Gillette removed his glasses. "I said before that I was alarmed so many recent assassinations have been attributed to Cain—attributed *here* to Cain—when it seems to me that the most accomplished assassin of our time—perhaps in history—has been relegated to a comparatively minor role. I think that's wrong. I think Carlos is the man we should be concentrating on. What's happened to *Carlos?*"

"I question your judgment, Alfred," said the Monk. "Carlos's time has passed, Cain's moved in. The old order changes; there's a new and, I suspect, far more deadly shark in the waters."

"I can't agree with that," said the man from National Security, his owl-eyes boring into the elder statesman of the intelligence community. "Forgive me, David, but it strikes me as if Carlos himself were manipulating this committee.

To take the attention away from himself, making us concentrate on a subject of much less importance. We're spending all our energies going after a toothless sand shark while the hammerhead roams free."

"No one's forgetting Carlos," objected Manning. "He's simply not as active as Cain's been."

"Perhaps," said Gillette icily, "that's exactly what Carlos wants us to believe. And, by God, we believe it."

"Can you doubt it?" asked Abbott. "The record of Cain's accomplishments is staggering."

"Can I doubt it?" repeated Gillette. "That's the question, isn't it? But can any of us be sure? That's also a valid question. We now find out that both the Pentagon and the Central Intelligence Agency have been literally operating independently of each other, without even conferring as to the accuracy of their sources."

"A custom rarely breached in this town," said Abbott, amused.

Again the congressman from Oversight interrupted. "What are you trying to say, Mr. Gillette?"

"I'd like more information about the activities of one Ilich Ramirez Sanchez. That's—"

"Carlos," said the congressman. "I remember my reading. I see. Thank you. Go on, gentlemen."

Manning spoke quickly. "May we get back to Zurich, please. Our recommendation is to go after Cain now. We can spread the word in the *Verbrecherwelt*, pull in every informer we have, request the cooperation of the Zurich police. We can't afford to lose another day. The man in Zurich *is* Cain."

"Then what was Brussels?" The CIA's Knowlton asked the question as much of himself as anyone at the table. "The method was Cain's, the informants unequivocal. What was the purpose?"

"To feed you false information, obviously," said Gillette. "And before we make any dramatic moves in Zurich, I suggest that each of you comb the Cain files and recheck every source given you. Have your European stations pull in every informant who so miraculously appeared to offer information. I have an idea you might find something you didn't expect: the fine Latin hand of Ramirez Sanchez."

"Since you're so insistent on clarification, Alfred," interrupted Abbott, "why not tell us about the unconfirmed occurrence that took place six months ago. We seem to be in a quagmire here; it might be helpful."

For the first time during the conference, the abrasive delegate from the National Security Council seemed to hesitate. "We received word around the middle of August from a reliable source in Aix-en-Provence that Cain was on his way to Marseilles."

"August?" exclaimed the colonel. "Marseilles? That was Leland! Ambassador Leland was shot in Marseilles. In August!"

"But Cain didn't fire that rifle. It was a Carlos kill; that *was* confirmed.

Bore-markings matched with previous assassinations, three descriptions of an unknown dark-haired man on the third and fourth floors of the waterfront warehouse, carrying a satchel. There was never any doubt that Leland was murdered by Carlos."

"For Christ's sake," roared the officer. "That's after the fact, after the kill! No matter whose, there was a contract out on Leland—hadn't that occurred to you? If we'd known about Cain, we might have been able to cover Leland. He was military property! Goddamn it, he might be alive today!"

"Unlikely," replied Gillette calmly. "Leland wasn't the sort of man to live in a bunker. And given his life-style, a vague warning would have served no purpose. Besides, had our strategy held together, warning Leland would have been counterproductive."

"In what way?" asked the Monk harshly.

"It's your fuller explanation. Our source was to make contact with Cain during the hours of midnight and three in the morning in the rue Sarrasin on August 23. Leland wasn't due until the twenty-fifth. As I say, had it held together we would have taken Cain. It didn't; Cain never showed up."

"And your *source* insisted on cooperating solely with *you,*" said Abbott. "To the exclusion of all others."

"Yes," nodded Gillette, trying but unable to conceal his embarrassment. "In our judgment, the risk to Leland had been eliminated—which in terms of Cain turned out to be the truth—and the odds for capture greater than they'd ever been. We'd finally found someone willing to come out and identify Cain. Would any of you have handled it any other way?"

Silence. This time broken by the drawl of the astute congressman from Tennessee.

"Jesus Christ Almighty . . . what a bunch of bullshitters."

Silence, terminated by the thoughtful voice of David Abbott.

"May I commend you, sir, on being the first honest man sent over from the Hill. The fact that you are not overwhelmed by the rarefied atmosphere of these highly classified surroundings is not lost on any of us. It's refreshing."

"I don't think the congressman fully grasps the sensitivity of—"

"Oh, shut up, Peter," said the Monk. "I think the congressman wants to say something."

"Just for a bit," said Walters. "I thought you were all over twenty-one; I mean, you *look* over twenty-one, and by then you're supposed to know better. You're supposed to be able to hold intelligent conversations, exchange information while respecting confidentiality, and look for common solutions. Instead, you sound like a bunch of kids jumping on a goddamn carousel, squabbling over who's going to get the cheap brass ring. It's a hell of a way to spend taxpayers' money."

"You're oversimplifying, Congressman," broke in Gillette. "You're talking about a utopian fact-finding apparatus. There's no such thing."

"I'm talking about reasonable men, sir. I'm a lawyer, and before I came up to this godforsaken circus, I dealt with ascending levels of confidentiality every day of my life. What's so damn new about them?"

"And what's your point?" asked the Monk.

"I want an explanation. For over eighteen months I've sat on the House Assassination Subcommittee. I've plowed through thousands of pages, filled with hundreds of names and twice as many theories. I don't think there's a suggested conspiracy or a suspected assassin I'm not aware of. I've lived with those names and those theories for damn near two years, until I didn't think there was anything left to learn."

"I'd say your credentials were very impressive," interrupted Abbott.

"I thought they might be; it's why I accepted the Oversight chair. I thought I could make a realistic contribution, but now I'm not so sure. I'm suddenly beginning to wonder what I *do* now."

"Why?" asked Manning apprehensively.

"Because I've been sitting here listening to the four of you describe an operation that's been going on for three years, involving networks of personnel and informants and major intelligence posts throughout Europe—all centered on an assassin whose 'list of accomplishments' is staggering. Am I substantively correct?"

"Go on," replied Abbott quietly, holding his pipe, his expression rapt. "What's your question?"

"Who is he? Who the hell is this Cain?"

16

The silence lasted precisely five seconds, during which time eyes roamed other eyes, several throats were cleared, and no one moved in his chair. It was as if a decision were being reached without discussion: evasion was to be avoided. Congressman Efrem Walters, out of the hills of Tennessee by way of the Yale Law Review, was not to be dismissed with facile circumlocution that dealt with the esoterica of clandestine manipulations. Bullshit was out.

David Abbott put his pipe down on the table, the quiet clatter his overture. "The less public exposure a man like Cain receives the better it is for everyone."

"That's no answer," said Walters. "But I assume it's the beginning of one."

"It is. He's a professional assassin—that is, a trained expert in wide-ranging methods of taking life. That expertise is for sale, neither politics nor personal motivation any concern to him whatsoever. He's in business solely to make a profit—and his profits escalate in direct ratio to his reputation."

The congressman nodded. "So by keeping as tight a lid as you can on that reputation you're holding back free advertising."

"Exactly. There are a lot of maniacs in this world with too many real or imagined enemies who might easily gravitate to Cain if they knew of him. Unfortunately, more than we care to think about already have; to date thirty-eight killings can be directly attributed to Cain, and some twelve to fifteen are probables."

"That's his list of 'accomplishments'?"

"Yes. And we're losing the battle. With each new killing his reputation spreads."

"He was dormant for a while," said Knowlton of the CIA. "For a number of months recently we thought he might have been taken himself. There were several probables in which the killers themselves were eliminated; we thought he might have been one of them."

"Such as?" asked Walters.

"A banker in Madrid who funneled bribes for the Europolitan Corporation for government purchases in Africa. He was shot from a speeding car on the Paseo de la Castellana. A chauffeur-bodyguard gunned down both driver and killer; for a time we believed the killer was Cain."

"I remember the incident. Who might have paid for it?"

"Any number of companies," answered Gillette, "who wanted to sell gold-plated cars and indoor plumbing to instant dictators."

"What else? Who else?"

"Sheik Mustafa Kalig in Oman," said Colonel Manning.

"He was reported killed in an abortive coup."

"Not so," continued the officer. "There was no attempted coup; G-Two informants confirmed that. Kalig was unpopular, but the other sheiks aren't fools. The coup story was a cover for an assassination that could tempt other professional killers. Three troublesome nonentities from the Officer Corps were executed to lend credence to the lie. For a while, we thought one of them was Cain; the timing corresponds to Cain's dormancy."

"Who would pay Cain for assassinating Kalig?"

"We asked ourselves that over and over again," said Manning. "The only possible answer came from a source who claimed to know, but there was no way to verify it. He said Cain did it to prove it could be done. By him. Oil sheiks travel with the tightest security in the world."

"There are several dozen other incidents," added Knowlton. "Probables that fall into the same pattern where highly protected figures were killed, and sources came forward to implicate Cain."

"I see." The congressman picked up the summary page for Zurich. "But from what I gather you don't know who he is."

"No two descriptions have been alike," interjected Abbott. "Cain's apparently a virtuoso at disguise."

"Yet people have seen him, talked to him. Your sources, the informants, this man in Zurich; none of them may come out in the open and testify, but surely you've interrogated them. You've got to have come up with a composite, with *something.*"

"We've come up with a great deal," replied Abbott, "but a consistent description isn't part of it. For openers, Cain never lets himself be seen in daylight. He holds meetings at night, in dark rooms or alleyways. If he's ever met more than one person at a time—as Cain—we don't know about it. We've been told he never stands, he's always seated—in a dimly lit restaurant, or a corner chair, or parked car. Sometimes he wears heavy glasses, sometimes none at all; at one rendezvous he may have dark hair, on another white or red or covered by a hat."

"Language?"

"We're closer here," said the CIA director, anxious to put the Company's research on the table. "Fluent English and French, and several Oriental dialects."

"Dialects? What dialects? Doesn't a language come first?"

"Of course. It's root-Vietnamese."

"Viet—" Walters leaned forward. "Why do I get the idea that I'm coming to something you'd rather not tell me?"

"Because you're probably quite astute at cross-examination, counselor." Abbott struck a match and lit his pipe.

"Passably alert," agreed the congressman. "Now, what is it?"

"Cain," said Gillette, his eyes briefly, oddly, on David Abbott. "We know where he came from."

"Where?"

"Out of Southeast Asia," answered Manning, as if sustaining the pain of a knife wound. "As far as we can gather, he mastered the fringe dialects so as to be understood in the hill country along the Cambodian and Laos border routes, as well as in rural North Vietnam. We accept the data; it fits."

"With what?"

"Operation Medusa." The colonel reached for a large, thick manila envelope on his left. He opened it and removed a single folder from among several inside; he placed it in front of him. "That's the Cain file," he said, nodding at the open envelope. "This is the Medusa material, the aspects of it that might in any way be relevant to Cain."

The Tennessean leaned back in his chair, the trace of a sardonic smile creasing his lips. "You know, gentlemen, you slay me with your pithy titles. Incidentally, that's a beaut; it's very sinister, very ominous. I think you fellows take a course in this kind of thing. Go on, Colonel. What's this Medusa?"

Manning glanced briefly at David Abbott, then spoke. "It was a clandestine outgrowth of the search-and-destroy concept, designed to function behind enemy lines during the Vietnam war. In the late sixties and early seventies, units of American, French, British, Australian and native volunteers were formed into teams to operate in territories occupied by the North Vietnamese. Their priorities were the disruption of enemy communications and supply lines, the pinpointing of prison camps and, not the least, the assassination of village leaders known to be cooperating with the Communists, as well as the enemy commanders whenever possible."

"It was a war-within-a-war," broke in Knowlton. "Unfortunately, racial appearances and languages made participation infinitely more dangerous than, say, the German and Dutch undergrounds, or the French Resistance in World War Two. Therefore, Occidental recruitment was not always as selective as it might have been."

"There were dozens of these teams," continued the colonel, "the personnel ranging from old-line navy chiefs who knew the coastlines to French plantation owners whose only hope for reparations lay in an American victory. There were British and Australian drifters who'd lived in Indochina for years, as well as highly motivated American army and civilian intelligence career officers. Also, inevitably, there was a sizable faction of hard-core criminals. In the main, smugglers— men who dealt in running guns, narcotics, gold and diamonds throughout the entire South China Sea area. They were walking encyclopedias when it came to night landings and jungle routes. Many we employed were runaways or fugitives from the States, a number well-educated, all resourceful. We needed their expertise."

"That's quite a cross-section of volunteers," interrupted the congressman. "Old-line navy and army; British and Australian drifters, French colonials, and platoons of thieves. How the hell did you get them to work together?"

"To each according to his greeds," said Gillette.

"Promises," amplified the colonel. "Guarantees of rank, promotions, pardons, outright bonuses of cash, and, in a number of cases, opportunities to steal funds from the operation itself. You see, they all had to be a little crazy; we understood that. We trained them secretly, using codes, methods of transport, entrapment and killing—even weapons Command Saigon knew nothing about. As Peter mentioned, the risks were incredible—capture resulting in torture and execution; the price was high and they paid it. Most people would have called them a collection of paranoiacs, but they were geniuses where disruption and assassination were concerned. Especially assassination."

"What was the price?"

"Operation Medusa sustained over ninety percent casualties. But there's a catch—among those who didn't come back were a number who never meant to."

"From that faction of thieves and fugitives?"

"Yes. Some stole considerable amounts of money from Medusa. We think Cain is one of those men."

"Why?"

"His *modus operandi*. He's used codes, traps, methods of killing and transport that were developed and specialized in the Medusa training."

"Then for Christ's sake," broke in Walters, "you've got a direct line to his identity. I don't care where they're buried—and I'm damn sure you don't want them made public—but I assume records were kept."

"They were, and we've extracted them all from the clandestine archives, inclusive of this material here." The officer tapped the file in front of him. "We've studied everything, put rosters under microscopes, fed facts into computers—everything we could think of. We're no further along than when we began."

"That's incredible," said the congressman. "Or incredibly incompetent."

"Not really," protested Manning. "Look at the man; look at what we've had to work with. After the war, Cain made his reputation throughout most of East Asia, from as far north as Tokyo down through the Philippines, Malaysia and Singapore, with side trips to Hong Kong, Cambodia, Laos and Calcutta. About two and a half years ago reports began filtering in to our Asian stations and embassies. There was an assassin for hire; his name was Cain. Highly professional, ruthless. These reports started growing with alarming frequency. It seemed that with every killing of note, Cain was involved. Sources would phone embassies in the middle of the night, or stop attachés in the streets, always with the same information. It was Cain, Cain was the one. A murder in Tokyo; a car blown up in Hong Kong; a narcotics caravan ambushed in the Triangle; a banker shot in Calcutta; an ambassador assassinated in Moulmein; a Russian technician or an American businessman killed in the streets of Shanghai itself. Cain was everywhere, his name whispered by dozens of trusted informants in every vital intelligence sector. Yet no one—not one single person in the entire east Pacific area—would come forward to give us an identification. Where were we to begin?"

"But by this time hadn't you established the fact that he'd been with Medusa?" asked the Tennessean.

"Yes. Firmly."

"Then with the individual Medusa dossiers, damn it!"

The colonel opened the folder he had removed from the Cain file. "These are the casualty lists. Among the white Occidentals who disappeared from Operation Medusa—and when I say disappeared, I mean vanished without a trace—are the following. Seventy-three Americans, forty-six French, thirty-nine and twenty-four Australians and British respectively, and an estimated fifty white male contacts recruited from neutrals in Hanoi and trained in the field—most of *them* we never knew. Over two hundred and thirty possibilities; how many are blind alleys? Who's alive? Who's dead? Even if we learned the name of every man who actually survived, who is he now? What is he? We're not even sure of Cain's nationality. We think he's American, but there's no proof."

"Cain's one of the side issues contained in our constant pressure on Hanoi to trace MIAs," explained Knowlton. "We keep recycling these names in with the division lists."

"And there's a catch with that, too," added the army officer. "Hanoi's counterintelligence forces broke and executed scores of Medusa personnel. They were aware of the operation, and we never ruled out the possibility of infiltration.

Hanoi knew the Medusans weren't combat troops; they wore no uniforms. Accountability was never required."

Walters held out his hand. "May I?" he said, nodding at the stapled pages.

"Certainly." The officer gave them to the congressman. "You understand of course that those names still remain classified, as does the Medusa Operation itself."

"Who made that decision?"

"It's an unbroken executive order from successive presidents based on the recommendation of the Joint Chiefs of Staff. It was supported by the Senate Armed Services Committee."

"That's considerable firepower, isn't it?"

"It was felt to be in the national interest," said the CIA man.

"In this case, I won't argue," agreed Walters. "The specter of such an operation wouldn't do much for the glory of Old Glory. We don't train assassins, much less field them." He flipped through the pages. "And somewhere here just happens to be an assassin we trained and fielded and now can't find."

"We believe that, yes," said the colonel.

"You say he made his reputation in Asia, but moved to Europe. When?"

"About a year ago."

"Why? Any ideas?"

"The obvious, I'd suggest," said Peter Knowlton. "He overextended himself. Something went wrong and he felt threatened. He was a white killer among Orientals, at best a dangerous concept; it was time for him to move on. God knows his reputation *was* made; there'd be no lack of employment in Europe."

David Abbott cleared his throat. "I'd like to offer another possibility based on something Alfred said a few minutes ago." The Monk paused and nodded deferentially at Gillette. "He said that we had been forced to concentrate on a 'toothless sand shark while the hammerhead roamed free,' I believe that was the phrase, although my sequence may be wrong."

"Yes," said the man from NSC. "I was referring to Carlos, of course. It's not Cain we should be after. It's Carlos."

"Of course. Carlos. The most elusive killer in modern history, a man many of us truly believe has been responsible—in one way or another—for the most tragic assassinations of our time. You were quite right, Alfred, and, in a way, I was wrong. We cannot afford to forget Carlos."

"Thank you," said Gillette. "I'm glad I made my point."

"You did. With me, at any rate. But you also made me think. Can you imagine the temptation for a man like Cain, operating in the steamy confines of an area rife with drifters and fugitives and regimes up to their necks in corruption? How he must have envied Carlos; how he must have been jealous of the faster, brighter, more luxurious world of Europe. How often did he say to himself, 'I'm better than Carlos.' No matter how cold these fellows are, their egos are immense. I suggest he went to Europe to find that better world . . . and to dethrone Carlos. The pretender, sir, wants to take the title. He wants to be champion."

Gillette stared at the Monk. "It's an interesting theory."

"And if I follow you," interjected the congressman from Oversight, "by tracking Cain we may come up with Carlos."

"Exactly."

"I'm not sure *I* follow," said the CIA director, annoyed. "Why?"

"Two stallions in a paddock," answered Walters. "They tangle."

"A champion does not give up the title willingly." Abbott reached for his pipe. "He fights viciously to retain it. As the congressman says, we continue to track Cain, but we must also watch for other spoors in the forest. And when and if we find Cain, perhaps we should hold back. Wait for Carlos to come after him."

"Then take both," added the military officer.

"Very enlightening," said Gillette.

The meeting was over, the members in various stages of leaving. David Abbott stood with the Pentagon colonel, who was gathering together the pages of the Medusa folder; he had picked up the casualty sheets, prepared to insert them.

"May I take a look?" asked Abbott. "We don't have a copy over at Forty."

"Those were our instructions," replied the officer, handing the stapled pages to the older man. "I thought they came from you. Only three copies. Here, at the Agency, and over at the Council."

"They did come from me." The silent Monk smiled benignly. "Too damn many civilians in my part of town."

The colonel turned away to answer a question posed by the congressman from Tennessee. David Abbott did not listen; instead his eyes sped rapidly down the columns of names; he was alarmed. A number had been crossed out, accounted for. Accountability was the one thing they could not allow. Ever. Where *was* it? He was the only man in that room who knew the name, and he could feel the pounding in his chest as he reached the last page. The name was there.

Bourne, Jason C.—Last known station: Tam Quan. What in God's name *had happened?*

René Bergeron slammed down the telephone on his desk; his voice only slightly more controlled than his gesture. "We've tried every café, every restaurant and bistro she's ever frequented!"

"There's not a hotel in Paris that has him registered," said the gray-haired switchboard operator, seated at a second telephone by a drafting board. "It's been more than two hours now; she could be dead. If she's not, she might well wish she were."

"She can only tell him so much," mused Bergeron. "Less than we could; she knows nothing of the old men."

"She knows enough; she's called Parc Monceau."

"She's relayed messages; she's not certain to whom."

"She knows why."

"So does Cain, I can assure you. And he would make a grotesque error with

Parc Monceau." The designer leaned forward, his powerful forearms tensing as he locked his hands together, his eyes on the gray-haired man. "Tell me, again, everything you remember. Why are you so sure he's Bourne?"

"I don't know that. I said he was Cain. If you've described his methods accurately, he's the man."

"Bourne *is* Cain. We found him through the Medusa records. It's why you were hired."

"Then he's Bourne, but it's not the name he used. Of course, there were a number of men in Medusa who would not permit their real names to be used. For them, false identities were guaranteed; they had criminal records. He would be one of those men."

"Why him? Others disappeared. You disappeared."

"I could say because he was here in Saint-Honoré and that should be enough. But there's more, much more. I watched him function. I was assigned to a mission he commanded; it was not an experience to be forgotten, nor was he. That man could be—*would* be—your Cain."

"Tell me."

"We parachuted at night into a sector called Tam Quan, our objective to bring out an American named Webb who was being held by the Viet Cong. We didn't know it, but the odds against survival were monumental. Even the flight from Saigon was horrendous; gale-force winds at a thousand feet, the aircraft vibrating as if it would fall apart. Still, he ordered us to jump."

"And you did?"

"His gun was pointed at our heads. At each of us as we approached the hatchway. We might survive the elements, not a bullet in our skulls."

"How many were there of you?"

"Ten."

"You could have taken him."

"You didn't know him."

"Go on," said Bergeron, concentrating; immobile at the desk.

"Eight of us regrouped on the ground; two, we assumed, had not survived the jump. It was amazing that I did. I was the oldest and hardly a bull, but I knew the area; it was why I was sent." The gray-haired man paused, shaking his head at the memory. "Less than an hour later we realized it was a trap. We were running like lizards through the jungle. And during the nights he went out alone through the mortar explosions and the grenades. To kill. Always coming back before dawn to force us closer and closer to the base camp. I thought at the time, sheer suicide."

"Why did you do it? He had to give you a reason; you were Medusans, not soldiers."

"He said it was the only way to get out alive, and there was logic to that. We were far behind the lines; we needed the supplies we could find at the base camp—if we could take it. He said we had to take it; we had no choice. If any argued, he'd put a bullet in his head—we knew it. On the third night we took the camp and found the man named Webb more dead than alive, but breathing. We also found the two missing members of our team, very much alive and stunned at what had happened. A white man and a Vietnamese; they'd been paid by the Cong to trap us—trap him, I suspect."

"Cain?"

"Yes. The Vietnamese saw us first and escaped. Cain shot the white man in the head. I understand he just walked up to him and blew his head off."

"He got you back? Through the lines?"

"Four of us, yes, and the man named Webb. Five men were killed. It was during that terrible journey back that I thought I understood why the rumors might be true—that he was the highest-paid recruit in Medusa."

"In what sense?"

"He was the coldest man I ever saw, the most dangerous, and utterly unpredictable. I thought at the time it was a strange war for him; he was a Savonarola, but without religious principle, only his own odd morality which was centered about himself. All men were his enemies—the leaders in particular—and he cared not one whit for either side." The middle-aged man paused again, his eyes on the drafting board, his mind obviously thousands of miles away and back in time. "Remember, Medusa was filled with diverse and desperate men. Many were paranoid in their hatred of Communists. Kill a Communist and Christ smiled— odd examples of Christian teaching. Others—such as myself—had fortunes stolen from us by the Viet Minh; the only path to restitution was if the Americans won the war. France had abandoned us at Dien Bien Phu. But there were dozens who saw that fortunes could be made from Medusa. Pouches often contained fifty to seventy-five thousand American dollars. A courier siphoning off half during ten, fifteen runs, could retire in Singapore or Kuala Lumpur or set up his own narcotics network in the Triangle. Beyond the exorbitant pay—and frequently the pardoning of past crimes—the opportunities were unlimited. It was in this group that I placed that very strange man. He was a modern-day pirate in the purest sense."

Bergeron unlocked his hands. "Wait a minute. You used the phrase, 'a mission he commanded.' There were military men in Medusa; are you sure he wasn't an American officer?"

"American, to be sure, but certainly not army."

"Why?"

"He hated all aspects of the military. His scorn for Command Saigon was in every decision he made; he considered the army fools and incompetents. At one point orders were radioed to us in Tam Quan. He broke off the transmission and told a regimental general to have sex with himself—he would not obey. An army officer would hardly do that."

"Unless he was about to abandon his profession," said the designer. "As Paris abandoned you, and you did the best you could, stealing from Medusa, setting up your own hardly patriotic activities—wherever you could."

"My country betrayed me before I betrayed her, René."

"Back to Cain. You say Bourne was not the name he used. What was it?"

"I don't recall. As I said, for many, surnames were not relevant. He was simply 'Delta' to me."

"Mekong?"

"No, the alphabet, I think."

" 'Alpha, Bravo, Charlie . . . Delta,' " said Bergeron pensively in English. "But in many operations the code word 'Charlie' was replaced by 'Cain,' because 'Charlie' had become synonymous with the Cong. 'Charlie' became 'Cain.' "

"Quite true. So Bourne dropped back a letter and assumed 'Cain.' He could have chosen 'Echo' or 'Foxtrot' or 'Zulu.' Twenty-odd others. What's the difference? What's your point?"

"He chose Cain deliberately. It was symbolic. He wanted it clear from the beginning."

"Wanted what clear?"

"That Cain would replace Carlos. *Think.* 'Carlos' is Spanish for Charles—Charlie. The code word 'Cain' was substituted for 'Charlie'—Carlos. It was his intention from the start. Cain would replace Carlos. And he wanted Carlos to know it."

"*Does* Carlos?"

"Of course. Word goes out in Amsterdam and Berlin, Geneva and Lisbon, London and right here in Paris. Cain is available; contracts can be made, his price lower than Carlos's fee. He erodes! He constantly erodes Carlos's stature."

"Two matadors in the same ring. There can only be one."

"It will be Carlos. We've trapped the puffed-up sparrow. He's somewhere within two hours of Saint-Honoré."

"But where?"

"No matter. We'll find him. After all, he found us. He'll come back; his ego will demand it. And then the eagle will sweep down and catch the sparrow. Carlos will kill him."

The old man adjusted his single crutch under his left arm, parted the black drape and stepped into the confessional booth. He was not well; the pallor of death was on his face, and he was glad the figure in the priest's habit beyond the transparent curtain could not see him clearly. The assassin might not give him further work if he looked too worn to carry it out; he needed work now. There were only weeks remaining and he had responsibilities. He spoke.

"Angelus Domini."

"Angelus Domini, child of God," came the whisper. "Are your days comfortable?"

"They draw to an end, but they are made comfortable."

"Yes. I think this will be your last job for me. It is of such importance, however, that your fee will be five times the usual. I hope it will be of help to you."

"Thank you, Carlos. You know, then."

"I know. This is what you must do for it, and the information must leave this world with you. There can be no room for error."

"I have always been accurate. I will go to my death being accurate now."

"Die in peace, old friend. It's easier. . . . You will go to the Vietnamese Embassy and ask for an attaché named Phan Loc. When you are alone, say the following words to him: 'Late March 1968 Medusa, the Tam Quan sector. Cain was there. Another also.' Have you got that?"

" 'Late March 1968 Medusa, the Tam Quan sector. Cain was there. Another also.' "

"He'll tell you when to return. It will be in a matter of hours."

17

"I think it's time we talked about a *fiche confidentielle* out of Zurich."

"My God!"

"I'm not the man you're looking for."

Bourne gripped the woman's hand, holding her in place, preventing her from running into the aisles of the crowded, elegant restaurant in Argenteuil, a few miles outside of Paris. The pavane was over, the gavotte finished. They were alone; the velvet booth a cage.

"Who *are* you?" The Lavier woman grimaced, trying to pull her hand away, the veins in the cosmeticized neck pronounced.

"A rich American who lives in the Bahamas. Don't you believe that?"

"I should have known," she said, "no charges, no check—only cash. You didn't even look at the bill."

"Or the prices before that. It's what brought you over to me."

"I was a fool. The rich always look at prices, if only for the pleasure of dismissing them." Lavier spoke while glancing around, looking for a space in the aisles, a waiter she might summon. Escape.

"Don't," said Jason, watching her eyes. "It'd be foolish. We'd both be better off if we talked."

The woman stared at him, the bridge of hostile silence accentuated by the hum of the large, dimly lit, candelabraed room and the intermittent eruptions of quiet laughter from the nearby tables. "I ask you again," she said. "Who are you?"

"My name isn't important. Settle for the one I gave you."

"Briggs? It's false."

"So's Larousse, and that's on the lease of a rented car that picked up three killers at the Valois Bank. They missed there. They also missed this afternoon at the Pont Neuf. He got away."

"Oh, God!" she cried, trying to break away.

"I said *don't!*" Bourne held her firmly, pulling her back.

"If I scream, monsieur?" The powdered mask was cracked with lines of venom now, the bright red lipstick defining the snarl of an aging, cornered rodent.

"I'll scream louder," replied Jason. "We'd both be thrown out, and once outside I don't think you'll be unmanageable. Why not talk? We might learn something from each other. After all, we're employees, not employers."

"I have nothing to say to you."

"Then I'll start. Maybe you'll change your mind." He lessened his grip cautiously. The tension remained on her white, powdered face, but it, too, was lessened as the pressure of his fingers was reduced. She was ready to listen. "You paid a price in Zurich. We paid, too. Obviously more than you did. We're after the same man; we know why *we* want him." He released her. "Why do you?"

She did not speak for nearly half a minute, instead, studying him in silence, her eyes angry yet frightened. Bourne knew he had phrased the question accurately; for Jacqueline Lavier not to talk to him would be a dangerous mistake. It could cost her her life if subsequent questions were raised.

"Who is 'we?' " she asked.

"A company that wants its money. A great deal of money. He has it."

"He did not earn it, then?"

Jason knew he had to be careful; he was expected to know far more than he did. "Let's say there's a dispute."

"How could there be? Either he did or he did not, there's hardly a middle ground."

"It's my turn," said Bourne. "You answered a question with a question and I didn't avoid you. Now, let's go back. Why do you want him? Why is the private telephone of one of the better shops in Saint-Honoré put on a *fiche* in Zurich?"

"It was an accommodation, monsieur."

"For whom?"

"Are you mad?"

"All right, I'll pass on that for now. We think we know anyway."

"Impossible!"

"Maybe, maybe not. So it was an accommodation . . . to kill a man?"

"I have nothing to say."

"Yet a minute ago when I mentioned the car, you tried to run. That's saying something."

"A perfectly natural reaction." Jacqueline Lavier touched the stem of her wineglass. "I arranged for the rental. I don't mind telling you that because there's no evidence that I did so. Beyond that I know nothing of what happened." Suddenly she gripped the glass, her mask of a face a mixture of controlled fury and fear. "Who *are* you people?"

"I told you. A company that wants its money back."

"You're interfering! Get out of Paris! Leave this alone!"

"Why should we? We're the injured party; we want the balance sheet corrected. We're entitled to that."

"You're entitled to nothing!" spat Mme. Lavier. "The error was yours and you'll pay for it!"

"Error?" He had to be *very* careful. It was here—right below the hard surface—the eyes of the truth could be seen beneath the ice. "Come off it. Theft isn't an error committed by the victim."

"The error was in your *choice,* monsieur. You chose the wrong man."

"He stole millions from Zurich," said Jason. "But you know that. He took millions, and if you think you're going to take them from him—which is the same as taking them from us—you're very much mistaken."

"We want no money!"

"I'm glad to know it. Who's 'we?' "

"I thought you said you knew."

"I said we had an idea. Enough to expose a man named Koenig in Zurich; d'Amacourt here in Paris. If we decide to do that, it could prove to be a major embarrassment, couldn't it?"

"Money? Embarrassment? These are *not issues.* You are consumed with stupidity, all of you! I'll say it again. Get out of Paris. Leave this alone. It is not your concern any longer."

"We don't think it's yours. Frankly, we don't think you're competent."

"*Competent?*" repeated Lavier, as if she did not believe what she had heard. "That's right."

"Have you any idea what you're *saying?* Whom you're *talking* about?"

"It doesn't matter. Unless you back off, my recommendation is that we come out loud and clear. Mock up charges—not traceable to us, of course. Expose Zurich, the Valois. Call in the Sûreté, Interpol . . . anyone and anything to create a manhunt—a massive manhunt."

"You *are* mad. And a fool."

"Not at all. We have friends in very important positions; we'll get the information first. We'll be waiting at the right place at the right time. We'll take him."

"You *won't* take him. He'll disappear again! Can't you *see* that? He's in Paris and a network of people he cannot know are looking for him. He may have escaped once, twice; but not a third time! He's trapped now. We've trapped him!"

"We don't want you to trap him. That's not in our interests." It was almost the moment, thought Bourne. Almost, but not quite; her fear had to match her anger. She had to be detonated into revealing the truth. "Here's our ultimatum, and we're holding you responsible for conveying it—otherwise you'll join Koenig and d'Amacourt. Call off your hunt tonight. If you don't we'll move first thing in the morning; we'll start shouting. Les Classiques'll be the most popular store in Saint-Honoré, but I don't think it'll be the right people."

The powdered face cracked. "You wouldn't dare! How dare you? Who are you to say this?!"

He paused, then struck. "A group of people who don't care much for your Carlos."

The Lavier woman froze, her eyes wide, stretching the taut skin into scar tissue. "You *do* know," she whispered. "And you think you can oppose him? You think you're a match for Carlos?"

"In a word, yes."

"You're *insane*. You don't give ultimatums to Carlos."

"I just did."

"Then you're dead. You raise your voice to *anyone* and you won't last the day. He has men everywhere; they'll cut you down in the street."

"They might if they knew whom to cut down," said Jason. "You forget. No one does. But they know who you are. And Koenig, and d'Amacourt. The minute we expose you, you'd be eliminated. Carlos couldn't afford you any longer. But no one knows me."

"You forget, monsieur. I do."

"The least of my worries. Find me . . . after the damage is done and before the decision is made regarding your own future. It won't be long."

"This is madness. You come out of nowhere and talk like a madman. You cannot do this!"

"Are you suggesting a compromise?"

"It's conceivable," said Jacqueline Lavier. "Anything is possible."

"Are you in a position to negotiate it?"

"I'm in a position to convey it . . . far better than I can an ultimatum. Others will relay it to the one who decides."

"What you're saying is what I said a few minutes ago: we can talk."

"We can talk, monsieur," agreed Mme. Lavier, her eyes fighting for her life.

"Then let's start with the obvious."

"Which is?"

Now. The truth.

"What's Bourne to Carlos? Why does he want him?"

"What's *Bourne*—" The woman stopped, venom and fear replaced by an expression of absolute shock. "*You* can ask *that?*"

"I'll ask it again," said Jason, hearing the pounding echoes in his chest. "What's Bourne to Carlos?"

"He's Cain! You know it as well as we do. He was your error, your choice! You chose the wrong man!"

Cain. He heard the name and the echoes erupted into cracks of deafening thunder. And with each crack, pain jolted him, bolts searing one after another through his head, his mind and body recoiling under the onslaught of the name. Cain. Cain. The mists were there again. The darkness, the wind, the explosions.

Alpha, Bravo, Cain, Delta, Echo, Foxtrot. . . . Cain, Delta. Delta, Cain. Delta . . . Cain.

Cain is for *Charlie.*

Delta is for *Cain!*

"What is it? What's wrong with you?"

"Nothing." Bourne had slipped his right hand over his left wrist, gripping it, his fingers pressed into his flesh with such pressure he thought his skin might break. He had to do *something;* he had to stop the trembling, lessen the noise, repulse the pain. He had to *clear his mind.* The eyes of the truth were staring at him; he could not look away. He was there, he was home, and the cold made him shiver. "Go on," he said, imposing a control on his voice that resulted in a whisper; he could not help himself.

"Are you ill? You're very pale and you're—"

"I'm fine," he interrupted curtly. "I said, go *on.*"

"What's there to tell you?"

"Say it all. I want to hear it from you."

"Why? There's nothing you don't know. You chose Cain. You dismissed Carlos; you think you can dismiss him now. You were wrong then and you are wrong now."

I will kill you. I will grab your throat and choke the breath out of you. Tell me! For Christ's sake, tell me! At the end, there is only my beginning! I must know it.

"That doesn't matter," he said. "If you are looking for a compromise—if only to save your life—tell me why we should listen. Why is Carlos so adamant . . . so paranoid . . . about Bourne? Explain it to me as if I hadn't heard it before. If you don't, those names that shouldn't be mentioned will be spread all over Paris, and you'll be dead by the afternoon."

Lavier was rigid, her alabaster mask set. "Carlos will follow Cain to the ends of the earth and kill him."

"We know that. We want to know why."

"He has to. Look to yourself. To people like you."

"That's meaningless. You don't know who we are."

"I don't have to. I know what you've done."

"Spell it out!"

"I did. You picked Cain over Carlos—that was your error. You chose the wrong man. You paid the wrong assassin."

"The wrong . . . assassin."

"You were not the first, but you will be the last. The arrogant pretender will be killed here in Paris, whether there is a compromise or not."

"We picked the wrong assassin . . ." The words floated in the elegant, perfumed air of the restaurant. The deafening thunder receded, angry still but far away in the storm clouds; the mists were clearing, circles of vapor swirling around him. He began to see, and what he saw was the outlines of a monster. Not a myth, but a monster. Another monster. There were two.

"Can you doubt it?" asked the woman. "Don't interfere with Carlos. Let him take Cain; let him have his revenge." She paused, both hands slightly off the table; Mother Rat. "I promise nothing, but I *will* speak for you, for the loss your people have sustained. It's possible . . . only possible, you understand . . . that your contract might be honored by the one you should have chosen in the first place."

"The one we should have chosen. . . . Because we chose the wrong one."

"You see that, do you not, monsieur? Carlos should be *told* that you see it. Perhaps . . . only perhaps . . . he might have sympathy for your losses if he were convinced you saw your error."

"That's your compromise?" said Bourne flatly, struggling to find a line of thought.

"Anything is possible. No good can come from your threats, I can tell you that. For any of us, and I'm frank enough to include myself. There would be only pointless killing; and Cain would stand back laughing. You would lose not once, but twice."

"If that's true . . ." Jason swallowed, nearly choking as dry air filled the vacuum in his dry throat, "then I'll have to explain to my people why we . . . chose . . . the . . . wrong man." *Stop it! Finish the statement. Control yourself.* "Tell me everything you know about Cain."

"To what purpose?" Lavier put her fingers on the table, her bright red nail polish ten points of a weapon.

"If we chose the wrong man, then we had the wrong information."

"You heard he was the equal of Carlos, no? That his fees were more reasonable, his apparatus more contained, and because fewer intermediaries were involved there was no possibility of a contract being traced. Is this not so?"

"Maybe."

"Of course it's so. It's what everyone's been told and it's all a lie. Carlos's strength is in his far-reaching sources of information—*infallible* information. In his elaborate system of reaching the right person at precisely the right moment prior to a kill."

"Sounds like too many people. There were too many people in Zurich, too many here in Paris."

"All blind, monsieur. Every one."

"Blind?"

"To put it plainly, I've been part of the operation for a number of years, meeting in one way or another dozens who have played their minor roles—none is major. I have yet to meet a single person who has ever spoken to Carlos, much less has any idea who he is."

"That's Carlos. I want to know about Cain. What *you* know about Cain." *Stay controlled. You cannot turn away. Look at her. Look at her!*

"Where shall I begin?"

"With whatever comes to mind first. Where did he come from?" *Do not look away!*

"Southeast Asia, of course."

"Of course . . ." *Oh, God.*

"From the American Medusa, we know that . . ."

Medusa! The winds, the darkness, the flashes of light, the pain. . . . The pain ripped through his skull now; he was not where he was, but where he had been. A world away in distance and time. The pain. Oh, Jesus. The pain . . .

Tao!

Che-sah!
Tam Quan!
Alpha, Bravo, Cain . . . Delta.
Delta . . . Cain!
Cain is for Charlie.
Delta is for Cain.

"What is it?" The woman looked frightened; she was studying his face, her eyes roving, boring into his. "You're perspiring. Your hands are shaking. Are you having an attack?"

"It passes quickly." Jason pried his hand away from his wrist and reached for a napkin to wipe his forehead.

"It comes with the pressures, no?"

"With the pressures, yes. Go on. There isn't much time; people have to be reached, decisions made. Your life is probably one of them. Back to Cain. You say he came from the American . . . Medusa."

"*Les mercenaires du diable,*" said Lavier. "It was the nickname given Medusa by the Indochina colonials—what was left of them. Quite appropriate, don't you think?"

"It doesn't make any difference what I think. Or what I know. I want to hear what *you* think, what *you* know about Cain."

"Your attack makes you rude."

"My impatience makes me impatient. You say we chose the wrong man; if we did we had the wrong information. *Les mercenaires du diable.* Are you implying that Cain is French?"

"Not at all, you test me poorly. I mentioned that only to indicate how deeply we penetrated Medusa."

"'We' being the people who work for Carlos."

"You could say that."

"I will say that. If Cain's not French, what is he?"

"Undoubtedly American."

Oh, God! "Why?"

"Everything he does has the ring of American audacity. He pushes and shoves with little or no finesse, taking credit where none is his, claiming kills when he had nothing to do with them. He has studied Carlos's methods and connections like no other man alive. We're told he recites them with total recall to potential clients, more often than not putting himself in Carlos's place, convincing fools that it was *he,* not Carlos, who accepted and fulfilled the contracts." Lavier paused. "I've struck a chord, no? He did the same with you—your people—yes?"

"Perhaps." Jason reached for his own wrist again, as the statements came back to him. Statements made in response to clues in a dreadful game.

Stuttgart. Regensburg. Munich. Two kills and a kidnapping, Baader accreditation. Fees from U. S. sources. . . .

Teheran? Eight kills. Divided accreditation—Khomeini and PLO. Fee, two million. Southwest Soviet sector.

Paris? . . . All contracts will be processed through Paris.
Whose contracts?
Sanchez . . . Carlos.

". . . always such a transparent device."

The Lavier woman had spoken; he had not heard her. "What did you say?"

"You were remembering, yes? He used the same device with you—your people. It's how he gets his assignments."

"Assignments?" Bourne tensed the muscles in his stomach until the pain brought him back to the table in the candelabraed dining room in Argenteuil. "He gets assignments, then," he said pointlessly.

"And carries them out with considerable expertise; no one denies him that. His record of kills is impressive. In many ways, he is second to Carlos—not his equal, but far above the ranks of *les guérilleros.* He's a man of immense skill, extremely inventive, a trained lethal weapon out of Medusa. But it is his arrogance, his lies at the expense of Carlos that will bring him down."

"And that makes him American? Or is it your bias? I have an idea you like American money, but that's about all they export that you do like." *Immense skill; extremely inventive; a trained lethal weapon. . . . Port Noir, La Ciotat, Marseilles, Zurich, Paris.*

"It is beyond prejudice, monsieur. The identification is positive."

"How did you get it?"

Lavier touched the stem of her wineglass, her red-tipped index finger curling around it. "A discontented man was bought in Washington."

"Washington?"

"The Americans also look for Cain—with an intensity approaching Carlos's, I suspect. Medusa has never been made public, and Cain might prove to be an extraordinary embarrassment. This discontented man was in a position to give us a great deal of information, including the Medusa records. It was a simple matter to match the names with those in Zurich. Simple for Carlos, not for anyone else."

Too simple, thought Jason, not knowing why the thought struck him. "I see," he said.

"And you? How did you find him? Not Cain, of course, but Bourne."

Through the mists of anxiety, Jason recalled another statement. Not his, but one spoken by Marie. "Far simpler," he said. "We paid the money to him by means of a shortfall deposit into one account, the surplus diverted blindly into another. The numbers could be traced; it's a tax device."

"Cain permitted it?"

"He didn't know it. The numbers were paid for . . . as you paid for different numbers—telephone numbers—on a *fiche.*"

"I commend you."

"It's not required, but everything you know about Cain is. All you've done so far is explain an identification. Now, go on. Everything you know about this man Bourne, everything you've been told." *Be careful. Take the tension from your voice. You are merely . . . evaluating data. Marie, you said that. Dear, dear Marie. Thank God you're not here.*

"What we know about him is incomplete. He's managed to remove most of the vital records, a lesson he undoubtedly learned from Carlos. But not all; we've pieced together a sketch. Before he was recruited into Medusa, he supposedly was a French-speaking businessman living in Singapore, representing a collective of American importers from New York to California. The truth is he had been dismissed by the collective, which then tried to have him extradited back to the States for prosecution; he had stolen hundreds of thousands from it. He was known in Singapore as a reclusive figure, very powerful in contraband operations, and extraordinarily ruthless."

"Before that," interrupted Jason, feeling again the perspiration breaking out on his hairline. "Before Singapore. Where did he *come* from?" *Be careful! The images! He could see the streets of Singapore. Prince Edward Road, Kim Chuan, Boon Tat Street, Maxwell, Cuscaden.*

"Those are the records no one can find. There are only rumors, and they are meaningless. For example, it was said that he was a defrocked Jesuit, gone mad; another speculation was that he had been a young, aggressive investment banker caught embezzling funds in concert with several Singapore banks. There's nothing concrete, nothing that can be traced. Before Singapore, nothing."

You're wrong, there was a great deal. But none of that is part of it. . . . There is a void, and it must be filled, and you can't help me. Perhaps no one can; perhaps no one should.

"So far, you haven't told me anything startling," said Bourne, "nothing relative to the information I'm interested in."

"Then I don't know what you want! You ask me questions, press for details, and when I offer you answers you reject them as immaterial. What *do* you want?"

"What do you know about Cain's . . . work? Since you're looking for a compromise, give me a reason for it. If our information differs, it would be over what he's done, wouldn't it? When did he first come to your attention? Carlos's attention? *Quickly!*"

"Two years ago," said Mme. Lavier, disconcerted by Jason's impatience, annoyed, frightened. "Word came out of Asia of a white man offering a service astonishingly similar to the one provided by Carlos. He was swiftly becoming an industry. An ambassador was assassinated in Moulmein; two days later a highly regarded Japanese politician was killed in Tokyo prior to a debate in the Diet. A week after that a newspaper editor was blown out of his car in Hong Kong, and in less than forty-eight hours a banker was shot on a street in Calcutta. Behind each one, Cain. Always Cain." The woman stopped, appraising Bourne's reaction. He gave none. "Don't you see? He was *everywhere.* He raced from one kill to another, accepting contracts with such rapidity that he had to be indiscriminate. He was a man in an enormous hurry, building his reputation so quickly that he shocked even the most jaded professionals. And no one doubted that *he* was a professional, least of all Carlos. Instructions were sent: find out about this man, learn all you can. You see, Carlos understood what none of us did, and in less than twelve months he was proven correct. Reports came from informers in Manila, Osaka, Hong Kong and Tokyo. Cain was moving to Europe, they said; he would make Paris itself his base of operations. The challenge was clear, the gauntlet thrown. Cain was out to destroy Carlos. He would become the *new* Carlos, his services *the* services required by those who sought them. As *you* sought them, monsieur."

"Moulmein, Tokyo, Calcutta . . ." Jason heard the names coming from his lips, whispered from his throat. Again they were floating, suspended in the perfumed air, shadows of a past forgotten. "Manila, Hong Kong . . ." He stopped, trying to clear the mists, peering at the outlines of strange shapes that kept racing across his mind's eye.

"These places and many others," continued Lavier. "That was Cain's error, his error still. Carlos may be many things to many people, but among those who have benefited from his trust and generosity, there is loyalty. His informers and hirelings are not so readily for sale, although Cain has tried time and again. It is said that Carlos is swift to make harsh judgments, but, as they also say, better a Satan one knows than a successor one doesn't. What Cain did not realize—does not realize now—is that Carlos's network is a vast one. When Cain moved to Europe, he did not know that his activities were uncovered in Berlin, Lisbon, Amsterdam . . . as far away as Oman."

"Oman," said Bourne involuntarily. "Sheik Mustafa Kalig," he whispered, as if to himself.

"Never proven!" interjected the Lavier woman defiantly. "A deliberate smoke-screen of confusion, the contract itself fiction. He took credit for an internal murder; no one could penetrate that security. A lie!"

"A lie," repeated Jason.

"So many lies," added Mme. Lavier contemptuously. "He's no fool, however; he lies quietly, dropping a hint here and there, knowing that they will be exaggerated in the telling into substance. He provokes Carlos at every turn, promoting himself at the expense of the man he would replace. But he's no match for Carlos; he takes contracts he cannot fulfill. You are only one example; we hear there have been several others. It's said that's why he stayed away for months, avoiding people like yourselves."

"Avoiding people . . ." Jason reached for his wrist; the trembling had begun again, the sound of distant thunder vibrating in far regions of his skull. "You're . . . sure of that?"

"Very much so. He wasn't dead; he was in hiding. Cain botched more than one assignment; it was inevitable. He accepted too many in too short a time. Yet whenever he did, he followed an abortive kill with a spectacular, unsolicited one, to uphold his stature. He would select a prominent figure and blow him away, the assassination a shock to everyone, and unmistakably Cain's. The ambassador traveling in Moulmein was an example; no one had called for his death. There were two others that we know of—a Russian commissar in Shanghai and more recently a banker in Madrid. . . ."

The words came from the bright red lips working feverishly in the lower part of the powdered mask facing him. He heard them; he had heard them before. He had *lived* them before. They were no longer shadows, but remembrances of that forgotten past. Images and reality were fused. She began no sentence he could not finish, nor could she mention a name or a city or an incident with which he was not instinctively familiar.

She was talking about . . . him.

Alpha, Bravo, Cain, Delta . . .

Cain is for Charlie, and Delta is for Cain.

Jason Bourne was the assassin called Cain.

There was a final question, his brief reprieve from darkness two nights ago at the Sorbonne. Marseilles. August 23.

"What happened in Marseilles?" he asked.

"Marseilles?" the Lavier woman recoiled. "How *could* you? What lies were you told? What *other* lies?"

"Just tell me what happened."

"You refer to Leland, of course. The ubiquitous ambassador whose death *was* called for—paid for, the contract accepted by Carlos."

"What if I told you that there are those who think Cain was responsible?"

"It's what he wanted *everyone* to think! It was the ultimate insult to Carlos—to steal the kill from him. Payment was irrelevant to Cain; he only wanted to show the world—our world—that he could get there first and do the job for which Carlos had been paid. But he didn't, you know. He had nothing to do with the Leland kill."

"He was there."

"He was trapped. At least, he never showed up. Some said he'd been killed, but since there was no corpse, Carlos didn't believe it."

"How was Cain supposedly killed?"

Madame Lavier retreated, shaking her head in short, rapid movements. "Two men on the waterfront tried to take credit, tried to get paid for it. One was never seen again; it can be presumed Cain killed him, if it *was* Cain. They were dock garbage."

"What was the trap?"

"The *alleged* trap, monsieur. They claimed to have gotten word that Cain was to meet someone in the rue Sarrasin a night or so before the assassination. They say they left appropriately obscure messages in the street and lured the man they were convinced was Cain down to the piers, to a fishing boat. Neither trawler nor skipper were seen again, so they may have been right—but as I say, there was no proof. Not even an adequate description of Cain to match against the man led away from the Sarrasin. At any rate, that's where it ends."

You're wrong. That's where it began. For me.

"I see," said Bourne, trying again to infuse naturalness into his voice. "Our information's different naturally. We made a choice on what we thought we knew."

"The *wrong* choice, monsieur. What I've told you is the truth."

"Yes, I know."

"Do we have our compromise, then?"

"Why not?"

"*Bien.*" Relieved, the woman lifted the wineglass to her lips. "You'll see, it will be better for everyone."

"It . . . doesn't really matter now." He could barely be heard, and he knew it. What did he say? What had he just said? Why did he say it? . . . The mists were closing in again, the thunder getting louder; the pain had returned to his temples. "I mean . . . I mean, as you say, it's better for everyone." He could feel—*see*—Lavier's eyes on him, studying him. "It's a reasonable solution."

"Of course it is. You are not feeling well?"

"I said it was nothing; it'll pass."

"I'm relieved. Now, would you excuse me for a moment?"

"No." Jason grabbed her arm.

"*Je vous prie, monsieur.* The powder room, that is all. If you care to, stand outside the door."

"We'll leave. You can stop on the way." Bourne signaled the waiter for a check.

"As you wish," she said, watching him.

He stood in the darkened corridor between the spills of light that came from recessed lamps in the ceiling. Across the way was the ladies' room, denoted by small, uncapitalized letters of gold that read FEMMES. Beautiful people—stunning women, handsome men—kept passing by; the orbit was similar to that of Les Classiques. Jacqueline Lavier was at home.

She had also been in the ladies' room for nearly ten minutes, a fact that would have disturbed Jason had he been able to concentrate on the time. He could not; he was on fire. Noise and pain consumed him, every nerve ending raw, exposed, the fibers swelling, terrified of puncture. He stared straight ahead, a history of dead men behind him. The past was in the eyes of truth; they had sought him out and he had seen them. Cain . . . *Cain* . . . *Cain.*

He shook his head and looked up at the black ceiling. He had to function; he could not allow himself to keep falling, plunging into the abyss filled with darkness and high wind. There were decisions to make. . . . No, they were made; it was a question now of implementing them.

Marie. Marie? Oh, God, my love, we've been so wrong!

He breathed deeply and glanced at his watch—the chronometer he had traded for a thin gold piece of jewelry belonging to a marquis in the south of France. *He is a man of immense skill, extremely inventive.* . . . There was no joy in that appraisal. He looked across at the ladies' room.

Where was Jacqueline Lavier? Why didn't she come out? What could she hope to accomplish remaining inside? He had had the presence of mind to ask the maître d' if there was a telephone there; the man had replied negatively, pointing to a booth by the entrance. The Lavier woman had been at his side; she heard the answer, understanding the inquiry.

There was a blinding flash of light. He lurched backward, recoiling into the wall, his hands in front of his eyes. The pain! Oh, Christ! His eyes were on fire!

And then he heard the words, spoken through the polite laughter of well-dressed men and women walking casually about the corridor.

"In memory of your dinner at Roget's, monsieur," said an animated hostess, holding a press camera by its vertical flashbar. "The photograph will be ready in a few minutes. Compliments of Roget."

Bourne remained rigid, knowing that he could not smash the camera, the fear of another realization sweeping over him. "Why me?" he asked.

"Your fiancée requested it, monsieur," replied the girl, nodding her head toward the ladies' room. "We talked inside. You are most fortunate; she is a lovely lady. She asked me to give you this." The hostess held out a folded note; Jason took it as she pranced away toward the restaurant entrance.

Your illness disturbs me, as I'm sure it does you, my new friend. You may be what you say you are, and then again you may not. I shall have the answer in a half hour or so. A telephone call was made by a sympathetic diner, and that photograph is on its way to Paris. You cannot stop it any more than you can stop those driving now to Argenteuil. If we, indeed, have our compromise, neither will disturb you—as your illness disturbs me—and we shall talk again when my associates arrive.

It is said that Cain is a chameleon, appearing in various guises, and most convincing. It is also said that he is prone to violence and to fits of temper. These are an illness, no?

He ran down the dark street in Argenteuil after the receding roof light of the taxi; it turned the corner and disappeared. He stopped, breathing heavily, looking in all directions for another; there were none. The doorman at Roget's had told him a cab would take ten to fifteen minutes to arrive; why had not monsieur requested one earlier? The trap was set and he had walked into it.

Up ahead! A light, another taxi! He broke into a run. He had to stop it; he had to get back to Paris. To Marie.

He was back in a labyrinth, racing blindly, knowing, finally, there was no escape. But the race would be made alone; that decision was irrevocable. There would be no discussion, no debate, no screaming back and forth—arguments based in love and uncertainty. For the certainty had been made clear. He knew who he was . . . what he had been; he was guilty as charged—as suspected.

An hour or two saying nothing. Just watching, talking quietly about anything but the truth. Loving. And then he would leave; she would never know when and he could never tell her why. He owed her that; it would hurt deeply for a while, but the ultimate pain would be far less than that caused by the stigma of Cain.

Cain!

Marie. Marie! What have I done?

"Taxi! Taxi!"

18

Get out of Paris! Now! Whatever you're doing, stop it and get out! . . . Those are orders from your government. They want you out of there. They want him isolated.

Marie crushed out her cigarette in the ashtray on the bedside table, her eyes falling on the three-year-old issue of *Potomac Quarterly,* her thoughts briefly on the terrible game Jason had forced her to play.

"I won't listen!" she said to herself out loud, startled at the sound of her own voice in the empty room. She walked to the window, the same window he had faced, looking out, frightened, trying to make her understand.

I have to know certain things . . . enough to make a decision . . . but maybe not everything. A part of me has to be able . . . to run, disappear. I have to be able to say to myself, what was isn't any longer, and there's a possibility that it never was because I have no memory of it. What a person can't remember didn't exist . . . for him.

"My darling, my darling. Don't let them do this to you!" Her spoken words did not startle now, for it was as though he were there in the room, listening, heeding his own words, willing to run, disappear . . . with her. But at the core of her understanding she knew he could not do that; he could not settle for a half-truth, or three-quarters of a lie.

They want him isolated.

Who were *they?* The answer was in Canada and Canada was cut off, another trap.

Jason was right about Paris; she felt it, too. Whatever it was, was here. If they could find one person to lift the shroud and let him see for himself he was being manipulated, then other questions might be manageable, the answers no longer pushing him toward self-destruction. If he could be convinced that whatever unremembered crimes he had committed, he was a pawn for a much greater single crime, he might be able to walk away, disappear with her. Everything *was* relative. What the man she loved had to be able to say to himself was not that the past no longer existed, but that it had, and he could live with it, and put it to rest. That was the rationalization he needed, the conviction that whatever he had been was far less than his enemies wanted the world to believe, for they would not use him otherwise. He was the scapegoat, his death to take the place of another's. If he could only *see* that; if she could only convince him. And if she did not, she would lose him. They would take him; they would kill him.

They.

"Who *are* you?" she screamed at the window, at the lights of Paris outside. "*Where* are you?"

She could feel a cold wind against her face as surely as if the panes of glass had melted, the night air rushing inside. It was followed by a tightening in her throat, and for a moment she could not swallow . . . could not breathe. The moment passed and she breathed again. She was afraid; it had happened to her before, on their first night in Paris, when she had left the café to find him on the steps of the Cluny. She had been walking rapidly down the Saint-Michel when it happened: the cold wind, the swelling of the throat . . . at that moment she had not been able to breathe. Later she thought she knew why; at that moment also, several blocks away inside the Sorbonne, Jason had raced to a judgment that in minutes he would reverse—but he had reached it then. He had made up his mind he would not come to her.

"Stop it!" she cried. "It's crazy," she added, shaking her head, looking at her watch. He had been gone over five hours; where was he? *Where was he?*

Bourne got out of the taxi in front of the seedily elegant hotel in Montparnasse. The next hour would be the most difficult of his briefly remembered life—a life that was a void before Port Noir, a nightmare since. The nightmare would continue, but he would live with it alone; he loved her too much to ask her to live it with him. He would find a way to disappear, taking with him the evidence that tied her to Cain. It was as simple as that; he would leave for a nonexistent rendezvous and not return. And sometime during the next hour he would write her a note:

It's over. I've found my arrows. Go back to Canada and say nothing for both our sakes. I know where to reach you.

The last was unfair—he would never reach her—but the small, feathered hope had to be there, if only to get her on a plane to Ottawa. In time—with time—their weeks together would fade into a darkly kept secret, a cache of brief riches to be uncovered and touched at odd quiet moments. And then no more, for life was lived for active memories; the dormant ones lost meaning. No one knew that better than he did.

He passed through the lobby, nodding at the *concierge,* who sat on his stool behind the marble counter, reading a newspaper. The man barely looked up, noting only that the intruder belonged.

The elevator rumbled and groaned its way up to the fifth floor. Jason breathed deeply and reached for the gate; above all he would avoid dramatics—no alarms raised by words or by looks. The chameleon had to merge with his quiet part of the forest, one in which no spoors could be found. He knew what to say; he had thought about it carefully as he had the note he would write.

"Most of the night walking around," he said, holding her, stroking her dark red hair, cradling her head against his shoulder . . . and aching, "chasing down cadaverous clerks, listening to animated nonsense, and drinking coffee disguised as sour mud. Les Classiques was a waste of time; it's a zoo. The monkeys and the peacocks put on a hell of a show, but I don't think anyone really knows anything. There's one outside possibility, but he could simply be a sharp Frenchman in search of an American mark."

"He?" asked Marie, her trembling diminished.

"A man who operated the switchboard," said Bourne, repelling images of blinding explosions and darkness and high winds as he pictured the face he did not know but knew so well. That man now was only a device; he pushed the images away. "I agreed to meet him around midnight at the Bastringue on rue Hautefeuille."

"What did he say?"

"Very little, but enough to interest me. I saw him watching me while I was asking questions. The place was fairly crowded, so I could move around pretty freely, talk to the clerks."

"Questions? What questions did you ask?"

"Anything I could think of. Mainly about the manager, or whatever she's called. Considering what happened this afternoon, if she were a direct relay to Carlos, she should have been close to hysterics. I saw her. She wasn't; she behaved as if nothing had happened except a good day in the shop."

"But she *was* a relay, as you call it. D'Amacourt explained that. The *fiche.*"

"Indirect. She gets a phone call and is told what to say before making another call herself." Actually, Jason thought, the invented assessment was based on reality. Jacqueline Lavier was, indeed, an indirect relay.

"You couldn't just walk around asking questions without seeming suspicious," protested Marie.

"You can," answered Bourne, "if you're an American writer doing an article on the stores in Saint-Honoré for a national magazine."

"That's very good, Jason."

"It worked. No one wants to be left out."

"What did you learn?"

"Like most of those kinds of places, Les Classiques has its own clientele, all wealthy, most known to each other and with the usual marital intrigues and adulteries that go with the scene. Carlos knew what he was doing; it's a regular answering service over there, but not the kind listed in a phone book."

"People told you that?" asked Marie, holding his arms, watching his eyes.

"Not in so many words," he said, aware of the shadows of her disbelief. "The accent was always on this Bergeron's talent, but one thing leads to another. You can get the picture. Everyone seems to gravitate to that manager. From what I've gathered, she's a font of social information, although she probably couldn't tell me anything except that she did someone a favor—an accommodation—and that someone will turn out to be someone else who did another favor for another someone. The source could be untraceable, but it's all I've got."

"Why the meeting tonight at Bastringue?"

"He came over to me when I was leaving and said a very strange thing." Jason did not have to invent this part of the lie. He had read the words on a note in an elegant restaurant in Argenteuil less than an hour ago. "He said, 'You may be what you say you are, and then again you may not.' That's when he suggested a drink later on, away from Saint-Honoré." Bourne saw her doubts receding. He had done it; she accepted the tapestry of lies. And why not? He was a man *of immense skill, extremely inventive.* The appraisal was not loathsome to him; he was Cain.

"He may be the one, Jason. You said you only needed one; he could be it!"

"We'll see." Bourne looked at his watch. The countdown to his departure had begun; he could not look back. "We've got almost two hours. Where did you leave the attaché case?"

"At the Meurice. I'm registered there."

"Let's pick it up and get some dinner. You haven't eaten, have you?"

"No . . ." Marie's expression was quizzical. "Why not leave the case where it is? It's perfectly safe; we wouldn't have to worry about it."

"We would if we had to get out of here in a hurry," he said almost brusquely, going to the bureau. *Everything was a question of degree now, traces of friction gradually slipping into speech, into looks, into touch. Nothing alarming, nothing based on false heroics; she would see through such tactics. Only enough so that later she would understand the truth when she read his words. "It's over. I've found my arrows. . . ."*

"What's the matter, darling?"

"Nothing." The chameleon smiled. "I'm just tired and probably a little discouraged."

"Good heavens, why? A man wants to meet you confidentially late at night, a man who operates a switchboard. He could lead you somewhere. And you're convinced you've narrowed Carlos's contact down to this woman; she's bound to be able to tell you *something*—whether she wants to or not. In a macabre way, I'd think you'd be elated."

"I'm not sure I can explain it," said Jason, now looking at her reflection in the mirror. "You'd have to understand what I found there."

"What you found?" A question.

"What I found." A statement. "It's a different world," continued Bourne, reaching for the bottle of scotch and a glass, "different people. It's soft and beautiful and frivolous, with lots of tiny spotlights and dark velvet. Nothing's taken seriously except gossip and indulgence. Any one of those giddy people— including that woman—could be a relay for Carlos and never know it, never even suspect it. A man like Carlos would use such people; anyone like him would, including *me*. . . . That's what I found. It's discouraging."

"And unreasonable. Whatever you believe, those people make very conscious decisions. That indulgence you talk of demands it; they think. And you know what *I* think? I think you *are* tired, and hungry, and need a drink or two. I wish you could put off tonight; you've been through enough for one day."

"I can't do that," he said sharply.

"All right, you can't," she answered defensively.

"Sorry, I'm edgy."

THE BOURNE IDENTITY 959

"Yes. I know." She started for the bathroom. "I'll freshen up and we can go. Pour yourself a stiff one, darling. Your teeth are showing."

"Marie?"

"Yes?"

"Try to understand. What I found there upset me. I thought it would be different. Easier."

"While you were looking, I was waiting, Jason. Not knowing. That wasn't easy either."

"I thought you were going to call Canada. Didn't you?"

She held her place for a moment. "No," she said. "It was too late."

The bathroom door closed; Bourne walked to the desk across the room. He opened the drawer, took out stationery, picked up the ballpoint pen and wrote the words:

It's over. I've found my arrows. Go back to Canada and say nothing for both our sakes. I know where to reach you.

He folded the stationery, inserted it into an envelope, holding the flap open as he reached for his billfold. He took out both the French and the Swiss bills, slipping them behind the folded note, and sealed the envelope. He wrote on the front: MARIE.

He wanted so desperately to add: *My love, my dearest love.*

He did not. He could not.

The bathroom door opened. He put the envelope in his jacket pocket. "That was quick," he said.

"Was it? I didn't think so. What are you doing?"

"I wanted a pen," he answered, picking up the ballpoint. "If that fellow has anything to tell me I want to be able to write it down."

Marie was by the bureau; she glanced at the dry, empty glass. "You didn't have your drink."

"I didn't use the glass."

"I see. Shall we go?"

They waited in the corridor for the rumbling elevator, the silence between them awkward, in a real sense unbearable. He reached for her hand. At the touch she gripped his, staring at him, her eyes telling him that her control was being tested and she did not know why. Quiet signals had been sent and received, not loud enough or abrasive enough to be alarms, but they were there and she had heard them. It was part of the countdown, rigid, irreversible, prelude to his departure.

Oh God, I love you so. You are next to me and we are touching and I am dying. But you cannot die with me. You must not. I am Cain.

"We'll be fine," he said.

The metal cage vibrated noisily into its recessed perch. Jason pulled the brass grille open, then suddenly swore under his breath.

"Oh, Christ, I forgot!"

"What?"

"My wallet. I left it in the bureau drawer this afternoon in case there was any trouble in Saint-Honoré. Wait for me in the lobby." He gently swung her through the gate, pressing the button with his free hand. "I'll be right down." He closed the grille; the brass latticework cutting off the sight of her startled eyes. He turned away and walked rapidly back toward the room.

Inside, he took the envelope out of his pocket and placed it against the base of the lamp on the bedside table. He stared down at it, the ache unendurable.

"Goodbye, my love," he whispered.

Bourne waited in the drizzle outside the Hotel Meurice on the rue de Rivoli, watching Marie through the glass doors of the entrance. She was at the front desk, having signed for the attaché case, which had been handed to her over the counter. She was now obviously asking a mildly astonished clerk for her bill, about to pay for a room that had been occupied less than six hours. Two minutes passed before the bill was presented. Reluctantly; it was no way for a guest at the Meurice to behave. Indeed, all Paris shunned such inhibited visitors.

Marie walked out on the pavement, joining him in the shadows and the mistlike drizzle to the left of the canopy. She gave him the attaché case, a forced smile on her lips, a slight breathless quality in her voice.

"That man didn't approve of me. I'm sure he's convinced I used the room for a series of quick tricks."

"What did you tell him?" asked Bourne.

"That my plans had changed, that's all."

"Good, the less said the better. Your name's on the registration card. Think up a reason why you were there."

"Think up? . . . I should think up a reason?" She studied his eyes, the smile gone.

"I mean we'll think up a reason. Naturally."

"Naturally."

"Let's go." They started walking toward the corner, the traffic noisy in the street, the drizzle in the air fuller, the mist denser, the promise of heavy rain imminent. He took her arm—not to guide her, not even out of courtesy—only to touch her, to hold a part of her. There was so little time.

I am Cain. I am death.

"Can we slow down?" asked Marie sharply.

"What?" Jason realized he had been practically running; for a few seconds he had been back in the labyrinth, racing through it, careening, feeling, and not feeling. He looked up ahead and found an answer. At the corner an empty cab had stopped by a garish newsstand, the driver shouting through an open window to the dealer. "I want to catch that taxi," said Bourne, without breaking stride. "It's going to rain like hell."

They reached the corner, both breathless as the empty cab pulled away, swinging left into rue de Rivoli. Jason looked up into the night sky, feeling the wet pounding on his face, unnerved. The rain had arrived. He looked at Marie in the gaudy lights of the newsstand; she was wincing in the sudden downpour. No. She was not wincing; she was staring at something . . . staring in disbelief, in shock. In horror. Without warning she screamed, her face contorted, the fingers of her right hand pressed against her mouth. Bourne grabbed her, pulling her head into the damp cloth of his topcoat; she would not stop screaming.

He turned, trying to find the cause of her hysterics. Then he saw it, and in that unbelievable split half-second he knew the countdown was aborted. He had committed the final crime; he could not leave her. Not now, not yet.

On the first ledge of the newsstand was an early-morning tabloid, black headlines electrifying under the circles of light:

SLAYER IN PAIRS

WOMAN SOUGHT IN ZURICH KILLINGS

SUSPECT IN RUMORED THEFT OF MILLIONS

Under the screaming words was a photograph of Marie St. Jacques.

"Stop it!" whispered Jason, using his body to cover her face from the curious newsdealer, reaching into his pocket for coins. He threw the money on the counter, grabbed two papers, and propelled her down the dark, rainsoaked street.

They were both in the labyrinth now.

Bourne opened the door and led Marie inside. She stood motionless, looking at him, her face pale and frightened, her breathing erratic, and audible mixture of fear and anger.

"I'll get you a drink," said Jason, going to the bureau. As he poured, his eyes strayed to the mirror and he had an overpowering urge to smash the glass, so despicable was his own image to him. What the hell had he *done?* Oh God! *I am Cain. I am death.*

He heard her gasp and spun around, too late to stop her, too far away to lunge and tear the awful thing from her hand. Oh, Christ, he had forgotten! She had found the envelope on the bedside table, and was reading his note. Her single scream was a searing, terrible cry of pain.

"Jasonnnn! . . ."

"Please! No!" He raced from the bureau and grabbed her. "It doesn't matter! It doesn't count anymore!" He shouted helplessly, seeing the tears swelling in her eyes, streaking down her face. *"Listen* to me! That was before, not now."

"You were leaving! My God, you were *leaving* me!" Her eyes went blank, two blind circles of panic. "I knew it! I felt it!"

"I *made* you feel it!" he said, forcing her to look at him. "But it's over now. I won't leave you. Listen to me. I won't leave you!"

She screamed again. "I couldn't breathe! . . . It was so cold!"

He pulled her to him, enveloping her. "We have to begin again. Try to understand. It's different now—and I can't change what was—but I won't leave you. Not like this."

She pushed her hands against his chest, her tear-stained face angled back, begging, "Why, Jason? Why?"

"Later. Not now. Don't say anything for a while. Just hold me; let me hold you."

The minutes passed, hysteria ran its course and the outlines of reality came back into focus. Bourne led her to the chair; she caught the sleeve of her dress on the frayed lace. They both smiled, as he knelt beside her, holding her hand in silence.

"How about that drink?" he said finally.

"I think so," she replied, briefly tightening her grip on his hand as he got up from the floor. "You poured it quite a while ago."

"It won't go flat." He went to the bureau and returned with two glasses half filled with whiskey. She took hers. "Feeling better?" he asked.

"Calmer. Still confused . . . frightened, of course. Maybe angry, too, I'm not sure. I'm too afraid to think about that." She drank, closing her eyes, her head pressed back against the chair. "Why did you do it, Jason?"

"Because I thought I had to. That's the simple answer."

"And no answer at all. I deserve more than that."

"Yes, you do, and I'll give it to you. I have to now because you have to hear it; you have to understand. You have to protect yourself."

"Protect—"

He held up his hand, interrupting her. "It'll come later. All of it, if you like. But the first thing we have to do is know what happened—not to *me*, but to *you*. That's where we have to begin. Can you do it?"

"The newspaper?"

"Yes."

"God knows, I'm interested," she said, smiling weakly.

"Here." Jason went to the bed where he had dropped the two papers. "We'll both read it."

"No games?"

"No games."

They read the long article in silence, an article that told of death and intrigue in Zurich. Every now and then Marie gasped, shocked at what she was reading; at other times she shook her head in disbelief. Bourne said nothing. He saw the hand of Ilich Ramirez Sanchez. *Carlos will follow Cain to the ends of the earth. Carlos will kill him.* Marie St. Jacques was expendable, a baited decoy that would die in the trap that caught Cain.

I am Cain. I am death.

The article was, in fact, two articles—an odd mixture of fact and conjecture, speculations taking over where evidence came to an end. The first part indicated a Canadian government employee, a female economist, Marie St. Jacques. She was placed at the scene of three murders, her fingerprints confirmed by the Canadian government. In addition, police found a hotel key from the Carillon du Lac, apparently lost during the violence on the Guisan Quai. It was the key to Marie St. Jacques' room, given to her by the hotel clerk, who remembered her well—remembered what appeared to him to be a guest in a highly disturbed state of anxiety. The final piece of evidence was a handgun discovered not far from the Steppdeckstrasse, in an alley close by the scene of two other killings. Ballistics held it to be the murder weapon, and again there were fingerprints, again confirmed by the Canadian government. They belonged to the woman, Marie St. Jacques.

It was at this point that the article veered from fact. It spoke of rumors along the Bahnhofstrasse that a multimillion-dollar theft had taken place by means of a computer manipulation dealing with a numbered, confidential account belonging to an American corporation called Treadstone Seventy-One. The bank was also named; it was of course the Gemeinschaft. But everything else was clouded, obscure, more speculation than fact.

According to "unnamed sources," an American male holding the proper codes transferred millions to a bank in Paris, assigning the new account to specific individuals who were to assume rights of possession. The assignees were waiting in Paris, and upon clearance, withdrew the millions and disappeared. The success of the operation was traced to the American's obtaining the accurate codes to the Gemeinschaft account, a feat made possible by penetrating the bank's numerical sequence related to year, month and day of entry, standard procedure for confidential holdings. Such an analysis could only be made through the use of sophisticated computer techniques and a thorough knowledge of Swiss banking practices. When questioned, an officer of the bank, Herr Walther Apfel, acknowledged that there was an ongoing investigation into matters pertaining to the American company, but pursuant to Swiss law, "the bank would have no further comment—to anyone."

Here the connection to Marie St. Jacques was clarified. She was described as a government economist extensively schooled in international banking procedures, as well as a skilled computer programmer. She was suspected of being an accomplice, her expertise necessary to the massive theft. And there *was* a male suspect; she was reported to have been seen in his company at the Carillon du Lac.

Marie finished the article first and let the paper drop to the floor. At the sound, Bourne looked over from the edge of the bed. She was staring at the wall, a strange pensive serenity having come over her. It was the last reaction he expected. He finished reading quickly, feeling depressed and hopeless—for a moment, speechless. Then he found his voice and spoke.

"Lies," he said, "and they were made because of me, because of who and what I am. Smoke you out, they find me. I'm sorry, sorrier than I can ever tell you."

Marie shifted her eyes from the wall and looked at him. "It goes deeper than lies, Jason," she said. "There's too much truth for lies alone."

"Truth? The only truth is that you were in Zurich. You never touched a gun, you were never in an alley near the Steppdeckstrasse, you didn't lose a hotel key and you never went near the Gemeinschaft."

"Agreed, but that's not the truth I'm talking about."

"Then what is?"

"The Gemeinschaft, Treadstone Seventy-One, Apfel. Those are true and the fact that any were mentioned—especially Apfel's acknowledgment—is incredible. Swiss bankers are cautious men. They don't ridicule the laws, not this way; the jail sentences are too severe. The statutes pertaining to banking confidentiality are among the most sacrosanct in Switzerland. Apfel could go to prison for years for saying what he did, for even alluding to such an account, much less confirming it by name. Unless he was ordered to say what he did by an authority powerful enough to contravene the laws." She stopped, her eyes straying to the wall again. "Why? Why was the Gemeinschaft or Treadstone or Apfel ever made part of the story?"

"I told you. They want me and they know we're together. Carlos knows we're together. Find you, he finds me."

"No, Jason, it goes beyond Carlos. You really *don't* understand the laws in Switzerland. Not even a Carlos could cause them to be flaunted this way." She looked at him, but her eyes did not see him; she was peering through her own mists. "This isn't one story, it's two. Both are constructed out of lies, the first connected to the second by tenuous speculation—public speculation—on a banking crisis that would never be made public, unless and until a thorough and private investigation proved the facts. And that second story—the patently false statement that millions were stolen from the Gemeinschaft—was tacked onto the equally false story that I'm wanted for killing three men in Zurich. It was added. Deliberately."

"Explain that, please."

"It's there, Jason. Believe me when I tell you that; it's right in front of us."

"What is?"

"Someone's trying to send us a message."

19

The army sedan sped south on Manhattan's East River Drive, headlights illuminating the swirling remnants of a late-winter snowfall. The major in the back seat dozed, his long body angled into the corner, his legs stretched out diagonally across the floor. In his lap was a briefcase, a thin nylon cord attached to the handle by a metal clamp, the cord itself strung through his right sleeve and down his inner tunic to his belt. The security device had been removed only twice in the past nine hours. Once during the major's departure from Zurich, and again with his arrival at Kennedy Airport. In both places, however, U.S. government personnel had been watching the customs clerks—more precisely, watching the briefcase. They were not told why; they were simply ordered to observe the inspections, and at the slightest deviation from normal procedures—which meant any undue interest in the briefcase—they were to intercede. With weapons, if necessary.

There was a sudden, quiet ringing; the major snapped his eyes open and brought his left hand up in front of his face. The sound was a wrist alarm; he pressed the button on his watch and squinted at the second radium dial of his two-zoned instrument. The first was on Zurich time, the second, New York; the alarm had been set twenty-four hours ago, when the officer had received his cabled orders. The transmission would come within the next three minutes. That is, thought the major, it would come if Iron Ass was as precise as he expected his subordinates to be. The officer stretched, awkwardly balancing the briefcase, and leaned forward, speaking to the driver.

"Sergeant, turn on your scrambler to 1430 megahertz, will you please?"

"Yes, sir." The sergeant flipped two switches on the radio panel beneath the dashboard, then twisted the dial to the 1430 frequency. "There it is, Major."

"Thanks. Will the microphone reach back here?"

"I don't know. Never tried it, sir." The driver pulled the small plastic microphone from its cradle and stretched the spiral cord over the seat. "Guess it does," he concluded.

Static erupted from the speaker, the scrambling transmitter electronically scanning and jamming the frequency. The message would follow in seconds. It did.

"Treadstone? Treadstone, confirm, please."

"Treadstone receiving," said Major Gordon Webb. "You're clear. Go ahead."

"What's your position?"

"About a mile south of the Triborough, East River Drive," said the major.

"Your timing is acceptable," came the voice from the speaker.

"Glad to hear it. It makes my day . . . sir."

There was a brief pause, the major's comment not appreciated. "Proceed to 139 East Seventy-first. Confirm by repeat."

"One-three-niner East Seventy-first."

"Keep your vehicle out of the area. Approach on foot."

"Understood."

"Out."

"Out." Webb snapped the transmission button in place and handed the microphone back to the driver. "Forget that address, Sergeant. Your name's on a very short file now."

"Gotcha', Major. Nothing but static on that thing anyway. But since I don't know where it is and these wheels aren't supposed to go there, where do you want to be dropped off?"

Webb smiled. "No more than two blocks away. I'd go to sleep in the gutter if I had to walk any further than that."

"How about Lex and Seventy-second?"

"Is that two blocks?"

"No more than three."

"If it's three blocks you're a private."

"Then I couldn't pick you up later, Major. Privates aren't cleared for this duty."

"Whatever you say, Captain." Webb closed his eyes. After two years, he was about to see Treadstone Seventy-One for himself. He knew he should feel a sense of anticipation; he did not. He felt only a sense of weariness, of futility. *What had happened?*

The incessant hum of the tires on the pavement below was hypnotic, but the rhythm was broken by sharp intrusions where concrete and wheels were not compatible. The sounds evoked memories of long ago, of screeching jungle noises woven into a single tone. And then the night—that night—when blinding lights and staccato explosions were all around him, and below him, telling him he was about to die. But he did not die; a miracle wrought by a man had given his life back to him . . . and the years went on, that night, those days never to be forgotten. *What the hell had happened?*

"Here we are, Major."

Webb opened his eyes, his hand wiping the sweat that had formed on his forehead. He looked at his watch, gripped his briefcase and reached for the handle of the door.

"I'll be here between 2300 and 2330 hours, Sergeant. If you can't park, just cruise around and I'll find you."

"Yes, sir." The driver turned in his seat. "Could the major tell me if we're going to be driving any distance later?"

"Why? Have you got another fare?"

"Come on, sir. I'm assigned to you until you say otherwise, you know that. But these heavy-plated trucks use gas like the old-time Shermans. If we're going far I'd better fill it."

"Sorry." The major paused. "Okay. You'll have to find out where it is, anyway, because I don't know. We're going to a private airfield in Madison, New Jersey. I have to be there no later than one hundred hours."

"I've got a vague idea," said the driver. "At 2330, you're cutting it pretty close, sir."

"OK—2300, then. And thanks." Webb got out of the car, closed the door and waited until the brown sedan entered the flow of traffic on Seventy-second Street. He stepped off the curb and headed south to Seventy-first.

Four minutes later he stood in front of a well-kept brownstone, its muted, rich design in concert with those around it in the tree-lined street. It was a quiet street, a monied street—old money. It was the last place in Manhattan a person would suspect of housing one of the most sensitive intelligence operations in the country. And as of twenty minutes ago, Major Gordon Webb was one of only eight or ten people in the country who knew of its existence.

Treadstone Seventy-One.

He climbed the steps, aware that the pressure of his weight on the iron grids embedded in the stone beneath him triggered electronic devices that in turn activated cameras, producing his image on screens inside. Beyond this, he knew little, except that Treadstone Seventy-One never closed; it was operated and monitored twenty-four hours a day by a select few, identities unknown.

He reached the top step and rang the bell, an ordinary bell, but not for an ordinary door, the major could see that. The heavy wood was riveted to a steel plate behind it, the decorative iron designs in actuality the rivets, the large brass knob disguising a hotplate that caused a series of steel bolts to shoot across into steel receptacles at the touch of a human hand when the alarms were turned on. Webb glanced up at the windows. Each pane of glass, he knew, was an inch thick, capable of withstanding the impact of .30 caliber shells. Treadstone Seventy-One was a fortress.

The door opened and the major involuntarily smiled at the figure standing there, so totally out of place did she seem. She was a petite, elegant-looking, gray-haired woman with soft aristocratic features and a bearing that bespoke monied gentility. Her voice confirmed the appraisal; it was mid-Atlantic, refined in the better finishing schools and at innumerable polo matches.

"How good of you to drop by, Major. Jeremy wrote us that you might. Do come in. It's such a pleasure to see you again."

"It's good to see you again, too," replied Webb, stepping into the tasteful foyer, finishing his statement when the door was closed, "but I'm not sure where it was we met before."

The woman laughed. "Oh, we've had dinner ever so many times."

"With Jeremy?"

"Of course."

"Who's Jeremy?"

"A devoted nephew who's also your devoted friend. Such a nice young man; it's a pity he doesn't exist." She took his elbow as they walked down a long hallway. "It's all for the benefit of neighbors who might be strolling by. Come along now, they're waiting."

They passed an archway that led to a large living room; the major looked inside. There was a grand piano by the front windows, harp beside it; and everywhere— on the piano and on polished tables glistening under the spill of subdued lamps— were silver-framed photographs, mementos of a past filled with wealth and grace. Sailboats, men and women on the decks of ocean liners, several military portraits. And, yes, two candid shots of someone mounted for a polo match. It was a room that belonged in a brownstone on this street.

They reached the end of the hallway; there was a large mahogany door, bas-relief and iron ornamentation part of its design, part of its security. If there was an infrared camera, Webb could not detect the whereabouts of the lens. The gray-haired woman pressed an unseen bell; the major could hear a slight hum.

"Your friend is here, gentlemen. Stop playing poker and go to work. Snap to, Jesuit."

"Jesuit?" asked Webb, bewildered.

"An old joke," replied the woman. "It goes back to when you were probably playing marbles and snarling at little girls."

The door opened and the aged but still erect figure of David Abbott was revealed. "Glad to see you, Major," said the former Silent Monk of Covert Services, extending his hand.

"Good to be here, sir." Webb shook hands. Another elderly, imposing-looking man came up beside Abbott.

"A friend of Jeremy's, no doubt," said the man, his deep voice edged with humor. "Dreadfully sorry time precludes proper introductions, young fellow. Come along, Margaret. There's a lovely fire upstairs." He turned to Abbott. "You'll let me know when you're leaving, David?"

"Usual time for me, I expect," replied the Monk. "I'll show these two how to ring you."

It was then that Webb realized there was a third man in the room; he was standing in the shadows at the far end, and the major recognized him instantly. He was Elliot Stevens, senior aide to the president of the United States—some said his alter ego. He was in his early forties, slender, wore glasses and had the bearing of unpretentious authority about him.

". . . it'll be fine." The imposing older man who had not found time to introduce himself had been speaking; Webb had not heard him, his attention on the White House aide. "I'll be waiting."

"Till next time," continued Abbott, shifting his eyes kindly to the gray-haired woman. "Thanks, Sister Meg. Keep your habit pressed. And down."

"You're still wicked, Jesuit."

The couple left, closing the door behind them. Webb stood for a moment, shaking his head and smiling. The man and woman of 139 East Seventy-first belonged to the room down the hall, just as that room belonged in the brownstone, all a part of the quiet, monied, tree-lined street. "You've known them a long time, haven't you?"

"A lifetime, you might say," replied Abbott. "He was a yachtsman we put to good use in the Adriatic runs for Donovan's operations in Yugoslavia. Mikhailovitch once said he sailed on sheer nerve, bending the worst weather to his will. And don't let Sister Meg's graciousness fool you. She was one of Intrepid's girls, a piranha with very sharp teeth."

"They're quite a story."

"It'll never be told," said Abbott, closing the subject. "I want you to meet Elliot Stevens. I don't think I have to tell you who he is. Webb, Stevens. Stevens, Webb."

"That sounds like a law firm," said Stevens amiably, walking across the room, hand extended. "Nice to know you, Webb. Have a good trip?"

"I would have preferred military transport. I hate those damned commercial airlines. I thought a customs agent at Kennedy was going to slice the lining of my suitcase."

"You look too respectable in that uniform," laughed the Monk. "You're obviously a smuggler."

"I'm still not sure I understand the uniform," said the major, carrying his briefcase to a long hatch table against the wall, and unclipping the nylon cord from his belt.

"I shouldn't have to tell you," answered Abbott, "that the tightest security is often found in being quite obvious on the surface. An army intelligence officer prowling around undercover in Zurich at this particular time could raise alarms."

"Then I don't understand, either," said the White House aide, coming up beside Webb at the table, watching the major's manipulations with the nylon cord and the lock. "Wouldn't an obvious presence raise even more shrill alarms? I thought the assumption of undercover was that discovery was less probable."

"Webb's trip to Zurich was a routine consulate check, predated on the G-Two schedules. No one fools anybody about those trips; they're what they are and nothing else. Ascertaining new sources, paying off informants. The Soviets do it all the time; they don't even bother to hide it. Neither do we, frankly."

"But that *wasn't* the purpose of this trip," said Stevens, beginning to understand. "So the obvious conceals the unobvious."

"That's it."

"Can I help?" The presidential aide seemed fascinated by the briefcase.

"Thanks," said Webb. "Just pull the cord through."

Stevens did so. "I always thought it was chains around the wrist," he said.

"Too many hands cut off," explained the major, smiling at the White House man's reaction. "There's a steel wire running through the nylon." He freed the briefcase and opened it on the table, looking around at the elegance of the furnished library-den. At the rear of the room was a pair of French doors that apparently led to an outside garden, an outline of a high stone wall seen dimly through the panes of thick glass. "So this is Treadstone Seventy-One. It isn't the way I pictured it."

"Pull the curtains again, will you please, Elliot?" Abbott said. The presidential aide walked to the French doors and did so. Abbott crossed to a bookcase, opened the cabinet beneath it, and reached inside. There was a quiet whir; the entire bookcase came out of the wall and slowly revolved to the left. On the other side was an electronic radio console, one of the most sophisticated Gordon Webb had seen. "Is this more what you had in mind?" asked the Monk.

"Jesus . . ." The major whistled as he studied the dials, calibrations, cable patches and scanning devices built into the panel. The Pentagon war rooms had far more elaborate equipment, but this was the miniaturized equal of most well-structured intelligence stations.

"I'd whistle, too," said Stevens, standing in front of the dense curtain. "But Mr. Abbott already gave me my personal sideshow. That's only the beginning. Five more buttons and this place looks like a SAC base in Omaha."

"Those same buttons also transform this room back into a graceful East Side library." The old man reached inside the cabinet; in seconds the enormous console was replaced by bookshelves. He then walked to the adjacent bookcase, opened the cabinet beneath and once again put his hand inside. The whirring began; the bookcase slid out, and shortly in its place were three tall filing cabinets.

The Monk took out a key and pulled out a file drawer. "I'm not showing off, Gordon. When we're finished, I want you to look through these. I'll show you the switch that'll send them back. If you have any problems, our host will take care of everything."

"What am I to look for?"

"We'll get to it; right now I want to hear about Zurich. What have you learned?"

"Excuse me, Mr. Abbott," interrupted Stevens. "If I'm slow, it's because all this is new to me. But I was thinking about something you said a minute ago about Major Webb's trip."

"What is it?"

"You said the trip was predated on the G-Two schedules."

"That's right."

"Why? The major's obvious presence was to confuse Zurich, not Washington. Or was it?"

The Monk smiled. "I can see why the president keeps you around. We've never doubted that Carlos has bought his way into a circle or two—or ten—in Washington. He finds the discontented men and offers them what they do not have. A Carlos could not exist without such people. You must remember, he doesn't merely sell death, he sells a nation's secrets. All too frequently to the Soviets, if only to prove to them how rash they were to expel him."

"The president would want to know that," said the aide. "It would explain several things."

"It's why you're here, isn't it?" said Abbott.

"I guess it is."

"And it's a good place to begin for Zurich," said Webb, taking his briefcase to an armchair in front of the filing cabinets. He sat down, spreading the folds inside the case at his feet, and took out several sheets of paper. "You may not doubt Carlos is in Washington, but I can confirm it."

"Where? Treadstone?"

"There's no clear proof of that, but it can't be ruled out. He found the *fiche*. He altered it."

"Good God, how?"

"The how I can only guess; the who I know."

"Who?"

"A man named Koenig. Until three days ago he was in charge of primary verifications at the Gemeinschaft Bank."

"Three days ago? Where is he now?"

"Dead. A freak automobile accident on a road he traveled every day of his life. Here's the police report; I had it translated." Abbott took the papers, and sat down in a nearby chair. Elliot Stevens remained standing; Webb continued. "There's something very interesting there. It doesn't tell us anything we don't know, but there's a lead I'd like to follow up."

"What is it?" asked the Monk, reading. "This describes the accident. The curve, speed of vehicle, apparent swerving to avoid a collision."

"It's at the end. It mentions the killing at the Gemeinschaft, the bolt that got us off our asses."

"It does?" Abbott turned the page.

"Look at it. Last couple of sentences. See what I mean?"

"Not exactly," replied Abbott, frowning. "This merely states that Koenig was employed by the Gemeinschaft where a recent homicide took place . . . . and he had been a witness to the initial gunfire. That's all."

"I don't think it is 'all,' " said Webb. "I think there was more. Someone started to raise a question, but it was left hanging. I'd like to find out who has his red pencil on the Zurich police reports. He could be Carlos's man; we know he's got one there."

The Monk leaned back in the chair, his frown unrelieved. "Assuming you're right, why wasn't the entire reference deleted?"

"Too obvious. The killing *did* take place; Koenig *was* a witness; the investigating officer who wrote up the report might legitimately ask why."

"But if he had speculated on a connection wouldn't he be just as disturbed that the speculation was deleted?"

"Not necessarily. We're talking about a bank in Switzerland. Certain areas are officially inviolable unless there's proof."

"Not always. I understood you were very successful with the newspapers."

"*Un*officially. I appealed to prurient journalistic sensationalism, and—although it damn near killed him—got Walther Apfel to corroborate halfway."

"Interruption," said Elliot Stevens. "I think this is where the Oval Office has to come in. I assume by the newspapers you're referring to the Canadian woman."

"Not really. That story was already out; we couldn't stop it. Carlos is wired into the Zurich police; they issued that report. We simply enlarged on it and tied her to an equally false story about millions having been stolen from the Gemeinschaft." Webb paused and looked at Abbott. "That's something we have to talk about; it may not be false after all."

"I can't believe that," said the Monk.

"I don't *want* to believe it," replied the major. "Ever."

"Would you mind backing up?" asked the White House aide, sitting down opposite the army officer. "I have to get this very clear."

"Let me explain," broke in Abbott, seeing the bewilderment on Webb's face. "Elliot's here on orders from the president. It's the killing at the Ottawa airport."

"It's an unholy mess," said Stevens bluntly. "The prime minister damn near told the president to take our stations out of Nova Scotia. He's one angry Canadian."

"How did it come down?" asked Webb.

"Very badly. All they know is that a ranking economist at National Revenue's Treasury Board made discreet inquiries about an unlisted American corporation and got himself killed for it. To make matters worse, Canadian Intelligence was told to stay out of it; it was a highly sensitive U. S. operation."

"Who the hell did *that?*"

"I believe I've heard the name Iron Ass bandied about here and there," said the Monk.

"General Crawford? Stupid son of a bitch—stupid iron-assed son of a bitch!"

"Can you imagine?" interjected Stevens. *"Their* man gets killed and *we* have the gall to tell them to stay out."

"He was right, of course," corrected Abbott. "It had to be done swiftly, no room for misunderstanding. A clamp had to be put on instantly, the shock sufficiently outrageous to stop everything. It gave me time to reach MacKenzie Hawkins—Mac and I worked together in Burma; he's retired but they listen to him. They're cooperating now and that's the important thing, isn't it?"

"There are other considerations, Mr. Abbott," protested Stevens.

"They're on different levels, Elliot. We working stiffs aren't on them; we don't have to spend time over diplomatic posturing. I'll grant you those postures are necessary, but they don't concern us."

"They do concern the president, sir. They're part of his every working-stiff day. And that's why I have to go back with a very clear picture." Stevens paused, turning to Webb. "Now, please, let me have it again. Exactly what did you do and why? What part did we play regarding this Canadian woman?"

"Initially not a goddamn thing; that was Carlos's move. Someone very high up in the Zurich police is on Carlos's payroll. It was the Zurich police who mocked up the so-called evidence linking her to the three killings. And it's ludicrous; she's no killer."

"All right, all right," said the aide. "That was Carlos. Why did he do it?"

"To flush out Bourne. The St. Jacques woman and Bourne are together."

"Bourne being this assassin who calls himself Cain, correct?"

"Yes," said Webb. "Carlos has sworn to kill him. Cain's moved in on Carlos all over Europe and the Middle East, but there's no photograph of Cain, no one really knows what he looks like. So by circulating a picture of the woman—and let me tell you, it's in every damn newspaper over there—someone may spot her. If she's found, the chances are that Cain—Bourne—will be found too. Carlos will kill them both."

"All right. Again, that's Carlos. Now what did *you* do?"

"Just what I said. Reached the Gemeinschaft and convinced the bank into confirming the fact that the woman might—just might—be tied with a massive theft. It wasn't easy, but it was their man Koenig who'd been bribed, not one of our people. That's an internal matter; they wanted a lid on it. Then I called the papers and referred them to Walther Apfel. Mysterious woman, murder, millions stolen; the editors leaped at it."

"For Christ's sake, why?" shouted Stevens. "You used a citizen of another country for a U.S. intelligence strategy! A staff employee of a closely allied government. Are you out of your minds? You only exacerbated the situation, you sacrificed her!"

"You're wrong," said Webb. "We're trying to save her life. We've turned Carlos's weapon against him."

"How?"

The Monk raised his hand. "Before we answer we have to go back to another question," he said. "Because the answer to that may give you an indication of how restricted the information must remain. A moment ago I asked the major how Carlos's man could have found Bourne—found the *fiche* that identified Bourne as Cain. I think I know, but I want him to tell you."

Webb leaned forward. "The Medusa records," he said, quietly, reluctantly.

"Medusa . . . ?" Stevens' expression conveyed the fact that the Medusa had been the subject of early White House confidential briefings. "They're buried," he said.

"Correction," intruded Abbott. "There's an original and two copies, and they're in vaults at the Pentagon, the CIA and the National Security Council. Access to them is limited to a select group, each one among the highest-ranking members of his unit. Bourne came out of Medusa; a cross-checking of those names with the bank records would produce his name. Someone gave them to Carlos."

Stevens stared at the Monk. "Are you saying that Carlos is . . . wired into . . . men like that? It's an extraordinary charge."

"It's the only explanation," said Webb.

"But why would Bourne ever use his own name?"

"It was necessary," replied Abbott. "It was a vital part of the portrait. It had to be authentic; everything had to be authentic. Everything."

"Authentic?"

"Maybe you'll understand now," continued the major. "By tying the St. Jacques woman into millions supposedly stolen from the Gemeinschaft Bank, we're telling Bourne to surface. He knows it's false."

"Bourne to *surface?*"

"The man called Jason Bourne," said Abbott, getting to his feet and walking slowly toward the drawn curtains, "is an American intelligence officer. There is no Cain, not the one Carlos believes. He's a lure, a trap for Carlos; that's who he is. Or was."

The silence was brief, broken by the White House man. "I think you'd better explain. The president has to know."

"I suppose so," mused Abbott, parting the curtains, looking absently outside. "It's an insoluble dilemma, really. Presidents change, different men with different temperaments and appetites sit in the Oval Office. However, a long-range intelligence strategy doesn't change, not one like this. Yet an offhand remark over a glass of whiskey in a postpresidential conversation, or an egotistical phrase in a memoir, can blow that same strategy right to hell. There isn't a day that we don't worry about those men who have survived the White House."

"*Please,*" interrupted Stevens. "I ask you to remember that I'm here on the orders of *this* president. Whether you approve or disapprove doesn't matter. He has the right by law to know; and in his name I insist on that right."

"Very well," said Abbott, still looking outside. "Three years ago we borrowed a page from the British. We created a man who never was. If you recall, prior to the Normandy invasion British Intelligence floated a corpse into the coast of

Portugal, knowing that whatever documents were concealed on it would find their way to the German Embassy in Lisbon. A life was created for that dead body; a name, a naval officer's rank; schools, training, travel orders, driver's license, membership cards in exclusive London clubs and a half-dozen personal letters. Scattered throughout were hints, vaguely worded allusions, and a few very direct chronological and geographical references. They all pointed to the invasion taking place a hundred miles away from the beaches at Normandy, and six weeks off the target date in June. After panicked checks were made by German agents all over England—and, incidentally, controlled and monitored by MI Five—the High Command in Berlin bought the story and shifted a large part of their defenses. As many as were lost, thousands upon thousands of lives were saved by that man who never was." Abbott let the curtain fall into place and walked wearily back to his chair.

"I've heard the story," said the White House aide. "And?"

"Ours was a variation," said the Monk, sitting down wearily. "Create a living man, a quickly established legend, seemingly everywhere at once, racing all over Southeast Asia, outdoing Carlos at every turn, especially in the area of sheer numbers. Whenever there was a killing, or an unexplained death, or a prominent figure involved in a fatal accident, there was Cain. Reliable sources—paid informants known for accuracy—were fed his name; embassies, listening posts, entire intelligence networks were repeatedly funneled reports that concentrated on Cain's rapidly expanding activities. His 'kills' were mounting every month, sometimes it seemed weekly. He was everywhere . . . and he *was*. In all ways."

"You mean this Bourne was?"

"Yes. He spent months learning everything there was to learn about Carlos, studying every file we had, every known and suspected assassination with which Carlos was involved. He pored over Carlos's tactics, his methods of operation, everything. Much of *that* material has never seen the light of day, and probably never will. It's explosive—governments and international combines would be at each others' throats. There was literally nothing Bourne did not know—that could be *known*—about Carlos. And then he'd show himself, always with a different appearance, speaking any of several languages, talking about things to selected circles of hardened criminals that only a professional killer would talk about. Then he'd be gone, leaving behind bewildered and often frightened men and women. They had seen Cain; he existed, and he was ruthless. That was the image Bourne conveyed."

"He's been underground like this for *three years?*" asked Stevens.

"Yes. He moved to Europe, the most accomplished white assassin in Asia, graduate of the infamous Medusa, challenging Carlos in his own yard. And in the process he saved four men marked by Carlos, took credit for others Carlos had killed, mocked him at every opportunity . . . always trying to force him out in the open. He spent nearly three years living the most dangerous sort of lie a man can live, the kind of existence few men ever know. Most would have broken under it; and that possibility can never be ruled out."

"What kind of man is he?"

"A professional," answered Gordon Webb. "Someone who had the training and the capability, who understood that Carlos had to be found, stopped."

"But three *years* . . .?"

"If that seems incredible," said Abbott, "you should know that he submitted to surgery. It was like a final break with the past, with the man he was in order to become a man he wasn't. I don't think there's any way a nation can repay a man like Bourne for what he's done. Perhaps the only way is to give him the chance to succeed—and by God I intend to do that." The Monk stopped for precisely two seconds, then added, "If it *is* Bourne."

It was as if Elliot Stevens had been struck by an unseen hammer. "What did you say?" he asked.

"I'm afraid I've held this to the end. I wanted you to understand the whole picture before I described the gap. It may *not* be a gap—we just don't know. Too many things have happened that make no sense to us, but we don't know. It's the reason why there can be absolutely no interference from other levels, no diplomatic sugar pills that might expose the strategy. We could condemn a man to death, a man who's given more than any of us. If he succeeds, he can go back to his own life, but only anonymously, only without his identity ever being revealed."

"I'm afraid you'll have to explain that," said the astonished presidential aide.

"Loyalty, Elliot. It's not restricted to what's commonly referred to as the 'good guys.' Carlos has built up an army of men and women who are devoted to him. They may not know him but they revere him. However, if he can take Carlos—or trap Carlos so we can take him—then vanish, he's home free."

"But you say he may *not* be Bourne!"

"I said we don't know. It *was* Bourne at the bank, the signatures were authentic. But is it Bourne now? The next few days will tell us."

"If he surfaces," added Webb.

"It's delicate," continued the old man. "There are so many variables. If it isn't Bourne—or if he's turned—it could explain the call to Ottawa, the killing at the airport. From what we can gather, the woman's expertise *was* used to withdraw the money in Paris. All Carlos had to do was make a few inquiries at the Canadian Treasury Board. The rest would be child's play for him. Kill her contact, panic her, cut her off, and use her to contain Bourne."

"Were you able to get word to her?" asked the major.

"I tried and failed. I had Mac Hawkins call a man who also worked closely with the St. Jacques woman, a man named Alan somebody-or-other. He instructed her to return to Canada immediately. She hung up on him."

"God*damn* it!" exploded Webb.

"Precisely. If we could have gotten her back, we might have learned so much. She's the key. Why is she with him? Why he with her? Nothing makes sense."

"Less so to me!" said Stevens, his bewilderment turning into anger. "If you want the president's cooperation—and I promise nothing—you'd better be clearer."

Abbott turned to him. "Some six months ago Bourne disappeared," he said. "Something happened; we're not sure what, but we can piece together a probability. He got word into Zurich that he was on his way to Marseilles. Later—too late—we understood. He'd learned that Carlos had accepted a contract on Howard Leland, and Bourne tried to stop it. Then nothing; he vanished. Had he been killed? Had he broken under the strain? Had he . . . given up?"

"I can't accept that," interrupted Webb angrily. "I won't accept it!"

"I know you won't," said the Monk. "It's why I want you to go through that file. You know his codes; they're all in there. See if you can spot any deviations in Zurich."

"Please!" broke in Stevens. "What do you *think?* You must have found something concrete, something on which to base a judgment. I need that, Mr. Abbott. The president needs it."

"I wish to heaven I had," replied the Monk. "What have we found? Everything and nothing. Almost three years of the most carefully constructed deception in our records. Every false act documented, every move defined and justified; each man and woman—informants, contacts, sources—given faces, voices, stories to tell. And every month, every week just a little bit closer to Carlos. Then nothing. Silence. Six months of a vacuum."

"Not now," countered the president's aide. "That silence was broken. By whom?"

"That's the basic question, isn't it?" said the old man, his voice tired. "Months of silence, then suddenly an explosion of unauthorized, incomprehensible activity. The account penetrated, the *fiche* altered, millions transferred—by all appearances, stolen. Above all, men killed and traps set for other men. But for whom, *by* whom?" The Monk shook his head wearily. "Who *is* the man out there?"

20

The limousine was parked between two streetlamps, diagonally across from the heavy ornamental doors of the brownstone. In the front seat sat a uniformed chauffeur; such a driver at the wheel of such a vehicle not an uncommon sight on the tree-lined street. What was unusual, however, was the fact that two other men remained in the shadows of the deep back seat, neither making any move to get out. Instead, they watched the entrance of the brownstone, confident that they could not be picked up by the infrared beam of a scanning camera.

One man adjusted his glasses, the eyes beyond his thick lenses owl-like, flatly suspicious of most of what they surveyed. Alfred Gillette, director of Personnel Screening and Evaluation for the National Security Council, spoke. "How gratifying to be there when arrogance collapses. How much more so to be the instrument."

"You really dislike him, don't you?" said Gillette's companion, a heavy-shouldered man in a black raincoat whose accent was derived from a Slavic language somewhere in Europe.

"I loathe him. He stands for everything I hate in Washington. The right schools, houses in Georgetown, farms in Virginia, quiet meetings at their clubs. They've got their tight little world and you don't break in—they run it all. The *bastards*. The superior, self-inflated *gentry* of Washington. They use other men's intellects, other men's work, wrapping it all into decisions bearing their imprimaturs. And if you're on the outside, you become part of that amorphous entity, a 'damn fine staff.'"

"You exaggerate," said the European, his eyes on the brownstone. "You haven't done badly down there. We never would have contacted you otherwise."

Gillette scowled. "If I haven't done badly, it's because I've become indispensable to too many like David Abbott. I have in my head a thousand facts they couldn't possibly recall. It's simply easier for them to place me where the questions are, where problems need solutions. Director of Personnel Screening and Evaluation! They created that title, that post, for me. Do you know why?"

"No, Alfred," replied the European, looking at his watch, "I don't know why."

"Because they don't have the patience to spend hours poring over thousands of résumés and dossiers. They'd rather be dining at Sans Souci, or preening in front of Senate committees, reading from pages prepared by others—by those unseen, unnamed 'damn fine staffs.'"

"You're a bitter man," said the European.

"More than you'll know. A lifetime doing the work those bastards should have done for themselves. And for what? A title and an occasional lunch where my brains are picked between the shrimp and the entrée! By men like the supremely arrogant David Abbott; they're nothing without people like me."

"Don't underestimate the Monk. Carlos doesn't."

"How could he? He doesn't know what to evaluate. Everything Abbott does is shrouded in secrecy; no one knows how many mistakes he's made. And if any come to light, men like me are blamed for them."

The European shifted his gaze from the window to Gillette. "You're very emotional, Alfred," he said coldly. "You must be careful about that."

The bureaucrat smiled. "It never gets in the way: I believe my contributions to Carlos bear that out. Let's say I'm preparing myself for a confrontation I wouldn't avoid for anything in the world."

"An honest statement," said the heavy-shouldered man.

"What about you? You found me."

"I knew what to look for." The European returned to the window.

"I mean *you*. The work you do. For Carlos."

"I have no such complicated reasoning. I come out of a country where educated men are promoted at the whim of morons who recite Marxist litany by rote. Carlos, too, knew what to look for."

Gillette laughed, his flat eyes close to shining. "We're not so different after all. Change the bloodlines of our Eastern establishment for Marx and there's a distinct parallel."

"Perhaps," agreed the European, looking again at his watch. "It shouldn't be long now. Abbott always catches the midnight shuttle, his every hour accounted for in Washington."

"You're sure he'll come out alone?"

"He always does, and he certainly wouldn't be seen with Elliot Stevens. Webb and Stevens will also leave separately; twenty-minute intervals is standard for those called in."

"How did you find Treadstone?"

"It wasn't so difficult. You contributed, Alfred; you were part of a damn fine staff." The man laughed, his eyes on the brownstone. "Cain was out of Medusa, you told us that, and if Carlos's suspicions are accurate, that meant the Monk, we knew *that*; it tied him to Bourne. Carlos instructed us to keep Abbott under twenty-four-hour surveillance; something had gone wrong. When the gunshots in Zurich were heard in Washington, Abbott got careless. We followed him here. It was merely a question of persistence."

"That led you to Canada? To the man in Ottawa?"

"The man in Ottawa revealed himself by looking for Treadstone. When we learned who the girl was, we had the Treasury Board watched, her section watched. A call came from Paris; it was she, telling him to start a search. We don't know why, but we suspect Bourne may be trying to blow Treadstone apart. If he's turned, it's one way to get out and keep the money. It doesn't matter. Suddenly, this section head no one outside the Canadian government had ever heard of was transformed into a problem of the highest priority. Intelligence communiqués were burning the wires. It meant Carlos was right; *you* were right, Alfred. There is no Cain. He's an invention, a trap."

"From the beginning," insisted Gillette. "I told you that. Three years of false reports, sources unverified. It was all there."

"From the beginning," mused the European. "Undoubtedly the Monk's finest creation . . . until something happened and the creation turned. Everything's turning; it's all coming apart at the seams."

"Stevens' being here confirms that. The president insists on knowing."

"He has to. There's a nagging suspicion in Ottawa that a section head at the Treasury Board was killed by American Intelligence." The European turned from the window and looked at the bureaucrat. "Remember, Alfred, we simply want to know what happened. I've given you the facts as we've learned them; they're irrefutable and Abbott cannot deny them. But they must be presented as having been obtained independently by your own sources. You're appalled. You demand an accounting; the entire intelligence community has been duped."

"It has!" exclaimed Gillette. "Duped and used. No one in Washington knows about Bourne, about Treadstone. They've excluded everyone; it *is* appalling. I don't have to pretend. Arrogant bastards!"

"Alfred," cautioned the European, holding up his hand in the shadows, "do remember whom you're working for. The threat cannot be based on emotion, but in cold professional outrage. He'll suspect you instantly; you must dispel those suspicions just as swiftly. *You* are the accuser, not he."

"I'll remember."

"Good." Headlight beams bounced through the glass. "Abbott's taxi is here. I'll take care of the driver." The European reached to his right and flipped a switch beneath the armrest. "I'll be in my car across the street, listening." He spoke to the chauffeur. "Abbott will be coming out any moment now. You know what to do."

The chauffeur nodded. Both men got out of the limousine simultaneously. The driver walked around the hood as if to escort a wealthy employer to the south side of the street. Gillette watched through the rear window; the two men stayed together for several seconds, then separated, the European heading for the approaching cab, his hand held up, a bill between his fingers. The taxi would be sent away; the caller's plans had changed. The chauffeur had raced to the north side of the street and was now concealed in the shadows of a staircase two doors away from Treadstone Seventy-One.

Thirty seconds later Gillette's eyes were drawn to the door of the brownstone. Light spilled through as an impatient David Abbott came outside, looking up and down the street, glancing at his watch, obviously annoyed. The taxi was late and he had a plane to catch; precise schedules had to be followed. Abbott walked down the steps, turning left on the pavement, looking for the cab, expecting it. In seconds he would pass the chauffeur. He did, both men well out of camera range.

The interception was quick, the discussion rapid. In moments, a bewildered David Abbott climbed inside the limousine and the chauffeur walked away into the shadows.

"You!" said the Monk, anger and disgust in his voice. "Of all people, *you.*"

"I don't think you're in any position to be disdainful . . . much less arrogant."

"What you've *done!* How *dare* you? Zurich. The Medusa records. It was you!"

"The Medusa records, yes. Zurich, yes. But it's not a question of what *I've* done; it's what you've done. We sent our own men to Zurich, telling them what to look for. We found it. His name is Bourne, isn't it? He's the man you call Cain. The man you invented."

Abbott kept himself in check. "How did you find this house?"

"Persistence. I had you followed."

"You had *me* followed? What the hell did you think you were *doing?*"

"Trying to set a record straight. A record you've warped and lied about, keeping the truth from the rest of us. What did you think *you* were doing?"

"Oh, my God, you damn fool!" Abbott inhaled deeply. "Why did you do it? Why didn't you come to me yourself?"

"Because you'd have done nothing. You've manipulated the entire intelligence community. Millions of dollars, untold thousands of man hours, embassies and stations fed lies and distortions about a killer that never existed. Oh, I recall your words—what a challenge to Carlos! What an irresistible *trap* is what it was! Only we were your pawns too, and as a responsible member of the Security Council, I resent it deeply. You're all alike. Who elected you God so you could break the rules—no, not just the rules, the laws—and make us look like fools?"

"There was no other way," said the old man wearily, his face a drawn mass of crevices in the dim light. "How many know? Tell me the truth."

"I've contained it. I gave you that."

"It may not be enough. Oh, Christ!"

"It may not last, period," said the bureaucrat emphatically. "I want to know what happened."

"What happened?"

"To this grand strategy of yours. It seems to be . . . falling apart at the seams."

"Why do you say that?"

"It's perfectly obvious. You've lost Bourne; you can't find him. Your Cain has disappeared with a fortune banked for him in Zurich."

Abbott was silent for a moment. "Wait a minute. What put you on to it?"

"You," said Gillette quickly, the prudent man rising to the baited question. "I must say I admired your control when that ass from the Pentagon spoke so knowingly of Operation Medusa . . . sitting directly across from the man who created it."

"History." The old man's voice was strong now. "That wouldn't have told you anything."

"Let's say it was rather unusual for you not to *say* anything. I mean, who at that table knew more about Medusa than you? But you didn't say a word, and that started me thinking. So I objected strenuously to the attention being paid this assassin, Cain. You couldn't resist, David. You had to offer a very plausible reason to continue the search for Cain. You threw Carlos into the hunt."

"It was the truth," interrupted Abbott.

"Certainly it was; you knew when to use it and I knew when to spot it. Ingenious. A snake pulled out of Medusa's head, groomed for a mythical title. The contender jumps into the champion's ring to draw the champion out of his corner."

"It was sound, sound from the beginning."

"Why not? As I say, it was ingenious, even down to every move made by his own people against Cain. Who better to relay those moves to Cain but the one man on the Forty Committee who's given reports on every covert operations conference. You used us all!"

The Monk nodded. "Very well. To a point you're right, there've been degrees of abuse—in my opinion, totally justified—but it's not what you think. There are checks and balances; there always are, I wouldn't have it any other way. Tread-stone is comprised of a small group of men among the most trustworthy in the government. They range from Army G-Two to the Senate, from the CIA to Naval Intelligence, and now, frankly, the White House. Should there be any true abuse, there's not one of them that would hesitate to put a stop to the operation. None has ever seen fit to do so, and I beg you not to do so either."

"Would I be made part of Treadstone?"

"You *are* part of it now."

"I see. What happened? Where is Bourne?"

"I wish to God we knew. We're not even sure it *is* Bourne."

"You're not even sure of *what?*"

"*I see. What happened? Where is Bourne?*"

"*I wish to God we knew. We're not even sure it is Bourne.*"

"*You're not even sure of what?*"

The European reached for the switch on the dashboard and snapped it off. "That's it," he said. "That's what we had to know." He turned to the chauffeur beside him. "Quickly, now. Get beside the staircase. Remember, if one of them comes out, you have precisely three seconds before the door is closed. Work fast."

The uniformed man got out first; he walked up the pavement toward Tread-stone Seventy-One. From one of the adjacent brownstones, a middle-aged couple were saying loud goodbyes to their hosts. The chauffeur slowed down, reached into his pocket for a cigarette and stopped to light it. He was now a bored driver, whiling away the hours of a tedious vigil. The European watched, then unbuttoned his raincoat and withdrew a long, thin revolver, its barrel enlarged by a silencer. He switched off the safety, shoved the weapon back into his holster, got out of the car and walked across the street toward the limousine. The mirrors had been angled properly; by staying in the blind spot there was no way either man inside could see him approach. The European paused briefly for the rear trunk, then swiftly, hand extended, lunged for the right front door, opened it and spun inside, leveling his weapon over the seat.

Alfred Gillette gasped, his left hand surging for the door handle; the European snapped the four-way lock. David Abbott remained immobile, staring at the invader.

"Good evening, Monk," said the European. "Another, whom I'm told often assumes a religious habit, sends you his congratulations. Not only for Cain, but for your household personnel at Treadstone. The Yachtsman, for instance. Once a superior agent."

Gillette found his voice; it was a mixture of a scream and a whisper. "What *is* this? Who *are* you?" he cried, feigning ignorance.

"Oh come now, old friend. That's not necessary," said the man with the gun. "I can see by the expression on Mr. Abbott's face that he realizes his initial doubts about you were accurate. One should always trust one's first instincts, shouldn't one, Monk? You were right, of course. We found another discontented man; your system reproduces them with alarming rapidity. He, indeed, gave us the Medusa files, and they did, indeed, lead us to Bourne."

"What are you doing?!" screamed Gillette. "What are you *saying!*"

"You're a bore, Alfred. But you were always part of a damn fine staff. It's too bad you didn't know which staff to stay with; your kind never do."

"You! . . ." Gillette rose bodily off the seat, his face contorted.

The European fired his weapon, the cough from the barrel echoing briefly in the soft interior of the limousine. The bureaucrat slumped over, his body crumbling to the floor against the door, owl-eyes wide in death.

"I don't think you mourn him," said the European.

"I don't," said the Monk.

"It *is* Bourne out there, you know. Cain turned; he broke. The long period of silence is over. The snake from Medusa's head decided to strike out on his own. Or perhaps he was bought. That's possible too, isn't it? Carlos buys many men, the one at your feet now, for example."

"You'll learn nothing from me. Don't try."

"There's nothing to learn. We know it all. Delta, Charlie . . . Cain. But the names aren't important any longer; they never were, really. All that remains is the final isolation—removing of the man-monk who makes the decisions. You. Bourne is trapped. He's finished."

"There are others who make decisions. He'll reach them."

"If he does, they'll kill him on sight. There's nothing more despicable than a man who's turned, but in order for a man to turn, there has to be irrefutable proof that he was yours to begin with. Carlos has the proof; he *was* yours, his origins as sensitive as anything in the Medusa files."

The old man frowned; he was frightened, not for his life, but for something infinitely more indispensable. "You're out of your mind," he said. "There is no proof."

"That was the flaw, *your* flaw. Carlos is thorough; his tentacles reach into all manner of hidden recesses. You needed a man from Medusa, someone who had lived and disappeared. You chose a man named Bourne because the circumstances of his disappearance had been obliterated, eliminated from every existing record—or so you believed. But you didn't consider Hanoi's own field personnel who had infiltrated Medusa; those records exist. On March 25, 1968, Jason Bourne was executed by an American Intelligence officer in the jungles of Tam Quan."

The Monk lunged forward; there was nothing left but a final gesture, a final defiance. The European fired.

The door of the brownstone opened. From the shadows beneath the staircase the chauffeur smiled. The White House aide was being escorted out by the old man who lived at Treadstone, the one they called the Yachtsman; the killer knew that meant the primary alarms were off. The three-second span was eliminated.

"So good of you to drop by," said the Yachtsman, shaking hands.

"Thank you very much, sir."

Those were the last words either man spoke. The chauffeur aimed above the walled brick railing, pulling the trigger twice, the muffled reports indistinguishable from the myriad if distant sounds of the city. The Yachtsman fell back inside; the White House aide clutched his upper chest, reeling into the door frame. The chauffeur spun around the brick railing and raced up the steps, catching Stevens' body as it plummeted down. With bull-like strength, the killer lifted the White House man off his feet, hurling him back through the door into the foyer beyond the Yachtsman. Then he turned to the interior border of the heavy, steel-plated door. He knew what to look for; he found it. Along the upper molding, disappearing into the wall, was a thick cable, stained the color of the doorframe. He closed the door part way, raised his gun and fired into the cable. The spit was followed by an eruption of static and sparks; the security cameras were blown out, screens everywhere now dark.

He opened the door to signal; it was not necessary. The European was walking rapidly across the quiet street. Within seconds he had climbed the steps and was inside, glancing around the foyer and the hallway—the door at the end of the hallway. Together both men lifted a rug from the foyer floor, the European closing the door on its edge, welding cloth and steel together so that a two-inch space remained, the security bolts still in place. No backup alarms could be raised.

They stood erect in silence; both knew that if the discovery was going to be made, it would be made quickly. It came with the sound of an upstairs door opening, followed by footsteps and words that floated down the staircase in a cultured female voice.

"Darling! I just noticed, the damn camera's on the fritz. Would you check it, please?" There was a pause; then the woman spoke again. "On second thought why not tell David?" Again the pause, again with precise timing. "Don't bother the Jesuit, darling. Tell David!"

Two footsteps. Silence. A rustle of cloth. The European studied the stairwell. A light went out. David. Jesuit . . . Monk!

"Get her!" he roared at the chauffeur, spinning around, his weapon leveled at the door at the end of the hallway.

The uniformed man raced up the staircase; there was a gunshot; it came from a powerful weapon—unmuffled, unsilenced. The European looked up; the chauffeur was holding his shoulder, his coat drenched with blood, his pistol held out, spitting repeatedly up the well of the stairs.

The door at the end of the hallway was yanked open, the major standing there in shock, a file folder in his hand. The European fired twice; Gordon Webb arched backward, his throat torn open, the papers in the folder flying out behind him. The man in the raincoat raced up the steps to the chauffeur; above, over the railing, was the gray-haired woman, dead, blood spilling out of her head and neck. "Are you all right? Can you move?" asked the European.

The chauffeur nodded. "The bitch blew half my shoulder off, but I can manage."

"You have to!" commanded his superior, ripping off his raincoat. "Put on my coat. I want the Monk in here! Quickly!"

"Jesus! . . ."

"Carlos wants the Monk in here!"

Awkwardly the wounded man put on the black raincoat and made his way down the staircase around the bodies of the Yachtsman and the White House aide. Carefully, in pain, he let himself out the door and down the front steps.

The European watched him, holding the door, making sure the man was sufficiently mobile for the task. He was; he was a bull whose every appetite was satisfied by Carlos. The chauffeur would carry David Abbott's corpse back into the brownstone, no doubt supporting it as though helping an aging drunk for the benefit of anyone in the street; and then he would somehow contain his bleeding long enough to drive Alfred Gillette's body across the river, burying him in a swamp. Carlos's men were capable of such things; they were all bulls. Discontented bulls who had found their own causes in a single man.

The European turned and started down the hallway; there was work to do. The final isolation of the man called Jason Bourne.

It was more than could be hoped for, the exposed files a gift beyond belief. Included were folders containing every code and method of communication ever used by the mythical Cain. Now not so mythical, thought the European as he gathered the papers together. The scene was set, the four corpses in position in the peaceful, elegant library. David Abbott was arched in a chair, his dead eyes in shock, Elliot Stevens at his feet; the Yachtsman was slumped over the hatch table, an overturned bottle of whiskey in his hand, while Gordon Webb sprawled on the floor, clutching his briefcase. Whatever violence had taken place, the setting indicated that it had been unexpected; conversations interrupted by abrupt gunfire.

The European walked around in suede gloves, appraising his artistry, and it *was* artistry. He had dismissed the chauffeur, wiped every door handle, every knob, every gleaming surface of wood. It was time for the final touch. He walked to a table where there were brandy glasses on a silver tray, picked one up and held it to the light; as he expected, it was spotless. He put it down and took out a small, flat, plastic case from his pocket. He opened it and removed a strip of transparent tape, holding it, too, up to the light. There they were, as clear as portraits—for they were portraits, as undeniable as any photograph.

They had been taken off a glass of Perrier, removed from an office at the Gemeinschaft Bank in Zurich. They were the fingerprints of Jason Bourne's right hand.

The European picked up the brandy glass and, with the patience of the artist he was, pressed the tape around the lower surface, then gently peeled it off. Again he held the glass up; the prints were seen in dull perfection against the light of the table lamp.

He carried the glass over to a corner of the parquet floor and dropped it. He knelt down, studied the fragments, removed several, and brushed the rest under the curtain.

They were enough.

21

"Later," said Bourne, throwing their suitcases on the bed. "We've got to get out of here."

Marie sat in the armchair. She had reread the newspaper article again, selecting phrases, repeating them. Her concentration was absolute; she was consumed, more and more confident of her analysis.

"I'm right, Jason. Someone *is* sending us a message."

"We'll talk about it later; we've stayed here too long as it is. That newspaper'll be all over this hotel in an hour, and the morning papers may be worse. It's no time for modesty; you stand out in a hotel lobby, and you've been seen in this one by too many people. Get your things."

Marie stood up, but made no other move. Instead, she held her place and forced him to look at her. "We'll talk about several things later," she said firmly. "You were leaving me, Jason, and I want to know why."

"I told you I'd tell you," he answered without evasion, "because you have to know and I mean that. But right now I want to get out of here. Get your things, goddamn it!"

She blinked, his sudden anger having its effect. "Yes, of course," she whispered.

They took the elevator down to the lobby. As the worn marble floor came into view, Bourne had the feeling they were in a cage, exposed and vulnerable; if the machine stopped, they would be taken. Then he understood why the feeling was so strong. Below on the left was the front desk, the *concierge* sitting behind it, a pile of newspapers on the counter to his right. They were copies of the same tabloid Jason had put in the attaché case Marie was now carrying. The *concierge* had taken one; he was reading it avidly; poking a toothpick between his teeth, oblivious to everything but the latest scandal.

"Walk straight through," said Jason. "Don't stop, just go right to the door. I'll meet you outside."

"Oh, my God," she whispered, seeing the *concierge*.

"I'll pay him as quickly as I can."

The sound of Marie's heels on the marble floor was a distraction Bourne did not want. The *concierge* looked up as Jason moved in front of him, blocking his view.

"It's been very pleasant," he said in French, "but I'm in a great hurry. I have to drive to Lyon tonight. Just round out the figure to the nearest five hundred francs. I haven't had time to leave gratuities."

The financial distraction accomplished its purpose. The *concierge* reached his totals quickly; he presented the bill. Jason paid it and bent down for the suitcases, glancing up at the sound of surprise that exploded from the *concierge*'s gaping mouth. The man was staring at the pile of newspapers on his right, his eyes on the photograph of Marie St. Jacques. He looked over at the glass doors of the entrance; Marie stood on the pavement. He shifted his astonished gaze to Bourne; the connection was made, the man inhibited by sudden fear.

Jason walked rapidly toward the glass doors, angling his shoulder to push them open, glancing back at the front desk. The *concierge* was reaching for a telephone.

"Let's go!" he cried to Marie. "Look for a cab!"

They found one on rue Lecourbe, five blocks from the hotel. Bourne feigned the role of an inexperienced American tourist, employing the inadequate French that had served him so well at the Valois Bank. He explained to the driver that he and his *petite amie* wanted to get out of central Paris for a day or so, someplace where they could be alone. Perhaps the driver could suggest several places and they would choose one.

The driver could and did. "There's a small inn outside Issy-les-Moulineaux, called La Maison Carrée," he said. "Another in Ivry sur Seine, you might like. It's very private, monsieur. Or perhaps the Auberge du Coin in Montrouge; it's very discreet."

"Let's take the first," said Jason. "It's the first that came to your mind. How long will it take?"

"No more than fifteen, twenty minutes, monsieur."

"Good." Bourne turned to Marie and spoke softly. "Change your hair."

"What?"

"Change your hair. Pull it up or push it back, I don't care, but change it. Move out of sight of his mirror. Hurry up!"

Several moments later Marie's long auburn hair was pulled severely back, away from her face and neck, fastened with the aid of a mirror and hairpins from her purse into a tight chignon. Jason looked at her in the dim light.

"Wipe off your lipstick. All of it."

She took out a tissue and did so. "All right?"

"Yes. Have you got an eyebrow pencil?"

"Of course."

"Thicken your eyebrows; just a little bit. Extend them about a quarter of an inch; curve the ends down just a touch."

Again she followed his instructions. "Now?" she asked.

"That's better," he replied, studying her. The changes were minor but the effect major. She had been subtly transformed from a softly elegant, striking woman into a harsher image. At the least, she was not on first sight the woman in the newspaper photograph and that was all that mattered.

"When we reach Moulineaux," he whispered, "get out quickly and stand up. Don't let the driver see you."

"It's a little late for that, isn't it?"

"Just do as I say."

Listen to me. I am a chameleon called Cain and I can teach you many things

I do not care to teach you, but at the moment I must. I can change my color to accommodate any backdrop in the forest, I can shift with the wind by smelling it. I can find my way through the natural and the manmade jungles. Alpha, Bravo, Charlie, Delta. . . . Delta is for Charlie and Charlie is for Cain. I am Cain. I am death. And I must tell you who I am and lose you.

"My darling, what is it?"

"What?"

"You're looking at me; you're not breathing. Are you all right?"

"Sorry," he said, glancing away, breathing again. "I'm figuring out our moves. I'll know better what to do when we get there."

They arrived at the inn. There was a parking lot bordered by a post-and-rail fence on the right; several late diners came out of the lattice-framed entrance in front. Bourne leaned forward in the seat.

"Let us off inside the parking area, if you don't mind," he ordered, offering no explanation for the odd request.

"Certainly, monsieur," said the driver, nodding his head, then shrugging, his movements conveying the fact that his passengers were, indeed, a cautious couple. The rain had subsided, returning to a mistlike drizzle. The taxi drove off. Bourne and Marie remained in the shadows of the foliage at the side of the inn until it disappeared. Jason put the suitcases down on the wet ground. "Wait here," he said.

"Where are you going?"

"To phone for a taxi."

The second taxi took them into the Montrouge district. This driver was singularly unimpressed by the stern-faced couple who were obviously from the provinces, and probably seeking cheaper lodgings. When and if he picked up a newspaper and saw a photograph of a French-Canadiènne involved with murder and theft in Zurich, the woman in his back seat now would not come to mind.

The Auberge du Coin did not live up to its name. It was not a quaint village inn situated in a secluded nook of the countryside. Instead, it was a large, flat, two-story structure a quarter of a mile off the highway. If anything, it was reminiscent of motels the world over that blighted the outskirts of cities; commerciality guaranteeing the anonymity of their guests. It was not hard to imagine various appointments by the scores that were best left to erroneous registrations.

So they registered erroneously and were given a plastic room where every accessory worth over twenty francs was bolted into the floor or attached with headless screws to lacquered formica. There was, however, one positive feature to the place; an ice machine down the hall. They knew it worked because they could hear it. With the door closed.

"All right, now. Who would be sending us a message?" asked Bourne, standing, revolving the glass of whiskey in his hand.

"If I knew, I'd get in touch with them," she said, sitting at the small desk, chair turned, legs crossed, watching him closely. "It could be connected with why you were running away."

"If it was, it was a trap."

"It was no trap. A man like Walther Apfel didn't do what he did to accommodate a trap."

"I wouldn't be so sure of that." Bourne walked to the single plastic armchair and sat down. "Koenig did; he marked me right there in the waiting room."

"He was a bribed foot-soldier, not an officer of the bank. He acted alone. Apfel couldn't."

Jason looked up. "What do you mean?"

"Apfel's statement had to be cleared by his superiors. It was made in the name of the bank."

"If you're so sure, let's call Zurich."

"They don't want that. Either they haven't the answer or they can't give it. Apfel's last words were that they would have no further comment. To anyone. That too, was part of the message. We're to contact someone else."

Bourne drank; he needed the alcohol, for the moment was coming when he would begin the story of a killer named Cain. "Then we're back to whom?" he said. "Back to the trap."

"You think you know who it is, don't you?" Marie reached for her cigarettes on the desk. "It's why you were running, isn't it?"

"The answer to both questions is yes." *The moment had come. The message was sent by Carlos. I am Cain and you must leave me. I must lose you. But first there is Zurich and you have to understand.* "That article was planted to find me."

"I won't argue with that," she broke in, surprising him with the interruption. "I've had time to think; they know the evidence is false—so patently false it's ridiculous. The Zurich police fully expect me to get in touch with the Canadian Embassy now—" Marie stopped, the unlit cigarette in her hand. "My God, Jason, that's what they want us to do!"

"Who wants us to do?"

"Whoever's sending us the message. They know I have no choice but to call the embassy, get the protection of the Canadian government. I didn't think of it because I've already *spoken* to the embassy, to what's his name—Dennis Corbelier—and he had absolutely nothing to tell me. He only did what I asked him to do; there was nothing else. But that was *yesterday*, not *today*, not *tonight.*" Marie started for the telephone on the bedside table.

Bourne rose quickly from the chair and intercepted her, holding her arm. "Don't," he said firmly.

"Why not?"

"Because you're wrong."

"I'm right, Jason! Let me prove it to you."

Bourne moved in front of her. "I think you'd better listen to what I have to say."

"No!" she cried, startling him. "I don't want to hear it. Not now!"

"An hour ago in Paris it was the only thing you wanted to hear. Hear it!"

"No! An hour ago I was dying. You'd made up your mind to run. Without me. And I know now it will happen over and over again until it stops for you.

You hear words, you see images, and fragments of things come back to you that you can't understand, but because they're there you condemn yourself. You always *will* condemn yourself until someone proves to you that whatever you were . . . there are others using you, who will sacrifice you. But there's also someone else out there who wants to help you, help us. That's the message! I know I'm right. I want to prove it to you. *Let* me!"

Bourne held her arms in silence, looking at her face, her lovely face filled with pain and useless hope, her eyes pleading. The terrible ache was everywhere within him. Perhaps it was better this way; she would see for herself, and her fear would make her listen, make her understand. There was nothing for them any longer. *I am Cain* . . . "All right, you can make the call, but it's got to be done my way." He released her and went to the telephone; he dialed the Auberge du Coin's front desk. "This is room 341. I've just heard from friends in Paris; they're coming out to join us in a while. Do you have a room down the hall for them? Fine. Their name is Briggs, an American couple. I'll come down and pay in advance and you can let me have the key. Splendid. Thank you."

"What are you doing?"

"Proving something to you," he said. "Get me a dress," he continued. "The longest one you've got."

"What?"

"If you want to make your call, you'll do as I tell you."

"You're crazy."

"I've admitted that," he said, taking trousers and a shirt from his suitcase. "The dress, please."

Fifteen minutes later, Mr. and Mrs. Briggs's room, six doors away and across the hall from room 341, was in readiness. The clothes had been properly placed, selected lights left on, others not functioning because the bulbs had been removed.

Jason returned to their room; Marie was standing by the telephone. "We're set."

"What have you done?"

"What I wanted to do; what I had to do. You can make the call now."

"It's very late. Suppose he isn't there?"

"I think he will be. If not, they'll give you his home phone. His name was in the telephone logs in Ottawa; it had to be."

"I suppose it was."

"Then he will have been reached. Have you gone over what I told you to say?"

"Yes, but it doesn't matter; it's not relevant. I know I'm not wrong."

"We'll see. Just say the words I told you. I'll be right beside you listening. Go ahead."

She picked up the phone and dialed. Seven seconds after she reached the embassy switchboard, Dennis Corbelier was on the line. It was quarter past one in the morning.

"Christ almighty, where *are* you?"

"You were expecting me to call, then?"

"I was hoping to hell you would! This place is in an uproar. I've been waiting here since five o'clock this afternoon."

"So was Alan. In Ottawa."

"Alan who? What are you talking about? Where the hell *are* you?"

"First I want to know what you have to tell me."

"*Tell* you?"

"You have a message for me, Dennis. What is it?"

"What is *what*? What message?"

Marie's face went pale. "I didn't kill anyone in Zurich. I wouldn't . . ."

"Then for God's sake," interrupted the attaché, "get *in* here! We'll give you all the protection we can. No one can touch you here!"

"Dennis, listen to me! You've been waiting there for my call, haven't you?"

"Yes, of course."

"Someone told you to wait, isn't that true?"

A pause. When Corbelier spoke, his voice was subdued. "Yes, he did. They did."

"What did they tell you?"

"That you need our help. Very badly."

Marie resumed breathing. "And they want to help us?"

"By us," replied Corbelier, "you're saying he's with you, then?"

Bourne's face was next to hers, his head angled to hear Corbelier's words. He nodded.

"Yes," she answered. "We're together, but he's out for a few minutes. It's all lies; they told you that, didn't they?"

"All they said was that you had to be found, protected. They *do* want to help you: they want to send a car for you. One of ours. Diplomatic."

"Who are they?"

"I don't know them by name; I don't have to. I know their rank."

"Rank?"

"Specialists, FS-Five. You don't get much higher than that."

"You trust them?"

"My God, yes! They reached me through Ottawa. Their orders came from Ottawa."

"They're at the embassy now?"

"No, they're outposted." Corbelier paused, obviously exasperated. "Jesus Christ, Marie—where *are* you?"

Bourne nodded again, she spoke.

"We're at the Auberge du Coin in Montrouge. Under the name of Briggs."

"I'll get that car to you right away."

"No, Dennis!" protested Marie, watching Jason, his eyes telling her to follow his instructions. "Send one in the morning. First thing in the morning—four hours from now, if you like."

"I can't *do* that! For your own sake."

"You have to; you don't understand. He was trapped into doing something and he's frightened; he wants to run. If he knew I called you, he'd be running now. Give me time. I can convince him to turn himself in. Just a few more hours. He's confused, but underneath he knows I'm right." Marie said the words, looking at Bourne.

"What kind of a son of a bitch is he?"

"A terrified one," she answered. "One who's being manipulated. I need the time. Give it to me."

"Marie . . . ?" Corbelier stopped. "All right, first thing in the morning. Say . . . six o'clock. And, Marie, they want to help you. They *can* help you."

"I know. Good night."

"Good night."

Marie hung up.

"Now, we'll wait," Bourne said.

"I don't know what you're proving. Of course he'll call the FS-Fives, and of course they'll show up here. What do you expect? He as much as admitted what he was going to do, what he thinks he has to do."

"And these diplomatic FS-Fives are the ones sending us the message?"

"My guess is they'll take us to who is. Or if those sending it are too far away, they'll put us in touch with them. I've never been surer of anything in my professional life."

Bourne looked at her. "I hope you're right, because it's your whole life that concerns me. If the evidence against you in Zurich isn't part of any message, if it was put there by experts to find me—if the Zurich police *believe* it—then I'm that terrified man you spoke about to Corbelier. No one wants you to be right more than I do. But I don't think you are."

At three minutes past two, the lights in the motel corridor flickered and went out, leaving the long hallway in relative darkness, the spill from the stairwell the only source of illumination. Bourne stood by the door of their room, pistol in hand, the lights turned off, watching the corridor through a crack between the door's edge and the frame. Marie was behind him, peering over his shoulder; neither spoke.

The footsteps were muffled, but there. Distinct, deliberate, two sets of shoes cautiously climbing the staircase. In seconds, the figures of two men could be seen emerging out of the dim light. Marie gasped involuntarily; Jason reached over his shoulder, his hand gripping her mouth harshly. He understood; she had recognized one of the two men, a man she had seen only once before. In Zurich's Steppdeckstrasse, minutes before another had ordered her execution. It was the blond man they had sent up to Bourne's room, the expendable scout brought now to Paris to spot the target he had missed. In his left hand was a small pencil light, in his right a long-barreled gun, swollen by a silencer.

His companion was shorter, more compact, his walk not unlike an animal's tread, shoulders and waist moving fluidly with his legs. The lapels of his topcoat were pulled up, his head covered by a narrow- brimmed hat, shading his unseen face. Bourne stared at this man; there was something familiar about him, about the figure, the walk, the way he carried his head. What was it? What *was* it? He knew him.

But there was not time to think about it; the two men were approaching the door of the room reserved in the name of Mr. and Mrs. Briggs. The blond man held his pencil light on the numbers, then swept the beam down toward the knob and the lock.

What followed was mesmerizing in its efficiency. The stocky man held a ring of keys in his right hand, placing it under the beam of light, his fingers selecting a specific key. In his left hand he gripped a weapon, its shape in the spill revealing an outsized silencer for a heavy-calibered automatic, not unlike the powerful Sternlicht Luger favored by the Gestapo in World War Two. It could cut through webbed steel and concrete, its sound no more than a rheumatic cough, ideal for taking enemies of the state at night in quiet neighborhoods, nearby residents unaware of any disturbance, only of disappearance in the morning.

The shorter man inserted the key, turned it silently, then lowered the barrel of the gun to the lock. Three rapid coughs accompanied three flashes of light; the wood surrounding any bolts shattered. The door fell free; the two killers rushed inside.

There were two beats of silence, then an eruption of muffled gunfire, spits and white flashes from the darkness. The door was slammed shut; it would not stay closed, falling back as louder sounds of thrashing and collision came from within the room. Finally a light was found; it was snapped on briefly, then shot out in fury, a lamp sent crashing to the floor, glass shattering. A cry of frenzy exploded from the throat of an infuriated man.

The two killers rushed out, weapons leveled, prepared for a trap, bewildered that there was none. They reached the staircase and raced down as a door to the right of the invaded room opened. A blinking guest peered out, then shrugged and went back inside. Silence returned to the darkened hallway.

Bourne held his place, his arm around Marie St. Jacques. She was trembling, her head pressed into his chest, sobbing quietly, hysterically, in disbelief. He let the minutes pass, until the trembling subsided and deep breaths replaced the sobs. He could not wait any longer; she had to see for herself. See completely, the impression indelible; she had to finally understand. *I am Cain. I am death.*

"Come on," he whispered.

He led her out into the hallway, guiding her firmly toward the room that was now his ultimate proof. He pushed the broken door open and they walked inside.

She stood motionless, both repelled and hypnotized by the sight. In an open doorway on the right was the dim silhouette of a figure, the light behind it so muted only the outline could be seen, and only then when the eyes adjusted to the strange admixture of darkness and glow. It was the figure of a woman in a long gown, the fabric moving gently in the breeze of an open window.

Window. Straight ahead was a second figure, barely visible but there, its shape an obscure blot indistinctly outlined by the wash of light from the distant highway. Again, it seemed to move, brief, spastic flutterings of cloth—of arms.

"Oh, God," said Marie, frozen. "Turn on the lights, Jason."

"None of them work," he replied. "Only two table lamps; they found one." He walked across the room cautiously and reached the lamp he was looking for; it was on the floor against the wall. He knelt down and turned it on; Marie shuddered.

Strung across the bathroom door, held in place by threads torn from a curtain, was her long dress, rippling from an unseen source of wind. It was riddled with bullet holes.

Against the far window, Bourne's shirt and trousers had been tacked to the frame, the panes by both sleeves smashed, the breeze rushing in, causing the fabric to move up and down. The white cloth of the shirt was punctured in a half-dozen places, a diagonal line of bullets across the chest.

"There's your message," said Jason. "Now you know what it is. And now I think you'd better listen to what I have to say."

Marie did not answer him. Instead, she walked slowly to the dress, studying it as if not believing what she saw. Without warning, she suddenly spun around, her eyes glittering, the tears arrested. "No! It's wrong! Something's terribly wrong! Call the embassy."

"What?"

"Do as I say. Now!"

"Stop it, Marie. You've got to understand."

"No, goddamn you! *You've* got to understand! It wouldn't happen this way. It couldn't."

"It did."

"Call the embassy! Use that phone over there and call it now! Ask for Corbelier. *Quickly,* for God's sake! If I mean anything to you, do as I ask!"

Bourne could not deny her. Her intensity was killing both herself and him. "What do I tell him?" he asked, going to the telephone.

"Get him first! *That's* what I'm afraid of . . . oh, God, I'm frightened!"

"What's the number?"

She gave it to him; he dialed, holding on interminably for the switchboard to answer. When it finally did, the operator was in panic, her words rising and falling, at moments incomprehensible. In the background he could hear shouts, sharp commands voiced rapidly in English and in French. Within seconds he learned why.

Dennis Corbelier, Canadian attaché, had walked down the steps of the embassy on the avenue Montaigne at 1:40 in the morning and had been shot in the throat. He was dead.

"There's the other part of the message, Jason," whispered Marie, drained, staring at him. "And now I'll listen to anything you have to say. Because there *is* someone out there trying to reach you, trying to help you. A message *was* sent, but not to us, not to me. Only to you, and only you were to understand it."

22

One by one the four men arrived at the crowded Hilton Hotel on Sixteenth Street in Washington, D.C. Each went to a separate elevator, taking it two or three floors above or below his destination, walking the remaining flights to the correct level. There was no time to meet outside the limits of the District of Columbia; the crisis was unparalleled. These were the men of Treadstone Seventy-One—those that remained alive. The rest were dead, slaughtered in a massacre on a quiet, tree-lined street in New York.

Two of the faces were familiar to the public, one more than the other. The first belonged to the aging senator from Colorado, the second was Brigadier General I. A. Crawford—Irwin Arthur, freely translated as Iron Ass—acknowledged spokesman for Army Intelligence and defender of the G-2 data banks. The other two men were virtually unknown except within the corridors of their own operations. One was a middle-aged naval officer, attached to Information Control, 5th Naval District. The fourth and last man was a forty-six-year-old veteran of the Central Intelligence Agency, a slender, coiled spring of anger who walked with a cane. His foot had been blown off by a grenade in Southeast Asia; he had been a deep-cover agent with the Medusa operation at the time. His name was Alexander Conklin.

There was no conference table in the room; it was an ordinary double occupancy with the standard twin beds, a couch, two armchairs, and a coffee table. It was an unlikely spot to hold a meeting of such consequence; there were no spinning computers to light up dark screens with green letters, no electronic communications equipment that would reach consoles in London or Paris or Istanbul. It was a plain hotel room, devoid of everything but four minds that held the secrets of Treadstone Seventy-One.

The senator sat on one end of the couch, the naval officer at the other. Conklin lowered himself into an armchair, stretching his immobile limb out in front of him, the cane between his legs, while Brigadier General Crawford remained standing, his face flushed, the muscles of his jaw pulsing in anger.

"I've reached the president," said the senator, rubbing his forehead, the lack of sleep apparent in his bearing. "I had to; we're meeting tonight. Tell me everything you can, each of you. You begin, General. What in the name of God happened?"

"Major Webb was to meet his car at 2300 hours on the corner of Lexington and Seventy-second Street. The time was firm, but he didn't show up. By 2330 the driver became alarmed because of the distance to the airfield in New Jersey. The sergeant remembered the address—mainly because he'd been told to forget it—drove around and went to the door. The security bolts had been jammed and the door just swung open; all the alarms had been shorted out. There was blood on the foyer floor, the dead woman on the staircase. He walked down the hallway into the operations room and found the bodies."

"That man deserves a very quiet promotion," said the naval officer.

"Why do you say that?" asked the senator.

Crawford replied. "He had the presence of mind to call the Pentagon and insist on speaking with covert transmissions, domestic. He specified the scrambler frequency, the time and the place of reception, and said he had to speak with the sender. He didn't say a word to anyone until he got me on the phone."

"Put him in the War College, Irwin," said Conklin grimly, holding his cane. "He's brighter than most of the clowns you've got over there."

"That's not only unnecessary, Conklin," admonished the senator, "but patently offensive. Go on, please, General."

Crawford exchanged looks with the CIA man. "I reached Colonel Paul McClaren in New York, ordered him over there, and told him to do absolutely nothing until I arrived. I then phoned Conklin and George here, and we flew up together."

"I called a Bureau print team in Manhattan," added Conklin. "One we've used before and can trust. I didn't tell them what we were looking for, but I told them to sweep the place and give what they found only to me." The CIA man stopped, lifting his cane in the direction of the naval officer. "Then George fed them thirty-seven names, all men whose prints we knew were in the FBI files. They came up with the one set we didn't expect, didn't want . . . didn't believe."

"Delta's," said the senator.

"Yes," concurred the naval officer. "The names I submitted were those of anyone—no matter how remote—who might have learned the address of Treadstone, including, incidentally, all of us. The room had been wiped clean; every surface; every knob, every glass—except one. It was a broken brandy glass, only a few fragments in the corner under a curtain, but it was enough. The prints were there: third and index fingers, right hand."

"You're absolutely positive?" asked the senator slowly.

"The prints can't lie, sir," said the officer. "They were there, moist brandy still on the fragments. Outside of this room, Delta's the only one who knows about Seventy-first Street."

"Can we be sure of that? The others may have said something."

"No possibility," interrupted the brigadier general. "Abbott would never have revealed it, and Elliot Stevens wasn't given the address until fifteen minutes before he got there, when he called from a phone booth. Beyond that, assuming the worst, he would hardly ask for his own execution."

"What about Major Webb?" pressed the senator.

"The major," replied Crawford, "was radioed the address solely by me after he landed at Kennedy Airport. As you know, it was a G-Two frequency and scrambled. I remind you, he also lost his life."

"Yes, of course." The aging senator shook his head. "It's unbelievable. *Why?*"

"I should like to bring up a painful subject," said Brigadier General Crawford. "At the outset I was not enthusiastic about the candidate. I understood David's reasoning and agreed he was qualified, but if you recall, he wasn't my choice."

"I wasn't aware we had that many choices," said the senator. "We had a man—a qualified man, as you agreed—who was willing to go in deep cover for an indeterminate length of time, risking his life every day, severing all ties with his past. How many such men exist?"

"We might have found a more balanced one," countered the brigadier. "I pointed that out at the time."

"You pointed out," corrected Conklin, "your own definition of a balanced man, which *I*, at the time, pointed out was a crock."

"We were both in Medusa, Conklin," said Crawford angrily yet reasonably. "You don't have exclusive insights. Delta's conduct in the field was continuously and overtly hostile to command. I was in a position to observe that pattern somewhat more clearly than you."

"Most of the time he had every right to be. If you'd spent more time in the field and less in Saigon you would have understood that. *I* understood it."

"It may surprise you," said the brigadier, holding his hand up in a gesture of truce, "but I'm not defending the gross stupidities often rampant in Saigon—no one could. I'm trying to describe a pattern of behavior that could lead to the night before last on Seventy-first Street."

The CIA man's eyes remained on Crawford; his hostility vanished as he nodded his head. "I know you are. Sorry. That's the crux of it, isn't it? It's not easy for me; I worked with Delta in half a dozen sectors, was stationed with him in Phnom Penh before Medusa was even a gleam in the Monk's eye. He was never the same after Phnom Penh; it's why he went into Medusa, why he was willing to become Cain."

The senator leaned forward on the couch. "I've heard it, but tell me again. The president has to know everything."

"His wife and two children were killed on a pier in the Mekong River, bombed and strafed by a stray aircraft—nobody knew which side's—the identity never uncovered. He hated that war, hated everybody in it. He snapped." Conklin paused, looking at the brigadier. "And I think you're right, General. He snapped again. It was in him."

"What was?" asked the senator sharply.

"The explosion, I guess," said Conklin. "The dam burst. He'd gone beyond his limits and the hate took over. It's not hard; you have to be very careful. He killed those men, that woman, like a madman on a deliberate rampage. None of them expected it except perhaps the woman who was upstairs, and she probably heard the shouts. He's not Delta anymore. We created a myth called Cain, only it's not a myth any longer. It's really him."

"After so many months . . ." The senator leaned back, his voice trailing off. "Why did he come back? From where?"

"From Zurich," answered Crawford. "Webb was in Zurich, and I think he's the only one who could have brought him back. The 'why' we may never know unless he expected to catch all of us there."

"He doesn't know who we are," protested the senator. "His only contacts were the Yachtsman, his wife, and David Abbott."

"And Webb, of course," added the general.

"Of course," agreed the senator. "But not at Treadstone, not even him."

"It wouldn't matter," said Conklin, tapping the rug once with his cane. "He knows there's a board; Webb might have told him we'd all be there, reasonably expecting that we would. We've got a lot of questions—six months' worth, and now several million dollars. Delta would consider it the perfect solution. He could take us and disappear. No traces."

"Why are you so certain?"

"Because, one, he was *there,*" replied the intelligence man, raising his voice. "We have his prints on a glass of brandy that wasn't even finished. And, two, it's a classic trap with a couple of hundred variations."

"Would you explain that?"

"You remain silent," broke in the general, watching Conklin, "until your enemy can't stand it any longer and exposes himself."

"And we've become the enemy? *His* enemy?"

"There's no question about it now," said the naval officer. "For whatever reasons, Delta's turned. It's happened before—thank heaven not very often. We know what to do."

The senator once more leaned forward on the couch. "What *will* you do?"

"His photograph has never been circulated," explained Crawford. "We'll circulate it now. To every station and listening post, every source and informant we have. He has to go somewhere, and he'll start with a place he knows, if only to buy another identity. He'll spend money; he'll be found. When he is, the orders will be clear."

"You'll bring him in at once?"

"We'll kill him," said Conklin simply. "You don't bring in a man like Delta, and you don't take the risk that another government will. Not with what he knows."

"I can't tell the president that. There are laws."

"Not for Delta," said the agent. "He's beyond the laws. He's beyond salvage."

"Beyond—"

"That's right, Senator," interrupted the general. "Beyond salvage. I think you know the meaning of the phrase. You'll have to make the decision whether or not to define it for the president. It might be better to—"

"You've got to explore *everything,*" said the senator, cutting off the officer. "I spoke to Abbott last week. He told me a strategy was in progress to reach Delta. Zurich, the bank, the naming of Treadstone; it's all part of it, isn't it?"

"It is, and it's over," said Crawford. "If the evidence on Seventy-first Street isn't enough for you, that should be. Delta was given a clear signal to come in. He didn't. What more do you want?"

"I want to be absolutely certain."

"I want him dead." Conklin's words, though spoken softly, had the effect of a sudden, cold wind. "He not only broke all the rules we each set down for ourselves—no matter what—but he sunk into the pits. He reeks; he *is* Cain. We've used the name Delta so much—not even Bourne, but Delta—that I think we've forgotten. Gordon Webb was his brother. Find him. Kill him."

BOOK
THREE

23

It was ten minutes to three in the morning when Bourne approached the Auberge du Coin's front desk, Marie continuing directly to the entrance. To Jason's relief, there were no newspapers on the counter, but the late night clerk behind it was in the same mold as his predecessor in the center of Paris. He was a balding, heavy-set man with half-closed eyes, leaning back in a chair, his arms folded in front of him, the weary depression of his interminable night hanging over him. But this night, thought Bourne, would be one he'd remember for a long time to come—beyond the damage to an upstairs room, which would not be discovered until morning. A relief night clerk in Montrouge had to have transportation.

"I've just called Rouen," said Jason, his hands on the counter, an angry man, furious with uncontrollable events in his personal world. "I have to leave at once and need to rent a car."

"Why not?" snorted the man, getting out of the chair. "What would you prefer, monsieur? A golden chariot or a magic carpet?"

"I beg your pardon?"

"We rent rooms, not automobiles."

"I *must* be in Rouen before morning."

"Impossible. Unless you find a taxi crazy enough at this hour to take you."

"I don't think you understand. I could sustain considerable losses and embarrassment if I'm not at my office by eight o'clock. I'm willing to pay generously."

"You have a problem, monsieur."

"Surely there's someone here who would be willing to lend me his car for, say . . . a thousand, fifteen hundred francs."

"A thousand . . . *fifteen hundred,* monsieur?" The clerk's half-closed eyes widened until his skin was taut. "In cash, monsieur?"

"Naturally. My companion would return it tomorrow evening."

"There's no rush, monsieur."

"I beg your pardon? Of course, there's really no reason why I couldn't hire a taxi. Confidentiality can be paid for."

"I wouldn't know where to *reach* one," interrupted the clerk in persuasive frenzy. "On the other hand, my Renault is not so new, perhaps, and perhaps, not the fastest machine on the road, but it is a serviceable car, even a worthy car."

The chameleon had changed his colors again, had been accepted again for someone he was not. But he knew now who he was and he understood.

Daybreak. But there was no warm room at a village inn, no wallpaper mottled by the early light streaking through a window, filtered by the weaving leaves outside. Rather, the first rays of the sun spread up from the east, crowning the French countryside, defining the fields and hills of Saint-Germain-en-Laye. They sat in the small car parked off the shoulder of a deserted back road, cigarette smoke curling out through the partially open windows.

He had begun that first narrative in Switzerland with the words *My life began six months ago on a small island in the Mediterranean called Ile de Port Noir.* . . .

He had begun this with a quiet declaration: *I'm known as Cain.*

He had told it all, leaving out nothing he could remember, including the terrible images that had exploded in his mind when he had heard the words spoken by Jacqueline Lavier in the candlelabraed restaurant in Argenteuil. Names, incidents, cities . . . assassinations.

"Everything fit. There wasn't anything I didn't know, nothing that wasn't somewhere in the back of my head, trying to get out. It was the truth."

"It *was* the truth," repeated Marie.

He looked closely at her. "We were wrong, don't you see?"

"Perhaps. But also right. You were right, and I was right."

"About what?"

"You. I have to say it again, calmly and logically. You offered your life for mine before you knew me; that's not the decision of a man you've described. If that man existed, he doesn't any longer." Marie's eyes pleaded, while her voice remained controlled. "You said it, Jason. 'What a man can't remember doesn't exist. For him.' Maybe that's what you're faced with. Can you walk away from it?"

Bourne nodded; the dreadful moment had come. "Yes," he said. "But alone. Not with you."

Marie inhaled on her cigarette, watching him, her hand trembling. "I see. That's your decision, then?"

"It has to be."

"You will heroically disappear so I won't be tainted."

"I have to."

"Thank you very much, and who the hell do you think you are?"

"What?"

"Who the *hell* do you think you *are?*"

"I'm a man they call Cain. I'm wanted by governments—by the police—from Asia to Europe. Men in Washington want to kill me because of what they think I know about this Medusa; an assassin named Carlos wants me shot in the throat because of what I've done to him. Think about it for a moment. How long do you think I can keep running before someone in one of those armies out there finds me, traps me, *kills* me? Is that the way you want your life to end?"

"Good God, no!" shouted Marie, something obviously very much on her analytical mind. "I intend to rot in a Swiss prison for fifty years or be hanged for things I never did in Zurich!"

"There's a way to take care of Zurich. I've thought about it; I can do it."

"How?" She stabbed out her cigarette in the ashtray.

"For God's sake, what difference does it make? A confession. Turning myself in, I don't know yet, but I can *do* it! I can put your life back together. I *have* to put it back!"

"Not that way."

"Why not?"

Marie reached for his face, her voice now soft once more, the sudden stridency gone. "Because I've just proved my point again. Even the condemned man—so sure of his own guilt—should see it.The man called Cain would never do what you just offered to do. For anyone."

"I *am* Cain!"

"Even if I were forced to agree that you were, you're not now."

"The ultimate rehabilitation? A self-induced lobotomy? Total loss of recall? That happens to be the truth, but it won't stop anyone who's looking for me. It won't stop him—them—from pulling a trigger."

"That happens to be the worst, and I'm not ready to concede it."

"Then you're not looking at the facts."

"I'm looking at two facts you seem to have disregarded. I can't. I'll live with them for the rest of my life because I'm responsible. Two men were killed in the same brutal way because they stood between you and a message someone was trying to send you. Through me."

"You saw Corbelier's message. How many bullet holes were there? Ten, fifteen?"

"Then he was used! You heard him on the phone and so did I. He wasn't lying; he was trying to help us. If not you, certainly me."

"It's . . . possible."

"Anything's possible. I have no answers, Jason, only discrepancies, things that can't be explained—that *should* be explained. You haven't once, ever, displayed a need or a drive for what you say you might have been. And without those things a man like that couldn't be. Or you couldn't be *him.*"

"I'm him."

"Listen to me. You're very dear to me, my darling, and that could blind me, I know it. But I also know something about myself. I'm no wide-eyed flower child; I've seen a share of this world, and I look very hard and very closely at those who attract me. Perhaps to confirm what I like to think are my values—and they *are* values. Mine, nobody else's." She stopped for a moment and moved away from him. "I've watched a man being tortured—by himself and by others—and he won't cry out. You may have silent screams, but you won't let them be anyone else's burden but your own. Instead, you probe and dig and try to understand. And that, my friend, is not the mind of a cold-blooded killer, any more than what you've done and want to do for me. I don't know what you were before, or what crimes you're guilty of, but they're not what you believe—what others want you to believe. Which brings me back to those values I spoke of. I know myself. I couldn't love the man you say you are. I love the man I know you are. You just confirmed it again. No killer would make the offer you just made. And that offer, sir, is respectfully rejected."

"You're a goddamn fool!" exploded Jason. "I can help you; you can't help me! Leave me *something* for Christ's sake!"

"I won't! Not that way . . ." Suddenly Marie broke off. Her lips parted. "I think I just did," she said, whispering.

"Did what?" asked Bourne angrily.

"Give us both something." She turned back to him. "I just said it; it's been there a long time. 'What others want you to believe . . .' "

"What the hell are you talking about?"

"Your crimes . . . what others want you to believe are your crimes."

"They're there. They're mine."

"Wait a minute. Suppose they were there but they *weren't* yours? Suppose the evidence was planted—as expertly as it was planted against me in Zurich—but it belongs to someone else. Jason—you don't *know* when you lost your memory."

"Port Noir."

"That's when you began to build one, not when you lost it. *Before* Port Noir; it could explain so much. It could explain *you,* the contradiction between you and the man people think you are."

"You're wrong. Nothing could explain the memories—the images—that come back to me."

"Maybe you just remember what you've been told," said Marie. "Over and over and over again. Until there was nothing else. Photographs, recordings, visual and aural stimulae."

"You're describing a walking, functioning vegetable who's been brainwashed. That's not me."

She looked at him, speaking gently. "I'm describing an intelligent, very ill man whose background conformed with what other men were looking for. Do you know how easily such a man might be found? They're in hospitals everywhere, in private sanitoriums, in military wards." She paused, then continued quickly. "That newspaper article told another truth. I'm reasonably proficient with computers; anyone doing what I do would be. If I were looking for a curve-example that incorporated isolated factors, I'd know how to do it. Conversely, someone looking for a man hospitalized for amnesia, whose background incorporated specific skills, languages, racial characteristics, the medical data banks could provide candidates. God knows, not many in your case; perhaps only a few, perhaps only one. But one man was all they were looking for, all they needed."

Bourne glanced at the countryside, trying to pry open the steel doors of his mind, trying to find a semblance of the hope she felt. "What you're saying is that I'm a reproduced illusion," he said, making the statement flatly.

"That's the end effect, but it's not what I'm saying. I'm saying it's possible you've been manipulated. Used. It would explain so much." She touched his hand. "You tell me there are times when things want to burst out of you—blow your head apart."

"Words—places, names—they trigger things."

"Jason, isn't it possible they trigger the false things? The things you've been told over and over again, but you can't relive. You can't see them clearly, because they're *not* you."

"I doubt it. I've seen what I can do. I've done them before."

"You could have done them for other reasons! . . . *Goddamn you,* I'm fighting for my life! For *both* our lives! . . . All right! You can *think,* you can *feel.* Think *now, feel* now! Look at me and tell me you've looked inside yourself, inside your thoughts and feelings, and you know without a doubt you're an assassin called Cain! If you can do that—*really* do that—then bring me to Zurich, take the blame for everything, and get out of my life! But if you can't, stay with me and let me help you. And love me, for God's sake. *Love* me, Jason."

Bourne took her hand, holding it firmly, as one might an angry, trembling child's. "It's not a question of feeling or thinking. I saw the account at the Gemeinschaft; the entries go back a long time. They correspond with all the things I've learned."

"But that account, those entries, could have been created yesterday, or last week, or six months ago. Everything you've heard and read about yourself could be part of a pattern designed by those who want you to take Cain's place. You're *not* Cain, but they want you to think you are, want others to think you are. But there's someone out there who knows you're not Cain and he's trying to tell you. I have my proof, too. My lover's alive, but two friends are dead because they got between you and the one who's sending you the message, who's trying to save your life. They were killed by the same people who want to sacrifice you to Carlos in place of Cain. You said before that everything fit. It didn't, Jason, but *this* does! It explains *you.*"

"A hollow shell who doesn't even own the memories he thinks he has? With demons running around inside kicking hell out of the walls? It's not a pleasant prospect."

"Those aren't demons, my darling. They're parts of you—angry, furious, screaming to get out because they don't belong in the shell you've given them."

"And if I blow that shell apart, what'll I find?"

"Many things. Some good, some bad, a great deal that's been hurt. But Cain won't be there, I promise you that. I believe in you, my darling. Please don't give up."

He kept his distance, a glass wall between them. "And if we're wrong? Finally wrong? What then?"

"Leave me quickly. Or kill me. I don't care."

"I love you."

"I know. That's why I'm not afraid."

"I found two telephone numbers in Lavier's office. The first was for Zurich, the other here in Paris. With any luck, they can lead me to the one number I need."

"New York? Treadstone?"

"Yes. The answer's there. If I'm not Cain, someone at that number knows who I am."

They drove back to Paris on the assumption that they would be far less obvious among the crowds of the city than in an isolated country inn. A blond-haired man wearing tortoise-shell glasses, and a striking but stern-faced woman, devoid of makeup, and with her hair pulled back like an intense graduate student at the Sorbonne, were not out of place in Montmartre. They took a room at the Terrasse on the rue de Maistre, registering as a married couple from Brussels.

In the room, they stood for a moment, no words necessary for what each was seeing and feeling. They came together, touching, holding, closing out the abusive world that refused them peace, that kept them balancing on taut wires next to one another, high above a dark abyss; if either fell, it was the end for both.

Bourne could not change his color for the immediate moment. It would be false, and there was no room for artifice. "We need some rest," he said. "We've got to get some sleep. It's going to be a long day."

They made love. Gently, completely, each with the other in the warm, rhythmic comfort of the bed. And there was a moment, a foolish moment, when adjustment of an angle was breathlessly necessary and they laughed. It was a quiet laugh, at first even an embarrassed laugh, but the observation was there, the appraisal of foolishness intrinsic to something very deep between them. They held each other more fiercely when the moment passed, more and more intent on sweeping away the awful sounds and the terrible sights of a dark world that kept them spinning in its winds. They were suddenly breaking out of that world, plunging into a much better one where sunlight and blue water replaced the darkness. They raced toward it feverishly, furiously, and then they burst through and found it.

Spent, they fell asleep, their fingers entwined.

Bourne woke first, aware of the horns and the engines in the Paris traffic below in the streets. He looked at his watch; it was ten past one in the afternoon. They had slept nearly five hours, probably less than they needed, but it was enough. It *was* going to be a long day. Doing what, he was not sure; he only knew that there were two telephone numbers that had to lead him to a third. In New York.

He turned to Marie, breathing deeply beside him, her face—her striking, lovely face—angled down on the edge of the pillow, her lips parted, inches from his lips. He kissed her and she reached for him, her eyes still closed.

"You're a frog and I'll make you a prince," she said in a sleep-filled voice. "Or is it the other way around?"

"As expanding as it may be; that's not in my present frame of reference."

"Then you'll have to stay a frog. Hop around, little frog. Show off for me."

"No temptations. I only hop when I'm fed flies."

"Frogs eat flies? I guess they do. Shudder; that's awful."

"Come on, open your eyes. We've both got to start hopping. We've got to start hunting."

She blinked and looked at him. "Hunting for what?"

"For me," he said.

From a telephone booth on the rue Lafayette, a collect call was placed to a number in Zurich by a Mr. Briggs. Bourne reasoned that Jacqueline Lavier would have wasted no time sending out her alarms; one had to have been flashed to Zurich.

When he heard the ring in Switzerland, Jason stepped back and handed the phone to Marie. She knew what to say.

She had no chance to say it. The international operator in Zurich came on the line.

"We regret that the number you have called is no longer in service."

"It was the other day," broke in Marie. "This is an emergency, operator. Do you have another number?"

"The telephone is no longer in service, madame. There is no alternate number."

"I may have been given the wrong one. It's most urgent. Could you give me the name of the party who had this number?"

"I'm afraid that's not possible."

"I told you; it's an emergency! May I speak with your superior, please?"

"He would not be able to help you. This number is an unpublished listing. Good afternoon, madame."

The connection was broken. "It's been disconnected," she said.

"It took too goddamn long to find that out," replied Bourne, looking up and down the street. "Let's get out of here."

"You think they could have traced it here? In Paris? To a public phone?"

"Within three minutes an exchange can be determined, a district pinpointed. In four, they can narrow the blocks down to half a dozen."

"How do you know that?"

"I wish I could tell you. Let's go."

"Jason. Why not wait out of sight? And watch?"

"Because I don't know what to watch for and they do. They've got a photograph to go by; they could station men all over the area."

"I don't look anything like the picture in the papers."

"Not you. Me. Let's go!"

They walked rapidly within the erratic ebb and flow of the crowds until they reached the boulevard Malesherbes ten blocks away, and another telephone booth, this with a different exchange from the first. This time there were no operators to go through; this was Paris. Marie stepped inside, coins in her hand and dialed; she was prepared.

But the words that came over the line so astonished her:

"La résidence du Général Villiers. Bonjour? . . . Allô? Allô?"

For a moment Marie was unable to speak. She simply stared at the telephone. *"Je m'excuse,"* she whispered. *"Une erreur."* She hung up.

"What's the matter?" asked Bourne, opening the glass door. "What happened? Who was it?"

"It doesn't make sense," she said. "I just reached the house of one of the most respected and powerful men in France."

24

"André François Villiers," repeated Marie, lighting a cigarette. They had returned to their room at the Terrasse to sort things out, to absorb the astonishing information. "Graduate of Saint-Cyr, hero of the Second World War, a legend in the Resistance, and, until his break over Algeria, De Gaulle's heir-apparent. Jason, to connect such a man with Carlos is simply unbelievable."

"The connection's there. Believe it."

"It's almost too difficult. Villiers is old-line honor-of-France, a family traced back to the seventeenth century. Today he's one of the ranking deputies in the National Assembly—politically to the right of Charlemagne, to be sure—but very much a law-and-order army man. It's like linking Douglas MacArthur to a Mafia hit man. It doesn't make sense."

"Then let's look for some. What was the break with De Gaulle?"

"Algeria. In the early sixties, Villiers was part of the OAS—one of the Algerian colonels under Salan. They opposed the Evian agreements that gave independence to Algeria, believing it rightfully belonged to France."

" 'The mad colonels of Algiers,' " said Bourne, as with so many words and phrases, not knowing where they came from or why he said them.

"That means something to you?"

"It must, but I don't know what it is."

"*Think,*" said Marie. "Why should the 'mad colonels' strike a chord with you? What's the first thing that comes to your mind? Quickly!"

Jason looked at her helplessly, then the words came. "Bombings . . . infiltrations. *Provocateurs.* You study them; you study the mechanisms."

"*Why?*"

"I don't know."

"Are decisions based on what you learn?"

"I guess so."

"What kind of decisions? You decide *what?*"

"Disruptions."

"What does that mean to you? Disruptions."

"I don't know! I can't think!"

"All right . . . all right. We'll go back to it some other time."

"There isn't time. Let's get back to Villiers. After Algeria, what?"

"There was a reconciliation of sorts with De Gaulle; Villiers was never directly implicated in the terrorism, and his military record demanded it. He returned to France—was welcomed, really—a fighter for a lost but respected cause. He resumed his command, rising to the rank of general, before going into politics."

"He's a working politician, then?"

"More a spokesman. An elder statesman. He's still an entrenched militarist, still fumes over France's reduced military stature."

"Howard Leland," said Jason. "There's your connection to Carlos."

"How? Why?"

"Leland was assassinated because he interfered with the Quai D'Orsay's arms buildups and exports. We don't need anything more."

"It seems incredible, a man like that . . ." Marie's voice trailed off; she was struck by recollection. "His son was murdered. It was a political thing, about five or six years ago."

"Tell me."

"His car was blown up on the rue du Bac. It was in all the papers everywhere. *He* was the working politician, like his father a conservative, opposing the socialists and Communists at every turn. He was a young member of parliament, an obstructionist where government expenditures was concerned, but actually quite popular. He was a charming aristocrat."

"Who killed him?"

"The speculation was Communist fanatics. He'd managed to block some legislation or other favorable to the extreme left wing. After he was murdered, the ranks fell apart and the legislation passed. Many think that's why Villiers left the army and stood for the National Assembly. That's what's so improbable, so contradictory. After all, his son *was* assassinated; you'd think the last person on earth he'd want to have anything to do with was a professional assassin."

"There's also something else. You said he was welcomed back to Paris because he was never *directly* implicated in the terrorism."

"If he was," interrupted Marie, "it was buried. They're more tolerant of passionate causes over here where country and the bed are concerned. And he was a legitimate hero, don't forget that."

"But once a terrorist, always a terrorist, don't you forget that."

"I can't agree. People change."

"Not about some things. No terrorist ever forgets how effective he's been; he lives on it."

"How would you know that?"

"I'm not sure I want to ask myself right now."

"Then don't."

"But I *am* sure about Villiers. I'm going to reach him." Bourne crossed to the bedside table and picked up the telephone book. "Let's see if he's listed or if that number's private. I'll need his address."

"You won't get near him. If he's Carlos's connection, he'll be guarded. They'll kill you on sight; they have your photograph, remember?"

"It won't help them. I won't be what they're looking for. Here it is. Villiers, A. F. Parc Monceau."

"I still can't believe it. Just knowing whom she was calling must have put the Lavier woman in shock."

"Or frightened her to the point where she'd do anything."

"Doesn't it strike you as odd that she'd be given that number?"

"Not under the circumstances. Carlos wants his drones to know he isn't kidding. He wants Cain."

Marie stood up. "Jason? What's a 'drone'?"

Bourne looked up at her. "I don't know . . . Someone who works blind for somebody else."

"Blind? Not seeing?"

"Not knowing. Thinking he's doing one thing when he's really doing something else."

"I don't understand."

"Let's say I tell you to watch for a car at a certain street corner. The car never shows up, but the fact that you're there tells someone else who's watching for you that something else has happened."

"Arithmetically, an untraceable message."

"Yes, I guess so."

"That's what happened in Zurich. Walther Apfel was a drone. He released that story about the theft not knowing what he was really saying."

"Which was?"

"It's a good guess that you were being told to reach someone you know very well."

"Treadstone Seventy-One," said Jason. "We're back to Villiers. Carlos found me in Zurich through the Gemeinschaft. That means he had to know about Treadstone; it's a good chance that Villiers does too. If he doesn't, there may be a way of getting him to find out for us."

"How?"

"His name. If he's everything you say he is, he thinks pretty highly of it. The honor-of-France coupled with a pig like Carlos might have an effect. I'll threaten to go to the police, to the papers."

"He'd simply deny it. He'd say it's outrageous."

"Let him. It isn't. That was his number in Lavier's office. Besides, any retraction will be on the same page as his obituary."

"You still have to get to him."

"I will. I'm part chameleon, remember?"

The tree-lined street in Parc Monceau seemed familiar somehow, but not in the sense that he had walked it before. Instead, it was the atmosphere. Two rows of well-kept stone houses, doors and windows glistening, hardware shining, staircases washed clean, the lighted rooms beyond filled with hanging plants. It was a monied street in a wealthy section of the city, and he knew he had been exposed to one like it before, and that exposure *had* meant something.

It was 7:35 in the evening, the March night cold, the sky clear, and the chameleon dressed for the occasion. Bourne's blond hair was covered by a cap, his neck concealed beneath the collar of a jacket that spelled out the name of a messenger service across the back. Slung over his shoulder was a canvas strap attached to a nearly empty satchel; it was the end of this particular messenger's run. He had two or three stops to make, perhaps four or five, if he thought they were necessary; he would know momentarily. The envelopes were not really envelopes at all, but brochures advertising the pleasures of the Bateaux Mouche, picked up from a hotel lobby. He would select at random several houses near General Villiers' residence and deposit the brochures in mail slots. His eyes would record everything they saw, one thing sought above everything else. What kind of security arrangements did Villiers have? Who guarded the general and how many were there?

And because he had been convinced he would find either men in cars or other men walking their posts, he was startled to realize there was no one. André François Villiers, militarist, spokesman for his cause, and the prime connection to Carlos, had no external security arrangements whatsoever. If he was protected, that protection was solely within the house. Considering the enormity of his crime, Villiers was either arrogant to the point of carelessness or a damn fool.

Jason climbed the steps of an adjacent residence, Villiers' door no more than twenty feet away. He deposited the brochure in the slot, glancing up at the windows of Villiers' house, looking for a face, a figure. There was no one.

The door twenty feet away suddenly opened. Bourne crouched, thrusting his hand beneath his jacket for his gun, thinking *he* was a damn fool; someone more observant than he had spotted him. But the words he heard told him it wasn't so. A middle-aged couple—a uniformed maid and a dark-jacketed man—were talking in the doorway.

"Make sure the ashtrays are clean," said the woman. "You know how he dislikes ashtrays that are stuffed full."

"He drove this afternoon," answered the man. "That means they're full now."

"Clean them in the garage; you've got time. He won't be down for another ten minutes. He doesn't have to be in Nanterre until eight-thirty."

The man nodded, pulling up the lapels of his jacket as he started down the steps. "Ten minutes," he said aimlessly.

The door closed and silence returned to the quiet street. Jason stood up, his hand on the railing, watching the man hurry down the sidewalk. He was not sure where Nanterre was, only that it was a suburb of Paris. And if Villiers was driving there himself, and if he was alone, there was no point in postponing confrontation.

Bourne shifted the strap on his shoulder and walked rapidly down the steps, turning left on the pavement. Ten minutes.

Jason watched through the windshield as the door opened and General of the Army André François Villiers came into view. He was a medium-sized, barrel-chested man in his late sixties, perhaps early seventies. He was hatless, with close-cropped gray hair and a meticulously groomed white chin beard. His bearing was unmistakably military, imposing his body on the surrounding space, entering it by breaking it, invisible walls collapsing as he moved.

Bourne stared at him, fascinated, wondering what insanities could have possibly driven such a man into the obscene world of Carlos. Whatever the reasons, they had to be powerful, for *he* was powerful. And that made him dangerous—for he was respected and had the ears of his government.

Villiers turned, speaking to the maid and glancing at his wristwatch. The woman nodded, closing the door, as the general walked briskly down the steps and around the hood of a large sedan to the driver's side. He opened the door and climbed in, then started the engine and rolled slowly out into the middle of the street. Jason waited until the sedan reached the corner and turned right; he eased the Renault away from the curb and accelerated, reaching the intersection in time to see Villiers turn right again a block east.

There was a certain irony in the coincidence, an omen if one could believe in such things. The route General Villiers chose to the outlying suburb of Nanterre included a stretch of back road in the countryside nearly identical to the one in Saint-German-en-Laye, where twelve hours ago Marie had pleaded with Jason not to give up—his life or hers. There were stretches of pastureland, fields that fused into the gently rising hills, but instead of being crowned by early light, these were washed in the cold, white rays of the moon. It occurred to Bourne that this stretch of isolated road would be as good a spot as any on which to intercept the returning general.

It was not difficult for Jason to follow at distances up to a quarter of a mile, which was why he was surprised to realize he had practically caught up with the old soldier. Villiers had suddenly slowed down and was turning into a graveled drive cut out of the woods, the parking lot beyond illuminated by floodlights. A sign, hanging from two chains on a high-angle post, was caught in the spill: L'ARBALÈTE. The general was meeting someone for dinner at an out-of-the-way restaurant, not *in* the suburb of Nanterre, but close by. In the country.

Bourne drove past the entrance and pulled off the shoulder of the road, the right side of the car covered by foliage. He had to think things out. He had to control himself. There was a fire in his mind; it was growing, spreading. He was suddenly consumed by an extraordinary possibility.

Considering the shattering events—the enormity of the embarrassment experienced by Carlos last night at the motel in Montrouge, it was more than likely that André Villiers had been summoned to an out-of-the-way restaurant for an emergency meeting. Perhaps even with Carlos *himself*. If that was the case, the premises would be guarded, and a man whose photograph had been distributed to those guards would be shot the instant he was recognized. On the other hand, the chance to observe a nucleus belonging to Carlos—or Carlos himself—was an opportunity that might never come again. He had to get inside L'Arbalète. There was a compulsion within him to take the risk. *Any* risk. It was crazy! But then he was not sane. Sane as a man with a memory was sane. *Carlos. Find Carlos! God in heaven, why?*

He felt the gun in his belt; it was secure. He got out and put on his topcoat, covering the jacket with the lettering across the back. He picked up a narrow-brimmed hat from the seat, the cloth soft, angled down all sides; it would cover his hair. Then he tried to remember if he had been wearing the tortoise-shell glasses when the photograph was taken in Argenteuil. He had not; he had removed them at the table when successive bolts of pain had seared through his head, brought on by words that told him of a past too familiar, too frightening to face. He felt his shirt pocket; the glasses were there if he needed them. He pressed the door closed and started for the woods.

The glare of the restaurant floodlights filtered through the trees, growing brighter with each several yards, less foliage to block the light. Bourne reached the edge of the short patch of forest, the graveled parking lot in front of him. He was at the side of the rustic restaurant, a row of small windows running the length of the building, flickering candles beyond the glass illuminating the figures of the diners. Then his eyes were drawn to the second floor—although it did not extend the length of the building, but only halfway, the rear section an open terrace. The enclosed part, however, was similar to the first floor. A line of windows, a bit larger, perhaps, but still in a row, and again glowing with candles. Figures were milling about, but they were different from the diners below.

They were all men. Standing, not sitting; moving casually, glasses in hands, cigarette smoke spiraling over their heads. It was impossible to tell how many—more than ten, less than twenty, perhaps.

There *he* was, crossing from one group to another, the white chin beard a beacon, switching on and off as it was intermittently blocked by figures nearer the windows. General Villiers had, indeed, driven out to Nanterre for a meeting, and the odds favored a conference that dealt with the failures of the past forty-eight hours, failures that permitted a man named Cain to remain alive.

The odds. What were the odds? Where were the guards? How many, and where were their stations? Keeping behind the edge of the woods, Bourne side-stepped his way toward the front of the restaurant, bending branches silently, his feet over the underbrush. He stood motionless, watching for men concealed in the foliage or in the shadows of the building. He saw none and retraced his path, breaking new ground until he reached the rear of the restaurant.

A door opened, the spill of light harsh, and a man in a white jacket emerged. He stood for a moment, cupping his hands, lighting a cigarette. Bourne looked to the left, to the right, above to the terrace; no one appeared. A guard stationed in the area would have been alarmed by the sudden light ten feet below the conference. There were no guards outside. Protection found—as it had to be at Villiers' house in Parc Monceau—within the building itself.

Another man appeared in the doorway, also wearing a white jacket, but with the addition of a chef's hat. His voice was angry, his French laced with the guttural dialect of Gascony. "While you piss off, we sweat! The pastry cart is half empty. Fill it. *Now*, you bastard!"

The pastry man turned and shrugged; he crushed out his cigarette and went back inside, closing the door behind him. The light vanished, only the wash of the moon remained, but it was enough to illuminate the terrace. There was no one there, no guard patrolling the wide double doors that led to the inside room.

Carlos. Find Carlos. Trap Carlos. Cain is for Charlie, and Delta is for Cain.

Bourne judged the distance and the obstacles. He was no more than forty feet from the rear of the building, ten or twelve below the railing that bordered the terrace. There were two vents in the exterior wall, vapor escaping from both, and next to them a drainpipe that was within reach of the railing. If he could scale the pipe and manage to get a toehold in the lower vent, he would be able to grab a rung of the railing and pull himself up to the terrace. But he could do none of this wearing the topcoat. He took it off, placing it at his feet, the soft-brimmed hat on top, and covered both with underbrush. Then he stepped to the edge of the woods and raced as quietly as possible across the gravel to the drainpipe.

In the shadows he tugged at the fluted metal; it was strongly in place. He reached as high as he could, then sprang up, gripping the pipe, his feet pressed into the wall, peddling one on top of the other until his left foot was parallel to the first vent. Holding on, he slipped his foot into the recess and propelled himself further up the drain. He was within eighteen inches of the railings; one surge launched from the vent and he could reach the bottom rung.

The door crashed open beneath him, white light shooting across the gravel into the woods. A figure plummeted out, weaving to maintain its balance, followed by the white-haired chef, who was screaming.

"You piss-ant! You're drunk, that's what you are! You've been drunk the whole shit-filled night! Pastries all over the dining room floor. Everything a mess. Get out, you'll not get a *sou!*"

The door was pulled shut, the sound of a bolt unmistakably final. Jason held on to the pipe, arms and ankles aching, rivulets of sweat breaking out on his forehead. The man below staggered backward, making obscene gestures repeatedly with his right hand for the benefit of the chef who was no longer there. His glazed eyes wandered up the wall, settling on Bourne's face. Jason held his breath as their eyes met; the man stared, then blinked and stared again. He shook his head, closing his lids, then opened them wide, taking in the sight he was not entirely sure was there. He backed away, lurching into a sideslip and a forward walk, obviously deciding that the apparition halfway up the wall was the result of his pressured labors. He weaved around the corner of the building, a man more at peace with himself for having rejected the foolishness that had assaulted his eyes.

Bourne breathed again, letting his body slump against the wall in relief. But it was only for a moment; the ache in his ankle had descended to his foot, a cramp forming. He lunged, grabbing the iron bar that was the base of the railing with his right hand, whipping his left up from the drainpipe, joining it. He pressed his knees into the shingles and pulled himself slowly up the wall until his head was over the edge of the terrace. It was deserted. He kicked his right leg up to the ledge, his right hand reaching for the wrought-iron top; balanced, he swung over the railing.

He was on a terrace used for dining in the spring and summer months, a tiled floor that could accommodate ten to fifteen tables. In the center of the wall separating the enclosed section from the terrace were the wide double doors he had seen from the woods. The figures inside were now motionless, standing still, and for an instant Jason wondered whether an alarm had been set off—whether they were waiting for him. He stood immobile, his hand on his gun; nothing happened. He approached the wall, staying in the shadows. Once there, he pressed his back against the wood and edged his way toward the first door until his fingers touched the frame. Slowly, he inched his head to the pane of glass level with his eyes and looked inside.

What he saw was both mesmerizing and not a little frightening. The men were in lines—three separate lines, four men to a line—facing André Villiers, who was addressing them. Thirteen men in all, twelve of them not merely standing, but standing at attention. They were old men, but not merely old men; they were old soldiers. None wore uniforms; instead in each lapel they wore ribbons, regimental colors above decorations for valor and rank. And if there was one all-pervasive note about the scene, it, too, was unmistakable. These were men used to command—used to power. It was in their faces, their eyes, in the way they listened—respect rendered, but not blindly, judgment ever present. Their bodies were old, but there was strength in that room. Immense strength. That was the frightening aspect. If these men belonged to Carlos, the assassin's resources were not only far-reaching, they were extraordinarily dangerous. For these were not ordinary men; they were seasoned professional soldiers. Unless he was grossly mistaken, thought Bourne, the depth of experience and range of influence in that room was staggering.

The mad colonels of Algiers—what was left of them? Men driven by memories of a France that no longer existed, a world that was no more, replaced by one they found weak and ineffectual. Such men could make a pact with Carlos, if only for the covert power it gave them. Strike. Attack. Dispatch. Decisions of life and death that were once a part of their fabric, brought back by a force that could serve causes they refused to admit were no longer viable. Once a terrorist, always a terrorist, and assassination was the raw core of terror.

The general was raising his voice; Jason tried to hear the words through the glass. They became clearer.

"... our presence will be felt, our purpose understood. We are together in our stand, and that stand is immovable; we *shall* be heard! In memory of all those who have fallen—our brothers of the tunic and the cannon—who laid down their lives for the glory of France. We shall force our beloved country to remember, and in their names to remain strong, lackey to no one! Those who oppose us will know our anger. In this, too, we are united. We pray to Almighty God that those who have gone before us have found peace, for we are still in conflict. . . . Gentlemen: I give you Our Lady—our France!"

There was a unison of muttered approvals, the old soldiers remaining rigidly at attention. And then another voice was raised, the first five words sung singly, joined at the sixth by the rest of the group.

Allons enfants de la patrie,
Le jour de gloire est arrivé . . .

Bourne turned away, sickened by the sight and the sounds inside that room. Lay waste in the name of glory; the death of fallen comrades perforce demands further death. It is required; and if it means a pact with Carlos, so be it.

What disturbed him so? Why was he suddenly swept by feelings of anger and futility? What triggered the revulsion he felt so strongly? And then he knew. He hated a man like André Villiers, despised the men in that room. They were all old men who made war, stealing life from the young . . . and the very young.

Why were the mists closing in again? Why was the pain so acute? There was no time for questions, no strength to tolerate them. He had to push them out of his mind and concentrate on André François Villiers, warrior and warlord, whose causes belonged to yesterday but whose pact with an assassin called for death today.

He would trap the general. Break him. Learn everything he knew, and probably kill him. Men like Villiers robbed life from the young and the very young. They did not deserve to live. *I am in my labyrinth again, and the walls are imbedded with spikes. Oh, God, they hurt.*

Jason climbed over the railing in the darkness and lowered himself to the drainpipe, each muscle aching. Pain, too, had to be erased. He had to reach a deserted stretch of road in the moonlight and trap a broker of death.

25

Bourne waited in the Renault, two hundred yards east of the restaurant entrance, the motor running, prepared to race ahead the instant he saw Villiers drive out. Several others had already left, all in separate cars. Conspirators did not advertise their association, and these old men were conspirators in the truest sense. They had traded whatever honors they had earned for the lethal convenience of an assassin's gun and an assassin's organization. Age and bias had robbed them of reason, as they had spent their lives robbing life . . . from the young and the very young.

What was it? Why won't it leave me? Some terrible thing is deep inside me, trying to break out, trying I think to kill me. The fear and the guilt sweep through me . . . but of what and for what I do not know. Why should these withered old men provoke such feelings of fear and guilt . . . and loathing?

They were war. They were death. On the ground and from the skies. From the skies . . . from the skies. Help me, Marie. For God's sake, help me!

There it was. The headlights swung out of the drive, the long black chassis reflecting the wash of the floodlights. Jason kept his own lights off as he pulled out of the shadows. He accelerated down the road until he reached the first curve, where he switched on the headlights and pressed the pedal to the floor. The isolated stretch in the countryside was roughly two miles away; he had to get there quickly.

It was ten past eleven, and as three hours before the fields swept into the hills, both bathed in the light of the March moon, now in the center of the sky. He reached the area; it *was* feasible. The shoulder was wide, bordering a pasture, which meant that both automobiles could be pulled off the road. The immediate objective, however, was to get Villiers to stop. The general was old but not feeble; if the tactic were suspect, he would break over the grass and race away. Everything was timing, and a totally convincing moment of the unexpected.

Bourne swung the Renault around in a U-turn, waited until he saw the headlights in the distance, then suddenly accelerated, swinging the wheel violently back and forth. The automobile careened over the road—an out-of-control driver, incapable of finding a straight line, but nevertheless speeding.

Villiers had no choice; he slowed down as Jason came racing insanely toward him. Then abruptly, when the two cars were no more than twenty feet from colliding, Bourne spun the wheel to the left, braking as he did so, sliding into a skid, tires screeching. He came to a stop, the window open, and raised his voice in an undefined cry. Half shout, half scream; it could have been the vocal explosion of an ill man or a drunk man, but the one thing it was not was threatening. He slapped his hand on the frame of the window and was silent, crouching in the seat, his gun on his lap.

He heard the door of Villiers' sedan open and peered through the steering wheel. The old man was not visibly armed; he seemed to suspect nothing, relieved only that a collision had been avoided. The general walked through the beams of the headlights to the Renault's left window, his shouts anxious, his French the interrogating commands of Saint-Cyr.

"What's the meaning of this? What do you think you're doing? Are you all right?" His hands gripped the base of the window.

"Yes, but you're not," replied Bourne in English, raising the gun.

"What . . ." The old man gasped, standing erect. "Who are you and what is this?"

Jason got out of the Renault, his left hand extended above the barrel of the weapon. "I'm glad your English is fluent. Walk back to your car. Drive it off the road."

"And if I refuse?"

"I'll kill you right now. It wouldn't take much to provoke me."

"Do these words come from the Red Brigades? Or the Paris branch of the Baader-Meinhof?"

"Why? Could you countermand them if they did?"

"I spit at them! And you!"

"No one's ever doubted your courage, General. Walk to your car."

"It's not a matter of courage!" said Villiers without moving. "It's a question of logic. You'll accomplish nothing by killing me, less by kidnapping me. My orders are firm, fully understood by my staff and my family. The Israelis are absolutely right. There can be no negotiations with terrorists. Use your gun, garbage! Or get out of here!"

Jason studied the old soldier, suddenly, profoundly uncertain, but not about to be fooled. It would be in the furious eyes that stared at him. One name soaked in filth coupled with another name heaped with the honors of his nation would cause another kind of explosion; it would be in the eyes.

"Back at that restaurant, you said France shouldn't be a lackey to anyone. But a general of France became someone's lackey. General André Villiers, messenger for Carlos. Carlos's contact, Carlos's soldier, Carlos's lackey."

The furious eyes did grow wide, but not in any way Jason expected. Fury was suddenly joined by hatred, not shock, not hysteria, but deep, uncompromising abhorrence. The back of Villiers' hand shot up, arching from his waist, the crack against Bourne's face sharp, accurate, painful. It was followed by a forward slap, brutal, insulting, the force of the blow reeling Jason back on his feet. The old man moved in, blocked by the barrel of the gun, but unafraid, undeterred by its presence, consumed only with inflicting punishment. The blows came one after another, delivered by a man possessed.

"Pig!" screamed Villiers. "Filthy, detestable pig! Garbage!"

"I'll shoot! I'll kill you! Stop it!" But Bourne could not pull the trigger. He was backed into the small car, his shoulders pressed against the roof. Still the old man attacked, his hands flying out, swinging up, crashing down.

"Kill me if you can—if you *dare! Dirt! Filth!*"

Jason threw the gun to the ground, raising his arms to fend off Villiers' assault. He lashed his left hand out, grabbing the old man's right wrist, then his left, gripping the left forearm that was slashing down like a broadsword. He twisted both violently, bending Villiers into him, forcing the old soldier to stand motionless, their faces inches from each other, the old man's chest heaving.

"Are you telling me you're *not* Carlos's man? Are you denying it?"

Villiers lunged forward, trying to break Bourne's grip, his barrel-like chest smashing into Jason. "I revile you! *Animal!*"

"*Goddamn* you—yes or no?"

The old man spat in Bourne's face, the fire in his eyes now clouded, tears welling. "Carlos killed my son," he said in a whisper. "He killed my only son on the rue du Bac. My son's life was blown up with five sticks of dynamite on the rue du Bac!"

Jason slowly reduced the pressure of his fingers. Breathing heavily, he spoke as calmly as he could.

"Drive your car into the field and stay there. We have to talk, General. Something's happened you don't know about, and we'd both better learn what it is."

"Never! Impossible! It could not happen!"

"It happened," said Bourne, sitting with Villiers in the front seat of the sedan.

"An incredible mistake has been made! You don't know what you're saying!"

"No mistake—and I do know what I'm saying because I found the number myself. It's not only the right number, it's a magnificent cover. Nobody in his right mind would connect you with Carlos, especially in light of your son's death. Is it common knowledge he was Carlos's kill?"

"I would prefer different language, monsieur."

"Sorry. I mean that."

"Common knowledge? Among the Sûreté, a qualified yes. Within military intelligence and Interpol, most certainly. I read the reports."

"What did they say?"

"It was presumed that Carlos did a favor for his friends from his radical days. Even to the point of allowing them to appear silently responsible for the act. It was politically motivated, you know. My son was a sacrifice, an example to others who opposed the fanatics."

"Fanatics?"

"The extremists were forming a false coalition with the socialists, making promises they had no intention of keeping. My son understood this, exposed it, and initiated legislation to block the alignment. He was killed for it."

"Is that why you retired from the army and stood for election?"

"With all my heart. It is customary for the son to carry on for the father . . ." The old man paused, the moonlight illuminating his haggard face. "In this matter, it was the father's legacy to carry on for the son. He was no soldier, nor I a politician, but I am no stranger to weapons and explosives. His causes were molded by me, his philosophy reflected my own, and he was killed for these things. My decision was clear to me. I would carry on our beliefs into the political arena and let his enemies contend with me. The soldier was prepared for them."

"More than one soldier, I gather."

"What do you mean?"

"Those men back there at the restaurant. They looked like they ran half the armies in France."

"They did, monsieur. They were once known as the angry young commanders of Saint-Cyr. The Republic was corrupt, the military incompetent, the Maginot a joke. Had they been heeded in their time, France would not have fallen. They became the leaders of the Resistance; they fought the Boche and Vichy all through Europe and Africa."

"What do they do now?"

"Most live on pensions, many obsessed with the past. They pray to the Virgin that it will never be repeated. In too many areas, however, they see it happening. The military is reduced to a sideshow, Communists and socialists in the Assembly forever eroding the strength of the services. The Moscow apparatus runs true to form; it does not change with the decades. A free society is ripe for infiltration, and once infiltrated the changes do not stop until that society is remade into another image. Conspiracy is everywhere; it cannot go unchallenged."

"Some might say that sounds pretty extreme itself."

"For what? Survival? Strength? Honor? Are these terms too anachronistic for you?"

"I don't think so. But I can imagine a lot of damage being done in their names."

"Our philosophies differ and I don't care to debate them. You asked me about my associates and I answered you. Now, please, this incredible misinformation of yours. It's appalling. You don't know what it's like to lose a son, to have a child killed."

The pain comes back to me and I don't know why. Pain and emptiness, a vacuum in the sky . . . from the sky. Death in and from the skies. Jesus, it hurts. It. What is it?

"I can sympathize," said Jason, his hands gripped to stop the sudden trembling. "But it fits."

"Not for an instant! As you said, no one in his right mind would connect me to Carlos, least of all the killer pig himself. It's a risk he would not take. It's unthinkable."

"Exactly. Which is why you're being used; it *is* unthinkable. You're the perfect relay for final instructions."

"Impossible! How?"

"Someone at your phone is in direct contact with Carlos. Codes are used, certain words spoken to get that person on the phone. Probably when you're not there, possibly when you are. Do you answer the telephone yourself?"

Villiers frowned. "Actually, I don't. Not that number. There are too many people to be avoided, and I have a private line."

"Who does answer it?"

"Generally the housekeeper, or her husband who serves as part butler, part chauffeur. He was my driver during my last years in the army. If not either of them, my wife, of course. Or my aide, who often works at my office at the house; he was my adjutant for twenty years."

"Who else?"

"There is no one else."

"Maids?"

"None permanent; if they're needed, they're hired for an occasion. There's more wealth in the Villiers name than in the banks."

"Cleaning woman?"

"Two. They come twice a week and not always the same two."

"You'd better take a closer look at your chauffeur and the adjutant."

"Preposterous! Their loyalty is beyond question."

"So was Brutus', and Caesar outranked you."

"You can't be serious."

"I'm goddamned serious. And you'd better believe it. Everything I've told you is the truth."

"But then you haven't really told me very much, have you? Your name, for instance."

"It's not necessary. Knowing it could only hurt you."

"In what way?"

"In the very remote chance that I'm wrong about the relay—and that possibility barely exists."

The old man nodded the way old men do when repeating words that have stunned them to the point of disbelief. His lined face moved up and down in the moonlight. "An unnamed man traps me on a road at night, holds me under a gun, and makes an obscene accusation—a charge so filthy, I wish to kill him—and he expects me to accept his word. The word of a man without a name, with no face I recognize, and no credentials offered other than the statement that Carlos is hunting him. Tell me why should I believe this man?"

"Because," answered Bourne. "He'd have no reason to come to you if *he* didn't believe it was the truth."

Villiers stared at Jason. "No, there's a better reason. A while ago, you gave me my life. You threw down your gun, you did not fire it. You could have. Easily. You chose, instead, to plead with me to talk."

"I don't think I pleaded."

"It was in your eyes, young man. It's always in the eyes. And often in the voice, but one must listen carefully. Supplication can be feigned, not anger. It is either real or it's a posture. Your anger was real . . . as was mine." The old man gestured toward the small Renault ten yards away in the field. "Follow me back to Park Monceau. We'll talk further in my office. I'd swear on my life that you're wrong about both men, but then as you pointed out, Caesar was blinded by false devotion. And indeed he did outrank me."

"If I walk into that house and someone recognizes me, I'm dead. So are you."

"My aide left shortly past five o'clock this afternoon and the chauffeur, as you call him, retires no later than ten to watch his interminable television. You'll wait outside while I go in and check. If things are normal, I'll summon you; if they're not, I'll come back out and drive away. Follow me again. I'll stop somewhere and we'll continue."

Jason watched closely as Villiers spoke. "Why do you want me to go back to Parc Monceau?"

"Where else? I believe in the shock of unexpected confrontation. One of those men is lying in bed watching television in a room on the third floor. And there's another reason. I want my wife to hear what you have to say. She's an old soldier's woman and she has antennae for things that often escape the officer in the field. I've come to rely on her perceptions; she may recognize a pattern of behavior once she hears you."

Bourne had to say the words. "I trapped you by pretending one thing; you can trap me by pretending another. How do I know Parc Monceau isn't a trap?"

The old man did not waver. "You have the word of a general officer of France, and that's all you have. If it's not good enough for you, take your weapon and get out."

"It's good enough," said Bourne. "Not because it's a general's word, but because it's the word of a man whose son was killed in the rue du Bac."

The drive back into Paris seemed far longer to Jason than the journey out. He was fighting images again, images that caused him to break out into sweat. And pain, starting at his temples, sweeping down through his chest, forming a knot in his stomach—sharp bolts pounding until he wanted to scream.

Death in the skies . . . from the skies. Not darkness, but blinding sunlight. No winds that batter my body into further darkness, but instead silence and the stench of jungle and . . . riverbanks. Stillness followed by the screeching of birds and the screaming pitch of machines. Birds . . . machines . . . racing downward out of the sky in blinding sunlight. Explosions. Death. Of the young and the very young.

Stop it! Hold the wheel! Concentrate on the road but do not think! Thought is too painful and you don't know why.

They entered the tree-lined street in Parc Monceau. Villiers was a hundred feet ahead, facing a problem that had not existed several hours ago: there were many more automobiles in the street now, parking at a premium.

There was, however, one sizable space on the left, across from the general's house; it could accommodate both their cars. Villiers thrust his hand out the window, gesturing for Jason to pull in behind him.

And then it happened. Jason's eyes were drawn by a light in a doorway, his focus suddenly rigid on the figures in the spill; the recognition of one so startling and so out of place he found himself reaching for the gun in his belt.

Had he been led into a trap after all? Had the word of a general officer of France been worthless?

Villiers was maneuvering his sedan into place. Bourne spun around in the seat, looking in all directions; there was no one coming toward him, no one closing in. It was *not* a trap. It was something else, part of what was happening about which the old soldier knew nothing.

For across the street and up the steps of Villiers' house stood a youngish woman—a striking woman—in the doorway. She was talking rapidly, with small anxious gestures, to a man standing on the top step, who kept nodding as if accepting instructions. That man was the gray-haired, distinguished-looking switchboard operator from Les Classiques. The man whose face Jason knew so well, yet did not know. The face that had triggered other images . . . images as violent and as painful as those which had ripped him apart during the past half hour in the Renault.

But there was a difference. This face brought back the darkness and torrential winds in the night sky, explosions coming one after another, sounds of a staccato gunfire echoing through the myriad tunnels of a jungle.

Bourne pulled his eyes away from the door and looked at Villiers through the windshield. The general had switched off his headlights and was about to get out of the car. Jason released the clutch and rolled forward until he made contact with the sedan's bumper. Villiers whipped around in his seat.

Bourne extinguished his own headlights and turned on the small inside roof light. He raised his hand—palm downward—then raised it twice again, telling the old soldier to stay where he was. Villiers nodded and Jason switched off the light.

He looked back over at the doorway. The man had taken a step down, stopped by a last command from the woman. Bourne could see her clearly now. She was in her middle to late thirties, with short dark hair, stylishly cut, framing a face that was bronzed by the sun. She was a tall woman, statuesque, actually, her figure tapered, the swell of her breasts accentuated by the sheer, close-fitting fabric of a long white dress that heightened the tan of her skin. If she was part of the house, Villiers had not mentioned her, which meant she was not. She was a visitor who knew when to come to the old man's home; it would fit the strategy of relay-removed-from-relay. And that meant she had a contact in Villiers' house. The old man had to know her, but how well? The answer obviously was not well enough.

The gray-haired switchboard operator gave a final nod, descended the steps and walked rapidly down the block. The door closed, the light of the carriage lamps shining on the deserted staircase and the glistening black door with the brass hardware.

Why did those steps and that door mean something to him? Images. Reality that was not real.

Bourne got out of the Renault, watching the windows, looking for the movement of a curtain; there was nothing. He walked quickly to Villiers' car; the front window was rolled down, the general's face turned up, his thick eyebrows arched in curiosity.

"What in heaven's name are you doing?" he asked.

"Over there, at your house," said Jason, crouching on the pavement. "You saw what I just saw."

"I believe so. And?"

"Who was the woman? Do you know her?"

"I would hope to God I did! She's my wife."

"Your *wife?*" Bourne's shock was on his face. "I thought you said . . . I thought you said she was an *old* woman. That you wanted her to listen to me because over the years you'd learned to respect her judgment. In the field, you said. That's what you *said.*"

"Not exactly. I said she was an *old soldier's* woman. And I do, indeed, respect her judgment. But she's my second wife—my very much younger second wife—but every bit as devoted as my first, who died eight years ago."

"Oh, my God . . ."

"Don't let the disparity of our ages concern you. She is proud and happy to be the second Madame Villiers. She's been a great help to me in the Assembly."

"I'm sorry," whispered Bourne. "Christ, I'm sorry."

"What about? You mistook her for someone else? People frequently do; she's a stunning girl. I'm quite proud of her." Villiers opened the door as Jason stood up on the pavement. "You wait here," said the general, "I'll go inside and check; if everything's normal, I'll open the door and signal you. If it isn't I'll come back to the car and we'll drive away."

Bourne remained motionless in front of Villiers, preventing the old man from stepping forward. "General, I've got to ask you something. I'm not sure how, but I have to. I told you I found your number at a relay drop used by Carlos. I didn't tell you where, only that it was confirmed by someone who admitted passing messages to and from contacts of Carlos." Bourne took a breath, his eyes briefly on the door across the street. "Now I've got to ask you a question, and please think carefully before you answer. Does your wife buy clothes at a shop called Les Classiques?"

"In Saint-Honoré?"

"Yes."

"I happen to know she does not."

"Are you sure?"

"Very much so. Not only have I never seen a bill from there, but she's told me how much she dislikes its designs. My wife is very knowledgeable in matters of fashion."

"Oh, Jesus."

"What?"

"General, I can't go inside that house. No matter what you find, I can't go in there."

"Why not? What are you saying?"

"The man on the steps who was talking to your wife. He's from the drop; it's Les Classiques. He's a contact to Carlos."

The blood drained from André Villiers' face. He turned and stared across the tree-lined street at his house, at the glistening black door and the brass fittings that reflected the light of the carriage lamps.

The pockmarked beggar scratched the stubble of his beard, took off his thread-bare beret and trudged through the bronze doors of the small church in Neuilly-sur-Seine.

He walked down the far right aisle under the disapproving glances of two priests. Both clerics were upset; this was a wealthy parish and, biblical compassion notwithstanding, wealth did have its privileges. One of them was to maintain a certain status of worshiper—for the benefit of other worshipers—and this elderly, disheveled derelict hardly fit the mold.

The beggar made a feeble attempt to genuflect, sat down in a pew in the second row, crossed himself and knelt forward, his head in prayer, his right hand pushing back the left sleeve of his overcoat. On his wrist was a watch somewhat in contradistinction to the rest of his apparel. It was an expensive digital, the numbers large and the readout bright. It was a possession he would never be foolish enough to part with, for it was a gift from Carlos. He had once been twenty-five minutes late for confession, upsetting his benefactor, and had no other excuse but the lack of an accurate timepiece. During their next appointment, Carlos had pushed it beneath the translucent scrim separating sinner from holy man.

It was the hour and the minute. The beggar rose and walked toward the second booth on the right. He parted the curtain and went inside.

"Angelus Domini."

"Angelus Domini, child of God." The whisper from behind the black cloth was harsh. "Are your days comfortable?"

"They are made comfortable . . ."

"Very well," interrupted the silhouette. "What did you bring me? My patience draws to an end. I pay thousands—hundreds of thousands—for incompetence and failure. What happened in Montrouge? Who was responsible for the lies that came from the embassy in the Montaigne? Who accepted them?"

"The Auberge du Coin was a trap, yet not one for killing. It is difficult to know exactly what it was. If the attaché named Corbelier repeated lies, our people are convinced he was not aware of it. He was duped by the woman."

"He was duped by Cain! Bourne traces each source, feeding each false information, thus exposing each and confirming the exposure. But why? To whom? We know what and who he is now, but he relays nothing to Washington. He refuses to surface."

"To suggest an answer," said the beggar, "I would have to go back many years, but it's possible he wants no intereference from his superiors. American Intelligence has its share of vacillating autocrats, rarely communicating fully with each other. In the days of the cold war, money was made selling information three and four times over to the same stations. Perhaps Cain waits until he thinks there is only one course of action to be taken, no differing strategies to be argued by those above."

"Age hasn't dulled your sense of maneuver, old friend. It's why I called upon you."

"Or perhaps," continued the beggar, "he really has turned. It's happened."

"I don't think so, but it doesn't matter. Washington thinks he has. The Monk is dead, they're all dead at Treadstone. Cain is established as the killer."

"The Monk?" said the beggar. "A name from the past; he was active in Berlin, in Vienna. We knew him well, healthier for it from a distance. There's your answer, Carlos. It was always the Monk's style to reduce the numbers to as few as possible. He operated on the theory that his circles were infiltrated, compromised. He must have ordered Cain to report only to him. It would explain Washington's confusion, the months of silence."

"Would it explain ours? For months there was no word, no activity."

"A score of possibilities. Illness, exhaustion, brought back for new training. Even to spread confusion to the enemy. The Monk had a cathedralful of tricks."

"Yet before he died he said to an associate that he did *not* know what had happened. That he wasn't even certain the man *was* Cain."

"Who was the associate?"

"A man named Gillette. He was our man, but Abbott couldn't have known it."

"Another possible explanation. The Monk had an instinct about such men. It was said in Vienna that David Abbott would distrust Christ on the mountain and look for a bakery."

"It's possible. Your words are comforting; you look for things others do not look for."

"I've had far more experience; I was once a man of stature. Unfortunately I pissed away the money."

"You still do."

"A profligate—what can I tell you?"

"Obviously something else."

"You're perceptive, Carlos. We should have known each other in the old days."

"Now you're presumptuous."

"Always. You know that I know you can swat my life away at any moment you choose, so I must be of value. And not merely with words that come from experience."

"What have you got to tell me?"

"This may not be of great value, but it is something. I put on respectable clothes and spent the day at the Auberge du Coin. There was a man, an obese man—questioned and dismissed by the Sûreté—whose eyes were too unsteady. And he perspired too much. I had a chat with him, showing him an official NATO identification I had made in the early fifties. It seems he negotiated the rental of an automobile at three o'clock yesterday morning. To a blond man in the company of a woman. The description fits the photograph from Argenteuil."

"A rental?"

"Supposedly. The car was to be returned within a day or so by the woman."

"It will never happen."

"Of course not, but it raises a question, doesn't it? Why would Cain go to the trouble of obtaining an automobile in such a fashion?"

"To get as far away as possible as rapidly as possible."

"In which case the information *has* no value," said the beggar. "But then there are so many ways to travel faster less conspicuously. And Bourne could hardly trust an avaricious night clerk; he might easily look for a reward from the Sûreté. Or anyone else."

"What's your point?"

"I suggest that Bourne could have obtained that car for the sole purpose of following someone here in Paris. No loitering in public where he might be spotted, no rented cars that could be traced, no frantic searches for elusive taxis. Instead, a simple exchange of license plates and a nondescript black Renault in the crowded streets. Where would one begin to look?"

The silhouette turned. "The Lavier woman," said the assassin softly. "And everyone else he suspects at Les Classiques. It's the only place he has to start. They'll be watched, and within days—hours perhaps—a nondescript black Renault will be seen and he'll be found. Do you have a full description of the car?"

"Down to three dents in the left rear fender."

"Good. Spread the word to the old men. Comb the streets, the garages, the parking lots. The one who finds it will never have to look for work again."

"Speaking of such matters . . ."

An envelope was slipped between the taut edge of the curtain and the blue felt of the frame. "If your theory proves right, consider this a token."

"I *am* right, Carlos."

"Why are you so convinced?"

"Because Cain does what you would do, what I would have done—in the old days. He must be respected."

"He must be killed," said the assassin. "There's symmetry in the timing. In a few days it will be the twenty-fifth of March. On March 25, 1968, Jason Bourne was executed in the jungles of Tam Quan. Now, years later—nearly to the day—another Jason Bourne is hunted, the Americans as anxious as we are to see him killed. I wonder which of us will pull the trigger this time."

"Does it matter?"

"*I* want him," whispered the silhouette. "He was never real, and that's his crime against me. Tell the old men that if any find him, get word to Parc Monceau but do nothing. Keep him in sight, but do *nothing!* I want him alive on the twenty-fifth of March. On March 25 I'll execute him myself and deliver his body to the Americans."

"The word will go out immediately."

"Angelus Domini, child of God."

"Angelus Domini," said the beggar.

26

The old soldier walked in silence beside the younger man down the moonlit path in the Bois de Boulogne. Neither spoke, for too much had already been said— admitted, challenged, denied and reaffirmed. Villiers had to reflect and analyze, to accept or violently reject what he had heard. His life would be far more bearable if he could strike back in anger, attack the lie and find his sanity again.

But he could not do that with impunity; he was a soldier and to turn away was not in him.

There was too much truth in the younger man. It was in his eyes, in his voice, in his every gesture that asked for understanding. The man without a name was not lying. The ultimate treason was in Villiers' house. It explained so many things he had not dared to question before. An old man wanted to weep.

For the man without a memory there was little to change or invent; the chameleon was not called upon. His story was convincing because the most vital part was based in the truth. He had to find Carlos, learn what the assassin knew; there would be no life for him if he failed. Beyond this he would say nothing. There was no mention of Marie St. Jacques, or the Ile de Port Noir, or a message being sent by person or persons unknown, or a walking hollow shell that might or might not be someone he was or was not—who could not even be sure that the fragments of memories he possessed were really his own. None of this was spoken of.

Instead, he recounted everything he knew about the assassin called Carlos. That knowledge was so vast that during the telling Villiers stared at him in astonishment, recognizing information he knew to be highly classified, shocked at new and startling data that was in concert with a dozen existing theories, but to his ears never before put forth with such clarity. Because of his son, the general had been given access to his country's most secret files on Carlos, and nothing in those records matched the younger man's array of facts.

"This woman you spoke with in Argenteuil, the one who calls my house, who admitted being a courier to you . . ."

"Her name is Lavier," Bourne interrupted.

The general paused. "Thank you. She saw through you; she had your photograph taken."

"Yes."

"They had no photograph before?"

"No."

"So as you hunt Carlos, he in turn hunts you. But you have no photograph; you only know two couriers, one of which was at my house."

"Yes."

"Speaking with my wife."

"Yes."

The old man turned away. The period of silence had begun.

They came to the end of the path, where there was a miniature lake. It was bordered with white gravel, benches spaced every ten to fifteen feet, circling the water like a guard of honor surrounding a grave of black marble. They walked to the second bench. Villiers broke his silence.

"I should like to sit down," he said. "With age there comes a paucity of stamina. It often embarrasses me."

"It shouldn't," said Bourne, sitting down beside him.

"It shouldn't," agreed the general, "but it does." He paused for a moment, adding quietly, "Frequently in the company of my wife."

"That's not necessary," said Jason.

"You mistake me." The old man turned to the younger, "I'm not referring to the bed. There are simply times when I find it necessary to curtail activities—leave a dinner party early, absent myself on weekends to the Mediterranean, or decline a few days on the slopes in Gstaad."

"I'm not sure I understand."

"My wife and I are often apart. In many ways we live quite separate lives, taking pleasure, of course, in each other's pursuits."

"I still don't understand."

"Must I embarrass myself further?" said Villiers. "When an old man finds a stunning young woman anxious to share his life, certain things are understood, others not so readily. There is, of course, financial security and in my case a degree of public exposure. Creature comforts, entry into the great houses, easy friendship with the celebrated; it's all very understandable. In exchange for these things, one brings a beautiful companion into his home, shows her off among his peers—a form of continuing virility, as it were. But there are always doubts." The old soldier stopped for several moments; what he had to say was not easy for him. "Will she take a lover?" he continued softly. "Does she long for a younger, firmer body, one more in tune with her own? If she does, one can accept it—even be relieved, I imagine—hoping to God she has the sense to be discreet. A cuckolded statesman loses his constituency faster than a sporadic drunk; it means he's fully lost his grip. There are other worries. Will she abuse his name? Publicly condemn an adversary whom one is trying to convince? These are the inclinations of the young; they are manageable, part of the risks in the exchange. But there is one underlying doubt that if proved justified cannot be tolerated. And that is if she is part of a design. From the beginning."

"You've felt it then?" asked Jason quietly.

"Feelings are not reality!" shot back the old soldier vehemently. "They have no place in observing the field."

"Then why are you telling me this?"

Villiers' head arched back, then fell forward, his eyes on the water. "There could be a simple explanation for what we both saw tonight. I pray there is, and I shall give her every opportunity to provide it." The old man paused again. "But in my heart I know there isn't. I knew it the moment you told me about Les Classiques. I looked across the street, at the door of my house, and suddenly a number of things fell painfully into place. For the past two hours I have played the devil's advocate; there is no point in continuing. There was my son before there was this woman."

"But you said you trusted her judgment. That she was a great help to you."

"True. You see, I wanted to trust her, desperately wanted to trust her. The easiest thing in the world is to convince yourself that you're right. As one grows old it is easier still."

"What fell into place for you?"

"The very help she gave me, the very trust I placed in her." Villiers turned and looked at Jason. "You have extraordinary knowledge about Carlos. I've studied those files as closely as any man alive, for I would give more than any man alive to see him caught and executed, I alone the firing squad. And as swollen as they are, those files do not approach what you know. Yet your concentration is solely on his kills, his methods of assassination. You've overlooked the other side of Carlos. He not only sells his gun, he sells a country's secrets."

"I know that," Bourne said. "It's not the side—"

"For example," continued the general, as if he had not heard Jason. "I have access to classified documents dealing with France's military and nuclear security. Perhaps five other men—all above suspicion—share that access. Yet with damning regularity we find that Moscow has learned this, Washington that, Peking something else."

"You discussed those things with your wife?" asked Bourne, surprised.

"Of course not. Whenever I bring such papers home, they are placed in a vault in my office. No one may enter that room except in my presence. There is only one other person who has a key, one other person who knows the whereabouts of the alarm switch. My wife."

"I'd think that would be as dangerous as discussing the material. Both could be forced from her."

"There was a reason. I'm at the age when the unexpected is a daily occurrence; I commend you to the obituary pages. If anything happened to me she is instructed to telephone the Conseiller Militaire, go down to my office, and stay by that vault until the security personnel arrive."

"Couldn't she simply stay by the door?"

"Men of my years have been known to pass away at their desks." Villiers closed his eyes. "All along it was she. The one house, the one place, no one believed possible."

"Are you sure?"

"More than I dare admit to myself. She was the one who insisted on the marriage. I repeatedly brought up the disparity of our ages, but she would have none of it. It was the years together, she claimed, not those that separated our birth dates. She offered to sign an agreement renouncing any claims to the Villiers estate and, of course, I would have none of that, for it was proof of her commitment to me. The adage is quite right: The old fool is the complete fool. Yet there were always the doubts; they came with the trips, with the unexpected separations."

"Unexpected?"

"She has many interests, forever demanding her attention. A Franco-Swiss museum in Grenoble, a fine arts gallery in Amsterdam, a monument to the Resistance in Boulogne-sur-Mer, an idiotic oceanography conference in Marseilles. We had a heated argument over that one. I needed her in Paris; there were diplomatic functions I had to attend and wanted her with me. She would not stay. It was as though she were being ordered to be here and there and somewhere else at a given moment."

Grenoble—near the Swiss border, an hour from Zurich. Amsterdam. Boulogne-sur-Mer—on the Channel, an hour from London. Marseilles . . . Carlos.

"When was the conference in Marseilles?" asked Jason.

"Last August, I believe. Toward the latter part of the month."

"On August 26, at five o'clock in the afternoon, Ambassador Howard Leland was assassinated on the Marseilles waterfront."

"Yes, I know," said Villiers. "You spoke of it before. I mourn the passing of the man, not his judgments." The old soldier stopped; he looked at Bourne. "My *God,*" he whispered. "She had to be with him. Carlos summoned her and she came to him. She *obeyed.*"

"I never went this far," said Jason. "I swear to you I thought of her as a relay—a blind relay. I never went this far."

Suddenly, from the old man's throat came a scream—deep and filled with agony and hatred. He brought his hands to his face, his head arched back once again in the moonlight; and he wept.

Bourne did not move; there was nothing he could do. "I'm sorry," he said.

The general regained control. "And so am I," he replied finally. "I apologize."

"No need to."

"I think there is. We will discuss it no further. I shall do what has to be done."

"Which is?"

The soldier sat erect on the bench, his jaw firm. "You can ask that?"

"I have to ask it."

"Having done what she's done is no different from having killed the child of mine she did not bear. She pretended to hold his memory dear. Yet she was and is an accomplice to his murder. And all the while she committed a second treason against the nation I have served throughout my life."

"You're going to kill her?"

"I'm going to kill her. She will tell me the truth and she will die."

"She'll deny everything you say."

"I doubt it."

"That's crazy!"

"Young man, I've spent over half a century trapping and fighting the enemies of France, even when they were Frenchmen. The truth will be heard."

"What do you think she's going to do? Sit there and listen to you and calmly agree that she's guilty?"

"She'll do nothing calmly. But she'll agree; she'll proclaim it."

"Why would she?"

"Because when I accuse her she'll have the opportunity to kill me. When she makes the attempt, I will have my explanation, won't I?"

"You'd take that risk?"

"I must take it."

"Suppose she doesn't make the attempt, doesn't try to kill you?"

"That would be another explanation," Villiers said. "In that unlikely event, I should look to my flanks if I were you, monsieur." He shook his head. "It will not happen. We both know it, I far more clearly than you."

"Listen to me," insisted Jason. "You say there was your son first. Think of him! Go after the killer, not the accomplice. She's an enormous wound for you, but he's a greater wound. Get the man who killed your son! In the end, you'll get both. Don't confront her; not yet. Use what you know against Carlos. Hunt him with me. No one's ever been this close."

"You ask more than I can give," said the old man.

"Not if you think about your son. If you think of yourself, it is. But not if you think of the rue du Bac."

"You are excessively cruel, monsieur."

"I'm right and you know it."

A high cloud floated by in the night sky, briefly blocking the light of the moon. Darkness was complete; Jason shivered. The old soldier spoke, resignation in his voice.

"Yes, you are right," he said. "Excessively cruel and excessively right. It's the killer, not the whore, who must be stopped. How do we work together? Hunt together?"

Bourne closed his eyes briefly in relief. "Don't do anything. Carlos has to be looking for me all over Paris. I've killed his men, uncovered a drop, found a contact. I'm too close to him. Unless we're both mistaken, your telephone will get busier and busier. I'll make sure of it."

"How?"

"I'll intercept a half a dozen employees of Les Classiques. Several clerks, the Lavier woman, Bergeron maybe, and certainly the man at the switchboard. They'll talk. And so will I. That phone of yours will be busy as hell."

"But what of me? What do I do?"

"Stay home. Say you're not feeling well. And whenever that phone rings, stay near whoever else answers. Listen to the conversation, try to pick up codes, question the servants as to what was said to them. You could even listen in. If you hear something, fine, but you probably won't. Whoever's on the line will know you're there. Still, you'll frustrate the relay. And depending upon where your wife is—"

"The whore is," broke in the old soldier.

"—in Carlos's hierarchy, we might even force him to come out."

"Again, how?"

"His lines of communication will be disrupted. The secure, unthinkable relay will be interfered with. He'll demand a meeting with your wife."

"He would hardly announce the whereabouts."

"He has to tell *her*." Bourne paused, another thought coming into focus. "If the disruption is severe enough, there'll be that one phone call, or that one person you don't know coming to the house, and shortly after, your wife will tell you she has to go somewhere. When it happens insist she leave a number where she can be reached. Be firm about it; you're not trying to stop her from going, but you *must* be able to reach her. Tell her anything—use the relationship *she* developed. Say it's a highly sensitive military matter you can't talk about until you get a clearance. Then you want to discuss it with her before you render a judgment. She might jump at it."

"What will it serve?"

"She'll be telling you where she is. Maybe where Carlos is. If not Carlos, certainly others closer to him. Then reach me. I'll give you a hotel and a room number. The name on the registry is meaningless, don't bother about it."

"Why don't you give me your real name?"

"Because if you ever mentioned it—consciously or unconsciously—you'd be dead."

"I'm not senile."

"No, you're not. But you're a man who's been hurt very badly. As badly as a person can be hurt, I think. *You* may risk your life; I won't."

"You're a strange man, monsieur."

"Yes. If I'm not there when you call, a woman will answer. She'll know where I am. We'll set up timing for messages."

"A woman?" the general drew back. "You've said nothing about a woman, or anyone else."

"There is no one else. Without her I wouldn't be alive. Carlos is hunting both of us; he's tried to kill both of us."

"Does she know about me?"

"Yes. She's the one who said it couldn't be true. That you couldn't be allied with Carlos. I thought you were."

"Perhaps I'll meet her."

"Not likely. Until Carlos is taken—if he *can* be taken—we can't be seen with you. Of all people, not you. Afterwards—if there is an afterwards—you may not want to be seen with us. With me. I'm being honest with you."

"I understand that and I respect it. In any event, thank this woman for me. Thank her for thinking I could be no part of Carlos."

Bourne nodded. "Can you be sure your private line isn't tapped?"

"Absolutely. It is swept on a regular basis; all the telephones restricted by the Conseiller are."

"Whenever you expect a call from me, answer the phone and clear your throat twice. I'll know it's you. If for any reason you can't talk, tell me to call your secretary in the morning. I'll call back in ten minutes. What's the number?"

Villiers gave it to him. "Your hotel?" asked the general.

"The Terrasse. Rue de Maistre, Montmartre. Room 420."

"When will you begin?"

"As soon as possible. Noon, today."

"Be like a wolfpack," said the old soldier, leaning forward, a commander instructing his officer corps. "Strike swiftly."

27

"She was *so* charming, I simply *must* do something for her," cried Marie in ebullient French into the telephone. "Also for the sweet young man; he was of such help. I tell you, the dress was a *succès fou!* I'm *so* grateful."

"From your descriptions, madame," replied the cultured male voice on the switchboard at Les Classiques, "I'm sure you mean Janine and Claude."

"Yes, of course. Janine and Claude, I remember now. I'll drop each a note with a token of my thanks. Would you by any chance know their last names? I mean, it seems so crass to address envelopes simply to 'Janine' and 'Claude.' Rather like sending missives to servants, don't you think? Could you ask Jacqueline?"

"It's not necessary, madame. I know them. And may I say that madame is as sensitive as she is generous. Janine Dolbert and Claude Oreale."

"Janine Dolbert and Claude Oreale," repeated Marie, looking at Jason. "Janine is married to that cute pianist, isn't she?"

"I don't believe Mademoiselle Dolbert is married to anyone."

"Of course. I'm thinking of someone else."

"If I may, madame, I didn't catch *your* name."

"How silly of me!" Marie thrust the phone away and raised her voice. "Darling, you're back, and so soon! That's marvelous. I'm talking to those lovely people at Les Classiques. . . . Yes, right away, my dear." She pulled the phone to her lips. "Thank you *so* much. You've been *very* kind." She hung up. "How'd I do?"

"If you ever decide to get out of economics," said Jason, poring through the Paris telephone book, "go into sales. I bought every word you said."

"Were the descriptions accurate?"

"To a cadaver and a very limp wrist. Nice touch, the pianist."

"It struck me that if she were married, the phone would be in her husband's name."

"It isn't," interrupted Bourne. "Here it is. Dolbert, Janine, rue Losserand." Jason wrote down the address. "Oreale, that's with an *O*, like the bird, isn't it? Not *Au.*"

"I think so." Marie lit a cigarette. "You're really going to go to their homes?"

Bourne nodded. "If I picked them up in Saint-Honoré, Carlos will have it watched."

"What about the others? Lavier, Bergeron, whoever-he-is on the switchboard."

"Tomorrow. Today's for the groundswell."

"The what?"

"Get them all talking. Running around saying things that shouldn't be said. By closing time, word will be spread through the store by Dolbert and Oreale.

I'll reach two others tonight; they'll call Lavier and the man at the switchboard. We'll have the first shock wave, and then the second. The general's phone will start ringing this afternoon. By morning the panic should be complete."

"Two questions," said Marie, getting up from the edge of the bed and coming toward him. "How are you going to get two clerks away from Les Classiques during store hours? And what people will you reach tonight?"

"Nobody lives in a deep freeze," replied Bourne, looking at his watch. "Especially in *haute couture*. It's 11:15 now; I'll get to Dolbert's apartment by noon and have the superintendent reach her at work. He'll tell her to come home right away. There's an urgent, very personal problem she'd better deal with."

"What problem?"

"I don't know, but who hasn't got one?"

"You'll do the same with Oreale?"

"Probably even more effective."

"You're outrageous, Jason."

"I'm deadly serious," said Bourne, his finger once again sliding down a column of names. "Here he is. Oreale, Claude Giselle. No comment. Rue Racine. I'll reach him by three; when I'm finished he'll head right back to Saint-Honoré and start screaming."

"What about the other two? Who are they?"

"I'll get names from either Oreale or Dolbert, or both. They won't know it, but they'll be giving me the second shock wave."

Jason stood in the shadows of the recessed doorway, in rue Losserand. He was fifteen feet from the entrance to Janine Dolbert's small apartment house where moments before a bewildered and suddenly richer *surintendant* had obliged a well-spoken stranger by calling Mademoiselle Dolbert at work and telling her that a gentleman in a chauffeured limousine had been around twice asking for her. He was back again; what should the *surintendant* do?

A small black taxi pulled up to the curb, and an agitated, cadaverous Janine Dolbert literally jumped out. Jason rushed from the doorway, intercepting her on the pavement, only feet from the entrance.

"That was quick," he said, touching her elbow. "So nice to see you again. You were very helpful the other day."

Janine Dolbert stared at him, her lips parted in recollection, then astonishment. "*You.* The American," she said in English. "Monsieur Briggs, isn't it? Are you the one who—"

"I told my chauffeur to take an hour off. I wanted to see you privately."

"Me? What could you possibly wish to see me about?"

"Don't you know? Then why did you race back here?"

The wide eyes beneath the short, bobbed hair were fixed on his, her pale face paler in the sunlight. "You're from the House of Azur, then?" she asked tentatively.

"I could be." Bourne applied a bit more pressure to her elbow. "And?"

"I've delivered what I promised. There will be nothing more, we agreed to that."

"Are you sure?"

"Don't be an idiot! You don't know Paris *couture*. Someone will get furious with someone else and make bitchy comments in your own studio. What strange deviations! And when the fall line comes out, with you parading half of Bergeron's designs before *he* does, how long do you think I can stay at Les Classiques? I'm Lavier's number two girl, one of the few who has access to her office. You'd better take care of me as you promised. In one of your Los Angeles shops."

"Let's take a walk," said Jason, gently propelling her. "You've got the wrong man, Janine. I've never heard of the House of Azur, and haven't the slightest interest in stolen designs—except where the knowledge can be useful."

"Oh, my God . . ."

"Keep walking." Bourne gripped her arm. "I said I wanted to talk to you."

"About what? What do you want from me? How did you get my name?" The words came rapidly now, the phrases overlapping. "I took an early lunch hour and must return at once; we're very busy today. Please—you're hurting my arm."

"Sorry."

"What I said; it was foolishness. A lie. On the floor, we've heard rumors; I was testing you. *That's* what I was doing, I was testing you!"

"You're very convincing. I'll accept that."

"I'm loyal to Les Classiques. I've always been loyal."

"It's a fine quality, Janine. I admire loyalty. I was saying that the other day to . . . what's his name? . . . that nice fellow on the switchboard. What *is* his name? I forget."

"Philippe," said the salesclerk, frightened, obsequious. "Philippe d'Anjou."

"That's it. Thank you." They reached a narrow, cobblestone alleyway between two buildings. Jason guided her into it. "Let's step in here for a moment, just so we're off the street. Don't worry, you won't be late. I'll only take a few minutes of your time." They walked ten paces into the narrow enclosure. Bourne stopped; Janine Dolbert pressed her back against the brick wall. "Cigarette?" he asked, taking a pack from his pocket.

"Thank you, yes."

"He lighted it for her, noting that her hand trembled. "Relaxed now?"

"Yes. No, not really. What do you want, Monsieur Briggs?"

"To begin with, the name's not Briggs, but I think you should know that."

"I don't. Why should I?"

"I was sure Lavier's number one girl would have told you."

"Monique?"

"Use last names, please. Accuracy's important."

"Brielle, then," said Janine frowning curiously. "Does she know you?"

"Why not ask her?"

"As you wish. What *is* it, monsieur?"

Jason shook his head. "You really *don't* know, do you? Three-quarters of the employees at Les Classiques are working with us and one of the brightest wasn't even contacted. Of course it's possible someone thought you were a risk; it happens."

"*What* happens? What risk? Who *are* you?"

"There isn't time now. The others can fill you in. I'm here because we've never received a report from you, and yet you speak to prime customers all day long."

"You *must* be clearer, monsieur."

"Let's say I'm the spokesman for a group of people—American, French, English, Dutch—closing in on a killer who's murdered political and military leaders in each of our countries."

"*Murdered?* Military, political . . ." Janine's mouth gaped, the ash of her cigarette breaking off, spilling over her rigid hand. "What *is* this? What are you *talking* about? I've heard none of this!"

"I can only apologize," said Bourne softly, sincerely. "You should have been contacted several weeks ago. It was an error on the part of the man before me. I'm sorry; it must be a shock to you."

"It *is* a shock, monsieur," whispered the salesclerk, her concave body tensed, a bent, lacquered reed against the brick. "You speak of things beyond my understanding."

"But now *I* understand," interrupted Jason. "Not a word from you about anyone. Now it's clear."

"It's not to me."

"We're closing in on Carlos. The assassin known as Carlos."

"*Carlos?*" The cigarette fell from Dolbert's hand, the shock complete.

"He's one of your most frequent customers, all the evidence points to it. We've narrowed the probabilities down to eight men. The trap is set for sometime in the next several days, and we're taking every precaution."

"Precaution . . .?"

"There's always the danger of hostages, we all know that. We anticipate gunfire, but it will be kept to a minimum. The basic problem will be Carlos himself. He's sworn never to be taken alive; he walks the streets wired up to explosives calculated to be in excess of a thousand-pound bomb. But we can handle that. Our marksmen will be on the scene; one clean shot to the head and it'll be all over."

"*Une seule balle . . .*"

Suddenly Bourne looked at his watch. "I've taken up enough of your time. You've got to get back to the shop and I have to get back to my post. Remember, if you see me outside, you don't know me. If I come into Les Classiques, treat me as you would any rich client. *Except* if you've spotted a customer you think may be our man; then don't waste time telling me. Again, I'm sorry about all this. It was a breakdown in communications, that's all. It happens."

"*Une rupture . . . ?*"

Jason nodded, turned in place, and began walking rapidly out of the alleyway toward the street. He stopped and glanced back at Janine Dolbert. She was comatose against the wall; for her the elegant world of *haute couture* was spinning wildly out of orbit.

Philippe d'Anjou. The name meant nothing to him, but Bourne could not help himself. He kept repeating it silently trying to raise an image . . . as the face of the gray-haired switchboard operator gave rise to such violent images of darkness and flashes of light. *Philippe d'Anjou.* Nothing. Nothing at all. Yet there had been something, something that caused Jason's stomach to knot, the muscles taut and inflexible, a flat panel of hard flesh constricted . . . by the darkness.

He sat by the front window and the door of a coffee shop on the rue Racine, prepared to get up and leave the moment he saw the figure of Claude Oreale arrive at the doorway of the ancient building across the street. His room was on the fifth floor, in a flat he shared with two other men, reached only by climbing a worn, angular staircase. When he did arrive, Bourne was sure he would not be walking.

For Claude Oreale, who had been so effusive with Jacqueline Lavier on another staircase in Saint-Honoré, had been told by a toothless landlady over the phone to get his *sale gueule* back to rue Racine and put a stop to the screaming and smashing of furniture that was taking place in his fifth-floor flat. Either he would stop it or the gendarmes would be called; he had twenty minutes to show up.

He did so in fifteen. His slight frame, encased in a Pierre Cardin suit—rear flap fluttering in the headwind—could be seen racing up the sidewalk from the nearby Métro exit. He avoided collisions with the agility of an out-of-shape broken-field runner trained by the Ballets Russe. His thin neck was thrust forward several inches in front of his vested chest, his long dark hair a flowing mane parallel to the pavement. He reached the entrance and gripped the railing, leaping up the steps and plunging into the shadows of the foyer.

Jason walked rapidly out of the coffee shop and raced across the street. Inside, he ran to the ancient staircase then started up the cracked steps. From the fourth floor landing, he could hear the pounding on the door above.

"Ouvrez! Ouvrez! Vite, nom de Dieu!" Oreale stopped, the silence within perhaps more frightening than anything else.

Bourne climbed the remaining steps until he could see Oreale between the bars of the railing and the floor. The clerk's frail body was pressed into the door, his hands on either side, fingers spread, his ear against the wood, his face flushed. Jason shouted in guttural, bureaucratic French, as he rushed up into view. "Sûreté! Stay exactly where you are, young man. Let's not have any unpleasantness. We've been watching you and your friends. We know about the darkroom."

"No!" screamed Oreale. "It has nothing to do with me, I swear it! *Darkroom?*"

Bourne raised his hand. "Be quiet, Don't shout so!" He immediately followed his commands by leaning over the railing and looking below.

"You can't involve me!" continued the salesclerk. "I'm not involved! I've told them over and over again to get rid of it all! One day they'll kill themselves. Drugs are for idiots! My God, it's quiet. I think they're dead!"

Jason stood up from the railing and approached Oreale, his palms raised. "I told you to shut up," he whispered harshly. "Get inside there and be quiet! This was all for the benefit of that old bitch downstairs."

The salesclerk was transfixed, his panic suspended in silent hysteria. "What?"

"You've got a key," said Bourne. "Open up and get inside."

"It's bolted," replied Oreale. "It's always bolted during these times."

"You damn fool, we had to *reach* you! We had to get you here without anyone knowing why. Open that door. Quickly!"

Like the terrified rabbit he was, Claude Oreale fumbled in his pocket and found the key. He unlocked the door and pushed it open as a man might entering a storage vault filled with mutilated corpses. Bourne propelled him through the doorframe, stepped inside and closed the door.

What could be seen of the flat belied the rest of the building. The fair-sized living room was filled with sleek, expensive furniture, dozens of red and yellow velvet pillows scattered about on couches, chairs and the floor. It was an erotic room, a luxurious sanctuary in the midst of debris.

"I've only got a few minutes," said Jason. "No time for anything but business."

"Business?" asked Oreale, his expression flat-out paralyzed. "This . . . this darkroom? *What* darkroom?"

"Forget it. You had something better going."

"What business?"

"We received word from Zurich and we want you to get it to your friend Lavier."

"Madame Jacqueline? My *friend?*"

"We can't trust the phones."

"What phones? The word? *What* word?"

"Carlos is right."

"Carlos? Carlos who?"

"The assassin."

Claude Oreale screamed. He brought his hand up to his mouth, bit the knuckle of his index finger and screamed. "What are you *saying?*"

"Be quiet!"

"Why are you saying it to *me?*"

"You're number five. We're counting on you."

"Five *what? For* what?"

"To help Carlos escape the net. They're closing in. Tomorrow, the next day, perhaps the day after that. He's to stay away; he's *got* to stay away. They'll surround the shop, marksmen every ten feet. The crossfire will be murderous; if he's in there it could be a massacre. Every one of you. Dead."

Oreale screamed again, his knuckle red. "Will you *stop* this! I don't know what you're talking about! You're a maniac and I won't hear another word—I haven't heard *anything*. Carlos, crossfire . . . massacres! God, I'm suffocating . . . I need air!"

"You'll get money. A lot of it, I imagine. Lavier will thank you. Also d'Anjou."

"D'Anjou? He loathes me! He calls me a peacock, insults me every chance he gets."

"It's his cover, of course. Actually, he's very fond of you—perhaps more than you know. He's number six."

"What are these *numbers?* Stop talking numbers!"

"How else can we distinguish between you, allocate assignments? We can't use names."

"Who can't?"

"All of us who work for Carlos."

The scream was ear-shattering, as the blood trickled from Oreale's finger. "I won't *listen!* I'm a couturier, an *artist!*"

"You're number five. You'll do exactly as we say or you'll never see this passion pit of yours again."

"*Aunghunn!*"

"Stop screaming! We appreciate you; we know you're all under a strain. Incidentally, we don't trust the bookkeeper."

"Trignon?"

"First names only. Obscurity's important."

"Pierre, then. He's hateful. He deducts for telephone calls."

"We think he's working for Interpol."

"Interpol?"

"If he is, you could all spend ten years in prison. *You'd* be eaten alive, Claude."

"*Aunghunn!*"

"Shut up! Just let Bergeron know what we think. Keep your eyes on Trignon, especially during the next two days. If he leaves the store for any reason, watch out. It could mean the trap's closing." Bourne walked to the door, his hand in his pocket. "I've got to get back, and so do you. Tell numbers one through six everything I told you. It's vital the word be spread."

Oreale screamed again, hysterically again. "Numbers! Always *numbers!* What *number?* I'm an artist, not a number!"

"You won't have a face unless you get back there as fast as you got here. Reach Lavier, d'Anjou, Bergeron. As quickly as you can. Then the others."

"*What* others?"

"Ask number two."

"Two?"

"Dolbert. Janine Dolbert."

"*Janine*. Her, too?"

"That's right. She's two."

The salesclerk flung his arms wildly above him in helpless protest.

"This is madness! Nothing makes sense!"

"Your life does, Claude," said Jason simply. "Value it. I'll be waiting across the street. Leave here in exactly three minutes. And don't use the phone; just leave and get back to Les Classiques. If you're not out of here in three minutes I'll have to return." He took his hand out of his pocket. In it was his gun.

Oreale expunged a lungful of air, his face ashen as he stared at the weapon. Bourne let himself out and closed the door.

The telephone rang on the bedside table. Marie looked at her watch; it was 8:15 and for a moment she felt a sharp jolt of fear. Jason had said he would call at 9:00. He had left La Terrasse after dark, around 7:00, to intercept a salesclerk named Monique Brielle. The schedule was precise, to be interrupted only in emergency. Had something happened?

"Is this room 420?" asked the deep male voice on the line.

Relief swept over Marie; the man was André Villiers. The general had called late in the afternoon to tell Jason that panic had spread through Les Classiques; his wife had been summoned to the phone no less than six times over the span of an hour and a half. Not once, however, had he been able to listen to anything of substance; whenever he had picked up the phone, serious conversation had been replaced by innocuous banter.

"Yes," said Marie. "This is 420."

"Forgive me, we did not speak before."

"I know who you are."

"I'm also aware of you. May I take the liberty of saying thank you."

"I understand. You're welcome."

"To substance. I'm telephoning from my office, and, of course, there's no extension for this line. Tell our mutual friend that the crisis has accelerated. My wife has taken to her room, claiming nausea, but apparently she's not too ill to be on the phone. On several occasions, as before, I picked up only to realize that they were alert for any interference. Each time I apologized rather gruffly, saying I expected calls. Frankly, I'm not at all sure my wife was convinced, but of course she's in no position to question me. I'll be blunt, mademoiselle. There is unspoken friction building between us, and beneath the surface, it is violent. May God give me strength."

"I can only ask you to remember the objective," broke in Marie. "Remember your son."

"Yes," said the old man quietly. "My son. And the whore who claims to revere his memory. I'm sorry."

"It's all right. I'll convey what you've told me to our friend. He'll be calling within the hour."

"Please," interrupted Villiers. "There's more. It's the reason I had to reach you. Twice while my wife was on the telephone the voices held meaning for me.

The second I recognized; a face came to mind instantly. He's on a switchboard in Saint-Honoré."

"We know his name. What about the first?"

"It was strange. I did not know the voice, there was no face to go with it, but I understood why it was there. It was an odd voice, half whisper, half command, an echo of itself. It was the command that struck me. You see, that voice was not having a conversation with my wife; it had issued an order. It was altered the instant I got on the line, of course; a prearranged signal for a swift goodbye, but the residue remained. That residue, even the tone, is well known to any soldier; it is his means of emphasis. Am I being clear?"

"I think so," said Marie gently, aware that if the old man was implying what she thought he was, the strain on him had to be unbearable.

"Be assured of it, mademoiselle," said the general, "it was the killer pig." Villiers stopped, his breathing audible, the next words drawn out, a strong man close to weeping. "He was . . . *instructing . . . my . . . wife . . .*" The old soldier's voice cracked. "Forgive me the unforgiveable. I have no right to burden you."

"You have every right," said Marie, suddenly alarmed. "What's happening has to be terribly painful for you, made worse because you have no one to talk to."

"I am talking to you, mademoiselle. I shouldn't, but I am."

"I wish we could keep talking. I wish one of us could be with you. But that's not possible and I know you understand that. Please try to hold on. It's terribly important that no connection be made between you and our friend. It could cost you your life."

"I think perhaps I have lost it."

"*Ça, c'est absurde,*" said Marie sharply, an intended slap in the old soldier's face. "*Vous êtes un soldat. Arrêtez ça immédiatement!*"

"*C'est l'institutrice qui corrige le mauvais élève. Vous avez bien raison.*"

"*On dit que vous êtes un géant. Je le crois.*" There was silence on the line; Marie held her breath. When Villiers spoke she breathed again.

"Our mutual friend is very fortunate. You are a remarkable woman."

"Not at all. I just want my friend to come back to me. There's nothing remarkable about that."

"Perhaps not. But I should also like to be your friend. You reminded a very old man of who and what he is. Or who and what he once was, and must try to be again. I thank you for a second time."

"You're welcome . . . my friend." Marie hung up, profoundly moved and equally disturbed. She was not convinced Villiers could face the next twenty-four hours, and if he could not, the assassin would know how deeply his apparatus had been penetrated. He would order every contact at Les Classiques to run from Paris and disappear. Or there would be a bloodbath in Saint-Honoré, achieving the same results.

If either happened, there would be no answers, no address in New York, no message deciphered, nor the sender found. The man she loved would be returned to his labyrinth. And he would leave her.

28

Bourne saw her at the corner, walking under the spill of the streetlight toward the small hotel that was her home. Monique Brielle, Jacqueline Lavier's number one girl, was a harder, more sinewy version of Janine Dolbert; he remembered seeing her at the shop. There was an assurance about her, her stride the stride of a confident woman, secure in the knowledge of her expertise. Very unflappable. Jason could understand why she was Lavier's number one. Their confrontation would be brief, the impact of the message startling, the threat inherent. It was time for the start of the second shock wave. He remained motionless and let her pass on the sidewalk, her heels clicking martially on the pavement. The street was not crowded, but neither was it deserted; there were perhaps a half dozen people on the block. It would be necessary to isolate her, then steer her out of earshot of any who might overhear the words, for they were words that no messenger would risk being heard. He caught up with her no more than thirty feet from the entrance to the small hotel; he slowed his pace to hers, staying at her side.

"Get in touch with Lavier right away," he said in French, staring straight ahead.

"Pardon? What did you say? Who are you, monsieur?"

"Don't stop! Keep walking. Past the entrance."

"You know where I *live?*"

"There's very little we don't know."

"And if I go straight inside? There's a doorman—"

"There's also Lavier," interrupted Bourne. "You'll lose your job and you won't be able to find another in Saint-Honoré. And I'm afraid that will be the least of your problems."

"Who *are* you?"

"Not your enemy." Jason looked at her. "Don't make me one."

"*You.* The American! Janine . . . Claude Oreale!"

"Carlos," completed Bourne.

"Carlos? What is this *madness?* All afternoon, nothing but Carlos! And *numbers!* Everyone has a number no one's heard of! And talk of traps and men with guns! It's crazy!"

"It's happening. Keep walking. Please. For your own sake."

She did, her stride less sure, her body stiffened, a rigid marionette uncertain of its strings. "Jacqueline spoke to us," she said, her voice intense. "She told us it was all insane, that it—*you*—were out to ruin Les Classiques. That one of the other houses must have paid you to ruin us."

"What did you expect her to say?"

"You are a hired provocateur. She told us the truth."

"Did she also tell you to keep your mouth shut? Not to say a word about any of this to anyone?"

"Of course."

"Above all," ran on Jason as if he had not heard her, "not to contact the police, which under the circumstances would be the most logical thing in the world to do. In some ways, the *only* thing to do."

"Yes, naturally . . ."

"Not naturally," contradicted Bourne. "Look, I'm just a relay, probably not much higher than you. I'm not here to convince you, I'm here to deliver a message. We ran a test on Dolbert; we fed her false information."

"Janine?" Monique Brielle's perplexity was compounded by mounting confusion. "The things she said were incredible! As incredible as Claude's hysterical screaming—the things *he* said. But what she said was the opposite of what he said."

"We know; it was done intentionally. She's been talking to Azur."

"The House of Azur?"

"Check her out tomorrow. Confront her."

"Confront her?"

"Just do it. It could be tied in."

"With what? Interpol? Traps? This is the same craziness! Nobody knows what you're talking about!"

"Lavier knows. Get in touch with her right away." They approached the end of the block; Jason touched her arm. "I'll leave you here at the corner. Go back to your hotel and call Jacqueline. Tell her it's far more serious than we thought. Everything's falling apart. Worst of all, someone has turned. Not Dolbert, not one of the clerks, but someone more highly placed. Someone who knows everything."

"Turned? What does that mean?"

"There's a traitor in Les Classiques. Tell her to be careful. Of everyone. If she isn't, it could be the end for all of us." Bourne released her arm, then stepped off the curb and crossed the street. On the other side he spotted a recessed doorway and quickly stepped inside.

He inched his face to the edge and peered out, looking back at the corner. Monique Brielle was halfway down the block, rushing toward the entrance of her hotel. The first panic of the second shock wave had begun. It was time to call Marie.

"I'm worried, Jason. It's tearing him apart. He nearly broke down on the phone. What happens when he looks at her? What must he be feeling, thinking?"

"He'll handle it," said Bourne, watching the traffic on the Champs-Elysées from inside the glass telephone booth, wishing he felt more confident about André Villiers. "If he doesn't, I've killed him. I don't want it on my head, but that's what I'll have done. I should have shut my goddamn mouth and taken her myself."

"You couldn't have done that. You saw d'Anjou on the steps; you couldn't have gone inside."

"I could have thought of something. As we've agreed, I'm resourceful—more than I like to think about."

"But you are doing something! You're creating panic, forcing those who carry out Carlos's orders to show themselves. Someone's got to stop the panic, and even you said you didn't think Jacqueline Lavier was high enough. Jason, you'll see someone and you'll know. You'll get him! You will!"

"I hope so; Christ, I hope so! I know exactly what I'm doing, but every now and then . . ." Bourne stopped. He hated saying it, but he had to—he had to say it to her. "I get confused. It's as if I'm split down the middle, one part of me saying 'Save yourself,' the other part . . . God help me . . . telling me to 'Get Carlos.' "

"It's what you've been doing from the beginning, isn't it?" said Marie softly.

"I don't *care* about Carlos!" shouted Jason, wiping away the sweat that had broken out on his hairline, aware, too, that he was cold. "It's driving me crazy," he added, not sure whether he had said the words out loud or to himself.

"Darling, come back."

"What?" Bourne looked at the telephone, again not sure whether he had heard spoken words, or whether he had wanted to hear them, and so they were there. *It was happening again. Things were and they were not. The sky was dark outside, outside a telephone booth on the Champs-Elysées. It had once been bright, so bright, so blinding. And hot, not cold. With screeching birds and screaming streaks of metal . . .*

"Jason!"

"What?"

"Come back. Darling, *please* come back."

"Why?"

"You're tired. You need rest."

"I have to reach Trignon. Pierre Trignon. He's the bookkeeper."

"Do it tomorrow. It can wait until tomorrow."

"No. Tomorrow's for the captains." *What was he saying? Captains. Troops. Figures colliding in panic. But it was the only way, the only way. The chameleon was a . . . provocateur.*

"Listen to me," said Marie, her voice insistent. "Something's happening to you. It's happened before; we both know that, my darling. And when it does, you have got to stop, we know that, too. Come back to the hotel. Please."

Bourne closed his eyes, the sweat was drying and the sounds of the traffic outside the booth replaced the screeching in his ears. He could see the stars in the cold night sky, no more blinding sunlight, no more unbearable heat. It had passed, whatever it was.

"I'm all right. Really, I'm okay now. A couple of bad moments, that's all."

"Jason?" Marie spoke slowly, forcing him to listen. "What caused them?"

"I don't know."

"You just saw the Brielle woman. Did she say something to you? Something that made you think of something else?"

"I'm not sure. I was too busy figuring out what to say myself."

"Think, darling!"

Bourne closed his eyes, trying to remember. Had there been something? Something spoken casually or so rapidly that it was lost at the moment? "She called me a *provocateur,"* said Jason, not understanding why the word came back to him. "But then, that's what I am, aren't I? That's what I'm doing."

"Yes," agreed Marie.

"I've got to get going," continued Bourne. "Trignon's place is only a couple of blocks from here. I want to reach him before ten."

"Be careful." Marie spoke as if her thoughts were elsewhere.

"I will. I love you."

"I believe in you," said Marie St. Jacques.

The street was quiet, the block an odd mixture of shops and flats indigenous to the center of Paris, bustling with activity during the day, deserted at night.

Jason reached the small apartment house listed in the telephone directory as Pierre Trignon's residence. He climbed the steps and walked into the neat, dimly lit foyer. A row of brass mailboxes was on the right, each one above a small spoked circle through which a caller raised his voice loudly enough to identify himself. Jason ran his finger along the printed names below the slots: M. PIERRE TRIG-NON—42. He pushed the tiny black button twice; ten seconds later there was a crackling of static.

"Oui?"

"Monsieur Trignon, s'il vous plaît?"

"Ici."

"Télégramme, monsieur. Je ne peux pas quitter ma bicyclette."

"Télégramme? Pour moi?"

Pierre Trignon was not a man who often received telegrams; it was in his astonished tone. The rest of his words were barely distinguishable, but a female voice in the background was in shock, equating a telegram with all manner of horrendous disasters.

Bourne waited outside the frosted glass door that led to the apartment house interior. In seconds he heard the rapid clatter of footsteps growing louder as someone—obviously Trignon—came rushing down the staircase. The door swung open, concealing Jason; a balding, heavy-set man, unnecessary suspenders creasing the flesh beneath a bulging white shirt, walked to the row of mailboxes, stopping at number 42.

"Monsieur Trignon?"

The heavy-set man spun around, his cherubic face set in an expression of helplessness. "A telegram! I have a telegram!" he cried. "Did you bring me a telegram?"

"I apologize for the ruse, Trignon, but it was for your own benefit. I didn't think you wanted to be questioned in front of your wife and family."

"*Questioned?*" exclaimed the bookkeeper, his thick, protruding lips curled, his eyes frightened. "*Me?* What about? What is this? Why are you here at my home? I'm a law-abiding citizen!"

"You work in Saint-Honoré? For a firm called Les Classiques?"

"I do. Who are you?"

"If you prefer, we can go down to my office," said Bourne.

"Who *are* you?"

"I'm a special investigator for the Bureau of Taxation and Records, Division of Fraud and Conspiracy. Come along—my official car is outside."

"Outside? Come along? I have no jacket, no coat! My wife. She's upstairs expecting me to bring back a telegram. A telegram!"

"You can send her one if you like. Come along now. I've been at this all day and I want to get it over with."

"Please, monsieur," protested Trignon. "I do not insist on going anywhere! You said you had questions. Ask your questions and let me go back upstairs. I have no wish to go to your office."

"It might take a few minutes," said Jason.

"I'll ring through to my wife and tell her it's a mistake. The telegram's for old Gravet; he lives here on the first floor and can barely read. She will understand."

Madame Trignon did not understand, but her shrill objections were stilled by a shriller Monsieur Trignon. "There, you see," said the bookkeeper, coming away from the mailslot, the strings of hair on his bald scalp matted with sweat. "There's no reason to go anywhere. What's a few minutes of a man's life? The television shows will be repeated in a month or two. Now, what in God's name *is* this, monsieur? My books are immaculate, totally immaculate! Of course I cannot be responsible for the accountant's work. That's a separate firm; *he's* a separate firm. Frankly, I've never liked him; he swears a great deal, if you know what I mean. But then, who am I to say?" Trignon's hands were held out palms up, his face pinched in an obsequious smile.

"To begin with," said Bourne, dismissing the protestations, "do not leave the city limits of Paris. If for any reason, personal or professional, you are called upon to do so, notify us. Frankly, it will not be permitted."

"Surely you're joking, monsieur!"

"Surely I'm not."

"I have no reason to leave Paris—nor the money to do so—but to say such a thing to me is unbelievable. What have I done?"

"The Bureau will subpoena your books in the morning. Be prepared."

"Subpoena? For what cause? Prepared for what?"

"Payments to so-called suppliers whose invoices are fraudulent. The merchandise was never received—was never meant to be received—the payments, instead, routed to a bank in Zurich."

"Zurich? I don't know what you're talking about! I've prepared no checks for Zurich."

"Not directly, we know that. But how easy it was for you to prepare them for nonexistent firms, the monies paid, then wired to Zurich."

"Every invoice is initialed by Madame Lavier! I pay *nothing* on my own!"

Jason paused, frowning. "Now it's you who are joking," he said.

"On my word! It's the house policy. Ask anyone! Les Classiques does not pay a *sou* unless authorized by Madame."

"What you're saying, then, is that you take your orders directly from her."

"But naturally!"

"Whom does she take orders from?"

Trignon grinned. "It is said from God, when not the other way around. Of course, that's a joke, monsieur."

"I trust you can be more serious. Who are the specific owners of Les Classiques?"

"It is a partnership, monsieur. Madame Lavier has many wealthy friends; they have invested in her abilities. And, of course, the talents of René Bergeron."

"Do these investors meet frequently? Do they suggest policy? Perhaps advocate certain firms with which to do business?"

"I wouldn't know, monsieur. Naturally, everyone has friends."

"We may have concentrated on the wrong people," interrupted Bourne. "It's quite possible that you and Madame Lavier—as the two directly involved with the day-to-day finances—are being used."

"Used for what?"

"To funnel money into Zurich. To the account of one of the most vicious killers in Europe."

Trignon convulsed, his large stomach quivering as he fell back against the wall. "In the name of God, what are you *saying?*"

"Prepare yourselves. Especially you. You prepared the checks, no one else."

"Only upon approval!"

"Did you ever check the merchandise against the invoices?"

"It's not my job!"

"So, in essence you issued payments for supplies you never saw."

"I never see anything! Only invoices that have been initialed. I pay only on those!"

"You'd better find every one. You and Madame Lavier had better start digging up every backup in your files. Because the two of you—especially you—will face the charges."

"Charges? What charges?"

"For a lack of a specific writ, let's call it accessory to multiple homicide."

"Multiple—"

"Assassination. The account in Zurich belongs to the assassin known as Carlos.

You, Pierre Trignon, and your current employer, Madame Jacqueline Lavier, are directly implicated in financing the most sought-after killer in Europe. Ilich Ramirez Sanchez. Alias Carlos."

"Aughhhh! . . ." Trignon slid down to the foyer floor, his eyes in shock, his puffed features twisted out of shape. "All afternoon . . ." he whispered. "People running around, hysterical meetings in the aisles, looking at me strangely, passing my cubicle and turning their heads. Oh, my *God.*"

"If I were you, I wouldn't waste a moment. Morning will be here soon, and with it possibly the most difficult day of your life." Jason walked to the outside door and stopped, his hand on the knob. "It's not my place to advise you, but if I were you, I'd reach Madame Lavier at once. Start preparing your joint defense—it may be all you have. A public execution is not out of the question."

The chameleon opened the door and stepped outside, the cold night air whipping across his face.

Get Carlos. Trap Carlos. Cain is for Charlie and Delta is for Cain.

False!

Find a number in New York. Find Treadstone. Find the meaning of a message. Find the sender.

Find Jason Bourne.

Sunlight burst through the stained-glass windows as the clean-shaven old man in the dated suit of clothes rushed down the aisle of the church in Neuilly-sur-Seine. The tall priest standing by the rack of novena candles watched him, struck by a feeling of familiarity. For a moment the cleric thought he had seen the man before, but could not place him. There had been a disheveled beggar yesterday, about the same size, the same . . . No, this old man's shoes were shined, his white hair combed neatly, and the suit of clothes, although from another decade, were of good quality.

"Angelus Domini," said the old man, as he parted the curtains of the confessional booth.

"Enough!" whispered the silhouetted figure behind the scrim. "What have you learned in Saint-Honoré?"

"Little of substance, but respect for his methods."

"Is there a pattern?"

"Random, it would appear. He selects people who know absolutely nothing and instigates chaos through them. I would suggest no further activity at Les Classiques."

"Naturally," agreed the silhouette. "But what's his purpose?"

"Beyond the chaos?" asked the old man. "I'd say it was to spread distrust among those who do know something. The Brielle woman used the words. She said the American told her to tell Lavier there was 'a traitor' inside, a patently false statement. Which of them would dare? Last night was insane, as you know. The bookkeeper, Trignon, went crazy. Waiting until two in the morning outside

Lavier's house, literally assaulting her when she returned from Brielle's hotel, screaming and crying in the street."

"Lavier herself did not behave much better. She was barely in control when she called Parc Monceau; she was told not to call again. No one is to call there . . . ever again. *Ever.*"

"We received the word. The few of us who know the number have forgotten it."

"Be sure you have." The silhouette moved suddenly; there was a ripple in the curtain. "Of *course* to spread distrust! It follows chaos. There's no question about it now. He'll pick up the contacts, try to force information from them and when one fails, throw him to the Americans and go on to the next. But he'll make the approaches alone; it's part of his ego. He *is* a madman. And obsessed."

"He may be both," countered the old man, "but he's also a professional. He'll make sure the names are delivered to his superiors in the event he does fail. So regardless of whether you take him or not, *they* will be taken."

"They will be dead," said the assassin. "But not Bergeron. He's far too valuable. Tell him to head for Athens; he'll know where."

"Am I to assume I'm taking the place of Parc Monceau?"

"*That* would be impossible. But for the time being you will relay my final decisions to whomever they concern."

"And the first person I reach is Bergeron. To Athens."

"Yes."

"So Lavier and the colonial, d'Anjou, are marked, then?"

"They are marked. Bait rarely survives, and they will not. You may also relay another message, to the two teams covering Lavier and d'Anjou. Tell them I'll be watching them—all the time. There can be no mistakes."

It was the old man's turn to pause, to bid silently for attention. "I've saved the best for last, Carlos. The Renault was found an hour and a half ago in a garage in Montmartre. It was brought in last night."

In the stillness the old man could hear the slow, deliberate breathing of the figure beyond the cloth. "I assume you've taken measures to have it watched—even now at the moment—and followed—even now at the moment."

The once-bespoken beggar laughed softly. "In accord with your last instructions, I took the liberty of hiring a friend, a friend with a sound automobile. He in turn has employed three acquaintances, and together they are on four six-hour shifts on the street outside the garage. They know nothing, of course, except that they are to follow the Renault at any hour of day or night."

"You do not disappoint me."

"I can't afford to. And since Parc Monceau was eliminated, I had no telephone number to give them but my own, which as you know, is a rundown café in the Quarter. The owner and I were friends in the old days, the better days. I could reach him every five minutes for messages and he would never object. I know where he got the money to pay for his business, and whom he had to kill to get it."

"You've behaved well, you have value."

"I also have a problem, Carlos. As none of us are to call Parc Monceau, how can I reach you? In the event I must. Say, for instance, the Renault."

"Yes, I'm aware of the problem. Are you aware of the burden you ask for?"

"I would much prefer not to have it. My only hope is that when this is over and Cain is dead, you will remember my contributions and rather than killing me, change the number."

"You *do* anticipate."

"In the old days it was my means of survival."

The assassin whispered seven figures. "You are the only man alive who has this number. Naturally it is untraceable."

"Naturally. Who would expect an old beggar to have it?"

"Every hour brings you closer to a better standard of living. The net is closing; every hour brings him nearer to one of several traps. Cain will be caught, and an imposter's body will be thrown back to the bewildered strategists who created him. They counted on a monstrous ego and he gave it to them. At the end, he was only a puppet, an expendable puppet. Everyone knew it but him."

Bourne picked up the telephone. "Yes?"

"Room 420?"

"Go ahead, General."

"The telephone calls have stopped. She's no longer being contacted—not at least by telephone. Our couple was out and the phone rang twice. Both times she asked me to answer it. She really wasn't up to talking."

"Who called?"

"The chemists with a prescription and a journalist requesting an interview. She couldn't have known either."

"Did you get the impression she was trying to throw you off by having you take the calls?"

Villiers paused, his reply laced with anger. "It was there, the effect less than subtle insofar as she mentioned she might be having lunch out. She said she had a reservation at the George Cinq, and I could reach her there if she decides to go."

"If she does, I want to get there first."

"I'll let you know."

"You said she's not being contacted by phone. 'Not at least by telephone,' I think you said. Did you mean something by that?"

"Yes. Thirty minutes ago a woman came to the house. My wife was reluctant to see her but nevertheless did so. I only saw her face for a moment in the parlor, but it was enough. The woman was in panic."

"Describe her."

Villiers did.

"Jacqueline Lavier," said Jason.

"I thought it might be. From the looks of her, the wolfpack was eminently successful; it was obvious she had not slept. Before taking her into the library, my wife told me she was an old friend in a marriage crisis. A fatuous lie; at her age there are no crises left in marriage, only acceptance and extraction."

"I can't understand her going to your house. It's too much of a risk. It doesn't make sense. Unless she did it on her own, knowing that no further calls were to be made."

"These things occurred to me," said the soldier. "So I felt the need of a little air, a stroll around the block. My aide accompanied me—a doddering old man taking his limited constitutional under the watchful eye of an escort. But my eyes, too, were watchful. Lavier was followed. Two men were seated in a car four houses away, the automobile equipped with a radio. Those men did not belong to the street. It was in their faces, in the way they watched my house."

"How do you know she didn't come with them?"

"We live on a quiet street. When Lavier arrived, I was in the sitting room having coffee, and heard her running up the steps. I went to the window in time to see a taxi drive away. She came in a taxi; she was followed."

"When did she leave?"

"She hasn't. And the men are still outside."

"What kind of car are they in?"

"Citroën. Gray. The first three letters of the license plate are *NYR.*"

"Birds in the air, following a contact. Where do the birds come from?"

"I beg your pardon. What did you say?"

Jason shook his head. "I'm not sure. Never mind. I'm going to try to get out there before Lavier leaves. Do what you can to help me. Interrupt your wife, say you have to speak with her for a few minutes. Insist her 'old friend' stay; say anything, just make sure she doesn't leave."

"I will do my best."

Bourne hung up and looked at Marie, standing by the window across the room. "It's working. They're starting to distrust each other. Lavier went to Parc Monceau and she was followed. They're beginning to suspect their own."

" 'Birds in the air," said Marie. "What did you mean?"

"I don't know; it's not important. There isn't time."

"I think it *is* important, Jason."

"Not now." Bourne walked to the chair where he had dropped his topcoat and hat. He put them on quickly and went to the bureau, opened the drawer and took out the gun. He looked at it for a moment, remembering. The images were there, the past that was his whole yet not his whole at all. Zurich. The Bahnhofstrasse and the Carillon du Lac; the Drei Alpenhäuser and the Löwenstrasse; a filthy boardinghouse on the Steppdeckstrasse. The gun symbolized them all, for it had once nearly taken his life in Zurich.

But this was Paris. And everything started in Zurich was in motion.

Find Carlos. Trap Carlos. Cain is for Charlie and Delta is for Cain.

False! Goddamn you, false!

Find Treadstone. Find a message. Find a man.

29

Jason remained in the far corner of the back seat as the taxi entered Villiers' block in Parc Monceau. He scanned the cars lining the curb; there was no gray Citroën, no license with the letters NYR.

But there was Villiers. The old soldier was standing alone on the pavement, four doors away from his house.

Two men . . . in a car four houses away from my house.

Villiers was standing now where that car had stood; it was a signal.

"Arrêtez, s'il vous plaît," said Bourne to the driver. *"Le vieux là-bas. Je veux parler avec lui."* He rolled down the window and leaned forward. *"Monsieur?"*

"In English," replied Villiers, walking toward the taxi, an old man summoned by a stranger.

"What happened?" asked Jason.

"I could not detain them."

"Them?"

"My wife left with the Lavier woman. I was adamant, however. I told her to expect my call at the George Cinq. It was a matter of the utmost importance and I required her counsel."

"What did she say?"

"That she wasn't sure she'd be at the George Cinq. That her friend insisted on seeing a priest in Neuilly-sur-Seine, at the Church of the Blessed Sacrament. She said she felt obliged to accompany her."

"Did you object?"

"Strenuously. And for the first time in our life together, she stated the thoughts in my own mind. She said, 'If it's your desire to check up on me, André, why not call the parish? I'm sure someone might recognize me and bring me to a telephone.' Was she testing me?"

Bourne tried to think. "Perhaps. Someone would see her there, she'd make sure of it. But bringing her to a phone might be something else again. When did they leave?"

"Less than five minutes ago. The two men in the Citroën followed them."

"Were they in your car?"

"No. My wife called a taxi."

"I'm going out there," said Jason.

"I thought you might," said Villiers. "I looked up the address of the church."

Bourne dropped a fifty-franc note over the back of the front seat. The driver grabbed it. "It's important to me to reach Neuilly-sur-Seine as fast as possible. The Church of the Blessed Sacrament. Do you know where it is?"

"But of course, monsieur. It is the most beautiful parish in the district."

"Get there quickly and there'll be another fifty francs."

"We shall fly on the wings of blessed angels, monsieur!"

They flew, the flight plan jeopardizing most of the traffic in their path.

"There are the spires of the Blessed Sacrament, monsieur," said the victorious driver, twelve minutes later, pointing at three soaring towers of stone through the windshield. "Another minute, perhaps two if the idiots who should be taken off the street will permit. . . ."

"Slow down," interrupted Bourne, his attention not on the spires of the church but on an automobile several cars ahead. They had taken a corner and he had seen it during the turn; it was a gray Citroën, two men in the front seat.

They came to a traffic light; the cars stopped. Jason dropped the second fifty-franc note over the seat and opened the door. "I'll be right back. If the light changes, drive forward slowly and I'll jump in."

Bourne got out, keeping his body low, and rushed between the cars until he saw the letters. NYR; the numbers following were 768, but for the moment they were inconsequential. The taxi driver had earned his money.

The light changed and the row of automobiles lurched forward like one elongated insect pulling its shelled parts together. The taxi drew alongside; Jason opened the door and climbed in. "You do good work," he said to the driver.

"I'm not sure I know the work I am doing."

"An affair of the heart. One must catch the betrayer in the act."

"In *church*, monsieur? The world moves too swiftly for me."

"Not in traffic," said Bourne. They approached the final corner before the Church of the Blessed Sacrament. The Citroën made the turn, a single car between it and a taxi, the passengers indistinguishable. Something bothered Jason. The surveillance on the part of the two men was too open, far too obvious. It was as if Carlos's soldiers wanted someone in that taxi to know they were there.

Of course! Villiers' wife was in that cab. With Jacqueline Lavier. And the two men in the Citroën wanted Villiers' wife to know they were behind her.

"There is the Blessed Sacrament," said the driver, entering the street where the church rose in minor medieval splendor in the center of a manicured lawn, crisscrossed by stone paths and dotted with statuary. "What shall I do, monsieur?"

"Pull into that space," ordered Jason, gesturing at a break in the line of parked cars. The taxi with Villiers' wife and the Lavier woman stopped in front of a path guarded by a concrete saint. Villiers' stunning wife got out first, extending her hand for Jacqueline Lavier, who emerged, ashen, on the pavement. She wore large, orange-rimmed sunglasses and carried a white purse, but she was no longer elegant. Her crown of silver-streaked hair fell in straight, disassociated lines down the sides of her death-white mask of a face, and her stockings were torn. She was at least three hundred feet away, but Bourne felt he could almost hear the erratic gasping for breath that accompanied the hesitant movements of the once regal figure stepping forward in the sunlight.

The Citroën had proceeded beyond the taxi and was now pulling to the curb. Neither man got out, but a thin metal rod, reflecting the glare of the sun, began rising out of the trunk. The radio antenna was being activated, codes sent over a guarded frequency. Jason was mesmerized, not by the sight and the knowledge of what was being done, but by something else. Words came to him, from where he did not know, but they were there.

Delta to Almanac, Delta to Almanac. We will not respond. Repeat, negative, brother.

Almanac to Delta. You will respond as ordered. Abandon, abandon. That is final.

Delta to Almanac. You're final, brother. Go fuck yourself. Delta out, equipment damaged.

Suddenly the darkness was all around him, the sunlight gone. There were no soaring towers of a church reaching for the sky; instead there were black shapes of irregular foliage shivering beneath the light of iridescent clouds. Everything was moving, *everything was moving;* he had to move with the movement. To remain immobile was to die. *Move!* For Christ's sake, *move!*

And take them *out.* One by *one.* Crawl in closer; overcome the fear—the terrible fear—and reduce the numbers. That was all there was to it. Reduce the numbers. The Monk had made that clear. Knife, wire, knee, thumb; you know the points of damage. Of death.

Death is a statistic for the computers. For you it is survival.

The Monk.

The *Monk?*

The sunlight came again, blinding him for a moment, his foot on the pavement, his gaze on the gray Citroën a hundred yards away. But it was difficult to see; why was it so difficult? Haze, mist . . . not darkness now but impenetrable mist. He was hot; no, he was cold. Cold! He jerked his head up, suddenly aware of where he was and what he was doing. His face had been pressed against the window; his breath had fogged the glass.

"I'm getting out for a few minutes," said Bourne. "Stay here."

"All day, if you wish, monsieur."

Jason pulled up the lapels of his topcoat, pushed his hat forward and put on the tortoise-shell glasses. He walked alongside a couple toward a religious sidewalk bazaar, breaking away to stand behind a mother and child at the counter. He had a clear view of the Citroën, the taxi which had been summoned to Parc Monceau was no longer there, dismissed by Villiers' wife. It was a curious decision on her part, thought Bourne; cabs were not that available.

Three minutes later the reason was clear . . . and disturbing. Villiers' wife came striding out of the church, walking rapidly, her tall, statuesque figure drawing admiring glances from strollers. She went directly to the Citroën, spoke to the men in front, then opened the rear door.

The purse. A *white* purse! Villiers' wife was carrying the purse that only minutes before had been clutched in the hands of Jacqueline Lavier. She climbed into the Citroën's back seat and pulled the door shut. The sedan's motor was switched on and gunned, prelude to a quick and sudden departure. As the car rolled away, the shiny metal rod that was the vehicle's antenna became shorter and shorter, retracting into its base.

Where was Jacqueline Lavier? Why had she given her purse to Villiers' wife? Bourne started to move, then stopped, instinct warning him. A trap? If Lavier was followed, those following her might also be trailed—and not by him.

He looked up and down the street, studying the pedestrians on the sidewalk, then each car, each driver and passenger, watching for a face that did not belong, as Villiers had said of the two men in the Citroën had not belonged in Parc Monceau.

There were no breaks in the parade, no darting eyes or hands concealed in outsized pockets. He was being overly cautious; Neuilly-sur-Seine was not a trap for him. He moved away from the counter and started for the church.

He stopped, his feet suddenly clamped to the pavement. A priest was coming out of the church, a priest in a black suit, a starched white collar and a black hat that partially covered his face. He had seen him before. Not long ago, not in a forgotten past, but recently. Very recently. Weeks, days . . . hours, perhaps. Where was it? *Where?* He knew him! It was in the walk, in the tilt of his head, in the wide shoulders that seemed to glide in place above the fluid movement of his body. He was a man with a gun! Where *was* it?

Zurich? The Carillon du Lac? Two men breaking through the crowds, converging, brokering death. One wore gold-rimmed glasses; it was not he. That man was dead. Was it that other man in the Carillon du Lac? Or in the Guisan Quai? An animal, grunting, wild-eyed in rape. Was it he? Or someone else. A dark-coated man in the corridor at the Auberge du Coin where the lights had been shorted out, the spill from the staircase illuminating the trap. A reverse trap where that man had fired his weapon in darkness at shapes he thought were human. Was it *that* man?

Bourne did not know, he only knew that he had seen the priest before, but not as a priest. As a man with a gun.

The killer in the priestly dark suit reached the end of the stone path and turned right at the base of the concrete saint, his face briefly caught in the sunlight. Jason froze; the *skin*. The killer's skin was dark, not tanned by the sun, but by birth. A Latin skin, its hue tempered generations ago by ancestors living in or around the Mediterranean. Forebears who migrated across the globe . . . across the seas.

Bourne stood paralyzed by the shock of his own certainty. He was looking at Ilich Ramirez Sanchez.

Get Carlos. Trap Carlos. Cain is for Charlie and Delta is for Cain.

Jason tore at the front of his coat, his right hand grasping the handle of the gun in his belt. He started running on the pavement, colliding with the backs and chests of strollers, shouldering a sidewalk vendor out of his way, lurching past a beggar digging into a wire trash—The *beggar!* The beggar's hand surged into his pocket; Bourne spun around in time to see the barrel of an automatic emerge from the threadbare coat, the sun's rays bouncing off the metal. The beggar had a gun! His gaunt hand raised it, weapon and eyes steady. Jason lunged into the street, careening off the side of a small car. He heard the spits of the bullets above him and around him, piercing the air with sickening finality. Screams, shrill and in pain, came from unseen people on the sidewalk. Bourne ducked between two automobiles and raced through the traffic to the other side of the street. The beggar was running away; an old man with eyes of steel was racing into the crowds, into oblivion.

Get Carlos. Trap Carlos. Cain is . . .!

Jason spun again and lurched again, propelling himself forward, throwing everything in his path out of his way, racing in the direction of the assassin. He stopped, breathless, confusion and anger welling in his chest, sharp bolts of pain returning to his temples. Where *was* he? Where was *Carlos!* And then he saw him; the killer had climbed behind the wheel of a large black sedan. Bourne ran back into the traffic, slamming hoods and trunks as he threaded his way insanely toward the assassin. Suddenly he was blocked by two cars that had collided. He spread his hands on a glistening chrome grille and leaped sideways over the impacted bumpers. He stopped again, his eyes searing with pain at what he saw, knowing it was pointless to go on. He was too late. The large black sedan had found a break in the traffic, and Ilich Ramirez Sanchez sped away.

Jason crossed back to the far pavement as the shrieking of police whistles turned heads everywhere. Pedestrians had been grazed or wounded or killed; a beggar with a gun had shot them.

Lavier! Bourne broke into a run again, back toward the Church of the Blessed Sacrament. He reached the stone path under the eye of the concrete saint and spun left, racing toward the arched, sculptured doors and the marble steps. He ran up and entered the Gothic church, facing racks of flickering candles, fused rays of colored light streaming down from the stained-glass windows high in the dark stone walls. He walked down the center aisle, staring at the worshipers, looking for streaked silver hair and a mask of a face laminated in white.

The Lavier woman was nowhere to be seen, yet she had not left; she was somewhere in the church. Jason turned, glancing up the aisle; there was a tall priest walking casually past the rack of candles. Bourne sidestepped his way through a cushioned row, emerged on the far right aisle and intercepted him.

"Excuse me, Father," he said. "I'm afraid I've lost someone."

"No one is lost in the house of God, sir," replied the cleric, smiling.

"She may not be lost in spirit, but if I don't find the rest of her, she'll be very upset. There's an emergency at her place of business. Have you been here long, Father?"

"I greet those of our flock who seek assistance, yes. I've been here for the better part of an hour."

"Two women came in a few minutes ago. One was extremely tall, quite striking, wearing a light-colored coat, and I think a dark kerchief over her hair.

The other was an older lady, not as tall, and obviously not in good health. Did you by any chance see them?"

The priest nodded. "Yes. There was sorrow in the older woman's face, she was pale and grieving."

"Do you know where she went? I gather her younger friend left."

"A devoted friend, may I say. She escorted the poor dear to confession, helping her inside the booth. The cleansing of the soul gives us all strength during the desperate times."

"To confession?"

"Yes—the second booth from the right. She has a compassionate father confessor, I might add. A visiting priest from the archdiocese of Barcelona. A remarkable man, too; I'm sorry to say this is his last day. He returns to Spain . . ." The tall priest frowned. "Isn't that odd? A few moments ago I thought I saw Father Manuel leave. I imagine he was replaced for a while. No matter, the dear lady is in good hands."

"I'm sure of it," said Bourne. "Thank you, Father. I'll wait for her." Jason walked down the aisle toward the row of confessional booths, his eyes on the second, where a small strip of white fabric proclaimed occupancy; a soul was being cleansed. He sat down in the front row, then knelt forward, angling his head slowly around so he could see the rear of the church. The tall priest stood at the entrance, his attention on the disturbance in the street. Outside, sirens could be heard wailing in the distance, drawing closer.

Bourne got up and walked to the second booth. He parted the curtain and looked inside, seeing what he expected to see. Only the method had remained in question.

Jacqueline Lavier was dead, her body slumped forward, rolled to the side, supported by the prayer stall, her mask of a face upturned, her eyes wide, staring in death at the ceiling. Her coat was open, the cloth of her dress drenched in blood. The weapon was a long, thin, letter opener, plunged in above her left breast. Her fingers were curled around the handle, her lacquered nails the color of her blood.

At her feet was a purse—not the white purse she had clutched in her hands ten minutes earlier, but a fashionable Yves St. Laurent, the precocious initials stamped on the fabric, an escutcheon of the *haute couture*. The reason for it was clear to Jason. Inside were papers identifying this tragic suicide, this overwrought woman so burdened with grief she took her own life while seeking absolution in the eyes of God. Carlos was thorough, brilliantly thorough.

Bourne closed the curtain and stepped away from the booth. From somewhere high in a tower, the bells of the morning Angelus rang splendidly.

The taxi wandered aimlessly through the streets of Neuilly-sur-Seine, Jason in the back seat, his mind racing.

It was pointless to wait, perhaps deadly to do so. Strategies changed as conditions changed, and they had taken a deadly turn. Jacqueline Lavier had been followed, her death inevitable but out of sequence. Too soon; she was still valuable. Then Bourne understood. She had not been killed because she had been disloyal to Carlos, rather because she had disobeyed him. She had gone to Parc Monceau—that was her indefensible error.

There was another known relay at Les Classiques, a gray-haired switchboard operator named Philippe d'Anjou, whose face evoked images of violence and darkness, and shattering flashes of light and sound. He had been in Bourne's past, of that Jason was certain, and because of that, the hunted had to be cautious; he could not know what that man meant to him. But he was a relay, and he, too, would be watched, as Lavier had been watched, additional bait for another trap, dispatch demanded when the trap closed.

Were these the only two? Were there others? An obscure, faceless clerk, perhaps, who was not a clerk at all but someone else? A supplier who spent hours in Saint-Honoré legitimately pursuing the cause of *haute couture*, but with another cause far more vital to him. Or her. Or the muscular designer, René Bergeron, whose movements were so quick and . . . *fluid.*

Bourne suddenly stiffened, his neck pressed back against the seat, a recent memory triggered. *Bergeron.* The darkly tanned skin, the wide shoulders accentuated by tightly rolled-up sleeves . . . shoulders that floated in place above a tapered waist, beneath which strong legs moved swiftly, like an animal's, a cat's.

Was it possible? Were the other conjectures merely phantoms, compounded fragments of familiar images he had convinced himself might be Carlos? Was the assassin—unknown to his relays—deep inside his own apparatus, controlling and shaping every move? Was it *Bergeron?*

He had to get to a telephone right away. Every minute he lost was a minute removed from the answer, and too many meant there would be no answer at all. But he could not make the call himself; the sequence of events had been too rapid, he had to hold back, store his own information.

"The first telephone booth you see, pull over," he said to the driver, who was still shaken by the chaos at the Church of the Blessed Sacrament.

"As you wish, monsieur. But if monsieur will please try to understand, it is past the time when I should report to the fleet garage. Way past the time."

"I understand."

"There's a telephone."

"Good. Pull over."

The red telephone booth, its quaint panes of glass glistening in the sunlight, looked like a large dollhouse from the outside and smelled of urine on the inside. Bourne dialed the Terrasse, inserted the coins and asked for room 420. Marie answered.

"What happened?"

"I haven't time to explain. I want you to call Les Classiques and ask for René Bergeron. D'Anjou will probably be on the switchboard; make up a name and tell him you've been trying to reach Bergeron on Lavier's private line for the past hour or so. Say it's urgent, you've got to talk to him."

"When he gets on, what do I say?"

"I don't think he will, but if he does, just hang up. And if d'Anjou comes on the line again, ask him when Bergeron's expected. I'll call you back in three minutes."

"Darling, are you all right?"

"I've had a profound religious experience. I'll tell you about it later."

Jason kept his eyes on his watch, the infinitesimal jumps of the thin, delicate sweep hand too agonizingly slow. He began his own personal countdown at thirty seconds, calculating the heartbeat that echoed in his throat as somewhere around two and a half per second. He started dialing at ten seconds, inserted the coins at four, and spoke to the Terrasse's switchboard at minus-five. Marie picked up the phone the instant it began to ring.

"What happened?" he asked. "I thought you might still be talking."

"It was a very short conversation. I think d'Anjou was wary. He may have a list of names of those who've been given the private number—I don't know. But he sounded withdrawn, hesitant."

"What did he say?"

"Monsieur Bergeron is on a fabric search in the Mediterranean. He left this morning and isn't expected back for several weeks."

"It's possible I may have just seen him several hundred miles from the Mediterranean."

"Where?"

"In church. If it *was* Bergeron, he gave absolution with the point of a very sharp instrument."

"What are you talking about?"

"Lavier's dead."

"Oh, my God! What are you going to do?"

"Talk to a man I think I knew. If he's got a brain in his head, he'll listen. He's marked for extinction."

30

"D'Anjou."

"Delta? I wondered when . . . I think I'd know your voice anywhere."

He had said it! The name had been spoken. The name that meant nothing to him, and yet somehow everything. D'Anjou knew. Philippe d'Anjou was part of the unremembered past. Delta. Cain is for Charlie and Delta is for Cain. Delta. Delta. Delta! He had known this man and this man had the answer! Alpha, Bravo, Cain, Delta, Echo, Foxtrot . . .

Medusa.

"Medusa," he said softly, repeating the name that was a silent scream in his ears.

"Paris is not Tam Quan, Delta. There are no debts between us any longer. Don't look for payment. We work for different employers now."

"Jacqueline Lavier's dead. Carlos killed her in Neuilly-sur-Seine less than thirty minutes ago."

"Don't even try. As of two hours ago Jacqueline was on her way out of France. She called me herself from Orly Airport. She's joining Bergeron—"

"On a fabric search in the Mediterranean?" interrupted Jason.

D'Anjou paused. "The woman on the line asking for René. I thought as much. It changes nothing. I spoke with her; she called from Orly."

"She was told to tell you that. Did she sound in control of herself?"

"She was upset, and no one knows why better than you. You've done a remarkable job down here, Delta. Or Cain. Or whatever you call yourself now. Of course she wasn't herself. It's why she's going away for a while."

"It's why she's dead. You're next."

"The last twenty-four hours were worthy of you. This isn't."

"She was followed; you're being followed. Watched every moment."

"If I am it's for my own protection."

"Then why is Lavier dead?"

"I don't believe she is."

"Would she commit suicide?"

"Never."

"Call the rectory at the Church of the Blessed Sacrament in Neuilly-sur-Seine. Ask about the woman who killed herself while taking confession. What have you got to lose? I'll call you back."

Bourne hung up and left the booth. He stepped off the curb, looking for a cab. The next call to Philippe d'Anjou would be made a minimum of ten blocks away. The man from Medusa would not be convinced easily, and until he was, Jason would not risk electronic scanners picking up even the general location of the call.

Delta? I think I'd know your voice anywhere. . . . Paris is not Tam Quan. Tom Quan . . . Tom Quan, Tom Quan! Cain is for Charlie and Delta is for Cain. Medusa!

Stop it! Do not think of things that . . . you cannot think about. Concentrate on what *is.* Now. *You.* Not what others say you are—not even what you may think you are. Only the now. And the now is a man who can give you answers.

We work for different employers. . . .

That was the key.

Tell me! For Christ's sake, tell me! Who is it? Who is my employer, d'Anjou?

A taxi swerved to a stop perilously close to his kneecaps. Jason opened the door and climbed in. "Place Vendôme," he said, knowing it was near Saint-Honoré. It was imperative to be as close as possible to put in motion the strategy that was rapidly coming into focus. He had the advantage; it was a matter of using it for a dual purpose. D'Anjou had to be convinced that those following him were his executioners. But what those men could not know was that another would be following *them.*

The Vendôme was crowded as usual, the traffic wild as usual. Bourne saw a telephone booth on the corner and got out of the taxi. He went inside the booth and dialed Les Classiques; it had been fourteen minutes since he had called from Neuilly-sur-Seine.

"D'Anjou?"

"A woman took her own life while at confession, that's all I know."

"Come on, you wouldn't settle for that. Medusa wouldn't settle for that."

"Give me a moment to put the board on hold." The line went dead for roughly four seconds. D'Anjou returned. "A middle-aged woman with silver and white hair, expensive clothing, and a St. Laurent purse. I've just described ten thousand women in Paris. How do I know you didn't take one, kill her, make her the basis of this call?"

"Oh, sure. I carried her into the church like a pieta, blood dripping in the aisles from her open stigmata. Be reasonable, d'Anjou. Let's start with the obvious. The purse wasn't hers; she carried a white leather handbag. She'd hardly be likely to advertise a competing house."

"Lending credence to my belief. It was *not* Jacqueline Lavier."

"Lends more to mine. The papers in that purse identified her as someone else. The body will be claimed quickly; no one touches Les Classiques."

"Because you say so?"

"No. Because it's the method used by Carlos in five kills I can name." *He could. That was the frightening thing.* "A man is taken out, the police believing he's one person, the death an enigma, killers unknown. Then they find out he's someone else, by which time Carlos is in another country, another contract fulfilled. Lavier was a variation of that method, that's all."

"Words, Delta. You never said much, but when you did, the words were there."

"And if you were in Saint-Honoré three or four weeks from now—which you won't be—you'd see how it ends. A plane crash or a boat lost in the Mediterranean. Bodies charred beyond recognition or simply gone. The identities of the dead, however, clearly established. Lavier and Bergeron. But only one is really dead—Madame Lavier. Monsieur Bergeron is privileged—more than you ever knew. Bergeron is back in business. And as for you, you're a statistic in the Paris morgue."

"And you?"

"According to the plan I'm dead too. They expect to take me through you."

"Logical. We're both from Medusa, they know that—Carlos knows that. It's to be assumed you recognized me."

"And you me?"

D'Anjou paused. "Yes," he said. "As I told you, we work for different employers now."

"That's what I want to talk about."

"No talking, Delta. But for old times' sake—for what you did for us all in Tam Quan—take the advice of a Medusan. Get out of Paris or you're that dead man you just mentioned."

"I can't do that."

"You should. If I have the opportunity I'll pull the trigger myself and be well paid for it."

"Then I'll give you that opportunity."

"Forgive me if I find that ludicrous."

"You don't know what I want or how much I'm willing to risk to get it."

"Whatever you want you'll take risks for it. But the real danger will be your enemy's. I know you, Delta. And I must get back to the switchboard. I'd wish you good hunting but—"

It was the moment to use the only weapon he had left, the sole threat that might keep d'Anjou on the line. "Whom do you reach for instructions now that Parc Monceau is out?"

The tension was accentuated by d'Anjou's silence. When he replied, his voice was a whisper. *"What did you say?"*

"It's why she was killed, you know. Why you'll be killed, too. She went to Parc Monceau and she died for it. You've been to Parc Monceau and you'll die for it, too. Carlos can't afford you any longer; you simply know too much. Why should he jeopardize such an arrangement? He'll use you to trap me, then kill you and set up another Les Classiques. As one Medusan to another, can you doubt it?"

The silence was longer now, more intense than before. It was apparent that the older man from Medusa was asking himself several hard questions. "What do you want from me? Except me. You should know hostages are meaningless. Yet you provoke me, astonish me with what you've learned. I'm no good to you dead or alive, so what is it you want?"

"Information. If you have it, I'll get out of Paris tonight and neither Carlos nor you will ever hear from me again."

"What information?"

"You'll lie if I ask for it now. I would. But when I see you, you'll tell me the truth."

"With a wire around my throat?"

"In the middle of a crowd?"

"A crowd? Daylight?"

"An hour from now. Outside the Louvre. Near the steps. At the taxi stand."

"The Louvre? Crowds? Information you think I have that will send you away? You can't reasonably expect me to discuss my employer."

"Not yours. Mine."

"Treadstone?"

He knew. Philippe d'Anjou had the answer. Remain calm. Don't let your anxiety show.

"Seventy-One," completed Jason. "Just a simple question and I'll disappear.

And when you give me the answer—the truth—I'll give you something in exchange."

"What could I possibly want from you? Except you?"

"Information that may let you live. It's no guarantee, but believe me when I tell you, you won't live without it. *Parc Monceau,* d'Anjou."

Silence again. Bourne could picture the gray-haired former Medusan staring at his switchboard, the name of the wealthy Paris district echoing louder and louder in his mind. There was death from Parc Monceau and d'Anjou knew it as surely as he knew the dead woman in Neuilly-sur-Seine was Jacqueline Lavier.

"What might that information be?" asked d'Anjou.

"The identity of your employer. A name and sufficient proof to have sealed in an envelope and given to an attorney, to be held throughout your natural life. But if your life were to end unnaturally, even accidentally, he'd be instructed to open the envelope and reveal the contents. It's protection, d'Anjou."

"I see," said the Medusan softly. "But you say men watch me, follow me."

"Cover yourself," said Jason. "Tell them the truth. You've got a number to call, haven't you?"

"Yes, there's a number, a man." The older man's voice rose slightly in astonishment.

"Reach him, tell him exactly what I said . . . except for the exchange, of course. Say I contacted you, want a meeting with you. It's to be outside the Louvre in an hour. The truth."

"You're insane."

"I know what I'm doing."

"You usually did. You're creating your own trap, mounting your own execution."

"In which event you may be amply rewarded."

"Or executed myself, if what you say is so."

"Let's find out if it is. I'll make contact with you one way or another, take my word for it. They have my photograph; they'll know it when I do. Better a controlled situation than one in which there's no control at all."

"Now I hear Delta," said d'Anjou. "He doesn't create his own trap; he doesn't walk in front of a firing squad and ask for a blindfold."

"No, he doesn't," agreed Bourne. "You don't have a choice, d'Anjou. One hour. Outside the Louvre."

The success of any trap lies in its fundamental simplicity. The reverse trap by the nature of its single complication must be swift and simpler still.

The words came to him as he waited in the taxi in Saint-Honoré down the street from Les Classiques. He had asked the driver to take him around the block twice, an American tourist whose wife was shopping in the strip of *haute couture.* Sooner or later she would emerge from one of the stores and he would find her.

What he found was Carlos's surveillance. The rubber-capped antenna on the black sedan was both the proof and the danger signal. He would feel more secure if that radio transmitter were shorted out, but there was no way to do it. The alternative was misinformation. Sometime during the next forty-five minutes Jason would do his best to make sure the wrong message was sent over that radio. From his concealed position in the back seat, he studied the two men in the car across the way. If there was anything that set them apart from a hundred other men like them in Saint-Honoré, it was the fact that they did not talk.

Philippe d'Anjou walked out onto the pavement, a gray homburg covering his gray hair. His glances swept the street, telling Bourne that the former Medusan had covered himself. He had called a number; he had relayed his startling information; he knew there were men in a car prepared to follow him.

A taxi, apparently ordered by phone, pulled up to the curb. D'Anjou spoke to the driver and climbed inside. Across the street an antenna rose ominously out of its cradle; the hunt was on.

The sedan pulled out after d'Anjou's taxi; it was the confirmation Jason needed. He leaned forward and spoke to the driver. "I forgot," he said irritably. "She said it was the Louvre this morning, shopping this afternoon. Christ, I'm half an hour late! Take me to the Louvre, will you please?"

"Mais oui, monsieur, Le Louvre."

Twice during the short ride to the monumental façade that overlooked the Seine, Jason's taxi passed the black sedan, only to be subsequently passed by it. The proximity gave Bourne the opportunity to see exactly what he needed to see. The man beside the driver in the sedan spoke repeatedly into the hand-held radio microphone. Carlos was making sure the trap had no loose spikes; others were closing in on the execution ground.

They came to the enormous entrance of the Louvre. "Get in line behind those other taxis," said Jason.

"But they wait for fares, monsieur. I have a fare; *you* are my fare. I will take you to the—"

"Just do as I say," said Bourne, dropping fifty francs over the seat.

The driver swerved into the line. The black sedan was twenty yards away on the right; the man on the radio had turned in the seat and was looking out the left rear window. Jason followed his gaze and saw what he thought he might see. Several hundred feet to the west in the huge square was a gray automobile, the car that had followed Jacqueline Lavier and Villiers' wife to the Church of the Blessed Sacrament and sped the latter away from Neuilly-sur-Seine after she had escorted Lavier to her final confession. Its antenna could be seen retracting down into its base. Over on the right, Carlos's soldier no longer held the microphone. The black sedan's antenna was also receding; contact had been made, visual sighting confirmed. Four men. These were Carlos's executioners.

Bourne concentrated on the crowds in front of the Louvre entrance, spotting the elegantly dressed d'Anjou instantly. He was pacing slowly, cautiously, back and forth by the large block of white granite that flanked the marble steps on the left.

Now. It was time to send the misinformation.

"Pull out of the line," ordered Jason.

"*What*, monsieur?"

"Two hundred francs if you do exactly what I tell you. Pull out and go to the front of the line, then make two left turns, heading back up the next aisle."

"I don't understand, monsieur!"

"You don't have to. Three hundred francs."

The driver swung right and proceeded to the head of the line, where he spun the wheel, sending the taxi to the left toward the row of parked cars. Bourne pulled the automatic from his belt, keeping it between his knees. He checked the silencer, twisting the cylinder taut.

"Where do you wish to go, monsieur?" asked the bewildered driver as they entered the aisle heading back toward the entrance to the Louvre.

"Slow down," said Jason. "That large gray car up ahead, the one pointing to the Seine exit. Do you see it?"

"But of course."

"Go around it slowly, to the right." Bourne slid over to the left side of the seat and rolled down the window, keeping his head and the weapon concealed. He would show both in a matter of seconds.

The taxi approached the sedan's trunk, the driver spinning the wheel again. They were parallel. Jason thrust his head and his gun into view. He aimed for the gray sedan's right rear window and fired, five spits coming one after another, shattering the glass, stunning the two men, who screamed at each other, lurching below the window frames to the floor of the front seat. But they had seen him. That was the misinformation.

"Get out of here!" yelled Bourne to the terrified driver, as he threw three hundred francs over the seat and wedged his soft felt hat into the well of the rear window. The taxi shot ahead toward the stone gates of the Louvre.

Now.

Jason slid back across the seat, opened the door and rolled out to the cobblestone pavement, shouting his last instructions to the driver. "If you want to stay alive, get out of here!"

The taxi exploded forward, engine gunning, driver screaming. Bourne dove between two parked cars, now hidden from the gray sedan, and got up slowly, peering between the windows. Carlos's men were quick, professional, losing no moment in the pursuit. They had the taxi in view, the cab no match for the powerful sedan, and in that taxi was the target. The man behind the wheel pulled the car into gear and raced ahead as his companion held the microphone, the antenna rising from its recess. Orders were being shouted to another sedan nearer the great stone steps. The speeding taxi swerved out into the street by the Seine, the large gray car directly behind it. As they passed within feet of Jason, the expressions on the two men's faces said it all. They had Cain in their sights, the trap had closed and they would earn their pay in a matter of minutes.

The reverse trap by the nature of its single complication must be swift and simpler still. . . .

A matter of minutes. . . . He had only a matter of moments if everything he believed was so. D'Anjou! The contact had played his role—his minor role—and was expendable—as Jacqueline Lavier had been expendable.

Bourne ran out from between the two cars toward the black sedan; it was no more than fifty yards ahead. He could see the two men; they were converging on Philippe d'Anjou, who was still pacing in front of the short flight of marble steps. One accurate shot from either man and d'Anjou would be dead, Treadstone Seventy-One gone with him. Jason ran faster, his hand inside his coat, gripping the heavy automatic.

Carlos's soldiers were only yards away, now hurrying themselves, the execution to be quick, the condemned man cut down before he understood what was happening.

"*Medusa!*" roared Bourne, not knowing why he shouted the name rather than d'Anjou's own. "Medusa—*Medusa!*"

D'Anjou's head snapped up, shock on his face. The driver of the black sedan had spun around, his weapon leveled at Jason, while his companion moved toward d'Anjou, his gun aimed at the former Medusan. Bourne dove to his right, the automatic extended, steadied by his left hand. He fired in midair, his aim accurate; the man closing in on d'Anjou arched backward as his stiffened legs were caught in an instant of paralysis; he collapsed on the cobblestones. Two spits exploded over Jason's head, the bullets impacting into metal behind him. He rolled to his left, his gun again steady, directed at the second man. He pulled the trigger twice; the driver screamed, an eruption of blood spreading across his face as he fell.

Hysteria swept through the crowds. Men and women screamed, parents threw themselves over children, others ran up the steps through the great doors of the Louvre, as guards tried to get outside. Bourne got to his feet, looking for d'Anjou. The older man had lunged behind the block of white granite, his gaunt figure now crawling awkwardly in terror out of his sanctuary. Jason raced through the panicked crowd, shoving the automatic into his belt, separating the hysterical bodies that stood between himself and the man who could give him the answers. Treadstone. *Treadstone!*

He reached the gray-haired Medusan. "Get up!" he ordered. "Let's get out of here!"

"Delta! . . . It was Carlos's man! I know him, I've *used* him! He was going to kill me!"

"I know. Come on! Quickly! Others'll be coming back; they'll be looking for us. Come *on!*"

A patch of black fell across Bourne's eyes, at the corner of his eyes. He spun around, instinctively shoving d'Anjou down as four rapid shots came from a gun held by a dark figure standing by the line of taxis. Fragments of granite and marble exploded all around them. It was *him!* The wide, heavy shoulders that floated in space, the tapered waist outlined by a form-fitting black suit . . . the dark-skinned face encased in a white silk scarf below the narrow-brimmed black hat. Carlos!

Get Carlos! Trap Carlos! Cain is for Charlie and Delta is for Cain!

False!

Find Treadstone! Find a message; for a man! Find Jason Bourne!

He was going mad! Blurred images from the past converged with the terrible reality of the present, driving him insane. The doors of his mind opened and closed, crashing open, crashing shut; light streaming out one moment, darkness the next. The pain returned to his temples with sharp, jarring notes of deafening thunder. He started after the man in the black suit with the white silk scarf wrapped around his face. Then he saw the eyes and the barrel of the gun, three dark orbs zeroed in on him like black laser beams. Bergeron? . . . Was it Bergeron? *Was* it? Or Zurich . . . or . . . No time!

He feigned to his left, then dove to the right, out of the line of fire. Bullets splattered into stone, the screeches of richochets following each explosion. Jason spun under a stationary car; between the wheels he could see the figure in black racing away. The pain remained but the thunder stopped. He crawled out on the cobblestones, rose to his feet and ran back toward the steps of the Louvre.

What had he done? D'Anjou was gone! How had it happened? The reverse trap was no trap at all. His own strategy had been used against him, permitting the only man who could give him the answers to escape. He had followed Carlos's soldiers, but Carlos had followed *him!* Since Saint-Honoré. It was all for nothing; a sickening hollowness spread through him.

And then he heard the words, spoken from behind a nearby automobile. Philippe d'Anjou came cautiously into view.

"Tam Quan's never far away, it seems. Where shall we go, Delta? We can't stay here."

They sat inside a curtained booth in a crowded café on the rue Pilon, a back street that was hardly more than an alley in Montmartre. D'Anjou sipped his double brandy, his voice low, pensive.

"I shall return to Asia," he said. "To Singapore or Hong Kong or even the Seychelles, perhaps. France was never very good for me; now it's deadly."

"You may not have to," said Bourne, swallowing the whiskey, the warm liquid spreading quickly, inducing a brief, spatial calm. "I meant what I said. You tell me what I want to know. I'll give you—" He stopped, the doubts sweeping over him; no, he would say it. "I'll give you Carlos's identity."

"I'm not remotely interested," replied the former Medusan, watching Jason closely. "I'll tell you whatever I can. Why should I withhold anything? Obviously I won't go to the authorities, but if I have information that could help you take Carlos, the world would be a safer place for me, wouldn't it? Personally, however, I wish no involvement."

"You're not even curious?"

"Academically, perhaps, for your expression tells me I'll be shocked. So ask your questions and then astonish me."

"You'll be shocked."

Without warning d'Anjou said the name quietly. "Bergeron?"

Jason did not move; speechless, he stared at the older man. D'Anjou continued.

"I've thought about it over and over again. Whenever we talk I look at him and wonder. Each time, however, I reject the idea."

"Why?" Bourne interrupted, refusing to acknowledge the Medusan's accuracy.

"Mind you, I'm not sure—I just feel it's wrong. Perhaps because I've learned more about Carlos from René Bergeron than anyone else. He's obsessed by Carlos; he's worked for him for years, takes enormous pride in the confidence. My problem is that he talks *too* much about him."

"The ego speaking through the assumed second party?"

"It's possible, I suppose, but inconsistent with the extraordinary precautions Carlos takes, the literally impenetrable wall of secrecy he's built around himself. I'm not certain, of course, but I doubt it's Bergeron."

"You said the name. I didn't."

D'Anjou smiled. "You have nothing to be concerned about, Delta. Ask your questions."

"I thought it *was* Bergeron. I'm sorry."

"Don't be, for he may be. I told you, it doesn't matter to me. In a few days I'll be back in Asia, following the franc, or the dollar, or the yen. We Medusans were always resourceful, weren't we?"

Jason was not sure why, but the haggard face of André Villiers came to his mind's eye. He had promised himself to learn what he could for the old soldier. He would not get the opportunity again.

"Where does Villiers' wife fit in?"

D'Anjou's eyebrows arched. "Angélique? But of course—you said Parc Monceau, didn't you? How—"

"The details aren't important now."

"Certainly not to me."

"What about her?" pressed Bourne.

"Have you looked at her closely? The skin?"

"I've been close enough. She's tanned. Very tall and very tanned."

"She keeps her skin that way. The Riviera, the Greek Isles, Costa del Sol, Gstaad; she is never without a sun-drenched skin."

"It's very becoming."

"It's also a successful device. It covers what she is. For her there is no autumn or winter pallor, no lack of color in her face or arms or very long legs. The attractive hue of her skin is always there, because it would be there in any event. With or without Saint-Tropez or the Costa Brava or the Alps."

"What are you talking about?"

"Although the stunning Angélique Villiers is presumed to be Parisian, she's not. She's Hispanic. Venezuelan, to be precise."

"Sanchez," whispered Bourne. "Ilich Ramirez Sanchez."

"Yes. Among the very few who speak of such things, it is said she is Carlos's first cousin, his lover since the age of fourteen. It is rumored—among those very few people—that beyond himself, she is the only person on earth he cares about."

"And Villiers is the unwitting drone?"

"Words from Medusa, Delta?" D'Anjou nodded. "Yes, Villiers is the drone. Carlos's brilliantly conceived wire into many of the most sensitive departments of the French government, including the files on Carlos himself."

"Brilliantly conceived," said Jason, remembering. "Because it's unthinkable."

"Totally."

Bourne leaned forward, the interruption abrupt. "Treadstone," he said, both hands gripping the glass in front of him. "Tell me about Treadstone Seventy-One."

"What can *I* tell *you?*"

"Everything they know. Everything Carlos knows."

"I don't think I'm capable of doing that. I hear things, piece things together, but except where Medusa's concerned, I'm hardly a consultant, much less a confidant."

It was all Jason could do to control himself, curb himself from asking about Medusa, about Delta and Tam Quan; the winds in the night sky and the darkness and the explosions of light that blinded him whenever he heard the words. He could not; certain things had to be assumed, his own loss passed over, no indication given. The priorities. Treadstone. Treadstone Seventy-One . . .

"What have you heard? What have you pieced together?"

"What I heard and what I pieced together were not always compatible. Still, obvious facts were apparent to me."

"Such as?"

"When I saw it was you, I knew. Delta had made a lucrative agreement with the Americans. Another lucrative agreement, a different kind than before, perhaps."

"Spell that out, please."

"Eleven years ago, the rumors out of Saigon were that the ice-cold Delta was the highest-paid Medusan of us all. Surely, you were the most capable *I* knew, so I assumed you drove a hard bargain. You must have driven an infinitely harder one to do what you're doing now."

"Which is? From what you've heard."

"What we know. It was confirmed in New York. The Monk confirmed it before he died, that much I was told. It was consistent with the pattern since the beginning."

Bourne held the glass, avoiding d'Anjou's eyes. The Monk. *The Monk. Do not ask. The Monk is dead, whoever and whatever he was. He is not pertinent now.* "I repeat," said Jason, "what is it they think they know I'm doing?"

"Come, Delta, *I'm* the one who's leaving. It's pointless to—"

"*Please,*" interrupted Bourne.

"Very well. You agreed to become Cain. The mythical killer with an unending list of contracts that never existed, each created out of whole cloth, given substance by all manner of reliable sources. Purpose. To challenge Carlos—'eroding his stature at every turn' was the way Bergeron phrased it—to undercut his prices, spread the word of his deficiencies, your own superiority. In essence, to draw out Carlos and take him. This was your agreement with the Americans."

Rays of his own personal sunlight burst into the dark corners of Jason's mind. In the distance, doors were opening, but they were still too far away and opened only partially. But there was light where before there was only darkness.

"Then the Americans are—" Bourne did not finish the statement, hoping in brief torment that d'Anjou would finish it for him.

"Yes," said the Medusan. "Treadstone Seventy-One. The most controlled unit of American intelligence since the State Department's Consular Operations. Created by the same man who built Medusa. David Abbott."

"The Monk," said Jason softly, instinctively, another door in the distance partially open.

"Of course. Who else would he approach to play the role of Cain but the man from Medusa known as Delta? As I say, the instant I saw you, I knew it."

"A role—" Bourne stopped, the sunlight growing brighter, warm not blinding.

D'Anjou leaned forward. "It's here, of course, that what I heard and what I pieced together was incompatible. It was said that Jason Bourne accepted the assignment for reasons I knew were not true. I was there, they were not; they could not know."

"What did they say? What did you hear?"

"That you were an American intelligence officer, possibly military. Can you imagine? *You.* Delta! The man filled with contempt for so much, not the least of which was for most things American. I told Bergeron it was impossible, but I'm not sure he believed me."

"What did you tell him?"

"What I believed. What I still believe. It wasn't money—no amount of money could have made you do it—it had to be something else. I think you did it for the same reason so many others agreed to Medusa eleven years ago. To clean a slate somewhere, to be able to return to something you had before, that was barred to you. I don't know, of course, and I don't expect you to confirm it, but that's what I think."

"It's possible you're right," said Jason, holding his breath, the cool winds of release blowing into the mists. *It made sense. A message was sent. This could be it. Find the message. Find the sender. Treadstone!*

"Which leads us back," continued d'Anjou, "to the stories about Delta. Who was he? What was he? This educated, oddly quiet man who could transform himself into a lethal weapon in the jungles. Who stretched himself and others beyond endurance for no cause at all. We never understood."

"It was never required. Is there anything else you can tell me? Do they know the precise location of Treadstone?"

"Certainly. I learned it from Bergeron. A residence in New York City, on East Seventy-first Street. Number 139. Isn't that correct?"

"Possibly . . . Anything else?"

"Only what you obviously know, the strategy of which I admit eludes me."

"Which is?"

"That the Americans think you turned. Better phrased, they want Carlos to believe they think you turned."

"Why?" *He was closer. It was here!*

"The story is a long period of silence coinciding with Cain's inactivity. Plus stolen funds, but mainly the silence."

That was it. The message. The silence. The months in Port Noir. The madness in Zurich, the insanity in Paris. No one could possibly know what had happened. He was being told to come in. To surface. You were right, Marie, my love, my dearest love. You were right from the beginning.

"Nothing else, then?" asked Bourne, trying to control the impatience in his voice, anxious now beyond any anxiety he had known to get back to Marie.

"It's all I know—but please understand, I was never told that much. I was brought in because of my knowledge of Medusa—and it was established that Cain was from Medusa—but I was never part of Carlos's inner circle."

"You were close enough. Thank you." Jason put several bills on the table and started to slide across the booth.

"There's one thing," said d'Anjou. "I'm not sure it's relevant at this point, but they know your name is not Jason Bourne."

"What?"

"March 25. Don't you remember, Delta? It's only two days from now, and the date's very important to Carlos. Word has been spread. He wants your corpse on the twenty-fifth. He wants to deliver it to the Americans on that day."

"What are you trying to say?"

"On March 25, 1968, Jason Bourne was executed at Tam Quan. You executed him."

31

She opened the door and for a moment he stood looking at her, seeing the large brown eyes that roamed his face, eyes that were afraid yet curious. She knew. Not the answer, but that there *was* an answer, and he had come back to tell her what it was. He walked into the room; she closed the door.

"It happened," she said.

"It happened." Bourne turned and reached for her. She came to him and they held each other, the silence of the embrace saying more than any spoken words. "You were right," he whispered finally, his lips against her soft hair. "There's a great deal I don't know—may never know—but you were right. I'm not Cain because there is no Cain, there never was. Not the Cain they talk about. He never existed. He's a myth invented to draw out Carlos. I'm that creation. A man from Medusa called Delta agreed to become a lie named Cain. I'm that man."

She pulled back, still holding him. "Cain is for Charlie . . .' " She said the words quietly.

"And Delta is for Cain," completed Jason. "You've heard me say it?"

Marie nodded. "Yes. One night in the room in Switzerland you shouted it in your sleep. You never mentioned Carlos; just Cain . . . Delta. I said something to you in the morning about it, but you didn't answer me. You just looked out the window."

"Because I didn't understand. I still don't, but I accept it. It explains so many things."

She nodded again. "The *provocateur*. The code words you use, the strange phrases, the perceptions. But why? Why *you*?"

" 'To clean a slate somewhere.' That's what he said."

"Who said?"

"D'Anjou."

"The man on the steps in Parc Monceau? The switchboard operator?"

"The man from Medusa. I knew him in Medusa."

"What did he say?"

Bourne told her. And as he did, he could see in her the relief he had felt in himself. There was a light in her eyes, and a muted throbbing in her neck, sheer joy bursting from her throat. It was almost as if she could barely wait for him to finish so she could hold him again.

"Jason!" she cried, taking his face in her hands. "Darling, my darling! My friend has come back to me! It's everything we knew, everything we felt!"

"Not quite everything," he said, touching her cheek. "I'm Jason to you, Bourne to me, because that's the name I was given, and have to use it because I don't have any other. But it's not mine."

"An invention?"

"No, he was real. They say I killed him in a place called Tam Quan."

She took her hands away from his face, sliding them to his shoulders, not letting him go. "There had to have been a reason."

"I hope so. I don't know. Maybe it's the slate I'm trying to clean."

"It doesn't matter," she said, releasing him. "It's in the past, over ten years ago. All that matters now is that you reach the man at Treadstone, because they're trying to reach you."

"D'Anjou said word was out that the Americans think I've turned. No word from me in over six months, millions taken out of Zurich. They must think I'm the most expensive miscalculation on record."

"You can explain what happened. You haven't knowingly broken your agreement; on the other hand you can't go on. It's impossible. All the training you received means nothing to you. It's there only in fragments—images and phrases that you can't relate to anything. People you're supposed to know, you don't know. They're faces without names, without reasons for being where they are or what they are."

Bourne took off his coat and pulled the automatic from his belt. He studied the cylinder—the ugly, perforated extension of the barrel that guaranteed to reduce the decibel count of a gunshot to a spit. It sickened him. He walked to the bureau, put the weapon inside and pushed the drawer shut. He held on to the knobs for a moment, his eyes straying to the mirror, to the face in the glass that had no name.

"What do I say to them?" he asked. "This is Jason Bourne calling. Of course I know that's not my name because I killed a man named Jason Bourne, but it's the one you gave me. . . . I'm sorry, gentlemen, but something happened to me on the way to Marseilles. I lost something—nothing you can put a price on—just my memory. Now, I gather we've got an agreement, but I don't remember what it is, except for crazy phrases like 'Get Carlos!' and 'Trap Carlos!' and something about Delta being Cain and Cain is supposed to replace Charlie and Charlie is really Carlos. Things like that, which may lead you to think I do remember. You might even say to yourselves, 'We've got one prime bastard here. Let's put him away for a couple of decades in a very tight stockade. He not only took us, but worse, he could prove to be one hell of an embarrassment.' " Bourne turned from the mirror and looked at Marie. "I'm not kidding. What do I say?"

"The truth," she answered. "They'll accept it. They've sent you a message; they're trying to reach you. As far as the six months is concerned, wire Washburn in Port Noir. He kept records—extensive, detailed records."

"He may not answer. We had our own agreement. For putting me back together he was to receive a fifth of Zurich, untraceable to him. I sent him a million American dollars."

"Do you think that would stop him from helping you?"

Jason paused. "He may not be able to help himself. He's got a problem; he's a drunk. Not a drinker. A drunk. The worst kind; he knows it and likes it. How long can he live with a million dollars? More to the point, how long do you think those waterfront pirates will let him live once they find out?"

"You can still prove you were there. You were ill, isolated. You weren't in contact with *anyone.*"

"How can the men at Treadstone be sure? From their view I'm a walking encyclopedia of official secrets. I *had* to be to do what I've done. How can they be certain I haven't talked to the wrong people?"

"Tell them to send a team to Port Noir."

"It'll be greeted with blank stares and silence. I left that island in the middle of the night with half the waterfront after me with hooks. If anyone down there made any money out of Washburn, he'll see the connection and walk the other way."

"Jason, I don't know what you're driving at. You've got your answer, the answer you've been looking for since you woke up that morning in Port Noir. What more do you want?"

"I want to be careful, that's all," said Bourne abrasively. "I want to 'look before I leap' and make damn sure the 'stable door is shut' and 'Jack be nimble, Jack be quick, Jack jump over the candlestick—but for Christ's sake don't fall into the fire!' How's that for *remembering?*" He was shouting; he stopped.

Marie walked across the room and stood in front of him. "It's very good. But that's not it, is it? Being careful I mean."

Jason shook his head. "No, it isn't," he said. "With each step I've been afraid, afraid of the things I've learned. Now, at the end, I'm more frightened than ever. If I'm not Jason Bourne, who am I really? What have I left back there? Has that occurred to you?"

"In all its ramifications, my darling. In a way, I'm far more afraid than you. But I don't think that can stop us. I wish to God it could, but I know it can't."

The attaché at the American Embassy on the avenue Gabriel walked into the office of the First Secretary and closed the door. The man at the desk looked up.

"You're sure it's him?"

"I'm only sure he used the key words," said the attaché, crossing to the desk, a red-bordered index card in his hand. "Here's the flag," he continued, handing the card to the First Secretary. "I've checked off the words he used, and if that flag's accurate, I'd say he's genuine."

The man behind the desk studied the card. "When did he use the name Treadstone?"

"Only after I convinced him that he wasn't going to talk with anyone in U. S. Intelligence unless or until he gave me a damn good reason. I think he thought it'd blow my mind when he said he was Jason Bourne. When I simply asked him what I could do for him, he seemed stuck, almost as if he might hang up on me."

"Didn't he say there was a flag out for him?"

"I was waiting for it but he never said it. According to that eight-word sketch—'Experienced field officer. Possible defection or enemy detention'—he could have just said the word 'flag' and we would have been in sync. He didn't."

"Then maybe he's not genuine."

"The rest fits, though. He *did* say D.C.'s been looking for him for more than six months. That was when he used the name Treadstone. He was from Treadstone; that's supposed to be the explosive. He also told me to relay the code words Delta, Cain and Medusa. The first two are on the flag, I checked them off. I don't know what Medusa means."

"I don't know what *any* of this means," said the First Secretary. "Except that my orders are to hightail it down to communications, clear all scrambler traffic to Langley and get a sterile patch to a spook named Conklin. Him I've heard of: a mean son of a bitch who got his foot blown off ten or twelve years ago in Nam. He pushes very strange buttons over at the Company. Also he survived the purges, which leads me to think he's one man they don't want roaming the streets looking for a job. Or a publisher."

"Who do you think this Bourne is?" asked the attaché. "I've never seen such a concentrated but formless hunt for a person in my whole eight years away from the States."

"Someone they want very badly." The First Secretary got up from the desk. "Thanks for this. I'll tell D.C. how well you handled it. What's the schedule? I don't suppose he gave you a telephone number."

"No way. He wanted to call back in fifteen minutes, but I played the harried bureaucrat. I told him to call me in an hour or so. That'd make it past five o'clock, so we could gain another hour or two by my being out to dinner."

"I don't know. We can't risk losing him. I'll let Conklin set up the game plan. He's the control on this. No one makes a move on Bourne unless it's authorized by him."

Alexander Conklin sat behind the desk in his white-walled office in Langley, Virginia, and listened to the embassy man in Paris. He was convinced; it *was* Delta. The reference to Medusa was the proof, for it was a name no one would know *but* Delta. The bastard! He was playing the stranded agent, his controls at the Treadstone telephone not responding to the proper code words—whatever they were—because the dead could not talk. He was using the omission to get himself off the meathook! The sheer nerve of the bastard was awesome. Bastard, *bastard!*

Kill the controls and use the kills to call off the hunt. Any kind of hunt. How many men had done it before, thought Alexander Conklin. He had. There had been a source-control in the hills of Huong Khe, a maniac issuing maniacal orders, certain death for a dozen teams of Medusans on a maniacal hunt. A young intelligence officer named Conklin had crept back into Base Camp Kilo with a North Vietnamese rifle, Russian caliber, and had fired two bullets into the head of a maniac. There had been grieving and harsher security measures put in force, but the hunt was called off.

There had been no fragments of glass found in the jungle paths of Base Camp Kilo, however. Fragments with fingerprints that irrefutably identified the sniper as an Occidental recruit from Medusa itself. There were such fragments found on Seventy-first Street, but the killer did not know it—Delta did not know it.

"At one point we seriously questioned whether he was genuine," said the embassy's First Secretary, rambling on as if to fill the abrupt silence from Washington. "An experienced field officer would have told the attaché to check for a flag, but the subject didn't."

"An oversight," replied Conklin, pulling his mind back to the brutal enigma that was Delta-Cain. "What are the arrangements?"

"Initially Bourne insisted on calling back in fifteen minutes, but I instructed lower-level to stall. For instance, we could use the dinner hour . . ." The embassy man was making sure a Company executive in Washington realized the perspicacity of his contributions. It would go on for the better part of a minute; Conklin had heard too many variations before.

Delta. Why had he turned? The madness must have eaten his head away, leaving only the instincts for survival. He had been around too long; he knew that sooner or later they would find him, kill him. There was never any alternative; he understood that from the moment he turned—or broke—or whatever it was. There was nowhere to hide any longer; he was a target all over the globe. He could never know who might step out of the shadows and bring his life to an end. It was something they all lived with, the single most persuasive argument against turning. So another solution had to be found: survival. The biblical Cain was the first to commit fratricide. Had the mythical name triggered the obscene decision, the strategy itself? Was it as simple as that? God knew it was the perfect solution. Kill them all, kill your brother.

Webb gone, the Monk gone, the Yachtsman and his wife . . . who could deny the instructions Delta received, since these four alone relayed instructions to him? He had removed the millions and distributed them as ordered. Blind recipients he had assumed were intrinsic to the Monk's strategy. Who was Delta to question the Monk? The creator of Medusa, the genius who had recruited and created him. Cain.

The perfect solution. To be utterly convincing, all that was required was the death of a brother, the proper grief to follow. The official judgment would be rendered. Carlos had infiltrated and broken Treadstone. The assassin had won, Treadstone abandoned. The *bastard!*

". . . so basically I felt the game plan should come from you." The First Secretary in Paris had finished. He was an ass, but Conklin needed him; one tune had to be heard while another was being played.

"You did the right thing," said a respectful executive in Langley. "I'll let our people over here know how well you handled it. You were absolutely right; we need time, but Bourne doesn't realize it. We can't tell him, either, which makes it tough. We're on sterile, so may I speak accordingly?"

"Of course."

"Bourne's under pressure. He's been . . . detained . . . for a long period of time. Am I clear?"

"The Soviets?"

"Right up to the Lubyanka. His run was made by means of a double-entry. Are you familiar with the term?"

"Yes, I am. Moscow thinks he's working for them now."

"That's what they think." Conklin paused. "And we're not sure. Crazy things happen in the Lubyanka."

The First Secretary whistled softly. "That's a basket. How are you going to make a determination?"

"With your help. But the classification priority is so high it's above embassy, even ambassadorial level. You're on the scene; you were reached. You can accept the condition or not, that's up to you. If you do, I think a commendation might come right out of the Oval Office."

Conklin could hear the slow intake of breath from Paris.

"I'll do whatever I can, of course. Name it."

"You already did. We want him stalled. When he calls back, talk to him yourself."

"Naturally," interrupted the embassy man.

"Tell him you relayed the codes. Tell him Washington is flying over an officer-of-record from Treadstone by military transport. Say D.C. wants him to keep out of sight and away from the embassy; every route is being watched. Then ask him if he wants protection, and if he does, find out where he wants to pick it up. But don't send anyone; when you talk to me again I'll have been in touch with someone over there. I'll give you a name then and an eye-spot you can give to him."

"Eye-spot?"

"Visual identification. Something or someone he can recognize."

"One of your men?"

"Yes, we think it's best that way. Beyond you, there's no point in involving the embassy. As a matter of fact, it's vital we don't, so whatever conversations you have shouldn't be logged."

"I can take care of that," said the First Secretary. "But how is the one conversation I'm going to have with him going to help you determine whether he's a double-entry?"

"Because it won't be one; it'll be closer to ten."

"Ten?"

"That's right. Your instructions to Bourne—from us through you—are that he's to check in on your phone every hour to confirm the fact that he's in safe territory. Until that last time, when you tell him the Treadstone officer has arrived in Paris and will meet with him."

"What will that accomplish?" asked the embassy man.

"He'll keep moving . . . if he's not ours. There are a half a dozen known deep-cover Soviet agents in Paris, all with tripped phones. If he's working with Moscow, the chances are he'll use at least one of them. We'll be watching. And if that's the way it turns out, I think you'll remember the time you spent all night at the embassy for the rest of your life. Presidential commendations have a way of raising a career man's grade level. Of course, you don't have too much higher to go . . ."

"There's higher, Mr. Conklin," interrupted the First Secretary.

The conversation was over; the embassy man would call back after hearing from Bourne. Conklin got up from the chair and limped across the room to a gray filing cabinet against the wall. He unlocked the top panel. Inside was a stapled folder containing a sealed envelope bearing the names and locations of men who could be called upon in emergencies. They had once been good men, loyal men, who for one reason or another could no longer be on a Washington payroll. In all cases it had been necessary to remove them from the official scene, relocate them with new identities—those fluent in other languages frequently given citizenship by cooperating foreign governments. They had simply disappeared.

They were the outcasts, men who had gone beyond the laws in the service of their country, who often killed in the interests of their country. But their country could not tolerate their official existence; their covers had been exposed, their actions made known. Still, they could be called upon. Monies were constantly funneled to accounts beyond official scrutiny, certain understandings intrinsic to the payments.

Conklin carried the envelope back to his desk and tore the marked tape from the flap; it would be resealed, remarked. There was a man in Paris, a dedicated man who had come up through the officer corps of Army Intelligence, a lieutenant colonel by the time he was thirty-five. He could be counted on; he understood national priorities. He had killed a left-wing cameraman in a village near Hue a dozen years ago.

Three minutes later he had the man on the line, the call unlogged, unrecorded. The former officer was given a name and a brief sketch of defection, including a covert trip to the United States during which the defector in question on special assignment had eliminated those controlling the strategy.

"A double-entry?" asked the man in Paris. "Moscow?"

"No, not the Soviets," replied Conklin, aware that if Delta requested protection, there would be conversations between the two men.

"It was a long-range deep cover to snare Carlos."

"The assassin?"

"That's right."

"You may *say* it's not Moscow, but you won't convince *me*. Carlos was trained in Novgorod and as far as I'm concerned he's still a dirty gun for the KGB."

"Perhaps. The details aren't for briefing, but suffice it to say we're convinced our man was bought off; he's made a few million and wants an unencumbered passport."

"So he took out the controls and the finger's pointed at Carlos, which doesn't mean a damn thing but give him another kill."

"That's it. We want to play it out, let him think he's home free. Best, we'd like an admission, whatever information we can get, which is why I'm on my way over. But it's definitely secondary to taking him out. Too many people in too many places were compromised to put him where he is. Can you help? There'll be a bonus."

"My pleasure. And keep the bonus, I hate fuckers like him. They blow whole networks."

"It's got to be airtight; he's one of the best. I'd suggest support, at least one."

"I've got a man from the Saint-Gervais worth five. He's for hire."

"Hire him. Here are the particulars. The control in Paris is an embassy blind; he knows nothing but he's in communication with Bourne and may request protection for him."

"I'll play it," said the former intelligence officer. "Go ahead."

"There's not much more for the moment. I'll take a jet out of Andrews. My ETA in Paris will be anywhere between eleven and twelve midnight your time.

I want to see Bourne within an hour or so after that and be back here in Washington by tomorrow. It's tight, but that's the way it's got to be."

"That's the way it'll be, then."

"The blind at the embassy is the First Secretary. His name is . . ."

Conklin gave the remaining specifics and the two men worked out basic ciphers for their initial contact in Paris. Code words that would tell the man from the Central Intelligence Agency whether or not any problems existed when they spoke. Conklin hung up. Everything was in motion exactly the way Delta would expect it to be in motion. The inheritors of Treadstone would go by the book, and the book was specific where collapsed strategies and strategists were concerned. They were to be dissolved, cut off, no official connection or acknowledgment permitted. Failed strategies and strategists were an embarrassment to Washington. And from its manipulative beginnings, Treadstone Seventy-One had used, abused and maneuvered every major unit in the United States Intelligence community and not a few foreign governments. Very long poles would be held when touching any survivors.

Delta knew all this, and because he himself had destroyed Treadstone, he would appreciate the precautions, anticipate them, be alarmed if they were not there. And when confronted he would react in false fury and artificial anguish over the violence that had taken place in Seventy-first Street. Alexander Conklin would listen with all his concentration, trying to discern a genuine note, or even the outlines of a reasonable explanation, but he knew he would hear neither. Irregular fragments of glass could not beam themselves across the Atlantic, only to be concealed beneath a heavy drape in a Manhattan brownstone, and fingerprints were more accurate proof of a man having been at a scene than any photograph. There was no way they could be doctored.

Conklin would give Delta the benefit of two minutes to say whatever came to his facile mind. He would listen, and then he would pull the trigger.

32

"Why are they doing it?" asked Jason, sitting down next to Marie in the packed café. He had made the fifth telephone call, five hours after having reached the embassy. "They want me to keep running. They're forcing me to run, and I don't know why."

"You're forcing yourself," said Marie. "You could have made the calls from the room."

"No, I couldn't. For some reason they want me to know that. Each time I call, that son of a bitch asks me where I am now, am I in 'safe territory'? Silly goddamn phrase, 'safe territory.' But he's saying something else. He's telling me that every contact must be made from a different location, so that no one outside or inside could trace me to a single phone, a single address. They don't want me in custody, but they want me on a string. They want me, but they're afraid of me; it doesn't make sense!"

"Isn't it possible you're imagining these things? No one said anything remotely like that."

"They didn't have to. It's in what they didn't say. Why didn't they just tell me to come right over to the embassy? Order me. No one could touch me there; it's U. S. territory. They didn't."

"The streets are being watched; you were told that."

"You know, I accepted that—blindly—until about thirty seconds ago when it struck me. By whom? Who's watching the streets?"

"Carlos, obviously. His men."

"You know that and I know that—at least we can assume it—but they don't know that. I may not know who the hell I am or where I came from, but I know what's happened to me during the past twenty-four hours. They don't."

"They could assume too, couldn't they? They might have spotted strange men in cars, or standing around too long, too obviously."

"Carlos is brighter than that. And there are lots of ways a specific vehicle could get quickly inside an embassy's gate. Marine contingents everywhere are trained for things like that."

"I believe you."

"But they didn't do that; they didn't even suggest it. Instead, they're stalling me, making me play games. Goddamn it, why?"

"You said it yourself, Jason. They haven't heard from you in six months. They're being very careful."

"Why this way? They get me inside those gates, they can do whatever they want. They control me. They can throw me a party or throw me into a cell. Instead, they don't want to touch me, but they don't want to lose me either."

"They're waiting for the man flying over from Washington."

"What better place to wait for him than in the embassy?" Bourne pushed back his chair. "Something's wrong. Let's get out of here."

It had taken Alexander Conklin, inheritor of Treadstone, exactly six hours and twelve minutes to cross the Atlantic. To go back he would take the first Concorde flight out of Paris in the morning, reach Dulles by 7:30 Washington time and be at Langley by 9:00. If anyone tried to phone him or asked where he had spent the night, an accommodating major from the Pentagon would supply a false answer. And a First Secretary at the embassy in Paris would be told that if he ever mentioned having had a single conversation with the man from Langley, he'd be descaled to the lowest attaché on the ladder and shipped to a new post in Tierra del Fuego. It was guaranteed.

Conklin went directly to a row of pay phones against the wall and called the embassy. The First Secretary was filled with a sense of accomplishment.

"Everything's according to schedule, Conklin," said the embassy man, the absence of the previously employed Mister a sign of equality. The Company executive was in Paris now, and turf was turf. "Bourne's edgy. During our last communication he repeatedly asked why he wasn't being told to come in."

"He did?" At first Conklin was surprised; then he understood. Delta was feigning the reactions of a man who knew nothing of the events on Seventy-first Street. If he had been told to come to the embassy, he would have bolted. He knew better; there could be no official connection. Treadstone was anathema, a discredited strategy, a major embarrassment. "Did you reiterate that the streets were being watched?"

"Naturally. Then he asked me who was watching them. Can you imagine?"

"I can. What did you say?"

"That he knew as well as I did, and all things considered I thought it was counterproductive to discuss such matters over the telephone."

"Very good."

"I rather thought so."

"What did he say to that? Did he settle for it?"

"In an odd way, yes. He said, 'I see.' That's all."

"Did he change his mind and ask for protection?"

"He's continued to refuse it. Even when I insisted." The First Secretary paused briefly. "He doesn't want to be watched, does he?" he said confidentially.

"No, he doesn't. When do you expect his next call?"

"In about fifteen minutes."

"Tell him the Treadstone officer has arrived." Conklin took the map from his pocket; it was folded to the area, the route marked in blue ink. "Say the rendezvous has been set for one-thirty on the road between Chevreuse and Rambouillet, seven miles south of Versailles at the Cimetière de Noblesse."

"One-thirty, road between Chevreuse and Rambouillet . . . the cemetery. Will he know how to get there?"

"He's been there before. If he says he's going by taxi, tell him to take the normal precautions and dismiss it."

"Won't that appear strange? To the driver, I mean. It's an odd hour for mourning."

"I said you're to 'tell him' that. Obviously he won't take a taxi."

"Obviously," said the First Secretary quickly, recovering by volunteering the unnecessary. "Since I haven't called your man here, shall I call him now and tell him you've arrived?"

"I'll take care of that. You've still got his number?"

"Yes, of course."

"Burn it," ordered Conklin. "Before it burns you. I'll call you back in twenty minutes."

A train thundered by in the lower level of the Métro, the vibrations felt throughout the platform. Bourne hung up the pay phone on the concrete wall and stared for a moment at the mouthpiece. Another door had partially opened somewhere in the distance of his mind, the light too far away, too dim to see inside. Still, there were images. On the road to Rambouillet . . . through an archway of iron latticework . . . a gently sloping hill with white marble. Crosses—large, larger, mausoleums . . . and statuary everywhere. Le Cimetière de Noblesse. A cemetery, but far more than a resting place for the dead. A drop, but even more than that. A place where conversations took place amid burials and the lowering of caskets. Two men dressed somberly as the crowds were dressed somberly, moving between the mourners until they met among the mourners and exchanged the words they had to say to each other.

There was a face, but it was blurred, out of focus; he saw only the eyes. And that unfocused face and those eyes had a name. David . . . Abbott. The Monk. The man he knew but did not know. Creator of Medusa and Cain.

Jason blinked several times and shook his head as if to shake the sudden mists away. He glanced over at Marie, who was fifteen feet to his left against the wall, supposedly scanning the crowds on the platform, watching for someone possibly watching him. She was not; she was looking at him herself, a frown of concern across her face. He nodded, reassuring her; it was not a bad moment for him. Instead, images had come to him. He had been to that cemetery; somehow he would know it. He walked toward Marie; she turned and fell in step beside him as they headed for the exit.

"He's here," said Bourne. "Treadstone's arrived. I'm to meet him near Rambouillet. At a cemetery."

"That's a ghoulish touch. Why a cemetery?"

"It's supposed to reassure me."

"Good God, how?"

"I've been there before. I've met people there . . . a man there. By naming it as the rendezvous—an unusual rendezvous—Treadstone's telling me he's genuine."

She took his arm as they climbed the steps toward the street. "I want to go with you."

"Sorry."

"You can't exclude me!"

"I have to, because I don't know what I'm going to find there. And if it's not what I expect, I'll want someone on my side."

"Darling, that doesn't make sense! I'm being hunted by the police. If they find me, they'll send me back to Zurich on the next plane; you said so yourself. What good would I be to you in Zurich?"

"Not you. Villiers. He trusts us, he trusts you. You can reach him if I'm not back by daybreak or haven't called explaining why. He can make a lot of noise, and God knows he's ready to. He's the one backup we've got, the only one. To be more specific, his wife is—through him."

Marie nodded, accepting his logic. "He's ready," she agreed. "How will you get to Rambouillet?"

"We have a car, remember? I'll take you to the hotel, then head over to the garage."

He stepped inside the elevator of the garage complex in Montmartre and pressed the button for the fourth floor. His mind was on a cemetery somewhere between Chevreuse and Rambouillet, on a road he had driven over but had no idea when or for what purpose.

Which was why he wanted to drive there now, not wait until his arrival corresponded more closely to the time of rendezvous. If the images that came to his mind were not completely distorted, it was an enormous cemetery. Where precisely within those acres of graves and statuary was the meeting ground? He would get there by one, leaving a half hour to walk up and down the paths looking for a pair of headlights or a signal. Other things would come to him.

The elevator door scraped open. The floor was three-quarters filled with cars, deserted otherwise. Jason tried to recall where he had parked the Renault; it was in a far corner, he remembered that, but was it on the right or the left? He started tentatively to the left; the elevator had been on his left when he had driven the car up several days ago. He stopped, logic abruptly orienting him. The elevator had been on his left when he had entered, not after he had parked the car; it had been diagonally to his right then. He turned, his movement rapid, his thoughts on a road between Chevreuse and Rambouillet.

Whether it was the sudden, unexpected reversal of direction or an inexperienced surveillance, Bourne neither knew or cared to dwell upon. Whichever, the moment saved his life, of that he was certain. A man's head ducked below the hood of a car in the second aisle on his right; that man had been watching him. An experienced surveillance would have stood up, holding a ring of keys he had presumably picked up from the floor, or checked a windshield wiper, then walked away. The one thing he would not do was what this man did; risk being seen by ducking out of sight.

Jason maintained his pace, his thoughts concerned on this new development. Who was this man? How had he been found? And then both answers were so clear, so obvious he felt like a fool. The clerk at the Auberge du Coin.

Carlos had been thorough—as he was always thorough—every detail of failure examined. And one of those details was a clerk on duty during a failure. Such a man bore scrutiny, then questioning; it would not be difficult. The show of a knife or a gun would be more than sufficient. Information would pour from the night clerk's trembling lips, and Carlos's army ordered to spread throughout the city, each district divided into sectors, hunting for a specific black Renault. A painstaking search, but not impossible, made easier by the driver, who had not bothered to switch license plates. For how many unbroken hours had the garage been watched? How many men were there? Inside, outside? How soon would others arrive? Would Carlos arrive?

The questions were secondary. He had to get out. He could do without the car, perhaps, but the resulting dependency on unknown arrangements might cripple him; he needed transportation and he needed it now. No taxi would drive a stranger to a cemetery on the outskirts of Rambouillet at one o'clock in the morning, and it was no time to rely on the possibility of stealing a car in the streets.

He stopped, taking cigarettes and matches from his pockets; then, striking a match, he cupped his hands and angled his head to protect the flame. In the corner of his eye he could see a shadow—squareshaped, stocky; the man once more had lowered himself, now behind the trunk of a nearer automobile.

Jason dropped to a crouch, spun to his left and lunged out of the aisle between two adjacent cars, breaking his fall with the palms of his hands, the maneuver made in silence. He crawled around the rear wheels of the automobile on his right, arms and legs working rapidly, quietly, down the narrow alley of vehicles, a spider scurrying across a web. He was behind the man now; he crept forward toward the aisle and rose to his knees, inching his face along smooth metal, and peered beyond a headlight. The heavy-set man was in full view, standing erect. He was evidently bewildered, for he moved hesitantly closer toward the Renault, his body low again, squinting to see beyond the windshield. What he saw frightened him further; there was nothing, no one. He gasped, the audible intake of breath a prelude to running. He had been tricked; he knew it and was not about to wait around for the consequences—which told Bourne something else. The man had been briefed on the driver of the Renault, the danger explained. The man began to race toward the exit ramp.

Now. Jason sprang up and ran straight ahead across the aisle, between the cars to the second aisle, catching up with the running man, hurling himself at his back and throwing him to the concrete floor. He hammerlocked the man's thick neck, crashing the outsized skull into the pavement, the fingers of his left hand pressed into the man's eye sockets.

"You have exactly five seconds to tell me who's outside," he said in French, remembering the grimacing face of another Frenchman in an elevator in Zurich. There had been men outside then, men who wanted to kill him then, on the Bahnhofstrasse. "Tell me! *Now!*"

"A man, one man, that's all!"

Bourne relocked the neck, digging his fingers deeper into the eyes. "Where?"

"In a car," spat out the man. "Parked across the street. My God, you're choking me! You're blinding me!"

"Not yet. You'll know it when and if I do both. What kind of car?"

"Foreign. I don't know. Italian, I think. Or American. I don't *know.* Please! My eyes!"

"Color!"

"Dark! Green, blue, very dark. Oh my *God!*"

"You're Carlos's man, aren't you?"

"Who?"

Jason yanked again, pressed again. "You heard me—you're from Carlos!"

"I don't know any Carlos. We call a man; there is a number. That's all we do."

"Has he been called?" The man did not reply; Bourne dug his fingers deeper. "Tell me!"

"Yes. I *had* to."

"When?"

"A few minutes ago. The coin telephone on the second ramp. My God! I can't see."

"Yes, you can. Get up!" Jason released the man, pulling him to his feet. "Get over to the car. Quickly!" Bourne pushed the man back between the stationary automobiles to the Renault's aisle. The man turned, protesting, helpless. "You heard me. Hurry!" shouted Jason.

"I'm only earning a few francs."

"Now you can drive for them." Bourne shoved him again toward the Renault.

Moments later the small black automobile careened down an exit ramp toward a glass booth with a single attendant and the cash register. Jason was in the back seat, his gun pressed against the man's bruised neck. Bourne shoved a bill and his dated ticket out the window; the attendant took both.

"Drive!" said Bourne. "Do exactly what I told you to do!"

The man pressed the accelerator, and the Renault sped out through the exit. The man made a screeching U-turn in the street, coming to a sudden stop in front of a dark green Chevrolet. A car door opened behind them; running footsteps followed.

"*Jules? Que se passe-t-il? C'est toi qui conduis?*" A figure loomed in the open window.

Bourne raised his automatic, pointing the barrel at the man's face. "Take two steps back," he said in French. "No more, just two. And then stand still." He tapped the head of the man named Jules. "Get out. Slowly."

"We were only to follow you," protested Jules, stepping out into the street. "Follow you and report your whereabouts."

"You'll do better than that," said Bourne, getting out of the Renault, taking his map of Paris with him. "You're going to drive me. For a while. Get in your car, both of you!"

Five miles outside of Paris, on the road to Chevreuse, the two men were ordered out of the car. It was a dark, poorly lighted, third-grade highway. There had been no stores, buildings, houses, or road phones for the past three miles.

"What was the number you were told to call?" demanded Jason. "Don't lie. You'd be in worse trouble."

Jules gave it to him. Bourne nodded and climbed into the seat behind the wheel of the Chevrolet.

The old man in the threadbare overcoat sat huddled in the shadows of the empty booth by the telephone. The small restaurant was closed, his presence there an accommodation made by a friend from the old days, the better days. He kept looking at the instrument on the wall, wondering when it would ring. It was only a question of time, and when it did he would in turn make a call and the better days would return permanently. He would be the one man in Paris who was the link to Carlos. It would be whispered among the other old men, and respect would be his again.

The high-pitched sound of the bell burst from the telephone, echoing off the walls of the deserted restaurant. The beggar climbed out of the booth and rushed to the phone, his chest pounding with anticipation. It was the signal. Cain was cornered! The days of patient waiting merely a preface to the fine life. He lifted the phone out of its curved recess.

"Yes?"

"It's Jules!" cried the breathless voice.

The old man's face turned ashen, the pounding in his chest growing so loud he could barely hear the terrible things being said. But he had heard enough.

He was a dead man.

White-hot explosions joined the vibrations that took hold of his body. There was no air, only white light and deafening eruptions surging up from his stomach to his head.

The beggar sank to the floor, the cord stretched taut, the phone still in his hand. He stared up at the horrible instrument that carried the terrible words. What could he do? What in the name of God would he *do*?

Bourne walked down the path between the graves, forcing himself to let his mind fall free as Washburn had commanded a lifetime ago in Port Noir. If ever he had to be a sponge, it was now; the man from Treadstone had to understand. He was trying with all his concentration to make sense out of the unremembered, to find meaning in the images that came to him without warning. He had not broken whatever agreement they had; he had not turned, or run. . . . He was a cripple; it was as simple as that.

He had to find the man from Treadstone. Where inside those fenced acres of silence would he be? Where did he expect *him* to be? Jason had reached the cemetery well before one, the Chevrolet a faster car than the broken-down Renault. He had passed the gates, driven several hundred yards down the road, pulled off onto the shoulder and parked the car reasonably out of sight. On his way back to the gates it had started to rain. It was a cold rain, a March rain, but a quiet rain, little intrusions upon the silence.

He passed a cluster of graves within a plot bordered by a low iron railing, the centerpiece an alabaster cross rising eight feet out of the ground. He stood for a moment before it. Had he been here before? Was another door opening for him in the distance? Or was he trying too desperately to find one? And then it came to him. It was not this particular grouping of gravestones, not the tall alabaster cross, nor the low iron railing. It was the rain. *A sudden rain. Crowds of mourners gathered in black around a burial site, the snapping of umbrellas. And two men coming together, umbrellas touching, brief, quiet apologies muttered, as a long brown envelope exchanged hands, pocket to pocket, unnoticed by the mourners.*

There was something else. An image triggered by an image, feeding upon itself, seen only minutes ago. Rain cascading down white marble; not a cold, light rain, but a downpour, pounding against the wall of a glistening white surface . . . and columns . . . rows of columns on all sides, a miniature replica of an ancient treasure.

On the other side of the hill. Near the gates. A white mausoleum, someone's scaled-down version of the Parthenon. He had passed it less than five minutes before, looking at it but not seeing it. *That* was where the sudden rain had taken place, where two umbrellas had touched and an envelope been delivered. He squinted at the radium dial of his watch. It was fourteen minutes past one; he started running back up the path. He was still early; there was time left to see a car's headlights, or the striking of a match or . . .

The beam of a flashlight. It was there at the bottom of the hill and it was moving up and down, intermittently swinging back at the gates as though the holder were concerned that someone might appear. Bourne had an almost uncontrollable urge to race down between the rows of graves and statuary, shouting at the top of his voice. *I'm here! It's me. I understand your message. I've come back! I have so much to tell you . . . and there is so much you must tell me!*

But he did not shout and he did not run. Above all else, he had to show control, for what afflicted him was so uncontrollable. He had to appear completely lucid—sane within the boundaries of his memory. He began walking down the hill in the cold light rain, wishing his sense of urgency had allowed him to remember a flashlight.

The flashlight. Something was odd about the beam of light five hundred feet below. It was moving in short vertical strokes, as if in emphasis . . . as if the man holding it were speaking emphatically to another.

He was. Jason crouched, peering through the rain, his eyes struck by a sharp, darting reflection of light that shot out whenever the beam hit the object in front of it. He crept forward, his body close to the ground, covering practically a hundred feet in seconds, his gaze still on the beam and the strange reflection. He could see more clearly now; he stopped and concentrated. There were two men, one holding the flashlight, the other a short-barreled rifle, the thick steel of the gun known only too well to Bourne. At distances of up to thirty feet it could blow a man six feet into the air. It was a very odd weapon for an officer-of-record sent by Washington to have at his command.

The beam of light shot over to the side of the white mausoleum; the figure holding the rifle retreated quickly, slipping behind a column no more than twenty feet away from the man holding the flashlight.

Jason did not have to think; he knew what he had to do. If there was an explanation for the deadly weapon, so be it, but it would not be used on him. Kneeling, he judged the distance and looked for points of sanctuary, both for concealment and protection. He started out, wiping the rain from his face, feeling the gun in his belt that he knew he could not use.

He scrambled from gravestone to gravestone, statue to statue, heading to his right, then angling gradually to his left until the semicircle was nearly complete. He was within fifteen feet of the mausoleum; the man with the murderous weapon was standing by the left corner column, under the short portico to avoid the rain. He was fondling his gun as though it were a sexual object, cracking the breach, unable to resist peering inside. He ran his palm over the inserted shells, the gesture obscene.

Now. Bourne crept out from behind the gravestone, hands and knees propelling him over the wet grass until he was within six feet of the man. He sprang up, a silent, lethal panther hurling dirt in front of him, one hand surging for the barrel of the rifle, the other for the man's head. He reached both, grabbed both, clasping the barrel in the fingers of his left hand, the man's hair in his right. The head snapped back, throat stretched, sound muted. He smashed the head into the white marble with such force that the expulsion of breath that followed signified a severe concussion. The man went limp, Jason supporting him against the wall, permitting the unconscious body to slip silently to the ground between the columns. He searched the man, removing a .357 Magnum automatic from a leather case sewn into his jacket, a razor-sharp scaling knife from a scabbard on his belt and a small .22 revolver from an ankle holster. Nothing remotely government issue; this was a hired killer, an arsenal on foot.

Break his fingers. The words came back to Bourne; they had been spoken by a man in gold-rimmed glasses in a large sedan racing out of the Steppdeckstrasse. There was reason behind the violence. Jason grabbed the man's right hand and bent the fingers back until he heard the cracks; he did the same with the left, the man's mouth blocked, Bourne's elbow jammed between the teeth. No sound emerged above the sound of the rain, and neither hand could be used for a weapon or as a weapon, the weapons themselves placed out of reach in the shadows.

Jason stood up and edged his face around the column. The Treadstone officer now angled the light directly into the earth in front of him. It was the stationary signal, the beam a lost bird was to home into; it might be other things also—the next few minutes would tell. The man turned toward the gate, taking a tentative step as though he might have heard something, and for the first time Bourne saw the cane, observed the limp. The officer-of-record from Treadstone Seventy-One was a cripple . . . as he was a cripple.

Jason dashed back to the first gravestone, spun behind it and peered around the marble edge. The man from Treadstone still had his attention on the gates. Bourne glanced at his watch; it was 1:27. Time remained. He pushed himself away from the grave, hugging the ground until he was out of sight, then stood up and ran, retracing the arch back to the top of the hill. He stood for a moment, letting his breathing and his heartbeat resume a semblance of normalcy, then reached into his pocket for a book of matches. Protecting it from the rain, he tore off a match and struck it.

"Treadstone?" he said loud enough to be heard from below.

"Delta!"

Cain is for Charlie and Delta is for Cain. Why did the man from Treadstone use the name Delta rather than Cain? Delta was no part of Treadstone; he had disappeared with Medusa. Jason started down the hill, the cold rain whipping his face, his hand instinctively reaching beneath his jacket, pressing the automatic in his belt.

He walked onto the stretch of lawn in front of the white mausoleum. The man from Treadstone limped toward him, then stopped, raising his flashlight, the harsh beam causing Bourne to squint and turn his head away.

"It's been a long time," said the crippled officer, lowering the light. "The name's Conklin, in case you've forgotten."

"Thank you. I had. It's only one of the things."

"One of what things?"

"That I've forgotten."

"You remembered this place, though. I figured you would. I read Abbott's logs; it was here where you last met, last made a delivery. During a state burial for some minister or other, wasn't it?"

"I don't know. That's what we have to talk about first. You haven't heard from me in over six months. There's an explanation."

"Really? Let's hear it."

"The simplest way to put it is that I was wounded, shot, the effects of the wounds causing a severe . . . dislocation. Disorientation is a better word, I guess."

"Sounds good. What does it mean?"

"I suffered a memory loss. Total. I spent months on an island in the Mediterranean—south of Marseilles—not knowing who I was or where I came from. There's a doctor, an Englishman named Washburn, who kept medical records. He can verify what I'm telling you."

"I'm sure he can," said Conklin, nodding. "And I'll bet those records are massive. Christ, you paid enough!"

"What do you mean?"

"We've got a record, too. A bank officer in Zurich who thought he was being tested by Treadstone transferred a million and a half Swiss francs to Marseilles for an untraceable collection. Thanks for giving us the name."

"That's part of what you have to understand. I didn't know. He'd saved my life, put me back together. I was damn near a corpse when I was brought to him."

"So you decided a million-odd dollars was a pretty fair ballpark figure, is that it? Courtesy of the Treadstone budget."

"I told you, I didn't *know.* Treadstone didn't exist for me; in many ways it still doesn't."

"I forgot. You lost your memory. What was the word? Disorientation?"

"Yes, but it's not strong enough. The word is amnesia."

"Let's stick to disorientation. Because it seems you oriented yourself straight into Zurich, right to the Gemeinschaft."

"There was a negative surgically implanted near my hip."

"There certainly was; you insisted on it. A few of us understood why. It's the best insurance you can have."

"I don't know what you're talking about. Can't you understand *that?*"

"Sure. You found the negative with only a number on it and right away you assumed the name of Jason Bourne."

"It didn't *happen* that way! Each day it seemed I learned something, one step at a time, one revelation at a time. A hotel clerk called me Bourne; I didn't learn the name Jason until I went to the bank."

"Where you knew exactly what to do," interrupted Conklin. "No hesitation at all. In and out, four million gone."

"Washburn told me what to do!"

"Then a woman came along who just happened to be a financial whiz kid to tell you how to squirrel away the rest. And before that you took out Chernak in the Löwenstrasse and three men *we* didn't know but figured they sure as hell knew you. And here in Paris, another shot in a bank transfer truck. Another associate? You covered every track, every goddamned track. Until there was only one thing left to do. And you—you son of a bitch—you did it."

"Will you *listen* to me! Those men tried to kill me; they've been hunting me since Marseilles. Beyond that, I honestly *don't know* what you're talking about. Things come to me at times. Faces, streets, buildings; sometimes just images I can't place, but I know they mean something, only I can't relate to them. And names—there are names, but then no faces. Goddamn you—I'm an *amnesiac!* That's the truth!"

"One of those names wouldn't be Carlos, would it?"

"Yes, and you know it. That's the point; you know much more about it than *I* do. I can recite a thousand facts about Carlos, but I don't know *why.* I was told by a man who's halfway back to Asia by now I had an agreement with Treadstone. The man worked for Carlos. He said Carlos knows. That Carlos was closing in on me, that you put out the word that I'd turned. He couldn't understand the strategy, and I couldn't tell him. You thought I'd turned because you didn't hear from me, and I couldn't reach you because I didn't know who you were. I *still* don't know who you are!"

"Or the Monk, I suppose."

"Yes, yes . . . the Monk. His name was Abbott."

"Very good. And the Yachtsman? You remember the Yachtsman, don't you? And his wife?"

"Names. They're there, yes. No faces."

"Elliot Stevens?"

"Nothing."

"Or . . . Gordon Webb." Conklin said the name quietly.

"What?" Bourne felt the jolt in his chest, then a stinging, searing pain that drove through his temples to his eyes. *His eyes were on fire! Fire! Explosions and darkness, high winds and pain. . . . Almanac to Delta! Abandon, abandon! You will respond as ordered. Abandon!* "Gordon . . ." Jason heard his own voice, but it was far away in a faraway wind. He closed his eyes, the eyes that burned so, and tried to push the mists away. Then he opened his eyes and was not at all surprised to see Conklin's gun aimed at his head.

"I don't know how you did it, but you did. The only thing left to do and you did it. You got back to New York and blew them all away. You butchered them, you son of a bitch. I wish to Christ I could bring you back and see you strapped into an electric chair, but I can't, so I'll do the next best thing. I'll take you myself."

"I haven't been in New York for months. Before then, I don't know—but not in the last half-year."

"Liar! Why didn't you do it *really* right? Why didn't you time your goddamn stunt so you could get to the funerals? The Monk's was just the other day; you would have seen a lot of old friends. And your *brother's*! Jesus God Almighty! You could have escorted his wife down the aisle of the church. Maybe delivered the eulogy, that'd be the kicker. At least speak well of the brother you killed."

"Brother? . . . *Stop* it! For Christ's sake, stop it!"

"Why should I? Cain lives! We made him and he came to life!"

"I'm not *Cain.* He never *was!* I never *was!*"

"So you *do* know! *Liar! Bastard!*"

"Put that gun away. I'm telling you, put it down!"

"No chance. I swore to myself I'd give you two minutes because I wanted to hear what you'd come up with. Well, I've heard it and it smells. Who gave *you* the right? We all lose things; it goes with the job, and if you don't like the goddamned job you get out. If there's no accommodation you fade; that's what I thought you did, and I was willing to pass on you, to convince the others to *let* you fade! But no, you came back, and turned your gun on us."

"No! It's not true!"

"Tell that to the laboratory techs, who have eight fragments of glass that spell out two prints. Third and index fingers, right hand. You were there and you butchered five people. You—one of *them*—took out your guns—plural—and blew them away. Perfect setup. Discredited strategy. Varied shells, multiple bullets, *infiltration.* Treadstone's aborted and you walk out free."

"No, you're wrong! It was Carlos. Not me, *Carlos.* If what you're saying took place on Seventy-first Street, it was him! He knows. They know. A residence on Seventy-first Street. Number 139. They know about it!"

Conklin nodded, his eyes clouded, the loathing in them seen in the dim light, through the rain. "So perfect," he said slowly. "The prime mover of the strategy blows it apart by making a deal with the target. What's your take besides the four million? Carlos give you immunity from his own particular brand of persecution? You two make a lovely couple."

"That's crazy!"

"And accurate," completed the man from Treadstone. "Only nine people alive knew that address before seven-thirty last Friday night. Three of them were killed, and we're the other four. If Carlos found it, there's only one person who could have told him. *You.* "

"How *could* I? I didn't know it. I *don't* know it!"

"You just said it." Conklin's left hand gripped the cane; it was a prelude to firing, steadying a crippled foot.

"Don't!" shouted Bourne, knowing the plea was useless, spinning to his left as he shouted, his right foot lashing out at the wrist that held the gun. *Che-sah!* was the unknown word that was the silent scream in his head. Conklin fell back, firing wildly in the air, tripping over his cane. Jason spun around and down, now hammering his left foot at the weapon; it flew out of the hand that held it.

Conklin rolled on the ground, his eyes on the far columns of the mausoleum, expecting an explosion from the gun that would blow his attacker into the air. No! The man from Treadstone rolled again. Now to the right, his features in shock, his wild eyes focused on—There was someone else!

Bourne crouched, diving diagonally backward as four gunshots came in rapid succession, three screeching ricochets spinning off beyond sound. He rolled over and over and over, pulling the automatic from his belt. He saw the man in the rain; a silhouetted figure rising above a gravestone. He fired twice; the man collapsed.

Ten feet away Conklin was thrashing on the wet grass, both hands spreading frantically over the ground, feeling for the steel of a gun. Bourne sprang up and raced over; he knelt beside the Treadstone man, one hand grabbing the wet hair, the other holding his automatic, its barrel pressed into Conklin's skull. From the far columns of the mausoleum came a prolonged, shattering scream. It grew steadily, eerily in volume, then stopped.

"That's your hired shotgun," said Jason, yanking Conklin's head to the side. "Treadstone's taken on some very strange employees. Who was the other man? What death row did you spring him from?"

"He was a better man than you ever were," replied Conklin, his voice strained, the rain glistening on his face, caught in the beam of the fallen flashlight six feet away on the ground. "They all are. They've all lost as much as you lost, but they never turned. We can count on them!"

"No matter what I say, you won't believe me. You don't *want* to believe me!"

"Because I know what you are—what you *did*. You just confirmed the whole damn thing. You can kill me, but they'll get you. You're the worst kind. You think you're special. You always did. I saw you after Phnom Penh—*everybody* lost out there, but that didn't count with you. It was only you, just *you!* Then in Medusa! No rules for Delta! The animal just wanted to kill. And that's the kind that turns. Well, I lost too, but I never turned. Go on! Kill me! Then you can go back to Carlos. But when I don't come back, they'll know. They'll come after you and they won't stop until they get you. Go on! Shoot!"

Conklin was shouting, but Bourne could hardly hear him. Instead he had heard two words and the jolts of pain hammered at his temples. *Phnom Penh! Phnom Penh. Death in the skies, from the skies. Death of the young and the very young. Screeching birds and screaming machines and the deathlike stench of the jungle . . . and a river. He was blinded again, on fire again.*

Beneath him the man from Treadstone had broken away. His crippled figure was crawling in panic, lunging, his hands surging through the wet grass. Jason blinked, trying to force his mind to come back to him. Then instantly he knew he had to point the automatic and fire. Conklin had found his gun and was raising it. But Bourne could not pull the trigger.

He dove to his right, rolling on the ground, scrambling toward the marble columns of the mausoleum. Conklin's gunshots were wild, the crippled man unable to steady his leg or his aim. Then the firing stopped and Jason got to his feet, his face against the smooth wet stone. He looked out, his automatic raised; he had to kill this man, for this man would kill him, kill Marie, link them both to Carlos.

Conklin was hobbling pathetically toward the gates, turning constantly, the gun extended, his destination a car outside in the road. Bourne raised his automatic, the crippled figure in his gunsight. A split half-second and it would be over, his enemy from Treadstone dead, hope found with that death, for there were reasonable men in Washington.

He could not do it; he could not pull the trigger. He lowered the gun, standing helpless by the marble column as Conklin climbed into his car.

The car. He had to get back to Paris. There was a way. It had been there all along. *She* had been there!

He rapped on the door, his mind racing, facts analyzed, absorbed and discarded as rapidly as they came to him, a strategy evolving. Marie recognized the knock; she opened the door.

"Dear God, look at you! What happened?"

"No time," he said, rushing toward the telephone across the room. "It was a trap. They're convinced I turned, sold out to Carlos."

"*What?*"

"They say I flew into New York last week, last Friday. That I killed five people . . . among them a brother." Jason closed his eyes briefly. "There was a brother— *is* a brother. I don't know, I can't think about it now."

"You never left Paris! You can prove it!"

"How? Eight, ten hours, that's all I'd need. And eight or ten hours unaccounted for is all *they* need now. Who's going to come forward?"

"I will. You've been with me."

"They think you're part of it," said Bourne, picking up the telephone and dialing. "The theft, the turning, Port Noir, the whole damn thing. They've locked you into me. Carlos engineered this down to the last fragment of a fingerprint. Christ! Did he put it together!"

"What are you doing? Whom are you calling?"

"Our backup, remember? The only one we've got. Villiers. Villiers' *wife*. She's the one. We're going to take her, break her, put her on a hundred racks if we have to. But we won't have to; she won't fight because she can't win. . . . Goddamn it, why doesn't he answer?"

"The private phone's in his office. It's three in the morning. He's probably—"

"He's on! General? Is that you?" Jason had to ask; the voice on the line was oddly quiet, but not the quiet of interrupted sleep.

"Yes, it is I, my young friend. I apologize for the delay. I've been upstairs with my wife."

"That's whom I'm calling about. We've got to move. *Now*. Alert French Intelligence, Interpol and the American Embassy but tell them not to interfere until I've seen her, talked to her. We have to talk."

"I don't think so, Mr. Bourne. . . . Yes, I know your name, my friend. As for your talking to my wife, however, I'm afraid that's not possible. You see, I've killed her."

33

Jason stared at the hotel room wall, at the flock paper with the faded designs that spiraled into one another in meaningless contortions of worn fabric. "Why?" he said quietly into the phone. "I thought you understood."

"I tried, my friend," said Villiers, his voice beyond anger or sorrow. "The saints know I tried, but I could not help myself. I kept looking at her . . . seeing the son she did not bear behind her, killed by the pig animal that was her mentor. My whore was someone else's whore . . . the animal's whore. It could not be otherwise, and as I learned, it was not. I think she saw the outrage in my eyes, heaven knows it was there." The general paused, the memory painful now. "She not only saw the outrage, but the truth. She saw that I knew. What she was, what she had been during the years we'd spent together. At the end, I gave her the chance I told you I would give her."

"To kill you?"

"Yes. It wasn't difficult. Between our beds is a nightstand with a weapon in the drawer. She lay on her bed, Goya's Maja, splendid in her arrogance, dismissing me with her private thoughts, as I was consumed by my own. I opened the drawer for a book of matches and walked back to my chair and my pipe, leaving the drawer open, the handle of the gun very much in evidence.

"It was my silence, I imagine, and the fact that I could not take my eyes off her that forced her to acknowledge me, then concentrate on me. The tension between us had grown to the point where very little had to be said to burst the floodgates, and—God help me—I said it. I heard myself asking, 'Why did you do it?' Then the accusation became complete. I called her my whore, the whore that killed my son.

"She stared at me for several moments, her eyes breaking away once to glance at the open drawer and the gun . . . and the telephone. I stood up, the embers in my pipe glowing, loose . . . *chauffé au rouge.* She spun her legs off the bed, put both hands into that open drawer and took out the gun. I did not stop her, instead I had to hear the words from her own lips, hear my own indictment of myself as well as hers. What I heard will go to my grave with me, for there will be honor left by my person and the person of my son. We will not be scorned by those who've given less than us. Never."

"General . . ." Bourne shook his head, unable to think clearly, knowing he had to find the seconds in order to find his thoughts. "General, what happened? She gave you my name. How? You've got to tell me that. *Please.*"

"Willingly. She said you were an insignificant gunman who wished to step into the shoes of a giant. That you were a thief out of Zurich, a man your own people disowned."

"Did she say who those people were?"

"If she did I didn't hear. I was blind, deaf, my rage uncontrolled. But you have nothing to fear from me. The chapter is closed, my life over with a telephone call."

"No!" Jason shouted. "Don't do that! Not now."

"I must."

"Please. Don't settle for Carlos's whore. Get Carlos! Trap Carlos!"

"Reaping scorn on my name by lying with that whore? Manipulated by the animal's slut?"

"Goddamn you—what about your *son?* Five sticks of dynamite on rue du Bac!"

"Leave him in peace. Leave me in peace. It's over."

"It's *not* over! Listen to me! Give a moment, that's all I ask." The images in Jason's mind raced furiously across his eyes, clashing, supplanting one another. But these images had meaning. Purpose. He could feel Marie's hand on his arm, gripping him firmly, somehow anchoring his body to a mooring of reality. "Did anyone hear the gunshot?"

"There was no gunshot. The *coup de grâce* is misunderstood in these times. I prefer its original intent. To still the suffering of a wounded comrade or a respected enemy. It is not used for a whore."

"What do you mean? You said you killed her."

"I strangled her, forcing her eyes to look into mine as the breath went out of her body."

"She had your gun on you . . ."

"Ineffective when one's eyes are burning from the loose embers of a pipe. It's immaterial now; she might have won."

"She *did* win if you let it stop here! Can't you see that? Carlos wins! She broke you! And you didn't have the brains to do anything but choke her to death! You talk about *scorn?* You're buying it all; there's nothing left but scorn!"

"Why do you persist, Monsieur Bourne?" asked Villiers wearily. "I expect no charity from you, nor from anyone. Simply leave me alone. I accept what is. You accomplish nothing."

"I will if I can get you to listen to me! Get Carlos, trap Carlos! How many times do I have to say it? He's the one you want! He squares it all for you! And he's the one I need! Without him I'm dead. *We're* dead. For God's sake, *listen to me!*"

"I would like to help you, but there's no way I can. Or will, if you like."

"There is." The images came into focus. He knew where he was, where he was going. The meaning and the purpose came together. "Reverse the trap. Walk away from it untouched, with everything you've got in place."

"I don't understand. How is that possible?"

"You didn't kill your wife. *I* did!"

"Jason!" Marie screamed, clutching his arm.

"I know what I'm doing," said Bourne. "For the first time, I really know what I'm doing. It's funny, but I think I've known it from the beginning."

Parc Monceau was quiet, the street deserted, a few porch lights shimmering in the cold, mistlike rain, all the windows along the row of neat, expensive houses dark, except for the residence of André François Villiers, legend of Saint-Cyr and Normandy, member of France's National Assembly . . . wife killer. The front windows above and to the left of the porch glowed dimly. It was the bedroom wherein the master of the house had killed the mistress of the house, where a memory-ridden old soldier had choked the life out of an assassin's whore.

Villiers had agreed to nothing; he had been too stunned to answer. But Jason had driven home his theme, hammered the message with such repeated emphasis that the words had echoed over the telephone. Get Carlos! Don't settle for the killer's whore! Get the man who killed your son! The man who put five sticks of dynamite in a car on rue du Bac and took the last of the Villiers line. He's the one you want. Get him!

Get Carlos. Trap Carlos. Cain is for Charlie and Delta is for Cain. It was so clear to him. There was no other way. At the end, it was the beginning—as the beginning had been revealed to him. To survive he had to bring in the assassin; if he failed, he was a dead man. And there would be no life for Marie St. Jacques. She would be destroyed, imprisoned, perhaps killed, for an act of faith that became an act of love. Cain's mark was on her, embarrassment avoided with her removal. She was a vial of nitroglycerine balanced on a highwire in the center of an unknown ammunition depot. Use a net. Remove her. A bullet in the head neutralizes the explosives in her mind. She cannot be heard!

There was so much Villiers had to understand, and so little time to explain, the explanation itself limited both by a memory that did not exist and the current state of the old soldier's mind. A delicate balance had to be found in the telling, parameters established as to time and the general's immediate contributions. Jason understood; he was asking a man who held his honor above all things to lie to the world. For Villiers to do that, the objective had to be monumentally honorable.

Get Carlos!

There was a second, ground floor entrance to the general's home, to the right of the steps, beyond a gate, where deliveries were made to the downstairs kitchen. Villiers had agreed to leave the gate and the door unlatched. Bourne had not bothered to tell the old soldier that it did not matter; that he would get inside in any event, a degree of damage intrinsic to his strategy. But first there was the risk that Villiers' house was being watched, there being good reasons for Carlos to do so, and equally good reasons not to do so. All things considered, the assassin might decide to stay as far away from Angélique Villiers as possible, taking no chance that one of his men could be picked up, thus proving his connection, the Parc Monceau connection. On the other hand, the dead Angélique was his cousin and lover . . . *the only person on earth he cares about.* Philippe d'Anjou.

D'Anjou! Of course there'd be someone watching—or two or ten! If d'Anjou had gotten out of France, Carlos could assume the worst; if the man from Medusa had not, the assassin would know the worst. The colonial would be broken, every word exchanged with Cain revealed. Where? Where were Carlos's men? Strangely enough, thought Jason, if there was no one posted in Parc Monceau on this particular night, his entire strategy was worthless.

It was not; they were there. In a sedan—the same sedan that had raced through the gates of the Louvre twelve hours ago, the same two men—killers who were the backups of killers. The car was fifty feet down the street on the left-hand side, with a clear view of Villiers' house. But were those two men slumped down in the seat, their eyes awake and alert, all that were there? Bourne could not tell; automobiles lined the curbs on both sides of the street. He crouched in the shadows of the corner building, diagonally across from the two men in the stationary sedan. He knew what had to be done, but he was not sure how to do it. He needed a diversion, alarming enough to attract Carlos's soldiers, visible enough to flush out any others who might be concealed in the street or on a rooftop, or behind a darkened window.

Fire. Out of nowhere. Sudden, away from Villiers' house, yet close enough and startling enough to send vibrations throughout the quiet, deserted, tree-lined street. Vibrations . . . sirens; explosive . . . explosions. It could be done. It was merely a question of equipment.

Bourne crept back behind the corner building into the intersecting street and ran silently to the nearest doorway, where he stopped and removed his jacket and topcoat. Then he took off his shirt, ripping the cloth from collar to waist; he put both coats on again, pulling up the lapels, buttoning the topcoat, the shirt under his arm. He peered into the night rain, scanning the automobiles in the street. He needed gasoline, but this was Paris and most fuel tanks would be locked. Most, but not all; there had to be an unsecured top among the line of cars at the curb.

And then he saw what he wanted to see directly up ahead on the pavement, chained to an iron gate. It was a motorbike, larger than a street scooter, smaller than a cycle, its gas tank a metal bubble between handlebars and seat. The top would have a chain attached, but it was unlikely to have a lock. Eight liters of fuel was not forty; the risk of any theft had to be balanced against the proceeds, and two gallons of gas was hardly worth a 500 franc fine.

Jason approached the bike. He looked up and down the street; there was no one, no sounds other than the quiet spattering of the rain. He put his hand on the gas tank top and turned it; it unscrewed easily. Better yet, the opening was relatively wide, the gas level nearly full. He replaced the top; he was not yet ready to douse his shirt. Another piece of equipment was needed.

He found it at the next corner, by a sewer drain. A partially dislodged cobblestone, forced from its recess by a decade of careless drivers jumping the curb. He pried it loose by kicking his heel into the slice that separated it from its jagged wall. He picked it up along with a smaller fragment and started back toward the motorbike, the fragment in his pocket, the large brick in his hand. He tested its weight . . . tested his arm. It would do; both would do.

Three minutes later he pulled the drenched shirt slowly out of the gas tank, the fumes mingling with the rain, the residue of oil covering his hands. He wrapped the cloth around the cobblestone, twisting and crisscrossing the sleeves, tying them firmly together, holding his missile in place. He was ready.

He crept back to the edge of the building at the corner of Villiers' street. The two men in the sedan were still low in the front seat, their concentration still on Villiers' house. Behind the sedan were three other cars, a small Mercedes, a dark brown limousine and a Bentley. Directly across from Jason, beyond the Bentley, was a white stone building, its windows outlined in black enamel. An inside hallway light spilled over to the casement bay windows on either side of the staircase; the left was obviously a dining room; he could see chairs and a long table in the additional light of a rococo sideboard mirror. The windows of that dining room with their splendid view of the quaint, rich Parisian street would do.

Bourne reached into his pocket and pulled out the rock; it was barely one-fourth the size of the gas-drenched brick, but it would serve the purpose. He inched around the corner of the building, cocked his arm and threw the stone as far as he could above and beyond the sedan.

The crash echoed throughout the quiet street. It was followed by a series of cracks as the rock clattered across the hood of a car and dropped to the pavement. The two men in the sedan bolted up. The man next to the driver opened his door, his foot plunging down to the pavement, a gun in his hand. The driver lowered the window, then switched on the headlights. The beams shot forward, bouncing back in blinding reflection off the metal and the chrome of the automobile in front. It was a patently stupid act, serving only to point up the fear of the men stationed in Parc Monceau.

Now. Jason raced across the street, his attention on the two men, whose hands were covering their eyes, trying to see through the glare of the reflected light. He reached the trunk of the Bentley, the cobblestone brick under his arm, a matchbook in his left hand, a cluster of torn-off matches in his right. He crouched, struck the matches, lowered the brick to the ground, then picked it up by an extended sleeve. He held the burning matches beneath the gas-soaked cloth; it burst instantly into flame.

He rose quickly, swinging the brick by the sleeve, and dashed over the curb, hurling his missile toward the bulging framework of the casement window with all his strength, racing beyond the edge of the building as impact was made.

The crash of shattering glass was a sudden intrusion on the rainsoaked stillness of the street. Bourne raced to his left across the narrow avenue, then back toward Villiers' block, again finding the shadows he needed. The fire spread, fanned by the wind from the broken window, leaping up into the willowy backing of the drapes. Within thirty seconds the room was a flaming oven, the fire magnified by the huge sideboard mirror. Shouts erupted, windows lighted up nearby, then farther down the street. A minute passed and the chaos grew. The door of the flaming house was yanked open and figures appeared—an elderly man in a nightshirt, a woman in a negligée and one slipper—both in panic.

Other doors opened, other figures emerged, adjusting from sleep to chaos, some racing toward the fire-swept residence—a neighbor was in trouble. Jason ran diagonally across the intersection, one more running figure in the rapidly gathering crowd. He stopped where he had started only minutes before, by the edge of the corner building, and stood motionless, trying to spot Carlos's soldiers.

He had been right; the two men were not the only guards posted in Parc Monceau. There were four men now, huddling by the sedan, talking rapidly, quietly. No, five. Another walked swiftly up the pavement, joining the four.

He heard sirens. Growing louder, drawing nearer. The five men were alarmed. Decisions had to be made; they could not all remain where they were. Perhaps there were arrest records to consider.

Agreement. One man would stay—the fifth man. He nodded and walked rapidly across the street to Villiers' side. The others climbed into the sedan, and as a fire engine careened up the street, the sedan curved out of its parking place and sped past the red behemoth racing in the opposite direction.

One obstacle remained: the fifth man. Jason rounded the building, spotting him halfway between the corner and Villiers's house. It was now a question of timing and shock. Bourne broke into a loping run, similar to that used by the people heading toward the fire, his head angled back toward the corner, running partially backward, a figure melting into the surrounding pattern, only the direction in conflict. He passed the man; he had not been noticed—but he *would* be noticed if he continued to the downstairs gate of Villiers' house and opened it. The man was glancing back and forth, concerned, bewildered, perhaps frightened by the fact that now he was the only patrol in the street. He was standing in front of a low railing; another gate, another downstairs entrance to another expensive house in Parc Monceau.

Jason stopped, taking two rapid sidesteps toward the man, then pivoted, his balance on his left foot, his right lashing out at the fifth man's midsection, pummeling him backward over the iron rail. The man shouted as he fell down into the narrow concrete corridor. Bourne leaped over the railing, the knuckles of his right hand rigid, the heels of both feet pushed forward. He landed on the man's chest, the impact breaking the ribs beneath him, his knuckles smashing into the man's throat. Carlos's soldier went limp. He would regain consciousness long after someone removed him to a hospital. Jason searched the man; there was a single gun strapped to his chest. Bourne took it out and put it into his topcoat pocket. He would give it to Villiers.

Villiers. The way was clear.

He climbed the staircase to the third floor. Halfway up the steps he could see a line of light at the bottom of the bedroom door; beyond that door was an old man who was his only hope. If ever in his life—remembered and unremembered—he had to be convincing, it was now. And his conviction was real—there was no room for the chameleon now. Everything he believed was based on one fact. Carlos had to come after him. It was the truth. It was the trap.

He reached the landing and turned to his left toward the bedroom door. He paused for a moment, trying to dismiss the echo in his chest; it was growing louder, the pounding more rapid. *Part of the truth, not all of it.* No invention, simply omission.

An agreement . . . a contract . . . with a group of men—honorable men—who were after Carlos. That was all Villiers had to know; it was what he had to accept. He could not be told he was dealing with an amnesiac, for in that loss of memory might be found a man of dishonor. The legend of Saint-Cyr, Algeria and Normandy would not accept that; not now, here, at the end of his life.

Oh, God, the balance was tenuous! The line between belief and disbelief so thin . . . as thin as it was for the man-corpse whose name was not Jason Bourne.

He opened the door and stepped inside, into an old man's private hell. Outside, beyond draped windows, the sirens raged and the crowds shouted. Spectators in an unseen arena, jeering the unknown, oblivious to its unfathomable cause.

Jason closed the door and stood motionless. The large room was filled with shadows, the only light a bedside table lamp. His eyes greeted by a sight he wished he did not have to see. Villiers had dragged a high-backed desk chair across the room and was sitting on it at the foot of the bed, staring at the dead woman sprawled over the covers. Angélique Villiers' bronzed head was resting on the pillow, her eyes wide, bulging out of their sockets. Her throat was swollen, the flesh a reddish purple, the massive bruise having spread throughout her neck. Her body was still twisted, in contrast to the upright head, contorted in furious struggle, her long bare legs stretched out, her hips turned, the negligée torn, her breasts bursting out of the silk—even in death, sensual. There had been no attempt to conceal the whore.

The old soldier sat like a bewildered child, punished for an insignificant act, the meaningful crime having escaped his tormentor's reasoning, and perhaps his own. He pulled his eyes away from the dead woman and looked at Bourne.

"What happened outside?" he asked in a monotone.

"Men were watching your house. Carlos's men, five of them. I started a fire up the block; no one was hurt. All but one man left; I took him out."

"You're resourceful, Monsieur Bourne."

"I'm resourceful," agreed Jason. "But they'll be back. The fire'll be out and they'll come back; before then, if Carlos puts it together, and I think he will. If he does, he'll send someone in here. He won't come himself, of course, but one of his guns will be here. When that man finds you . . . and her . . . he'll kill you. Carlos loses her, but he still wins. He wins a second time; he's used you through her and at the end he kills you. He walks away and you're dead. People can draw whatever conclusions they like, but I don't think they'll be flattering."

"You're very precise. Assured of your judgment."

"I know what I'm talking about. I'd prefer not to say what I'm going to say, but there's no time for your feelings."

"I have none left. Say what you will."

"Your wife told you she was French, didn't she?"

"Yes. From the south. Her family was from Loures Barouse, near the Spanish border. She came to Paris years ago. Lived with an aunt. What of it?"

"Did you ever meet her family?"

"No."

"They didn't come up for your marriage?"

"All things considered, we thought it would be best not to ask them. The disparity of our ages would have disturbed them."

"What about the aunt here in Paris?"

"She died before I met Angélique. What's the point of all this?"

"Your wife wasn't French. I doubt there was even an aunt in Paris, and her family didn't come from Loures Barouse, although the Spanish border has a certain relevance. It could cover a lot, explain a lot."

"What do you mean?"

"She was Venezuelan. Carlos's first cousin, his lover since she was fourteen. They were a team, have been for years. I was told she was the only person on earth he cared about."

"A whore."

"An assassin's instrument. I wonder how many targets she set up. How many valuable men are dead because of her."

"I cannot kill her twice."

"You can use her. Use her death."

"The insanity you spoke of?"

"The only insanity is if you throw your life away. Carlos wins it all; he goes on using his gun . . . and sticks of dynamite . . . and you're one more statistic. Another kill added to a long list of distinguished corpses. *That's* insane."

"And you're the reasonable man? You assume the guilt for a crime you did not commit? For the death of a whore? Hunted for a killing that was not yours?"

"That's part of it. The essential part, actually."

"Don't talk to me of insanity, young man. I beg you, leave. What you've told me gives me the courage to face Almighty God. If ever a death was justified, it was hers by my hand. I will look into the eyes of Christ and swear it."

"You've written yourself out, then," said Jason, noticing for the first time the bulge of a weapon in the old man's jacket pocket.

"I will not stand trial, if that's what you mean."

"Oh, that's perfect, General! Carlos himself couldn't have come up with anything better. Not a wasted motion on his part; he doesn't even have to use his own gun. But those who count will know he did it; he caused it."

"Those who count will know nothing. *Une affaire de coeur . . . une grave maladie . . .* I am not concerned with the tongues of killers and thieves."

"And if I told the truth? Told why you killed her?"

"Who would listen? Even should you live to speak. I'm not a fool, Monsieur Bourne. You are running from more than Carlos. You are hunted by many, not just one. You as much as told me so. You would not tell me your name . . . for my own safety, you claimed. When and if this was over, you said, it was *I* who might not care to be seen with *you*. Those are not the words of a man in whom much trust is placed."

"You trusted me."

"I told you why," said Villiers, glancing away, staring at his dead wife. "It was in your eyes."

"The truth?"

"The truth."

"Then look at me now. The truth is still there. On that road to Nanterre, you told me you'd listen to what I had to say because I gave you your life. I'm trying to give it to you again. You can walk away free, untouched, go on standing for the things you say are important to you, were important to your son. You can win! . . . Don't mistake me, I'm not being noble. Your staying alive and doing what I ask is the only way I can stay alive, the only way I'll ever be free."

The old soldier looked up. "Why?"

"I told you I wanted Carlos because something was taken from me—something very necessary to my life, my sanity—and he was the cause of it. That's the truth—I believe it's the truth—but it's not the whole truth. There are other people involved, some decent, some not, and my agreement with them was to get Carlos, trap Carlos. They want what you want. But something happened that I can't explain—I won't try to explain—and those people think I betrayed them. They think I made a pact with Carlos, that I stole millions from them and killed others who were my links to them. They have men everywhere, and the orders are to execute me on sight. You were right: I'm running from more than Carlos. I'm hunted by men I don't know and can't see. For all the wrong reasons. I didn't do the things they say I did, but no one wants to listen. I have no pact with Carlos—you know I don't."

"I believe you. There's nothing to prevent me from making a call on your behalf. I owe you that."

"How? What are you going to say? 'The man known to me as Jason Bourne has no pact with Carlos. I know this because he exposed Carlos's mistress to me, and that woman was my wife, the wife I choked to death so as not to bring dishonor to my name. I'm about to call the Sûreté and confess my crime—although, of course, I won't tell them why I killed her. Or why I'm going to kill myself.' . . . Is that it, General? Is that what you're going to say?"

The old man stared silently at Bourne, the fundamental contradiction clear to him. "I cannot help you then."

"Good. Fine. Carlos wins it all. She wins. You lose. Your son loses. Go on—call the police, then put the barrel of the gun in your goddamn mouth and blow your goddamn head off! Go *on!* That's what you want! Take yourself out, lie down and *die!* You're not good for anything else anymore. You're a self-pitying old, *old man!* God knows you're no match for Carlos. No match for the man who placed five sticks of dynamite in rue du Bac and killed your son."

Villiers' hands shook; the trembling spread to his head. "Do not do this. I'm telling you, do not *do* this."

"Telling me? You mean you're giving me an order? The little old man with the big brass buttons is issuing a *command?* Well, forget it! I don't take orders from men like you! You're frauds! You're worse than all the people you attack; at least they have the stomachs to do what they say they're going to do! You *don't.* All you've got is wind. Words and wind and self-serving bromides. Lie down and *die,* old man! But don't give me an order!"

Villiers unclasped his hands and shot out of the chair, his racked body now trembling. "I told you. No more!"

"I'm not interested in what you tell me. I was right the first time I saw you. You belong to Carlos. You were his lackey alive and you'll be his lackey dead."

The old soldier's face grimaced in pain. He pulled out his gun, the gesture pathetic, the threat, however, real. "I've killed many men in my time. In my profession it was unavoidable, often disturbing. I don't want to kill you now, but I will if you disregard my wishes. Leave me. Leave this house."

"That's terrific. You must be wired into Carlos's head. You kill me, he sweeps the board!" Jason took a step forward, aware of the fact that it was the first movement he had made since entering the room. He saw Villiers' eyes widen; the gun shook, its oscillating shadow cast against the wall. A single half ounce of pressure and the hammer would plunge forward, bullet finding its mark. For in spite of madness of the moment, the hand that held that weapon had spent a lifetime gripping steel; it would be steady when the instant came. If it came. That was the risk Bourne had to take. Without Villiers, there was nothing; the old man had to understand. Jason suddenly shouted: "Go *on!* Fire. *Kill* me. Take your orders from Carlos! You're a soldier. You've got your orders. Carry them out."

The trembling in Villiers' hand increased, the knuckles white as the gun rose higher, its barrel now leveled at Bourne's head. And then Jason heard the whisper from an old man's throat.

" '*Vous êtes un soldat . . . arrêtez . . . arrêtez.*' "

"What?"

"I am a soldier. Someone said that to me recently, someone very dear to you." Villiers spoke quietly. "She shamed an old warrior into remembering who he was . . . who he had been. *'On dit que vous êtes un géant. Je le crois.'* She had the grace, the kindness to say that to me also. She had been told I was a giant, and she believed it. She was wrong—Almighty God, she was wrong—but I shall try." André Villiers lowered the gun; there was dignity in the submission. A soldier's dignity. A giant's. "What would you have me do?"

Jason breathed again. "Force Carlos into coming after me. But not here, not in Paris. Not even in France."

"Where then?"

Jason held his place. "Can you get me out of the country? I should tell you, I'm wanted. My name and description by now are on every immigration desk and border check in Europe."

"For the wrong reasons?"

"For the wrong reasons."

"I believe you. There are ways. The Conseiller Militaire has ways and will do as I ask."

"With an identity that's false? Without telling them why?"

"My word is enough. I've earned it."

"Another question. That aide of yours you talked about. Do you trust him— *really* trust him?"

"With my life. Above all men."

"With another's life? One you correctly said was very dear to me?"

"Of course. Why? You'll travel alone?"

"I have to. She'd never let me go."

"You'll have to tell her something."

"I will. That I'm underground here in Paris, or Brussels, or Amsterdam. Cities where Carlos operates. But she has to get away; our car was found in Montmartre. Carlos's men are searching every street, every flat, every hotel. You're working with me now; your aide will take her into the country—she'll be safe there. I'll tell her that."

"I must ask the question now. What happens if you don't come back?"

Bourne tried to keep the plea out of his voice. "I'll have time on the plane. I'll write out everything that's happened, everything that I . . . remember. I'll send it to you and you make the decisions. With her. She called you a giant. Make the right decisions. Protect her."

" *'Vous êtes un soldat . . . arrêtez.'* You have my word. She'll not be harmed."

"That's all I can ask."

Villiers threw the gun on the bed. It landed between the twisted bare legs of the dead woman; the old soldier coughed abruptly, contemptuously, his posture returning. "To practicalities, my young wolfpack," he said, authority coming back to him awkwardly, but with definition. "What's this strategy of yours?"

"To begin with, you're in a state of collapse, beyond shock. You're an automaton walking around in the dark, following instructions you can't understand but have to obey."

"Not very different from reality, wouldn't you say?" interrupted Villiers. "Before a young man with truth in his eyes forced me to listen to him. But how is this perceived state brought about? And why?"

"All you know—all you remember—is that a man broke into your house during the fire and smashed his gun into your head; you fell unconscious. When you woke up you found your wife dead, strangled, a note by her body. It's what's in the note that's driven you out of your mind."

"What would that be?" asked the old soldier cautiously.

"The truth," said Jason. "The truth you can't ever permit anyone to know. What she was to Carlos, what he was to her. The killer who wrote the note left a telephone number, telling you that you could confirm what he's written. Once you were satisfied, you could destroy the note and report the murder any way you like. But for telling you the truth—for killing the whore who was so much a part of your son's death—he wants you to deliver a written message."

"To Carlos?"

"No. He'll send a relay."

"Thank God for that. I'm not sure I could go through with it, knowing it was him."

"The message will reach him."

"What is it?"

"I'll write it out for you; you can give it to the man he sends. It's got to be exact, both in what it says and what it doesn't say." Bourne looked over at the dead woman, at the swelling in her throat. "Do you have any alcohol?"

"A drink?"

"No. Rubbing alcohol. Perfume will do."

"I'm sure there's rubbing alcohol in the medicine cabinet."

"Would you mind getting it for me? Also a towel, please."

"What are you going to do?"

"Put my hands where your hands were. Just in case, although I don't think anyone will question you. While I'm doing that, call whomever you have to call to get me out. The timing's important. I have to be on my way before you call Carlos's relay, long before you call the police. They'd have the airports watched."

"I can delay until daybreak, I imagine. An old man's state of shock, as you put it. Not much longer than that. Where will you go?"

"New York. Can you do it? I have a passport identifying me as a man named George Washburn. It's a good job."

"Making mine far easier. You'll have diplomatic status. Preclearance on both sides of the Atlantic."

"As an Englishman? The passport's British."

"As a NATO accommodation. Conseiller channels; you are part of an Anglo-American team engaged in military negotiations. We favor your swift return to the United States for further instructions. It's not unusual, and sufficient to get you rapidly past both immigration points."

"Good. I've checked the schedules. There's a seven A.M. flight, Air France to Kennedy."

"You'll be on it." The old man paused; he had not finished. He took a step toward Jason. "Why New York? What makes you so certain Carlos will follow you to New York?"

"Two questions with different answers," said Bourne. "I have to deliver him where he marked me for killing four men and a woman I didn't know . . . one of those men very close to me, very much a part of me, I think."

"I don't understand you."

"I'm not sure I do, either. There's no time. It'll all be in what I write down for you on the plane. I have to prove *Carlos knew.* A building in New York. Where it all took place; they've got to understand. He *knew* about it. Trust me."

"I do. The second question, then. Why will he come after you?"

Jason looked again at the dead woman on the bed. "Instinct, maybe. I've killed the one person on earth he cares about. If she were someone else and Carlos killed her, I'd follow him across the world until I found him."

"He may be more practical. I think that was your point to me."

"There's something else," replied Jason, taking his eyes away from Angélique Villiers. "He has nothing to lose, everything to gain. No one knows what he looks like, but he knows me by sight. Still, he doesn't know my state of mind. He's cut me off, isolated me, turned me into someone I was never meant to be. Maybe he was too successful; maybe I'm mad, insane. God knows killing *her* was insane. My threats are irrational. How much more irrational am I? An irrational man, an insane man, is a panicked man. He can be taken out."

"Is your threat irrational? Can you be taken out?"

"I'm not sure. I only know I don't have a choice." *He did not. At the end it was as the beginning. Get Carlos. Trap Carlos. Cain is for Charlie and Delta is for Cain. The man and the myth were finally one, images and reality fused. There was no other way.*

Ten minutes had passed since he had called Marie, lied to Marie, and heard the quiet acceptance in her voice, knowing it meant she needed time to think. She had not believed him, but she believed *in* him,; she, too, had no choice. And he could not ease her pain; there had been no time, there *was* no time. Everything was in motion now, Villiers was downstairs calling an emergency number at France's Conseiller Militaire, arranging for a man with a false passport to fly out of Paris with diplomatic status. In less than three hours a man would be over the Atlantic, approaching the anniversary of his own execution. It was the key; it was the trap. It was the last irrational act, insanity the order of that date.

Bourne stood by the desk; he put down the pen and studied the words he had written on a dead woman's stationery. They were the words a broken, bewildered old man was to repeat over the telephone to an unknown relay who would demand the paper and give it to Ilich Ramirez Sanchez.

I killed your bitch whore and I'll come back for you. There are seventy-one streets in the jungle. A jungle as dense as Tam Quan, but there was a path you missed, a vault in the cellars you did not know about—just as you never knew about me on the day of my execution eleven years ago. One other man knew and you killed him. It doesn't matter. In that vault are documents that will set me free. Did you think I'd become Cain without that final protection? Washington won't dare touch me! It seems right that on the date of Bourne's death, Cain picks up the papers that guarantee him a very long life. You marked Cain. Now I mark you. I'll come back and you can join the whore.

Delta

Jason dropped the note on the desk and walked over to the dead woman. The alcohol was dry, the swollen throat prepared. He bent down and spread his fingers, placing his hands where another's had been placed.

Madness.

34

Early light broke over the spires of the church in Levallois-Perret in northwest Paris, the March morning cold, the night rain replaced by mist. A few old women, returning to their flats from all-night cleaning shifts in the city proper, trudged in and out of the bronze doors, holding railings and prayer books, devotions about to begin or finished with, precious sleep to follow before the drudgery of surviving the daylight hours. Along with the old women were shabbily dressed men—most also old, others pathetically young—holding overcoats together, seeking the warmth of the church, these clutching bottles in their pockets, precious oblivion extended, another day to survive.

One old man, however, did not float in the trancelike movements of the others. He was an old man in a hurry. There was reluctance—even fear, perhaps—in his lined, sallow face, but no hesitation in his progress up the steps and through the doors, past the flickering candles and down the far left aisle of the church. It was an odd hour for a worshiper to seek confession; nevertheless this old beggar went directly to the first booth, parted the curtain and slipped inside.

"Angelus Domini . . ."

"Did you *bring* it?" the whisper demanded, the priestly silhouette behind the curtain trembling with rage.

"Yes. He thrust it in my hand like a man in a stupor, weeping, telling me to get out. He's burned Cain's note to him and says he'll deny everything if a single word is ever mentioned." The old man shoved the pages of writing paper under the curtain.

"He used her stationery—" The assassin's whisper broke, a silhouetted hand brought to a silhouetted head, a muted cry of anguish now heard behind the curtain.

"I urge you to remember, Carlos," pleaded the beggar. "The messenger is not responsible for the news he bears. I could have refused to hear it, refused to bring it to you."

"How? *Why?* . . ."

"Lavier. He followed her to Parc Monceau, then both of them to the church. I saw him in Neuilly-sur-Seine when I was your point. I told you that."

"I know. But *why?* He could have used her in a hundred different ways! Against me! Why *this?*"

"It's in his note. He's gone mad. He was pushed too far, Carlos. It happens; I've seen it happen. A man on a double-entry, his source-controls taken out; he has no one to confirm his initial assignment. Both sides want his corpse. He's stretched to the point where he may not even know who he is any longer."

"He knows . . ." The whisper was drawn out in quiet fury. "By signing the name Delta, he's telling me he knows. We both know where it comes from, where *he* comes from."

The beggar paused. "If that's true, then he's still dangerous to you. He's right. Washington won't touch him. It may not want to acknowledge him, but it will call off its hangmen. It may even be forced to grant him a privilege or two in return for his silence."

"The papers he speaks of?" asked the assassin.

"Yes. In the old days—in Berlin, Prague, Vienna—they were called 'final payments.' Bourne uses 'final protection,' a minor variance. They were papers drawn up between a primary source-control and the infiltrator, to be used in the event the strategy collapsed, the primary killed, no other avenues open to the agent. It was not something you would have studied in Novgorod; the Soviets had no such accommodations. Soviet defectors, however, insisted upon them."

"They were incriminating, then?"

"They had to be to some degree. Generally in the area of who was manipulated. Embarrassment is always to be avoided; careers are destroyed by embarrassment. But then, I don't have to tell you that. You've used the technique brilliantly."

" 'Seventy-one streets in the jungle . . .' " said Carlos, reading from the paper in his hand, an icelike calm imposed on his whisper. "A jungle as dense as Tam Quan.' . . . This time the execution will take place as scheduled. Jason Bourne will not leave *this* Tam Quan alive. By any other name, Cain will be dead, and Delta will die for what he's done. Angélique—you have my word." The incantation stopped, the assassin's mind racing to the practical. "Did Villiers have any idea when Bourne left his house?"

"He didn't know. I told you, he was barely lucid, in as much a state of shock as with his telephone call."

"It doesn't matter. The first flights to the United States began within the past hour. He'll be on one. I'll be in New York with him, and I won't miss this time.

My knife will be waiting, its blade a razor. I'll peel his face away; the Americans will have their Cain without a face! Then they can give this Bourne, this Delta, whatever name they care to."

The blue-striped telephone rang on Alexander Conklin's desk. Its bell was quiet, the understated sound lending an eerie emphasis. The blue-striped telephone was Conklin's direct line to the computer rooms and data banks. There was no one in the office to take the call.

The Central Intelligence executive suddenly rushed limping through the door, unused to the cane provided him by G-2, SHAPE, Brussels, last night when he had commandeered a military transport to Andrews Field, Maryland. He threw the cane angrily across the room as he lurched for the phone. His eyes were bloodshot from lack of sleep, his breath short; the man responsible for the dissolution of Treadstone was exhausted. He had been in scrambler-communication with a dozen branches of clandestine operations—in Washington and overseas—trying to undo the insanity of the past twenty-four hours. He had spread every scrap of information he could cull from the files to every post in Europe, placed agents in the Paris-London-Amsterdam axis on alert. Bourne was alive and dangerous; he had tried to kill his D.C. control; he could be anywhere within ten hours of Paris. All airports and train stations were to be covered, all underground networks activated. Find him! *Kill him!*

"Yes?" Conklin braced himself against the desk and picked up the phone.

"This is Computer Dock 12," said the male voice efficiently. "We may have something. At least, State doesn't have any listing on it."

"*What,* for Christ's sake?"

"The name you gave us four hours ago. Washburn."

"What about it?"

"A George P. Washburn was pre-cleared out of Paris and into New York on an Air France flight this morning. Washburn's a fairly common name; he could be just a businessman with connections, but it was flagged on the readout, and since the status was NATO-diplomatic, we checked with State. They never heard of him. There's no one named Washburn involved with any ongoing NATO negotiations with the French government from any member nation."

"Then how the hell was he pre-cleared? Who gave him the diplomatic?"

"We checked back through Paris; it wasn't easy. Apparently it was an accommodation of the Conseiller Militaire. They're a quiet bunch."

"The Conseiller? Where do they get off clearing *our* people?"

"It doesn't have to be 'our' people or 'their' people; it can be anybody. Just a courtesy from the host country, and that was a French carrier. It's one way to get a decent seat on an overbooked plane. Incidentally, Washburn's passport wasn't even U.S. It was British."

There's a doctor, an Englishman named Washburn . . . It *was* him! It was Delta, and France's Conseiller had cooperated with him. But why New York? What was in New York for him? And who placed so high in Paris would accommodate Delta? What had he told them? Oh, Christ! How *much* had he told them?

"When did the flight get in?" asked Conklin.

"Ten thirty-seven this morning. A little over an hour ago."

"All right," said the man whose foot had been blown off in Medusa, as he slid painfully around the desk into his seat. "You've delivered, and now I want this scratched from the reels. Delete it. Everything you gave me. Is that clear?"

"Understood, sir. Deleted, sir."

Conklin hung up. New York. *New York?* Not Washington, but New York! There was nothing in New York any longer. Delta knew that. If he was after someone in Treadstone—if he was after *him*—he would have taken a flight directly to Dulles. What was in New York?

And why had Delta deliberately used the name Washburn? It was the same as telegraphing a strategy; he knew the name would be picked up sooner or later ... Later ... *After* he was inside the gates! Delta was telling whatever was left of Treadstone that he was dealing from strength. He was in a position to expose not only the Treadstone operation, but he could go God knows how much further. Whole networks he had used as Cain, listening posts and ersatz consulates that were no more than electronic espionage stations ... even the bloody specter of Medusa. His connection inside the Conseiller was his proof to Treadstone how high up he had traveled. His signal that if he could reach within so rarefied a group of strategists, nothing could stop him. Goddamn it, stop him from *what?* What was the point? He had the millions; he could have faded!

Conklin shook his head, remembering. There had been a time when he would have let Delta fade; he had told him so twelve hours ago in a cemetery outside of Paris. A man could take only so much, and no one knew that better than Alexander Conklin, once among the finest covert field officers in the intelligence community. Only so much; the sanctimonious bromides about still being alive grew stale and bitter with time. It depended on what you were before, what you became with your deformity. Only so much ... But Delta did *not* fade! He came back with insane statements, insane demands ... crazy tactics no experienced intelligence officer would even contemplate. For no matter how much explosive information he possessed, no matter how high he penetrated, no sane man walked back into a minefield surrounded by his enemies. And all the blackmail in the world could not bring you back. ...

No sane man. No *sane* man. Conklin sat slowly forward in his chair.

I'm not Cain. He never was. I never was! I wasn't in New York. ... It was Carlos. Not me, Carlos! If what you're saying took place on Seventy-first Street, it was him. He knows!

But Delta *had* been at the brownstone on Seventy-first Street. Prints—third and index fingers, right hand. And the method of transport was now explained: Air France, Conseiller cover ... Fact: Carlos could not have known.

Things come to me ... faces, streets, buildings. Images I can't place ... I know a thousand facts about Carlos, but I don't know why!

Conklin closed his eyes. There was a phrase, a simple code phrase that had been used at the beginning of Treadstone. What was it? It came from Medusa . . . *Cain is for Charlie and Delta is for Cain.* That was it. Cain for *Carlos.* Delta-Bourne became the Cain that was the decoy for Carlos.

Conklin opened his eyes. Jason Bourne was to replace Ilich Ramirez Sanchez. That was the entire strategy of Treadstone Seventy-One. It was the keystone to the whole structure of deception, the parallax that would draw Carlos out of position into their sights.

Bourne. Jason Bourne. The totally unknown man, a name buried for over a decade, a piece of human debris left in a jungle. But he *had* existed; that, too, was part of the strategy.

Conklin separated the folders on his desk until he found the one he was looking for. It had no title, only an initial and two numbers followed by a black *X*, signifying that it was the only folder containing the origins of Treadstone.

T-71 X. The birth of Treadstone Seventy-One.

He opened it, almost afraid to see what he knew was there.

Date of execution. Tam Quan Sector. March 25 . . .

Conklin's eyes moved to the calendar on his desk.

March 24.

"Oh, my God," he whispered, reaching for the telephone.

Dr. Morris Panov walked through the double doors of the psychiatric ward on the third floor of Bethesda's Naval Annex and approached the nurses' counter. He smiled at the uniformed aide shuffling index cards under the stern gaze of the head floor nurse standing beside her. Apparently the young trainee had misplaced a patient's file—if not a patient—and her superior was not about to let it happen again.

"Don't let Annie's whip fool you," said Panov to the flustered girl. "Underneath those cold, inhuman eyes is a heart of sheer granite. Actually, she escaped from the fifth floor two weeks ago but we're all afraid to tell anybody."

The aide giggled; the nurse shook her head in exasperation. The phone rang on the desk behind the counter.

"Will you get that, please, dear," said Annie to the young girl. The aide nodded and retreated to the desk. The nurse turned to Panov. "Doctor Mo, how am I ever going to get anything through their heads with you around?"

"With love, dear Annie. With love. But don't lose your bicycle chains."

"You're incorrigible. Tell me, how's your patient in Five-A? I know you're worried about him."

"I'm still worried."

"I hear you stayed up all night."

"There was a three A.M. movie on television I wanted to see."

"Don't do it, Mo," said the matronly nurse. "You're too young to end up in there."

"And maybe too old to avoid it, Annie. But thanks."

Suddenly Panov and the nurse were aware that he was being paged, the wide-eyed trainee at the desk speaking into the microphone.

"Dr. Panov, please. Telephone for—"

"*I'm* Dr. Panov," said the psychiatrist in a *sotto voce* whisper to the girl. "We don't want anyone to know. Annie Donovan here's really my mother from Poland. Who is it?"

The trainee stared at Panov's ID card on his white coat; she blinked and replied. "A Mr. Alexander Conklin, sir."

"Oh?" Panov was startled. Alex Conklin had been a patient on and off for five years, until they both had agreed he'd adjusted as well as he was ever going to adjust—which was not a hell of a lot. There were so many, and so little they can do for them. Whatever Conklin wanted had to be relatively serious for him to call Bethesda and not the office. "Where can I take this, Annie?"

"Room One," said the nurse, pointing across the hall. "It's empty. I'll have the call transferred."

Panov walked toward the door, an uneasy feeling spreading through him.

"I need some very fast answers, Mo," said Conklin, his voice strained.

"I'm not very good at fast answers, Alex. Why not come in and see me this afternoon?"

"It's not me. It's someone else. Possibly."

"No games, please. I thought we'd gone beyond that."

"No games. This is a Four-Zero emergency, and I need help."

"Four-Zero? Call in one of your staff men. I've never requested that kind of clearance."

"I can't. That's how tight it is."

"Then you'd better whisper to God."

"Mo, *please!* I only have to confirm possibilities, the rest I can put together myself. And I don't have five seconds to waste. A man may be running around ready to blow away ghosts, anyone he thinks is a ghost. He's already killed very real, very important people and I'm not sure he knows it. Help me, help *him!*"

"If I can. Go ahead."

"A man is placed in a highly volatile, maximum stress situation for a long period of time, the entire period in deep cover. The cover itself is a decoy—very visible, very negative, constant pressure applied to maintain that visibility. The purpose is to draw out a target similar to the decoy by convincing the target that the decoy's a threat, forcing the target into the open. . . . Are you with me so far?"

"So far," said Panov. "You say there's been constant pressure on the decoy to maintain a negative, highly visible profile. What's been his environment?"

"As brutal as you can imagine."

"For how long a period of time?"

"Three years."

"Good God," said the psychiatrist. "No breaks?"

"None at all. Twenty-four hours a day, three hundred and sixty-five days a year. Three years. Someone not himself."

"When will you damn fools learn? Even prisoners in the worst camps could be themselves, talk to others who were themselves—" Panov stopped, catching his own words and Conklin's meaning. "That's your point, isn't it?"

"I'm not sure," answered the intelligence officer. "It's hazy, confusing, even contradictory. What I want to ask is this. Could such a man under these circumstances begin to . . . believe he's the decoy, assume the characteristics, absorb the mocked dossier to the point where he believes it's him?"

"The answer to that's so obvious I'm surprised you ask it. Of course he could. Probably would. It's an unendurably prolonged performance that can't be sustained unless the belief becomes a part of his everyday reality. The actor never off the stage in a play that never ends. Day after day, night after night." The doctor stopped again, then continued carefully. "But that's not really your question, is it?"

"No," replied Conklin. "I go one step further. Beyond the decoy. I have to; it's the only thing that makes sense."

"Wait a minute," interrupted Panov sharply. "You'd better stop there, because I'm not confirming any blind diagnosis. Not for what you're leading up to. No way, Charlie. That's giving you a license I won't be responsible for—with or without a consultation fee."

" 'No way . . . *Charlie.*' Why did you say that, Mo?"

"What do you mean, why did I say it? It's a phrase. I hear it all the time. Kids in dirty blue jeans on the corner; hookers in my favorite saloons."

"How do you know what I'm leading up to?" said the CIA man.

"Because I had to read the books and you're not very subtle. You're about to describe a classic case of paranoid schizophrenia with multiple personalities. It's not just your man assuming the role of the *decoy,* but the decoy himself transferring *his* identity to the one he's after. The *target.* That's what you're driving at, Alex. You're telling me your man is three people: himself, decoy and target. And I repeat. No way, Charlie. I'm not confirming anything remotely like that without an extensive examination. That's giving you rights you can't have: three reasons for dispatch. No way!"

"I'm not asking you to confirm anything! I just want to know if it's *possible.* For Christ's sake, Mo, there's a lethally experienced man running around with a gun, killing people he claims he didn't know, but whom he worked with for three years. He denies being at a specific place at a specific time when his own fingerprints prove he was there. He says images come to him—faces he can't place, names he's heard but doesn't know from where. He claims he was never the decoy; it was never him! But it was! It *is!* Is it *possible?* That's all I want to know. Could the stress and time and the everyday pressures break him like this? Into three?"

Panov held his breath for a moment. "It's possible," he said softly. "If your facts are accurate, it's possible. That's all I'll say, because there are too many other possibilities."

"Thank you." Conklin paused. "A last question. Say there was a date—a month and a day—that was significant to the mocked dossier—the decoy's dossier."

"You'd have to be more specific."

"I will. It was the date when the man whose identity was taken for decoy was killed."

"Then obviously not part of the working dossier, but known to your man. Am I following you?"

"Yes, he knew it. Let's say he was there. Would he remember it?"

"Not as the decoy."

"But as one of the other two?"

"Assuming the target was also aware of it, or that he'd communicated it through his transference, yes."

"There's also a place where the strategy was conceived, where the decoy was created. If our man was in the vicinity of that place, and the date of death was close at hand, would he be drawn to it? Would it surface and become important to him?"

"It would if it was associated with the original place of death. Because the decoy was born there; it's possible. It would depend on who he was at the moment."

"Suppose he was the target?"

"And knew the location?"

"Yes, because another part of him had to."

"Then he'd be drawn to it. It would be a subconscious compulsion."

"Why?"

"To kill the decoy. He'd kill everything in sight, but the main objective would be the decoy. Himself."

Alexander Conklin replaced the phone, his nonexistent foot throbbing, his thoughts so convoluted he had to close his eyes again to find a consistent strain. He had been wrong in Paris . . . in a cemetery outside of Paris. He had wanted to kill a man for the wrong reasons, the right ones beyond his comprehensions. He *was* dealing with a madman. Someone whose afflictions were not explained in twenty years of training, but were understandable if one thought about the pains and the losses, the unending waves of violence . . . all ending in futility. No one knew anything really. Nothing made sense. A Carlos was trapped, killed today, and another would take his place. Why did we do it . . . David?

David. I say your name finally. We were friends once, David . . . Delta. I knew your wife and your children. We drank together and had a few dinners together in far-off posts in Asia. You were the best foreign service officer in the Orient and everyone knew it. You were going to be the key to the new policy, the one that was around the corner. And then it happened. Death from the skies in the Mekong.

You turned, David. We all lost, but only one of us became Delta. In Medusa. I did not know you that well—drinks and a dinner or two do not a close companion make—but few of us become animals. You did, Delta.

And now you must die. Nobody can afford you any longer. None of us.

"Leave us, please," said General Villiers to his aide, as he sat down opposite Marie St. Jacques in the Montmartre café. The aide nodded and walked to a table ten feet away from the booth; he would leave but he was still on guard. The exhausted old soldier looked at Marie. "Why did you insist on my coming here? He wanted you out of Paris. I gave him my word."

"Out of Paris, out of the race," said Marie, touched by the sight of the old man's haggard face. "I'm sorry. I don't want to be another burden for you. I heard the reports on the radio."

"Insanity," said Villiers, picking up the brandy his aide had ordered for him. "Three hours with the police, living a terrible lie, condemning a man for a crime that was mine alone."

"The description was accurate, uncannily accurate. No one could miss him."

"He gave it to me himself. He sat in front of my wife's mirror and told me what to say, looking at his own face in the strangest manner. He said it was the only way. Carlos could only be convinced by my going to the police, creating a manhunt. He was right, of course."

"He was right," agreed Marie, "but he's not in Paris, or Brussels, or Amsterdam."

"I beg your pardon?"

"I want you to tell me where he's gone."

"He told you himself."

"He lied to me."

"How can you be certain?"

"Because I know when he tells me the truth. You see, we both listen for it."

"You both . . .? I'm afraid I don't understand."

"I didn't think you would; I was sure he hadn't told you. When he lied to me on the phone, saying the things he said so hesitantly, knowing I knew they were lies, I couldn't understand. I didn't piece it together until I heard the radio reports. Yours and another. That description . . . so complete, so total, even to the scar on his left temple. Then I knew. He wasn't going to stay in Paris, or within five hundred miles of Paris. He was going far away—where that description wouldn't mean very much—where Carlos could be led, delivered to the people Jason had his agreement with. Am I right?"

Villiers put down the glass. "I've given my word. You're to be taken to safety in the country. I don't understand the things you're saying."

"Then I'll try to be clearer," said Marie, leaning forward. "There was another report on the radio, one you obviously didn't hear because you were with the police or in seclusion. Two men were found shot to death in a cemetery near Rambouillet this morning. One was a known killer from Saint-Gervais. The other was identified as a former American Intelligence officer living in Paris, a highly controversial man who killed a journalist in Vietnam and was given the choice of retiring from the army or facing a court-martial."

"Are you saying the incidents are related?" asked the old man.

"Jason was instructed by the American Embassy to go to that cemetery last night to meet with a man flying over from Washington."

"*Washington?*"

"Yes. His agreement was with a small group of men from American Intelligence. They tried to kill him last night; they think they have to kill him."

"Good God, why?"

"Because they can't trust him. They don't know what he's done or where he's been for a long period of time and he can't tell them." Marie paused, closing her eyes briefly. "He doesn't know who he is. He doesn't know who *they* are; and the man from Washington hired other men to kill him last night. That man wouldn't listen; they think he's betrayed them, stolen millions from them, killed men he's never heard of. He hasn't. But he doesn't have any clear answers, either. He's a man with only fragments of a memory, each fragment condemning him. He's a near total amnesiac."

Villiers' lined face was locked in astonishment, his eyes pained in recollection. "For all the wrong reasons . . .' He said that to me. 'They have men everywhere . . . the orders are to execute me on sight. I'm hunted by men I don't know and can't see. For all the wrong reasons.' "

"For *all* the wrong reasons," emphasized Marie, reaching across the narrow table and touching the old man's arm. "And they do have men everywhere, men ordered to kill him on sight. Wherever he goes, they'll be waiting."

"How will they know where he's gone?"

"He'll tell them. It's part of his strategy. And when he does, they'll kill him. He's walking into his own trap."

For several moments Villiers was silent, his guilt overwhelming. Finally he spoke in a whisper. "Almighty God, what have I done?"

"What you thought was right. What he convinced you was right. You can't blame yourself. Or him, really."

"He said he was going to write out everything that had happened to him, everything that he remembered . . . How painful that statement must have been for him! I can't wait for that letter, mademoiselle. We can't wait. I must know everything you can tell me. Now."

"What can you do?"

"Go to the American Embassy. To the ambassador. Now. *Everything.*"

Marie St. Jacques withdrew her hand slowly as she leaned back in the booth, her dark red hair against the banquette. Her eyes were far away, clouded with the mist of tears. "He told me his life began for him on a small island in the Mediterranean called Ile de Port Noir. . . ."

The secretary of state walked angrily into the office of the director of Consular Operations, the department's section dealing with clandestine activities. He strode across the room to the desk of the astonished director, who rose at the sight of this powerful man, his expression a mixture of shock and bewilderment.

"Mr. Secretary? . . . I didn't receive any message from your office, sir. I would have come upstairs right away."

The secretary of state slapped a yellow legal pad down on the director's desk. On the top page was a column of six names written with the broad strokes of a felt-tipped pen.

BOURNE

DELTA

MEDUSA

CAIN

CARLOS

TREADSTONE

"What is this?" asked the secretary. "What the hell *is* this?"

The director of Cons-Op leaned over the desk. "I don't know, sir. They're names, of course. A code for the alphabet—the letter D—and a reference to Medusa; that's still classified, but I've heard of it. And I suppose the 'Carlos' refers to the assassin; I wish we knew more about him. But I've never heard of 'Bourne' or 'Cain' or 'Treadstone.' "

"Then come up to my office and listen to a tape of a telephone conversation that I've just had with Paris and you'll learn all about them!" exploded the secretary of state. "There are extraordinary things on that tape, including killings in Ottawa and Paris, and some very strange dealings our First Secretary in the Montaigne had with a CIA man. There's also outright lying to the authorities of foreign governments, to our *own* intelligence units, and to the European newspapers—with neither the knowledge nor the consent of the Department of State! There's been a global deception that's spread misinformation throughout more countries than I want to think about. We're flying over, under a deep-diplomatic, a Canadian woman—an economist for the government in Ottawa who's wanted for murder in Zurich. We're being *forced* to grant asylum to a fugitive, to subvert the laws—because if that woman's telling the truth, we've got our ass in a sling! I want to know what's been going on. Cancel everything on your calendar—and I mean *everything.* You're spending the rest of the day and all night if you have to digging this damn thing out of the ground. There's a man walking around who doesn't know who he is, but with more classified information in his head than ten intelligence computers!"

It was past midnight when the exhausted director of Consular Operations made the connection; he had nearly missed it. The First Secretary at the embassy in Paris, under threat of instant dismissal, had given him Alexander Conklin's name. But Conklin was nowhere to be found. He had returned to Washington on a military jet out of Brussels in the morning, but had signed out of Langley at 1:22 in the afternoon, leaving no telephone number—not even an emergency number—where he could be reached. And from what the director had learned about

Conklin, that omission was extraordinary. The CIA man was what was commonly referred to as a shark-killer; he directed individual strategies throughout the world where defection and treason were suspected. There were too many men in too many stations who might need his approval or disapproval at any given moment. It was not logical he would sever that cord for twelve hours. What was also unusual was the fact that his telephone logs had been scratched; there were none for the past two days—and the Central Intelligence Agency had very specific regulations concerning those logs. Traceable accountability was the new order of the new regime. However, the director of Cons-Op had learned one fact: Conklin had been attached to Medusa.

Using the threat of State Department retaliation, the director had requested a closed circuit readout of Conklin's logs for the past five weeks. Reluctantly, the Agency beamed them over and the director had sat in front of a screen for two hours, instructing the operators at Langley to keep the tape repeating until he told them to stop.

Eighty-six logicals had been called, the word Treadstone mentioned; none had responded. Then the director went back to the possibles; there was an army man he had not considered because of his well-known antipathy to the CIA. But Conklin had telephoned him twice during the space of twelve minutes a week ago. The director called his sources at the Pentagon and found what he was looking for: Medusa.

Brigadier General Irwin Arthur Crawford, current ranking officer in charge of Army Intelligence data banks, former commander, Saigon, attached to covert operations—still classified. *Medusa.*

The director picked up the conference room phone; it bypassed the switchboard. He dialed the brigadier's home in Fairfax, and on the fourth ring, Crawford answered. The State Department man identified himself and asked if the general cared to return a call to State and be put through for verification.

"Why would I want to do that?"

"It concerns a matter that comes under the heading of Treadstone."

"I'll call you back."

He did so in eighteen seconds, and within the next two minutes the director had delivered the outlines of State's information.

"There's nothing there we don't know about," said the brigadier. "There's been a control committee on this from the beginning, the Oval Office given a preliminary summation within a week of the inauguration. Our objective warranted the procedures, you may be assured of that."

"I'm willing to be convinced," replied the man from State. "Is this related to that business in New York a week ago? Elliot Stevens—that Major Webb and David Abbott? Where the circumstances were, shall we say, considerably altered?"

"You were aware of the alterations?"

"I'm the head of Cons-Op, General."

"Yes, you would be . . . Stevens wasn't married; the rest understood. Robbery and homicide were preferable. The answer is affirmative."

"I see . . . Your man Bourne flew into New York yesterday morning."

"I know. We know—that is Conklin and myself. We're the inheritors."

"You've been in touch with Conklin?"

"I last spoke to him around one o'clock in the afternoon. Unlogged. He insisted on it, frankly."

"He's checked out of Langley. There's no number where he can be reached."

"I know that, too. Don't try. With all due respect, tell the Secretary to back away. You back away. Don't get involved."

"We *are* involved, General. We're flying over the Canadian woman by diplomatic."

"For God's sake, why?"

"We were forced to; she forced us to."

"Then keep her in isolation. You've *got* to! She's *our* resolve, we'll be responsible."

"I think you'd better explain."

"We're dealing with an *insane* man. A multiple schizophrenic. He's a walking firing squad; he could kill a dozen innocent people with one outburst, one explosion in his own head, and he wouldn't know why."

"How do you know?"

"Because he's already killed. That massacre in New York—it was *him*. He killed Stevens, the Monk, Webb—above all, Webb—and two others you never heard of. We understand now. He *wasn't* responsible, but that can't change anything. Leave him to us. To Conklin."

"Bourne?"

"Yes. We have proof. Prints. They were confirmed by the Bureau. It was him."

"Your man would leave prints?"

"He did."

"He couldn't have," said the man from State finally.

"What?"

"Tell me, where did you come up with the conclusion of insanity? This multiple schizophrenia or whatever the hell you call it."

"Conklin spoke to a psychiatrist—one of the best—an authority on stress-breakdowns. Alex described the history—and it was brutal. The doctor confirmed our suspicions, Conklin's suspicions."

"He *confirmed* them?" asked the director, stunned.

"Yes."

"Based on what Conklin said? On what he *thought* he knew?"

"There's no other explanation. Leave him to us. He's our problem."

"You're a damn fool, General. You should have stuck to your data banks or maybe more primitive artillery."

"I resent that."

"Resent it all you like. If you've done what I think you've done, you may not have anything left but resentment."

"Explain that," said Crawfore harshly.

"You're not dealing with a madman, or with insanity, or with any goddamned multiple schizophrenia—which I doubt you know any more about than I do. You're dealing with an *amnesiac,* a man who's been trying for months to find out who he is and where he comes from. And from a telephone tape we've got over here, we gather he tried to tell you—tried to tell Conklin, but Conklin wouldn't listen. None of you would *listen* . . . You sent a man out in deep cover for three years—three *years*—to pull in Carlos, and when the strategy broke, you assumed the worst."

"Amnesia? . . . No, you're wrong! I spoke to Conklin; he *did* listen. You don't understand; we both knew—"

"I don't want to hear his name!" broke in the director of Consular Operations.

The general paused. "We both knew . . . Bourne . . . years ago. I think you know from where; you read the name off to me. He was the strangest man I ever met, as close to being paranoid as anyone in that outfit. He undertook missions—risks—no sane man would accept. Yet he never asked for anything. He was filled with so much hate."

"And that made him a candidate for a psychiatric ward ten years later?"

"Seven years," corrected Crawford. "I tried to prevent his selection in Treadstone. But the Monk said he was the best. I couldn't argue with that, not in terms of expertise. But I made my objections known. He was psychologically a borderline case; we knew why. I was proven right. I stand on that."

"You're not going to stand on anything, General. You're going to fall right on your iron ass. Because the Monk was right. Your man *is* the best, with or without a memory. He's bringing in Carlos, delivering him right to your goddamn front door. That is, he's bringing him in unless you kill Bourne first." Crawford's low, sharp intake of breath was precisely what the director was afraid he might hear. He continued. "You can't reach Conklin, can you?" he asked.

"No."

"He's gone under, hasn't he? Made his own arrangements, payments funneled through third and fourth parties unknown to each other, the source untraceable, all connections to the Agency and Treadstone obliterated. And by now there are photographs in the hands of men Conklin doesn't know, wouldn't recognize if they held him up. Don't talk to me about firing squads. Yours is in place, but you can't see it—you don't know where it is. But it's prepared—a half a dozen rifles ready to fire when the condemned man comes into view. Am I reading the scenario?"

"You don't expect me to answer that," said Crawford.

"You don't have to. This is Consular Operations; I've been there before. But you were right about one thing. This *is* your problem; it's right back in your court. We're not going to be touched by you. That's my recommendation to the

Secretary. The State Department can't afford to know who you are. Consider this call unlogged."

"Understood."

"I'm sorry," said the director, meaning it, hearing the futility in the general's voice. "It all blows up sometimes."

"Yes. We learned that in Medusa. What are you going to do with the girl?"

"We don't even know what we're going to do with you yet."

"That's easy. Eisenhower at the summit: 'What U-Twos?' We'll go along; no preliminary summation. Nothing. We can get the girl off the Zurich books."

"We'll tell her. It may help. We'll be making apologies all over the place; with her we'll try for a very substantial settlement."

"Are you *sure?*" interrupted Crawford.

"About the settlement?"

"No. The amnesia. Are you positive?"

"I've listened to that tape at least twenty times, heard her voice. I've never been so sure of anything in my life. Incidentally, she got in several hours ago. She's at the Pierre Hotel under guard. We'll bring her down to Washington in the morning after we figure out what we're going to do."

"Wait a minute!" The general's voice rose. "Not tomorrow! She's here . . .? Can you get me clearance to see her?"

"Don't dig that grave of yours any deeper, General. The fewer names she knows, the better. She was with Bourne when he was calling the embassy; she's aware of the First Secretary, probably Conklin by now. He may have to take the fall himself. Stay out of it."

"You just told me to *play* it out."

"Not this way. You're a decent man; so am I. We're professionals."

"You don't understand! We have photographs, yes, but they may be useless. They're three years old, and Bourne's changed, changed drastically. It's why Conklin's on the scene—where I don't know—but he's there. He's the only one who's seen him, but it was night, raining. She may be our only chance. She's been with him—living with him for weeks. She *knows* him. It's possible that she'd recognize him before anyone else."

"I don't understand."

"I'll spell it out. Among Bourne's many, many talents is the ability to change his appearance, melt into a crowd or a field or a cluster of trees—be where you can't see him. If what you say is so, he wouldn't remember, but we used to have a word for him in Medusa. His men used to call him . . . a chameleon."

"That's your Cain, General."

"It was our Delta. There was no one like him. And that's why the girl can help. Now. Clear me! Let me see her, talk to her."

"By clearing you, we acknowledge you. I don't think we can do that."

"For God's sake, you just said we were decent men! Are we? We can save his life! Maybe. If she's with me and we find him, we can get him out of there!"

"There? Are you telling me you know exactly where he's going to be?"

"Yes."

"How?"

"Because he wouldn't go anywhere else."

"And the time span?" asked the incredulous director of Consular Operations. "You know *when* he's going to be there?"

"Yes. Today. It's the date of his own execution."

35

Rock music blared from the transistor radio with tin-like vibrations as the long-haired driver of the Yellow Cab slapped his hand against the rim of the steering wheel and jolted his jaw with the beat. The taxi edged east on Seventy-first Street, locked into the line of cars that began at the exit on the East River Drive. Tempers flared as engines roared in place and cars lurched forward only to slam to sudden stops, inches away from bumpers in front. It was 8:45 in the morning, New York's rush hour traffic as usual a contradiction in terms.

Bourne wedged himself into the corner of the back seat and stared at the tree-lined street beneath the rim of his hat and through the dark lenses of his sunglasses. He had *been* there; it was all indelible. He had walked the pavements, seen the doorways and the storefronts and the walls covered with ivy—so out of place in the city, yet so right for this street. He had glanced up before and had noticed the roof gardens, relating them to a gracious garden several blocks away toward the park, beyond a pair of elegant French doors at the far end of a large . . . complicated . . . room. That room was inside a tall, narrow building of brown, jagged stone, with a column of wide, lead-paned windows rising four stories above the pavement. Windows made of thick glass that refracted light both inside and out in subtle flashes of purple and blue. Antique glass, perhaps, ornamental glass . . . bulletproof glass. A brownstone residence with a set of thick outside steps. They were odd steps, unusual steps, each level crisscrossed with black ridges that protruded above the surface, protecting the descender from the elements. Shoes going down would not slip on ice or snow . . . and the weight of anyone climbing up would trigger electronic devices inside.

Jason knew that house, knew they were coming closer to it. The echo in his chest accelerated and became louder as they entered the block. He would see it any moment, and as he held his wrist, he knew why Parc Monceau had struck such chords in his mind's eye. That small part of Paris was so much like this short stretch of the Upper East Side. Except for an isolated intrusion of an unkempt stoop or an ill-conceived whitewashed façade, they could be identical blocks.

He thought of André Villiers. He had written down everything he could remember since a memory had been given him in the pages of a notebook hastily purchased at Charles de Gaulle Airport. From the first moment when a living, bullet-ridden man had opened his eyes in a humid, dingy room on Ile de Port Noir through the frightening revelations of Marseilles, Zurich and Paris—especially Paris, where the specter of an assassin's mantle had fallen over his shoulders, the expertise of a killer proven to be his. By any standards, it was a confession, as damning in what it could not explain as in what it described. But it was the truth as he knew the truth, infinitely more exculpatory after his death than before it. In the hands of André Villiers it would be used well; the right decisions would be made for Marie St. Jacques. That knowledge gave him the freedom he needed now. He had sealed the pages in an envelope and mailed it to Parc Monceau from Kennedy Airport. By the time it reached Paris he would be alive or he would be dead; he would kill Carlos or Carlos would kill him. Somewhere on that street—so like a street thousands of miles away—a man whose shoulders floated rigidly above a tapered waist would come after him. It was the only thing he was absolutely sure of; he would do the same. Somewhere on that street . . .

There it was! It was *there,* the morning sun bouncing off the black enameled door and the shiny brass hardware, penetrating the thick, lead-paned windows that rose like a wide column of glistening, purplish blue, emphasizing the ornamental splendor of the glass, but not its resistance to the impacts of high-powered rifles and heavy-calibered automatic weapons. He was *here,* and for reasons—emotions—he could not define, his eyes began to tear and there was a swelling in his throat. He had the incredible feeling that he had come back to a place that was as much a part of him as his body or what was left of his mind. Not a home; there was no comfort, no serenity found in looking at that elegant East Side residence. But there was something else—an overpowering sensation of—*return.* He was back at the beginning, *the* beginning, at both departure and creation, black night and bursting dawn. Something was happening to him; he gripped his wrist harder, desperately trying to control the almost uncontrollable impulse to jump out of the taxi and race across the street to that monstrous, silent structure of jagged stone and deep blue glass. He wanted to leap up the steps and hammer his fist against the heavy black door.

Let me in! I am here! You must let me in! Can't you understand?
I AM INSIDE!

Images welled up in front of his eyes; jarring sounds assaulted his ears. A jolting, throbbing pain kept exploding at his temples. He was inside a dark room—*that* room—staring at a screen, at other, inner images that kept flashing on and off in rapid, blinding succession.

Who is he? Quickly. You're too late! You're a dead man. Where is this street? What does it mean to you? Whom did you meet there? What? Good. Keep it simple; say as little as possible. Here's a list: eight names. Which are contacts?

Quickly! Here's another. Methods of matching kills. Which are yours? . . . No, no, no! Delta might do that, not Cain! You are not Delta, you are not you! You are Cain. You are a man named Bourne. Jason Bourne! You slipped back. Try again. Concentrate! Obliterate everything else. Wipe away the past. It does not exist for you. You are only what you are here, became here!

Oh, God. Marie had said it.

Maybe you just know what you've been told. . . . Over and over and over again. Until there was nothing else. . . . Things you've been told . . . but you can't relive . . . because they're not you.

The sweat rolled down his face, stinging his eyes, as he dug his fingers into his wrist, trying to push the pain and the sounds and the flashes of light out of his mind. He had written Carlos that he was coming back for hidden documents that were his . . . "final protection." At that time, the phrase had struck him as weak; he had nearly crossed it out, wanting a stronger reason for flying to New York. Yet instinct had told him to let it stand; it was a part of his past . . . somehow. Now he understood. His identity was inside that house. His *identity*. And whether Carlos came after him or not, he had to find it. He *had* to!

It was suddenly insane! He shook his head violently back and forth trying to suppress the compulsion, to still the screams that were all around him—screams that were his screams, his voice. *Forget Carlos. Forget the trap. Get inside that house! It was there; it was the beginning!*

Stop it!

The irony was macabre. There was no final protection in that house, only a final explanation for himself. And it was meaningless without Carlos. Those who hunted him knew it and disregarded it; they wanted him dead because of it. But he was so close . . . he had to find it. It was there.

Bourne glanced up; the long-haired driver was watching him in the rearview mirror. "Migraine," said Jason curtly. "Drive around the block. To this block again. I'm early for my appointment. I'll tell you where to let me off."

"It's your wallet, mister."

The brownstone was behind them now, passed quickly in a sudden, brief break in the traffic. Bourne swung around in the seat and looked at it through the rear window. The seizure was receding, the sights and sound of personal panic fading; only the pain remained, but it too would diminish, he knew that. It had been an extraordinary few minutes. Priorities had become twisted; compulsion had replaced reason, the pull of the unknown had been so strong that for a moment or two he had nearly lost control. He could not let it happen again; the trap itself was everything. He had to see that house again; he had to study it again. He had all day to work, to refine his strategy, his tactics for the night, but a second, calmer appraisal was in order now. Others would come during the day, closer appraisals. The chameleon in him would be put to work.

Sixteen minutes later it was obvious that whatever he intended to study no longer mattered. Suddenly, everything was different, everything had changed. The line of traffic in the block was slower, another hazard added to the street.

A moving van had parked in front of the brownstone; men in coveralls stood smoking cigarettes and drinking coffee, putting off that moment when work was to commence. The heavy black door was open and a man in a green jacket, the moving company's emblem above the left pocket, stood in the foyer, a clipboard in his hand. Treadstone was being dismantled! In a few hours it could be gutted, a shell! It couldn't be! They had to stop!

Jason leaned forward, money in his hand, the pain gone from his head; all was movement now. He had to reach Conklin in Washington. Not later—not when the chess pieces were in place—but right now! Conklin had to tell them to stop! His entire strategy was based on darkness . . . always darkness. The beam of a flashlight shooting out of first one alleyway, then another, then against dark walls and up at darkened windows. Orchestrated properly, swiftly, darting from one position to another. An assassin would be drawn to a stone building at night. At *night.* It would happen at night! Not now! He got out.

"Hey, mister!" yelled the driver through the open window.

Jason bent down. "What is it?"

"I just wanted to say thanks. This makes my—"

A *spit.* Over his shoulder! Followed by a cough that was the start of a scream. Bourne stared at the driver, at the stream of blood that had erupted over the man's left ear. The man was dead, killed by a bullet meant for his fare, fired from a window somewhere in that street.

Jason dropped to the ground, then sprang to his left spinning toward the curb. Two more spits came in rapid succession, the first imbedded in the side of the taxi, the second exploding the asphalt. It was unbelievable! He was marked before the hunt had begun! Carlos was *there.* In position! He or one of his men had taken the high ground, a window or a rooftop from which the entire street could be observed. Yet the possibility of indiscriminate death caused by a killer in a window or on a rooftop was crazy; the police would come, the street blocked off, even a reverse trap aborted. And Carlos was *not* crazy! It did not make sense. Nor did Bourne have the time to speculate; he had to get out of the trap . . . the reverse trap. *He had to get to that phone.* Carlos was here! At the doors of Treadstone! He had brought him back. He had actually brought him back! It was his proof!

He got to his feet and began running, weaving in and out of the groups of pedestrians. He reached the corner and turned right—the booth was twenty feet away, but it was also a target. He could not use it.

Across the street was a delicatessen, a small rectangular sign above the door: TELEPHONE. He stepped off the curb and started running again, dodging the lurching automobiles. One of them might do the job Carlos had reserved for himself. That irony, too, was macabre.

"The Central Intelligence Agency, sir, is fundamentally a fact-finding organization," said the man on the line condescendingly. "The sort of activities you describe are the rarest part of our work, and frankly blown out of proportion by films and misinformed writers."

"Goddamn it, *listen* to me!" said Jason, cupping the mouthpiece in the crowded delicatessen. "Just tell me where Conklin is. It's an emergency!"

"His office already told you, sir. Mr. Conklin left yesterday afternoon and is expected back at the end of the week. Since you say you know Mr. Conklin, you're aware of his service-related injury. He often goes for physical therapy—"

"Will you *stop* it! I saw him in Paris—outside of Paris—two nights ago. He flew over from Washington to meet me."

"As to that," interrupted the man in Langley, "when you were transferred to this office, we'd already checked. There's no record of Mr. Conklin having left the country in over a year."

"Then it's buried! He was there! You're looking for codes," said Bourne desperately. "I don't have them. But someone working with Conklin will recognize the words. Medusa, Delta, Cain . . . Treadstone! Someone *has* to!"

"No one does. You were told that."

"By someone who doesn't. There are those who do. Believe me!"

"I'm sorry. I really—"

"Don't hang up!" There was another way; one he did not care to use, but there was nothing else. "Five or six minutes ago, I got out of a taxi on Seventy-first Street. I was spotted and someone tried to take me out."

"Take . . . you out?"

"Yes. The driver spoke to me and I bent down to listen. That movement saved my life, but the driver's dead, a bullet in his skull. That's the truth, and I know you have ways of checking. There are probably half a dozen police cars on the scene by now. Check it out. That's the strongest advice I can give you."

There was a brief silence from Washington. "Since you asked for Mr. Conklin—at least used his name—I'll follow this up. Where can I reach you?"

"I'll stay on. This call's on an international credit card. French issue, name of Chamford."

"Chamford? You said—"

"*Please.*"

"I'll be back."

The waiting was intolerable, made worse by a stern Hassid glaring at him, fingering coins in one hand, a roll in another, and crumbs in his stringy, unkempt beard. A minute later the man in Langley was on the line, anger replacing compromise.

"I think this conversation has come to an end, Mr. Bourne or Chamford, or whatever you call yourself. The New York police were reached; there's no such incident as you described on Seventy-first Street. And you were right. We do have ways of checking. I advise you that there are laws about such calls as this, strict penalties involved. Good day, sir."

There was a click; the line went dead. Bourne stared at the dial in disbelief. For months the men in Washington had searched for him, wanted to kill him for the silence they could not understand. Now, when he presented himself— presented them with the sole objective of his three-year agreement—he was dismissed. They still would not listen! But that man *had* listened. And he had come back on the line denying a death that had taken place only minutes ago. It could not be . . . it was *insane*. It had *happened*.

Jason put the phone back on the hook, tempted to bolt from the crowded delicatessen. Instead, he walked calmly toward the door, excusing himself through the rows of people lined up at the counter, his eyes on the glass front, scanning the crowds on the sidewalk. Outside, he removed his topcoat, carrying it over his arm, and replaced the sunglasses with his tortoise-shells. Minor alterations, but he would not be where he was going long enough for them to be a major mistake. He hurried across the intersection toward Seventy-first Street.

At the far corner he fell in with a group of pedestrians waiting for the light. He turned his head to the left, his chin pressed down into his collarbone. The traffic was moving but the taxi was gone. It had been removed from the scene with surgical precision, a diseased, ugly organ cut from the body, the vital functions in normal process. It showed the precision of a master assassin, who knew precisely when to go in swiftly with a knife.

Bourne turned quickly, reversing his direction, and began walking south. He had to find a store; he had to change his outer skin. The chameleon could not wait.

Marie St. Jacques was angry as she held her place across the room from Brigadier General Irwin Arthur Crawford in the suite at the Pierre Hotel. "You wouldn't listen!" she accused. "None of you would listen. Have you any idea what you've *done* to him?"

"All too well," replied the officer, the apology in his acknowledgment, not his voice. "I can only repeat what I've told you. We didn't know what to listen *for*. The differences between the appearance and the reality were beyond our understanding, obviously beyond his own. And if beyond his, why not ours?"

"He's been trying to reconcile the appearance and reality, as you call it, for seven months! And all you could do was send out men to kill him! He tried to *tell* you. What kind of people *are* you?"

"Flawed, Miss St. Jacques. Flawed but decent, I think. It's why I'm here. The time span's begun and I want to save him if I can, if *we* can."

"God, you make me sick!" Marie stopped, she shook her head and continued softly. "I'll do whatever you ask, you know that. Can you reach this Conklin?"

"I'm sure I can. I'll stand on the steps of that house until he has no choice *but* to reach me. He may not be our concern, however."

"Carlos?"

"Perhaps others."

"What do you mean?"

"I'll explain on the way. Our main concern now—our *only* concern now—is to reach Delta."

"Jason?"

"Yes. The man you call Jason Bourne."

"And he's been one of you from the beginning," said Marie. "There were no slates to clean, no payments or pardons bargained for?"

"None. You'll be told everything in time, but this is *not* the time. I've made arrangements for you to be in an unmarked government car diagonally across from the house. We have binoculars for you; you know him better than anyone now. Perhaps you'll spot him. I pray to God you do."

Marie went quickly to the closet and got her coat. "He said to me one night that he was a chameleon . . ."

"He remembered?" interrupted Crawford.

"Remembered what?"

"Nothing. He had a talent for moving in and out of difficult situations without being seen. That's all I meant."

"Wait a minute." Marie approached the army man, her eyes suddenly riveted on his again. "You say we have to reach Jason, but there's a better way. Let him come to us. To *me*. Put me on the steps of that house. He'll see *me*, get word to me!"

"Giving whoever's out there two targets?"

"You don't know your own man, General. I said 'get word to me.' He'll send someone, pay a man or a woman on the street to give me a message. I know him. He'll do it. It's the surest way."

"I can't permit it."

"Why not? You've done everything else stupidly! Blindly! Do one thing intelligently!"

"I can't. It might even solve problems you're not aware of, but I can't do it."

"Give me a reason."

"If Delta's right, if Carlos has come after him and is in the street, the risk is too great. Carlos knows you from photographs. He'll kill you."

"I'm willing to take that risk."

"I'm not. I'd like to think I'm speaking for my government when I say that."

"I don't think you are, frankly."

"Leave it to others. May we go, please?"

"General Service Administration," intoned a disinterested switchboard operator.

"Mr. J. Petrocelli, please," said Alexander Conklin, his voice tense, his fingers wiping the sweat from his forehead as he stood by the window, the telephone in his hand. "Quickly, please!"

"Everybody's in a hurry—" The words were shorted out, replaced by the hum of a ring.

"Petrocelli, Reclamation Invoice Division."

"What are you people *doing?*" exploded the CIA man, the shock calculated, a weapon.

The pause was brief. "Right now, listening to some nut ask a stupid question."

"Well, listen further. My name's Conklin, Central Intelligence Agency, Four-Zero clearance. You *do* know what that means?"

"I haven't understood anything you people've said in the past ten years."

"You'd better understand this. It took me damn near an hour, but I just reached the dispatcher for a moving company up here in New York. He said he had an invoice signed by you to remove all the furniture from a brownstone on Seventy-first Street—139, to be exact."

"Yeah, I remember that one. What about it?"

"Who gave you the order? That's *our* territory. We removed our equipment last week, but we did not—repeat, did *not*—request any further activity."

"Just hold it," said the bureaucrat. "I saw that invoice. I mean, I read it before I signed it; you guys make me curious. The order came directly from Langley on a priority sheet."

"*Who* in Langley?"

"Give me a moment and I'll tell you. I've got a copy in my out file; it's here on my desk." The crackling of paper could be heard on the line. It stopped and Petrocelli returned. "Here it is, Conklin. Take up your beef with your own people in Administrative Controls."

"They didn't know what they were doing. Cancel the order. Call up the moving company and tell them to clear out! Now!"

"Blow smoke, spook."

"What?"

"Get a written priority requisition on my desk before three o'clock this afternoon, and it may—just may—get processed tomorrow. Then we'll put everything back."

"Put everything *back?*"

"That's right. You tell us to take it out, we take it out. You tell us to put it back, we put it back. We have methods and procedures to follow just like you."

"That equipment—everything—was on loan! It wasn't—*isn't*—an Agency operation."

"Then why are you calling me? What have you got to do with it?"

"I don't have time to explain. Just get those people out of there. Call New York and get them out! Those are Four-Zero orders."

"Make them a hundred and four and you can still blow smoke. Look, Conklin, we both know you can get what you want if I get what I need. Do it right. Make it legitimate."

"I can't involve the Agency!"

"You're not going to involve me, either."

"Those people have got to get out! I'm telling you—" Conklin stopped, his eyes on the brownstone below and across the street, his thoughts suddenly paralyzed. A tall man in a black overcoat had walked up the concrete steps; he turned and stood motionless in front of the open door. It was *Crawford.* What was he doing? What was he doing *here?* He had lost his senses; he was out of his mind! He was a stationary target; he could break the trap!

"Conklin? Conklin . . .?" The voice floated up out of the phone as the CIA man hung up.

Conklin turned to a stocky man six feet away at an adjacent window. In the man's large hand was a rifle, a telescopic sight secured to the barrel. Alex did not know the man's name and he did not want to know it; he had paid enough not to be burdened.

"Do you see that man down there in the black overcoat standing by the door?" he asked.

"I see him. He's not the one we're looking for. He's too old."

"Get over there and tell him there's a cripple across the street who wants to see him."

Bourne walked out of the used clothing store on Third Avenue, pausing in front of the filthy glass window to appraise what he saw. It would do; everything was coordinated. The black wool knit hat covered his head to the middle of his forehead; the wrinkled, patched army field jacket was several sizes too large; the red-checked flannel shirt, the wide-bulging khaki trousers and the heavy work shoes with the thick rubber soles and huge rounded toes were all of a piece. He only had to find a walk to match the clothing. The walk of a strong, slow-witted man whose body had begun to show the effects of a lifetime of physical strain, whose mind accepted the daily inevitability of hard labor, reward found with a six-pack at the end of the drudgery.

He would find that walk; he had used it before. Somewhere. But before he searched his imagination, there was a phone call to make; he saw a telephone booth up the block, a mangled directory hanging from a chain beneath the metal shelf. He started walking, his legs automatically more rigid, his feet pressing weight on the pavement, his arms heavy in their sockets, the fingers of his hands slightly spaced, curved from years of abuse. A set, dull expression on his face would come later. Not now.

"Belkins Moving and Storage," announced an operator somewhere in the Bronx.

"My name is Johnson," said Jason impatiently but kindly. "I'm afraid I have a problem, and I hope you might be able to help me."

"I'll try, sir. What is it?"

"I was on my way over to a friend's house on Seventy-first Street—a friend who died recently, I'm sorry to say—to pick up something I'd lent him. When I got there, your van was in front of the house. It's most embarrassing, but I think your men may remove my property. Is there someone I might speak to?"

"That would be a dispatcher, sir."

"Might I have his name, please?"

"What?"

"His name."

"Sure. Murray. Murray Schumach. I'll connect you."

Two clicks preceded a long hum over the line.

"Schumach."

"Mr. Schumach?"

"That's right."

Bourne repeated his embarrassing tale. "Of course, I can easily obtain a letter from my attorney, but the item in question has little or no value—"

"What is it?"

"A fishing rod. Not an expensive one, but with an old-fashioned casting reel, the kind that doesn't get tangled every five minutes."

"Yeah, I know what you mean. I fish out of Sheepshead Bay. They don't make them reels like they used to. I think it's the alloys."

"I think you're right, Mr. Schumach. I know exactly in which closet he kept it."

"Oh, what the hell—a fishing rod. Go up and see a guy named Dugan, he's the supervisor on the job. Tell him I said you could have it, but you'll have to sign for it. If he gives you static, tell him to go outside and call me; the phone's disconnected down there."

"A Mr. Dugan. Thank you very much, Mr. Schumach."

"Christ, that place is a ballbreaker today!"

"I beg your pardon?"

"Nothing. Some whacko called telling us to get out of there. And the job's firm, cash guaranteed. Can you believe it?"

Carlos. Jason could believe it.

"It's difficult, Mr. Schumach."

"Good fishing," said the Belkins man.

Bourne walked west on Seventieth Street to Lexington Avenue. Three blocks south he found what he was looking for: an army-navy surplus store. He went inside.

Eight minutes later he came out carrying four brown, padded blankets and six wide canvas straps with metal buckles. In the pockets of his field jacket were two ordinary road flares. They had been there on the counter looking like something they were not, triggering images beyond memory, back to a moment of time when there had been meaning and purpose. And anger. He slung the equipment over his left shoulder and trudged up toward Seventy-first Street. The chameleon was heading into the jungle, a jungle as dense as the unremembered Tam Quan.

It was 10:48 when he reached the corner of the tree-lined block that held the secrets of Treadstone Seventy-One. He was going back to the beginning—his beginning—and the fear that he felt was not the fear of physical harm. He was prepared for that, every sinew taut, every muscle ready; his knees and feet, hands and elbows weapons, his eyes trip-wire alarms that would send signals to those weapons. His fear was far more profound. He was about to enter the place of his birth and he was terrified at what he might find there—remember there.

Stop it! The trap is everything. Cain is for Charlie and Delta is for Cain!

The traffic had diminished considerably, the rush hour over, the street in the doldrums of midmorning quiescence. Pedestrians strolled now, they did not hasten; automobiles swung leisurely around the moving van, angry horns replaced by brief grimaces of irritation. Jason crossed with the light to the Treadstone side; the tall, narrow structure of brown, jagged stone and thick blue glass was fifty yards down the block. Blankets and straps in place, an already weary, slow-witted laborer walked behind a well-dressed couple toward it.

He reached the concrete steps as two muscular men, one black, one white, were carrying a covered harp out the door. Bourne stopped and called out, his words halting, his dialect coarse.

"Hey! Where's Doogan?"

"Where the hell d'you t'ink?" replied the white, angling his head around. "Sittin' in a fuckin' chair."

"He ain't gonna lift nothin' heavier than that clipboard, man," added the black. "He's an *executive,* ain't that right, Joey?"

"He's a crumbball, is what he is. Watcha' got there?"

"Schumach sent me," said Jason. "He wanted another man down here and figured you needed this stuff. Told me to bring it."

"Murray the menace!" laughed the black. "You new, man? I ain't seen you before. You come from shape-up?"

"Yeah."

"Take that shit up to the executive," grunted Joey, starting down the steps. "He can *allocate* it, how about that Pete? *Allocate*—you like it?"

"I love it, Joey. You a regular dictionary."

Bourne walked up the reddish brown steps past the descending movers to the door. He stepped inside and saw the winding staircase on the right, and the long narrow corridor in front of him that led to another door thirty feet away. He had climbed those steps a thousand times, walked up and down that corridor thousands more. He had come back, and an overpowering sense of dread swept through him. He started down the dark, narrow corridor; he could see shafts of sunlight bursting through a pair of French doors in the distance. He was approaching the room where Cain was born. *That* room. He gripped the straps on his shoulder and tried to stop the trembling.

Marie leaned forward in the back seat of the armor-plated government sedan, the binoculars in place. Something had happened; she was not sure what it was, but she could guess. A short, stocky man had passed by the steps of the brownstone a few minutes ago, slowing his pace as he approached the general, obviously saying something to him. The man had then continued down the block and seconds later Crawford had followed him.

Conklin had been found.

It was a small step if what the general said was true. Hired gunmen, unknown to their employer, he unknown to them. Hired to kill a man . . . for all the wrong reasons! Oh, God, she loathed them all! Mindless, stupid men. Playing with the lives of other men, knowing so little, thinking they knew so much.

They had not listened! They never listened until it was too late, and then only with stern forbearance and strong reminders of what might have been—had things been as they were perceived to be, which they were not. The corruption came from blindness, the lies from obstinacy and embarrassment. Do not embarrass the powerful; the napalm said it all.

Marie focused the binoculars. A Belkins man was approaching the steps, blankets and straps over his shoulder, walking behind an elderly couple, obviously residents of the block out for a stroll. The man in the field jacket and the black knit hat stopped; he began talking to two other movers carrying a triangular-shaped object out the door.

What was it? There was something . . . something odd. She could not see the man's face; it was hidden from view, but there was something about the neck, the angle of the head . . . what was it? The man started up the steps, a blunt man, weary of his day before it had begun . . . a slovenly man. Marie removed the binoculars; she was too anxious, too ready to see things that were not there.

Oh, God, my love, my Jason. Where are you? Come to me. Let me find you. Do not leave me for these blind, mindless men. Do not let them take you from me.

Where was Crawford? He had promised to keep her informed of every move, everything. She had been blunt. She did not trust him, any of them; she did not trust their intelligence, that word spelled with a lower-case *i.* He had promised . . . where *was* he?

She spoke to the driver. "Will you put down the window, please. It's stifling in here."

"Sorry, miss," replied the civilian-clothed army man. "I'll turn on the air conditioning for you, though."

The windows and doors were controlled by buttons only the driver could reach. She was in a glass and metal tomb in a sun-drenched, tree-lined street.

"I don't believe a word of it!" said Conklin, limping angrily across the room back to the window. He leaned against the sill, looking out, his left hand pulled up to his face, his teeth against the knuckle of his index finger. "Not a goddamned word!"

"You don't want to believe it, Alex," countered Crawford. "The solution is so much easier. It's in place, and so much simpler."

"You didn't hear that tape. You didn't hear Villiers!"

"I've heard the woman; she's all I have to hear. She said we didn't listen . . . you didn't listen."

"Then she's lying!" Awkwardly Conklin spun around. "Christ, of course she's lying! Why wouldn't she? She's his woman. She'll do anything to get him off the meathook."

"You're wrong and you know it. The fact that he's here proves you're wrong, proves I was wrong to accept what you said."

Conklin was breathing heavily, his right hand trembling as he gripped his cane. "Maybe . . . maybe we, maybe . . ." He did not finish; instead he looked at Crawford helplessly.

"We ought to let the solution stand?" asked the officer quietly. "You're tired, Alex. You haven't slept for several days; you're exhausted. I don't think I heard that."

"No." The CIA man shook his head, his eyes closed, his face reflecting his disgust. "No, you didn't hear it and I didn't say it. I just wish I knew where the hell to begin."

"I do," said Crawford, going to the door and opening it. "Come in, please."

The stocky man walked in, his eyes darting to the rifle leaning against the wall. He looked at the two men, appraisal in his expression. "What is it?"

"The exercise has been called off," Crawford said. "I think you must have gathered that."

"What exercise? I was hired to protect him." The gunman looked at Alex. "You mean you don't need protection anymore, sir?"

"You know exactly what we mean," broke in Conklin. "All signals are off, all stipulations."

"What stipulations? I don't know about any stipulations. The terms of my employment are very clear. I'm protecting you, sir."

"Good, fine," said Crawford. "Now what we have to know is who else out there is protecting him."

"Who else where?"

"Outside this room, this apartment. In other rooms, on the street, in cars, perhaps. We have to *know.*"

The stocky man walked over to the rifle and picked it up. "I'm afraid you gentlemen have misunderstood. I was hired on an individual basis. If others were employed, I'm not aware of them."

"You *do* know them!" shouted Conklin. "Who *are* they? *Where* are they?"

"I haven't any idea . . . sir." The courteous gunman held the rifle in his right arm, the barrel angled down toward the floor. He raised it perhaps two inches, no more than that, the movement barely perceptible. "If my services are no longer required, I'll be leaving."

"Can you *reach* them?" interrupted the brigadier. "We'll pay generously."

"I've already been paid generously, sir. It would be wrong to accept money for a service I can't perform. And pointless for this to continue."

"A man's life is at stake out there!" shouted Conklin.

"So's mine," said the gunman, walking to the door, the weapon raised higher. "Goodbye, gentlemen." He let himself out.

"*Jesus!*" roared Alex, swinging back to the window, his cane clattering against a radiator. "What do we *do?*"

"To start with, get rid of that moving company. I don't know what part it played in your strategy, but it's only a complication now."

"I can't. I tried. I didn't have anything to do with it. Agency Controls picked up our sheets when we had the equipment taken out. They saw that a store was being closed up and told GSA to get us the hell out of there."

"With all deliberate speed," said Crawford, nodding. "The Monk covered that equipment by signature; his statement absolves the Agency. It's in his files."

"That'd be fine if we had twenty-four hours. We don't even know if we've got twenty-four minutes."

"We'll still need it. There'll be a Senate inquiry. Closed, I hope. . . . Rope off the street."

"What?"

"You heard me—rope off the street! Call in the police, tell them to rope everything off!"

"Through the Agency? This is domestic."

"Then *I* will. Through the Pentagon, from the Joint Chiefs, if I have to. We're standing around making excuses, when it's right in front of our eyes! Clear the street, rope it off, bring in a truck with a public address system. Put *her* in it, put her on a *microphone!* Let her say anything she likes, let her scream her head off. She was right. He'll come to *her!*"

"Do you know what you're saying?" asked Conklin. "There'll be questions. Newspapers, television, radio. Everything will be exposed. Publicly."

"I'm aware of that," said the brigadier. "I'm also aware that she'll do it for us if this goes down. She may do it anyway, no matter what happens, but I'd rather try to save a man I didn't like, didn't approve of. But I respected him once, and I think I respect him more now."

"What about another man? If Carlos is really out there, you're opening the gates for him. You're handing him his escape."

"We didn't create Carlos. We created Cain and we abused him. We took his mind and his memory. We owe him. Go down and get the woman. I'll use the phone."

Bourne walked into the large library with the sunlight streaming through the wide, elegant french doors at the far end of the room. Beyond the panes of glass were the high walls of the garden . . . all around him objects too painful to look at; he knew them and did not know them. They were fragments of dreams—but solid, to be touched, to be felt, to be used—not ephemeral at all. A long hatch table where whiskey was poured, leather armchairs where men sat and talked, bookshelves that housed books and other things—concealed things—that appeared with the touch of buttons. It was a room where a myth was born, a myth that had raced through Southeast Asia and exploded in Europe.

He saw the long, tubular bulge in the ceiling and the darkness came, followed by flashes of light and images on a screen and voices shouting in his ears.

Who is he? Quick. You're too late! You're a dead man! Where is this street? What does it mean to you? Whom did you meet there? . . . Methods of kills. Which are yours? No! . . . You are not Delta, you are not you! . . . You are only what you are here, became here!

"Hey! Who the hell are *you?*" The question was shouted by a large, red-faced man seated in an armchair by the door, a clipboard on his knees. Jason had walked right past him.

"You Doogan?" Bourne asked.

"Yeah."

"Schumach sent me. Said you needed another man."

"What for? I got five awready, and this fuckin' place has hallways so tight you can't hardly get through 'em. They're climbing asses now."

"I don't know. Schumach sent me, that's all I know. He told me to bring this stuff." Bourne let the blankets and the straps fall to the floor.

"Murray sends new junk? I mean, that's new."

"I don't—"

"I know, I *know!* Schumach sent you. Ask Schumach."

"You can't. He said to tell you he was heading out to Sheepshead. Be back this afternoon."

"Oh, that's great! He goes fishing and leaves me with the shit. . . . You're new. You a crumbball from the shape-up?"

"Yeah."

"That Murray's a beaut. All I need's another crumbball. Two wiseass stiffs and now four crumbballs."

"You want me to start in here? I can start in here."

"No, asshole! Crumbballs start at the top, you ain't heard? It's further away, *capisce?*"

"Yeah, I *capisce.*" Jason bent down for the blankets and the straps.

"Leave that junk here—you don't need it. Get upstairs, top floor, and start with the single wood units. As heavy as you can carry, and don't give me no union bullshit."

Bourne circled the landing on the second floor and climbed the narrow staircase to the third, as if drawn by a magnetic force beyond his understanding. He was being pulled to another room high up in the brownstone, a room that held both the comfort of solitude and the frustration of loneliness. The landing above was dark, no lights on, no sunlight bursting through windows anywhere. He reached the top and stood for a moment in silence. Which room was it? There were three doors, two on the left side of the hallway, one on the right. He started walking slowly toward the second door on the left, barely seen in the shadows. That was it; it was where thoughts came in the darkness . . . memories that haunted him, pained him. Sunlight and the stench of the river and the jungle . . . screaming machines in the sky, screaming down from the sky. *Oh, God, it hurt!*

He put his hand on the knob, twisted it and opened the door. Darkness, but not complete. There was a small window at the far end of the room, a black shade pulled down, covering it, but not completely. He could see a thin line of sunlight, so narrow it barely broke through, where the shade met the sill. He walked toward it, toward that thin, tiny shaft of sunlight.

A scratch! A scratch in the darkness! He spun, terrified at the tricks being played on his mind. But it was not a trick! There was a diamondlike flash in the air, light bouncing off steel.

A knife was slashing up at his face.

"I would willingly see you die for what you've done," said Marie, staring at Conklin. "And that realization revolts me."

"Then there's nothing I can say to you," replied the CIA man, limping across the room toward the general. "Other decisions could have been made—by him and by you."

"Could they? Where was he to start? When that man tried to kill him in Marseilles? In the rue Sarrasin? When they hunted him in Zurich? When they shot at him in Paris? And all the while he didn't know why. What was he to do?"

"Come out! Goddamn it, come out!"

"He did. And when he did, you tried to kill him."

"You were there! You were with him. You had a memory."

"Assuming I knew whom to go to, would you have listened to me?"

Conklin returned her gaze. "I don't know," he answered, breaking the contact between them and turning to Crawford. "What's happening?"

"Washington's calling me back within ten minutes."

"But what's *happening?*"

"I'm not sure you want to hear it. Federal encroachment on state and municipal law-enforcement statutes. Clearances have to be obtained."

"Jesus!"

"Look!" The army man suddenly bent down to the window. "The truck's leaving."

"Someone got through," said Conklin.

"Who?"

"I'll find out." The CIA man limped to the phone; there were scraps of paper on the table, telephone numbers written hastily. He selected one and dialed. "Give me Schumach . . . please . . . Schumach? This is Conklin, Central Intelligence. Who gave you the word?"

The dispatcher's voice on the line could be heard halfway across the room. "What word? Get off my back! We're on that job and we're going to finish it! Frankly I think you're a whacko—"

Conklin slammed down the phone. "Christ . . . oh, *Christ!*" His hand trembled as he gripped the instrument. He picked it up and dialed again, his eyes on another scrap of paper. "Petrocelli. Reclamations," he commanded. "Petrocelli? Conklin again."

"You faded out. What happened?"

"No time. Level with me. That priority invoice from Agency Controls. Who signed it?"

"What do you mean, who signed it? The top cat who always signs them. McGivern."

Conklin's face turned white. "That's what I was afraid of," he whispered, as he lowered the phone. He turned to Crawford, his head quivering as he spoke. "The order to GSA was signed by a man who retired two weeks ago."

"Carlos . . ."

"Oh, God!" screamed Marie. "The man carrying the blankets, the straps! The way he held his head, his neck. Angled to the right. It was him! When his head hurts, he favors the right. It was Jason! He went *inside.*"

Alexander Conklin turned back to the window, his eyes focused on the black enameled door across the way. It was closed.

The hand! The skin . . . the dark eyes in the thin shaft of light. *Carlos!*

Bourne whipped his head back as the razorlike edge of the blade sliced the flesh under his chin, the eruption of blood streaming across the hand that held the knife. He lashed his right foot out, catching his unseen attacker in the kneecap, then pivoted and plunged his left heel into the man's groin. Carlos spun, and again the blade came out of the darkness, now surging toward him, the line of assault directly at his stomach. Jason sprang back off the ground, crossing his wrists, slashing downward, blocking the dark arm that was an extension of the handle. He twisted his fingers inward, yanking his hands together, vicing the forearm beneath his blood-soaked neck and wrenched the arm diagonally up. The knife creased the cloth of his field jacket and once above his chest. Bourne spiraled the arm downward, twisting the wrist now in his grip, crashing his shoulder into the assassin's body, yanking again as Carlos plunged sideways off balance, his arm pulled half out of its socket.

Jason heard the clatter of the knife on the floor. He lurched toward the sound, at the same time reaching into his belt for his gun. It caught on the cloth; he rolled on the floor, but not quickly enough. The steel toe of a shoe crashed into the side of his head—his temple—and shock waves bolted through him. He rolled again, faster, faster, until he smashed into the wall; coiling upward on his knee, trying to focus through the weaving, obscure shadows in the near total darkness. The flesh of a hand was caught in the thin line of light from the window; he lunged at it, his own hands now claws, his arms battering rams. He gripped the hand, snapping it back, breaking the wrist. A scream filled the room.

A scream and the hollow, lethal cough of a gunshot. An icelike incision had been made in Bourne's upper left chest, the bullet lodged somewhere near his shoulder blade. In agony, he crouched and sprang again, pummeling the killer with a gun into the wall above a sharp-edged piece of furniture. Carlos lunged away as two more muted shots were fired wildly. Jason dove to his left, freeing his gun, leveling it at the sounds in the darkness. He fired, the explosion deafening, useless. He heard the door crash shut; the killer had raced out into the hallway.

Trying to fill his lungs with air, Bourne crawled toward the door. As he reached it, instinct commanded him to stay at the side and smash his fist into the wood at the bottom. What followed was the core of a terrifying nightmare. There was a short burst of automatic gunfire as the paneled wood splintered, fragments flying across the room. The instant it stopped, Jason raised his own weapon and fired diagonally through the door; the burst was repeated. Bourne spun away, pressing his back against the wall; the eruption stopped and he fired again. There were now two men inches from each other, wanting above all to kill each other. *Cain is for Charlie and Delta is for Cain. Get Carlos. Trap Carlos. Kill Carlos!*

And then they were not inches from each other. Jason heard racing footsteps, then the sounds of a railing being broken as a figure lurched down the staircase. Carlos was racing below; the pig-animal wanted support; he was hurt. Bourne wiped the blood from his face, from his throat, and moved in front of what was left of the door. He pulled it open and stepped out into the narrow corridor, his gun leveled in front of him. Painfully he made his way toward the top of the dark staircase. Suddenly he heard shouts below.

"What the hell *you doin' man? Pete! Pete!*"

Two metallic coughs filled the air.

"Joey! *Joey!*"

A single spit was heard; bodies crashed to a floor somewhere below.

"Jesus! *Jesus,* Mother of—!"

Two metallic coughs again, followed by a guttural cry of death. A third man was killed.

What had that third man said? *Two wiseass stiffs and now four crumbballs.* The moving van was a Carlos operation! The assassin had brought two soldiers with him—the first three crumbballs from the shape-up. Three men with weapons, and he was one with a single gun. Cornered on the top floor of the brownstone. Still Carlos was inside. *Inside.* If he could get out, it would be Carlos who was cornered! If he could get out. *Out!*

There was a window at the front end of the hallway, obscured by a black shade. Jason veered toward it, stumbling, holding his neck, creasing his shoulder so to blunt the pain in his chest. He ripped the shade from its spindle; the window was small, the glass here, too, thick, prismatic blocks of purple and blue light shooting through it. It was unbreakable, the frame riveted in place; there was no way he could smash a single pane. And then his eyes were drawn below to Seventy-first Street. The moving van was gone! Someone had to have driven it away . . . one of Carlos's soldiers! That left two. *Two* men, not three. And he was on the high ground; there were always advantages on the high ground.

Grimacing, bent partially over, Bourne made his way to the first door on the left; it was parallel to the top of the staircase. He opened it and stepped inside. From what he could see it was an ordinary bedroom: lamps, heavy furniture, pictures on the walls. He grabbed the nearest lamp, ripped the cord from the wall and carried it out to the railing. He raised it above his head and hurled it down, stepping back as metal and glass crashed below. There was another burst of gunfire, the bullets shredding the ceiling, cutting a path in the plaster. Jason screamed, letting the scream fade into a cry, the cry into a prolonged desperate wail, and then silence. He edged his way to the rear of the railing. He waited. Silence.

It happened. He could hear the slow, cautious footsteps; the killer had been on the second floor landing. The footsteps came closer, became louder; a faint shadow appeared on the dark wall. *Now.* Bourne sprang out of his recess and fired four shots in rapid succession at the figure on the staircase; a line of bullet holes and eruptions of blood appeared diagonally across the man's collar. The killer spun, roaring in anger and pain as his neck arched back and his body plummeted

THE BOURNE IDENTITY 1141

down the steps until it was still, sprawled faceup across the bottom three steps. In his hands was a deadly automatic field machine gun with a rod and brace for a stock.

Now. Jason ran over to the top of the staircase and raced down, holding the railing, trying to keep whatever was left of his balance. He could not waste a moment; he might not find another. If he was going to reach the second floor it was now, in the immediate aftermath of the soldier's death. And as he leaped over the dead body, Bourne knew it was a soldier; it was not Carlos. The man was tall and his skin was white, very white, his features Nordic or northern European, in no way Latin.

Jason ran into the hallway of the second floor, seeking the shadows, hugging the wall. He stopped, listening. There was a sharp scrape in the distance, brief scratch from below. He knew what he had to do now. The assassin was on the first floor. And the sound had not been deliberate; it had not been loud enough or prolonged enough to signify a trap. Carlos was injured—a smashed kneecap or a broken wrist could disorient him to the point where he might collide with a piece of furniture or brush against a wall with a weapon in his hand, briefly losing his balance as Bourne was losing his. It was what he needed to know.

Jason dropped to a crouch and crept back to the staircase, to the dead body sprawled across the steps. He had to pause for a moment; he was losing strength, too much blood. He tried to squeeze the flesh at the top of his throat and press the wound in his chest—anything to stem the bleeding. It was futile; to stay alive he had to get out of the brownstone, away from the place where Cain was born. Jason Bourne . . . there was no humor in the word association. He found his breath again, reached out and pried the automatic weapon from the dead man's hands. He was ready.

He was dying and he was ready. *Get Carlos. Trap Carlos . . . Kill Carlos!* He could not get out; he knew that. Time was not on his side. The blood would drain out of him before it happened. The end was the beginning: Cain was for Carlos and Delta was for Cain. Only one agonizing question remained: who was Delta? It did not matter. It was behind him now; soon there would be the darkness, not violent but peaceful . . . freedom from that question.

And with his death Marie would be free, his love would be free. Decent men would see to it, led by a decent man in Paris whose son had been killed on rue du Bac, whose life had been destroyed by an assassin's whore. Within the next few minutes, thought Jason, silently checking the clip in the automatic weapon, he would fulfill his promise to that man, carry out the agreement he had with men he did not know. By doing both, the proof was his. Jason Bourne had died once on this day; he would die again but would take Carlos out with him. He was ready.

He lowered himself to a prone position and crept hands over elbows toward the top of the staircase. He could smell the blood beneath him, the sweet, bland odor penetrating his nostrils, informing him of a practicality. Time *was* running out. He reached the top step, pulling his legs up under him, digging into his pocket for one of the road flares he had purchased at the army-navy store on Lexington Avenue. He knew now why he had felt the compulsion to buy them. He was back in the unremembered Tam Quan, forgotten except for brilliant, blinding flashes of light. The flares had reminded him of that fragment of memory; they would light up a jungle now.

He uncoiled the waxed fuse from the small round recess in the flare head, brought it to his teeth and bit through the cord, shortening the fuse to less than an inch. He reached into his other pocket and took out a plastic lighter; he pressed it against the flare, gripping both in his left hand. Then he angled the rod and the brace of the weapon into his right shoulder, shoving the curved strip of metal into the cloth of his blood-soaked field jacket; it was secure. He stretched out his legs and, snakelike, started down the final flight of steps, head below, feet above, his back scraping the wall.

He reached the midpoint of the staircase. Silence, darkness, all the lights had been extinguished . . . Lights? *Light?* Where were the rays of sunlight he had seen in that hallway only minutes ago? They had streamed through a pair of french doors at the far end of the room—that room—beyond the corridor, but he could see only darkness now. The door had been shut; the door beneath him, the only other door in that hallway, was also closed, marked by a thin shaft of light at the bottom. Carlos was making him choose. Behind which door? Or was the assassin using a better strategy? Was he in the darkness of the narrow hallway itself?

Bourne felt a stabbing jolt of pain in his shoulder blade, then an eruption of blood that drenched the flannel shirt beneath his field jacket. Another warning: there was very little time.

He braced himself against the wall, the weapon leveled at the thin posts of the railing, aimed down into the darkness of the corridor. *Now!* He pulled the trigger. The staccato explosions tore the posts apart as the railing fell, the bullets shattering the walls and the door beneath him. He released the trigger, slipping his hand under the scalding barrel, grabbing the plastic lighter with his right hand, the flare in his left. He spun the flint; the wick took fire and he put it to the short fuse. He pulled his hand back to the weapon and squeezed the trigger again, blowing away everything below. A glass chandelier crashed to a floor somewhere; singing whines of ricochets filled the darkness. And then—*light!* Blinding light as the flare ignited, firing the jungle, lighting up the trees and the walls, the hidden paths and the mahogany corridors. The stench of death and the jungle was everywhere, and he was there.

Almanac to Delta. Almanac to Delta. Abandon, abandon!

Never. Not now. Not at the end. Cain is for Carlos and Delta is for Cain. Trap Carlos. Kill Carlos!

Bourne rose to his feet, his back pressed against the wall, the flare in his left hand, the exploding weapon in his right. He plunged down into the carpeted underbrush, kicking the door in front of him open, shattering silver frames and trophies that flew off tables and shelves into the air. Into the trees. He stopped;

there was no one in that quiet, soundproof, elegant room. No one in the jungle path.

He spun around and lurched back into the hallway, puncturing the walls with a prolonged burst of gunfire. No one.

The door at the end of the narrow, dark corridor. Beyond was the room where Cain was born. Where Cain would die, but not alone.

He held his fire, shifting the flare to his right hand beneath the weapon, reaching into his pocket for the second flare. He pulled it out, and again uncoiled the fuse and brought it to his teeth, severing the cord, now millimeters from its point of contact with the gelatinous incendiary. He shoved the first flare to it; the explosion of light was so bright it pained his eyes. Awkwardly, he held both flares in his left hand and, squinting, his legs and arms losing the battle for balance, approached the door.

It was open, the narrow crack extending from top to bottom on the lock side. The assassin was accommodating, but as he looked at that door, Jason instinctively knew one thing about it that Carlos did not know. It was a part of his past, a part of the room where Cain was born. He reached down with his right hand, bracing the weapon between his forearm and his hip, and gripped the knob.

Now. He shoved the door open six inches and hurled the flares inside. A long staccato burst from a Sten gun echoed throughout the room, throughout the entire house, a thousand dead sounds forming a running chord beneath, as sprays of bullets imbedded in a lead shield backed by a steel plate in the door.

The firing stopped, a final clip expended. *Now.* Bourne whipped his hand back to the trigger, crashed his shoulder into the door and lunged inside, firing in circles as he rolled on the floor, swinging his legs counterclockwise. Gunshots were returned wildly as Jason honed his weapon toward the source. A roar of fury burst from blindness across the room; it accompanied Bourne's realization that the drapes had been drawn, blocking out the sunlight from the french doors. Then why was there so much light . . . magnified light beyond the sizzling blindness of the flares? It was overpowering, causing explosions in his head, sharp bolts of agony at his temples.

The *screen!* The huge screen was pulled down from its bulging recess in the ceiling, drawn taut to the floor, the wide expanse of glistening silver a white-hot shield of ice-cold fire. He plunged behind the large hatch table to the protection of a copper dry bar; he rose and jammed the trigger back, in another burst—a final burst. The last clip had run out. He hurled the weapon by its rod-stock across the room at the figure in white overalls and a white silk scarf that had fallen below his face.

The *face!* He knew it! He had seen it before! Where . . . where? Was it Marseilles? Yes . . . no! Zurich? Paris? Yes *and* no! Then it struck him at that instant in the blinding, vibrating light, that the face across the room was known to many, not just him. But from where? *Where?* As so much else, he knew it and did not know it. But he *did* know it! It was only the name he could not find!

He spiraled back off his feet, behind the heavy copper dry bar. Gunshots came, two . . . three, the second bullet tearing the flesh of his left forearm. He pulled his automatic from his belt; he had three shots left. One of them had to find its mark—Carlos. There was a debt to pay in Paris, and a contract to fulfill, his love far safer with the assassin's death. He took the plastic lighter from his pocket, ignited it and held it beneath a bar rag suspended from a hook. The cloth caught fire; he grabbed it and threw it to his right, as he dove to his left. Carlos fired at the flaming rag, as Bourne spun to his knees, leveling his gun, pulling the trigger twice.

The figure buckled but did not fall. Instead, he crouched, then sprang like a white panther diagonally forward, his hands outstretched. What was he *doing?* Then Jason knew. The assassin gripped the edge of the huge silver screen, ripping it from its metal bracket in the ceiling, pulling it downward with all his weight and strength.

It floated down above Bourne, filling his vision, blocking everything else from his mind. He screamed as the shimmering silver descended over him, suddenly more frightened of it than of Carlos or of any other human being on the earth. It terrified him, infuriated him, splitting his mind in fragments; images flashed across his eyes and angry voices shouted in his ears. He aimed his gun and fired at the terrible shroud. As he slashed his hand against it wildly, pushing the rough silver cloth away, he understood. He had fired his last shot, his *last.* As a legend named Cain, Carlos knew by sight and by sound every weapon on earth; he had counted the gunshots.

The assassin loomed above him, the automatic in his hand aimed at Jason's head. "Your execution, Delta. On the day scheduled. For everything you've done."

Bourne arched his back, rolling furiously to his right; at least he would die in motion! Gunshots filled the shimmering room, hot needles slicing across his neck, piercing his legs, cutting up to his waist. Roll, *roll!*

Suddenly the gunshots stopped, and in the distance he could hear repeated sounds of hammering, the smashing of wood and steel, growing louder, more insistent. There was a final deafening crash from the dark corridor outside the library, followed by men shouting, running, and beyond them somewhere in the unseen, outside world, the insistent whine of sirens.

"In here! He's in *here!*" screamed Carlos.

It was insane! The assassin was directing the invaders directly toward him, *to* him! Reason was madness, nothing on earth made sense!

The door was crashed open by a tall man in a black overcoat; someone was with him, but Jason could not see. The mists were filling his eyes, shapes and sounds becoming obscured, blurred. He was rolling in space. Away . . . away.

But then he saw the one thing he did not want to see. Rigid shoulders that floated above a tapered waist raced out of the room and down the dimly lit corridor. *Carlos.* His screams had sprung the trap open! He had *reversed* it! In the chaos he had trapped the stalkers. He was *escaping!*

"Carlos . . ." Bourne knew he could not be heard; what emerged from his bleeding throat was a whisper. He tried again, forcing the sound from his stomach. "It's *him*. It's . . . *Carlos!*"

There was confusion, commands shouted futilely, orders swallowed in consternation. And then a figure came into focus. A man was limping toward him, a cripple who had tried to kill him in a cemetery outside of Paris. There was nothing left! Jason lurched. crawling toward the sizzling, blinding flare. He grabbed it and held it as though it were a weapon, aiming it at the killer with a cane.

"Come on! Come *on!* Closer, you bastard! I'll burn your eyes out! You think you'll kill me, you *won't!* I'll kill you! I'll burn your eyes!"

"You don't understand," said the trembling voice of the limping killer. "It's me, Delta. It's Conklin. I was wrong."

The flare singed his hands, his eyes! . . . *Madness. The explosions were all around him now, blinding, deafening, punctuated by ear-splitting screeches from the jungle that erupted with each detonation.*

The jungle! Tam Quan! The wet, hot stench was everywhere, but they had reached it! The base camp was theirs!

An explosion to his left; he could see it! High above the ground, suspended between two trees, the spikes of a bamboo cage. The figure inside was moving. He was alive! Get to him, reach him!

A cry came from his right. Breathing, coughing in the smoke, a man was limping toward the dense underbrush, a rifle in his hand. It was him, the blond hair caught in the light, a foot broken from a parachute jump. The bastard! A piece of filth who had trained with them, studied the maps with them, flown north with them . . . all the time springing a trap on them! A traitor with a radio who told the enemy exactly where to look in that impenetrable jungle that was Tam Quan.

It was Bourne! Jason Bourne. Traitor, garbage!

Get him! Don't let him reach others! Kill him! Kill Jason Bourne! He is your enemy! Fire!

He did not fall! The head that had been blown apart was still there. Coming toward him! What was happening? Madness. Tam Quan . . .

"Come with us," said the limping figure, walking out of the jungle into what remained of an elegant room. *That* room. "We're not your enemies. Come with us."

"Get *away* from me!" Bourne lunged again, now back to the fallen screen. It was his sanctuary, his shroud of death, the blanket thrown over a man at birth, a lining for his coffin. "You are my enemy! I'll take you all! I don't care, it doesn't matter! Can't you understand!? I'm *Delta!* Cain is for Charlie and Delta is for Cain! What more do you want from me? I was and I *was* not! I am and I *am* not! Bastards, *bastards!* Come on! Closer!"

Another voice was heard, a deeper voice, calmer, less insistent. "Get her. Bring her in."

Somewhere in the distance the sirens reached a crescendo, and then they stopped. Darkness came and the waves carried Jason up to the night sky, only to hurl him down again, crashing him into an abyss of watery violence. He was entering an eternity of weightless . . . memory. An explosion filled the night sky now, a fiery diadem rose above black waters. And then he heard the words, spoken from the clouds, filling the earth.

"Jason, my love. My only love. Take my hand. Hold it. Tightly, Jason. Tightly, my darling."

Peace came with the darkness.

EPILOGUE

Brigadier General Crawford put the file folder down on the couch beside him. "I don't need this," he said to Marie St. Jacques, who sat across from him in a straightback chair. "I've gone over it and over it, trying to find out where we missed."

"You presumed where no one should," said the only other person in the hotel suite. He was Dr. Morris Panov, psychiatrist; he stood by the window, the morning sun streaming in, putting his expressionless face in shadow. "I allowed you to presume, and I'll live with it for the rest of my life."

"It's nearly two weeks now," said Marie impatiently. "I'd like specifics. I think I'm entitled to them."

"You are. It was an insanity called clearance."

"Insanity," agreed Panov.

"Protection, also," added Crawford. "I subscribe to that part. It has to continue for a very long time."

"Protection?" Marie frowned.

"We'll get to it," said the general, glancing at Panov. "From everyone's point of view, it's vital. I trust we all accept that."

"Please! Jason—who is he?"

"His name is David Webb. He was a career foreign service officer, a specialist in Far Eastern affairs, until his separation from the government five years ago."

"Separation?"

"Resignation by mutual agreement. His work in Medusa precluded any sustained career in the State Department. 'Delta' was infamous and too many knew he was Webb. Such men are rarely welcome at the diplomatic conference tables. I'm not sure they should be. Visceral wounds are reopened too easily with their presence."

"He was everything they say? In Medusa?"

"Yes. I was there. He was everything they say."

"It's hard to believe," said Marie.

"He'd lost something very special to him and couldn't come to grips with it. He could only strike out."

"What was that?"

"His family. His wife was a Thai; they had two children, a boy and a girl. He was stationed in Phnom Penh, his house on the outskirts, near the Mekong River. One Sunday afternoon while his wife and children were down at their dock, a stray aircraft circled and dove, dropping two bombs and strafing the area. By the time he reached the river the dock was blown away, his wife and children floating in the water, their bodies riddled."

"Oh, God," whispered Marie. "Whom did the plane belong to?"

"It was never identified. Hanoi disclaimed it; Saigon said it wasn't ours. Remember, Cambodia was neutral; no one wanted to be responsible. Webb had to strike out; he headed for Saigon and trained for Medusa. He brought a specialist's intellect to a very brutal operation. He became Delta."

"Was that when he met d'Anjou?"

"Later on, yes. Delta was notorious by then. North Vietnamese Intelligence had put an extraordinary price on his head, and it's no secret that among our own people a number hoped they'd succeed. Then Hanoi found out that Webb's younger brother was an army officer in Saigon, and having studied Delta—knowing the brothers were close—decided to mount a trap; they had nothing to lose. They kidnapped Lieutenant Gordon Webb and took him north, sending back a Cong informant with word that he was being held in the Tam Quan sector. Delta bit; along with the informer—a double agent—he formed a team of Medusans who knew the area and picked a night when no aircraft should have left the ground to fly north. D'Anjou was in the unit. So was another man Webb didn't know about; a white man who'd been bought by Hanoi, an expert in communications who could assemble the electronic components of a high-frequency radio in the dark. Which is exactly what he did, betraying the unit's position. Webb broke through the trap and found his brother. He also found the double agent and the white man. The Vietnamese escaped in the jungle; the white man didn't. Delta executed him on the spot."

"And that man?" Marie's eyes were riveted on Crawford.

"Jason Bourne. A Medusan from Sydney, Australia; a runner of guns, narcotics and slaves throughout all Southeast Asia; a violent man with a criminal record who was nevertheless highly effective—if the price were high enough. It was in Medusa's interests to bury the circumstances of his death; he became an MIA from a specialized unit. Years later, when Treadstone was being formed and Webb called back, it was Webb himself who took the name of Bourne. It fit the requirements of authenticity, traceability. He took the name of the man who'd betrayed him, the man he had killed in Tam Quan."

"Where was he when he was called back for Treadstone?" asked Marie. "What was he doing?"

"Teaching in a small college in New Hampshire. Living an isolated life, some said destructive. For him." Crawford picked up the file folder. "Those are the essential facts, Miss St. Jacques. Other areas will be covered by Dr. Panov, who's made it clear that my presence is not required. There is, however, one remaining detail which must be thoroughly understood. It's a direct order from the White House."

"The protection," said Marie, her words a statement.

"Yes. Wherever he goes, regardless of the identity he assumes or the success of his cover, he'll be guarded around the clock. For as long as it takes—even if it never happens."

"Please explain that."

"He's the only man alive who's ever seen Carlos. *As* Carlos. He knows his identity, but it's locked away in his mind, part of an unremembered past. We understand from what he says that Carlos is someone known to many people—a visible figure in a government somewhere, or in the media, or international banking or society. It fits with a prevalent theory. The point is one day that identity may come into focus for Webb. We realize you've had several discussions with Dr. Panov. I believe he'll confirm what I've said."

Marie turned to the psychiatrist. "Is it true, Mo?"

"It's possible," said Panov.

Crawford left and Marie poured coffee for the two of them. Panov went to the couch where the brigadier had been sitting.

"It's still warm," he said, smiling. "Crawford was sweating right down to his famous backsides. He has every right to, they all do."

"What's going to happen?"

"Nothing. Absolutely nothing until I tell them they can go ahead. And that may not be for months, a couple of years for all I know. Not until he's ready."

"For what?"

"The questions. And photographs—volumes of them. They're compiling a photographic encyclopedia based on the loose description he gave them. Don't get me wrong; one day he'll have to begin. He'll want to; we'll all want him to. Carlos has to be caught, and it's not my intention to blackmail them into doing nothing. Too many people have given too much; *he's* given too much. But right now he comes first. His head comes first."

"That's what I mean. What's going to happen to him?"

Panov put down his coffee. "I'm not sure yet. I've too much respect for the human mind to deal you chicken soup psychology; there's too damn much of it floating around in the wrong hands. I've been in on all the conferences—I insisted upon that—and I've talked to the other shrinks and the neurosurgeons. It's true we can go in with a knife and reach the storm centers, reduce the anxieties, bring a kind of peace to him. Even bring him back to what he was, perhaps. But it's not the kind of peace he wants . . . and there's a far more dangerous risk. We might wipe away too much, take away the things he has found—will *continue* to find. With care. With time."

"Time?"

"I believe it, yes. Because the pattern's been established. There's growth, the pain of recognition and the excitement of discovery. Does that tell you something?"

Marie looked into Panov's dark, weary eyes; there was a light in them. "All of us," she said.

"That's right. In a way, he's a functioning microcosm of us all. I mean, we're all trying to find out who the hell we are, aren't we?"

Marie went to the front window in the cottage on the waterfront, with the rising dunes behind it, the fenced-off grounds surrounding it. And guards. Every fifty feet a man with a gun. She could see him several hundred yards down the beach; he was scaling shells over the water, watching them bounce across the waves that gently lapped into the shore. The weeks had been good to him, for him. His body was scarred but whole again, firm again. The nightmares were still there, and moments of anguish kept coming back during the daylight hours, but somehow it was all less terrifying. He was beginning to cope; he was beginning to laugh again. Panov had been right. Things were happening to him; images were becoming clearer, meaning found where there had been no meaning before.

Something had happened *now!* Oh, *God,* what *was* it? He had thrown himself into the water and was thrashing around, shouting. Then, suddenly, he sprang out, leaping over the waves onto the beach. In the distance, by the barbed-wire fence, a guard spun around, a rifle whipped up under an arm, a hand-held radio pulled from a belt.

He began racing across the wet sand toward the house, his body lurching, swaying, his feet digging furiously into the soft surface, sending up sprays of water and sand behind him. *What was it?*

Marie froze, prepared for the moment they knew might come one day, prepared for the sound of gunfire.

He burst through the door, chest heaving, gasping for breath. He stared at her, his eyes as clear as she had ever seen them. He spoke softly, so softly she could barely hear him. But she did hear him.

"My name is David . . ."

She walked slowly toward him.

"Hello, David," she said.